THE ANGELS WEEP
&
A TIME TO DIE

Wilbur Smith was born in Central Africa in 1933. He was educated at Michaelhouse and Rhodes University.

He became a full-time writer in 1964 after the successful publication of *When the Lion Feeds*, and has since written thirty novels, all meticulously researched on his numerous expeditions worldwide. His books are now translated into twenty-six languages.

He owns a farm and game reserve and has an abiding concern for the peoples and wildlife of his native continent, an interest strongly reflected in his novels.

Also by Wilbur Smith

THE COURTNEYS
When the Lion Feeds
The Sound of Thunder
A Sparrow Falls
Birds of Prey
Monsoon
Blue Horizon

THE COURTNEYS OF AFRICA
The Burning Shore
Power of the Sword
Rage
Golden Fox

THE BALLANTYNE NOVELS
A Falcon Flies
Men of Men
The Leopard Hunts in Darkness

Also

The Dark of the Sun
Shout at the Devil
Gold Mine
The Diamond Hunters
The Sunbird
Eagle in the Sky
The Eye of the Tiger
Cry Wolf
Hungry as the Sea
Wild Justice
Elephant Song
River God
The Seventh Scroll
Warlock

WILBUR SMITH

The Angels
Weep
&
A Time to Die

PAN BOOKS

The Angels Weep first published 1982 by William Heinemann.
First published by Pan Books 1981
A Time to Die first published 1989 by William Heinemann.
First published by Pan Books 1990

This omnibus edition published 2005 by Pan Books
an imprint of Pan Macmillan Ltd
Pan Macmillan, 20 New Wharf Road, London N1 9RR
Basingstoke and Oxford
Associated companies throughout the world
www.panmacmillan.com

ISBN 0 330 44099 3

Copyright © Wilbur Smith 1982, 1989

. The right of Wilbur Smith to be identified as the
author of this work has been asserted by him in accordance
with the Copyright, Designs and Patents Act 1988.

1 3 5 7 9 8 6 4 2

A CIP catalogue record for this book is available from
the British Library.

Printed and bound in Great Britain by
Mackays of Chatham plc, Chatham, Kent

THE ANGELS
WEEP

This book is for my beloved wife

Danielle Antoinette

But man, proud man,
Dress'd in a little brief authority,
Most ignorant of what he's most assur'd,
His glassy essence, like an angry ape,
Plays such fantastic tricks before high heaven
As make the angels weep.

Measure for Measure
William Shakespeare

PART ONE

William Shakespeare

PART ONE

PART ONE

Three horsemen rode out from the edge of the forest with a restrained eagerness that not even weary weeks of constant searching could dull.

They reined in, stirrup to stirrup, and looked down into another shallow valley. Each stalk of the dry winter grass bore a fluffy seed-head of a lovely pale rose colour, and the light breeze stirred them and made them dance, so that the herd of sable antelope in the gut of the valley seemed to float belly-deep in a bank of swirling pink mist.

There was a single herd bull. He stood almost fourteen hands tall at the withers. His satiny back and shoulders were black as a panther's, but his belly and the intricate designs of his face-mask were the startling iridescent white of mother-of-pearl. His great ridged horns, curved like Saladin's scimitar, swept back to touch his croup, and his neck was proudly arched as that of a blood Arabian stallion. Long ago hunted to extinction in his former southern ranges, this noblest of all the antelopes of Africa had come to symbolize for Ralph Ballantyne this wild and beautiful new land between the Limpopo and the wide green Zambezi rivers.

The great black bull stared arrogantly at the horsemen on the ridge above him, then snorted and tossed his war-like head. Thick dark mane flying, sharp hooves clattering over the stony ground, he led his chocolate-coloured brood mares at a gallop up and over the far ridge, leaving the watching men mute at their grandeur and their beauty.

Ralph Ballantyne was first to rouse himself and he turned in the saddle towards his father.

'Well, Papa,' he asked, 'do you recognize any landmarks?'

'It was more than thirty years ago,' Zouga Ballantyne

3

murmured, a little frown of concentration puckering an arrowhead in the centre of his forehead, 'thirty years, and I was riddled with malaria.' Then he turned to the third rider, the little wizened Hottentot, his companion and servant since those far-off days. 'What do you think, Jan Cheroot?'

The Hottentot lifted the battered regimental cap from his head, and smoothed the little peppercorns of pure white wool that covered his scalp. 'Perhaps—'

Ralph cut in brusquely, 'Perhaps it was all merely a fever dream.'

The frown on his father's handsome bearded features sharpened, and the scar upon his cheek flushed from bone-porcelain to rose, while Jan Cheroot grinned with anticipation; when these two were together it was better entertainment than a cock-fight any day.

'Damn it, boy,' Zouga snapped. 'Why don't you go back to the wagons and keep the women company.' Zouga drew the thin chain from his fob pocket and dangled it before his son's face. 'There it is,' he snapped, 'that's the proof.'

On the ring of the chain hung a small bunch of keys, and other oddments, a gold seal, a St Christopher, a cigar-cutter and an irregular lump of quartz the size of a ripe grape. This last was mottled like fine blue marble and starred through its centre with a thick wedge of gleaming native metal.

'Raw red gold,' said Zouga. 'Ripe for the picking!'

Ralph grinned at his father, but it was an insolent and provocative grin, for he was bored. Weeks of wandering and fruitless searching were not Ralph's style at all.

'I always suspected that you picked that up from a pedlar's stall on the Grand Parade at Cape Town, and that it's only fool's gold anyway.'

The scar on his father's cheek turned a darker furious red, and Ralph laughed delightedly and clasped Zouga's shoulder.

'Oh, Papa, if I truly believed that, do you think I would waste weeks of my time? What with the railroad building and the dozen other balls I am juggling, would I be here, instead of in Johannesburg or Kimberley?'

He shook Zouga's shoulder gently, the smile no longer mocking. 'It's here – we both know it. We could be standing on the reef at this very moment, or it could be just over the next ridge.'

Slowly the heat went out of Zouga's scar, and Ralph went on evenly. 'The trick, of course, is to find it again. We could stumble over it in the next hour, or search another ten years.'

Watching father and son, Jan Cheroot felt a small prick of disappointment. He had seen them fight once before, but that was long ago. Ralph was now in the full prime of his manhood, almost thirty years of age, accustomed to handling the hundreds of rough men that he employed in his transport company and his construction teams, handling them with tongue and boot and fist. He was big and hard and strutty as a game cock, but Jan Cheroot suspected that the old dog would still be able to roll the puppy in the dust. The praise name that the Matabele had given Zouga Ballantyne was 'Bakela', the Fist, and he was still fast and lean. Yes, Jan Cheroot decided regretfully, it would still be worth watching, but perhaps another day, for already the flare of tempers had faded and the two men were again talking quietly and eagerly, leaning from their saddles towards each other. Now they seemed more like brothers, for although the family resemblance was unmistakable, yet Zouga did not seem old enough to be Ralph's father. His skin was too clear and unlined, his eye too quick and vital and the faint lacing of silver in his golden beard might have been merely the bleaching of the fierce African sun.

'If only you had been able to get a sun-sight, the other observations you made were all so accurate,' Ralph lamented. 'I was able to go directly to every cache of ivory that you left that year.'

'By that time the rains had started.' Zouga shook his

5

head. 'And, by God, how it rained! We hadn't seen the sun for a week, every river was in full spate, so we were marching in circles, trying to find a ford—' He broke off, and lifted the reins in his left hand. 'But I've told the tale a hundred times. Let's get on with the search,' he suggested quietly, and they trotted down off the ridge into the valley, Zouga stooping from the saddle to examine the ground for chips of broken reef, or swivelling slowly to survey the skyline to try and recognize the shape of the crests or the blue loom of a distant kopje against the towering African sky, where the silver fair-weather cumulus sailed high and serene.

'The only definite landmark we have to work on is the site of the ruins of Great Zimbabwe,' Zouga muttered. 'We marched eight days due westwards from the ruins.'

'Nine days,' Jan Cheroot corrected him. 'You lost one day when Matthew died. You were in fever. I had to nurse you like a baby, and we were carrying that damned stone bird.'

'We couldn't have made good more than ten miles a day,' Zouga ignored him. 'Eight days' march, not more than eighty miles.'

'And Great Zimbabwe is there. Due east of us now.' Ralph reined in his horse as they came out on the next ridge. 'That is the Sentinel.' He pointed at a rocky kopje, the distant blue summit shaped like a crouching lion. 'The ruins are just beyond, I would never mistake that view.'

For both father and son the ruined city had a special significance. There within the massive stone-built walls Zouga and Jan Cheroot had found the ancient graven bird images that had been abandoned by the long-vanished inhabitants. Despite the desperate straits to which they had been reduced by fever and the other hardships of the long expedition from the Zambezi river in the north, Zouga had insisted on carrying away with him one of the statues.

Then many years later it had been Ralph's turn. Guided by his father's diary and the meticulous sextant observations

6

that it contained, Ralph had once again won through to the deserted citadel. Though he had been pursued by the border impis of Lobengula, the Matabele king, he had defied the king's taboo on the holy place and had spirited away the remaining statues. Thus all three men had intimate knowledge of those haunting and haunted ruins, and as they stared at the far hills that marked the site, they were silent with their memories.

'I still wonder, who were the men who built Zimbabwe?' Ralph asked at last. 'And what happened to them?' There was an uncharacteristic dreamy tone to his voice, and he expected no answer. 'Were they the Queen of Sheba's miners? Was this the Ophir of the Bible? Did they carry the gold they mined to Solomon?'

'Perhaps we will never know.' Zouga roused himself. But we do know they valued gold as we do. I found gold foil and beads and bars of bullion in the courtyard of Great Zimbabwe, and it must be within a few miles of where we stand that Jan Cheroot and I explored the shafts that they drove into the earth, and found the broken reef piled in dumps ready for crushing.' Zouga glanced across at the little Hottentot. 'Do you recognize any of this?'

The dark pixie face wrinkled up like a sun-dried prune as Jan Cheroot considered. 'Perhaps from the next ridge,' he muttered lugubriously, and the trio rode down into the valley that looked like a hundred others they had crossed in the preceding weeks.

Ralph was a dozen strides ahead of the others, cantering easily, swinging his mount to skirt a thicket of the dense wild ebony, when abruptly he stood in the stirrups, snatched his hat from his head and waved it high.

'Tally ho!' he yelled. 'Gone away!'

And Zouga saw the burnt gold flash of fluid movement across the far slope of open ground.

'Three of the devils!' Ralph's excitement and his loathing were clear in the pitch and timbre of his voice. 'Jan Cheroot,

7

you turn 'em on the left! Papa, stop them crossing the ravine!'

The easy manner of command came naturally to Ralph Ballantyne, and the two older men accepted it as naturally, while none of them questioned for an instant why they should destroy the magnificent animals that Ralph had flushed from the ebony thicket. Ralph owned two hundred wagons, each drawn by sixteen draught oxen. King's Lynn, Zouga's estates, taken up with the land grants that the British South Africa Company had issued to the volunteers who had destroyed the Matabele king's impis, covered many tens of thousands of acres that were stocked with the pick of the captured Matabele breeding herds running with blood bulls imported from Good Hope and old England.

Father and son were both cattlemen, and they had suffered the terrible depredations of the lion prides which infested this lovely land north of the Limpopo and Shashi rivers. Too often they had heard their valuable and beloved beasts bellowing in agony in the night, and in the dawn found their ravaged carcasses. To both of them, lions were the worst kind of vermin, and they were elated with this rare chance of taking a pride in broad daylight.

Ralph yanked the repeating Winchester rifle from the leather scabbard under his left knee, as he urged the chestnut gelding into full gallop after the big yellow cats. The lion had been the first away, and Ralph had only a glimpse of him, sway-backed and swing-bellied, the dense dark ruff of his mane fluffed out with alarm, padding majestically on heavy paws into the scrub. The older lioness followed him swiftly. She was lean and scarred from a thousand hunts, blue with age across the shoulders and back. She went away at a bounding gallop. However, the younger lioness, unaccustomed to men, was bold and curious as a cat. She was still faintly cub-spotted across her creamy gold belly, and she turned on the edge of the thicket to snarl at the pursuing horseman. Her ears lay flat against her skull, her furry pink tongue curled out over her fangs, and her whiskers were white and stiff as porcupine quills.

Ralph dropped his reins onto the gelding's neck, and the horse responded instantly by plunging to a dead stop and freezing for the shot, only the scissoring of his ears betraying his agitation.

Ralph tossed up the Winchester and fired as the buttplate slapped into his shoulder. The lioness grunted explosively as the bullet thumped into her shoulder, angled for the heart. She went up in a high sunfishing somersault, roaring in her death frenzy. She fell and rolled on her back, tearing at the scrub with fully extended yellow claws, and then stretching out in a last shuddering convulsion before slumping into the softness of death.

Ralph pumped a fresh round into the chamber of the Winchester, and gathered up the reins. The gelding leaped forward.

Out on the right Zouga was pounding up the lip of the ravine, leaning forward in the saddle, and at that moment the second lioness broke into the open ahead of him, going for the deep brush-choked ravine at a driving run, and Zouga fired still at full gallop. Ralph saw dust spurt under the animal's belly.

'Low and left. Papa is getting old,' Ralph thought derisively, and brought the gelding crashing down to a stiff-legged halt. Before he could fire, Zouga had shot again, and the lioness collapsed and rolled like a yellow ball on the stony earth, shot through the neck a hand's span behind the ear.

'Bully for you!' Ralph laughed with excitement, and kicked his heels into the gelding's flank as they charged up the slope, shoulder to shoulder.

'Where is Jan Cheroot?' Zouga shouted, and as if in reply they heard the clap of rifle fire in the forest on the left, and they swung the horses in that direction.

'Can you see him?' Ralph called.

The bush was thicker ahead of them, and the thorn branches whipped at their thighs as they passed. There was a second shot, and immediately afterwards the furious ear-numbing roars of the lion mingled with Jan Cheroot's shrill squeals of terror.

'He is in trouble!' Zouga called anxiously, as they burst out of the thick scrub.

Before them there lay parkland, fine open grass beneath the tall flat-topped acacia trees along the crest of the ridge. A hundred yards ahead Jan Cheroot was tearing along the crest, twisted in the saddle to look over his shoulder, his face a mask of terror, his eyes huge and glistening white. He had lost his hat and rifle, but he was lashing his mount across the neck and shoulders, although the animal was already at a wild uncontrolled gallop.

The lion was a dozen strides behind them, but gaining with each elastic bound as though they were standing still. Its heaving flank was painted slick and shiny with bright new blood, shot through the guts, but the wound had not crippled nor even slowed the beast. Rather it had maddened him, so that the solid blasts of sound from his throat sounded like the thunder of the skies.

Ralph swerved his gelding to try and intercept the little Hottentot, and alter the angle to give himself an open shot at the lion, but at that moment the cat came up out of its flat snaking charge, reared up over the bunched and straining quarters of the horse and raked them with long curved talons so that the sweat-darkened hide opened in deep parallel wounds, and the blood smoked from them in a fine crimson cloud.

The horse shrieked and lashed out with its hind hooves, catching the lion in his chest, so that he reeled and lost a stride. Immediately he gathered himself and came again, quartering in beside the running horse, his eyes inscrutably yellow as he prepared to leap astride the panic-driven animal.

'Jump, Jan Cheroot!' Ralph yelled. The lion was too close to risk a shot. 'Jump, damn you!' But Jan Cheroot did not appear to have heard him, he was clinging helplessly to the tangled flying mane, paralysed with fear.

The lion rose lightly into the air, and settled like a huge yellow bird on the horse's back, crushing Jan Cheroot beneath his massive, blood-streaked body. At that instant, horse and rider and lion seemed to disappear into the very earth, and there was only a swirling column of dust to mark where they had been. Yet the shattering roars of the enraged animal and Jan Cheroot's howls of terror grew even louder as Ralph galloped up to the point on the ridge where they had disappeared.

With the Winchester in one hand he kicked his feet from the stirrup irons and jumped from the saddle, letting his own momentum throw him forward until he stood on the edge of a sheer-sided pitfall at the bottom of which lay a tangle of heaving bodies.

'The devil is killing me!' screamed Jan Cheroot, and Ralph could see him pinned beneath the body of the horse. The horse must have broken its neck in the fall, it was a lifeless heap with head twisted up under its shoulder and the lion was ripping the carcass and saddle, trying to reach Jan Cheroot.

'Lie still,' Ralph shouted down at him. 'Give me a clear shot!'

But it was the lion that heard him. He left the horse and came up the vertical side of the pit with the ease of a cat climbing a tree, his glossy muscular hindquarters driving him lightly upwards and his pale yellow eyes fastened upon Ralph as he stood on the lip of the deep hole.

Ralph dropped on one knee to steady himself for the shot, and aimed down into the broad golden chest. The jaws were wide open, the fangs long as a man's forefinger and white as polished ivory, the deafening clamour from the open throat dinned into Ralph's face. He could smell the

11

rotten-flesh taint of the lion's breath and flecks of hot saliva splattered against his cheeks and forehead.

He fired, and pumped the loading-handle and fired again, so swiftly that the shots were a continuous blast of sound. The lion arched backwards, hung for a long moment from the wall of the pit, and then toppled and fell back upon the dead horse.

Now there was no movement from the bottom of the pit, and the silence was more intense than the shattering uproar that had preceded it.

'Jan Cheroot, are you all right?' Ralph called anxiously.

There was no sign of the little Hottentot, he was completely smothered by the carcasses of horse and lion.

'Jan Cheroot, can you hear me?'

The reply was in a hollow, sepulchral whisper. 'Dead men cannot hear – it's all over, they have got old Jan Cheroot at last.'

'Come out from under there,' Zouga Ballantyne ordered, as he stepped up to Ralph's shoulder. 'This is no time to play the clown, Jan Cheroot.'

R alph dropped a coil of manilla rope down to Jan Cheroot, and between them they hauled him and the saddle from the dead horse to the surface.

The excavation into which Jan Cheroot had fallen was a deep narrow trench along the crest of the ridge. In places it was twenty feet deep, but never more than six feet wide. Mostly it was choked with creepers and rank vegetation, but this could not disguise the certainty that it had been dug by men.

'The reef was exposed along this line,' Zouga guessed, as they followed the edge of the old trench, 'the ancient miners simply dug it out and did not bother to refill.'

12

'How did they blast the reef?' Ralph demanded. 'That's solid rock down there.'

'They probably built fires upon it, and then quenched it with water. The contraction cracked the rock.'

'Well, they seem to have taken out every grain of the ore body and left nary a speck for us.'

Zouga nodded. 'They would have worked out this section first, and then when the reef pinched out they would have started sinking potholes along the strike to try and intercept it again.' Zouga turned to Jan Cheroot and demanded, 'Now do you recognize this place, Jan Cheroot?' And when the Hottentot hesitated, he pointed down the slope. 'The swamp in the valley down there, and the teak trees—'

'Yes, yes.' Jan Cheroot clapped his hands, and his eyes twinkled with delight. 'This is the same place where you killed the bull elephant – the tusks are on the stoep at King's Lynn.'

'The ancient dump will be just ahead.' Zouga hurried forward.

He found the low mound covered by grass, and went down on his knees to scrabble amongst the grass roots, picking out the chips of white sugar quartz, examining each one swiftly and discarding it. Occasionally he wet one with his tongue, held it to the sunlight to try and highlight the sparkle of metal, then frowned and shook his head with disappointment.

At last he stood and wiped his hands on his breeches.

'It's quartz all right, but the ancient miners must have hand-sorted this dump. We will have to find the old shafts if we want to see visible gold in the ore.'

From the top of the ancient dump Zouga orientated himself rapidly.

'The carcass of the bull elephant fell about there,' he pointed, and to confirm it Jan Cheroot searched in the grass and lifted a huge thighbone, dry and white as chalk, and at last after thirty years beginning to crumble.

'He was the father of all elephant,' Jan Cheroot said reverently. 'There will never be another like him, and it was he that led us to this place. When you shot him he fell here to mark it for us.'

Zouga turned a quarter-circle and pointed again. 'The ancient shaft where we buried old Matthew will be there.'

Ralph recalled the elephant hunt as his father had described it in his celebrated book *A Hunter's Odyssey*. The black gunbearer had not flinched from the great bull elephant's charge, but had stood it down and handed Zouga the second gun, sacrificing his own life for that of his master. So Ralph understood and remained silent, as Zouga went down on one knee beside the rock pile that marked the gunbearer's grave.

After a minute, Zouga rose and dusted off his knee, and said simply, 'He was a good man.'

'Good, but stupid,' Jan Cheroot agreed. 'A wise man would have run.'

'And a wise man would have chosen a better grave,' Ralph murmured. 'He is plumb in the centre of a gold reef. We will have to dig him out.'

But Zouga frowned. 'Let him lie. There are other shafts along the strike.' He turned away, and the others followed him. A hundred yards farther on, Zouga stopped again. 'Here!' he called with satisfaction. 'The second shaft – there were four of them altogether.'

This opening had also been refilled with chunks of native rock. Ralph shrugged off his jacket, propped his rifle against the bole of the nearest tree and climbed down into the shallow depression until he stooped over the narrow blocked entrance.

'I'm going to open it up.'

They worked for half an hour, prising loose the boulders with a branch of a leadwood and manhandling them aside

14

until they had exposed the square opening to the shaft. It was narrow, so narrow that only a child could have passed through it. They knelt and peered down into it. There was no telling how deep it was, for it was impenetrably black in the depths and it stank of damp, of fungus and bats, and of rotting things.

Ralph and Zouga stared into the opening with a horrid fascination.

'They say the ancients used child slaves or captured Bushmen in the workings,' Zouga murmured.

'We have to know if the reef is down there,' Ralph whispered. 'But no grown man—' he broke off and there was another moment of thoughtful silence, before Zouga and Ralph glanced at each other and smiled, and then both their heads turned in unison towards Jan Cheroot.

'Never!' said the little Hottentot fiercely. 'I am a sick old man. Never! You will have to kill me first!'

Ralph found a stump of candle in his saddlebag, while Zouga swiftly spliced together the three coils of rope used for tethering the horses, and Jan Cheroot watched their preparation like a condemned man watching the construction of the gallows.

'For twenty-nine years, since the day I was born, you have been telling me of your courage and daring,' Ralph reminded him, as he placed an arm around Jan Cheroot's shoulder and led him gently back to the mouth of the shaft.

'Perhaps I exaggerated a little,' Jan Cheroot admitted, as Zouga knotted the rope under his armpits and strapped a saddlebag around his tiny waist.

'You, who have fought wild men and hunted elephant and lion – what can you fear in this little hole? A few snakes, a little darkness, the ghosts of dead men, that's all.'

'Perhaps I exaggerated more than a little,' Jan Cheroot whispered huskily.

'You are not a coward are you, Jan Cheroot?'

'Yes,' Jan Cheroot nodded fervently. 'That is exactly what I am, and this is no place for a coward.'

Ralph drew him back, struggling like a hooked catfish on the end of the rope, lifted him easily and lowered him into the shaft. His protests faded gradually as Ralph paid out the rope.

Ralph was measuring the rope across the reach of his outstretched arms. Reckoning each span at six feet, he had lowered the little Hottentot a little under sixty feet before the rope went slack.

'Jan Cheroot!' Zouga bellowed down the shaft.

'A little cave.' Jan Cheroot's voice was muffled and distorted by echoes. 'I can just stand. The reef is black with soot.'

'Cooking fires. The slaves would have been kept down there,' Zouga guessed, 'never seeing the light of day again until they died.' Then he raised his voice. 'What else?'

'Ropes, plaited grass ropes, and buckets, leather buckets like we used on the diamond diggings at New Rush—' Jan Cheroot broke off with an exclamation. 'They fall to pieces when I touch them, just dust now.' Faintly they could hear Jan Cheroot sneezing and coughing in the dust he had raised and his voice was thickened and nasal as he went on, 'Iron tools, something like an adze,' and when he called again they could hear the tremor in his voice. 'Name of the great snake, there are dead men here, dead men's bones. I am coming up – pull me up!'

Staring down the narrow shaft, Ralph could see the light of the candle flame wavering and trembling at the bottom.

'Jan Cheroot, is there a tunnel leading off from the cave?'

'Pull me up.'

'Can you see a tunnel?'

'Yes, now will you pull me up?'

'Not until you follow the tunnel to the end.'

'Are you mad? I would have to crawl on hands and knees.'

'Take one of the iron tools with you, to break a piece off the reef.'

'No. That is enough. I go no farther, not with dead men guarding this place.'

'Very well,' Ralph bellowed into the hole, 'then I will throw the end of the rope down on top of you.'

'You would not do that!'

'After that I will put the rocks back over the entrance.'

'I am going.' Jan Cheroot's voice had a desperate edge, and once again the rope began slithering down into the shaft like a serpent into its nest.

Ralph and Zouga squatted beside the shaft, passing their last cheroot back and forth and waiting with ill grace and impatience.

'When they deserted these workings, they must have sealed the slaves in the shaft. A slave was a valuable chattel, so that proves they were still working the reef and that they left in great haste.' Zouga paused, cocked his head to listen and then said, 'Ah!' with satisfaction. From the depths of the earth at their feet came the distant clank of metal tool on living rock. 'Jan Cheroot has reached the working-face.'

However, it was many minutes more before they saw the wavering candle light in the bottom of the pit again and Jan Cheroot's pleas, quavering and pitiful, came up to them.

'Please, Master Ralph, I have done it. Now will you pull me up, please?'

Ralph stood with one booted foot on each side of the shaft, and hauled in the rope hand over hand. The muscles of his arms bulged and subsided under the sleeves of his thin cotton shirt, as he lifted the Hottentot and his burden to the surface without a pause, and when he had finished, Ralph's breathing was still even and quiet and there was not a single bead of perspiration on his face.

'So, Jan Cheroot, what did you find?'

Jan Cheroot was coated all over with fine pale dust through which his sweat had cut muddy runnels and he stank of bat guano and the mushroom odour of long-deserted caves. With hands that still shook with fear and exhaustion, he opened the flap of the saddlebag at his waist.

'This is what I found,' he croaked, and Zouga took a lump of the raw rough rock from him.

It had a crystalline texture, that glittered like ice and was marbled with blue and riven by minute flaws and fissures, some of which had cracked through under the pounding of the iron adze with which Jan Cheroot had hacked it from the rock face. However, the shattered fragments of shining quartz were held together by the substance that had filled every crack and fault line in the ore. This cement was a thin malleable layer of bright metal, that twinkled in the sunlight when Zouga wet it with the tip of his tongue.

'By God, Ralph, will you look at that!' And Ralph took it from his father's hand with the reverence of a worshipper receiving the sacrament.

'Gold!' he whispered, and it sparkled at him, that lovely yellow smile that had captivated men almost from the time they had first stood upon their hind legs.

'Gold!' Ralph repeated.

To find this glimmer of precious metal they had laboured most of their lives, father and son, they had ridden far and, in the company of other freebooters, had fought bloody battles, had helped destroy a proud nation and hunt a king to a lonely death.

Led by a sick man with swollen crippled heart and grandiose dreams, they had seized a vast land that now bore that giant's name, Rhodesia, and they had forced the land to yield up, one by one, its riches. They had taken its wide sweet pastures and lovely mountain ranges, its forests of fine native timber, its herds of sleek cattle, its legions of sturdy black men who for a pittance would provide the thews to

18

gather in the vast harvest. And now at last they held the ultimate treasure in their hands.

'Gold!' Ralph said for the third time.

They struck their pegs along the ridge, cutting them from the living acacia trees that oozed clear sap from the axe cuts, and they hammered them into the hard earth with the flat of the blade. Then they built cairns of stone to mark the corner of each claim.

Under the Fort Victoria Agreement, which both of them had signed when they volunteered to ride against Lobengula's impis, they were each entitled to ten gold claims. This naturally did not apply to Jan Cheroot. Despite the fact that he had ridden into Matabeleland with Jameson's flying column and shot down the Matabele *amadoda* at the Shangani river and the Bembesi crossing with as much gusto as had his masters, yet he was a man of colour, and as such he could not share the spoils.

In addition to the booty to which Zouga and Ralph were entitled under the Victoria Agreement, both of them had bought up many blocks of claims from the dissolute and spendthrift troopers of Jameson's conquering force, some of whom had sold for the price of a bottle of whisky. So between them they could peg off the entire ridge and most of the valley bottoms on each side of it.

It was hard work, but urgent, for there were other prospectors abroad, one of whom could have followed their tracks. They worked through the heat of noon and by the light of the moon until sheer exhaustion forced them to drop their axes and sleep where they fell. On the fourth evening, they could stop at last, content that they had secured the entire reef for themselves. There was no gap between their pegs into which another prospector could jump.

19

'Jan Cheroot, there is only one bottle of whisky left,' Zouga groaned, and stretched his aching shoulders, 'but tonight I am going to let you pour your own dop.'

They watched with amusement the elaborate precautions which Jan Cheroot took to get the last drop into his brimming mug. In the process, the line around the bottom that marked his daily grog ration was entirely ignored, and when the mug was full, he did not trust the steadiness of his own hand but slurped up the first mouthful on all fours like a dog.

Ralph retrieved the bottle, and ruefully considered the remnants of the liquor before pouring a dram for his father and himself.

'The Harkness Mine,' Zouga gave them the toast.

'Why do you call it that?' Ralph demanded, when he lowered his mug and wiped his moustache with the back of his hand.

'Old Tom Harkness gave me the map that led me to it,' Zouga replied.

'We could find a better name.'

'Perhaps, but that's the one I want.'

'The gold will be just as bright, I expect,' Ralph capitulated, and carefully moved the whisky bottle out of the little Hottentot's reach, for Jan Cheroot had drained his mug already. 'I am glad we are doing something together again, Papa.' Ralph settled down luxuriously against his saddle.

'Yes,' Zouga agreed softly. 'It's been too long since we worked side by side in the diamond pit at New Rush.'

'I know just the right fellow to open up the workings for us. He is a top man, the best on the Witwatersrand goldfields, and I'll have my wagons bringing up the machinery before the rains break.'

It was part of their agreement that Ralph would provide the men and machinery and money to run the Harkness Mine when Zouga led him to it. For Ralph was a rich man. Some said he was already a millionaire, though Zouga knew

20

that was unlikely. Nevertheless, Zouga remembered that Ralph had provided the transport and commissariat for both the Mashonaland column and the Matabeleland expedition against Lobengula, and for each he had been paid huge sums by Mr Rhodes' British South Africa Company, not in cash but in company shares. Like Zouga himself, he had speculated by buying up original land grants from the thriftless drifters that made up the bulk of the original column and had paid them in whisky, carried up from the railhead in his own wagons. Ralph's Rhodesia Lands Company owned more land than did even Zouga himself.

Ralph had also speculated in the shares of the British South Africa Company. In those heady days when the column first reached Fort Salisbury, he had sold shares that Mr Rhodes had issued to him at £1 for the sum of £3-15s-0d on the London stock market. Then, when the pioneers' vaunting hopes and optimism had withered on the sour veld and barren ore bodies of Mashonaland, and Rhodes and Jameson were secretly planning their war against the Matabele king, Ralph had re-purchased British South Africans at eight shillings. He had then seen them quoted at £8 when the column rode into the burning ruins of Lobengula's kraal at GuBulawayo and the Company had added the entire realm of the Matabele monarch to its possessions.

Now, listening to his son talk with that infectious energy and charisma which even those hard days and nights of physical labour on the claims could not dull, Zouga reflected that Ralph had laid the telegraph lines from Kimberley to Fort Salisbury, that his construction gangs were at this moment laying the railway lines across the same wilderness towards Bulawayo, that his two hundred wagons carried trade goods to more than a hundred of Ralph's own trading-posts scattered across Bechuanaland and Matabeleland and Mashonaland, that as of today Ralph was a half-owner of a gold mine that promised to be as rich as any on the fabulous Witwatersrand.

Zouga smiled to himself as he listened to Ralph talk in the flickering firelight, and he thought suddenly, 'Damn it, but they might be right after all – the puppy might just possibly be a millionaire already.' And his pride was tinged with envy. Zouga himself had worked and dreamed from long before Ralph was born, had made sacrifices and had suffered hardships that still made him shudder when he thought about them, all for much lesser reward. Apart from this new reef, all he had to show for a lifetime of striving was King's Lynn and Louise – and then he smiled. With those two possessions, he was richer than Mr Rhodes would ever be.

Zouga sighed and tilted his hat forward over his eyes, and with Louise's beloved face held firmly in the eye of his mind he drifted into sleep, while across the fire Ralph still talked quietly, for himself more than for his father, and conjured up new visions of wealth and power.

It was two full days' ride back to the wagons, but they were still half a mile from the camp when they were spotted, and a joyous tide of servants and children and dogs and wives came clamouring out to greet them.

Ralph spurred forward and leaned low from the saddle to sweep Cathy up onto the pommel so violently that her hair tumbled into her face and she shrieked breathlessly until he silenced her with a kiss full on the mouth, and he held the kiss unashamedly while little Jonathan danced impatiently around the horse shouting, 'Me too! Lift me up, too, Papa!'

When at last he broke the kiss, Ralph held her close still, and his stiff dark moustache tickled her ear as he whispered, 'The minute I get you into the tent, Katie my love, we will give that new mattress of yours a stiff test.'

She flushed a richer tone of pink and tried to slap his cheek, but the blow was light and loving. Ralph chuckled, then reached down and picked Jonathan up by one arm and dropped him into the gelding's croup behind the saddle.

The boy wrapped his arms around Ralph's waist and demanded in a high piping voice: 'Did you find gold, Papa?'

'A ton.'

'Did you shoot any lions?'

'A hundred.'

'Did you kill any Matabele?'

'The season's closed,' Ralph laughed, and ruffled his son's dark thick curls, but Cathy scolded quickly.

'That's a wicked thing to ask your father, you blood-thirsty little pagan.'

Louise followed the younger woman and the child at a more sedate pace, stepping lightly and lithely in the thick dust of the wagon road. Her hair was drawn back from her broad forehead and hung down her back to the level of her waist in a thick braid. It emphasized the high arches of her cheekbones.

Her eyes had changed colour again. It always fascinated Zouga to see the shifts of her mood reflected in those huge slanted eyes. Now they were a lighter softer blue, the colour of happiness. She stopped at the horse's head and Zouga stepped down from the stirrup and lifted the hat from his head, studying her gravely for a moment before he spoke.

'Even in such a short time I had forgotten how truly beautiful you are,' he said.

'It was not a short time,' she contradicted him. 'Every hour I am away from you is an eternity.'

It was an elaborate camp, for this was Cathy and Ralph's home. They owned no other, but like gypsies moved to where the pickings were richest. There were four wagons outspanned under the tall arched wild fig trees on the bank of the river above the ford. The tents were of new snowy canvas, one of which, set a little apart, served for ablution. This contained a galvanized iron bath in which one could stretch out full length. There was a servant whose sole duty was to tend the forty-gallon drum on the fire behind the tent and to deliver unlimited quantities of hot water, day and night. Another smaller tent beyond held a commode whose seat Cathy had hand-painted with cupids and bouquets of roses, and beside the commode she had placed the ultimate luxury, scented sheets of soft coloured paper in a sandalwood box.

There were horse-hair mattresses on each cot, comfortable canvas chairs to sit on, and a long trestle-table to eat off under the fly of the open-sided dining tent. There were canvas coolers for the champagne and lemonade bottles, food safes screened with insect-proof gauze, and thirty servants. Servants to cut wood and tend fires, servants to wash and iron so that the women could change their clothing daily, others to make the bed and sweep up every fallen leaf from the bare ground between the tents and then sprinkle it with water to lay the dust, one to wait exclusively upon Master Jonathan, to feed him and bathe him and ride him on a shoulder or sing to him when he grew petulant. Servants to cook the food and to wait upon the table, servants to light the lanterns and lace up the flies of the tents at nightfall and even one to empty the bucket of the hand-painted commode whenever the little bell tinkled.

Ralph rode in through the gate of the high thornbush stockade that surrounded the entire camp to protect it from the nocturnal visits of the lion prides. Cathy was still on the saddle in front of him and his son up behind.

He looked about the camp with satisfaction, and squeezed Cathy's waist. 'By God, it's good to be home, a hot bath, and you can scrub my back, Katie.' He broke off, and exclaimed with surprise. 'Damn it, woman! You might have warned me!'

'You never gave me a chance,' she protested.

Parked at the end of the row of wagons was a closed coach, a vehicle with sprung wheels, the windows fitted with teak shutters that could be raised against the heat. The body of the coach was painted a cool and delightful green under the dust and dried mud of hard travel, the doors were picked out in gold leaf and the high wheels piped with the same gold. The interior was finished in glossy green leather with gold tassels on the curtains. There were fitted leather and brass steamer trunks strapped to the roof rack, and beyond the coach in Ralph's kraal of thornbush, the big white mules, all carefully matched for colour and size, were feeding on bundles of fresh grass that Ralph's servants had cut along the river bank.

'How did Himself find us?' Ralph demanded, as he let Cathy down to the ground. He did not have to ask who the visitor was, this magnificent equipage was famous across the continent.

'We are camped only a mile from the main road up from the south,' Cathy pointed out tartly. 'He could hardly miss us.'

'And he has his whole gang with him, by the looks of it,' Ralph muttered. There were two dozen blood horses in the kraal with the white mules.

'All the king's horses and all the king's men,' Cathy agreed, and at that moment Zouga hurried in through the gate with Louise on his arm. He was as excited by their visitor as Ralph was irritated.

'Louise tells me that he has broken his journey especially to talk to me.'

'You had better not keep him waiting then, Papa,' Ralph grinned sardonically. It was strange how all men, even the aloof and cool-headed Major Zouga Ballantyne, came under the spell that their visitor wove. Ralph prided himself that he alone was able to resist it, although at times it required a conscious effort.

Zouga was striding eagerly down the row of wagons towards the inner stockade with Louise skipping to keep up with him. Ralph dawdled deliberately, admiring the remarkable animals that Jonathan had moulded from river clay and now paraded for his approbation.

'Beautiful hippos, Jon-Jon! Not hippo? Oh, I see, the horns fell off, did they? Well then, they are the most beautiful, fattest hornless kudu that I have ever seen.'

Cathy tugged at his arm at last. 'You know he wants to speak to you also, Ralph,' she urged, and Ralph swung Jonathan up onto his shoulder, took Cathy on his other arm, for he knew that such a display of domesticity would irritate the man they were going to meet, and sauntered into the inner stockade of the camp.

The canvas sides of the dining marquee had been rolled up to allow the cool afternoon breeze to blow through it, and there were half a dozen men seated at the long trestle-table. In the centre of the group was a hulking figure, dressed in an ill-fitting jacket of expensive English cloth that was closed to the top button. The knot of his necktie had slipped and the colours of Oriel College were dulled with the dust of the long road up from the diamond city of Kimberley.

Even Ralph, whose feelings for this ungainly giant of a man were ambivalent, hostility mixed with a grudging admiration, was shocked by the changes that a few short years had wrought on him. The meaty features seemed to have sagged from the raw bones of his face, his colour was high and unhealthy. He was barely forty years of age, yet his moustache and sideburns had faded from ruddy blond to dull silver, and he looked fifteen years older. Only the pale blue eyes retained their force and mystic visionary glitter.

'Well, how are you, Ralph?' His voice was high and clear, incongruous in such a big body.

'Good afternoon, Mr Rhodes,' Ralph replied, and despite himself let his son slip from his shoulder and lowered him gently to the ground. Instantly the child darted away.

'How is my railway progressing, while you are out here enjoying yourself?'

'Ahead of schedule and below budget,' Ralph countered the barely veiled rebuke, and with a small effort broke the hypnotic gaze of those blue eyes and glanced at the men who flanked Mr Rhodes.

On his right was the great man's shadow, small, narrow-shouldered and as neatly dressed as his master was untidy. He had the prim but nondescript features of a schoolmaster, and receding wispy hair, but keen and acquisitive eyes that gave the lie to the rest of it.

'Jameson,' Ralph nodded coolly at him, using neither Doctor Leander Starr Jameson's title nor the more familiar and affectionate 'Doctor Jim'.

'Young Ballantyne.' Jameson slightly emphasized the diminutive and gave it a faintly derogatory twist. From the very first, their hostility had been mutual and instinctive.

From Rhodes' left rose a younger man with straight back and broad shoulders, an open handsome face and a friendly smile which showed big even white teeth.

'Hello, Ralph.' His handshake was firm and dry, his Kentucky accent easy and pleasant.

'Harry, I was speaking of you this very morning.' Ralph's pleasure was obvious, and he glanced at Zouga. 'Papa, this is Harry Mellow, the best mining engineer in Africa.'

Zouga nodded. 'We have been introduced.' And father and son exchanged a glance of understanding.

This young American was the one that Ralph had chosen to develop and operate the Harkness Mine. It meant little to Ralph that Harry Mellow, like most of the bright young bachelors of special promise in southern Africa, already worked for Cecil John Rhodes. Ralph intended to find the bait that would tempt him away.

'We must talk later, Harry,' he murmured, and turned to another young man seated at the end of the table.

'Jordan,' he exclaimed. 'By God, it's good to see you.'

The two brothers met and embraced, and Ralph made no effort to hide his affection, but then everybody loved Jordan.

They loved him not only for his golden beauty and gentle manner, but also for his many talents and for the warmth and real concern that he extended to all about him.

'Oh Ralph, I have so much to ask, and so much to tell you.' Jordan's delight was as intense as Ralph's.

'Later, Jordan,' Mr Rhodes broke in querulously. He did not like to be interrupted, and he waved Jordan back to his seat. Jordan went instantly. He had been Mr Rhodes' private secretary since he was nineteen years of age, and obedience to his master's least whim was part of his nature by now.

Rhodes glanced at Cathy and Louise. 'Ladies, I am sure you will find our discourse tedious, and you have urgent chores to attend to, I am certain.'

Cathy glanced up at her husband, and saw Ralph's quick annoyance at the artless presumption with which Mr Rhodes had taken over his camp and all within it. Surreptitiously Cathy squeezed his hand to calm him, and felt Ralph relax slightly. There was a limit to even Ralph's defiance. He might not be in Rhodes' employ, but the railway contract and a hundred cartage routes depended upon this man.

Then Cathy looked across at Louise, and saw that she was as piqued by the dismissal. There was a blue spark in her eyes and a faint heat under the fine freckles on her cheeks, but her voice was level and cool as she replied for both Cathy and herself, 'Of course you are correct, Mr Rhodes. Will you please excuse us.'

It was well known that Mr Rhodes was uncomfortable in the presence of females. He employed no female servants, would not allow a painting nor statue of a woman to decorate his ornate mansion at Groote Schuur in the Cape of Good Hope, he would not even employ a married man in a position close to his person, and immediately discharged even the most trusted employee who took the unforgivable plunge into matrimony. 'You cannot dance to a woman's whims and serve me at the same time,' he would explain as he fired an offender.

Now Rhodes beckoned Ralph. 'Sit here, where I can see you,' he commanded, and immediately turned back to Zouga, and began rapping out questions. His questions cut like the lash of a stock whip, but the attention with which he listened to the replies was evidence of the high regard he had for Zouga Ballantyne. Their relationship went back many years, to the early days of the diamond diggings at Colesberg kopje which had since been renamed Kimberley after the colonial secretary who accepted it into Her Majesty's dominions.

On those diggings Zouga had once worked claims which had yielded up the fabulous 'Ballantyne Diamond', but now Rhodes owned those claims, as he owned every single claim on the fields. Since then, Rhodes had employed Zouga as his personal agent at the kraal of Lobengula, King of the Matabele, for he spoke the language with colloquial fluency. When Doctor Jameson had led his flying column in that swift and victorious strike against the king, Zouga had ridden with him as one of his field officers and had been the first man into the burning kraal of GuBulawayo after the king had fled.

After Lobengula's death, Rhodes had appointed Zouga 'Custodian of Enemy Property', and Zouga had been responsible for rounding up the captured herds of Matabele cattle and redistributing them as booty to the company and to Jameson's volunteers.

Once Zouga had completed that task, Rhodes would have appointed him Chief Native Commissioner, to deal with the indunas of the Matabele, but Zouga had preferred to retire to his estates at King's Lynn with his new bride, and had let the job go to General Mungo St John. However, Zouga was still on the Board of the British South Africa Company, and Rhodes trusted him as he did few other men.

'Matabeleland is booming, Mr Rhodes,' Zouga reported. 'You will find Bulawayo is almost a city already, with its own school and hospital. There are already more than six hundred white women and children in Matabeleland, a sure sign that your settlers are here to stay at last. All the land grants have been taken up, and many of the farms are already being worked. The bloodstock from the Cape is taking to the local conditions and breeding well with the captured Matabele cattle.'

'What about the minerals, Ballantyne?'

'Over ten thousand claims have been registered, and I have seen some very rich crushings.' Zouga hesitated, glanced at Ralph, and when he nodded, turned back to Rhodes. 'Within the last few days, my son and I have rediscovered and pegged the ancient workings I first stumbled on in the sixties.'

'The Harkness Mine,' Rhodes nodded heavily, and even Ralph was impressed by the range and grasp of his mind. 'I remember your original description in *The Hunter's Odyssey*. Did you sample the reef?'

In reply, Zouga placed a dozen lumps of quartz upon the table in front of him, and the raw gold glistened so that the men around the table craned forward in rapt fascination. Mr Rhodes turned one of the samples in his big mottled hands before passing it to the American engineer.

'What do you make of these, Harry?'

'It will go fifty ounces a ton,' Harry whistled softly. 'Perhaps too rich, like Nome and Klondike.' The American looked up at Ralph. 'How thick is the reef? How broad is the strike?'

Ralph shook his head. 'I don't know, the workings are too narrow to get into the face.'

'This is quartz, of course, not the banket reef like we have on the Witwatersrand,' Harry Mellow murmured.

The banket reef was named after the sweetmeat of toffee and nuts and almonds and cloves which the conglomerated reef so much resembled. It was made up of the thick sedimentary beds of ancient buried lakes, not as rich in gold as this chip of quartz, but many feet thick and extending as wide as the broad lakes had once stretched, a mother lode which could be mined for a hundred years without exhausting its reserves.

'It's too rich,' Harry Mellow repeated, fondling the sample of quartz. 'I can't believe that it will be more than a stringer a few inches thick.'

'But if it isn't?' Rhodes demanded harshly.

The American smiled quietly. 'Then you will not only control nearly all the diamonds in the world, Mr Rhodes, but most of the gold as well.'

His words were a sharp reminder to Ralph that the British South Africa Company owned fifty per cent royalty in every ounce of gold mined in Matabeleland, and Ralph felt his resentment return in full force. Rhodes and his ubiquitous BSA Company were like a vast octopus that smothered the efforts and the fortunes of all lesser men.

'Will you allow Harry to ride with me for a few days, Mr Rhodes, so that he can examine the strike?' Ralph's irritation sharpened the tone of his request, so that Rhodes' big shaggy head lifted quickly and his pale blue eyes seemed to search out his soul for a moment before he nodded, and then with a mercurial change of direction abandoned the subject of gold and shot his next question at Zouga.

'The Matabele indunas – how are they behaving themselves?'

This time Zouga hesitated. 'They have grievances, Mr Rhodes.'

'Yes?' The swollen features coagulated into a scowl.

'The cattle, naturally enough, are the main source of trouble,' Zouga said quietly, and Rhodes cut him off brusquely.

'We captured less than 125,000 head of cattle, and we returned 40,000 of those to the tribe.'

Zouga did not remind him that the return was made only after the strongest representation by Robyn St John, Zouga's own sister. Robyn was the missionary doctor at Khami

Mission Station and she had once been Lobengula's closest friend and adviser.

'Forty thousand head of cattle, Ballantyne! A most generous gesture by the Company!' Rhodes repeated portentously, and again he did not add that he had made this return in order to avert the famine which Robyn St John had warned him would decimate the defeated Matabele nation, and which would have surely brought the intervention of the Imperial government in Whitehall, and possibly the revocation of the Royal Charter under which Rhodes' Company ruled both Mashonaland and Matabeleland. Not such an outstanding act of charity, after all, Ralph thought wryly.

'After giving back those cattle to the indunas, we were left with less than eighty-five thousand head, the Company barely recouped the cost of the war.'

'Still the indunas claim they were given back only inferior beasts, the old and barren cows and scrub bulls.'

'Damn it, Ballantyne, the volunteers earned the right to first pick from the herds. Quite naturally, they chose the prime stock.' He shot out his right fist with the forefinger aimed like a pistol at Zouga's heart. 'They do say that our own herds, chosen from the captured cattle, are the finest in Matabeleland.'

'The indunas don't understand that,' Zouga answered.

'Well then, the least they should understand is that they are a conquered nation. Their welfare depends on the goodwill of the victors. They extended no such consideration to the tribes that they conquered when they lorded it across the continent. Mzilikazi slew a million defenceless souls when he devastated the land south of the Limpopo, and Lobengula, his son, called the lesser tribes his dogs, to kill or cast into slavery as the whim took him. They must not whine now at the bitter taste of defeat.'

Even gentle Jordan, at the end of the table, nodded at

this. 'To protect the Mashona tribes from Lobengula's depredations was one of the reasons why we marched on GuBulawayo,' he murmured.

'I said that they had grievances,' Zouga pointed out. 'I did not say that they were justified.'

'Then what else do they have to complain of?' Rhodes demanded.

'The Company police. The young Matabele bucks whom General St John has recruited and armed are strutting through the kraals, usurping the power of the indunas, taking their pick of the young girls—'

Again Rhodes interrupted. 'Better that than a resurrection of the fighting impis under the indunas. Can you imagine twenty thousand warriors in impi under Babiaan and Gandang and Bazo? No, St John was right to break the power of the indunas. As Native Commissioner, it is his duty to guard against resurgence of the Matabele fighting tradition.'

'Especially in view of the events that are in train south of where we now sit.' Dr Leander Starr Jameson spoke for the first time since he had greeted Ralph, and Rhodes turned to him swiftly.

'I wonder if this is the time to speak of that, Doctor Jim.'

'Why not? Every man here is trustworthy and discreet. We are all committed to the same bright vision of Empire, and the Lord knows, we are in no danger of being overheard. Not in this wilderness. What better time than now to explain why the Company police must be made even stronger, must be better armed and trained to the highest degree of readiness?' Jameson demanded.

Instinctively Rhodes glanced at Ralph Ballantyne, and Ralph raised one eyebrow, a cynical and mildly challenging gesture that seemed to decide Rhodes.

'No, Doctor Jim,' he spoke decisively. 'There will be another time for that.' And when Jameson shrugged and capitulated, Rhodes turned to Jordan. 'The sun is setting,' he said, and Jordan rose obediently to charge the glasses. The sundowner whisky was already a traditional ending to the day in this land north of the Limpopo.

The brilliant white gems of the Southern Cross hung over Ralph's camp, dimming the lesser stars, and sprinkling the bald domes of the granite kopjes with a pearly light as Ralph picked his way towards his tent. He had inherited his father's head for liquor, so that his step was even and steady. It was ideas, not whisky, which had inebriated him.

He stooped through the fly of the darkened tent and sat down on the edge of the cot. He touched Cathy's cheek.

'I am awake,' she said softly. 'What time is it?'

'After midnight.'

'What kept you so long?' she whispered, for Jonathan slept just beyond the canvas screen.

'The dreams and boasts of men drunk with power and success.' He grinned in the dark and dragged off his boots. 'And by God, I did my fair share of dreaming and boasting.' He stood to strip off his breeches. 'What do you think of Harry Mellow?' he asked, with an abrupt change of pace.

'The American? He is very—' Cathy hesitated. 'I mean, he seems to be manly and rather nice.'

'Attractive?' Ralph demanded. 'Irresistible to a young woman?'

'You know I don't think like that,' Cathy protested primly.

'The hell you don't,' Ralph chuckled, and as he kissed her, he covered one of her round breasts with his cupped hand. Through the thin cotton nightdress it felt taut as a ripening melon. She struggled genteelly to free her lips from his and to prise his fingers loose, but he held her fast and

34

after a few seconds she struggled no more, and instead she slipped her arms around the back of his neck.

'You smell of sweat and cigars and whisky.'

'I'm sorry.'

'Don't be, it's lovely,' she purred.

'Let me take off my shirt.'

'No, I'll do it for you.'

Much later Ralph lay upon his back with Cathy snuggled down against his bare chest.

'How would you like to have your sisters come down from Khami?' he asked suddenly. 'They enjoy camp life, but even more, they like to escape from your mother.'

'It was I who wanted to invite the twins,' she reminded him sleepily. 'You were the one who said they were too – unsettling.'

'Actually, I said they were too rowdy and boisterous,' he corrected her, and she raised her head and looked at him in the faint moonlight that filtered through the canvas.

'A change of heart—' She thought about it for a moment, aware that her husband always had good reason for even his most unreasonable suggestions.

'The American,' she exclaimed, with such force that behind the canvas screen Jonathan stirred and whimpered. Instantly, Cathy dropped her voice to a fierce whisper. 'Not even you would use my own sisters – you wouldn't, would you?'

He pulled her head down onto his chest again. 'They are big girls now. How old are they?'

'Eighteen.' She wrinkled her nose as his damp, curly chest hairs tickled it. 'But, Ralph—'

'Old maids, already.'

'My own sisters – you wouldn't use them?'

'They never get to meet decent young men at Khami. Your mother frightens them all off.'

'You are awful, Ralph Ballantyne.'

'Would you like a demonstration of just how awful I can be?'

She considered that for a moment, and then, 'Yes, please,' she giggled softly.

'One day I will be riding with you,' Jonathan said. 'Won't I, Papa?'

'One day, soon,' Ralph agreed, and ruffled the child's dark curling head. 'Now I want you to take care of your mother while I am away, Jon-Jon.'

Jonathan nodded, his face pale and set, the tears grimly restrained.

'Promise?' Ralph squeezed the small warm body that he held on his lap, and then he stooped from the saddle and stood the child beside Cathy, and Jonathan took her hand protectively, though he did not reach to her hip.

'I promise, Papa,' he said, and gulped, staring up at his father on the tall horse.

Ralph touched Cathy's cheek lightly with his fingertips.

'I love you,' she said softly.

'My beautiful Katie.' And it was true. The first yellow rays of sunlight in her hair turned it into a bright halo and she was serene as a madonna in the deep fastness of their love.

Ralph spurred away, and Harry Mellow swung his horse in beside him. It was a fine red thoroughbred from Mr Rhodes' private stable, and he rode like a plainsman. At the edge of the forest both men turned to look back. The woman and child still stood at the gate of the stockade.

'You are a lucky man,' Harry said softly.

'Without a good woman, there is no today, and without a son there is no tomorrow,' Ralph agreed.

36

The vultures were still hunched in the tree-tops, although the bones of the lions had been picked clean and scattered across the stony ground of the ridge. They had to digest the contents of their bloated bellies before they could soar away, and their dark misshapen bodies against the clear winter sky guided Ralph and Harry the last few miles to the ridge of the Harkness claims.

'It looks promising,' Harry gave his guarded judgement that first night as they squatted beside the camp fire. 'The country rock is in contact with the reef. You could have a reef that continues to real depth, and we have traced the strike for over two miles. Tomorrow I will mark out the spots where you must sink your prospect holes.'

'There are mineralized ore bodies right across this country,' Ralph told him. 'The continuation of the great gold crescent of the Witwatersrand and Pilgrims Rest and Tati goldfields curves right across here—' Ralph broke off. 'But you have the special gift, I have heard them say you can smell gold at fifty miles.'

Harry dismissed the suggestion with a deprecating wave of his coffee mug, but Ralph went on, 'And I have the wagons and capital to grubstake a prospecting venture, and to develop the finds that are made. I like you, Harry, I think we would work well together, the Harkness Mine first, and after that, who knows, the whole bloody country, perhaps.'

Harry started to speak, but Ralph put a hand on his forearm to stop him.

'This continent is a treasure chest. The Kimberley diamond fields and the Witwatersrand banket, side by side, all the diamond and gold in the one bucket – who would ever have believed it?'

'Ralph.' Harry shook his head. 'I have already thrown in my lot with Mr Rhodes.'

Ralph sighed, and stared into the flames of the fire for a full minute. Then he relit the stump of his dead cheroot, and began to argue and cajole in his plausible and convincing way. An hour later as he rolled into his blanket, he repeated his offer.

'Under Rhodes you will never be your own man. You will always be a servant.'

'You work for Mr Rhodes, Ralph.'

'I contract to him, Harry, but the profit or loss is mine. I still own my soul.'

'And I don't,' Harry chuckled.

'Come in with me, Harry. Find out what it feels like to bet your own cards, to calculate your own risks, to give the orders, instead of taking them. Life is all a game, Harry, and there is only one way to play it, flat out.'

'I'm Rhodes' man.'

'When the time comes, then we will talk again,' Ralph said and pulled the blanket over his head. Within minutes his breathing was slow and regular.

In the morning Harry marked the sites for the prospect bores with cairns of stone, and Ralph realized how cunningly he was quartering the extended line of the reef to pick it up again at depth. By noon Harry had finished, and as they up-saddled, Ralph made a swift calculation and realized it would be another two days before Cathy's twin sisters could arrive at the base camp from Khami Mission.

'Seeing that we have come so far, we should make a sweep out towards the east before turning back. God knows what we could find – more gold, diamonds.' And when Harry hesitated, 'Mr Rhodes will have gone on to Bulawayo already. He'll be holding court there for the next month at least, he won't even miss you.'

Harry thought for a moment, then grinned like a schoolboy about to bunk his classes to raid the orchard. 'Let's go!' he said.

They rode slowly, and at each river course they dismounted to pan the gravel from the bottom of the stagnant green pools. Wherever the bedrock outcropped above the overburden of earth, they broke off samples. They searched out the burrows of ant-bear and porcupine, and the nests of the swarming white termites to find what grains and chippings they had brought up from depth.

On the third day, Harry said, 'We've picked up a dozen likely shows of colour. I particularly liked those crystals of beryllium, they are a good pointer to emerald deposits.'

Harry's enthusiasm had increased with each mile ridden, but now they had reached the end of the outward leg of their eastward sweep, and even Ralph realized that it was time to turn back. They had been out five days from the base camp, they had exhausted their coffee and sugar and meal, and Cathy would be anxious by now.

They took one last look at the country that they must leave unexplored for the time being.

'It's beautiful,' Harry murmured. 'I have never seen a more magnificent land. What is the name of that range of hills?'

'That's the southern end of the Matopos.'

'I have heard Mr Rhodes speak of them. Aren't they the sacred hills of the Matabele?'

Ralph nodded. 'If I believed in witchcraft—' he broke off and chuckled with embarrassment. 'There is something about those hills.'

There was the first rosy flush of the sunset in the western sky, and it turned the smooth polished rock of those distant brooding hills to pink marble, while their crests were garlanded with fragile twists of cloud coloured by the softly slanting rays to ivory and ashes.

'There is a secret cave hidden in there where a witch who presided over the tribes used to live. My father took in a commando and destroyed her at the beginning of the war against Lobengula.'

'I have heard the story, it is one of the legends, already.'

'Well, it's true. They say—' Ralph broke off and studied the tall and turreted range of rock with a thoughtful expression. 'Those are not clouds, Harry,' he said at last. 'That's smoke. Yet there are no kraals in the Matopos. It could be a bush-fire, but I don't think so, it's not on a broad front.'

'Then where is the smoke coming from?'

'That is what we are going to find out,' Ralph replied, and before Harry could protest, he had started his horse, and was cantering across the plains of pale winter grass towards the high rampart of bare granite that blocked off the horizon.

A Matabele warrior sat aloof from the men who swarmed about the earthen kilns. He sat in the meagre shade of a twisted cripple-wood tree. He was lean, so that the rack of his ribs showed through the covering of elastic muscle under his cloak. His skin was burned by the sun to the deep midnight black of carved ebony, and it was glossed with health, like the coat of a race-trained thoroughbred, blemished only by the old healed gunshot wounds on his chest and back.

He wore a simple kilt and cloak of tanned leather, no feathers nor war rattles, no regimentals of fur nor plumes of marabou stork upon his bared head. He was unarmed, for the white men had made roaring bonfires of the long rawhide shields and carried away the broad silver assegais by the wagon-load; they had confiscated also the Martini-Henry rifles with which the Company had paid King Lobengula for the concession to all the mineral wealth beneath this land.

On his head the warrior wore the headring of the induna; it was of gum and clay, woven permanently into his own hair and black and hard as iron. This badge of rank announced to the world that he had once been a councillor of Lobengula, the last king of the Matabele. The simple ring declared his royal bloodline, the Zanzi blood of the Kumalo tribe, running back pure and unbroken to old Zululand, a thousand miles and more away in the south.

Mzilikazi had been this man's grandfather; Mzilikazi who had defied the tyrant Chaka and led his people away towards the north. Mzilikazi, the little chief who had slaughtered a million souls on that terrible northward march, and in the process had become a mighty emperor, as powerful and cruel as Chaka had ever been. Mzilikazi, his grandfather, who had finally brought his nation to this rich and beautiful land, who had been the first to enter these magical hills and to listen to the myriad weird voices of the Umlimo, the Chosen One, the witch and oracle of the Matopos.

Lobengula, son of Mzilikazi, who ruled the Matabele after the old king's death, had been the young man's blood uncle. It was Lobengula who had granted him the honours of the induna's headring, and appointed him commander of one of the elite fighting impis. But now Lobengula was dead, and the young induna's impi had been blown to nothing by the Maxim guns on the bank of the Shangani river, and the same Maxim guns had branded him with those deeply dimpled cicatrices upon his trunk.

His name was Bazo, which means 'the axe', but more often now men spoke of him as 'the Wanderer'. He had sat beneath the cripple-wood tree all that day, watching the ironsmiths perform their rites, for the birth of iron was a mystery to all but these adepts. The smiths were not Matabele, but were members of an older tribe, an ancient people whose origins were somehow interwoven with those haunted and ruined stone walls of Great Zimbabwe.

Although the new white masters and their queen beyond the seas had decreed that the Matabele no longer own *amaholi*, slaves, yet these Rozwi ironsmiths were still the dogs of the Matabele, still performed their art at the behest of their warlike masters.

The ten oldest and wisest of the Rozwi smiths had selected the ore from the quarry, deliberating over each fragment like vain women choosing ceramic beads from the trader's stock. They had judged the iron ore for colour and weight, for the perfection of the metal it contained and for its purity from foreign matter, and then they had broken up the ore upon the rock anvils until each lump was the perfect size. While they worked with care and total preoccupation, some of their apprentices were cutting and burning the tree trunks in the charcoal pits, controlling the combustion with layers of earth and finally quenching it with clay pots of water. Meanwhile, yet another party of apprentices made the long journey to the limestone quarries and returned with the crushed catalyst in leather bags slung upon the backs of the baggage bullocks. When the master smiths had grudgingly approved the quality of charcoal and limestone, then the building of the rows of clay kilns could begin.

Each kiln was shaped like the torso of a heavily pregnant woman, like a fat, domed belly, in which the layers of iron ore and charcoal and limestone would be packed. At the lower end of the kiln was the crotch guarded by symbolically truncated clay thighs between which was the narrow opening into which would be introduced the buckhorn nozzle of the leather bellows.

When all was ready, the head smith chopped the head off the sacrificed rooster, and passed down the line of kilns, sprinkling them with hot blood while he chanted the first of the ancient incantations to the spirit of iron.

Bazo watched with fascination, and a prickle of superstitious awe on his skin, as fire was introduced through the vaginal openings of the kilns, the magical moment of impregnation which was greeted with a joyous cry by the assembled smiths. Then the young apprentices pumped the leather bellows in a kind of religious ecstasy, singing the hymns which ensured the success of the smelting and set the rhythm for the work on the bellows. When each fell back exhausted, there was another to take his place and keep the steady blast of air driving deeply into the kiln.

A faint haze of smoke hung over the workings; like sea fret on a still summer's day, it rose to eddy slowly around the tall bald peaks of the hills. Now at last it was time to draw the smelting, and as the head smith freed the clay plug from the first kiln, a joyous shout of thanksgiving went up from the assembly at the bright glowing rush of the molten metal from the womb of the furnace.

Bazo found himself trembling with excitement and wonder, as he had when his first son had been born in one of the caves in these self-same hills.

'The birth of the blades,' he whispered aloud, and in his imagination he could already hear the dinning of the hammers as they beat out the metal, and the sizzling hiss of the quenching that would set the temper of the edge and point of the broad stabbing spears.

A touch on his shoulder startled him from his reverie, and he glanced up at the woman who stood over him, and then he smiled. She wore the leather skirt, decorated with beads, of the married woman, but there were no bangles nor bracelets on her smooth young limbs.

Her body was straight and hard, her naked breasts symmetrical and perfectly proportioned. Although she had already suckled a fine son, they were not marred by stretch marks. Her belly was concave as a greyhound's, while the skin was smooth and drum-tight. Her neck was long and graceful, her nose straight and narrow, her eyes slanted above the Egyptian arches of her cheekbones. Her features were those of a statuette from the tomb of some long-dead pharaoh.

'Tanase,' said Bazo, 'another thousand blades.' Then he saw her expression and broke off. 'What is it?' he asked with quick concern.

'Riders,' she said. 'Two of them. White men coming from the southern forests, and coming swiftly.'

Bazo rose in a single movement, quick as a leopard alarmed by the approach of the hunters. Only now his full height and the breadth of his shoulders were evident, for he towered a full head over the ironsmiths about him. He lifted the buckhorn whistle that hung on a thong about his neck and blew a single sharp blast. Immediately all the scurry and bustle amongst the kilns ceased and the master smith hurried to him.

'How long to draw the rest of the smelting and break down the kilns?' Bazo demanded.

'Two days, oh Lord,' answered the iron-worker, bobbing respectfully. His eyes were bloodshot from the smoke of the furnace, and the smoke seemed to have stained his cap of white woolly hair to dingy yellow.

'You have until dawn—'

'Lord!'

'Work all night, but screen the fires from the plain.' Bazo turned from him and strode up the steep incline to where twenty other men waited below the granite cap of the hill.

Like Bazo, they wore only simple leather kilts, and were unarmed, but their bodies were tempered and fined down by war and the training for war, and there was the warrior's arrogance in their stance as they rose to acknowledge their induna and their eyes were bright and fierce. There was no doubt that these were Matabele, not *amaholi* dogs.

'Follow!' ordered Bazo, and led them at a trot along the lower contour of the hill. There was a narrow cave in the base of the cliff, and Bazo drew aside the hanging creepers that screened the mouth and stopped into the gloomy interior. The cave was only ten paces deep, and it ended abruptly in a scree of loose boulders.

Bazo gestured and two of his men went up to the end wall of the cave and rolled aside the boulders. In the recess beyond there was the glint of polished metal like the scales of a slumbering reptile. As Bazo moved out of the entrance, the slanting rays of the setting sun struck deeply into the cave, lighting the secret arsenal. The assegais were stacked in bundles of ten and bound together with rawhide thongs.

The two warriors lifted out a bundle, broke the thongs and swiftly passed the weapons down the line of men, until each was armed. Bazo hefted the stabbing spear. The shaft was of polished red heartwood of mukusi, the blood-wood tree. The blade was hand-forged, wide as Bazo's palm and long as his forearm. He could have shaved the hair from the back of his hand with the honed edge.

He had felt naked until that moment, but now, with the familiar weight and balance in his hand, he was a man again. He gestured to his men to roll the boulders back into place covering the cache of bright new blades, and then he led them back along the path. On the shoulder of the hill, Tanase waited for him on the ledge of rock which commanded a wide view across the grassy plains, and beyond them the blue forests dreamed softly in the evening light.

'There,' she pointed, and Bazo saw them instantly.

Two horses, moving at an easy canter. They had reached the foot of the hills and were riding along them, scouting for an easy route. The riders peered up at the tangle of boulders and at the smooth pearly sheets of granite which offered no foothold.

There were only two access trails to the valley of the ironsmiths, each of them narrow and steep, with necks which could be easily defended. Bazo turned and looked back. The smoke from the kilns was dissipating, there were only a few pale ribbons twisting along the grey granite cliffs. By morning there would be nothing to lead a curious traveller to the secret place, but there was still an hour of daylight, less perhaps, for the night comes with startling rapidity in Africa above the Limpopo river.

'I must delay them until dark,' Bazo said. 'I must turn them before they find the path.'

'If they will not be turned?' Tanase asked softly, and in reply Bazo merely altered his grip on the broad assegai in his right hand, and then quickly drew Tanase back off the rocky ledge, for the horsemen had halted and one of them, the taller and broader man, was carefully sweeping the hillside with a pair of binoculars.

'Where is my son?' Bazo asked.

'At the cave,' Tanase replied.

'You know what to do if—' he did not have to go on, and Tanase nodded.

'I know,' she said softly, and Bazo turned from her and went bounding down the steep pathway with twenty armed *amadoda* at his back.

At the narrow place which Bazo had marked, he stopped. He did not have to speak, but at a single gesture of his free hand his men slipped off the narrow trail and disappeared into the crevices and cracks of the gigantic boulders that stood tall on either hand. In seconds there was no sign of them, and Bazo broke off a branch from one of the dwarfed trees that grew in a rocky pocket, and he ran back, sweeping the trail of all sign that might alert a wary man to the ambush. Then he placed his assegai on a shoulder-high ledge beside the path and covered it with the green branch. It was within easy reach if he were forced to guide the white riders up the trail.

'I will try to turn them, but if I cannot, wait until they reach this place,' he called to the hidden warriors. 'Then do it swiftly.'

His men were spread out for two hundred paces along both sides of the trail, but they were concentrated here at the bend. A good ambush must have depth to it, so if a victim breaks through the first rank of attackers, there will be others waiting for him beyond. This was a good ambush: in bad ground on a steep narrow trail where a horse could not turn readily nor go ahead at full gallop. Bazo nodded to himself with satisfaction, then unarmed and shieldless he went springing down the trail towards the plain, agile as a klipspringer over the rough track.

'It will be dark in half an hour,' Harry Mellow called after Ralph. 'We should find a place to camp.'

'There must be a path,' Ralph rode with one fist on his hip and the felt hat pushed back on his head, looking up the wild cliff.

'What do you expect to find up there?'

'I don't know, and that's the devil of it.' Ralph grinned over his shoulder. He was unprepared and twisted off balance, so when his horse shied violently under him, he almost lost a stirrup and had to grab at the pommel of the saddle to prevent himself going over, but at the same time he yelled to Harry.

'Cover me!' and with his free hand Ralph tugged the Winchester rifle from its leather boot under his knee. His horse was rearing and skittering in a tight circle so he could not get the rifle up. He knew that he was blocking Harry's line of fire, and that for those long seconds he was completely defenceless, and he swore helplessly, anticipating a rush of dark spearmen out of the broken rock and scrub at the foot of the cliff.

Then he realized there was only one man, and that he was unarmed, and again he yelled at Harry, with even more urgency, for he had heard the clash of the breech block behind him as the American loaded and cocked.

'Hold it! Don't shoot!'

The gelding reared again, but this time Ralph jerked it down and then stared at the tall black man who had stepped

47

so silently and unexpectedly out of the crevice of a fractured granite block.

'Who are you?' he demanded, his voice rasping with the shock, which still screwed his guts into a ball and charged his veins with a quick rush of blood. 'Damn you, I nearly shot you.' Ralph caught himself, and this time repeated in fluent Sindebele, the Matabele language, 'Who are you?'

The tall man in the plain leather cloak inclined his head slightly, but his body remained absolutely still, the empty hands hanging at his side.

'What manner of question is that,' he asked gravely, 'for one brother to ask another?'

Ralph stared at him. Taking in the induna's headring on his brow and the gaunt features, scored and riven by the crags and deep lines of some terrible suffering, a sorrow or an illness that must have transported this man to the frontiers of hell itself. It moved Ralph deeply to look upon that riven face, for there was something, the fierce dark eyes and the tone of the deep measured voice that was so familiar, and yet so altered as to be unrecognizable.

'Henshaw,' the man spoke again, using Ralph Ballantyne's Matabele praise name. 'Henshaw, the Hawk, do you not know me? Have these few short years changed us so?'

Ralph shook his head in disbelief, and his voice was full of wonder. 'Bazo, it is not you – surely, it is not you? Did you not after all die with your impi at Shangani?' Ralph kicked both feet out of the stirrups and jumped to the ground. 'Bazo. It is you!' He ran to embrace the Matabele. 'My brother, my black brother,' he said, and there was the lift and lilt of pure joy in his voice.

Bazo accepted the embrace quietly, his hands still hanging at his sides, and at last Ralph stood back and held him at arm's length.

'At Shangani, after the guns were still, I left the wagons and walked out across the open pan. Your men were there, the Moles-that-burrow-under-a-mountain.' That was the name that King Lobengula himself had given to Bazo's impi, *Izimvukuzane Ezembintaba*. 'I knew them by their red shields, by the plumes of the marabou stork and the headbands of fur from the burrowing mole.' These were the regimentals bestowed upon the impi by the old king, and Bazo's eyes turned luminous with the agony of memory as Ralph went on. 'Your men were there, Bazo, lying upon each other like the fallen leaves of the forest. I searched for you, rolling the dead men onto their backs to see their faces, but there were so many of them.'

'So many,' Bazo agreed, and only his eyes betrayed his emotion.

'And there was so little time to look for you,' Ralph explained quietly. 'I could only search slowly, with care, for some of your men were *fanisa file*.' It was an old Zulu trick to sham dead on the battlefield and wait for the enemy to come out to loot and count the kill. 'I did not want an assegai between my shoulder-blades. Then the laager broke up and the wagons rolled on towards the king's kraal. I had to leave.'

'I was there,' Bazo told him, and drew aside the leather cloak. Ralph stared at the dreadful scars, and then dropped his gaze, while Bazo covered his torso again. 'I was lying amongst the dead men.'

'And now?' Ralph asked. 'Now that it is all over, what are you doing here?'

'What does a warrior do when the war is over, when the impis are broken and disarmed, and the king is dead?' Bazo shrugged. 'I am a hunter of wild honey now.' He glanced up the cliff at where the last smoke wisps were blending into the darkening sky as the sun touched the tops of the western forest. 'I was smoking a hive when I saw you coming.'

'Ah!' Ralph nodded. 'It was that smoke that led us to you.'

'Then it was fortunate smoke, my brother Henshaw.'

'You still call me brother?' Ralph marvelled gently.

'When it might have been I who fired the bullets—' He did not complete the sentence, but glanced down at Bazo's chest.

'No man can be held to account for what he does in the madness of battle,' Bazo answered. 'If I had reached the wagons that day,' he shrugged, 'you might be the one who carried the scars.'

'Bazo,' Ralph gestured to Harry to ride forward, 'this is Harry Mellow, he is a man who understands the mystery of the earth, who can find the gold and the iron which we seek.'

'Nkosi, I see you.' Bazo greeted Harry gravely, calling him 'Lord' and not allowing his deep resentment to show for an instant. His king had died and his nation had been destroyed by the weird passion of the white men for that accursed yellow metal.

'Bazo and I grew up together on the Kimberley diamond fields. I have never had a dearer friend,' Ralph explained quickly, and then turned impetuously back to Bazo. 'We have a little food, you will share it with us, Bazo.' This time Ralph caught the shift in Bazo's gaze, and he insisted. 'Camp with us here. There is much to talk about.'

'I have my woman and my son with me,' Bazo answered. 'They are in the hills.'

'Bring them,' Ralph told him. 'Go quickly, before darkness falls, and bring them down into camp.'

B azo alerted his men with the dusk call of the francolin, and one of them stepped out of the ambush onto the path.

'I will hold the white men at the foot of the hills for tonight,' Bazo told him quietly. 'Perhaps I can send them away satisfied, without trying to find the valley. However, warn the ironsmiths that the kilns must be quenched by dawn tomorrow, there must be no shred of smoke.'

Bazo went on giving his orders, the finished weapons and freshly smelted metal to be hidden and the paths swept clear of spoor, the ironsmiths to retreat along the secret path deeper into the hills, the Matabele guards to cover their retreat. 'I will follow you when the white men have gone. Wait for me at the peak of the Blind Ape.'

'Nkosi.' They saluted him, and slipped away, silent as the night-prowling leopard, into the failing light. Bazo took the fork in the path, and when he reached the rocky spur on the prow of the hill, there was no need for him to call. Tanase was waiting for him with the boy carried on her hip, the roll of sleeping-mats upon her head and the leather grain-bag slung on her back.

'It is Henshaw,' he told her, and heard the serpentine hiss of her breath. Though he could not see her expression, he knew what it must be.

'He is the spawn of the white dog who violated the sacred places—'

'He is my friend,' Bazo said.

'You have taken the oath,' she reminded him fiercely. 'How can any white man still be your friend?'

'He was my friend, then.'

'Do you remember the vision that came to me, before the powers of divination were torn from me by this man's father?'

'Tanase,' Bazo ignored the question, 'we must go down to him. If he sees my wife and my son are with me, then there will be no suspicions. He will believe that we are indeed hunting the honey of wild bees. Follow me.' He turned back down the trail, and she followed him closely, and her voice sank to a whisper, of which he could clearly hear every word. He did not look back at her, but he listened.

'Do you remember my vision, Bazo? On the first day that

51

I met this man whom you call the Hawk, I warned you. Before the birth of your son, when the veil of my virginity was still unpierced, before the white horsemen came with their three-legged guns that laugh like the river demons that live in the rocks where the Zambezi river falls. When you still called him "brother" and "friend", I warned you against him.'

'I remember.' Bazo's own voice had sunk as low as hers.

'In my vision I saw you high upon a tree, Bazo.'

'Yes,' he whispered, going on down the trail without looking back at her. There was a superstitious tremor in Bazo's voice now, for his beautiful young wife had once been the apprentice of the mad sorcerer, Pemba. When Bazo at the head of his impi had stormed the sorcerer's mountain stronghold, he had hacked off Pemba's head and taken Tanase as a prize of war, but the spirits had claimed her back.

On the eve of the wedding-feast when Bazo would have taken the virgin Tanase as his first bride, as his senior wife, an ancient wizard had come down out of the Matopos Hills and led her away, and Bazo had been powerless to intervene, for she had been the daughter of the dark spirits and she had come to her destiny in these hills.

'The vision was so clear that I wept,' Tanase reminded him, and Bazo shivered.

In that secret cave in the Matopos the full power of the spirits had descended upon Tanase, and she had become the Umlimo, the chosen one, the oracle. It was Tanase, speaking in the weird voices of the spirits, who had warned Lobengula of his fate. It was Tanase who had foreseen the coming of the white men with their wonderful machines that turned the night to noon day, and their little mirrors that sparkled like stars upon the hills, speeding messages vast distances across the plains. No man could doubt that she had once had the power of the oracle, and that in her mystic trances she had been able to see through the dark veils of the future for the Matabele nation.

However, these strange powers had depended upon her maidenhead remaining unpierced. She had warned Bazo of this, pleading with him to strip her of her virginity and rid her of these terrible powers, but he had demurred, bound by law and custom, until it had been too late and the wizards had come down from the hills to claim her.

At the beginning of the war which the white men had carried so swiftly to Lobengula's kraal at GuBulawayo, a small band had detached from the main army; they were the hardest and cruellest, led by Bakela the Fist, himself a hard fierce man. They had ridden swiftly into these hills. They had followed the secret path that Bakela had discovered twenty-five years or so before, and galloped to the secret cavern of the Umlimo. For Bakela knew the value of the oracle, knew how sacred she was, and how her destruction would throw the Matabele nation into despair. Bakela's riders had shot down the guardians of the caverns, and forced their way within. Two of Bakela's troopers had found Tanase, young and lovely and naked in the deepest recesses of the cave, and they had violated her, savagely tearing the maidenhead that she had once offered so lovingly to Bazo. They had rutted upon her until her virgin blood splattered the floor of the cavern and her screams had guided Bakela to them.

He had driven his men off her with fist and boot, and when they were alone, he had looked down upon Tanase where she lay bloodied and broken at his feet. Then strangely, this hard fierce man had been overcome with compassion. Though he had ridden this dangerous road for the sole purpose of destroying the Umlimo, yet the bestial behaviour of his troopers had weakened his resolve, had placed some burden of recompense upon him.

Bakela must have known that with her virginity torn

from her she had lost her powers, for he told her: 'You, who were Umlimo, are Umlimo no longer.' He had accomplished her destruction without using rifle or sword, and he turned and strode from the dark cavern, leaving her life in exchange for her virginity and the loss of her dark powers.

She had told the story to Bazo many times, and he knew that the mists of time had closed before her eyes and that now they shrouded the future from her, but no man could doubt that she had once possessed the power of the Sight.

Thus Bazo shivered briefly, and he felt the ghost fingers touching the nape of his neck as Tanase went on in her husky whisper.

'I wept, Bazo my lord, when I saw you upon the high tree, and while I wept, the man you call Henshaw the Hawk was looking up at you – and smiling!'

They ate cold bully beef straight from the cans, using the blade of a hunting knife to spoon it out, and passing the cans from hand to hand. There was no coffee, so they washed down the glutinous mess with sun-warmed draughts from the felt-covered water bottles, and then Ralph shared out his remaining cheroots with Harry Mellow and Bazo. They lit them with burning twigs from the fire and smoked in silence for a long time.

Close at hand a hyena warbled and sobbed in the darkness, drawn by the firelight and the smell of food, while further out across the plain, the lions were hunting, sweeping towards the moonrise, not roaring before the kill but coughing throatily to keep in contact with the other animals in the pride.

Tanase, with the child on her lap, sat at the edge of the firelight, aloof from the men, and they ignored her. It would have offended Bazo if they had paid undue attention to her, but now Ralph took the cheroot from his mouth and glanced in her direction.

'What is your son's name?' he asked Bazo, and there was a heartbeat of hesitation before Bazo replied.

'He is called Tungata Zebiwe.'

Ralph frowned quickly, but checked the harsh words that rose to his lips. Instead he said, 'He is a fine boy.'

Bazo held out his hand towards the child, but Tanase restrained him for a moment with a quiet ferocity.

'Let him come to me,' Bazo ordered sharply, and reluctantly Tanase let the sleepy child stagger to his father and climb into his arms.

He was a pretty, dark toffee colour, with a pot belly and chubby limbs. Except for the bracelets of copper wire at his wrists and a single string of beads around his waist, he was stark naked. His hair was a dark fluffy cap and his eyes were owlish with sleep as he stared at Ralph.

'Tungata Zebiwe,' Ralph repeated his name, and then leaned across to stroke his head. The child made no attempt to pull away, nor did he show any trace of alarm, but in the shadows Tanase hissed softly and reached out as if to take the child back, then dropped her hand again.

'The Seeker after what has been stolen,' Ralph translated the child's name, and caught the mother's dark eyes. 'The Seeker after justice – that is a heavy duty to place upon one so young,' he said quietly. 'You would make him an avenger of injustice inflicted before his birth?'

Then smoothly Ralph seemed to change to a different subject.

'Do you remember, Bazo, the day we first met? You were a green youth sent by your father and his brother the king to work on the diamond fields. I was even younger and greener, when my father and I found you in the veld and he signed you to a three-year labour contract, before any other digger could put his brand on you.'

The lines of suffering and sorrow that marred Bazo's features seemed to smooth away as he smiled, and for a few moments he was that young guileless and carefree youth again.

'It was only later I found out that the reason Lobengula sent you and thousands of other young bucks like you to the fields was to bring home as many fat diamonds as you could steal.' They both laughed, Ralph ruefully and Bazo with a vestige of his youthful glee.

'Lobengula must have hidden a great treasure somewhere. Jameson never did find those diamonds when he captured GuBulawayo.'

'Do you remember the hunting falcon, Scipio?' Bazo asked.

'And the giant spider that won us our first gold sovereigns at the Kimberley spider-fights,' Ralph continued, and they chatted animatedly, recalling how they had worked shoulder to shoulder in the great diamond pit, and the mad diversions with which they had broken the dreadful monotony of that brutal labour.

Not understanding the language, Harry Mellow rolled in his blanket and pulled the corner of it over his head. In the shadows Tanase sat, still as a beautiful ebony carving, not smiling when the men laughed but with her eyes fastened on their lips as they spoke.

Abruptly Ralph changed the subject again. 'I have a son also,' he said. 'He was born before the war, so he is a year or two older than yours.'

The laughter dried immediately, and although Bazo's expression was neutral, his eyes were wary.

'They could be friends, as we are friends,' Ralph suggested, and Tanase looked protectively towards her son, but Bazo did not reply.

'You and I could work side by side once more,' Ralph went on. 'Soon I will have a rich gold mine in the forests yonder, and I will need a senior induna in charge of the hundreds of men who will come to work.'

'I am a warrior,' said Bazo, 'no longer a mine labourer.'

'The world changes, Bazo,' Ralph answered softly. 'There are no longer any warriors in Matabeleland. The shields are burned. The assegai blades are broken. The eyes are no longer red, Bazo, for the wars are finished. The eyes are white now, and there will be peace in this land for a thousand years.'

Bazo was silent.

'Come with me, Bazo. Bring your son to learn the white man's skills. One day he will read and write, and be a man of consequence, not merely a hunter of wild honey. Forget this sad name you have given him, and find another. Call him a joyous name and bring him to meet my own son. Together they will enjoy this beautiful land, and be brothers as we once were brothers.'

Bazo sighed then. 'Perhaps you are right, Henshaw. As you say, the impis are disbanded. Those who were once warriors now work on the roads that Lodzi is building.' The Matabele always had difficulty in pronouncing the sound of 'R', thus Rhodes was 'Lodzi', and Bazo was referring to the system of conscripted labour which the Chief Native Commissioner, General Mungo St John, had introduced in Matabeleland. Bazo sighed again. 'If a man must work, it is better that he work in dignity at a task of importance with somebody whom he respects. When will you begin to dig for your gold, Henshaw?'

'After the rains, Bazo. But come with me now. Bring your woman and your son—'

Bazo held up one hand to silence him. 'After the rains, after the great storms, we will talk again, Henshaw,' Bazo said quietly, and Tanase nodded her head and for the first time she smiled, an odd little smile of approval. Bazo was right to dissemble and to lull Henshaw with vague promises.

With her specially trained sense of awareness, Tanase recognized that despite the direct gaze of his green eyes and his open, almost childlike smile, this young white man was harder and more dangerous than even Bakela, his father.

'After the great storms,' Bazo had promised him, and that had a hidden meaning. The great storm was the secret thing that they were planning.

'First there are things that I must do, but once they are done, I will seek you out,' Bazo promised.

B azo led up the steep gradient of the narrow pathway through the deep gut of the granite hills. Tanase followed a dozen paces behind him. The roll of sleeping-mats and the iron cooking-pot were carried easily on her head, and her spine was straight and her step fluid and smooth to balance the load. The boy skipped at her side, singing a childish nonsense in a high piping chant. He was the only one unaffected by the brooding menace of this dark valley. The scrub on each side of the path was dense and armed with vicious thorn. The silence was oppressive, for no bird sang and no small animal rustled the leaves.

Bazo stepped lightly across the boulders in the bed of the narrow stream that crossed the trail and paused to look back as Tanase scooped a handful of the cool water and held it to the boy's lips. Then they went on.

The path ended abruptly against a sheer cliff of pearly granite, and Bazo stopped and leaned on the light throwing-spear, the only weapon that the white administrator in Bulawayo allowed a black man to carry to protect himself and his family against the predators which infested the wilderness. It was a frail thing, not an instrument of war like the broad stabbing assegai.

Leaning his weight on the spear, Bazo looked up the tall cliff. There was a watchman's thatched hut on a ledge just below the summit, and now a quavering old man's voice challenged him.

'Who dares the secret pass?' Bazo lifted his chin and answered in a bull-bellow which sent the echoes bouncing from the cliffs.

'Bazo, son of Gandang. Bazo, Induna of the Kumalo blood royal.'

Then, not deigning to await the reply, Bazo stepped through the convoluted portals of granite, into the passage-way that split the cliff.

The passage was narrow, barely wide enough for two grown men to walk shoulder to shoulder, and the floor was clean white sand with chips of bright mica that sparkled and crunched like sugar under his bare feet. The passage twisted like a maimed serpent, and then abruptly debouched into a sweeping valley of lush green, bisected by a tinkling stream that spilled from the rock-face near where Bazo stood.

The valley was a circular basin a mile or so across, completely walled in by the high cliffs. In its centre was a tiny village of thatched huts, but as Tanase came out of the mouth of the secret passage and stopped beside Bazo, both of them looked beyond the village to the opposite wall of the valley.

In the base of the cliff, the low wide opening of a cavern snarled at them like a toothless mouth. Neither of them spoke for many minutes as they stared across at the sacred cave, but the memories came crowding back upon both of them. In that cavern Tanase had undergone the frightful indoctrination and initiation which had transformed her into the Umlimo, and on the rocky floor she had suffered the cruel abuse that had stripped her of her powers, and made her an ordinary woman once more.

Now in that cavern another being presided in Tanase's place as spiritual head of the nation, for the powers of the Umlimo never die, but are passed on from one initiate to another, as they had been from forgotten times when the ancients had built the great stone ruins of the Zimbabwe.

'Are you ready?' Bazo asked at last.

'I am ready, lord,' she replied, and they started down towards the village. But before they reached it, they were met by a weird procession of creatures, some of them barely recognizable as human, for they crawled on all fours and whined and yapped like animals. There were ancient withered crones with empty dugs flapping against their bellies, pretty little girls with pubescent breast-buds and blank unsmiling faces, old men with deformed limbs who dragged themselves in the dust, and slim mincing youths with well-formed muscular bodies and mad eyes that rolled back into their skulls, all of them decked with the gruesome parapher-nalia of the necromancer and wizard, bladders of lion and crocodile, skin of python and bird, skulls and teeth of ape, of man, and of beast. They ringed Bazo and Tanase, prancing and mewling and leering, until Bazo felt his skin itching with the insects of loathing and he lifted his son high on his shoulder away from their touching, prying hands.

Tanase was unperturbed, for this fantastic throng had once been her own retinue, and she stood expressionless as one of the horrible witches crawled to her and slobbered and frothed over her bare feet. Dancing and chanting, the guardians of the Umlimo led the two wanderers into the village, and then disappeared, slipping away into the thatched huts.

However, they were not alone. In the centre of the village stood a *setenghi*, an airy open-sided hut of white mopani poles, and a roof of neat thatch. In the shade of the *setenghi* there were men waiting, but these were entirely different from the strange throng which had met them at the entrance of the village.

Each of these men sat upon a low carved stool. Though some of them were grossly fat and others skinny and stooped, they were all of them surrounded by an almost palpable air of dignity and authority. Though some were white-headed with snowy woollen beards and deeply wrinkled faces and others were in the prime of their life and powers, they all of them wore upon their heads the simple black headring of gum and clay.

Here assembled in the secret valley of the Umlimo were what was left of the leaders of the Matabele nation, men who had once stood at the head of the fighting impis as they formed the bull-formation of encircling horns and crushing chest. Some of them, the eldest, remembered the exodus from the south driven by the mounted Boer horsemen; they had fought as young men under great Mzilikazi himself and still wore with pride the tassels of honour which he had awarded to them.

All of them had sat upon the councils of King Lobengula, son of great Mzilikazi, and had been on the Hills of the Indunas that fateful day when the king had stood before the assembled regiments and had faced eastward, the direction from which the column of wagons and white soldiers was entering Matabeleland. They had shouted the royal salute 'Bayete!' as Lobengula poised his great swollen body on gout-distorted legs and then defiantly hurled the toy spear of kingship at the invaders who were still out of sight beyond the blue horizon. These were the indunas who had led their fighting men past the king in review singing his praises and the battle hymns of the regiments, saluting Lobengula for the last time, and then going out to where the Maxim guns waited for them behind the wagon-sides and plaited thorn bush walls of the white men's laager.

In the midst of this distinguished assembly sat three men – the three surviving sons of Mzilikazi, the noblest and most revered of all the indunas. Somabula, on the left, was the eldest, victor of a hundred fierce battles, the warrior for whom the lovely Somabula forests had been named. On the right was Babiaan, wise and brave. The honourable scars laced his torso and limbs. However, it was the man in the centre who rose from his ornately carved stool of wild ebony and came out into the sunlight.

'Gandang, my father, I see you and my heart sings,' cried Bazo.

'I see you, my son,' said Gandang, his handsome face made almost beautiful by the joy that lit it, and when Bazo knelt before him, he touched his head in blessing, and then raised him up with his own hand.

'Baba!' Tanase clapped her hands respectfully before her face, and when Gandang nodded his acknowledgement, she withdrew quietly to the nearest hut, where she could listen from behind the thin reed wall.

It was not for a woman to attend the high councils of the nation. In the time of the kings, a lesser woman would have been speared to death for daring to approach an *indaba* such as this. Tanase, however, was the one that had once been the Umlimo, and she was still the mouth-piece of the chosen one. Besides which, the world was changing, the kings had passed, the old customs were dying with them, and this woman wielded more power than any but the highest of the assembled indunas. Nevertheless, she made the gesture of retiring to the closed hut, so as not to offend the memory of the old ways.

Gandang clapped his hands and the slaves brought a stool and a baked clay beerpot to Bazo. Bazo refreshed himself with a long draught of the thick tart bubbling gruel and then he greeted his fellow indunas in strict order of their seniority, beginning with Somabula and going slowly down the ranks; and while he did so he found himself mourning their pitiful shrunken numbers, only twenty-six of them were left.

'Kamuza, my cousin.' He looked across at the twenty-sixth and most junior of the indunas. 'My sweetest friend, I see you.'

Then Bazo did something that was without precedent, he

62

came to his feet and looked over their heads, and went on with the formal greetings.

'I greet you, Manonda, the brave!' he cried. 'I see you hanging on the branch of the mkusi tree. Dead by your own hand, choosing death rather than to live as a slave of white men.'

The assembled indunas glanced over their own shoulders, following the direction of Bazo's gaze with expressions of superstitious awe.

'Is that you, Ntabene? In life they called you the Mountain, and like a mountain you fell on the banks of the Shangani. I greet you, brave spirit.'

The assembled indunas understood then. Bazo was calling the roll of honour, and they took up the greeting in a deep growl.

'*Sakubona*, Ntabene.'

'I see you, Tambo. The waters of the Bembesi crossing ran red with your blood.'

'*Sakubona*, Tambo,' growled the indunas of Kumalo.

Bazo threw aside his cloak and began to dance. It was a swaying sensuous dance and the sweat sprang to gloss his skin and the gunshot wounds glowed upon his chest like dark jewels. Each time he called the name of one of the missing indunas, he lifted his right knee until it touched his chest, and then brought his bare foot down with a crash upon the hard earth, and the assembly echoed the hero's name.

At last Bazo sank down upon his stool, and the silence was fraught with a kind of warlike ecstasy. Slowly all their heads turned until they were looking at Somabula, the eldest, the most senior. The old induna rose and faced them, and then, because this was an *indaba* of the most weighty consequences, he began to recite the history of the Matabele nation. Though they had all heard it a thousand times since their infancy, the indunas leaned forward avidly. There was no written word, no archives to store this history, it must be remembered verbatim to be passed on to their children, and their children's children.

The story began in Zululand a thousand miles to the south, with the young warrior Mzilikazi defying the mad tyrant Chaka, and fleeing northwards with his single impi from the Zulu might. It followed his wanderings, his battles with the forces that Chaka sent to pursue him, his victories over the little tribes which stood in Mzilikazi's path. It related how he took the young men of the conquered tribes into his impis and gave the young women as wives to his warriors. It recorded the growth of Mzilikazi from a fugitive and rebel, to, first, a little chieftain, then to a great war chief, and at last to a mighty king.

Somabula related faithfully the terrible M'fecane, the destruction of a million souls as Mzilikazi laid waste to the land between the Orange river and the Limpopo. Then he went on to tell of the coming of the white men, and the new method of waging war. He conjured up the squadrons of sturdy little ponies with bearded men upon their backs, galloping into gunshot range, then wheeling away to reload before the amadoda could carry the blade to them. He retold how the impis had first met the rolling fortresses, the squares of wagons lashed together with trek chains, the thorn branches woven into the spokes of the wheels and into every gap in the wooden barricade, and how the ranks of Matabele had broken and perished upon those walls of wood and thorn.

His voice sank mournfully as he told of the exodus northwards, driven by the grim bearded men on horseback. He recalled how the weaklings and the infants had died on that tragic trek, and then Somabula's voice rose joyfully as he described the crossing of the Limpopo and the Shashi rivers and the discovery of this beautiful bountiful land beyond.

By then Somabula's voice was strained and hoarse, and

he sank down onto his stool and drank from the beerpot while Babiaan, his half-brother, rose to describe the great days, the subjugation of the surrounding tribes, the multiplication of the Matabele cattle-herds until they darkened the sweet golden grasslands, the ascension of Lobengula, 'the one who drives like the wind', to the kingship, the fierce raids when the impis swept hundreds of miles beyond the borders, bringing home the plunder and the slaves, that made the Matabele great. He reminded them how the regiments, plumed and befurred, carrying their great colour-matched war shields had paraded before the king like the endless flow of the Zambezi river; how the maidens danced at the Festival of First Fruits, bare-breasted and anointed with shiny red clay, bedecked with wild flowers and beads. He described the secret showing of the treasure, when Lobengula's wives smeared his vast body with thick fat and then stuck the diamonds to it, diamonds stolen by the young bucks from the great pit that the white men had dug far to the south.

Listening to the telling of it, the indunas remembered vividly how the uncut stones had glowed on the king's gross body like a coat of precious mail, or like the armoured scales of some wondrous mythical reptilian monster. In those days how great had been the king, how uncountable his herds, how fierce and warlike the young men and how beautiful the girls – and they nodded and exclaimed in approbation.

Then Babiaan sank down and Gandang rose from his stool. He was tall and powerful, a warrior in the late noon of his powers, his nobility unquestioned, his courage tested and proven a hundred times, and as he took up the tale, his voice was deep and resonant.

He told how the white men had come up from the south. To begin with there were only one or two of them begging small favours, to shoot a few elephant, to trade their beads and bottles for native copper and ivory. Then there were more of them, and their demands were more insistent, more worrisome. They wanted to preach a strange three-headed god, they wanted to dig holes and search for the yellow metal and the bright stones. Deeply troubled, Lobengula had come to this place in the Matopos, and the Umlimo had warned him that when the sacred bird images flew from the ruins of Great Zimbabwe, then there would be no more peace in the land.

'The stone falcons were stolen from the sacred places,' Gandang reminded them, 'and Lobengula knew then that he could no more resist the white men than his father, Mzilikazi, had been able to.'

Thus the king had chosen the most powerful of all the white petitioners, 'Lodzi', the big blue-eyed man who had eaten up the diamond mines and who was the induna of the white queen across the sea. Hoping to make him an ally, Lobengula had entered into a treaty with Lodzi; in exchange for gold coins and guns, he had granted to him a charter to dig for the buried treasures of the earth exclusively in Lobengula's eastern dominions.

However, Lodzi had sent a great train of wagons with hard fighting men like Selous and Bakela, leading hundreds of young white men armed like soldiers to take possession of the Charter lands. Sorrowfully, Gandang recited the long list of grievances and the breaking of faith, which had culminated in the clatter of Maxim guns, in the destruction of the king's kraal at Bulawayo, and the flight of Lobengula towards the north.

Finally, he described Lobengula's death. Broken-hearted and sick, the king had taken poison, and Gandang himself had laid the body in a secret cave overlooking the valley of the Zambezi, and he had placed all the king's possessions around him, his stool, his head-pillow of ivory, his sleeping-mat and fur kaross, his beerpots and beef-bowls, his guns and his war shield, his battle-axe and stabbing-spear, and at the last the little clay pots of glittering diamonds he had laid at Lobengula's gout-distorted feet. When all was done, Gandang had walled up the entrance to the cave, and slaughtered the slaves who had done the work. Then he had led the shattered nation back southwards into captivity.

At the last words, Gandang's hands fell to his sides, his chin sank onto the broad scarred and muscled chest, and a desolate silence descended upon them. At last one of the indunas in the second rank spoke. He was a frail old man with all the teeth missing from his upper jaw. His lower lids drooped away from his watery eyeballs so that the inner flesh showed like pink velvet and his voice was scratchy and breathless.

'Let us choose another king,' he began, but Bazo interrupted him.

'A king of slaves, a king of captives?' He laughed abruptly, scornfully. 'There can be no king until there is a nation once again.'

The ancient induna sank back, and gummed his toothless mouth, blinking about him miserably, his mind altering direction in the way of old men. 'The cattle,' he murmured, 'they have taken our cattle.'

The others hummed in angry assent. Cattle were the only true wealth; gold and diamonds were white men's baubles, but cattle were the foundation of the nation's welfare.

'One-Bright-Eye sends unblooded young bucks of our own people to lord it in the kraals—' complained another. 'One-Bright-Eye' was the Matabele name for General Mungo St John, the Chief Native Commissioner of Matabeleland.

'These Company police are armed with guns, and they show no respect for the custom and the law. They laugh at the indunas and the tribal elders, and they take the young girls into the bushes—'

'One-Bright-Eye orders all our *amadoda*, even those of

67

Zanzi blood, respected warriors and the fathers of warriors to labour like lowly *amaholi*, like dirt-eating slaves, digging his roads.'

The litany of their wrongs, real and fancied, was recited yet again by a succession of angry indunas, while only Somabula and Babiaan and Gandang and Bazo sat aloof.

'Lodzi has burned our shields and snapped the blades of the stabbing-spears. He has refused our young men the ancient right to raid the Mashona when all the world knows that the Mashona are our dogs to kill or let live as we choose.'

'One-Bright-Eye has disbanded the impis, and now no man knows who has the right to take a wife, nobody knows which maize field belongs to which village and the people squabble like sickly children over the few scrawny beasts that Lodzi has returned to us.'

'What must we do?' cried one, and then another strange and unprecedented thing happened. All of them, even Somabula, looked towards the tall scarred young man they called the Wanderer, and they waited expectantly for no one knew what.

Bazo made a sign with one hand and Tanase stooped out through the entrance of the reed hut. Clad only in the brief leather apron, slim and straight and supple, she carried the roll of sleeping-mat in her arms, and she knelt before Bazo and unrolled the mat on the earth at his feet.

The nearest indunas who could see what was concealed in the roll grunted with excitement. Bazo took it up in both hands and held it high. It caught the light, and now they all gasped. The design of the blade was by King Chaka himself; the metal had been beaten out and polished to burning silver by the skilled smiths of the Rozwi, and the bloodwood shaft had been bound with copper wire and the coarse black hairs from the tail-tuft of a bull elephant.

'Jee!' hissed one of the indunas, the deep drawn-out war chant of the fighting impis, and the others took up the cry, swaying slightly to the force of it, their faces lighting with the first ecstasy of the fighting madness.

Gandang put a halt to it. He sprang to his feet and the chant broke off as he made an abrupt gesture.

'One blade will not arm the nation, one blade will not prevail against the little three-legged guns of Lodzi.'

Bazo rose and stood facing his father.

'Take it in your hands, Baba,' he invited, and Gandang shook his head angrily, but he could not take his eyes off the weapon.

'Feel how the heft of it can make a man of even a slave,' Bazo insisted quietly, and this time Gandang stretched out his right hand. His palm was bloodless white with tension and his fingers trembled as they closed around the grip.

'Still it is only one blade,' he insisted, but he could not resist the feel of the beautiful weapon and he stabbed into the air with it.

'There are a thousand like this,' Bazo whispered.

'Where?' Somabula barked.

'Tell us where,' clamoured the other indunas, but Bazo goaded them.

'By the time that the first rains fall, there will be five thousand more. At fifty places in the hills the smiths are at work.'

'Where?' Somabula repeated. 'Where are they?'

'Hidden in the caves of these hills.'

'Why were we not told?' Babiaan demanded.

Bazo answered, 'There would have been those who doubted it could be done, those who counselled caution and delay, and there was no time for talk.'

Gandang nodded. 'We all know he is right, defeat has turned us into chattering old women. But now,' he handed the assegai to the man beside him, 'feel it!' he ordered.

'How will we assemble the impis?' the man asked, turning the weapon in his hands. 'They are scattered and broken.'

'That is the task of each of you. To rebuild the impis,

and to make certain that they are ready when the spears are sent out.'

'How will the spears reach us?'

'The women will bring them, in bundles of thatching-grass, in rolls of sleeping-mats.'

'Where will we attack? Will we strike at the heart, at the great kraal the white men have built at GuBulawayo?'

'No.' Bazo's voice rose fiercely. 'That was the madness which destroyed us before. In our rage we forgot the way of Chaka and Mzilikazi, we attacked into the strength of the enemy, we went in across good shooting ground onto the wagons where the guns waited.' Bazo broke off, and bowed his head towards the senior indunas. 'Forgive me, Baba, the puppy should not yap before the old dog barks. I speak out of turn.'

'You are no puppy, Bazo,' Somabula growled. 'Speak on!'

'We must be the fleas,' Bazo said quietly. 'We must hide in the white man's clothing and sting him in the soft places until we drive him to madness. But when he scratches, we will move on to another soft place.

'We must lurk in darkness and attack in the dawn, we must wait for him in the bad ground and probe his flanks and his rear.' Bazo never raised his voice, but all of them listened avidly. 'Never must we run in against the walls of the laager, and when the three-legged guns begin to laugh like old women, we must drift away like the morning mist at the first rays of the sun.'

'This is not war,' protested Babiaan.

'It is war, Baba,' Bazo contradicted, 'the new kind of war, the only kind of war which we can win.'

'He is right,' a voice called from the ranks of indunas. 'That is the way it must be.'

They spoke up, one after the other, and no man argued against Bazo's vision, until the turn came back to Babiaan.

'My brother Somabula has spoken the truth, you are no puppy, Bazo. Tell us only one thing more, when will it be?'

'That I cannot tell you.'

'Who can?'

Bazo looked down at Tanase, who still knelt at his feet.

'We have assembled in this valley for good reason,' Bazo told them. 'If all agree, then my woman who is an intimate of the Umlimo, and an initiate of the mysteries, will go up to the sacred cavern to take the oracle.'

'She must go immediately.'

'No, Baba.' Tanase's lovely head was still bowed in deep respect. 'We must wait until the Umlimo sends for us.'

There were places where the scars had knotted into hard lumps in Bazo's flesh. The machine-gun bullets had done deep damage. One arm, fortunately not the spear arm, was twisted and shortened, permanently deformed. After hard marching or exercise with the weapons of war, or after the nervous tension of planning and arguing and persuading others to his views, the torn and lumpy flesh often seized up in agonizing spasms.

Kneeling beside him in the little reed hut, Tanase could see the cramped muscles and rigid contraction of sinews under his dark skin twisted like living black mambas trying to escape from a silken bag. With strong tapered fingers, she worked the ointment of fat and herbs into the crested muscle down his spine and the shoulder-blades, following the rubbery contractions up his neck to the base of his skull. Bazo groaned at the sweet agony of her bone-hard fingers, but slowly he relaxed and the knotted muscles subsided.

'You are good for me in so many ways,' he murmured.

'I was born for no other reason,' she answered, but Bazo sighed and shook his head slowly.

'You and I were both born for some purpose which is still hidden from us. We know that – we are different, you and I.'

She touched his lips with her finger to still him. 'We will come back to that on the morrow.'

She placed both hands on his shoulders and drew him backwards, until he lay flat on the reed mat, and she began to work on his chest and the rigid muscles of his flat hard belly.

'Tonight there is only us,' she repeated, in the throaty purr of a lioness at the kill, delighting in the power she could wield over him with the mere pressure of her finger-tips, and yet at the same time consumed by a tenderness so deep that she felt her chest crushing beneath the weight of it. 'Tonight we are all the world.' She leaned forward and touched the bullet-wounds with the tip of her tongue and his arousal was so massive that she could not encompass it within the span of her thumb and long pink-lined fingers.

He tried to sit up, but she held him down with a light pressure against his chest, then she slipped the drawstring of her apron and with a single movement straddled him, both of them crying out involuntarily at the heat and terrible yearning of each other's bodies. Then they were swept away together in a sudden exquisite fury.

When it had passed, she cradled his head against her bosom, and crooned to him like an infant, until his breathing was deep and regular in the dark hut. Even then, though she was silent, she did not sleep with him but lay and marvelled that such rage and compassion could possess her at the same moment in time.

'I will never know peace again,' she realized suddenly. 'And nor will he.' And she mourned for the man she loved, and for the need to goad and drive him on towards the destiny that she knew awaited both of them.

On the third day the messenger of the Umlimo came down from the cavern to where the indunas waited in the village.

The messenger was a pretty girl-child with a solemn expression and old wise eyes. She was on the very edge of puberty with the hard little stones already forming in her mulberry-dark nipples and the first light fuzz shading the deep cleft in the angle of her thighs. Around her neck she wore a talisman that only Tanase recognized. It was a sign that one day this child in her turn would take on the sacred mantle of the Umlimo and preside in the gruesome cavern in the cliff above the village.

Instinctively the child looked to Tanase where she squatted to one side of the ranks of men, and with her eyes and a secret hand sign of the initiates, Tanase indicated Somabula, the senior induna. The child's indecision was merely a symptom of the swift degeneration of Matabele society. In the time of the kings no one, child nor adult, would have been in any doubt as to the order of precedence.

When Somabula rose to follow the messenger, his half-brothers rose with him, Babiaan on one hand and Gandang on the other.

'You also, Bazo,' Somabula said, and though Bazo was younger and more junior than some of them, none of the other indunas protested at his inclusion in the mission.

The child-witch took Tanase's hand, for they were sisters of the dark spirits, and the two of them led the way up the steep path. The mouth of the cavern was a hundred paces wide, but the roof was barely high enough to clear a man's head. Once long ago the opening had been fortified with blocks of dressed stone, worked in the same fashion as the walls of Great Zimbabwe, but these had been tumbled into rough piles, leaving gaps like those in an old man's teeth.

The little party halted involuntarily. The four indunas hung back and drew closer together, as though to take comfort from each other. Men who had wielded the assegai in a hundred bloody battles and run onto the guns of the white men's laager were fearful now as they faced the dark entrance.

In the silence a voice spoke suddenly from above them, emanating from the bare cliff-face of smooth lichen-streaked granite. 'Let the indunas of royal Kumalo enter the sacred place!' They were the quavering discordant tones of an ancient bedlam, and the four warriors looked up fearfully, but there was no living thing to be seen, and none of them could summon the courage to reply.

Tanase had felt the child's hand quiver slightly in her grip at the ventriloquist effort of projection, and only Tanase was so attuned to the ways of the witches that she knew how the art of the voices was taught to the apprentices of the Umlimo. The child was already highly skilled, and Tanase shuddered involuntarily as she realized what other fearful skills she must have mastered, what other gruesome ordeals and terrible agonies she must already have endured. In a moment of empathy she squeezed the child's narrow cool hand, and together they stepped through the ruined portals.

Behind them the four noble warriors crowded with the temerity of children, peering around them anxiously and stumbling on the uneven footing. The throat of the cavern narrowed, and Tanase thought with a flash of grim humour that it was as well that the light was too bad for the indunas to make out clearly the walls on either hand, for even their warlike courage might have been unequal to the horror of the catacombs.

In a bygone age that the verbal history of the Rozwi and the Karanga tribes could no longer recount, generations before bold Mzilikazi led his tribe into these hills, another plundering marauder had passed this way. It might have been Manatassi, the legendary conquering queen, at the head of her merciless hordes, laying waste to the land and slaughtering everything in her path, sparing neither woman nor child nor even the domestic animals.

The threatened tribes had taken refuge in this valley, but the marauders had burst through the narrow pass and the miserable host had fled into their final sanctuary in this cavern. The roof overhead was still coated with soot, for the marauders had not deemed it worthwhile to lay siege to the cavern. They had pulled down the protecting wall and blocked the entrance with piles of green brush and wood. Then they had put in fire. The entire tribe had perished, and smoke had mummified their remains. So they had lain down the years in banks and heaps, piled as high as the low roof.

As Tanase's party went forward, from somewhere ahead of them a faint bluish light grew in intensity, until Bazo exclaimed suddenly and pointed to the wall of human debris beside him. In places, the parchment-like flesh had peeled away so that the ivory skulls grinned at them, and the contorted skeletal arms seemed to wave a macabre salutation as they passed. The indunas were bathed in sweat, despite the cool gloom, and their expressions were awed and sickly.

Tanase and the child followed the twisting pathway with unerring familiarity, and came out at last above a deep natural amphitheatre. A single ray of sunlight burned down from a narrow crack in the domed cavern roof. On the floor of the amphitheatre was an open fireplace, and a tendril of pale blue smoke twisted slowly upwards towards the opening high above. Tanase and the child led them down the rock steps to the smooth sandy floor of the amphitheatre, and at her gesture the four indunas sank down gratefully and squatted facing the smouldering fire.

Tanase released the child's hand, and sat a little to one side and behind the men. The child crossed to the far wall and took a handful of herbs from one of the big round clay pots that stood there. She threw the handful upon the fire

75

and immediately a great yellow cloud of acrid smoke billowed upwards, and as it slowly cleared, the indunas started and exclaimed with superstitious dread.

A grotesque figure faced them from across the flames. It was an albino, with silver-white leprous skin. It was a woman, for the great pale breasts were massively pendulous, the nipples a painful boiled pink colour. She was stark naked and her dense public bush was white as frost-struck winter grass, and above it her belly hung in loose balconies of fat. Her forehead was low and sloped backwards, her mouth was wide and thin so that she appeared toadlike. Across her broad and flattened nose and her pale cheeks, the unpigmented skin had erupted in a tender raw rash. Her thickened forearms were folded across her belly and her thighs, splotched with large ginger-coloured freckles, were wide-spread as she knelt on a mat of zebra skin and regarded the men before her fixedly.

'I see you, oh Chosen One,' Somabula greeted her. Despite an enormous effort of will, his voice trembled.

The Umlimo made no response, and Somabula rocked back on his heels and was silent. The girl-child was busy amongst the pots, and now she came forward and knelt beside the gross albino, proffering the clay pipe she had prepared.

The Umlimo took the long reed stem between her thin silvery lips, and the girl lifted a live coal from the fire with her bare hands and placed it on the vegetable ball in the bowl of the pipe. It began to glow and splutter and the Umlimo drew a slow lungful and then let the aromatic smoke trickle out of her simian nostrils. Immediately the heavy sweetish odour of *insanghu* carried to the waiting men.

The oracle was induced in different ways. Before Tanase had lost the power, it had descended spontaneously upon her, throwing her into convulsive fits, while the spirit voices struggled to escape from her throat. However, this grotesque successor had to resort to the wild hemp pipe. The seeds and flowers of the *Cannabis sativa* plant, crushed in the green and moulded into sun-dried balls, were her key to the spirit world.

She smoked quietly, a dozen short inhalations without allowing the smoke to escape, holding it in until her pale face seemed to swell and the pink pupils of her eyes glazed over. Then she expelled the smoke with an explosive exhalation, and started again. The indunas watched her with such fascination that they did not at first notice the soft scratching sound on the cavern floor. It was Bazo who at last started and grunted with shock, and involuntarily grasped his father's forearm. Gandang exclaimed and began to rise in horror and alarm, but Tanase's voice arrested him.

'Do not move. It is dangerous,' she whispered urgently, and Gandang sank back and froze into stillness.

From the dark recesses in the back of the cavern a lobster-like creature scuttled across the pale sandy floor towards where the Umlimo squatted. The firelight glinted on the glossy armoured carapace of the creature as it reached the Umlimo, and then began to climb up her bloated silver-white body. It paused in her lap, with the long segmented tail lifting and pulsing, its spiderlike legs hooked into the Umlimo's coarse white pubic curls, before it began climbing again, up over her bulging belly, hanging from one drooping pale breast like some evil fruit on the bough, upwards it climbed, onto her shoulder and then it reached the angle of her jaw below the ear.

The Umlimo remained unperturbed, sipping little puffs of the narcotic smoke from the mouthpiece of her pipe, her pink eyes staring blindly at the indunas. The huge glittering insect crawled up her temple and then sideways until it stopped in the centre of her crusted and scabbed forehead, where it hung upside down, and the long scorpion tail, longer than a man's forefinger, arched up over its horny back.

The Umlimo began to mutter and mumble and a rime of white froth bubbled onto her raw lips. She said something in a strange language, and the scorpion on her forehead pulsed its long segmented tail, and from the point of the red fang at the tip a clear drop of venom welled and sparkled like a jewel in the dim light.

The Umlimo spoke again, in a hoarse strained voice and an unintelligible language.

'What does she say?' Bazo whispered, turning his head towards Tanase. 'What language does she use?'

'She speaks in the secret tongue of the initiates,' Tanase murmured. 'She is inviting the spirits to enter and take control of her body.'

The albino reached up slowly and took the scorpion off her forehead. She held the head and body within her closed fist, only the long tail whipped furiously from side to side, and she brought it down slowly and held it to her own breast. The scorpion struck, and the rigid thorn fang buried itself deeply in her obscene pink flesh. The Umlimo's face did not alter, and the scorpion struck again and again, leaving little red punctures in the soft breast.

'She will die!' gasped Bazo.

'Let her be,' hissed Tanase. 'She is not like other women. The poison will not harm her – it serves only to open her soul to the spirits.'

The albino lifted the scorpion from her bosom, and dropped it into the flames of the fire where it writhed and withered into a little charred speck, and suddenly the Umlimo uttered an unearthly shriek.

'The spirits enter,' Tanase whispered.

The Umlimo's mouth gaped open, and little glassy strings of saliva drooled from her chin, while three or four wild voices seemed to issue from her throat simultaneously, each trying to drown out the others, voices of men and women and animals, until at last one rose above them, and silenced the others. It was a man's voice, and it spoke in the mystical

78

tongue; even its modulation and cadence were totally alien, but Tanase quietly translated for them.

'When the noon sun goes dark with wings, and the trees are bare of leaves in the springtime, then, warriors of Matabele, put an edge to your steel.'

The four indunas nodded. They had heard this prophecy before, for the Umlimo was often repetitious and always she was obscure. They had puzzled over the same words before. It was this message that Bazo and Tanase had carried to the scattered peoples of the Matabele during their wandering from kraal to kraal.

The gross albino seer grunted and threshed her arms, as though struggling with an invisible adversary. The pale pink eyes jerked in her skull, out of kilter with each other, so that she squinted and leered, and she ground her teeth together with a sound like a hound worrying a bone.

The girl-child rose quietly from where she squatted amongst the pots, and she leaned over the Umlimo and dashed a pinch of pungent red powder into her face. The Umlimo's paroxysm eased, the clenched jaw fell open and another voice spoke, a guttural, blurred sound, barely human, using the same weird dialect, and Tanase strained forward to catch each syllable and then repeated calmly:

'When the cattle lie with their heads twisted to touch their flank, and cannot rise, then warriors of Matabele take heart, for the time will be nigh.'

This time there was a slight difference in the wording of the prophecy from the one that they had heard before, and all of them pondered it silently as the Umlimo fell forward onto her face and flopped limply as a boneless jellyfish. Slowly all movement of the albino's body ceased, and she lay like death.

Gandang made as if to rise, but Tanase hissed a warning, and he arrested the movement and they waited, the only sound in the cavern was the click and rustle of the fire and the flirt of bats' wings high against the domed roof.

Then another convulsion ran down the Umlimo's back, and her spine arched, her hideous face lifted, but this time her voice was childlike and sweet, and she spoke in the Matabele language for all of them to understand.

'When the hornless cattle are eaten up by the great cross, let the storm begin.'

Her head sagged forward, and the child covered her with a kaross of fluffy jackal furs.

'It is over,' said Tanase. 'There will be no more.'

Thankfully the four indunas rose, and crept back along the gloomy pathway through the catacombs, but as they saw the glimmer of sunlight through the entrance ahead, so their steps quickened, until they burst out in the valley with such indecent and undignified haste that they avoided each other's eyes.

That night, sitting in the open-sided *setenghi* on the floor of the valley, Somabula repeated the prophecies of the Umlimo to the assembled indunas. They nodded over the first two familiar riddles, and as they had a hundred times before, they delved inconclusively for the meaning, and then agreed: 'We will find the meaning when the time is appointed – it is always the way.'

Then Somabula went on to relate the third prophecy of the Umlimo, the new and unfamiliar riddle: 'When the hornless cattle are eaten up by the great cross.'

The indunas took snuff and passed the beerpots from hand to hand, as they talked and argued the hidden meaning, and only when they had all spoken did Somabula look beyond them to where Tanase sat holding the child under her leather cloak to protect him from the night chill.

'What is the true meaning, woman?' he asked.

'Not even the Umlimo herself knows that,' Tanase replied, 'but when our ancestors first saw the white man riding up from the south, they believed that their mounts were hornless cattle.'

'Horses?' Gandang asked thoughtfully.

'It may be so,' Tanase agreed. 'Yet a single word of the Umlimo may have as many meanings as there are crocodiles in the Limpopo river.'

'What is the cross, the great cross, of the prophecy?' Bazo asked.

'The cross is the sign of the white men's three-headed god,' Gandang answered. 'My senior wife, Juba, the little Dove, wears that sign about her neck, given to her by the missionary at Khami when she poured water on her head.'

'Is it possible that the white men's god will eat up the white men's horses?' doubted Babiaan. 'Surely he is their protector, not their destroyer.'

And the discussion passed from elder to elder, while the watchfire burned low and over the valley the vast shining firmament of the heavens turned with weighty dignity.

To the south of the valley, amongst the other heavenly bodies, burned a group of four great white stars that the Matabele called the 'Sons of Manatassi'. They told how Manatassi, that terrible queen, had birth-strangled her offspring with her own hands, so that none of them might ever challenge her monarchy. According to the legend, the souls of the little ones had ascended to shine on high, eternal witness to the cruelty of their dam.

Not one of the indunas knew that the name by which the white men knew these same stars was the Southern Cross.

R alph Ballantyne was wrong when he predicted to Harry Mellow that by the time they returned to the base camp Mr Rhodes and his entourage would have moved on to Bulawayo. For as they rode in through the gates of the stockade, he saw the magnificent mule coach still parked where he had last seen it, and beside it were a dozen other decrepit and travel-worn vehicles: Cape carts and surreys, even a bicycle with worn tyres replaced by strips of buffalo-hide.

'Mr Rhodes has set up court here,' Cathy explained furiously, as soon as she and Ralph were alone in the bath tent. 'I have made the camp too comfortable by half, and he has taken it over from me.'

'As he does everything else,' Ralph remarked philosophically, as he stripped off his stinking shirt, and flung it into the far corner. 'I've slept in that for five nights, by God, the laundry boy will have to beat it to death with a club before he gets it into the tub.'

'Ralph, you aren't taking it seriously,' Cathy stamped her foot in frustration. 'This is my home. The only home I have, and now do you know what that – what Mr Rhodes told me?'

'Have we got any more soap?' Ralph demanded as he hopped on one leg to free his breeches. 'One bar will not be enough.'

'He said, "Jordan will be in charge of the kitchens while we are here, Mrs Ballantyne, he knows my tastes." What do you think of that?'

'Jordan is a damned fine cook.' Ralph lowered himself gingerly into the bath, and grunted as his naked buttocks touched the nearly boiling surface.

'I have been forbidden my own kitchen.'

'Get in!' Ralph ordered, and she broke off and stared at him incredulously.

'What did you say?' she demanded, but in reply he seized her ankle and toppled Cathy shrieking her protests on top of himself. Steaming water and suds splattered the canvas walls of the tent, and when he released her at last, she was sodden to the waist.

'Your dress is soaked,' he pointed out complacently; 'now you have no choice – take it off!'

Naked, she sat with her back to him in the galvanized

bath with her knees drawn up under her chin, and her damp hair piled on top of her head, but still she continued her protest.

'Even Louise could bear the man's arrogance and misogyny no longer. She made your father take her back to King's Lynn, so now I have to bear him on my own!'

'You always were a brave girl,' Ralph told her and ran the soapy flannel caressingly down her smooth back.

'And now the word has gone out to every dead-beat and drifter in Matabeleland that he is here and they are riding in from every direction for the free whisky.'

'Mr Rhodes is a generous man,' Ralph agreed, and tenderly slid the soapy flannel over her shoulder and down the front.

'It is your whisky,' said Cathy, and caught his wrist before the flannel could reach its obvious destination.

'The man has an infernal nerve.' For the first time Ralph showed some emotion. 'We will have to get rid of him. That whisky is worth £10 a bottle in Bulawayo.' Ralph managed to slip the flannel a little further south.

'Ralph, that tickles.' Cathy wriggled.

'When are your twin sisters arriving?' He ignored her protest.

'They sent a runner ahead, they should be here before nightfall. Ralph, give me that flannel immediately!'

'We will see how steely Mr Rhodes' nerves really are—'

'Ralph I can do that myself, thank you kindly, give me the flannel!'

'And we will also see how sharp Harry Mellow's reflexes are—'

'Ralph, are you crazy? We are in the bath!'

'We will take care of both of them with one stroke.'

'Ralph, you can't! You can't – not in the bath!'

'We will have Jordan out of your kitchen, Harry Mellow overseer of the Harkness Mine and Mr Rhodes on his way to Bulawayo an hour after those two arrive—'

'Ralph, darling, do stop talking. I can't concentrate on two things at once,' Cathy murmured.

The tableau at the trestle-table in the dining tent seemed unaltered since Ralph had last seen it, rather like one of the productions at Madame Tussaud's Waxworks. Mr Rhodes even wore the same clothing as he dominated the tent with his expansive charisma.

Only the bit players seated in the position of petitioners facing the long table had changed. These were a motley bunch of out-of-luck prospectors, concession-seekers, and impecunious promoters of ambitious ventures, who had been attracted by Mr Rhodes' reputation and millions like jackal and hyena to the lion's kill.

It was the mode in Matabeleland to display one's individuality by adopting eccentric headgear, and the selection which faced Mr Rhodes across the table included a Scottish bonnet with an eagle feather pinned to the brim by a yellow cairngorm, a tall brushed beaver girt with a green St Patrick's ribbon, and a magnificent embroidered Mexican sombrero, the owner of which was relating a meandering tale of woe which Mr Rhodes cut short. He did not enjoy listening as much as he did talking.

'So then, you've had enough of Africa, have you? But you haven't the passage money?' he asked brusquely.

'That's it exactly, Mr Rhodes, you see my old mother—'

'Jordan, give the fellow a chitty to see him home, and charge it to me personally.' He waved away the man's thanks, and looked up as Ralph came into the tent.

'Harry tells me your trip was a great success. He panned your crushings from the Harkness reef at thirty ounces a ton, that's thirty times richer than the best banket reef of the Witwatersrand. I think we should open a bottle of champagne. Jordan, don't we have a few bottles of the Pommery '87 left?'

'At least I'm not providing the champagne as well as the whisky,' Ralph thought cynically, as he lifted his glass to the toast. 'The Harkness Mine.' He joined the dutiful chorus and the moment he had drunk he turned on Dr Leander Starr Jameson.

'What is this about the mining laws?' he demanded. 'Harry tells me you are adopting the American mining code.'

'Do you have any objection?' Jameson flushed, and his sandy moustache bristled.

'That code was drawn up by lawyers to keep themselves in fat fees in perpetuity. The new Witwatersrand laws are simpler and a million times more workable. By God, isn't it enough that your Company royalty will rob us of fifty per cent of our profits?' As Ralph said it, it dawned upon him that the American mining code would be a smoke-screen behind which the artful Rhodes could manoeuvre at will.

'Remember, young Ballantyne,' Jameson stroked his moustache, and blinked piously. 'Remember who the country belongs to. Remember who paid the costs of the occupation of Mashonaland and who financed the Matabele war.'

'Government by a commercial company.' Despite himself, Ralph felt his anger rising again and he clenched his hands on the table in front of him. 'A company that owns the police force and the courts. And if I have a dispute with your Company, who will decide it – surely not the BSA Company's own magistrate?'

'There are precedents.' Mr Rhodes' tone was reasonable and placatory, but his eyes were not. 'The British East India Company—' And Ralph's reply crackled:

'The British government eventually had to take India

away from those pirates Clive, Hastings and that ilk, for corruption and oppression of the natives. The sepoy rising was the logical outcome of their administration.'

'Mr Ballantyne.' Mr Rhodes' voice always went shrill when he was excited or angry. 'I am going to ask you to withdraw those remarks, they are historically inaccurate, and by implication insulting.'

'I withdraw, unreservedly.' Ralph was angry with himself now, he was usually much too cool-headed to allow himself to be provoked. There was no possible profit to be gained from a head-on collision with Cecil John Rhodes. His smile was easy and friendly as he went on. 'I am sure we will have no need of the services of a Company magistrate.'

Mr Rhodes answered his smile with the same ease, but there was a steely blue flicker in his eyes as he raised his glass. 'To a deep mine and a deeper relationship,' he said, and only one other person in the tent recognized it as a challenge.

Jordan moved restlessly in his camp chair at the back of the tent. He knew these two men so well, loved both so dearly. Ralph his brother had been with him through all that lonely and tempestuous childhood, his protector and his comfort in the bad times and his joyous friend through the good.

Looking at his brother now, and comparing Ralph to himself, it seemed impossible that two brothers could be so different. Where Jordan was blond and slim and graceful, Ralph was dark and muscled and powerful; where Jordan was gentle and self-effacing, Ralph was hard and bold and as hawk-fierce as his Matabele praise-name implied. Instinctively Jordan looked from him to the big burly figure facing him across the camp table.

Here Jordan's feelings went beyond love itself to a kind of religious fervour. He did not really see the physical changes that a few short years had wrought in this god-head of his existence: the thickening of Mr Rhodes' already bulky body, the bloating and coarsening of features already mottled with cyanosis caused by the labouring of the damaged heart, the reddish-blond curls receding swiftly now and slashed with grey at the temples. The way a loving woman places little store on the appearance of the man she has chosen as her own, so Jordan saw far beyond the marks of suffering and sickness and the racing years. He saw to the steely core of the man, the ultimate source of his immense power and brooding presence.

Jordan wanted to cry out to his beloved brother, to run to him and physically restrain him from the folly of turning this giant of a soul into an enemy. He had seen other men do just that, and be ruthlessly crushed.

Then with a sickening slide in the pit of his stomach, he knew which side he would cast his lot if that dreaded confrontation ever forced a choice upon him. He was Mr Rhodes' man, beyond brotherly ties and family loyalties, to the very end of life itself, he was Mr Rhodes' man.

He sought desperately for some plausible excuse to break the tension between the two most important persons in his life, but relief came from beyond the stockade, in the delighted cries of the servants, the hysterical barking of the camp dogs, the crunch of cartwheels and the excited shrieks of more than one woman. Jordan was the only one watching Ralph's face, so he caught the sly and smug expression as his brother rose.

'It seems we have more visitors,' Ralph said, and the twins came into the inner stockade.

Victoria came first, as Ralph had expected that she would. She came on long shapely legs, outlined beneath the whirl and boil of her thin cotton skirts, barefoot in defiance of all ladylike pretensions, carrying her shoes in one hand, and Jonathan riding on her hip. The child was squeaking like a warthog piglet that has lost the teat.

'Vicky! Vicky, did you bring me anything?'

'A kiss on the cheek and a slap on the behind.' Vicky

laughed, and hugged him. Her laughter was loud and gay and unaffected, her mouth was a little too large, but her lips were velvety as rose petals and sweetly shaped, her teeth were large and square and white as bone-china porcelain, and as she laughed her tongue, furry pink as that of a cat, curled between them. Her eyes were green and wide-spaced, her skin was that lustrous silky English perfection that neither sun nor massive doses of anti-malarial quinine could mar. She would have been striking, even without the dense tresses of copper-blonde hair, ruffled by the wind, and wild as the sea, that tumbled about her face and shoulders.

She riveted the attention of every man there, even Mr Rhodes, but it was to Ralph she ran, holding his son on her hip still, and she threw her free arm around his neck. She was so tall that she had only to stand on her toes to reach his lips. The kiss was not long held, but her lips were soft and wet, the pressure of her breasts through her cotton blouse was springy and elastic and warm against his chest, and her thighs against his sent a shock up his spine, so that Ralph broke the embrace, and for an instant her green eyes mocked him, dared him to something that she did not fully understand, revelling in this heady sense of power over all mankind that she had not yet tested to its limits.

Then she tossed Jonathan to Ralph and whirled away to run barefoot down the tent and launched herself into Jordan's arms.

'Darling Jordan, oh, how we have missed you!' She forced him into a prancing jig around the stockade, shaking out her shining hair and carolling joyously.

Ralph glanced at Mr Rhodes, and when he saw his expression of shock and unease, he grinned and released Jonathan, letting him race across to cling to Vicky's skirt and add his shrill voice to the uproar, then he turned to greet the second twin.

Elizabeth was as tall as Vicky, but darker. Her hair was

polished mahogany, shot through with sparks of burgundy and her skin was sun-kindly, gilded to the colour of a tiger's eyes. She was slim as a dancer, with a narrow waist and shoulders supporting a long heron neck, and her breasts were smaller than Vicky's, yet elegantly pointed, and though her voice was soft and her laughter a throaty purr, yet there was a mischievous quirk to her lips, a jaunty tilt to her head and a measured sexual candour and awareness to the gaze of her wild honey eyes.

She and Cathy were arm in arm, but now she slipped out of her elder sister's embrace and presented herself to Ralph.

'My favourite brother-in-law,' she murmured, and looking into her eyes Ralph was reminded that though her voice was softer, and her manner seemingly more restrained than that of her twin, yet Elizabeth was always the instigator and prime mover in any mischief that the pair conjured up. This close, her true beauty was apparent, less flamboyant than Vicky's perhaps, but the balance of her features and the depths beyond those golden-brown eyes were more disturbing.

She kissed Ralph, and the contact was as brief but even less sisterly than had been the elder twin's embrace, and as she drew back from it, she slanted her eyes with a pretence of innocence, that was more deadly than any brazening. Ralph broke the electric contact, and looked to Cathy, making a comical moue of resignation, and hoping that she still believed his studied avoidance of the twins was because he found them boisterous and childish.

Flushed and panting, Vicky released Jordan, placed her hands on her hips and asked Ralph, 'Ralph, are you not going to present us to the company?'

'Mr Rhodes, may I present my sisters-in-law,' said Ralph with relish.

'Oh, the famous Mr Rhodes,' Vicky gushed theatrically, but there were little green sparks in her eyes. 'It is such an honour to meet the conqueror of the Matabele nation, because, you see, King Lobengula was a personal friend of our family.'

'Please excuse my sister, Mr Rhodes.' Elizabeth curtsied, and her expression was demure. 'She intends no discourtesy, but our parents were the first missionaries to the Matabele, and our father sacrificed his life trying to help Lobengula while your troops were pursuing him to his death. My mother—'

'Young lady, I am fully aware who your mother is,' Mr Rhodes forestalled her sharply.

'Oh good,' Vicky chimed sweetly. 'Then you will appreciate the gift that she asked me to present to you.'

Vicky reached into the deep pocket of her long skirt and brought out a thin volume. It was bound in cardboard, not morocco leather, and the quality of the yellow paper was coarse and matt. She laid it on the trestle-table in front of Mr Rhodes, and when he saw the title his heavy jaw clamped closed. Even Ralph quailed slightly. He had counted on the twins providing an unsettling influence, but he had not expected them to be so instantly explosive.

The book was entitled *Trooper Hackett of Matabeleland*, by *Robyn Ballantyne*, for the twins' mother wrote and published under her maiden name. There was probably not a man in the stockade who had not already read the slim volume, or at least heard of its contents, and if Vicky had thrown a live mamba on the table, their consternation could not have been more intense.

The contents of the book were so dangerous that three reputable London publishers had rejected it, and finally Robyn St John had published it privately and created an immediate sensation. In six months it had sold almost two hundred thousand copies, and had been treated to extensive reviews in almost every influential newspaper both at home in England and abroad in the colonies.

The frontispiece of the book set the tone for the text

that followed. It was a murky photograph that depicted a dozen white men in BSA Company uniform standing under the spreading branches of a tall wild teak tree and looking up at the corpses of four semi-naked Matabele hanging by their necks from the topmost branches. There was no caption to the photograph, and the faces of the white men were too indistinct to be recognizable.

Now Mr Rhodes reached out and opened the book at the gruesome illustration. 'Those are four Matabele indunas who were wounded at the battle of Bembesi, and who committed suicide by hanging, rather than surrender to our forces,' he growled. 'They are not the victims of some atrocity as this scurrilous piece of offal implies.'

Mr Rhodes closed the book with a snap, and Elizabeth exclaimed sweetly, 'Oh, Mr Rhodes, Mama will be so disappointed that you did not enjoy her little story.'

The book described the fictional adventures of Trooper Hackett of the BSA Company expeditionary force, and his whole-hearted participation in the slaughter of the Matabele with machine-gun fire, the pursuit and shooting down of the fleeing survivors, the burning of the kraals, the looting of Lobengula's cattle and the rape of the young Matabele girls. Then Trooper Hackett is separated from his squadron and spends the night alone on a wild kopje, and while huddled over his camp-fire a mysterious white stranger comes out of the night and joins him at the fire. Hackett remarks, 'Ah, you have been in the wars, too, I see,' leaning forward and inspecting the stranger's feet. 'By God! Both of them! And right through – you must have had a bad time of it!'

And the stranger replies, 'It all happened a very long time ago,' then the reader is left in no doubt as to whom he is dealing with, especially when the author describes his beautiful gentle countenance and his all-seeing blue eyes. Abruptly the stranger breaks into a florid injunction to young Hackett.

'Take a message to England. Go to that great people and demand of them: "Where is the sword that was given into your hand, that with it you might enforce justice and deal out mercy? How came you to give it up into the hands of men whose search is gold, whose thirst is wealth, to whom the souls and bodies of their fellow men are counters in a game, men who have transformed the sword of a great people into a tool to burrow for gold, as the snouts of swine for earth nuts?"'

It was little wonder, Ralph smiled to himself, that Mr Rhodes pushed the book away and wiped the hand that had touched it on the lapel of his rumpled Norfolk jacket.

'Oh, Mr Rhodes,' murmured Vicky, angel-faced and wide-eyed. 'At the least you must read the inscription that Mama dedicated to you.' She retrieved the discarded volume, opened the flyleaf and read aloud, '"For Cecil John Rhodes, without whose endeavours this book would never have been written."'

Mr Rhodes rose from his seat with ponderous dignity.

'Ralph,' he said quietly. 'Thank you for your hospitality. Dr Jim and I will be getting on to Bulawayo, I think. We have spent too long here as it is.' Then he looked across at Jordan. 'The mules are well rested. Jordan, is there a moon tonight?'

'There will be a good moon tonight,' Jordan replied promptly, 'and there are no clouds so we will have a good light for the road.'

'Can we be ready to leave by this evening, then?'

It was a command, and Mr Rhodes did not wait for a reply, but stalked out of the stockade towards his own tent, and the little doctor followed him stiffly. The moment they were gone, the twins burst into merry tinkling laughter and hugged each other ecstatically.

'Mama would have been proud of you, Victoria Isabel—'

'Well, I am not.' Jordan's voice cut through their hilarity.

He was white-faced and shaking with anger. 'You are ill-mannered and silly little girls.'

'Oh Jordan,' Vicky wailed and seized his hands. 'Don't be cross. We love you so.'

'Oh yes, we do. Both of us.' Elizabeth took his other hand, but he pulled away from them.

'You do not have any idea in those giddy little heads how dangerous a game you are playing, not only for yourselves.' He strode away from them, but paused for a moment in front of Ralph. 'Nor do you, Ralph.' His expression softened, and he placed his hand on Ralph's shoulder. 'Please be more careful – for my sake, if not for your own.' Then he followed his master from the stockade.

Ralph pulled the gold hunter from the inner pocket of his waistcoat and made a show of inspecting it.

'Well,' he announced to the twins, 'sixteen minutes to clear the camp. That must be a new record even for you two.' He returned the watch to his pocket and put one arm around Cathy's shoulders. 'There you are, Katie my love, there is your home again without a single stranger.'

'That is not quite the case,' murmured a soft Kentucky accent, and Harry Mellow rose from the log he had been using as a seat and removed the slouch hat from his curly head. The twins stared at him for a startled instant, then flashed each other a look of complete accord and a remarkable transformation came over them. Liza smoothed her skirts and Vicky pushed back the dense dangling tresses from her face and their expressions became grave and their comportment ladylike.

'You may present the young gentleman, cousin Ralph,' said Vicky in accents so refined as to make Ralph glance at her to confirm it was the same girl speaking.

When the mule coach drove through the outer gates of the stockade, there was one member of Mr Rhodes' party who was not aboard.

'What did you tell Mr Rhodes?' Cathy asked, hanging onto Ralph's arm as they watched the coach rolling away, a dark shadow on the moon-silver road.

'I told him that I needed Harry for a day or two more to help me lay out the development for the Harkness.' Ralph lit his last cheroot of the day and they began the leisurely stroll around the camp that was a little ritual of their life together. It was their time of contentment and delicious anticipation, the time when they talked over the events of the day just past and planned for the one ahead, at the same time touching each other as they walked, her hand in the crook of his arm, their hips sliding against each other, a closeness which would soon lead naturally and sweetly to the wide soft cot in the bell tent.

'Was that true?' Cathy asked.

'Semi-true,' he admitted. 'I need him for longer than a day or two, more like ten or twenty years.'

'If you succeed, you will be one of the few men to get the better of Mr Rhodes, and he will not like it.'

Ralph stopped her and commanded. 'Listen!'

From the inner stockade there was the orange glow of the fire and the sound of a banjo being played with such rare skill that the limpid notes shimmered and ran into each other; like some exotic birdsong, it rose to an impossible crescendo and then ceased so abruptly that the utter stillness trembled in the air for many seconds before the night chorus of the cicadas in the trees, which had been shamed to silence by the vaunting instrument, hesitantly recommenced. With it mingled the patter of soft palms and the twins' unfeigned exclamations of delight.

'He is a man of many talents, your Harry Mellow.'

'The chief of them is that he can spot gold in a filled tooth across a polo field. However, I have no doubt your little sisters will come to cherish others of his accomplishments.'

'I should send them to bed,' Cathy murmured.

'Don't be the wicked elder sister,' Ralph admonished, and the music started again, but this time Harry Mellow's soaring baritone led and the twins picked up the refrain in their true clear voices.

'Leave the poor creatures alone, they have enough of that at home.' Ralph led her away.

'It's my duty,' Cathy protested half-heartedly.

'If it's duty you are after,' Ralph chuckled, 'then, by God, woman, I have another more pressing duty for you to perform!'

He lay stretched out on his back on the cot, and watched her prepare for bed in the lamplight. It had taken her a long time to forget her upbringing as the child of Christian missionaries and to allow him to watch her, but now she had come to enjoy it, and she had flaunted a little before him, until he grinned and leaned out of the cot to crush out the cheroot, then lifted both hands towards her.

'Come here, Katie!' he ordered, but she hung back provocatively.

'Do you know what I want?'

'Not, but I know what I want.'

'I want a home—'

'You have a home.'

'With thatch and brick walls, and a real garden.'

'You have a garden, the most beautiful garden in the world, and it stretches from the Limpopo to the Zambezi.'

'A garden with roses and geraniums.' She came to him, and he lifted the sheet. 'Will you build me a home, Ralph?'

'Yes.'

'When?'

'When the railroad is finished.'

She sighed softly. He had made the same promise while he was laying the telegraph line, and that was before Jonathan was born, but she knew better than to remind

95

him. Instead, she slipped under the sheet, and strangely his arms, as they closed around her, became home for that moment.

In the southern springtime on the shores of one of the great lakes that lie in the hot depths of the Rift Valley, that mighty geological fault that splits the shield of the African continent like the stroke of an axe, there occurred at that time a bizarre hatching.

The egg masses of *Schistocerca gregaria*, the desert locust, that were buried in the loose earth along the edge of the lake, released their flightless nymphs. The eggs had been laid in unusually propitious conditions of weather and environment. The swarms of breeding insects had been concentrated by unseasonable winds upon the papyrus banks of the lake, a vast food supply that heightened their fecundity. When the time came for them to spawn, another chance wind pushed them *en masse* onto a dry friable terrain of the correct acidity to protect the egg masses from fungus infection while the mild humidity drifting up from the lake ensured perfectly elastic egg-casings from which the hatching nymphs were able to escape readily.

In other less fortuitous seasons the loss and wastage might be as high as ninety-nine per cent, but this year the kindly earth rendered up such a multitude of nymphs that it could not contain them. Though the hatching ground was almost fifty square miles, the insects were forced to crawl upon each other's backs in layers and drifts and banks ten and twenty deep, so that the surface of the desert seemed to become a single seething organism, monstrous and terrifying.

The constant agitation and stimulation of contact with their siblings wrought a miraculous change in this teeming tide of nymphs. Their colour turned from the drab desert brown of their kind to a vivid orange and metallic midnight black. Their metabolic rate surged and they became hyperactive and nervous. Their hind legs grew longer and more powerful, their wings developed with startling rapidity, and they entered the gregarious phase. When they had moulted for the last time and their newly fledged wings had dried, the last chance fluke of weather occurred. The tropical clouds along the valley escarpment blew away, and a terrible sun beat down upon the crawling mass of insects, the valley became an oven, and the entire swarm of mature locusts took spontaneously to the air.

In that baptism to flight, the heat that their bodies had sucked up from the baking earth of the valley was increased even further by their muscular activity. They could not stop, and they winged southwards in a cloud that eclipsed the sun, and stretched from horizon to horizon.

In the cool of the evening this mighty cloud sank to earth and the trees of the forest could not bear their weight. Branches as thick as a man's waist snapped off under the clinging masses of insects. In the morning the rising heat spurred them into flight once more, and they rose to darken the heavens and left the forest stripped bare of its tender spring foliage, so that the empty twisted branches looked like the limbs of cripples in a strange dead landscape.

Southwards the endless flights poured across the sky, until far below them the silver ribbon of water that was the Zambezi river glinted dully in the shadow of their passing.

The whitewashed walls of Khami Mission Station burned in the noon sunlight with the eye-aching brilliance of bleached bone. The family dwelling, surrounded by wide shaded verandas, and roofed with thick dark thatch, stood a little apart from the church and its attendant buildings, but all of them seemed to crouch below the line of wooded hills, the way that chickens huddle below the hen when there is a hawk in the sky.

From the front steps of the house, the gardens stretched down past the well to the little stream. At first, nearer the house, there were roses and bougainvillaea, poinsettia and banks of phlox, that formed bright bold slashes of colour against a veld still brown from the long dry winter just passed; but nearer the stream the fields of maize were tended by convalescents from the mission clinic, and soon on the tall green plants the immature cobs would begin to set. Between the rows of corn the earth was hidden beneath the dark green umbrella leaves of new pumpkin plants. These fields fed the hundreds of hungry mouths, the family and servants and sick and converts who came from all over Matabeleland to this tiny oasis of hope and succour.

On the veranda of the main house, at a bare hand-planed table of heavy mukwa wood, the family was seated at the midday meal. It was a meal of steaming salted maize bread baked in the leaves and washed down with *maas*, the cool thick soured milk from a stone jug, and, in the opinion of the twins, the grace that preceded it was disproportionately long for such frugal fare. Vicky fidgeted and Elizabeth sighed at a volume that was carefully calculated not to exceed the knife edge beyond which it would attract her mother's wrath.

Doctor Robyn St John, the doyenne of Khami Mission, had dutifully thanked the Almighty for His bounty but was going on, in conversational tones, to point out to Him that a little rain soon would help pollination of the immature cobs in the field and ensure a continuation of that bounty. Robyn's eyes were closed, and her features were relaxed and serene, her skin was almost as unlined as that of Victoria's. Her dark hair had the same russet highlights as Elizabeth's, but there was just a fine silver mist at her temples to betray her age.

'Dear Lord,' she said, 'in Your wisdom You have allowed our best cow, Buttercup, to lose her milk. We submit to Your will which surpasses all understanding, but we do need milk if this little mission is going to continue to work to Your glory—' Robyn paused to let that sink in. 'Amen!' said Juba from the far end of the table.

Since her conversion to Christianity, Juba had taken to covering her huge black melon-sized breasts with a high-buttoned man's under-vest, and amongst the necklaces of ostrich shell and bright ceramic trade beads around her neck hung a simple crucifix of rolled gold on a fine chain. Apart from that she was still dressed in the traditional costume of a high-ranking Matabele matron.

Robyn opened her eyes and smiled at her. They were companions of many years, since Robyn had rescued her from the hold of the Arab slaving dhow in the Mozambique channel, long before the birth of any of the children, when both of them had been young and unmarried; but it had only been shortly before his destruction by the Company forces that King Lobengula had at last given his permission for Juba's conversion to the Christian faith.

Juba, the little Dove – how she had changed since those far-off days. Now she was the senior wife of Gandang, one of the great indunas of the Matabele nation, brother of King Lobengula himself, and she had borne him twelve sons, the eldest of whom was Bazo, the Axe, himself an induna. Four of her younger sons had died in front of the Maxim machine-guns at the Shangani river and the Bembesi crossing. Nevertheless, as soon as that brief cruel little war had ended, Juba had returned to Khami Mission and to Robyn.

Now she smiled back at Robyn. Her face was a glossy full moon, the silky black skin stretched tightly over the layers of fat. Her dark eyes sparkled with a lively intelligence, and her teeth were a perfect and unblemished white. On her vast lap, within the circle of her arms, each as thick as a man's thigh, she held Robyn St John's only son.

Robert was not quite two years old, a thin child, without his father's rugged bone structure but with the same strange yellow-flecked eyes. His skin was sallow from regular doses of anti-malarial quinine. Like many infants born of a mother on the verge of menopause, there was a quaint old-fashioned solemnity about him, like a little old gnome who had already lived a hundred years. He watched his mother's face as though he had understood each word she uttered.

Robyn closed her eyes again, and the twins who had perked up at the prospect of a final amen glanced at each other, and slumped with resignation.

'Dear Lord, Thou knowest of the great experiment upon which Thy humble servant will embark before this day ends, and we are certain of Your understanding and protection during the dangerous days ahead.'

Juba's understanding of the English language was just sufficient to follow this injunction, and the smile faded from her face. Even the twins looked up again, both of them so troubled and unhappy that when Robyn sounded the long-awaited 'Amen', neither of them reached for the platters or jugs.

'Victoria, Elizabeth, you may begin,' Robyn had to prompt them, and they chewed dismally for a while.

'You never told us it was to be today,' Vicky spoke up at last.

'The young girl from Zama's kraal is a perfect subject, she started her chills an hour ago, I expect her fever to peak before sundown.'

'Please, Mama.' Elizabeth jumped up from her seat and knelt beside Robyn with both arms around her waist, her expression stricken. 'Please don't do it.'

'Now don't be a silly girl, Elizabeth,' Robyn told her firmly. 'Return to your seat and eat your food.'

'Lizzie is right.' Vicky had tears in her green eyes. 'We don't want you to do this. It's so dangerous, so horrible.'

Robyn's expression softened a little, and she placed one

100

narrow but strong brown hand on Elizabeth's head. 'Sometimes we have to do things that frighten us. It's God's test of our strength and faith.' Robyn stroked the lustrous dark hair back from Elizabeth's forehead. 'Your grandfather, Fuller Ballantyne—'

'Grandfather was touched,' Vicky cut in quickly. 'He was crazy mad.'

Robyn shook her head. 'Fuller Ballantyne was a great man of God, there were no limits to his vision and courage. It is only the mean little people who call such men mad. They doubted him, as they now doubt me, but as he did, I shall prove the truth,' she said firmly.

The previous year Robyn had, in her professional capacity as Medical Superintendent of Khami Mission, submitted a paper to the British Medical Association in which she set out the conclusions of twenty years' study of tropical malarial fever.

At the beginning of the paper she had scrupulously acknowledged the work of Charles Louis Alphonse Laveran who was the first to isolate the malarial parasite under microscopic examination, but then Robyn had gone on to postulate that the periodic paroxysms of chill and fever that characterized the disease were coincident with the segmentation of these parasites in the patient's bloodstream.

The august members of the British Medical Association were well aware of Robyn's reputation as a political trouble-stirrer, a radical who flew in the face of their conservative convictions. They had never forgiven nor forgotten that she had impersonated a man to attend medical school and had desecrated their exclusive masculine preserve by obtaining her medical qualification under false colours. They recalled with pain the furore and scandal that she had conjured up when the governors of St Matthew's Hospital, London, where she had received her training, had attempted, quite reasonably, to revoke her doctorate. Sourly they had looked on as she published a series of highly successful books, culminating in the infamous *Trooper Hackett of Matabeleland*, a vicious attack on the Company in which a great deal of the association's funds were invested.

Naturally the honourable members of such an august body were above such mundane emotions as envy and malice, so none of them had grudged her the princely royalties from her publications, and when some of Robyn's outrageous theories on tropical diseases had finally been proven accurate, and after they had been brought under pressure by Oliver Wicks who was Robyn's champion and editor of the *Standard*, they had magnanimously retracted their previous refutations. Nevertheless, when Dr Robyn St John, previously Codrington, *née* Ballantyne, finally succeeded in hoisting and hanging herself on her own audacity and presumption, the members of the British Medical Association would not be numbered amongst the company of her mourners.

Thus, they read the first part of Robyn's latest paper on malarial fever with mild alarm. Her theory on the coincidence of parasite segmentation and patient temperature-change could only add lustre to her reputation. Then, with mounting joy, they came to the second part, and realized that once more she had placed herself and her reputation in jeopardy. Since Hippocrates had first described the disease, in the fifth century BC, it had been an uncontested fact that malaria, as its name implied, was transmitted by the foul airs of swampy ground and poisonous nights. Robyn St John postulated that this was fallacy, and that it was transmitted from a sufferer to a healthy victim by the physical transfer of blood. Then, incredibly, her paper went on to suggest that the carrier agents were the flying mosquitoes that were usually associated with the swamps and marshy ground where the disease proliferated. As proof, Robyn cited her discovery, by microscopic examination, of the malarial parasite in the stomach contents of the insects.

Offered such an opportunity, her peers in the British

Medical Association had been unable to resist the temptation to embark on an orgy of derision. 'Doctor St John should not allow her penchant for lurid fiction to intrude upon the sacred grounds of medical research,' wrote one of her more charitable critics. 'There is not the remotest shred of evidence that any disease can be transferred in the blood, and to look to the agency of flying insects to affect this mischief is not far removed from belief in vampires and werewolves.'

'They scoffed at your grandfather also.' Robyn's chin was up now as she addressed her family, and in this mood the strength and determination of her features were daunting. 'When he refuted their belief that yellow jack was an infectious or a contagious disease, they challenged him to provide proof.'

The twins had heard this piece of family history a dozen times before, so they both paled in anticipatory nausea.

'He went into that fever hospital where all those eminent surgeons were gathered, and he collected a crystal glass of the yellow vomit from one of the patients who was dying of the disease, and he toasted his fellow surgeons with the glass and then he quaffed it down in front of them all.'

Vicky covered her own mouth, and Elizabeth gagged softly and turned icy pale.

'Your grandfather was a courageous man, and I am his daughter,' Robyn said simply. 'Now eat up your lunch. I expect you both to assist me this afternoon.'

Behind the church stood the new ward that Robyn had built since the death of her first husband in the Matabele war. It was an open-sided godown with low waist-high walls. The thatched roof was supported on upright poles of mopani. In hot weather the breeze could blow through the structure unhindered, but in the rains or when it turned cold, then woven grass mats could be unrolled to close in the walls.

The sleeping-mats were laid out in rows upon the clay floor, no attempt being made to separate families, so that healthy spouses and offspring were camped with the sick and suffering. Robyn had found it better to turn the ward into a bustling community rather than have her patients pine to death. However, the arrangement was so congenial and the food so good, that it had been difficult to persuade patients to leave after their cure had been effected, until Robyn had hit upon the ruse of sending all convalescents, and their families, to work in the fields or at building the new wards. This had dramatically reduced the clinic's population to manageable proportions.

Robyn's laboratory stood between the church and the ward. It was a small rondavel with adobe walls, and a single window. Shelves and a workbench ran around the entire curved inside wall. In pride of place stood Robyn's new microscope, purchased with the royalties of *Trooper Hackett*, and beside it her working journal, a thick leather-bound volume in which she was now noting her preliminary observations.

'Subject: Caucasian female at present in good health—' she wrote in her firm neat hand, but she looked up irritably with pen poised at Juba's tragic tone and mournful expression.

'You swore on oath to the great King Lobengula that you would care for his people after he was gone. How can you honour that promise if you are dead, Nomusa?' Juba asked in Sindebele, using Robyn's Matabele praise name 'Nomusa – Girl Child of Mercy'.

'I am not going to die, Juba,' Robyn snapped irritably. 'And for the love of all things holy, take that look off your face.'

'It is never wise to provoke the dark spirits, Nomusa.'

'Juba is right, Mama,' Vicky supported her. 'You have

104

deliberately stopped taking quinine, not a single tablet in six weeks, and your own observations have shown the danger of blackwater fever is increased—'

'Enough!' Robyn slapped the table with the flat of her hand. 'I will listen to no more.'

'All right,' Elizabeth agreed. 'We won't try and stop you again, but if you become dangerously ill, should we ride into Bulawayo to fetch General St John?'

Robyn threw her pen onto the open page so the ink splattered and she leaped to her feet.

'You will do no such thing, do you hear me, girl? You will not go near that man.'

'Mama, he is your husband,' Vicky pointed out reasonably.

'And he is Bobby's father,' Elizabeth said quickly.

'And he loves you,' Vicky gabbled it out before Robyn could stop her.

Robyn was white-faced and shaking with anger and some other emotion that prevented her speaking for a moment, and Elizabeth took advantage of her uncharacteristic silence.

'He is such a strong—'

'Elizabeth!' Robyn found her voice, and it rang like steel from the scabbard. 'You know I have forbidden discussion of that man.' She sat back at the desk, picked up the pen and for a long minute the scratching of her nib was the only sound in the room, but when she spoke again, Robyn's voice was level and businesslike. 'While I am incapacitated, Elizabeth will write up the journal – she has the better handwriting. I want hourly entries, no matter how grave the situation.'

'Very well, Mama.'

'Vicky, you will administer treatment, but not before the cycle has been established beyond any chance of refutation. I have prepared a written list of instructions for you to follow, should I become insensible.'

'Very well, Mama.'

'And me, Nomusa?' Juba asked softly. 'What must I do?'

Robyn's expression softened then, and she laid her hand on the other woman's forearm.

'Juba, you must understand that I am not reneguing on my promise to take care of your people. What I will accomplish with this work is a final understanding of a disease that has ravaged the Matabele and all people of Africa since the beginning of time. Trust me, dear friend, this is a long step towards freeing your people and mine of this terrible scourge.'

'I wish there was another way, Nomusa.'

'There is not.' Robyn shook her head. 'You asked what you should do to help; will you stay with me, Juba, to give me comfort?'

'You know I will,' Juba whispered, and hugged Robyn to her. Robyn seemed slim and girlish in that vast embrace, and Juba's sobs shook them both.

The black girl lay on her sleeping-mat against the low wall of the ward. She was of marriageable age, for when she cried out in delirium and threw aside the fur kaross, her naked body was fully matured, with a wide fertile spread of hips and hard-thrusting nipples to her breasts, but the heat of fever was burning her up. Her skin looked as brittle as parchment, her lips were grey and cracked, and her eyes glittered with the unnatural brilliance of the fever that was rushing down upon her.

Robyn pressed her hand into the girl's armpit, and exclaimed, 'She is like a furnace, the poor child is at the climax,' and she pulled her hand away and covered her with the thick soft kaross. 'I think this is the moment. Juba, take her shoulders. Vicky, hold her arm, and you, Elizabeth, bring the bowl.'

The girl's bare arm protruded from under the kaross, and

Vicky held her at the elbow while Robyn slipped a tourniquet of whiplash leather over her forearm and twisted it up until the blood vessels in the Matabele girl's wrist swelled up, purple black and hard as unripe grapes.

'Come on, child,' Robyn snapped at Elizabeth, and she proferred the white enamel basin and drew back the cloth that covered it. Her hand was trembling.

Robyn picked up the syringe. The barrel of brass had a narrow glass inset running down its length. Robyn detached the hollow needle from the nipple at the end, and at the same time with the thumb of her free hand she pumped up the veins in the girl's wrist with a stroking motion, and then pierced the skin with an angled stab of the thick needle. She found the vein almost immediately, and a thin jet of dark red venous blood shot from the open end of the needle and pattered onto the clay floor. Robyn fitted the syringe nipple into the needle, and slowly withdrew the plunger, watching intently as the fever-hot blood flowed into the brass barrel and showed through the glass inset.

'I am taking two cubic centimetres,' she murmured, as the line of moving red reached the graduation stamped in the brass, and she jerked the needle from the girl's skin and staunched the blood that followed it with the pressure of her thumb, dropped the syringe back into the bowl, and released the loop of the tourniquet.

'Juba,' she said, 'give her the quinine now and stay with her until she starts to sweat.' Robyn rose with a swirl of skirts, and the twins had to run to keep up with her as she crossed to her laboratory.

As soon as they were in the circular room, Robyn slammed the door.

'We must be quick,' she said, unbuttoning the cuff of her leg-of-mutton sleeve, and rolling it high. 'We must not allow any organisms in the blood to deteriorate.' And she offered her arm to Vicky who looped the tourniquet around it and began twisting it up tightly.

'Make a note of the time,' Robyn ordered.

'Seventeen minutes past six,' said Elizabeth, standing beside her and holding the enamel basin, while she stared with a controlled horror at the blue veins under the pale skin of her mother's arm.

'We will use the basilic vein,' Robyn said in a matter-of-fact tone, and took a fresh needle from the case on the desk.

Robyn bit her lip at the prick, but went on probing gently down towards her own swollen vein until suddenly there was an eruption of blood from the open end of the needle, and Robyn grunted with satisfaction and reached for the charged syringe.

'Oh Mama!' cried Vicky, unable to restrain herself longer.

'Do be quiet, Victoria.'

Robyn fitted the syringe into the needle, and without any dramatic pause or portentous words, expelled the still hot blood from the fever-struck Matabele girl into her own vein.

She withdrew the needle, and rolled down her sleeve in businesslike fashion.

'All right,' she said. 'If I am right – and I am – we can expect the first paroxysm in forty-eight hours.'

The full-sized billiard table was the only one in Africa north of the Kimberley Club, and south of Shepheard's Hotel in Cairo. It had been transported in sections three hundred miles from the railhead, and Ralph Ballantyne's bill for cartage had been £112. However, the proprietor of the Grand Hotel had recouped his costs a dozen times over since he had set up the massive slate top on its squat teak legs in the centre of his saloon bar.

The table was a source of pride to every citizen of Bulawayo. Somehow it seemed to symbolize the transition from barbarism to civilization, that subjects of Queen

Victoria should be striking the ivory balls across the green baize on the same spot where a few short years previously a pagan black king had conducted his grisly 'smelling-out' ceremonies and gruesome executions.

The crowd of spectators in the bar room, that lined all the walls and even stood on the long barcounter for a better view of the game, were nearly all men of substance, for they had won their grants and gold claims by riding into this land in Doctor Jim's conquering column. They each owned three thousand acres of the sweet-pastured veld, and their share of the herds of Lobengula's captured cattle grazed upon them. Many of them had already driven their claim pegs into the rich surface reefs in which visible gold gleamed in the white Matabeleland sunlight.

Of course some of the reefs were unpayable stringers, yet already Ed Pearson had pegged an ancient working between the Hwe Hwe and Tshibgiwe rivers that had panned samples at five ounces the ton. He called it the 'Globe and Phoenix', and Harry Mellow, acting on Mr Rhodes' instructions, had surveyed the reef and estimated that there were 2 million tons of reserves, making it the richest gold mine in existence, except possibly for Ralph Ballantyne's Harkness Mine further south with its estimated 5 million tons of reserves at an incredible twenty ounces to the ton.

There was rich red gold and the good Lord alone knew what other treasure buried in this earth, and the mood was optimistic and boisterous. Bulawayo was a boom town and the spectators encouraged the two billiard players with raucous banter and extravagant wagers.

General Mungo St John chalked his cue carefully and then wiped the blue dust from his fingers with a silk handkerchief. He was a tall man with wide shoulders and narrow hips, but as he moved around the green table he favoured one long powerful leg, an old gunshot injury, an affliction that no man dared mention in his presence.

He was coatless, with gold expanders holding his white

linen shirtsleeves above the elbows, and his waistcoat was embroidered with silver and gold metallic thread. On a lesser man, such theatrical dress would have looked ostentatious, but on Mungo St John it was correct as an emperor's ermine and purple.

He paused at the corner of the table and surveyed the lie of the ivory balls. His single eye had a predatory gleam to it, tawny yellow and strangely flecked, like the eye of an eagle. The empty socket of the other eye was covered with a black cloth patch and it gave him the air of a genteel pirate as he smiled across the table at his opponent.

'Cannon and losing hazard off red,' Mungo St John announced calmly, and there was a roar of comment in which a dozen voices were offering odds of five to one and better against the play, and Harry Mellow grinned boyishly, and tipped his head in reluctant admiration of the big man's audacity.

The game they were playing was 'Zambezi nominated three cushion', which is as far from ordinary billiards as the little gecko lizards on the bar room rafters were from the big gnarled twenty-foot mugger crocodiles of the Zambezi pools. It was a local variation of the game, combining the most difficult elements of English and French billiards. The player's cue ball had to strike three cushions of the table before completing a scoring coup, but in addition to this monstrous condition, the player had to announce beforehand exactly how he intended scoring. This prevented him executing a fluke score, and if he did make an unannounced and therefore unintended winning stroke, he was penalized the points he should have won. It was a tough game. The stakes between the players were £5 a point, but naturally the players and the spectators were free to offer side bets for or against the players making their nominated coup. With players of the calibre of Harry Mellow and Mungo St John on the table, there was £1,000 or more riding on each stroke, and the voices that shouted the odds and those that accepted them were hoarse with tension.

Mungo St John replaced the long black cheroot between his teeth and he made a little tripod with the fingers of his left hand, then he laid the polished maplewood cue into the notch of his thumb and forefinger. There was a final flurry of bets, and then a silence fell over the crowded room. The air was blue with tobacco smoke, and the faces that strained forward were flushed and sweating. Mungo St John lined up his white cue ball with his single bright eye, and across the table Harry Mellow took a slow breath and held it. If Mungo succeeded with the cannon, it scored two points, and another three points for the hazard off red, but that was not all that was at stake, for Harry had placed a side bet of £50 against the score. He stood to lose or win over 100 guineas.

Mungo St John's face was grave as a professor of philosophy considering the riddle of the universe as he made a gentle practice stroke that he arrested with the leather button at the tip of the long cue almost touching the white ivory ball. Then he drew back the cue deliberately to its full travel. At the instant that he launched the stroke the voice of a young woman cut through the bated silence of watching men.

'General St John, you must come quickly.'

There were only one hundred white women in the entire vast land north of the Shashi and south of the Zambezi rivers, of which probably ninety were already married and most of the others spoken for. A voice with such lovely ringing tones could have turned every male head down both sides of the Champs-Elysées, but in the billiard saloon of the Grand Hotel of woman-starved Bulawayo, it had the effect of a close-range broadside of grapeshot. A waiter dropped a tray laden with schooners of beer, a heavy wooden bench toppled over backwards with a shattering crash as the six men seated upon it sprang to attention like guardsmen, an inebriated transport rider toppled backwards off the counter on top of the barman who instinctively swung a round-arm punch at him, missed and swept a row of whisky bottles off the shelf.

The sudden uproar in the deep silence would have unnerved a marble statue of Zeus, but Mungo St John completed his stroke with an almost creamy smoothness, his single yellow eye unblinking in the calm handsome face as it followed the flight of the ball from the tip of his cue. The white ball thumped crisply against the far cushion, doubled the table and the spin hooked it through the corner, striking the cushion at an angle that bled the speed off the ivory. It came trundling back and Mungo St John lifted his left hand to let it pass under his nose; it touched the other white ball with just sufficient force to deflect it a hair's breadth and send it on to kiss the red ball like a lover. The contact robbed the cue ball of the last of its impetus, and it hovered on the edge of the corner pocket for a weary moment and then dropped soundlessly into the net.

It was a perfect cannon and losing hazard, nominated and executed, and a thousand pounds had been won and lost in those few seconds, but every man in the room except Mungo St John was staring at the doorway in a kind of mesmeric trance. Mungo St John lifted his cue ball from the net, and re-spotted it, then as he chalked his cue again, he murmured, 'Victoria, my dear, there are times when even the prettiest young lady should remain silent.' Once again he stooped over the table. 'Pot red,' he announced, and the company was so entranced by the tall coppery-haired girl in their midst, that no bet was offered nor accepted, but as Mungo St John took his cue back for the next stroke, Victoria spoke again.

'General St John, my mother is dying.'

This time Mungo St John's head flew up, his single eye wide with shock, and the white ball screwed off down the table in a violent miscue as he stared at Vicky. Mungo let the wooden cue drop with a clatter onto the floor and he ran from the bar room.

Vicky went on standing in the doorway of the bar room for a few seconds. Her hair was tangled into thick ropes on her shoulders by the wind, and her breathing was still so rough that her breasts heaved tantalizingly under her thin cotton blouse. Her eyes swept the sea of grinning, ingratiating faces, and then stopped when they reached the tall figure of Harry Mellow in his dark riding-boots and breeches and the faded blue shirt open at his throat to show a nest of crisp curls in the vee. Vicky flushed and turned to hurry back through the doorway.

Harry Mellow tossed his cue to the barman, and shoved his way through the disappointed crowd. By the time he reached the street, Mungo St John, still bareheaded and in shirtsleeves, was mounted on a big bay mare, but leaning from the saddle to talk urgently to Vicky, who stood at his stirrup.

Mungo looked up and saw Harry. 'Mr Mellow,' he called, 'I would be obliged if you could see my stepdaughter safely out of town. I am needed at Khami.' Then he put his heels into the mare's flanks, and she jumped away at a dead run down the dusty street.

Vicky was climbing up onto the driving-seat of a rickety little cart drawn by two diminutive donkeys with drooping melancholy ears, and on the seat beside her sat the mountainous black figure of a Matabele woman.

'Miss Codrington,' Harry called urgently. 'Please wait.'

He reached the wheel of the cart with a few long strides and looked up at Vicky.

'I have wanted to see you again – so very much.'

'Mr Mellow,' Vicky lifted her chin haughtily, 'the road to Khami Mission is clearly signposted, you could not possibly have lost your way.'

'Your mother ordered me off the Mission Station – you know that damned well.'

113

'Please do not use strong language in my presence, sir,' said Vicky primly.

'I apologize, but your mother does have a reputation. They say she fired both barrels at one unwanted visitor.'

'Well,' Vicky admitted, 'that is true, but he *was* one of Mr Rhodes' hirelings, and it *was* birdshot, and she *did* miss with one barrel.'

'Well, I am one of Mr Rhodes' hirelings, and she might have upped to buckshot, and the practice might have improved her shooting.'

'I like a man of determination. A man who takes what he wants – and damn the consequences.'

'That is strong language, Miss Codrington.'

'Good day to you, Mr Mellow.' Vicky shook up the donkeys, and they stumbled into a dejected trot.

The little cart reached the outskirts of the new town, where the dozen or so brick buildings gave way to grass huts and tattered dusty canvas shelters and where the wagons of the transport riders were parked wheel to wheel on both sides of the track, still laden with the bags, bolts and bales that they had carried up from the railhead. Vicky was sitting upright on the cart, looking straight ahead but anxiously she told Juba out of the side of her mouth, 'Tell me if you see him coming, but don't let him see you looking.'

'He comes,' Juba announced comfortably. 'He comes like a cheetah after a gazelle.'

Vicky heard the beat of galloping hooves from behind, but she merely sat a little straighter.

'Hau!' Juba smiled with nostalgic sadness. 'The passion of a man. My husband ran fifty miles without stopping to rest or drink, for in those days my beauty drove men mad.'

'Don't stare at him, Juba.'

'He is so strong and impetuous, and he will make such fine sons in your belly.'

'Juba!' Vicky flushed scarlet. 'That is a wicked thing for a

114

Christian lady even to think. I shall probably send him back anyway.'

Juba shrugged and chuckled. 'Ah! Then he will make those fine sons elsewhere. I saw him looking at Elizabeth when he came to Khami.'

Vicky's blushes turned a deeper, angrier shade. 'You are an evil woman, Juba—' But before she could go on Harry Mellow reined in his rangey gelding beside the cart.

'Your stepfather placed you in my care, Miss Codrington, and it is therefore my duty to see you home as swiftly as possible.'

He reached into the cart, and before she realized his intentions, he had whipped a long sinewy arm around her waist, and as she kicked and shrieked with surprise, he swung her up onto the horse's rump behind his saddle.

'Hold on!' he ordered. 'Tightly!' And instinctively she threw both arms around his lean hard body. The way it felt shocked her so that she relaxed her grip and leaned back just as Harry urged the gelding forward and Vicky came so perilously close to flying backwards over his haunches into the dusty track that she snatched at Harry with renewed fervour, and tried to close her mind and shut off her body from these unfamiliar sensations. Her training warned her that anything that raised such a warmth in the base of her stomach, made the skin of her forearms prickle so, and rendered her breathless and deliriously lightheaded, must be unholy and wicked.

To distract herself she examined the fine hairs that grew down the back of his neck, and the soft silky skin behind his ears, and found yet another sensation rising in her throat, a kind of choking suffocating tenderness. She had an almost unbearable compulsion to press her face against the faded blue shirt and breathe in the virile smell of his body. It had the sharp odour of steel struck against flint, underlaid with a warmer scent like the first raindrops on sun-baked earth.

Her confusion was dispelled abruptly by the realization that the gelding was still in a flying gallop and at this pace the journey back to Khami would be brief indeed.

'You are punishing your mount, sir.' Her voice quavered and played her false, so Harry turned his head.

'I cannot hear you.'

She leaned unnecessarily close so that her loose hair touched his cheek and her lips brushed his ear.

'Not so fast,' she repeated.

'Your mother—'

' – is not that ill.'

'But you told General St John—'

'Do you think Juba and I would have left Khami if there was the least danger?'

'St John?'

'It was a fine excuse to get them together again. So romantic, we should allow them a little time alone.'

Harry reined the gelding down to a more sedate pace, but instead of relaxing her grip Vicky wriggled a little closer.

'My mother does not recognize her own feelings,' she explained. 'Sometimes Lizzie and I have to take things into our own hands.'

Even as she said it, Vicky regretted having mentioned her twin's name. She had also noticed Harry Mellow look at Elizabeth on his only visit to Khami Mission, and she had seen Elizabeth look straight back. After Harry had left Khami in some haste with her mother's ultimate farewells ringing in his ears, Vicky had attempted to negotiate with her sister an agreement that Elizabeth would not encourage further smouldering glances from Mr Mellow. In reply Elizabeth had smiled in that infuriating way she had. 'Don't you think we should let Mr Mellow decide on that?'

If Harry Mellow had been attractive before, Elizabeth's unreasonable tenacity had made him irresistible now, and instinctively Vicky tightened her grip around his waist. At the same time she saw the wooden kopjes that marked

Khami Mission Station looming ahead above the low scrubby bush, and she felt a sinking dread. Soon Harry would be confronted with Elizabeth's honey-brown eyes and that soft dark flood of hair pierced with russet stars of light.

This was the only time in her entire life that Vicky could remember being free from surveillance, without her mother or Juba or, particularly, her twin being within earshot or touching distance. It was an exhilarating sensation added to all the other unfamiliar and clamorous sensations which assailed her, and the last restraints of her strict religious upbringing were swept away in this sudden reckless rebellious mood. She realized with an unerring woman's instinct that she could have what she so dearly wanted, but only if she took direct bold action, and took it immediately.

'It is a sad and bitter thing that a woman should be alone, when she loves somebody so.'

Her voice had sunk to a low purr, and it affected Harry so that he brought the horse down to a walk.

'God did not mean a woman to be alone,' she murmured, and saw the blood come up under the soft skin behind his ears, 'nor a man either,' she went on, and slowly he turned his head and looked into her green eyes.

'It is so hot in the sun,' Vicky whispered, holding his gaze. 'I should like to rest for a few minutes in the shade.'

He lifted her down from the saddle, and she stood close to him still, without averting her eyes from his face.

'The wagon dust has covered everything and left us no clean place to sit,' she said. 'Perhaps we should try further from the road?'

And she took his hand, and quite naturally led him through the soft pale knee-high grass towards one of the mimosa trees. Beneath its spreading feathery branches they would be out of sight of any chance traveller upon the road.

Mungo St John's mare was lathered in dark streaks down her shoulders and his riding-boots were splattered with blown froth from her gaping jaws as he drove her over the top of the neck between the kopjes, and without pause pushed her down towards the white Mission buildings. The mare's hoof beats rang against the hills and echoed from the mission walls, and Elizabeth's slim skirted figure appeared on the wide veranda of the homestead. She shaded her eyes to peer up the slope at Mungo, and when she recognized him, hurried down the steps into the sunlight.

'General St John, oh, thank God you have come.' She ran to take the mare's head.

'How is she?' There was a wild, driven look upon Mungo's bony features. He kicked his feet from the stirrups and jumped down to seize Elizabeth by the shoulders and shake her in his anxiety.

'It started as a game, Vicky and I wanted you to come to Mama because she needs you – she wasn't bad, just a little go of fever.'

'Damn you, girl,' Mungo shouted at her, 'what has happened?'

At his tone the tears that Elizabeth had been holding back broke with a sob and streamed down her cheeks. 'She has changed – it must be the girl's blood – she is burning up with the girl's blood.'

'Pull yourself together.' Mungo shook her again. 'Come on, Lizzie, this isn't like you.'

Elizabeth gulped once, and then her voice steadied. 'She injected blood from a fever patient into herself.'

'From a black girl? In God's name, why?' Mungo demanded, but did not wait for her reply. He left Elizabeth and ran up onto the veranda, and burst in through the door to Robyn's bedroom, but he stopped before he reached the bed.

In the small closed room, the stink of fever was as rank as that of a sty, and the heat from the body in the narrow cot had condensed on the glass of the single window like steam from a kettle of boiling water. Crouched beside the cot like a puppy at its master's feet was Mungo's son. Robert looked up at his father with huge solemn eyes, and his mouth twisted in the thin pale face.

'Son!' Mungo took another step towards the cot, but the child leaped to his feet and silently he darted for the door, ducking nimbly under Mungo's outstretched hand, and his bare feet slapped on the veranda as he raced away. For a moment Mungo yearned after him, and then he shook his head and instead he went to the cot. He stood over it and looked down at the still figure upon it.

Robyn had wasted until the bones of her skull seemed to rise through the pale flesh of her cheeks and forehead. Her eyes were closed, and sunk into deep leaden-purple sockets. Her hair, laced with silver at the temples, seemed dry and brittle as the winter grasses of the parched veld, and as he leaned to touch her forehead, a paroxysm of shivering took her that rattled the iron bedstead and her teeth chattered so violently that it seemed they must shatter like porcelain. Under Mungo's fingers her skin was almost painfully hot to the touch, and he looked up sharply at Elizabeth who stood beside him with a stricken expression.

'Quinine?' he demanded.

'I have given her more than I should, a hundred grains since this morning, but there is no response.' Elizabeth broke off, reluctant to tell him the worst.

'Yes, what is it?'

'Before this, Mama had not taken quinine for six weeks. She wanted to give the fever a chance to strike, and to prove her theory.'

Mungo stared at her aghast. 'But, her own studies—' He shook his head in disbelief. 'She has shown herself, that

119

abstinence followed by massive doses—' He could not go on, as though the words might conjure up the spectre he feared most.

Elizabeth had anticipated his fears. 'Her pallor,' she whispered, 'the total lack of response to the quinine – I am so afraid.'

Instinctively Mungo put his arm around Elizabeth's shoulders, and for a few seconds she shrank against him. Mungo had always enjoyed a special relationship with the twins, they had always been his willing accomplices and secret allies at Khami Mission, from the first day that he had arrived, dying of the suppurating gunshot wound in his leg. Though they had been barely pubescent at that time, the twins had not been proof against the strange mesmeric effect he had on women of all ages.

'Vicky and I tempted fate by telling you that Mama was dying.'

'That's enough.' He shook her gently. 'Has she passed water?' And then, roughly, to cover the embarrassment between them, 'Has she urinated?'

'Not since last night.' Elizabeth shook her head miserably, and he pushed her towards the door.

'We must force her to take liquid. There is a bottle of Cognac in my saddlebag. Get lemons from the garden, a bowl of sugar and a big jug of boiling water.'

Mungo held Robyn's head, while Elizabeth forced small sips of the steaming liquid between her white lips, and Robyn fought them in her delirium, hounded and driven by the terrible phantoms of malarial fever.

Then, as they worked, the icy chills that had racked Robyn's body gave way abruptly to a baking heat that desiccated her, and though she did not recognize either Mungo or Elizabeth, she drank thirstily from their hands, gulping and choking in her eagerness, even though she was so weak that when she tried to lift her head, it lolled and rolled to one side, so that Mungo had to steady her. His hands, powerful and brutal-looking, were strangely tender and gentle as he cupped her chin and wiped away the drops that dribbled from her lips.

'How much has she taken?' he asked.

'Over four pints,' Elizabeth answered, checking the level in the jug.

The light in the room altered as evening began to fall, and Elizabeth stood up and held her back as she went to the door and looked across the veranda at the road that led down from the neck.

'Vicky and Juba should have been home before now,' she said, but her mother cried out again, and she closed the door and hurried back to the cot.

Suddenly, as she knelt beside Mungo, she became aware of the sharp ammoniacal odour that pervaded the room. She averted her eyes and said softly, 'I must change her.'

But Mungo did not rise. 'She is my wife,' he said. 'Neither Vicky nor Juba is here, and you will need help.'

Elizabeth nodded and drew down the bedclothes, and then whispered huskily, 'Oh sweet God.'

'It is what we feared,' Mungo said quietly, hopelessly.

The skirts of Robyn's nightdress were rucked up high around her pale girlish thighs. They were sodden, as was the thin mattress beneath her, but it was not the sulphur yellow urine stain that they had hoped to see. Staring bleakly at the soiled bed clothes, Mungo recalled the piece of callous doggerel that he had heard the troopers of Jameson's column sing:

> 'Black as the angel
> Black as the ace,
> When the fever waters flow
> They are as black as disgrace.
> Soon we'll lay him down below,
> And chuck dirt in his face.'

The reeking stain was black, black as old congealing blood, the drainage from kidneys that were trying to purge the bloodstream of the wild-fire anaemia that was coursing through Robyn's body, the destruction of the red corpuscles that was the cause of the dreadful pallor. For the malaria had been transmuted to something infinitely more evil and deadly.

As they both stared helplessly at it, there was a commotion on the veranda and the door burst open. Victoria stood at the threshold. She was transformed, glowing from within, charged with that strange fragile beauty of a young woman awakened for the first time to the wonder and mystery of love.

'Where have you been, Vicky?' Elizabeth asked. Then she saw the tall young man in the doorway behind her twin. She realized what Harry Mellow's bemused yet proud expression meant. She felt no resentment, no envy, only a small quick pleasure for Vicky. Elizabeth had never wanted Harry Mellow; she had teased her sister by pretending interest but her own love was for a man she could never have, she had long ago resigned herself to that. She was happy for Vicky, but sad for herself, and Vicky misinterpreted her expression.

'What is it?' The glow faded from Vicky's lovely face, and she lifted a hand to her bosom as though to stem the panic that rose within her. 'What has happened, Lizzie? What is it?'

'Blackwater,' Elizabeth answered flatly. 'Mother has blackwater fever.'

She did not have to elaborate. The twins had lived their lives on a hospital station. They knew that the disease was peculiarly selective. It attacked only white persons, and Robyn's researches had linked that peculiarity to the use of quinine, which was restricted almost entirely to the whites. Robyn had treated fifty or more cases at the mission over the years. At first it had been the old ivory hunters and itinerant traders, then more recently the troopers of Jameson's column and the new settlers and prospectors that were swarming across the Limpopo river.

The twins knew that of those fifty cases of blackwater, only three had survived. The rest of them lay in the little cemetery beyond the river. Their mother was under virtual sentence of death, and Vicky flew to the bedside and knelt beside her.

'Oh, Mama,' she whispered, stricken with guilt. 'I should have been here.'

Juba heated rounded river stones in the open fire and wrapped them in blankets. They packed them around Robyn's body, and then covered her with four karosses of wild fur. She fought weakly to throw off the covers, but Mungo held her down. Despite the internal heat of the fever and the external temperature of the hot stones trapped under the furs, her skin was burning dry and her eyes had the flat blind glitter of water-worn rock crystal.

Then as the sun touched the tree-tops and the light in the room turned to sombre orange, the fever broke and oozed from the pores of her marble pale skin like the juice of crushed sugar cane from the press. The sweat came up in fat shining beads across her forehead and chin, each drop joining with the others until they ran in thick oily snakes back into her hair, soaking it as though she had been held under water. It ran into her eyes, faster than Mungo could wipe it away. It poured down her neck and wetted and matted the fur of the kaross. It soaked through the thin mattress and pattered like rain on the hard dry floor below.

The temperature of her body plunged dramatically, and when the sweat had passed, Juba and the twins sponged her naked body. She had dehydrated and wasted, so that the rack of her ribs stood out starkly, and her pelvis formed a bony hollowed basin. They handled her with exaggerated care, for any rough movement might rupture the delicate damaged walls of the renal blood vessels and bring on the torrential haemorrhage which so often ended this disease.

When they had finished, they called Mungo back from where he was sitting with Harry Mellow on the stoep of the Mission. Robyn was comatose. Mungo set the lantern on the floor so that the feeble light would not trouble her.

'I will call you if there is any change.' He sent the women away and sat on the stool beside the cot.

Robyn sank slowly during the night, as the disease destroyed her blood, and in the dawn light she looked as though she had been sucked by some monstrous vampire. He knew she was dying, and he took her hand, and she did not stir.

A soft rustle at the door made Mungo turn his head. Robert, his son, stood in the door. His nightshirt was threadbare and patched, too tight under the armpits and the skirts were up above his knees. His thick tangled curls flopped onto the broad pale forehead, and he stared at Mungo unblinkingly, owl-eyed from sleep.

Mungo sat very still, for he sensed that any movement would put the child to flight like a frightened wild animal. He waited a hundred beats of his own heart, and at last the child shifted his gaze to his mother's face, and for the first time there was expression in his eyes. Slowly, a pace at a time, he crossed to the bed, and hesitantly reached out to touch his mother's cheek. Robyn opened her eyes. Already they were glazed and sightless, looking beyond the dark frontiers which she had reached.

'Mummy,' said Robert. 'Please don't die, Mummy.'

Robyn's eyes flickered from side to side, and then miraculously they focused on Robert's face. She tried to lift her hand, but it merely twitched and then relaxed again.

'Listen to me. If you die,' Mungo said harshly, and her

eyes swivelled to him, 'if you die,' he repeated deliberately, 'the child will be mine.'

For the first time she recognized him. He could see it, and his words had reached her. He saw the anger come alive in her eyes, saw the enormous effort that she made to speak, but she could make no sound, only her lips formed a single word.

'Never!'

'Then live,' he challenged her. 'Live, damn you!' And he saw her begin to fight again.

Robyn's life-forces rose and sank to the dreadful tides of the disease, baking fever followed icy chills, and the long exhausted coma followed the bursting sweats. At times she raved in delirium, assailed by fantasies and demons from the past. Sometimes she looked at Mungo St John and saw him as he had been so long ago, on the quarter-deck of his beautiful Baltimore clipper *Huron*, when Robyn had been in her early twenties.

'So handsome,' she whispered. 'So devilishly, impossibly handsome.'

Then she was lucid for brief periods, and the fever added strength to her anger.

'You killed him – you killed him, and he was a saint,' she whispered, her voice light but shaking with fury, and Mungo could not quieten her. 'He was my husband, and you sent him across the river to where you knew the Matabele assegais waited. You killed my husband as surely as if you had driven the blade through his heart with your own hand.'

Then her mood changed again. 'Please, will you never let me be at peace?' she pleaded, her voice so weak that he had to lean over her to catch her words. 'You know I cannot resist you, yet everything you stand for is an offence against me and my God, against me and the lost and leaderless people that have been given into my care.'

'Drink,' he ordered. 'You must drink.' And she struggled weakly as he held the jug to her lips.

Then the disease would tighten its grip upon her and sweep her away into the burning fever mists, where there was no sense and no reality. The days and nights swung past in a blur. Sometimes Mungo would start awake – to find it was past midnight, and one of the twins was sleeping in the chair on the other side of the bed. He would rise, numbed with fatigue, to force Robyn to drink again.

'Drink,' he whispered to her. 'Drink, or die.'

Then he sank back into his own chair, and when he awoke again it was dawn, and his son stood beside the chair, staring into his face. As he opened his eyes, the boy darted away again, and when he called after him, Robyn whispered fiercely from the cot:

'You will never have him – never!'

Sometimes in the noonday, when Robyn was lying pale and silent, resting between the periodic onslaughts of the fever, Mungo could sleep for a few hours on the pallet set at the far end of the veranda, until Juba or one of the twins called him. 'It has begun again.' And he hurried to the cot and goaded and coaxed her from her lethargy and forced her to go on fighting.

Sometimes, sitting beside the cot, his own bony features now gaunt and haggard, he wondered at himself. He had possessed a hundred women more beautiful than this in his lifetime. He was well aware of the strange attraction he could still wield over any woman, and yet he had chosen this one, this one whom he could never possess. The one who hated him as fiercely as she loved him; who had conceived his son in a soul-consuming passion, and yet kept him from the child with all her determination. She was the one who had demanded that Mungo marry her, yet vehemently denied him the duty of a wife, who would not allow him in her presence except now when she was too weak to resist, or on those rare occasions when her lust for him overcame her conscience and her revulsion.

He remembered one of those occasions only a month or so previously, when he had wakened in the backroom of his mud-brick hut on the outskirts of Bulawayo. There was a candle burning, and Robyn stood beside the camp-bed that was the only item of furniture in his room. She must have ridden through the darkness and the wilderness to reach him.

'God forgive me!' she had whispered, and fallen upon him in a frenzy of desire.

In the first light she had left him exhausted and stunned, and when he had followed her out to Khami Mission the next day, she had met him on the veranda armed with a shotgun and he had known instinctively that if he tried to mount the steps to touch her, she would have killed him. He had never seen such loathing as there was in her eyes, for herself as much as for him.

Endlessly she had written to the newspapers, at home and in the Cape, denouncing almost every proclamation he made as Chief Native Commissioner of Matabeleland. She had attacked his conscripted labour policy which provided the ranchers and the miners with the black men they desperately needed to ensure the continuance and the prosperity of this new land. She had condemned the levy of his native police force he used to keep order over the tribe. Once she had even stormed into an *indaba* he was holding with the tribal indunas and harangued them in fluent Sindebele in his presence, calling the indunas 'old women' and 'cowards' for submitting to the authority of Mungo and the British South Africa Company. Then not an hour later, she had waited beside the path, in thick bush near the ford of the river, and had waylaid him as he rode back from the *indaba*. Naked as wild animals, they had made love upon her saddle blanket in the veld, and the fury of it came so

127

close to mutual destruction that it left him shaken and appalled.

'I hate you, oh God, how I hate you,' she had whispered, her eyes full of tears, as she mounted her horse again and galloped away, heedless of the thorns that ripped at her skirts.

Her exhortations to the indunas were blatant incitement to rebellion and bloody revolution, while in her book *Trooper Hackett of Matabeleland*, in which she mentioned Mungo by name, the words she put into his mouth and the actions she ascribed to him were a most virulent slander. Mr Rhodes and other directors of the BSA Company had urged Mungo to take legal action against her.

'Against my own wife, sir?' He had slanted his single eye and smiled ruefully. 'What a fool I would appear.'

She was the most implacable and remorseless adversary he had ever known, and yet the thought of her dead desolated him, so that each time she sank back towards the abyss, so he sank with her, and when she rallied, so his spirits soared to match her.

Yet the play of emotion and the way in which he drained his own reserves to sustain her wearied him to the very core of his soul, and it went on and on, without respite, day after day – until finally Elizabeth broke in on the few hours of deathlike sleep which he allowed himself. He heard the emotion that shook her voice and saw the tears in her eyes.

'It's over, General St John,' she said, and he flinched as though she had struck him across the face, and staggered groggily to his feet. He felt his own tears sting the rims of his eyes.

'I cannot believe it.' Then he realized that Elizabeth was smiling through her tears, and she was proffering the enamelled pot she held in both hands.

It stank of ammonia and the peculiar rotting odour of the disease, but the colour of the fluid had changed, from the deadly black of Guinness stout to the light golden of Pilsner beer.

'It's over,' Elizabeth repeated. 'Her water has cleared. She's safe. Thank God, she's safe.'

By that afternoon Robyn was well enough once more to order Mungo St John to leave Khami Mission, and the following morning she tried to rise from the cot to enforce that order.

'I cannot allow my son to come under your evil influences for another day.'

'Madam—' he started, but she swept his protest aside.

'So far I have resolved not to tell the child about you. He does not know that his father once commanded the most notorious slaving fleet that ever made the middle passage. He does not know of the thousands of damned souls, innocent children of Africa, whom you carried away to a far continent. He does not yet understand that it was you, and your ilk, that waged bloody and unprovoked war upon Lobengula and the Matabele nation, nor that you are the instrument of cruel oppression over them – but unless you leave, I shall change that resolve.' Her voice crackled with some of its old force, and Juba had to hold her by the shoulders. 'I order you to leave Khami immediately.'

The effort left Robyn white and panting, and under Juba's gentle chubby hands she sank back against the bolster, and Elizabeth whispered to Mungo:

'She might have a relapse. Perhaps it would be best.'

The corner of Mungo's mouth twisted up in that mocking grin that Robyn remembered so well, but in the golden depths of his single eye there was a shadow, a regret or a terrible loneliness, Robyn could not be sure.

'Your servant, ma'am.' He gave her an exaggerated bow, and strode from the sick room. Robyn listened to his footsteps crossing the veranda and going down the steps. Only then did she push Juba's hands away and roll on her side to face the blank whitewashed wall.

At the crest, where the path ran through a saddle between the thickly forested hills, Mungo St John reined in his mare, and looked back. The veranda of the homestead was deserted and he sighed and picked up the reins again and faced ahead down the road into the north, but he did not shake up the mare. Instead he frowned, and lifted his chin to look into the heavens.

The northern sky was dark. It was as though a heavy curtain fell from the high heaven to the earth. It was not a cloud, for it had a peculiar density and body to it, like the poisonous plankton of the mysterious red tide which he had seen sweeping across the surface of the southern Atlantic, spreading death and desolation wherever it touched.

Yet Mungo had never seen anything like this. The magnitude of it challenged the imagination. It reached in a great arc around half the horizon, and even as he watched, it swept towards the sun which stood near its noon zenith.

Far north Mungo had seen the khamsin winds raise the mighty sandstorms over the Sahara, yet he realized there was not a sand desert within a thousand miles which could generate such a phenomenon. This was beyond his experience, and his puzzlement turned to alarm as he realized the speed at which this thing was bearing down upon him.

The fringes of the dark veil touched the rim of the sun and the white noon light altered. The mare fidgeted uncomfortably under Mungo, and a troop of guinea fowl, that had been chittering in the grass beside the track, fell silent. Swiftly the murky tide flooded the heavens, and the sun turned a sullen orange, like a disc of heated metal from the smithy's forge, and a vast shadow fell upon the land.

A silence had fallen upon the world. The murmurous insect chorus from the forest was stilled, the tinking and cheeping of small birds in the scrub had died away, sounds that were the background song of Africa, unnoticed until they were gone.

Now the stillness was oppressive. The mare nodded her

head and the tinkle of her curb chain sounded jarringly loud. The spreading curtain thickened and smothered the sky, the shadow deepened.

Now there was a sound. A faint and distant sibilance like the wind shifting the sugary white sands of the desert dunes. The sun glowed dully as the ashes of a dying camp-fire.

The faint hissing sound gathered strength, like the hollow echo in a seashell held to the ear, and the filtered sunlight was a weird purplish glow. Mungo shivered with a kind of religious awe, though the heat of noon seemed even more oppressive in the gloom.

The strange rustling sound mounted swiftly, became a deep humming flutter, and then the rush of high winds; and the sun was gone, blotted out completely. Out of the half-light he saw it coming low across the forest, sweeping towards him in twisting columns like some monstrous fog-bank.

With a low roar of millions upon millions of wings, it was upon him. It struck like a volley of grapeshot from a cannon, driving into his face, the impact of each horny-winged body striking with a numbing shock that broke his skin and drew blood.

He flung up his hands to protect his face, and the startled mare reared, and it was a miracle of horsemanship that he kept his seat. He was half-blinded and dazed by the rushing torrent of wings about his head, and he snatched at the air, and they were so thick that he caught one of the flying insects.

It was almost twice as long as his forefinger, wings a glaring orange slashed with intricate designs of black. The thorax was covered in horny armour, and from the helmeted head stared the bulging multiple eyes, yellow as polished topaz, and the long back legs were fanged with red-tipped thorns. It kicked convulsively in his hand, piercing the skin and leaving a fine line of blood droplets upon it.

He crushed it and it crackled and exploded in a burst of

yellow juice. 'Locusts!' He looked up again, marvelling at their multitudes. 'The third plague of Egypt,' he spoke aloud, then swung the mare away from the onrushing wall of flying bodies, and put his heels into her, driving her at a gallop back down the hill towards the Mission. The locust cloud flew faster than the mare could go at a full gallop, so he rode in semi-darkness, surrounded by the great drumming roar of wings.

A dozen times he almost lost the track, so dense was the swarm in the air around him. They settled on his back and crawled over him, the sharp feet needling his exposed skin. As soon as he struck them away, others took their place, and he had a sense of horror, of being overwhelmed and drowned in a seething cauldron of living organisms.

Ahead of him the buildings of Khami Mission loomed out of the darkened noon day. The twins and servants were gathered on the veranda, paralysed with astonishment, and he flung himself off the mare and ran towards them.

'Get every person who can walk down into the fields. Take pots, drums – anything they can bang to make a noise, blankets to wave—'

The twins recovered swiftly. Elizabeth pulled a shawl over her head to protect it and ran out into the swirling storm of locusts towards the church and the wards, while Vicky disappeared into the kitchen and came out carrying a nest of iron pots.

'Good girl,' Mungo gave her a quick hug. 'When this is over I want a word about you and Harry.' He snatched the largest pot from her. 'Come on.'

With a suddenness that brought them up short from a dead run, the air cleared and the sunlight was so white and blinding that they had to shield their eyes against it.

It was no release, for the entire heaven-high cloud of locusts had sunk to the earth, and though the sky was blue and high, the fields and the forest were transformed. The tallest trees looked like grotesquely coloured haystacks, seething heaps of orange and black. The branches swayed and sagged to the unbearable weight of tiny bodies, and every few seconds there was a sharp crack as a branch snapped and came crashing down. Before their eyes the standing corn flattened under the onslaught, and the very earth crawled with the myriad clicking, rustling bodies.

They ran into the fields, a hundred frantic human figures, banging the metal pots and flapping the coarse grey hospital blankets, and in front of each of them the insects rose in a brief puff of wings and resettled as they passed.

Now the air was raucous with a new sound. The excited shrieks of thousands of birds gorging upon the swarm. There were squadrons of jet-black drongos with long forked tails, starlings of iridescent malachite green, rollers and bee-eaters in jewelled colours of turquoise and sunlight yellow, carmine and purple, jinking and whirling in full flight, ecstatic with greed. The storks strode knee-deep through the living carpet, marabous with horrific scaly heads, woolly-necked storks with scarves of fluffy white, saddle-bills with yellow medallions decorating their long red and black beaks, all of them pecking hungrily at the living banquet.

It did not last long, less than an hour. Then, as abruptly as it had settled, the great swarm roared spontaneously into the air as though it were a single creature. Once again an unnatural dusk fell across the earth as the sun was obliterated, and a false dawn followed as the clouds thinned and winged away southwards. In the empty fields, the human figures seemed tiny and insignificant as they stared about them in horror. They did not recognize their home.

The maize fields were reduced to bare brown earth, even the coarse pithy stalks of the corn had been devoured. The rose bushes around the homestead were merely brown sticks. The peach and apple blossom in the orchards was gone and bare twisted branches seemed to be an echo of winter, even

133

the indigenous forests on the hills and the thick riverine bush along the banks of the Khami river had been devastated.

There was no trace of green, no leaf nor blade of grass untouched in the wide brown swathe of destruction that the swarm had blazed through the heart of Matabeleland.

Juba travelled with two female attendants. It was a symptom of the decline that had come upon the Matabele nation. There was a time, before the occupation of the Company, when a senior wife of one of the great indunas of the House of Kumalo would have had an entourage of forty women in waiting, and fifty plumed and armed *amadoda* to see her safely to her husband's kraal. Now Juba carried her own sleeping-mat balanced upon her head, and despite her great and abundant flesh, she moved with an extraordinary lightness and grace, her back straight and her head on high.

She had shed the woollen vest, now that she was away from the Mission, although she still wore the crucifix around her neck. Her huge naked breasts swung and bounced with youthful elasticity. They had been anointed with fat and shone in the sunlight, and her legs flashed under the short cowhide apron as she moved at a gait between a trot and a glide, that covered the dusty track at surprising speed.

The two attendants, both young newly married women from Juba's kraal, followed her closely, but they were silent, not singing nor laughing. Instead they turned their heads from side to side under their burdens to stare in awe at the bleak and denuded land around them. The locust swarms had passed this way also. The bare crippled trees were devoid of insect or bird life. The sun had already scorched the exposed earth and it was crumbling into dust and blowing away on the little eddies of wind.

They came up over a low rise, and involuntarily stopped and drew closer together, not even laying down their bundles, so complete was their horrified fascination at what lay ahead of them. Once it had been the great regimental kraal of the Inyati impi which Gandang commanded. Then, by the decree of the Native Commissioner at Bulawayo, the impi had been disbanded and scattered. The kraal had been destroyed by fire. However, when the women had last seen it, new growth of grass had begun to cover the scars, but now it had been stripped away by the locust swarms and the circular black banks of ash lay exposed once again. They invoked memories of a past grandeur, and the new kraal built to house Gandang and his close family was tiny and insignificant in comparison.

It lay a mile down the bank of the Inyati river, and the pasture in between was destroyed. The spring rains had not yet filled the river and the sandbanks were silvery white, the polished water-worn boulders glittered like reptile scales in the sunlight. The new kraal itself seemed deserted, and the cattle-pens were empty.

'They have taken the cattle again,' said Ruth, the handsome young woman who stood beside Juba. She was not yet twenty years of age, and although she had already worn the headdress of the married woman for two seasons, she had not yet conceived. It was the secret terror that she was barren that had driven her to convert to Christianity – three gods as omnipotent as the ones which Juba had described to her would certainly not allow one of their own to remain childless. She had been baptized by Nomusa almost a full moon previously, and her name had been changed by her new gods and Nomusa from Kampu to Ruth. Now she was most anxious to rejoin her husband, one of Gandang's nephews, and to put to the test the efficacy of her new religion.

'No,' Juba told her shortly. 'Gandang will have sent the herds eastwards to find new pasture.'

135

'The *amadoda* – where are the men?'

'Perhaps they have gone with the cattle.'

'That is work for boys, not men.'

Juba snorted. 'Since One-Bright-Eye has taken their shields, our men are merely *mujiba*.'

The *mujiba* were the herdboys, not yet initiated into their fighting regiments, and Juba's companions were shamed by the truth of her words. It was true that their men had been disarmed, and that the cattle and slave raids which had been the main activity and diversion of the *amadoda* had been forbidden. At least their own husbands were blooded warriors, they had washed their spears in the blood of Wilson's troopers on the banks of the Shangani river in the one beautiful killing, the one small Matabele victory of that war, but what would become of the younger men, now that a whole way of life had been denied them? Would they ever be able to win on the battlefield the right to go in to the women, and take a wife? Or would the customs and laws under which they had lived all their lives fall into disregard and disuse? And if they did, then what would become of the nation?

'The women are still here,' Juba pointed out the rows of workers in the brown denuded cornfields. They swayed in rhythm to the swing of the hoes.

'They are replanting the fields,' Ruth said.

'It is too late,' Juba muttered, 'there will be no harvest to celebrate at the dance of the first fruits this season.' Then she roused herself. 'Let us go down.'

At one of the shallow pools between the sandbanks, they laid aside their headloads and shed their aprons. In the cool green water they washed away the sweat and dust of the road. Ruth found a buffalo creeper that had escaped the locusts and she picked yellow flowers to twine into head-pieces for all of them.

The women in the fields saw them as they came up the

bank and ran shrieking with delight to greet them, jostling each other in their eagerness to make obeisance to Juba.

'*Mamewethu*', they called her, as they bowed and clapped their hands in deep respect. They took her load from her and two of her grandchildren came forward shyly to hold each of her hands. Then, singing the songs of welcome, the little procession filed up to the kraal.

Not all the men had left. Gandang sat under the bare branches of the wild fig tree on his carved stool of chiefship and Juba hurried to kneel before him.

He smiled down at her fondly, nodding comfortably at her protestations of duty and devotion. Then as an extraordinary mark of his feeling for her, he lifted her with his own hand and seated her on the mat which one of his junior wives spread before him. He waited while she refreshed herself from the big clay beerpot that another wife knelt to hand her.

Then he waved the women and children away, and alone at last the two of them leaned their heads together and talked like the beloved companions that they were.

'Nomusa is well?' Gandang asked. He did not share Juba's deep love for the woman doctor at Khami Mission, in fact he viewed with deep suspicion this alien religion that his senior wife had adopted. It was Gandang's impi that had caught Wilson's little patrol on the banks of the Shangani river during the war and slain them to a man. Amongst the corpses, stripped naked by his warriors so that the shocking mulberry-coloured assegai wounds in their white flesh were exposed, had lain the body of the woman missionary's first husband. There could never be love where there had been blood. However, Gandang respected the white woman. He had known her as long as he had known Juba, and he had watched her unflagging efforts to champion and protect the Matabele people. She had been friend and adviser to the old King Lobengula, and she had brought comfort to thousands of sick and dying Matabele, so now his concern was genuine. 'Has she thrown aside the evil spirits that she brought upon herself by drinking the girl's blood?'

It was inevitable that the accounts of Robyn's experiment with the transference of malaria would become garbled and take on the aura of witchcraft.

'She did not drink the girl's blood.' Juba tried to explain that the taking of blood had been for the good of the Matabele nation, but because she did not understand it completely herself, her explanation was unconvincing. She saw the doubt in Gandang's eyes, and she abandoned the effort.

'Bazo, the Axe?' she asked instead. 'Where is he?' Her first-born son was also her favourite.

'In the hills with all the other young men,' Gandang answered.

The Matopos Hills were always the refuge of the Matabele in time of danger and trouble, and Juba leaned forward anxiously to ask, 'There has been trouble?'

Gandang shrugged in reply. 'In these times there is always trouble.'

'From whence does it come?'

'One-Bright-Eye sent word with his *kanka* – with his jackals – that we must provide two hundred young men to work on the new gold mine in the south that belongs to Henshaw, the Hawk.'

'You did not send the men?'

'I told his *kanka*.' The derogatory name for the Company native police likened them to the little scavengers that followed the lion for the scraps, and expressed the hatred that the Matabele felt for these traitors. 'I told them that the white men had deprived me of my shield and assegai and my honour as an induna, therefore I had lost the right to command my young men to dig the white men's holes for them or to build their roads.'

'And now One-Bright-Eye comes?'

138

Juba spoke with resignation. She knew all the moves that must be made: the command, the defiance, the confrontation. She had watched it all before, and now she was sick of men's pride and men's wars and the death and maiming and suffering.

'Yes,' Gandang agreed. 'Not all the *kanka* are traitors and one has sent word that One-Bright-Eye is on the road, with fifty men – and so the young men have gone into the hills.'

'But you stay here to meet him?' Juba asked. 'Unarmed and alone, you wait for One-Bright-Eye and fifty armed men?'

'I have never run from any man,' Gandang said simply, 'never in my life.'

And Juba felt her pride and her love choke her as she looked into the stern handsome face, and noticed as if for the first time the hoar-frost sparkling on the dark cap of his hair above the headring.

'Gandang, my lord, the old times have passed. Things change. The sons of Lobengula work as house-boys in the kraal of Lodzi far away in the south beside the great water. The impis are scattered, and there is a new and gentle god in the land, the god Jesus. Everything has changed, and we must change with it.'

Gandang was silent a long time, staring out across the river as though he had not heard her speak. Then he sighed and took a little red snuff from the buckhorn that hung on a thong around his neck. He sneezed and wiped his eyes, and looked at her.

'Your body is part of my body,' he said. 'Your first-born son is my son. If I do not trust you, then I cannot trust myself. So I tell you, that the old times will come again.'

'What is this, Lord?' Juba asked. 'What strange words are these?'

'The words of the Umlimo. She has called forth an oracle. The nation will be free and great again—'

'The Umlimo sent the impis onto the guns at Shangani

139

and Bembesi,' Juba whispered bitterly. 'The Umlimo preaches war and death and pestilence. There is a new god now. The god Jesus of peace.'

'Peace?' Gandang asked bitterly. 'If that is the word of this god, then the white men do not listen very well to their own. Ask the Zulu of the peace they found at Ulundi, ask the shade of Lobengula of the peace they brought with them to Matabeleland.'

Juba could not reply, for again she had not fully understood when Nomusa explained, and she bowed her head in resignation. After a while, when Gandang was certain that she had accepted what he had said, he went on:

'The oracle of the Umlimo is in three parts – and already the first has come to pass. The darkness at noon, the wings of the locust, and the trees bare of leaves in the springtime. It is happening and we must look to our steel.'

'The white men have broken the assegais.'

'In the hills there has been a new birthing of steel.' Involuntarily Gandang lowered his voice to a whisper. 'The forges of the Rozwi smiths burn day and night and the molten iron runs copiously as the waters of the Zambezi.'

Juba stared at him. 'Who has done this?'

'Bazo, your own son.'

'The wounds of the guns are still fresh and bright upon his body.'

'But he is an induna of Kumalo,' Gandang whispered proudly, 'and he is a man.'

'One man,' Juba replied. 'One man only, where are the impis?'

'Preparing in secret, in the wild places, re-learning the skills and arts which they have not yet forgotten.'

'Gandang, my lord, I feel my heart beginning to break again, I feel my tears gathering like the rainstorms of summer. Must there always be war?'

'You are a daughter of Matabele, of pure Zanzi blood from the south. Your father's father followed Mzilikazi, your father spilled his blood for him, as your own son did for Lobengula – do you have to ask that question?'

She was silent, knowing how futile it was to argue with him when there was that glitter in his eyes. When the fighting madness was in him, there was no room for reason.

'Juba, my little Dove, there will be work for you when the prophecy of the Umlimo comes to full term.'

'Lord?' she asked.

'The women must carry the blades. They will be bound up in rolls of sleeping-mats and in bundles of thatching-grass, and carried on the heads of the women to where the impis are waiting.'

'Lord.' Her voice was neutral, and she dropped her eyes from his hard glittering gaze.

'The white men and their *kanka* will not suspect the women, they will let them pass freely upon the road,' Gandang went on. 'You are the mother of the nation now that the king's wives are dead and scattered. It will be your duty to assemble the young women, to train them in their duty, and to see them place the steel in the hands of the warriors at the time that the Umlimo has foreseen, the time when the hornless cattle are eaten up by the cross.'

Juba was reluctant to reply, afraid to conjure up his wrath. He had to demand her answer.

'You have heard my word, woman, and you know your duty to your husband and your people.'

Then only Juba lifted her head and looked deeply into his dark fierce eyes.

'Forgive me, Lord. This time I cannot obey you. I cannot help to bring fresh sorrow upon the land. I cannot bear to hear again the wails of the widows and orphans. You must find another to carry the bloody steel.'

She had expected his anger. She could have weathered that, as she had a hundred times before, but she saw in his eyes something that had never been there before. It was contempt, and she did not know how she could bear it. When Gandang stood up without another word and stalked away towards the river, she wanted to run after him and throw herself at his feet, but then she remembered the words of Nomusa.

'He is a gentle God, but the way He sets for us is hard beyond the telling of it.'

And Juba found that she could not move. She was trapped between two worlds and two duties, and she felt as though it was tearing her soul down the middle.

Juba sat alone under the bare wild fig tree the rest of the day. She sat with her arms folded across her great glossy breasts, and she rocked herself silently, as though the movement might comfort her as it would a fretful child, but there was no surcease in either movement or thought, so it was with relief that at last she looked up and saw her two attendants kneeling before her. She did not know how long they had been there. She had not even heard them come up, so rapt had she been in her sorrow and confusion.

'I see you, Ruth,' she said, nodding at the Christian girl and her companion, 'and you too, Imbali, my little Flower. What is it that makes you look so sad?'

'The men have gone into the hills,' whispered Ruth.

'And your hearts have gone with them,' Juba smiled at the two young women. It was a fond yet sad smile, as though she remembered her own youthful bodily passions and regretted that the flames had burned so low.

'I have dreamed of nothing but my beautiful man, every lonely night we have been away,' murmured Ruth.

'And of the fine son he will make with you,' Juba chuckled. She knew the girl's desperate need, and teased her lovingly. 'Lelesa, the lightning stroke, your man is well named.'

142

Ruth hung her head. 'Do not mock me, *Mamewethu*,' she murmured pitifully, and Ruth turned to Imbali.

'And you, little Flower, is there no bee to tickle your petals either?'

The girl giggled and covered her mouth and squirmed with embarrassment.

'If you need us, *Mamewethu*,' Ruth said earnestly, 'then we will stay with you.'

Juba kept them in an agony of suspense for a few seconds longer.

How firm and nubile was their young flesh, how sweetly shaped their young bodies, how eager were their great dark eyes, how vast their hunger for all that life had to offer. Juba smiled again and clapped her hands.

'Be gone,' she said, 'both of you. There are those that need you more than I do. Away with you both, follow your men into the hills.'

The girls squealed with delight, and throwing aside all ceremony, they embraced Juba joyously.

'You are the sunshine and the moon,' they told her, and then they fled to their huts to prepare for the journey, and for a little while Juba's own sorrow was lightened. But at the fall of night when no young wife came to summon her to Gandang's hut, it returned in full strength, and she wept alone on her sleeping-mat until at last sleep came over her, but then there were dreams – dreams full of the glow of flames and the smell of rotting flesh, and she cried out in her sleep, but there was no one to hear and awaken her.

General Mungo St John reined in and looked around him at the devastated forests. There was no cover, the locusts had seen to that, and it would make his task more difficult.

He lifted the slouch hat from his head and mopped his forehead. This was the suicide month. The great cumulus cloud banks heaved up heaven high along the horizon and the heat shivered and wavered in mirage above the bare baked earth. Mungo carefully readjusted the black patch over his empty eye-socket, and turned in the saddle to look back at the file of men that followed him.

There were fifty of them, all Matabele, but wearing a bizarre motley of traditional and European dress. Some wore patched moleskin breeches, and others tasselled fur aprons. Some were barefoot, others wore rawhide sandals and a few even sported hobnailed boots without socks or puttees. Most of them were bare-chested, though a few wore cast-off tunics or tattered shirts. There was, however, one single item of uniform that was common to them all. It was worn on a chain around the left arm above the elbow, a polished brass disc engraved with the words: 'BSA Co. Police.'

They were each of them armed with a new repeating Winchester rifle, and a bandolier of brass cartridges. Their legs were dusty to the knees, for they had made a hard fast march southwards, keeping up easily with Mungo St John's trotting mount. Mungo looked them over with grim satisfaction. Despite the lack of cover, he believed that the speed of their advance must take the kraals by surprise.

It was like one of his slaving expeditions on the west coast, so long ago, before that damned Lincoln and the Royal bloody Navy had cut off the multi-million-dollar trade. By God, those had been the days. The swift approach march, the encirclement of the village and the dawn rush with the slavers' clubs cracking against woolly black skulls. Mungo roused himself. Was it a sign of age to hark back so often to the long-ago? he wondered.

'Ezra,' he called his sergeant to come up to him. He was the only other mounted man in the column. He rode a swaybacked grey with a rough coat.

Ezra was a hulking Matabele with a scarred cheek, memento of a mining accident in the great diamond pit at Kimberley, six hundred miles to the south. It was there that he had adopted his new name and learned his English.

'How far ahead is Gandang's kraal?' Mungo asked him in that language.

'That far,' Ezra swept his arm through an arc of the sky, indicating two hours or so of the sun's passage.

'All right,' Mungo nodded. 'Send the scouts out. But I want no mistakes. Explain to them again that they must cross the Inyati river upstream of the kraal and circle out to wait in the foothills.'

'Nkosi,' Ezra nodded.

'Tell them they must seize anybody who runs from the kraal, and bring them in.'

The business of translating every command irked Mungo, and for the hundredth time since he had crossed the Limpopo, he resolved to study the Sindebele language.

Ezra saluted Mungo with an exaggerated flourish, an imitation of the British soldiers he had watched from the barred window of his cell while he was serving his sentence for diamond theft, and turned in the saddle to shout the orders to the men who followed the two horsemen.

'Warn them that they must be in position before dawn. That is when we will ride in.'

Mungo unstrapped the felt-covered water-bottle from the pommel of his saddle and unscrewed the stopper.

'They are ready, Nkosi,' the sergeant reported.

'Very well, Sergeant, send them away,' said Mungo, and raised the water-bottle to his lips.

For many seconds after waking, Juba believed that the screams of the women and the whimpering of the children were all part of her nightmares, and she pulled the fur kaross over her head.

Then there was a crash as the door to the hut was broken open, a rush of bodies into the dark interior, and Juba came fully awake and threw off the kaross. Rough hands seized her and though she screamed and struggled, she was dragged naked into the open. The sky was paling with the dawn and the constables had piled fresh logs on the fire, so that Juba recognized the white man immediately, and she shrank back into the safety of the crowd of sobbing, wailing women before he could notice her.

Mungo St John was in a fury, bellowing at his sergeant, striding backwards and forwards beyond the fire, slapping his riding-whip against his glossy boot. His face was flushed a dark crimson like the wattles of the waddling black *singisi*, the grotesque turkey buzzard of the veld, and his single eye blazed in the firelight.

'Where are the men? I want to know where the men have gone!'

Sergeant Ezra came hurrying down the rank of cringing women, peering into their faces. He stopped in front of Juba, recognizing her instantly, one of the *grandes dames* of the tribe; as she drew herself to her full height, even in her total and massive nudity she was dignified and queenly. She expected some mark of respect, some gesture of courtesy from him, but instead the sergeant seized her wrist and twisted her arm up so viciously that she was forced to her knees.

'Where are the *amadoda?*' he hissed at her. 'Where have the men gone?'

Juba choked down the sob of agony in her throat, and croaked, 'It is true there are no men here, for certainly the ones who wear the little brass bangles of Lodzi on their arms are not men—'

'Cow,' hissed the sergeant, 'fat black cow.' And he jerked her arm upwards, forcing her face into the dirt.

'Enough, *kanka*!' A voice cut through the hubbub, and the tone and power of it commanded instant silence. 'Let the woman be.'

Involuntarily the sergeant released Juba and stepped back, and even Mungo St John halted his furious pacing.

Gandang stalked into the firelight, and though he wore only his headring and a short loincloth, he was as menacing as a prowling lion, and the sergeant fell back in front of him. Juba struggled to her feet, rubbing her wrist, but Gandang did not even glance at her. He strode to Mungo St John and asked:

'What is it that you seek, white man, coming into my kraal like a thief in the night?'

Mungo looked to the sergeant for a translation.

'He says you are a thief,' the sergeant told him, and Mungo jerked up his chin and glared at Gandang.

'Tell him he knows what I come for, tell him I want two hundred strong young men.'

And Gandang retreated immediately into the studied defensive obtuseness of Africa, which few Europeans know how to counter, and which infuriated a man like St John who could not even understand the language, and who had to submit to the laborious process of translation. The sun was well up when Gandang repeated the question he had first asked almost an hour before.

'Why does he want my young men to come to him? They are content here.'

And Mungo's clenched fists shook with the effort of restraint.

'All men must work,' the sergeant translated, 'it is the law of the white men.'

'Tell him,' Gandang retorted, 'that it is not the way of Matabele. The *amadoda* see no dignity nor great virtue in digging in the dirt. That is for women and *amaholi*.'

147

'The induna says that his men will not work,' the sergeant translated maliciously, and Mungo St John could endure no more of it. He took a swift pace forward and slashed the riding whip into the induna's face.

Gandang blinked, but he neither flinched nor raised his hand to touch the shining tumescent welt that rose swiftly across his cheek. He made no effort to staunch the thin trickle of blood from his crushed lip that snaked down his chin, but he let it drip onto his naked chest.

'My hands are empty now, white man,' he said, in a whisper that was more penetrating than a bellow, 'but they will not always be so.' And he turned towards his hut.

'Gandang,' Mungo St John shouted after him. 'Your men will work if I have to hunt them down and chain them like animals.'

The two girls followed the path at a smooth swinging trot that did not disturb the balance of the large bundles they carried upon their heads. In the bundles there were special gifts for their men, salt and stamped corn, snuff and beads and lengths of trade calico for loincloths that they had wheedled out of Nomusa's store at Khami Mission. They were both in high spirits, for they had passed out of the swathe of destruction left by the locust swarms, and the acacia forests were a golden yellow haze of spring bloom murmurous with bees.

Ahead of them rose the first pearly granite domes, and amongst them they would find the men, so they called gaily to each other, silly girlish banter, and their laughter was sweet as the tinkle of bells. It carried far ahead of them. They skirted the base of a tall cliff, and without pausing to rest started up the natural steps of grey stone. It led them upwards into a steep ravine which would eventually take them to the summit.

Imbali was leading, her round hard haunches swaying under the short skirt as she skipped over the uneven footing, and Ruth who was every bit as eager followed her closely into the angle where the path turned sharply between two huge round boulders that had rolled down from above.

Imbali stopped so abruptly that Ruth almost ran into her, and then she hissed with alarm.

A man stood in the centre of the path. Although he was unmistakably a Matabele, the girls had never seen him before. The stranger wore a blue shirt, and on his upper arm sparkled a round brass disc. In his hand he carried a rifle. Quickly Ruth glanced behind her and hissed again. Another armed man had stepped out from the shaded angle of the boulder and cut off their retreat. He was smiling, but there was nothing in that smile to reassure the girls. They lowered the bundles from their heads and shrank closer to each other.

'Where are you going, pretty little kittens?' asked the smiling *kanka*. 'Are you going to search for a tomcat?'

Neither of the girls answered. They stared at him with big frightened eyes.

'We will go with you.' The smiling *kanka* was so broad across the chest, his legs so muscular, that he appeared to be deformed. His teeth were very white and big as those of a horse, but the smile never reached his eyes. His eyes were small and cold and dead-looking.

'Lift your bundles, kittens, and lead us to the cats.'

Ruth shook her head. 'We go only to search for medicine roots, we do not understand what you want of us.'

The *kanka* came closer. His thick legs were bowed, and they gave him a peculiar rolling gait. Suddenly he kicked over Ruth's bundle, and it burst open.

'Ah!' he smiled coldly. 'Why do you carry such gifts, if you go to search for *muti*?'

Ruth dropped to her knees, and scrabbled amongst the rocks to retrieve the spilled corn and scattered beads. The *kanka* dropped his hand onto her back and stroked her lustrous black skin.

'Purr, little kitten,' he grinned, and Ruth froze, crouched at his feet with her hands filled with spilled grain.

The *kanka* ran his fingers lightly up and placed his hand upon the nape of her neck. His hand was huge, the knuckles enlarged, the fingers thick and powerful. Ruth began to tremble as the fingers encircled her neck.

The *kanka* looked up at his companion, who still guarded the pathway, and the two of them exchanged a glance. Imbali saw and understood.

'She is a bride,' she whispered. 'Her husband is the nephew of Gandang. Take care, *kanka*.'

The man ignored her. He lifted Ruth to her feet by the neck, and twisted her face towards him.

'Take us to where the men are hiding.'

Ruth stared at him silently for a second, and then suddenly and explosively she spat into his face. The frothy spittle spattered his cheeks and dripped from his chin.

'*Kanka!*' she hissed. 'Traitor jackal!'

The man never stopped smiling. 'That is what I wanted you to do,' he told her, and hooked his finger into the string of her skirt and snapped it. The skirt fell around her ankles.

He held her by the scruff and she struggled and covered her groin with both hands. The *kanka* looked at her naked body and his breathing changed.

'Watch the other,' he told his companion and tossed his Winchester rifle to him. The second constable caught it by the stock and prodded Imbali with the barrel until she backed up against the high granite boulder.

'Our time will come very soon,' he assured her, and turned his head to watch the other couple, at the same time holding Imbali pinned against the rock.

The *kanka* dragged Ruth off the path, but for only a few paces, and the scrub that screened them was thin and leafless.

'My man will kill you,' cried Ruth. They could hear everything on the path, even the sound of the *kanka*'s ragged breathing.

'Then give me good value, if I must pay with my life,' he chuckled, and then gasped with pain. 'So kitten, you have sharp claws.' And there was the clap of a blow on soft flesh, the sound of struggling, the bushes heaved and loose pebbles rolled away down the slope.

The constable guarding Imbali strained for a glimpse of what was happening. His lips were open and he licked them. He could make out blurred movement through the leafless branches, and then there was the sound of a body falling heavily to earth and the breath being driven violently from Ruth's lungs by a crushing weight.

'Hold still, kitten,' the *kanka* panted. 'You make me angry. Lie still,' and abruptly Ruth screamed. It was the shrill ringing cry of an animal in mortal agony, repeated again and again, and the *kanka* grunted. 'Yes. There, yes,' and then snuffed like a boar at the trough, and there was a soft rhythmic slapping sound, and Ruth kept screaming.

The man guarding Imbali propped the spare rifle against the boulder and stepped off the path, and with the barrel of his own Winchester parted the branches and stared. His face seemed to swell and darken with passion, his whole attention concentrated on what he was watching.

With the second constable's attention so distracted, Imbali sidled along the granite, and then paused for an instant to gather herself before darting away. She had reached the angle of the pathway before the man turned and saw her.

'Come back!' he shouted.

'What is it?' the *kanka* demanded from behind the bushes in a thick tortured voice.

'The other one, she is running.'

'Stop her,' the *kanka* bellowed, and his companion ran to the corner.

151

Imbali was fifty paces down the hillside, flying like a gazelle over the rough ground, driven by her terror. The man thumbed back the hammer of his Winchester, flung the butt to his shoulder and fired wildly, without aiming. It was a fluke shot. It caught the girl in the small of the back and the big soft lead slug tore out through her belly. She collapsed and rolled down the steep pathway, her limbs tumbling about loosely.

The constable lowered the rifle. His expression was shocked and unbelieving. Slowly, hesitantly, he went down to where the girl lay. She was on her back. Her eyes were open, and the exit wound in her flat young stomach gaped hideously, her torn entrails bulged from it. The girl's eyes switched to his face, the terror in them flared up for an instant, and then slowly faded into utter blankness.

'She is dead.' The *kanka* had left Ruth, and come down the path. He had left his apron in the bushes. His blue shirt-tails flapped around his bare legs.

Both of them stared down at the dead girl.

'I did not mean it,' said the *kanka* with the hot rifle in his hands.

'We cannot let the other one go back to tell what has happened,' his companion replied, and turned back up the pathway. As he passed, he picked up his own rifle from where it leaned against the rock. He stepped off the path, behind the thin screen of bushes.

The other man was still staring into Imbali's blank eyes when the second shot rang out. He flinched to the crack of it, and lifted his head. As the echoes lapped away amongst the granite cliffs, the *kanka* stepped back onto the path. He ejected the spent cartridge case from the breech and it pinged against the rock.

'Now we must find a story for One-Bright-Eye, and for the indunas,' he said quietly, and strapped the fur apron back around his thick waist.

They brought the two girls back to Gandang's kraal on the back of the police sergeant's grey horse. Their legs dangled down one side and their arms down the other. They had wrapped a grey blanket around their naked bodies, as though ashamed of the wounds upon them, but the blood had soaked through and dried black upon it, and the big metallic green flies swarmed joyously upon the stains.

In the centre of the kraal, the sergeant gestured to the *kanka* who led the grey, and he turned back and cut the line that secured the girl's ankles. The corpses were immediately unbalanced and slid head-first to the swept bare earth. They fell without dignity in an untidy tumble of bare limbs, like game brought in from the hunting veld for skinning and dressing out.

The women had been silent until then, but now they began the haunting ululation of mourning, and one of them scooped a handful of dust and poured it over her own head. The others followed her example, and their cries brought out the gooseflesh down the arms of the sergeant, though his expression remained neutral and his voice level as he spoke to Gandang.

'You have brought this sadness on your people, old man. If you had obeyed the wishes of Lodzi and sent in your young men, as is your duty, these women would have lived to bear sons.'

'What crime did they commit?' Gandang asked, and watched his senior wife come forward to kneel beside the bloody dust-smeared bodies.

'They tried to kill two of my police.'

'Hau!' Gandang expressed his scornful disbelief, and the sergeant's voice rasped with anger for the first time.

'My men caught them and forced them to lead them to where the *amadoda* are hiding. At last night's camp, when my men were asleep, they would have thrust sharpened sticks into their earholes to the brain, but my men sleep lightly, and when they awoke, the women ran into the night and my men had to stop them.'

For a long moment Gandang stared at the sergeant, and his eyes were so terrible that Ezra turned away to watch the senior wife as she knelt beside one of the girls. Juba closed the slack jaws, and then gently wiped the congealed blood from Ruth's lips and nostrils.

'Yes,' Gandang advised Ezra. 'Look well, white man's jackal, remember this thing for all the days that are left to you.'

'Dare you threaten me, old man?' the sergeant blustered.

'All men must die,' Gandang shrugged, 'but some die sooner and more painfully than others.' And Gandang turned and walked back to his hut.

G andang sat alone by the small smoky fire in his hut. Neither the broiled beef nor white maize cakes in the platter at his side had been touched. He stared into the flames, and listened to the wailing of the women and the beat of the drums.

He knew that Juba would come to tell him when the girls' bodies had been bathed and wrapped in the green skin of the freshly slaughtered ox. As soon as it was light, it would be his duty to supervise the digging of the grave in the centre of the cattle kraal, so he was not surprised when there was a soft scratching at the doorway and he called softly to Juba to enter.

She came to kneel at his side. 'All is ready for the morning, my husband.'

He nodded, and they were silent for a while, and then Juba said, 'I wish to sing the Christian song that Nomusa has taught me when the girls are put into the earth.'

He inclined his head in acquiescence, and she went on.

154

'I wish also that you would dig their graves in the forest so that I may place crosses over them.'

'If that is the way of your new god,' he agreed again, and now he rose and crossed to his sleeping-mat in the far corner.

'Nkosi,' Juba remained kneeling. 'Lord, there is something else.'

'What is it?' He looked back at her. His beloved features remote and cold.

'I, and my women, will carry the steel as you bid me,' she whispered. 'I made an oath with my finger in the wound in Ruth's flesh. I will carry the assegais to the *amadoda*.'

He did not smile, but the coldness went out of his eyes, and he held out one hand to her. Juba rose and went to him, and he took her hand and led her to the sleeping-mat.

B azo came down out of the hills three days after the girls had been placed in the earth, under the bare spreading branches of a giant mimosa at a place which overlooked the river. There were two young men with him, and the three of them went directly to the graves with Juba guiding them. After a while, Bazo left the two young bridegrooms to mourn their women and he went back to where his father waited for him under the fig tree.

After he had made his dutiful greetings, they drank from the same beerpot, passing it back and forth between them in silence, and when it was empty Gandang sighed.

'It is a terrible thing.'

Bazo looked up at him sharply. 'Rejoice, my father. Thank the spirits of your ancestors,' he said. 'For they have given us a greater bargain than we could ever have wished for.'

'I do not understand this.' Gandang stared at his son.

'For two lives – lives of no importance, lives that would have been spent in vain and empty-headed frivolity – for this insignificant price, we have kindled a fire in the belly of the nation. We have steeled even the weakest and most cowardly of our *amadoda*. Now when the time comes, we know that there will be no hesitating. Rejoice, my father, at the gift we have been given.'

'You have become a ruthless man,' Gandang whispered at last.

'I am proud that you should find me so,' Bazo replied. 'And if I am not ruthless enough for the work, then my son or his son, in their time, will be.'

'You do not trust the oracle of the Umlimo?' Gandang demanded. 'She has promised us success.'

'No, my father.' Bazo shook his head. 'Think carefully on her words. She has told us only to make the attempt. She promised us nothing. It is with us alone to succeed or fail. That is why we must be hard and relentless, trusting nobody, looking for any advantage, and using it to the full.'

Gandang thought about that for a while, then sighed again.

'It was not like this before.'

'Nor will it ever be again. It has changed, Baba, and we must change with it.'

'Tell me what else there is to be done,' Gandang invited. 'What way can I help to bring success?'

'You must order the young men to come down out of the hills and to go in to work as the white men are bidding.'

Gandang considered the question without speaking.

'From now until the hour, we must become fleas. We must live under the white men's cloak, so close to the skin that he does not see us, so close that he forgets we are there waiting to sting.'

Gandang nodded at the sense of it, but there was a fathomless regret in his eyes. 'I liked it better when we formed the bull, with the horns outflung to surround the enemy and the veterans massed in the centre to crush them. I loved the closing in when we went in singing the praise song of the regiment, when we made our killing in the sunlight with our plumes flying.'

'Never again, Baba,' Bazo told him. 'Never again will it be like that. In the future we will wait in the grass like the coiled puff-adder. We may have to wait a year or ten, a lifetime or more – perhaps we may never see it, my father. Perhaps it will be our children's children who strike from the shadows with other weapons than the silver steel that you and I love so well, but it is you and I that will open the road for them to follow, the road back to greatness.'

Gandang nodded, and there was a new light in his eyes, like the first glow of the dawn. 'You see very clearly, Bazo. You know them so well, and you are right. The white man is strong in every way except patience. He wants it all to happen today. While we know how to wait.'

They were silent again, sitting with their shoulders just touching, and the fire had burned low before Bazo stirred.

'I will be gone by daylight,' he said.

'Where?' Gandang asked.

'East to the Mashona.'

'For what reason?'

'They also must prepare for the day.'

'You seek aid from Mashona dogs, from the very eaters of dirt?'

'I seek aid wherever it can be found,' said Bazo simply. 'Tanase says that we will find allies beyond our borders, beyond the great river. She speaks even of allies from a land so cold that the waters there turn hard and white as salt.'

'Is there such a land?'

'I do not know. I know only that we must welcome any ally, from wherever they may come. For Lodzi's men are hard, fierce fighters. You and I both have learned that well.'

All the windows of the mule coach were open and the shutters were lowered so that Mr Rhodes could converse freely with the men who rode in close attendance upon each side. They were the aristocracy of this new land, only a dozen or so of them, but between them they owned vast tracts of fertile, virgin country, sprawling herds of native cattle, and blocks of mineral claims beneath which lay dreams of uncountable wealth.

The man in the luxurious carriage, drawn by a team of five matched white mules, was their head. In his capacity as a private citizen, he enjoyed such wealth and power as was usually only commanded by kings. His Company owned a land which was bigger than the United Kingdom and Ireland put together, which he administered by decree as a private estate. He controlled the world's production of diamonds through a cartel that he had made as powerful as an elected government. He owned outright the mines that produced ninety-five per cent of the world's diamonds. On the fabulous Witwatersrand gold fields, his influence was not as great as it might have been, for he had passed up many opportunities to acquire claims along the strike, where the gold-rich banket reef had once stood proud above the surrounding grassland, sharp and black as a shark's dorsal fin, before the miners had whittled it away.

'I do not sense the power in this reef,' he had said once, as he stood on the outcrop, staring at it moodily with those pale Messianic blue eyes. 'I can sit on the lip of the great hole at Kimberley and I know just how many carats are coming up with each load, but this—' He had shaken his head and gone back to his horse, turning his back on £100 million in pure gold.

When, finally, he had been forced to accept the true potential of the 'Ridge of White Waters' and was on the very point of hurrying back to pick up what few properties were still available, a tragic accident had distracted him. His dearest friend, a fine and beautiful young man named

Neville Pickering, his companion and partner of many years, had been thrown from his horse and dragged.

Rhodes had stayed at Kimberley to nurse him, and then when Neville died, to mourn him. The great opportunities had slipped away from Rhodes in those weeks. Yet still he had at last founded his Consolidated Goldfields Company upon the reef, and though it was nothing like his De Beers Consolidated Mines Company, nor the gold empire that his old rival J. B. Robinson had built, yet at the end of the last financial year it had paid a dividend of 125 per cent.

His fortune was such that when, on a whim, he decided to pioneer the farming of deciduous fruit in southern Africa, he had instructed one of his managers to purchase the entire Franschhoek valley.

'Mr Rhodes, it will cost a million pounds,' the manager had demurred.

'I did not ask for your estimate,' Rhodes replied testily. 'I simply gave you an order – buy it!'

That was his private life, but his public life was no less spectacular.

He was a privy councillor to the queen, and thus could speak directly to the men who steered the greatest empire the world had ever known. In truth, some of them were less than sympathetic to him. Gladstone had once remarked, 'I know only one thing about Mr Rhodes. He has made a great deal of money in a very short time. This does not fill me with any overwhelming confidence.'

The rest of the British nobility were less critical, and whenever he visited London, he was the darling of society, lords and dukes and earls flocked to him, for there were lucrative directorships on the Board of the BSA Company to be filled, and a single word from Mr Rhodes could lead to a killing on the stock exchange.

Added to all this, Mr Rhodes was the elected prime minister of Cape Colony, sure of the vote of every English-speaking citizen and through the good offices of his old friend Hofmeyr and his Afrikander Bond, sure of most of the Dutch-speaking votes as well.

Thus, as he lolled on the green leather seat of his coach, dressed untidily in a rumpled high-buttoned suit, the knot of his Oriel College necktie slipping a little, he was at the very zenith of his wealth and power and influence.

Seated opposite him, Jordan Ballantyne was pretending to study the shorthand notes that Mr Rhodes had just dictated, but over the pad he was watching his master with a shadow of concern in his sensitive long-lashed eyes. Although the flat brim of his hat kept Mr Rhodes' eyes in shadow and prevented Jordan from reading any trace of pain in them, yet his colour was high and unhealthy, and though he spoke with all his old force, he was sweating more heavily than the early morning cool warranted.

Now he raised his voice, calling in that high, almost petulant tone, 'Ballantyne!' And Zouga Ballantyne spurred his horse up beside the window and leaned attentively from the saddle.

'Tell me, my dear fellow,' Rhodes demanded. 'What is this new building to be?'

He pointed at the freshly opened foundation trenches and the stacks of red burned brick piled on the corner plot at the intersection of two of Bulawayo's wide and dusty streets.

'That's the new synagogue,' Zouga told him.

'So my Jews have come to stay!' Mr Rhodes said with a smile, and Zouga suspected that Mr Rhodes had known precisely what those foundations were for, but had asked the question to pave the way for his own witticism. 'Then my new country will be all right, Ballantyne. They are the birds of good omen, who would never roost in a tree marked for felling.'

Zouga chuckled dutifully, and they went on talking while Ralph Ballantyne, riding in the bunch, watched them with such interest that he neglected the lady riding beside him, until she tapped him on the forearm with her crop.

'I said, it will be interesting to see what happens when we reach Khami,' Louise repeated, and Ralph's attention jerked back to his stepmother. She rode astride, the only woman he knew that did so, and though she wore ankle-length divided skirts, her seat was elegant and sure. Ralph had seen her out-ride his own father, beating him in a gruelling point-to-point race over rough terrain. That had been in Kimberley, before the trek to the north and this land, but the years had treated Louise kindly indeed. Ralph smiled to himself as he recalled the youthful crush he had been smitten with when he first saw her driving her phaeton and pair of golden palominos down Kimberley's crowded main street. That was so many years ago, and though she had married his father since then, he still felt a special affection for her that was definitely neither filial nor dutiful. She was only a few years older than he was, and the Blackfoot Indian blood in her veins gave her beauty a certain timeless element.

'I cannot imagine that even Robyn, my honoured aunt and mother-in-law, would use the occasion of her youngest daughter's marriage for political advantage,' Ralph said.

'Are you confident enough to wager on that, a guinea, say?' Louise asked with a flash of even white teeth, but Ralph threw back his head and laughed.

'I have learned my lesson – I'll never bet against you again.' Then he dropped his voice. 'Besides, I don't really have that much faith in my mother-in-law's restraint.'

'Then why on earth does Mr Rhodes insist on going to the wedding? He must know what to expect.'

'Well, firstly, he owns the land the Mission is built upon, and, secondly, he probably feels that the ladies of Khami Mission are depriving him of a valued possession.' Ralph lifted his chin to indicate the bridegroom who rode a

161

little ahead of the group. Harry Mellow had a flower in his button-hole, a gloss on his boots and a grin upon his lips.

'He hasn't lost him,' Louise pointed out.

'He fired him as soon as he realized he couldn't talk Harry out of it.'

'But he is such a talented geologist, they say he can smell gold a mile away.'

'Mr Rhodes does not approve of his young men marrying, no matter how talented.'

'Poor Harry, poor Vicky, what will they do?'

'Oh, it's all arranged,' Ralph beamed.

'You?' she hazarded.

'Who else?'

'I should have known. In fact it would not surprise me to learn that you engineered the whole business,' Louise accused, and Ralph looked pained.

'You do me a grave injustice, Mama.' He knew she did not like that title and used it deliberately, to tease her. Then Ralph looked ahead and his expression changed like a bird-dog scenting the pheasant.

The wedding party had ridden out past the last new buildings and shanties of the town, onto the broad rutted wagon road. Coming towards them, up from the south, was a convoy of transport wagons. There were ten of them, so strung out that the furthest of them were marked only by columns of fine white dust rising above the flat-topped acacia trees. On the nearest wagon-tent Louise could already read the company name, 'RHOLANDS', the shortened form of 'Rhodesian Lands and Mining Co', which Ralph had chosen as the umbrella for his multitudinous business activities.

'Damn me,' he exclaimed happily. 'Old Isazi has brought them in five days ahead of schedule. That little black devil is a miracle.' He tipped his hat in apology to Louise. 'Business calls. Excuse me, please, Mama.' And he galloped ahead, swinging off his horse as he came level with the lead wagon, and embracing the diminutive figure in cast-off military-style jacket who skipped at the flank of the bullock team brandishing a thirty-foot-long trek whip.

'What kept you so long, Isazi?' Ralph demanded. 'Did you meet a pretty Matabele girl on the road?'

The little Zulu driver tried not to grin, but the network of wrinkles that covered his face contracted and there was a puckish sparkle in his eyes.

'I can still deal with a Matabele girl and her mother and all her sisters in the time it would take you to inspan a single ox.'

It was not only a declaration of virility, but also an oblique reference to Ralph's skill as a teamsman. Isazi had taught him all he knew of the open road, but still treated Ralph with the indulgent condescension usually reserved for a small boy.

'No, little Hawk, I did not want to rob you of too much bonus money by bringing them in more than five days ahead.'

This was a gentle reminder of what Isazi expected in his next pay packet.

Now the little Zulu, with the headring granted him by King Cetewayo before the battle of Ulundi still upon his snowy head, stood back and looked at Ralph with the speculative eye he usually reserved for a bullock.

'Hau, Henshaw, what finery is this?' He glanced at Ralph's suit and English boots, and at the sprig of mimosa blossom in Ralph's button-hole. 'Even flowers like a simpering maiden at her first dance. And what is that under your coat, surely the Nkosikazi is the one who carries the babies in your family?'

Ralph glanced down at his own midriff. Isazi was being unfair, there was barely a trace of superfluous flesh there, nothing that a week of hard hunting would not remove, but Ralph sustained the banter that they both enjoyed.

'It is the privilege of great men to wear fine apparel and eat good food,' he said.

'Then fall to, little Hawk with fine feathers.' Isazi shook his head disapprovingly. 'Eat your fill. While wiser men do the real work, you play like a boy.' His tone belied the warmth of his smile, and Ralph clasped his shoulder.

'There was never a driver like you, Isazi, and there probably never will be again.'

'Hau, Henshaw, so I have taught you something, even if only to recognize true greatness when you see it,' Isazi chuckled at last, and put the long lash up into the air with a report like a shot of cannon, and called to his oxen.

'Come, Fransman, you black devil! Come, Sathan, my darling. *Pakamisa*, pick it up!'

Ralph mounted and backed his horse off the road and watched his laden wagons trundle by. There was £3,000 of profit in that single convoy for him, and he had 200 wagons, plying back and forth across the vast sub-continent. Ralph shook his head in awe as he remembered the single elderly eighteen-footer that he and Isazi had driven out of Kimberley that first time. He had purchased it on borrowed money, and laden it with trade goods that he did not own.

'A long road and a hard one,' he said aloud, as he wheeled his horse and kicked it into a gallop in pursuit of the mule coach and the wedding party.

He fell in again beside Louise, and she started from a reverie as though she had not even noticed his absence.

'Dreaming,' he accused her, and she spread the fingers of one graceful hand in admission of guilt, and then lifted it to point.

'Do look, Ralph. How beautiful it is!'

A bird flitted across the track ahead of the coach. It was a shrike with a shiny black back, and a breast of a stunning crimson that burned in the white sunlight like a precious ruby.

'How beautiful it all is,' she exulted as the bird disappeared into the scrub, and Louise turned in the saddle to take in the whole horizon with a sweep of her arm that made the tassels of her white buckskin jacket flutter. 'Do you know, Ralph, that King's Lynn is the very first real home I have ever known.' And only then Ralph realized that they were still on his father's land. Zouga Ballantyne had used up the entire fortune he had won from the blue ground of Kimberley's pit to buy the land grants of the drifters and never-contents amongst Doctor Jameson's troopers who had ridden into Matabeleland in the expeditionary force that had defeated Lobengula. Each of them had been entitled to four thousand acres of his choice, and some of them had sold that right to Zouga Ballantyne for as little as the price of a bottle of whisky.

It would take a rider on a good horse three days to ride around the boundary of King's Lynn. The home that Zouga had built for Louise stood on one of those distant hills, overlooking the wide plain of acacia trees and sweet grass, its thick golden thatch and burned brick blending with the shading grove of tall trees, as though it had always been there.

'This beautiful land will be so good to us,' she whispered, her voice husky and her eyes brimming with an almost religious joy. 'Vicky will be married today, and her children will grow strong here. Perhaps—' She broke off and a little cloud passed behind her eyes. She had not yet given up all hope of bearing Zouga's child. Every night, after his gentle loving, she would lie with her hands clasped over her stomach, and her thighs clenched as if to hold his seed within her and she would pray, while he slept quietly beside her. 'Perhaps—' but it would be ill-omened to even mention it and she changed it, 'perhaps one day Jonathan or one of your sons yet unborn will be the master of King's Lynn.' She reached across and laid her hand on his forearm. 'Ralph, I have his strange premonition that our descendants will live here for ever.'

Ralph smiled fondly at her and covered her hand with his. 'Well, now, my dear Louise, even Mr Rhodes himself only gives it four thousand years. Will you not settle for that?'

'Oh you!' She struck him playfully on the shoulder. 'Will you never be serious!' And then she exclaimed, and turned her horse out of the procession.

Under one of the flat-topped acacias beside the track, stood a pair of Matabele boys, neither of them older than ten years. They wore only the little *mutsha* loincloths, and hung their heads shyly as Louise greeted them in fluent rippling Sindebele. King's Lynn employed dozens of these *mujiba* to tend the vast herds of native cattle and the fine breeding bulls that Zouga had brought up from the south. These were but two of them, yet Louise knew them by name, and their faces shone with genuine affection as they returned her greeting.

'I see you also, Balela.' The praise name the Matabele servants of King's Lynn had given her meant 'the One who brings Clear and Sunny Skies' and the two children waited expectantly, answering her questions dutifully, until Louise at last reached into the pocket of her skirt and dropped a morsel of candy into each of their cupped pink palms.

They scampered back to their herds, cheeks bulging like those of squirrels, and their eyes huge with delight.

'You spoil them,' Ralph chided her, as she rejoined him.

'They are our people,' she said simply, and then almost regretful: 'here is the boundary. I hate to leave our own land.'

And the wedding procession passed the simple roadside peg, and rode onto the land of Khami Mission Station. However, it was almost an hour later that the mules hauled the coach up the steep track, through thick bush, and paused to blow on the level neck of ground high above the whitewashed church and its attendant buildings.

It seemed as though an army was encamped in the valley.

Jordan jumped down from the coach, shrugging off the cotton dust-coat that had protected his beautiful dove-grey suit, and smoothing his dense golden curls as he crossed to his brother.

'What on earth is going on, Ralph?' he demanded. 'I never expected anything like this.'

'Robyn has invited half the Matabele nation to the wedding and the other half invited themselves.' Ralph smiled down at his brother. 'Some of them have trekked a hundred miles to be here, every patient she has ever treated, every convert she ever turned, every man, woman and child who ever came to beg a favour or advice, everyone who ever called her "Nomusa" – they are all here, and they have all brought their families and friends. It's going to be the greatest jollification since Lobengula held the last *Chawala* ceremony back in '93.'

'But who is going to feed them all?' Jordan went immediately to the logistics.

'Oh, Robyn can afford to blow a few of her royalties, and I sent her a gift of fifty head of slaughter-bullocks. Then they do say that Gandang's wife, old fat Juba, has brewed a thousand gallons of her famous *twala*. They will be bloated as pythons and overflowing with good cheer.' Ralph punched his brother's arm affectionately. 'Which reminds me that I have worked up a fair old thirst myself, let's get on with it.'

The road was lined on both sides with hundreds of singing maidens, all of them decked with beads and flowers; their skin was anointed with fat and clay so that it shone like cast bronze in the sunlight. Their short aprons swirled about their thighs as they stamped and swayed, and their naked bosoms bounced and joggled.

'By God, Jordan, have you ever seen such a fine display?' Ralph teased his brother, well aware of his prudish and reserved attitude to all women. 'That pair over there would keep your ears warm in a blizzard, I warrant!'

Jordan blushed and quickly made his way back to join his master, as the girls crowded about the carriage and the mules were reduced to a walk.

One of the girls recognized Mr Rhodes.

'Lodzi!' she called, and her cry was taken up by the others. 'Lodzi! Lodzi!'

Then they saw Louise. 'Balela, we see you. Welcome, Balela,' they sang, clapping and swaying. 'Welcome, the One who brings Clear and Sunny Skies.'

Then they recognized Zouga, and they cried, 'Come in peace, the Fist.' And then to Ralph, 'We see you, little Hawk, and our eyes are white with joy.'

Zouga lifted his hat and waved it over his head. 'By God,' he murmured to Louise, 'I wish Labouchère and the damned Aborigine Protection Society could be here to see this.'

'They are happy and secure as they never were under Lobengula's bloody rule,' Louise agreed, 'this land will be kind to us, I feel it deep in my heart.'

From the back of his horse, Ralph could look over the heads of the girls. There were very few men in the crowd, and they hung back at the fringe of the press of black bodies. However, a face caught Ralph's attention, a single solemn face amongst all the smiles.

'Bazo!' Ralph called and waved, and the young induna looked at him steadily, still without smiling.

'We will talk later,' Ralph shouted, and then he was past, swept along by the throng down the avenue of tall dark green spathodea trees with their flaming orange blossoms.

When they reached the lawns, the dancing black girls fell back, for, by unspoken accord, these were reserved for the white guests. There were a hundred or so gathered below the wide thatched veranda. Cathy was there, for she had ridden out three days before to help with the preparations. She was slender and cool in a dress of yellow muslin and the straw hat upon her dark head was wide as a wagon-wheel and loaded with artificial flowers of bright-coloured silk that Ralph had ordered from London.

Jonathan let out a shriek when he saw Ralph, but Cathy held his hand firmly to prevent him being trampled in the crowd that surged forward to engulf the bridegroom in a storm of greetings and good cheer. Ralph left his horse, and came through the crowd, and Cathy almost lost her hat in the violence of his embrace. She had to snatch desperately at it, and then she froze and the colour drained from her face.

The door of the mule coach had opened, Jordan jumped down and set the step.

'Ralph,' Cathy blurted, clinging to his arm. 'It's him! What's he doing here?'

Mr Rhodes' bulk had appeared in the doorway of the carriage, and a shocked hush fell upon them all.

'Oh Ralph, what will Mama say? Couldn't you have stopped him?'

'Nobody stops him,' Ralph murmured, without releasing her. 'Besides this is going to be better than a cock-fight, any day.'

As he said it, Robyn St John, drawn by the commotion, came out onto the step of the homestead. Her face, still flushed from the heat of the stove, was radiant with a smile of welcome for her latest guests, but the smile shrivelled when she recognized the man in the doorway of the carriage. She stiffened, and the flush receded from her face, leaving it icy pale.

'Mr Rhodes,' she said clearly in the silence. 'I am delighted that you have come to Khami Mission.'

Mr Rhodes' eyes flickered as though she had slapped him across the face. He had expected anything but that, and he inclined his head with cautious gallantry, but Robyn went on:

'Because it gives me a heaven-sent opportunity to order you not to set a foot over my threshold.'

Mr Rhodes bowed with relief, he did not like unresolved positions over which he had no control.

'Let us grant that your jurisdiction reaches that far,' he agreed. 'But this side of that threshold, the ground on which I stand belongs to the BSA Company of which I am Chairman—'

'No, sir,' Robyn denied hotly, 'the Company has granted me the usufruct—'

'A fine legal point.' Mr Rhodes shook his head gravely. 'I will ask my Administrator to give us a ruling on that.' The Administrator was Doctor Leander Starr Jameson. 'But in the meantime, I should like to raise a glass to the happiness of the young couple.'

'I assure you, Mr Rhodes, that you will not be served refreshment at Khami.'

Mr Rhodes nodded at Jordan, and he hurried back to the mule coach. In a flurry of activity he supervised the uniformed servants who unpacked the camp chairs and tables and placed them in the shade of the tender growth that the spathodea trees had put out since the locust plague.

As Mr Rhodes and his party settled themselves, Jordan fired the cork from the first bottle of champagne and spilled a frothy deluge into a crystal glass, and Robyn St John disappeared abruptly from the veranda.

Ralph placed Jonathan in Cathy's arms. 'She's up to something,' he said, and sprinted across the lawns. He vaulted over the low veranda wall and burst into the living-room just as Robyn lifted the shotgun down from its rack above the fireplace.

'Aunt Robyn, what are you doing?'

'Changing the cartridges, taking out the birdshot and putting in big loopers!'

'My darling mother-in-law, you cannot do that,' Ralph protested, and edged towards her.

'Not use big loopers?' Robyn circled him warily, keeping

out of reach, holding the shotgun with its ornate curly hammers at the level of her chest.

'You cannot shoot him.'

'Why not?'

'Think of the scandal.'

'Scandal and I have been travelling companions as long as I can remember.'

'Then think of the mess,' Ralph urged her.

'I'll do it on the lawn,' Robyn said, and Ralph knew that she meant it. He sought desperately for inspiration, and found it.

'Number Six!' he cried, and Robyn froze and stared at him.

'Number Six, "Thou shalt not kill".'

'God was not speaking of Cecil Rhodes,' Robyn said, but her eyes wavered.

'If the Almighty was allowing open season on specified targets, I'm sure He would have put in a footnote.' Ralph pursued his advantage, and Robyn sighed and turned back to the leather cartridge bag on its hook.

'Now what are you doing?' Ralph demanded suspiciously.

'Changing back to birdshot,' Robyn muttered. 'God didn't say anything about flesh wounds.' But Ralph seized the stock of the shotgun and with only a token of resistance Robyn relinquished it.

'Oh, Ralph,' she whispered. 'The effrontery of that man. I wish I was allowed to swear.'

'God will understand,' Ralph encouraged her.

'Damn him to bloody hell!' she said.

'Better?'

'Not much.'

'Here,' he said, and slipped the silver flask from his back pocket.

She took a swallow, and blinked at the tears of anger that stung her eyes.

'Better?'

'A little,' she admitted. 'What must I do, Ralph?'

'Conduct yourself with frosty dignity.'

'Right.' She lifted her chin determinedly and marched back onto the veranda.

Under the spathodea trees, Jordan had donned a crisp white apron and tall chef's cap, and was serving champagne and huge golden Cornish pasties to whoever wanted them. The veranda, which had been crowded with guests before the arrival of the mule coach, was now deserted, and there was a jovial throng around Mr Rhodes.

'We will start cooking the sausage,' Robyn told Juba. 'Get your girls busy.'

'They aren't even married yet, Nomusa,' Juba protested. 'The wedding is not until five o'clock—'

'Feed them,' Robyn ordered. 'I'll back my sausage against Jordan Ballantyne's pasties to bring 'em back.'

'And I'll put my money on Mr Rhodes' champagne to keep 'em there,' Ralph told her. 'Can you match it?'

'I haven't a drop, Ralph,' Robyn admitted. 'I have beer and brandy, but not champagne.'

With a single glance, Ralph caught the eye of one of the younger guests on the lawn. He was the manager of Ralph's General Dealer's shop in Bulawayo. He read Ralph's expression, and hurried up the steps to his side, listened intently to his instructions for a few seconds, and then ran to his horse.

'Where did you send him?' Robyn demanded.

'A convoy of my wagons arrived today. They will not have unloaded yet. We'll have a wagon full of bubbly out here within a few hours.'

'I'll never be able to repay you for this, Ralph.'

For a moment Robyn considered him, and then for the first time ever she stood on tiptoe and gave him a light dry kiss on the lips, before hurrying back to her kitchen.

Ralph's wagon hove over the hill at a dramatic moment. Jordan was down to his last bottle of champagne, the empty green bottles formed an untidy hillock behind his stall, and the crowd had already begun to drift across to the barbecue pits on which Robyn's celebrated spiced beef sausage was sizzling in clouds of aromatic steam.

Isazi brought the wagon to a halt below the veranda, and, like a conjuror, drew back the canvas hood to reveal the contents. The crowd flocked away to leave Mr Rhodes sitting alone beside his fancy coach.

Within minutes Jordan sidled up beside his brother.

'Ralph, Mr Rhodes would like to purchase a few cases of your best champagne.'

'I'm not selling in job lots. Tell him it's a full wagon or nothing.' Ralph smiled genially. 'At twenty pounds a bottle.'

'That's piracy,' Jordan gasped.

'It's also the only available champagne in Matabeleland.'

'Mr Rhodes will not be pleased.'

'I'll be pleased enough for both of us,' Ralph assured him. 'Tell him it's cash, in advance.'

While Jordan went with the bad news to his master, Ralph sauntered across to the bridegroom and put one arm around his shoulder.

'Be grateful to me, Harry my boy. Your wedding is going to be a hundred-year legend, but have you told the lovely Victoria about her honeymoon yet?'

'Not yet,' Harry Mellow admitted.

'Wise decision, laddie. Wankie's country does not have the appeal of the bridal suite at the Mount Nelson Hotel in Cape Town.'

'She will understand,' Harry said with more force than belief.

'Of course she will,' Ralph agreed, and turned to meet Jordan who returned brandishing the cheque which Mr Rhodes had scribbled on a tattered champagne label.

173

'How charmingly appropriate,' Ralph murmured, and tucked it into his top pocket. 'I'll send Isazi back to fetch the next wagon.'

The rumour of wagonloads of free champagne for all at Khami Mission turned Bulawayo into a ghost town. Unable to compete with these prices, the barman of the Grand Hotel closed down his deserted premises and joined the exodus southwards. As soon as the news reached them, the umpires called 'stumps' on the cricket match being played on the police parade ground, and the twenty-two players still in their flannels formed a guard of honour for Isazi's wagon, while behind them followed what remained of the town's population on horse, cycle or foot.

The little Mission church could hold only a fraction of the invited and uninvited, the rest of them overflowed into the grounds, though the heaviest concentrations were always to be found around the two widely separated champagne wagons. Copious draughts of warm champagne had made the men sentimentally boisterous and many of the women loudly weepy, so a thunderous acclaim greeted the bride when she at last made her appearance on the Mission veranda.

On her brother-in-law's arm, and attended by her sisters, Victoria made her way down the alley that opened for her across the lawn.

She was pretty enough to begin with, with her green eyes shining and the vivid coppery mass of her hair upon the white satin of her dress, but when she returned the same way, this time on the arm of her new husband, she was truly beautiful.

'All right,' Ralph announced. 'It's all legal – now the party can truly begin.'

He signalled to the band, a hastily assembled quartet led by Matabeleland's only undertaker on the fiddle, and they launched into a spirited Gilbert and Sullivan. This was the only sheet music available north of the Limpopo. Each member of the quartet provided his own interpretation of *The Mikado*, so that the dancers could waltz or polka to it as the inclination and the champagne dictated.

By dawn of the following day, the party had started to warm up, and the first fist-fight broke out behind the church. However, Ralph settled it by announcing to the shirtsleeved contestants, 'This will never do, gentlemen, it is an occasion of joy and goodwill towards all mankind.' And then before they realized his intention, he dropped them on their backs in quick succession with a left and right swing that neither of them saw coming. Then he helped them solicitously back onto their feet and led them weaving groggily to the nearest drink wagon.

By dawn on the second day, the party was in full swing. The bride and bridegroom, reluctant to miss a moment of the fun, had not yet left on their honeymoon and were leading the dancing under the spathodea trees. Mr Rhodes, who had rested during the night in the mule coach, now emerged and ate a hearty breakfast of bacon and eggs cooked by Jordan over the open fire, washed it down with a tumbler of champagne, and was moved to oratory. He stood on the driver's seat of the coach and spoke with all his usual eloquence and charisma honed to an edge by a sense of occasion and his own burning belief in his subject.

'My Rhodesians,' he addressed his audience, and they took it as an endearment rather than a claim to ownership, and loved him for it. 'Together you and I have made a great leap forward towards the day when the map of Africa will be painted pink from Cape Town to Cairo, when this fair continent will be set beside India, a great diamond beside a lustrous ruby, in the crown of our beloved Queen—'

They cheered him, the Americans and Greeks and Italians and Irish as loudly as the subjects of the 'beloved Queen' herself.

Robyn St John endured half an hour of these sentiments before she lost control of the frosty dignity that Ralph had

175

counselled, and from the veranda of the homestead she began a counter reading of her own, as yet unpublished, poetry:

'Mild melancholy and sedate he stands
Tending another's herds upon the field.
His father's once, where now the white man builds
His home and issues forth his proud commands.
His dark eyes flash not, his listless hand
Leans on the shepherd staff, no more he wields
The gleaming steel, but to the oppressor yields—'

Her high, clear voice rang over Mr Rhodes'; heads turned back and forth between the two of them like the spectators at a tennis match.

'This is only a beginning,' Mr Rhodes raised his volume, 'a great beginning, yes, but a beginning nonetheless. There are ignorant and arrogant men, not all of them black,' and even the dullest listener recognized that the allusion was to old Kruger, the Boer president of the South African Republic in the Transvaal, 'who must be allowed the opportunity to come beneath the shield of the *pax britannica* of their own free will, rather than be driven to it by force of arms.'

His audience was once again entranced, until Robyn selected another of her works in matching warlike mood, and let fly with:

'He scorns the hurt, nor regards the scar
Of recent wound, but burnishes for war
His assegai and targe of buffalo-hide.
Is he a rebel? Yes, it is a strife
Between the black-skinned raptor and the white.
A savage? Yes, though loath to aim at life
Evil for evil fierce he doth requite.
A heathen? Teach him then thy better creed,
Christian! If thou deserv'st that name indeed!'

The audience's critical faculty was dulled by two days and two nights of revelry and they applauded Robyn's impassioned delivery with matching fervour, though the sense of it was thankfully lost upon them.

'The Lord save us,' Ralph groaned, 'from emetic jingoism and aperient scansion!' And he wandered away down the valley to get out of earshot of the competing orators, carrying a bottle of Mr Rhodes' champagne in one hand, and with his son perched upon his shoulder. Jonathan wore a sailor suit with Jack Tar collar, and a straw boater on his head; the ribbon hung down his back, and he clucked and urged his father on with his heels as though he was astride a pony.

There were fifty head of slaughter-oxen and a thousand gallon pots of Juba's beer to account for, and the black wedding guests were giving the task their dedicated attention. Down here the dancing was even more energetic than that under the spathodea trees, the young men were leaping and twisting and stamping until the dust swirled waist-high about them and the sweat cut runnels down their naked backs and chests. The girls swayed and shuffled and sang, and the drummers hammered out their frenetic rhythms until they dropped exhausted, and others snatched up the wooden clubs to beat the booming hollowed-out tree-trunks. While Jonathan, on Ralph's back, squealed with delight, one of the slaughter-oxen, a heavy hump-backed red beast, was dragged out of the kraal. A spearsman ran forward and stabbed it through the carotid and jugular. With a mournful bellow the animal collapsed, kicking spasmodically. The butchers swarmed over the carcass, flaying off the hide in a single sheet, delving for the titbits, the kidneys and liver and tripes, throwing them wet and shiny onto the live coals, hacking through the rack of ribs, slicing off thick steaks and heaping them on the racks over the cooking-fire.

Half raw, running with fat and juice, the meat was stuffed into eager mouths and the beerpots tilted to the hot blue summer sky. One of the cooks tossed Ralph a ribbon of tripe, scorched from the fierce flames, and with the contents still adhering to the stomach lining. Without a visible qualm, Ralph stripped away the lining and bit off a chunk of the sweet white flesh beneath.

'*Mushle!*' he told the cook. 'Good! Very good.' And passed up a sliver to the child on his back. 'Eat it, Jon-Jon, what doesn't kill you, makes you fat,' and his son obeyed with noisy relish, and agreed with his father's verdict.

'*Mushle*, it's really *mush*, Papa.'

Then the dancers surrounded them, prancing and whirling, challenging Ralph. Ralph sat Jonathan on the fence of the cattle kraal, where he had a grandstand view. Then he strode into the centre and set himself in the heroic posture of the Nguni dancer. Bazo had taught him well when they were striplings, and now he raised his right knee as high as his shoulder and brought his booted foot down on the hard earth with a crash, and the other dancers hummed in encouragement and approbation.

'Jee! Jee!'

Ralph leaped and stamped and postured, and the other dancers were pressed to match him, the women clapped and sang and on the kraal fence Jonathan howled with excitement and pride.

'Look at my daddy!'

His shirt soaked with sweat, his chest heaving, chuckling breathlessly, Ralph dropped out at last and lifted Jonathan back onto his shoulder. The two of them went on, greeting by name those they recognized in the throng, accepting a proffered morsel of beef or a swallow of tart gruel-thick beer, until at last on the rise beyond the kraal, seated on a log, aloof from the dancers and revellers, Ralph found the man he was seeking.

'I see you, Bazo the Axe,' he said, and sat down on the log beside him, set the champagne bottle between them and passed Bazo one of the cheroots for which he had developed a taste so long ago on the diamond fields. They smoked in silence, watching the dancers and the feasting until Jonathan grew restless and edged away to seek more exciting occupation, and found it immediately.

He was confronted by a child a year or so younger than he was. Tungata, son of Bazo, son of Gandang, son of great Mzilikazi, was stark naked except for the string of bright ceramic beads around his hips. His navel popped out in the centre of his fat little belly, his limbs were sturdy, dimpled knees and bracelets of healthy fat at his wrists. His face was round and smooth and glossy, his eyes huge and solemn as he examined Jonathan with total fascination.

Jonathan returned his scrutiny with equal candour, and made no attempt to pull away as Tungata reached and touched the collar of his sailor suit.

'What is your son's name?' Bazo asked, watching the children with an inscrutable expression on his dark features.

'Jonathan.'

'What is the meaning of that name?'

'The gift of God,' Ralph told him.

Jonathan suddenly took the straw hat from his own head and placed it upon that of the Matabele princeling. It made such an incongruous picture, the beribboned boater on the head of the naked black boy with his pot belly and little uncircumcised penis sticking out under it at a jaunty angle, that both men smiled involuntarily. Tungata gurgled with glee, seized Jonathan's hand and dragged him away unprotestingly into the throng of dancers.

The lingering warmth of that magical moment between the children thawed the stiffness between the two men. Fleetingly, they recaptured the rapport of their young manhood. They passed the champagne bottle back and forth, and when it was empty, Bazo clapped his hands and Tanase came to kneel dutifully before him and offered a clay pot of bubbling brew. She never looked up at Ralph's face, and she withdrew as silently as she had come.

179

At noon she returned to where the two men were still deep in conversation. Tanase led Jonathan by one hand and Tungata, still with the straw hat on his head, by the other. Ralph, who had forgotten all about him, started violently when he saw his son. The child's beatific grin was almost masked by layers of grime and beef fat. His sailor suit was the victim of the marvellous games which he and his newly found companion had invented. The collar hung by a thread, the knees were worn through, and Ralph recognized some of the stains as ash and ox blood and mud and fresh cow dung. He was less certain of the others.

'Oh my God,' Ralph groaned, 'your mother will strangle us both.' He picked up his son gingerly. 'When will I see you again, old friend?' he asked Bazo.

'Sooner than you think,' Bazo replied softly. 'I told you I would work for you again when I was ready.'

'Yes,' Ralph nodded.

'I am ready now,' said Bazo simply.

Victoria was amazingly gracious in her acceptance of the change of honeymoon venue, when Harry Mellow explained shamefacedly, 'Ralph has this idea. He wants to follow up one of the African legends, at a place called Wankie's country, near the great falls that Doctor Livingstone discovered on the Zambezi river. Vicky, I know how you looked forward to Cape Town and to seeing the sea for the first time, but—'

'I've lived without the sea for twenty years, a little longer won't hurt much.' And she took Harry's hand. 'Wherever thou goest, my love, Wankie's country, Cape Town, or the North Pole, just as long as we are together.'

The expedition was conducted in Ralph Ballantyne's usual style, six wagons and forty servants to convey the two families northwards through the magnificent forests of northern Matabeleland towards the great Zambezi river. The weather was mild and the pace leisurely. The country teemed with wild game, and the newly-weds billed and cooed and made such languorous eyes at each other that it was infectious.

'Just whose honeymoon is this?' Cathy mumbled in Ralph's ear one lazy loving morning.

'Action first, questions later,' Ralph replied, and Cathy chuckled in a throaty self-satisfied way and cuddled back down in the feather mattress of the wagon bed.

At evening and mealtimes, Jonathan had to be forcibly removed from the back of the pony that Ralph had given him for his fifth birthday, and Cathy anointed the saddle-sores on his buttocks with Zambuk.

They reached Wankie's village on the twenty-second day and for the first time since leaving Bulawayo, the idyllic mood of the caravan bumped back to earth.

Under the reign of King Lobengula, Wankie had been a renegade and outlaw. Lobengula had sent four separate punitive impis to bring his severed head back to GuBulawayo, but Wankie had been as cunning as he was insolent, as slippery as he was mendacious, and the impis had all returned empty-handed to face the king's wrath.

After Lobengula's defeat and death, Wankie had brazenly set himself up as chieftain of the land between the Zambezi and the Gwaai rivers, and he demanded tribute of those who came to trade or hunt the elephant herds that had been driven into the bad lands along the escarpment of the Zambezi valley, where the tsetse fly turned back the horse-men and only the hardiest would go in on foot to chase the great animals.

Wankie was a handsome man in his middle age, open-faced and tall, with the air of the chief he claimed to be, and he accepted the gift of blankets and beads that Ralph presented to him with no effusive gratitude, enquired pol-itely after Ralph's health and that of his father, and brothers and sons, and then waited like a crocodile at the drinking place for Ralph to come to the real purpose of his visit.

'The stones that burn?' he repeated vaguely, his eyes hooded as he pondered, seeming to search his memory for such an extraordinary subject, and then quite artlessly he remarked that he had always wanted a wagon. Lobengula had owned a wagon, and therefore Wankie believed that every great chief should have one, and he turned on his stool and glanced pointedly at Ralph's six magnificent Cape-built eighteen-footers outspanned in the glade below the kraal.

'That damned rogue has the cheek of a white man,' Ralph protested bitterly to Harry Mellow across the camp-fire. 'A wagon, no less. Three hundred pounds of any man's money.'

'But, darling, if Wankie can guide you, won't it be a bargain price?' Cathy asked mildly.

'No. I'm damned if I'll give in to him. A couple of blankets, a case of brandy, but not a three hundred pound-wagon.'

'Damned right, Ralph,' Harry chuckled. 'I mean we got Long Island for that price—'

He was interrupted by a discreet cough behind him. Bazo had come across silently from the other fire where the drivers and servants were bivouacked.

'Henshaw,' he started, when Ralph acknowledged him. 'You told me that we had come here to hunt buffalo to make trek riems from their hides,' he accused. 'Did you not trust me?'

'Bazo, you are my brother.'

'You lie to your brothers?'

'If I had spoken of the stones that burn in Bulawayo, we would have had a hundred wagons following us when we left town.'

'Did I not tell you that I had led my impi over these hills, chasing the same hairless baboon upon whom you now shower gifts?'

'You did not tell me,' Ralph replied, and Bazo moved on hastily from that subject. He was not proud of his campaign against Wankie, the only one during all the years that he had been induna of the 'Moles' which had not ended in complete success. He still recalled the old king's recriminations – would that he could ever forget them.

'Henshaw, if you had spoken to me, we would not have had to waste our time and demean ourselves by parleying with this son of thirty fathers, this unsavoury jackal-casting, this—'

Ralph cut short Bazo's opinion of their host, by standing up and seizing Bazo's shoulders. 'Bazo, can you lead us there? Is that what you mean? Can you take us to the stones that burn?'

Bazo inclined his head, in assent. 'And it will not cost you a wagon, either,' he replied.

They rode into a red and smoky dawn through the open glades in the forest. Ahead of them the buffalo herds opened to give them passage and closed behind them as they passed. The huge black beasts held their wet muzzles high, the massive slaty bosses of horn giving them a ponderous dignity, and they stared in stolid astonishment as the horsemen passed within a few hundred paces, and then returned unalarmed to graze. The riders barely glanced at them, their attention was fastened instead on Bazo's broad bullet-scarred back as he led them at an easy trot towards the low line of flat-topped hills that rose out of the forest ahead.

On the first slope they tethered the horses, and climbed, while above them the furry little brown klipspringer, swift as chamois, flew sure-footed up the cliffs and from the summit an old dog baboon barked his challenge down at them. Though they ran at the slope, they could not keep up with Bazo, and he was waiting for them halfway up on a ledge above which the cliff rose sheer to the summit. He made no dramatic announcement, but merely pointed with his chin. Ralph and Harry stared, unable to speak, their chests heaving and their shirts plastered to their backs with sweat from the climb.

There was a horizontal seam, twenty foot thick, sandwiched in the cliff face. It ran along the cliff as far as they could see in each direction, black as the darkest night and yet glittering with a strange greenish iridescence in the slanted rays of the early sun.

'This was the only thing we lacked in this land,' Ralph said quietly. 'The stones that burn, black gold – now we have it all.'

Harry Mellow went forward and laid his hand upon it reverently, as though he were a worshipper touching the relic of a saint in some holy place.

'I have never seen coal of this quality in a seam so deep, not even in the Kentucky hills.'

Suddenly he snatched his hat off his head and with a wild Indian whoop threw it far out down the slope.

'We are rich!' he shouted. 'Rich! Rich! Rich!'

'Better than working for Mr Rhodes?' Ralph asked, and Harry grabbed his shoulders and the two of them spun together in a yelling, stomping dance of jubilation on the narrow ledge, while Bazo leaned against the seam of black coal and watched them unsmilingly.

It took them two weeks to survey and peg their claims, covering all the ground beneath which the seams of coal might be buried. Harry shot the lines with his theodolite, and Bazo and Ralph worked behind him with a gang of axemen driving in the pegs and marking the corners with cairns of loose stones.

While they worked, they discovered a dozen other places in the hills where the deep rich seams of glittering coal were exposed at the surface.

'Coal for a thousand years,' Harry predicted. 'Coal for the railways and the blast furnaces, coal to power a new nation.'

On the fifteenth day the two of them traipsed back to camp at the head of their bone-weary gang of Matabele.

Victoria, deprived of her new husband for two weeks, was as palely forlorn as a young widow in mourning, but by breakfast the following day she had regained her fine high colour and the sparkle in her eyes as she hovered over Harry, replenishing his coffee cup and heaping his plate with slices of smoked warthog and piles of rich yellow scrambled ostrich egg.

Sitting at the head of the breakfast table set under the giant msasa trees, Ralph called to Cathy:

'Break out a bottle of champagne, Katie my sweeting, we have something to celebrate,' and he saluted them with a brimming mug. 'Ladies and gentlemen, I give you a toast to the gold of the Harkness Mine and the coal of the Wankie field, and to the riches of both!'

They laughed and clinked their mugs and drank the toast.

'Let's stay here for ever,' said Vicky. 'I'm so happy. I don't want it to end.'

'We'll stay a little longer,' Ralph agreed, with his arm about Cathy's waist. 'I told Doctor Jim we were coming up here to hunt buffalo. If we don't bring a few wagon-loads of hides back with us, the little doctor is going to start wondering.'

The evening wind came softly out of the east. Ralph knew that at this season it would hold steadily during the night, and increase with the warmth of the sun.

He sent out two teams of his Matabele, each team armed with a package of Swan Vestas and leading a span of trek oxen. They moved out eastwards and by dawn they had reached the bank of the Gwaai river. Here they felled two big dried-out thorn trees and hooked the trek chains onto the trunks.

When they put fire into the branches, the dried wood burned like a torch and the oxen panicked. The drivers ran beside each span, keeping them galloping in opposite directions, heading across the wind, dragging the blazing trees behind them and spreading a trail of sparks and flaring twigs through the tall dry grass. Within an hour, there was a forest fire burning across a front of many miles, with the wind behind it roaring down towards the long open vlei where Ralph's wagons were outspanned. The smoke billowed heaven-high, a vast dun pall.

Ralph had roused the camp before first light, and he supervised the back-burn while the dew on the vlei subdued the flames and made them manageable. The Matabele put fire into the grass on the windward side of the open vlei and let it burn to the forest line on the far side. Here they beat it out before it could take hold of the trees.

Isazi rolled his wagons out onto the blackened still-hot earth, and formed them into a square with his precious oxen penned in the centre. Then, for the first time, they had a chance to pause and look eastward. The dark smoke cloud of the forest fire blotted out the dawn, and their island of safety seemed suddenly very small in the path of that terrible conflagration. Even the mood of the usually cheerful Matabele was subdued, and they kept glancing uneasily at the boiling smoke line as they honed their skinning knives.

'We will be covered with soot,' Cathy complained. 'Everything will be filthy.'

'And a little singed, like as not,' Ralph laughed, as he and Bazo checked the spare horses and slipped the rifles into their scabbards.

Then he came to Cathy and with an arm about her shoulders, told her, 'You and Vicky are to stay in the wagons. Don't leave them, whatever happens. If you get a little warm, splash water on yourselves, but don't leave the wagons.'

Then he sniffed the wind, and caught the first whiff of

smoke. He winked at Harry, who had Vicky in his arms in a lingering farewell.

'I'll bet my share of the Wankie field against yours.'

'None of your crazy bets, Ralph Ballantyne,' Vicky cut in quickly. 'Harry has a wife to support now!'

'A guinea, then!' Ralph moderated the wager.

'Done!' agreed Harry.

They shook hands on it and swung up into the saddles.

Bazo led up Ralph's spare horse, with a rifle in the scabbard and a bandolier of bright brass cartridges looped to the pommel.

'Keep close, Bazo,' Ralph told him, and looked across at Harry. He had his own Matabele outrider and spare horse close behind him.

'Ready?' Ralph asked, and Harry nodded, and they trotted out of the laager.

The acrid stink of smoke was strong on the wind now, and the horses flared their nostrils nervously and stepped like cats over the hot ash of the back-burn.

'Just look at them!' Harry's voice was awed.

The herds of buffalo had begun moving down-wind ahead of the bush-fire. Gradually one herd had merged with another, a hundred becoming five hundred, then a thousand. Then the thousand began multiplying, the westward movement becoming faster, black bodies packing closer, the earth beginning to tremble faintly under the iron-black hooves. Now every few minutes one of the herd bulls, an animal so black and solid that he seemed to be hewn from rock, would stop and turn back, stemming the moving tide of breeding cows. He would lift his mighty horned head with its crenellated bosses and snuffle the east wind into his wet nostrils, blink at the sting of the smoke, turn again and break into a heavy swinging trot; and his cows would be infected by his agitation, while the red calves bawled in bewilderment and pressed to the flanks of their dams.

Now the herds were being compressed against each other.

The huge beasts, the largest of them a ton and a half of flesh and bone, were moving shoulder to shoulder and muzzle to tail across a front almost a mile wide. The leaders came cascading out of the forest onto the edge of the vlei, while the serried ranks reached back into the looming dust and were hidden by the twisted silver trunks of the msasa trees.

Ralph knotted the scarf up over his nose and mouth, and pulled his hat low over his eyes.

'Harry, my lad, every one that falls this side of the wagons,' he made a wide gesture, 'is mine. Everything that side is yours.'

'And a guinea on the bag,' Harry agreed. He levered a cartridge into the breech of his Lee Enfield rifle and with one of his wild Indian whoops clapped his heels into his horse's flanks and drove straight at the nearest beasts.

Ralph let him go, and held his own horse down to a trot. Gently he angled in towards the rolling herds, careful not to spook them prematurely, letting them concentrate on the flames behind rather than the hunter ahead. This way he got in really close, and picked out a good bull in the front rank. He leaned into the rifle, and aimed into the barrel of the thick neck, just where the bald scabby hide creased at the front of the shoulder.

The shot was almost drowned by the din of pounding hooves and bawling calves, but the bull dropped his nose to the earth, and somersaulted over it, sliding on his back, kicking convulsively in his death agony, and bellowing as mournfully as a foghorn in a winter gale. The herds plunged into full gallop.

Steering his mount with his heels and toes, leaving both hands free to load and aim and fire, Ralph pressed in against the wall of dark bodies in gargantuan flight. Sometimes he was so close that the rifle muzzle was merely inches from a monstrous neck or shoulder, and the muzzle flash was quick and bright as a lance as it buried itself in the thick black hide. At each crash of the rifle, another beast went down, for at that range an experienced huntsman could make a butchery of it. He fired until the hammer fell on an empty chamber, and then crammed fresh rounds into the magazine, and fired again as fast as he could pump the loading handle, not lifting the butt from his shoulder nor his eye from the sights.

The barrel was smoking hot, each shot now recoiling viciously into his shoulder, so that his teeth cracked together in his jaws and the forefinger of his right hand was bleeding, a flap of loose skin torn from the second joint by the trigger guard, so he was seconds slow on the reload, and then he was firing again. Deafened by gunfire, each shot was a muted popping in his abused eardrums, and the uproar of the galloping, bawling, bellowing herd was dreamlike and far away. His vision was dulled by the head-high bank of dust, and, as they tore once more into the forest, by the sombre shadows of the tree-tops that met overhead. He was bleeding from chin and lip and forehead where stones as big as acorns had been thrown into his face by the flying hooves ahead of him. Still he loaded and fired and reloaded. He had long ago lost all count of the bag and the endless herd still pressed close on both flanks of his floundering horse.

Suddenly one bandolier was empty, a hundred rounds fired, he realized with surprise, and Ralph pulled a fresh one from his saddlebag, instinctively ducking under a long branch and straightening up to find an enormous bull galloping half a length ahead of him.

It seemed to Ralph's distorted vision to be the monarch of all buffalo, with a spread of horns wider than a man could reach, heavy as one of the granite boulders of the Matopos, so old that the points were worn blunt and rounded. His rump and back were grey and bald with age, the bush ticks hanging in blue grapelike bunches in the deep folds of skin on each side of his huge swinging testicles.

Ralph's horse, almost blown now, could not hold him and the bull was pulling away strongly, his huge quarters

bunching and contracting, cloven hooves driving almost
hock-deep into the soft sandy earth under the immense
weight of his body. Ralph stood in the stirrups and aimed
for the spine at the base of the bull's long tufted tail as it
lashed his own sides in the fury of his run.

At the instant that Ralph fired, a branch snatched at his
shoulder and the shot flew wide, socking meatily into the
round black haunch. The bull tripped and checked, catching
himself before he went down, swinging abruptly aside with
blood spurting down his hind legs. Ralph gathered his
exhausted horse to follow him, but another thick grey tree-
trunk sprang out of the dust clouds ahead and forced him to
turn hard the other way to avoid it. Rough bark grazed his
knee and the bull was lost in the ranks of racing animals
and the billowing dust.

'Let him go,' Ralph shouted aloud. There was no chance
that he could find a single animal again in this multitude.
He cranked another cartridge into the scorching breech of
his rifle, and shot a sleek red queen through the back of the
skull, and an instant later knocked her half-grown calf down
with a bullet through the shoulder.

The rifle was empty and he began to reload, concentrating all his attention on the task, until suddenly some instinct
warned him and he glanced up.

The wounded bull had turned back to hunt him.

It came out of the gloom like a black avalanche, goring
the laggards out of its way, to cut a path for itself through
the racing black river of animals. Its nose was high, the
muzzle glistening wetly, and long silver strings of mucus
dangled from the flaring nostrils. It came quartering in and
the dusty earth exploded in pale puffs under the savagely
driving hooves.

'Come boy!' Ralph yelled desperately at his tired gelding,
gathering him with knees and reins, turning him away from
the bull's charge and at the same time cramming a cartridge
into the loading slot of the Winchester.

The bull closed in a crabbing rush, and Ralph swivelled the rifle and fired point-blank into the gigantic head, knowing there would be no time for another shot. The bull's head flinched and a splinter of slaty grey horn tore from the huge round bosses, and then the bull steadied himself, moving with the grace of a gazelle on his huge front legs. His head dropped. Ralph could have reached out and touched the crest of shaggy hide between his shoulders, instead he jerked his near leg from the stirrup and lifted his knee as high as his chin, just as the bull hooked the massive horns at the gelding's flank. At the place where Ralph's knee had been a moment before, the blunt tip of a black horn crashed into the horse's chest.

Ralph heard the ribs crackle and snap like dry sticks, and the air from the gelding's lungs was driven out of his throat in a whistling scream. Horse and rider were lifted high. The gelding was still screaming at the agony of his collapsed chest as Ralph was thrown clear. The rifle spun from his hand and he landed on his hip and shoulder and rolled to his knees. His right leg was numbed by the shock, it pinned him for precious seconds.

The buffalo was braced over the fallen gelding, front legs splayed, armoured head low, blood dribbling and trickling down its massive muscled quarters, and now it hooked at the horse, catching him in the soft of his belly and splitting him open like a cod on a fishwife's block. Soft, wet entrails, slippery as cooked spaghetti, were wrapped around the blunt point, and as the bull tossed his head, he stripped them out of the gaping belly cavity. The horse kicked once more, and then was still.

Dragging his right leg, Ralph crawled towards the base of a wild teak.

'Bazo!' he screamed. 'Bring the rifle! Bring the horse! Bazo!'

He could hear the shrill of panic and terror in his own voice, and the bull heard it also. It left the horse, and Ralph heard the splayed hooves thudding into the sandy earth, heard the snort of its breath and smelled the rank bovine reek of the animal. He howled again and dragged himself to his feet, hopping on his good leg. He knew he was not going to reach the mopani and he whirled to face the enraged bull.

It was so close that he could see the wet trail of tears from the corners of its pink-shot piggy little eyes running down the shaggy black cheeks, and the spongy tongue, splotched pink and grey, lolling from its jaws as it bellowed at him. The head went down to hook him and split him, as it had the horse, but at that instant another voice bellowed in Sindebele:

'Hau! Thou uglier than death!' The bull checked, and pivoted on his stubby forelegs. 'Come, thou witches' curse!'

Bazo was taking the bull off him, he galloped in out of the rolling dust, dragging the spare horse on its lead rein, and he angled in now across the bull's front, taunting it with his voice and flapping his monkey-skin cloak in its face. The bull accepted the lure of the cloak, put his nose down, and went after it. The horse that Bazo rode was still fresh, and it skittered out of the arc of the great swinging head, and the bull's polished horn glinted at the top of its lunge.

'Henshaw,' Bazo yelled, 'take the spare horse.' And he dropped the lead rein, sending the free horse down on Ralph, still at full gallop.

Ralph crouched in its path, and the grey mare saw him and swerved at the last moment, but Ralph leaped for the saddle, and got a hold on the pommel. For a dozen strides he hopped beside the mare, his feet skimming the ground as she carried him away. Then he gathered himself and swung his weight up across her back. His buttocks thumped onto the saddle, and he did not waste time groping for the stirrups. He yanked the spare rifle from the scabbard under his knee, and kicked the mare around after the great black bull.

The beast was intent on Bazo still, chasing him in a grotesque lumbering charge which covered the ground with uncanny speed. At that moment a low branch caught the half-naked Matabele induna a ringing crack across the shoulder and side of the head.

He was thrown sideways, the monkey-skin cloak flew away, flapping like an overfed black crow, and Bazo slid further until he was hanging upside down, his head almost brushing the ground between his mount's slashing hooves.

Coming up on the bull's blood-splattered quarters, Ralph fired into its back, probing for the spine in the mountain of black hide and bulging muscle. He fired with a mechanical action, cranking the loading handle, and the recoil dinned in upon his ears, so he could barely hear the heavy lead bullets slapping into the bull's body with a sound like a housewife beating a carpet. One of his bullets found the pumping lungs, for there was a sudden torrent of frothy blood blown from both the bull's nostrils, and the wild charge broke down into a short hampered trot.

Ralph came up alongside it, and it turned the great head and looked at him through eyes that swam with the tears of its death agony. Ralph reached across and almost touched the broad forehead under the beetling horns with the muzzle of the rifle. The bull flung his head back from the brain shot, and it dropped silently onto its knees. It never moved again.

Ralph galloped on and caught the bridle of Bazo's running horse. He yanked it down to a halt.

'Only a Matabele rides with his head in the stirrups and his feet in the saddle,' he gasped, and pulled Bazo upright.

The dark skin was smeared from Bazo's forehead by the rough bark of the branch, the raw flesh was pale pink and droplets of clear lymph welled up out of it like seed pearls.

'Henshaw, my little Hawk,' he replied thickly. 'You screamed so loudly I thought you were losing your virginity – with a horn, from behind.'

Ralph spluttered with shaky laughter, almost hysterical with the relief from terror and mortal danger. Bazo shook his head to clear it, his eyes came back into focus, and his grin was wicked.

'Go back to the women, Henshaw, for you cry like a maiden. Give me your gun and I will win your guinea for you.'

'See if you can keep up,' Ralph told him, and booted his horse into a run. The reaction from terror came upon him in a kind of atavistic madness, the wild soaring passion of the hunter, and he fell upon the galloping herds in a murderous frenzy.

The bushfire overtook them and put an end to the slaughter at last. Ralph and Bazo were almost caught between the enveloping arms of flame, but they broke through with the manes of their horses frizzled and stinking from the heat and Ralph's shirt scorched in brown patches. Then from the sanctuary of the back-burn, they watched in awe as the fire swept by on either side. It was a gale of heat that whirled burning branches aloft, and crashed from tree to tree, leaping a gap a hundred feet wide with a deep whooshing roar and bursting the next tree asunder as though it had been hit by a lyddite shell from a howitzer.

The flames sucked the air away so that they gasped for breath, and the heat went deep into their lungs, so they coughed like hemp-smokers. It seared the exposed skin of their faces, seemed to dry the moisture from their eyeballs and dazzle their vision as though they were staring into the fierce orb of the sun itself.

Then the fire was gone, burning away into the west, and they were silent and shaken, awed by the grandeur of its passing and by their own insignificance in the face of such elemental power.

It was the following morning before the earth had cooled sufficiently for the skinners to go out to work. The carcasses of the buffalo were half-roasted, the hair burned away on the upper side, yet untouched on the side where they had lain against the earth. The skinners worked in a landscape like a hellish vision of Hieronymus Bosch, a desolate and blackened earth, grotesquely twisted bare trees, with the hideous shapes of the vultures crouched in the upper branches.

One team of skinners rolled the huge carcasses and made the shallow incisions around the neck, down the limbs and swollen bellies, then the next team hooked on the bullock teams and stripped off the skin in a single slab, while the third team scooped the coarse white rock salt over the wet hides and spread them in the sun.

By the second day, the air was thick with the reek of hundreds of rotting carcasses; and the chorus of cries and howls and croakings of the scavengers was a fitting accompaniment to the scene. Although the dun palls of smoke had cleared, the sky was dark once again with wings, the glossy sable pinions of the crows, the quick sharp stabbing wings of the little kites and the great majestic spread of the vultures.

Around each naked carcass, stripped of its hide and with the obscene pink bellies massively swollen with gases, the hyena whooped and chuckled and the little dog-like jackal darted in nervously to snatch up a titbit of offal. The vultures hopped and flapped and squabbled, pecking at each other with steely hooked beaks, forcing their way through the enlarged anus of the cadaver into the belly cavern.

The tall black and white marabou storks, solemn as undertakers, stalked in with their bright greedy eyes set in the naked face-mask. Their crops were naked of feathers also; pink and scalded-looking, they dangled down in front of the throat like the swollen genitalia of some repulsive albino. With their long and powerful bills, they would rip off a strip of flesh on which the greenish iridescent sheen of putrefaction was already blooming. Then they pointed the bill at the sky, gaping and straining with the effort of gobbling the morsel down on top of their already gorged crop.

The stink of rotting, scorched flesh and the smell of the scavengers wafted down on the little circle of wagons, and kept the women from sleep.

'Ralph, can we leave here tomorrow?' Cathy whispered.

'Why?' he asked sleepily. 'You like it here, you said so.'

'Not any more,' she answered, and then after a while, 'Ralph, if we go on burning and killing like this, how long will it last?'

He was so startled that he heaved himself on one elbow and peered at her in the candlelight.

'What on earth are you talking about, girl?'

'When the animals are all gone, this will no longer be the land I know and love.'

'Gone?' He shook his head in sympathy, as though for an idiot child. 'Gone? By God, Katie, you saw the herds out there. They are countless, limitless. They are as thick as that all the way north to Khartoum. We could hunt like that every day, and not scratch the surface. No, Katie, they will never go.'

'How many did you kill?' she asked quietly.

'Me? Two hundred and fourteen, thirty-two more than your esteemed brother-in-law.' Ralph lay back comfortably, and pulled her head down onto his chest. 'And that cost the cocky bastard a guinea of his ill-gotten loot.'

'Between you, almost four hundred – in a single day's hunting, Ralph.' Her voice was so low that he barely heard it, but his own became rough with impatience.

'Damn it, Katie, I need the skins. They are mine to take if I want them. That's all there is to it. Now, go to sleep, silly girl.'

If anything, Ralph Ballantyne's estimate of the buffalo herds was conservative. Probably never had any large mammal been so prolifically massed upon the earth's face in all of its history. From the great Sud where the infant Nile weaves its way through fathomless swamps of floating papyrus, southwards over the wide savannahs of eastern and central Africa, down to the Zambezi and beyond to the golden glades and forests of Matabeleland, the vast black herds roamed.

They were very seldom hunted by the primitive tribes. They were too swift and fierce and powerful for their bows and spears. The digging of a pitfall large and deep enough to trap such an enormous beast was a labour that few of the tribesmen thought about seriously enough to interrupt their dancing and beer-drinking and cattle-raidings. The Arab travellers into the interior were not interested in such coarse game, rather they were intent on capturing and chaining the tender young black maidens and youths for the markets at Malindi and Zanzibar, or in hunting the wrinkled grey elephant for their curved ivory tusks. Very few European travellers, bearing their sophisticated weapons, had yet ventured into these remote lands, and even the huge prides of lion which followed the herds could not check their natural multiplication.

The grasslands were blackened by the huge bovine beasts. Some herds, twenty or thirty thousand strong, were so dense that the animals in the rear literally starved, for the pasturage was destroyed by the forerunners before they could reach it. Weakened by their own vast multitudes, they were ripe for the pestilence that came out of the north.

It came out of Egypt. It was the same plague that Moses' God Jehovah had inflicted on the Pharaoh of Egypt. It was the *Peste bovine*, the rinderpest, a virus disease which attacks all the ruminants, but of those the most susceptible are the bovines: buffalo and domestic cattle. The stricken animals are blinded and choked by the discharge from the mucous membranes. Mucus pours in thick ropes from their nostrils and jaws. The discharge is highly infectious and contagious, and it persists on the pasturage over which the animal has passed long after its host has perished.

The course of the disease is rapid and irreversible. The mucous discharges are swiftly followed by profuse diarrhoea and dysentery, with the beasts straining to evacuate even after their bowels are purged of all but bloody slime. Then when at last the animal goes down and no longer has the strength to rise, the convulsions twist the horned head back and around, until the nose touches the flank. That is the position in which they die.

The rinderpest passed with the speed of a gale wind across the continent, so that in places where the concentrations of buffalo were heaviest, a herd of ten thousand great horned animals was wiped out between the dawn and the sunset of a single day. The carcasses lay so thickly on the denuded savannah that they were touching each other like shoals of poisoned sardine washed up on a beach. Over this carnage hung the characteristic fetid odour of the disease with which soon mingled the stench of putrefaction, for even the teeming flocks of vultures and packs of gluttonous hyena could not devour one thousandth part of this awful windfall.

This gale of disease and death blew southwards, swallowing up the blundering, bellowing herds – southwards until at last it reached the Zambezi. Even that wide stretch of swirling green water could not check the pestilence. It was carried to the far bank in the bulging crops of the vultures and carrion storks, and was scattered upon the pasture in the faeces that they voided in flight.

The dreadful gale began again, southwards it moved, ever southwards.

Isazi, the little Zulu driver, was always the first awake in the laager. It gave him satisfaction to be alert and aware when others half his age still slept.

He left his mat and he went to the watch-fire. It was nothing but a pile of fluffy white ash, but Isazi moved the blackened tips of the logs together, crushed a few dry leaves of the ilala palm between them and leaned close to blow upon it. The ash flew away, and a coal glowed sullenly before the palm leaf popped into a cheery little flame. The logs took and Isazi warmed his palms for a moment, and then left the circle of wagons and wandered down to where the oxen were penned.

Isazi loved his bullocks as some men love their children or their dogs. He knew each by name. He knew their separate natures, their strengths and their weaknesses. He knew which of them would try to turn out of the span when the going got tough or the footing soft, and he knew those with great hearts and special intelligence. Of course, he had his favourites, like the huge red wheeler he had christened Dark Moon for his huge soft eyes, an ox who had held a loaded eighteen-footer against the flood of the Shashi when the mud bank was crumbling under his hooves, or Dutchman, the black and white dappled lead ox that he had trained to come like a dog to his whistle and lead the others to their place in the span.

Isazi chuckled lovingly, as he opened the thorn bush gate of the temporary kraal and whistled for Dutchman. In the pre-dawn gloom, a beast coughed, and the sound had a peculiarly harrowing quality that struck a chill into Isazi's guts. A healthy bullock did not cough that way.

He stood in the opening of the kraal, hesitating to go in, then he smelled something that he had never smelled before. Faint though the whiff of it was, it made his gorge rise. It smelled like a beggar's breath or a leper's sores. He had to force himself to go forward against the smell and his own dread.

'Dutchman,' he called. 'Where are you, my beauty?'

There was the explosive spluttering sound of a beast racked by dysentery, and Isazi ran towards it. Even in the bad light he recognized the bulky dappled shape. The bullock was lying down.

Isazi ran to it. 'Up,' he called. '*Vusa, thandwa!* Get up, my darling.' For a beast only lies down when it has given up hope.

The bullock heaved convulsively, but did not come to its feet. Isazi dropped to his knees, and placed his arm around its neck. The neck was twisted back at an awkward unnatural angle. The velvety muzzle pressed into the beast's flank. The muscles under the sleek skin were convulsed as rigidly as cast iron.

Isazi ran his hands down the beast's neck, feeling the fierce heat of fever. He touched the cheek, and it was slick and wet. Isazi lifted his hand to his own nose. It was coated with a thick slime and the little Zulu gagged at the smell of it. He scrambled to his feet, and backed away fearfully until he reached the gate. Then he whirled and ran to the wagons.

'Henshaw,' he yelled wildly. 'Come quickly, little Hawk.'

'Flame lilies,' Ralph Ballantyne growled. His face was congested with black angry blood, as he strode through the kraal. The lily was a lovely flower of crimson edged with gold that grew on a bright green bush that tempted any grazing animal that did not know them.

'Where are the herdboys? Bring those bloody *mujiba* here.' He stopped beside the twisted carcass of Dark Moon, a trained wheeler like this was worth £50. It was not the only dead ox, eight others were down and as many more were sickening.

Isazi and the other drivers dragged in the herders. They were terrified children, the eldest on the verge of puberty, the youngest ten years old, their immature groins covered only by a scrap of *mutsha* cloth, their little round buttocks naked.

'Don't you know what a flame lily is?' Ralph shouted at them. 'It's your job to watch for poison plants and keep the oxen off them. I'm going to thrash the skin off your black backsides to teach you.'

'We saw no lilies,' the eldest boy declared stoutly, and Ralph rounded on him.

'You cocky little bastard.'

In Ralph's hand was a sjambok of hippo hide. It was almost five foot long, thicker than a man's thumb at the butt and tapering to whip cord at the tip. It had been cured to the lovely amber colour of a meerschaum pipe.

'I'll teach you to look to the oxen, instead of sleeping under the nearest tree.'

Ralph swung the lash around the back of the child's legs. It hissed like a puff-adder, and the boy screamed at the cut of it. Ralph seized his wrist, and held him up for a dozen more strokes across the legs and buttocks. Then he let him go and grabbed the next *mujiba*. The child danced to the tune of the sjambok, howling at each cut.

'All right.' Ralph was satisfied at last. 'Get the healthy animals into the span.'

There were only sufficient oxen left to make up three teams. Ralph was forced to abandon half of the wagons, with their loads of salted buffalo hides, and they trekked on southwards as the sun came up over the horizon.

Within an hour another ox had fallen in the traces, with its nose twisted back against its side. They cut it loose and left it lying beside the track. Half a mile further two more bullocks went down. Then they began dropping so regularly that by noon Ralph was forced to abandon two more wagons, and the last one rolled on with a depleted span dragging it. Long ago Ralph's rage had given way to bewilderment. It was clear that this was no ordinary case of veld poisoning. None of his drivers had seen anything to equal it, and there was not even a precedent in the whole vast body of African folklore.

'It is a *tagathi*,' Isazi gave his opinion. He had seemed to shrink with grief for his beloved bullocks, so now he was a mournful little black gnome of a man. 'This is a terrible witchcraft.'

'By God, Harry,' Ralph led his new brother-in-law out of earshot of the women. 'We'll be lucky to get even the one wagon home. There are a few bad river drifts to cross yet. We had better ride ahead and try to pick an easier crossing on the Lupane river.'

The river was only a few miles ahead, they could already make out the dark green of the forest along its course. Ralph and Harry rode side by side, both of them worried and anxious.

'Five wagons lying out here,' Ralph muttered moodily. 'At three hundred pounds each, to say nothing of the cattle I've lost—' He broke off and sat up very straight in the saddle.

They had come out onto another open glade beside the river, and Ralph was staring across it at the three huge dappled giraffe. With the stilt legs of herons and the long graceful necks of swans, they were the strangest looking of all Africa's mammals. Their huge eyes were soft and sorrowful, their heads, strangely ugly-beautiful, were topped not by true horns but by outgrowths of bone covered with skin and hair. Their gait had the same deliberate slow motion of a chameleon, and yet a big bull would weigh a ton and stand eighteen feet tall. They were mute, no extremity of pain or passion could induce a whisper of sound from their swanlike throats. Their heart was large as a drum to pump as high as that head, and the arteries of the neck were fitted with valves to prevent the brain exploding under the pressure when the giraffe stooped, splay-legged, to drink.

These three animals were moving in single file across the

vlei. The old stink-bull leading them was almost black with age, the cow that followed was splotched with reddish fawn, and the half-grown calf was a lovely soft beige.

The calf was dancing. Ralph had never seen anything like it. It was swaying, and turning in slow and elegant pirouettes, the neck twisting and untwisting, swinging first to one side then to the other. Every few paces the mother turned back anxiously to watch its offspring, and then torn between duty and maternal love, swung again to follow the old bull. At last, quite slowly, with a kind of weary grace, the calf slumped to the grassy earth, and lay in a tangle of long limbs. The mother hovered for a minute or two, and then in the way of the wilderness, deserted the weak and went on after her mate.

Ralph and Harry rode up, slowly, almost reluctantly, to where the calf lay. Only when they reached it were they aware of the fatal mucous discharge from jaws and nostrils, and the diarrhoea painting the dappled hind-quarters. They stared at the corpse in disbelief, until suddenly Harry wrinkled his nose and sniffed.

'That smell, the same as the oxen—' he started, and suddenly realization dawned upon him. 'A murrain,' he whispered. 'By the sweet name of the Virgin, Harry, it's some kind of plague. It is wiping out everything, game and oxen.' Under his deep tan, Ralph had turned a muddy colour. 'Two hundred wagons, Harry,' he whispered, 'almost four thousand bullocks. If this thing goes on spreading, I'm going to lose them all.' He reeled in the saddle so that he had to clutch at the pommel for his balance. 'I'll be finished. Wiped out – all of it.' His voice trembled with self-pity, and then a moment later he shook himself like a wet spaniel, sloughing off despair, and colour rushed back into his darkly handsome face.

'No, I'm not,' he said fiercely. 'I'm not finished yet, not without a fight anyway.' And he whirled to face Harry. 'You'll have to bring the women back to Bulawayo alone,' he ordered. 'I'm taking the four best horses.'

'Where are you going?' Harry asked.

'Kimberley.'

'What for?'

But Ralph had pivoted his horse like a polo pony, and was lying along its neck as he raced back towards the single wagon that had just come out of the forest behind them. Even as he reached it, one of the lead oxen collapsed and lay convulsed in the traces.

I sazi did not go to the kraal the following dawn. He was afraid of what he would find. Bazo went in his place.

They were all dead. Every single bullock. They were already stiff and cold as statues, locked in that dreadful final convulsion. Bazo shivered, and pulled his monkey-skin cloak more closely around his shoulders. It was not the dawn chill, but the icy finger of superstitious awe that had touched him.

'When the cattle lie with their heads twisted to touch their flank, and cannot rise—' he repeated aloud the exact words of the Umlimo, and his dread was carried away by the jubilant rush of his warlike spirits. 'It is happening, just as it was prophesied.'

Never before had the Chosen One's words been so unequivocal. He should have seen it immediately, but the whirlwind of events had confused him so that it was only now that the true significance of this fatal plague had come upon him. Now he wanted to leave the laager, and run southwards, day and night, without stopping, until he reached that secret cavern in the sacred hills.

He wanted to stand before the assembled indunas and tell them: 'You who doubted, believe now the words of the Umlimo. You with milk and beer in your bellies, put a stone in their place.'

He wanted to go from mine to farm to the new villages the white men were building where his comrades now laboured with pick and shovel instead of the silver blade, wearing the ragged cast-offs of their masters rather than the plumes and kilts of the regiment.

He wanted to ask them, 'Do you remember the war song of the *Izimvukuzane Ezembintaba*, the Moles-that-burrow-under-a-mountain? Come, you diggers of the other men's dirt, come rehearse the war song of the Moles with me.'

But it was not yet full term, there was the third and final act of the Umlimo's prophecy to unfold, and until then Bazo, like his old comrades, must play the white man's servant. With an effort, he masked his savage joy, withdrawing behind the inscrutable face of Africa. Bazo left the kraal of dead bullocks and went to the remaining wagon. The white women and the child were asleep within the body of the vehicle, and Harry Mellow was lying wrapped in his blanket under the chassis where the dew could not wet him.

Henshaw had deserted them late the previous afternoon, before they had even reached the bank of the Lupani river. He had chosen four horses, the swiftest and strongest. He had charged Bazo most strictly with the task of leading the little party back to Bulawayo on foot, then he had kissed his wife and son, shaken hands briefly with Harry Mellow, and galloped away southwards towards the drift on the Lupani, leading the three spare horses on a long rein and riding like a man chased by wild dogs.

Now Bazo stooped beside the wagon and spoke slowly and clearly to the blanket-wrapped figure beneath it. Though Harry Mellow's grasp of Sindebele improved each day, it was still equivalent to that of a five-year-old and Bazo had to be sure he understood.

'The last of the oxen is dead. One horse was killed by the buffalo, and Henshaw has taken four.'

Harry Mellow sat up quickly and made the decision. 'That leaves one mount each for the women, and Jon-Jon can ride up behind one of them. The rest of us will walk. How long back to Bulawayo, Bazo?'

Bazo shrugged eloquently. 'If we were an impi, fast and fit, five days. But at the pace of a white man in boots—'

They looked like refugees, each servant carrying bundles of only the most essential stores upon his head, and strung out in a long straggling line behind the two horses. The women were hampered by their long skirts whenever they walked to rest the horses, and Bazo could not contain himself to this pace. He ranged far ahead of the others and once he was out of sight and well beyond earshot, he pranced and stamped, stabbing with an imaginary assegai at a non-existent adversary, and accompanying the *giya*, the challenge dance, with the fighting chant of his old impi.

> 'Like a mole in the earth's gut
> Bazo found the secret way—'

The first verse of the song commemorated the impi's assault on the mountain stronghold of Pemba, the wizard, when so long ago Bazo had climbed the subterranean passage to the top of the cliff. It was as a reward for this feat that Lobengula had promoted Bazo to induna, had given him the headring, and allowed him to 'go in to the women' and choose Tanase as his wife.

Dancing alone in the forest, Bazo sang the other verses. Each of them had been composed after a famous victory, all except the last. That verse was the only one that had never been sung by the full regiment in battle array. It was the verse for the last charge of the Moles, when with Bazo at their head, they had run onto the laager on the banks of the Shangani river. Bazo had composed it himself, as he lay in the cave of the Matopos, near unto death with the mortification of the bullet wounds in his body.

> 'Why do you weep, widows of Shangani,
> When the three-legged guns laugh so loudly?

Why do you weep, little sons of the Moles,
When your fathers did the king's bidding?'

Now suddenly there was another verse. It came into
Bazo's head complete and perfect, as though it had been
sung ten thousand times before.

'The Moles are beneath the earth,
"Are they dead?" asked the daughters of Mashobane.
Listen, pretty maids, do you not hear
Something stirring, in the darkness?'

And Bazo, the Axe, shouted it to the msasa trees in their
soft mantles of red leaves, and the trees bowed slightly to
the east wind, as though they, too, were listening.

R alph Ballantyne stopped at King's Lynn. He threw
the reins to Jan Cheroot, the old Hottentot hunter.
'Water them, old man, and fill the grain bags for
me. I will be away again in an hour.'

Then he ran up onto the veranda of the sprawling
thatched homestead, and his stepmother came out to meet
him, her consternation turning to delight, when she recognized him.

'Oh Ralph, you startled me—'

'Where is my father?' Ralph demanded, as he kissed her
cheek, and Louise's expression changed to match the gravity
of his.

'In the north section, they are branding the calves – but
what is it, Ralph? I haven't seen you like this.'

He ignored the question. 'The north section, that's six
hours' ride. I cannot spare the time to go to him.'

'It's serious,' she decided. 'Don't torture me, Ralph.'

'I'm sorry.' He laid his hand on her arm. 'There is some dreadful murrain sweeping down out of the north. It hit my cattle on the Gwaai river, and we lost them all, over one hundred head in twelve hours.'

Louise stared at him. 'Perhaps—' she whispered, but he cut across her brusquely.

'It's killing everything, giraffe and buffalo and oxen, only the horses have not been touched yet. But, by God, Louise, I saw buffalo lying dead and stinking on each side of the track as I rode southwards yesterday. Animals that had been strong and healthy the day before.'

'What must we do, Ralph?'

'Sell,' he answered. 'Sell all the cattle at any price, before it reaches us.' He turned and shouted to Jan Cheroot. 'Bring the notebook from my saddlebag.'

While he scribbled a note for his father, Louise asked, 'When did you last eat?'

'I cannot remember.'

He ate the slabs of cold venison and raw onion and strong cheese on slices of stone-ground bread, and washed it down with a jug of beer, while he gave Jan Cheroot his instructions. 'Speak to nobody else but my father. Tell nobody else of this thing. Go swiftly, Jan Cheroot.' But Ralph was up in the saddle and away before the little Hottentot was ready to ride.

Ralph circled wide of the town of Bulawayo, to avoid meeting an acquaintance and to reach the telegraph line at a lonely place, well away from the main road. Ralph's own construction gangs had laid the telegraph line, so he knew every mile of it, every vulnerable point and how most effectively to cut off Bulawayo and Matabeleland from Kimberley and the rest of the world.

He tethered his horses at the foot of one of the telegraph poles and shinned up it to the cluster of porcelain insulators and the gleaming copper wires. He used a magnus hitch on a leather thong to hold the ends of the wire from falling to earth, and then cut between the knots. The wire parted with a singing twang, but the thong held, and when he climbed down to the horses and looked up, he knew it would need a skilled linesman to detect the break.

He flung himself back into the saddle, and booted the horse into a gallop. At noon he intersected the road and turned southwards along it. He changed horses every hour, and rode until it was too dark to see the tracks. Then he knee-haltered the horses, and slept like a dead man on the hard ground. Before dawn, he ate a hunk of cheese and a slice of the rough bread Louise had put into his saddlebag, and was away again with the first softening of the eastern sky.

At mid-morning, he turned out of the track, and found the telegraph line where it ran behind a flat-topped kopje. He knew the Company linesmen hunting for the first break in the line would be getting close to it by now, and there may be somebody in the telegraph office in Bulawayo anxious to send a report to Mr Rhodes about the terrible plague that was ravaging the herds.

Ralph cut the line in two places and went on. In the late afternoon, one of his horses broke down. It had been ridden too hard, and he turned it loose beside the road. If a lion did not get it, then perhaps one of his drivers would recognize the brand.

The next day, fifty miles from the Shashi river, he met one of his own convoys coming up from the south. There were twenty-six wagons in the charge of a white overseer. Ralph stopped only long enough to commandeer the man's horses, leave his own exhausted animals with him, and then he rode on. He cut the telegraph lines twice more, once on each side of the Shashi river, before he reached the railhead.

He came upon his surveyor first, a red-haired Scot. With a gang of blacks, they were working five miles ahead of the main crews, and cutting the lines for the rails. Ralph did not even dismount.

'Did you get the telegraph I sent you from Bulawayo, Mac?' he demanded without wasting time on greetings.

'Nowt, Mr Ballantyne.' The Scot shook his dusty curls. 'Not a word from the north in five days – they say the lines are down, longest break I've heard of.'

'Damn it to hell,' Ralph swore furiously, to cover his relief. 'I wanted you to hold a truck for me.'

'If you hurry, Mr Ballantyne, sir, there is an empty string of trucks going back today.'

Five miles further on Ralph reached the railhead. It was crossing a wide flat plain dotted with thorn scrub. The boil of activity seemed incongruous in this bleak, desolate land on the edge of the Kalahari Desert. A green locomotive huffed columns of silver steam high into the empty sky, shunting the string of flat-topped bogies to the end of the glistening silver rails. Teams of singing black men, dressed only in loincloths, but armed with crowbars, levered the steel rails over the side of the trucks and as they fell in a cloud of pale dust, another team ran forward to lift and set the tracks onto the teak sleepers.

The foremen levelled them with cast-iron wedges and the hammer boy followed them, driving in the steel spikes with ringing blows. Half a mile back was the construction headquarters. A square sweat box of wood and corrugated iron that could be moved up each day. The chief engineer was in his shirtsleeves, sweating over a desk made of condensed-milk cases nailed together.

'What is your mileage?' Ralph demanded from the door of the shack.

'Mr Ballantyne, sir,' the engineer jumped up. He was an inch taller than Ralph, bull-necked and with thick hairy forearms, but he was afraid of Ralph. You could see it in his eyes. It gave Ralph a flicker of satisfaction, he was not trying to be the most popular man in Africa. There was no prize for that. 'We didn't expect you, not until the end of the month.'

'I know. What's your mileage?'

'We have had a few snags, sir.'

'By God, man, do I have to kick it out of you?'

'Since the first of the month,' the engineer hesitated. He had proved to himself that there was no profit in lying to Ralph Ballantyne. 'Sixteen miles.'

Ralph crossed to the survey map, and checked the figures. He had noted the beacon numbers of the railhead as he passed.

'Fifteen miles and six hundred yards, isn't sixteen,' he said.

'No, sir. Almost sixteen.'

'Are you satisfied with that?'

'No, sir.'

'Nor am I.' That was enough, Ralph told himself, any more would decrease the man's usefulness, and there wasn't a better man to replace him, not between here and the Orange river.

'Did you get my telegraph from Bulawayo?'

'No, Mr Ballantyne. The lines have been down for days.'

'The line to Kimberley?'

'That is open.'

'Good. Get your operator to send this.'

Ralph stooped over the message pad and scribbled quickly.

'For Aaron Fagan, attorney at law, De Beers Street, Kimberley. Arriving early tomorrow 6th. Arrange urgent noon meeting with Rough Rider from Rholand.'

Rough Rider was the private code for Roelof Zeederberg, Ralph's chief rival in the transport business. Zeederberg's express coaches plied from Delagoa to Algoa Bay, from the goldfields of Pilgrims Rest to Witwatersrand, to the railhead at Kimberley.

While his telegraph operator tapped it out on the brass and teak instrument, Ralph turned back to his engineer.

'All right, what were the snags that held you up, and how can we beat them?'

'The worst is the bottle-neck at Kimberley shunting-yards.'

For an hour they worked, and at the end of it the locomotive whistled outside the shack. They went out, still arguing and planning. Ralph tossed his saddlebag and blanket-roll onto the first flat car, and held the train for ten minutes longer while he arranged the final details with his engineer.

'From now on you will get your hardware faster than you can nail it down,' he promised grimly, as he vaulted up onto the bogie and waved at the driver.

The whistle sent a jet of steam spurting into the dry desert air, and the locomotive wheels spun and then gripped with a jolt, and the long string of empty cars began to trundle southwards, building up speed rapidly. Ralph found a corner of the truck out of the wind, and rolled into his blanket. Eight days' ride from the Lupani river to the railhead. It had to be some sort of record.

'But there is no prize for that either,' he grinned wearily, pulled his hat over his eyes and settled down to listen to the song of the wheels over the ties. 'We have got to hurry. We have got to hurry.' And then just before he fell asleep, the song changed: 'The cattle are dying. The cattle are dead,' sang the wheels over and over again, but even that could not keep him awake one second longer.

They pulled into the shunting-yards at Kimberley, sixteen hours later. It was just past four in the morning.

Ralph jumped down off the bogie as the locomotive slowed for the points, and with his saddlebags slung over his shoulder, trudged up De Beers Street. There was a light on in the telegraph office and Ralph beat on the wooden hatch until the night operator peered out at him like a barn owl from its nest.

'I want to send an urgent telegraph to Bulawayo.'

'Sorry, mate, the line is down.'

'When will it be open again?'

'God knows, it's been out for six days already.'

Ralph was still grinning as he swaggered into the lobby of Diamond Lil's Hotel.

The night clerk was new. He did not recognize Ralph. He saw a tall lean sunburned man, whose stained and dusty clothing hung loosely on him. That wild ride had burned off all Ralph's excess flesh. He had not shaved since leaving the Lupani, and his boots were scuffed almost through the uppers by the brushing of the thorn scrub as he had ridden through it. Locomotive soot had darkened his face and reddened his eyes, and the clerk recognized a drifter when he saw one.

'I'm sorry, sir,' he said. 'The hotel is full.'

'Who is in the Blue Diamond suite?' Ralph asked affably.

'Sir Randolph Charles,' the clerk's voice was filled with reverence.

'Get him out,' said Ralph.

'I beg your pardon?' the clerk reared back, and his expression was frosty. Ralph reached across the desk, and took him by his watered silk cravat, and drew him closer.

'Get him out of my suite,' Ralph repeated, his lips an inch from the man's ear. 'Quickly!'

It was at that moment that the day clerk came into the reception office.

'Mr Ballantyne,' he cried with a mixture of alarm and feigned pleasure as he rushed to the rescue of his colleague. 'Your permanent suite will be ready in a minute.' Then he hissed in the night clerk's other ear. 'Clear that suite immediately, or he'll do it for you.'

The Blue Diamond had one of the very few bathrooms

in Kimberley with laid-on hot water. Two black servants stoked the boiler outside the window to keep steam whistling from the valve while Ralph lay chin-deep and adjusted a trickle of scalding water with his big toe on the tap. At the same time he shaved his jaws with a straight razor, working by touch and scorning the mirror. The day clerk had supervised the removal of Ralph's steamer trunk from the box-room, and hovered over the valets as they pressed the suits and tried to improve upon the perfect shine of the boots that they unpacked from the trunk.

At five minutes before noon, Ralph, smelling of brilliantine and eau de Cologne, marched into Aaron Fagan's office. Aaron was a thin stooped man, with threadbare hair brushed straight back from a deep intellectual forehead. His nose was beaked, his mouth full and sensitive and his sloe-eyes aware and bright.

He played a cruel game of kalabriasz, giving no quarter, and yet there was a compassionate streak in his nature which Ralph valued as highly as any of his other qualities. If he had known what Ralph intended at this moment, he would have tried to dissuade him, but after having put the case against it, he would then have gone ahead and drawn up a contract as mercilessly as he would have elevated his jasz and menel for a winning coup at kalabriasz.

Ralph didn't have time to argue ethics with him now, so as they embraced and patted each other's shoulder-blades affectionately, he forestalled the question by asking: 'Are they here?' and then pushing open the door to the inner office.

Roelof and Doel Zeederberg did not rise as he entered and neither they nor Ralph made any attempt to shake hands. They had clashed viciously, but indecisively, on too many occasions.

'So, Ballantyne, you want to waste our time again?' Roelof's accent was still thick with his Swedish ancestry, but under his pale ginger brows, his eyes were quick with interest.

'My dear Roelof,' Ralph protested, 'I would never do that. All I want is that we should resolve this tariff on the new Matabeleland route before we put each other out of business.'

'Ja!' Doel agreed sarcastically. 'That's a good thought, like my mother-in-law should love me.'

'We are willing to listen, for a few minutes anyway.' Roelof's tone was casual, but his interest was quicker still.

'One of us should buy the other out, and set his own tariffs,' said Ralph blandly, and the brothers glanced at each other involuntarily. Roelof made a fuss of relighting his dead cigar to hide his astonishment.

'You are asking yourselves why?' Ralph said. 'You want to know why Ralph Ballantyne wants to sell out.' Neither brother denied it; they waited quietly as vultures in the tree-tops.

'The truth is this, I have over-extended myself in Mata-beleland. The Harkness Mine—'

The lines of tension around Roelof's mouth smoothed out. They had heard about the mine, the talk on the Johannesburg stock exchange floor was that it would cost £50,000 to bring it into production.

'I am behind on the railway contract for Mr Rhodes,' Ralph went on quietly and seriously. 'I need cash.'

'You had a figure in mind?' Roelof asked, and took a puff on the cigar.

Ralph nodded and gave it to him, and Roelof choked on his smoke. His brother pounded him between his shoulders until he regained his breath, and then Roelof chuckled and shook his head.

'Ja,' he said. 'That's good. That's a very good one.'

'It looks as though you were right,' Ralph agreed. 'I am wasting your time.' He pushed back his chair and stood up.

'Sit down.' Roelof stopped laughing. 'Sit down and let's talk,' he said briskly, and by the following noon Aaron Fagan had drawn up the contract in his own hand.

It was very simple. The purchasers accepted the attached statement of assets as complete and correct. They agreed to take over all existing contracts of carriage and the responsibility of all goods at present in transit. The seller gave no guarantees. The purchase price was in cash, no share transfers were involved, and the effective date was that of the signatures – walk out, walk in.

They signed in the presence of their attorneys, and then both parties, accompanied by their legal counsellors, crossed the street to the main branch of the Dominion Colonial and Overseas Bank where the cheque of Zeederberg Bros was presented and duly honoured by the manager. Ralph swept the bundles of five-pound notes into his carpet bag, tipped his hat to the brothers Zeederberg.

'Good luck to you, gentlemen,' and then he took Aaron Fagan's arm and led him in the direction of Diamond Lil's Hotel.

Roelof Zeederberg massaged the bald spot on his crown. 'I suddenly have this strange feeling,' he murmured uneasily as he watched them go.

The next morning, Ralph left Aaron Fagan at the door of his office.

'You'll be hearing from the good brothers Zeederberg again sooner than you expect,' he warned him affably. 'Try not to bother me with their accusations, there's a good fellow.' He sauntered away across the Market Square, leaving Aaron staring after him thoughtfully.

Ralph's progress was slow, half a dozen acquaintances stopped him to enquire solicitously after his health, and then seek confirmation of the sale of his transport company, or to find out if he intended making a public issue of Harkness Mine shares.

'Give me a nod when you decide, Ralph.'

'Any help I can give, it will be my pleasure, Mr Ballantyne.'

Rumours of the 'payable' values of the Harkness ore put it as high as sixty ounces to the ton, and everybody he met wanted to be let in, so it took him almost an hour to cover the five hundred yards to the offices of the De Beers Consolidated Mines Company.

It was a magnificent edifice, a temple dedicated to the worship of diamonds. The open balconies on all three floors were laced with white grilles of delicate ironwork, the walls were of redbrick with corners picked out in worked stone blocks, the windows were of stained glass and the doors were oiled teak with polished brass fittings.

Ralph signed his name in the visitors' book and a uniformed janitor with white gloves led him up the spiral staircase to the top floor. There was a brass plate on the teak door, a name only, with no title to accompany it: 'Mr Jordan Ballantyne'. But the grandeur of the office beyond the door gave some indication of Jordan's importance in the hierarchy of De Beers Diamond Company.

The double windows looked out over the Kimberley mine; the excavation was almost a mile across, and it was impossible even from this height to see into its depth. It seemed as though a meteor had struck and ploughed this crater through the earth's crust. Each day saw it driven deeper and deeper still, as the miners followed the fabulous cone of blue kimberlite conglomerate downwards. Already that hole had delivered up almost ten million carats of fine diamonds, and Mr Rhodes' Company owned it all.

Ralph merely glanced once at this view of the pit in which he had spent most of his youth grovelling and scratching for the elusive stones, and then he surveyed the room appraisingly. The panelling was of seasoned oak, the intricate carving worked by craftsmen, the carpets over the floor were silk Qum, and the books in the shelves were matching sets bound in morocco and stamped in gold leaf.

There was the sound of running water from the open door of the bathroom, and a voice asked, 'Who is it?'

Ralph spun his hat onto the stand, and turned to face the door as Jordan came through it. He was in his shirt-sleeves with protectors over his cuffs, his shirt was the finest Irish linen and the cravat under his stock was watered silk. He was drying his hands on a monogrammed towel, but he froze when he saw Ralph, then he threw the towel aside and crossed to him with three long lithe strides and a cry of delight.

At last Ralph broke the brotherly embrace and held Jordan off at arm's length to study him.

'Always the dandy,' Ralph teased him, and ruffled his thick fashionably dressed golden curls.

No amount of brotherly familiarity could dim the fact that Jordan was still one of the most handsome men that Ralph had ever met. No, he was more than handsome, he was beautiful, and his evident pleasure at seeing Ralph heightened the glow of his skin and the lively sparkle of green behind his long curved fringe of lashes. As always, his younger brother's charisma and gentle nature recaptivated Ralph.

'And you,' Jordan laughed, 'you look so hard and brown and lean, what on earth happened to that prosperous paunch?'

'I left it on the road from Matabeleland.'

'Matabeleland!' Jordan's expression changed. 'Then you'll have brought the terrible news with you.' Jordan hurried to the leather-topped desk. 'The telegraph line has been down for over a week, this is the first message to come through. I finished decoding it not an hour ago.'

He handed Ralph the flimsy, and he scanned it swiftly. The translation was written in Jordan's fair hand between the lines of teleprinting. The addressee was 'Jove', Mr Rhodes' private code name, and it was from General Mungo St John in his capacity as acting Administrator of Matabeleland in the absence of Doctor Jameson.

'Outbreak of cattle disease reported from northern Matabeleland. Losses sixty per cent repeat sixty per cent. Company veterinarian recognizes symptoms similar to *Peste bovine* epidemic Italy 1880. Disease also known as rinderpest. No known treatment. Possible losses 100 per cent failing isolation and control. Urgently request authority to destroy and burn all cattle in central province to prevent southward spread.'

While he feigned astonishment and shock at the first paragraph, Ralph ran his eye swiftly down the remaining text. It was a rare opportunity to read a decoded BSA Company report; the fact that Jordan had handed it to him was a measure of his agitation.

There were lists of police strengths and dispositions, summaries of monies held and dispensed, administrative requisitions, recommendations for trading-licences, and the roster of mineral claims filed in Bulawayo. Ralph passed the sheet back to his brother with a suitably solemn expression.

At the head of the roster of new claims, he had seen a block of forty square miles registered in the name of Wankie Coal Mining Company. That was the name that he and Harry Mellow had agreed upon for their company, and Ralph glowed with satisfaction that did not show on his face. Harry must have got the women and Jonathan safely back to Bulawayo, and he had wasted no time in filing the claims. Once again Ralph congratulated himself on his choice of partner and brother-in-law. The only prickle of uncertainty was the rider to the roster that St John had sent.

Advise soonest Company policy regarding coal and base metals claims – register 198 in favour of Wankie Coal Mining Co. held in abeyance pending clarification.

The claims were filed but not yet confirmed; however, Ralph would have to worry about that later. Right now, he had to concentrate on Jordan's apprehensions.

'Papa is right in the path of this thing, this rinderpest. He has worked so hard all his life, and had such rotten luck – oh Ralph, it can't happen to him, not again.' Jordan stopped as another thought occurred to him. 'And you, too. How many bullock teams did you have in Matabeleland, Ralph?'

'None.'

'None? I don't understand.'

'I sold every last ox and wagon to the Zeederbergs.'

Jordan stared at him. 'When?' he asked at last.

'Yesterday.'

'When did you leave Bulawayo, Ralph?'

'What has that got to do with it?' Ralph demanded.

'The telegraph lines – they were cut, you know, deliberately. In four places.'

'Extraordinary, who would have done a thing like that?'

'I don't even dare to ask.' Jordan shook his head. 'And on second thoughts, I don't want to know when you left Bulawayo, or whether or not Papa sold his stock as suddenly as you did yours.'

'Come on, Jordan, I'll take you to lunch at the club. A bottle of bubbly will console you for belonging to a family of rogues and for working for another.'

The Kimberley Club had a most undistinguished façade. Since its foundation, it had been enlarged twice, and the additions were glaringly apparent, unbaked Kimberley brick abutting upon galvanized iron and finally fired redbrick. The iron roof was unpainted, but there were strange little touches of pretension, the white picket fence, the front door glazed in Venetian glass.

Until a man had become a member, he could not consider himself truly to have arrived in South Africa. Membership was so prized that Barney Barnato, who despite his millions had been steadfastly blackballed, was finally tempted to sell out his diamond holdings to Mr Rhodes only after he had been promised the coveted membership as part of the deal. Even then, with the pen in his hand, Barnato had hesitated over signing the contract.

'How do I know they still won't chuck me out again, as soon as I've signed?'

'My dear fellow, we will make you a life governor,' Mr Rhodes assured him, offering the final plum that was irresistible to the little slum-born Cockney.

On his first night as a member of the club, Barnato strode up to the long bar dressed like a theatrical impresario, and ordered a round of drinks for all, then flashed a magnificent ten-carat blue-white diamond ring on his third finger.

'What do you gents think of that, hey?'

One of the members studied it for a moment, and remarked, 'Clashes awfully with the colour of your fingernails, old boy.' Then ignoring the proffered drink, he sauntered through to the billiard room, and everybody except Barney Barnato and the barman trooped out after him. It was that kind of club.

Ralph's and Jordan's own membership had been assured as soon as they came of age. For not only was their father a founder member and a life governor, but he was also a holder of the Queen's commission and a gentleman. These things counted at the Kimberley Club ahead of vulgar wealth. The porter greeted the brothers by name, and put their cards up on the 'in' board. The barman behind the long bar poured Jordan a pink gin and Indian tonic, without being ordered, though he turned to Ralph apologetically.

'We don't see you often enough, Mr Ralph. Is it still Glenlivet whisky, sir, water and no ice?'

In the dining-room they both ordered from the carving trolley, juicy young lamb, with the subtle taste of the Karroo herbs on which it had barely been weaned, served with parsleyed baby new potatoes. Jordan declined the champagne that Ralph suggested.

'I am a working man,' he smiled, 'my tastes are simpler than yours, something like Château Margaux '73 would suit me better.'

The twenty-year-old claret cost four times more than any champagne on the wine list.

'By God!' said Ralph ruefully. 'Under that urban veneer, you are a true Ballantyne, after all.'

'And you must be neck-deep in filthy lucre after that timely sale. It's my brotherly duty to help you get rid of it.'

'Fire sale price,' Ralph demurred, but nodded in appreciation of the claret. They ate in contented silence for a few minutes, then Ralph picked up his glass.

'What does Mr Rhodes think of the coal deposits that Harry and I pegged?' he asked mildly, pretending to study the ruby lights in the wine, but watching his brother's reaction.

He saw the corners of Jordan's mouth quiver with surprise, saw his eyes flare with some other emotion which he could not read before it was masked, then Jordan lifted a pink morsel of the lamb on the silver fork, chewed it fastidiously and swallowed before he asked:

'Coal?'

'Yes, coal!' Ralph agreed. 'Harry Mellow and I pegged a huge deposit of high-grade coal in northern Matabeleland – haven't you seen the filing yet? Hasn't the Board approved the register? You must know about it, Jordan.'

'What a fine wine this is.' Jordan inhaled the bouquet. 'A big, spicy perfume.'

'Oh, of course, the telegraph line has been down. You haven't received it yet?'

'Ralph, I happen to know through my spies,' Jordan said carefully, and Ralph leaned closer to him, 'that the club secretary has just received a twenty-pound Stilton from Fortnum's. It should be perfect after the voyage.'

'Jordan.' Ralph stared at him, but Jordan would not look up.

'You know I can't say anything,' he whispered miserably, so instead they ate the Stilton on water biscuits and accompanied it with a port from the cask that was not listed on the wine card, its existence known only to the privileged members.

At last Jordan took the gold hunter from his fob pocket.

'I should be getting back, Mr Rhodes and I are leaving for London at noon tomorrow. There is a great deal to do before we go.'

However, as they stepped out of the front door of the club, Ralph took his brother's elbow firmly and steered him into De Beers Road, lulling him with a flow of family gossip until they were opposite a pretty redbrick cottage almost hidden by dog roses, its diamond-paned windows curtained with frilled lace, and its demure little sign on the gate:

'French dressmakers. *Haute Couture*.
Continental Seamstresses. Specialities for
individual tastes.'

Before Jordan had realized what his brother was about, Ralph had lifted the latch of the gate and was leading him down the walk. Ralph felt that on top of good food and wine, the company of one of the young ladies whom Diamond Lil chose with such taste and care to ornament Rose Cottage could not fail to soften and relax the tongue of even such a loyal servant as Jordan into indiscreet comment on his master's affairs.

Jordan took one pace beyond the gate, before he pulled back from Ralph's grasp with unnecessary violence.

'Where are you going?' he demanded. He had gone as pale as though a mamba had crossed the path at his feet. 'Do you know what this place is?'

'Yes, I do,' Ralph nodded. 'It's the only whorehouse I know of where a doctor checks the goods on offer at least once a week.'

'Ralph, you can't go in there.'

'Oh, come now, Jordie,' Ralph smiled, and took his arm again. 'It's me, your brother Ralph. You don't have to put on a show. A salty young bachelor like you, by God, I'll bet there is a plaque on the wall above every bed in there with your name on it—' He stopped, as he recognized Jordan's real consternation. 'What is it, Jordie?' For once Ralph was uncertain of himself. 'Don't tell me you have never had your cuff turned back for you by one of Lil's seamstresses?'

'I have never set foot in that place.' Jordan shook his head vehemently. He had gone pale and his lips trembled. 'And nor should you, Ralph. You are a married man!'

'Oh Lord, Jordie, don't be daft, lad. Even a solid diet of caviar and champagne can pall after a while. A hunk of country ham and a jug of rough cider makes a nice change.'

'That's your business,' Jordan flashed at him. 'And I don't propose to stand in the street in front of this – this institution, discussing it.'

He turned on his heel and strode away down the sidewalk a half-dozen paces before looking back over his shoulder.

'You would do better to consult your lawyer about your damned coal than—' Jordan broke off with a stricken expression, clearly horrified by his indiscretion, then he hurried away towards Market Square.

Ralph's jaw hardened, his eyes went cold and hard as polished emeralds. He had got his hint from Jordan, and it

224

hadn't cost him the price of one of Diamond Lil's fancy girls either. The lace curtain in the front window of Rose Cottage lifted, and a pretty dark-eyed lass with a creamy oval face and soft red mouth smiled out at him, shaking her ringlets in invitation to enter.

'Sit on it, dearie,' Ralph told her grimly. 'And keep it warm for me. I'll be back later.'

He ground out the half-smoked Romeo y Julieta under his heel, and strode away towards Aaron Fagan's office building.

A aron Fagan called them the 'wolf pack'.
'Mr Rhodes keeps them chained in specially constructed kennels, but lets them run every now and then, just to get a little taste of human flesh.'

They did not look particularly lupine. There were four of them, soberly dressed men whose ages ranged from late thirties to mid-fifties.

Aaron introduced each of them individually, and then collectively. 'These gentlemen are the De Beers Company permanent legal advisers. I think I am correct in saying that they also act on behalf of the British South Africa Company?'

'That is correct, Mr Fagan,' said the senior counsellor, and his colleagues arranged themselves down the opposite side of the long table. Each of them placed his pigskin folder of papers neatly in front of him, and then, like a rehearsed vaudeville team, they looked up in unison. It was only then that Ralph recognized the wolf-like glitter in their eyes.

'In what way can we be of assistance?'

'My client is seeking clarification of the mining laws promulgated by the BSA Company,' Aaron replied, and two hours later Ralph was groping desperately through a maze of jargon and convoluted legal side-roads as he tried to follow the discussion, and his irritation was becoming increasingly obvious.

Aaron made a silent plea for patience, and with an effort Ralph stopped the angry words reaching his lips, instead he hunched further down in his chair, and in a deliberately boorish gesture of defiance, he placed one boot on the polished table top amongst the scattered legal papers and crossed his other ankle on top of it.

For another hour he listened, sinking lower and still lower in his chair and scowling at the lawyers opposite him, until Aaron Fagan asked humbly: 'Does that mean in your opinion my client has not fulfilled the requirements of Section 27 B Clause Five read in conjunction with Section 7 Bis?'

'Well, Mr Fagan, we would first have to examine the question of due performance as set out in Section 31,' replied the pack leader carefully, smoothing his moustache and glancing at his assistants who nodded brightly again in concert. 'In terms of that section—'

Abruptly Ralph reached the far frontier of his patience. He brought his boots down off the table onto the floor with a crash that startled the four grey-suited men across the table. One of them knocked his folder onto the floor, and papers flew like the feathers when a red caracal cat gets into the henhouse.

'I may not know the difference between "due performance" and the aperture between your buttocks,' announced Ralph in a voice that made the leader pale and shrink in size. Like all men of words, he had a horror of violence, and that was what he sensed in the gaze with which Ralph fixed him. 'However, I do know a wagonload of horse manure when I see one. And this, gentlemen, is grade-one horse manure you are giving me.'

'Mr Ballantyne.' One of the younger assistants was bolder

than his chief. 'I must protest your use of language! Your insinuation—'

'It is not an insinuation,' Ralph rounded on him. 'I am telling you outright that you are a bunch of bandits, is that still not clear enough? How about robbers then, or pirates?'

'Sir—' The assitant sprang to his feet, flushed with indignation, and Ralph reached across the table and caught him by the front of his stock. He twisted it sharply, cutting off the man's protest before it emerged.

'Pray be silent, my good fellow, I am speaking,' Ralph admonished him, and then went on, 'I am sick of dealing with little thieves. I want to speak to the head bandit. Where is Mr Rhodes?'

At that moment a locomotive down in the shunting-yards whistled. The sound only just carried even in the silence which followed Ralph's question, and Ralph remembered Jordan's excuse for ending lunch the previous day. He released the struggling lawyer so abruptly that the man collapsed back into his chair, fighting for breath.

'Aaron,' Ralph demanded. 'What time is it?'

'Eight minutes of noon.'

'He was fobbing me off – the cunning bastard was fobbing me off!'

Ralph whirled and ran from the boardroom.

There were half a dozen horses at the hitching rack outside the front of the De Beers building. Without checking his speed, Ralph decided on a big strong-looking bay and ran to it. He clinched the girth, unhitched the reins, and turned its head out into the road.

'Hey, you,' shouted the janitor. 'That's Sir Randolph's mount!'

'Tell Sir Randolph he can have his suite back,' Ralph

227

called, and vaulted to the saddle. It had been a good choice, the bay drove strongly between his knees. They galloped past the mine stagings, through the gap between the hillocks formed by the high tailing dumps and Ralph saw Mr Rhodes' private train.

It was already crossing the points at the southern end of the yards and running out into the open country. The locomotive was hauling four coaches, steam spurted from the pistons of the driving wheels with each stroke. The signal arm was down and the lights were green. The locomotive was picking up speed swiftly.

'Come boy,' Ralph encouraged the bay, swinging it towards the barbed-wire fence beside the track. The horse steadied himself, pricking his ears forward as he judged the wire. Then he went for it boldly. 'Oh good boy.' Ralph lifted him with hands and knees.

They flew over it with two feet to spare and landed neatly. There was flat open ground ahead, and the railway tracks curved slightly. Ralph aimed to cut the curve. He lay against the horse's neck, watching the stony ground for holes. Five hundred yards ahead the train was pulling gradually away from them, but the bay ran on gamely.

Then the locomotive hit the gradient of the Magersfontein Hills and the huffing of the boiler changed its beat and slowed. They caught it a quarter of a mile from the crest, and Ralph pushed the bay in close enough for him to lean from the saddle and grab the handrail of the rear balcony on the last coach. Ralph swung across the gap and scrambled up onto the balcony. He looked back. The bay was already grazing contentedly on the Karroo bush beside the tracks.

'Somehow, I knew you were coming.' Ralph turned quickly. Jordan was standing in the door of the coach. 'I even had a bed made up for you in one of the guest compartments.'

'Where is he?' Ralph demanded.

'Waiting for you in the saloon. He watched your dare-devil riding with interest. I won a guinea on you.'

Ostensibly the train was for the use of all the directors of De Beers, though none of them, apart from the Chairman of the Board, had yet shown the temerity to exercise that right.

The exteriors of the coaches and the locomotive were varnished in chocolate brown and gold. The interiors were as luxurious as unlimited expenditure could make them, from the fitted Wilton carpets and cut-glass chandeliers in the saloon to the solid gold and onyx fittings in the bathrooms.

Mr Rhodes was slumped in a buttoned calf-leather chair beside the wide picture window in his private car. There were sheaves of paper on the Italian gold-embossed leather top of his bureau, and a crystal glass of whisky at his elbow. He looked tired and ill. His face was bloated and blotched with livid purple. There was more silver than ruddy gold in his moustache and wavy hair now, but his eyes were still that pale fanatical blue and his voice high and sharp.

'Sit down, Ballantyne,' he said. 'Jordan, get your brother a drink.'

Jordan placed a silver tray with a ship's decanter, a Stuart crystal glass and a matching claret jug of water on the table beside Ralph. While he did so, Mr Rhodes addressed himself once more to the papers in front of him.

'What is the most important asset of any nation, Ballan-tyne?' he demanded suddenly, without looking up again.

'Diamonds?' suggested Ralph mockingly, and he heard Jordan draw breath sharply behind him.

'Men,' said Mr Rhodes, as though he had not heard. 'Young, bright men, imbued during the most susceptible period of their lives with the grand design. Young men like you, Ralph, Englishmen with all the manly virtues.' Mr Rhodes paused. 'I am endowing a series of scholarships in my will. I want these young men to be chosen carefully and sent to Oxford University.' For the first time he looked up at Ralph. 'You see, it is utterly unacceptable that a man's noblest thoughts should cease, merely because the man dies. These will be my living thoughts. Through these young men, I shall live for ever.'

'How will you select them?' Ralph asked, intrigued despite himself by this design for immortality, devised by a giant with a crippled heart.

'I am working on that now.' Rhodes rearranged the papers on his bureau. 'Literary and scholastic achievement, of course, success at manly sports, powers of leadership.'

'Where would you find them?' For the moment, Ralph had set aside his anger and frustration. 'From England, all of them?'

'No, no,' Mr Rhodes shook his shaggy leonine head. 'From every corner of the Empire – Africa, Canada, Australia, New Zealand, even from America. Thirteen from America each year, one for every state.'

Ralph suppressed a smile. The colossus of Africa, of whom Mark Twain had written 'When he stands on Table Mountain, his shadow falls on the Zambezi', had blind spots in his vast scheming mind. He still believed that America consisted of the original thirteen states. Such small imperfections gave Ralph courage to face him, to oppose him. He did not touch the decanter at his elbow. He would need all his wits to find any other weakness to exploit.

'And after men?' Rhodes asked. 'What is the next most precious asset of a new land? Diamonds, as you suggest, or gold perhaps?' He shook his head. 'It is the power that drives the railways, that turns the mine headgears, that fuels the blast furnaces, the power that makes all the wheels go round. Coal.'

Then they were both silent, staring at each other. Ralph felt every muscle in his body under stress, the hackles at the back of his neck rising in an atavistic passion. The young bull facing up to the herd bull in their first trial of strength.

'It is very simple, Ralph, the coal deposits in Wankie's country must be retained in responsible hands.'

'The hands of the British South Africa Company?' Ralph asked grimly.

Mr Rhodes did not have to reply. He merely went on staring into Ralph's eyes.

'By what means will you take them?' Ralph broke the silence.

'By any means that are necessary.'

'Legal or otherwise?'

'Come on, Ralph, you know it is totally within my power to legalize anything I do in Rhodesia.' Not Matabeleland or Mashonaland, Ralph noted, but Rhodesia. The megalomanic dream of grandeur was complete. 'Of course, you will be compensated – land, gold claims – whatever you choose. What will it be, Ralph?'

Ralph shook his head. 'I want the coal deposits that I discovered and that I pegged. They are mine. I will fight you for them.'

Rhodes sighed and pinched the bridge of his nose. 'Very well, I withdraw my offer of compensation. Instead, let me point out a few facts to you of which you are probably unaware. There are two Company linesmen who have sworn an affidavit before the Administrator in Bulawayo that they saw you personally cutting telegraph lines south of the town on Monday the fourth at 4 p.m.'

'They are lying,' said Ralph, and turned to look at his brother. Only he could have made the deduction and pointed it out to Mr Rhodes. Jordan sat quietly in an armchair at the end of the saloon. He did not look up from the shorthand pad on his lap, and his beautiful face was serene. Ralph tasted the sourness of treachery on the back of his tongue, and he turned back to face his adversary.

'They may be lying,' Mr Rhodes agreed softly. 'But they are prepared to testify under oath.'

'Malicious damage to Company property,' Ralph raised an eyebrow. 'Is that a capital offence now?'

'You still do not understand, do you? Any contract made under a deliberate misrepresentation can be set aside by a court of law. If Roelof Zeederberg could prove that when you and he signed your little agreement, you were fully aware of the epidemic of rinderpest which is sweeping Rhodesia,' (that name again) 'and that you had committed a criminal act to keep that fact from him—' Mr Rhodes did not finish. Instead he sighed again and rubbed his chin, the silver stubble rasped under his thumb. 'On the fourth, your father, Major Zouga Ballantyne, sold five thousand head of breeding stock to Gwaai Cattle Ranches, one of my own companies. Three days later, half of them were dead of rinderpest, and the rest will soon be destroyed by the Company anti-rinderpest measures. Already Zeederberg Brothers have lost sixty per cent of the bullocks you sold them, they have two hundred wagons and their loads stranded on the great north road. Don't you see, Ralph, both your contract of sale and your father's could be declared null and void. Both of you forced to refund the purchase monies you received and to take back thousands of dead and dying animals.'

Ralph's face was stony, but his skin had yellowed like a man five days in fever. Now with a jerky movement he poured the crystal tumbler half full of whisky, and he swallowed a mouthful as though it were broken glass. Mr Rhodes let the subject of rinderpest lie between them like a coiled adder, and he seemed to go off in another direction.

'I hope that my legal advisers followed my instructions and apprised you of the mining and prospecting laws that have been adopted for the Charter territories. We have decided to apply the American law, as opposed to the Transvaal law.' Mr Rhodes sipped from his glass, and then twisted it between his fingers. The base had left a wet circle on the expensive Italian leather. 'There are some peculiar features of these American laws. I doubt that you have had an opportunity to study all of them, so I will take the liberty of pointing one out to you. In terms of Section 23, any mineral claim pegged between sunset of one day and sunrise of the following day shall be void and the title in those claims liable to be set aside by an order of the mining commissioner. Did you know that?'

Ralph nodded his head. 'They told me.'

'There is an affidavit on the Administrator's desk at this moment, made in the presence of a Justice of the Peace by one Jan Cheroot, a Hottentot in the domestic service of Major Zouga Ballantyne, to the effect that certain claims registered by the Rhodesian Land and Mining Company, of which you are the major shareholder, which claims are known as the Harkness Mine, were pegged during the hours of darkness, and therefore liable to be declared void.'

Ralph started so that his glass rattled against the silver tray, and whisky slopped over the rim.

'Before you chastise this unfortunate Hottentot, let me hasten to assure you that he believed he was acting in the best interests of you and his master when he swore this affidavit.'

This time the silence drew out for many minutes, while Mr Rhodes peered out of the window at the bleak tree-less sunbleached spaces of the Karroo under a milky blue sky.

Then quite suddenly Mr Rhodes spoke again. 'I understand that you have already committed yourself to the purchase of mining machinery for the Harkness Mine, and that you have signed personal sureties for over thirty thousand pounds. The choice before you is simple enough then. Give up all claim to the Wankie coal deposits, or lose not only them, but the Zeederberg contract and the Harkness claims. Walk away still a rich man by any standards, or—'

Ralph let the unfinished statement rest for ten beats of his racing heart, and then he asked: 'Or?'

'Or else I will destroy you, utterly,' said Mr Rhodes. Calmly he met the ferocious hatred in the eyes of the young man before him. He was inured by now both to adulation and to hatred, such things were meaningless when measured against the grand design of his destiny. Yet he could afford a placating word.

'You must understand that there is nothing personal in this, Ralph,' he said. 'I have nothing but admiration for your courage and determination. As I said earlier, it is in young men like you that I place my hope for the future. No, Ralph, it is not personal. I simply cannot allow anything or anybody to stand in my way. I know what has to be done, and there is so little time left in which to do it.'

The instinct to kill came upon Ralph in a black unholy rage. He could clearly imagine his fingers locked into the swollen throat, feel his thumbs crushing the larynx from which that shrill cruel voice rose. Ralph closed his eyes and fought off his rage. He threw it off the way a man throws off a sodden cloak when he comes in from the storm, and when he opened his eyes again, he felt as though his whole life had changed. He was icy calm, the tremor gone from his hands, and his voice was level.

'I understand,' he nodded. 'In your place I would probably do the same thing. Shall we ask Jordan to draw up the contract making over any rights I or my partners might have in the Wankie coalfields to the BSA Company, and in consideration thereof the BSA Company irrevocably confirms my rights in the claims known as the Harkness Mine.'

Mr Rhodes nodded approvingly. 'You will go far, young man. You are a fighter.' Then he looked up at Jordan. 'Do it!' he said.

The locomotive roared on into the night, and despite the tons of lead that had been placed over the axles to soften the ride for Mr Rhodes, the carriages lurched rhythmically and the ties clattered harshly under the steel wheels.

Ralph sat by the window in his stateroom. The goose-down coverlet was drawn back invitingly on the double bed behind the green velvet curtains, but it had no attraction for him. He was still fully dressed, though the ormolu clock on the beside table showed the time as three o'clock in the morning. He was drunk, yet unnaturally clear-headed, as though his rage had burned up the alcohol as soon as he swallowed it.

He stared out of the window. There was a full moon standing over the strangely shaped purple kopjes along the horizon, and every once in a while the beat of the wheels changed to a ringing gong as they crossed another low steel bridge over a dry river course in which the sugary sand glowed like molten silver in the moonlight.

Ralph had sat through dinner at Mr Rhodes' board, listening to his high, jarring voice parading a succession of weird and grandiose ideas, interspersed with sudden startling truths or shop-worn old maids' platitudes that spilled endlessly out of the big man with the lumpy, ungainly body.

The only reason why Ralph managed to control his emotions and keep a good face, the reason why he even managed to nod in agreement or smile at one of Mr Rhodes' sallies, was the realization that he had uncovered another of his adversary's weaknesses. Mr Rhodes lived in a stratum so high above other men, he was so cushioned by his vast wealth, so blinded by his own visions, that he did not seem even to realize that he had made a mortal enemy. If he did think at all of Ralph's feelings, it was to suppose that he had already discounted the loss of the Wankie coalfields, and accepted it as philosophically and impersonally as Mr Rhodes himself had.

Even so, the choice food and noble wines were tasteless as sawdust, and Ralph swallowed them with difficulty and experienced a surge of relief when Mr Rhodes finally declared the evening ended in his usual abrupt manner by pushing back his chair without warning and rising to his feet. Only then he paused for a moment to examine Ralph's face.

'I measure a man by the style in which he faces adversity,' he said. 'You will do, young Ballantyne.'

In that moment Ralph had come close, once again, to losing control, but then Mr Rhodes had left the saloon with his bearlike gait, leaving the two brothers together at the table.

'I am sorry, Ralph,' Jordan had said simply. 'I tried to warn you once. You should not have challenged him. You should not have forced me to choose between you and him. I have put a bottle of whisky in your stateroom. We will reach the village of Matjiesfontein in the morning. There is a first-rate hotel run by a fellow called Logan. You can wait there for the northbound train to take you back to Kimberley tomorrow evening.'

Now the whisky bottle was empty, Ralph looked at it with astonishment. He should have been comatose from the amount that he had drunk. It was only when he tried to stand that his legs cheated him, and he fell against the washstand. He steadied himself, and peered into his own image in the mirror.

It was not the face of a drunkard. His jaw was hard-edged, his mouth firm, his eyes dark and angry. He pulled back from the mirror, glanced at the bed, and knew that he could not sleep, not even now when he was almost burned out with rage and hatred. Suddenly he wanted surcease, a short oblivion, and he knew where to find it. At the far end of the saloon, behind the tall double doors of intricate marquetry work, was an array of bottles, the finest and most exotic liquors gathered from every civilized land – that was where he could find oblivion.

Ralph crossed his stateroom, fumbled with the door catch and stepped out. The cold Karroo night air flicked his hair and he shivered in his shirtsleeves, and then weaved down the narrow corridor towards the saloon. He bumped first one shoulder and then the other against the polished teak bulkheads, and cursed his own clumsiness. He crossed the open balcony between coaches, clutching at the handrail to steady himself, eager to get out of the wind. As he entered the corridor of the second coach, one of the doors slid open ahead of him, and a shaft of yellow light outlined the slim and graceful figure that stepped through.

Jordan had not seen his brother. He paused in the doorway and looked back into the stateroom beyond. His expression was as soft and as loving as that of a mother leaving her sleeping infant. Gently, with exaggerated care, he closed the sliding door so as not to make the least sound. Then he turned and found himself face to face with Ralph.

Like his brother, Jordan was coatless, but his shirt was unbuttoned down to the silver buckle of his breeches; the cuffs of his sleeves were not linked as though the garment had been thrown on carelessly, and Jordan's feet were bare, very white and elegantly shaped against the dark-toned carpet.

None of this surprised Ralph. He expected that, like himself, Jordan was hungry or visiting the heads. He was too fuddled to ponder on it, and was about to invite Jordan to come with him to find another bottle, when he saw the expression on Jordan's face.

He was instantly transported back fifteen years in time, to the thatched bungalow of his father's camp near the great pit of the Kimberley mine where he and Jordan had passed most of their youth. One night, that long ago, Ralph had surprised his brother in a childish act of onanism, and had seen that same expression, that stricken dread and guilt, upon his lovely face.

Now again Jordan was transfixed, rigid and pale, staring at Ralph with huge terrified eyes, his hand raised as though to shield his throat. Suddenly Ralph understood. He recoiled in horror and found the door onto the balcony closed behind him. He flattened his back against it, unable to speak for infinite seconds, while they stared at each other. When at last Ralph regained his voice, it was rough as though he had run a hard race.

'By God, now I know why you have no use for whores, for you are one yourself.'

Ralph turned and tore open the door, he ran out onto the balcony and looked about him wildly, like a creature in a trap, and saw the clean moon-washed spaces of the open veld. He kicked open the gate of the balcony, swung down the steps, and let himself drop into the night.

The earth hit him with crushing force and he rolled down the ballasting and came to rest face down in the harsh scrub beside the tracks. When he lifted his head, the red running-lights of the caboose were dwindling away into the south, and the sound of the wheels was already muted, by distance.

Ralph pushed himself up, and limped and staggered away into the empty veld. Half a mile from the tracks he fell to his knees again, and gagged and retched as he vomited up the whisky and his own disgust. The dawn was an unearthly orange wash behind a crisp black cut-out of flat-topped hills. Ralph lifted his face to it, and he spoke aloud.

'I swear I will have him. I swear that I will destroy this monster, or destroy myself in the attempt.'

At that moment the rim of the sun pushed up above the hills and hurled a brazen dart of light into Ralph's face as though a god had been listening, and had sealed the pact with flame.

'My father killed a great elephant upon this spot. The tusks stand on the stoep at King's Lynn,' Ralph said quietly. 'And I shot a fine lion here myself. It seems strange that things like that will never happen again at this place.'

Beside him Harry Mellow straightened up from the theodolite, and for a moment his face was grave.

'We have come to conquer the wilderness,' he said. 'Soon there will be a high headgear reaching up into the sky, and if the Harkness reef runs true, one day a town with schools and churches, hundreds perhaps thousands of families. Isn't that what we both want?'

Ralph shook his head. 'I would be getting soft if I did not. It just seems strange, when you look at it now.'

The low valleys were still blowing with the soft pink grasses, the timber along the ridges was tall, the tree trunks silver in the sunlight, but even as they watched one of them shivered against the sky and then toppled with a rending crackling roar. The Matabele axemen swarmed over the fallen giant to lop off the branches and for a moment longer the shadow of regret lingered in Ralph's eyes, then he turned away.

'You have picked a good site,' he said, and Harry followed the direction of his gaze.

'Knobs Hill,' he laughed.

The thatch and daub hut was sited so that it would not overlook the compound for the black labourers. Instead it had a breathtaking view over the forest to where the southern escarpment dipped away into infinite blue distances. A tiny feminine figure came out of the hut, her apron a merry spot of tulip yellow against the raw red earth which Vicky hoped would one day be a garden. She saw the two men below her and waved.

'By God, that girl has done wonders.' Harry lifted his hat above his head to acknowledge the greeting, his expression fondly besotted. 'She copes so well, nothing upsets her – not even the cobra in the lavatory this morning – she just up and blasted it with a shotgun. Of course, I'll have to fix the seat.'

'It's her life,' Ralph pointed out. 'Put her in a city and she'd probably be in tears in ten minutes.'

'Not my girl,' said Harry proudly.

'All right, you made a good choice,' Ralph agreed, 'but it's bad form to boost your own wife.'

'Bad form?' Harry shook his head wonderingly. 'You limeys!' he said, and stooped to put his eye back to the lens of the theodolite.

'Leave that damn thing for a minute.' Ralph pinched his shoulder lightly. 'I didn't ride three hundred miles to look at your backside.'

'Fine.' Harry straightened. 'I'll let the work lie. What do you want to talk about?'

'Show me how you decided on the site of your No.1 shaft,' Ralph invited, and they went down the valley, while Harry pointed out the factors which had led him to choose the spot.

'The ancient trenches are inclined at just over forty degrees, and we have three layers of schists over-running. Now I extended out the strike of the ancient reef, and we put in the potholes here—'

The exploratory potholes were narrow vertical shafts, each under a gantry of raw native timber, spaced out in a straight line along the slope of the hill.

'We went down a hundred feet on five of them, down through the friable levels, and we picked up the upper schist layer again—'

'Schist isn't going to make us rich.'

'No, but the reef's still under it.'

'How do you know?'

'You hired me for my nose.' Harry chuckled. 'I can smell it.' And led Ralph on. 'So you see this is the only logical spot for the main shaft. I reckon to intersect the reef again at three hundred feet and once we are on it we can stope it out.'

A small gang of black men were clearing the collar area of the reef and Ralph recognized the tallest of them.

'Bazo,' he cried, and the induna straightened up and rested on his pick handle.

'Henshaw,' he greeted Ralph gravely. 'Have you come to watch the real men at work?'

Bazo's flat hard muscle shone like wet anthracite, and running sweat had left snaking trails down it.

'Real men?' Ralph asked. 'You promised me two hundred, and you have brought me twenty.'

'The others are waiting,' Bazo promised. 'But they will not come if they cannot bring their women with them. One-Bright-Eye wants the women to stay in the villages.'

'They can bring their women, as many as they wish. I will speak to One-Bright-Eye. Go to them. Choose the strongest and the best. Bring me your old comrades from the Moles impi, and tell them I will pay them well and feed them better, and they can bring their women and breed strong sons to work my mines.'

'I will leave in the morning,' Bazo decided. 'And be back before the moon shows its horns again.'

When the two white men moved on down the survey line, Bazo watched them for a while, his face expressionless and his eyes inscrutable, then he looked at his gang and nodded.

They spat on their palms, hefted their pick-axes and Bazo sang out the opening chorus of the work chant.

'*Ubunyonyo bu ginye entudhla.* The little black ants can eat up the giraffe.'

Bazo had composed the line beside the corpse of a giraffe struck down by the rinderpest, and untouched by all the gorged scavengers of the veld except a colony of the black safari ants which had cleaned the cadaver down to the bone. The significance of it had stayed with Bazo; how, by

241

persistence, even the greatest are overcome, and the seemingly innocent line of gibberish was now insidiously preparing the minds of the *amadoda* who laboured under him. At the invocation they swung the picks on high, standing shoulder to shoulder, the crescent-headed tools silhouetted against the flat blue of the sky.

'*Guga mzimba!*' they replied in soaring chorus. '*Sala nhliziyo*. Though our bodies are worn out, our hearts are constant.'

And then together the humming 'Jee!' as the pick-heads hissed downwards in unison, and with a crash buried themselves in the iron earth.

Each man levered his pick-head free, took one step forward and braced himself as Bazo sang: 'The little black ants can eat up the giraffe.'

And again the act was repeated, and again, and a hundred times more, while the sweat was flung from their bodies and the red dust flew.

B azo loped along at a deceptively easy gait that never varied, though the hills were steep and the valleys abrupt. His spirits were joyous, he had not truly realized how much the labours of the last weeks had galled until he was released from them. Once long ago he had worked with pick and shovel in the yellow diamond pit at Kimberley. Henshaw had been his companion then, and the two of them had made a game of the brutal endless labour. It had built their muscles and made them strong, but had caged and cramped their spirits, until neither of them could suffer it longer, and they had escaped together.

Since those days Bazo had known the savage joy and the divine madness of that terrible moment that the Matabele call the 'closing in'. He had stood against the king's enemies and killed in the sunlight with his regimental plumes flying.

He had won honours and the respect of his peers. He had sat on the king's council with the induna's headring on his brow, and he had come to the brink of the black river and briefly looked beyond it into the forbidden land that men call death, and now he had learned a new truth. It was more painful for a man to go backwards than it is for him to go forward. The drudgery of menial labour rankled the more now for the glories that had preceded it.

The path dropped away towards the river and disappeared into the dense dark green vegetation like a serpent into its hole. Bazo followed it down and stopped into the gloomy tunnel, and then froze. Instinctively his right hand reached for the non-existent assegai on its leather thong under the grip of the long shield that also was not there – so hard do old habits die. The shield had long ago been burned on the bonfires with ten thousand other shields, and the steel snapped in half on the anvils of the BSA Company blacksmiths.

Then he saw this was no enemy that came towards him down the narrow tunnel of riverine bush, and his heart bounded almost painfully against his ribs.

'I see you, Lord,' Tanase greeted him softly.

She was slim and upright as the young girl he had captured at the stronghold of Pemba the wizard, the same long graceful legs and clinched-in waist, the same heron's neck like the stem of a lovely black lily.

'Why are you so far from the village?' he demanded, as she knelt dutifully before him, and clapped her hands softly at the level of her waist.

'I saw you on the road, Bazo, son of Gandang.'

And he opened his mouth to question her further, for he had come swiftly, then he changed his mind and felt the little superstitious prickle of insect feet along the nape of his neck. Sometimes still there were things about this woman that disquieted him, for she had not been stripped of all her occult powers in the cave of the Umlimo.

'I see you, Lord,' Tanase repeated. 'And my body calls to yours the way a hungry infant fresh roused from sleep frets for the breast.'

He lifted her up, and held her face between his hands to examine it as though he had picked a rare and beautiful flower in the forest. It had taken much to accustom himself to the way she spoke of their secret bodily desires. He had been taught that it was unseemly for a Matabele wife to show pleasure in the act of generation, and to speak of it the way a man does. Instead she should be merely a pliant and unprotesting vessel for her husband's seed, ready whenever he was, and unobtrusive and self-effacing when he was not.

Tanase was none of these things. At first she had shocked and horrified him with some of the things she had learned in her apprenticeship for the dark mysteries. However, shock had turned to fascination as she had unfolded each skill before him.

She had potions and perfumes that could rouse a man even when he was exhausted and wounded from the battle-field, she had tricks of voice and eyes that bit like an arrowhead. Her fingers could find unerringly the spots beneath his skin at places on his body of which even he was unaware, upon which she played like the keys of the marimba, making him more man than he had even dreamed was possible. Her own body she could use more skilfully than he could wield his shield and long bright steel and deal as telling blows. She could make each separate muscle of her body move and tighten in complete freedom from the muscles around it. At will she could bring him to precipitous rushing release or keep him hovering high as a black-shouldered kite when it hunts on sharply stabbing pinions.

'We have been too long apart,' she whispered, with that combination of voice and slant of wide Egyptian eyes that tripped his breath and made his heart race. 'I came to meet you alone, so we could be free for a while of your son's clamorous adoration and the eyes of the villagers.' And she led him off the track, and unclasped her leather cloak to spread it on the soft bed of fallen leaves.

Long after the storm had passed, and the aching tension had left his body, when his breathing was deep and even again and his eyelids drooped with the deeply contented lassitude that follows the act of love, she raised herself on her elbow above him, and with a kind of reverential wonder traced out the planes of his face with the tip of one finger, and then said softly: 'Bayete!'

It was the greeting that is made only to a king, and he stirred uncomfortably and his eyes opened wide. He looked at her, and knew that expression. Their loving had not softened her, and made her sleepy, as it had done him. That royal greeting had not been a jest.

'Bayete!' she said again. 'The sound of it troubles you, my fine sharp-bladed axe. But why should it do so?'

Suddenly Bazo felt the insects of fear and superstition crawling on his skin again, and he was angry and afraid. 'Do not talk like this, woman. Do not offend the spirits with your silly girlish prattlings.'

She smiled, but it was a cruel catlike smile, and she repeated. 'Oh Bazo, the bravest and the strongest, why do you then start so at my girlish words? You in whose veins runs the purest blood of Zanzi? Son of Gandang, the son of Mzilikazi, do you dream perchance of the little redwood spear that Lobengula carried in his hand? Son of Juba, whose great-grandfather was mighty Diniswayo, who was nobler even than his protégé Chaka, who became King of Zulu, do you not feel the royal blood coursing in your veins, does it make you itch for things you dare not even speak aloud?'

'You are mad, woman, the mopani bees have entered your head and driven you mad.'

But Tanase smiled still with her lips close to his ear, and she touched his eyelids with her soft pink fingertip.

'Do you not hear the widows of Shangani and Bembesi

245

crying aloud, "Our father Lobengula is gone, we are orphans with no one to protect us." Do you not see the men of Matabeleland with empty hands entreat the spirits? "Give us a king," they cry. "We must have a king."'

'Babiaan,' whispered Bazo. 'Somabula and Gandang. They are Lobengula's brothers.'

'They are old men, and the stone has fallen out of their bellies, the fire has gone out in their eyes.'

'Tanase, do not speak so.'

'Bazo, my husband, my king, do you not see to whom the eyes of all the indunas turn when the nation is in council?'

'Madness,' Bazo shook his head.

'Do you not know whose word they wait upon now, do you not see how even Babiaan and Somabula listen when Bazo speaks?'

She laid the palm of her hand over his mouth to still his protests, and then in one swift movement she had mounted and straddled him again, and miraculously he was ready and more than ready for her, and she cried out fiercely:

'Bayete, son of kings! Bayete, father of kings, whose seed will rule when the white men have been swallowed again by the ocean which spewed them up.'

And with a shuddering cry he felt as though she had drawn the very life force from his guts, and left in its place a dreadful haunting longing, a fire in his blood, that would not be assuaged until he held in his hand the little redwood spear that was the symbol of the Nguni monarch.

They went side by side, hand in hand, which was a curious thing, for a Matabele wife always walks behind her husband with the roll of the sleeping-mat balanced upon her head. But they were like children caught up in a kind of delirious dream, and when they reached the crest of the pass, Bazo took her in his arms and held her to his breast in an embrace that he had never used before.

'If I am the axe, then you are the cutting edge, for you are a part of me, but the sharpest part.'

'Together, Lord, we will hack through anything that stands in our way,' she answered fiercely, and then she pulled out from the circle of his arms and lifted the flap of the beaded pouch upon her belt.

'I have a gift to make your brave heart braver and your will as hard as your steel.' She took something soft and grey and fluffy from her pouch, and stood before him on tiptoe, reaching high with both arms to bind the strip of fur around his forehead. 'Wear this moleskin for the glory that was and that shall be again, induna of the Moles-who-burrowed-under-a-hill. One day soon, we will change it for a headband of spotted gold leopard skin, with royal blue heron feathers set upon it.'

She took his hand and they started down from the hilltop, but they did not reach the grassy plain before Bazo stopped again and inclined his head to listen. There was a faint popping sound on the small dry breeze, like the bubbles bursting in a pot of boiling porridge.

'Guns,' he said. 'Still far away, but many of them.'

'It is so, Lord,' Tanase replied. 'Since you left, the guns of One-Bright-Eye's *kanka* have been busy as the tongues of the old women at a beer-drink.'

'There is a terrible pestilence sweeping through the land.' General Mungo St John had selected a clay anthill as a rostrum from which to address his audience. 'It passes from one animal to the next, as a bush-fire jumps from tree to tree. Unless we can contain it, all the cattle will die.'

Below the anthill, Sergeant Ezra was translating loudly,

while the listening tribesmen squatted silently facing them. There were almost two thousand of them, the occupants of all the villages that had been built along both banks of the Inyati river to replace the regimental kraals of Lobengula's impi.

The men were in the foremost ranks, their faces expressionless but their eyes watchful; behind them were the youths and boys not yet admitted to the rank of warrior. These were the *mujiba*, the herdboys, whose daily life was intimately interwoven with the herds of the tribe. The present *indaba* concerned them as much as it did the elders. There were no women present, for it was a matter of cattle, of the nation's wealth.

'It is a great sin to try to hide your cattle, as you have done. To drive them into the hills or the thick forest. These cattle carry with them the seeds of the pestilence,' Mungo St John explained, and waited for his sergeant to translate, before going on. 'Lodzi and I are very angry with these deceptions. There will be heavy fines for those villages which hide their cattle, and as further punishment, I will double the work quotas for the men, so that you will work like *amaholi*, like slaves you will toil, if you attempt to defy the word of Lodzi.' Mungo St John paused again, and lifted the black eye-patch to wipe away the sweat that trickled down from under the wide-brimmed slouch hat. Drawn by the lowing herds in the thornbush kraal, the big shiny green flies swarmed, and the place stank of cow dung and unwashed humanity. Mungo found himself impatient with the necessity of trying to explain his actions to this silent unresponsive throng of half-naked savages, for he had already repeated this same warning at thirty other *indabas* across Matabeleland. His sergeant finished the translation and glanced up at him expectantly.

Mungo St John pointed to the mass of cattle penned in the thorn kraal behind him. 'As you have seen, it is of no avail to try to hide the herds. The native police track them down.' Mungo stopped again, and frowned in annoyance. In the second row, a Matabele buck had risen and was facing him quietly.

He was a tall man, finely muscled, although one arm seemed deformed, for it was twisted from the shoulder at an awkward angle. Though the body was that of a man in his full prime, the face was eroded and ravaged, as though by grief or pain, and was aged before its time. On the neat cap of dense curls, the man wore the headring of an induna, and around his forehead a headband of grey fur.

'Baba, my father,' said the induna. 'We hear your words, but like children we do not understand them.'

'Who is this fellow?' Mungo demanded of Sergeant Ezra, and nodded when he heard the reply. 'I know about him. He is a troublemaker.' Then to Bazo, raising his voice, 'What is so strange about what I say? What is it that puzzles you?'

'You say, Baba, that the sickness will kill the cattle – so before it does, you will shoot them dead. You say, Baba, that to save our cattle you must kill them for us.'

The quiet ranks of Matabele stirred for the first time. Though their expressions were still impassive, here a man coughed and there another shuffled his bare feet in the dust or yet another flicked his switch at the circling flies. No man laughed, not one mocked with word or smile, but it was mockery nonetheless, and Mungo St John sensed it. Behind those inscrutable black African faces, they were gleefully following the mock humble questions of the young induna with the old worn face.

'We do not understand such deep wisdom, Baba, please be kind and patient with your children and explain it to us. You say that if we try to hide our cattle, then you will confiscate them from us to pay the heavy fines that Lodzi demands. You say in the same breath, Baba, that if we are obedient children and bring the cattle to you, then you will shoot them and burn them up.'

In the packed ranks an elderly whitebeard who had taken snuff sneezed loudly, and there was immediately an epidemic of sneezing and coughing. Mungo St John knew they were encouraging the young induna in this sly impudence.

'Baba, gentle Father, you warn us that you will double our work quotas, and we will be as slaves. This is another matter which escapes from us, for is a man who works one day at another's command less a slave than he who works two days? Is not a slave merely a slave – and is not a free man truly free? Baba, explain to us the degrees of slavery.'

There was a faint humming sound now, like the sound of a hive at noon, and though the lips of the Matabele facing Mungo St John did not move, he saw that their throats trembled slightly. They were beginning to drum, it was the prelude and unchecked it would be followed by the deep ringing 'Jee! Jee!' of the chant.

'I know you, Bazo,' Mungo St John shouted. 'I hear and mark your words. Be sure that Lodzi also will hear them.'

'I am honoured, little Father, that my humble words will be carried to the great white father, Lodzi.'

This time there were cunning and wicked grins on the faces of the men around Bazo.

'Sergeant,' Mungo St John shouted. 'Bring that man to me!'

The big sergeant leaped forward with the brass badge of his rank glittering on his upper arm, but as he did so the ranks of silent Matabele rose to their feet and closed up. No man raised a hand, but the sergeant's forward rush was smothered and he struggled in the crowd as though in living black quicksand, and when he reached the place where Bazo had been, the induna was gone.

'Very well,' Mungo St John nodded grimly, when the sergeant reported back to him. 'Let him go. It will wait for another day, but now we have work to do. Get your men into position.'

A dozen armed black police trotted forward and formed

a line facing the throng of tribesmen, holding their rifles at high port. At the same time the rest of the contingent climbed up onto the thorny walls of the kraal and at the command they pumped cartridges into the breeches of the repeating Winchester rifles.

'Let it begin,' Mungo nodded, and the first volley of rifle fire thundered out.

The black constables were firing down into the milling mass of cattle in the kraal, and at each shot a beast would fling its horned head high and collapse, to be hidden at once by the others. The smell of fresh blood maddened the herd and it surged wildly against the thorn barrier, the din of the blood-bellow was deafening, and from the ranks of watching Matabele went up a mourning howl of sympathy.

These animals were their wealth and their very reason for existence. As *mujiba* they had attended the birthings in the veld, and helped to beat off the hyena and the other predators. They knew each animal by name and loved them with that special type of love that will make the pastoral man lay down his own life to protect his herds.

In the front rank was a warrior so old that his legs were thin as those of the marabou stork and whose skin was the colour of a tobacco pouch and puckered in a network of fine wrinkles. It seemed there was no moisture left in his dried-out ancient frame, and yet fat heavy tears rolled down his withered cheeks as he watched the cattle shot down. The crash of rifle fire went on until sunset, and when it at last was silent, the kraal was filled with carcasses. They lay upon each other in deep windrows like the wheat after the scythes have passed. Not a single Matabele had left the scene, they watched in silence now, their mourning long ago silenced.

'The carcasses must be burned,' Mungo St John strode down the front rank of warriors. 'I want the carcasses covered with wood. No man is spared this labour, neither the sick nor the old. Every man will wield an axe, and when they are covered, I will put the fire to it myself.'

'What is the mood of the people?' Bazo asked softly, and Babiaan, the senior of all the old king's councillors, answered him. It was not lost on the others in the packed beehive thatched hut that Babiaan's tone was respectful.

'They are sick with grief,' said Babiaan. 'Not since the death of the old king has there been such despair in their hearts as now that the cattle are being killed.'

'It is almost as though the white men wish to plunge the assegai in their own breast.' Bazo nodded. 'Each cruel deed strengthens us, and confirms the prophecy of the Umlimo. Can there be one amongst you who still has doubts?'

'There are no doubts. We are ready now,' replied Gandang, his father, and yet he also looked to Bazo for confirmation, and waited for his reply.

'We are not ready.' Bazo shook his head. 'We will not be ready until the third prophecy of the Umlimo has come to pass.'

'"When the hornless cattle are eaten up by the cross",' Somabula whispered. 'We saw the cattle destroyed today, those that the pestilence has spared.'

'That is not the prophecy,' Bazo told them. 'When it comes, there will be no doubt in our minds. Until that time we must continue with the preparations. What is the number of the spears, and where are they held?'

One by one the other indunas stood and each made his report. They listed the numbers of warriors that were trained and ready, where each group was situated and how soon they could be armed and in the field.

When the last one had finished, Bazo went through the form of consulting the senior indunas, and then gave the field commanders their objectives.

'Suku, induna of the Imbezu impi. Your men will sweep the road from the Malundi drift southwards to Gwanda mine. Kill anybody you find upon the road, cut the copper

252

wires at each pole. The *amadoda* working at the mine will be ready to join you when you reach there. There are twenty-eight whites at Gwanda, including the women and the family at the trading-post. Afterwards, count the bodies to make certain that none has escaped.'

Suku repeated the orders, word-perfectly, displaying the phenomenal recall of the illiterate who cannot rely on written notes, and Bazo nodded and turned to the next commander to give him his instructions and to hear them recited back to him.

It was long after midnight before all of them had received and repeated their orders, and then Bazo addressed them again.

'Stealth and speed are our only allies. No warrior will carry a shield, for the temptation to drum upon it in the old way would be too strong. Steel alone, silent steel. There will be no singing the war songs when you run, for the leopard does not growl before he springs. The leopard hunts in darkness, and when he enters the goatshed he spares nothing – as easily as he rips the throat from the billy, he kills also the nanny and the kids.'

'Women?' asked Babiaan sombrely.

'Even as they shot down Ruth and Imbali,' Bazo nodded.

'Children?' asked another induna.

'Little white girls grow up to bear little white boys, and little white boys in their turn grow up to carry guns. When a wise man finds a mamba's lair, he kills the snake and crushes the eggs under foot.'

'Will we spare none?'

'No,' Bazo confirmed quietly, but there was something in his voice that made Gandang, his father, shiver. He recognized the moment when the real power shifted from the old bull to the younger. Indisputably, Bazo was now their leader.

So it was Bazo who said at last, '*Indaba pelile!* The meeting is finished!' And one by one the indunas saluted him and left the hut and slipped away into the night, and when the last was gone, the screen of goatskins at the back was pushed aside and Tanase stepped out and came to Bazo.

'I am so proud,' she whispered, 'that I want to weep like a silly girl.'

It was a long column, counting the women and children, almost a thousand human beings. It was strung out over a mile, winding like a maimed adder down out of the hills. Again custom was being flouted, for although the men led, they were burdened with grainbags and cooking-pots. Of old, they would have carried only their shield and weapons. There were more than the two hundred strong men that Bazo had promised Henshaw.

The women came after them. Many of the men had brought more than one wife and some as many as four. Even the very young girls, those not yet in puberty, carried rolls of sleeping-mats balanced upon their heads, and the mothers had their infants slung upon their hips so that they could suckle from a fat black breast while on the march. Juba's roll of matting was as heavy as any of them. However, despite her great bulk, the younger women had to step out to keep pace with her. Her high clear soprano led the singing.

Bazo came back along the column at an easy lope, unmarried girls turned their heads, careful not to unbalance their burdens, to watch him as he passed, and then they whispered and giggled amongst themselves, for though he was ravaged and scarred, the aura of power and purpose that surrounded him was intensely attractive to even the youngest and flightiest of them.

Bazo came level with Juba, and fell in at her side.

'*Mamewethu.*' He greeted her respectfully. 'The burdens of your young girls will be a little lighter after we cross the river. We will leave three hundred assegais concealed in the millet-bins and buried under the goatshed of Suku's people.'

'And the rest of them?' Juba asked.

'Those we will take with us to the Harkness Mine. A place of concealment has been prepared. From there your girls will take them out a few at a time to the outlying villages.'

Bazo started back towards the head of the column, but Juba called him back.

'My son, I am troubled, deeply troubled.'

'It grieves me, little Mother. What troubles you?'

'Tanase tells me that all the white folk are to be kissed with steel.'

'All of them,' Bazo nodded.

'Nomusa, who is more than a mother to me, must she die also, my son? She is so good and kind to our people.'

Gently Bazo took her by the arm and led her off the path, where they could not be overheard.

'That very kindness which you speak of makes her the most dangerous of all of them,' Bazo explained. 'The love that you bear for her weakens us all. If I say to you, "We will spare this one," then you will ask, "Can we not also spare her little son, and her daughters and their children?"' Bazo shook his head. 'No, I tell you truly, if I were to spare one of them, it would be One-Bright-Eye himself.'

'One-Bright-Eye!' Juba started. 'I do not understand. He is cruel and fierce, without understanding.'

'When our warriors look on his face and hear his voice, they are reminded once again of all the wrongs we have suffered, and they become strong and angry. When they look upon Nomusa, they become soft and hesitant. She must be amongst the very first to die, and I will send a good man to do that work.'

'You say they must all die?' Juba asked. 'This one, that comes now. Will he die also?' Juba pointed ahead, where the path wound lazily beneath the spreading flat-topped acacia trees. There was a horseman cantering towards them from the direction of the Harkness Mine and even at this distance there was no mistaking the set of his powerful shoulders and his easy and yet arrogant seat in the saddle. 'Look at him!' Juba went on. 'It was you who gave him the praise name of "little Hawk". You have often told me how as youths you worked shoulder to shoulder, and ate from the same pot. You were proud when you described the wild falcon that you caught and trained together.' Juba's voice sank lower. 'Will you kill this man that you call your brother, my son?'

'I will let no other do it,' Bazo affirmed. 'I will do it with my own hand, to make sure it is swift and clean. And after him I will kill his woman and his son. When that is done, there will be no turning back.'

'You have become a hard man, my son,' Juba whispered, with terrible shadows of regret in her eyes and an ache in her voice.

Bazo turned away from her, and stepped back onto the path. Ralph Ballantyne saw him and waved his hat above his head.

'Bazo,' he laughed, as he rode up. 'Will I ever learn never to doubt you? You bring me more than the two hundred you promised.'

R alph Ballantyne crossed the southern boundary of King's Lynn, but it was another two hours' riding before he made out the milky grey loom of the homestead kopjes on the horizon.

The veld through which he rode was silent now, and almost empty. It chilled Ralph so that his expression was gloomy and his thoughts dark. Where several months ago his father's herds of plump multicoloured cattle had grazed, the new grass was springing up again dense and green and untrodden, as though to veil the white bones with which the earth was strewn so thickly.

Only Ralph's warning had saved Zouga Ballantyne from complete financial disaster. He had managed to sell off some small portion of his herds to Gwaai Cattle Ranches, a BSA Company subsidiary, before the rinderpest struck King's Lynn, but he had lost the rest of his cattle, and their bones gleamed like strings of pearls amongst the new green grass.

Ahead of Ralph amongst the mimosa trees was one of his father's cattle-posts, and Ralph stood in the saddle and shaded his eyes, puzzled by the haze of pink dust which hung over the old stockade. The dust had been raised by hooves and there was the sharp crack of a trek whip, a sound that had not been heard in Matabeleland for many months.

Even at a distance, he recognized the figures silhouetted upon the railing of the stockade like a pair of scraggly old crows.

'Jan Cheroot!' he called as he rode up. 'Isazi! What are you two old rogues playing at?'

They grinned at him delightedly, and scrambled down to greet him.

'Good Lord!' Ralph's astonishment was unfeigned as he realized what the animals in the stockade were. The curtains of thick dust had hidden them until this minute. 'Is this how you spend your time when I am away, Isazi? Whose idea is this?'

'Bakela, your father's.' Isazi's expression instantly became melancholy. 'And it is a stupid idea.'

The flat sleek animals were striped in vivid black and white, their manes stiff as the bristles in a chimney-sweep's broom.

'Zebras, by God!' Ralph shook his head. 'How did you round them up?'

257

'We used up a dozen good horses chasing them,' Jan Cheroot explained, his leathery yellow features wrinkled with disapproval.

'Your father hopes to replace the trek oxen with these dumb donkeys. They are as wild and unreasonable as a Venda virgin. They bite and kick until you get them in the traces and then they lie down and refuse to pull.' Isazi spat with disgust.

It was manifest folly to try to bridge in a few short months the vast gap between wild animal and domesticated beast of burden. It had taken millennia of selection and breeding to develop the doughty courage, the willing heart and strong back of the draught bullock. It was a measure of the settlers' desperate need for transport that Zouga should even make the attempt.

'Isazi.' Ralph shook his head. 'When you have finished this boy's game, I have man's work for you at the railhead camp.'

'I will be ready to go with you when you return,' Isazi promised enthusiastically. 'I am sick to the stomach with striped donkeys.'

Ralph turned to Jan Cheroot. 'I want to talk to you, old friend.' When they were well beyond the stockade, he asked the little Hottentot, 'Did you put your mark on a Company paper saying that we had pegged the Harkness claims in darkness?'

'I would never let you down,' Jan Cheroot declared proudly. 'General St John explained to me, and I put my mark on the paper to save the claims for you and the major.' He saw Ralph's expression, and demanded anxiously, 'I did the right thing?'

Ralph leaned out of the saddle and clasped the bony old shoulder. 'You have been a good and loyal friend to me all my life.'

'From the day you were born,' Jan Cheroot declared.

'When your mama died, I fed you, and held you on my knee.'

Ralph opened his saddlebag, and the old Hottentot's eyes gleamed when he saw the bottle of Cape brandy.

'Give a dram to Isazi,' Ralph told him, but Jan Cheroot clasped the bottle to his bosom as though it were a first-born son.

'I wouldn't waste good brandy on a black savage,' he declared indignantly, and Ralph laughed and rode on towards the homestead of King's Lynn.

Here there was all the bustle and excitement that he had expected. There were horses that Ralph did not recognize in the paddock below the big thatched house, and amongst them the unmistakable matched white mules of Mr Rhodes' equipage. The coach itself stood under the trees in the yard, its paintwork asparkle and harness-wear carefully stacked on the racks in the saddle-room beside the stables. Ralph felt his anger flare up when he saw it. His hatred burned like a bellyful of cheap wine, and he could taste the acid of it at the back of his throat. He swallowed hard to control it as he dismounted.

Two black grooms ran to take his horse. One of them unstrapped his blanket-roll, his saddlebags and rifle scab-bard, and ran with them up towards the big house. Ralph followed him, and he was halfway across the lawns when Zouga Ballantyne came out onto the wide stoep, and with a linen table-napkin shaded his eyes against the glare. He was still chewing from the luncheon table.

'Ralph, my boy. I didn't expect you until evening.'

Ralph ran up the steps and they embraced, and then Zouga took his arm and led him down the veranda. The walls were hung with trophies of the chase, the long twisted horns of kudu and eland, the gleaming black scimitars of sable and roan antelope, and guarding each side of the double doors that led into the dining-room were the immense tusks of the great bull elephant that Zouga Ballantyne had shot on the site of the Harkness Mine. These heavy curved shafts of ivory were as tall as a man standing on tiptoe could reach, and thicker than a fat lady's thigh.

Zouga and Ralph passed between them into the dining-room. Under the thatch it was cool and dark after the brilliant white glare of noon. The floor was of hand-sawn wild teak, and the roof beams of the same material. Jan Cheroot had made the long refectory table and the chairs with seats of leather thonging from timber cut on the estate, but the glinting silver was from the Ballantyne family home at King's Lynn in England, a tenuous link between two places of the same name and yet of such dissimilar aspect.

Zouga's empty chair was at the far end of the long table, and facing it down the long board was the familiar massive brooding figure that raised his shaggy head as Ralph came in from the stoep.

'Ah, Ralph, it's good to see you.' It amazed Ralph that there was no rancour in either Mr Rhodes' voice or eyes. Could he have truly put the dispute over the Wankie coalfields out of his mind, as though it had never happened? With an effort, Ralph matched his own reaction to the other man's.

'How are you, sir?' Ralph actually smiled as he gripped the broad hand with its hard prominent knuckles. The skin was cool, like that of a reptile, the effect of the poor circulation of the damaged heart. Ralph was pleased to release it, and pass on down the length of the long table. He was not certain that he could long conceal his true feelings from the close scrutiny of those pale hypnotic eyes.

They were all there. The suave little doctor at Mr Rhodes' right hand, his appropriate station.

'Young Ballantyne,' he said coldly, offering his hand without rising.

'Jameson!' Ralph nodded familiarly, knowing that the

deliberate omission of the title would rankle with him as much as the condescending 'young' had annoyed Ralph.

On Mr Rhodes' other hand was a surprising guest. It was the first time that Ralph had ever seen General Mungo St John at King's Lynn. There had once been a relationship between the lean grizzled soldier with the dark and wicked single eye and Louise Ballantyne, Ralph's stepmother. That had been many years ago, long before Ralph had left Kimberley for the north.

Ralph had never entirely fathomed that relationship, nor somehow the breath of scandal clouding it. But it was significant that Louise Ballantyne was not in the room, and that there was no place set at the table for her. If Mr Rhodes had insisted that St John was present at this gathering, and Zouga Ballantyne had agreed to invite him, then there was a compelling reason for it. Mungo St John flashed that wolfish smile at Ralph as they shook hands. Despite the family complications, Ralph had always had a sneaking admiration for this romantically piratical figure, and his answering smile was genuine.

The stature of the other men at the table confirmed the importance and significance of this gathering. Ralph guessed that the meeting was being held here to preserve the absolute secrecy that they could not have assumed in the town of Bulawayo. He guessed also that every guest had been personally selected and invited by Mr Rhodes, rather than by his father.

Apart from Jameson and St John, there was Percy Fitzpatrick, a partner of the Corner House mining group, and prominent representative of the Witwatersrand Chamber of Mines, the organ of the gold barons of Johannesburg. He was a lively and personable young man with a fair complexion and ruddy hair and moustache, whose chequered career had included bank clerk, transport rider, citrus farmer, guide to Lord Randolph Churchill's Africa expedition, author and mining magnate. Many years later Ralph would reflect on the irony of this extraordinary man's claim to immortality being founded on a sentimental book about a dog called Jock.

Beyond Fitzpatrick sat the Honourable Bobbie White, who had just visited Johannesburg at Mr Rhodes' suggestion. He was a handsome and pleasant young aristocrat, the type of Englishman that Mr Rhodes preferred. He was also a staff officer and a career soldier as his mess tunic revealed.

Next to him sat John Willoughby, second-in-command of the original pioneer column, which had taken occupation of Fort Salisbury and Mashonaland. He had also ridden with Jameson's column that had destroyed Lobengula, and his Willoughby's Consolidated Company owned almost one million acres of prime pastoral land in Rhodesia, a rival to Ralph's Rholands Company, so their greetings were guarded.

Then there was Doctor Rutherford Harris, the first secretary of the British South Africa Company and a member of Mr Rhodes' political party in which he represented the Kimberley constituency in the Cape Parliament. He was a taciturn grey man with a sinister cast of eye, and Ralph mistrusted him as one of Mr Rhodes' slavish minions.

At the end of the table, Ralph came face to face with his brother Jordan, and he hesitated for just a fraction of a second, until he saw the desperate appeal in Jordan's gentle eyes. Then he gripped his brother's hand briefly, but he did not smile and his voice was cool and impersonal as he greeted him like a mere acquaintance, and then took the place that a servant in a white Kanza uniform and scarlet sash had hurriedly laid beside Zouga at the head of the table.

The animated conversation that Ralph had interrupted was resumed with Mr Rhodes orchestrating and directing it.

'What about your trained zebras?' he demanded of Zouga, who shook his golden beard.

'It was a desperate measure and doomed from the outset. But when you consider that out of the hundred thousand head of cattle that we had in Matabeleland before the rinderpest, only five hundred or so have survived, any chance seemed worth taking.'

'They say that the Cape buffalo have been wiped out utterly and completely by the disease,' Doctor Jameson suggested. 'What do you think, Major?'

'Their losses have been catastrophic. Two weeks ago I rode as far north as the Pandamatenga river, where a year ago I counted herds of over five thousand together. This time I saw not a single living beast. Yet I cannot believe they are now extinct. I suspect that somewhere out there are scattered survivors, the ones that had a natural immunity, and I believe that they will breed.'

Mr Rhodes was not a sportsman; he had once said of his own brother Frank, 'Yes, he's a good fellow, he hunts and he fishes – in other words, he is a perfect loafer,' and this conversation about wild game bored him almost immediately. He changed it by turning to Ralph.

'Your railway line – what is the latest position, Ralph?'

'We are still almost two months ahead of our schedule,' Ralph told him with a touch of defiance. 'We crossed the Matabeleland border fifteen days ago – I expect as we sit here that the railhead has reached the trading-post at Plumtree already.'

'It's as well,' Rhodes nodded. 'We shall have urgent need of your line in a very short while.' And he and Doctor Jim exchanged a conspiratorial glance.

When they had all relished Louise's bread and butter pudding, thick with nuts and raisins and running with wild honey, Zouga dismissed the servants, and poured the Cognac himself, while Jordan carried around the cigars. As they settled back in their seats, Mr Rhodes made one of his startlingly abrupt changes of subject and pace, and Ralph was immediately aware that the true purpose for which he had been summoned to King's Lynn was about to be revealed.

'There is not one of you who does not know that my life's task is to see the map of Africa painted red from Cape Town to Cairo. To deliver this continent to our Queen as another jewel in her crown.' His voice that had been irritable and carping up until now, took on a strange mesmeric quality. 'We men of the English-speaking Anglo-Saxon race are the first among nations, and destiny has imposed a sacred duty upon us – to bring the world to peace under one flag and one great monarch. We must have Africa, all of it, to add to our Queen's dominions. Already my emissaries have gone north to the land between the Zambezi and the Congo rivers to prepare the way.' Rhodes broke off and shook his head angrily. 'But all this will be of no avail if the southern tip of the continent eludes us.'

'The South African Republic,' said Jameson. 'Paul Kruger and his little banana republic in the Transvaal.' His voice was low but bitter.

'Do not be emotive, Doctor Jim,' Rhodes remonstrated mildly. 'Let us concern ourselves merely with the facts.'

'And what are the facts, Mr Rhodes?' Zouga Ballantyne leaned forward eagerly from the head of the table.

'The facts are that an ignorant old bigot, who believes that the rabble of illiterate Dutch nomads that he leads are the new Israelites, specifically chosen by their Old Testament God – this extraordinary personage sits astride a vast stretch of the richest part of the African continent, like an unkempt and savage hound with a bone, and growls at all efforts at progress and enlightenment.'

They were all silenced by this bitter invective, and Mr Rhodes looked around at their faces before he went on.

'There are thirty-eight thousand Englishmen on the goldfields of Witwatersrand, Englishmen who pay nineteen of every twenty pounds of the revenue that flows into Kruger's coffers, Englishmen who are responsible for every bit of civilization in that benighted little republic, and yet Kruger denies them the franchise, they are taxed mercilessly and denied representation. Their petitions for the vote are greeted in the Volksraad by the contemptuous derision of a motley assembly of untutored oafs.' Rhodes glanced at Fitzpatrick. 'Am I being unfair, Percy? You know these people, you live with them on a day-to-day basis. Is my description of the Transvaal Boer accurate?'

Percy Fitzpatrick shrugged. 'Mr Rhodes is correct. The Transvaal Boer is a different animal from his Cape cousins. The Cape Dutch have had the opportunity of absorbing some of the qualities of the English way of life. By comparison they are an urbane and civilized people, while the Transvaaler has unfortunately lost none of the traits of his Dutch ancestry: he is slow, obstinate, hostile, suspicious, cunning and malevolent. It galls a man to be told to go to hell by that ilk, especially when we ask only for our rights as free men, the right to vote.'

Mr Rhodes, not long to be denied the floor, went on.

'Not only does Kruger insult our countrymen, but he plays other more dangerous games. He has discriminated against British goods with punitive tariffs. He has given trade monopolies in all essential mining goods, even dynamite, to members of his family and government. He is blatantly arming his burghers with German guns and building a corps of German Krupp artillery, and he is openly flirting with the Kaiser.' Rhodes paused. 'A German sphere of influence in the midst of Her Majesty's domains would forever damn our dreams of a British Africa. The Germans do not have our altruism.'

'All that good yellow gold going to Berlin,' Ralph mused softly, and immediately regretted having spoken, but Mr Rhodes did not seem to have heard, for he went on.

'How to reason with a man like Kruger? How can one even talk to a man who still believes implicitly that the earth is flat?'

Mr Rhodes was sweating again, although it was cool in the room. His hand shook so that as he reached for his glass, he knocked it over, and the golden cognac spread across the polished table-top. Jordan rose quickly and mopped it up before it could cascade into Mr Rhodes' lap, and then he took a silver pillbox from his fob pocket, and from it placed a white tablet close to Mr Rhodes' right hand. The big man took it, and still breathing heavily, placed it under his tongue. After a few moments his breathing eased and he could speak again.

'I went to him, gentlemen. I went to Pretoria to see Kruger at his own home. He sent a message with a servant, that he could not see me that day.'

They had all of them heard this story, their surprise was only that Mr Rhodes could recount such a humiliating incident. President Kruger had sent a black servant to one of the richest and most influential men in the world with this message:

'I am rather busy at the moment. One of my burghers has come to discuss a sick ox with me. Come back on Tuesday.'

'God knows,' Doctor Jim intervened to break the embarrassed silence. 'Mr Rhodes has done everything a reasonable man could. To risk further insult from this old Boer could bring discredit not only on Mr Rhodes personally, but on our Queen and her Empire.' The little doctor paused and looked at each of his listeners in turn. Their faces were rapt, they waited intently for his next words. 'What can we do about it? What *must* we do about it?'

Mr Rhodes shook himself, and looked at the young staff officer in his resplendent mess kit.

'Bobbie?' he said in invitation.

'Gentlemen, you may be aware that I have just returned

266

from the Transvaal.' Bobbie White lifted a leather briefcase from the floor beside his chair to the table, and from it produced a sheaf of crisp white paper. He passed a sheet to every man at the table.

Ralph glanced at his copy, and started slightly. It was the order of battle of the army of the South African Republic. His surprise was so intense that he missed the first part of what Bobbie White was saying.

'The fort at Pretoria is under repair and extension. The walls have been breached for this purpose and will be entirely vulnerable to a small determined force.' Ralph had to force himself to believe what he was hearing. 'Apart from the corps of artillery, there is no regular standing army. As you can see from the paper before you, the Transvaal depends upon its citizen commandos for defence. It requires four to six weeks for them to assemble into an effective force.'

Bobbie White finished his recital, and Mr Rhodes turned from him to Percy Fitzpatrick.

'Percy?' he invited.

'You know what Kruger calls those of us whose capital and resources have developed his gold-mining industry for him? He calls us the "Uitlanders", the "Outlanders", the "Foreigners". You know also that we Outlanders have elected our own representatives, which we call the "Johannesburg Reform Committee". I have the honour to be one of the elected members of that Committee, and so I speak for every Englishman in the Transvaal.' He paused and carefully dressed his moustache with his forefinger, and then went on. 'I bring you two messages. The first is short and simple. It is, "We are determined and united to the cause. You may rely upon us to the utmost."'

The men about the table nodded, but Ralph felt his skin tingle. They were taking this seriously – it was not some boyish nonsense. They were plotting one of the most audacious acts of piracy in history. He kept his expression serious and calm with an enormous effort as Fitzpatrick went on.

'The second message is in the form of a letter signed by all the members of the Reform Committee. With your permission I shall read it to you. It is addressed to Doctor Jameson in his capacity as Administrator of Rhodesia, and it reads as follows:

'Dear Sir,   Johannesburg.
The position of matters in this state has become so critical that we are assured that at no distant period there will be a conflict between the Transvaal government and the Uitlander population . . .'

As the letter unfolded, Ralph recognized that it was a justification for armed insurrection.

'A foreign corporation of Germans and Hollanders is controlling our destinies, and in conjunction with the Boer leaders endeavouring to cast them in a mould which is wholly alien to the genius of the British peoples . . .'

They were going to try to take by force of arms the richest gold reef in existence, Ralph sat bemused.

'When our petition for franchise was debated in the Transvaal Volksraad, one member challenged the Uitlanders to fight for the rights they asked for, and not a single member spoke against him. The Transvaal government has called into existence all the elements necessary for armed conflict.
It is under these circumstances that we feel constrained to call upon you, as an Englishman, to come to our aid should a disturbance arise. We guarantee any

expense you may incur by helping us, and we ask you to believe that nothing but sternest necessity has prompted this appeal.'

Percy Fitzpatrick looked up at Doctor Jim, and then finished.

'It is signed by all the members of the committee, Leonard, Phillips, Mr Rhodes' brother Francis, John Hays Hammond, Farrar and by myself. We have not dated it.'

At the head of the table, Zouga Ballantyne let out his breath in a low whistle, but nobody else spoke while Jordan rose and passed down the table re-filling each glass from the crystal decanter. Mr Rhodes was slumped forward over the table, his chin resting on the heel of his hand, staring out of the windows down across the lawns towards the far blue line of hills, the Hills of the Indunas, where once the Matabele king's kraal had stood. Everybody at the table waited for him, until at last he sighed heavily.

'I much prefer to find a man's price, and pay it, rather than to fight him, but we are not dealing with a normal man here. God save us all from saints and fanatics, give me a solid rogue every time.' His head turned towards Doctor Jameson, and the dreaming blue eyes focused. 'Doctor Jim,' he invited, and the little doctor rode his chair back on its hind legs and thrust his hands deep into his pockets.

'We will need to send five thousand rifles and a million rounds of ammunition into Johannesburg.'

Intrigued and fascinated despite himself, Ralph interrupted to ask, 'Where will you – where will we get those? They are not common trade goods.'

Doctor Jim nodded. 'That's a good question, Ballantyne. The rifles and ammunition are already in the mine stores of De Beers at Kimberley.'

Ralph blinked, the plot was far advanced, further than he had believed possible. Then he recalled the little doctor's

269

suspicious behaviour at the base camp from which they had discovered the Harkness reef. They must have been busy for months. He must find out all the details.

'How will we get them into Johannesburg? They'll have to be smuggled in, and it's a bulky shipment—'

'Ralph,' Mr Rhodes smiled. 'You didn't really believe you were invited here for a social luncheon. Who would you judge to be the most experienced of us in shipping weapons? Who carried the Martini rifles to Lobengula? Who is the shrewdest transport operator on the sub-continent?'

'Me?' Ralph was startled.

'You,' agreed Mr Rhodes, and as Ralph stared at him, he felt a sudden unholy excitement welling up within him. He was to be at the centre of this fantastic conspiracy, privy to every detail. His mind began to race, he knew intuitively that this was one of the opportunities that comes a man's way once in a lifetime, and he had to wring from it every last advantage.

'You will do it, of course?' A small shadow passed across the penetrating blue eyes.

'Of course,' said Ralph, but the shadow persisted. 'I am an Englishman. I know my duty,' Ralph went on quietly and sincerely, and he saw the shadow clear from Mr Rhodes' eyes. That was something he could believe in, something he could trust. He turned back to Doctor Jameson.

'I'm sorry,' Mr Rhodes said. 'We interrupted you.' And Jameson went on:

'We will raise a mounted force of around six hundred picked men here—' and he looked at John Willoughby and Zouga Ballantyne, both of them proven soldiers. 'I will rely heavily on you two.' And Willoughby nodded, but Zouga frowned and asked,

'Six hundred men will take weeks to ride from Bulawayo to Johannesburg.'

'We will not start from Bulawayo,' Jameson replied evenly. 'I have the approval of the British government to maintain a mobile armed force in Bechuanaland, on the railway concession strip which runs down the border of the Transvaal. The force is for the protection of the railway, but it will be based at Pitsani, a mere one hundred and eighty miles from Johannesburg. We can be there in fifty hours' hard riding, long before the Boers could raise any kind of resistance.'

It was at that moment that Ralph realized that it was feasible. Given Doctor Leander Starr Jameson's legendary luck, they could pull it off. They could take the Transvaal with the same ease as they had seized Matabeleland from Lobengula.

By God, what a prize that would be! A billion pounds sterling in gold, annexed to Rhodes' own land, Rhodesia. After that everything else was possible – British Africa, a whole continent. Ralph was stunned at the magnitude of the design.

It was Zouga Ballantyne again who unerringly identified the fatal flaw in the scheme. 'What is the position of Her Majesty's government? Will they support us?' he asked. 'Without them it will all be in vain.'

'I have just returned from London,' Mr Rhodes replied. 'While I was there I dined with the colonial secretary, Mr Joseph Chamberlain. As you know, he has instilled a new spirit of vigour and determination into Downing Street. He is in complete sympathy with the plight of our subjects in Johannesburg. He is also fully aware of the dangers of German intervention in southern Africa. Let me just assure you all that Mr Chamberlain and I understand each other. I can say no more at this stage, you must trust me.'

If that is true, Ralph thought, then the chances of complete success were better than even. The swift thrust to the heart of the unprepared enemy, the uprising of armed citizenry, the appeal to a magnanimous British government, and finally the annexation.

As he listened to the planning, Ralph was swiftly calculating the consequences of the successful outcome of the plot. The chief of these were that the British South Africa Company and De Beers Consolidated Diamond Company would become the richest and most powerful commercial enterprises on the face of the earth, and they were Mr Rhodes' *alter ego*. Ralph's anger and hatred returned so fiercely that his hands trembled, and he had to place them carefully in his lap, but still he could not prevent himself glancing at his younger brother.

Jordan was staring at Mr Rhodes with such an expression of naked adoration that Ralph was certain that every other man at the table must see it too, and he was sickened with shame. He need not have concerned himself, they were all caught up in the glory and grandeur of one man's dream, carried forward by the charisma and compelling leadership of the shaggy colossus at the head of the table.

Yet it was still Zouga the pragmatic soldier who probed for flaws and faults.

'Doctor Jim, will you be raising all six hundred men here in Rhodesia?' he asked.

'For reasons of secrecy and expediency, we cannot raise them in Cape Colony, or anywhere else, for that matter,' Jameson nodded. 'With the rinderpest scourge having swept away their fortunes, there will be that number and more of young Rhodesians eager to enlist if only for the pay and the rations, and all of them will be good fighting men who rode against the Matabele.'

'Do you think it wise to leave this country stripped bare of its able-bodied men?'

Mr Rhodes frowned quickly as he intervened. 'It would be only for a few short months, and we do not have an enemy to fear, do we?'

'Don't we?' Zouga asked. 'There are tens of thousands of Matabele—'

'Oh come now, Major,' Jameson cut in. 'The Matabele are a defeated and disorganized rabble. General St John will be acting Administrator of the territory in my absence, perhaps he is the best person to set your fears at rest.'

They all looked to the tall man at Jameson's side, and Mungo St John removed the long cheroot from his mouth and smiled, crinkling the corner of his single eye.

'I have two hundred armed native police whose loyalty is unquestioned. I have informers placed in every large Matabele village who will give me warning of any stirrings. No, Major, I give you my assurance that the only enemy we need take into account is the obstinate old Boer in Pretoria.'

'I accept that from a soldier of General St John's calibre,' said Zouga simply, and turned back to Mr Rhodes. 'Can we discuss the details of raising this force: how much money do we have at our disposal?'

Ralph watched their faces as they planned and argued, and with surprise saw that his own father's was as greedy and eager as any of them. Whatever words came from their mouths, Ralph thought, whatever they seem to be talking about, what they are actually talking about is money.

Suddenly Ralph remembered that dawn over the barren Karroo, when he had knelt alone in the desert and sworn an oath, calling on God to witness it, and he now had to use all his will-power to prevent himself from looking up at Mr Rhodes. He knew that this time he could not conceal it from him, so he kept his eyes on the crystal glass of cognac in front of him, while he strove for self-control and forced himself to think dispassionately.

If it were possible to destroy this giant of a man, was it not also possible to destroy his Company, to wrest from it the powers of government and the land rights and the mineral rights that it held over all Rhodesia?

Ralph felt the thrill of it humming through his blood as he realized that this might be not only the chance for fierce vengeance, but also for vast fortune, within his grasp. If the plot failed, then the shares of the gold-mining companies involved, Corner House mining group, Rand Mines, Consolidated Goldfields, would all crash with it. A simple bear coup on the Johannesburg stock exchange could net millions of pounds.

Ralph Ballantyne felt a sense of awe at the magnitude of the prospect that faced him, a prospect of power and wealth such as he had never dreamed of until this moment. He almost missed the question, and looked up when Mr Rhodes repeated it.

'I said, how soon can you leave for Kimberley to take charge of the shipments, Ralph?'

'Tomorrow,' Ralph replied evenly.

'I knew we could rely upon you,' Mr Rhodes nodded.

R alph had lingered deliberately to be the last to leave King's Lynn.

Now he and his father stood on the veranda and watched the dust column raised by Mr Rhodes' mule coach dwindling away down the hill. Ralph leaned against one of the whitewashed pillars that supported the roof, with his sunbrowned muscular arms folded across his chest and his eyes crinkled against the spiralling smoke of the cheroot between his teeth.

'You aren't naïve enough to accept young Percy's estimate of the Boers, are you, Papa?'

Zouga chuckled. 'Slow, suspicious, malevolent and all that nonsense.' He shook his head. 'They ride hard and shoot straight, they have fought every black tribe south of the Limpopo—'

'Not to mention our own soldiers,' Ralph reminded him. 'Majuba Hill, 1881, General Colley and ninety of his men are buried on the peak, the Boers didn't lose a single man.'

'They are good soldiers,' Zouga admitted, 'but we will have surprise on our side.'

'However, you do agree that it will be an act of international banditry, Papa?' Ralph removed the cheroot from his mouth and tapped off the ash. 'We won't have one shred of moral justification for it.'

Ralph watched the scar on Zouga's cheek turn white as bone-china. It was an infallible barometer of his mood.

'I do not understand,' Zouga said, but they both knew he understood perfectly.

'It's robbery,' Ralph persisted. 'Not just a little footpaddery, but robbery on the grand scale. We are plotting to steal a country.'

'Did we then steal this land from the Matabele?' Zouga demanded.

'That was different,' Ralph smiled. 'They were pagan savages, but here we are planning to overthrow a government of fellow Christians.'

'When we consider the greater good of the Empire,' Zouga's scar had turned from icy white to crimson.

'Empire, Papa?' Ralph was still smiling. 'If there are two people who should be entirely honest with each other, they are you and me. Look at me, and tell me straight that there will be no profit in it for us – other than the satisfaction of having done our duty to the Empire.'

But Zouga did not look at him. 'I am a soldier—'

'Yes,' Ralph cut him short. 'But you are also a rancher who has just come through the rinderpest. You managed to sell five thousand head of cattle, but we both know that was not enough. How much do you owe, Papa?'

After a moment's hesitation, Zouga told him grudgingly. 'Thirty thousand pounds.'

'Do you have any expectation of paying off those debts?'
'No.'

'Not unless we take the Transvaal?'

Zouga did not reply, but the scar faded and he sighed.

'All right,' Ralph told him. 'I just wanted to be certain that I was not alone in my motives.'

275

'You will go through with it?' Zouga asked.

'Don't worry, Papa. We'll come out of it, I promise you that.' Ralph pushed himself away from the pillar, and called to the grooms to bring his horse.

From the saddle he looked down at his father and for the first time noticed how the weariness of age had faded the green of his eyes.

'My boy, just because some of us will be rewarded for our endeavours, it does not mean that the enterprise is not a noble one. We are the servants of the Empire, and faithful servants are entitled to a fair wage.'

Ralph reached down and clasped his shoulder, then he picked up the reins and rode down the hill through the acacia forests.

The railhead was feeling its way up the escarpment, like a cautious adder, often following the ancient elephant roads, for these huge beasts had pioneered the easiest gradients and the gentlest passes. It had left the swollen baobabs and yellow fever trees of the Limpopo basin far below and the forests were lovelier, the air sweeter, and the streams clearer and colder.

Ralph's base camp had moved up with the railhead into one of the secluded valleys, just out of earshot of the hammers of the gangs driving the steel spikes into the teak railway sleepers. The spot had many of the charms of the remote wilderness. In the evenings a herd of sable antelope came down to feed in the grass glade below the camp, and the barking of baboons from the hills roused them each dawn. Yet the telegraph hut at the railhead was ten minutes' stroll away, around the foot of the wooded hill, and the locomotive bringing up the rails and sleepers from Kimberley delivered as well the latest copy of *The Diamond Fields*

Advertiser, and any other small luxuries that the camp required.

In an emergency Cathy would have the railway overseer and any men of his gang to call upon, while the camp itself was protected by twenty loyal Matabele servants and Isazi, the little Zulu driver, who pointed out modestly that he alone was worth twenty more of the bravest Matabele. In the unlikely event of Cathy becoming lonely or bored, the Harkness Mine was only thirty miles away, and Harry and Vicky promised to ride across every weekend.

'Can't we come with you, Daddy?' Jonathan pleaded. 'I could help you, really I could.'

Ralph lifted him into his lap. 'One of us has to stay and look after Mama,' he explained. 'You are the only one I can trust.'

'We can take her with us,' Jonathan suggested eagerly, and Ralph had a vision of his wife and child in the midst of an armed revolution, with barricades in the streets and Boer commandos ravaging the countryside.

'That would be very nice, Jon-Jon,' Ralph agreed, 'but what about the new baby? What happens if the stork arrives here while we are all away and there is nobody to sign for your little sister?'

Jonathan scowled. He was already developing a healthy dislike for this not yet arrived but eternally present female personage. She seemed to stand squarely in the way of every pleasant prospect or exciting plan, both parents managed to introduce his darling sister into almost every conversation, and his mother spent much of the time formerly devoted to Master Jonathan's interests in knitting and sewing or just sitting smiling to herself. She no longer went out riding with him each morning and evening, nor indulged in those rowdy romps which he enjoyed so heartily. Jonathan had in fact already consulted Isazi on the possibility of getting a message to the stork and telling him not to bother, that they had changed their minds. However, Isazi had not been very encouraging, although he had promised to have a word with the local witchdoctor on Jonathan's behalf.

Now confronted once more with that ubiquitous female, Jonathan capitulated with poor grace.

'Well, can I come with you when my baby sister is here to look after Mama?'

'I tell you what, old fellow, I'll do better than that. How would you like to go on a big boat across the sea?' This was the kind of talk Jonathan preferred, and his face lit up.

'Can I sail it?' he demanded.

'I'm sure the captain will let you help him,' Ralph chuckled. 'And when we get to London, we will stay in a big hotel and we will buy all sorts of presents for your mama.'

Cathy dropped her knitting into her lap, and stared at him in the lamplight.

'What about me?' Jonathan demanded. 'Can we buy all sorts of presents for me too?'

'And for your baby sister,' Ralph agreed. 'Then when we come back we will go to Johannesburg and we will buy a big house, with shining chandeliers and marble floors.'

'And stables for my pony.' Jonathan clapped his hands.

'And a kennel for Chaka.' Ralph ruffled his curls. 'And you will go to a fine brick school with lots of other little boys.' Jonathan's grin wavered slightly, that was perhaps carrying things a little too far, but Ralph stood him on his feet again, slapped his backside lightly and told him, 'Now go and kiss your mother goodnight, and ask her to tuck you up in your cot.'

Cathy hurried back from the nursery tent, moving with the appealing awkwardness of her pregnancy into the fire-light, and she came to where Ralph sat in the canvas folding chair with his boots stretched to the blaze, and the whisky glass in his hand. She stopped behind his chair, put both arms around his neck and, with her lips pressed to his cheek, whispered: 'Is it true, or are you just teasing me?'

'You have been a good brave girl for long enough. I'm going to buy you a home that you didn't dare even dream about.'

'With chandeliers?'

'And a carriage to take you to the opera.'

'I don't know if I like opera – I've never been to one.'

'We'll find out in London, won't we?'

'Oh Ralph, I'm so happy I think I could cry. But why now? What has happened to make it all change?'

'Something is going to happen before Christmas that is going to change our lives. We are going to be rich.'

'I thought we were already rich?'

'I mean really rich, the way Robinson and Rhodes are rich.'

'Can you tell me what it is?'

'No,' he said simply. 'But you only have a few short weeks to wait, just until Christmas.'

'Oh, darling,' she sighed. 'Will you be away that long, I miss you so.'

'Then let's waste no more precious time talking.' He stood up, picked her up in his arms and carried her carefully to the bell tent under the spreading wild fig tree.

In the morning Cathy stood with Jonathan beside her, holding his hand to restrain him, and they looked up at Ralph on the foot-plate of the big green locomotive.

'We always seem to be saying goodbye.' She had to raise her voice above the hiss of steam from the driving wheels and the roar of the flames in the firebox.

'It's the last time,' Ralph promised her.

How handsome and gay he was, it made her heart swell until it threatened to choke her.

'Come back to me as soon as you can.'

'I will, just as soon as I can.' The engine-driver pulled

down the brass throttle-handle and the huff of steam drowned Ralph's next words.

'What? What did you say?' Cathy trotted heavily beside the locomotive as it began to trundle down the steel tracks.

'Don't lose the letter,' he repeated.

'I won't,' she promised, and then the effort of keeping level with the rolling locomotive became too much. She came up short, and waved with the white lace handkerchief until the curve in the southbound tracks carried the train out of sight beyond the heel of a kopje, and the last mournful sob of its steam whistle died on the air. Then she turned back to where Isazi waited with the trap. Jonathan wrested his hand from hers and raced ahead to scramble up onto the seat.

'Can I drive them, Isazi?' he pleaded, and Cathy felt a prick of anger at the fickleness of boyhood – one moment tearful and bereft, the next shrieking with the prospect of handling the reins.

As she settled onto the buttoned leather rear seat of the trap, she slipped her hand into the pocket of her apron to check that the sealed envelope that Ralph had left with her was still safe. She drew it out and read the tantalizing instruction he had written upon the face: 'Open only when you receive my telegraph.'

She was about to return it to her pocket; then she bit her lip, fighting the temptation, and at last ran her fingernail under the flap, splitting it open and drew out the folded sheet.

'Upon receiving my telegraph, you must send the following telegraph immediately and urgently: "To Major Zouga Ballantyne. Headquarters of Rhodesian Horse Regiment at Pitsani Bechuanaland: YOUR WIFE MRS LOUISE BALLANTYNE GRAVELY ILL RETURN IMMEDIATELY KINGS LYNN."'

Cathy read the instruction twice and suddenly she was deadly afraid.

'Oh my mad darling, what are you going to do?' she whispered, and Jonathan urged the horses into a trot back along the track towards the camp.

T he workshops of the Simmer and Jack gold mine stood below the steel headgear on the crest of the ridge. The town of Johannesburg sprawled away in the low valley, and over the further rounded hills. The workshop was roofed and walled with corrugated iron, and the concrete floor was stained with black puddles of spilled engine oil. It was oven-hot under the iron, and beyond the big double sliding doors at the end of the shed the sunlight of early summer was blinding.

'Close the doors,' Ralph Ballantyne ordered, and two of the small group went to struggle with the heavy wood and iron structures, grunting and sweating with unaccustomed physical effort. With the doors closed, it was gloomy as a Gothic cathedral, and the white beams of sunlight through chinks in the iron walls were filled with swirling dust motes.

Down the centre of the floor stood a row of fifty yellow drums. Stencilled on each lid in black paint were the words: 'Heavy Duty Engine Oil. 44 gals.'

Ralph slipped off his beige linen jacket, pulled down the knot of his necktie and rolled up his shirtsleeves. He selected a two-pound hammer and a cold chisel from the nearest workbench and started to hack open the lid of the nearest drum. The four other men crowded closer to watch. The hammer strokes echoed hollowly about the long shed. The yellow paint flew off in tiny flakes beneath the chisel, and the raw metal was bright as newly minted shillings.

At last Ralph prised open the half-severed lid, and bent

it back. The surface of the oil glimmered glutinous and coal-black in the poor light; Ralph thrust his right arm into it as far as the elbow, and drew out a long oilskin-wrapped bundle dripping with the thick oil. He carried it to the workbench, and slit the binding with the chisel, and there were exclamations of satisfaction as he stripped away the covering.

'The very latest Lee Metford bolt-action rifles firing the new smokeless cordite load. There is no other rifle in the world to match it.'

They passed the weapon from hand to hand, and when it reached Percy Fitzpatrick, he rattled the bolt, opening and closing it rapidly.

'How many?'

'Ten to a drum,' Ralph answered. 'Fifty drums.'

'And the rest of them?' demanded Frank Rhodes. He was as unlike his younger brother as Ralph was to Jordan. A tall lean man with deepset eyes and high cheekbones, his greying hair receding from a deep bony forehead.

'I can bring through a shipment every week for the next five weeks,' Ralph told him, wiping his greasy hands on a ball of cotton waste.

'Can you do it quicker than that?'

'Can you clean and distribute them quicker than that?' Ralph countered, and without waiting for a reply, turned to John Hays Hammond, the brilliant American mining engineer whom he trusted more than Mr Rhodes' effete brother.

'Have you decided on the final plan of action?' he asked. 'Mr Rhodes will want to know when I return to Kimberley.'

'We will seize the Pretoria fort and the arsenal as our first objective,' Hays Hammond told him, and they fell into a detailed discussion with Ralph scribbling notes on the back of a cigarette packet. When at last Ralph nodded and stuffed the packet into his back pocket, Frank Rhodes demanded:

'What is the news from Bulawayo?'

'Jameson has his men, over six hundred of them. They

are mounted and armed. He will be ready to move southwards to Pitsani on the last day of the month, that's his latest report.' Ralph shrugged on his jacket again. 'It will be wiser if we are not seen together.'

He returned to shake hands with each of them, but when he reached Colonel Frank Rhodes, he could not resist the temptation to add, 'It would also be wiser, Colonel, if you could limit your telegraph messages to essentials only. The code you are using, the daily references to this fictitious gold-mine flotation of yours is enough to attract the attention of even the most dimwitted of the Transvaal police agents, and we know for certain that there is one in the Johannesburg telegraph office.'

'Sir, we have indulged in no unnecessary traffic,' Frank Rhodes replied stiffly.

'Then how do you rate your latest effort? *"Are the six hundred northern shareholders in a position to take up their debentures?"*' Ralph mimicked his prim old maidish diction, then nodded farewell and went out to where his horse was tethered, and rode down the road to Fordsberg Dip and the city.

E lizabeth rose at a glance from her mother, and began to gather up the soup bowls.

'You haven't finished, Bobby,' she told her young brother.

'I'm not hungry, Lizzie,' the child protested. 'It tastes funny.'

'You always have an excuse not to eat, Master Robert,' Elizabeth scolded him. 'No wonder you are so skinny, you'll never grow up strong and tall like your papa.'

'That's enough, Elizabeth,' Robyn spoke sharply. 'Leave the boy, if he's not hungry. You know he isn't well.'

Elizabeth glanced at her mother, then dutifully stacked

Robert's bowl with the others. None of the girls had ever been allowed to leave food, not even when they were giddy with malaria, but she had learned not to protest the unfairness of Robyn's indulgence of her only son. With the kerosene lantern in her other hand, Elizabeth went out of the back door and crossed to the thatched kitchen hut.

'It is time she had a husband.' Juba shook her head mournfully. 'She needs a man in her bed and a baby to her breast to make her smile.'

'Don't talk nonsense, Juba,' snapped Robyn. 'There will be time for that later. She is doing important work here, I could not let her go. She is as good as a trained doctor.'

'The young men come out from Bulawayo one after the other, and she sends them all away,' Juba went on, ignoring Robyn's injunction.

'She's a sensible, serious girl,' Robyn agreed.

'She is a sad girl, with a secret.'

'Oh Juba, not every woman wants to spend her life as some man's chattel,' Robyn scoffed.

'Do you remember when she was a girl?' Juba went on unperturbed. 'How bright she was, how she shone with joy, how she sparkled like a drop of morning dew.'

'She has grown up.'

'I thought it was the tall young rock-finder, the man from across the sea who took Vicky away.' Juba shook her head. 'It was not him. She laughed at Vicky's wedding, and it was not the laughter of a girl who has lost her love. It is something else,' Juba decided portentously, 'or somebody else.'

Robyn was about to protest further, but she was interrupted by the sound of excited voices in the darkness outside the door, and she stood up quickly.

'What is it?' she called. 'What is happening out there, Elizabeth?' and the flame of the lantern came bobbing back across the yard, lighting Elizabeth's flying feet but leaving her face in darkness.

'Mama! Mama! Come quickly!' Her voice rang with excitement. Elizabeth burst in through the door.

'Control yourself, girl.' Robyn shook her shoulder, and Elizabeth took a deep breath.

'Old Moses has come up from the village – he says that there are soldiers, hundreds of soldiers riding past the church.'

'Juba, get Bobby's coat.' Robyn took her woollen shawl and her cane down from behind the door. 'Elizabeth, give me the lantern!'

Robyn led the family down the driveway under the dark spathodea trees, past the godowns of the hospital, towards the church. They went in a small tight group, with Bobby bundled up in a woollen coat riding on Juba's fat hip, but before they reached the church, there were many other dark figures hurrying along in the darkness around them.

'They are coming out of the hospital.' Juba was righteously indignant. 'And tomorrow they will all be sick again.'

'You'll never stop them.' Elizabeth sighed with resignation. 'Curiosity killed the cat.' And then she exclaimed, 'There they are! Moses was right – just look at them!'

The starlight was bright enough to reveal the torrent of dark horsemen pouring down the road from the neck of hills. They rode two abreast and a length between each rank. It was too dark to see their faces under the broad brims of their slouch hats, but a rifle barrel stuck up like an accuser's finger behind each man's shoulder, silhouetted against the frosty fields of stars that filled the heavens. The deep dust of the track muffled the hooves to a soft floury puffing sound, but the saddles squeaked with the rub of dubbined leather and a curb chain tinkled as a horse snorted softly and tossed its head.

Yet the quiet was uncanny for such a multitude. No voice raised above a whisper, no orders to close up, not even the usual low warning, "Ware hole!' of massed horsemen moving in formation across unfamiliar terrain in darkness. The head of the column reached the fork in the road below the church, but took the lefthand turning, the old wagon road towards the south.

'Who are they?' Juba asked with a thrill of superstitious awe in her voice. 'They look like ghosts.'

'Those aren't ghosts,' Robyn said flatly. 'Those are Jameson's tin soldiers, that's his new Rhodesian Horse Regiment.'

'Why are they taking the old road?' Elizabeth, too, spoke in a whisper, infected by Juba and by the unnatural quiet. 'And why are they riding in the dark?'

'This stinks of Jameson – and his master.' Robyn stepped forward to the edge of the road and called loudly, lifting the lantern above her head, 'Where are you going?'

A low voice from the column answered her: 'There and back to see how far it is, missus!' and there were a few low chuckles, but the column flowed on past the church without a check.

In the centre of the column were the transports, seven wagons drawn by mules, for the rinderpest had left no draught-oxen. After the wagons came eight two-wheeled carts with canvas covers over the Maxim machine-guns, and then three light field guns, relics of Jameson's expeditionary force that had captured Bulawayo a few short years ago. The tail of the column was again made up of mounted men, two abreast.

It took almost twenty minutes for them all to pass the church, and then the silence was complete, with just the taint of dust in the air as a reminder of their going. The patients from the hospital began to slip away from the roadside, back into the darker shadows beneath the spathodea trees, but the little family group stayed on silently, waiting for Robyn to move.

'Mummy, I am cold,' Bobby whined at last, and Robyn roused herself.

'I wonder what devilry they are up to now,' she murmured, and led them back up the hill towards the homestead.

'The beans will be cold by now,' Elizabeth complained, as she hurried back into the kitchen hut, while Robyn and Juba climbed up the steps onto the stoep.

Juba let Bobby down from her hip, and he scampered back into the warm lamplight of the dining-room. Juba was about to follow him, but Robyn stopped her with a hand upon her forearm. The two women stood together, close and secure in the love and companionship they bore each other. They looked out across the valley, in the direction in which the dark and silent horsemen had disappeared.

'How beautiful it is!' Robyn murmured. 'I always think of the stars as my friends, they are so constant, so well remembered, and tonight they are so close.' She lifted her hand as though to pluck them from the firmament. 'There is Orion, and there is the bull.'

'And there Manatassi's four sons,' Juba said, 'the poor murdered babes.'

'The same stars,' Robyn hugged Juba closer to her, 'the same stars shine upon us all, even though we know them by different names. You call those four white stars Manatassi's Sons – but we call them the Cross. The Southern Cross.'

She felt Juba start and then begin to shiver, and Robyn's voice was instantly concerned.

'What is it, my little Dove?' she asked.

'Bobby was right,' whispered Juba. 'It is cold, we should go in now.' She sat silent during the rest of the meal, but when Elizabeth took Bobby through to his bedroom, she said simply, 'Nomusa, I must go back to the village.'

'Oh Juba, you have only just returned, whatever is the matter?'

'I have a feeling, Nomusa, a feeling in my heart that my husband needs me.'

'Men,' said Robyn bitterly. 'If we could only be shot of all of them – life would be so much simpler if we women ran the world.'

'It is the sign,' whispered Tanase, holding her son to her bosom, and the light from the small smoky little fire in the centre of the hut left her eyes in shadow like those of a skull. 'It is always the way with the prophecy of the Umlimo, the meaning becomes clear only when the events come to pass.'

'The wings in the dark noon,' Bazo nodded, 'and the cattle with their heads twisted to touch their flanks, and now—'

'And now the cross has eaten up the hornless cattle, the horsemen have gone south in the night. It is the third, the last sign for which we waited,' Tanase exulted softly. 'The spirits of our ancestors urge us on. The time of waiting is over.'

'Little Mother, the spirits have chosen you to make their meaning clear. Without you we would never have known what the white men call those four great stars. Now the spirits have other work for you. You are the one who knows where they are, you know how many are at Khami Mission.'

Juba looked at her husband, and her lips trembled, her great dark eyes were swimming with tears. Gandang nodded to her to speak.

'There is Nomusa,' she whispered. 'Nomusa, who is more than a mother and a sister to me. Nomusa who cut the chain that held me in the slave ship—'

'Put those thoughts from your mind,' counselled Tanase gently. 'There is no place for them now. Tell us who else is at the Mission.'

'There is Elizabeth, my gentle sad Lizzie, and Bobby, who I carry upon my hip.'

'Who else?' Tanase insisted.

'There are no others,' Juba whispered.

Bazo looked at his father.

'They are yours, all of them at Khami Mission. You know what must be done.'

Gandang nodded, and Bazo turned back to his mother.

'Tell me, sweet little Mother.' His voice sank to a soothing rumble. 'Tell me about Bakela, the Fist, and his woman. What news do you have of him?'

'Last week he was in the big house at King's Lynn, he and Balela, the One who brings Clear and Sunny Skies.'

Bazo turned to one of the other indunas who sat in the rank behind Gandang.

'Suku!'

The induna rose on one knee.

'Baba?' he asked.

'Bakela is yours, and his woman,' Bazo told him. 'And when you have done that work, go on to Hartley Hills and take the miners there, there are three men, and a woman with four whelps.'

'Nkosi Nkulu,' the induna acknowledged the order, and no one queried or demurred when he called Bazo, 'Nkosi Nkulu! King!'

'Little Mother, where is Henshaw and his woman, who is the daughter of Nomusa?'

'Nomusa had a letter from her, three days ago. She is at the railhead, she and the boy. She carries an infant, which will be born about the time of the *Chawala* festival. She wrote of her great joy and happiness.'

'And Henshaw?' Bazo asked patiently. 'What of Henshaw?'

'In the letter she said he was with her, the source of her happiness. He may still be with her.'

'They are mine,' Bazo said. 'They and the five white men who are at the railhead. Afterwards we will sweep up the wagon road and take the two men and the woman and three children at Antelope Mine.' He went on quietly allocating a task to each of his commanders, each farm and lonely mine was given to one of them with a recountal of the victims to be expected there, the telegraph lines were to be cut, the native police were to be executed, the drifts were to be guarded, all the wagon roads had to be swept for travellers, firearms collected, and livestock carried off and hidden. When he had finished, he turned to the women.

'Tanase, you will see to it that all our own women and children go into the ancient place of sanctuary, you yourself will lead them into the sacred hills of the Matopos. You will make certain that they stay in small groups, each well separated from the others, and the *mujiba*, the young boys not yet initiated, will watch from the hilltops against the coming of the white men. The women will have the potions and the *muti* ready for those of our men who are wounded.'

'Nkosi Nkulu,' said Tanase after each instruction, and she watched his face, trying not to let her pride and her wild exultation show. 'King!' she called him, as the other indunas had done.

Then the telling of it was over, and they waited for one thing more. The silence in the hut was strained and intense, the white of eyes gleaming in faces of polished ebony, as they waited, and at last Bazo spoke.

'By tradition, on the night of the *Chawala* moon, the sons and daughters of Mashobane, of Mzilikazi, and of Lobengula, should celebrate the Festival of the First Fruits. This season there will be no cobs of corn to reap, for the locusts have reaped them for us. This season there will be no black bull for the young warriors to kill with their bare hands, for the rinderpest has done their work for them.'

Bazo slowly looked about the circle of their faces.

'So on the night of this *Chawala* moon, let it begin. Let the storm rage. Let the eyes turn red. Let the young men of Matabele run!'

'Jee!' hummed Suku in the second rank of indunas, and 'Jee!' old Babiaan took up the war chant, and then they were all swaying together with their throats straining and their eyes bulging redly in the firelight with the divine fighting madness coming down upon them.

The ammunition was the most time-consuming of the stores to handle, and Ralph was limited to twenty trusted men to do the work for him.

There were 10,000 rounds in each iron case, with the W.D. and arrow impressed upon its lid. They were secured with a simple clip that could be knocked open with a rifle butt. The British army always learned its lesson the hard way. They had learned this one at Isandhlwana, the Hill of the Little Hand, on the frontier of Zululand when Lord Chelmsford left 1,000 men at his base camp, while he took a flying column to bring the Zulu indunas to battle. Avoiding contact with the column, the indunas doubled back and stormed the base camp. Only when the swarming impis broke through the perimeter did the quartermasters realize that Chelmsford had taken the keys for the ammunition chests with him. Isazi, Ralph's little Zulu driver, had given him an eye-witness account of the end.

'They were tearing at the boxes with axes, with bayonets and with their bare hands. They were swearing and screaming with rage and chagrin when we brought the assegais to them, and at the last they tried to defend themselves with their empty rifles.' Isazi's eyes had gone misty with the memory, the way an old man recalls a lost love. 'I tell you, little Hawk, they were brave men and it was a beautiful stabbing.'

Nobody could be certain how many Englishmen had died at the Little Hand, for it was almost a year before

Chelmsford retook the field, but it was one of the most terrible disasters of British military history, and immediately after it the War Office redesigned their ammunition chests.

Now the fact that the .303 ammunition was packed in these WD chests was some indication of how deep was the understanding between Mr Rhodes and the colonial secretary in Whitehall. However, the bulk packets had to be broken down and repacked in waxed paper. One hundred rounds to the packet, then these had to be soldered into tin sheets before going into the oil drums. It was an onerous task and Ralph was pleased to escape for a few hours from the workshops of the De Beers Consolidated Mines Company where it was being done.

Aaron Fagan was waiting for him in his office, with his coat on and his Derby hat in his hand.

'You are becoming a secretive fellow, Ralph,' he accused. 'Couldn't you have given me some idea of what you expect?'

'You will learn that soon enough,' Ralph promised, and put a cheroot between his lips. 'All I want to know from you is that this fellow is trustworthy, and discreet.'

'He is the eldest son of my own sister,' Aaron bridled, and Ralph struck a Vesta to the end of the cheroot to calm him.

'That is all very well, but can he keep his mouth shut?'

'I will stake my life on it.'

'You may have to,' Ralph told him drily. 'Well, let us go to visit this paragon.'

David Silver was a plump young man with a pink scrubbed complexion, gold-rimmed pince-nez and his hair glossy with brilliantine and parted down the centre so that his scalp gleamed in the division like the scar of a sword-cut. He deferred courteously to his Uncle Aaron, and went to pains to make certain that both his guests were comfortable, that their chairs were arranged with the light from the windows falling from behind and that each of them had an ashtray beside him and a cup of tea in his hand.

'It's orange pekoe,' he pointed out modestly, as he settled beside his desk. Then he placed his fingertips together, pursed his lips primly and looked expectantly at Ralph.

While Ralph briefly explained his requirements, he nodded his head brightly and made little sucking sounds of encouragement.

'Mr Ballantyne – ' he kept nodding like a mandarin doll when Ralph had finished – 'that is what we stockbrokers – ' he spread his hand deprecatingly – 'in our jargon call a "bear position" or "selling short". It is quite a commonplace transaction.'

Aaron Fagan squirmed a little in his chair, and glanced apologetically at Ralph. 'David, I think Mr Ballantyne knows—'

'No, no,' Ralph raised a hand to Aaron, 'please let Mr Silver continue. I am sure his discourse will be enlightening.' His expression was solemn, but his eyes twinkled with amusement. The irony was lost on David Silver and he accepted Ralph's invitation.

'It is an entirely short-term speculative contract. I always make a point of mentioning this to any of my clients who contemplate entering into one. To be entirely truthful, Mr Ballantyne, I do not approve of this speculation. I always feel that the stock exchange is a venue for legitimate investment, a market where capital can meet and mate with legitimate enterprise. It should not have been made into a bookmakers' turf where sportsmen bet on dark horses.'

'That is a very noble thought,' Ralph agreed.

'I am glad you see it that way.' David Silver puffed out his cheeks pompously. 'However, to return to the operation of selling shares short. The client enters the market and offers to sell shares of a specified company which he does not possess, at a price below the current market price, for delivery at some future date, usually one to three months ahead.'

'Yes,' Ralph nodded solemnly. 'I think I follow so far.'

'Naturally, the expectation of the bear operator is that the shares will fall considerably in value before he is obliged to deliver them to the purchaser. From his point of view the larger the fall in value the greater will be his profit.'

'Ah!' said Ralph. 'An easy way to make money.'

'On the other hand' – David Silver's plump features became stern – 'should the shares rise in value the bear operator will incur considerable losses. He will be forced to re-enter the market and buy shares at the inflated prices to make good his delivery to the purchaser, and naturally he will be paid only the previously agreed price.'

'Naturally!'

'Now you can see why I try to discourage my clients from engaging in these dealings.'

'Your uncle assured me that you were a prudent man.'

David Silver looked smug. 'Mr Ballantyne, I think you should know that there is a buoyant mood in the market. I have heard it rumoured that some of the Witwatersrand companies will be reporting highly elevated profits this quarter. In my view this is the time to buy gold shares, not to sell them.'

'Mr Silver, I am a terrible pessimist.'

'Very well.' David Silver sighed with the air of a superior being inured to the intractability of the common man. 'Will you tell me exactly what you have in mind, please, Mr Ballantyne?'

'I want to sell the shares of two companies short,' Ralph told him. 'Consolidated Goldfields and the British South Africa Company.'

An air of vast melancholy came over David Silver. 'You have chosen the strongest companies on the board, those are Mr Rhodes' enterprises. Did you have a figure in mind, Mr Ballantyne? The minimum lot that can be traded is one hundred shares—'

'Two hundred thousand,' said Ralph mildly.

'Two hundred thousand pounds!' gasped David Silver.

'Shares,' Ralph corrected him.

'Mr Ballantyne.' Silver had paled. 'BSA is standing at twelve pounds and Consolidated at eight. If you sell two hundred thousand shares – well, that is a transaction of two million pounds.'

'No, no!' Ralph shook his head. 'You misunderstand me.'

'Thank the good Lord for that.' A little colour flowed back into David Silver's chubby cheeks.

'I meant not two hundred thousand in total, but two hundred thousand in each company. That is four million pounds' worth altogether.'

David Silver sprang to his feet with such alacrity that his chair flew back against the wall with a crash, and for a moment it seemed that he might try to escape out into the street.

'But,' he blubbered, 'but—' And then he could think of no further protest. His pince-nez misted and his lower lip stuck out like a sulky child's.

'Sit down,' Ralph ordered gently, and he sank back miserably into his chair.

'I will have to ask you to make a deposit,' Silver made one last effort.

'How much will you need?'

'Forty thousand pounds.'

Ralph opened his cheque-book on the edge of the desk, and took one of David Silver's pens from the rack. The squeak of the nib was the only sound in the hot little office, until Ralph sat back and fanned the cheque to dry the ink.

'There is just one thing more,' he said. 'Nobody outside these four walls, nobody is ever to know that I am the principal in this transaction.'

'You have my word.'

'Or your testicles,' Ralph warned him, as he leaned close to hand him the cheque, and though he smiled, his eyes were such a cold green that David Silver shivered, and he felt a sharp pang of anticipation in his threatened parts.

It was a typical highveld Boer homestead set on a rocky ridge above an undulating treeless plain of silver grass. The roof was of galvanized corrugated iron which had begun to rust through in patches. The house was surrounded by wide verandas, and the whitewash was discoloured and flaking from the wall. There was a windmill on a skeletal tower behind the house. The vanes blurred against the pale cloudless sky, spinning in the dry dusty wind, and at each weary crank of the plunger, a cupful of cloudy green water spilled into the circular concrete cistern beside the kitchen door.

There was no attempt at a garden or lawn. A dozen scrawny speckled fowls scratched at the bare baked earth, or perched disconsolately on the derelict Cape wagon and the other ruined equipment that always seemed to ornament the yard of every Boer homestead. On the side of the prevailing wind stood a tall Australian eucalyptus tree with the old bark hanging in tatters from the silver trunk like the skin of a moulting serpent. In its scant shade were tethered eight sturdy brown ponies.

As Ralph dismounted below the veranda, a pack of mongrel hounds came snapping and snarling about his boots, and he scattered them yelping and howling with a few kicks and a hissing cut from his hippo-hide sjambok.

'U kom 'n bietjie laat, meneer.' A man had come out onto the veranda. He was in shirtsleeves with braces holding up the baggy brown trousers that left his bare ankles exposed. On his feet, he wore rawhide velskoen without socks.

'Jammer,' Ralph apologized for being late. Using the simplified form of Dutch, which the Boer called the taal, the language.

The man held the door open for Ralph and he stooped through it into the windowless living-room. It smelled of stale smoke and dead ash from the open fireplace. The floor was covered with rush mats and animal-skins. There was a single table down the centre of the room, of heavy crudely fashioned dark wood. There was a single hanging on the wall opposite the fireplace, an embroidered copy of the ten commandments in High Dutch script. The only book in the room lay open on the bare table-top. It was an enormous Dutch Bible with leather cover and bindings of brass.

On leather-thonged chairs, eight men sat down the length of both sides of the table. They all looked up at Ralph as he entered. There was not a man amongst them younger than fifty years old, for the Boers valued experience and acquired wisdom in their leaders. Most of them were bearded and all of them wore rough hard-worn clothing, and were solemn and unsmiling. The man who had greeted Ralph followed him in and silently indicated an empty chair. Ralph sat down and every shaggy bearded head turned away from him towards the figure at the end of the table.

He was the biggest man in the room, monumentally ugly, as a bulldog or one of the great anthropoids is ugly. His beard was a grey scraggly fringe, but his upper lip was shaven. His face hung in folds and bags, the skin was darkly burned by ten thousand fierce African suns, and it was lumped and stained with warts and with the speckles of benign skin cancer, like the foxing on the pages of a very old book. One eyelid drooped to give him a crafty suspicious expression. His toffee-brown eyes had also been affected by the white sun glare of Africa, and by the scouring dust of the hunting veld and the battlefield, so they were now perpetually bloodshot, sore and inflamed-looking. His people called him Oom Paul, Uncle Paul, and held him in only slightly less veneration than they did their Old Testament God.

Paul Kruger began to read aloud again from the open Bible before him. He read slowly, followed the text with his finger. The thumb was missing from his hand. It had been blown off by a bursting gunbarrel thirty years before. His voice was a rumbling *basso profundo*.

'Nevertheless the people be strong that dwell in the land, and the cities are walled and very great: and moreover we saw the children of the Anak there ... And Caleb stilled the people, and said: Let us go up at once and possess it, for we are well able to overcome it.'

Ralph watched him intently, studying the huge slumped body, the shoulders so wide that the ugly head seemed to perch upon them like a bedraggled bird on a mountaintop, and he thought of the legend that surrounded this strange man.

Paul Kruger had been nine years old when his father and uncles had packed their wagons and gathered their herds and trekked northwards, away from British rule, driven on by the memory of their folk heroes hanged at Slachters Nek by the Redcoats. The Krugers trekked from the injustice of having their slaves turned free, from the English black circuit courts, from judges who did not speak their language, from taxes levied on land that was theirs and from the foreign troops who seized their beloved herds to pay those taxes.

The year had been 1835 and on that hard trek Paul Kruger became a man at an age when most boys are still playing with kites and marbles. Each day he was given a single bullet and a charge of powder and sent out to provide meat for the family. If he failed to bring back a buck, his father beat him. He became, by necessity, an expert marksman.

It was one of his duties to scout ahead for water and good grazing, and to lead the caravan to it. He became a skilled horseman and developed an almost mystical affinity for the veld, and the herds of fat-tailed sheep and multi-hued cattle that were his family's wealth. Like a Matabele *mujiba*, he knew every beast by name, and could pick out an ailing animal from the herd at a mile distant.

When Mzilikazi, the Matabele emperor, sent his impis

with their long shields swarming down upon the little caravan of wagons, little Paul took his place with the other men at the barricades. There were thirty-three Boer fighting men inside the circle of wagons. The wagon trucks were lashed together with trek chains, and the openings between the wheels latticed with woven thorn-branches.

The Matabele *amadoda* were uncountable. Regiment after regiment they charged, hissing their deep ringing 'Jee!' They attacked for six hours without respite, and when the bullets ran low, the Boer women smelted and cast lead in the midst of the battle. When the Matabele fell back at last, their dead lay chest-deep around the wagons and little Paul had become a man, for he had killed a man – many men.

Strangely, it was another four years before he killed his first lion, sending a hardened ball through its heart as it sprang upon his horse's back. By now he was able to test a new horse by galloping it over broken ground. If it fell, young Paul would land catlike, on his feet, shake his head with disapproval, and walk away. When hunting buffalo, he would mount facing his horse's tail so as to have a steadier shot when the beasts chased his horse, as they invariably did. This unusual seat in no way hampered his control of the horse, and he could change to face ahead so swiftly and smoothly as not to upset his mount's stride in full gallop.

About this time he showed a gift of extra-sensory powers. Before a hunt, standing at his horse's head, he would go into a self-induced trance and begin describing the surrounding countryside and the wild animals in it. 'One hour's ride to the north there is a small muddy pan. A herd of quagga are drinking there, and five fat eland are coming down the path to the water. On the hill above it, under a camel-thorn tree, a pride of lion are resting, *'n ou swart maanhaar*, an old blackmane, and two lionesses. In the valleys beyond, three giraffe.' The hunters would find the animals, or the signs they had left, exactly as young Paul described them.

At sixteen, he was entitled, as a man, to ride off two

farms, as much land as a horseman could encircle in a day. Each of them was approximately sixteen thousand acres. They were the first of the vast land-holdings he acquired and held during his lifetime, sometimes bartering sixteen thousand acres of prime pasture for a plough or a bag of sugar.

At twenty he was a field cornet, an elected office which was something between magistrate and sheriff; at such tender years to be chosen by men who venerated age marked him as somebody unusual. About this time, he ran a foot race against a horseman on a picked steed over a course of a mile, and won by a length. Then during a battle against the black chief Sekukuni, the Boer General was shot through the head and tumbled over the edge of the kopje. The General was a big bulky man, two hundred and forty pounds weight, but Paul Kruger leaped down the krans, picked up the body and ran back up the hillside under the musket-fire of Sekukuni's men.

When he set off to claim his bride, he found his way blocked by the wide Vaal river in raging spate, the carcasses of cattle and wild game rolling by in the flood. Despite cries of warning from the ferryman, and without even removing his boots, he urged his horse into the brown waters and swam across. Flooded rivers would not stop a man like Paul Kruger.

After having fought Moshesh and Mzilikazi, and every other warlike tribe south of the Limpopo river, after having burned Dr David Livingstone's mission on the suspicion that he was supplying arms to the tribes, after having fought even his own people, the rebellious Boers of the Orange Free State, he was made Commandant-in-Chief of the army, and still later the President of the South African Republic.

It was this indomitable, courageous, immensely physically powerful, ugly, obstinate, devout and cantankerous old man, rich in land and herds, who now lifted his head from the

Bible and finished his reading with a simple injunction to the men who waited upon him attentively.

'Fear God, and distrust the English,' he said, and closed the Bible.

Then still without taking his bloodshot eyes from Ralph's face, he bellowed with shocking force, 'Bring coffee!' and a coloured maid bustled in with a tin tray loaded with steaming mugs. The men around the table exchanged pouches of black Magaliesberg shag, and charged their pipes, watching Ralph with closed and guarded expressions. Once the oily blue smoke had veiled the air, Kruger spoke again.

'You asked to see me, *mijn heer?*'

'Alone,' said Ralph.

'These men I trust.'

'Very well.'

They used the *taal.* Ralph knew that Kruger could speak English with some fluency, and that he would not do so as a matter of principle. Ralph had learned to speak the *taal* on the diamond-diggings. It was the simplest of all European languages, suited to the everyday life of an uncomplicated society of hunters and farmers, though even they, for the purposes of political discussion or worship, fell back upon the sophistication of High Dutch.

'My name is Ballantyne.'

'I know who you are. Your father was the elephant-hunter. A strong man, they say, and straight – but you,' and now a world of loathing entered the old man's tone, 'you belong to that heathen, Rhodes.' And though Ralph shook his head, he went on, 'Do not think I have not heard his blasphemies. I know that when he was asked if he believed there was a God, he replied,' and here he broke into heavily accented English for the first time, '"I give God a fifty-fifty chance of existing."' Kruger shook his head slowly. 'He will pay for that one day, for the Lord has commanded, "Thou shalt not take My name in vain."'

'Perhaps that day of payment is already at hand,' said Ralph softly. 'And perhaps you are God's chosen instrument.'

'Do you dare to blaspheme, also?' the old man demanded sharply.

'No,' Ralph shook his head. 'I come to deliver the blasphemer into your hands.' And he laid an envelope on the dark wood, then with a flick slid it down the length of the table until it lay in front of the president. 'A list of the arms he has sent secretly into Johannesburg, and where they are held. The names of the rebels who intend to use them. The size and force of the commando gathered on your borders at Pitsani, the route they will take to join the rebels in Johannesburg, and the date on which they intend to ride.'

Every man at the table had stiffened with shock, only the old man still puffed calmly at his pipe. He made no effort to touch the envelope.

'Why do you come to me with this?'

'When I see a thief about to break into a neighbour's home, I take it as my duty to warn him.'

Kruger removed the pipe from his mouth and flicked a spurt of yellow tobacco juice from the stem onto the dung-floor beside his chair.

'We are neighbours,' Ralph explained. 'We are white men living in Africa. We have a common destiny. We have many enemies, and one day we may be required to fight them together.'

Kruger's pipe gurgled softly, but nobody spoke again for fully two minutes, until Ralph broke the silence.

'Very well then,' he said. 'If Rhodes fails, I will make a great deal of money.'

Kruger sighed, and nodded. 'All right, now I believe you at last, for that is an Englishman's reason for treachery.' And he picked up the envelope in his brown gnarled old hand. 'Goodbye, *mijn heer*,' he said softly.

Cathy had taken to her paintbox again. She had put it away when Jon-Jon was born, but now there was time for it once more, However, this time she was determined to make a more serious work of it, instead of sugary family portraits and pretty landscapes.

She had begun a study of the trees of Rhodesia, and already had a considerable portfolio of them. First she painted the entire tree, making as many as twenty studies of typical specimens before settling on a representative example, and then to the master painting she added detailed drawings of the leaves, the flowers and the fruits, which she rendered faithfully in watercolours; finally she pressed actual leaves and blooms and gathered the seeds, then wrote a detailed description of the plant.

Very soon she had realized her own ignorance, and had written to Cape Town and London for books on botany, and for Linnaeus' *Systema Naturae* for plants. Using these, she was training herself to become a competent botanist. Already she had isolated eight trees that had not been previously described, and she had named one for Ralph 'Terminalia Ralphii' and another for Jonathan who had climbed to the upper branches to bring down its pretty pink flowers for her.

When she diffidently sent some of her dried specimens and a folio of drawings to Sir Joseph Hooker at Kew Gardens, she received an encouraging letter, complimenting her on the standard of her artwork and confirming her classifications of the new species. With the letter was an autographed copy of his *Genera Plantarum*, 'to a fellow student of nature's wonders', and it had become the start of a fascinating correspondence. The new hobby was one that could be practised side by side with Jon-Jon's bird-nesting activities, and it helped fill the dreary days when Ralph was away, although now she had difficulty keeping up with Jon-Jon, her swollen belly reducing her to an undignified waddle. She had to leave all the climbing and rock-scrambling to him.

This morning they were working one of the kloofs of the hills above the camp where they had found a beautiful spreading tree with strange candelabra of fruit on the upper branches. Jonathan was twenty feet above ground, edging out to snatch a laden branch when Cathy heard voices calling in the thick bush that clogged the mouth of the kloof. She swiftly rebuttoned her blouse and dropped her skirts down over her bare legs – the heat was oppressive in the confined gulley between the hills and she had been sitting on the bank and dabbling her feet in the trickle of the stream.

'Yoo hoo!' she yelled, and the telegraph-operator came sweating and scrambling up the steep side.

He was a dismal shrimp of a man, with a bald head and protruding eyes, but he was also one of Cathy's most fervent admirers. The arrival of a telegraph for her was an excuse for him to leave his hut and seek her out. He waited adoringly with his hat in his hands, as she read the message.

'Passage reserved Union Castle leaving Cape Town for London March 20th stop open envelope and follow instructions carefully stop home soon love Ralph.'

'Will you send a telegraph for me, Mr Braithwaite?'

'Of course, Mrs Ballantyne, it will be a great pleasure.' The little man blushed like a girl and hung his head bashfully.

Cathy wrote out the message recalling Zouga Ballantyne to King's Lynn on a sheet of her sketchpad, and Mr Braithwaite clutched it to his concave chest like a holy talisman.

'Happy Christmas, Mrs Ballantyne,' he said, and Cathy started. The days had gone by so swiftly, she had not realized that the year 1895 was so far gone. Suddenly the prospect of Christmas alone in the wilderness, another Christmas without Ralph, appalled her.

'Happy Christmas, Mr Braithwaite,' she said, hoping he

would leave before she began to cry. Her pregnancy made her so weak and weepy – if only Ralph would come back. If only . . .

Pitsani was not a town nor even a village. It was a single trading-store, standing forlornly in the flat sandveld on the edge of the Kalahari Desert that stretched away 1,500 miles into the west. However, it was only a few miles to the frontier of the Transvaal, but no fence nor border-post marked the division. The country was so flat and featureless and the scrub so low, that the rider could see the trading-store from a distance of seven miles, and around it, shimmering like ghosts in the heat mirage, the little cone-shaped white tents of an army encamped.

The rider had pushed his horse mercilessly along the thirty miles from the railway at Mafeking, for he bore an urgent message. He was an unlikely choice for a peace messenger, for he was a soldier and a man of action. His name was Captain Maurice Heany, a handsome man with dark hair and moustaches and flashing eyes. He had served with Carrington's horse and the Bechuana police, and in the Matabele war he had commanded a troop of mounted infantry. He was a hawk and he bore the message of a dove. The sentries picked up his dust from two miles out and there was a small bustle as the guard was called out.

When Heany trotted into the camp all its senior officers were already gathered at the command tent, and Doctor Jameson himself came forward to shake his hand and lead him into the tent where they were screened from curious eyes. Zouga Ballantyne poured Indian tonic onto a dram of gin, and brought it to him.

'Sorry, Maurice, this is not the Kimberley Club, I'm afraid we have no ice.'

'Ice or not, you have saved my life.'

They knew each other well. Maurice Heany had been one of Ralph Ballantyne's and Harry Johnston's junior partners when they had contracted to bring the original pioneer column into Mashonaland.

Heany drank and wiped his moustache before looking up at John Willoughby, and the little doctor. He was in a quandary as to whom he should address his message to, for although Willoughby was the regimental commander and Zouga Ballantyne his second-in-command, and although Doctor Jameson was officially only a civilian observer, they all knew with whom the ultimate decision-making and authority lay.

Jameson smoothed his embarrassment by ordering directly, 'Well then, out with it, man.'

'It's not good news, Doctor Jim. Mr Rhodes is utterly determined that you must remain here until after the Reform Committee has captured Johannesburg.'

'When will that be?' Jameson demanded bitterly. 'Just look at these!' He picked up a sheaf of telegraph flimsies from the camp table. 'A new telegraph every few hours, in Frank Rhodes' execrable code. Take this one, yesterday.' Jameson read aloud: '"*It is absolutely necessary to delay floating until company letterhead agreed upon*".' Jameson dropped the telegraphs back on the table with disgust. 'This ridiculous quibbling over what flag to fly. Damn me, but if we aren't doing this for the Union Jack, then what are we doing it for?'

'It is rather like the timorous bride who, having set the date, views the approach of the wedding day with delicious confusion.' Zouga Ballantyne smiled. 'You must remember that our friends on the Reform Committee in Johannesburg are more used to stock deals and financial speculation than the use of steel. Like the blushing virgin, they may need a little judicial forcing.'

'That's it exactly.' Doctor Jameson nodded. 'And yet Mr Rhodes is concerned that we should not move ahead of them.'

'There is one other thing that you should know.' Heaney hesitated. 'It does seem that the gentlemen in Pretoria are aware that something is afoot. There is even talk that there is a traitor amongst us.'

'That is unthinkable,' snapped Zouga.

'I agree with you, Zouga,' Doctor Jim nodded. 'It is much more likely that these damned puerile telegraphs of Frank Rhodes have come to old Kruger's notice.'

'Be that as it may, gentlemen. The Boers are making certain preparations – it is even possible that they have already called out their commandos in the Rustenburg and Zeerust divisions.'

'If that is the case,' Zouga said softly, 'then we have a choice. We can either move immediately, or we can all go home to Bulawayo.'

Doctor Jameson could not remain seated any longer, he jumped up from his canvas chair and began pacing up and down the tent with quick jerky little strides. They all watched in silence until he stopped in the opening of the tent and stared out across the sun-scorched plain towards the eastern horizon beneath which lay the great golden prize of the Witwatersrand. When at last he turned to face them, they could see that he had reached his decision.

'I am going,' he said.

'Thought you would,' murmured Zouga.

'What are you going to do?' Jameson asked as softly.

'Going with you,' said Zouga.

'Thought you would,' said Jameson, and then glanced at Willoughby who nodded.

'Good! Johnny will you call the men out? I would like to speak to them before we ride – and, Zouga, will you see to it that the telegraph lines are all cut? I don't want ever to see another one of those communications from Frankie. Anything more he has to say, he can tell me face to face when we reach Johannesburg.'

'They've got Jameson!' The cry echoed through the elegant hush of the Kimberley Club, like a Hun war-cry at the gates of Rome.

The consternation was immediate and overwhelming. Members boiled out of the long bar into the marbled lobby, and surrounded the news-crier. Others from the reading-room lined the banisters, shouting their queries down the stair-well. In the dining-room someone bumped into the carving-wagon in his haste to reach the lobby, and sent it crashing on its side while the joint rolled across the floor with roast potatoes preceding it like a squad of footmen.

The bearer of the news was one of the prosperous Kimberley diamond-buyers, a profession no longer referred to as 'kopje-walloping', and such was his agitation that he had forgotten to remove his straw boater when entering the club portals. An offence that at another time would have merited a reprimand from the committee.

Now he stood in the centre of the lobby, hat firmly on his head and reading spectacles sliding to the end of his empurpled nose, a symptom of his excitement and agitation. He was reading from a copy of *The Diamond Fields Advertiser*, the ink of which was so fresh that it smeared his fingers: 'Jameson raises White Flag at Doornkop after sixteen killed in fierce fighting. Doctor Jameson, I have the honour to meet you. General Cronje accepts surrender.'

Ralph Ballantyne had not left his seat at the head of the corner table, although his guests had deserted him to join the rush into the lobby. He signalled the distracted wine waiter to refill his glass, and then helped himself to another spoonful of the *sole bonne femme*, while he waited for his guests to return. They came trooping back, led by Aaron Fagan, like a funeral party returning from the cemetery.

'The Boers must have been waiting for them—'

'Doctor Jim walked straight into it—'

'What on earth did the man think he was doing?'

Chairs rasped and every one of them reached for his glass the moment he was seated.

'He had six hundred and sixty men and guns. By God, it was a carefully planned thing then.'

'There will be a few tales to tell.'

'And heads to roll, no doubt.'

'Doctor Jim's luck has run out at last.'

'Ralph, your father is amongst the prisoners!' Aaron was reading the newsprint.

For the first time Ralph showed emotion. 'That's not possible.' He snatched the paper from Aaron's hand, and stared at it in agony.

'What happened?' he muttered. 'Oh God, what has happened?' But somebody else was yelling in the lobby.

'Kruger has arrested all the members of the Reform Committee – he has promised to have them tried for their lives.'

'The gold mines!' another said clearly in the ensuing silence, and instinctively every head lifted to the clock on the wall above the dining-room entrance. It was twenty minutes to two. The stock exchange re-opened on the hour. There was another rush, this time out of the club doors. On the sidewalk, hatless members shouted impatiently for their carriages, while others set out at a determined trot towards the stock exchange buildings.

The club was almost deserted, not more than ten diners were left at the tables. Aaron and Ralph were alone at the corner table. Ralph still held the list of prisoners in his hand.

'I cannot believe it,' he whispered.

'It's a catastrophe. What can possibly have possessed Jameson?' Aaron agreed.

It seemed that the worst had happened, nothing could match the dreadful tidings that they had received so far, but then the club secretary came out of his office ashen-faced, and stood in the doorway of the dining-room.

'Gentlemen,' he croaked. 'I have some more terrible news. It has just come through on the wire. Mr Rhodes has offered his resignation as prime minister of Cape Colony. He has also offered to resign from the chairmanship of the Charter Company, of De Beers and of Consolidated Goldfields.'

'Rhodes,' Aaron whispered. 'Mr Rhodes was in it. It's a conspiracy – the Lord only knows what will be the final consequences of this thing, and who Mr Rhodes will bring down with him.'

'I think we should order a decanter of port,' said Ralph, as he pushed his plate away from him. 'I'm not hungry any more.'

He thought about his father in a Boer prison, and suddenly an image come into his mind of Zouga Ballantyne in a white shirt, his hands bound behind his back, his gold- and silver-laced beard sparkling in the sunlight, the whitewashed wall at his back, regarding the rank of riflemen in front of him with those calm green eyes of his. Ralph felt nauseated and the rare old port tasted like quinine on his tongue. He set the glass down.

'Ralph.' Aaron was staring at him across the table. 'The bear transaction, you sold the shares of Charter and Consolidated short, and your position is still open.'

'I have closed all your transactions,' said David Silver. 'I averaged out BSA shares at a little over seven pounds, that gives you a profit, after commission and levy, of almost four pounds a share. You did even better on the Consolidated Goldfields transactions, they were the worst hit in the crash, from eight pounds when you began selling them short they dropped to almost two pounds when it looked as though Kruger was going to seize the mining companies of the Witwatersrand in retaliation.' David Silver broke off and looked at Ralph with awe. 'It is the kind of killing which becomes a legend on the floor, Mr Ballantyne. The frightful risk you took,' he shook his head in admiration. 'What courage! What foresight!'

'What luck!' said Ralph impatiently. 'Do you have my difference cheque?'

'I have.' David Silver opened the black leather valise in his lap and brought from it a snowy white envelope sealed with a rosette of scarlet wax.

'It is counter-signed and guaranteed by my bank.' David laid it reverently upon his Uncle Aaron's desk-top. 'The total is,' and he breathed it like a lover, 'one million and fifty-eight pounds eight shillings and sixpence. After the one that Mr Rhodes paid to Barney Barnato for his claims in the Kimberley mine, it is the largest cheque ever drawn in Africa, south of the equator – what do you say to that, Mr Ballantyne!'

Ralph looked at Aaron in the chair behind the desk. 'You know what to do with it. Just be certain it can never be traced back to me.'

'I understand,' Aaron nodded, and Ralph changed the subject.

'Has there been an answer to my telegraph yet? My wife is not usually so slow in replying.' And because Aaron was an old friend, who loved the gentle Cathy as much as any of her many admirers, Ralph went on to explain. 'She is within two months of her time. Now that the dust of

Jameson's little adventure has begun to settle and there is no longer any danger of war, I must get Cathy down here, where she can have expert medical attention.'

'I'll send my clerk to the telegraph office.' Aaron rose and crossed to the door of the outer office, to give his instructions. Then he looked back at his nephew. 'Was there anything else, David?' The little stockbroker started. He had been staring at Ralph Ballantyne with the glow of hero-worship in his eyes. Now he hastily assembled his papers, and stuffed them into his valise, before coming and offering his soft white hand to Ralph.

'I cannot tell you what an honour it has been to be associated with you, Mr Ballantyne. If there is ever anything at all I can do for you—'

Aaron had to shoo him out of the door.

'Poor David,' he murmured, as he came back to the desk. 'His very first millionaire, it's a watershed in any young stockbroker's life.'

'My father—' Ralph did not even smile.

'I'm sorry, Ralph. There is nothing more we can do. He will go back to England in chains with Jameson and the others. They are to be imprisoned in Wormwood Scrubs until they are called to answer the charge.' Aaron selected a sheet of paper from the pile on his desk. '"*That they, with certain other persons in the month of December 1895, in South Africa, within Her Majesty's dominions, did unlawfully prepare and fit out a military expedition to proceed against the dominions of a certain friendly state, to wit, the South African Republic, contrary to the provisions of the Foreign Enlistment Act of 1870.*"'

Aaron laid down the paper and shook his head. 'There is nothing any of us can do now.'

'What will happen to them? It's a capital offence—'

'Oh no, Ralph, I am sure it won't come to that.'

Ralph sank down in his chair and stared moodily out of the window, for the hundredth time castigating himself for not having anticipated that Jameson would cut the telegraph lines before marching on Johannesburg. The recall that Cathy had sent to Zouga Ballantyne, the fiction that Louise was gravely ill, had never reached him and Zouga had ridden into the waiting Boer commandos with the rest of them.

If only, Ralph thought, and then his thoughts were interrupted. He looked up expectantly as the clerk came hesitantly into the office.

'Has there been a reply from my wife?' Ralph demanded, and the man shook his head.

'Begging your pardon, Mr Ballantyne, sir, but there has not.' He hesitated, and Ralph urged him:

'Well, man, what is it? Spit it out, there's a good fellow.'

'It seems that all the telegraph lines to Rhodesia have been down since noon on Monday.'

'Oh, so that is it.'

'No, Mr Ballantyne, that's not all. There has been a message from Tati on the Rhodesian border. It seems a rider got through this morning.' The clerk gulped. 'This messenger seems to have been the only survivor.'

'Survivor!' Ralph stared at him. 'What does that mean? What on earth are you talking about?'

'The Matabele have risen. They are murdering all the whites in Rhodesia – man, woman and child, they are being slaughtered!'

'Mummy, Douglas and Suss aren't here. There is nobody to get me breakfast.' Jon-Jon came into the tent while Cathy was still brushing out her hair, and twisting it up into thick braids.

'Did you call for them?'

'I called and called.'

'Tell one of the grooms to go down and fetch them, darling.'

'The grooms aren't here also.'

'The grooms aren't here either,' Cathy corrected him and stood up. 'All right, then, let's go and see about your breakfast.'

Cathy stepped out into the dawn. Overhead the sky was a lovely dark rose colour shaded to ripe orange in the east, and the bird chorus in the trees above the camp was like the tinkle of silver bells. The camp-fire had died to a puddle of grey powdery ash and had not been replenished.

'Put some wood on, Jon-Jon,' Cathy told him and crossed to the kitchen hut. She frowned with annoyance. It was deserted. She took down a tin from the gauzed meat-safe and then looked up as the doorway darkened.

'Oh Isazi,' she greeted the little Zulu. 'Where are the other servants?'

'Who knows where a Matabele dog will hide himself when he is needed?' Isazi asked contemptuously. 'They have most likely spent the night dancing and drinking beer and now their heads are too heavy to carry.'

'You'll have to help me,' said Cathy. 'Until the cook gets here.'

After breakfast in the dining-tent, Cathy called Isazi from the fire again.

'Have any of them come back yet?'

'Not yet, Nkosikazi.'

'I want to go down to the railhead. I hope there is a telegraph from Henshaw. Will you put the ponies into the trap, Isazi.'

Then for the first time she noticed the little frown of concern on the old Zulu's wrinkled features.

'What is it?'

'The horses – they are not in the kraal.'

'Where are they then?'

'Perhaps one of the *mujiba* took them out early, I will go to find them.'

'Oh, it doesn't matter.' Cathy shook her head. 'It's only a short walk to the telegraph office. The exercise will be good for me.' And she called to Jonathan, 'Fetch my bonnet for me, Jon-Jon.'

'Nkosikazi, it is perhaps not wise, the little one—'

'Oh don't fuss,' Cathy told him fondly, and took Jonathan's hand. 'If you find the ponies in time you can come and fetch us.' Then swinging her bonnet by its ribbon and with Jonathan skipping beside her, she started along the track that led around the side of the wooded hill towards the railhead.

There was no clamour of hammers on steel. Jonathan noticed it first.

'It's so quiet, Mama.' And they stopped to listen.

'It's not Friday,' Cathy murmured. 'Mr Mac can't be paying the gangs.' She shook her head, still not alarmed. 'That's strange.' And they went on.

At the corner of the hill they stopped again, and Cathy held her bonnet up to shade her eyes from the low sun. The railway lines ran away southward, glistening like the silken threads of a spider's web, but below them they ended abruptly at the raw gash of the cut line through the bush. There was a pile of teak sleepers at the railhead and a smaller bundle of steel rails, the service locomotive was due up from Kimberley this afternoon to replenish those materials. The sledgehammers and shovels were in neat stacks where the shift had left them at dusk the night before. There was no human movement around the railhead.

'That's even stranger,' said Cathy.

'Where is Mr Henderson, Mama?' Jonathan asked. His voice was unusually subdued. 'Where are Mr Mac and Mr Braithwaite?'

'I don't know. They must still be in their tents.'

The tents of the white surveyor and the engineer and his supervisors were grouped just beyond the square galvanized iron shack of the telegraph. There was no sign of life around the hut nor between the neat pyramids of canvas, except for a single black crow which sat on the peak of one of them.

Its hoarse cawing reached them faintly, and as Cathy watched, it spread its black wings and flapped heavily to earth at the entrance of the tent.

'Where are all the hammer-boys?' Jonathan piped, and suddenly Cathy shivered.

'I don't know, darling.' Her voice cracked and she cleared her throat. 'We will go and find out.' She realized she had spoken too loudly, and Jonathan shrank against her legs.

'Mummy, I'm frightened.'

'Don't be a silly boy,' Cathy told him firmly, and dragging him by the hand, she started down the hill.

By the time she reached the telegraph hut, she was moving as fast as her big round belly would allow, and her breathing in her own ears was deafening.

'Stay here.' She did not know what prompted her to leave Jonathan at the steps of the veranda, but she went up alone to the door of the telegraph hut.

The door was ajar. She pushed it fully open.

Mr Braithwaite sat beside his table facing the doorway. He was staring at her with those pale popping eyes, and his mouth hung open.

'Mr Braithwaite,' Cathy said, and at the sound of her voice there was a hum like a swarm of bees taking flight, and the big cobalt blue flies that had covered his shirt-front rose in a cloud into the air, and Cathy saw that his belly was a gaping mushy red pit, and that his entrails hung in ropes down between his knees into a tangle on the floor under the desk.

Cathy shrank back against the door. She felt her legs turn rubbery under her and black shadows wheeled through her vision like the wings of bats at sundown. One of the metallic blue flies settled on her cheek and crawled sluggishly down towards the corner of her mouth.

Cathy leaned forward slowly and retched explosively, and her breakfast spattered on the wooden floor between her feet. She backed away slowly out of the door, shaking her head and trying to wipe the sickly sweet taste of vomit from her lips. She almost tripped on the steps, and sat down heavily. Jonathan ran to her, and clung to her arm.

'What happened, Mummy?'

'I want you to be a brave little man,' she whispered.

'Are you sick, Mummy?' The child shook her arm with agitation, and Cathy found it difficult to think.

She realized what had caused the hideous mutilation of the corpse in the hut. The Matabele always disembowelled their victims. It was a ritual that released the spirit of the dead man, and allowed it to go on to its Valhalla. To leave the belly pouch was to trap the victim's shade upon the earth and have it return to haunt the slayer.

Mr Braithwaite had been split by the razor-sharp edge of a Matabele assegai and his hot entrails had been plucked from him like those of a chicken. It was the work of a Matabele war party.

'Where is Mr Henderson, Mummy?' Jon-Jon demanded shrilly. 'I am going to his tent.'

The big burly engineer was one of Jonathan's favourite friends, and Cathy caught his arm.

'No, Jon-Jon – don't go!'

'Why not?'

The crow had screwed up its courage at last and now it hopped into the opening of the engineer's tent and disappeared. Cathy knew what had attracted it.

'Please be quiet, Jon-Jon,' Cathy pleaded. 'Let Mummy think.'

The missing servants. They had been warned, of course, as had the Matabele construction gangs. They knew that a war party was out, and they had faded away – and a horrifying thought struck Cathy. Perhaps the servants, her own people, were part of the war party. She shook her head violently. No, not them. These must be some small band of renegades, not her own people.

They would have struck at dawn, of course, for it was the

317

favourite hour. They had caught Henderson and his foreman asleep in the tents. Only the faithful little Braithwaite had been at his machine. The telegraph machine – Cathy started up – the telegraph was her one link with the outside world.

'Jon-Jon, stay here,' she ordered, and crept back towards the door of the hut.

She steeled herself, and then glanced into the interior, trying not to look at the little man in the chair. One quick glance was enough. The telegraph machine had been ripped from the wall and smashed into pieces on the floor of the hut. She reeled back and leaned against the iron wall beside the door, clutching her swollen stomach with both hands, forcing herself to think again.

The war party had struck the railhead and then disappeared back into the forest – and then she remembered the missing servants. The camp, they had not disappeared, they would be circling up through the trees towards the camp. She looked around her desperately, expecting at any moment to see the silent black files of plumed warriors come padding out of the thick bush.

The Service train from Kimberley was due late that afternoon, ten hours from now, and she was alone, except for Jonathan. Cathy sank down on her knees, reached for him and clung to him with the strength of despair, and only then realized that the boy was staring through the open doorway.

'Mr Braithwaite is dead!' Jonathan said matter-of-factly. Forcibly, she turned his head away. 'They are going to kill us too, aren't they, Mummy?'

'Oh Jon-Jon!'

'We need a gun. I can shoot. Papa taught me.'

A gun – Cathy looked towards the silent tents. She did not think she had the courage to go into one of them, not even to find a weapon. She knew what carnage to expect there.

A shadow fell over her and she screamed.

'Nkosikazi. It is me.'

Isazi had come down the hill as silently as a panther.

'The horses are gone,' he said, and she motioned him to look into the telegraph hut.

Isazi's expression did not change.

'So,' he said quietly, 'the Matabele jackals can still bite.'

'The tents,' Cathy whispered. 'See if you can find a weapon.'

Isazi went with the lithe swinging run of a man half his age, ducking from one tent-opening to another, and when he came back to her, he carried an assegai with a broken shaft.

'The big one fought well. He was still alive, with his guts torn out of him and the crows were eating them. He could no longer speak, but he looked at me. I have given him peace. But there are no guns – the Matabele have taken them.'

'There are guns at the camp,' Cathy whispered.

'Come, Nkosikazi,' he lifted her tenderly to her feet and Jonathan manfully took her other arm, though he did not reach to her armpit.

The first pain hit Cathy before they reached the thick bush at the edge of the cut line, and it doubled her over. They held her while the paroxysm lasted, Jonathan not understanding what was happening, but the little Zulu was grave and silent.

'All right.' Cathy straightened up at last, and tried to wipe the long tendrils of her hair off her face, but they were plastered there by her own sweat.

They went up on the track at Cathy's pace. Isazi was watching the forest on both sides for the dark movement of warriors, and he carried the broken assegai in his free hand with an underhand stabbing grip.

Cathy gasped and staggered as the next pain caught her.

319

This time they could not hold her and she went down on her knees in the dust. When it passed, she looked up at Isazi.

'They are too close together. It is happening.'

He did not have to reply.

'Take Jonathan to the Harkness Mine.'

'Nkosikazi, the train—'

'The train will be too late. You must go.'

'Nkosikazi – you, what will become of you?'

'Without a horse, I could never reach the Harkness. It is almost thirty miles. Every moment you waste now wastes the boy's life.'

He did not move.

'If you can save him, Isazi, then you save part of me. If you stay here, we will all die. Go. Go quickly!' she urged.

Isazi reached for Jonathan's hand, but he jerked away.

'I won't leave my mummy.' His voice rose hysterically. 'My daddy said I must look after my mummy.'

Cathy gathered herself. It took all her determination to perform the most difficult task of her young life. She hit Jonathan open-handed across the face, back and forth, with all her strength. The child staggered away from her. The vivid crimson outlines of her fingers rising on the pale skin of his cheeks. She had never struck his face before.

'Do as I tell you,' Cathy blazed at him furiously. 'Go with Isazi this very instant.'

The Zulu snatched up the child, and looked down at her for a moment longer.

'You have the heart of a lioness. I salute you, Nkosikazi.' And he went bounding away into the forest, carrying Jonathan with him. In seconds he had disappeared and then only did she let the sobs come shaking and choking up her throat.

She thought then that being entirely alone is the hardest thing in life to bear. She thought of Ralph, and she had never loved nor wanted him the way she did at that moment. It seemed for a time that she had used the last grain of her courage to strike her only child, and to send him away for a faint chance of salvation. She would be content to stay here, kneeling in the dust in the early sunlight until they came for her with the cruel steel.

Then from somewhere deep within her she found the strength to rise and hobble on up the path. At the heel of the hill, she looked down at the camp. It looked so quiet and orderly. Her home. The smoke from the camp-fire rose like a pale grey feather into the still morning air, so welcoming, so safe; illogically she felt that if she could only reach her tent then it would be all right.

She started and she had not gone a dozen paces, before she felt something burst deep within her, and then the abrupt hot rush down the inside of her legs as her waters broke and poured from her. She struggled on, hampered by her sodden skirts, and then, unbelievably, she had reached her own tent.

It was so cool and dark within, like a church, she thought, and again her legs gave way beneath her. She crawled painfully across the floor, and her hair came tumbling down and blinded her. She groped her way to the wagon chest set at the foot of the big camp cot, and threw the hair out of her eyes as she rested against it.

The lid was so heavy that it took all her strength, but at last it fell open with a crash. The pistol was tucked under the crocheted white bedcovers, that she had hoarded for the home that Ralph would one day build for her. It was a big service Webley revolver. She had only fired it once, with Ralph steadying her from behind, holding her wrists against the recoil.

Now it needed both her hands to lift it out of the chest. She was too tired to climb onto the cot. She sat with her back against the chest, both her legs straight out in front of her flat against the floor, and she held the pistol with both hands in her lap.

She must have dozed, for when she started awake, it was to hear the whisper of feet against the bare earth. She looked up. There was the shadow of a man silhouetted by the slanting rays of the sun against the white canvas of the tent like a figure in a magic lantern show. She lifted the pistol and aimed at the entrance. The ugly black weapon wavered uncertainly in her grip, and a man stepped through the flap.

'Oh, thank God.' Cathy let the pistol fall into her lap. 'Oh thank God, it's you,' she whispered and let her head fall forward. The thick curtain of her hair fell open, splitting down the back of her head, exposing the pale skin at the tender nape of her neck. Bazo looked down at it. He saw a soft pulse throbbing beneath the skin.

Bazo wore only a kilt of civet-tails, and about his forehead a band of mole-skin – no feathers nor tassels. His feet were bare. In his left hand he held a broad stabbing assegai. In his right he carried a knobkerrie like the mace of a medieval knight. The handle was of polished rhinoceros horn, three feet long, and the head was a ball of heavy leadwood studded with hand-forged nails of native iron.

When he swung the knobkerrie, all the strength of his wide shoulders was behind the blow, and his point of aim was the pulse in the pale nape of Cathy's neck.

Two of his warriors came into the tent and flanked Bazo, their eyes were still glazed with the killing madness. They also wore the mole-skin headbands, and they looked down at the crumpled body on the floor of the tent. One of the warriors changed his grip on the assegai, ready for the cutting stroke.

'The woman's spirit must fly,' he said.

'Do it!' Bazo said, and the warrior stooped and worked quickly, expertly.

'There is life within her,' he said. 'See! It moves yet.'

'Still it!' Bazo ordered, and left the tent, striding out into the sunlight.

'Find the boy,' he ordered his men who waited there. 'Find the white cub.'

The driver of the locomotive was terrified. They had stopped for a few minutes at the trading-post beside the tracks at Plumtree siding, and he had seen the bodies of the storekeeper and his family lying in the front yard.

Ralph Ballantyne thrust the muzzle of the rifle between his shoulder-blades, and marched him back to the cab, forcing him to go on northwards, deeper and deeper into Matabeleland.

They had come all the way from the Kimberley shunting-yards with the loco throttle wide open, and Ralph had spelled the stoker on the footplate, shovelling the lumpy black coal into the firebox with a monotonous rhythm, bare-chested and sweating in the furnace glare, the coal dust blackening his face and arms like those of a chimney-sweep, his palms wet and raw from the burst blisters.

They had clipped almost two hours off the record run to the railhead. As they came roaring around the bend between the hills and saw the iron roof of the telegraph shack, Ralph hurled the shovel aside and clambered onto the side of the cab to peer ahead.

His heart leaped joyfully against his ribs, there was movement around the hut and between the tents, there was life here! Then his heart dropped as swiftly as it had risen, as he recognized the skulking dog-like shapes.

The hyena were so intent on squabbling over the things they had dragged out of the tents, that they were totally unafraid. It was only when Ralph started shooting that they scattered. He knocked down half a dozen of the loathsome beasts before the rifle was empty. He ran from the hut to each tent in turn, and then back to the locomotive. Neither the driver nor the fireman had left the cab.

'Mr Ballantyne, these murdering bloody 'eathen will be back at any minute—'

'Wait!' Ralph shouted at him, and scrambled up the side of the cattle-truck behind the coal buggy. He knocked out the locking-pins and the door came crashing down to form a drawbridge.

Ralph led the horses out of the truck. There were four of them, one already saddled, the best mounts he had been able to find. He paused only long enough to clinch the girth, and then swung up into the saddle with the rifle still in his hand.

'I'm not going to wait here,' the driver yelled. 'Christ Almighty, those niggers are animals, man, animals.'

'If my wife and son are here, I'll need to get them back. Give me one hour,' Ralph asked.

'I'm not waiting another minute. I'm going back.' The driver shook his head.

'You can go to hell then,' Ralph told him coldly.

He kicked his horse into a gallop, and dragging the spare mounts on the lead-rein behind him, took the track up the side of the kopje towards the camp.

As he rode, he thought once more that perhaps he should have listened to Aaron Fagan, perhaps he should have recruited a dozen other horsemen in Kimberley to go with him. But he knew that he would never have been able to abide the few hours that he would have needed to find good men. As it was, he had left Kimberley less than half an hour after he had received the telegraph from Tati – just long enough to fetch his Winchester, fill the saddlebags with ammunition, and take the horses from Aaron's stables to the shunting-yard.

Before he turned the angle of the hill, he glanced back over his shoulder. The locomotive was already huffing back along the curve of the rails towards the south. Now, as far as he knew, he might be the only white man left alive in Matabeleland.

Ralph galloped into the camp. They had been there already. The camp had been looted, Jonathan's tent had collapsed, his clothing was scattered and trampled into the dust.

'Cathy,' Ralph shouted, as he dismounted. 'Jon-Jon! Where are you?'

Paper rustled under his feet and Ralph looked down. Cathy's portfolio of drawings had been thrown down and had burst open, the paintings of which she was so proud were torn and crumpled. Ralph picked up one of them, it was of the lovely dark scarlet trumpet flowers of *Kigelia africana*, the African sausage tree. He tried to smooth out the rumpled sheet, and then realized the futility of that gesture.

He ran on to their living-tent, and ripped open the flap.

Cathy lay on her back with her unborn child beside her. She had promised Ralph a daughter – and she had kept her promise.

He fell on his knees beside her, and tried to lift her head, but her body had set into an awful rigidity, she was stiff as a carven statue in marble. As he lifted her, he saw the great cup-shaped depression in the back of her skull.

Ralph backed away, and then flung himself out of the tent.

'Jonathan,' he screamed. 'Jon-Jon! Where are you?'

He ran through the camp like a madman.

'Jonathan! Please, Jonathan!'

When he found no living thing, he stumbled into the forest up onto the slope of the kopje.

'Jonathan! It's Daddy. Where are you, my darling?'

Dimly in his anguish he realized that his cries might bring the *amadoda*, as the bleat of the goat brings the leopard, and suddenly he wanted that to happen with all his soul.

'Come!' he yelled into the silent forest. 'Come on. Come and find me also!' And he stopped to fire the Winchester into the air, and listen to the echoes go bounding away down the valley.

At last he could run and scream no more, and he came up panting against the bole of one of the forest trees.

'Jonathan,' he croaked. 'Where are you, my baby?'

Slowly he turned down and went down the hill. He moved like a very old man.

At the edge of the camp, he stopped and peered short-sightedly at something that lay in the grass, then he stopped and picked it up. He turned it over and over in his hands, and then balled it into his fist. His knuckles turned white with the strength of his grip. What he held was a headband of softly tanned mole-skin.

Still holding the scrap of fur in his hand, he went into the camp to prepare his dead for burial.

Robyn St John woke to the soft scratching on the shutter of her bedroom, and she raised herself on one elbow.

'Who is it?' she called.

'It is me, Nomusa.'

'Juba, my little Dove, I did not expect you!'

Robyn slipped out of bed and crossed to the window. When she opened the shutter, the night was opalescent with moonlight, and Juba was huddled below the sill.

'You are so cold.' Robyn took her arm. 'You'll catch your death. Come inside immediately. I'll fetch a blanket.'

'Nomusa, wait.' Juba caught her wrist. 'I must go.'

'But you have only just arrived.'

'Nobody must know that I was here, please tell nobody, Nomusa.'

'What is it? You are shaking—'

'Listen, Nomusa. I could not leave you – you are my mother and sister and friend, I could not leave you.'

'Juba—'

'Do not speak. Listen for a minute,' Juba pleaded. 'I have so little time.'

It was only then that Robyn realized that it was not the chill of night that shook Juba's vast frame. She was racked with sobs of fear and of dread.

'You must go, Nomusa. You and Elizabeth and the baby. Take nothing with you, leave this very minute. Go into Bulawayo, perhaps you will be safe there. It is your best chance.'

'I don't understand you, Juba. What nonsense is this?'

'They are coming Nomusa. They are coming. Please hurry.'

Then she was gone. She moved swiftly and silently for such a big woman, and she seemed to melt into the moon shadows under the spathodea trees. By the time Robyn had found her shawl and run down the veranda, there was no sign of her.

Robyn hurried down towards the hospital bungalows, stumbling once on the verge of the path, calling with increasing exasperation.

'Juba, come back here! Do you hear me? I won't stand any more of this nonsense!'

She stopped at the church, uncertain which path to take.

'Juba! Where are you?'

The silence was broken only by the yipping of a jackal up on the hillside above the Mission. It was answered by another on the peak of the pass where the road to Bulawayo crossed the hills.

'Juba!'

The watch-fire by the hospital bungalow had burned out. She crossed to it, and threw on to it a log from the woodpile. The silence was unnatural. The log caught and flared. In its light she climbed the steps of the nearest bungalow.

The sleeping-mats of the patients were in two rows, facing each other down each wall, but they were deserted. Even the most desperately ill had gone. They must have been carried away, for some of them had been past walking.

Robyn hugged the shawl around her shoulders. 'Poor ignorant heathen,' she said aloud. 'Another witchcraft scare, they will run from their own shadows.'

She turned sorrowfully away, and walked through the darkness back towards the house. There was a light burning in Elizabeth's room, and as Robyn climbed the steps of the veranda, the door opened.

'Mama! Is that you?'

'What are you doing, Elizabeth?'

'I thought I heard voices.'

Robyn hesitated, she did not want to alarm Elizabeth, but then she was a sensible child, and unlikely to go into hysteria over a bit of Matabele superstition.

'Juba was here. There must be another witchcraft scare. She ran off again.'

'What did she say?'

'Oh, just that we should go in to Bulawayo to escape some sort of danger.'

Elizabeth came out onto the veranda in her nightdress, carrying the candle.

'Juba is a Christian, she doesn't dabble in witchcraft.' Elizabeth's tone was concerned. 'What else did she say?'

'Just that,' Robyn yawned. 'I'm going back to bed.' She started along the veranda, and then stopped. 'Oh, the others have all run off. The hospital is empty. It's most annoying.'

'Mama, I think we should do as Juba says.'

'What do you mean by that?'

'I think we should go in to Bulawayo immediately.'

'Elizabeth, I thought better of you.'

'I have an awful feeling. I think we should go. Perhaps there is real danger.'

'This is my home. Your father and I built it with our own

hands. There is no power on earth that will force me to leave it,' Robyn said firmly. 'Now go back to bed. With no help, we are going to have a busy day tomorrow.'

They squatted in long silent ranks in the long grass below the crest of the hills. Gandang moved quietly down the ranks, stopping occasionally to exchange a word with an old comrade in arms. To revive a memory of another waiting before a battle of long ago.

It was strange to sit upon the bare earth during the waiting time. In the old days they would have sat on their shields, the long dappled shields of iron-hard oxhide, squatting upon them not for comfort but to hide their distinctive shape from a watchful enemy until the moment came to strike terror into his belly and steel into his heart; squatting upon them also to prevent some young buck in the throes of the divine madness from prematurely drumming upon the rawhide with his assegai and giving warning of the waiting impi.

It was strange also not to be decked out in the full regimentals of the Inyati impi, the plumes and furs and tassels of cow-tails, the war rattles at ankle and wrist, the tall headdress that turned a man into a giant. They were dressed like neophytes, like unblooded boys, with only their kilts about their waists, but the scars upon their dark bodies and the fire in their eyes gave the lie to that impression.

Gandang felt himself choking with a pride that he once thought he would never experience again. He loved them, he loved their fierceness and their valour, and though his face was quiet and expressionless, the love shone through in his eyes.

They picked it up and gave it back to him a hundred times. 'Baba!' they called him in their soft deep voices. 'Father, we thought we would never fight at your shoulder again,' they said. 'Father, those of your sons who die today will be forever young.'

Across the neck of the hills a jackal wailed mournfully and was answered from close at hand. The impi was in position, lying across the Khami hills like a coiled mamba, waiting and watchful and ready.

There was a glow in the sky now. The false dawn, that would be followed by the deeper darkness before the true dawn. The deep darkness that the *amadoda* loved and used so well.

They stirred quietly, and grounded the shaft of assegai between their heels, ready for the order: 'Up my children. It is the time of the spears.'

This time the order did not come, and the true dawn flushed the sky with blood. In its light the *amadoda* looked at each other.

One of the senior warriors, who had won Gandang's respect on fifty battlefields, spoke for all of them. He went to where Gandang sat alone to one side of the impi.

'Baba, your children are confused. Tell us why we wait.'

'Old friend, are your spears so thirsty for the blood of women and babes, that they cannot wait for richer fare?'

'We can wait as long as you command it, Baba. But it is hard.'

'Old friend, I am baiting for a leopard with a tender goat,' Gandang told him, and let his chin sink back on the great muscles of his chest.

The sun pushed up and gilded the tree-tops along the hills, and still Gandang did not move, and the silent ranks waited behind him in the grass.

A young warrior whispered to another. 'Already the storm has begun. Everywhere else our brethren are busy. They will mock us when they hear how we sat on the hilltop—'

One of the older men hissed a rebuke at him, and the young warrior fell silent, but further down the ranks another youngster shifted on his haunches and his assegai tapped against that of his neighbour. Gandang did not raise his head.

Then from the hilltop a wild francolin called. 'Qwaali! Qwaali!' The sharp penetrating cry was a characteristic sound of the veld, only a sharp ear would have detected anything strange about this one.

Gandang rose to his feet. 'The leopard comes,' he said quietly, and stalked up to the vantage point from which he could look down the full length of road that led to the town of Bulawayo. The sentry who had sounded the call of the wild pheasant pointed wordlessly with the hilt of his assegai.

There was an open coach and a troop of horsemen upon the road. Gandang counted them, eleven riding hard, coming directly out towards the Khami hills. The figure that led them was unmistakable, even at this distance. The height in the saddle, the alert set of head, the long stirrups.

'Hau! One-Bright-Eye!' Gandang greeted him softly. 'I have waited many long moons for you.'

General Mungo St John had been awakened in the middle of the night. In his nightshirt he had listened to the hysterical outpourings of a coloured servant who had escaped from the trading-store on the Ten-Mile Drift. It was a wild tale of slaughter and burning, and the man's breath smelled of good Cape brandy.

'He's drunk,' said Mungo St John flatly. 'Take him away, and give him a good thrashing.'

The first white man got into town three hours before dawn. He had been stabbed through the thigh and his left arm was broken in two places by blows from a knobkerrie. He was clinging to his horse's neck with his good arm.

'The Matabele are out!' he screamed. 'They are burning the farms—' and he slid out of the saddle in a dead faint.

331

By first light there were fifty wagons formed into a laager in the market square; without oxen to draw them, they had been manhandled into position. All the town's women and children had been brought into the laager and put to work making bandages, reloading ammunition, and baking hard bread against a siege. The few able-bodied men that Doctor Jameson had not taken with him into captivity in the Transvaal were swiftly formed into troops, and horses and rifles were found for those who lacked them.

In the midst of the bustle and confusion, Mungo St John had commandeered a fast open coach with a coloured driver, picked out the most likely and best mounted troop of horsemen, and using his authority as acting Administrator given them the order.

'Follow me!'

Now he reined in on the crest of the hills above Khami Mission, at the point where the track was narrowest and the tall yellow grass and the forest hemmed it in like a wall on each side, and he shaded his single eye.

'Thank God!' he whispered. The thatched roofs of the Mission that he expected to see billowing with smoke and flame stood serenely in the quiet green valley beyond.

The horses were sweating and blowing from the pull up the hills, and the coach had lagged two hundred paces behind Mungo. As soon as it came up, without giving a moment's rest to the mules, Mungo shouted, 'Troop, forward!' and spurred away down the track, with his troopers clattering behind him.

Robyn St John came out of the thatched rondavel that was her laboratory, and as soon as she recognized the man that led the column, she placed her hands upon her boyish hips and lifted her chin angrily.

'What is the meaning of this intrusion, sir?' she demanded.

'Madam, the Matabele tribe is in full rebellion. They are murdering women and children, burning the homesteads.'

Robyn took a step backwards protectively, for Robert had come pale-faced from the clinic to hang onto her skirts.

'I have come to take you and your children to safety.'

'The Matabele are my friends,' said Robyn. 'I have nothing to fear from them. This is my home. I do not intend leaving it.'

'I do not have time to indulge your predilection for obstructive disputation, madam,' he said grimly, and stood in the stirrups.

'Elizabeth!' he bellowed, and she came onto the veranda of the homestead. 'The Matabele are in revolt. We are all in mortal danger. You have two minutes to gather what personal items your family may need—'

'Take no heed of him, Elizabeth,' Robyn shouted angrily. 'We are staying here.'

Before she realized his intention, Mungo had pricked his horse with a spur, backing it up towards the laboratory doorway; then he stooped from the saddle and caught Robyn about the waist. He swung her up over the pommel of the saddle, with her backside in the air and her skirts around her hips. She kicked and yelled with outrage, but he walked his horse alongside the open coach and with a heave of his shoulder dumped her in another flurry of petticoats onto the back seat.

'If you do not stay there, madam, I will not hesitate to have you bound. It will be most undignified.'

'I will never forgive you for this!' she panted through white lips, but she could see he meant the threat seriously.

'Robert,' Mungo St John ordered his son, 'go to your mother. Immediately!'

The child scampered to the coach and climbed into it.

'Elizabeth!' Mungo St John bellowed again. 'Hurry, girl. All our lives depend on haste now.'

Elizabeth ran out onto the veranda with a bundle over her shoulder.

'Good girl!' Mungo St John smiled at her. So pretty and

brave and level-headed, she had always been one of his favourites. He jumped down to boost her into the coach, and then vaulted back into the saddle.

'Troop, Walk. March! Trot!' he ordered, and they wheeled out of the yard.

The coach was in the rear of the column. The ten troopers in double ranks ahead of it, and five lengths out in front of them again rode Mungo St John. Despite herself, Elizabeth was thrilled and deliciously fearful. It was all so different from the quiet monotonous round of life at Khami Mission, the armed men, the urgency and tension in each of them, the dark threat of the unknown surrounding them, the romance of the faithful husband riding through the valley of the shadow of death to save his beloved woman. How noble and dashing he looked at the head of the column, how easily he sat his horse, and when he turned to look back at the coach, how reckless was his smile – there was only one other man in all the world to match him. If only it had been Ralph Ballantyne come to save her alone! The thought was sinful, and she put it away quickly, and to distract herself looked back down the hill.

'Oh, Mama!' she cried, jumping up in the swaying coach, pointing wildly. 'Look!'

The Mission was burning. The thatch of the church stood in a tall beacon of leaping flame. Smoke was curling out of the homestead, and as they stared in horror, they saw tiny dark human figures running down the pathway under the spathodea trees, carrying torches of dry grass. One of them stopped to hurl his torch onto the roof of the clinic.

'My books,' whispered Robyn. 'All my papers. My life's work.'

'Don't look, Mama.' Elizabeth sank down beside her on the seat, and they clung to each other like lost children.

The little column reached the crest of the pass; without a pause the weary horses plunged down the far side – and the Matabele came simultaneously from both sides of the

334

track. They rose out of the grass in two black waves, and the humming roar of their war chant swelled like the sound of an avalanche gathering momentum down a steep mountainside.

The troopers had been riding with their carbines cocked, the butts resting on their right thighs, but so swift was the rush of Matabele that only a single volley rippled down the column. It made no impression upon the black wave of humanity, and then as the horses reared and whinnied with terror, the troopers were dragged from their saddles, and stabbed through and through, ten and twenty times. The warriors were mad with blood lust. They swarmed over the bodies, snarling and howling, like the hounds tearing the carcass of the fox.

A huge sweat-shining warrior seized the coloured driver by the leg, and plucked him off the driver's seat of the coach, and while he was still in the air another warrior transfixed him on the broad silver blade of an assegai.

Only Mungo St John, five lengths ahead of the column, broke clear. He had taken a single assegai-thrust through the side, and the blood streamed down one leg of his breeches, down his riding-boot and dripped from the heel.

He still sat high in the saddle, and he looked back over his shoulder. He looked over the heads of the Matabele straight into Robyn's eyes. It was only for an instant, and then he had wheeled his horse, and he drove back into the mass of black warriors, riding for the coach. He fired his service pistol into the face of a warrior who leaped to catch his horse's head, but from the other side another Matabele stabbed upwards overhanded, deeply into his armpit. Mungo St John grunted and spurred onwards.

'I'm here!' he shouted to Robyn. 'Don't worry, my darling—' and a warrior stabbed him through the belly. He doubled over. His horse went down, sharp steel driven through its heart, and it seemed that it was all over, but miraculously Mungo St John rose to his feet and stood foursquare with the pistol in his hand. His eye-patch had been torn from his head, and the empty eye-socket glared so demoniacally, that for a moment the warriors fell back and he stood in their midst with the terrible spear wounds in his chest and belly running red.

Gandang stepped out of the press, and a silence fell upon them all. The two men stood face to face for a long second, Mungo tried to lift the pistol, but his strength failed him, and then Gandang drove the silver blade through the centre of Mungo St John's chest and it shot a hand's span out of his back.

Gandang stood over the body and placed one foot upon Mungo St John's chest and pulled the blade free. It made a sucking sound like a boot in thick mud. It was the only sound, and after it was silence. The silence was even more terrible than the war chant and the screams of dying men.

The dense press of black bodies hemmed in the coach, and hid the corpses of the dead troopers. The *amadoda* formed a ring around where Mungo St John lay upon his back, his features still twisted into a grimace of rage and agony. His one eye glaring at the enemy he could no longer see.

One at a time the warriors lifted their heads and stared at the huddle of women and a child in the open body of the coach. The very air was charged with menace, their eyes were glazed with the killing madness, and blood still splattered their arms and chests and speckled their faces like a macabre war paint. The ranks swayed like prairie grass touched by a little breeze. In the rear a single voice began to hum, but before it could spread, Robyn St John rose to her feet and from the height of the coach looked down upon them. The hum died out into silence.

Robyn reached forward and picked up the reins. The Matabele watched her and still not one of them moved. Robyn flicked the reins, and the mules started forward at a walk.

Gandang, son of Mzilikazi, senior induna of the Matabele, stepped off the track, and behind him the ranks of his *amadoda* opened. The mules passed slowly down the lane between them, stepping daintily over the mutilated corpses of the troopers. Robyn stared straight ahead, holding the reins stiffly. Just once as she drew level with where Mungo St John lay, she glanced down at him, and then looked ahead again.

Slowly, the coach rolled on down the hill, and when Elizabeth looked back again, the road was deserted.

'They have gone, Mama,' she whispered, and only then did she realize that Robyn was shaking with silent sobs.

Elizabeth put her arm around her shoulders, and for a moment Robyn leaned against her.

'He was a terrible man, but, oh God forgive me, I loved him so,' she whispered, and then she straightened up and urged the mules into a trot towards Bulawayo.

Ralph Ballantyne rode through the night, taking the difficult and direct path through the hills rather than the broad wagon road. The spare horses were loaded with food and blankets that he had salvaged from the railhead camp. He led them at a walk over the rocky terrain, husbanding them for whatever efforts lay ahead of them.

He rode with his rifle across his lap, loaded and cocked. Every half hour or so, he halted his horse and fired three spaced rifle shots into the starry sky. Three shots, the universal recall signal. When the echoes had muttered and rumbled away down the hills, he listened carefully, twisting slowly in the saddle to cover every direction, and then he called, yelling his despair into the silences of the wilderness.

'Jonathan! Jonathan!'

Again he rode on slowly through the darkness, and when

the dawn came he watered the horses at a stream and let them graze for a few hours, sitting on an antheap to guard them, munching biscuit and bully, and listening.

It was strange how many of the sounds of the bush could seem like the cries of a human child to someone who listened wishfully. The mournful 'quay' of a grey lourie brought Ralph to his feet with his heart hammering, the screech of a meercat, even the wail of the wind in the tree-tops disturbed him.

In mid-morning he up-saddled and rode again. He knew that in daylight there was greater danger of running into a Matabele patrol, but the prospect had no terrors. He found himself welcoming it. Deep inside him was a cold dark area, a place that he had never visited before, and now as he rode on, he explored it and found there such hatred and anger as he had never believed was possible. Riding slowly through the lovely forests in the clean white sunshine, he discovered that he was a stranger to himself; until this day he had never known what he was, but now he was beginning to find out.

He reined in his horse on the crest of a high bare ridge, where watching Matabele eyes could have seen him from afar silhouetted against the blue, and deliberately he fired another three single shots. When no file of running warriors came to the summons, his hatred and anger were stronger still.

An hour after noon, he climbed the ridge of the ancients where Zouga had killed the great elephant and looked down onto the Harkness Mine.

The buildings had been burned. On the far ridge the walls that Harry Mellow had built for Vicky were still standing, but the empty windows were like the eyes of a skull. The roof beams were stark and blackened, some of them collapsed beneath the weight of charred thatch. The gardens were trampled, and the lawns were strewn with the debris of two young lives – the brass bedstead with stuffing bursting out of the torn mattress, the chests of Vicky's dowry broken open and the contents scorched and scattered.

Further down the valley the mine store and office had been burned also. The stacks of blackened goods still smouldered, and there was the stink of burning rubber and leather on the air. There was another smell mingled with it, a smell like greasy pork cooking, the first time Ralph had smelled human flesh roasting, but instinctively he knew what it was, and he felt his stomach heave.

In the trees about the burned-out buildings roosted the hunch-backed vultures. There were hundreds of these disgusting birds, from the big black vultures with their bald red heads to the dirty brown birds with obscene woollen caps covering their long necks. Amongst the vultures were the carrion storks, the raucous crows and the little wheeling black kites. It must be a rich banquet to attract such a gathering.

Ralph rode down off the crest and almost immediately found the first bodies. Matabele warriors, he saw with grim satisfaction, they had crawled away to die of their wounds. Harry Mellow had held out better than the construction gang at the railhead.

'That he should have taken a thousand of the black butchers with him,' Ralph hoped aloud, and rode on cautiously with his rifle at the ready.

He dismounted behind the ruins of the mine store and tethered the horses with a slippery hitch, ready for a quick run. Here there were more dead Matabele, lying amid their own broken and discarded weapons. The ash was still hot, and three or four corpses lay within the shell of the store. They had been burned to unrecognizable black mounds, and the smell of pork was overpowering.

Holding his rifle at high port, Ralph stepped carefully through the ash and debris towards the corner of the building. The squawk and flap of the vultures and the scavengers covered any small sounds he might make, and he was ready to meet the sudden charge of warriors that might be lying in ambush for him. He steeled himself also to the discovery of the corpses of Harry and pretty blonde little Vicky. Burying his own mutilated loved ones had not hardened him to the horror of what he knew he would find here.

He reached the corner of the building, removed his hat and carefully peeked around the wall.

There were two hundred yards of open ground between the burned-out store and the open mouth of the No. 1 adit shaft that Harry had driven into the side of the hill. The open ground was heaped with dead warriors. There were piles and skeins of them, drifts and windrows of them. Some were twisted into agonized sculptures of black limbs and some of them lay singly, as though resting, curled into the foetal position. Most of them had been ripped and gnawed by the birds and the jackals, but others were untouched.

This killing ground gave Ralph a bitter feeling of pleasure.

'Good for you, Harry my boy,' he whispered.

Ralph was about to step into the open, when his eardrums cracked with the brutal disruption of passing shot, so close that he felt his own hair flap against his forehead. He reeled back behind the shelter of the wall, shaking his head to clear the insect humming in his ears. That bullet must have missed by an inch or less, good shooting for a Matabele sniper. They were notoriously poor marksmen.

He had been careless. The piles of dead warriors had distracted him, he had presumed that the impi had finished its bloody business and gone on, a stupid presumption.

He crouched low and ran back down the length of the burned building, sweeping his open flank with an eye sharpened by the hot rush of adrenalin through his veins. The Matabele loved the encircling movement: if they were

340

out front, then they would soon be in his rear, up there amongst the trees.

He reached the horses, slipped the tether and led them over the hot ash into the shelter of the walls. From the saddlebag he took a fresh bandolier of ammunition and slung it over his other shoulder, criss-crossing his chest like a Mexican bandit, and muttering to himself.

'All right, you black bastards, let's burn some powder.'

One corner of the stone wall had collapsed where the unbaked Kimberley brick had not been able to withstand the heat. The opening was jagged, it would break the silhouette of his head and the rear wall would prevent back lighting. Carefully he peered out over the bloody ground. They were well concealed, probably in the bush above the mine shaft.

Then with a start of surprise he realized that the mouth of the adit shaft had been barricaded, it was blocked with baulks of timber and what looked like sacks of maize.

They were in the mineshaft – but that didn't make sense, he puzzled. Yet it was confirmed immediately. There was a vague shadowy movement beyond the barricade in the throat of the shaft, and another bullet sang off the lip of the wall under Ralph's nose, blinding him with brick dust.

He ducked down, and wiped his swimming eyes. Then he filled his lungs and bellowed.

'Harry! Harry Mellow!'

There was silence, even the vultures and the jackals quieted by the shocking burst of gunfire.

'Harry – it's me, Ralph.'

There was a faint answering shout, and Ralph jumped up, vaulted over the broken wall and ran towards the shaft. Harry Mellow was racing towards him, jumping over the piles of dead Matabele, a wide grin on his face. They met halfway, and embraced with the violence of relief, wordlessly pounding each other's backs, and then before he could speak, Ralph looked over the big American's shoulder.

Other figures had emerged from behind the rude barricade. Vicky dressed in men's breeches and shirt, with a rifle in her hand and coppery hair tangled around her shoulders. At her side Isazi, the diminutive Zulu driver, and another even smaller figure ran ahead of them both. The child ran with both arms pumping, and face screwed up.

Ralph caught him up and hugged him to his chest, pressing his haggard unshaven cheek against the boy's velvet skin.

'Jonathan,' he croaked, and then his voice failed. The feel of the child's warm little body, and the milky puppy smell of his sweat was almost too painful to be borne.

'Daddy.' Jon-Jon pulled back his head, and his face was pale and stricken.

'I couldn't look after Mummy. She wouldn't let me.'

'That's all right, Jon-Jon,' Ralph whispered. 'You did your best—'

And then he was crying. The terrible dry hacking sobs of a man driven to the far frontiers of his love.

Though he hated to let the child out of his arms for a moment, Ralph sent Jonathan to help Isazi feed the horses at the entrance to the shaft. Then he drew Vicky and Harry Mellow aside and in the gloom of the tunnel where they could not see his face, he told them simply:

'Cathy is dead.'

'How?' Harry broke the stunned silence. 'How did she die?'

'Badly,' Ralph told them. 'Very badly. I don't want to say any more.'

Harry held Vicky while she wept and when her first sharp grief was over, Ralph went on, 'We can't stay here. We have a choice, the railhead or Bulawayo.'

'Bulawayo may be burned and sacked by now,' Harry pointed out.

'And there may be an impi between here and the railhead,' said Ralph. 'But if Vicky wants to try and reach the railhead, we can send her and Jon-Jon south on the first train that gets through.'

'Then?' Harry asked. 'What then?'

'Then I am riding to Bulawayo. If they are still alive, then they'll want fighting men to stay that way.'

'Vicky?' Harry hugged his wife.

'My mother and my family are at Bulawayo. This is the land of my birth – I'm not running away.' She wiped the wetness off her cheeks with her thumbs. 'I'm coming with you to Bulawayo.'

Ralph nodded. He would have been surprised if she had agreed to go south.

'We will ride as soon as we have eaten.'

They took the wagon road northwards and it was a dismal route. The derelict wagons abandoned during the rinderpest were as regular as milestones. The wagon canvas was already rotted to tatters, the cargoes looted, and scattered on the grass, shattered cases and broken boxes and rusting tins. In the traces of some of the wagons the mummified remains of the oxen lay where they had fallen, heads twisted back in the convulsions that had killed them.

Then at intervals they came upon death and destruction that was fresher and more poignant. One of the Zeederbergs' express coaches in the middle of the track, with the mules speared to death and, festooned from the branches of a thorn-tree, the disembowelled bodies of the driver and his passengers.

At the drift of the Inyati river the blackened walls of the trading-post was all that were left standing. Here there was a macabre twist to the usual mutilation of the dead. The naked bodies of the Greek shopkeeper's wife and her three daughters had been laid in a neat row in the front yard with the shafts of the knobkerries thrust up into their private parts. The shopkeeper himself had been beheaded, and his trunk thrown onto the fire. His head, fixed on an assegai, leered at them in the centre of the road. Ralph covered Jon-Jon's face with his coat, and held him close as they rode past.

Ralph sent Isazi ahead to scout the drift and he found it defended. Ralph closed up the little party and they took it at a gallop, catching the dozen or so Matebele *amadoda* by surprise, shooting four of them down as they ran to their weapons, and thundering up the far bank together in the dust and gunsmoke. They were not followed, though Ralph, hoping they might be, turned back and lay in ambush beside the road.

Ralph held Jonathan in his lap during the night, starting awake every few minutes from nightmares in which Cathy screamed and pleaded for mercy. In the dawn he found that without realizing it, he had taken the mole-skin headband from his jacket and held it balled in his fist. He put it back in his pocket and buttoned the flap, as though it was something rare and precious.

They rode on northwards all that day, past the little one-man gold mines and the homesteads where men and their families had begun to carve a life out of the wilderness. Some of them had been taken completely by surprise. They were still clad in the remnants of their night-clothes. One little boy even clutched his teddy bear while his dead mother reached out to him with fingers that did not quite touch his sodden curls.

Others had sold their lives dearly, and the dead Matabele were flung like woodchips from a sawmill in a wide circle around the burned-out homesteads. Once they found dead *amadoda* but no white bodies. There were tracks of horses and a vehicle heading out northwards.

'The Andersons. They got away,' Ralph said. 'Please God, they are in Bulawayo by now.'

Vicky wanted to take the old wagon road, past Khami Mission, but Ralph would not do so.

'If they are there, it's too late. You've seen enough. If they got away, we'll find them in Bulawayo.'

So they rode into the town of Bulawayo in the early morning of the third day. The barricades opened to let them pass into the huge central laager in the town square, and the townspeople thronged around the horses, shouting questions.

'Are the soldiers coming?'

'When are the soldiers coming?'

'Did you see my brother? He was at the Antelope Mine—'

'Have you any news?'

When she saw Robyn waving to her from the top of one of the wagons in the market square, Vicky wept again for the first time since leaving the Harkness Mine. Elizabeth jumped down from the wagon and pushed her way through the crowd to Ralph's horse.

'Cathy?' she asked.

Ralph shook his head and saw his own sorrow reflected in her clear dark honey-coloured eyes. Elizabeth reached up and lifted Jon-Jon down from the front of the saddle.

'I'll look after him, Ralph,' she said softly.

The family was installed in a corner of the central laager. Under Robyn's and Louise's direction, the single wagon had been turned into a crowded but adequate home.

On the first day of the rising, Louise and Jan Cheroot, the little Hottentot, had brought the wagon in from King's Lynn. One of the survivors from the Matabele attack at Victoria Mine had galloped past the homestead, shouting a barely coherent warning as he went by.

Louise and Jan Cheroot, already alerted by the desertion of the Matabele labourers and servants, had taken time to pack the wagon with a load of essentials, tinned food and blankets and ammunition, and they had driven into Bulawayo, Jan Cheroot handling the traces, and Louise sitting on top of the load with a rifle in her hands. Twice they had seen small war parties of Matabele at a distance, but a few warning shots had kept them there, and they reached the town amongst the very first refugees.

. Thus the family did not have to rely on the charity of the townsfolk, like so many others who had arrived in Bulawayo with only a lathered horse and an empty rifle.

Robyn had set up a clinic under a canvas awning beside the wagon and had been asked by the Siege Committee to supervise the health and sanitation of the laager. While Louise had quite naturally taken charge of the other women in the laager, setting up a system by which all food stocks and other essential supplies were pooled and rationed, delegating the care of the half-dozen orphans to foster mothers, and organizing the other activities, from an entertainment committee, to lessons in loading ammunition and handling firearms for those gentlewomen who did not already have those skills.

Ralph left Vicky to break the news of Cathy's death to her mother, gave Jon-Jon into Elizabeth's care and set off across the laager to find a member of the Siege Committee.

It was after dark when Ralph got back to the wagon. Surprisingly, there was a brittle air of festivity upon the town. Despite the terrible bereavements that most families had suffered, despite the threat of dark impis gathering just beyond the walls of the laager, yet the cries of the children playing hide-and-go-seek amongst the wagons, the merry notes of a concertina, the laughter of women and the cheerful blaze of the watch-fires might have been those of a picnic in happier times.

Elizabeth had bathed both Jonathan and Robert, so they

glowed pinkly and smelled of carbolic soap, and now as they ate their dinner at the camp table, she was telling them a story that made their eyes big as marbles in the lamplight.

Ralph smiled his thanks at her, and summoned Harry Mellow with an inclination of his head.

The two men sauntered off on a seemingly casual circuit of the darkening laager. They walked with their heads close together, while Ralph told Harry quietly, 'The Siege Committee seem to be doing a good job. They have held a census of the laager already, and they reckon there are six hundred and thirty two women and children and nine hundred and fifteen men. The defence of the town seems to be on good footing, but nobody has yet thought of anything but defence. They were delighted to hear that their plight is known in Kimberley and Cape Town. I gave them the first news that they have had from outside the territory since the rising began – ' Ralph drew on his cheroot – 'and they seemed to think it was as good as a couple of regiments of cavalry on their way already. We both know that isn't so.'

'It will take months to get troops up here.'

'Jameson and his officers are on their way to England for trial, and Rhodes has been summoned to a court of inquiry.' Ralph shook his head. 'And there is worse news. The Mashona tribes have risen in concert with the Matabele.'

'Good God.' Harry stopped dead and seized Ralph's arm. 'The whole territory – all at the same time? This thing has been carefully planned.'

'There has been heavy fighting in the Mazoe valley and in the Charter and Lomagundi districts around Fort Salisbury.'

'Ralph, how many have these savages murdered?'

'Nobody knows. There are hundreds of scattered farms and mines out there. We have to reckon on at least five hundred men, women and children dead.'

They walked on in silence for a while. Once a sentry challenged them, but recognized Ralph.

'Heard you got through, Mr Ballantyne – are the soldiers coming?'

'Are the soldiers coming?' Ralph muttered, when they were past. 'That's what they all ask from the Siege Committee downwards.' They reached the far end of the laager and Ralph spoke quietly to the guard there.

'All right, Mr Ballantyne, but keep your eyes open. Those murdering heathen are all over.'

Ralph and Harry passed through the gateway into the town. It was utterly deserted. Everyone had been moved into the central laager. The thatch and daub shanties were dark and silent, and the two men walked down the centre of the broad dusty main street until the buildings petered out on either hand; they stopped and stood staring out into the scrubland.

'Listen!' said Ralph. A jackal yipped down near the Umguza stream, and was answered from the shadows of the acacia forest out in the south.

'Jackal,' said Harry, but Ralph shook his head.

'Matabele!'

'Will they attack the town?'

Ralph did not reply immediately. He was staring out into the veld, and he had something in his hands that he was teasing like a string of Greek worry beads. 'There are probably twenty thousand fighting bucks out there. They have got us bottled up here, and sooner or later, when they have massed their impis and plucked up their courage, they will come. They will come long before the soldiers can get here.'

'What are our chances?'

Ralph wrapped the thing he held in his hand around one finger, and Harry saw it was a strip of drab fur. 'We have got four Maxim guns, but there are six hundred women and children, and out of the nine hundred men, half are not fit to hold a rifle. The best way to defend Bulawayo is not to sit in the laager and wait for them—'

Ralph turned away and they went back along the silent street. 'They wanted me to join the Siege Committee, and I told them I did not like sieges.'

'What are you going to do, Ralph?'

'I am going to get together a small group of men. Those who know the tribe and the land, those who can shoot straight and talk Sindebele well enough to pass as natives – and we are going to go out there in the Matopos Hills, or wherever else they are hiding, and we are going to start killing Matabele.'

Isazi brought in fourteen men. They were all Zulus from the south, drivers and wagon-boys from the Zeeder-berg Company who had once worked for Rholands Transport, but had been stranded in Bulawayo by the rinderpest.

'I know you can drive an eighteen-ox span,' Ralph nodded at the circle of their faces as they squatted around the fire passing the red tin of 'Wrights No. 1 Best Stuff' that Ralph had provided, from hand to hand. 'I also know that any one of you can eat his own weight in *sadza* maize porridge in one sitting, and wash it down with enough beer to stun a rhinoceros, but can you fight?'

And Isazi answered for them all, using the patient tone usually reserved for an obtuse child.

'We are Zulu.' It was the only reply necessary.

J an Cheroot brought in six more, all of them Cape boys, with mixed Bushman and Hottentot blood, like Jan Cheroot himself.

'This one is named Grootboom, the big tree.' Ralph thought he looked more like a Kalahari Desert thornbush, dark, dry and thorny. 'He was a corporal in the Fifty-second Foot at Cape Town Fort. He is my nephew.'

'Why did he leave Cape Town?'

Jan Cheroot looked pained. 'There was a dispute over a lady. A man had his gizzard slit. They accused my dear nephew of the dastardly deed.'

'Did he do it?'

'Of course he did. He is the best man with a knife that I know – after me,' Jan Cheroot declared modestly.

'Why do you want to kill Matabele?' Ralph asked him in Sindebele, and the Hottentot answered him fluently in the same language.

'It is work I understand and enjoy.'

Ralph nodded and turned to the next man.

'It is possible that this one is even more closely related to me,' Jan Cheroot introduced him. 'His name is Taas, and his mother was a great beauty. She owned a famous shebeen at the foot of Signal Hill above Cape Town docks. At one time she and I were dear and intimate friends, but then the lady had many friends.'

The prospective recruit had the flat nose and high cheekbones, the oriental eyes and the same waxen smooth skin as Jan Cheroot – if he was one of Jan Cheroot's bastards and had spent his boyhood in Cape Town's notorious dockland, then he should be a good man in a fight. Ralph nodded.

'Five shillings a day,' he said. 'And a free box to bury you in if the Matabele catch you.'

J ameson had taken many hundreds of horses south with him, and the Matabele had swept the horses off the farms. Maurice Gifford had already taken 160 mounted men down towards Gwanda to bring in any survivors who might be cut off on the outlying farms and mines, and still be holding out. While Captain George Grey had formed a troop of mounted infantry, 'Grey's Scouts', with most of the mounts that remained. The four mounts that Ralph had brought in with him were fine beasts, and he had managed to buy six more at exorbitant prices, £100 for an animal that would have fetched £15 on a good day at Kimberley market, but there were no others. He lay awake long after midnight under the wagon worrying about it while above him Robyn and Louise slept with the two girls and the children on the wagon truck under the canvas tent.

Ralph's eyes were closed, and a few feet away Harry Mellow was breathing deeply and regularly drowning out any small sounds. Yet even in his preoccupation, Ralph became aware of another presence near him in the darkness. He smelled it first, the taint of woodsmoke and cured animal furs and the odour of the fat with which a Matabele warrior anoints his body.

Ralph slipped his right hand up under the saddle he was using for a pillow, and his fingers touched the chequered walnut butt of his Webley pistol.

'Henshaw,' whispered a voice he did not recognize, and Ralph whipped his left arm around a thick corded neck and at the same moment thrust the muzzle of the pistol into the man's body.

'Quickly,' he grated. 'Who are you, before I kill you?'

'They told me you were quick and strong.' The man was speaking Sindebele. 'Now I believe it.'

'Who are you?'

'I have brought you good men and the promise of horses.'

Neither of them had spoken above a whisper.

'Why do you come like a thief?'

'Because I am Matabele, the white men will kill me if they find me here. I have come to take you to these men.'

Ralph released him carefully, and reached for his boots.

They left the laager and slipped through the silent deserted town. Ralph had spoken only once more.

'You know that I will kill you if this is treachery.'

'I know it,' replied the Matabele.

He was tall, as tall as Ralph but even heavier built, and once when he glanced back at Ralph the moonlight showed the silky sheen of scar tissue slashed across his cheek beneath his right eye.

In the yard of one of the last houses of the town, close to the open veld, yet screened from it by the wall that some houseproud citizen had erected to protect his garden, there were twelve more Matabele *amadoda* waiting. Some of them wore fur kilts while others were dressed in ragged Western cast-offs.

'Who are these men?' Ralph demanded. 'Who are you?'

'My name is Ezra, Sergeant Ezra. I was Sergeant to One-Bright-Eye who the impis killed at Khami Hills. These men are all Company police.'

'The Company police have been disbanded and disarmed,' Ralph said.

'Yes, they have taken away our guns. They say they do not trust us. That we may go over to the rebels.'

'Why do you not?' Ralph said. 'Some of your brothers have. They say a hundred of the Company police have gone over, and taken their rifles with them.'

'We cannot – even if we had wished to.' Ezra shook his head. 'Have you heard of the killing of two Matabele women near the Inyati river? A woman called Ruth and another called Little Flower, Imbali?'

Ralph frowned. 'Yes, I remember.'

'It was these men, and I was their sergeant. The induna

352

named Gandang has asked that we be taken to him alive. He wishes personally to supervise the manner of our deaths.'

'I want men who can kill the women of the Matabele as easily as they killed ours,' said Ralph. 'Now what of these horses?'

'The horses captured by the Matabele at Essexvale and Belingwe are being held in the hills at a place I know of.'

L ong before the curfew bell, they had all slipped out of the central laager singly and in pairs, Jan Cheroot and his Cape boys taking the horses with them, and by the time Ralph and Harry Mellow strolled down the main street as though they were taking the evening air before returning to the laager for dinner, the others were all gathered in the walled garden at the end of the street.

Sergeant Ezra had brought the kilts and spears and knobkerries, and Jan Cheroot had the big black three-legged pot of beef fat and lampblack boiled to a paste. Ralph and Harry and the Hottentots stripped naked and smeared each other with the rancid mixture, taking care to work it in around the back of the ears, the knees and elbows, and below the eyes where pale skin might show.

By the time the curfew bell in the Anglican church began to toll, they were all dressed in the kilts of Matabele *amadoda*. Ralph and Harry covered their hair, which would have betrayed them, with headdresses of black widow-bird feathers. Isazi and Jan Cheroot strapped the rawhide bootees over the hooves of the horses, while Ralph gave his final orders, speaking in Sindebele, the only language they would use during the entire raid.

They left the town in the sudden darkness between sunset and moonrise, the hoofbeats of the horses deadened by the rawhides, and Ezra's Matabele running at the stirrups on silent bare feet. After the first hour, Ralph muttered a curt order to the Matabele and they took a stirrup-leather and hung from it, a man on each side of the horses. The pace of the march never slackened below a canter. They swept south and eastwards, until the crenellated crests of the Matopos Hills were outlined against the moon-pale sky.

A little after midnight Ezra grunted.

'This is the place!'

Ralph rose in the stirrups and raised his right arm. The column bunched up and dismounted. Jan Cheroot's reputed bastard, Taas, came to take the horses, while Jan Cheroot himself checked his men's weapons.

'I will put them against the firelight for you,' Ralph whispered to him. 'Watch for my signal.'

Then Ralph smiled at Isazi, his teeth glinting in the shiny black mask of his daubed face. 'There will be no prisoners. Lie close, but beware of Jan Cheroot's bullets.'

'Henshaw, I want to go in with you.'

Harry Mellow spoke in Sindebele, and Ralph answered him in the same language.

'You shoot better than you talk. Go with Jan Cheroot.'

At another order from Ralph, every one of them reached into the leather pouch on his hip and brought out a white cow-tail tassel necklace. They were the recognition insignia, that might prevent them killing each other in the press of the fighting. Only Ralph added another ornament to his dress. From his hip pouch he brought the strip of mole-skin and bound it around his upper arm; then he hefted the heavy assegai and leadwood knobkerrie and nodded at Ezra.

'Lead!'

The line of Matabele, with Ralph running in second place, trotted at a traverse across the slope of the hill. As they turned the southern buttress, they saw the red glow of a watch-fire in the valley below. Ralph sprinted past Ezra to the front of the line. He filled his lungs and began to sing.

'Lift the rock under which sleeps the serpent.
Lift the rock and let the Mamba loose.
The Mamba of Mashobane has silver fangs of steel.'

It was one of the fighting songs of the Insukamini impi, and behind him the line of Matabele picked up the refrain in their deep melodious voices. It resounded from the hills and woke the camp in the valley. Naked figures, risen from the sleeping-mats, threw wood on the fires, and the red glow lit the underside of the acacia trees so they formed a canopy like a circus tent overhead.

Ezra had estimated there were forty *amadoda* guarding the horses, but there were more than that already gathered around the fires and every second more flocked into the bivouac, the outposts coming in to see what was causing the commotion. Ralph had planned for that. He wanted no stragglers. They must be concentrated, so that his riflemen could fire into the bunch, making one bullet do the work of three or four. Ralph trotted into the Matabele encampment.

'Who commands here?' Ralph broke off the battle-song, and demanded in a bellow. 'Let the commander stand forth to hear the word I bring from Gandang.' He knew from the account that Robyn had given him of the massacre on the Khami Hills that the old induna was one of the leaders of the uprising. His choice of name had the effect he had hoped for.

'I am Mazui.' A warrior stepped forward respectfully. 'I wait for the word of Gandang, son of Mzilikazi.'

'The horses are no longer safe in this place. The white men have learned where they are. At the rise of the sun we will take them deeper into the hills,' Ralph told him. 'To a place that I shall show you.'

'It shall be done.'

'Where are the horses?'

'They are in the kraal, guarded by my *amadoda*, safe from the lions.'

'Bring in all your pickets,' Ralph ordered, and the commander shouted an order and then turned back to Ralph eagerly.

'What news is there of the fighting?'

'There has been a great battle,' Ralph launched into a fanciful account, miming the fighting in the traditional way, leaping and shouting and stabbing in the air with his assegai.

'Thus we came upon the rear of the horsemen, and thus and thus we stabbed them—' His own Matabele gave him a chorus of long drawn-out 'Jee' and leaped and postured with him.

The audience was enraptured, beginning to stamp and sway in sympathy with Ralph and his Matabele. The sentries and pickets had come in from the periphery of the camp. No more hurrying black figures emerged from the shadows. They were all here – a hundred, perhaps a hundred and twenty, not more, Ralph estimated, against his forty men. Not unfair odds, Jan Cheroot's Cape boys were all first-rate marksmen, and Harry Mellow with a rifle was worth five ordinary men.

From close at hand, on the first slope of the hill, a nightjar called. It was a musical quavering cry, that sounded like 'Good Lord, deliver us'; this pious sentiment gave the bird its popular name, the Litany bird. It was the signal which Ralph had been listening for. He felt a bleak satisfaction that Jan Cheroot had followed his orders so strictly. From the position on the slope, Jan Cheroot would have the crowd of *amadoda* silhouetted against the firelight.

Making it all part of the dance, Ralph whirled away, still prancing and stamping, opening a distance of twenty paces between himself and the nearest Matabele. Here Ralph ended his dance abruptly with his arms spread like a crucifix. He stood deathly still staring at his audience with wild eyes, and a silence fell upon them all.

Slowly Ralph raised his arms above his head. He stood like that for a moment, a heroic figure glistening with fat, every muscle in his arms and chest standing proud, the kilt of civet-tails hanging to his knees, the collar of white cow-tails around his neck, his charm against the death that lurked in the darkness beyond the firelight. His blackened features were twisted into a ferocious grimace that held the watchers spellbound. The dancing and singing had served its purpose well. It had distracted the *amadoda*, and masked any noise that the Zulus and Hottentots might have made while moving into position around the bivouac.

Now suddenly Ralph let out a demoniacal howl that made the *amadoda* shudder, and he dropped his arms – the signal for which Harry and Jan Cheroot were waiting.

The curtains of darkness were torn aside by the blast of massed rifle fire. The range was point-blank, the muzzles almost touching the press of dark naked bodies. It smashed into them, a single bullet churning through belly and chest and spine, bringing down four men, stopping only when the slug broke up against one of the heavy bones of pelvis or femur.

So unexpected was the assault, that the mass of warriors milled aimlessly, receiving three volleys from the repeating Winchesters, before they broke and ran. More than half of them were down already, and many of those still on their feet were wounded. They ran on top of Isazi's Zulus, and piled up against them like water on a dam wall. Ralph heard the great shouts of '*Ngidla!* I have eaten!' as the Zulus put in the steel, and heard the screams of the dying men.

Now at last the Matabele were rallying, closing up shoulder to shoulder to meet the thin line of Zulus and overrun it. It was the moment Ralph had waited for. He led his own Matabele racing across their rear and flung them at the naked undefended backs of the struggling warriors.

Long ago, as boys on the Kimberley diamond-workings, Bazo had taught Ralph the art of spearsmanship. Ralph had been as skilful with the broad blade as any of the Matabele youths who were his companions. However, it was one thing to practise the long under-handed killing stroke, and another actually to send the point into living flesh.

Ralph was unprepared for the sensation of the steel in his hand running in and slowing against the sucking resistance, feeling the steel touch and grate on bone, and the haft kick in his hand as his victims bucked and convulsed at the agony. It felt like the butt of the rod when a salmon makes its first run.

Instinctively Ralph twisted the blade in the man's body, the way Bazo had taught him, maximizing the tissue damage and breaking the vacuum that held the steel – then he jerked it clear, and for the first time felt the fine hot spray of blood from the wound fly into his face and splatter his right arm and chest.

He stepped over the dying man who thrashed on the earth, and sank the steel again and then again. The smell of blood and the screams maddened him, but it was a cold fierce madness that magnified his vision and slowed down the micro-seconds of mortal combat, so that he saw the counter-thrust and turned his adversary's blade aside with contemptuous ease, using the momentum of his shoulders to drive his own point through the Matabele guard and into the notch formed by the joint of his collar-bones at the base of his throat. The man's breath whistled over his severed vocal cords, and he dropped his assegai and seized Ralph's blade with his bare hands. Ralph pulled it back, and the razor edges cut to the bone of the man's fingers, and his hands fell open nervelessly as the Matabele dropped to his knees.

Ralph leaped over him and poised to thrust again.

'Henshaw!' a voice screamed in his face. 'It is me!' and through his madness Ralph saw the white cow-tail tassels about the neck and held the stroke; the two lines of attackers had met.

'It is over,' Isazi panted, and Ralph looked about him in bewilderment. It had happened so swiftly. He shook his head to free the cold vice of fighting madness that gripped it.

They were all down, though a few of them still twisted and twitched and groaned.

'Isazi, finish them!' Ralph ordered, and watched the Zulus begin the grim work, passing quickly from body to body, feeling for the pulse below the ear and if they found it, stilling it with a quick thrust.

'Ralph,' Harry came scrambling down the slope at the head of the Cape boys. 'By God, that was one—'

'No English,' Ralph warned him, then raising his voice. 'We will take the horses now. Bring the spare bridles and lead-reins.'

There were fifty-three fine horses in the thornbush kraal. Most of them carried the BSA Company brand. Each of the unmounted Zulus and Matabele selected a mount, and the remaining animals were put onto lead-reins.

In the meantime the Cape boys were going over the field with the speed and precision of born footpads, selecting the rifles that could be used and throwing the ancient Martini-Henrys and muzzle-loaders and knobkerries onto the fire, snapping the assegai blades in the fork of a tree. The loot they discovered, cutlery and crockery and clothing of European manufacture, proved that this impi had taken part in the depredations of the first few days of the rising. That, too, was thrown upon the flames. Within an hour of the first rifle-shot, they were moving out again. This time every man was well mounted, and the spare horses followed at a canter on the lead-reins.

They rode down the main street of Bulawayo in the uncertain grey light of pre-dawn. In the front rank Ralph and Harry had scrubbed most of the blackening from their faces, but to make certain they did not draw the fire of a jittery sentry, they carried a flag made from Harry Mellow's white flannel undershirt.

The inhabitants of the laager tumbled out of their beds

to gape and question, and then as they began to realize that this little cavalcade heralded the first retaliation against the slaughter and arson committed by the tribes, the cheering began and rose into joyous hysteria.

While Vicky and Elizabeth proudly served them a double ration breakfast under the wagon awning, Ralph and Harry received an endless string of well-wishers, of tearful widows whose husbands had perished under the Matabele assegais, bringing thanks and a half-dozen eggs or a freshly baked cake, of wistful boys come merely to stare at the heroes, and of keen young men demanding eagerly, 'Is this where we sign up to join Ballantyne's Scouts?'

There were shrieks of delight as Judy set about her long-suffering husband with her baton. The children in the front row clapped their hands as the blows cracked upon Punch's wooden head and his grotesquely humped back, and the bells on his cap jingled.

Swimming valiantly against the mainstream of sentiment, Jon-Jon's face was red as Punch's hooked nose and screwed up with outrage. 'Hit her back!' he howled, bouncing up and down. 'She's only a girl!'

'Spoken like a true Ballantyne,' Ralph laughed, at the same time forcibly restraining his son from leaping into the fray on the side of down-trodden mankind.

Elizabeth sat beyond Jon-Jon, with Robert on her lap. The child's sickly face was solemn and he sucked dedicatedly upon his thumb like an elderly gnome upon his pipe. In contrast, Elizabeth was radiant with a childlike joy, her cheeks flushed and her eyes shining, as she egged Judy on to further excesses.

A shining lock of her hair had come loose from the tortoiseshell comb and lay against the tender velvety skin of her temple, half curled around the lobe of her ear. Her ear was a faint pink, and so thin and delicately shaped that the sunlight showed through it as though it were made from some rare bone-china. The same sunlight made the burgundy sparks flare like electricity in her thick dark tresses.

It drew Ralph's attention from the marionettes, and he watched her covertly over Jonathan's curly head. Her laughter was a throaty purr, natural and unashamed, and Ralph laughed again in sympathy. She turned her head and for a moment Ralph looked deeply into her eyes. It was like looking into a bowl of hot honey. He seemed to be able to see into limitless depths that were flecked with gold. Then Elizabeth dropped the veil of dark curved lashes over them, and looked back at the tiny stage, but she was no longer laughing. Instead her lower lip trembled and a dark flush of blood washed up her throat.

Feeling strangely guilty and shaken, Ralph quickly fastened his own eyes, if not his attention, on the squawking, battling marionettes. The sketch ended, to Jonathan's vast satisfaction, with Judy being led away to some nameless but richly deserved fate by a policeman in Mr Peel's blue helmet, and the mild bespectacled little bookkeeper of Meikles Store came out from behind his candy-striped screen with the glove puppets still upon his hands, to take his bows.

'He looks just like Mr Kipling,' Elizabeth whispered, 'and he has the same bloodthirsty and violent imagination.'

Ralph felt a rush of gratitude towards her that she should gloss over that unexpected moment of awkwardness so gracefully. He picked up the boys, sat one upon each shoulder, and they followed the dispersing audience across the laager.

Upon his father's shoulder, Jonathan chattered like a flock of starlings, explaining to Bobby the finer points of the play which were clearly too subtle for any lesser intelligence than his own to follow. However, both Ralph and Elizabeth walked in silence.

When they reached the wagon, Ralph slid both children

to the ground and they scampered away. Half-heartedly, Elizabeth made to follow them, but stopped and turned back to him when Ralph spoke.

'I don't know what I would have done without you – you've been wonderfully kind—' He hesitated. 'Without Cathy—' He saw the pain in her eyes and broke off. 'I just wanted to thank you.'

'You don't have to do that, Ralph,' she answered quietly. 'Anything you need – I'll always be here to help.' Then her reserve cracked, she started to speak again, but her lips trembled and she turned away sharply and followed the two boys into the wagon.

Ralph had paid siege prices for the bottle of whisky by scrawling a cheque on the label from a bully beef tin for £20. He took it hidden under his coat to where Isazi and Jan Cheroot and Sergeant Ezra sat together beside a fire away from their men.

They swilled the coffee grounds out of their enamel mugs and proffered them for a good dram of the whisky and sipped in silence for a while, all of them staring into the camp-fire flames, letting the warmth of the spirit spread out through their bodies.

At last Ralph nodded at Sergeant Ezra, and the big Matabele began to speak quietly.

'Gandang and his Inyati impi are still waiting in the Khami Hills – he has twelve hundred men. They are all blooded warriors, Babiaan is bivouacked below the Hills of the Indunas with six hundred. He could be here in an hour—' Quickly Ezra recounted the positions of the impis, the names of their indunas, and the mood and mettle of their warriors.

'What of Bazo and his Moles?' At last Ralph asked the question that concerned him most, and Ezra shrugged.

'We do not have word of them. I have my best men in the hills, searching for them. Nobody knows where the Moles have gone.'

'Where will we strike next?' Ralph asked the question rhetorically, musing as he stared in the fire. 'Will it be at Babiaan in the Hills of the Indunas, or Zama with his thousand lying across the Mangiwe Road?'

Isazi coughed in polite disagreement, and when Ralph glanced up at him, he said, 'Last night I sat at one of Babiaan's camp-fires, eating his meat, and listening to his men talk. They spoke of our attack upon the camp of the horses, and how the indunas had warned them in future to be on their guard against all strangers, even though they wore the furs and feathers of the fighting impis. We will not work the same trick twice.'

Jan Cheroot and Ezra grunted in agreement, and the little Hottentot inverted his mug to prove it empty, and glanced significantly at the bottle between Ralph's feet. Ralph poured again, and as he cupped the mug in his hands and inhaled the pungent perfume of the spirit, his mind went back to that afternoon – to the laughter of the children and a lovely young girl whose hair burned with soft fires in the sunlight.

His voice was rough and ugly. 'Their women and children,' he said. 'They will be hidden in the caves and the secret valleys of the Matopos. Find them!'

There were five small boys under the bank of the stream. They were all stark naked, and their legs were coated to above the knees with slick yellow clay. They laughed and squabbled good-naturedly as they dug the clay out of the bank with sharpened sticks and packed it into crudely woven reed baskets.

Tungata Zebiwe, 'The Seeker after what has been Stolen',

was the first to climb out of the stream, lugging the heavy basket to a shady place where he squatted and set to work. The others straggled up the bank after him and seated themselves in a circle.

Tungata took a handful of clay from his basket and rolled it into a thick soft sausage between his pink palms. Then he moulded it with practised skill, forming the humped back and sturdy legs. When it was complete, he set the body carefully between his knees on a slab of dried bark; then turned his attention to sculpting the head separately with curved red devil thorns for the horns and chips of waterworn rock-crystal for the eyes. He attached the head to the thick neck, sticking out his tongue with concentration as he adjusted it to a proud angle, and then he sat back and studied it with a critical eye.

'*Inkunzi Nkulu!*' he hailed his creation. 'Great Bull!'

Grinning with delight, he carried the clay beast to the antheap, and set it on its bark base to dry in the sun. Then he hurried back to begin making the cows and calves for his herd. As he worked, he mocked the creations of the other boys, comparing them to his own great herd bull, and grinning cheekily at their retorts.

Tanase watched him from the shadows. She had come silently down the path through the thick riverine bush, led on by the tinkling of child-laughter, and the happy banter. Now she was reluctant to interrupt this magical moment.

In the sadness and striving, in the menace and smoke of war, it seemed that all joy and laughter had been forgotten. It needed the resilience and vision of a child to remind her of what had once been – and what might be again. She felt a suffocating weight of love overwhelm her, followed almost immediately by a formless dread. She wanted to rush to the child and take him in her arms, to hold him tightly to her bosom and protect him from – she was not sure what.

Then Tungata looked up and saw her, and came to her carrying the clay bull with shy pride.

'See what I have made.'

'It is beautiful.'

'It is for you, Umame, I made it for you.'

Tanase took the offering. 'He is a fine bull, and he will breed many calves,' she said, and her love was so strong that the tears scalded her eyelids. She did not want the child to see it.

'Wash the clay off your legs and arms,' she told him. 'We must go up to the cave.'

He skipped beside her on the path, his body still wet from the river, his skin glistening with a velvety black sheen, laughing delightedly when Tanase set the clay bull upon her head, walking straight-backed and hips swinging, to balance the load.

They came up the path to the base of the cliff. It was not truly a cave, but a long low overhang of the cliff face. They were not the first to use it as a home. The rocky roof was blackened with the soot of innumerable cooking-fires, and the back wall was decorated with the ancient paintings and engravings of the little yellow Bushmen who had hunted here long before Mzilikazi led his impis into these hills. They were wonderful pictures of rhinoceros and giraffe and gazelle, and of the little stick figures, armed with bows and outsized genitalia, who hunted them.

There were almost five hundred persons living in this place, one of the secret safe places of the tribe, where the women and the children were sent when war or some other catastrophe threatened the Matabele. Though the valley was steep and narrow, there were five escape routes, hidden paths scaling the cliffs or narrow clefts through the granite, which made it impossible for an enemy to trap them in the gut of the valley.

The stream provided fresh clear water for drinking, thirty milch cows that had survived the rinderpest provided *mass*, the soured milk which was one of the tribe's staples. And when they marched in, every woman had borne upon her head a leather grain-bag. The locusts had depleted the harvest, but with careful planning they could exist here for many months.

The women were spread out down the length of the rock shelter, busy with their separate tasks. Some of them were stamping the corn in mortars carved from a dried tree-trunk, using a heavy wooden pestle that they swung up with both hands above their head and then let drop of its own weight into the cup of the mortar, clapping their hands and then seizing the club to lift it for the next stroke. Others were plaiting bark cloth for sleeping-mats, or tanning wild animals' skins, or stringing ceramic beads. Over it all hung the faint blue mist of the cooking-fires, and the sweet hum of women's voices, interspersed with the gurgling and chirping of black babes who crawled naked on the rocky floor, or hung like fat limpets from their mothers' breasts.

Juba was at the far end of the shelter, imparting to two of her daughters and the new wife of one of her middle sons the delicate secrets of beer-brewing. The sorghum grain had been soaked and had germinated, now came the drying and grinding of the yeast. It was an absorbing task, and Juba did not become aware of the presence of her senior daughter-in-law and her eldest grandson until they stood over her. Then she looked up, and her smile split the great round of her face.

'My mother,' Tanase knelt before her respectfully. 'I must speak with you.'

Juba struggled to rise, but was pinned by her own vast weight. Her daughters took an elbow each and heaved her upright. Once she was on her feet, she moved with surprising agility, swept Tungata onto her hip and carried him easily along the pathway. Tanase fell in beside her.

'Bazo has sent for me,' Tanase told her. 'There is dissension amongst the indunas, Bazo needs the words of the Umlimo made clear. Without that the struggle will fall into vacillation and talk. We will lose all that we have won so dearly.'

'Then you must go, my child.'

'I must go swiftly, I cannot take Tungata with me.'

'He is safe here, I will look after him. When do you leave?'

'Immediately.'

Juba sighed and nodded. 'So be it.'

Tanase touched the child's cheek. 'Obey your grand-mother,' she said softly, and like a shadow was gone around the bend of the narrow pathway.

Tanase passed through the granite portals that guarded the valley of the Umlimo. She had only her memories of this place for travelling companions, and they were not good company. Yet when she went down the path, she walked straight, with a kind of antelope grace, her long limbs swinging freely and her head held high on the long heron's neck.

As soon as she entered the little cluster of huts in the bottom of the valley, her trained senses were immediately aware of the tensions and angers that hung over the place like a sickly miasma over a fever swamp. She could feel the anger and frustration in Bazo when she knelt before him, and made her dutiful obeisance. She knew so well what those knots of tense muscle at the points of his clenched jaw and the reddish glaze in his eyes meant.

Before she rose, she had noted how the indunas had drawn into two separate groups. On one side the elders, and facing them the young and headstrong were ranged about Bazo. She crossed the space between them and knelt before Gandang and his white-headed brothers, Somabula and Babiaan.

'I see you, my child.' Gravely Gandang acknowledged her greeting, and then the abruptness with which he broached the real reason for her summons warned Tanase of its dire import.

'We wish you to speak to us on the meaning of the Umlimo's latest prophecy.'

'My lord and father, I am no longer an intimate of the mysteries—'

Impatiently Gandang brushed aside her disclaimer. 'You understand more than anyone outside that dreadful cave. Listen to the words of the Umlimo, and discourse faithfully upon them.'

She bowed her head in acquiescence, but at the same time turned slightly so that she had Bazo at the very edge of her vision.

'The Umlimo spake thus: "Only a foolish hunter blocks the opening of the cave from which the wounded leopard seeks to escape."' Gandang repeated the prophecy, and his brothers nodded at the accuracy of his rendition.

Veiling her eyes behind thick black lashes, Tanase turned her head the breadth of a finger. Now she could see Bazo's right hand as it rested on his bare thigh. She had taught him the rudiments of the secret sign language of the initiates. His forefinger curled and touched the first joint of his thumb. It was a command.

'Remain silent!' said that gesture. 'Speak not!' She made the signal of comprehension and acknowledgement, with the hand that hung at her side. Then she raised her head.

'Was that all, Lord?' she asked of Gandang.

'There is more,' he answered. 'The Umlimo spake a second time: "The hot wind from the north will scorch the weeds in the fields, before the new corn can be planted. Wait for the north wind."' All the indunas leaned forward eagerly, and Gandang told her, 'Speak to us of the meaning.'

'The meaning of the Umlimo's words is never clear at once. I must ponder on it.'

'When will you tell us?'

'When I have an answer.'

'Tomorrow morning?' Gandang insisted.

'Perhaps.'

'Then you will spend the night alone, that your meditation be not disturbed,' Gandang ordered.

'My husband,' Tanase demurred.

'Alone,' Gandang repeated sharply. 'With a guard on the door of your hut.'

The guard that was set upon her hut was a young warrior, not yet married, and because of it he was that much more susceptible to the wiles of a beautiful woman. When he brought the bowl of food to Tanase, she smiled in such a way that he lingered at the door of the hut. When she offered him a choice morsel, he glanced outside guiltily and then came to take it from her hand.

The food had a strange bitter taste, but he did not want to give offence, so he swallowed it manfully. The woman's smile promised things that the young warrior could barely believe possible, but when he tried to answer her provocative sallies, his voice slurred strangely in his own ears, and he was overcome with a lassitude such that he had to close his eyes for a moment.

Tanase replaced the stopper on the buckhorn bottle she had concealed in her palm, and stepped quietly over the guard's sleeping form. When she whistled, Bazo came swiftly and silently to where she waited by the stream.

'Tell me, Lord,' she whispered, 'that which you require of me.'

When she returned to the hut, the guard still slept deeply. She propped him in the doorway with his weapon across his lap. In the morning his head would ache, but he would not be eager to tell the indunas how he had spent the night.

'I have thought deeply on the words of the Umlimo,' Tanase knelt before the indunas, 'and I read meaning into the parable of the foolish hunter who hesitates in the entrance of the cave.'

Gandang frowned as he guessed the slant of her reply, but she went on calmly.

'Would not the brave and skilled hunter go boldly into the cave where the animal lurks, and slay it?' One of the elder indunas hissed with disagreement, and sprang to his feet.

'I say that the Umlimo has warned us to leave the road to the south open, so that the white men with all their women and chattels may leave this land for ever,' he shouted, and immediately Bazo was on his feet facing him.

'The white men will never leave. The only way to rid ourselves of them is to bury them.' There was a roar of approval from the younger indunas grouped around Bazo, but he lifted his hand to silence them.

'If you leave the south road open, it will certainly be used – by the soldiers who march up it with their little three-legged guns.'

There were angry cries of denial and encouragement.

'I say to you that we are the hot wind from the north, that the Umlimo prophesied, we are the ones who will scorch the weeds—'

The shouts that drowned him out showed just how deeply the nation's leaders were divided, and Tanase felt the blackness of despair come down upon her. Gandang rose to his feet, and such was the weight of tradition and custom that even the wildest and fiercest of the young indunas fell silent.

'We must give the white men a chance to leave with their women. We will leave the road open for them to go, and we will wait in patience for the hot wind, the miraculous wind from the north that the Umlimo promises to blow our enemies away—'

Bazo alone had not squatted respectfully to the senior induna, and now he did something that was without precedent. He interrupted his father, and his voice was full of scorn.

'You have given them chance enough,' said Bazo. 'You have let the woman from Khami and all her brats go free. I ask you one question, my father, is what you propose kindness or is it cowardice?'

They gasped, for when a son could speak thus to his father, then the world that once they all had known and understood was now changed. Gandang looked at Bazo across the small space that separated them, which was a gulf neither of them would ever be able once again to bridge. Though he was still tall and erect, there was such sorrow in Gandang's eyes that made him seem as old as the granite hills that surrounded them.

'You are no longer my son,' he said simply.

'And you are no longer my father,' Bazo said, and turning on his heel, strode from the hut. First Tanase, and then, one after another, the young indunas stood up and followed Bazo out into the sunlight.

An outrider came in at full gallop and brought his horse up so sharply that it reared and sawed its head against the bit.

'Sir, there is large party of rebels coming up the road ahead,' he shouted urgently.

'Very well, trooper.' The Honourable Maurice Gifford, officer commanding troops B and D of the Bulawayo field force, touched the brim of his slouch hat with a gloved hand in acknowledgement. 'Go forward and keep them under observation.' Then he turned in the saddle. 'Captain Dawson, we will put the wagons into laager under those trees, there will be a good field of fire for the Maxim from there – I will take out fifty mounted men to engage the enemy.'

It really was a piece of astonishing good luck to run into a group of rebels so close to Bulawayo. After weeks of scouring the countryside, Gifford and his 160 troopers had managed to gather in thirty or so survivors from the isolated villages and trading-posts, but so far they had not had even a chance of a scrap with the Matabele. Leaving Dawson to prepare the laager, Gifford spurred down the Bulawayo road at the head of fifty of his best men.

Gifford was the youngest son of an earl, a handsome young aristocrat and junior officer in a famous guards regiment. He had been spending his leave on a spot of shooting in Africa, and had been fortunate enough to have his holiday enlivened by a native uprising. The general opinion of the Honourable M. Gifford was that he was frightfully keen, and a damned fine young fellow, bound to go a long way.

He reined in his horse at the crest of the rise, and held up his gloved right hand to halt the troop.

'There they are, sir,' cried the outrider. 'Bold as brass.'

The Honourable Maurice Gifford polished the lenses of his binoculars on the tail of his yellow silk scarf, and then held the glasses to his eyes.

'They are all mounted,' he said, 'and jolly well mounted at that,' he murmured. 'But, I say, what a murderous-looking bunch of ruffians.'

The approaching horsemen were half a mile away, a straggling mob, dressed in war kilts and headdresses, armed with a weird assortment of modern and primitive weapons.

'Troop, into extended order, left and right wheel,' Gifford ordered. 'Sergeant, we will use the slope to charge them, and then disengage and attempt to draw them within range of the Maxim.'

'Begging your pardon, sir,' the sergeant mumbled, 'but isn't that a white man leading them?'

Gifford lifted the binoculars and peered through them again. 'The devil it is!' he muttered. 'But the fellow is dressed in furs and things.'

The fellow gave him a cheery wave, as he rode up at the head of his motley gang.

"Morning, you aren't Maurice Gifford by any chance?'

'I am sir,' Gifford replied frostily. 'And who are you, if I may be so bold as to ask?'

'The name's Ballantyne, Ralph Ballantyne.' The fellow gave him an engaging grin. 'And these gentlemen,' with his thumb he indicated those who followed him, 'are Ballantyne's Scouts.'

Maurice Gifford looked them over with distaste. It was impossible to tell their racial origins, for they were all painted with fat and clay to look like Matabele, and they wore cast-offs and tribal dress. Only this fellow Ballantyne had left his face its natural colour, probably to identify himself to the Bulawayo field force, but it was equally probable that he would blacken it as soon as he had what he wanted from them. He was not shy about making his wants known, either.

'A requisition, Mr Gifford,' he said, and handed over a folded and sealed note from his belt pouch.

Gifford bit on the finger of his glove, and drew it off his right hand, before he accepted the note and broke the seal.

'I cannot let you have my Maxim, sir,' he exclaimed as he read. 'I have a duty to protect the civilians in my care.'

'You are only four miles from the laager at Bulawayo and the road is clear of Matabele. We have just swept it for you. There is no longer any danger to your people.'

'But—' said Gifford.

'The requisition is signed by Colonel William Napier, officer commanding the Bulawayo field force. I suggest you take the matter up with him, when you reach Bulawayo.' Ralph was still smiling. 'In the meantime, we are rather pressed for time. We will just relieve you of the Maxim, and trouble you no further.'

Gifford crumpled the note, and glared impotently at Ralph, then shifted his ground.

'You and your men appear to be wearing enemy uniform,' he accused. 'That is in contravention of the articles of war, sir.'

'Read the articles to the indunas, Mr Gifford, particularly those dealing with the murder and torture of non-combatants.'

'There is no call for an Englishman to descend to the level of the savages he is fighting,' said Gifford loftily. 'I have had the honour to meet your father, Major Zouga Ballantyne. He is a gentleman. I wonder what he would say about your conduct.'

'My father and his fellow conspirators, all of them English gentlemen, are presently standing trial on charges of having waged war against a friendly government. However, I will certainly solicit his opinion of my conduct at the first available opportunity. Now if you will send your sergeant back with us to hand over the Maxim, I will bid you good day, Mr Gifford.'

They unloaded the Maxim from its cart, removed the tripod and ammunition boxes, and loaded them onto three pack-horses.

'How did you get Napier to sign away one of his precious Maxims?' Harry Mellow demanded, as he clinched the straps on the pack-saddles.

'Sleight of hand,' Ralph winked at him. 'The pen is mightier—'

'You forged the requisition,' Harry stared at him. 'They'll shoot you.'

'They'll have to catch me first.'. Ralph turned and bellowed to his Scouts, 'Troop, mount! Walk march, forward!'

There was no doubt that he was a wizard. A wizened little fellow, not much taller than Tungata or any of his companions, but he was painted in the most marvellous colours, zigzags of crimson and white and black across his face and chest.

When he first appeared out of the bush beside the stream in the secret valley, the children were frozen with terror. But before they could recover their wits sufficiently to run, the little painted wizard uttered such a string of cries and grunts, imitating horse and eagle and chacma baboon, at the same time prancing and flapping and scratching, that their terror turned to fascination.

Then from the sack over his shoulder, the wizard dug out a huge lump of rock sugar candy. He sucked it noisily, and the children who had not tasted sugar in weeks drew closer and watched him with glistening dark eyes. He proffered the lump of sugar to Tungata who edged forward, snatched it and scampered back. The little wizard laughed in such an infectious manner, that the other children laughed with him and swarmed forward to grab at the fresh lumps of candy he offered. Surrounded by laughing, clapping children, the little wizard climbed the path up the side of the valley to the rock shelter.

The women, lulled and reassured by the sounds of happy children, came to crowd about the little wizard, to stare and giggle, and the boldest to ask him:

'Who are you?'

'Where do you come from?'

'What is in the sack?'

In reply to the last question, the wizard drew out a handful of coloured ribbons, and the younger women shrieked with feminine vanity and tied them at their wrists and throats.

'I bring gifts and happy tidings,' the wizard cackled. 'Look what I bring you.'

There were steel combs, and small round mirrors, a little

box that played sweet tinkling music – they crowded about him, utterly enchanted. 'Gifts and happy tidings,' sang the wizard.

'Tell us! Tell us!' they chanted.

'The spirits of our forefathers have come to aid us. They have sent a divine wind to eat up the white men, as the rinderpest ate up the cattle. All the white men are dead!'

'The *amakiwa* are dead!'

'They have left behind them all these wonderful gifts. The town of Bulawayo is empty of white men, but these things are there for all to take. As much as you will – but hurry, all the men and women of the Matabele are going there. There will be nothing left for those who come after. Look, look at these beautiful pieces of cloth, there are thousands of them. Who wants these pretty buttons, these sharp knives? Those who want them must follow me!' sang the wizard. 'For the fighting is over! The white men are dead! The Matabele have triumphed, who wants to follow me?'

'Lead us, little Father,' they begged him. 'We will follow you.'

Still digging out gewgaws and trifles from the sack, the painted wizard started down towards the end of the narrow valley, and the women snatched up their little ones, strapped them to their backs with strips of cloth, called to the older children and hurried after the wizard.

'Follow me, people of Mashobane!' he chirped. 'Your time of greatness has come. The prophecy of the Umlimo is fulfilled. The divine wind from the north has blown the *amakiwa* away.'

Tungata, almost hysterical with excitement and dread that he would be left behind, hurried down the length of the rock shelter, until he saw the huge beloved figure squatting against the back wall of rock.

'Grandmother,' he squeaked. 'The wizard has pretty things for us all. We must hurry!'

Over the millennia the stream had cut a narrow twisted exit from the bowel of the valley, with high cliffs on each side. The granite was painted with rich orange and yellow lichens. Compressed into this chasm the stream fell in smoking cascades of white water, before debouching into a shallower wider valley in the lower foothills.

The valley was filled with fine grass, the colour of a ripening wheat field. The pathway clung to the edge of the chasm, with a perilous drop to foaming white water on one hand and with the cliff rising sheer on the other. Then the gradient became more gentle and the path emerged into the quiet valley below. Rainwater had scarred the side of the lower valley with deep dongas, natural entrenchments, and one of these afforded an ideal emplacement for the Maxim.

Ralph had two of his troopers set it up with the thick water-jacketed barrel just clearing the lip of the donga. There were 2,000 rounds of ammunition in the oblong boxes, stacked beside the weapon. While Harry Mellow cut branches of thornbrush to screen the Maxim, Ralph paced off the ranges in front of the donga and set up a cairn of loose stones beside the footpath.

He came scrambling back up the slope, and told Harry, 'Set the sights for three hundred yards.'

Then he went down the length of the donga, giving his orders to each man, and making him repeat them to ensure there was no misunderstanding.

'When Jan Cheroot reaches the cairn, the Maxim will fire. Wait for the Maxim, then open up on the back of the column, and move your fire forward.'

Sergeant Ezra nodded, and levered a cartridge into the breech of the Winchester. He screwed up his eyes, judging the wind-deflection by the swaying of the grasstops and the feel of it against his face. Then he settled his elbow on the earthen parapet of the gulley, and laid his scarred cheek against the butt.

Ralph returned along the donga to where Harry Mellow was preparing the Maxim. He watched while Harry twisted the elevation screw to raise the barrel slightly to the 300 yard setting, and then swung the gun left and right in its tripod to make certain that the traverse was free and clear.

'Load one,' Ralph ordered, and Taas, who was loading, fed the brass tag of the cartridge-belt into the open breech. Harry let the loading handle fly back and the mechanism clattered harshly.

'Load two!' He pumped the handle a second time, pulling the belt through, and the first round was extracted from the belt and fed smoothly into the breech.

'Ready!' Harry looked up at Ralph.

'Now all we have to do is wait.'

Ralph nodded, and opened the pouch on his hip. From it he took the strip of brown mole-skin and bound it carefully about his right arm above the elbow. Then they settled down to wait.

They waited in the sunlight, and it beat down upon their greasy naked backs, until their sweat oozed from clogged pores and the flies came swarming gleefully to it. They waited while the sun made its noon, and then began to slip down the farther side of the sky.

Abruptly, Ralph raised his head, and at the movement a little stirring rippled down the row of marksmen lining the lip of the donga. There was a sound of many voices at a distance, and they woke echoes from the lichen-stained cliffs that guarded the entrance to the gorge. Then there was singing, sweet children's voices, the sound of it rose and filled with each fluke of the wind and each turn in the rocky passage.

From the entrance to the gorge a diminutive figure came dancing. The weird pattern of red and black and white paints disguised Jan Cheroot's flat pug-like features, and the buttery yellow of his skin, but there was no mistaking his sprightly step, and the way he carried his head at a birdlike angle. The sack of pretties that he had used as bait was long ago empty and had been discarded.

He scampered down the path towards the stone cairn which Ralph had built, and behind him came the Matabele. So eager were they that they crowded three or four abreast, and jostled each other to keep pace with the Pied Piper that led them.

'More then I had hoped,' Ralph whispered, but Harry Mellow did not look at him. The coating of black fat covered the pallor of his face, but his eyes were stricken as he stared fixedly over the sights of the Maxim.

The long column of Matabele was still emerging from the gorge, but Jan Cheroot was almost level with the cairn.

'Ready,' Ralph grated.

Jan Cheroot reached the cairn, and then with a miraculous twinkling movement, he disappeared as though a pitfall had sucked him in.

'Now!' said Ralph.

Not a man in the long line of riflemen moved. They were all staring down into the valley.

'Now!' Ralph repeated.

The head of the column had stopped in bewilderment at Jan Cheroot's abrupt disappearance, and those behind pushed forward.

'Open fire!' Ralph ordered.

'I can't do it,' whispered Harry, sitting behind the gun with both hands on the grips.

'Damn you!' Ralph's voice shook. 'They slit Cathy's belly open, and tore my daughter out of her womb. Kill them, damn you!'

'I can't,' Harry choked, and Ralph seized his shoulder and dragged him backwards.

He dropped down behind the gun in his place, and grabbed the double pistol grips. With his forefingers he hooked the safety-locks open, and then pressed his thumbs down on the chequered firing-button. The Maxim gun began its hellish fluttering roar, and the empty brass cartridge-cases spewed in a bright stream from the breech.

Peering through the drifts of blue gunsmoke, Ralph slowly traversed the gun from left to right, sweeping the pathway from the mouth of the gorge to the stone cairn, and from the donga on each side of him the repeating Winchesters added their thunder to the din. The gunfire almost, but not quite, drowned out the sounds from the valley below.

J uba could not keep pace with the younger women, nor with the racing children. She lagged further and further behind, with Tungata urging her on anxiously.

'We will be too late, Grandmother. We must hurry.'

Before they reached the gorge at the end of the valley, Juba was wheezing and staggering, all her rolls of shining fat wobbling at each heavy pace, and she was seeing patches of darkness before her eyes.

'I must rest,' she panted, and sank down beside the path. The stragglers streamed past her, laughing and joshing her as they entered the gorge.

'Ah, little Mother, do you want to climb up on my back?'

Tungata waited beside her, hopping from one foot to the other, wringing his hands with impatience.

'Oh Grandmother, just a little farther—'

When at last the patches of darkness cleared from her vision, she nodded at him, and he seized her hands and threw all the weight of his tiny body into levering her upright.

Now, as Juba hobbled along the path, they were the very last in the file, but they could hear the laughter and chanting far ahead, magnified by the funnel of the gorge. Tungata ran forward, and then drawn by his duty, skipped back to Juba's hand again.

'Please, Grandmother – oh please!'

Twice more Juba was forced to stop. They were all alone now, and the sunlight did not penetrate the depths of the narrow gorge. It was shadowy and the cold coming up from the dashing white waters chilled even Tungata's high spirits.

The two of them came around the bend, and looked out between the high granite portals into the open sunlit grassy bowl beyond.

'There they are!' Tungata cried with relief.

The pathway through the yellow grassland was thick with people, but, like a column of safari ants on the march that had come against an impossible obstacle, the head of the line was bunching and milling.

'Hurry, Grandmother, we can catch up!'

Juba heaved her bulk upright and hobbled towards the welcoming warm sunlight.

At that moment the air around her head began to flutter as though a bird had been trapped within her skull. For a moment she thought that it was a symptom of her exhaustion, but then she saw the masses of human figures ahead of her begin to swirl and tumble and boil like dust-motes in a whirlwind.

Although she had never heard it before, she had listened when the warriors who had fought at Shangani and the Bembesi crossing described the little three-legged guns that chattered like old women. Armed suddenly by reserves of strength that she never believed she possessed, Juba seized Tungata and blundered back up the gorge like a great cow elephant in flight.

R alph Ballantyne sat on the edge of his camp cot. There was a lighted candle set in its own wax on the upturned tea-chest that served as a table, and a half-filled whisky bottle and enamel mug beside it.

Ralph frowned at the open page of his journal, trying to focus in the flickering yellow candlelight. He was drunk. The bottle had been full half an hour before. He picked up the mug and drained it, set it down and poured from the bottle again. A few drops spilled onto the empty page of his journal. He wiped them away with his thumb and studied the wet mark it left with a drunkard's ponderous concentration. He shook his head, to try and clear it, then he picked up his pen, dipped it and carefully wiped off the excess ink from the nib.

He wrote laboriously and where the ink touched the wetness left by the spilled whisky, it spread in a soft blue fan shape on the paper. That annoyed him inordinately, and he flung the pen down and deliberately filled the enamel mug to the brim. He drank it, pausing twice for breath, and when the mug was empty, he held it between his knees, with his head bowed over it.

After a long time, and with an obvious effort, he lifted his head again, and re-read what he had written, his lips forming the words, like a schoolboy with his first reader.

'War makes monsters of us all.'

He reached for the bottle again, but knocked it on its side and the golden brown spirit glugged into a puddle on the lid of the tea-chest. He fell back on the cot and closed his eyes, his legs dangling to the floor and one arm thrown over his face protectively.

Elizabeth had put the boys to bed in the wagon, and crawled into the cot below theirs, careful not to disturb her own mother. Ralph had not eaten dinner with the family, and he had sent Jonathan back with a rough word when he had gone across to the tent to fetch his father to the meal.

Elizabeth lay on her side under the woollen blanket, and

her eye was level with the laced-up opening in the canvas hood, so she could see out. The candle was still burning in Ralph's tent, but, in the corner of the laager, the tent that Harry and Vicky shared had been in darkness for an hour. She closed her eyes and tried to force herself to sleep, but she was so restless that beside her Robyn St John sighed petulantly and rolled over. Elizabeth opened her eyes again and peered surreptitiously through the canvas slit. The candle was still burning in Ralph's tent.

Gently she eased herself out from under the blanket, watching her mother the while. She picked up her shawl from the lid of the chest, and clambered silently down to the ground.

With the shawl about her shoulders, she sat on the disselboom of the wagon. There was still only a sheet of canvas between her and where her mother lay. She could clearly hear the rhythm of Robyn's breathing. She judged when she sank deeply below the level of consciousness, for her breathing made a soft glottal rattle in the back of her throat.

The night was warm, and the laager almost silent; a puppy yapped unhappily from the far end, and closer at hand a baby's hungry wail was swiftly gagged by a mother's teat. Two of the sentries met at the nearest corner of the laager, and their voices murmured for a while. Then they parted and she saw the silhouette of a slouch hat against the night sky as one of them passed close to where she sat.

The candle still burned in the tent, and it must be past midnight by now. The flame drew her as though she were a moth. She rose and crossed to the tent. Silently, almost furtively. She lifted the flap and slipped in, letting it drop closed behind her.

Ralph lay on his back on the steel cot, his booted feet dangled to the ground, and one arm covered his face. He was making an unhappy little whimpering sound in his sleep. The candle was guttering, burned down into a puddle of its own molten wax, and the smell of spilled whisky was sharp and pungent. Elizabeth crossed to the tea-chest, and set the fallen bottle upright. Then the open page of the journal caught her attention, and she read the big uneven scrawl: 'War makes monsters of us all.'

It gave her a pang of pity so sharp that she closed the leatherbound journal quickly, and looked at the man who had written that agonized heart-cry. She wanted to reach across and touch his unshaven cheek, but instead she hitched her nightdress in a businesslike fashion and squatted beside the cot. She undid the straps of his riding-boots, and then, taking them one at a time between her knees, she pulled them off his feet. Ralph muttered and flung the arm off his face, rolling away from the candlelight. Gently Elizabeth lifted his legs and swung them up onto the cot. He groaned and curled into a foetal position.

'Big baby,' she whispered, and smiled to herself. Then she could resist no longer and she stroked the thick dark lock of hair off his forehead. His skin was fever-hot, moist with sweat, and she laid her palm against his cheek. His dark new beard was stiff and harsh, the feel of it sent electric prickles shooting up her arm. She pulled her hand away, and, once more businesslike, unfolded the blanket from the foot of the cot and drew it up over his body.

She leaned over him to settle it under his chin, but he rolled over again and before she could jump back, one hard muscular arm wrapped over her shoulder. She lost her balance and fell against his chest, and the arm pinned her helplessly.

She lay very still, her heart pounding wildly. After a minute the grip of his arm relaxed, and gently she tried to free herself. At her first movement, the arm locked about her, with such savage strength that her breath was driven from her lungs with a gasp.

Ralph mumbled, and brought his other hand over, and she convulsed with shock as it settled high up on the back of her thigh. She dared not move. She knew she could not break the grip of his restraining arm. She had never expected him to be so powerful, she felt as helpless as an unweaned infant, totally in his power. She felt the hand behind her begin to fumble and grope upwards – and then she sensed the moment when he became conscious.

The hand slid up to the nape of her neck, and her head was pulled forward with a gentle but irresistible force until she felt the heat and the wetness of his mouth spread over hers. He tasted of whisky and something else, a yeasty musky man taste, and without her volition, her own lips melted and spread to meet his.

Her senses spun like wheels of flame behind her closed eyelids, the sensations were so tumultuous, that for long moments she did not realize that he had swept her nightdress up to the level of her shoulder-blades, and now his fingers, hard as bone, and hot as fire, ran in a long slow caress down the cleft of her naked buttocks and then settled into the soft curve where they joined her thighs. It galvanized her.

Her breath sobbed in her throat, and she struggled to be free, to escape from the torture of her own wild wanting, of her cruel need for him, and from his skilful insistent fingers. He held her easily, his mouth against the soft of her throat, and his voice was hoarse and rough.

'Cathy!' he said. 'My Katie! I missed you so!'

Elizabeth stopped struggling. She lay against him like a dead woman. No longer fighting, no longer even breathing.

'Katie!' His hands were desperate to find her, but she was dead, dead.

He was fully awake now. His hands left Elizabeth's body and came up to her face. He cupped her head in his hands, and lifted it. He looked at her uncomprehendingly for a long moment, and then she saw the green change in his eyes.

'Not Cathy!' he whispered.

She opened his fingers gently and stood up beside the cot.

'Not Cathy,' she said softly. 'Cathy has gone, Ralph.'

She stooped over the guttering candle, cupped one hand behind it, and blew it out. Then she stood upright again in the sudden total darkness. She unfastened the bodice of her nightdress, shrugged it over her shoulders and let it fall around her ankles. She stepped out of it and lay down on the cot beside Ralph. She took his unresisting hand and replaced it where it had been before.

'Not Cathy,' she whispered. 'Tonight it's Elizabeth. Tonight and for ever more.' And she placed her mouth over his.

When at last she felt him fill all the sad and lonely places within her, her joy was so intense that it seemed to crush and bruise her soul and she said: 'I love you. I have always loved you – I will always love you.'

Jordan Ballantyne stood beside his father on the platform of the Cape Town railway station. They were both stiff and awkward in the moment of parting.

'Please don't forget to give my,' Jordan hesitated over the choice of words, 'my very warmest regards to Louise.'

'I am sure she will be pleased,' said Zouga. 'I have not seen her for so long—' Zouga broke off.

The separation from his wife had drawn out over the long months of his trial in the Queen's Bench Division of the High Court before the Lord Chief Justice, Baron Pollock, Mr Justice Hawkins, and a special jury. The Lord Chief Justice had shepherded a reluctant jury towards the inevitable verdict.

'I direct you that, in accordance with the evidence and your answers to the specific questions I have put to you, you ought to find a verdict of guilty against all the defendants.' And he had his way.

'The sentence of the Court, therefore, is that as to you

Leander Starr Jameson, and as to you John Willoughby, that you be confined for a period of fifteen months' imprisonment without hard labour. That you, Major Zouga Ballantyne, have three months' imprisonment without hard labour.'

Zouga had served four weeks of his sentence in Holloway, and with the balance remitted, had been released to the dreadful news that in Rhodesia the Matabele had risen and that Bulawayo was under siege.

The voyage southwards down the Atlantic had been agonizing, he had had no word of Louise, nor of King's Lynn, and his imagination conjured up horrors that were nourished by tales of slaughter and mutilation. Only when the Union Castle mailboat had docked that morning in Cape Town Harbour were his terrible anxieties relieved.

'She is safe in Bulawayo,' Jordan had answered his first question. Overcome with emotion, Zouga had embraced his youngest son, repeating, 'Thank God, oh thank God!' over and over again.

They had lunched together in the dining-room of the Mount Nelson Hotel and Jordan had given his father the latest intelligence from the north.

'Napier and the Siege Committee seem to have stabilized the situation. They have got the survivors into Bulawayo, and Grey and Selous and Ralph with their irregulars have given the rebels a few bloody knocks to keep them at a wary distance.

'Of course the Matabele have an absolutely free run of the territory outside the laagers at Bulawayo and Gwelo and Belingwe. They do as they please, though strangely enough they do not seem to have closed the road to the southern drifts. If you can reach Kimberley in time to join the relief column that Spreckley is taking through, you should be in Bulawayo by the end of the month – and Mr Rhodes and I will not be long in joining you.

'Spreckley will be taking through only essential supplies, and a few hundred men to stiffen the defence of Bulawayo until the imperial troops can get there. As you probably know, Major-General Sir Frederick Carrington has been chosen to command, and Mr Rhodes and I will be going up with his staff. I have no doubt we will bring the rebels to book very swiftly.'

Jordan kept up a monologue during the entire meal, to cover the embarrassment caused by the stares and the whispers of the other diners, who were deliciously scandalized by the presence of one of Jameson's freebooters in their midst. Zouga ignored the stir he was creating, and addressed himself to the meal and the conversation with Jordan until a young journalist from the *Cape Times*, clutching his shorthand pad, approached the table.

'I wonder if you would care to comment on the leniency of the sentences passed by the Lord Chief Justice.'

Only then did Zouga raise his head, and his expression was bleak.

'In the years ahead they will give medals and knighthoods to men who achieve exactly the same task that we attempted,' he said quietly. 'Now will you be kind enough to let us finish our lunch in peace.'

At the railway station Jordan fussed over making certain that Zouga's trunk was in the goods van and that he had a forward-facing seat in the last carriage. Then they faced each other awkwardly, as the guard blew his warning whistle.

'Mr Rhodes asked me to enquire whether you would still be good enough to act as his agent at Bulawayo?'

'Tell Mr Rhodes that I am honoured by his continued confidence.'

They shook hands and Zouga climbed into the coach.

'If you see Ralph—'

'Yes?' Zouga asked.

'Never mind.' Jordan shook his head. 'I hope you have a safe journey, Papa.'

Leaning from the carriage-window as the train pulled out

from the platform, Zouga studied the receding figure of his youngest son. He was a fine-looking young fellow, Zouga decided, tall and athletic, his grey three-piece suit in fashion, yet also in perfect understated taste – and yet there was something incongruous about him, an air of the lost waif, an aura of uncertainty and deep-rooted unhappiness.

'Damned nonsense,' Zouga told himself, and drew his head in and pulled up the window by its leather strap.

The locomotive built up speed across the Cape flats for its assault on the rampart of mountains that guarded the African continental shield.

J ordan Ballantyne cantered up the driveway towards the great white house, that crouched amongst its oaks and stone-pines on the lower slopes of the flat-topped mountain. He was pursued by a feeling of guilt. It was many years since he had neglected his duties for an entire day. Even a year ago it would have been unthinkable for him to do so. Every day, Sunday and public holidays notwithstanding, Mr Rhodes needed him close at hand.

The subtle change in their relationship was something that increased his feelings of guilt and introduced a darker more corrosive emotion. It had not been entirely necessary for him to spend the whole day with his father, from when the mailship worked her way into Table Bay, with the furious red dawn and the south-easter raging about her, until the northern express pulled out from under the glassed dome of Cape Town station. He could have slipped away and been back at his desk within a few hours, but he had tried to force a refusal out of Mr Rhodes, an acknowledgement of his own indispensability.

'Take a few days if you like, Jordan – Arnold will be able to handle anything that might come up.' Mr Rhodes had barely glanced up from the London papers.

'There is that new draft of Clause 27 of your will—' Jordan had tried to provoke him, and instead received the reply he most dreaded.

'Oh, give that to Arnold. It's time he understood about the scholarships. Anyway, it will give him a chance to use that newfangled Remington machine of his.'

Mr Rhodes' childlike pleasure in having his correspondence printed out swiftly and neatly on the caligraph was another source of disquiet to Jordan. Jordan had not yet mastered the caligraph's noisy keyboard, chiefly because Arnold's jealousy monopolized the machine. Jordan had ordered his own model shipped out to him, but it had to come from New York and it would be months yet before he could expect it to arrive.

Now Jordan reined in the big glossy bay at the steps to Groote Schuur's back stoep, and as he dismounted, he tossed the reins to the groom, and hurried into the house. He took the backstairs to the second floor, and went directly to his own room, unbuttoning his shirt and pulling the tails from his breeches as he kicked the door closed behind him.

He poured water from the Delft jug into the basin and splashed it onto his face. Then he dried on a fluffy white towel, tossed it aside and picked up the silver-handled brushes and ran them over his crisp golden curls. He was about to turn away from the mirror and find a fresh shirt when he stopped, and stared thoughtfully at his own image.

Slowly he leaned closer to the glass and touched his face with his fingertips. There were crows' feet at the outer corners of his eyes; he stretched the skin between his fingers but the lines persisted. He turned his head slightly, the light from the tall window showed up the pouches beneath his eyes.

'You only see them at that angle,' he thought, and then flattened his hair back from the peak of his forehead with the palm of his hand. There was the pearly gleam of his scalp through the thinning strands, and quickly he fluffed his hair up again.

He wanted to turn away, but the mirror had a dreadful fascination. He smiled: it was a grimace that lifted his upper lip. His left canine tooth was darker, definitely a darker grey than it had been a month before when the dentist had drilled out the nerve, and suddenly Jordan was overwhelmed by a cold penetrating despair.

'In less than two weeks' time I will be thirty years old – oh God, I'm getting old, so old and ugly. How can anyone still like me?'

He bore down hard on the sob that threatened to choke him, and turned away from the cruel glass.

In his office there was a note in the centre of the tooled morocco leather top of his desk, weighted down with the silver ink well.

'See me as soon as possible. C. J. R.'

It was in that familiar spiky scrawl, and Jordan felt a leap of his spirits. He picked up his shorthand pad, and knocked on the communicating door.

'Come!' the high-pitched voice commanded, and Jordan went through.

'Good evening, Mr Rhodes, you wanted to see me?'

Mr Rhodes did not reply at once, but went on making corrections to the typed sheet in front of him, crossing out a word and scrawling a substitute above it, changing a comma to a semi-colon, and while he worked, Jordan studied his face.

The deterioration was shocking. He was almost totally grey now, and the pouches below his eyes were a deep purple colour. His jowl had thickened and hung in a dewlap under his jawbone. His eyes were red-rimmed and their Messianic blue was blurred and diluted. All this in the six months or so since Jameson's disastrous raid, and Jordan's thoughts jumped back to that day that the news had come. Jordan had brought it to him in this same library.

There had been three telegrams. One from Jameson himself was addressed to Mr Rhodes' Cape Town office, not to the mansion at Groote Schuur, and so it had lain all weekend in the letterbox of the deserted building. It began, 'As I do not hear from you to the contrary—'

The second telegram was from the magistrate at Mafeking, Mr Boyes. It read in part, 'Colonel Grey has ridden with police detachments to reinforce Dr Jameson—'

The last telegram was from the commissioner of police at Kimberley. 'I deem it my duty to inform you that Dr Jameson, at the head of a body of armed men, has crossed the Transvaal border—'

Mr Rhodes had read the telegrams, meticulously arranging them on the top of his desk before him as he finished each.

'I thought I had stopped him,' he had kept muttering as he read. 'I thought he understood that he must wait.'

By the time he had finished reading, he had been pale as candlewax and the flesh seemed to have sagged from the bones of his face like unrisen dough.

'Poor old Jameson,' he had whispered at last. 'Twenty years we have been friends and now he goes and destroys me.' Mr Rhodes had leaned his elbows on the desk and placed his face in his hands. He had sat like that for many minutes and then said clearly: 'Well, Jordan, now I will see who my true friends are.'

Mr Rhodes had not slept for five nights after that. Jordan had lain awake in his own room down the passage and listened to the heavy tread back and forth across the yellow-wood floor, and then, long before the first light of dawn, Mr Rhodes would ring for him, and they would ride together for hours upon the slopes of Table Mountain before returning to the great white mansion to face the latest renunciations and rejections, to watch with a kind of helpless fascination his life and his work crumbling inexorably into dust about them.

Then Arnold had arrived to take his place as Jordan's assistant. His official title was second secretary, and Jordan had welcomed his assistance with the more mundane details of running the complex household. He had accompanied them on their visit to London in the aftermath of Jameson's misadventure, and remained firmly by Rhodes' side on the long return journey via the Suez Canel, Beira and Salisbury.

Now Arnold stood attentively beside Mr Rhodes' desk, handing him a sheet typed upon the caligraph, waiting while he read and corrected it, and then replacing it with a fresh sheet. With the rancid taste of envy, Jordan recognized, not for the first time, that Arnold possessed the clean blond good looks that Mr Rhodes so much admired. His demeanour was modest and frank, yet when he laughed, his entire being seemed to glow with some inner illumination. He had been up at Oriel, Mr Rhodes' old Oxford college, and it was more and more obvious that Mr Rhodes took pleasure and comfort in having him near by, as he had once taken from Jordan's presence.

Jordan waited quietly by the door, feeling strangely out of place in what he had come to think of as his own home, until Mr Rhodes handed the last corrected sheet to Arnold and looked up.

'Ah, Jordan,' he said. 'I wanted to warn you that I am advancing the date of my departure for Bulawayo. I think my Rhodesians need me. I must go to them.'

'I will see to it immediately,' Jordan nodded. 'Have you decided on a date, Mr Rhodes?'

'Next Monday.'

'We will take the express to Kimberley, of course?'

'You will not be accompanying me,' said Mr Rhodes flatly.

'I do not understand, Mr Rhodes.' Jordan made a helpless little gesture of incomprehension.

'I require utter loyalty and honesty in my employees.'

'Yes, Mr Rhodes, I know that.' Jordan nodded, and then

slowly his expression became uncertain and disbelieving. 'You are not suggesting that I have ever been disloyal or dishonest—'

'Get that file, please, Arnold,' Mr Rhodes ordered, and when he fetched it from the library table, he added, 'Give it to him.'

Arnold silently came across the thick silk and wool carpet, and offered the box-file to Jordan. As he reached for it, Jordan was aware, for the first time ever, of something other than openness and friendly concern in Arnold's eyes, it was a flash of vindictive triumph so vicious as to sting like the lash of a riding-whip across the face. It lasted for only a blink of time, and was gone so swiftly that it might never have been, but it left Jordan feeling utterly vulnerable and in dreadful danger.

He placed the folder on the table beside him, and opened the cover. There were at least fifty sheets in the folder. Most of them had been typed on the caligraph, and each was headed 'Copy of original.'

There were stockbrokers' buy and sell orders, for shares in De Beers and Consolidated Goldfields. The quantities of shares in the transactions were enormous, involving millions of sterling. The broking firm was Silver & Co., of whom Jordan had never heard, though they purported to conduct business in Johannesburg, Kimberley and London.

Then there were copies of statements from half a dozen banks, in the different centres where Silver & Co. had offices. A dozen or so entries on the statements had been underlined in red ink: 'Transfer to Rholands – £86,321 – 7s 9d. Transfer to Rholands – £146,821 – 9s 11d.'

The name shocked him, Ralph's company, and though he did not understand why, it increased his sense of peril.

'I don't understand what this has to do with me—' He looked up at Mr Rhodes.

'Your brother entered into a series of large bear transactions in those companies most drastically affected by the failure of Jameson's enterprise.'

'It would appear—' Jordan began uncertainly, and was interrupted by Mr Rhodes.

'It would appear that he has made profits in excess of a million pounds, and that he and his agents have gone to extreme lengths to disguise and conceal these machinations.'

'Mr Rhodes, why do you tell me this, why do you adopt that tone? He is my brother, but I cannot be held responsible—'

Mr Rhodes held up one hand to silence him. 'Nobody has accused you of anything yet – your eagerness to justify yourself is unbecoming.'

Then he opened the leatherbound copy of Plutarch's *Lives* which lay on one corner of his desk. There were three sheets of writing-paper lying between the pages. Mr Rhodes took out the sheets, and proffered the top one to Jordan.

'Do you recognize this?'

Jordan felt himself blushing agonizingly. At that moment he hated himself for ever having written this letter. He had done so in the terrible spiritual travail following the night of Ralph's discoveries and brutal accusation in the private pullman coach from Kimberley.

'It is the copy of a private letter that I wrote to my brother—' Jordan could not lift his eyes to meet those of Mr Rhodes. 'I do not know what possessed me to keep a copy of it.'

A paragraph caught his eye, and he could not prevent himself re-reading his own words.

'There is nothing I would not do to convince you of my continued affection, for only now, when I seem to have forfeited it, am I truly conscious of how much your regard means to me.'

He held the sheet possessively. 'This is a private and intimate communication,' he said in a low voice, which shook with shame and outrage. 'Apart from my brother, to whom it is addressed, nobody has the right to read it.'

'You do not deny that you are the author, then?'

'It would be vain of me to do so.'

'Indeed, it would,' Mr Rhodes agreed, and passed him the second sheet.

Jordan read on down the page in mounting bewilderment. The handwriting was his, but the words were not. So skilfully and naturally did they continue from the sentiments of the first page, however, that he found himself almost doubting his own recall. What he was reading was his own acquiescence to pass on to Ralph confidential and privileged information related to the planning and timing of Jameson's intervention in the Transvaal. '*I do agree that the contemplated venture is totally outside civilized law, and this has convinced me to give you my assistance – this and the moral debt that I feel that I owe to you.*'

Only then he noticed the slant and form of a letter that was not in his hand. The entire page was a skilful forgery. He shook his head wordlessly. He felt as though the fabric of his existence had been ripped through and through.

'That your conspiracy was successful, we know from the rich fruits your brother harvested,' said Mr Rhodes wearily, in the voice of a man so often betrayed that this no longer had the power to wound him. 'I congratulate you, Jordan.'

'Where did this come from?' The page shook in Jordan's hand. 'Where—' He broke off and looked up at Arnold, standing behind his master's shoulder. There was no trace of that vindictive triumph remaining; Arnold was grave and concerned – and unbearably handsome.

'I see,' Jordan nodded. 'It is a forgery, of course.'

Mr Rhodes made an impatient gesture. 'Really Jordan. Who would go to the trouble of forging bank statements that can readily be verified?'

'Not the bank statements, the letter.'

'You agreed it was yours.'

'Not this page, not this—'

Mr Rhodes' expression was remote, his eyes cold and unfeeling.

'I will have the bookkeeper come up from the town office to go over the household accounts with you, and to make an inventory. You will, of course, hand over your keys to Arnold. As soon as all that has been done, I will instruct the bookkeeper to issue you a cheque for three months' salary in lieu of notice, though I am certain you will understand my reluctance to provide you with a letter of recommendation. I would be obliged if you could remove yourself and your belongings from these premises before my return from Rhodesia.'

'Mr Rhodes—'

'There is nothing further that we have to discuss.'

Mr Rhodes and his entourage, Arnold amongst them, had left on the northern express for Kimberley and the Matabeleland railhead three weeks before. It had taken that long for Jordan to wind up the inventories and complete the household accounts.

Mr Rhodes had not spoken to Jordan again after that final confrontation. Arnold had relayed two brief instructions, and Jordan had retained his dignity and resisted the temptation to hurl bootless recriminations at his triumphant rival. He had only seen Mr Rhodes three times since that fateful evening, twice from his office window as he returned from those long aimless rides through the pine forests on the lower slopes of the mountain, and the third and final time as he climbed into the coach for the railway station.

Now, as he had been for three long weeks, Jordan was alone in the great deserted mansion. He had ordered the servants to leave early, and had personally checked the kitchens and rear areas, before locking up the doors. He moved slowly through the carpeted passageways carrying the oil-lamp in both hands. He wore the Chinese silk brocade dressing-gown that had been Mr Rhodes' personal gift to him on his twenty-fifth birthday. He felt burned out, blackened like a forest tree after the fire has passed, leaving the hollowed-out trunk continuing to smoulder within.

He was on a pilgrimage of farewell about the great house, and the memories that it contained. He had been present from the very first days of the planning to renovate and redecorate the old building. He had spent so many hours listening to Herbert Baker and Mr Rhodes, taking notes of their conversations and occasionally, at Mr Rhodes' invitation, making a suggestion.

It was Jordan who had suggested the motif for the mansion, a stylized representation of the stone bird from the ancient ruins of Rhodesia, the falcon of Zimbabwe. The great raptor, the pedestal on which it perched decorated with a shark's tooth pattern, adorned the banisters of the main staircase. It was worked into the polished granite of the huge bath in Mr Rhodes' suite, it formed a fresco around the walls of the dining-room and four replicas of the strange bird supported the corners of Mr Rhodes' desk.

The bird had been a part of Jordan's life from as far back as his earliest memories reached. The original statue had been taken by Zouga Ballantyne from the ancient temple, one of seven identical statues that he had discovered there. He had only been able to carry one of them. He had left the other birds lying in the ancient temple enclosure, and taken the best-preserved example.

Almost thirty years later Ralph Ballantyne had returned to Great Zimbabwe, guided by his father's journal and the map he had drawn. Ralph had found the six remaining statues lying in the temple enclosure of the ruins just as his father had left them, but Ralph had come prepared. He had loaded the statues onto the draught oxen he had brought with him and, despite the attempts of the Matabele guardians to prevent him, had escaped southwards across the Shashi river with his treasure. In Cape Town a syndicate of businessmen headed by the multi-millionaire, Barney Barnato, had purchased the relics from Ralph for a substantial sum, and had presented them to the South African Museum in Cape Town. The six statues were still on display to the public there. Jordan had visited the premises, and spent an hour standing transfixed before them.

However, his own personal magic was embodied in the original statue that his father had discovered, and which throughout his childhood had ridden as ballast over the rear wheel-truck of the family wagon, during their wanderings and travels across the vast African veld. Jordan had slept a thousand nights above the bird, and somehow its spirit had pervaded his own and taken possession of him.

When Zouga at last led the family to the Kimberley diamond-diggings, the bird statue had been unloaded from the wagon and placed under the camel-thorn tree which marked their last camp. When Jordan's mother, Aletta Ballantyne, had fallen sick with the deadly camp fever, and finally succumbed to the disease, the statue had come to play an even larger place in Jordan's life.

He had christened the bird Panes, after the goddess of the North American Indian tribes, and later he had avidly studied the lore of the great goddess Panes that Frazer had detailed in his *Golden Bough*, a study in magic and religion. He learned how Panes was a beautiful woman who had been taken up into the mountains. To the adolescent Jordan, Panes and the bird statue became confused with the image of his dead mother. Secretly he had developed a form of invocation to the goddess, and in the dead of night when all the other members of his family slept, he would creep out to make a small sacrifice of hoarded food to Panes and worship her with his own rituals.

When Zouga, financially reduced, had been forced to sell the bird to Mr Rhodes, the boy had been desolated – until the opportunity to enter Mr Rhodes' service and follow the goddess replaced the emptiness of his existence with not one but two deities: the goddess Panes and Mr Rhodes. Even after he was grown to manhood in Mr Rhodes' service, the statue continued to bulk large in Jordan's consciousness, though it was only very occasionally, in times of deep turmoil of the spirit, that he actually resorted to the childish rituals of worship.

Now he had lost the lodestone of his life, and irresistibly he was drawn towards the statue for the last time. Slowly he descended the curve of the main staircase. As he passed, he caressed the carved balustrades which were worked into faithful copies of the ancient bird.

The lofty entrance hallway below was floored with black and white marble slabs arranged in a chequer-board pattern. The main doors were in massive red teak, and the fittings were of burnished brass. The light of the lantern that Jordan carried sent grotesquely misshapen shadows flowing across the marble or fluttering like gigantic bats against the high carved ceiling. In the centre of the marble floor stood a heavy table, upon which were the silver trays for visiting-cards and mail. Between them was a tall decoration of dried protea blooms which Jordan had arranged with his own hands.

Jordan set the lamp of Sèvres porcelain upon the table like a ritual lantern upon a pagan altar. He stepped back from it and slowly raised his head. The original stone falcon of Zimbabwe stood in its high niche, guarding the entrance to Groote Schuur. Seeing it thus it was not possible to doubt the aura of magical power that invested the graven image. It seemed that the prayers and incantations of the long-dead priests of Zimbabwe still shimmered in the air about it, that the blood of the sacrifices steamed from the wavering shadows upon the marble floor, and that the prophecies of the Umlimo, the Chosen One of the ancient spirits, invested it with separate life.

Zouga Ballantyne had heard the prophecies from the Umlimo's lips and had faithfully recorded them in his journal. Jordan had re-read them a hundred times and could repeat them by rote, he had made them part of his own personal ritual and invocation to the goddess.

'There shall be no peace in the kingdom of the Mambos or the Monomatapa until they return. For the white eagle will war with the black bull until the stone falcons return to roost.'

Jordan looked up at the bird's proud, cruel head, at the sightless eyes which stared blankly towards the north, towards the land of the Mambos and the Monomatapa which men now called Rhodesia, and where the white eagle and the black bull were again locked in mortal conflict, and Jordan felt a sense of helplessness and emptiness, as though he were caught up in the coils of destiny and was unable to break free.

'Have pity on me, great Panes,' and he dropped to his knees. 'I cannot go. I cannot leave you or him. I have no place to go.'

In the lamplight his face was tinged with a faint greenish sheen, as though it had been carved from glacial ice. He lifted the porcelain lamp from the table, and held it high above his head with both hands.

'Forgive me, great Panes,' he whispered, and hurled the lamp against the panelled woodwork of the wall.

The lobby was plunged into darkness for a moment, as the flame of the shattered lamp fluttered to the very edge of extinction. Then it sent a ghostly blue light skittering across the surface of the spreading pool of oil. Suddenly the flames burned up strongly and touched the trailing edges of the long velvet drapes that covered the windows.

Still kneeling before the stone statue, Jordan coughed as the first wisps of smoke enveloped him. He was mildly surprised that, after the first burning sting of it in his lungs, there was so very little pain. The image of the falcon high above him slowly receded, dimmed by the tears that filled Jordan's eyes and by the dense swirling curtains of smoke.

The flames made a low drumming roar as they caught on the wooden panelling and shot to the ceiling. One of the heavy drapes burned through, and as it fell it spread open like the wings of an immense vulture. The fiery wings of thick velvet covered Jordan's kneeling figure and their weight bore him face down to the marble floor.

Already asphyxiated by the dense blue smoke, he did not even struggle and within seconds the mound of crumpled velvet was transformed into a funeral pyre, and the flames reached up joyously to lick against the base of the stone falcon in its high niche.

'Bazo has come down from the place of the Umlimo at last,' Isazi said quietly, and Ralph could not contain himself.

'Are you sure of this?' he demanded eagerly, and Isazi nodded.

'I have sat at the camp-fires of his impi, and with my own eyes have seen him, with the bullet scars shining like medals of silver upon his chest, with my own ears I have heard him harangue his *amadoda*, steeling them for the fighting which lies ahead.'

'Where is he, Isazi? Tell me where I can find him.'

'He is not alone.' Isazi was not about to spoil the dramatic impact of his report by prematurely divulging the bare bones of fact. 'Bazo has with him the witch, who is his woman. If Bazo is warlike, then this woman, Tanase, the favourite of the dark spirits, is bold and ruthless, driven by such bloody cruelty that the *amadoda* when they look upon her beauty shudder as though it is an unspeakable ugliness.'

'Where are they?' Ralph repeated.

'Bazo has with him the wildest and most reckless of the

young indunas, Zama and Kamuza, and they have brought their *amadoda*, three thousand of the fiercest and finest. With Bazo and Tanase at their head, these impis are as dangerous as the gut-stabbed lion, as deadly as the old bull buffalo circling in thick cover to lay for the unwary hunter—'

'God damn you, Isazi, we have waited long enough.' Ralph snarled at him. 'Tell me where he is.'

Isazi looked pained and deliberately took a little snuff. His eyes watered, then he sneezed delectably and wiped his nostrils on the palm of his hand.

'Gandang and Babiaan and Somabula are not with him.' Isazi took up his recital precisely at the point where Ralph had so boorishly interrupted him. 'I listened while the *amadoda* spoke of an *indaba* held many weeks back at the valley of the Umlimo. They say that the old indunas decided to wait for the divine intervention of the spirits, to leave the road southwards open for the white men to leave Matabeleland and to sit upon their shields until these things come to pass.'

Ralph made a gesture of disgusted resignation. 'Do not hurry in your telling of it, wise one,' he encouraged Isazi with weighted sarcasm. 'Do not spare us the smallest detail.'

Isazi nodded seriously, but his dark eyes sparkled and he tugged at his little goatee beard to prevent himself grinning.

'The bellies of the old indunas are cooling, they recall the Shangani and Bembesi battlefields. Their spies report that the laager here at Bulawayo is guarded by the three-legged guns. I tell you, Henshaw, that Bazo is the serpent's head. Cut it off and the body dies.' Isazi nodded sagely.

'Now will you tell me where Bazo is, my brave and wise old friend?'

Isazi nodded again in appreciation of Ralph's change of tone.

'He is very close,' Isazi said. 'Not two hours' march from where we sit.' Isazi made a wide gesture that took in the darkened laager about them. 'He lies with his three thousand *amadoda* in the Valley of the Goats.'

Ralph looked up at the segment of old moon that hung low down in the sky.

'Four days to new moon,' he murmured. 'If Bazo plans to attack the laager here, then it will be in the dark of the moon.'

'Three thousand men,' Harry Mellow murmured. 'There are fifty of us.'

'Three thousand. The *Moles* and the *Insukamini* and the *Swimmers*.' Sergeant Ezra shook his head. 'As Isazi has said, the fiercest and the finest.'

'We will take them,' said Ralph Ballantyne calmly. 'We will take them in the Valley of the Goats, two nights from now, and here is the way we will do it—'

B azo, son of Gandang, who had denied his father and defied the greater indunas of Kumalo, passed from one watch-fire to the next and beside him moved the slim and exquisitely graceful figure of his woman, Tanase.

Bazo reached the fire and stood tall above it. The flames lit his features from below, so that the cavities of his eyes were black caverns in the depths of which his eyes glinted like the coils of a deadly reptile. The light of the camp-fire picked out in harsh detail every line and crease that suffering had riven into his face. Around his forehead was bound the simple strip of mole-skin; he did not need the feathers of heron and paradise widowbirds to place the seal upon his majesty. The firelight glinted upon the great muscles of his chest and arms and his scars were the only regalia of honour that he wore.

Tanase's beauty was even more poignant when seen beside his ravaged features. Her naked breasts were strangely incongruous in these warlike councils, but beneath their satiny swelling they were hard as battle-forged muscle, and the sudden thrust of her nipples puckered and dark, large as the first joint of a man's little finger, were like the bosses in the centre of a war-shield.

As she stood at Bazo's shoulder in the firelight, her gaze was as fierce as any warrior there, and she looked up at her husband with a ferocious pride as he began to speak.

'I offer you a choice,' Bazo said. 'You can remain as you are, the dogs of the white men. You can stay as *amaholi*, the lowliest of slaves, or you can become once again *amadoda*—'

His voice was not raised, nor strained; it seemed to rumble up out of his throat, but it rang clearly to the highest part of the natural rocky amphitheatre, and the dark masses of warriors that filled the bowl stirred and sighed at the words.

'The choice is yours, but it must be made swiftly. This morning I have received runners from the south.' Bazo paused, and his listeners craned forward. There were three thousand of them squatting in massed ranks, but there was no sound from them as they waited for Bazo's next words.

'You have heard the fainthearted tell you that if we do not dispute the southern road, then the white men that are in Bulawayo will pack their wagons, take their women and go meekly down that road to the sea.' Still not a sound from the listening warriors.

'They were wrong – and now they are proven so. Lodzi has come,' said Bazo, and there was a sigh like the wind in the grass.

'Lodzi has come,' Bazo repeated. 'And with him the soldiers and the guns. They gather now at the head of the iron road that Henshaw built. Soon, very soon, they will begin the march up the road which we have left open for them. Before the new moon is half grown to its full, they will be in Bulawayo, and then you will truly be *amaholi*. You and your sons and their sons will toil in the white men's mines and herd the white men's herds.'

There was a growl, like a leopard when first it is roused, and it shook the dark ranks until Bazo lifted high the hand that held his silver assegai.

'That is not to be. The Umlimo has promised us that this land will once again belong to us, but it is our task to make this prophecy into reality. The gods do not favour those who wait for fruit to fall from the tree into their open mouths. My children, we will shake the tree.'

'Jee!' said a single voice from the massed ranks, and immediately the humming war chant was taken up by them all.

'Jee!' sang Bazo, stamping his right foot and stabbing the broad blade towards the moonless sky, and his men sang with him.

Tanase stood still as an ebony carving beside him, but her lips were parted softly, and her huge slanted eyes glowed like moons in the firelight.

At last Bazo spread his arm again, and waited for their silence. 'Thus it will be,' he said, and again the waiting warriors strained for every word. 'First we will eat up the laager at Bulawayo. It has always been the way of the Matabele to fall upon their enemy at that hour before the dawn, just before the first light of day – ' the warriors hummed softly in assent – 'and the white men know this is our way,' Bazo went on. 'Every morning, in the last deep darkness they stand to their guns, waiting for the leopard to walk into their trap. The *Matabele always come before the dawn*, they tell each other. *Always!* they say, but I tell you that this time it will be different, my children.'

Bazo paused and looked carefully into the faces of the men who squatted in the front rank.

'This time it will be in the hour before midnight, at the rise of the white star from the east.'

Standing before them in the old way, Bazo gave them their order of battle, and squatting in the black mass of half-naked bodies, his bare shoulders touching those of the *amadoda* on each side of him, his hair covered by the feather headdress and his face and body plastered with the mixture of fat and soot, Ralph Ballantyne listened to the detailed instructions.

'At this season, the wind will rise with the rise of the white star. It will come from the east, so from the east we will come also. Each one of you will carry upon his head a bundle of thatch grass and the green leaves of the msasa trees,' Bazo told them, and anticipating what was to come, Ralph felt the nerve ends in his fingertips tingle with the shock.

'A smoke-screen,' he thought. 'That's a naval tactic!'

'As soon as the wind rises, we will build a great fire.' Bazo confirmed it immediately. 'Each of you will throw his bundle upon it as he passes, and we will go forward in the darkness and the smoke. It will avail them not at all to shoot their rockets into the sky, for our smoke will blind the gunners.'

Ralph imagined how it might be, the warriors emerging from the impenetrable rolling bank of smoke, not visible until they were within stabbing range, swarming over the wall of wagons or creeping between the wheels. Three thousand of them coming in silently and relentlessly – even if the laager were warned and alerted, it would be almost impossible to stop them. The Maxims would be almost useless in the smoke, and the broad-bladed assegais the more effective weapon at such close range.

A vivid image of the slaughter burned into his brain, and he remembered Cathy's corpse, and imagined beside it the mutilated remains of Jonathan and of Elizabeth, her white smooth flesh as cruelly desecrated. His rage came strongly to arm him, and he stared down into the amphitheatre at the tall heroic figure with the ravaged face, laying out the terrible details of the massacre.

'We must leave not a single one of them. We must destroy the last reason why Lodzi should bring his soldiers. We will offer him only dead bodies, burned buildings and silver steel, if he makes the attempt.'

Then in his rage Ralph shouted with the other *amadoda*, and hummed the wild war chant, his features as contorted as theirs, and his eyes as wild.

'The *indaba* is ended,' Bazo told them at last. 'Go now to your sleeping-mats to refresh yourself for the morrow. When you rise with the sun, let your first task be to cut, each of you, a bundle of dry grass and green leaves as heavy as you can carry.'

Ralph Ballantyne lay beneath his fur kaross on a sleeping-mat of woven reeds, and listened to the camp settling into sleep about him. They had withdrawn into the narrower reaches of the valley. He saw the watch-fires dwindle, and the circles of their orange light shrink in upon them. He listened to the murmur of voices subside, and the breathing of the warriors near him changing, becoming deeper and more regular.

Here the Valley of the Goats was broken rocky defile, choked with thick thorn scrub, so that the impis could not concentrate in one place. They were spread out in pockets, down the length of the valley, fifty men or so in each small clearing, the narrow twisted paths through the thorn scrub overshadowed by the taller trees, which formed a canopy overhead.

The darkness became more menacing as the last fires died into powdery grey ash, and Ralph, lying beneath the fur blanket, gripped the haft of his assegai and judged his moment.

It came at last, and Ralph drew back the kaross stealthily. On all fours he crept to where the nearest warrior lay, groping gently for him. His fingers touched the bare skin of an arm. The warrior started awake at the touch, and sat bolt upright.

'Who is it?' he asked in a thick guttural voice, rough with sleep, and Ralph stabbed him in the stomach.

The man screamed. It was a cry of ringing mortal agony that bounded from the rocky sides of the valley, cutting through the silences of the night watch, and Ralph bellowed with him.

'Devils! Devils are killing me!' He rolled over and stabbed another warrior, wounding him so he yelled in surprise and pain.

'There are devils here!'

At fifty other watch-fires down the valley, the men of Ballantyne's Scouts were stabbing and screaming with Ralph.

'Defend yourselves, there are ghosts at work!'

'*Tagati!* Witchcraft! Beware the witches!'

'Kill the witches!'

'Witchcraft! Defend yourselves!'

'Run! Run! The devils are amongst us.'

Three thousand warriors, every one of them steeped from childhood in superstition and witchlore, awakened to the screams and wild cries of dying men, and the panic-stricken warnings yelled by men come face to face with the devil's legions. They awakened in blinding suffocating darkness, and seized their weapons and struck out in terror, yelling with fright and the comrades they wounded shrieked and struck back at them.

'I am wounded. Defend yourselves from the devils. Hah! Hah! The devils are killing me!'

The night was filled with running figures that collided and stabbed and cried.

'The valley is haunted!'

'The devils will kill us all!'

'Run! Run!'

Then from the head of the valley rose such a monstrous iron-lunged braying, such a cacophony that it could only be the voice of the great demon himself. *Tokoloshe*, the eater of men. It was a sound that drove terrified men over the last frontier of reason, into the realms of witless insensate pandemonium.

On his hands and knees, Ralph crawled down the narrow pathway, keeping below the level of the slashing spears, silhouetting the frantic figures of running men against the faint light of the stars, and when he stabbed up at them, he aimed for the groin and belly rather than the killing stroke, so that the men that he maimed added their cries to the uproar.

From the head of the valley, Harry Mellow blew another blaring blast on the brass foghorn, and it was echoed by the screams of men blundering up the sides of the valley and escaping into the open grassland beyond.

Ralph crept forward, listening for a single voice in the thousands. In the first few minutes hundreds of fleeing warriors, most of them unarmed, had escaped from the valley. In every direction they were disappearing into the night, and each second they were followed by others, men who would have unflinchingly charged into the smoking muzzles of the Maxim machine-guns, but who were reduced by fear of the supernatural to mindless panic-stricken children. Their cries faded with distance, and now at last Ralph heard the voice for which he had waited.

'Stand fast, the Moles,' it roared. 'Stand with Bazo. These are not demons.' And Ralph crept towards the sound.

In the clearing ahead of him, a camp-fire fed with fresh logs flared up sullenly, and Ralph recognized the tall figure with wide gaunt shoulders, and the slim woman at his side.

'This is white men's trickery,' she cried, beside her lord. 'Wait, my children.'

Ralph sprang up and ran through the dense scrub to them. 'Nkosi,' he cried. He did not have to disguise his

410

voice, it was rough and hoarse with dust and tension and battle-lust. 'Lord Bazo, I am with you! Let us stand together against this treachery.'

'Brave comrade!' Bazo greeted him with relief as Ralph loomed out of the dark. 'Stand back to back, form a ring in which each of us will guard the other, and call out to other brave men to join us.'

Bazo turned his back to Ralph, and drew the woman Tanase to his side. It was she who glanced back and recognized Ralph as he stooped.

'It is Henshaw,' she screamed, but her warning came too late. Before Bazo could turn back to face him, Ralph had changed his grip on the assegai, using it like a butcher's cleaver, and with a single stroke he hacked across the back of Bazo's legs, just above the ankles, and the Achilles' tendons parted with a soft rubbery popping sound. Bazo collapsed onto his knees, both legs crippled, pinned like a beetle to a board.

Ralph seized Tanase's wrist, jerked her out of the circle of firelight, and hurled her headlong to earth. Holding her easily, he tore off her short leather skirt and placed the point of the assegai in her groin.

'Bazo,' he whispered. 'Throw your spear upon the fire, or I will open your woman's secret parts as you opened those of mine.'

T he Scouts used the first glimmerings of the new day to move slowly down the valley in an extended line, finishing the wounded Matabele. While they worked, Ralph sent Jan Cheroot back to where they had left the horses to fetch the ropes. He was back within minutes with the heavy coils of new yellow manila over the saddles of the horses that he led.

'The Matabele have scattered back into the hills,' he

reported grimly. 'It will take a week for them to find each other and regroup.'

'We won't wait that long.'

Ralph took the ropes and began making the knots. The Scouts came in as he worked. They were scrubbing their assegai blades with handfuls of dried grass, and Sergeant Ezra told Ralph, 'We lost four men, but we found Kamuza, the induna of the Swimmers, and we counted over two hundred bodies.'

'Get ready to pull out,' Ralph ordered. 'What remains to be done will not take long.'

Bazo sat beside the remains of the fire. His arms were bound behind him with thongs of rawhide, and his legs were thrust straight out in front of him. He had no control over his feet, they flopped nervelessly like dying fish stranded on a receding tide, and the slow watery blood oozed from the deep gashes above his heels.

Tanase sat beside him. She was stark naked, and bound like him with her arms behind her back.

Sergeant Ezra stared at her body, and he murmured, 'We have worked hard all night. We have earned a little sport. Let me and my *kanka* take this woman into the bushes for a short while.'

Ralph did not bother to reply, but turned to Jan Cheroot instead. 'Bring the horses,' he ordered.

Tanase spoke to Bazo without moving her lips, in the way of the initiates.

'What is the business of the ropes, Lord? Why do they not shoot us, and have done?'

'It is the white man's way, the way that conveys the deepest disrespect. They shoot honoured enemies, and use the ropes on criminals.'

'Lord, on the day I first met this one you call Henshaw, I dreamed that you were high upon a tree and he looked up at you and smiled,' she whispered. 'It is strange that in that dream I did not see myself beside you upon that tree.'

412

'They are ready now,' said Bazo, and turned his head to her. 'With my heart I embrace you. You have been the fountainhead of my life.'

'I embrace you, my husband. I embrace you, Bazo, who will be the father of kings.'

She went on staring into his ravaged, ugly-beautiful face and she did not turn her head when Henshaw stood tall over them and said in a harsh tortured voice, 'I give you a better death than you gave to the ones I loved.'

T he ropes were of different lengths, so that Tanase hung slightly lower than her lord. The soles of her bare feet, suspended at the height of a man's head, were very white and her toes pointed straight at the earth like those of a little girl standing on tiptoe. Her long heron neck was twisted sharply to one side, so that she still seemed to listen for Bazo's voice.

Bazo's swollen face was lifted towards the yellow dawn sky, for the knot had ridden around under his chin. Ralph Ballantyne's face was lifted also as he stood at the base of the tall acacia tree in the bottom of the Valley of the Goats looking up at them.

In one other respect, Tanase's vision was unfulfilled – Ralph Ballantyne did not smile.

S o Lodzi came and with him came Major-General Carrington and Major Robert Stephenson Smyth Baden-Powell who would one day coin the motto 'Be Prepared', and behind them came the guns and the soliders. The women and children danced out from the laager at Bulawayo with bouquets of wild flowers for them, and they sang 'For they are jolly good fellows' and wept with joy.

413

The senior indunas of Kumalo, betrayed by the Umlimo's promises of divine intervention, uncertain and with the fire in their bellies swiftly cooling, squabbling amongst themselves and awed by the massive show of military force that they had provoked, withdrew slowly with their impis from the vicinity of Bulawayo.

The imperial troops sortied in great lumbering columns and swept the valleys and the open land. They burned the deserted villages and the standing crops and they drove away the few cattle that the rinderpest had spared. They shelled the hills where they suspected the Matabele might be hiding, and they rode their horses to exhaustion, chasing the elusive black shadows that flittered through the forest ahead of them. The Maxims fired until the water in the cooling-jackets boiled, but the range was nine hundred yards or more and the targets were as fleet as rabbits.

So the weeks dragged on and became months, and the soldiers tried to starve the Matabele and force them into a set-piece battle, but the indunas sulked in the broken ground and took refuge in the Matopos Hills where the guns and the soldiers dared not follow them.

Occasionally the Matabele caught an isolated patrol or a man on his own, once even the legendary Frederick Selous, elephant-hunter and adventurer extraordinary. Selous had dismounted to 'pot' one of the rebels that were disappearing over the ridge ahead, when a stray bullet grazed his pony, and his usually impeccably behaved animal bolted and left him stranded. Only then he realized that he had outridden the main body of his Scouts, and that the Matabele were instantly aware of his predicament. They turned back and coursed him like dogs on a hare.

It was a race the likes of which Selous had not run since his elephant-hunting days. The bare-footed and lightly equipped *amadoda* gained swiftly, so close at last that they freed their blades from the thongs and began that terrible humming war chant. Only then Lieutenant Windley,

Selous' second-in-command, spurred in and pulling his foot from the left stirrup, gave Selous the leather and galloped with him into the ranks of the oncoming Scouts.

At other times the swing of fortune was towards the soldiers, and they would surprise a foraging patrol of Matabele at a drift or in thick bush, and hang them from the nearest trees that would bear the weight.

It was an inconclusive cruel little war, that drew on and on. The military officers who were conducting the campaign were not businessmen, they did not think in terms of cost-efficiency, and the bill for the first three months was a million pounds of sterling, a cost of £5,000 per head of Matabele killed. The bill was for the account of Mr Cecil John Rhodes and his British South Africa Company.

In the Matopos Hills, the indunas were forced towards starvation, and in Bulawayo Mr Rhodes was forced just as inexorably towards bankruptcy.

The three riders moved in a cautious, mutually protective spread. They kept to the centre of the track, their rifles were loaded and cocked and carried at high port.

Jan Cheroot rode point, fifty yards ahead. His little woolly head turned tirelessly from side to side as he searched the bush on each side. Behind him came Louise Ballantyne, delighting in her escape from the confinements of the Bulawayo laager after these weary months. She rode astride, with all the *élan* of a natural horsewoman, and there was a feather in her little green cap, and when she turned to look back every few minutes, her lips parted in a loving smile. She was not yet accustomed to having Zouga with her once again, and she had constantly to reassure herself.

Zouga was fifty yards behind her, and he answered her smile in a way that wrenched something deep inside her.

He sat easy and straight in the saddle, the wide-brimmed slouch hat slanted over one eye. The sun had gilded away the pallor of Holloway gaol, and the silver and gold of his beard gave him the air of a Viking chieftain.

In that extended order they rode up from the grassy plains, under the high arched branches of the msasa trees, up the first slope of the hills and, as he reached the false crest, Jan Cheroot stood in his stirrups and shouted with relief and delight. Unable to contain themselves, Louise and Zouga cantered forward and reined in beside him.

'Oh, thank you, Lord,' Louise whispered huskily, and reached across for Zouga's hand.

'It's a miracle,' he said softly, and squeezed her fingers.

Ahead of them the mellow thatch of King's Lynn basked comfortably in the sunlight. It seemed to be the most beautiful sight either of them had ever looked upon.

'Untouched.' Louise shook her head in wonder.

'Must be the only homestead in Matabeleland that wasn't burned.'

'Oh come on, my darling,' she cried, with sudden ecstasy. 'Let's go back to our home.'

Zouga restrained her at the steps of the wide front porch, and made her stay in the saddle, her rifle at the ready, holding the reins of their horses while he and Jan Cheroot searched the homestead for any sign of Matabele treachery.

When Zouga came out onto the stoep again, he carried his rifle at the trail and smiled at her.

'It's safe!'

He helped her down from the saddle, and while Jan Cheroot led the horses away to stall feed them in the stables from the grainbags he had brought, Zouga and Louise went up the front steps hand in hand.

The thick ivory curves of the old bull elephant's tusks still framed the doorway to the dining-room, and Zouga stroked one of them as he passed.

'Your good luck charms,' Louise chuckled indulgently.

'The household gods,' he corrected her, and they passed between them into the house.

The house had been looted. They could not have expected less, but the books were still there, thrown from the shelves, some with their spines broken or with the leather boards damaged or gnawed by rats, but they were all there.

Zouga retrieved his journals and dusted them superficially with his silk scarf. There were dozens of them, the record of his life, meticulously handwritten and illustrated with ink drawings and coloured maps.

'It would have truly broken my heart to have lost these,' he murmured, piling them carefully on the library table and stroking one of the red morocco covers. The silver was lying on the dining-room floor, some of it battered, but most of it intact. It has no value to a Matabele.

They wandered through the rambling homestead, through the rooms that Zouga had added haphazardly to the original structure, and they found small treasures amongst the litter: a silver comb he had given her on their first Christmas together, the diamond and enamel dress studs which had been her birthday present to him. She handed them back to him and went up on tiptoe to offer her face to his kiss.

There was still crockery and glassware on the kitchen shelves, though all the pots and knives had been stolen and the doors to the pantry and storerooms had been broken off their hinges.

'It won't take much to fix,' Zouga told her. 'I can't believe how lucky we've been.'

Louise went out into the kitchen and found four of her red Rhode Island hens scratching in the dust. She called Jan Cheroot from the stable and begged a few handfuls of grain from the horses' feed-bags. When she clucked at the hens, they came in a flutter of wings to be fed.

The glass in the windows of the main bedroom was smashed, and wild birds had come through to roost in the rafters. The bedspread was stained with their excrement, but when Louise stripped it off, the linen and mattress beneath it were clean and dry.

Zouga put an arm around her waist, squeezed it and looked down at her, in the way she knew so well.

'You are a wicked man, Major Ballantyne,' she breathed huskily. 'But there are no curtains on the windows.'

'Fortunately there are still shutters.' He went to close them, while Louise folded back the sheet and then unfastened the top button of her blouse. Zouga returned in time to assist her with the others.

An hour later when they came out again onto the front stoep, they found Jan Cheroot had dusted off the chairs and table, and unpacked the picnic basket they had brought from Bulawayo. They drank fine Constantia wine and ate cold Cornish pasties, while Jan Cheroot waited upon them and regaled them with anecdotes and reminiscences of the exploits of Ballantyne's Scouts.

'There were none like us,' he declared modestly. 'Ballantyne's Scouts! The Matabele learned to know us well.'

'Oh, don't let's talk about war,' Louise pleaded.

But Zouga asked with good-natured sarcasm, 'What happened to all your heroes? The war still goes on, and we need men like you.'

'Master Ralph changed,' said Jan Cheroot, darkly. 'He changed just like that.' He snapped his fingers. 'From the day we caught Bazo at the Valley of the Goats, he wasn't interested any more. He never rode with the Scouts again, and within a week he had gone back to the railhead to finish building his railway. They say he will drive the first train into Bulawayo before Christmas, that's what they say.'

'Enough!' Louise declared. 'It's our first day at King's Lynn in almost a year. I will not have another word of war. Pour some wine, Jan Cheroot, and take a little sip for yourself.' Then she turned to Zouga. 'Darling, can't we leave Bulawayo and come back here?'

Zouga shook his head regretfully. 'I'm sorry, my love. I could not risk your precious life. The Matabele are still in rebellion, and this is so isolated—'

From the back of the house came the sudden shriek and cackle of alarmed poultry. Zouga broke off and jumped to his feet. As he reached for his rifle propped against the wall, he said softly but urgently, 'Jan Cheroot, go around the back of the stables. I'll come from the other side.' Then to Louise, 'Wait here, but be ready to run for the horses if you hear a shot.' And the two men slipped silently away down the veranda.

Zouga reached the corner of the wall below the main bedroom, just as there was another storm of squawks and cackles, and the beating of wings. He ducked around the corner, and sprinted down the thick whitewashed walls that protected the kitchen yard, and flattened himself beside the gate. Above the cacophony of terrified chickens and the flapping of wings, he heard a voice say, 'Hold that one! Do not let it go!'

The voice was Matabele, and almost immediately a half-naked figure ducked through the doorway beside Zouga, carrying a chicken in each hand.

One thing only prevented Zouga firing. The pendulous bare breasts that flapped against the Matabele's ribs as she ran. Zouga smashed the butt of his rifle between the woman's shoulders, knocking her to the earth, and he leaped over her body into the kitchen yard.

Beside the kitchen door stood Jan Cheroot. He held his rifle in one hand and in the other the skinny, naked, struggling body of a small black boy.

'Shall I knock his head in?' Jan Cheroot asked.

'You are no longer a member of Ballantyne's Scouts,' Zouga told him. 'Just keep a hold on him, but don't hurt him.' And he turned back to examine his own prisoner.

She was an elderly Matabele woman, almost on the point of starvation. She must once have been a big heavily fleshed woman, for her skin hung loosely upon her in folds and wrinkles. Once those breasts must have been the size of water melons, and almost bursting with fat, but now they were empty pouches that dangled almost to her navel. Zouga caught her wrist and hauled her to her feet. He marched her back into the kitchen yard, and he could clearly feel the bones of her arm through the wasted flesh.

Jan Cheroot was still holding the boy, and now Zouga studied him briefly. He also was skeletally thin, each rib and each knob of his spine poked through the skin, and his head seemed too big for his body, and his eyes too big for his head.

'Little bugger is starving,' said Zouga.

'That's one way of getting rid of them,' Jan Cheroot agreed, and at that moment Louise stepped into the kitchen doorway with the rifle still in her hand, and her expression changed the instant she saw the black woman.

'Juba,' she said. 'Is that you, Juba?'

'Oh Balela,' the Matabele woman whimpered. 'I had thought never to see the sunshine of your face again.'

'What now!' said Zouga grimly. 'We have caught ourselves a pretty prize, Jan Cheroot. The senior wife of the great and noble induna Gandang, and this puppy must be his grandson! I didn't recognize either of them, they are on their last legs.'

Tungata Zebiwe sat in his grandmother's bony lap and ate with a quiet frenzy, the total dedication of a starving animal. He ate the extra Cornish pasties from the picnic basket, then he ate the crusts that Zouga had left. Louise searched the saddlebags and found a battered tin of bully, and the child ate that also, stuffing the rich fatty meat into his mouth with both hands.

'That's right,' said Jan Cheroot sourly. 'Fatten him up

now, so we have to shoot him later.' And he went off sulkily to saddle the horses for the return to Bulawayo.

'Juba, little Dove,' Louise asked, 'are all the children like this?'

'The food is finished,' Juba nodded. 'All the children are like this, though some of the little ones are dead already.'

'Juba – is it not time that we women put an end to the foolishness of our men, before all the children are dead?'

'It is time, Balela,' Juba agreed. 'Time and past time.'

'Who is this woman?' Mr Rhodes asked, in that exasperated high-pitched voice that betrayed his agitation, and he peered at Zouga. His eyes seemed to have taken a new prominence as though they were being squeezed out of his skull.

'She is the senior wife of Gandang.'

'Gandang – he commanded the impi that massacred Wilson's patrol on the Shangani?'

'He was a half-brother to Lobengula. With Babiaan and Somabula he is the senior of all the indunas.'

'I don't suppose there is anything to lose by talking to them,' Mr Rhodes shrugged. 'This business will destroy us all if it goes on much longer. Tell this woman to take a message back that the indunas must lay down their arms and come in to Bulawayo.'

'I'm sorry, Mr Rhodes,' Zouga told him. 'They won't do that. They have had an *indaba* in the hills, all the indunas have spoken, and there is only one way.'

'What is that, Ballantyne?'

'They want you to go to them.'

'Me – personally?' Mr Rhodes asked softly.

'We will speak only to Lodzi, and he must come to us unarmed. He must come into the Matopos without the soldiers. He may bring three other men with him, but none of them must carry a weapon. If they do, we kill them immediately.' Zouga repeated the message that Juba had brought out of the hills for him, and Mr Rhodes closed his eyes and covered them with the palm of his hand. His voice wheezed painfully in his chest, so that Zouga had to lean forward to catch his words.

'In their power,' he said. 'Alone and unarmed, completely in their power.'

Mr Rhodes dropped his hand and stood up. He moved heavily to the opening of the tent. He clasped his hands behind his back, and rocked back on his heels. Outside in the hot dusty noon, a bugle sang the advance, and there was the distant sound of a cavalry troop leaving the laager, hooves and the rattle of lance butts in their hard leather boots.

Mr Rhodes turned back to Zouga. 'Can we afford to trust them?' he asked.

'Can we afford not to, Mr Rhodes?'

They left the horses at the place that had been agreed, in one of the myriad valleys in the granite hills that reared into broken crests and dropped into deep troughs like the frozen surf whipped up by a wild Atlantic gale. Zouga Ballantyne led from there, taking the twisted narrow footpath through dense brush, moving slowly and looking back every few paces at the shambling, bearlike figure that followed him.

When the path began to climb, Zouga stopped and waited for him to regain his breath. Mr Rhodes' face had taken on a bluish mottled appearance, and he was sweating heavily. However, after only a few minutes, he waved Zouga onwards impatiently.

Close behind Mr Rhodes followed the two others that

the indunas had stipulated. One was a journalist – Mr Rhodes was too much of a showman to miss an opportunity such as this – and the other was a doctor, for he realized that the assegais of the Matabele were not the only threat he faced, on this gruelling journey.

The shimmering heat of the Matopos Hills made the air above the granite surfaces dance and waver as though they were the plates of a wood-fired iron stove. The silence had a cloying suffocating texture that seemed almost tangible, and the sudden sharp bird calls that cut through it every few minutes served only to emphasize its intensity.

The scrub pressed in closely on each side of the track, and once Zouga saw a branch tremble and stir when there was no breeze. He strode on upwards with a measured pace, as though he were leading the guard of honour at a military funeral. The path turned sharply into a vertical crack in the highest point of the granite wall, and here Zouga waited again.

Mr Rhodes reached him and leaned against the heated granite with his shoulder while he wiped his face and neck with a white handkerchief. He could not speak for many minutes and then he gasped, 'Do you think they will come, Ballantyne?'

Farther down the valley, from the thickest bush, a robin called and Zouga inclined his head to listen. It was almost convincing mimicry.

'They are here before us, Mr Rhodes. The hills are alive with Matabele,' and he looked for fear in the pale blue eyes. When he found none, he murmured quietly, almost shyly, 'You are a brave man, sir.'

'A pragmatic one, Ballantyne.' And a smile twisted the swollen disease-ravaged face. 'It's always better to talk than to fight.'

'I hope the Matabele agree.' Zouga returned his smile and they went on into the vertical crack in the granite, passing swiftly through shadow into the sunlight once more, and below them was a basin in the granite. It was ringed by high ramparts of broken granite, and bare of any cover.

Zouga looked down into the little circular valley and all his soldier's instincts were offended.

'It's a trap,' he said. 'A natural killing-ground from which there is no escape.'

'Let us go down,' said Mr Rhodes.

In the middle of the basin was a low anthill, a raised platform of hard yellow clay, and instinctively the little group of white men made their way towards it.

'We might as well make ourselves comfortable,' Mr Rhodes panted, and sank down upon it. The other members of the party sat on each side of him – only Zouga remained upon his feet.

Though he kept his face impassive, his skin itched as the insects of dread crawled over it. This was the heart of the Matopos Hills, the sacred hills of the Matabele, their stronghold in which they would be at their bravest and most reckless. It was folly to come unarmed into this place, to throw themselves upon the mercy of the most savage and bloodthirsty tribe of a cruel wild continent. Zouga stood with his empty hands clasped behind his back, and turned slowly upon his heel, surveying the wall of rock that hemmed them in. He had not completed his circle before he said quietly:

'Well, gentlemen. Here they are!'

Without a sound, with no spoken command, the impis rose from their concealment, and formed a living barricade along the skyline. They stood in rank upon rank and shoulder to shoulder, completely encompassing the rocky valley. It was impossible to count their multitude, impossible even to guess at their thousands, but still the silence persisted as though their eardrums were filled with wax.

'Do not move, gentlemen,' Zouga cautioned them, and they waited in the sunlight. They waited while the silent impassive impis stood guard about them. Now no bird called and not the lightest breeze stirred the forest of feather headdresses and the kilts of fur.

At last the ranks opened and a group of men came through. The ranks closed behind them, and the little group came on down the path. These were the great princes of Kumalo, the Zanzi of royal blood – but how they were reduced.

They were all of them old men, with the hoarfrost of the years sparkling in their woolly caps of hair and in their beards. They were starved to the thinness of pariah dogs, with their warrior's muscles stringy and wasted, and their old bones showing through. Some of them had dirty blood-soaked bandages bound over their wounds, while the limbs and faces of others were scabbed with the sores that starvation and deprivation breed.

Gandang led them, and a pace behind him on either hand came his half-brothers Babiaan and Somabula, and behind them again the other sons of Mashobane, wearing the headrings of honour and carrying every one of them the broad silver killing blades and the tall rawhide shields that gave them their name Matabele, 'the People of the Long Shields'.

Ten paces in front of Zouga, Gandang stopped and grounded his shield, and the two men stared deeply into each other's eyes, and both of them were thinking of the day they had first met thirty years and more before.

'I see you, Gandang, son of Mzilikazi,' Zouga said at last.

'I see you, Bakela, the one who strikes with the fist.'

And behind Zouga Mr Rhodes ordered calmly, 'Ask him if it is to be war or peace.'

Zouga did not take his eyes from those of the tall emaciated induna.

'Are the eyes still red for war?' he asked.

Gandang's reply was a deep rumble, but it carried clearly to every induna who followed him, and it rose up to the massed ranks of warriors upon the heights.

'Tell Lodzi that the eyes are white,' he said, and he stooped and laid his shield and his assegai upon the ground at his feet.

Two Matabele, dressed only in loincloths, pushed the steel cocopan along the narrow-gauge railway tracks. When they reached the tip, one of them knocked out the retaining pin and the steel pan swivelled and spilled its five-ton load of sugary blue quartz in the funnel-shaped chute. The rock tumbled and rolled into the sizing box, and piled on the steel grating where another dozen Matabele fell upon it with ten-pound sledgehammers, and broke it up so that it could fall through the grating into the stamp boxes below.

The stamps were of massive cast iron; hissing steam drove them in a monotonous see-saw rhythm, pounding the ore to the consistency of talcum powder. The roar of the stamps was ear-numbing. A continuous stream of water, piped up from the stream in the valley below, sluiced the powdered ore out of the stamp boxes and carried it down the wooden gutters to the James tables.

In the low open-sided hut, Harry Mellow stood over the No. 1 table, and watched the flow of thick mud-laden water washing across the heavy copper sheet that was the tabletop. The top was inclined to allow the worthless mud to run to waste, and eccentric cams agitated the table gently to spread the flow and ensure that every particle of ore touched the coated surface of the table. Harry closed the screw valve, and diverted the flow of mud to the No. 2 table. Then he threw the lever and the agitation of the table ceased.

Harry glanced up at Ralph Ballantyne and Vicky who were watching him avidly, and he cocked a thumb to reassure them – the thunderous roar of the stamps drowned all conversation here – and then Harry stooped over the table once more. The tabletop was coated with a thick layer of quicksilver, and, using a wide spatula, Harry began scraping it off the copper and squeezing it into a heavy dark ball. One of the unique properties of mercury is its ability to mop up particles of gold the way that blotting paper sucks up ink.

When Harry had finished, he had a ball of amalgamated mercury twice the size of a baseball, that weighed almost forty pounds. He needed both hands to lift it. He carried it across to the thatched rondavel that served as laboratory and refinery for the Harkness Mine, and Ralph and Vicky hurried after him, and crowded into the tiny room behind him.

The three of them watched with utter fascination as the ball of amalgam began to dissolve and bubble in the retort over the intense blue flame of the primus stove.

'We cook off the mercury,' Harry explained, 'and condense it again, but what we have left behind is this.'

The boiling silver liquid reduced in quantity, and began to change in colour. They caught the first reddish-yellow promise, the gleam that has enchanted men for more than six thousand years.

'Just look at it!' Vicky clapped her hands with excitement, shaking out her thick coppery tresses, and her eyes shone as though with a reflection of the lustre of the precious liquid that she was watching. The last of the mercury boiled away, and left behind a deep glowing puddle of pure gold.

'Gold,' said Ralph Ballantyne. 'The first gold of the Harkness Mine.' And then he threw back his head and laughed. The sound startled them. They had not heard Ralph laugh since he had left Bulawayo, and while they stared at him, he seized both of them, Vicky in one arm and Harry in the other, and danced them out into the sunlight.

They danced in a circle, and the two men whooped and howled, Ralph like a highlander, and Harry like a Plains

Indian, while the Matabele hammer-boys broke off their labours and watched them, first with astonishment, and then chuckling in sympathy.

Vicky broke out of the circle first, panting and holding the first bulge of her pregnant tummy in both hands.

'You are mad!' she laughed breathlessly. 'Mad! Both of you! And I love you for it.'

The mix was fifty-fifty, half river-clay dug from the banks of the Khami and half yellow anthill clay, the adhesive qualities of which had been enhanced by the saliva of the termites which had carried it up through their subterranean tunnels to the surface. The clays were puddled in a pit beside the bottom well, the same well that Clinton Codrington, Robyn's first husband, and Jordan Ballantyne had dug together so long ago, even before the Charter Company's pioneers had first ridden into Matabeleland.

Two of the Mission converts cranked up each bucketful from the well, and spilled it into the mixing pit, another two shovelled in the clay and a dozen naked black children, led by Robert St John, made a game out of trampling the clay to the correct consistency. Robyn St John was helping pack the clay into the oblong wooden moulds, each eighteen inches by nine. A line of Mission boys and girls carried the filled moulds away to the drying ground, where they carefully turned out the wet bricks onto the beds of dry grass, and then hurried back with the empty moulds to have them refilled.

There were thousands of yellow bricks lying in long lines in the sun, but Robyn had calculated that they needed at least twenty thousand for the new church alone. Then of course they would have to cut all the timber and cure it, and in a month's time the thatch grass in the vleis would be tall enough to begin cutting.

Robyn straightened and placed her muddied yellow hand in the small of her back to ease the cramping muscles. A lock of grey-flecked hair had escaped from under the scarf she had knotted over her head, and there was a smear of mud down her cheek and neck, but the little runnels of her own sweat were eroding this away and staining the high collar of her blouse with it.

She looked up at the burned-out ruins of the Mission; the charred roof beams had fallen in and the heavy rains of the last wet season had dissolved the unbaked brick walls into a shapeless hillock. They would have to re-lay every brick, and lift every rafter into place again, and the prospect of all that grinding, unremitting labour gave Robyn St John a deep and exciting sense of anticipation. She felt as strong and alive as the young medical missionary who had first stepped onto this unforgiving African soil almost forty years before.

'Thy will be done, dear Lord,' she said aloud, and the Matabele girl beside her cried happily, 'Amen, Nomusa!'

Robyn smiled at her, and was about to bend once more to the brick moulds, when she started, shaded her eyes, and then picked up her skirts and rushed down the track towards the river, running like a young girl.

'Juba,' she cried. 'Where have you been? I have waited so long for you to come home.'

Juba set down the heavy load she carried balanced on her head, and came lumbering to meet her.

'Nomusa!' She was weeping as she hugged Robyn to her. Great fat oily tears slid down her cheeks and mingled with the sweat and mud on Robyn's face.

'Stop crying, you silly girl,' Robyn scolded her lovingly. 'You will make me start. Just look at you! How skinny you are, we will have to feed you up! And who is this?'

The black boy dressed only in a soiled loincloth came forward shyly.

'This is my grandson, Tungata Zebiwe.'

'I did not recognize him, he has grown so big.'

'Nomusa, I have brought him to you so that you can teach him to read and to write.'

'Well, the first thing we will have to do is give him a civilized name. We shall call him Gideon and forget that horrible vengeful name.'

'Gideon,' Juba repeated. 'Gideon Kumalo. And you will teach him to write?'

'We have a lot of work to do first,' Robyn said firmly. 'Gideon can go into the mud puddle with the other children and you can help me pack the moulds. We have to start all over, Juba, and build it all up from the beginning again.'

'I admire the grandeur and loneliness of the Matopos, and therefore I desire to be buried in the Matopos on the hill which I used to visit and which I called the "View of the World" in a square to be cut in the rock on the top of the hill and covered with a plain brass plate with these words thereon: "Here lie the remains of CECIL JOHN RHODES".'

So when at last the pumping of his diseased heart ceased, he came to Bulawayo once more along the railroad that Ralph Ballantyne had laid. The speical saloon coach in which his coffin rode was draped with purple and black, and at each town and siding along the way, those whom he had called 'my Rhodesians' brought wreaths to pile upon the casket. From Bulawayo the coffin was taken on a guncarriage into the Matopos Hills and the pure black bullocks that drew it plodded slowly up the rounded egg-shaped dome of granite that he had chosen.

Above the open sepulchre stood a tripod gantry, with

block and chain at the peak, and around it a dense throng of humanity: elegant gentlemen, uniformed officers, and ladies with black ribbons on their hats. Then, farther out, there stretched a vast black sea of half-naked Matabele, twenty thousand come to see him go down into the earth. At their head were the indunas who had met him near this same hill to treat for peace. There were Gandang and Babiaan and Somabula, all of them very old men now.

Gathered at the head of the grave were the men who had replaced them in real power, the administrators of the Charter Company, Milton and Lawley, and the members of the first Rhodesian Council. Ralph Ballantyne was amongst them with his young wife beside him.

Ralph's expression remained grave and tragic as the coffin was lowered on its chains into the gaping tomb, and the bishop read aloud the obituary that Mr Rudyard Kipling had composed:

'It is his will that he look forth
Across the world he won,
The granite of the ancient north,
Great spaces washed with sun.
There shall he patient take his seat
(As when the death he dared)
And there await a people's feet
In the paths that he prepared.'

As the heavy brass plaque was lowered into position, Gandang stepped out of the ranks of the Matabele, and lifted one hand.

'The father is dead,' he cried, and then in a single blast of sound, like the thunder of a tropical storm, the Matabele nation gave the salute they had never given to a white man before.

'Bayete!' they shouted as one man. 'Bayete!'

The salute to a king.

The funeral crowds dispersed, slowly, seemingly reluctantly. The Matabele drifted away like smoke amongst the valleys of their sacred hills, and the white folk followed the path down the face of the granite dome. Ralph helped Elizabeth over the uneven footing, and he smiled down at her.

'The man was a rogue, and you weep for him,' he teased her gently.

'It was all so moving,' Elizabeth dabbed at her eyes. 'When Gandang did that—'

'Yes. He fooled them all, even those he led into captivity. Damn me, but it's a good thing they buried him in solid rock and put a lid on him, or he would have squared the devil and got out of it at the last moment.'

Ralph turned her out of the stream of people, of mourners who were following the path.

'I told Isazi to bring the carriage round to the back of the hill, we don't want to be caught in the crush.'

Under their feet the granite was painted a vivid orange with lichen, and the little blue-headed lizards scuttled for cover in the crevices and then glared at them with their throats throbbing and the cockscomb crests of the monstrous heads fully erect. Ralph paused on the lower slope of the dome, where a twisted and deformed msasa tree had found precarious purchase in one of the crevices and he looked back up at the peak.

'So he's dead at long last, but his Company still governs us. I have work to do yet, work that may take the rest of my life.'

Then abruptly and uncharacteristically, Ralph shivered, although the sun was blazing hot.

'What is it, my dear?' Elizabeth turned to him with quick concern.

'Nothing,' he said. 'Perhaps I just walked over my own grave.' Then he chuckled. 'We'd best go down now before Jon-Jon drives poor Isazi completely out of his mind.'

He took her arm and led her down to where Isazi had parked the carriage in the shade, and from a hundred paces they picked up the piping of Jonathan's questions and speculations, each punctuated with a demanding: '*Uthini*, Isazi? What do you say, Isazi?'

And the patient reply: 'Eh-heh, *Bawu*. Yes, yes, little Gadfly.'

PART TWO

1977

The Land-Rover turned off the black-topped road, and as soon as it hit the dirt track, the pale dust boiled out from under its back wheels. It was an elderly vehicle, the desert-coloured paintwork was scored and scratched by thorn and branch down to the bare metal. Rock and sharp shale had bitten chunks of rubber out of the heavily lugged tyres.

The doors and the top were off and the cracked windshield lay flat on the bonnet, so that the wind swept over the two men in the front seat. Behind their heads stood the gun-rack. The forks, lined with foam rubber, held a formidable battery of weapons: two semi-automatic FN rifles, sprayed with dun and green camouflage paint, a short 9mm Uzi submachine-gun with the extra long magazine clipped on ready for instant use, and, still in its canvas slip-cover, a heavy Colt Sauer 'Grand African' whose .458 magnum cartridge could knock a bull elephant off its feet. From the uprights of the gun-rack dangled haversacks containing spare clips and magazines, and a damp canvas waterbottle. They swung harmoniously with each jolt and lurch of the Land-Rover.

Craig Mellow drove with his foot jamming the accelerator to the floorboards. Though the vehicle's body clattered and banged loosely, he had always serviced and tuned the engine himself, and the speedometer needle pressed against the stop pin at the end of the dial. There is only one way to go into an ambush, and that is flat out. Get through it as fast as possible, remembering always that they usually laid it out at least half a kilometre deep. Even at 150 K's an hour, that meant receiving fire for twelve seconds. In that time a good man with an AK 47 can get off three magazines of thirty rounds each.

Yes, the way to go in was fast – but, of course, a landmine was a beast of an entirely different colour. When they boosted one of those sweethearts with ten kilos of plastic, it kicked you and your vehicle fifty feet in the air and shot your spine out through the top of your skull.

So although Craig lounged comfortably on the hard leather seat, his eyes scoured the road ahead. This late in the day there had been traffic through ahead of him, and he drove for the diamond tracks in the dust, but he watched for an extraneous tuft of grass, an old cigarette packet or even a pat of dried cow-dung that could conceal the marks of a dig in the road. Of course, this close to Bulawayo he was in more danger from a drunken driver than from terrorist activity, but it was wise to nurture the habit.

Craig glanced sideways at his passenger, and jerked his thumb over his shoulder. The man swivelled in his seat and reached into the cool box in the back. He brought out two cans of Lion beer with the dew on them, and while he did so, Craig flicked his attention back to the road.

Craig Mellow was twenty-nine years old, although the floppy thatch of dark hair blowing all over his forehead, the innocent candour of his hazel eyes, and the vulnerable slant to his wide gentle mouth gave him the air of a small boy who expects to be unjustly reprimanded at any moment. He still wore the embroidered green shoulder flashes of a ranger in the Department of Wildlife and Nature Conservation on his khaki bush-shirt.

Beside him Samson Kumalo pulled the tabs off the beer cans. He wore the same uniform, but he was a tall Matabele with a deep intelligent forehead and a hard smooth-shaven lantern jaw. He ducked as a spurt of froth flew from the cans, and then handed one of them to Craig and kept one for himself. Craig saluted him with his can and swigged a mouthful, then licked the white moustache from his upper

438

lip, and put the Land-Rover to the twisting road up the Khami hills.

Before they reached the crest, Craig dropped the empty can into the plastic trash-bag that hung from the dash, and slowed the Land-Rover, looking for the turn-off.

Tall yellow grass hid the small faded sign.

KHAMI ANGLICAN MISSION
Staff Cottages. No through road.

It was at least a year since Craig had last driven this road and he almost missed it.

'Here it is!' Samson warned him, and he swung sharply onto the secondary track. It jinked through the forest, then came abruptly to the long straight avenue of spathodea trees that led down to the staff village. The trunks were thicker than a man's chest, and the dark green branches met overhead. At the head of the avenue, almost screened by the trees and the long grass, was a low whitewashed wall with a rusty wrought-iron gate. Craig pulled onto the verge and switched off the engine.

'Why are we stopping here?' Samson asked.

They always spoke English when they were alone; just as they always spoke Sindebele when anyone else was listening; just as Samson called him 'Craig' in private and 'Nkosi' or 'Mambo' at all other times. It was a tacit understanding between them, for in this tortured war-torn land, there were those who had taken Samson's fluent English as the mark of a 'cheeky mission boy', and recognized by the easy intimacy between the two men that Craig was that thing of doubtful loyalties, a *kaffir-lover**.

* 'Kaffir' is derived from the Arabic word for an infidel. During the nineteenth century, it denoted members of the southern African tribes. Without any derogatory bias it was employed by statesmen, eminent authors, missionaries and champions of the native peoples. Nowadays its use is the sure mark of the racial bigot.

'Why are we stopping at the old cemetery?' Samson repeated.

'All that beer.' Craig climbed out of the Land-Rover and stretched. 'I have to pump ship.'

He relieved himself against the battered front wheel, then went to sit on the low wall of the graveyard, swinging his long bare sun-browned legs. He wore khaki shorts and suede desert boots without socks, for the barbed seeds of arrow grass stick in knitted wool.

Craig looked down onto the roofs of Khami Mission Station that lay below the wooded hills. Some of the older buildings, dating back to before the turn of the century, were thatched, although the new school and hospital were tiled with red terracotta. However, the rows of low-cost housing in the compound were covered with unpainted corrugated asbestos. They made an unsightly grey huddle beside the lovely green of the irrigated fields. They offended Craig's aesthetic sense, and he looked away.

'Come on, Sam, let's get cracking—' Craig broke off and frowned. 'What the hell are you doing?'

Samson had gone through the wrought-iron gate into the walled cemetery and was urinating casually on one of the gravestones.

'Jesus, Sam, that's desecration.'

'An old family custom.' Samson shook himself and zipped up. 'My Grandpa Gideon taught it to me,' he explained, and then switched into Sindebele. 'Giving water to make the flower grow again,' he said.

'What the hell is that supposed to mean?'

'The man that lies down there killed a Matabele girl called Imbali, the Flower,' said Samson. 'My grandfather always pees on his grave whenever he passes this way.'

Craig's shock was gradually replaced by curiosity. He swung his legs over the wall, and went to stand beside Samson.

'Sacred to the memory of General Mungo St John, Killed during the Matabele Rebellion of 1896.'

Craig read the inscription aloud:

'Man hath no greater love than this that he
lay down his life for another.
Intrepid sailor, brave soldier, faithful
husband and devoted father.
Always remembered by his widow Robyn and
his son Robert.'

Craig combed the hair out of his eyes with his fingers, 'Judging by his advertising, he was one hell of a guy.'

'He was a bloody murderer – he, as much as any one man could, provoked the rebellion.'

'Is that so?'

Craig passed on to the next grave, and read that inscription.

'Here lie the mortal remains of
DOCTOR ROBYN ST JOHN, Née BALLANTYNE
Founder of Khami Mission,
Departed this life April 16th 1931, aged 94 years.
Well done thou good and faithful servant.'

He glanced back at Samson. 'Do you know who she was?'

'My grandfather calls her Nomusa, the Girl-Child of Mercy. She was one of the most beautiful people who ever lived.'

'Never heard of her either.'

'You should have, she was your great-great-grandmother.'

'I have never bothered much with the family history. Mother and father were second cousins, that's all I know. Mellows and Ballantynes for generations back – I've never sorted them all out.'

'"A man without a past, is a man without a future",' Samson quoted.

'You know, Sam, sometimes you get up my nose.' Craig grinned at him. 'You've got an answer for everything.'

He walked on down the row of old graves, some of them with elaborate headstones, doves and groups of mourning angles, and they were decked with faded artificial flowers in domes of clear glass. Others were covered with simple concrete slabs in which the lettering had eroded to the point of illegibility. Craig read those he could.

'ROBERT ST JOHN Aged 54 years
Son of Mungo and Robyn.'

'JUBA KUMALO Aged 83 years
Fly little Dove.'

And then he stopped as he saw his own surname.

'VICTORIA MELLOW Née CODRINGTON
Died 8th April 1936 aged 63 years
Daughter of Clinton and Robyn, wife of Harold.'

'Hey Sam, if you were right about the others, then this must have been my great-grandmother.'

There was a tuft of grass growing out of a crack through the slab, and Craig stooped and plucked it out. And as he did so, he felt a bond of affinity with the dust beneath that stone. It had laughed and loved and given birth that he might live.

'Hi there, Gran,' he whispered. 'I wonder what you were really like?'

'Craig, it's almost one o'clock,' Sam interrupted him.

'Okay, I'm coming.' But Craig lingered a few moments longer, held by that unaccustomed nostalgia. 'I'll ask Bawu,' he decided and went back to the Land-Rover.

He stopped again outside the first cottage of the village. The small yard was freshly raked and there were petunias in tubs on the veranda.

'Look here, Sam,' Craig began awkwardly. 'I don't know what you're going to do now. You could join the police, like I am doing. Perhaps we could work it that we were together again.'

'Perhaps,' Sam agreed expressionlessly.

'Or I could talk to Bawu about getting you a job at King's Lynn.'

'Clerk in the pay office?' Sam asked.

'Yea! I know.' Craig scratched his ear. 'Still, it's something.'

'I'll think about it,' Sam murmured.

'Hell, I feel bad, but you didn't have to come with me, you know. You could have stayed in the department.'

'Not after what they did to you.' Sam shook his head.

'Thanks, Sam.'

They sat silently for a while, then Sam climbed down and lugged his bag out of the back of the Land-Rover.

'I'll come out and see you as soon as I'm fixed up. We'll work something out,' Craig promised. 'Keep in touch, Sam.'

'Sure.' Sam held out his hand, and they shook briefly.

'*Hamba gashle*, go in peace,' Sam said.

'*Shala gashle*. Stay in peace.'

Craig started the Land-Rover and swung back the way they had come. As he drove up the avenue of spathodea, he glanced in the rear-view mirror. Sam was standing in the centre of the road with his bag on one shoulder, watching him go. There was a hollow feeling of bereavement in Craig's chest. The two of them had been together for so long.

'I'll work something out,' he repeated determinedly.

Craig slowed at the top of the rise as he always did here, anticipating his first glimpse of the homestead, but when it came it was with that little shock of disappointment.

Bawu had stripped the thatch off the room and replaced it with dull grey corrugated asbestos sheet. It had to be done, of course, an RPG-7 rocket fired into the thatch from outside the perimeter – and the whole building would have gone up like the fifth of November. Still Craig resented the change, just as he did the loss of the beautiful jacaranda trees. They had been planted by Bawu's grandfather, old Zouga Ballantyne who built King's Lynn back in the early 1890s. In spring their gentle rain of blue petals had carpeted the lawns, but they had been cut down to open a field of defensive fire around the house, and in their place now stood the ten-foot security fence of diamond mesh and barbed wire.

Craig drove down into the shallow dip below the main homestead towards the complex of offices, storerooms and tractor workshops which were the heart of the vast sprawling ranch. Before he was halfway down, a lanky figure appeared in the high doorway of the workshop, and stood with arms akimbo watching him approach.

'Hello, Grandpa.' Craig climbed out of the Land-Rover, and the old man frowned to cover his pleasure.

'How many times have I got to tell you, "Don't call me that!" You want people to think I'm old?' Jonathan Ballantyne was burned and dessicated by the sun to the consistency of biltong, the dark strips of dried venison that were such a Rhodesian delicacy.

It seemed that if you were to cut him, dust and not blood would pour from the wound, but his eyes were still a brilliant twinkling green and his hair was a dense white shock that fell to his collar at the back of his neck. It was one of his many conceits. He shampooed it every day, and brushed it with a pair of silver-backed brushes that stood on the table beside his bed.

'Sorry, Bawu.' Craig reverted to his Matabele name, the Gadfly, and seized the old man's hand. It was mere bone covered by cool dry skin, but the grip was startlingly strong.

'So you got yourself fired again,' Jonathan accused. Although his teeth were artificial, they were a neat fit, filling out the wizened cheeks, and he kept them so sparkling white as to match his hair and silvery moustache. Another of his conceits.

'I resigned,' Craig denied.

'You got fired.'

'It was close,' Craig admitted. 'But I beat them to it. I resigned.'

Craig was not really surprised that Jonathan already knew of his latest misfortune. Nobody knew how old Jonathan Ballantyne was for certain, the outside estimate was a hundred years, though eighty-plus was Craig's guess, but still nothing got by him.

'You can give me a lift up to the house.' Jonathan swung up easily onto the high passenger seat, and with relish began pointing out the additions to the defence of the homestead.

'I have put in twenty more Claymores on the front lawn.' Jonathan's Claymore mines were ten kilos of plastic explosive packed inside a drum of scrap-iron suspended on a pipe tripod. He could fire them electrically from his bedroom.

Jonathan was a chronic insomniac, and Craig had a bizarre mental picture of the old man spending every night sitting bolt upright in his nightshirt with his finger on the button praying for a terrorist to come within range. The war had added twenty years to his life. Jonathan hadn't had such a good time since the first battle of the Somme, where he had won his MC one lovely autumn morning by grenading three German machine-gun nests in quick succession. Secretly Craig believed that the first thing any ZIPRA* guerrilla recruit was taught when he began his basic training

* Zimbabwe People's Revolutionary Army.

was to give King's Lynn and the crazy old man who lived there the widest possible berth.

As they drove up through the gates in the security fence and were surrounded by a mixed pack of fearsome Rottweilers and Dobermann pinschers, Jonathan explained the latest refinements to his battle plan.

'If they come from behind the kopje, I'll let them get into the minefield, then take them in *enfilade*—'

He was still explaining and gesticulating as they climbed the steps to the wide veranda and he finished the briefing by adding darkly and mysteriously:

'I have just invented a secret weapon, I'm going to test it tomorrow morning. You can watch.'

'I'd enjoy that, Bawu,' Craig thanked him doubtfully. The last tests that Jonathan had conducted had blown all the windows out of the kitchens and flesh-wounded the Matabele cook.

Craig followed Jonathan down the wide shady veranda. The wall was hung with hunting trophies, the horns of buffalo and kudu and eland, and on each side of the double glass doors leading to the old dining-room, now the library, stood a pair of enormous elephant tusks, so long and curved that their tips almost met at the level of the ceiling above the doorway.

As he went through the door, Jonathan absentmindedly stroked one of them. There was a spot on the thick yellow curve that had been polished shiny by the touch of his fingers over the decades.

'Pour us each a gin, my boy,' he ordered. Jonathan had stopped drinking whisky on the day that Harold Wilson's government had imposed sanctions on Rhodesia. It was Jonathan's single-handed retaliatory attempt at disrupting the economy of the British Isles.

'By God, you've drowned it,' he complained, as he tasted the concoction, and dutifully Craig took his glass back to the imbuia cocktail cabinet and stiffened the gin component.

'That's a little better.' Jonathan settled himself behind his desk and placed the Stuart crystal tumbler in the centre of his leather and brass-bound blotter.

'Now,' he said. 'Tell me what happened this time.' And he fixed Craig with those bright green eyes.

'Well, Bawu, it's a long story. I don't want to bore you.' Craig sank down into the deep leather armchair and became intensely interested in the furnishings of the room which he had known since childhood. He read the titles on the spines of the morocco-bound books on the shelves, and studied the massed display of blue silk rosettes which the prize Afrikander bulls of King's Lynn had won at every agricultural show south of the Zambezi river.

'Shall I tell you what I heard? I heard you refused to obey the legitimate order of your superior, to wit the head game warden, and that thereafter you perpetrated a violence upon that worthy, or more specifically that you punched him in the head. Giving him the excuse to dismiss you for which he had probably been searching desperately since the first day you arrived in the Park.'

'The reports are exaggerated.'

'Don't give me that little-boy grin of yours, young man. This is not a matter of levity,' Jonathan told him sternly. 'Did you refuse to partake in the elephant cull, or did you not?'

'Have you ever been on a cull, Jon-Jon?' Craig asked softly. He only used his grandfather's pet name in moments of deep sincerity. 'The spotter plane picks a likely herd, say fifty animals, and radio talks us onto them. We go in the last mile or so on foot at a dead run. We get in very close, ten paces, so we are shooting uphill. We use the 458s to cannon them. What we do is pick out the old queens of the herd, because the younger animals love and respect them so

447

much that they won't leave them. We hit the queens first, head shots, of course, that gives us plenty of time to work on the others. We are pretty good at it by now. We drop them so fast that the heaps have to be pulled apart by tractors afterwards. That leaves the calves. It's interesting to watch a calf trying to lift its dead mother back onto her feet again with its tiny trunk.'

'It has to be done, Craig,' said Jonathan quietly. 'The parks are overstocked by thousands of animals.' But Craig seemed not to have heard.

'If the orphan calves are too young to survive, we hit them also, but if they are the right age, we round them up and sell them to a nice old man who takes them away and resells them to a zoo in Tokyo or Amsterdam, where they will stand behind bars with a chain around the foot and eat the peanuts that the tourists throw them.'

'It has to be done,' Jonathan repeated.

'He was taking kickbacks from the animal-dealers,' Craig said. 'So that we were ordered to leave orphans that were so young they only had a fifty-fifty chance of survival. So that we looked for herds with high percentages of small calves. He was taking bribes from the dealers.'

'Who? Not Tomkins, the head warden?' Jonathan exclaimed.

'Yes, Tomkins.' Craig stood up and took both their glasses to refill.

'Have you got proof?'

'No, of course I haven't,' Craig replied irritably. 'If I had I would have taken it straight to the minister.'

'So you just refused to cull.'

Craig flopped back in the chair, long bare legs sprawled and hair hanging in his eyes.

'That's not all. They are stealing the ivory from the cull. We are supposed to leave the big bulls, but Tomkins ordered us to hit anything with good ivory, and the tusks disappear.'

'No proof on that either, I suppose?' Jonathan asked drily.

'I saw the helicopter making the pick-up.'

'And you got the registration letters?'

'They were masked,' Craig shook his head, 'but it was a military machine. It's organized.'

'So you punched Tomkins?'

'It was beautiful,' said Craig dreamily. 'He was on his hands and knees trying to pick up his teeth that were scattered all over the floor of his office. I never worked out what he was going to do with them.'

'Craig, my boy, what did you hope to achieve? Do you think it will stop them, even if your suspicions are correct?'

'No, but it made me feel a lot better. Those elephant are almost human. I became pretty fond of them.'

They were both silent for a while and then Jonathan sighed. 'How many jobs is that now, Craig?'

'I wasn't keeping score, Bawu.'

'I can't believe that anybody with Ballantyne blood in his veins is totally lacking in either talent or ambition. Christ, boy, we Ballantynes are winners, look at Douglas, look at Roland—'

'I'm a Mellow, only half a Ballantyne.'

'Yes, I suppose that accounts for it. Your grandfather frittered away his share in the Harkness Mine, so when your father married my Jean he was almost a pauper. Good God, those shares would be worth ten million pounds today.'

'That was during the great depression of the Thirties – a lot of people lost money then.'

'We didn't – the Ballantynes didn't.'

Craig shrugged. 'No, the Ballantynes doubled up during the depression.'

'We are winners,' Jonathan repeated. 'But what happens to you now? You know my rule, you don't get a penny more from me.'

'Yes, I know that rule, Jon-Jon.'

'You want to try working here again? It didn't pan out so well last time, did it?'

'You are an impossible old bastard,' said Craig fondly. 'I love you, but I'd rather work for Idi Amin than for you again.'

Jonathan looked immensely pleased with himself. His image of himself as tough, ruthless and ready to kill, was another of his conceits. He would have been deeply insulted if anybody had called him easy-going or generous. The large anonymous donations he made to every charity, deserving or otherwise, were always accompanied by blood-curdling threats to anybody revealing his identity.

'So what are you going to do with yourself this time?'

'Well, I was trained as an armourer when I did my national service, and there is an armourer's berth open in the police. The way I see it, I'm going to be called up again anyway, so I might as well beat them to it and enlist.'

'The police,' Jonathan mused, 'that does have the virtue of being one of the few things you haven't tried yet. Get me another drink.'

While Craig poured gin and tonic, Jonathan put on his fiercest expression to cover his embarrassment and growled, 'Look here, boy, if you are really short, I'll bend the rule this once, and lend you a few dollars to tide you over. Strictly a loan though.'

'That's very decent of you, Bawu, but a rule is a rule.'

'I make 'em, I break 'em,' Jonathan glared at him. 'How much do you need?'

'You know those old books you wanted?' Craig murmured, as he put the old man's glass back in front of him, and an expression of intense cunning came into Jonathan's eyes which he tried in vain to conceal.

'What books?' His innocence was loaded.

'Those old journals.'

'Oh, those!' And despite himself Jonathan glanced at the bookshelves beside his desk upon which were displayed his collection of family journals. They stretched back over a hundred years, from the arrival of his grandfather, Zouga

Ballantyne, in Africa in 1860 up to the death of Jonathan's father, Sir Ralph Ballantyne, in 1929, but the sequence was broken by a few missing years, three volumes which had come down on Craig's side of the family, through old Harry Mellow, who had been Sir Ralph's partner and dearest friend.

For some perverse reason that Craig could not even understand himself, he had up until now resisted all the old man's blandishments and attempts to get his hands on them. It was probably because they were the one small lever he had on Jonathan that he had held out since they had come into his possession on his twenty-first birthday, the only item of any value in the inheritance from his long-dead father.

'Yes, those,' Craig nodded. 'I thought I might let you have them.'

'You must be hard pressed.' The old man tried not to let his glee shine through.

'Even more than usual,' Craig admitted.

'You waste—'

'Okay, Bawu. We've been down that road before,' Craig stopped him hurriedly. 'Do you want them?'

'How much?' Jonathan demanded suspiciously.

'Last time you offered me a thousand each.'

'I must have been soft.'

'Since then there has been a hundred per cent inflation—'

Jonathan loved to haggle. It enhanced his image of himself as hard and ruthless. Craig reckoned he was worth ten million. He owned King's Lynn and four other ranches. He owned the Harkness Mine which after eighty years in production was still producing 50,000 ounces of gold a year, and he had assets outside this beleaguered country, prudently stashed away over the years in Johannesburg, London and New York. Ten million was probably conservative, Craig realized, and set himself to bargain as hard as the old man.

At last they reached a figure with Jonathan grumbling, 'They're worth half of that.'

'There are two other conditions, Bawu.' And immediately Jonathan was suspicious again.

'Number one, you leave them to me in your will, the whole set, Zouga Ballantyne's and Sir Ralph's journals, all of them.'

'Roland and Douglas—'

'They are going to get King's Lynn and the Harkness and all the rest – that's what you told me.'

'Damn right,' he growled. 'They won't blow it all out the window like you would.'

'They can have it,' Craig grinned easily. 'They are Ballantynes as you say, but I want the journals.'

'What is your second condition?' Jonathan demanded.

'I want access to them now.'

'What do you mean?'

'I want to be able to read and study any of them whenever I want to.'

'What the hell, Craig, you have never given a damn about them before. I doubt you have even read the three you own.'

'I've glanced through them,' Craig admitted shame-facedly.

'And now?'

'I was up at Khami Mission this morning, in the old cemetery. There is a grave there, Victoria Mellow—'

Jonathan nodded. 'Aunty Vicky, Harry's wife, go on.'

'I had this strange feeling as I was standing there. Almost as though she was calling to me.' Craig plucked at the thick forelock over his eyes and could not look at his grandfather. 'And suddenly I wanted to find out more about her, and the others.'

They were both silent for a while, and then Jonathan nodded.

'All right, my boy, I accept your conditions. Both sets will be yours one day, and until then you can read them whenever you wish to.'

Jonathan had seldom been so pleased with a bargain. He had completed his sets after thirty years, and if the boy was serious about reading them, he had found a good home for them. The Lord knew, neither Douglas nor Roland was interested, and in the meantime perhaps the journals might draw Craig back to King's Lynn more often. He wrote out the cheque and signed it with a flourish, while Craig went out to the Land-Rover and dug the three leather-bound manuscripts from the bottom of his kitbag.

'I suppose you will spend it all on that boat,' Jonathan accused as he came in from the veranda.

'Some of it,' Craig admitted. He placed the books in front of the old man.

'You are a dreamer.' Jonathan slid the cheque across the desk.

'Sometimes I prefer dreams to reality.' Craig scrutinized the figures briefly, then buttoned the pink cheque into his top pocket.

'That's your trouble,' said Jonathan.

'Bawu, if you start lecturing me, I'm going to head straight back to town.'

Jonathan held up both hands in capitulation. 'All right,' he chuckled. 'Your old room is the way you left it, if you want to use it.'

'I have an appointment with the police recruiting officer on Monday, but I'll stay the weekend, if that's okay?'

'I'll ring Trevor this evening and fix the interview.'

Trevor Pennington was the assistant commissioner of police. Jonathan believed in starting at the top.

'I wish you wouldn't, Jon-Jon.'

'Don't be daft,' Jonathan snapped. 'You must learn to use every advantage, my boy, that's the way life works.'

Jonathan picked up the first of the three volumes of manuscript and gloatingly stroked it with his gnarled brown fingers.

'Now, you can leave me alone for a while,' he ordered, as he unfolded his wire-framed reading-glasses and perched them on his nose. 'They are playing tennis across at Queen's Lynn, I will see you back here for sundowners.'

Craig glanced back from the doorway, but Jonathan Ballantyne was hunched over the book, transported by the entries in yellow faded ink back to his childhood.

Although it shared a common seven-mile boundary with King's Lynn, Queen's Lynn was a separate ranch. Jonathan Ballantyne had added it to his holdings during the great depression of the 1930s, paying five cents on the dollar of its real worth. Now it formed the eastern spread of the Rholands Ranching Company.

It was the home of Jonathan's only surviving son, Douglas Ballantyne, and his wife Valerie. Douglas was the managing director of both Rholands and the Harkness Mine. He was also Minister of Agriculture in Ian Smith's UDI government, and with any luck he might be away on mysterious government or company business.

Douglas Ballantyne had once given Craig his honest appraisal. 'At heart you are a bloody hippie, Craig, you should get your hair cut and start bracing up, you can't go on dawdling through life and expecting Bawu and the rest of the family to carry you for ever.'

Craig pulled a sour face at the memory as he drove down past the stockyards of Queen's Lynn, and smelled the ammoniacal tang of cow-dung.

The huge Afrikander beasts were a uniform deep chocolate red, the bulls hump-backed and with swinging dewlaps that almost brushed the earth. This breed had made Rhodesian beef almost as renowned as the marbled beef of Kobe. As Minister of Agriculture it was Douglas Ballantyne's duty to see that, despite sanctions, the world was not deprived of this delicacy. The route that it took to the tables of the great restaurants of the world was via Johannesburg and Cape Town, where it perforce changed its name, but the connoisseurs recognized it and asked for it by its *nom de guerre*, their taste-buds probably piqued by the knowledge that they were eating forbidden fruits. Rhodesian tobacco and nickel and copper and gold all went out the same way, while petrol and diesel oil made the return trip. The popular bumper sticker said simply, 'Thank you, South Africa.'

Beyond the stock-pens and veterinary block, once again protected by the diamond mesh and barbed-wire security fence, lay the green lawns and banks of flowering shrubs and the blazing Pride of India trees of the gardens of Queen's Lynn. The windows had been covered with grenade screens and the servants would drop steel bullet-proof shutters into their slots before sunset, but here the defences had not been built with the same gusto as Bawu had shown at King's Lynn. They fitted unobtrusively into the gracious surroundings.

The lovely old house was very much as Craig remembered it from before the war, rosy red brick and wide cool verandas. The jacaranda trees that lined the long curved driveway were in full flower, like a mist bank of pale ethereal blue, and there were at least two dozen cars parked beneath them, Mercedes and Jaguars, Cadillacs and BMWs, their paintwork hazed with the red dust of Matabeleland. Craig concealed his venerable Land-Rover behind the tumble of red and purple bougainvillaea creeper, so as not to lower the tone of a Queen's Lynn Saturday. From habit he slung an FN rifle over his shoulder and wandered around the side of the house.

From ahead there came the sound of children's voices, gay as songbirds, and the genial scolding of their black nannies, punctuated by the sharp 'Pock! Pock!' of a long rally from the tennis courts.

Craig paused at the head of the terraced lawns. Children spilled and tumbled and chased each other in circles like puppies over the green grass. Nearer the yellow clay courts, their parents sprawled on spread rugs or sat at the shaded white tea-tables, under the brightly coloured umbrellas. They were bronzed young men and women in tennis whites, sipping tea or drinking beer from tall frosted glasses, calling ribald comment and advice to the players upon the courts. The only incongruous note was the row of machine pistols and automatic rifles beside the silver tea set and cream scones.

Someone recognized Craig and shouted, 'Hi Craig, long time no see,' and others waved, but there was just that faint edge of condescension in their manner reserved for the poor relative. These were the families with great estates, a closed club of the wealthy in which, for all their geniality, Craig would never have full membership.

Valerie Ballantyne came to meet him, slim-hipped and girlishly graceful in her short white tennis skirt. 'Craig, you are as thin as a bean pole.' He always brought out the maternal instincts in any female between eight and eighty.

'Hello, Aunty Val.'

She offered him a smooth cheek that smelled of violets. Despite her delicate air, Valerie was president of the Women's Institute, served on the committees of a dozen schools, charities and hospitals, and was a gracious, accomplished hostess.

'Uncle Douglas is in Salisbury. Smithy sent for him yesterday. He will be sorry to have missed you.' She took his arm. 'How is the Game Department?'

'It will probably survive without me.'

'Oh, no, Craig, not again!'

''Fraid so, Aunty Val.' He didn't really feel up to a discussion of his career at that moment. 'Do you mind if I get myself a beer?'

There was a group of men around the long trestle-table that did service as a bar. The group opened to let him in, but the conversation went straight back to a discussion of the latest raid that the Rhodesian security forces had made into Mozambique.

'I tell you, when we hit the camp, there was food still cooking on the fires, but they had run for it. We caught a few stragglers, but the others had been warned.'

'Bill is right, I had it from a colonel in intelligence, no names, no pack drill, but there is a bad security leak. A traitor near the top, the terrs are getting up to twelve hours' warning.'

'We haven't had a really good kill since last August when we took six hundred.'

The eternal war talk bored Craig. He sipped his beer and watched the play on the nearest court.

It was mixed doubles, and at that moment they changed ends.

Roland Ballantyne came around the net with his arm around his partner's waist. He was laughing, and his teeth were startlingly white and even in the deep tan of his face. His eyes were that peculiar Ballantyne green, like crème de menthe in a crystal glass, and although he wore his hair short, it was thick and wavy, bleached to honey-gold by the sun.

He moved like a leopard, with a lazy gliding gait, and the superb physical condition that was a prerequisite of any member of the Scouts glossed the muscles of his forearms and bare legs. He was only a year older than Craig, but his assurance always made Craig feel gawky and callow in comparison. Craig had once heard a girl he admired, a

457

young lady usually blasée and affectedly unimpressed, describe Roland Ballantyne as the most magnificent stud on show.

Now Roland saw him, and waved his racquet. 'Don't be vague, call for Craig!' he greeted him across the court, and then said something inaudible to the girl beside him. She chuckled and looked at Craig.

Craig felt the shock begin in the pit of his stomach and ripple outwards like a stone dropped into a still pool. He stared at her, petrified, unable to drag his eyes off her face. She stopped laughing, and for a moment longer returned his gaze, then she broke out of the circle of Roland's arm and went to the baseline, bouncing the ball lightly off her racquet and Craig was certain that her cheeks had flushed a shade pinker than the game had previously rouged them.

Still he could not take his eyes off her. She was the most perfect thing he had ever seen. She was tall, she reached almost to Roland's shoulder and he was six one. Her hair was cropped into a glossy cap of curls, that changed colour as the sunlight played upon it, from the burnished iridescence of obsidian to the rich dark glow of a noble burgundy wine held to the candlelight.

Her face was squarish, with a firm, perhaps stubborn, line to the jaw, but her mouth was wide and tender and humorous. Her eyes were wide-spaced and slanted to such a degree that they seemed just a touch squint. It gave her a vulnerable appealing air, but when she glanced at Roland, they took on a wicked taunting glint.

'Let's blast them, pardner,' she called, and the lift of her voice raised little goose bumps on Craig's forearms.

The girl turned her shoulders and hips away, tossed the yellow ball high as she went up on tiptoe and then swung back into the overhead stroke. The racquet sprang sharply and the ball blurred low across the net, and spurted white chalk from the centre line.

She crossed the court with quick dainty steps, and caught

the return on the volley. She tucked it away in the corner, and then glanced at Craig.

'Shot!' he called, his voice ringing hollowly in his own ears, and a little satisfied smile puckered the corner of her mouth.

She turned away and stooped to recover a loose ball. Her back was turned towards Craig, her feet slightly apart and she did not bend her knees. Her legs were long and shapely, and as her short pleated skirt popped up, he had a fleeting glimpse of thin lacy panties and the buttocks in them so neat and hard and symmetrical that he was reminded of a pair of ostrich eggs gleaming in the Kalahari sunlight.

Craig dropped his eyes guiltily as if he had played the peeping Tom. He felt light-headed and strangely breathless. He forced himself not to look back at the court, but his heart was pounding as though he had just run a cross-country, and the conversation around him seemed to be in a foreign language, relayed through a faulty transmitter. It did not make sense.

It seemed hours later that a hard muscular arm was thrown around his shoulders, and Roland's voice in his ear.

'You're looking well, old son.' At last Craig allowed himself to look around.

'The terrs haven't caught you yet, Roly?'

'No way, Sonny,' Roland hugged him. 'Let me introduce you to a girl who loves me.' Only Roland could make a remark like that sound witty and sophisticated. 'This is Bugsy. Bugsy, this is my favourite cousin, Craig, the well-known sex maniac.'

'Bugsy?' Craig looked into those strangely tilted eyes. 'It doesn't suit you.' He realized that they were not black, but a dark indigo blue.

'Janine,' she said. 'Janine Carpenter.' She held out her hand. It was slim and warm and moist from the game. He did not want to release it.

'I warned you,' Roland laughed. 'Stop molesting the girl and come and have a set with me, Sonny.'

'I haven't got togs.'

'All you need is shoes. We are the same size, I'll send a servant for a spare pair.'

Craig hadn't played for over a year. The lay-off seemed to have worked wonders. He had never played so well. The ball came off the sweet spot of his racquet so fast and clean that it felt as though he had clean missed it, and the top-spin pulled it down onto the baseline as though it were a magnet.

Effortlessly, he passed Roland on either side, and then dropped the ball so short that it left him stranded in mid-court. He hit first-time serves that nicked the line, and returned shots that usually he would not have bothered to chase, then he rushed the net and slaughtered Roland's best forehand.

He was loving it, so involved with the marvellous unaccustomed sense of power and of his own invincibility, that he had not even noticed that the stream of Roland Ballantyne's easy banter had long ago dried up – until he won another game and Roland said, 'Five games to love.'

Something in his tone reached Craig at last, and for the first time since they had begun playing, he really looked at Roland's face. It was a swollen ugly red. His jaw clenched so that there were lumps of muscle below his ears. His eyes were murderous green, and he was dangerous as a wounded leopard.

Craig looked away from him as they changed sides and he saw that their game had fascinated everybody. Even the older women had left the tea-tables and come down to the fence. He saw Aunty Val, with a nervous little smile on her lips. From hard experience, she recognized her son's mood.

Craig saw the sniggering smiles on the faces of the men. Roland had won his tennis half-blue at Oxford, and he had been Matabeleland singles champion three years running. They were enjoying this as much as Craig had been up until then.

Suddenly Craig felt appalled at his own success. He had never beaten Roland at anything, not a single contest of any sort, not even monopoly nor darts, not once in twenty-nine years. The elasticity and strength went out of his legs, and he stood on the baseline, just a long-legged gangling boy again, dressed in faded khaki shorts and worn tennis shoes without socks. He gulped miserably, pushed the hair out of his eyes, and crouched to receive service.

Across the net Roland Ballantyne was a tall athletic figure. He glared at Craig. Craig knew he was not seeing him, he was seeing an adversary, something to be destroyed.

'We Ballantynes are winners,' Bawu had said. 'We have got the instinct for the jugular.'

Roland seemed, impossibly, to grow even taller, and then he served. Craig began to move left, saw it was the wrong side and tried to change. His long legs tangled and he sprawled on the yellow clay. He stood up, retrieved his racquet, and went across to the other court. There was a bloody smear on his knee. Roland's next service crashed in, and he did not get a touch of his racquet to it.

When his turn came, he hit one into the net, and the next one off the wood. Roland broke his service three times in a row, and it went on like that.

'Match point,' Roland said. He was smiling again, gay and handsome and genial as he bounced the ball at his feet, and lined up for his final service. Craig felt that old heavy feeling in his limbs, the despair of the born loser.

He glanced off court. Janine Carpenter was looking directly at him, and in the instant before she smiled encouragingly, Craig saw the pity in those dark indigo eyes, and abruptly he was angry.

He socked Roland's service, double-handed, into the corner, and had it come back as hard. He crossed with his forehand, and Roland was grinning as he drove it back. Again Craig caught it perfectly, and even Roland was forced to lob. It came down from on high, floating helplessly, and Craig was under it, poised and coldly angry, and he hit it with all his weight and strength and despair. It was his best shot. After that he had nothing to follow. Roland trapped it on the bounce, before it could rise, and he punched it tantalizingly past Craig's right hip while he was twisted hopelessly off balance by the power of his own stroke.

Roland laughed, and vaulted easily over the net.

'Not bad, Sonny.' He put his arm patronizingly around Craig's shoulders. 'I'll know not to give you a start in future,' he said and led Craig off the court.

Those who had been gloatingly anticipating Roland's humiliation a few minutes before now crowded slavishly around him.

'Well played, Roly.'

'Great stuff.'

And Craig slipped away from them. He picked a clean white towel off the pile and wiped his neck and face. Trying not to look as miserable as he felt, he went to the deserted bar, and fished a beer out of the bath of crushed ice. He swallowed a mouthful, and it was so tart that it made his eyes swim. Through the tears he realized suddenly that Janine Carpenter was standing beside him.

'You could have done it,' she said softly. 'But you just gave up.'

'Story of my life.' He tried to sound gay and witty, like Roland, but it came out flat, and self-pityingly.

She seemed about to speak again, then shook her head and walked away.

Craig used Roland's shower and when he came out with the towel around his waist, Roland was in front of the full-length mirror adjusting the angle of his beret.

The beret was dark maroon with a brass cap-badge above the left ear. The badge was a brutish human head, with the forehead of a gorilla and the same broad flattened nose. The eyes were crossed grotesquely and the tongue protruded from between negroid lips, like a Maori carving of a war idol.

'When old Great-grandpa Ralph recruited the Scouts during the rebellion,' Roland had once explained to Craig, 'one of his better-known exploits was to catch the leader of the rebels, and to hang him from the top of an acacia tree. We have taken that as our regimental emblem – Bazo's hanged head. How do you like it?'

'Charming,' Craig had given his opinion. 'You always did have such exquisite taste, Roly.'

Roland had conceived the Scouts three years previously when the sporadic warfare of the earlier days had begun to intensify into the merciless internecine conflict of the present time. His original idea had been to gather a force of young white Rhodesians who could speak fluent Sindebele and reinforce them with young Matabele who had been with their white employers since childhood, men whose loyalty was unquestionable. He would train black and white elements into an elite strike-force that could move easily through the tribal trust areas amongst the peasant farmers, speaking their language and understanding their ways, able to impersonate innocent tribesmen or ZIPRA terrorists at will, able to meet the enemy at the border or drop onto him from the sky and take him on at the most favourable terms.

He had gone to General Peter Walls at Combined Services Headquarters. Of course, Bawu had made the usual phone calls to clear the way, and Uncle Douglas had put a word in Smithy's ear during a cabinet meeting. They had given Roland the go-ahead, and so Ballantyne's Scouts had been reborn, seventy years after the original troop was disbanded.

In the three years since then, Ballantyne's Scouts had cut their way into legend. Six hundred men who had been officially credited with two thousand kills, who had been five hundred miles over the border into Zambia to hit a ZIPRA training base; men who had sat at the village fires in the tribal trust lands listening to the chatter of the women who had just returned from carrying baskets of grain to the ZIPRA cadres in the hills, men who laid their ambushes and maintained them for five straight days, burying their own excrement beside them, waiting patiently and as unmoving as a leopard beside the water-hole, waiting for yet another good kill.

Roland turned from the mirror as Craig came into the bedroom. The pips of a full colonel sparkled on his shoulders, and over his heart the cluster of the silver cross was pinned below his dog-tab on the crisply ironed khaki bush-shirt.

'Help yourself to what you need, Sonny,' he invited, and Craig went to the built-in cupboard and selected a pair of flannels and a white cricket sweater with the colours of Oriel College around the neck. It seemed like coming home to be wearing Roland's cast-offs again, he had always been a year behind him.

'Mom tells me you've been fired again.'

'That's right.' Craig's voice was muffled by the sweater over his head.

'There's a billet for you with the Scouts.'

'Roly, I don't fancy the idea of putting piano wire around somebody's neck and plucking his head off.'

'We don't do that every day,' Roland grinned. 'Personally, I much prefer a knife, you can also use it to slice biltong when you aren't slitting throats. But seriously, Sonny, we could use you. You talk the lingo like one of them, and you are a real buff at blowing things up. We are short of blast bunnies.'

'When I left King's Lynn I swore an oath that I would never work for anyone in the family again.'

'The Scouts aren't family.'

'You are the Scouts, Roly.'

'I could have you seconded, you know that?'

'That wouldn't work.'

'No,' Roland agreed. 'You always were a stubborn blighter. Well, if you change your mind, let me know.' He knocked a cigarette half out of its soft pack and then pulled it the rest of the way with his lips. 'What do you think of Bugsy?' The cigarette waggled as he asked the question, and he flicked his gold Ronson to it.

'She's all right,' Craig said cautiously.

'Only all right?' Roland protested. 'Try magnificent, try sensational, wonderful, super-great – wax lyrical, for you're talking about the woman I love.'

'Number one thousand and ten on the list of the women you have loved,' Craig corrected.

'Steady, old son, this one I am going to marry.'

Craig felt a coldness come over his soul, and he turned away to comb his damp hair in the mirror.

'Did you hear what I said? I'm going to marry her.'

'Does she know?'

'I'm letting her ripen a little before I tell her.'

'Ask her, don't you mean ask her?'

'Old Roly tells 'em, he doesn't ask 'em. You are supposed to say, "Congratulations, I hope you will be very happy."'

'Congratulations, I hope you will be very happy.'

'That's my boy. Come on, I'll buy you a drink.'

They went down the long central corridor that bisected the house but before they reached the veranda, a telephone rang in the lobby and they heard Aunty Val's voice:

'I'll fetch him. Hold the line please,' and then louder, 'Roland, darling, it's Cheetah for you.'

465

Cheetah was the call-sign of Scout base. 'I'm coming, Mom.' Roland strode into the lobby and Craig heard him say, 'Ballantyne,' and then after a short silence, 'are you sure it's him? By Christ, this is the chance we have been waiting for. How soon can you get a chopper here? On its way? Good! Throw a net around the place, but don't go in until I get there. I want this baby myself.'

When he came back into the corridor, he was transformed. It was the same look as he had given Craig across the net, cold and dangerous and without mercy.

'Can you get Bugsy back to town for me, Sonny? We are going into a contact.'

'I'll look after her.'

Roland strode out onto the veranda. The last of the tennis guests were dispersing towards their vehicles, gathering up nannies and children as they went, shouting farewells and last-minute invitations for the coming week. There was a time when a gathering like this would not have broken up until after midnight, but now nobody drove the country roads after 4 p.m., the new witching hour.

Janine Carpenter was shaking hands and laughing with a couple from the neighbouring ranch.

'I'd love to come over,' she said, and then she looked up and saw Roland's expression. She hurried to him.

'What is it?'

'We are going in. Sonny will look after you. I'll call you.' He was searching the sky, already remote and detached, and then there was the whack, whack, whacking of helicopter rotors in the air and the machine came bustling in low over the kopje. She was painted in dull battle-brown, and there were two Scouts standing in the open belly port, one white and one black, both in bush camouflage and full webbing.

Roland ran down the lawns to meet her as she sank, and before she touched he jumped to link arms with his Matabele sergeant, and swung up into the cabin of the helicopter. As the machine rose and beat away, nose low

466

over the kopje, Craig caught a last glimpse of Roland. He had already replaced the beret with a soft bush hat, and his sergeant was helping him into his camouflage battle-smock.

'Roly said I was to see you home. I take it you live in Bulawayo?' Craig asked, as the helicopter disappeared and the sound of its rotors dwindled. It seemed to take an effort for her to bring her attention back to him.

'Yes, Bulawayo. Thanks.'

'We won't make it this evening, not before ambush hour. I was going to stay over at my grandpa's place.'

'Bawu?'

'You know him?'

'No, but I'd love to. Roly has kept me in fits with stories about him. Do you think there'd be a bed for me also?'

'There are twenty-two beds at King's Lynn.'

She perched on the seat of the old Land-Rover beside him, and the wind made her hair shimmer and flutter.

'Why does he call you Bugsy?' Craig had to raise his voice above the engine noise.

'I'm an entomologist,' she shouted back. 'You know, bugs and things.'

'Where do you work?' The cool evening air flattened her blouse against her chest, and she was very obviously not wearing a bra. She had small finely shaped breasts and the cold made her nipples stand out in little dark lumps under the thin cloth. It was difficult not to gawk.

'At the museum. Did you know that we have the finest collection of tropical and sub-tropical insects in existence, better than the Smithsonian or the Kensington Natural History Museum?'

'Bully for you.'

'Sorry, I can be a bore.'

'Never.'

She smiled her thanks, but changed the subject. 'How long have you known Roland?'

'Twenty-nine years.'

'How old are you?'

'Twenty-nine.'

'Tell me about him.'

'What's to tell about somebody who is perfect?'

'Try to think of something,' she encouraged him.

'Head boy at Michaelhouse. Captain of rugger and cricket. Rhodes scholarship to Oxford, Oriel scholar. Blues for rowing and cricket, half-blue for tennis, colonel in the Scouts, silver cross for valour, heir to twenty-million-plus dollars. You know, all the usual things.' Craig shrugged.

'You don't like him,' she accused.

'I love him,' he said. 'In a funny sort of way.'

'You don't want to talk about him any more?'

'I'd rather talk about you.'

'That suits me, what do you want to know?'

He wanted to make her smile again. 'Start at the time you were born and don't miss anything out.'

'I was born in a little village in Yorkshire, my daddy is the local veterinarian.'

'When? I said not to miss anything.'

She slanted her eyes mischievously. 'What is the local expression for an indeterminate date – some time before the rinderpest?'

'That was in the 1890s.'

'Okay,' she smiled again. 'I was born some time after the rinderpest.'

It was working, Craig realized. She liked him. She smiled more readily, and their banter was light and easy. Perhaps it was just wistful imagination, but he thought he detected the first sexual awareness in her manner, the way she held her head and moved her body, the way she – then abruptly he thought of Roland and felt the cold slide of despair.

Jonathan Ballantyne came out onto the veranda of King's Lynn, took one look at her, and went immediately into his role of the lustful roué.

He kissed her hand. 'You are the prettiest young lady that Craig has ever come up with – by a street.'

Some perverse streak made Craig deny it. 'Janine is Roly's friend, Bawu.'

'Ah,' the old man nodded. 'I should have known. Too much class for your taste, boy.'

Craig's marriage had lasted a little longer than one of his jobs, just over a year, but Bawu had not approved of Craig's choice, had said so before the wedding and after it, before the divorce and after it – and at every opportunity since then.

'Thank you, Mr Ballantyne.' Janine slanted her eyes at Jonathan.

'You may call me Bawu.' Jonathan gave her his ultimate accolade, made an arm for her and said, 'Come and see my Claymore mines, my dear.'

Craig watched them go off on a tour of the defences, another sure sign of Bawu's high favour.

'He has three wives buried up on the kopje,' Craig muttered ruefully, 'and is still as randy as an old goat.'

Craig woke to his bedroom door cracking back on its hinges, and Jonathan Ballantyne's cry.

'Are you going to sleep all day? It's four-thirty already.'

'Just because you haven't slept for twenty years, Bawu.'

'Enough of your lip, boy – today's the big day. Get that pretty little filly of Roland's and we'll all go down to test my secret weapon.'

'Before breakfast?' Craig protested, but excited as a child invited to a picnic, the old man had gone already.

It was parked at a prudent distance from the nearest building. The cook had threatened to resign if there were any more experiments conducted within blast range of his kitchen. It stood on the edge of a field of ripening seed maize, and it was surrounded by a small crowd of labourers and tractor drivers and clerks.

'What on earth is it?' Janine puzzled, as they crossed the ploughed land towards it, but before anyone could reply, a figure in greasy blue overalls detached itself from the crowd and hurried towards them.

'Mister Craig, thank goodness you are here. You've got to stop him.'

'Don't be a blithering old idiot, Okky,' Jonathan ordered. Okky van Rensburg had been chief mechanic on King's Lynn for twenty years. Behind his back Jonathan boasted that Okky could strip down a John Deere tractor, and build up a Cadillac and two Rolls Royce Silver Clouds out of the spare parts. He was a wiry grease-stained little monkey of a man. He ignored Jonathan's injunction to silence.

'Bawu's going to kill himself, unless somebody stops him.' He wrung his scarred blackened hands pitifully.

But already Jonathan was donning his helmet and fastening the strap under his chin. It was the same tin helmet that he had worn on that day in 1916 that he won his Military Cross, and the dent in the side had been made by a shard of German shrapnel. There was an unholy gleam in his eyes as he advanced upon the monstrous vehicle.

'Okky has converted a three-ton Ford truck,' he explained to Janine, 'lifted the chassis,' as though it were on stilts, the vehicle's body stood high above the huge lugged tyres, 'put in deflectors here,' he pointed out the heavy steel vee-shaped plates under the cab that would split the blast of a landmine, 'armoured the cab,' the body looked like a tiger tank, with steel hatches, a driver's slit and gunports for a heavy Browning machine-gun, 'but look what we have got on top!' At a glance it could have been mistaken for the conning tower of a nuclear submarine, and Okky was still wringing his hands.

'He's got twenty galvanized steel pipes filled with plastic explosive and thirty pounds of ball-bearings each.'

'Good Lord, Bawu.' Even Craig was horrified. 'The damn things will explode!'

'He has set them in blocks of concrete,' Okky moaned, 'and aimed them out on each side just like the cannons on one of Nelson's ships of the line. Ten on each side.'

'A twenty-gun Ford,' Craig breathed with awe.

'When I run into an ambush, I just press the button – and boom, a broadside of three hundred pounds of ball-bearings into the bastards,' Jonathan gloated openly. 'A whiff of grape, as old Bonaparte said.'

'He's going to blow himself to hell,' Okky moaned.

'Oh, do stop being an old woman,' Jonathan told him. 'And give me a leg up.'

'Bawu, this time I really do agree with Okky.' Craig tried to stop him, but the old man went up the steel ladder with the agility of a vervet monkey, and posed dramatically in the hatchway, like the commander of a panzer division.

'I'll let off one broadside at a time, the starboard side first.' Then his eyes lit on Janine. 'Would you like to be my co-pilot, my dear?'

'That is astonishingly civil of you, Bawu, but I think I'll get a better view from the irrigation ditch over there.'

'Then stand back everyone.' Jonathan made a wide imperious gesture of dismissal, and the Matabele labourers and drivers who had been witnesses to Jonathan's previous test took off like a brigade of Egyptian infantry departing from the Six-day War. Some of them were still running as they crossed the ridge of the kopje.

Okky reached the irrigation ditch half a dozen paces ahead of Craig and Janine, and then the three of them cautiously lifted their heads above the bank. Three hundred yards away, the grotesque Ford stood in monumental isolation in the middle of the ploughed land, and from the hatchway Jonathan gave them a cheery wave, and then disappeared.

They covered their ears with both hands and waited. Nothing happened.

'He's chickened out,' Craig said hopefully, and the hatch opened again. Jonathan's helmeted head reappeared, his face red with outrage.

'Okky, you son of a bitch, you disconnected the wiring,' he roared. 'You are fired, do you hear me? Fired!'

'Third time he has fired me this week,' Okky muttered morosely. 'It was the only way I could think of to stop him.'

'Hold on, my dear,' Jonathan addressed himself to Janine. 'I'll have it connected up in a jiffy.'

'Don't worry on my account, Bawu,' she yelled back, but he had disappeared again.

The minutes passed, each one a separate eternity, and their hopes gradually rose again.

'It's not going to work.'

'Let's get him out of there.'

'Bawu, we are coming to get you,' Craig cupped his hands and bellowed. 'And you'd better come quietly.'

He rose slowly out of the ditch, and at that moment the armoured Ford disappeared in a huge boiling cloud of smoke and dust. A sheet of white flame licked over the field of standing maize, scything it flat as though some monstrous combine-harvester had swept across it, and they were enveloped by such an appalling blast of sound, that Craig lost his balance and fell back into the ditch on top of the other two.

Frantically they scrambled to untangle themselves in the bottom of the ditch, and then looked out fearfully again across the ploughed field. The dreadful silence was broken only by the singing in their own ears, and the dwindling yelps of the old man's pack of savage Rottweilers and

Dobermann pinschers as they fled in utter panic back up the road towards the homestead. The field was obscured by a dense curtain of drifting blue smoke and red-brown dust.

They climbed up out of the ditch and stared into the smoke and dust, and the breeze blew it gently aside. The Ford lay upon its back. All four of its massive lugged tyres were pointing to the heavens as though in abject surrender.

'Bawu!' Craig cried and raced towards it. The gaping mouths of the pipe cannons were still oozing oily wreaths of smoke, but there was no other movement.

Craig wrestled the steel hatch open, and crawled into it on his hands and knees. The dark interior stank of acrid plastic explosive burn.

'Bawu!' He found him crumpled in the bottom of the cab, and he knew instantly that the old man was *in extremis*. The whole shape of his face had altered, and his voice was an unintelligible blur.

Craig caught him up in his arms and tried to drag him towards the hatch, but the old man fought him off with desperate strength, and at last Craig understood what he was saying.

'My teeth, blown my bloody teeth out!' He was back on his hands and knees searching desperately. 'Mustn't let her see me, find them, boy, find them.'

Craig found the missing plates under the driver's seat, and with them once more in place, Jonathan shot out of the hatchway and confronted Okky van Rensburg furiously.

'You made it top-heavy, you blithering old idiot.'

'You can't talk to me like that, Bawu, I don't work for you any longer. You fired me.'

'You're hired,' bellowed Jonathan. 'Now get that thing right way up again.'

Twenty sweating, singing Matabele heaved the Ford slowly upright and at last it flopped over onto its wheels again.

'Looks like a banana,' Okky remarked with obvious satisfaction. 'The recoil of your cannons has bent it almost double. You'll never get that chassis straight again.'

'There is only one way to straighten it,' Jonathan announced and began tightening the strap of his tin helmet again.

'What are you going to do, Jon-Jon?' Craig demanded anxiously.

'Fire the other broadside, of course,' said Jonathan grimly. 'That will knock it straight again.' But Craig seized one of his arms, Okky the other, and Janine murmured soothingly to him as they led him away to the waiting Land-Rover.

'Can you imagine Bawu reaching for the cigarette-lighter and hitting the wrong button while driving down Main Street,' Craig chortled, 'and letting that lot go through the front doors of the City Hall?'

They giggled over it the whole way back to town, and as they drove in past the lovely lawns of the municipal gardens, Craig suggested easily, 'Sunday evening in Bulawayo, you could suffer a nervous breakdown from the mad gaiety of it. Let me cook you one of my famous dinners on the yacht, and save you from it.'

'The yacht?' Janine was instantly intrigued. 'Here? Fifteen hundred miles from the nearest salt water?'

'I will say no more,' Craig declared. 'Either you come with me, or you will forever be consumed by unsatisfied curiosity.'

'A fate worse than death,' she agreed. 'And I have always been a good sailor. Let's go!'

Craig took the airport road but before they left the built-up area, he turned into one of the older sections of the town. Between two rundown cottages was an empty plot. It was screened from the road by the dense greenery of a row of ancient mango trees. Craig parked the Land-Rover under one of the mango trees, and led her deeper into an unkempt jungle of bougainvillaea and acacia trees, until she stopped abruptly and exclaimed:

'You weren't kidding. It's a real yacht.'

'They don't come any realer than that,' Craig agreed proudly. 'Livranos-designed, forty-five feet overall length, and every plank laid by my own lily-whites.'

'Craig, she's beautiful!'

'She will be one day when I finish her.'

The vessel stood on a wooden cradle, with baulks of timber chocking the sides. The deep keel and ocean-going hull lifted the stainless steel deck-railings fifteen feet above Janine's head as she ran forward eagerly.

'How do I get up?'

'There is a ladder round the other side.'

She scrambled up onto the deck, and called down. 'What is her name?'

'She hasn't got one yet.'

He climbed up into the cockpit beside her. 'When will you launch her, Craig?'

'The good Lord knows,' he smiled. 'There is a mountain of work to be done on her yet, and every time I run out of money, everything comes to a grinding halt.'

He was unlocking the hatch as he spoke, and the moment he swung it open Janine ducked down the companionway.

'It's cosy down here.'

'This is where I live.' He climbed down into the saloon after her and dropped his kitbag on the deck. 'I've finished her off below decks, the galley is through there. Two cabins each with double bunks, a shower and a chemical toilet.'

'It's beautiful,' Janine repeated, running her fingers over the varnished teak joinery, and then bouncing experimentally on the couches.

'Beats paying rent,' he agreed.

'What remains to be done?'

475

'Not much – engine, winches, rigging, sails, only about twenty thousand dollars' worth. However, I have just soaked Bawu for almost half of that.' He lit the gas refrigerator and then selected a tape and put it on the player.

Janine listened to the liquid purling piano for a few moments and then said, 'Ludwig van B., of course?'

'Of course, who else?'

Then with slightly less assurance, she said, 'The Pathétique Sonata?'

'Oh, very good.' He grinned as he found a bottle of Zonnebloem Riesling in one of the cupboards, 'and the *artiste*?'

'Oh, come on!'

'Give it a shot.'

'Kentner?'

'Not bad, but it's Pressler.' She pulled a face to show her mortification, and he drew the cork and half-filled the glasses with pale golden wine.

'Here's looking at you, kid.'

She sipped and murmured, 'Mmm! That's good.'

'Dinner!' Craig dived back into the cupboard. 'Rice and canned stuff. The potatoes and onions are three months old, growing sprouts already.'

'Macrobiotic,' she said. 'Good for you. Can I help?'

They worked happily shoulder to shoulder in the tiny galley, and every time they moved they brushed against each other. She smelled of scented soap, and when he looked down on top of her head, her curly hair was so dense and lustrous that he had an almost uncontrollable urge to bury his face in it. Instead he went to look for another bottle of wine.

He emptied four assorted cans into the pot, chopped onions and potatoes over the mixture and spooned in curry powder. He served it on a bed of rice.

'Delicious,' Janine declared. 'What do you call it?'

'Don't ask embarrassing questions.'

476

'When you launch her, where will you sail her?'

Craig reached over her head and brought down a chart and an Indian Ocean Pilot from the bookshelves.

'All right.' He pointed out a position on the chart. 'Here we are anchored in a secluded little cove on an island in the Seychelles. If you look out the porthole you will see the palm trees and the beaches whiter than sugar. Under us the water is so clear that we seem to be floating in air.'

Janine looked out of the porthole. 'You know what – you are right! There are the palm trees and I can hear guitars.'

When they finished eating they pushed the dishes aside, and pored over the books and charts.

'Where next? How about the Greek islands?'

'Too touristy.' She shook her head.

'Australia and the Barrier Reef?'

'Beauty!' She mimicked an Aussie accent. 'Can I go topless, sport?'

'Bottomless too, if you want.'

'Rude boy.'

The wine had flushed her cheeks, and put a sparkle in her eyes. She slapped his cheek lightly, and he knew he could kiss her then but before he moved, she said, 'Roland told me you were a dreamer.'

The name stopped him dead. He felt the coldness in his chest, and suddenly he was angry with her for spoiling the mood of the moment. He wanted to hurt her as she had just hurt him.

'Are you sleeping with him?' he asked, and she swayed back and stared at him with shock. Then her eyes slanted like those of a cat, and the rims of her nostrils turned bone-white with fury.

'What did you say?'

His own perversity would not let him turn back from the precipice, and he stepped out over it.

'I asked if you were sleeping with him.'

'Are you sure you want to know?'

'Yes.'

'All right, the answer is "yes", and it's bloody marvellous. Okay?'

'Okay,' he said miserably.

'Now you can take me home, please.'

They drove in complete silence except for her terse directions, and when he parked outside the three-storey block of apartments, he noticed that they were called Beau Vallon, the same as the Seychelles beach over which they had fantasized.

She climbed out of the Land-Rover. 'I'm grateful for the lift,' she said, and walked up the paved path towards the entrance of the building.

Before she reached it, she turned and came back. 'Do you know that you are a spoilt little boy?' she asked. 'And that you give up on everything, just like you did on the tennis court.'

This time she disappeared into the entrance of the building without looking back.

When he got back to the yacht, Craig put the charts and books away, then he cleaned the dishes, dried them, and stacked them in their racks. He thought he had left a bottle of gin in one of the cupboards, but he couldn't find it. There wasn't even any of the wine left. He sat in the saloon with the gaslight hissing softly over his head, and he felt numb and empty. There was no point in going to his bunk. He knew he would not sleep.

He unlaced the kitbag; the leather-bound journal that Jonathan had loaned him was on top. He opened it and began to read. It had been written in 1860. The writer was Zouga Ballantyne, Craig's great-great-grandfather.

After a while, Craig no longer felt numb and empty, for he was on the quarterdeck of a tall ship, running southwards down the green Atlantic towards a savage enchanted continent.

Samson Kumalo stood in the centre of the dusty track and watched Craig's beaten-up old Land-Rover growl away up the avenue of spathodea trees. When it took the turn past the old cemetery and disappeared, he picked up his bag and opened the garden gate of the staff cottage. He walked around the side of the building, and stopped below the back porch.

His grandfather, Gideon Kumalo, sat on a straight-backed kitchen chair. The walking-stick, carved like a twisted serpent, was propped between his feet and both his hands rested on the head. He was asleep, sitting upright in the uncomfortable chair in the blaze of the white sunlight.

'It is the only way I can get warm,' he had told Samson.

His hair was white and fluffy as cotton wool, the little goatee beard on the tip of his chin trembled with each gentle snore of his breathing. His skin seemed so thin and delicate, that it might tear like ancient parchment, and it was the same very dark amber colour. The network of wrinkles that covered it was cruelly exposed by the direct glare of the sun.

Careful not to block the old man's sunlight, Samson climbed the steps, set his bag aside and sat on the half-wall in front of him. He studied his face, and felt again that gentle suffocating feeling of love. It was more than the duty that any Matabele boy was taught to show to his elders, it went beyond the conventions of parental affection, for between the two of them was an almost mystical bond.

For almost sixty years Gideon Kumalo had been the assistant headmaster at Khami Mission School. Thousands of young Matabele boys and girls had grown up under his guidance, but none had been as special to him as his own grandson.

Suddenly the old man started and opened his eyes. They were milky-blue and sightless as those of a newborn puppy. He tilted his head at a blind listening angle. Samson held his breath and sat motionless, fearful that Gideon might have at last lost the sense of perception which was almost miraculous. The old man turned his head slowly the other way, and listened again. Samson saw his nostrils flare slightly as he sniffed the air.

'Is it you?' he asked in a rusty voice, like the squeak of an unoiled hinge. 'Yes, it is you, Vundla.' The hare has always played a prominent place in African folklore, the original of the legend of Br'er Rabbit that the slaves took to America with them. Gideon had nicknamed Samson after the lively clever little animal. 'Yes, it is you, my little Hare!'

'Baba!' Samson let his breath out and went down on one knee before him. Gideon groped for his head and caressed it.

'You have never been away,' he said. 'For you live always in my heart.'

Samson thought he might choke if he tried to speak. Silently he reached and took the thin fragile hands and held them to his lips.

'We should have a little tea,' Gideon murmured. 'You are the only one who can make it to my taste.'

The old man had a sweet tooth, and Samson placed six heaped teaspoons of brown sugar into the enamel mug before he poured the brew from the blackened tin kettle into it. Gideon cupped his hands around the mug, sipped noisily, and then smiled and nodded.

'Now tell me, little Hare, what has happened to you? I feel something in you, an uncertainty, like a man who has lost the path and seeks to find it again.'

He listened while Samson spoke, sipping and nodding. Then when he finished talking, he said: 'It is time you came back to the Mission to teach. You told me once that you could not teach the young people about life until you learned yourself. Have you learned yet?'

'I do not know, Baba. What can I teach them? That death stalks the land, that life is as cheap as a single bullet?'

'Will you always live with doubts, my dear grandson,

must you always look for the questions that have no answers? If a man doubts everything, then he will attempt nothing. The strong men of this world are the ones who are always certain of their own rightness.'

'Then perhaps I will never be strong, Grandfather.'

They finished the pot of tea and Samson brewed another. Even the melancholy of their conversation could not dim their pleasure in each other, and they basked in it until at last Gideon asked: 'What time is it?'

'Past four o'clock.'

'Constance will be off duty at five. Will you go down to the hospital to meet her?'

Samson changed into jeans and a light blue shirt, and left the old man on the porch. He went down the hill. At the gate of the high security fence that enclosed the hospital, he submitted to the body-search by the uniformed guards, and then went up past the post-operative wards, outside which the convalescent patients in blue dressing-gowns sat on the lawn in the sunlight. Many of them had limbs missing, for the Khami Hospital received many of the victims of land-mine explosion and other war injuries. All the patients were black. Khami Hospital was graded as African only.

At the reception desk in the main entrance hall, the two little Matabele nurses recognized him and chittered like sparrows with pleasure. Gently Samson tapped them for the current gossip of the Mission Station, the marriages and births, the deaths and courtships of this close-knit little community. He was interrupted by a sharp authoritative voice.

'Samson, Samson Kumalo!' and he turned to see the hospital superintendent striding purposefully down the wide corridor towards him.

Doctor Leila St John wore a white laboratory-coat with a row of ballpoint pens in the top pocket, and a stethoscope dangling from her neck. Under the open coat was a shapeless maroon sweater and a long skirt of crumpled Indian cotton in a gaudy ethnic design. Her feet were in thick green men's socks, and open sandals which buckled at the side. Her dark hair was stringy and lank, tied with leather thongs into two tails that stuck out on each side of her head above her prominent ears.

Her skin was unnaturally pale, inherited from her father, Robert St John. It was pock-marked with the cicatrices of ancient acne. Her horn-rimmed spectacles were square and mannish, and a cigarette dangled from the corner of her wide thin lips. She had a prim, serious old-fashioned face, but the gaze of her green eyes was direct and intense as she stopped in front of Samson and took his hand firmly.

'So the prodigal returns – to run off with one of my best theatre sisters, I have no doubt.'

'Good evening, Doctor Leila.'

'Are you still playing "boy" to your white settler?' she demanded. Leila St John had spent five years in detention in Gwelo political prison at the pleasure of the Rhodesian government. She had been there at the same time as Robert Mugabe who, from exile, now led the ZANU wing of the liberation army.

'Craig Mellow is a third-generation Rhodesian on both sides of his family. He is also my friend. He is not a settler.'

'Samson, you are an educated and highly capable man. All around you the world is melting in the crucible of change, history is being forged on the anvil of war. Are you content to waste the talents that God gave you and let other lesser men snatch the future from you?'

'I do not like war, Doctor Leila. Your father made me a Christian.'

'Only mad men do, but what other way is there to destroy the insensate violence of the capitalist imperialist system? What other way to meet the noble and legitimate aspirations of the poor, the weak and the politically oppressed?'

Samson glanced swiftly around the entrance hall, and she smiled.

'Don't worry, Samson. You are amongst friends here. True friends.' Leila St John glanced at her wristwatch. 'I must go. I will tell Constance to bring you to dinner. We will talk again.' She turned abruptly away, and the heels of her scuffed brown sandals clacked on the tiled floor as she hurried towards the double swing-doors marked 'Out-Patients'.

Samson found a seat on one of the long benches outside these doors, and waited amongst the sick and lame, the coughing and sniffing, the bandaged and the bleeding. The sharp antiseptic smell of the hospital seemed to permeate his clothes and skin.

Constance came at last. One of the nurses must have warned her, for her head turned eagerly from side to side and her dark eyes shone excitedly as she searched for him. He savoured the pleasure of seeing her for a moment or two longer before standing up from his seat on the bench.

Her uniform was crisply starched and ironed, the white apron stark upon the pink candy stripes, and her cap was perched at a jaunty angle. The badges of her grades – theatre sister, midwifery, and the others gleamed on her breast. Her hair was pulled up tightly and plaited into intricate patterns over her scalp, an arrangement which took many patient hours to perfect. Her face was round and smooth as a dark moon, the classical Nguni beauty with huge black eyes and sparkling white teeth in her welcoming smile.

Her back was straight, her shoulders narrow but strong. Her breasts under the white apron were good, her waist narrow and her hips broad and fecund. She moved with that peculiar African grace, as though she danced to music that she alone could hear.

She stopped in front of him. 'I see you, Samson,' she murmured. Suddenly shy, she dropped her eyes.

'I see you, my heart,' he replied as softly. They did not touch each other, for a display of passion in public was against custom and would have been distasteful to both of them.

They walked slowly up the hill together towards the cottage. Although she was not a blood relative of Gideon Kumalo, Constance had been one of his favourite students before his failing eyesight drove him into retirement. When his wife died, Constance had gone to live with him, to care for him and keep his house. It was there she had met Samson.

Though she chattered easily enough, relating the small happenings that had taken place in his absence, Samson sensed some reserve in her, and twice she glanced back along the path with something of fear in her eyes.

'What is it that troubles you?' he asked, as they paused at the garden gate.

'How did you know—' she began, and then answered herself. 'Of course you know. You know everything about me.'

'What is it that troubles you?'

'The "boys" are here,' Constance said simply, and Samson felt the chill on his skin so that the goose pimples rose upon his forearms.

The 'boys' and the 'girls' were the guerrilla fighters of the Zimbabwe revolutionary army.

'Here?' he asked. 'Here at the Mission?'

She nodded.

'They bring danger and the threat of death upon everybody here,' he said bitterly.

'Samson, my heart,' she whispered. 'I have to tell you. I could shirk my duty no longer. I have joined them at last. I am one of the "girls" now.'

They ate the evening meal in the central room of the cottage, which was kitchen, dining-room and sitting-room in one.

In place of a table-cloth, Constance covered the scrubbed deal table with sheets of the *Rhodesian Herald* newspaper. The columns of newsprint were interspersed with columns of blank paper, the editor's silent protest against the draconian decrees of the government censors. In the centre of it she placed a large pot of maize meal, cooked stiff and fluffy white and beside it a small bowl of tripes and sugar beans. Then she filled the old man's bowl, placed it in front of him, and put his spoon in his hand; sitting beside him throughout the meal, she tenderly directed his hand and wiped up his spillage.

From the wall the small black and white television set gave them a fuzzy image of the newscaster.

'In four separate contacts in Mashonaland and Matabeleland, twenty-six terrorists have been killed by the security forces in the past twenty-four hours. In addition, sixteen civilians were killed in crossfire and eight others were reported killed in a land-mine explosion on the Mrewa road. Combined Operations Headquarters regret to announce the death in action of two members of the security forces. The dead were Sergeant John Sinclair of the Ballantyne Scouts—'

Constance stood up and switched off the television set, then sat down again and spooned a little more meat and beans into Gideon's bowl.

'It is like a soccer match,' she said with a bitterness that Samson had never heard in her voice. 'Each evening they give us the score. Terrorists – 2: security forces – 26; we should fill in the coupons for the pools.' Samson saw that she was crying, and could think of nothing to say for her comfort.

'They give us the names and ages of the white soldiers, how many children they leave, but the others are only "terrorists", or "black civilians". Yet they have mothers and fathers and wives and children also.' She sniffed up her tears. 'They are Matabele as we are, they are our people. Death has become so easy, so commonplace in this land, but the ones that do not die, those will come to us here – our people, with their legs torn from their bodies or their brains damaged so that they become drooling idiots.'

'War is always crueller when the women and children are in it,' Gideon said in his dusty old voice. 'We kill their women, they kill ours.'

There was a soft scratching at the door, and Constance stood up and went quickly to it. She switched out the electric light before she opened it. Outside it was night, but Samson saw the silhouettes of two men in the darkened doorway. They slipped into the room, and there was the sound of the door closing. Then Constance switched on the light.

Two men stood against the wall. One glance was enough for Samson to know who they were. They were dressed in jeans and denim shirts, but there was an animal alertness about them, in the way they moved, in their quick bright restless eyes.

The elder of the two nodded at the other, who went quickly into the bedrooms, searched them swiftly and then came back to check the curtains over the windows, to make certain there was no chink between them. Then he nodded at the other man, and slipped out of the door again. The elder man sat down on the bench opposite Gideon Kumalo. He had finely boned features, with an Arab beakiness to his nose, but his skin was almost purple-black and his head was shaven bald.

'My name is Comrade Tebe,' he said quietly. 'What is your name, old father?'

'My name is Gideon Kumalo.' The blind man looked past his shoulder, his head cocked slightly.

'That is not the name your mother gave you, that is not how your father knew you.'

The old man began to tremble, and he tried three times to speak before the words came out.

'Who are you?' he whispered.

'That is not important,' the man said. 'We are trying to find who you are. Tell me, old man, have you ever heard the name Tungata Zebiwe? The Seeker after what has been Stolen, the Seeker after Justice?'

Now the old man began to shake so that he knocked the bowl from the table and it rang in narrowing circles on the concrete floor at his feet.

'How do you know that name?' he whispered. 'How do you know these things?'

'I know everything, old father. I even know a song. We will sing it together, you and I.'

And the visitor began to sing in soft, but thrilling baritone:

> 'Like a mole in the earth's gut,
> Bazo found the secret way—'

It was the ancient battle hymn of the 'Moles' impi, and the memories came crashing back upon Gideon Kumalo. In the way of very old men, he could remember in crystal detail the days of his childhood while the events of the previous week were already becoming hazy. He remembered a cave in the Matopos Hills and his father's never-forgotten face in the firelight, and the words of the song came back to him:

> 'The moles are beneath the earth.
> "Are they dead?" asked the daughters of
> Mashobane.'

Gideon sang in his scratchy old man's voice, and as he sang, the tears welled up out of his milky blind eyes, and ran unheeded down his cheeks.

'Listen pretty maids, do you not hear
Something stirring, in the darkness?'

When the song was ended, the visitor sat in silence while Gideon wiped away his tears. Then he said softly, 'The spirits of your ancestors call you, Comrade Tungata Zebiwe.'

'I am an old man, blind and feeble, I cannot respond to them.'

'Then you must send somebody in your place,' said the stranger. 'Someone in whose veins runs the blood of Bazo the Axe, and Tanase the witch.' Then the stranger turned slowly towards Samson Kumalo who sat at the head of the table, and he looked directly into Samson's eyes.

Samson stared back at him flatly. He was angry. He had known instinctively why the stranger had come. There were few Matabele who were university graduates, or who had his other obvious gifts. He had known for a long time now how badly they wanted him, and it had taken all his ingenuity to avoid them. Now at last they had found him and he was angry at them and at Constance. She had led them to him. He had noticed the way she had kept glancing up at the door during the meal. He knew now that she had told them that he was here.

On top of his anger he felt a weight of weary resignation. He knew that he could no longer resist them. He knew the risks that it would involve, not for himself alone. These were hard men, tempered in blood to a cruelty that was hard to imagine. He understood why the stranger had spoken first to Gideon Kumalo. It was to mark him. If now Samson refused to bend to them, then the old man was in terrible peril.

'You must send someone in your place.'

It was the age-old bargain, a life for a life. If Samson refused the bargain, he knew the old man's life was forfeit, and that even then that would not end the affair. They wanted him, they would have him.

'My name is Samson Kumalo,' he said. 'I am a Christian, and I abhor war and cruelty.'

'We know who you are,' said the stranger. 'And we know that in these times there is no place for softness.'

The stranger broke off as the door was pushed open a slit, and the second stranger who had been on watch outside in the night put his head into the room and said urgently,

'*Kanka!*' Just the one word, 'Jackals!' and he was gone.

Swiftly the elder stranger stood up, drew a 7.62mm Tokarev pistol from the waistband of his jeans, and at the same time switched out the light. In the darkness he whispered close to Samson's ear. 'The Bulawayo bus station. Two days from today at eight o'clock in the morning.'

Then Samson heard the latch of the door click, and the three of them were alone. They waited in the darkness for five minutes before Constance said, 'They have gone.' She switched on the light and began collecting the dishes and balling up the newsprint that had served as a table-cloth.

'Whatever alarmed the "boys" must have been a false alarm. The village is quiet. There is no sign of the security forces.'

Neither of the men answered and she made mugs of cocoa for them.

'There is a film on television at nine o'clock, *The Railway Children*.'

'I am tired,' Samson said. He was still angry with her.

'I am tired also,' Gideon whispered, and Samson helped him towards the front bedroom. He looked back from the doorway and Constance gave him such a pathetically appealing glance that he felt his anger towards her falter.

He lay in the narrow iron bed across from the old man, and in the darkness listened to the small sounds from the kitchen as Constance cleaned up and set out the breakfast for the next morning. Then the door to her small back bedroom closed.

Samson waited until the old man began to snore before

he rose silently. He draped the rough woollen blanket over his naked shoulders, left the bedroom and went to Constance's room. The door was unlocked. It swung open to his touch and he heard her sit up quickly in the bed.

'It is me,' he said quietly.

'Oh, I was so afraid you would not come.'

He reached out and touched her naked skin. It was cool and velvety soft. She took his fingers and drew him down towards her, and he felt the last vestige of his resentment shrivel away.

'I am sorry,' she whispered.

'It does not matter,' he said. 'I could not have hidden for ever.'

'You will go?'

'If I do not then they will take my grandfather, and that will not satisfy them.'

'That is not the reason you will go. You will go for the same reason that I did. Because I had to.'

The smooth length of her body was as naked as his own. When she moved, her breasts jostled against his chest, and he felt the heat beginning to flow through her.

'Are they taking you into the bush?' he asked.

'No. Not yet. I am ordered to remain here. There is to be work for me here.'

'I am glad.' He brushed her throat with his lips. In the bush her chances would be very slim. The security forces were maintaining a kill-ratio of over thirty to one.

'I heard Comrade Tebe give you an hour and a place. Do you think they will use you in the bush?'

'I do not know. I think they will take me for training first.'

'This may be our last night together for a long time,' she whispered, and he did not reply but traced her spine in its valley of velvety pliant muscle down to the deep cleft of her buttocks.

'I want you to place a son in my womb,' she whispered. 'I

want you to give me something to cherish while we are apart.'

'It is an offence against law and custom.'

'There is no law in this land except the gun, there is no custom except that which we care to observe.' Constance rolled under him and clasped him within her long hard limbs. 'Yet in the midst of all this death we must preserve life. Give me your child, my heart, give him to me tonight, for there may be no other nights for us.'

Samson woke in a blaze of nightmare. Light flooded the tiny room, striking through the threadbare curtain over the single window and casting harsh moving shadows on the bare whitewashed wall. Constance clung to him. Her body still hot and moist from their loving, and her eyes soft with sleep. From outside a monstrous distorted voice blared orders.

'This is the Rhodesian army. All people are to come out of their houses immediately. Do not run. Do not hide. No innocent person will be harmed. Come out of your houses immediately. Hold up your hands. Do not run. Do not attempt to hide.'

'Get dressed,' Samson told Constance. 'Then help me with the old man.'

She staggered, still half-asleep, to the corner cupboard and pulled a plain pink cotton shift down over her nude body. Then, barefoot, she followed Samson to the front bedroom. He was dressed only in a pair of khaki shorts and he was helping Gideon to rise. Outside the cottage the loudhailers were screeching in their metallic stentorian voices.

'Come out immediately. Innocent people will not be harmed. Do not run.'

Constance spread a woollen blanket over the old man's shoulders, then between them they led him through the living-room to the front porch. Samson unlocked the door and stepped out, holding both hands high, palms forward, and the blinding white beam of a searchlight fixed on him, so that he was forced to protect his face with one hand.

'Bring Grandfather.'

Constance led the old man out of the front door and the three of them stood close together in a pathetic huddle, blinded by the light and confused by the repeated bellow of the loudhailer.

'Do not run. Do not attempt to hide.'

The row of staff cottages had been surrounded. The searchlights beamed out of the darkness and picked out the little family groups of the teachers and nursing staff and their families as they clung together for comfort, most of them covered only with flimsy night-clothes or hastily draped blankets.

From the impenetrable darkness behind the searchlight, figures emerged, moving like panthers, alert and predatory. One of them vaulted over the veranda railing and flattened against the wall, using Samson's body to shield himself from the doorway and the windows.

'Three of you. Is that all?' he demanded in Sindebele. He was a lean, powerful-looking man in battle-smock and jungle hat. His face and hands were painted with night camouflage so it was impossible to tell whether he was black or white.

'Only three,' Samson replied.

The man had an FN rifle on his hip, the barrel swinging slightly to cover them all.

'If there is anybody in the building, say so quickly, otherwise they will be killed.'

'There is nobody.'

The soldier called an order and his troopers went in simultaneously through the back and front doors and side windows. They swept through the cottage in seconds, working as a skilled team, covering each other. Satisfied that it was clear, they scattered back into the darkness and left the three on the veranda.

'Do not move,' screeched the loudhailers. 'Stay where you are.'

In the darkness under the spathodea trees Colonel Roland Ballantyne took the unit reports as they came in. With each negative show, his frustration increased. Their information had been good and the scent hot. It was a scent he had followed often before. Comrade Tebe was one of their prime targets. He was a ZIPRA commissar who had been operating within Matabeleland for almost seven months now. They had been as close to him as this on three other occasions. It always seemed to be the same. The tip from one of the informers or from a member of the Scouts operating under civilian cover. *Tebe was in such and such a village*. They would move up silently and surround it, methodically closing every bolt-hole. Then in the darkness and bleakest hour of the night they would go in and sweep. Once they had taken two of his lieutenants, but Tebe was not with them. The regimental sergeant-major of the Scouts, Esau Gondele, had questioned the two terrorists while Roland watched. By dawn neither of them were able to stand up any longer but they had not spoken.

'Use the chopper,' Roland ordered.

They hovered at two thousand feet while Sergeant-Major Gondele hung the most defiant terrorist from the belly hatch, holding him by the webbing belt looped under his armpits.

'Tell me, my friend, where we will find your Comrade Tebe.'

The man twisted his head up sideways and tried to spit at Esau Gondele, but the down-draught of the spinning rotors had blown his spittle away. The sergeant-major had glanced at Roland, and when he nodded, opened his fist. The terrorist had fallen two thousand feet, turning slowly end over end. Perhaps he was past screaming or perhaps it was his final defiance, but he was utterly silent during the drop.

Sergeant-Major Gondele had reached for the second terrorist and looped a webbing under his armpits. As he lowered him out of the hatch, his bound feet dangling two thousand feet above the golden Matabele grasslands, the man had looked up and said, 'I will tell you.'

However, they had held out for just thirty minutes too long. When the Scouts hit the safe house in Hillside Location, Comrade Tebe had moved again.

Roland Ballantyne's frustration was corrosive. The week before, Comrade Tebe had left an explosive device in a supermarket chariot. It had killed seven people, all of them female, two of them under ten years of age. Roland wanted him very badly, so badly that when he realized that once again he had escaped, a kind of heavy black feeling closed down over half his mind.

'Bring the informer,' he ordered, and Esau Gondele spoke softly into the portable radio. Within minutes they heard the Land-Rover coming up the hill, and its headlights flickered through the trees of the forest.

'All right, Sergeant-Major. Get these people lined up.'

There were sixty or so of them lined up along the verge of the road in front of the long row of staff cottages. The searchlights trapped them in a stark and merciless glare. Colonel Roland Ballantyne vaulted up onto the back of the Land-Rover and held the bull-horn to his lips. He spoke in perfect colloquial Sindebele.

'The evil ones have been amongst you. They have left the stink of death on this village. They have come here to plan destruction, to kill and cripple you and your children. You should have come to us that we might protect you. Because you were afraid to ask for our help, you have brought even greater hardship upon yourselves.'

The long line of black people, men and women and children still in their night-clothes, stood stolidly and stoically as cattle in the crush. They were caught between the millstones of the guerrillas on one side and the security forces on the other. They stood in the white searchlights and listened.

'The government is your father. Like a good father it seeks to protect its children. However, there are stupid children amongst you. Those who conspire with the evil ones, those who feed them and give them news and warn them when we come. We know these things. We know who warned them.'

At Roland's feet, sitting on the cross-bench of the Land-Rover was a human figure. It was draped from head to foot in a single sheet of cloth so that it was impossible to tell whether it was a man or a woman. There were eye-holes cut in the hood of the cloth.

'We will now smell out the evil ones amongst you, those who give comfort to the death-bringers,' Roland told them.

The Land-Rover rolled slowly along the line of villagers, and as it drew level with each man or woman, the soldier shone his flashlight into the person's face at a range of only a few feet. In the open back of the vehicle, the mysteriously robed and masked figure stared out of the eye-holes in the sheet. The dark eyes gleamed in the reflected light of the flashlight as they examined each face.

The veiled informer sat unmovingly as the Land-Rover came on at a walking pace down towards where Samson and Constance supported the old man between them.

Without moving his lips, Samson asked her, 'Is it safe, do they know you?'

'I do not know,' she answered him.

'What can we do—' but by that time the Land-Rover was drawing level with where they stood, and Constance did not have time to reply.

In the rear of the vehicle, the masked figure moved for the first time. A long black arm shot out from under the sheet, and pointed directly into Constance's upturned face. Not a word was spoken, but two of the camouflaged Scouts stepped out of the darkness behind her and seized her arms.

'Constance!' Samson ran forward and reached for her. A rifle-butt smashed into his back at the level of his kidneys and flaming agony tore up his spine and burst against the roof of his skull. He dropped to his knees.

Pain distorted his vision, and the flashlight shone into his face, blinding him. He pushed himself upright with a violent effort, but found that the muzzle of an FN rifle was pressed into his stomach.

'We don't want you, my friend. Do not interfere in what does not concern you.'

The Scouts were leading Constance away. She went docilely. She seemed very small and helpless between the two tall soldiers in full battle-dress. She turned and looked back at Samson. Her great soft eyes clung to his face and her lips moved.

Then for an instant the body of the Land-Rover blocked the beam of the searchlight. Darkness enveloped the group, and a second later when the searchlight caught them again, Constance had broken away from her captors and she was running.

'No!' screamed Samson in terrible agony. He knew what was about to happen. 'Stop, Constance, stop.'

She flew like a lovely moth in the light, the pink of her dress flitting between the trunks of the spathodea trees, and then the bullets ripped chunks of white wet wood from the trees about her, and she was no longer swift and graceful; it was as though the moth's wings had been shredded by a spiteful child.

Four soldiers carried her body back, each of them holding a leg or an arm. Constance's head hung back almost to touch the ground, and the blood from her nostrils and mouth running down her cheeks was thick and black as treacle in the searchlights. They tossed her up into the back of the Land-Rover, where she lay in a tangle of dark limbs like a gazelle shot on the hunting veld.

Samson Kumalo walked down the main street of Bulawayo. The cool of the night still lingered and the shadows of the jacaranda trees threw tiger stripes across the blue macadam surface. He mingled easily with the lazy flow of humanity along the sidewalk, and he made no effort to avert his face as he passed a BSA police constable in his blue and khaki uniform and pith helmet on the corner of the park.

While he waited for the traffic lights, he watched the faces about him: the flat incurious expression of the Matabele, their eyes veiled defensively, the bright young white matrons in pretty floral dresses, going about their shopping with a handbag on one shoulder and a machine-pistol on the other. There were very few white men in the streets, and most of those too old for military service – the others were all uniformed and armed.

The traffic that crossed the intersection in front of him was mostly military. Since the imposition of economic sanctions, the gasolene ration had been reduced to a few litres a month. The farmers coming into town for the day drove the ungainly mine-proofed machines with blast-deflectors and armoured bodies.

Samson was aware for the first time since Constance's death of the true extent of his hatred as he watched their white faces. Before today there had been a numbness in him that was anaesthetic, but that was fading.

He carried no luggage, for a parcel would immediately have attracted attention and invited a body-search. He wore jeans and a short-sleeved shirt and gym shoes – no jacket that might have concealed a weapon; and like the other Matabele around him, his face was blank and expressionless. He was armed only with his hatred.

The lights changed and he crossed the road unhurriedly and turned down towards the bus station. Even this early it was crowded. There were patient queues of peasants waiting to make the journey back to the tribal trust lands. All of

497

them were loaded with their purchases, bags of meal and salt, tins of cooking-oil or paraffin, bundles of material and cardboard boxes of other luxuries, of matches and soap and candles. They squatted under the iron roofs of the shelters, chattering and laughing, chewing roasted maize cobs, drinking Coca-Cola, some of the mothers feeding their infants from the breast, or scolding their toddlers.

Every few minutes a bus would draw up in greasy clouds of diesel exhaust, to discharge a horde of passengers, and immediately they were replaced from the endless queues. Samson leaned against the wall of the public latrines. It was the most central position, and he settled himself to wait.

He did not at first recognize Comrade Tebe. He wore a filthy tattered blue overall with 'COHEN'S BUTCHERY' embroidered across the back in red letters. His careless stoop disguised his height, and an expression of moronic goodwill made him appear harmless.

He passed Samson without a glance in his direction, and entered the latrine. Samson waited a few seconds before he followed him. The toilet reeked of cheap tobacco smoke and stale urine. It was crowded and Comrade Tebe jostled against Samson and slipped a blue cardboard ticket into his hand.

In one of the cabinets Samson examined it. It was a single third-class ticket, Bulawayo to Victoria Falls. He took his place in the Victoria Falls queue five places behind Tebe. The bus was thirty-five minutes late, and there was the usual rush to heave luggage up onto the roof-racks and find a seat.

Tebe was in a window seat three rows ahead of Samson. He never looked round while the heavily loaded red bus lumbered out through the northern suburbs. They passed the long avenue of jacaranda trees that Cecil Rhodes had planted and which led up to the gabled State House on the hill above the town where once the royal kraal of Lobengula,

King of the Matabele, had stood. They passed the turn-off to the airport and reached the first road-block.

Every passenger was forced to dismount and identify his luggage. It was opened and searched by the constables manning the road-block, and then a random selection of men and women was made for body-searching. Neither Samson nor Tebe was amongst those selected and fifteen minutes later the bus was reloaded and allowed to pass.

As they roared on northwards, the acacia and savannah swiftly gave way to stately forest. Samson crouched on the hard bench and watched it pass. Ahead of him Tebe appeared to be sleeping. A little before noon they reached the stop for St Matthew's Mission on the Gwaai river at the edge of the Sikumi Forest Reserve. Most of the passengers fetched their luggage down from the roof-racks and trudged away along the web of footpaths that led into the forest.

'We will stop here one hour,' the uniformed driver told the others. 'You can make a fire and cook your meal.'

Tebe caught Samson's eye and sauntered away towards the little general dealer's store at the crossroads. When Samson followed him into the building, he did not at first find Tebe. Then he saw the door behind the counter was ajar, and the proprietor made a small gesture of invitation towards it. Tebe was waiting for him in the back room amongst the piles of maize sacks and dried skins, the cartons of carbolic soap and the crates of cold drinks.

He had shed the ragged overalls, and with them the character of the indolent labourer.

'I see you, Comrade Samson,' he said quietly.

'That is my name no longer,' Samson answered.

'What is your name?'

'Tungata Zebiwe.'

'I see you, Comrade Tungata,' Tebe nodded with satisfaction. 'You worked in the Game Department. You understand guns, do you not?'

Tebe did not wait for an answer. He opened one of the metal bins of ground meal that stood against the rear wall. He brought out a long bundle wrapped in a green plastic agricultural fertilizer bag and dusted off the powdery white meal. He undid the twine that secured it and handed the weapon that it contained to Tungata Zebiwe, who recognized it instantly. In the early days of the bush war, the security forces had mounted a publicity campaign to tempt informers to report the presence of guerrilla weapons in their villages. They had used television spots and newspaper advertisements. In the remote tribal trust areas they had made massive aerial drops of illustrated pamphlets, all offering a $5,000 reward for information leading to the recovery of a single one of these.

It was a 7.62mm automatic Kalashnikov (AK) assault rifle. Tungata took it in his hands and found it surprisingly heavy for its size. Unlike most NATO weapons, it was made not of metal-stamped components, but of milled steel. The butt and stock were of laminated wood.

'These are the magazines.' The Rhodesians called it the *Banana gun* because of these characteristic curved magazines. 'Loading the mags,' Tebe demonstrated, pushing the short light brass cartridges down into the mouth with his thumb. 'Try it.' Tungata was immediately competent, he had the second magazine loaded with its full thirty rounds in as many seconds.

'Good,' Tebe nodded again, the wisdom of his choice confirmed. 'Now to load the rifle. Like this.' He pressed the forward end of the magazine into the receiver slot and then tilted the rear end upwards. There was a click as the catch engaged.

In less than three minutes Tebe had demonstrated why the AK was the preferred weapon of guerrilla troops the world around. Its ease of operation and its robust construction made it ideal for the task. With a racial sneer, the

Rhodesians called it the only 'kaffir-proof' weapon in the shop.

'Selector up as far as it will go and it's safe,' Tebe finished the demonstration. 'Fully down is semi-automatic. In between is fully automatic.' He showed Tungata the two Cyrillic letters stamped in the block. 'AB,' he said. 'Russian for "Automatic". Take it.' He handed it to Tungata, and he watched while he loaded and cocked and unloaded swiftly and neatly. 'Yes, good. Remember the gun is heavy but it climbs quickly in automatic. Take a firm grip.'

Tebe rolled the weapon into a cheap grey blanket from which it could be freed instantly.

'The owner of this store is one of us,' Tebe said. 'He is even now loading supplies for us onto the bus. It is time for me to tell you why we are here, and where we are going.'

When Tungata and Tebe left the general dealer's store and sauntered towards the parked bus, the children had already arrived. There were almost sixty of them, the boys in khaki shirts and short pants, and the girls in blue gymslips with the green sash of St Matthew's Mission School around their waists. All of them were bare-footed. They were chattering and giggling with excitement at this unexpected outing, this delightful release from the tedium of the schoolroom. Tebe had said they were the Standard VIII pupils, which meant their average age would be fifteen years. All the girls appeared to be pubescent, full-breasted under the coarse cloth of their school uniforms. Under the direction of their class teacher, a young bespectacled Matabele, they were lining up beside the dusty red bus in an obedient and orderly manner. As soon as he saw Tebe, the teacher hurried to meet him.

'It is as you ordered, Comrade.'

'What did you tell the fathers at the Mission?'

'That it was a field exercise. That we would not return until after dark, Comrade.'

'Get the children into the bus.'

'Immediately, Comrade.'

The bus-driver, with his peaked cap perched authoritatively on his head, began to protest the influx of young passengers, none of them with a ticket, until Tebe stepped up behind him and pressed the Tokarev pistol into his ribs. Then he turned the pale grey of last night's camp-fire ashes and subsided into his seat. The children scrambled for seats beside the windows, and then looked up with expectant shining faces.

'We are going on an exciting journey,' the bespectacled teacher told them. 'You must do exactly as you are told. Do you understand?'

'We understand,' they replied in dutiful chorus.

Tebe touched the bus-driver on the shoulder with the barrel of the pistol.

'Drive northwards towards the Zambezi river and the Victoria Falls,' he ordered softly. 'If we should meet a security road-block, stop immediately and behave as you always do. Do you hear?'

'Yes,' mumbled the driver.

'I hear you, Comrade, and I will obey,' Tebe prompted him.

'I hear you, Comrade, and I will obey.'

'If you do not, then you will be the very first to die. I give you my word on it.'

Tungata sat on the bench seat at the very rear of the bus, with the blanket-wrapped AK on the floorboards at his feet. He had counted the children and made a list. There were fifty-seven of them, of which twenty-seven were girls. As he asked their names, he made his estimate of each one's brightness and leadership potential and marked the best on the list with a star. He was pleased that the bespectacled teacher confirmed his choice. He had selected four of the boys and a girl. She was fifteen years old, her name was Miriam and she was a slim pretty child with a quick smile and bright intelligent gaze. There was something in her that reminded him of Constance, and she sat beside him on the bench seat so that he could watch her respond to the first session of indoctrination.

While the bus roared on northwards beneath the marvellous vaulted roof of the forest, along the straight smooth macadamized highway, Comrade Tebe stood beside the driver's seat facing the upturned fresh young faces.

'What is my name?' he asked, and then he told them, 'I am Comrade Tebe. What is my name?'

'Comrade Tebe,' they cried.

'Who is Comrade Tebe? Comrade Tebe is your friend and your leader.'

'Comrade Tebe is our friend and our leader.'

Question and answer repeated again and again.

'Who is Comrade Tungata?'

'Comrade Tungata is our friend and our leader.'

The children's voices took on a strident fervour, and there was a mesmeric glitter in their eyes.

'What is the revolution?'

'The revolution is power to the people,' they shrieked, like Western children of the same age at a pop concert.

'Who are the people?'

'We are the people.'

'Who is the power?'

'We are the power.'

They swayed in their seats, transported into a state of ecstasy. By this time most of the girls were crying with wild joy.

'Who is Comrade Inkunzi?'

'Comrade Inkunzi is father of the revolution.'

'What is the revolution?'

'The revolution is power to the people.'

The catechism began again, and impossibly they were carried even higher on the wings of political fanaticism.

Tungata, himself strangely roused, wondered at the skill

and ease with which it was orchestrated. Higher still and higher Tebe carried them, until Tungata found himself shrieking with them in a wonderful catharsis of the hatred and grief which had festered within him since Constance's murder. He was shaking like a man in fever, and when the bus lurched and threw Miriam's slim barely matured body against him, he found himself instantly and painfully sexually aroused. It was strange, almost religious, madness that overwhelmed them all, and at the end Comrade Tebe gave them the song.

'This is the song which you will sing as you go into battle, it is the song of your glory, it is the song of the revolution.'

They sang it in their sweet true children's voices, the girls harmonizing and clapping in spontaneous rhythm:

'There are guns across the border
And your murdered fathers stir.
There are guns across the river
And your slave-born children weep.
There is a bloody moon arising
How long will freedom sleep?'

Now at last Tungata felt the tears break from his own eyes and pour in scalding streams down his face.

'There are guns in Angola
And a whisper on the wind.
There are guns in Maputo
And a rich red crop to reap.
There's a bloody moon arising
How long will freedom sleep?'

It left them stunned and exhausted, like the survivors of some terrible ordeal. Comrade Tebe spoke quietly to the bus-driver, and they turned off the main road onto a barely noticeable track into the forest. The bus was forced to slow down to a crawl, as it followed the serpentine track that jinked around the bigger trees and dipped through dry riverbeds. It was dark by the time they stopped. The track had petered out and most of the children were asleep. Tungata went down the bus waking them and moving them out.

The boys were sent to find firewood and the girls set to preparing a simple meal of maize meal and sweet tea. Tebe led Tungata aside and explained to him.

'We have entered the liberated area, the Rhodesians no longer patrol this strip of territory. From here we go on foot. It will be two days to the drifts. You will march in the rear of the column, be alert for deserters. Until we reach the river, there is always the danger from the faint-hearted. Now I will deal with the driver.'

Tebe led the subdued and terrified man away from the camp, with an arm around his shoulders. He returned alone twenty minutes later, by which time most of the children had eaten and had curled up like puppies on the bare earth beside the fires.

The girl Miriam came to them shyly with a bowl of maize cake and the two men sat close together while they ate. Tebe spoke with his mouth full. 'You think them babes.' He indicated the sleeping schoolchildren. 'Yet they learn swiftly and believe what they are taught without question. They have no concept of death, therefore they know no fear. They obey, and when they die there is no loss of trained men who cannot be replaced. The Simbas used them in the Congo, the Viet Cong used them against the Americans, they are the perfect fodder on which the revolution is nurtured.' He scraped out the bowl. 'If any of the girls is to your liking, you may use her. That is one of their duties.'

Tebe stood up. 'You will take the first watch. I will relieve you at midnight.' Still chewing, he walked away. At the nearest fire he squatted down beside where Miriam lay and whispered something to her. She stood up immediately, and followed him trustingly out of the firelight.

Later, when Tungata patrolled the perimeter of the sleeping camp, he heard a strangled little wail of pain from the darkness where Tebe and the girl lay. Then there was a sound of a blow, and the cry choked off into gentle sobbing. Tungata moved around to the opposite side of the camp, where he did not have to listen.

Before dawn Tungata drove the bus to the brink of the steep watercourse, and then, yelling with delight, the boys pushed it over the edge. The girls helped them gather branches and heap them over the vehicle until it was hidden from even a low-flying helicopter.

They moved out northwards at first light. Tebe took the point, keeping half a kilometre ahead of the column. The schoolmaster stayed with the children, enforcing the complete silence Tebe had ordered. Before they had covered a mile, he was sweating through the back of his shirt and his spectacles were misted over. Tungata came up behind them, carrying the AK at the trail, avoiding the footpath, staying in the dappled forest shade, stopping every few minutes to listen, and once every hour doubling back to lie beside the path and make certain they were not followed.

None of the skills of the game-ranger had deserted him. He found himself completely at ease, and in a strange sort of way he was happy. The future had taken care of itself. He was committed at last. There were no longer any doubts, no guilty sense of duty neglected, and the warrior blood of Gandang and Bazo flowed strongly in his veins.

At noon they rested for an hour. There were no fires and they ate cold maize cake and washed it down with muddy water from a water-hole in the mopani. The water tasted of the urine of the elephants who had bathed in it during the night. When Miriam brought his ration to Tungata, she could not look into his face, and when she walked away she moved carefully, as though favouring an injury.

In the afternoon they began to descend towards the Zambezi river, and the character of the bush altered. The grand forests gave way to more open savannah, and there was profuse sign of wild game. Circling out behind the column, Tungata surprised a solitary old sable antelope bull, with ebony and salt-white body and elegant back-swept horns. He stood noble and proud. Tungata felt a strange affinity with him, and when he took the wind and went away at a gallop, he left Tungata feeling enriched and strengthened.

Tebe halted the column in the middle of the afternoon and told them, 'We will be marching all night. You must rest now.'

Then for Tungata he drew a sketch-map in the dust with a twig.

'This is the Zambezi. Beyond it is Zambia. They are our allies. That is where we go. To the west is Botswana and the waterless land. We are moving parallel to its border, but before we reach the Zambezi we must cross the road between Victoria Falls and Kazungula. The Rhodesians patrol it. We must cross it in darkness. Then beyond it, along this bank of river the Rhodesians have laid their *cordon sanitaire*. It is a minefield to prevent us using the drifts. It is necessary to reach it at dawn.'

'How do we cross the minefield?'

'Our people will be waiting for us there to take us through. Now rest.'

Tungata woke with a hand on his shoulder, and was instantly alert.

'The girl,' Tebe whispered. 'The girl Miriam, she has run.'

'Did the schoolteacher not stop her?'

'She told him she was going to relieve herself.'

'She is not important,' Tungata suggested. 'Let her go.'

'She is not important,' Tebe agreed. 'But the example to the others is important. Take the spoor,' he ordered.

Miriam must have known the geography of this extreme northwestern corner of Matabeleland. Instead of going back, she had struck boldly northwards on the line of their march; clearly she was hoping to reach the Kazungula road while it was still light, and then she would go in to one of the Rhodesian patrols.

'How wise we were to follow her,' Tebe whispered, as soon as the line of the spoor was evident. 'The bitch would have called the *kanka* down on us within an hour.'

The girl had made no attempt to hide her spoor, and Tungata followed it at a run. He was superbly fit, for he had worked beside Craig Mellow in the bloody elephant culls, and ten miles was barely far enough to roughen his breathing. Comrade Tebe matched him stride for stride, leopard-quick and with cruel bleak eyes searching ahead.

They caught Miriam two miles before she reached the road. When she saw them behind her, she simply gave up. She sank onto her knees, and trembled so uncontrollably that her teeth rattled in her jaw. They stood over her, and she could not look up at them.

'Kill her,' Tebe ordered softly.

Tungata had known instinctively that it would happen this way, and yet his soul turned leaden and icy.

'We never give an order twice,' Tebe said, and Tungata changed his grip on the stock of the AK.

'Not with the rifle,' Tebe said. 'The road lies just beyond those trees. The Rhodesians could be here in minutes.'

He took a clasp-knife from his pocket and handed it to Tungata. Tungata propped his rifle against a mopani trunk, and opened the knife. He saw that the point of the blade had been snapped off, and when he tested the edge with his thumb, he found that Tebe had deliberately dulled the edge by rubbing it against a stone.

He felt appalled and sickened by what he was expected to do, and the manner in which he was expected to do it. He tried to hide his emotions, for Tebe was watching him curiously. He understood that he had been set a test, trial by cruelty, and Tungata knew that if he failed it, then he was as doomed as was the child, Miriam. Still stony-faced, Tungata pulled the leather belt from the loops of his jeans and used it to strap the girl's wrists together behind her back.

He stood behind her so that he did not have to look into the dark terrified eyes. He placed his knee between her shoulder-blades and pulled her chin back to expose the slender throat. Then he glanced once more at Tebe for a reprieve. There was no mercy there, and he began to work.

It took some minutes, with the damaged blade and the child struggling wildly, but at last the carotid artery erupted and he let her fall forward on her face. He was panting and bathed in his own rancid-smelling sweat, but the last vestiges of his previous existence as Samson Kumalo were burned away. At last he was truly Tungata Zebiwe, the Seeker after what has been Stolen – the Seeker after Vengeance.

He broke a bunch of leaves off the nearest mopani sapling and scrubbed his hands with it. Then he cleansed the blade by stabbing it into the earth. When he handed the knife back to Comrade Tebe, he met his eyes unflinchingly, and saw in them a spark of compassion and understanding.

'There is no going back now,' Tebe said, softly. 'At last you are truly one of us.'

They reached the road a little after midnight, and while the schoolmaster held the children in a quiet group in a copse beside it, Tebe and Tungata swept the verges for a kilometre in both directions, in case the Rhodesians had laid an ambush. When they found it clear, they took the children across at the point which Tungata had chosen where hard gravel approaches would hold no signs. Then Tungata went back and carefully swept the road surface with a broom of grass.

They reached the *cordon sanitaire* before the light. The minefield was forty miles long and one hundred yards deep. It contained over three million explosive devices, of various types, from the Claymores on trip-wires, to the plastic anti-personnel mines which would take off a limb, but would seldom kill outright. The object was to leave the enemy with a casualty to succour and nurse, a casualty who would never again be a fighting warrior.

The edge of the minefield was marked by a line of enamel discs set on stakes or nailed to the trunks of trees. They bore a red skull and crossbones device and the words 'Danger – Minefield'. Tebe ordered the children to lie flat in the dense brown grass, and to draw the stalks over them as concealment from the air. Then they settled to wait and Tebe explained to Tungata:

'The AP mines are laid in a certain pattern. There is a key to the pattern, but it is very difficult to discover and often there are deliberate flaws in it. It requires great skill and iron courage to enter the field and pick up the pattern, to identify exactly at which point one has come in, and to anticipate the sequence. The Claymores are different and need other tricks.'

'What tricks are those?'

'You will see when our guide comes.' But he did not come at dawn.

At noon Tebe said, 'We can only wait. It is certain death to go into the field alone.' There was no food or water, but he would not let the children move. 'It is something they would have had to learn anyway.' He shrugged. 'Patience is our weapon.'

The guide came in the late afternoon. Even Tungata did not know he was close until he was amongst them.

'How did you find us?'

'I cast along the edge of the road until I found where you had crossed.' The guide was not much older than any of the hijacked schoolchildren, but his eyes were those of an old man for whom life had no surprises left.

'You are late,' Tebe accused.

'There is a Rhodesian ambush on the drifts,' the guide shrugged. 'I had to go around.'

'When can you take us through?'

'Not until the dew falls.' The guide lay down beside Tungata. 'Not until the morning.'

'Will you explain to me the pattern of the mines?' Tungata asked, and the boy glanced across at Tebe. He nodded his permission.

'Think of the veins in the leaf of the mopani,' the guide began, and drew the lines in the dust. He talked for almost an hour with Tungata nodding and asking an occasional question.

When he had finished speaking, the boy laid his head on his folded arms and did not move again until dawn the following morning. It was a trick that they all learned, the trick of instant sleep and instant awakening. Those who did not learn it never lasted very long.

As soon as the light was strong enough, the guide crawled to the edge of the field. Tungata followed him closely. In his right hand the guide carried a sharpened spoke from a bicycle wheel, in the other a bunch of yellow plastic strips cut from a cheap shopping-bag. He crouched low against the earth, his head cocked like a sparrow.

'The dew,' he whispered. 'Do you see it?' and Tungata started. Just a few paces in front of them a string of sparkling diamond drops seemed suspended in the air a few inches above the earth.

The almost invisible trip-wire of a Claymore was lit up for them by its necklace of dew and by the first low rays of the sun. The guide marked it with a yellow strip and began to probe with the bicycle spoke. Within seconds he hit something in the loose friable earth, and with gentle fingers swept clear the grey circular top of an AP mine. He stood with it between his toes and reached out to probe again. He worked with amazing speed, and found three more mines.

'So, we have found the key,' he called to Tungata who lay at the edge of the field. 'Now we must be quick, before the dew dries.'

The young guide crawled boldly down the passageway to which he had discovered the entrance. He marked two more Claymore trip-wires before he reached the invisible turn in the passage. Here he probed again, and as soon as he confirmed the pattern, turned into the next zigzag.

It took him twenty-six minutes to open and mark the passage through to the far edge of the field. Then he came back and grinned at Tungata. 'Do you think you can do it now?'

'Yes,' Tungata replied without conceit, and the boy's cocky grin faded.

'Yes, I think you could – but always watch for the wild one. They put it there on purpose. There is no way to guard against it, except care.'

He and Tungata took the children through in groups of five, making them hold hands. At each Claymore, Tungata or the guide stood with a foot on each side of the trip-wires to make certain not one of them touched it as they passed.

On the last journey through, when Tungata was less than a dozen paces from safety, but while he was straddling the final trip-wire, they all heard the throb of an aircraft engine. It was coming up-river from the direction of the Victoria Falls, and it grew rapidly in volume. Tungata and the last three children were in the open. The temptation to run was almost irresistible.

'Do not move,' the young guide called desperately. 'Stay still, crouch down.' So they knelt in the middle of the open minefield, and the fine steel wire with its single plastic strip marker ran through the crotch of Tungata's legs. He was an inch away from violent death.

The aircraft noise built up swiftly, and then it roared over the tree-tops between them and the river. It was a silver-painted Beechcraft Baron with the letters 'RUAC' in black upon the fuselage.

'Rhodesian United Air Carriers,' the guide identified it. 'They take rich capitalist pig tourists to see the Smoke that Thunders.'

The machine was so low and close that they could see the pilot chatting to the woman passenger beside him, and then the plane banked away and was hidden again by the fronds of the ivory-nut palms growing along the banks of the Zambezi river. Slowly Tungata straightened up. He found his shirt was sticking to his body with perspiration.

'Move,' he said to the child beside him. 'But carefully.'

At the Victoria Falls the entire Zambezi river plunges over a precipitous ledge, and falls in a turmoil of thundering spray into the narrow gorge far below, giving it the African name 'the Smoke that Thunders'.

A few miles up-river from this incredible phenomenon, the drifts begin. For forty miles, up as far as the little border post at Kazungula, the wide river tumbles through rapids and then spreads into dawdling shallows. There are twelve places at which oxen can drag a wagon through to the north bank, or a man can wade across if he is willing to chance the Zambezi crocodiles, some of which weigh a ton and can tear the leg off a buffalo and swallow it whole.

'They have an ambush on the drifts,' the skinny little guide told Tungata. 'But they cannot guard them all. I know where they were this morning, but they may have moved. We will see.'

'Go with him,' Tebe ordered, and Tungata accepted it as a mark of trust.

That morning he learned from the little guide that to

survive it was necessary to use all the senses, not merely the ears and the eyes. The two of them moved in on the approaches to the nearest drift. They moved an inch at a time, searching and listening, sweeping the dense riverine scrub and the tangled lianas beneath the water-fattened trunks of the forest.

The guide's touch alerted Tungata, and they lay shoulder to shoulder on a bed of damp leaf-mould, utterly still but tense as coiled adders. It was only minutes later that Tungata realized that beside him the guide was snuffling the air. When he placed his lips on Tungata's ear, his whisper was a breath only.

'They are here.' Gently he drew Tungata back, and when they were clear he asked: 'Did you smell them?'

Tungata shook his head, and the guide grinned. 'Spearmint. The white officers cannot understand that the smell of toothpaste lingers for days.'

They found the next drift unguarded, and waited for darkness to take the children across, making them hold hands to form a living chain. On the far bank the guide would not let them rest. Although the children were shivering with cold in their sodden clothing, he forced them on.

'We are in Zambia at last, but we are not yet safe,' he warned. 'The danger is as great here as it is on the south bank. The *kanka* cross at will, and if they suspect us, they will come in hot pursuit.'

He kept them marching all that night, and half the following day, by which time the children were dragging and whining with hunger and fatigue. In the afternoon, the path brought them suddenly out of the forest to the wide cut of the main railway-line, and beside the track were half a dozen crude huts of canvas and rough-hewn poles. In the siding stood two cattle trucks.

'This is the ZIPRA recruiting-post,' the guide explained. 'For the moment you are safe.'

In the morning while the children were embarking into one of the cattle trucks, the skinny guide came to Tungata.

'Go in peace, Comrade. I have an instinct for those who will survive, and for those who will die in the bush. I think you will live to see the dream of glory fulfilled.' And he shook hands, the alternate grip of palm and thumb which was the sign of respect. 'I think we will meet again, Comrade Tungata.'

He was wrong. Months later, Tungata heard that the skinny little guide had walked into an ambush at the drifts. With half his stomach shot away, he had crept into an antbear hole and kept them off until his last round was fired. Then he had pulled the pin of a grenade and held it to his own chest.

The camp was two hundred miles north of the Zambezi. There were fifteen hundred recruits housed in the thatched barracks. Most of the instructors were Chinese. Tungata's instructor was a young woman named Wan Lok. She was short and broad, with the sturdy limbs of a peasant. Her face was flat and sallow, her eyes slitted and bright as those of a mamba, and she wore a cloth cap over her hair, and a baggy cotton uniform like a suit of pyjamas.

On the first day she made them run forty kilometres in the heat, carrying a forty-kilo pack. Equally burdened, she kept easily ahead of the strongest runners, except when she doubled-back to harangue and chivy on the stragglers. By that evening Tungata was no longer supercilious and scornful of being taught by a woman.

They ran every day after that, then they drilled with heavy wooden poles, and learned the discipline of Chinese shadow-boxing. They worked with the AK assault rifles until they could field-strip them while blindfolded and reassemble them in under fifteen seconds. They worked with the RPG-7 rocket-launchers and the grenades. They worked with bayonet and trench-knife. They learned to lay a landmine, and how to boost it with plastic explosive to destroy even a mine-proofed vehicle. They learned how to set a mine under the black top of a macadamized highway by tunnelling in from the verge. They learned to lay out an ambush on a forest path, or along a main road. They learned how to make a running defence in front of a superior fireforce, while delaying and harassing it, and they did all this on a daily ration of a scoop of maize meal and a handful of dried kapenta, the smelly little fish from Lake Kariba, that looked like English whitebait.

Zambia, their host country, had paid a high price for supporting their cause. The railway-line to the south that crossed the bridge over the Victoria Falls had been closed since 1973, and Rhodesian task forces had attacked and destroyed the bridges into Tanzania and Maputo, which were land-locked Zambia's only remaining lifeline to the outside world. The rations offered the guerrillas were sumptuous fare compared to those of the average Zambian citizen.

Starved to the leanness of greyhounds, and worked to the hardness of iron, half their nights were spent in the political rallies, the endless chanting and singing, and shouted massed responses to the commissar's catechism.

'What is the revolution?'

'The revolution is power to the people.'

'Who are the people?'

'Who is the power?'

After midnight they were allowed to stagger away to the thatched barracks and sleep – until the instructors woke them again at four o'clock in the morning.

After three weeks, Tungata was taken to the sinister isolated hut beyond the camp periphery. Surrounded by instructors and political commissars, he was stripped naked and forced to 'struggle'. While they shrieked the foulest abuse at him, calling him 'running dog of the racist capitalists' and 'counter-revolutionary' and 'imperialist reactionary', Tungata was driven to strip his soul as bare as his body.

He shouted aloud his confessions, he told them how he had worked with the capitalist tyrants, how he had denied his brethren, how he had doubted and back-slid and harboured reactionary and counter-revolutionary thoughts, how he had lusted for food and sleep, and had betrayed the trust of his comrades. They left him utterly exhausted and broken on the floor of the hut, then Wan Lok took him by the hand, as though she were his mother and he her child, and led him stumbling and weeping back to the barracks.

The next day he was allowed to sleep until noon and awoke feeling serene and strong. In the evening at the political rally, he was called to take his place in the front rank amongst the section-leaders.

A month later, Wan Lok summoned him to her sleeping-hut in the instructors' compound. She stood before him, a dumpy squat figure in her rumpled cotton uniform.

'Tomorrow you are going in,' she said, and took the cloth cap from her head.

He had never seen her hair before. It fell to her waist, as thick and black and liquid as a spill of crude oil.

'You will not see me again,' she said, and unbuttoned the front of her uniform. Her body was the colour of butter, hard and immensely powerful, but what startled and intrigued Tungata was that her pubic hair was as straight as that upon her head, without any kinking or curling. It excited him inordinately.

'Come,' she said, and led him to the thin mattress on the dirt floor of the hut.

They did not use the drifts on the return but they crossed the Zambezi in dugout canoes at the point where the river flowed into the immensity of Lake Kariba. In the moonlight the stark silhouettes of the drowned trees were silver and tortured as the limbs of lepers against the starry sky.

There were forty-eight of them in the cadre, under a political commissar and two young but battle-tempered captains. Tungata was one of the four section-leaders with ten men under him. Each of them, even the commissar, carried a sixty-kilo load beneath which they toiled like pregnant hunchbacks. There was no place for food in their packs, so they lived on lizards and bush rats, and the half-incubated eggs of wild birds. They competed with the hyena and vulture at lion kills for the putrefying scraps, and at night they visited the kraals of the black peasant farmers and emptied the grain bins.

They crossed the Chizarira Hills and struck southwards through trackless forest and waterless wilderness until they hit the Shangani river. They followed it southwards still, passing within a few kilometres of the lonely monument in the mopani forest which marks the spot where Allan Wilson and his patrol made their last heroic but futile stand against the impi of Gandang, son of Mzilikazi, brother of the last Matabele king, Lobengula.

When they came to the lands of the white farmers, their work began. On the dirt roads they laid the heavy land-mines that they had carried so far upon their backs. Freed of this onerous burden, they attacked the isolated white homesteads.

They hit four farmhouses in a single week, secure in the knowledge that the security forces were no longer moving to the rescue of a beleaguered homestead during the hours of darkness because they were aware that the attackers mined all the approach roads before commencing an attack. So the guerrillas had all night to finish the job and escape.

The technique was highly developed by this time. At dusk they poisoned the dogs and cut the ring-wire. Then they fired rockets into the windows and doorways and rushed the breaches they had made. At two farms they were held off by a dogged defence, but at the other two they penetrated. The horrors that they left behind them were a deliberate provocation to the rescuers who would come in at first light. What they found might drive the security forces to take out their shock and rage and frustration on the local black population, and in doing so drive them into the ZIPRA camp.

At last, after six weeks in the field, low on ammunition and explosives, they began to pull back, laying ambushes as they withdrew. They abandoned the first ambush after two fruitless days. However, at the second ambush on a remote country road, they were lucky.

They trapped a white farmer who was rushing his wife, suffering from a peritonitis following a burst appendix, to the local hospital. The farmer had his two teenage daughters in the vehicle with him. He almost broke through the ambush, but as the armoured vehicle passed Tungata's position, he jumped up and ran into the road behind it. He hit it in the soft rear section with an armour-piercing RPG-7 rocket at point-blank range.

The farmer and his eldest daughter were killed in the blast, but his sick wife and the younger daughter were still alive. The political commissar let the 'boys' have the dying women. They queued up and took them in the road beside the shattered vehicle, one after the other.

When Tungata did not join the line, the commissar condescended to explain, 'When a honey guide leads you to the hive, you must leave him a piece of the comb. Since the beginning of history, rape has always been one of the rewards of the conquerors. It makes them fight better, and it will madden the enemy.'

They left the road that night and moved back into the

hills, back towards the lake and sanctuary. Ballantyne's Scouts caught them in the middle of the following afternoon. There was very little warning. Just a tiny Cessna 210 spotter plane circling high overhead, and while the commissars and the captains were still shouting the orders to deploy and set up a perimeter, the Scouts came in.

The delivery vehicle was an ancient twin-engined Dakota that had seen service in the Western Desert during World War II. It was painted with grey non-reflective paint to thwart the infra-red seekers of SAM-7 missiles. It flew so low that it seemed to scrape the ragged rocky crests of the kopjes, and as its shadow momentarily blotted out the sun, the fighting men spewed out of the gaping belly-port.

The olive-green umbrellas of their parachutes popped open only seconds before they hit the ground. As the silk flared, they were down. They landed on their feet, and even before the parachutes settled softly in billowing folds, they had snapped their harnesses and were running forward, firing.

The commissar and both veteran captains were killed within the first three minutes, and the Scouts swept forward, rolling up the green panic-stricken guerrillas against the foot of the kopje. Tungata, acting without conscious thought, gathered the men closest to him and led them in a desperate counter-attack down a shallow donga that bisected the line of Scouts.

He heard the Scout commander give the order on the bull-horn. 'Green and red, hold on your position; blue, clean out that gulley.' The distorted voice echoed against the hills, but Tungata recognized it. He had last heard it at Khami Mission on the night Constance was murdered. It turned him cold and clear thinking.

He judged his moment finely, and then pulled out of the donga, under the whipping crackle of the FNs. His calm steadied the men with him, and he started the running defence as Wan Lok had taught him. They were in contact for three hours, in contact with élite battle-hardened troops, and Tungata kept his little band in hand and they counterattacked and laid AP mines behind them and held at every natural strongpoint, until it was dark. Then Tungata broke off the contact and pulled his men out. By that time there were only eight of them left and three of these were wounded.

Seven days later, in the morning before the dew dried, Tungata opened a passage through the *cordon sanitaire*, probing with a bayonet until he found the key to the pattern, and he took his men across the drifts. There were only five of them left. None of the wounded had been able to stand the pace, and Tungata had personally finished them with the commissar's Tokarev pistol to save them being interrogated by the pursuers.

In the town of Livingstone, on the north bank of the Zambezi opposite the Victoria Falls, Tungata reported to ZIPRA headquarters, and the commissar was astonished.

'But you were all killed. The Rhodesians claimed on the television—'

A driver in a black Mercedes with the party flag fluttering on the bonnet took Tungata up to the Zambian capital of Lusaka, and there in a safe house on a quiet street he was ushered into a sparsely furnished room where a man sat alone at a cheap pine desk.

'Baba!' Tungata recognized him immediately. 'Nkosi nkulu! Great Chief!'

The man laughed, a throaty bellow of sound. 'You may call me that when we are alone, but at other times you must call me Comrade Inkunzi.'

Inkunzi was the Sindebele word for a bull. It suited the man admirably. He was huge, with a chest like a beer-keg and a belly like a sack of grain. His hair was thick and white, all the things that the Matabele venerate, physical size and strength and the hair of age and wisdom.

'I have watched you with interest, Comrade Tungata. Indeed, it was I that sent to fetch you.'

'I am honoured, Baba.'

'You have richly repaid my faith.'

The big man settled lower in his chair and linked his fingers over the bulk of his stomach. He was silent for a while, studying Tungata's face, then abruptly he asked, 'What is the revolution?'

The reply, so often repeated, came instantly to Tungata's lips.

'The revolution is power to the people.'

Comrade Inkunzi's delighted bull-bellow crashed out again.

'The people are mindless cattle,' he laughed. 'They would not know what to do with power if anyone was fool enough to let them have it! No, no! It is time you learned the true answer.' He paused, and he was no longer smiling. 'The truth is that the revolution is power to the chosen few. The truth is that I am the head of those few, and that you, Commissar Comrade Tungata, are now one of them.'

C raig Ballantyne parked the Land-Rover and switched off the engine. He twisted the rear-view mirror on its goose-neck and used it to adjust the angle of his peaked uniform cap. Then he looked around at the elegant new building that housed the museum. It stood in the middle of the botanical gardens, surrounded by tall palms and green lawns and bright beds of geraniums and sweet-peas.

Craig realized that he was putting off the moment and clenched his jaw determinedly. He left the Land-Rover in the car park and climbed the front steps of the museum.

'Good morning, Sergeant.' The girl at the enquiries desk recognized the three stripes on the sleeve of his khaki and navy blue police uniform. Craig still felt vaguely ashamed of his rapid promotion.

'Don't be damned silly, boy,' Bawu had growled when he protested at the family influence. 'It's a technical appointment, Sergeant Armourer.'

'Hi!' Craig gave the girl his boyish grin, and her expression warmed instantly. 'I'm looking for Miss Carpenter.'

'I'm sorry. I don't know her.' The girl looked unhappy at having to disappoint him.

'But she works here,' Craig protested. 'Janine Carpenter.'

'Oh!' she brightened. 'You mean Doctor Carpenter. Is she expecting you?'

'Oh, I'm sure she knows I'm coming,' Craig assured her.

'She is in Room 211. Up the stairs, turn left, through the door that says "Staff Only", and it's the third door on the right.'

Craig pushed the door open at the invitation of 'Enter!' that greeted his knock. It was a long narrow room with skylights and fluorescent tubes overhead and the walls lined as high as the ceiling with shallow drawers, each with a pair of bright brass handles.

Janine stood at the bench table which ran down the centre of the room. She was dressed in blue jeans and a brightly checked lumberjack's woollen shirt.

'I didn't know you wore glasses,' Craig said. They gave her an air of owlish erudition, and she whipped them off her face and hid them behind her back.

'Well!' she greeted him. 'What do you want?'

'Look,' he said, 'I just had to find out what an entomologist does. I had this bizarre picture of you wrestling with tsetse flies and beating locusts to death with a club.' He closed the door quietly behind him and kept talking as he sidled up to the table beside her. 'I say, that looks interesting!'

She was like an affronted cat, back arched and every hair upon it erect, but slowly she relaxed.

'Slides,' she explained reluctantly. 'I am setting up

microscopic slides.' And then with fresh irritation in her voice, 'You know, you show the typical prejudice of the ignorant and uninformed layman. As soon as anyone mentions insects, you immediately think of pests like locusts and disease-carriers like tsetse flies.'

'Is that wrong?'

'*Hexapoda* is the largest class of the largest animal phylum, *Arthropoda*. It has literally hundreds of thousands of members, most of which are beneficial to man, and the pests are in the vast minority.'

He wanted to take her up on the 'vast minority' as a contradiction in terms, but his good sense for once prevailed. Instead he said, 'I never thought of that. How do you mean beneficial to man?'

'They pollinate plants, they scavenge and control pests, and they serve as food—' She was away, and after a few minutes, Craig's interest was no longer feigned. Like any dedicated specialist, she was fascinating while talking in her chosen field. Once she realized that he was a receptive and sympathetic audience, she became even more articulate.

The banks of shallow drawers contained the collection which she had boasted on their first meeting was the finest in the world. She showed Craig microscopic feather-winged beetles of the family *Ptiliidae* which were a mere one hundredth of an inch long and compared them to the monstrous African Goliath beetles. She showed him insects of exquisite jewelled beauty and others of repulsive ugliness. She showed him insects that imitated orchids and flowers and sticks and tree bark and snakes. There was a wasp that used a pebble as a tool, and a fly that, like a cuckoo, placed its eggs in the nest of another. There were ants that kept aphids as milch cows and farmed crops of fungus. She showed him insects that lived in glaciers and others that lived in the depths of the Sahara, some that lived in seawater and even larvae that existed in pools of crude petroleum where they devoured other insects trapped in the glutinous liquid.

She showed him dragonflies with twenty thousand eyes and ants that could lift a thousand times their own body weight; she explained bizarre forms of nutrition and reproduction, and such was her rapture that she forgot her vanity and put the horn-rimmed spectacles back on her nose. She looked so cute that Craig wanted to hug her.

At the end of two hours, she removed the spectacles and faced him defiantly. 'Okay,' she said. 'So I am primarily the curator of the collection of *Hexapoda*, but at the same time I am also a consultant to the Departments of Agriculture, Wildlife and Nature Conservation and Public Health. That's what entomologists do, mister – now what the hell do you do?'

'What I do is I go around inviting entomologists to lunch.'

'Lunch?' She looked vague. 'What is the time? My God, you've wasted my entire Saturday morning!'

'T-bone steaks,' he wheedled. 'I have just been paid.'

'Perhaps I am lunching with Roly,' she told him cruelly.

'Roly is in the bush.'

'How do you know that?'

'I phoned Aunty Val at Queen's Lynn to check.'

'You crafty blighter.' She laughed for the first time. 'Okay, I give up. Take me to lunch.'

The steaks were thick and juicy and the beer was icy cold, with dew running down the glass. They laughed a lot and at the end of the meal he asked, 'What do entomologists do on Saturday afternoons?'

'What do police sergeants do?' she countered.

'They go sleuthing up their family antecedents in weird and wonderful places – want to come along?'

She knew all about the Land-Rover by now, so she put a silk scarf around her head and dark glasses over her eyes to protect them from the wind, and Craig restocked the coolbox with crushed ice and beer. They drove out into the Rhodes Matopos National Park, into the enchanted hills where once the Umlimo had held sway and the Matabele had come for succour and sanctuary in the times of tribal disasters. The beauty of the place struck Janine to the heart.

'The hills look like those wonderful fairy castles along the banks of the Rhine.'

In the valleys there were herds of wild antelope, sable and kudu, as tame as sheep. They barely lifted their heads as the Land-Rover passed and then returned to graze.

It seemed that they had the hills to themselves, for few others would risk being alone on these dirt-surfaced roads in the very stronghold of Matabele tradition, but when Craig parked the Land-Rover in a shady grove beneath a massive bald dome of granite, an old Matabele guardian in the suntans and slouch hat of the Park Board came down to meet them and escort them as far as the gates that bore the inscription: 'Here are buried men who deserve well of their country.'

They climbed to the summit of the hill and there, guarded by stone sentinels of natural granite and covered by a heavy bronze plaque, they found the grave of Cecil John Rhodes.

'I know so little about him,' Janine confessed.

'I don't think anybody knew much about him,' Craig said. 'He was a very strange man, but when they buried him, the Matabele gave him the royal salute. He had some incredible power over other men.'

They went down the far side of the hill to the square mausoleum of stone blocks with its bronze frieze of heroic figures.

'Allan Wilson and his men,' Craig explained, 'they exhumed their bodies from the battlefield on the Shangani, and reburied them here.'

On the north wall of the memorial were the names of the dead and Craig ran his finger down the graven roll of honour and stopped at one name.

'The Rev. Clinton Codrington,' he read it aloud. 'He was my great-great-grandfather, a strange man, and his wife, my great-great-grandmother was a remarkable woman indeed. The two of them, Clinton and Robyn, founded the Mission Station at Khami. A few months after he was killed by the Matabele, she married the commander of the column who had ordered Clinton to his death, an American chap called St John. I bet there was some interesting hanky-panky there! A bit of hithering and thithering, a touch of to-ing and fro-ing.'

'They used to do it even in those days?' Janine asked. 'I thought it was a recent invention.'

They wandered on around the side of the hill and came to another grave. Over the grave stood a misshapen and dwarfed msasa tree that had taken precarious hold in a fault in the solid granite. Like the one on the summit, this grave also was covered by a heavy plate of weathered bronze, but the inscription read:

'Here lies the body of
SIR RALPH BALLANTYNE,
FIRST PRIME MINISTER OF SOUTHERN
RHODESIA.
He deserves well of his country.'

'Ballantyne,' she said. 'Must be an ancestor of Roly's.'

'A mutual ancestor of both of ours,' Craig agreed. 'Our great-grandfather, Bawu's papa. This is the real reason why we have driven out here.'

'What do you know about him?'

'A great deal, actually. I have just finished reading his personal journals. He was quite a lad. If they hadn't knighted him, they would probably have had to hang him. By his own secret confessions, he was an unqualified rogue, but a colourful one.'

'So that is where you get it from,' she laughed. 'Tell me more.'

'Funny thing, he was a sworn enemy of that other old rogue up there.' Craig pointed up the hill towards Cecil Rhodes' grave. 'And here they are buried almost side by side. Great-grandpa Ralph writes in his journal that he discovered the Wankie coalfield, but Rhodes cheated him out of it. He swore an oath to destroy Rhodes and his Company, he actually wrote that down! I'll show you! And he boasts that he succeeded. In 1923 the rule of Rhodes' British South Africa Company came to an end. Southern Rhodesia became a British colony, old Sir Ralph was its prime minister. He had made good his threat.'

They sat down, side by side, on the curbstone of the grave and he told her the funniest and most interesting of the stories that he had read in the secret journals, and she listened with fascination.

'It's strange to think that they are a part of us and we a part of them,' she whispered. 'That everything that is happening now had its roots in what they did and said.'

'Without a past there is no future,' Craig repeated the words of Samson Kumalo, then went on, 'that reminds me, I have something else I want to do before we go back to town.'

This time Craig did not have to be warned of the hidden turn-off, and he swung onto the track that led past the cemetery, down the avenues of spathodea trees to the whitewashed staff cottages of Khami Mission. The first cottage in the row was deserted. There were no curtains in the windows and when Craig climbed up onto the porch and peered in, he saw the rooms were bare.

'Who are you looking for?' Janine asked, when he came back to the Land-Rover.

'A friend.'

'A good friend?'

'The best friend I ever had.'

He drove on down the hill to the hospital and parked again. He left Janine in the Land-Rover and went into the lobby. A woman came striding to meet him. She wore a white laboratory coat, and her unnaturally pale face was set in a belligerent frown.

'I hope you haven't come here to harass and frighten our people,' she began. 'Here police mean trouble.'

'I'm sorry,' Craig glanced down at his uniform. 'It's a private matter. I am looking for a friend of mine. His family lived here. Samson Kumalo—'

'Oh,' the woman nodded. 'I recognize you now. You were Sam's employer. Well, he's gone.'

'Gone? Do you know where?'

'No,' flatly, and unhelpfully.

'His grandfather, Gideon—'

'He's dead.'

'Dead?' Craig was appalled. 'How?'

'He died of a broken heart – when your people murdered someone who was dear to him. Now, if there is nothing more you want to know, we don't like uniforms here.'

By the time they reached town it was late afternoon. Craig drove directly to his yacht without asking her permission, and when he parked under the mango trees, Janine made no comment, but climbed out and walked beside him to the ladderway.

Craig put a tape on the recorder and opened a bottle of wine, then he brought down Sir Ralph's leather-bound journal that Bawu had loaned him, and they sat side by side on the bench in the saloon and pored over it. The faded ink and pencil drawings that decorated the margins delighted Janine, and when she came to a description of the locust plagues of the 1890s, she was captivated.

'The old geezer had a good eye.' She studied his drawing of a locust. 'He might have been a trained naturalist, just look at the detail.'

She glanced up at him sitting close beside her. He looked like a puppy, an adoring puppy. She deliberately closed the leather-bound book without taking her eyes from his. He leaned closer to her, and she made no effort to pull away. He covered her lips with his own, and felt them soften and part. Her huge slanted eyes closed, and the lashes were long and delicate as butterflies' wings.

After a long time she whispered huskily, 'For God's sake, don't say anything stupid. Just keep right on doing what you are doing at the moment.'

He obeyed, and it was she who broke the silence. Her voice was shaky.

'I hope you had enough forethought to make the bunk wide enough for two.'

Still he said nothing, but lifted her up in his arms and took her to see for herself.

'Do you know, I didn't realize it could be like that.' There was wonder in his voice, as he stared down at her, leaning on one elbow. 'It was so good and natural and easy.'

She traced a fingertip over his bare chest, drawing little circles around his nipples. 'I like a hairy chest,' she purred.

'I mean – you know, I always felt it was such a solemn thing to do – after vows and declarations.'

'The sound of organ music?' she giggled. 'If you'll excuse the expression.'

'That's another thing,' he said. 'The only time I have ever heard you giggle is when you are doing it, or when you have just done it.'

'That's the only time I ever feel like giggling,' she agreed, and giggled again. 'Do be a pet and get the wineglasses.'

'Now what is so funny?' he demanded from the companion way.

'Your bottom is white and baby smooth – no, don't cover it.'

While he hunted in the galley cupboard, she called from the cabin, 'Do you have a tape of the "Pastoral".'

'I think so.'

'Put it on, pet.'

'Why?'

'I will tell you when you come back to bed.'

She was sitting at the head of the bunk, stark naked in the lotus position. He put one of the wineglasses in her hand, and after a short struggle managed to twist his own long legs into the lotus and sat facing her.

'So tell me,' he invited.

'Don't be dense, Craig – I mean isn't that just a perfect accompaniment?'

Another great storm of music and love swept over them, leaving them clinging helplessly to each other, and in the aching silence that followed, she tenderly stroked back the sweat-damp hair that had fallen into his eyes.

It was too much for him. 'I love you,' he blurted out. 'Oh God, I love you so!'

Almost roughly she pushed him aside, and sat up.

'You are a sweet funny boy, and a gentle considerate lover, but you do have an ungodly talent for saying stupid things at the wrong time.'

In the morning, she said, 'You made dinner, so I'll make breakfast,' and went to the galley wearing only one of his old shirts. She had to roll the sleeves up and the tails dangled below her knees.

'You've got enough eggs and bacon to open your own restaurant – were you expecting a visitor?'

'Not expecting, but hoping,' he called back from the shower. 'Make mine sunny side up!'

After breakfast she helped him install the big glittering

stainless-steel winches on the maindeck. It needed someone to hold the gusset plates in position while he drilled and bolted through from the other side.

'You are very handy, aren't you?' she said. They had to shout at each other, for he was working below deck while she was perched on the edge of the cockpit.

'It's kind of you to notice.'

'So I suppose you are a first-class armourer.'

'I'm pretty good.'

'Do you do what I suspect, fix up guns?'

'One of my duties.'

'How can you bring yourself to do it? Guns are so evil.'

'That is the typical prejudice of the ignorant and uninformed layman.' He turned her own words against her. 'Firearms are on one level highly functional and useful tools, and on another level they can be magnificent works of art. Man has always lavished some of his most creative instincts on his weapons.'

'But the way men use them!' she protested.

'For instance, they were used to prevent Adolf Hitler gassing the entire Jewish nation,' he pointed out.

'Oh come on, Craig. What are they being used for out there in the bush at this very moment?'

'Guns aren't evil, but some of the men who use them are. You could say the same about spanners.'

He tightened the bolts on the winch and stuck his head out of the hatch. 'That's enough for today – on the seventh day He rested – how about a beer?'

Craig had rigged a speaker in the cockpit and they lolled in the sun and drank beer and listened to the music.

'Look, Jan, I don't know a tactful way to put this, but I don't want you seeing anyone else, do you know what I mean?'

'There you go again.' Her eyes slanted and crackled like blue ice. 'Do shut up, Craig!'

'I mean after what has happened between us,' he ploughed on doggedly. 'I think we should—'

'Look, dear boy, you have a choice – make me mad again, or make me giggle again, what's it going to be.'

At lunchtime on Monday, she came up to police headquarters, and they ate his ham sandwiches while he showed her around the armoury, and despite herself, she was intrigued by the exhibits of captured weapons and explosives. He explained the operation of the various types of mines and how they could be detected and disarmed.

'You have to hand it to the terrs,' Craig admitted. 'The swine carry those things in on their backs, two hundred miles or so through the bush. Just try and pick that up, and you'll see what I mean.'

At last he took her through to a small back room. 'This is my special project. It's called T & I, trace and identify.' He gestured at the charts that covered the walls and the big boxes of empty cartridge-cases piled beside the workbench. 'After each contact with terrs our armourers sweep the area and pick up every used cartridge. Firstly they are checked for fingerprints. So if the terr has a record, then we can identify him immediately. If he has polished his rounds before loading or if we have no record of his fingerprints – we can still trace exactly which rifle fired the cartridge.'

He led her to the bench, and let her look into the low-power microscope that stood on it. 'The firing-pin in each rifle strikes an indentation into the cap of the cartridge which is as individual as a fingerprint. We can follow the career of each active terr in the field. We can make accurate estimates of how many there are and which are the hot ones.'

'The hot ones?' She looked up from the microscope.

'Out of every hundred terrs in the field, ninety or so of them hole up in good cover near a village which can supply them with food and young girls, and they try to keep out of danger and contact with our forces. But the hot ones are different. They are the tigers, the fanatics, the killers, these charts show their first team.'

He led her to the wall.

'Look at this one. We call him Primrose because his firing-pin leaves a mark like a flower. He has been in the bush for three years, and been in contact ninety-six times. That is almost once every ten days, he must be made of steel.'

Craig ran his finger down the chart.

'Here is another, we call him Leopard Paw, you can see why by the print of his rifle. He is a newcomer, his first time across the river, but he hit four farms and ran an ambush, then he went into contact with Roly's Scouts. Not many of them survive that, Roly's boys are incredible. They wiped out most of the cadre, but Leopard Paw fought like a veteran and got away with a bunch of his men. Roly's combat report says he lost four men to AP mines that Leopard Paw put down as he ran, and another six in the actual fighting – ten men. That's the heaviest casualties the Scouts have ever taken in any one contact.' Craig tapped the name on the chart. 'He is the hot one. We are going to hear more of this lad.'

Janine shuddered. 'It's awful – all this death and suffering. When will it ever end?'

'It started when man first stood up on his hind legs, it's not going to end tomorrow. Now let's talk about dinner tonight, I'll pick you up at your flat at seven, okay?'

She telephoned him at the armoury a little before five o'clock.

'Craig, don't come for me this evening.'

'Why not?'

'I won't be there.'

'What has happened?'

'Roly is back from the bush.'

Craig did a little work on the foredeck of the yacht,

placing the cleats for the jib sheets, but when it was too dark, he went below, and wandered around disconsolately. She had left her dark glasses on the table beside the bunk, and a lipstick on the edge of the wash-basin. The saloon still smelled of her perfume, and the two wineglasses stood together in the sink.

'I think I will get drunk,' he decided, but he had no tonic, and gin with plain water tasted awful. He tipped it into the sink, and put the 'Pastoral' on the tape, but the images it conjured up were too painful. He hit the 'stop' button.

He picked Sir Ralph's leather-bound journal off the table, and flicked through it. He had read it twice; he should have gone out to King's Lynn at the weekend, Bawu would have been expecting him to come for the next journal in the series. He started to read it again, and it was an immediate opiate for the loneliness.

After a while he searched in the drawer of the chart-table and found the ruled exercise book which he had used for drawing the layout of the cabins and galley. He tore out the used pages, and there were still over a hundred unused sheets. He sat down at the saloon table with an HB pencil from the navigation set, and stared at the first empty sheet for almost five minutes. Then he wrote:

'Africa crouched low on the horizon, like a lion in ambush, tawny and gold in the early sunlight, seared by the cold of the Benguela Current.

'Robyn Ballantyne stood by the ship's rail and stared towards it—'

Craig re-read what he had written, and felt a strange excitement, something he had never experienced before. He could actually see the young woman. He could see the way she stood with her chin lifted eagerly and the wind snapping and tangling her hair.

The pencil started to race across the empty page, and the woman moved in his mind and spoke aloud in his ears. He turned the page and wrote on, then, almost before he realized it, the exercise book was filled with his pointed peaky handwriting and outside the porthole by his head the day was lightening.

E ver since Janine Carpenter could remember, there had always been horses in her father's stables at the back of the veterinary dispensary. When she was eight her father had taken her out for the first time with the local hunt. Just after her twenty-second birthday, a few months before she had left home for Africa, she had been awarded her hunt buttons.

The mount that Roland Ballantyne had given her was a beautiful chestnut filly without any other marking. She was curried to a gloss so that she shone in the sunlight like wet red silk. Janine had ridden her often before. She was fleet and strong, and there was an accord between them.

Roland rode his stallion. It was an enormous black beast he called 'Mzilikazi' after the old king. The veins stood out under the skin of his shoulders and belly like living serpents. The great black bunch of his testicles was crudely and overpoweringly masculine. When he laid back his ears and bared his teeth, the mucous membrane in the corner of his savage eyes was the colour of blood. There was an arrogance and menace in him that frightened Janine, and yet excited her also. Horses and rider were of a pair.

Roland Ballantyne wore brown whipcord breeches and high boots boned to glossy perfection. The short sleeves of the crisp white shirt were stretched tightly across the hard smooth muscle of his upper arms. Janine was certain that he always wore white to contrast against the deep tan of his face and arms. She thought he was impossibly handsome, and that cruel and ruthless streak in him made him all the more attractive than mere good looks alone could ever do.

Last night in the bed in her bachelor flat she had asked him,

'How many men have you killed?'

'As many as necessary,' he had replied, and though she thought that she hated war and death and suffering, it excited her in a way she could not control. Afterwards he had laughed easily and said, 'You are a kinky little bitch, did you know that?' She had hated him for understanding and she had been desperately ashamed, and so angry that she had gone for his eyes with her nails. He had held her down effortlessly, and still chuckling he had whispered in her ear until she lost control again.

Now when she looked up at him riding beside her, she felt the lingering fear of him and the goose-flesh on her arms and the hard ball of excitement in the pit of her stomach.

They rode up to the top of the hills, and he reined the stallion down. It danced in a tight little circle, picking up its hooves delicately and tried to nuzzle her filly, but Roland pulled its head away and pointed at the horizons that fell away into blue distances in every direction.

'Everything you can see from here. Every blade of grass, every grain of earth, all of it belongs to the Ballantynes. We fought for it, we won it – it's ours and anyone who wants to take it away from us will have to kill me first.' The idea of anyone or anything doing that was ludicrous. He was a young god, one of the immortals.

He dismounted and led the horses to one of the tall msasa trees. He tied them, and then reached up and lifted her down from the saddle. He walked her to the edge of the precipice, and held her against him, her back to his chest, so that she could look out and see it all.

'There it is!' he said. 'Just look at it.'

It was beautiful, rich golden grasslands and graceful trees, waters that flowed in the small clear streams or shone like mirrors where the dam walls held them back, the tranquil herds of big red cattle, as red as the rich earth beneath their hooves, and arched above it all the high cloud-dappled blue of the African sky.

'It needs a woman to love it as I love it,' he said. 'A woman to breed fine sons to cherish it, to hold it as I will hold it.'

She knew what he was going to say then, and now that it was about to happen, she felt numbed and confused. She felt herself beginning to tremble against him.

'I want you to be that woman,' Roland Ballantyne said, and she began to weep uncontrollably.

T he NCOs of Ballantyne's Scouts clubbed together to give their colonel and his new lady an engagement party.

They held it in the sergeants' mess at the Thabas Indunas barracks. The officers and the wives of the regiment were all invited so that when Roland and Janine drove up in the Mercedes, there was a packed crowd waiting on the front veranda to meet them. Led by Sergeant-Major Gondele, they launched into a rollicking but untuneful rendition of 'For they are jolly good fellows'.

'Damn good thing you don't fight like you sing,' Roland told them. 'Your backsides would have more holes than a sieve by now.'

He treated them with a rough paternal severity and affection, the total easy assurance of the dominant male, and they worshipped him openly. Janine understood that. She would have been surprised if it were otherwise. What did surprise her was the brotherhood of the Scouts. The way that officers and men, black and white, were held together by an almost tangible bond of trust and accord.

She sensed that it was something stronger than even the strongest family ties, and later when she spoke to Roland about it, he replied simply, 'When your life depends on another man, you come to love him.'

They treated Janine with enormous respect, almost awe. They called her 'Donna' if they were Matabele and 'Ma'am' if they were white, and she responded immediately to them.

Sergeant-Major Gondele personally fetched her a gin that would have stunned an elephant, and looked hurt when she asked for a little more tonic. He introduced her to his wife. She was a pretty plump daughter of a senior Matabele tribal chief, 'which makes her a sort of princess', Roly explained. She had five sons, the exact number that Janine and Roly had decided upon, and she spoke excellent English, so she and Janine were immediately in deep and earnest conversation, from which Janine was at last distracted by a voice at her elbow.

'Doctor Carpenter, may I apologize for being late.' It was said in the perfectly modulated tones and classless accents of a BBC announcer or a graduate of the Royal Academy of Dramatic Art. Janine turned to face an elegant figure in the uniform of a wing commander of the Rhodesian Air Force.

'Douglas Hunt-Jeffreys,' he said, and offered her a narrow, almost femininely smooth hand. 'I was desolated by the prospect of not meeting the lovely lady of the gallant colonel.' He had the cultured vacuous features of a dilettante, and the uniform, no matter that it was perfectly tailored, looked out of place on his narrow shoulders. 'The whole regiment has been in a complete tizzy since we heard the monumental tidings.'

She knew instinctively that despite his appearance and his choice of words, he was not a gay. It was the way he held her hand, and the subtle glance that dropped down her body like a silken robe, and then came back to her face. She found her interest titillated, he was like a razor-blade wrapped in velvet. If she needed confirmation of his heterosexuality, it was the way in which Roland reappeared almost immediately at her side when he realized to whom she was speaking.

'Dougie, my old fruit,' Roland's smile had a white sharkish quality.

'Bon soir, mon brave.' The wing commander took the ivory cigarette-holder from between his teeth. 'I must say I didn't expect you to show such exquisite taste. Doctor Carpenter is utterly ravishing. I do approve, dear boy. I truly do.'

'Dougie has to approve everything we do,' Roland explained. 'He's our liaison with Combined Ops.'

'Doctor Carpenter and I have just discovered that we were almost neighbours, we are members of the same hunt, and she was at school with my little sister. I cannot understand how we haven't met before.'

Janine realized then, almost with disbelief, that Roland Ballantyne was jealous of her and this man. He took her arm, just above the elbow and with a light pressure steered her away.

'You will excuse us, Douglas. I want Bugsy to meet some of the lads—'

'Bugsy, forsooth!' Douglas Hunt-Jeffreys shook his head in pained disbelief. 'These colonials are all of them barbarians.' And he wandered away to find another gin and tonic.

'You don't like him?' Janine could not resist stirring Roland's jealousy a little.

'He's good at his job,' Roland said shortly.

'I thought he was rather cute.'

'Perfidious Albion,' he replied.

'What does that mean?'

'He is a pom.'

'So am I,' she said with a slight edge beneath her smile. 'And if you go back just a little, you are a pommy also, Roland Ballantyne.'

'The difference is you and I are good poms. Douglas Hunt-Jeffreys is a prick.'

'One of those. Oh goody!' And he laughed with her.

'If there is one thing of which I approve whole-heartedly, it's a blatant self-confessed nymphomaniac,' he said.

'Then we are going to get on very well together, you and I.' She hugged his arm in a gesture of reconciliation, and he led her to a group of young men at the end of the bar. With their cropped heads and fresh faces they looked like undergraduates, only their eyes held that flat pebbly look, she remembered Hemingway had called them 'machine-gunners' eyes'.

'Nigel Taylor, Nandele Zama, Peter Sinclair,' Roland introduced them. 'These lads almost missed the party. They only got back from the bush two hours ago. This morning they had a good contact near the Gwaai, twenty-six kills.'

Janine hesitated over her choice of words, and then said faintly, 'That's nice,' rather than 'Congratulations', both of which seemed grossly inappropriate for the passing of twenty-six human lives. It seemed to suffice, however.

'Will you be riding the colonel this evening, Donna?' the young Matabele sergeant asked eagerly, and Janine looked hurriedly to Roland for clarification. Even in such a close family environment it seemed a rather personal enquiry.

'Mess tradition,' Roland grinned at her discomfort. 'At midnight Sergeant-Major and I race down to the main gates and back. Princess Gondele will be his jockey, and I am afraid you will be rather expected to do the honours for me.'

'You are not as fat as Princess,' the young Matabele ran an appraising eye over Janine, 'I'm going to bet ten dollars on you, Donna.'

'Oh goodness. I do hope we don't let you down.'

By midnight the excitement was frenetic, of the peculiar quality that grips men who live their daily lives in mortal danger and who know that this stolen hour of joyous existence may be their last. They thrust bunches of banknotes into the hands of the adjutant who was official holder of bets, and crowded around their fancies to bolster them with raucous encouragement.

Princess and Janine were in stockinged feet with their skirts rucked up and tucked into their panties like little girls at the seaside, standing on a chair on each side of the main doors to the mess. Outside, the tarmac road down to the main gates was lit by the headlights of army vehicles parked along the verge, and lined with the overflow from the mess bar, all of them full of gin and rowdy enthusiasm.

On the bar Sergeant-Major Gondele and Roland were stripped down to breeches and jungle boots. Esau Gondele was a black giant, his shaven head like a cannonball, and his shoulders lumpy with muscle. Beside him even Roland looked like a boy, his chest untouched by the sun was very smooth and white.

'You trip me this time, S'arn-Major, and I'll tear your head off,' he warned, and Esau patted his shoulder soothingly.

'Sorry, boss. You ain't ever going to get close enough to trip.'

The adjutant took the last bets, and then mounted to the bar-top rather unsteadily with a service pistol in one hand and a glass in the other.

'Shut up, all of you. At the gun the two competitors will each consume a quart bottle of beer. When the bottle is empty they will be free to take up one of these beautiful young ladies.'

There was a storm of wolf-whistles and clapping.

'Do shut up, chaps!' The adjutant swaying precariously on the bar-top tried to look stern.

'We all know the rules.'

'Get on with it.'

The adjutant made a gesture of resignation, pointed the pistol at the ceiling, and pulled the trigger. There was a crash of shot and one of the roof lights went out. The adjutant's bald head was showered with fragments of the shattered bulb.

'I say, I forgot to change to blanks,' he murmured distractedly, but nobody took any further interest in him.

Sergeant-Major Gondele and Roland both had their heads thrown back, the base of the black bottles pointed at the roof, and their throats pulsed regularly as the frothing beer gushed down them. Gondele finished a second before Roland, leaped from the counter, emitted a great beer belch, and swept a squealing Princess up onto his shoulders. He was out of the doors before Janine could wrap her bare legs around Roland's neck.

Roland scorned the veranda stairs, and vaulted over the far railing. It was a four-foot drop to the lawn below, and Janine, a veteran of the hunt, only stayed on his shoulders by a fierce grip in his hair and a miracle of balance, but they had cut two yards off the big Matabele's lead. They stayed close behind him down the long curving drive, jungle boots pounding on the black tarmac with Roland grunting at each stride, and Janine bouncing and swaying on his shoulders. The spectators howled and leaned on the horns of the parked trucks so the noise was pandemonium.

They reached the main gates, and the black sentry recognized Roland and gave him a flourishing salute.

'At ease!' Roland told him as he turned in Gondele's wake.

'If you get a chance, pull Princess off,' he panted to Janine.

'That's cheating,' she protested breathlessly.

'This is war, baby.'

Gondele was breathing like a bull, lumbering up the hill with the headlights glistening on his burnished muscles, and still two paces behind him Roland ran with quick light steps. Janine could feel the strength flowing out of his body like electricity, but it was not that alone that started whittling the inches off Gondele's lead. It was that same rage to win that she had seen grip him on the courts at Queen's Lynn.

Then suddenly they were running side by side, straining their hearts and bodies beyond mere physical strength. It was at the end a contest of wills, a trial of who could bear the agony longest.

Janine looked across at Princess, and saw in her set expression that she expected Janine to foul her, both knew it was within the rules and she had heard Roland order Janine to do so.

'Don't worry,' Janine called to her, and got a flashing smile as a reward.

Shoulder to shoulder the two men came around the bend of the driveway; the lawn stretched to meet them, and beneath her Janine felt Roland make some almost mystical call on reserves that should not have existed. It was to her unthinkable that anyone could make such effort to win a childish contest – a normal man could not have done it, a totally sane man would not have done it. There was a wildness, a madness in Roland Ballantyne that frightened and at the same time elated her.

In the glare of the headlights and the roar of the crowd, Roland Ballantyne simply burned off the bigger stronger man and left him floundering half a dozen yards behind him as he leaped up the stairs, crashed through the mess doors and dropped Janine onto the bar-top.

His face was swollen and ugly red as he thrust it inches from hers. 'I told you to do something,' he snarled hoarsely. 'Don't you ever disobey me again, ever!' And in that moment she was truly afraid of him.

Then he went to Esau Gondele and the two of them threw their arms around each other and sobbed with laughter and exhaustion and staggered in a circle trying to lift each other off their feet. The adjutant thrust a roll of bank-notes into Roland's hand. 'Your winnings, sir,' he said, and Roland slapped it onto the bar counter. 'Come on, lads, help me drink it up,' he wheezed, still fighting for breath.

Esau Gondele took one sip of his beer and then poured the rest over Roland's head.

'Sorry, Nkosi,' he roared. 'But I've always wanted to do that.'

'This is, my dear, just a typical homely evening with Ballantyne's Scouts.' Janine looked around to find Douglas Hunt-Jeffreys beside her, with the ivory cigarette-holder between his teeth. 'Some time when the varsity rugger club atmosphere palls, and your intended is away in the bush, you might find a little civilized company makes a pleasant change.'

'The only thing about you that interests me is what makes you think I might be interested.'

'It takes one to recognize one, darling.'

'You are impertinent. I could tell Roland.'

'You could,' he agreed. 'But then I always like to live dangerously. Goodnight, Doctor Carpenter, I hope we meet again.'

They left the mess after two in the morning. Despite the alcohol he had taken, Roland drove as he always did, very fast and well. When they reached her apartment, he carried her up the stairs, despite her muted protests. 'You will wake everybody in the building!'

'If they sleep so lightly – just wait until I get you upstairs. They will be sending you lawyers' letters, or get-well cards.'

After he had made love to her, he fell instantly asleep. She lay next to him and watched his face in the orange and red flashes of the neon sign on the roof of the service station across the street. In relaxation he was even more beautiful than awake, but she found herself thinking suddenly of Craig Mellow, of his funniness and his gentleness.

'They are so different,' she thought. 'And yet I love them both now, each in a different way.'

545

It troubled her so that she fell asleep only as the dawn swamped the neon flashes on the bedroom curtains.

Roland seemed to waken her immediately. 'Breakfast, wench,' he ordered. 'I've got a meeting at nine o'clock at Combined Ops.'

They sat on her balcony, amongst her miniature forest of pot plants, and ate scrambled eggs and wild mushrooms.

'I know it's usually the bride's prerogative, Bugsy, but can we set a date for around the end of next month?'

'So soon? Can you tell me why?'

'Not all of it – but after that we will be going into quarantine, and I might be out of circulation for a while.'

'Quarantine?' She laid down her fork.

'When we start planning and training for a special operation we go into total isolation. There have been too many security leaks lately. Too often our boys have walked into a sucker punch. We have got a big one coming up, and the whole group will be quarantined in a special camp; nobody, not even myself, will be allowed outside contact, not even with parents or wives, until after the operation.'

'Where is this camp?'

'I cannot tell you, but if we spend the honeymoon at Victoria Falls as you wanted, it will suit me just fine. You can fly back here afterwards and I can go straight into quarantine.'

'Oh, darling, it's so soon. There will be so many arrangements to make. I don't know if Mummy and Daddy can get out here by then.'

'Telephone them.'

'All right,' she agreed. 'But I hate the thought of you having to leave so soon afterwards.'

'I know. It won't always be that way.' He looked at his watch. 'Time to go. I'll be a little late this evening, I want to talk to Sonny. I hear he's living in that boat of his again.'

She tried to cover her shock.

'Sonny? Craig, why do you want to see him?'

When Roland told her why, she could think of nothing to say. She went on staring at him in appalled silence.

J anine telephoned him at the police armoury as soon as she reached the museum.

'Craig, I have to see you.'

'Wonderful, I'll make the dinner.'

'No, no – immediately. You must get away.'

He laughed. 'I've only had this job a few months. Even for me it will be a record.'

'Tell them your mother is sick.'

'I'm an orphan.'

'I know, darling, but this is life and death.'

'What did you call me?'

'It slipped out.'

'Say it again.'

'Craig, don't be an idiot.'

'Say it.'

'Darling.'

'Where and when?'

'Half an hour at the bandstand in the gardens, and Craig it's bad news.' She hung up without letting him talk again.

She saw him first. He came at a lope, like a Saint Bernard puppy, with legs too long and his hair sticking out under the peak of his cap, a frown of worry crumpling up his face, but when he saw her sitting on the steps of the white-painted bandstand, the frown smoothed and his eyes lit with that special soft look that today she found too painful to bear.

'God,' he said. 'I had forgotten how lovely you are.'

'Let's walk.' She couldn't look at him, but when he took her hand, she could not bring herself to pull her fingers out of his.

Neither of them spoke again until they reached the river.

They stood on the bank and watched a little girl in a white dress and pink ribbons feeding breadcrumbs to the ducks.

'I had to tell you first,' she said. 'I owed you that at least.' She felt him go very still beside her, but still she could not look at him, yet she could not withdraw her hand from his.

'Before you say anything, I want to tell you again what I told you before. I love you, Jan.'

'Oh, Craig.'

'Do you believe me?'

She nodded and swallowed.

'All right, then, now you tell me what you called me to hear.'

'Roland has asked me to marry him.'

His hand began to tremble.

'And I said yes.'

'Why, Jan?'

She jerked her hand away at last. 'Damn you, why do you always have to do it?'

'Why?' he persisted. 'I know you love me. Why are you going to do it?'

'Because I love him more,' she said, still angry. 'If you were me, who would you marry?'

'When you put it that way,' he agreed. 'I suppose you are right.' Now at last she looked at him. He was very pale. 'Roly always was the winner. I hope you will be very happy, Jan.'

'Oh, Craig, I'm so sorry.'

'Yes, I know. So am I. Can we just leave it now, Jan. There is nothing more to say.'

'Yes, there is. Roland is coming to see you this evening. He is going to ask you to be his best man.'

Roland Ballantyne perched on the edge of the operations table. It was an enormous relief map of Matabeleland. The disposition of the security force elements was shown by small movable counters and their strength by a numbered card set into each counter like a menu-holder. Every branch of the force had its own colour – the Ballantyne Scouts were maroon. They were shown as 250 in Thabas Indunas barracks, but there was still a patrol of fifty near the Gwaai, involved in the hot pursuit of the survivors of the previous day's contact.

On the opposite side of the operations table Wing Commander Douglas Hunt-Jeffreys slapped the wooden pointer into the palm of the other hand.

'All right,' he nodded. 'This is for heads of staff only. Let's go over it from the beginning, please.'

There were just the two of them in the operations room, and the red security light above the steel door was burning.

'Code name Buffalo,' Roland said. 'The object of operation is the elimination of Josiah Inkunzi and/or one or all of his chiefs of staff – Tebe, Chitepo and Tungata.'

'Tungata?' Hunt-Jeffreys asked.

'A new one,' Roland explained.

'Go on, please.'

'We will cut them at the safe house in Lusaka, at some date after the fifteenth of November when we expect Inkunzi to return from a visit to Hungary and East Germany.'

'You will be able to get intelligence of his return?' Douglas asked, and when Roland nodded, 'Can you let me know your source?'

'That is not even for you, Dougie, my boy.'

'Very well, as long as you will be certain that Inkunzi is in residence before you move.'

'From now on let's call him Buffalo.'

'How will you go in?'

'We will go in overland. A column of Land-Rovers with

Zambian police markings and all personnel will wear Zambian police uniforms.'

Douglas raised an eyebrow. 'Geneva Convention?'

'Legitimate ruse of war,' Roland countered.

'They'll shoot you if they catch you.'

'They would do that anyway, uniforms or not. The answer will be not to let any of our lads get caught.'

'All right, you go in by road – which one?'

'Livingstone to Lusaka.'

'A long haul through hostile territory, and our air force has blown the bridges at Kaleya.'

'There is an alternative route upstream, there will be a guide waiting to take us through the bush to reach it.'

'So you have covered that bridge, but how do you cross the Zambezi?'

'There is a drift below Kazungula.'

'Which you have checked, of course?'

'On a dummy run. We took a vehicle across, using winch and floats, in nine minutes flat. We will have the entire task force across in under two hours. There is a track that will take us out onto the great north road fifty K's north of Livingstone.'

'What about re-supply?'

'The guide at Kaleya is a white maize farmer, he has fuel on his farm, and we will back up with helicopters.'

'I take it you will use the helicopters to evacuate if you are forced to abort the operation?'

Roland nodded. 'That's it, Dougie old bean. Pray it's not necessary.'

'Let's go on to personnel then. How many will you use?'

'Forty-five Scouts, that includes S'arn-Major and myself, and ten specialists.'

'Specialists?'

'We expect to find a pile of documents in Buffalo's HQ. Probably so much that we will not be able to bring it all back. We need at least four intelligence experts to evaluate on the spot, what to keep and what to burn. You pick them for us.'

'The other specialists?'

'Medicos, two of them. Henderson and his aide. We have used them before.'

'Good, who else?'

'Blast bunnies, to clear the house of booby-traps, to set our own when we leave, and to blow the bridges behind us on our way home.'

'Armourers from Salisbury?'

'I can get two good lads here in Bulawayo, one is a cousin of mine.'

'Fine, let me have a list of names.' Douglas carefully withdrew the stub of his cigarette from the ivory holder, crushed it out, and replaced it with a fresh tube from the packet of Gold Leaf.

'What about a site for the quarantine camp?' he asked. 'Have you given it some thought?'

'There is the Wankie Safari Lodge on the Dett vlei. It's two hours' drive from the Zambezi, and it has been on a caretaker basis since the Wankie strip was abandoned.'

'Five-star comfort – the Scouts are getting soft.' Douglas grinned mockingly. 'Okay, I'll see that you get it.' Douglas made a note and then looked up. 'Now let's go over the dates. How soon can you be ready to go?'

'Fifteenth of November. That gives us eight weeks to assemble the equipment, and rehearse the raid—'

'It probably also fits in rather well with the date of your wedding, doesn't it?' Douglas tapped the ivory holder against his teeth, and delighted in Roland Ballantyne's quick flare of temper.

'The timing of the raid has nothing to do with my private affairs, it will be dictated entirely by Buffalo's movements. In any event, my wedding will take place a week before the start of quarantine. Janine and I will spend our honeymoon at the Victoria Falls Hotel which is only two hours' drive from the camp at Wankie Safari Lodge. She will fly back to Bulawayo on the airway's scheduled flight, and I will go into quarantine directly from Vic Falls.'

Douglas lifted a defensive hand and grinned mockingly. 'I say, do keep your hair on, old man. Just a civil enquiry, that's all. By the way, I think my wedding invitation must have been lost in the post—' But Roland had returned to his list, and was studying it with all his attention.

Douglas Hunt-Jeffreys lay on the ample bed in the cool shuttered bedroom, and examined the naked woman who slept beside him. At first she had seemed a most unpromising subject, with her pale acne-scarred face and disconcerting staring eyes behind horn-rimmed spectacles, her abrupt, aggressive, almost mannish manner, and the smouldering intensity of the political militant. But stripped of her shapeless sweater and baggy skirts, of her thick woollen socks and crude leather sandals, she had a slim pale, almost girlish, body, with fine small breasts that Douglas found very much to his taste. When she removed the spectacles, her staring eyes softened into appealing unfocused myopia, and under Douglas' skilful lips and fingers, she unloosed a tumultuous physical response which had at first astonished and then delighted him. He found he could induce in her an epileptic passion, a state in which she was almost catatonic and totally susceptible to his will, her depravity limited only by the range of Douglas' fertile imagination.

'A murrain on beautiful women,' he smiled contentedly to himself. 'It's the ugly little ducklings who are the absolute ravers!'

They had met in the middle of the morning, and now it was – careful not to disturb her, Douglas checked his gold

Rolex – it was two o'clock in the afternoon. Even for Douglas, a marathon performance.

'Poor lamb is exhausted.' He craved a cigarette, but decided to give her ten minutes more. There was no hurry. He could afford to lie a little longer and leisurely review this case.

Like many good controllers, Douglas had found that a sexual relationship with his female agents, and occasionally even with some of his male agents, was an effective tool of manipulation, a short-cut to the dependencies and loyalties that were so desirable in his trade. This case was a perfect example. Without the physical lever Doctor Leila St John would be a difficult and unpredictable subject, whereas with it she had become one of his best agents ever.

Douglas Hunt-Jeffreys by a fluke of war was a born Rhodesian. His father had come out to Africa at the beginning of Hitler's war to command the Royal Air Force training station at Gwelo. He had met and married a local girl, and Douglas had been delivered in 1941 by the Air Force doctor. The family had returned to England at the end of his father's tour of duty, and Douglas had followed the well-worn family path to Eton, and then on to the Royal Air Force.

After that there had been an unusual diversion in his career, and he found himself in British military intelligence. Back in 1964, when Ian Smith came to power in Rhodesia, and started making the first threatening noises about breaking with Britain in a unilateral declaration of independence, Douglas Hunt-Jeffreys had been the perfect choice of an agent to place in the field. He had returned to Rhodesia, taking up his Rhodesian nationality, joined the Rhodesian Air Force and began immediately to mole his way up the ladder of command.

He was now chief co-ordinator for British intelligence throughout the territory, and Doctor Leila St John was one of his recruits. Naturally, she had no idea as to who was her ultimate employer; any suggestion of military intelligence, no matter to which country it belonged, would have sent her scampering up the nearest tree like a frightened cat. Douglas grinned lazily at his own imagery. Leila St John believed herself to be a member of a small courageous group of left-wing guerrillas, intent on wresting the land of her birth from its racialist fascist conquerors and delivering it unto the joys of Marxist communism.

On the other hand, the concern of Douglas Hunt-Jeffreys and his government was to arrive at the swiftest settlement acceptable to the United Nations and to the United States, France, West Germany and their other Western allies, and to withdraw from an embarrassing, untidy and costly situation with what dignity and despatch they could still muster, preferably leaving in charge the least objectionable of the African guerrilla leaders.

British and American intelligence appraisals showed that Josiah Inkunzi, despite all his extreme left-wing rhetoric and the military assistance which he had solicited and received from communist China and the Soviet bloc countries, was a pragmatist. From the Western viewpoint, he was far and away the least of many much greater evils; his elimination would clear the way for a horde of truly vicious Marxist monsters to take over and lead the nation-to-be Zimbabwe into the clutches of the big red bear.

A secondary consideration was that a successful Rhodesian assassination coup on Inkunzi would bolster the slowly flagging fighting resolve of the Rhodesian UDI government, and would render Ian Smith and his gang of right-wing cabinet ministers even less amenable to reason than they had been to date. No, it was absolutely essential that Josiah Inkunzi's life be protected at all costs, and Douglas Hunt-Jeffreys tickled the sleeping woman gently.

'Wake up, pussy cat,' he said. 'It's time to talk.'

She sat up and stretched, and then groaned softly and

touched herself cautiously. 'Ah!' she murmured huskily. 'I ache all over, inside and out, and it feels good.'

'Light each of us a cigarette,' he ordered, and she fitted one into his ivory holder with practised dexterity, lit it and placed it between his lips.

'When do you expect the next courier from Lusaka?' He blew a spinning smoke-ring that broke on her bosom like mist on a hilltop.

'Overdue,' she said. 'I told you about the Umlimo.'

'Oh, yes,' Douglas nodded. 'The spirit medium.'

'The arrangements to move her are all in hand, and Lusaka is sending a high party official, probably a commissar, to take charge of the transfer. He will arrive at any time.'

'It seems a lot of trouble to go to for a senile old witch-doctor.'

'She is the spiritual leader of the Matabele people,' Leila told him fiercely, 'her presence with the guerrilla army would be of incalculable value to their morale.'

'Yes, I understand, you explained the superstitions to me.' Douglas stroked her cheek soothingly and she subsided gradually. 'So they are sending a commissar. That's good, though it always puzzles me how they move back and forth across the border, in and out of the towns, and from one end of the country to the other, with so little trouble.'

'To the average white man, one black face looks the same as every other,' Leila explained. 'There is no system of passes or passports, every village is a base, nearly every black person an ally. As long as they do not carry arms or explosives, they can use the buses and railways, and pass through the road-blocks with impunity.'

'All right,' Douglas agreed. 'Just as long as what I have for you gets back to Lusaka as soon as possible.'

'By next week at the latest,' Leila promised.

'The Ballantyne Scouts are setting up a full-scale operation to cull Inkunzi and his staff at the safe house in Lusaka.'

'Oh my God, no!' Leila gasped with shock.

'Yes, I'm afraid so, unless we can warn him. Now here are the details. Memorize them, please.'

The rackety old bus came down the winding road through the hills, leaving behind it a long greasy black smear of diesel fumes which drifted sluggishly aside on the small breeze. The roof-racks were piled with bundles tied with rope and pieces of string, with cardboard boxes and cheap suitcases, with squawking chickens in cages of plaited bark and bent green twigs, and with other less readily identifiable packages.

The driver slammed on his brakes when he saw the road-block ahead, and the chattering and laughter of his passengers died into an uneasy silence. As soon as the bus stopped, the black passengers poured out of the forward entrance, and under the direction of the waiting armed police separated into groups according to their sex, men to one side, women and their children to the other. In the meantime, two black constables climbed aboard to search the empty bus for fugitives hiding under the seats or for hidden weapons.

Comrade Tungata Zebiwe was amongst the huddle of male passengers. He was dressed in a floppy hat, a ragged shirt and short khaki trousers, on his feet were filthy tennis shoes and his big toes protruded through the stained canvas uppers. He seemed typical of the unskilled itinerant labourers who made up the great bulk of the country's labour force; he was safe, just as long as the police check was cursory, but he had every reason to believe that this one would not be.

After crossing the Zambezi drifts in darkness, and negotiating the *cordon sanitaire*, he had made his way south through the abandoned strip and reached the main road near the collieries at Wankie. He was travelling alone, and carrying forged employment papers to show that he had been discharged two days previously from employment as a labourer at the collieries. It should have been enough to take him through any ordinary road-block.

However, two hours after he had boarded the crowded bus and when they were approaching the outskirts of Bulawayo, he realized suddenly that there was another ZIPRA courier amongst the passengers. She was a Matabele woman in her late twenties, who had been in the training camp with him in Zambia. She was also dressed like a peasant girl, and had an infant strapped upon her back in the traditional fashion. Tungata studied her surreptitiously as the bus roared southwards, hoping that she might not be carrying incriminating material. If she was, and if she was picked up at a road-block, then every other passenger in the bus would be subjected to full security scrutiny, which included fingerprints, and as a former Rhodesian government employee, Tungata's fingerprints were on the files.

The woman, although his ally and comrade, was a deadly danger to him now. She was a totally unimportant pawn, a mere courier, and she was expendable, but what was she carrying at the moment? He watched her surreptitiously, looking for any indication of her status, and then suddenly his attention focused on the infant strapped to the girl's back. With a swoop of dread in the pit of his stomach, Tungata realized the worst. The woman was active. If they took her, they would almost certainly take Tungata also.

Now, he lined up with the other male passengers for the body search by the black police members; on the far side of the bus the women passengers were forming a separate line. Women police would search them to the skin. The girl courier was in fifth place in the line, she was joggling the sleeping infant on her back, and its tiny head waggled from side to side. Tungata could wait no longer.

Abruptly he pushed his way to the front of the queue,

and spoke urgently but quietly to the black sergeant in charge of the search. Then Tungata pointed deliberately at the girl in the women's line. The girl saw the accuser's finger pointed at her, she looked about her, and then broke from the line and started to run.

'Stop her!' the sergeant bellowed, and the running girl loosed the strap of cloth that held the infant to her back and let the tiny black body fall to the earth. Freed of her burden, she raced for the line of thick thornbush along the verge of the road. However, the road-block had been laid to prevent just such an escape, and two police constables rose from concealment at the edge of the bush. The girl doubled back, but they had her trapped and a heavy blow with a gun-butt knocked her sprawling in the grass. They dragged her back, struggling and kicking, spitting and snarling, like a cat, and as she passed Tungata, she shrieked at him.

'Traitor, we will eat you! Jackal, you will die—'

Tungata stared at her with bovine indifference.

One of the constables picked up the naked infant from where the girl had abandoned it, and he exclaimed immediately.

'It's cold.' He turned the body gingerly, and the tiny limbs sprawled lifelessly. 'It's dead!' The constable's voice was shocked, and then he started again. 'Look! Look at this!'

The child's body had been gutted like that of a fish. The cut ran upwards from its groin, across its stomach, through the sternum of the chest to the base of the little throat and the wound had been closed with sacking twine and crude cobbled stitches. The white police captain, with a sickly expression on his face, snipped the stitches and the body cavity bulged open. It was packed with ropes of brown plastic explosive.

'All right.' The captain stood up. 'Hold them all. We will run a full check on every one of the bastards.'

Then the captain came to Tungata. 'Well done, friend.'

He clapped Tungata's shoulder. 'You can claim your reward from the main police station. Five thousand dollars – that's good, hey! You just give them this.' He scribbled on his notebook and tore off the sheet. 'That's my name and rank. I will witness your claim. One of our Land-Rovers will be going into Bulawayo in a few minutes – I'll see you get a lift into town.'

Tungata submitted docilely to the customary search by the guards at the gates to Khami Mission Hospital. He was still dressed in his labourer's rags, and carrying the forged discharge from the Wankie collieries.

One of the guards glanced at the work papers. 'What is wrong with you?'

'I have a snake in my stomach.'

Tungata clasped his hands over the offending organ. A snake in the stomach could mean anything from colic to duodenal ulcers.

The guard laughed. 'The doctors will cut out your mamba for you, go to the out-patients department.' He pointed out the side entrance, and Tungata went up the driveway with an ungainly sloppy gait.

The Matabele sister at the out-patient desk recognized him with a flicker of surprise, then her expression went dead-pan and she made out a card for him and waved him to one of the crowded benches. A minute or two later the black sister rose from the desk and crossed to the door marked 'Duty Doctor'. She went in and closed the door behind her.

When she came out again, she pointed at Tungata. 'You next!' she said.

Tungata shambled across the hall and went in through the same door. Leila St John came joyfully to meet him, as soon as he closed the door behind him.

'Comrade Commissar!' she whispered, and embraced him. 'I was so worried!' She kissed him on each cheek, and as she stepped back, Tungata had changed character from

559

dull-witted peasant to deadly warrior, tall and dangerously cold-faced.

'You have clothes for me?'

Behind the movable screen, Tungata changed swiftly and stepped out again buttoning the white laboratory-coat. On his lapel he wore a plastic dog-tag that identified him as 'DOCTOR G. J. KUMALO', which placed him immediately above idle suspicion.

'I would like to know what arrangements you have made,' he said, and seated himself facing Leila St John across her desk.

'I have had the Umlimo in our geriatric ward since she was brought in by her followers from the Matopos Reservation about six months ago.'

'What is her physical condition?'

'She is a very old lady – ancient, is perhaps the better word. I see no reason to doubt her claim that she is 120 years old. She was already a young woman when Cecil Rhodes' freebooters rode into Bulawayo and hunted King Lobengula to his death.'

'Her condition, please.'

'She was suffering from malnutrition, but I have had her on a nutritional drip and she is much stronger, though she cannot walk, nor is she in control of her bowels and bladder. She is an albino, and she suffers from a type of skin allergy, but I have been able to prescribe an antihistamine ointment which has given her a great deal of relief. Her hearing and eyesight are failing, but her heart and other vital organs are remarkably strong for her age. Moreover, her brain is sharp and clear. She appears to be totally lucid.'

'So she can travel?' Tungata insisted.

'She is eager to do so. It is her own prophecy that she must cross the great waters before the spears of the nation prevail.'

Tungata made an impatient gesture, and Leila St John interpreted it.

'You do not set any store by the Umlimo, and her predictions, do you, Comrade?'

'Do you, Doctor?' he asked.

'There are areas which our sciences have not yet penetrated. She is an extraordinary woman. I don't say I believe everything about her, but I am aware of a force within her.'

'It is our estimate that she will be extremely valuable as a propaganda weapon. The great majority of our people are still uneducated and superstitious. You still have not answered my question, Doctor. Can she travel?'

'I think she can. I have prepared medications for her to take on the journey. I have also made out medical certificates, which should be sufficient to see her safely through any security checks as far as the border with Zambia. I will provide one of my best medical orderlies, a black male nurse, to travel with her. I would go myself, but it would attract too much attention.'

Tungata was silent for a long time, his hard handsome features rapt in thought. He had such a presence of command and authority that Leila found herself waiting almost timidly for his next words, eager to respond whether they were command or question.

However, when he spoke, it was to muse softly. 'The woman is as valuable dead as alive, and dead she would be easier to handle, I presume you could preserve her body in formaldehyde or something of that nature.'

Despite herself, Leila was shocked, and yet strangely awed by the ruthlessness, excited by the man's deadly resolve.

'I pray that won't be necessary,' she whispered, staring at him. She had never met a man like this.

'I will see her first, then I will decide,' Tungata said quietly. 'I wish to do so immediately.'

There were three weird crones squatting outside the door of the private ward on the top floor in the south wing of the hospital. They were dressed in the dried skins of wild cat and jackal and python, and hung about the neck and waist with bottles and gourds and stoppered buckhorns, with dried goat-bladders and bone rattles, with phials and the leather bags that contained their divining bones.

'These are the old woman's followers,' Leila St John explained, 'they will not leave her.'

'They will,' said Tungata softly, 'when I decide that they will.'

One of them hopped towards him, whining and snivelling, reaching out to touch his leg with filth-encrusted fingers, and Tungata spurned her aside with his foot, and opened the door to the private ward. He went in, and Leila followed him and closed the door behind them. It was a small room with bare tiled floor and the walls were painted with a white gloss paint. There was a bedside locker with a stainless-steel tray of medicines and instruments upon it. The bed was on castors with an adjustable handle and screw at the foot. The head of the bed-frame was raised and the frail figure under the single sheet seemed no larger than a child. There was the glass bowl of a drip suspended above the bed, and a transparent plastic tube snaked down from it.

The Umlimo was asleep. Her unpigmented skin was a dusty pinkish grey, crusted with dark scabs that extended up over the pale bald scalp. The skin that covered her skull was so thin and fragile that the bone seemed to shine through it like a water-worn pebble beneath the surface of a mountain stream, but from her brow down to the edge of the white sheet beneath her chin, the skin was impossibly wrinkled and folded, like that of some prehistoric relic from the age of the great reptiles. Her mouth was open, the scabbed lips trembled with each breath, and there was a single yellow worn tooth left in the desiccated grey gums. She opened her eyes. They were pink as those of a white rabbit, sunk deeply in folds of grey skin, swimming in their own gummy mucus.

'Greetings, old Mother.' Leila went to her and touched

the age-ravaged cheek. 'I have a visitor for you,' she said in perfect Sindebele.

The old woman made a small keening sound in her throat, and she began to shake, her entire body taken by convulsions, as she stared at Tungata.

'Calm yourself, old Mother.' Leila was concerned. 'He will not harm you.'

The old woman lifted one arm from under the sheet. It was skeletal, the elbow-joint enlarged and distorted by arthritic processes, the hand was a claw, with lumpy knuckles and twisted fingers. She pointed them at Tungata.

'Son of kings,' she wailed, her voice surprisingly clear and strong, 'father of kings. King that will be, when the falcons return. Bayete, he that will be king, Bayete!' It was a royal salute, and Tungata went rigid with shock. His own skin-tone changed to dark grey, and little blisters of sweat burst out upon his brow. Leila St John fell back until she was against the wall. She stared at the frail old woman in the high steel bed. Spittle frothed on the thin scabbed lips, and the pink eyes rolled back into the ancient skull, yet the wailing voice rose higher.

'The falcons have flown afar. There will be no peace in the kingdoms of the Mambos or the Monomatopas until they return. He who brings the stone falcons back to roost shall rule the kingdoms.' Her voice rose to a shriek. 'Bayete, Nkosi nkulu. Hail, Mambo. Live for ever, Monomatopa.' The Umlimo greeted Tungata with all the titles of the ancient rulers, and then collapsed against the soft white pillows. Leila hurried back to her side, and placed her fingers over the sticklike wrist.

'She's all right,' she said after a moment, and looked up at Tungata. 'What do you want me to do?'

He shook himself like a man awakening from deep sleep, and with the sleeve of his white coat, wiped the icy sweat of superstitious dread from his forehead.

'Look after her well. Make sure she is ready to leave by

morning. We will take her north across the great river,'
he said.

Leila St John backed up her small Fiat into the
ambulance bay beside the casualty department, and
screened from curious eyes, Tungata slipped through
the back door and crouched down between the seats. Leila
spread a mohair travelling-rug over him and drove down to
the main gates. She spoke briefly to one of the guards, and
then swung the Fiat onto the branch road that led to the
superintendent's residence.

She spoke without looking back or moving her lips.

'No sign of security forces, not yet. It looks as though
your arrival has gone unnoticed, but we will take no
chances.'

She parked in the lean-to garage which had been added
to the old stone-walled building, and while she unloaded
her valise and a pile of files from the seat, she made certain
they were still not observed. The garden was screened from
the road and the thatched church by trellised creepers and
flowering shrubs.

She opened the side door to the house, and said, 'Please
keep low, and go in as quickly as you can.'

He ducked out of the Fiat, and she followed him into the
living-room. The shutters and curtains were drawn and it
was half-dark.

'My grandmother built this house after the original was
burned down during the 1896 troubles. Fortunately she took
precautions against the troubles of the future.'

Leila crossed the floor of sawn Rhodesian teak, the highly
polished surface of which was strewn with tanned animal
skins and hand-woven rugs in bold patterns and primary
colours.

She entered the walk-in stone fireplace and drew aside

564

the black grate. The floor of the fireplace was of slate flags, and she used the fire irons to prise and lift one of these. When Tungata stepped up beside her, he saw that she had exposed a square vertical shaft, into one wall of which were set stone steps.

'This was where Comrade Tebe was hiding that night?' Tungata asked. 'When the Scouts, the *kanka*, could not find him?'

'Yes, he was here. It would be best if you went down now.'

He dropped nimbly down the shaft and found himself in darkness. Leila closed the slate hatch and came down beside him. She groped along the wall and turned a switch. A bare electric bulb lit on the roof of the tiny stone cell. There was a deal table on which were stacked a few well-thumbed books, pushed beneath it was a low stool and there was a narrow truckle-bed against the far wall. A chemical toilet stood at its foot.

'Not very comfortable,' she apologized. 'But nobody will find you here.'

'I have had less luxurious accommodation,' he assured her. 'Now let us go over your arrangements.'

She had the medical certificates ready on the table, and she sat on the stool and wrote down his requirements for the transportation of the Umlimo as he dictated them.

When she had finished, he said, 'Memorize that and destroy it.'

'Very well.'

He watched while she went over the list carefully and then looked up.

'Now, there is a message for you to take to Comrade Inkunzi,' she said. 'It is from our friend in high places.'

'Give it to me,' he nodded.

'Ballantyne's Scouts, the *kanka*, they are planning a special operation. It is to destroy Comrade Inkunzi and his staff. Your own name is high on their list.'

565

Tungata's expression did not change. 'Do you have any details of their plans?'

'All the details,' she assured him. 'This is what they will do—'

She spoke slowly and deliberately for almost ten minutes, and he did not interrupt her. Even when she had finished, he was silent for many minutes, lying flat on his back on the bed, staring up at the electric bulb. Then she saw that his jaws clenched and that a smoky red tide seemed to have spread over his eyeballs. His voice, when he spoke, was thick with loathing.

'Colonel Roland Ballantyne. If we could get him! He is responsible for the deaths of over three thousand of our people – he and his *kanka*. In the camps they speak his name in whispers, as though he were some sort of demon. His name alone turns our bravest men to cowards. I have seen him and his butchers at work. Oh, if we could only take him.' He sat up and glared at her. 'Perhaps—' His voice was choked and slurred as though he was drunk with hatred. 'Perhaps this is our chance.'

He reached out and took Leila by the shoulders. His fingers dug deeply into her flesh and she winced and tried to draw away. He held her without effort.

'This woman of his. You say that she will fly from the Victoria Falls? Can you get me the date, the number of the flight, the exact time?'

She nodded, afraid of him now, terrified by his strength and fury.

'We have somebody in the airway booking-office,' she whispered, no longer trying to escape the agony of his grip. 'I can get it for you.'

'The bait,' he said, 'the tender lamb that will lure the leopard into the trap.'

S he brought him food and drink down the stone shaft and waited while Tungata ate.

For a while he ate in silence, then abruptly he returned to the subject of the Umlimo.

'The stone falcons,' he started, 'you heard what the old woman said?'

She nodded and he went on, 'Tell me what you know of these things.'

'Well, the stone falcons are the emblem on the flag. They are minted on the coinage of this country.'

'Yes, go on.'

'They are ancient carvings of bird figures. They were discovered in the ruins of Zimbabwe by the early white adventurers, and stolen by them. There is a legend that Lobengula tried to prevent them, but they were taken south.'

'Where are they now?' Tungata demanded.

'One of them was destroyed by fire when Cecil Rhodes' house at Groote Schuur was burned down, but the others, I'm not absolutely certain, but I think they are at Cape Town in South Africa.'

'Whereabouts?'

'In the museum, there.'

He grunted and went on eating steadily. When the bowl and mug were empty he pushed them aside and stared at her again with those smoky eyes.

'The words of the old woman,' he began and then paused.

'The prophecy of the Umlimo,' she went on for him, 'that the man who returned the falcons would rule this land, and that you were that man.'

'You will tell nobody what she said – do you understand me?'

'I will tell nobody,' she promised.

'You know that if you do, I will kill you.'

'I know that,' she said simply, and gathered the bowl and mug and replaced them on the tray.

She stood before him waiting, and when he did not speak again, she asked, 'Is there anything else?'

He went on staring at her, and she dropped her eyes.

'Do you wish me to stay?'

'Yes,' he said, and she turned to the light switch.

'Leave the light,' he ordered. 'I want to see your whiteness.'

The first time she cried out, it was in fear and pain, the second time – and the uncounted times after that – was in mindless, incoherent transports of ecstasy.

D ouglas Ballantyne had selected a dozen of the finest slaughter-beasts from the herds of King's Lynn and Queen's Lynn. The prime carcasses had hung in the cold room for three weeks until they were perfect. They were being barbecued whole on the open coal pits at the bottom of the gardens. The kitchen servants of Queen's Lynn worked in relays, turning the spits and basting the sizzling golden carcasses amidst clouds of fragrant steam.

There were three bands to provide continuous music. The caterers had been flown in with all their equipment from Johannesburg, and paid suitable danger-money for entering the war zone. The gardens of every homestead for fifty miles around had been ransacked for flowers and the marquees were filled with banks of floral decorations, of roses and poinsettia and dahlia in fifty blazing shades of colour.

Bawu Ballantyne had chartered a special aircraft to bring the liquor up from South Africa. There was a little over four tons' weight of fine wines and spirits. After searching his political conscience, Bawu had even decided to suspend his personal sanctions against the United Kingdom of Great Britain and Ireland for the duration of the wedding festivities, and had included one hundred cases of Chivas Regal whisky in the shipment. This was his most valuable contribution to the preparations, but there had been others.

He had transferred some of his most potent and cherished Claymore mines across from the King's Lynn defences and added them to the decorations in the Queen's Lynn gardens.

'You can never be too careful,' he explained darkly, when taxed with it. 'If there is a terr attack during the ceremony—' He made the motion of pressing a button, and the entire family shuddered at the thought of a mushroom-shaped cloud hanging over Queen's Lynn. It had taken all their combined powers of persuasion to get him to remove his pets.

He had then sneaked into the kitchens and added an extra six bottles of brandy to the mix for the wedding cake. Fortunately Valerie had made a final tasting and when she got her breath back, ordered the chef to bury it and start a new batch. From then on Bawu was banned from the kitchens in disgrace, and Douglas had drawn up a roster of family members to keep him under surveillance during the great day.

Craig had the first shift from nine in the morning when the two thousand invited guests started arriving until eleven when Craig would hand over to a cousin and assume his other duties as Roland's best man. Craig had helped the old man dress in his uniform from the Kaiser's war. A local tailor had been brought out to King's Lynn to make the alterations, and the results were surprising. Bawu looked dapper and spry with his Sam Browne belt and swagger-stick, and the double row of coloured ribbons on his chest.

Craig was proud of him as he took up his position on the front veranda, and looked over the crowded lawns, lifting his swagger-stick in acknowledgement of the affectionate cries of 'Hello, Uncle Bawu', brushing out his gleaming silver moustaches and tipping the peak of his cap at a more debonair angle over one eye.

'Damn me, boy,' he told Craig. 'This whole business

makes me feel quite romantic again. I haven't been married myself for nearly twenty years. I have a good mind to give it one last whirl!'

'There is always the widow Angus,' Craig suggested, and his grandfather was outraged.

'That old crow!'

'Bawu, she is rich and only fifty.'

'That's old, boy. Catch 'em young and train 'em well. That's my motto.' Bawu winked at him. 'Now how about that one?'

His choice was twenty-five years old, twice divorced already, wearing an unfashionable mini-skirt and casting a bold eye about her.

'You can introduce me.' Bawu gave his magnanimous permission.

'I think the prime minister wants to see you, Bawu.' Craig searched desperately for a distraction, before the pert little bottom under the mini-skirt was soundly pinched. Craig had seen the old man flirting before. He left Bawu, gin and tonic in hand, giving Ian Smith a few tips on international diplomacy.

'You have to remember that these fellows, Callaghan and his friends, are working class, Ian, my boy, you cannot treat them like gentlemen. They wouldn't understand that—'

And the prime minister, worn and tired and wan with his responsibilities, one eyelid drooping, his curly sandy hair receding, tried to hide his smile as he nodded.

'Quite right, Uncle Bawu, I'll remember that.'

Craig felt safe to leave him for ten minutes, sure that the old man's opinions of the British Labour government were good for at least that long, and he made his way swiftly through the crowds to where Janine's parents stood with a small group at the end of the veranda.

He insinuated himself unobtrusively into the circle, and studied Janine's mother out of the corner of his eye. It gave him a hollow aching feeling to recognize the same features, the jawline and deep forehead blurred only marginally by the passage of time. She had the same slanted eyes with the same appealing cat-like cast to them. She caught his gaze and smiled at him.

'Mrs Carpenter, I'm a good friend of Janine's. My name is Craig Mellow.'

'Oh yes, Jan wrote about you in her letters.' Her smile was warm, and her voice had haunting echoes of her daughter's. Craig found himself babbling away to her, and could not prevent it – until softly and compassionately she said:

'She told me you were such a nice person. I am sorry, I truly am.'

'I don't understand?' Craig stiffened.

'You love her very much, don't you?'

He stared at her miserably, unable to reply, and she touched his arm in understanding.

'Excuse me,' he blurted. 'Roland will be ready to dress, I must go.' He stumbled and almost fell on the veranda steps.

'By God, Sonny, where have you been? I thought you were going to let me go into contact on my own,' Roland shouted from the shower. 'Have you got the ring?'

They waited side by side, under the bower of fresh flowers in front of the makeshift altar which also was smothered with flowers. Roland wore full-dress uniform: the maroon beret with Bazo's head cap-badge, the colonel's crowns on his shoulders, the silver cross for valour on his breast, white gloves on his hands and the gilt and tasselled sword at his waist.

In his simple police uniform, Craig felt gauche and drab, like a sparrow beside a golden eagle, like a tabby cat beside a leopard, and the waiting seemed to go on for ever. Through it all, Craig clung to a hopeless notion that it was still not going to happen – that was the only way he could hold his despair at bay.

Then there was the triumphant swell of the bridal march,

and down both sides of the carpeted aisle from the house, the crowds stirred and hummed with excitement and anticipation. Craig felt his soul begin the final plunge into cold and darkness, he could not bring himself to look around. He stared straight ahead at the face of the priest. He had known him since childhood, but now he seemed a stranger, his face swam and wavered in Craig's vision.

Then he smelled Janine; even over the scent of the altar flowers he recognized her perfume, and he almost choked on the memories it evoked. He felt the train of her dress brush against his ankle, and he moved back slightly and turned so that he could see her for the last time.

She was on her father's arm. The veil covered her hair, and misted her face, but beneath its soft folds, he could see her eyes, those great slanted eyes, the dark indigo of a tropical sea, shining softly as she looked up at Roland Ballantyne.

'Dearly beloved, we are gathered together here in the sight of God, and in the face of this church, to join together this man and this woman in holy matrimony—'

Now Craig could not take his eyes from her face. She had never looked so lovely. She wore a crown of fresh violets, the exact colour of her eyes. He still hoped that it would not happen, that something would prevent it.

'Therefore if any man can show any just cause, why they may not lawfully be joined together, let him now speak—'

He wanted to call out, to stop it. He wanted to shout, 'I love her, she is mine,' but his throat was so dry and painful that he could not draw breath enough through it. Then, it was happening.

'I, Roland Morris, take thee, Janine Elizabeth, to have and to hold from this day forward—' Roly's voice was clear and strong and it raked Craig's soul to its very depths. After that, nothing else mattered. Craig seemed to be standing a little away from it all, as though all the laughter and joy was on the other side of a glass partition, the voices were strangely muted, even the light seemed dulled as though a cloud had passed across the sun.

He watched from the back of the crowd, standing under the jacaranda trees, while Janine came out onto the veranda still carrying her bouquet of violets, dressed in her blue going-away ensemble. She and Roland were still hand in hand, but now he lifted her onto a table-top and there were feminine shrieks of excitement as Janine poised to toss her bouquet.

In that moment, she looked over their heads, and saw Craig. The smile stayed on her lovely wide mouth, but something moved in her eyes, a dark shadow, perhaps of pity, perhaps even regret, then she threw the bouquet, one of her bridesmaids caught it, and Roland swept her down and away. Hand in hand, the two of them ran down the lawns to where the helicopter waited with its rotor already turning. They ran laughing, Janine clutching her wide-brimmed straw hat, and Roland trying to shield her from the storm of confetti that swirled around them.

Craig did not wait for the machine to bear them away. He returned to where he had left the old Land-Rover at the back of the stables. He drove back to the yacht. He stripped off his uniform, threw it onto the bunk, and pulled on a pair of silk jogging shorts. He went into the galley and from the refrigerator hooked out a can of beer. Sipping the froth, he went back into the saloon. A loner all his life, he had believed himself immune to the tortures of loneliness, and now he knew he had been mistaken.

By this time there was a stack of over fifty exercise books upon the saloon table, each of them filled from cover to cover with his pencilled scrawl. He sat down and selected a pencil from the bunch stuck into an empty coffee mug like porcupine quills. He began to write, and slowly the corrosive agony of loneliness receded and became merely a slow dull ache.

On Monday morning, when Craig walked into police

headquarters, on his way through to the armoury, the member-in-charge called him into his office.

'Craig, I've got movement papers for you. You are being detached on special assignment.'

'What is it?'

'Hell, I don't know. I just work here. Nobody tells me anything, but you are ordered to report to the area commander, Wankie, on twenty-eighth—' The inspector broke off and studied Craig's face. 'Are you feeling okay, Craig?'

'Yes, why do you ask?'

'You are looking bloody awful.' He considered for a few moments. 'I tell you what, if you sneak away from here on the twenty-fifth, you could give yourself a couple of days' break before reporting to your new assignment.'

'You are the only star in my firmament, George.' Craig grinned lopsidedly, and thought to himself, 'That's all I need, three days with nothing to do but feel sorry for myself.'

The Victoria Falls Hotel is one of those magnificent monuments to the great days of Empire. Its walls are as thick as those of a castle, but painted brilliant white. The floors are of marble, with sweeping staircases and colonnaded porticos, the ceilings are cathedral-high with fancy plaster-work and gently revolving fans. The terraces and lawns stretch down to the very brink of the abyss through which the Zambezi river boils in all its fury and grandeur.

Spanning the gorge is the delicate steel tracery of the arched bridge of which Cecil Rhodes ordered, 'I want the spray from the falls to wet my train as it passes on its way to the north.' The spray hangs in a perpetual snowy mantle over the chasm, twisting and folding upon itself as the breeze picks at it, and always there is the muted thunder of falling water like the sound of storm surf heard from afar.

When David Livingstone, the missionary explorer, first stood on the edge of the gorge and looked down into the sombre sunless depths, he said, 'Sights such as these must have been gazed upon by angels in their flight.' The Livingstone suite, which looks out upon this view, was named after him.

One of the black porters who carried up their luggage told Janine proudly, 'King Georgey slept here – and Missy Elizabeth, who is now the queen, with her sister Margaret when they were little girls.'

Roly laughed. 'Hell, what was good enough for King Georgey!' and he grossly overtipped the grinning porters and fired the cork from the bottle of champagne that waited for them in a silver ice-bucket.

They walked hand in hand along the enchanted path beside the Zambezi river, while the timid little spotted bushbuck scuttled away into the tropical undergrowth and the vervet monkeys scolded them from the tree-tops. They ran laughing hand in hand through the rain forests, under the torrential downpour of falling spray; Janine's hair melted down her face, and their sodden clothing clung to their bodies. When they kissed, standing on the edge of the high cliff, the rock trembled under their feet and the turmoil of air displaced by the volume of tumbling water buffeted them and flung the icy spray into their faces.

They cruised on the placid upper reaches of the river in the sunset, and they chartered a light aircraft to fly over the serpentine coiling and uncoiling gorge in the noon, and Janine clung to Roland in delicious vertigo as they skimmed the rocky lip of the gorge. They danced to the African steel band, under the stars, and the other guests who recognized Roland's uniform watched them with pride and affection. 'One of Ballantyne's Scouts,' they told each other, 'they are very special, the Scouts.' And they sent wine to their table in the manorial dining-room to mark their appreciation.

Roland and Janine lay late in bed in the mornings and

had their breakfast sent up to them. They played tennis and Roland lobbed his service and returned to her forehand. They lay in the sunlight beside the Olympic-sized pool and anointed each other with suncream. In their brief bathing-suits they were magnificently healthy clean young animals, and so obviously in love that they seemed charmed and set apart. In the evenings they sat under the umbrella spread of the great trees on the terrace and drank Pimms No. 1 cup, and experienced a marvellous sense of defiance in flaunting themselves to the full view of their mortal enemies on the far side of the gorge.

Then one day at dinner, the manager stopped at their table.

'I understand that you are leaving us tomorrow, Colonel Ballantyne. We shall miss you both.'

'Oh no!' Janine shook her head laughingly. 'We are staying until the twenty-sixth.'

'Tomorrow is the twenty-sixth, Mrs Ballantyne.'

The head porter had all their luggage piled at the hotel entrance and Roland was settling their bill. Janine waited for him under the portico. Suddenly she started as she recognized the battered old open Land-Rover that swung in through the gates, and parked in one of the open slots at the end of the lot.

Her first reaction, as she watched the familiar gawky figure untangle his long legs and flick the hair out of his eyes as he climbed out, was quick anger.

'He's come on purpose,' she thought. 'Just to try and spoil it all.'

Craig came ambling towards her with his hands thrust into his pockets, but when he was less than a dozen paces from where she stood, he recognized her and his confusion was obviously unfeigned.

'Jan,' he blushed furiously. 'Oh my God, I didn't know you'd be here.'

She felt her anger recede. 'Hello, Craig dear. No, it was a secret, until now.'

'I'm so dreadfully sorry—'

'Don't be, we are leaving anyway.'

'Sonny boy,' Roland came out of the doorway behind Janine and went to throw a brotherly arm around Craig's shoulders. 'You are ahead of time. How are you?'

'You knew I was coming?' Craig looked even more confused.

'I knew,' Roland admitted, 'but not so soon. You were supposed to report on the twenty-eighth.'

'George gave me a couple of days.' Since that first startled exchange, Craig had not looked at Janine again. 'I thought I would spend them here.'

'Good boy, you will need the rest. You and I are going to be doing a bit of work together. I tell you what, Sonny, let's have a quick drink. I'll explain it to you – some of it anyway.'

'Oh, darling,' Janine cut in swiftly, 'we don't have time. I'll miss the flight.' She could not bear the hurt and confusion in Craig's eyes another moment.

'Damn it, I suppose you are right.' Roland checked his watch. 'It will have to keep until I see you the day after tomorrow, Sonny,' and at that moment the airways' bus drove into the hotel driveway. Roland and Janine were the only passengers in the mini-bus out to the airport.

'Darling, when will I see you again?'

'Look, I can't say for sure, Bugsy, that depends on so many things.'

'Will you telephone me or write even?'

'You know I can't.'

'I know, but I will be at the flat, just in case.'

'I wish you would go out to live at Queen's Lynn – that's where you belong now.'

577

'My job—'

'The hell with your job. Ballantyne wives don't work.'

'Well, see here, Colonel, sir, this Ballantyne wife is going on working until—'

'Until?' he asked.

'Until you give me something better to do.'

'Like what?'

'Like a baby.'

'Is that a challenge?'

'Oh please, Colonel, sir, do take it as one.'

At the airport there was a cheerfully rowdy young crowd, all the men in uniform, come to see the aircraft leave. Most of them knew Roland and they plied him and Janine with drinks. It made the last minutes more bearable. Then suddenly they were standing at the gate and the air hostess was calling for boarding.

'I shall miss you so,' Janine whispered. 'I shall pray for you.'

He kissed her and held her so fiercely that she almost lost her breath.

'I love you,' Roland said.

'You never said that before.'

'No,' he agreed. 'Not to anybody before. Now, go, woman – before I do something stupid.'

She was the last in the straggling line of passengers that climbed the boarding-ladder into the elderly Viscount aircraft parked on the hard stand. She wore a white blouse with a daffodil-yellow skirt and flat sandals. There was a matching yellow scarf around her hair and a sling-bag over her shoulder. In the doorway of the aircraft at the top of the boarding-ladder, she looked back, shading her eyes as she searched for Roland, and when she found him she smiled and waved and then stepped through the fuselage door. The door closed and the boarding-ladder wheeled away. The Rolls-Royce Dart turbo-prop engines whined and fired, and the silver Viscount, with the flying Zimbabwe bird emblem on its tail, taxied downwind to its holding point.

Cleared for take-off, it lumbered back down the runway, and climbed slowly into the air. Roland watched it bank onto its southerly heading for Bulawayo, and then went back into the airport building, showed his pass to the guard at the door and climbed the steps to the control tower.

'What can we do for you, Colonel?' the assistant controller at the flight planning desk greeted him.

'I am expecting a helicopter flight coming in from Wankie to pick me up—'

'Oh, you are Colonel Ballantyne – yes, we have your bird on the plot. They were airborne twelve minutes ago. They will be here in an hour and ten minutes.'

While they were talking, the flight-controller at the picture windows was speaking quietly with the pilot of the departing Viscount.

'You are cleared to standard departure, unrestricted climb fifteen thousand feet. Over now to Bulawayo approach on 118 comma six. Goodday!'

'Understand standard departure unrestricted climb to flight level—'

The pilot's calm, almost bored voice broke off and the side-band hummed for a few seconds. Then the voice came back crackling with urgency. Roland spun away from the flight planning desk, and strode to the controller's console. He gripped the back of the controller's chair and through the tall windows stared up into the sky.

The high fair-weather clouds were already turning pink with the oncoming sunset, but the Viscount was out of sight, somewhere out there in the south. Roland's face was hard and terrible with anger and fear, as he listened to the pilot's voice grating out of the radio speakers.

The portable surface-to-air missile-launcher, designated SAM-7, is a crude-looking weapon almost indistinguishable from the bazooka anti-tank rocket launcher of World War II. It looks like a five-foot section of ordinary drainpipe, but the exhaust end is slightly flared into the mouth of a funnel. At the point of balance, there is a shoulder-plate below the barrel and an aiming and igniting device like a small portable AM radio set attached to the upper surface of the barrel.

The weapon is operated by two men. The loader simply places the missile in the exhaust breech of the barrel and, making sure the fins engage the slots, pushes it forward until its rim engages the electrical terminals and locks it into the firing-position. The missile weighs a little less than ten kilos. It has the conventional rocket shape, but in the front of the nose cone is an opaque glass eye, behind which is located the infra-red sensor. The tail-fins are steerable, enabling the rocket to lock onto and follow a moving target. The gunner settles the barrel across his shoulder, places the earphones on his head, and switches on the powerpack. In the earphones he hears the cyclic tone of his audio-warning. He tunes this down below the background infra-red count, so that it is no longer audible.

The weapon is now loaded and ready to fire. The gunner searches out his target through the cross-hatched gun-sight. As soon as an infra-red source is detected by the missile's sensor, the audio warning begins to sound and a tiny red bulb lights up in the eye-piece of the gun-sight to confirm that the missile is 'locked-on'. It remains only for the gunner to press the trigger in the pistol-type grip and the missile launches itself in relentless pursuit of its prey, steering itself to track it accurately through any turns or changes of altitude.

Tungata Zebiwe had held his cadre in position for four days. Apart from himself, there were eight of them and he had chosen each of them with extreme care. They were all

580

veterans of proven courage and determination, but, more importantly, they were all of superior intelligence and capable of operating under their own initiative. Every one of them had been trained in the use of the SAM-7 missile-launcher, in both roles of loader and gunner, and each of them carried one of the finned missiles in addition to their AK 47 assault rifles, and the usual complement of grenades and AP mines. Any two of them could make the attack, and had been thoroughly briefed to do so.

The wind direction would dictate the departure track of any aircraft leaving the main runway of Victoria Falls airport. Wind velocity would also affect the aircraft's altitude as it passed over any specific point on the extended centre-line and crosswind legs of its outward track. Fortunately for Tungata's calculations, the prevailing north-easterly wind had been blowing at a steady fifteen knots during the entire four days in which they had been in position.

He had chosen a small kopje, thickly wooded enough to give them good cover, but not so thick that it impeded the view over the surrounding tree-tops. From the peak in the early mornings, before the heat-haze and dust thickened, Tungata had been able to see the stationary silver cloud of spray that marked the Victoria Falls on the northern horizon.

Each afternoon they had practised the attack drill. Half an hour before the expected time of departure of the scheduled Viscount flight from Victoria Falls to Bulawayo, Tungata had moved them into position: six men in a ring below the summit to guard against surprise attack by security forces, and three men above them in the actual attack group.

Tungata himself was the gunner, and his loader and back-up loader had both been chosen for the acuteness of their hearing and the sharpness of their eyesight. On each of the three preceding afternoon drills, they had been able to hear the turbo-prop Rolls-Royce Dart engines minutes after take-off. They were in climb power-setting, and the whine was distinctive, it drew the eye to the tiny crucifix shape of the aircraft against the blue.

On the first afternoon, the Viscount had climbed almost directly over their kopje, at not more than eight thousand feet in altitude, and Tungata had locked on and tracked it until it passed out of sight and then out of hearing. The second afternoon the aircraft had passed at about the same altitude, but five miles to the east of their position. That was extreme range for the missile. The audio-signal had been weak and intermittent, and the lock-on bulb had glowed only fitfully. Tungata had to admit to himself that an attack would probably have failed. The third day the Viscount had been east of them again, three miles out. It would have been a good kill, so that the odds seemed to be about two to one in their favour.

This fourth day he moved the attack team into position on the summit fifteen minutes early, and tested the SAM launcher by aiming it at the lowering sun. It howled in his ears at the excitation of that immense infra-red source. Tungata switched off the powerpack and they settled down to wait, all their faces lifted to the sky.

His loader glanced at his wristwatch and murmured, 'They are late.'

Tungata hissed at him viciously. He knew they were late, and already the doubts were crowding in – flight delayed or cancelled, even a leak in their own security, the *kanka* might already be on their way.

'Listen!' said his loader, and seconds later he heard it also, the faint whistling whine in the northern sky.

'Ready!' he ordered, and settled the shoulder-plate into position and switched on the powerpack. The audio-warning had been pre-set, but he checked it again.

'Load!' he said. He felt the missile go into the breech and

weight the barrel slightly tail-heavy. He heard the clunk of the rim seating itself against the terminals.

'Loaded!' his No. 2 confirmed and tapped his shoulder.

He traversed left and right, making certain he was firmly settled, and his loader spoke again. '*Nansi!* There!' He extended his arm over Tungata's left shoulder, and pointed upwards with his forefinger. Tungata searched, and then caught the high silver spark as the sunlight reflected off burnished metal.

'Target identified!' he said, and heard his two loaders move aside softly to avoid the back-blast of the rocket.

The tiny speck grew swiftly in size, and Tungata saw that it was tracking to pass less than half a mile to the west of the hillock, and that it was at least a thousand feet lower than it had been on the preceding afternoons. It was in a perfect position for attack. He picked it up in the cross-wires of the gun-sight, and the missile howled lustfully in his earphones, a wicked sound like a wolf-pack hunting at full moon. The missile had sensed the infra-red burn from the exhausts of the Rolls-Royce engines. In the gun-sight the lock-on bulb burned like a fiery red Cyclops' eye, and Tungata pressed the trigger.

There was a stunning whoosh of sound, but almost no recoil from the weapon across his shoulder as it exhausted through the funnel vent in the rear. He was enveloped for micro-seconds in white fumes and whirling dust, but when they were whipped away by their own velocity, he saw the little silver missile going upwards into the blue on the feather of its own rocket vapours. It was like a hunting falcon bating from the gloved fist, going up to tower above its quarry. Its speed was dazzling, so that it seemed to dwindle miraculously into nothingness, and there was only the faint drumming rumble of its rocket-burn.

Tungata knew that there was no time for a second launch. By the time they could re-load, the Viscount would be well out of range. They stared up at the tiny shiny aircraft and the seconds seemed to flow with the slow viscosity of honey.

Then there was a little flick of liquid silver that distorted the perfect cruciform of the aircraft's wing profile. It popped open like a ripe cotton pod, and the Viscount seemed to lurch and yaw, then steady again. Seconds later they heard the crack of the strike to confirm what they had seen, and a hoarse roar of triumph burst up out of Tungata Zebiwe's throat.

As he watched, the Viscount banked into a gentle turn, then abruptly something large and black detached itself from the port wing, and fell away towards the earth. The aircraft dropped its nose sharply, and the engine noise rose into a shrill wild whine.

Standing in the control tower, staring out through the floor-to-ceiling non-reflective glass window into the mellow evening sky, and listening to the rapid tense exchanges between the flight controller and the Viscount pilot, Roland Ballantyne was held in a paralysing vice of helplessness and rage.

'Mayday! Mayday! Mayday! This is Viscount 782, do you copy, tower?'

'Viscount 782, what is the nature of your emergency?'

'We have taken a missile strike on our port engine housing. We are engine out.'

'Viscount 782, I query your assessment.'

The pilot's tension and stress flared. 'Damn you, tower, I was in 'Nam. It's a SAM hit, I tell you. I have activated the fire-extinguishers and we still have control. I am initiating a one hundred and eighty-degree turn!'

'We will have all emergency standby here, Viscount 782. What is your position?'

'We are eighty nautical miles outbound.' The pilot's voice cracked. 'Oh God! The port engine has gone. It's fallen clean out of her.'

There was a long silence. They knew the pilot was fighting for control of the crippled machine, fighting the asymmetrical thrust of the remaining engine which was trying to flip the Viscount over into a graveyard spiral, fighting the enormous weight transfer caused by the loss of the port engine. In the control tower they were all frozen in silent agony, and then the radio speaker crackled and croaked. 'Rate of descent three thousand feet a minute. Too fast. I can't hold her. We are going in. Trees, too fast. Too many trees. This is it! Oh mother, this is it!'

Then there was no more.

In the control tower Roland sprang back to the flight planning desk, and snapped at the assistant controller.

'Rescue helicopters!'

'There's only one helicopter within three hundred miles. That's your one coming in from Wankie.'

'The only one, are you sure?'

'They have all been pulled out for a special op. in the Vumba mountains, yours is the only one in this zone.'

'Get me in touch with it,' he ordered, and took the microphone from the controller as soon as contact was established.

'This is Ballantyne, we have lost a Viscount with forty-six crew and passengers,' he said.

'I copied the transmissions,' the helicopter pilot answered.

'You are the only rescue vehicle, what is your ETA?'

'I'm fifty minutes out.'

'What personnel do you have aboard?'

'I have Sergeant-Major Gondele and ten troopers.'

Roland had planned to rehearse night jump-landings during the return to Wankie. Gondele and his Scouts would be in full combat gear, and they would have Roland's personal pack and weapons aboard.

'I'll be waiting on the tarmac for your pick-up. We will have a doctor with us,' he said. 'This is Cheetah One standing by.'

J anine Ballantyne had the aisle seat, in the second last row on the port side of the Viscount. In the window seat was a teenage girl with braces on her teeth and her hair in pigtails. The girl's parents were in the seats directly in front of her.

'Did you go to the crocodile farm?' she demanded of Janine.

'We didn't get around to it,' Janine admitted.

'They have got a huge big croc there, he's five metres long. They call him Big Daddy,' the girl burbled.

The Viscount had stabilized in its climb attitude, and the seatbelt lights went out. From the seat behind Janine the blue-uniformed hostess stood up and went forward along the aisle.

Janine glanced across the aisle, across the two empty seats, through the Perspex porthole. The lowering sun was a big sullen red ball, wearing a moustache of purple cloud. The forest roof was a sea of dark green that spread away in all directions below them, its monotony broken by an occasional pimple of higher ground.

'My daddy bought me a T-shirt with Big Daddy on it, but it's in my case—'

There was a shattering crash, a great swirling silver cloud obscured the portholes, and the Viscount lurched so wildly that Janine was hurled painfully against her safety-belt. The air hostess was flung upwards against the roof of the cabin, and she fell back like a broken doll and lay twisted across the back of one of the empty seats. There was a cacophony of shrieks and screams from the passengers and the girl clung desperately to Janine's arm, shrilling incoherently. The cabin tilted sharply but smoothly as the aircraft banked, and then suddenly the Viscount plunged forward and swung viciously from side to side.

The safety-belt held Janine in her seat, but it felt like an insane roller-coaster ride down the sky. Janine leaned over and hugged the child to try and still her piercing screams. Although her head was being whipped from side to side, Janine got a glimpse out of the porthole, and saw the horizon turning like the spokes of a spinning-wheel, and it made her feel giddy and nauseated. Then abruptly she focused on the silver wing of the aircraft below her. Where the streamlined engine-nacelle had been was a ragged hole. Through it she could see the fluffy roof of the forest. The torn wing was flexing and twisting, she could see the wrinkles appearing in the smooth metal skin. Her ears were popping and creaking with the violent pressure-change, and the trees were rushing towards her in a sombre green blur.

She tore the child's arms from around her neck and forced her head down into her own lap. 'Hold your knees,' she shouted. 'Keep your face down.' And she did herself what she had ordered.

Then they hit, and there was a deafening rending, roaring, crashing tumult. She was flung mercilessly about in her seat, tumbled and battered, blinded and stunned and hammered by flying pieces of debris.

It seemed to go on for ever. She saw the roof above her clawed away and blinding sunlight struck her for an instant. Then it was gone, and something hit her across one shin. Clearly, above all the other sounds, she heard her own bone break, and the pain shot up her spine into her skull. End over end she was hurled, and then another blow in the back of the neck and her vision exploded into shooting sparks of light through a black singing void.

When she recovered consciousness, she was still in her seat, but hanging upside down from her safety-strap. Her face felt engorged with the blood that had flowed into it, and her vision wavered and swam like a heat mirage. Her head ached. It felt as though a red-hot nail was being driven into the centre of her forehead with a sledgehammer.

She twisted slowly, and saw that her broken leg was hanging down in front of her face, the toe pointing where the heel should have been.

'I will never walk again,' she thought, and the horror of it braced her. She reached for the release on the buckle of her safety-belt, and then remembered how many necks are broken from a release in the upside-down position. She hooked her elbow through the arm of her seat, and then lifted the release. Her hold on the seat flipped her as she fell and she landed on her hip with her broken leg twisted under her. The pain was too much and she lost consciousness again.

It must have been hours later that she woke again for it was almost dark. The silence was frightening. It took her many groggy seconds to realize where she was, for she was looking at grass and treetrunks and sandy earth.

Then she realized that the fuselage of the Viscount had been severed just in front of her seat, as though by a guillotine; the tail section was all that was left around her. Over Janine's head the body of the child who had been her seating partner still hung by its strap. Her arms dangled below her head, and her blonde pigtails pointed at the earth. Her eyes were wide open, and her face contorted with the terror in which she had died.

Janine used her elbows to crawl out of the shattered fuselage, dragging her leg behind her and she felt the coldness and nausea of shock sweep over her. Still on her stomach, she retched and vomited until she was too weak to do anything else but let herself sink back into the darkness in her head. Then she heard a sound in the silence, faint at first, but growing swiftly in volume.

It was the wackety-wackety-wack of a helicopter's rotors. She looked up at the sky, but it was shrouded by the roof of the forest overhead, and she realized that the last rays of daylight had gone and the swift African night was rushing down upon the earth.

'Oh please!' she screamed. 'Here I am. Please help me!' But the sound of the helicopter grew no louder, it seemed to pass only a few hundred metres from where she lay under the concealing trees, and then the sound of its rotors receded as swiftly as the darkness came on, and at last there was silence.

'A fire,' she thought. 'I must start a signal fire.'

She looked around her wildly, and almost within reach of where she lay was the crumpled body of the blonde girl's father who had been in the seat in front of her. She crawled to him, and touched his face, running her finger lightly over his eyelids. There was no flicker of response. She sobbed and drew back, and then steeled herself and returned once more to search the dead man's pockets. The disposable Bic plastic cigarette-lighter was in the side pocket of his jacket. At the first flick it gave her a pretty yellow flame, and she sobbed again – this time with relief.

Roland Ballantyne sat in the co-pilot's seat of the Super Frelon helicopter and peered down at the tree-tops only two hundred feet below him. It was so dark that the occasional clearing in the forest was a mere pale leprous patch. There was no definition in the tree-tops, they were a dark amorphous mattress. Even when the light had been stronger, the chances of spotting the wreckage below the tree-tops had been remote. Of course there was the possibility that part of a wing or tail-section had torn off and been left hanging high up, and in easy view. However, they could not trust to that.

At first they were looking for damage to the tree-tops, a blaze of lopped branches or the tell-tale white splotches of torn bark and raw wet wood. They were looking for a signal flare, or for smoke or the chance reflection of the late sun off bare metal, but then the light started to go. Now they were flying in desperation, waiting for, but not really believing, they would see a signal flare or a torch or even a fire.

Roland turned to the pilot and shouted in the rackety cabin.

'Landing lights. Switch them on!'

'They will overheat and burn out in five minutes,' the pilot bellowed back. 'No good!'

'One minute on, and one minute off to cool again,' Roland told him. 'Try it.' The pilot reached for the switch and below them the forest was lit with the cruel bluish-white glare of the phosphorous lamps. The pilot dropped even closer to the earth.

The shadows below the trees were stark and black. In one clearing they trapped a small herd of elephant. The animals were monstrous and unearthly in the flood of light, with their tentlike ears extended in alarm. Then the helicopter bore on and plunged them back into utter darkness.

Back and forth they flew, covering the corridor which the Viscount must have followed on her outward track, but that was one hundred nautical miles long and ten wide, one thousand square miles. It was full night now, and Roland glanced at the luminous dial of his wristwatch. It was nine o'clock, almost four hours since the Viscount had gone in. If there were survivors, they would be dying now, from the cold and shock, from loss of blood and internal injuries, while here in the main cabin of the Super Frelon there was a doctor, with twenty quarts of plasma, with blankets – with the chance of life.

Grimly Roland stared down into the brilliant circle of white light as it danced over the tree-tops like the spotlight over a theatrical stage, and there was a cold and desolate despair in him that seemed slowly to numb his limbs and paralyse his resolve. He knew she was down there, so close, so very close, and yet he was helpless.

Suddenly he bunched his right fist and slammed it into the metal partition at his side. The skin smeared from his knuckles and the pain shot up his arm to the shoulder, but the pain was a stimulant, and in it he found his anger again. He cupped the anger to him, the way a man shelters a candle-flame in a high wind.

In the seat beside him the pilot checked the time-lapse on his stopwatch and then switched off the landing lights to cool them. The blackness that followed was more intense for the brilliance that had preceded it. Roland's night-sight was destroyed, his vision filled with wriggling insects of starred light, and he was forced to cover his eyes with his hands for a few seconds to rest them and let them re-adjust.

So he did not see the tiny dull red spark down below him that showed through the forest tops for the smallest part of a second, and then was left behind as the Super Frelon roared back on the next leg of its search pattern.

Janine had gathered a pile of dried grass and twigs, and built them up into a cone ready for the flame of the lighter. It had been difficult work. She had dragged herself slowly backwards on her buttocks and hands, with her broken leg sliding along after her as she gathered the kindling from the nearest bushes. Each time her leg caught or twisted over an irregularity of the torn earth, she almost fainted again with the pain.

Once she had the fire ready, she had laid the plastic lighter beside it, and fallen back to rest. Almost immediately the night cold struck through her thin clothing and she began to shiver uncontrollably. It required an enormous effort of will to force herself to move again, but she started back towards the shattered tail-section of the Viscount. It was still just light enough to make out the trail of devastation that the main forward-section of the aircraft had smashed through the forest.

There were pieces of metal and burst luggage and bodies littered down this dreadful pathway, although the main wreckage, carried on by its own weight, was not in sight from where she lay.

Once again Janine called, 'Is anybody there, is anybody else alive?' But the night was silent. She dragged herself on.

The lighter tail-section in which Janine had been seated must have struck one of the larger trees as the fuselage broadsided, and it had been sheered off neatly. The whiplash of impact had broken the necks of the passengers around her – only the fact that Janine had been leaning forward with her face pressed into her lap had saved her.

Janine reached the severed tail end, and raised herself to peer in, avoiding looking at the body of the teenage girl which still hung upside-down from her inverted seat. The storage cupboards forward of the aircraft's galley had broken open and in the gloom she could make out a treasure-house of blankets and canned food and drink. She dragged herself inchingly towards it. The feel of a woollen blanket around her shoulders was a blessed boon, and then thirstily she drank two cans of bitter lemon before searching further through the spilled and jumbled contents of the storage cupboard.

She found the first-aid kit and splinted and strapped her

leg as best she could. The relief was immediate. There were disposable syringes and a dozen ampoules of morphine in the kit. The prospect of a surcease from agony was an acute temptation, but she knew it would dull her and inactivity or the inability to respond swiftly would be mortally dangerous in the long hours of darkness that lay ahead. She was still playing with the temptation when she heard the helicopter again.

It was coming swiftly towards her – she dropped the syringe and lunged clumsily towards the gaping hole in the fuselage. She tumbled out onto the dusty earth, a fall of almost three feet, and the pain of her leg anchored her for seconds. Then, through it, she heard the whistle and throbbing beat of the helicopter coming towards her.

She clawed her fingers into the earth, and bit into her bottom lip until she tasted blood in her mouth to subdue the pain as she dragged herself towards the pile of kindling. By the time she reached it, the helicopter engine was a vast roaring in her head, and the sky above the forest was lightening with a bluish-white glow. She flicked the plastic lighter, and held the tiny flame to the dried grass. It flared up swiftly.

She lifted her face to the sky and in the light of the fire and the growing glare of the landing-lights, her cheeks were smeared with dust and dried blood from the cut in her scalp, and wet with the new tears of mingled agony and hope that slid from under her swollen eyelids.

'Please,' she prayed. 'Oh sweet merciful God, please let them see me.'

The landing-lights grew stronger, dazzling, blinding – and then suddenly went out. Darkness struck her like a club. The sound of the helicopter passed over her, and she felt the buffeting down-draught of air from the rotors. For a brief instant she saw the black shark-like shape of it silhouetted against the stars – and then it was gone, and the sound of the spinning rotors sank swiftly into silence.

In that silence she heard her own wild shrieks of despair. 'Come back! You can't leave me! Please come back!'

She recognized the hysteria in her own voice, and thrust her fist into her mouth to gag it, but still the savage uncontrollable sobs racked her whole body, and the coldness of the night was made unbearable by the icy grip that despair had upon her.

She crawled closer to the fire. She had been able to gather only a few handfuls of twigs. It would not last long, but the cheerful yellow and orange flames gave her a brief warmth and a moment of comfort in which to regain control. She gave one last choking gasping sob and bit down upon it. She closed her eyes and counted slowly to ten, and felt herself steadying.

She opened her eyes, and across the fire from her, at the level of her own eyes, she saw a pair of canvas jungle boots. Slowly, she lifted her eyes and shaded them from the fire with one hand. She made out the form of a man, a tall man, and the flickering light of the fire lit his face. He was looking down at her with an expression she could not fathom, perhaps it was compassion.

'Oh, thank you, God,' Janine whispered. 'Oh, thank you.' She began to drag herself towards the man. 'Help me,' she croaked. 'My leg is broken – please help me.'

Standing on the peak of the kopje, Tungata Zebiwe watched the stricken aircraft tumble down the sky like a high-flying duck hit by shot. He threw the empty rocket-launcher aside, and he lifted both hands above his head, fists clenched, and shook them in triumph to the heavens.

'It is done,' he roared, 'they are dead!' His face was swollen with the raging blood of the berserker, and his eyes

594

were smoky like the glow of slag upon the tip, when it comes red-hot from the blast furnace.

Behind him his men shook their weapons above their heads, caught up like Tungata in the divine killing madness of the victors, the atavistic instinct come down from their forefathers who had formed the fighting bull, and raced in on the horns to the stabbing.

As they watched, the Viscount fell towards the forest top, and then at the very last moment it seemed to check. The nose of the tiny silver machine came up out of its death dive, and for a fleeting few seconds it seemed to fly parallel with the earth, but still sinking fast. Then it touched the tree-tops, and was instantly snatched from view, but the crash site was so close that Tungata had been able to hear, if only very faintly, the shattering impact of metal against trees and earth.

'Mark it!' Tungata sobered. 'Comrade, the hand-bearing compass! Get a fix on it!' He re-measured the distance with his eye. 'About six miles, we can be there by dark.'

They moved out from the base of the kopje in their running formation, in the haft and spearhead, the flanks covering the bearers of the heavy equipment and the point breaking trail and clearing for ambush. They moved fast, at a pace just below a jog-trot that would carry them seven kilometres to the hour. Tungata was running the point himself, and every fifteen minutes he halted and went down on one knee to check the bearing on the hand-compass. Then he was up, and with an overhead pump of his fist signalled the advance. They went on, swiftly and relentlessly.

As the light started to fade, they heard the helicopter, and Tungata gave the side-arm cut-out signal that dropped them into cover. The helicopter passed a mile to the east, and he got them up and took them on for ten minutes more, before stopping again.

He brought in his wing-men, and told them quietly, 'We are here, the machine is lying within a few hundred metres of us.'

They looked around them at the forest, the tall twisted columns of treetrunks seemed to reach as high as the darkening heaven. Through a chink in the leafy roof of the forest the evening star was a bright white prick of light.

'We will go into extended line,' Tungata told them, 'and sweep along the line of bearing.'

'Comrade Commissar, if we stay too late, we will not be able to reach the river tomorrow. The *kanka* will be here at first light,' one of his men pointed out diffidently.

'We will find the wreck,' Tungata said. 'Do not even think otherwise. That is why we have done this. To lay a trail for the *kanka* to follow. Now let us begin the search.'

They moved like grey wolves through the forest, Tungata keeping them in line and on direction with a code of bird-whistles like those of a nightjar. They went southwards for twenty minutes by his watch, and then he pivoted his line, and they went back, moving silently, bowed under their packs, but with the AK 47 rifles held at high port across their chests.

Twice more Tungata pivoted his line, and they searched back and forth, and the minutes drained away. It was past nine o'clock, there was a limit to how much longer he dared remain in the area of the wreck. His man had been right. First light would bring the avengers swarming out of the skies.

'One hour more,' he told himself aloud. 'We will search one hour more.' Yet he knew that to leave without laying a hot scent for the jackals to follow was to abandon the most important part of the operation. He had to entice Ballantyne and his *kanka* to the killing ground that he had chosen so carefully. He had to find the wreck, and leave something there for the *kanka* that would madden them, that would bring them rushing after him without regard to any of the consequences.

He heard the helicopter then, still far off, but coming back swiftly. Then he saw the glow of its landing-lights on the tree-tops, and he gave the signal to put his line into cover. The helicopter passed within half a kilometre of where they lay. Its glaring eye confused and jumbled up the shadows beneath the trees, making them run across the forest floor like ghostly fugitives.

Abruptly the light was quenched, but the memory of it left a hot red spot on the retina of Tungata's eyeballs. They listened to the engine beat dwindle, and then Tungata whistled his men to their feet, and they went forward once more. Within two hundred paces Tungata stopped again, and sniffed the dank cold air of the forest.

Wood smoke! His heart jumped against his ribs, and he gave the soft warbling bird-call that presaged danger. He slipped out of the shoulder-straps of his heavy backpack and lowered it gently to earth. Then the line went forward again, moving lightly and silently. Ahead of Tungata something large and pale loomed from the darkness. He flicked his flashlight on. It was the nose-section of the Viscount, the wings sheared off it, the fuselage shattered. It lay on its side, so that he could flash his beam through the windscreen into the cockpit. The dead crew were still strapped into their seats. Their faces were bloodless pale, their eyes staring and glassy.

The line of guerrillas moved on quickly down the swath that the machine had hacked from the forest for itself. It was strewn with wreckage and debris, with clothing from the burst luggage-hold, with books and newspapers that fluttered aimlessly in the small night breeze. In the litter, the corpses seemed strangely peaceful and relaxed. Tungata turned his flashlight into the face of a grey-haired middle-aged woman. She lay on her back with no visible injury.

Her skirts were tucked modestly down below her knees, and her hands relaxed at her sides. However, her false teeth had been flung from her mouth and it gave her the look of an ancient crone.

He passed her and went on. His men were stopping every few paces to hunt swiftly through the clothing of the dead, or to examine an abandoned handbag or briefcase. Tungata wanted a live one. He needed a live one, and the dead were scattered all about him.

'The smoke,' he whispered. 'I smelled smoke.'

And then ahead of him, at the very edge of the forest line, he saw a pretty little flower of flame, flickering and wavering in the gentle movement of air. He changed his grip on the rifle and slipped the selector onto semi-automatic fire. From the shadows he searched the area around the fire carefully and then stepped up to it. His jungle boots made no sound.

There was a woman lying beside the fire. She wore a thin yellow skirt, but it was stained with blood and dirt. The woman lay with her face in her arm. Her whole body was racked with gasping sobs. Her one leg below the skirt was roughly bound up with wooden splints and field bandages. Slowly she raised her head. In the feeble firelight her eyes were dark as those of a skull, and the pale skin, like her clothing, was smeared with blood and dirt. She raised her head very slowly until she was looking up at him, and then words came tumbling out of her swollen lips.

'Oh, thank you, God,' she blurted, and began to crawl towards Tungata, the leg slithering along behind her. 'Oh, thank you. Help me!' Her voice was so hoarse and broken that he could barely understand the words. 'My leg is broken – please help me!' She reached out and clasped his ankle.

'Please,' she blubbered, and he squatted down beside her.

'What is your name?' he asked very gently, and his tone touched her, but she could not think – could not even remember her own name.

He started to stand, but she reached out in dreadful fear of being left alone again. She seized his hand.

'Don't go, please! My name – I'm Janine Ballantyne.'

He patted her hand, almost tenderly, and he smiled. The quality of that smile warned her. It was savagely, joyfully triumphant. She snatched her hand away and pushed herself to her knees. She looked wildly about her. Then she saw the other dark figures that crowded out of the night around her. She saw their faces, the white gleam of teeth as they grinned down at her. She saw the guns in their hands and the glittering stare in their eyes.

'You,' she gasped. 'It's you!'

'Yes, Mrs Ballantyne,' Tungata said softly. 'It is us.'

He stood up and spoke to the men about him. 'I give her to you. She is yours. Use her – but do not kill her. On your own lives, do not kill her – I want to leave her here alive.'

Two of the men stepped forward and seized Janine's wrists. They dragged her away from the fire, behind the tail-section of the wreckage. The other comrades laid down their rifles and followed them. They were laughing and bickering quietly over the order of preference and beginning to loosen their clothing.

At first the screams from the darkness were so shrill and harrowing that Tungata turned away and squatted over the fire, feeding it with twigs to distract himself, but very soon there were no more screams, only the soft sound of sobbing, and the occasional sharper cry immediately muffled.

It went on for a long time, and Tungata's early disquiet was submerged and controlled. There was no passion or lust in this thing. It was an act of violence, of extreme provocation to a deadly enemy, an act of war, without guilt or compassion, and Tungata was a warrior.

One by one his men came back to the fire, adjusting their clothing. Strangely, they were subdued and stony-faced.

'Is it over?' Tungata looked up, and one of them stirred

and half rose, looking enquiringly at Tungata. Tungata nodded.

'Be quick then,' he said. 'It is only seven hours to first light.'

Not all of them went back behind the wreckage, but when they were ready to move out, Tungata did so.

Ballantyne's woman's naked white body was curled in the foetal position. She had chewed her lips until they were raw meat, and she blubbered softly and monotonously through them.

Tungata squatted beside her and took her face in his hands and twisted it up until he could look into her eyes. He shone his flashlight into them. They were the eyes of a wounded and terrified animal, perhaps she had already crossed over the line between sanity and madness. He could not be certain, so he spoke slowly as though to a retarded child.

'Tell them my name is Tungata Zebiwe, the Seeker after what has been Stolen – the Seeker after Justice, after Vengeance,' he said, and he stood up.

She tried to roll away from him, but pain stopped her and as she covered her groin with both hands he saw the thin spurt of fresh blood from between her fingers. He turned from her and picked up her stained yellow skirt from where it had been tossed over a bush. As he strode back to the fire, he stuffed the skirt into his pocket.

'*Lungela!*' he said. 'All right, it is done. Move out!'

At midnight the pilot yelled across at Roland Ballantyne. 'We are almost out of fuel, we must go back. They have a tanker waiting for us on the apron.'

For a few moments Roland did not seem to understand. In the greenish reflection of the instrument panel his face was expressionless, but his mouth was a thin cruel slash and his eyes were terrible.

'Go quickly,' he said. 'And get back here quickly.'

On the tarmac the Scouts' own doctor, Paul Henderson, was waiting to take over from the GP that Roland had picked up at Victoria Falls. Once he was aboard, Roland led Sergeant-Major Gondele a little apart from the other troopers.

'If only we could know which way the bastards are headed,' he murmured. 'Are they going south, or are they heading back for the river? Are they going to try the drifts – and if so, which one?'

Esau Gondele recognized in him the need to talk, to say something merely to take his mind off the horror of what awaited them out there in the dark forest.

'We won't be able to follow them with the bird,' he said. 'The forest is too thick. They would hear us from five miles and disappear.'

'We can't follow with the chopper,' Roland agreed. 'They have got a SAM-7 with them. They would chop us out of the sky. The helicopter could be suicide – only way is to cut their spoor and go after them on foot.'

'They will have a night's start, a full night.' Esau Gondele shook the great black cannonball of his head doubtfully.

'The cat cannot resist mauling the dead bird,' Roland said. 'Perhaps they have not yet started to run, perhaps they are drunk with blood, perhaps we can still take them.'

'Ready to go!' the pilot shouted as the fuel-tanker started up and backed away from the Super Frelon, and they ran back to the open port in the fuselage and scrambled aboard. The helicopter lifted swiftly, not wasting time in climbing, and roared away low over the dark bush.

At ten minutes to five o'clock the following morning, long before the sun had pushed up above the horizon, but when the light was already strong enough to make out shapes and colours, Roland slapped the pilot's shoulder and pointed to port. The pilot banked the Super Frelon sharply in that direction. It was a broken branch, the underside of the leaves were lighter in colour than those around it, it had been a flag to catch Roland's eye. Then there was another fleck of white, the raw stump of freshly broken branch sticking into the morning light. The pilot checked the Frelon, and they hovered fifty feet above it. They were staring down through the leafy canopy, and something white fluttered in the down-draught of the rotors.

'Go down!' Roland shouted, and as they sank lower, suddenly it was all there, broken wreckage and the debris of the dead, blowing aimlessly about in the windstorm of the rotors.

'There is a clearing!' Roland pointed, and as the helicopter settled towards it, the Scouts spilled out of her, jumping from fifteen feet to the earth and immediately spreading out into a defensive perimeter. Then Roland deployed them into a line of skirmishers and they went forward into the swath-line in quick rushes, ready to meet enemy fire. Within minutes they had cleared the area.

'Survivors!' Roland snapped. 'Search for survivors!'

They went back down the swath, and in the dawn light the carnage was horrific. Beside each corpse a Scout paused briefly, but they were cold and stiff and the men went on. Roland reached the nose-section, and glanced through the windscreen. There was nothing to do for the crew until the long green plastic body-bags arrived. He turned back, searching frantically, looking for a scrap of bright yellow, the colour of Janine's skirt.

'Colonel!' There was a faint shout from the forest edge.

Roland sprinted towards it. Sergeant-Major Gondele was standing by the shattered tail-section of the aircraft.

'What is it?' Roland demanded harshly, and then saw her.

Esau Gondele had covered Janine's naked body with a blue airways blanket from the wreck. She lay curled under it like a sleeping child with just her tousled head showing. Roland dropped on his knee and gently lifted the corner of the blanket. Her eyes were closed with swollen purple bruises and her lips were raw chewed flesh. For seconds he did not recognize her, and when he did, he believed that she was dead. He laid his open palm upon her cheek, and the skin was moist and warm.

She opened her eyes. They were mere slits in the abused flesh. She looked up at him, and the dull lifeless eyes were more frightening than her torn and battered flesh. Then the eyes came alive – with terror. Janine screamed, and there was the ring of madness in the sound.

'Darling.' Roland caught her up in his arms, but she fought him wildly, still screaming. Her eyes were mad and staring. Fresh blood oozed from the cracked scabs on her lips.

'Doctor!' Roland yelled. 'Here! On the double!' and it took all his strength to hold her. She had thrown off the blanket, and naked she kicked and lashed out at him.

Paul Henderson came at the run, and tore open his pack. He filled a syringe and muttered, 'Hold her still!' as he swabbed her skin. He pressed in the needle and squeezed the clear contents of the syringe into her arm. She went on fighting and screaming for almost a minute and then gradually quietened and relaxed.

The doctor took her from Roland's arms, and nodded to his assistant. The young medic orderly held up a blanket as a screen and the doctor laid Janine on another.

'Get out of here,' he snapped at Roland, and began his examination.

Roland picked up his rifle and stumbled to the tail-section of the Viscount. He leaned against it, and his breathing was hoarse and ragged, but slowly it eased and he pushed himself upright.

'Colonel, sir.' Esau Gondele appeared beside him. 'We have picked up their spoor, incoming and outgoing.'

'How long ago?'

'Five hours at the least, probably longer.'

'Be ready to move out. We are going after them.' Roland turned away from him. He needed to be alone just a little longer, he was not yet entirely under control.

Two of the Scouts came from the helicopter at a trot, carrying one of the yellow plastic body-moulded stretchers between them.

'Colonel!' Paul Henderson tucked the blue blanket carefully around Janine's body and then he and the orderly lifted her tenderly onto the yellow stretcher and tightened the straps to hold her. While the orderly prepared the plasma drip, the doctor led Roland a little aside.

'It's not very good news,' he said, softly.

'What did they do to her?' Roland asked, and Paul Henderson told him. Roland gripped the stock of the rifle so hard that his arms began to shudder and the muscle in his forearms stood out in ridges and hard knots.

'She is bleeding internally,' Henderson finished. 'I have to get her into theatre very quickly. A theatre that can handle this type of surgery, Bulawayo.'

'Take the helicopter,' Roland ordered brusquely.

They ran with the stretcher to the Super Frelon. The orderly holding the drip-bottle high.

'Colonel,' Henderson looked back. 'She is still conscious. If you want—' He did not finish. The little group waited for Roland beside the fuselage, not certain whether to load the stretcher aboard.

With a strange reluctance, Roland walked heavily towards them. The enemy had used his woman. She was one thing that was sacred. How many of them? The thought made him check, and he had to force himself to go on to where she lay on the stretcher. He looked down at her. Only her face showed above the blanket. It was grotesquely swollen, and her mouth was a raw red ruin. Her once-lustrous hair was stiff with filth and dried blood, but her eyes were clear. The drug had driven back the madness, and now she was looking up at him. Only the eyes were the same, dark indigo blue.

Painfully her damaged lips framed a word, but no sound came. It was his name she was trying to say.

'Roland!'

And his revulsion rushed upon him, he could not hold it back. How many of them had taken her that way, a dozen, more? She had been his woman, but that had been destroyed. He tried to fight it, but he felt nauseated, and quick cold sweat chilled his face. He tried to force himself to stoop over her, to kiss that terribly battered face, but he could not. He could not speak nor move, and slowly the light of recognition went out in her eyes. It was replaced by that dull empty look he had seen before, and then she closed the livid swollen lids over them and rolled her head slowly away from him.

'Take good care of her,' Roland muttered hoarsely, and they lifted the stretcher into the helicopter. Paul Henderson turned to him, his face twisted with pity and helpless anger, and he laid his hand on Roland's arm.

'Roly, it wasn't her fault,' he said.

'If you say anything more, I might kill you.' Roland's voice was thickened and coarsened by disgust and hatred.

Paul Henderson turned from him and clambered into the machine. Roland made a wind-up signal to the pilot in the bubble windscreen above him, and the big clumsy aircraft lifted noisily into the sky.

'Sergeant-Major,' Roland called. 'Take the spoor!' and he did not look back as the helicopter rose high into the pink dawn and then swung away southwards.

They went in deep formation, so that if they ran into an ambush, the tail could circle and outflank the attackers to free the head. They went at storming speed, much too fast for safety, going hard as marathon runners. Within the first hour Roland had ordered his Scouts to strip their packs. They abandoned everything but the radio set, their weapons and water-bottles and first-aid kits, and Roland pushed the pace still harder.

He and Esau Gondele took turns at point, the one dropping back each hour as the other came forward. They lost the spoor twice in stony ground but each time picked it up on the first cast ahead. It was running true and straight, and they had quickly made the number of the chase as nine men. Within two hours Roland knew each of them as individuals by the spoor they left behind them, the one with a nick in his left heel, flat-foot, long-one with a gap of over a metre in his stride, and each of the others with more subtle characteristics to differentiate them. He knew them, and he hungered for them.

'They are going for the drifts,' Esau Gondele grunted as he came up and took over the point from Roland. 'We should radio ahead and set a patrol for them.'

'There are twelve drifts, forty miles. A thousand men wouldn't do it.' Roland wanted them for himself, all nine of them. One look at his face and Esau Gondele realized that. He picked up the run of the spoor. They were crossing an open glade of golden grass. The chase had left a sweep line through the grass, the stems still bent in the direction of their flight, and the sunlight reflected at a different intensity from these. It was like following a highway. They went down it at a swinging easy run, and ahead of him Esau Gondele saw some of the grass stems springing upright again. They were that close already, and it wasn't yet noon. They had cut at least three hours off the lead that the ZIPRA cadres had upon them.

'We can catch them before the river – we can have them for ourselves,' Esau Gondele thought fiercely, and resisted the temptation to lengthen his stride. They could move no faster, an inch more on his stride would put a term on their endurance, whereas at this pace they could run the sun down and the moon up.

At two in the afternoon they lost the spoor again. They were on a long low ridge of black ironstone, and the ground took no prints. As soon as Esau Gondele lost contact, the line stopped dead, and went into a defensive attitude, only Roland moved up and knelt out on his flank, keeping good separation so that a single burst could not take them both.

'How does it look?' Roland brushed the tiny mopani bees from his eyes and nostrils. They were maddeningly persistent in their hunt for moisture.

'I think they are going straight in.'

'If they are going to twist, this is the place to do it,' Roland answered, he wiped his face on his forearm and the greasy camouflage paint came away in a dirty brown and green smear.

'If we cast ahead again we may lose half an hour,' Esau Gondele pointed out, 'three kilometres.'

'If we run blind we may lose more than that, we may never make them again.' Roland looked around thoughtfully at the mopani forest along the ridge. 'I don't like it,' he decided at last. 'We will make a cast.'

The two of them circled out beyond the ridge, and as Esau Gondele had warned, it cost them half an hour of their gain, but they did not make the cut. There was no spoor on the direct line that they had been following, the chase had turned.

'They can only have followed the ridge, we have a one-on-one choice. East is away from the drifts, I don't believe they would chance it. We will run the western ridge blind,' Roland decided, and they turned and went on harder than before, for they were rested and they had the lost half-hour to make up. Roland ran with doubt gnawing his guts, and rocky black ironstone crunching under his boots.

Esau Gondele was far out on his right flank, on the softer earth below the ridge, watching for the point where the chase left it and turned northwards towards the river again – if it ever did.

Roland could not cover the southern edge of the ridge as well, the ironstone belt was too wide. It would mean splitting his meagre forces. The south side was his blind side. If they had doubled, or turned eastwards, then he had lost them. The thought of that was unbearable. He clenched his jaws until they ached and it felt as though his teeth might splinter, and he checked his watch – they had been on the ridge forty-eight minutes. He was making the conversion of time to distance in his head when he saw the birds.

There were four of them, two brace of sandgrouse, and they were flighting in that peculiar quick-winged slant that made their intention unmistakable.

'They are going down to water,' Roland said aloud, and marked their descent below the tree-tops before signalling to Esau Gondele.

The water was a pothole in the mopani, a relic of the last rains. Twenty metres in diameter, most of it black mud, trampled by the game herds to the consistency of putty. The nine sets of man-prints were perfectly cast in it, going directly to the puddle of muddy water in the centre, and then once again heading directly northwards towards the river. They were onto the chase again, and Roland's hatred burned up brightly once more.

'Drain your bottles,' he ordered. There was no profit in adulterating what remained of their sweet water with that filthy coffee-coloured liquid in the pan. They drank greedily and then one man collected their bottles and went out across the mud to refill them. Roland would not risk more of his troopers than was necessary out there on the exposed pan.

It was almost four o'clock by the time they were ready to take the spoor again, and by Roland's reckoning, they were still ten miles from the river.

'We can't let them get across, Sergeant-Major,' he told him quietly. 'From now on we won't hold back, push all out.'

The pace was too hard, even for superbly trained athletes such as they were. If they ran into contact now, they would be blown, almost helpless during the long minutes it would take to recover – but they reached the Kazungula road unchallenged.

There had been no security patrol over the gravel surface for at least four hours. They found where the chase had taken the precaution of reconnoitring the road and sweeping away the signs of their crossing. That had cost them precious minutes, and the Scouts were within an ace of contact. The patch of earth where one of the terrorists had urinated was still muddy wet. The sandy earth had not had time to absorb it, nor the sun to evaporate it. They were minutes behind. It was folly to go in at the run, but as they crossed the road, Roland repeated, 'All out!' And when he saw the flicker of Esau Gondele's eyes as he looked back, Roland went on, 'Take number two, I will lead.'

He led at full run, hurdling the low thorn scrub in his path, relying only on his own speed to survive the first volley when they made the contact, knowing that even if the terrs took him out he could leave Esau Gondele and his men to finish it for him. Survival no longer was important to Roland, all that mattered was to make the contact and destroy them, as they had destroyed Janine.

Yet when he saw the flash of movement and colour in the scrub ahead of him, he went belly-down from full run and made two quick rolls to the side, to spoil the aim. He was onto the target an instant later, and fired a short burst, one light touch on the trigger and the FN hammered into his shoulder. Then as the echoes fled there was complete silence. No return fire, and his Scouts were down in cover behind him, not firing until they had a target.

He signalled Esau Gondele. 'Stay and cover me!' and went up on his feet, keeping low, rushing forward, jinking and twisting.

He dropped to the ground again beside a thornbush. In the thorny branches above his head was the thing that had drawn his fire. It flapped again on the hot little breeze off the river. It was a woman's skirt, soft fine cotton, bright buttercup yellow, but stained with dried blood and dirt.

Roland reached up and tore the skirt off the thorns, he bundled it in his fist and pressed his face into the cloth. Her perfume still lingered, very faintly but unmistakably. Roland found himself on his feet running forward with all his strength, with all his hatred, driven on by a madness that was at last out of control.

Ahead of him through the trees he saw the warning markers along the edge of the *cordon sanitaire*. The little red-painted skulls seemed to taunt him, to goad him on. He did not check as he passed them, nothing was going to stop him now, ahead of him stretched the minefield. Something smashed into the back of Roland's knees, and he was thrown to earth, the wind driven from his lungs, but immediately he was trying to struggle up. Esau Gondele tackled him again, dragged him back from the edge, and they swayed together, straining chest to chest.

'Let me go!' Roland panted. 'I have to—'

Esau Gondele got his right arm free and crashed his fist into Roland's face, into his cheek, knocking his head across, half-stunning him, then taking instant advantage of his shock by twisting his arm up between his shoulder-blades and dragging him back. Clear of the minefield, he threw Roland to earth again, and dropped down beside him, pinning him with one massive black arm.

'You crazy bastard, you'll get us all killed,' he snarled into Roland's face. 'You were into it already – just one more step—'

Roland stared at him uncomprehendingly, like a sleeper waking from a nightmare.

'They have gone through the *cordon*,' Esau hissed at him. 'They have got clear. It's finished. They have gone.'

'No,' Roland shook his head. 'They haven't got away. Get the radio up here. We can't let them get away.'

Roland used the security network, the calling channel was 129.7 megahertz.

'All units, this is Cheetah One – come in, any station,' he called quietly, but with the edge of desperation in his voice. The power on the set was only four watts, and Victoria Falls was thirty miles or so downriver. The only reply was the hum and burr of static.

He switched to the aviation frequencies, and tried Vic Falls approach on 126.9. Still no reply, he clicked over to tower and keyed the microphone.

'Tower, this is Cheetah One. Come in, please.'

There was a whisper, scratchy and faint.

'Cheetah One, this is Victoria Falls tower, you are transmitting on a restricted frequency.'

'Tower, we are a unit of Ballantyne's Scouts, we are in hot pursuit.'

'Cheetah One, is your chase the gang that Sammed the Viscount?'

'Tower, that's affirmative!'

'Cheetah One, you have our full co-operation.'

'I need a chopper to lift us over the *cordon sanitaire*. Do you have one on the plot?'

'Negative, Cheetah One. One fixed-wing aircraft available.'

'Stand by.'

Roland lowered the microphone, and stared out across the minefield. It was so narrow. It would take twenty seconds to cross it, but it might have been the Sahara.

'If they send a vehicle to pick us up – we can fly from Vic Falls and make a para-jump on the far bank,' Esau Gondele muttered beside his ear.

'No good. It will take two hours—' Roland broke off. 'By God, that's it!' He thumbed the key of the microphone.

'Tower, this is Cheetah One.'

'Go ahead, Cheetah One.'

'There is a police armourer at Victoria Falls Hotel. Name, Sergeant Craig Mellow. I want him dropped on my position soonest possible to open the minefield. Telephone the hotel.'

'Stand by, Cheetah One.' Tower's thin whisper faded and they lay in the sun and sweated, burned up by the heat and their hatred.

'Cheetah One, we have Mellow. He is already *en route* to the field. We will make the delivery with a silver Beechcraft Baron. RUAC markings. Give us a position and a recognition.'

'Tower, we are on the *cordon sanitaire*, estimate thirty miles upstream from the falls. We will give you a white phosphorous grenade.'

'Roger, Cheetah One. I understand white smoke marker. In view of SAM danger, we can only make one pass at low level. Expect delivery in twenty minutes.'

'Tower, we are running out of daylight, tell them to hurry it up, for God's sake, those bastards are going to get clean away.'

Esau Gondele had the grenade-launcher fitted to the muzzle of his FN rifle. They heard the faint beat of twin aircraft engines coming from downstream, and Roland touched Esau's arm.

'Ready?' he asked.

The sound of the engines built up swiftly. Roland raised

himself into a kneeling position and stared into the east. He saw the flash of silver just on the tree-tops and he tapped Esau's shoulder.

'Now!'

There was the crack of the blank cartridge and the grenade lobbed up and over in a lazy parabola, fired away from the minefield towards the Kazungula road. The grenade exploded, and a column of white smoke leaped above the brown sun-seared bush. The small twin-engine aircraft banked gently towards the marker, and then steadied again.

The passenger door had been removed, leaving a square opening above the wing root. In the opening crouched a familiar lanky figure with the cross-webbing of the parachute harness coming out of his crotch over his chest and shoulders. The bulky chute package dangled low against the back of his legs. He wore a paratrooper's helmet and goggles, but his legs were brown and bare and his feet were thrust into plain suede velskoen.

The Beechcraft was very low – perhaps too low. Roland felt a stab of anxiety, Sonny was no Scout. He had done his eight jumps for his paratrooper wings, but they were standard jumps from four thousand feet. The Beechcraft was barely two hundred feet above the bush. The pilot was taking no chances with incoming SAM fire.

'Make another pass,' Roland shouted. 'You are too low.'

He crossed his arms overhead, waving them off, but as he did it the wind-battered figure in the hatch of the Beechcraft dropped head-first over the trailing edge of the silver wing. The tail seemed to slash at him like an executioner's axe, skimming his back, and the long ribbon of the rip-cord flirted out behind him, still attached to the speeding machine like an umbilical cord.

Craig dropped like a stone towards the earth, and watching him Roland felt his breath jam in his throat. Abruptly the silk streamed from the chute pack, flared open with an audible snap like a whiplash and Craig was plucked violently erect, his legs rodding out stiffly under him, almost touching the earth. For a long second he seemed to be suspended there like a man on the gallows, and then he dropped and rolled on his back with his feet together but high above him. Another roll and he was on his feet, sawing the parachute cords to collapse the blooming silk mushroom.

Roland let his breath out. 'Bring him in,' he ordered.

Two of the Scouts hustled Craig forward, with a grip on each arm, forcing him to crouch and run. He dropped beside Roland who greeted him harshly. 'You have to get us through, Sonny, as quick as you can.'

'Roly, was Janine on the Viscount?'

'Yes, damn you, now get us through.'

Craig had opened his light pack, and was assembling his tools, probe and side-cutters and rolls of coloured tape, steel tape-measure and hand-compass.

'Is she alive?' Craig could not look at Roland's face for the answer, but he started to tremble as he heard it.

'She's alive, but only just—'

'Thank God, oh thank God,' Craig whispered, and Roland studied his face thoughtfully.

'I didn't realize that you felt that way, Sonny.'

'You never were very perceptive.' At last Craig looked up at him defiantly. 'I loved her from the first moment I saw her.'

'All right, then you will want to get these bastards as much as I do. Open that field, and hurry.' Roland signalled and his Scouts moved up quickly and lay along the edge of the minefield, their weapons pointing forward. Roland turned back to Craig.

'Ready?'

Craig nodded.

'You know the pattern?'

'You'd better pray I do.'

'Get in there, Sonny,' Roland ordered, and Craig stood

614

up and walked into the minefield and started to work with the probe and the tape-measure.

Roland contained his impatience for less than five minutes, then he called, 'Christ, Sonny, we have two hours of daylight – how long is this going to take?'

Craig did not even look around. He was stooped like a potato harvester, probing the earth gently, and the sweat had soaked through the back of his khaki shirt in a long dark stain.

'Can't you hurry it up?'

With all the concentration of a surgeon clamping off an artery, Craig snipped the piano-wire trip of a Claymore mine, and then laid the coloured tape on the earth behind him, as he moved forward a pace. It was their thread through the labyrinth that Craig was laying.

Craig probed again. He had chosen an unfortunate point to enter the pattern on an overlap of two separate systems. Ordinarily he would have retraced his steps along the coloured tape, and begun again at another point on the perimeter, but that could cost him precious time, perhaps as much as twenty minutes.

'Craig, you are bloody standing still,' Roland called. 'Christ, man, have you lost your nerve?'

Craig flinched at the accusation. He should have checked the pattern to his left, there should be an AP at a 30-degree angle from the last one he had found, and a twenty-four-inch gap between them, if he had correctly read the pattern. To check it would mean two minutes' work.

'Move, damn you, Mellow!' Roland's voice lashed him. 'Don't just stand there. Move!'

Craig steeled himself, the chance was three-to-one in his favour. He stepped forward one pace, and gingerly put his weight onto his left foot. It was firm. He took another pace, placing his right foot with the delicacy of a cat stalking a bird, firm again. Now the left foot, a droplet of sweat fell from his brow into his eye, flooding it and half-blinding him. He blinked it away and completed the step. Safe again.

There must be a Claymore mine on his right now. His legs were trembling, but he lowered himself into a squat. The wire, it wasn't there! He had mis-read the pattern. He was blind in the middle of the field, living on chance. He blinked his eyes rapidly, and then with a surge of relief he picked up the almost invisible wire exactly where it should have been. It seemed to quiver with tension like his own nerves. He reached out with the side-cutters, and had almost touched the wire when Roland's voice spoke just at his shoulder.

'Don't waste time—'

Craig started violently and jerked his hand away from the deadly wire. He looked back. Roland had followed the coloured tape marker; he had come out into the minefield, and he was down on one knee with his FN rifle across his thigh only a pace behind Craig. His face was masked with a thick layer of camouflage paint, like some primitive warrior from another time, savage and monstrous.

'I am going as fast as I dare.' Craig used his thumb to squeeze the heavy drops of nervous sweat from his eyebrows.

'You aren't,' Roland told him flatly. 'You have been in here almost twenty minutes, and you haven't moved twenty paces. It will be dark before we get through if you chicken it.'

'Damn you!' Craig whispered hoarsely.

'Yes,' Roland encouraged. 'Get mad. Get fighting mad.'

Craig reached forward and snipped the trip-wire. It made a tiny quivering spring like a guitar string lightly plucked with a fingernail.

'That's it, Sonny. Move!' Roland's voice was at his back, a low monotonous litany.

'Think of those bastards, Sonny. They are out there, running like rabid jackals. Think of them getting away.'

Craig moved forward, taking each pace more firmly.

'They killed everybody on that Viscount, Craig. Every-body, men and women and children. Everybody except her.' Roland did not use her name. 'They left her alive. But when I found her, she couldn't speak, Sonny. She could only scream and struggle like a wild animal.'

Craig stopped dead, and looked back. His face was icy pale.

'Don't stop, Sonny. Keep going.'

Craig stooped and probed quickly. The AP was there, exactly where it should be. He went forward into the corridor with quick short steps and Roland's dry cold whisper was in his ear.

'They had raped her, Sonny, all of them. Her leg was broken in the crash, but that didn't stop them. They got on top of her, like rutting animals one after the other.'

Craig found himself running forward up the invisible corridor, merely counting his paces, not using the tape-measure to check the length of it, not using the compass to measure the angle of the turn.

At the end he fell flat and stabbed frantically into the earth with the probe, but Roland's voice was there behind him.

'When they had all finished, they started again,' he whispered. 'But this time they rolled her over and sodomized her, Sonny—'

Craig heard himself sob with each stroke of the probe. He hit the casing of a mine lying just under the surface, and the force of the blow jarred his arm. He dropped the probe and scratched with his fingers into the earth, exposing the circular top of the AP mine. It was the size of one of those old-fashioned tins of fifty Players Navy Cut cigarettes. Craig lifted it out of its cavity, set it aside and went forward, but Roland's whisper followed relentlessly.

'One after the other they did it to her, Sonny, all except the last one. He couldn't manage it twice, so he took his bayonet and pushed that up her instead.'

'Stop it, Roly! For Chrissake, stop it!'

'You say you love her, Sonny – then hurry, for her sake, hurry!'

Craig found the second AP mine and plucked it from the earth, he hurled it away from him down the length of the minefield and it bounced and rolled like a rubber ball before disappearing into a clump of grass. It did not explode. Craig clawed his way forward, stabbing the probe ferociously as though into the heart of one of them, and he found the third mine, the last one in the ninety-degree corner of the corridor.

It was open all the way to the opposite perimeter of the minefield, where there would be two Claymore trip-wires. Craig jumped to his feet and ran down the corridor, with violent death only inches on each side of his flying feet. He was almost blinded by his own tears, and he sobbed in time to his run. He reached the end of the corridor and stopped. Only the trip-wires now, only the trip-wires of the Claymores and they would be through the *cordon sanitaire*.

'Well done, Sonny,' Roland's voice close behind, 'well done, you've got us through.'

Craig changed the side-cutters into his right hand and took one step more. He felt it move under the sole of his right foot, the almost infinitesimal give, as though he had stepped on a subterranean mole-run and it had collapsed.

'It shouldn't have been there,' he thought despairingly, and time seemed to be suspended.

He heard the click of the primer. It sounded like the release of a camera-shutter, but muted by the thin layer of sand over it.

'The wild one,' he thought, and still time was frozen. He had time to think. 'It's the wild one in the pattern.' And nothing happened, just that click. He felt a spring of hope. 'It's dud, it's a misfire.' He was going to get away with it.

Then the mine exploded under his right foot. It felt as though someone had hit him with a full swing of a crow-bar under the sole. There was no pain, just that stunning slam of shock into his foot, driven up his spine until his jaws clashed and he felt his tongue split between his teeth, bitten clean through.

No pain, just the deafening implosion of the shockwave into his eardrums, as though somebody had held a double-barrelled shotgun close to his head and fired both barrels together.

No pain, just the blinding rush of dust and smoke past his face, and then he was flung into the air as though he were the plaything of a callous giant, and he came down again on his belly. The wind driven from his lungs, so he wheezed for breath, his mouth filled with blood from his bitten tongue. His eyes were stinging from flying grit and smoke. He wiped them clear and Roland's face was in front of his, hazy and wavering like a heat mirage. Roland's lips were moving, but Craig could not hear the words. His ears buzzed viciously from the blast.

'It's all right, Roly,' he said, and his own voice was almost lost in the singing memory of the explosion. 'I'm all right,' Craig repeated.

He pushed himself up and rolled into a sitting position. His left leg stuck straight out ahead of him, the inside of the calf was lacerated and discoloured purple black from the explosion, and blood oozed from out of the opening of his short khaki pants, shrapnel must have flown up into his buttocks and lower belly, but the velskoen was still on his left foot. He tried to move his foot and it responded immediately, waggling at him reassuringly.

But there was something wrong. He was dazed and groggy, his ears still dinning, yet through it he realized there was something dreadfully wrong – and then gradually it dawned on him.

There was no right leg, just the short fat stump of it sticking out of the leg of his pants. The heat of the explosion had cauterized the raw end of the stump, and seared it white, the dead bloodless white of frostbite. He stared at it, and knew it was a trick of his eyesight, because he could *feel* his leg was still there. He tried to move the missing foot, and he *felt* it move, but there was nothing there.

'Roly.' Even through the din in his ears, he heard the high hysterical tone of his own voice. 'Roly, my leg. Oh God, my leg! It's gone!'

Then at last the blood came, bursting through the heat-seared flesh in bright arterial spurts.

'Roly, help me!'

Roland stepped over him, squatting with a foot on each side of Craig's body, his back to Craig, screening him from his own mutilated lower body. Roland unrolled the canvas wallet that contained his field medical kit, and strapped the tourniquet from it around the stump. The haemorrhage shrivelled and he bound the field-dressing over the stump. He worked quickly, with the dexterity of practice and experience, and the second that he finished, he swivelled to look into Craig's pale dusty sweat-streaked face.

'Sonny, the Claymores. Can you do the Claymores? For her sake, Sonny, try!'

Craig stared at him. 'Sonny – for Janine,' Roland whispered, and pulled him up into a sitting position. 'Try! For her sake, try!'

'Side-cutters!' Craig mumbled, staring with great hurt eyes at the blood-soaked turban that wrapped his stump. 'Find my side-cutters!'

Roland pressed the tool into his hand.

'Turn me onto my belly,' Craig said.

Roland rolled him carefully, and Craig began to slide himself forward; walking his elbows in the torn dusty earth, he dragged his one remaining leg over the shallow crater left by the exploding AP mine, and then stopped and reached forward. There was the guitar twang, as the first trip-wire parted in the jaws of the cutter, and, laboriously as a maimed insect squashed under a gardener's heel, Craig dragged himself onto the very edge of the minefield. For the last time he reached out. His hand was shaking wildly, and he seized his own wrist with his left hand to steady it; sobbing with the effort he guided the open jaws of the cutter over the hair-thin steel wire, and bore down. It went with a ping, and Craig dropped the tool.

'Okay, it's open,' he sobbed, and Roland pulled the lanyard out of the vee of his shirt, and lifted the whistle to his lips. He blew a single crisp blast, and pumped his arm over his head.

'Let's go!'

The Scouts came through the minefield at a run, keeping their rigid ten-pace separation, following the zigzag of the tape that Craig had laid down the corridor to guide them. As each one of them came to where Craig still lay on his belly, they jumped lightly over his back and melted away into the open bush, beyond the minefield, spreading out into their running formation. Roland lingered a second longer at Craig's side.

'I can't spare anyone to stay with you, Sonny.' He laid the medical kit beside his head. 'There is morphine for when it gets too bad.'

He laid something else beside the medical kit. It was a hand-grenade. 'The terrs may get to you before our boys do. Don't let them take you. A grenade is messy, but effective.' Then Roland leaned forward and kissed Craig on the forehead. 'Bless you, Sonny!' he said, and then he was on his feet going forward again at a run. Within seconds, the thick riverine Zambezi bush had swallowed him, and slowly Craig lowered his face into the crook of his arm.

Then, at last, the pain came at him like a ravening lion.

Commissar Tungata Zebiwe crouched in the bottom of the slit trench, and listened to the husky voice speaking from the portable radio.

'They are through the minefield, coming down to the river.'

His observers were on the north bank of the Zambezi, in carefully prepared positions from which they could sweep the opposite bank and the small heavily wooded islands that split the shallows of the wide river-course.

'How many?' Tungata asked into the microphone.

'No count yet.'

Of course, they would be mere flickers of movement in the darkening bush, impossible to get a head count, as they came forward in overlapping covering rushes. Tungata looked up at the sky, there was less than an hour before dark, he estimated, and felt a fresh onslaught of the doubts that had beset him ever since he had brought his cadre through the drifts almost three hours before.

Could he entice the pursuers into crossing the river? Without that, the destruction of the Viscount and all else that he had so far achieved would be halved in propaganda and psychological value against the enemy. He had to bring the Scouts across into the carefully prepared killing-ground. He had carried the woman's skirt and left it on the edge of the *cordon sanitaire* for just that purpose, to bring them on.

Yet he recognized that it would be an irrational act for any commander to take a small force across such a natural barrier as the Zambezi at the close of day with darkness only minutes away, into hostile territory against an enemy of unknown strength who must anticipate his arrival and who had been able to prepare for it at leisure. Tungata could not expect them to come – he could only hope.

It would depend chiefly upon who had command of the pursuers. The bait that he had laid to draw them in would be only truly effective on one man, the multiple rape and mutilation of the woman, the bloodied skirt would have their full effect only upon Colonel Roland Ballantyne himself. Tungata tried objectively to assess the chances that it was Ballantyne himself commanding the pursuit.

He had been at Victoria Falls Hotel, ZIPRA agents had made a positive identification. The woman had called herself Ballantyne, the Scouts were the nearest and most effective force in the area. Surely they must be the first to the site of the wreck, and surely Ballantyne would be with them. Tungata had to allow himself a better than even chance that his operation was working as planned.

Tungata's first confirmation that the pursuit was close had been a little before four o'clock that afternoon, when there had been one short burst of automatic fire from the south bank. At that moment, Tungata's cadre had just completed the crossing of the drift. They were still soaked and lying panting, like hunting-dogs too hard run, and Tungata had been chilled to realize how close the Scouts had been behind them, despite the many hours' start they had had and the fierce pace that Tungata had forced on his men. Twenty minutes more and they would have been caught on the south bank at the *cordon sanitaire*, and Tungata cherished no illusions as to what that would have meant. His men were the élite of the ZIPRA forces, but they were no match for Ballantyne's Scouts. On the south bank they would have been doomed, but now that they were across the Zambezi, the advantage had swung dramatically. Tungata's preparations to receive the pursuing force had taken fully ten days, and had been carried out with the full co-operation of the Zambian army and police force.

The radio crackled again and Tungata lifted the microphone to his lips and acknowledged curtly. The observer's voice was lowered, as though he feared it might carry to the dangerous quarry across the river.

'They have not attempted the crossing. Either they are waiting for dark, or they are not coming.'

'They must come,' Tungata whispered to himself, and then he keyed the microphone.

'Put up the flare,' he ordered.

'Stand by!' the observer answered, and Tungata lowered the microphone and looked up expectantly into the purple and rose of the evening sky. It was a risk, but then it had all been a risk, from the very moment they crossed the Zambezi carrying the SAM-7 launcher.

The signal flare streaked up into the sunset, and five hundred feet above the river it burst into a crimson ball of fire. Tungata watched it begin to sink gracefully towards the earth again. He found that he had driven his fingernails into the flesh of his palms with the strength of his grip upon the radio microphone.

The flare, fired so tantalizingly close to the river bank, from just behind the first line of trees on the north bank, could frighten them off and make them abandon the pursuit, or it could have the effect that Tungata hoped for. It could convince them how close they were to their quarry, and precipitate the cat-like reflex to follow anything that flees.

Tungata waited and the seconds dragged by. He shook his head, facing at last the prospect of failure, feeling the chill of it begin in the pit of his stomach and beginning to spread. Then the radio crackled, and the observer's voice was strained and hoarse:

'They are coming!' he said.

Tungata snatched the microphone to his lips. 'All units. Hold your fire. This is Comrade Tungata. Hold your fire.'

He had to pause then, his relief mixed with dread that at this last moment one of his nervous guerrillas might spring the trap prematurely. He had six hundred men deployed on the killing-ground, only regimental strength was sufficient for a detachment of *kanka*. With his own eyes Tungata had seen them fight, and anything less than odds of twenty to one in his favour would not be acceptable.

He had achieved his numerical advantage, but in his own

great numbers there was a concealed danger. Control was weakened, not all of his men were warriors of quality, amongst them there must be many of those who were nervous and susceptible to the mysterious aura, the almost superstitious awe, that surrounded the legend of Ballantyne's Scouts.

'All field commanders,' he kept repeating into the microphone, 'hold your fire. This is Commissar Comrade Tungata. Hold your fire.' Then he lowered the microphone and made one long last careful study of the ground in front of him.

The north bank of the river was almost a mile from where he waited. It was marked by a palisade of taller trees, the twisted trunks of great strangler figs and tall mkusi, their branches laden with trailing lianas, and higher even than these were the elegant bottle palms, their spiky fronds silhouetted against the blushing sunset. There was no glimpse of the river through this wall of lush growth.

Then abruptly the line of forest ended on this wide meadow-like opening. It was one of the Zambezi flood plains. In the rainy season, when the river burst its banks, this area would be inundated and transformed into a shallow lagoon filled with water-lilies and reeds, but now it had dried out, and the reeds had wilted and fallen, no longer providing cover for a pursuer, or a fugitive.

One of Tungata's main concerns had been to keep the soft surface of this wide pan uncontaminated by spoor and footprints. There had been a regiment encamped along its fringes for almost ten days now, a regiment digging the trench system and batteries for the mortars. Just one man wandering across the pan would have left a warning to the pursuers, but it had been kept clean.

The only spoor out there was that of the wild buffalo herds, of the dainty red puku antelope, and the tracks of nine men, the same tracks that led from the crash site of the Viscount, and which Tungata and his cadre had laid only three hours previously. These tracks emerged from the fringe of riverine bush and ran down the centre of the open flood plain to the higher forested ground on this side.

The carrier band of Tungata's radio hummed to life and the whisper of his observer warned, 'They are halfway across the drift.'

Tungata imagined the line of dark heads above the sunset-pink waters, looking like a string of beads on a bodice of velvet.

'How many?' Tungata asked.

'Twelve.'

Tungata felt a quick drop of disappointment. So few? He had hoped for more. He hesitated for a heartbeat before he asked: 'Is there a white officer?'

'Only one man in camouflage paint, he is at the head of the line.'

'It's Ballantyne,' Tungata told himself. 'It's the great jackal himself, it must be him.'

Again the voice spoke from the radio. 'They are across, into the trees. We have lost sight.'

Now, would they commit themselves to cross the flood plain? Tungata focused his night-glasses on the treeline. The specially ground and coated lens picked up every available ray of light – but still even through the lens the shapes of the trees and bushes beneath them were becoming indistinct. The sun had gone, and the last colours of the sunset were fading, the first stars were pricking the dark canopy of the night sky.

'They are still in the trees.' It was a different voice on the radio, deeper and harsher. One of the second line of observers covering the southernmost fringe of the pan.

Tungata gave another order into the microphone.

'Unscreen the fire!' he said quietly, and seconds later there was a tiny yellow glow of a camp-fire in the treeline furthest from the river. As Tungata stared at it through the night-glasses, a human figure passed in front of the low flames. It gave the perfect illusion of a quiet camp amongst the trees, where an unsuspecting quarry exhausted from the long chase, but believing themselves safe at last, were resting and preparing the evening meal. But was it too obvious a lure, Tungata wondered anxiously, was he relying too much upon the unbalanced rage of the pursuers?

His self-doubts were answered almost immediately. The gruff voice on the radio said suddenly, 'They have left the trees, they are crossing the pan.'

It was too dark now to make out anything at that range. He had to rely on the sighting of his forward posts, and he turned the luminous dial of his wristwatch so that he could see the sweep of the second-hand. The pan was one and a half kilometres across, at a run the Scouts would take approximately four minutes to cross it.

Without taking his eyes off the dial, Tungata spoke into the microphone. 'Mortars, stand by with star-shell.'

'Mortars, standing by!'

The second-hand completed its circuit of the dial, and started around again.

'Mortars, fire!' Tungata ordered.

From the forest behind him came that hollow clunking sound of three-inch mortars, and Tungata heard the flute of the mortar bombs rising swiftly overhead. Then suddenly, at the zenith of their trajectory, the star-shells burst.

They hung suspended on their tiny parachutes, and their light was a harsh electric blue. The open flood plain was illuminated like some gigantic sports stadium. The tiny group of running men in the centre were trapped in the naked glare, and their shadows on the earth beneath them seemed black and weighty as solid ironstone.

They went down instantly – but there was no cover. Even though they were flattened against the earth, their bodies formed sharply defined hummocks. But they were almost immediately obliterated by the leaping sheets of dust and flying clods of earth that sprang up around them like a bank of pale whirling fog. Tungata had six hundred men in the treeline surrounding the pan. All of them were firing now, and the hurricane of automatic fire swept over the huddled figures in the middle of the open pan.

From the mortar batteries set farther back in the forest, the bombs rose high over Tungata's head and then dropped into the open pan. The crack of their explosions added a sharp counterpoint to the background thunder of small-arms fire, and the mortar bursts jumped up like pale dust-devils in the light of the star-shells.

Nothing could live out there. The Scouts must long ago all be torn to shreds by shot and shrapnel, but still it went on and on, minute after minute, while more star-shells crackled into eye-searing bright sizzling blue light overhead.

Tungata panned his binoculars slowly over the drifting screen of dust and smoke. He could see no sign of life – and at last he shifted the microphone to order the ceasefire. But before he could speak, he saw movement, directly in front of his position, not two hundred paces distant, and out of the curtain of dust came two ghostly figures.

They came at a run, side by side, seeming to wade through the thick swamp of mortar-smoke and dust, and they appeared monstrous and inhuman in the stark light of the star-shells. One of them was a huge Matabele. He had lost his helmet and his head was round and black as a cannonball, his open mouth was a pink cave lined with ivory teeth, and his bull bellow rose above even that storm of gunfire. The other was a white man, the top of his battledress torn half off his body, exposing the pale flesh of chest and shoulders, but his face was daubed with fiendish streaks of dark green and brown paint.

The two of them were firing as they came on, and Tungata felt a stir of the superstitious dread that he had despised in his own troops, for they seemed immune to the storm of bullets through which they charged.

'Kill them!' Tungata heard his own voice screaming, and

a burst of FN fire from one of them kicked the top of the bank of loose earth in front of his slit trench.

Tungata ducked and ran to the gunner behind the heavy machine-gun at the end of the trench.

'Aim carefully,' he shouted, and the gunner fired a long thunderous burst, but the two figures ran on towards them unscathed.

Tungata pushed the man away from the gun and took his place. For infinite seconds he peered over the sights, making the tiny adjustments to the gun's elevation, and then he fired.

The tall Matabele was driven backwards, as though he had been hit by a runaway automobile, and then he seemed to disintegrate, breaking up like a straw man in a high wind as the bullets tore him to pieces. He melted into the surface of the pan.

The second man came on, running and firing, screaming an incoherent challenge, and Tungata swung the machine-gun onto him. He paused for a micro-second to make certain of his aim, and he saw the flash of hard white flesh through the gunsight, and the diabolically painted face above it.

Tungata fired, and the heavy gun pounded briefly in his hand, then jammed and was silent.

Tungata was frozen, completely in the grip of supernatural dread, for the man was still coming on. He had dropped his FN rifle, and half his shoulder was shot away. The shattered arm dangled uselessly at his side, but he was on his feet coming straight at Tungata.

Tungata jumped to his feet and pulled the Tokarev pistol from the webbing holster on his side. The man was almost at the trench now, not ten paces away, and Tungata pointed the pistol at him. He fired and saw the bullet strike in the centre of the naked white chest. The man dropped to his knees, no longer able to come forward, but straining to do so, reaching out towards his enemy with his one remaining arm, no sound coming out of the open blood-glutted mouth.

This close, despite the thick mask of camouflage paint, Tungata recognized him from that never-forgotten night at Khami Mission. The two men stared at each other for a second longer, and then Roland Ballantyne fell forward onto his face.

Slowly the great storm of gunfire from around the rim of the pan shrivelled and died away. Tungata Zebiwe climbed stiffly out of the trench and went to where Roland Ballantyne lay. With his foot he rolled him down the bank of earth onto his back, and with a sense of disbelief saw the eyelids quiver and then open slowly. In the light of the star-shells the green eyes that stared up at him still seethed with rage and hatred.

Tungata squatted beside the man, and said softly in English, 'Colonel Ballantyne, I am very pleased to meet you again.'

Then Tungata leaned forward, placed the muzzle of the Tokarev against his temple, just an inch in front of his earhole, and fired a bullet through Roland Ballantyne's brain.

The paraplegic section of St Giles' Hospital was a haven, a sanctuary into which Craig Mellow retreated gratefully.

He was more fortunate than some of the other inmates. He suffered only two journeys along the long green-painted corridor, the wheels of the trolley on which he lay squeaking unrhythmically, and the masked impersonal faces of the theatre sisters hovering above his, down through the double swing doors at the end, into the stink of asepsis and anaesthetic.

The first time they had built him a fine stump, with a thick cushion of flesh and skin around it to take the artificial limb. The second time they had removed most of the larger fragments of shrapnel that had peppered his crotch and buttocks and lower back. They had also searched, unsuccessfully, for some mechanical reason for the complete paralysis of his body below the waist.

His mutilated flesh recovered from the surgery with the rapidity of that of a healthy young animal, but the leg of plastic and stainless steel stood unused beside his bedside locker, and his arms thickened with muscle from lifting himself on the chain handles and from manipulating the wheelchair.

Swiftly he found his special niches in the sprawling old building and gardens. He spent much of his day in the therapeutic workshop working from the wheelchair. He stripped his old Land-Rover completely and rebuilt the engine, grinding the crankshaft and reboring the block. Then he converted it to hand controls, fitted handles and adapted the driver's seat to make it easier to swing his paralysed lower body in and out. He built a rack for the folding wheelchair where once the gun racks had been behind the front seat, and he resprayed the body a lustrous maroon colour.

When he finished work on the Land-Rover, he began designing and machining stainless-steel and bronze fittings for the yacht, working hour after hour on the lathes and drilling presses. While his hands were busy he found he could crowd out the haunting memories, so he lavished care and total concentration on the task, turning out small masterpieces in wood and metal.

In the evenings he had his reading and his writing, though he never read a newspaper, nor watched the television set in the hospital common room. He never took part with the other patients in any discussion of the fighting or of the complicated peace negotiations which commenced with such high hopes and broke down so regularly. That way, Craig could pretend to himself that the wolves of war were not still hunting across the land.

Only at night he could not control the tricks his mind and memory played upon him, and once again he sweated with terror in an endless minefield, with Roly's voice whispering obscenities in his ears, or he saw the electric glare of star-shells in the night sky above the river and heard the storm of gunfire. Then he would wake screaming, with the night nurse beside him, concerned and compassionate.

'It's all right, Craig, it was just one of your feemies. It's all right.' But it was not all right, he knew it would never be all right.

Aunty Valerie wrote to him. The one thing that tortured her and Uncle Douglas was that Roland's body had never been recovered. They had heard a horror story through the security forces' intelligence that Roland's bullet-riddled corpse had been put on public display in Zambia and that the guerrillas in the training camps had been invited to spit and urinate upon it to convince themselves that he was truly dead. Afterwards the body had been dumped into one of the pit latrines of the guerrilla training camp.

She hoped Craig would understand that neither she nor Uncle Douglas felt up to visiting him at present, but if there was anything he needed, he had only to write to them.

On the other hand, Jonathan Ballantyne came to visit Craig every Friday. He drove his old silver Bentley and brought a picnic-basket with him. It always contained a bottle of gin and half a dozen tonics. He and Craig shared it, in a sheltered nook at the end of the hospital gardens. Like Craig, the old man wanted to avoid the painful present, and they found escape together into the past. Each week Bawu brought one of the old family journals, and they discussed it avidly, Craig trying to glean every one of the old man's memories of those far-off days.

Only twice did they break their accord of forgetfulness and silence. Once Craig asked, 'Bawu, what has happened to Janine?'

632

'Valerie and Douglas wanted her to go and live at Queen's Lynn, when she was released from hospital, but she wouldn't go. As far as I know, she is still working at the museum.'

The next week it was Bawu who paused as he was about to climb back into the Bentley, and said, 'When they killed Roly, that was the first time I realized that we were going to lose this war.'

'Are we going to lose, Bawu?'

'Yes,' said the old man, and drove away leaving Craig in the wheelchair staring after the Bentley.

At the end of the tenth month at St Giles', Craig was sent for a series of tests that lasted four days. They X-rayed him and stuck electrodes to his body, they tested his eyesight and his reaction time to various stimuli, they scanned the surface of his skin for heat changes that would show nervous malfunction, they gave him a lumbar puncture and sucked out a sample of his spinal fluid. At the end of it, Craig was nervous and exhausted. That night he had another nightmare. He was lying in the minefield again, and he could hear Janine. She was in the darkness ahead of him. They were doing to her what Roland had described and she was screaming for him to help her. He could not move. When he woke at last, his sweat had formed a tepid puddle in the red rubber undersheet.

The next day the doctor in charge of his case told him, 'You did wonderfully in your tests, Craig, we are really proud of you. Now I am going to start a new course of treatment, I am sending you to Doctor Davis.'

Dr Davis was a young man with an intense manner and a disconcerting directness in his stare. Craig took an immediate dislike to him, sensing that he would seek to destroy the cocoon of peace which Craig had almost succeeded in weaving about himself. It was only after he had been in Davis' office for ten minutes that Craig realized that he was a psychiatrist.

'Look here, Doctor, I'm not a funny bunny.'

'No, you are not, but we think you might need a little help, Craig.'

'I am fine. I don't need help.'

'There is nothing wrong with your body or nervous system, we want to find out why you have no function in your lower body.'

'Listen, Doctor, I can save you a lot of trouble. The reason I can't move my stump and my one good kicker is that I stepped on an AP mine and it blew pieces of me all over the scenery.'

'Craig, there is a recognized condition, once they used to call it shell-shock—'

'Doctor,' Craig interrupted him. 'You say there is nothing wrong with me?'

'Your body has healed perfectly.'

'Fine, why didn't somebody tell me before?'

Craig wheeled his chair down the corridor to his room. It took him five minutes to pack his books and papers, then he wheeled himself out to the shiny maroon Land-Rover, slung his valise into the back, dragged himself up into the driver's seat, loaded the wheelchair into the rack behind him and drove out to the yacht.

In the St Giles' workshop he had designed and put together a system of pulley and hand winches to lift himself easily up the high side of the hull to deck-level. Now the other modifications to the yacht absorbed all his energy and ingenuity. Firstly he had to install grab handles to pull himself around the deck and cockpit and below decks. He sewed leather patches on the seat of his trousers and skidded around on his backside, as he adapted the galley and the head, lowered the bunk and rebuilt the chart-table to his new requirements. He worked with music blaring out from the speakers and a mug of gin within easy reach – music and liquor helped to chase away unwanted memories.

The yacht was a fortress. He left it only once a month,

when he went into town to pick up his police pension cheque, and to stock up his larder and his supply of writing-paper.

On one of these trips he found a second-hand typewriter, and a 'teach yourself to type' paperback. He screwed the carriage of the machine to a corner of the chart-table where it would be secure even in a gale at sea, and he began converting the mess of handwritten exercise books into neat piles of typescript; his speed built up with practice until he could make the keys chatter in time to the music.

Dr Davis, the psychiatrist, tracked him down at last, and Craig called down to him from the cockpit of the yacht.

'Look here, Doc, I realize now that you were right, I am a raving homicidal psychopath. If I were you, I wouldn't put a foot on that ladder.'

After that Craig rigged up a counter-balance so that he could pull the ladder up after him like a drawbridge. He let it down only for Bawu and each Friday they drank gin and built a little world of fantasy and imagination in which they both could hide.

Then Bawu came on a Tuesday. Craig was up on the foredeck reinforcing the stepping of the mainmast. The old man climbed out of the Bentley, and Craig's happy cry of welcome died on his lips. Bawu seemed to have shrivelled up. He looked ancient and fragile, like one of those unwrapped mummies in the Egyptology section of the British Museum. In the back of the Bentley was the Matabele cook from King's Lynn who had worked for the old man for forty years. Under Bawu's direction, the Matabele unloaded two large crates from the boot of the Bentley, and placed them in the goods lift.

Craig winched the crates up, and then lowered the lift for the old man. In the saloon Craig poured gin into the glasses, avoiding looking at his grandfather, embarrassed for his sake.

Bawu was truly an old man at last. His eyes were rheumy

and unfocused, his mouth slack so that he mumbled and sucked noisily at his lips. He spilled a dribble of gin down his shirt-front and didn't realize that he had done so. They sat in silence for a long time, the old man nodding to himself and making small incoherent grunts and burbles. Then suddenly he said:

'I've brought you your inheritance,' and Craig realized that the crates on the deck must contain the journals that they had haggled over. 'Douglas wouldn't know what to do with them anyway.'

'Thank you, Bawu.'

'Did I ever tell you about the time Mr Rhodes held me upon his lap?' Bawu asked with a disconcerting change of direction. Craig had heard the story fifty times before.

'No, you never did. I'd love to hear it, Bawu.'

'Well, it was during a wedding out at Khami Mission – must have been '95 or '96.' The old man bumbled on for ten minutes, before he lost the thread of the story entirely and lapsed into silence again.

Craig refilled the glasses, and Bawu stared at the opposite bulkhead, and suddenly Craig realized that tears were running down the withered old cheeks.

'What is it, Bawu?' he demanded with quick alarm. Those slow painful tears were a terrible thing to watch.

'Didn't you hear the news?' the old man asked.

'You know I never listen to the news.'

'It's over, my boy, all over. We have lost. Roly, you, all those young men, it was all for nothing – we have lost the war. Everything we and our fathers fought for, everything we won and built, it's all gone. We have lost it all over a table in a place called Lancaster House.'

Bawu's shoulders were shaking quietly, the tears still streaming down his face. Craig dragged himself across the saloon and lifted himself onto the bench beside him. He took Bawu's hand and held it. The old man's hand was thin and light and dry, like the dried bones of a dead seabird.

The two of them, old and young, sat holding hands like frightened children in an empty house.

O n the following Friday, Craig crawled out of his bunk early and did his housekeeping in anticipation of Bawu's regular visit. The previous day he had laid in half a dozen bottles of gin, so there was unlikely to be a drought, and he broke the seal on one of them and set it ready with the two glasses polished to a shine. Then he put the first three hundred pages of the typescript next to the bottle.

'It will cheer the old man up.' He had taken months to pluck up his courage sufficiently to tell Bawu what he was attempting. Now that another person was about to be allowed to read his typescript, Craig was seized by conflicting emotions; firstly by dread that it would all be judged as valueless, that he had wasted time and hope upon something of little worth, and secondly by a sharp resentment that the private world that he had created upon those blank white sheets was to be invaded by a trespasser, even one as beloved as Bawu.

'Anyway, somebody has to read it sometime,' Craig consoled himself and dragged himself down to the heads.

While he sat on the chemical toilet he could see his own face in the mirror above the hand-basin. For the first time in months he truly looked at himself. He had not shaved in a week, and the gin had left soft putty-coloured pouches under his eyes. The eyes themselves were hurt and haunted by terrible memories, and his mouth was twisted like that of a lost child on the verge of tears.

He shaved, and then switched on the shower and sat under it – revelling in the almost-forgotten sensation of hot suds. Afterwards, he combed his wet hair over his face and with the scissors trimmed it straight across the line of his eyebrows, then he scrubbed his teeth until the gums bled. He found a clean blue shirt, and then slid along the companionway, hoisted himself to deck-level, lowered the boarding-ladder, and found a place in the sun with his back against the coping of the cabin to wait for Bawu.

He must have dozed, for the sound of an automobile engine made him start awake, but it was not the whisper of the old man's Bentley, but the distinctive throb of a Volkswagen Beetle. Craig did not recognize the drab green vehicle, not the driver who parked it under the mango trees, and came hesitantly towards the yacht.

She was a dumpy little figure, of that indeterminate age that plain girls enter in their late twenties, and which carries them through to old age. She walked without pride, slumping as though to hide her breasts and the fact that she was a woman. Her skirt was bulky around her thick waist, and the low sensible shoes almost drew attention away from the surprisingly lovely lines of her calves and the graceful ankles.

She walked with her arms folded across her chest as though she was cold, even in the hot morning sunlight. She peered shortsightedly at the path through horn-rimmed spectacles, and her hair was long and lank, hanging straight and lustreless to hide her face, until she stood below the yacht side and looked up at Craig. Her skin was bad, like that of a teenager who was on junk food, and her face was plump, but with an unhealthy soft look, and a sickroom pallor.

Then she lifted the horn-rimmed spectacles from her face. The frames left little red indentations on each side of her nose, but the eyes, those huge slanted cat's-eyes with the strange little cast in them, those eyes so dark indigo blue as to be almost black – they were unmistakable.

'Jan,' Craig whispered. 'Oh God, Jan, is it you?'

She made a heart-breakingly feminine gesture of vanity – pushing the lank dull hair off her face, and dropped her eyes, standing awkwardly pigeon-toed in the dowdy skirt.

Her voice barely carried up to him. 'I'm sorry to bother you. I know how you must feel about me, but can I come up, please?'

'Please, Jan, please do.' He dragged himself to the rail and steadied the ladder for her.

'Hello,' he grinned at her shyly, as she reached the deck-level.

'Hello, Craig.'

'I'm sorry, I'd like to stand up, but you'll have to get used to talking down to me.'

'Yes,' she said. 'I heard.'

'Let's go down to the saloon. I'm expecting Bawu. It will be like old times.'

She looked away. 'You've done a lot of work, Craig.'

'She's almost finished,' he told her proudly.

'She's beautiful.' Janine went down from the cockpit into the saloon, and he lowered himself after her.

'We could wait for Bawu,' Craig said, as he placed a tape on the machine, instinctively avoiding Beethoven and selecting Debussy for a lighter happier sound. 'Or we could have a drink right now.' He grinned to cover his uneasiness and discomfort. 'And quite frankly I *need* one right away.'

Janine did not touch her glass, but sat staring at it.

'Bawu told me you were still working at the museum.'

She nodded, and Craig felt his chest constricted with helpless pity for her.

'Bawu will be here—' He searched desperately for something to say to her.

'Craig, I came to tell you something. The family asked me to come to you, they wanted somebody whom you knew to break the news.' Now she looked up from the glass. 'Bawu won't be coming today,' she said. 'He won't be coming ever again.'

After a long time Craig asked softly, 'When did it happen?'

'Last night, while he was sleeping. It was his heart.'

'Yes,' Craig murmured. 'His heart. It was broken – I knew that.'

'The funeral will be tomorrow at King's Lynn, in the afternoon. They want you to be there. We could go together, if you don't mind?'

T he weather changed during the night, and the wind went up into the southeast bringing with it the thin cold drizzling *guti* rain.

They laid the old man down amongst his wives and children and grandchildren in the little cemetery at the back of the hills. The rain on the freshly turned red earth piled beside the open grave made it seem as though the earth were bleeding from a mortal wound.

Afterwards, Craig and Janine drove back to Bulawayo in the Land-Rover.

'I'm staying at the same flat,' Janine said, as they drove through the park. 'Will you drop me there, please?'

'If I am alone now, I'll just get sad drunk,' Craig said. 'Won't you come back to the yacht, just for a little while, please?' Craig heard the pleading in his own voice.

'I'm not very good around people any more,' she said.

'Nor am I,' Craig agreed. 'But you and I aren't just people, are we?'

Craig made coffee for both of them, and brought it through from the galley. They sat opposite each other, and he found it difficult not to stare at her.

'I must look a sight,' she said, abruptly, and he did not know how to answer her.

'You will always be the most beautiful woman I have ever known.'

'Craig, did they tell you what happened to me?'

'Yes, I know.'

'Then you must know that I am not really a woman any more. I will never be able to let a man, any man, touch me again.'

'I can understand that.'

'That's one of the reasons that I never tried to see you again.'

'What are the other reasons?' he asked.

'That you would not wish to see me, to have anything to do with me.'

'That I don't understand.'

Janine was silent again, huddled on the bench seat, hugging herself with that protective gesture.

'Roly felt that way,' she blurted. 'After they were finished with me. When he found me there beside the wreck, when he realized what they had done to me, he could not even bear to touch me, not even to speak to me.'

'Jan—' Craig started, but she cut him off.

'It's all right, Craig. I didn't tell you to hear you deny it for me. I told you so that you would know about me. So that you would know that I have nothing left to offer a man that way.'

'Then I can tell you that, like you, I have nothing to offer a woman – that way.'

There was quick and real pain in her eyes. 'Oh Craig, my poor Craig – I didn't realize – I thought it was just one leg—'

'On the other hand, I can offer someone friendship and caring, and just about everything else.' He grinned at her. 'I can even offer a shot of gin.'

'I thought you didn't want to get drunk.' She smiled back at him gently.

'I said sad drunk, but we should give Bawu a little wake. He would have liked that.'

They sat facing each other across the saloon table, chatting in desultory fashion, both of them beginning to relax as the gin warmed them and gradually they recaptured some of that long-lost camaraderie that they had once enjoyed.

Janine explained her reasons for not accepting the invitation of Douglas and Valerie to live at Queen's Lynn. 'They look at me with such pity, that I start to feel it all over again. It would be like going into a state of perpetual mourning.'

He told her about St Giles', and the way he had absconded. 'They say it's not my legs, but my head that prevents me from walking. Either they are crazy or I am – I prefer to think that it's them.'

He had two steaks in the refrigerator, and he grilled them on the gas while she made a dressing for the salad, and while they worked he explained all the modifications that he had made to the layout of the yacht.

'With the roller boom, I would be able to shorten or make sail without leaving the cockpit,' he chatted on. 'I bet that I could manage her single-handed. It's a pity I'm not ever going to have the chance.'

'What do you mean?' She stopped with an onion in one hand and a knife in the other.

'My darling is never going to feel the kiss of salt water on her bottom,' he explained. 'They have impounded her.'

'Craig, I don't understand.'

'I applied to the exchange control authorities for a permit to ship her to the coast. You know what they are like, don't you?'

'I've heard they are pretty rough,' she answered.

'Rough? That's like calling Attila the Hun unkind. If you try to get out of the country, even as a legal emigrant, they allow you to take out only a thousand dollars' worth of goods or cash. Well, they sent an inspector round and he valued the yacht at two hundred and fifty thousand. If I want to take it out, I have to make a cash deposit of a quarter of a million dollars, a quarter of a million! I have a little over ten thousand dollars between me and prostitution, so until I come up with another two hundred and forty thousand, here I sit.'

'Craig, that's cruel. Couldn't you appeal? I mean in your special circumstances?' She stopped herself when she saw the little arrowhead of a frown appear between his eyes. Craig brushed over the reference to his disability.

'You can see their point of view, I suppose. Every white man in the country wants to get out before the big black baddies take over. We would strip the country bare if there was no control.'

'But, Craig, what are you going to do?'

'Stay here, I suppose. I don't have much alternative. I'll sit here and read Hiscock's *Voyaging Under Sail* and Mellor's *Cruising Safe and Simple*.'

'I wish there was something I could do to help.'

'There is. You can lay the table and hook a bottle of wine out of the cupboard.'

Janine left more than half her steak, and drank little of the wine, then she wandered across the saloon to examine his collection of tapes.

'Paganini's *Capricci*,' she murmured, 'now I know you are a masochist.' And then her attention was attracted to the neat square pile of the typescript on the shelf beside the tapes.

'What is this?' She turned the first few sheets, and then looked up at him. Those beautiful blue eyes in the once beautiful face, that was now swollen and distorted with fat and speckled about the chin with angry little blemishes, made his heart plunge. 'What is it?' And then, seeing his expression, 'Oh, I'm sorry. It's none of my business.'

'No!' he said, quickly. 'It's not that. It's just that I don't really know what it is—' He couldn't call it a book, and it would be pretentious to call it a novel. 'It's just something I have been fiddling with.'

Janine riffled the edges of the sheets. The pile was over twelve inches deep. 'It doesn't look like fiddling,' she chuckled, the first time he had heard her laugh since their reunion. 'To me it looks like deadly earnest!'

'It's a story I have been trying to write down.'

'May I read it?' she asked, and he felt panic rising in him.

'Oh, it wouldn't interest you.'

'How do you know?' She lugged the huge typescript to the table. 'May I read it?'

He shrugged helplessly. 'I don't think you will get far, but if you would like to try—'

She sat down and read the first page.

'It's still very rough, you must make allowances,' he said.

'Craig, you still don't know when to shut up, do you?' she said, without looking up. She turned the page.

He took the plates and glasses through to the galley and washed them, then he made coffee and brought the pot to the saloon table. Janine did not look up. He poured her a mug, and she did not look up from the page.

After a while he left her and slid through to his cabin. He stretched out on the bunk, and picked up the book he was reading from the bedside table. It was Crawford's *Mariners' Celestial Navigation*, and he began to wrestle distractedly with zenith distances and azimuth angles. He woke with Janine's hand on his cheek. She jerked her fingers away as he sat up hurriedly.

'What time is it?' he asked groggily.

'It's morning, I have to go. I didn't sleep all night. I don't know how I will get through work today.'

'Will you come back?' he demanded, coming full awake.

'I have to, I have to finish reading. I would take it with me, but I'd need a camel to carry it, it's so big.'

She stood over the bunk looking down at him, with a strange speculation in those slanted dark blue eyes.

'It's difficult to believe that was written by somebody I thought that I knew,' she mused softly. 'I realize that I really knew very little about you at all.' She glanced at her watch. 'Oh, my gosh! I have to fly!'

She parked the VW under the mango trees beside the yacht a little after five o'clock that evening.

'I have brought the steaks,' she called, 'and the wine.' She came up the ladder and ducked down into the saloon. Her voice floated up to him in the cockpit, 'But you'll have to cook them. I can't spare the time, I'm afraid.' By the time he got down into the saloon, she was already seated and completely engrossed in the massive typescript.

It was long past midnight when she turned the last page. When she had finished it, she sat quietly with her hands clasped in her lap, staring at the pile of paper silently.

Then when she looked up at him at last, her eyes were bright and wet with tears.

'It's magnificent,' she said quietly. 'It will take me a little time before I can get over it enough to talk about it rationally, and then I will want to read it again.'

The following evening, she brought a fat Cornish chicken. 'It's range-fed,' she told him. 'One more steak and you would start growing horns.'

She made a *coq au vin* and while they ate, she demanded an explanation of the characters in his typescript.

'Was Mr Rhodes really a homosexual?'

'There doesn't seem to be any other explanation,' he defended himself. 'So many great men are hounded to greatness by their own imperfections.'

'What about Lobengula? Was his first love really a captured white girl? Did he commit suicide? And Robyn Ballantyne – tell me more about her, did she impersonate a man to enrol in medical school? How much of that is true?'

'Does it matter?' Craig laughed at her. 'It's just a story, the way it might have been. I was just trying to portray an age, and the mood of that age.'

'Oh, yes, it does matter,' she said seriously. 'It matters very much to me. You have made it matter. It is as though I am a part of it – you have made me a part of it all.'

That night when it grew late, Craig said simply, 'I made

up the bunk in the forward cabin, it seems silly for you to drive all that way home.'

She stayed, and the following evening she brought a valise which she unpacked into the stowage of the forward cabin, and they settled slowly into a routine. She had first use of the shower and heads in the morning while he made the breakfast. He did the cleaning and made up the bunks while she did the shopping and any other errands for him during her lunchbreak. When she arrived back at the yacht in the evenings, she would change into a tee-shirt and jeans, then help him with the work on the yacht. She was particularly good at sanding and varnishing, she had more patience and dexterity than Craig did.

At the end of the first week, Craig suggested, 'It would save you a bundle if you gave up that flat of yours.'

'I'll pay you rent,' she agreed, and when he protested, 'Okay, then, I get the food and liquor – agreed?'

That night just after she had doused the gaslight in her cabin, she called through the dark saloon to his stern cabin.

'Craig, do you know, this is the first time that I feel safe since—' She did not finish.

'I know how you feel,' he assured her.

'Goodnight, Skipper.'

Yet it was only a few nights later that he came awake to her screams. They were so anguished, so tormented and heartrending, that for seconds he could not move; then he tumbled from his bunk and sprawled on the deck in his haste to get to her. He fumbled and found the switch to the fluorescent tube in the saloon, and then clawed himself down the companionway.

In the reflected light from the saloon, he saw her crouched in one corner of the cabin. Her bedclothes were hanging in untidy festoons from the bunk, her nightdress was rucked up around her naked thighs and her fingers formed a cage across her terrified contorted face.

He reached for her. 'Jan, it's all right. I'm here!' He

wrapped both arms around her, to try and still those dreadful cries of terror. Immediately she turned into a maddened animal, and she flew at him. Her nails slashed down his forehead, and had he not jerked away, he would have lost his eye; the bloody parallel wounds ended in his eyebrow, and thick dark blood oozed into his eye, half-blinding him. Her strength was out of all proportion to her size, he could not hold her, and the harder he tried, the wilder she became. She sank her teeth into his bare forearm, leaving a crescent-shaped bite-mark deep in his flesh.

He rolled away from her, and instantly she crawled back into the corner, and crouched there, keening and blubbering to herself, staring at him with glittering unseeing eyes. Craig felt his skin crawl and itch with dread and his own horror. Once again he tried to reach her, but at first advance she bared her teeth like a rabid dog and snarled at him.

He rolled out of the cabin and dragged himself into the saloon. Frantically he searched through the tapes and found Beethoven's 'Pastoral'. He pressed it into the slot and turned the volume up to the maximum. The magnificent music swamped the yacht.

Slowly the sounds from her cabin dwindled into silence, and then hesitantly Janine came into the companionway of the saloon. She held her arms crossed over her chest, but the madness was gone from her eyes.

'I had a dream,' she whispered, and came to sit at the table.

'I'll make some coffee,' he said.

In the galley he bathed his scratches and bites with cold water, and took the coffee through to her.

'The music—' she started, and then she saw his torn face. 'Did I do that?'

'It doesn't matter,' he said.

'I'm sorry, Craig,' she whispered. 'But you must not try to touch me. You see I am a little bit mad also. You mustn't try to touch me.'

647

Comrade Tungata Zebiwe, Minister for Trade, Tourism and Information in the Cabinet of the newly elected government of Zimbabwe, walked briskly along one of the narrow gravel pathways that meandered through the lush gardens of State House. His four bodyguards followed him at a respectful distance. They were all former members of his old ZIPRA cadre, each of them hardened veterans whose loyalty had been tested a hundred times. Now, however, they had changed the camouflage dungarees of the bush war for dark business suits and sunglasses, the new uniform of the political élite.

The daily pilgrimage on which Tungata was intent had become a ritual of his household. As one of the senior Cabinet ministers, he was entitled to luxurious quarters in one of the annexes of State House. It was an easy and congenial walk from there, through the gardens, past State House itself, to the *indaba* tree.

State House was a sprawling edifice with white walls and gables, arched in the tradition of the great homes of the Cape of Good Hope. It had been built on the instructions of that arch-imperialist Cecil John Rhodes. His taste for the big and barbaric showed in the design, and his sense of history in his choice of the site for State House. It was built on the spot where Lobengula's kraal had once stood before it was destroyed by Rhodes' marauders when they rode in to take possession of this land.

Beyond the great house, not two hundred paces from its wide verandas, stood a tree, a gnarled old wild plum enclosed and protected by a fence of iron palings. This tree was the object of Tungata's pilgrimage. He stopped in front of the iron palings, and his bodyguards hung back so as not to intrude on this private moment.

Tungata stood with his feet apart and his hands clasped lightly behind his back. He was dressed in a navy blue suit with a light chalk stripe. One of a dozen that Gieves and Hawkes of Savile Row had tailored for him during his last visit to London. It fitted his wide rangy shoulders to perfection and subtly emphasized his narrow waist and the length of his legs. He wore a snowy white shirt under it, his tie was maroon with the tiny buckle and bridle logo of Gucci picked out in blue. His shoes were by the same Italian house, and he wore his expensive Western clothes with the same *élan* as his forefathers had worn the blue heron's feathers and royal leopard pelts.

He removed the gold-rimmed aviator-type Polaroid glasses from his face, and as part of his personal ritual, read the inscription on the plaque that was riveted to the palings.

'Beneath this tree Lobengula, the last King
of the Matabele, held his court and sat in judgement.'

Then he looked up into the branches, as though in search of his ancestor's spirit. The tree was dying of old age, some of the central branches were black and dry, but from the rich red soil at its base new shoots were bursting into vibrant life.

Tungata saw the significance of that and he murmured to himself, 'They will grow as strong as the great tree once was – and I also am a shoot of the old king's stock.'

There was a light tread on the gravel path behind Tungata. He frowned as he turned, but the frown cleared as he saw who it was.

'Comrade Leila,' he greeted the white woman with the pale intense face.

'I am honoured that you call me that, Comrade Minister,' Leila came directly to him and held out her hand.

'You and your family have always been true friends of my people,' he told her simply, as he took her hand. 'Beneath this tree your grandmother, Robyn Ballantyne, met often with Lobengula, my great-great-uncle. She came at his invitation to give him advice and counsel.'

'Now, I come at your invitation, and you must believe

that I will always be yours to command.' He released her hand and turned back to the tree, his voice had a quiet reflective quality.

'You were with me when the Umlimo, the spirit medium of our people, made her final prediction. I thought it was right that you should be there when that prediction is brought to fruition.'

'The stone falcons have returned to roost,' Leila St John agreed softly. 'But that is not all the Umlimo's prophecy. She foresaw that the man who brought the falcons back to Zimbabwe would rule the land as once did the Mambos and Monomatopas, as once did your ancestors Lobengula and great Mzilikazi.'

Tungata turned slowly to face her once more.

'That is a secret that you and I share, Comrade Leila.'

'It will remain our secret, Comrade Tungata, but you and I both know that there will be need during the difficult years that lie ahead for a man as strong as Mzilikazi was strong.'

Tungata did not reply. He looked up into the branches of the ancient tree, and his lips moved in a silent supplication. Then he replaced the gold-rimmed glasses over his eyes, and turned back to Leila.

'The car is waiting,' he said.

It was a black bullet-proofed Mercedes 500. There were four police motorcycle outriders and a second smaller Mercedes for his bodyguards. The small convoy drove very fast, with the police sirens shrieking and wailing, and the colourful little ministerial pennant fluttering on the front of Tungata's Mercedes.

They went down the three-kilometre-long jacaranda-lined driveway that Cecil Rhodes had designed as the approach to his State House, and then crossed the main commercial section of Bulawayo, flying through the red lights at the junctions to the geometrical grid of roads and avenues, past the town square where the wagons had laagered during the rebellion when Bazo's impis had threatened the town, down along the wide avenue that bisected the meticulously groomed lawns of the public gardens, and at last turned off sharply and drew up in front of the modern three-storey museum building.

There was a red carpet laid down the front steps of the museum and a small gathering of dignitaries, headed by the Mayor of Bulawayo, the first Matabele ever to hold that position, and the curator of the museum.

'Welcome, Comrade Minister, on this historic occasion.'

They escorted him down the long corridor to the public auditorium. Every seat was already filled, and as Tungata entered, the entire gathering stood and applauded him, the whites in the gathering outdoing the Matabele as a positive demonstration of their goodwill.

Tungata was introduced to the other dignitaries on the speakers' platform. 'This is Doctor Van der Walt, curator of the Southern African Museum.'

He was a tall balding man with a heavy South African accent. Tungata shook hands with him briefly and unsmilingly. This man represented a nation that had actively opposed the people's republican army's march to glory. Tungata turned to the next in line.

She was a young white woman, and she was immediately familiar to Tungata. He stared at her sharply, not quite able to place her. She had gone very pale under his scrutiny, and her eyes were dark and terrified as those of a hunted animal. The hand in his was limp and cold, and trembled violently – still Tungata could not decide where he had seen her before.

'Doctor Carpenter is the curator of the Entomological Section.' The name meant nothing to Tungata, and he turned away from her, irritated by his own inability to place her. He took his seat in the centre of the platform facing the auditorium, and the South African Museum's curator rose to address the gathering.

'All the credit for the successful negotiation of the

exchange between our two institutions must go to the honourable minister who today honours us with his presence.' He was reading from a typed sheet, clearly anxious to have done with speaking and sit down again. 'It was at Minister Tungata Zebiwe's initiative that discussions first took place, and he sustained these during the difficult period when we appeared to be making little or no progress. Our great problem was in setting a relative value on two such diverse exhibits. On one hand you had one of the world's most extensive and exhaustive collections of tropical insects, representing many decades of dedicated collecting and classification, while on the other hand we had these unique artefacts from an unknown civilization.' Van der Walt seemed to be warming to his subject enough to look up from his prepared script. 'However, it was the honourable minister's determination to regain for his new nation a priceless part of its heritage that at last prevailed, and it is to his credit entirely that we are gathered here today.'

When at last Van der Walt sat down again, there was a polite splattering of applause, and then an expectant silence as Tungata Zebiwe rose to his feet. The minister had an immense presence, and without yet uttering a word, he transfixed them with his smoky unwavering gaze.

'My people have a saying that was passed down from the wise ones of our tribe,' he started in his deep rumbling voice. 'It is this: The white eagle has stooped on the stone falcons and cast them to earth. Now the eagle shall lift them up again and they will fly afar. There shall be no peace in the kingdoms of the Mambos or the Monomatopas until they return. For the white eagle will war with the black bull until the stone falcons return to roost.'

Tungata paused a moment, letting his words hang between them, heavy with portent. Then he went on. 'I am sure all of you here know the story of how the bird statues of Zimbabwe were seized by Rhodes' plunderers, and despite the efforts of my ancestors to prevent it, how they were carried away southwards across the Limpopo river.'

Tungata left the podium and strode to the curtained-off section at the back of the speakers' platform. 'My friends, my comrades,' he turned to face them once more. 'The stone falcons have returned to roost!' he said, and drew aside the curtains.

There was a long breathless silence and the audience stared avidly at the serried rank of tall soapstone carvings that was revealed. There were six of them, and they were those that Ralph Ballantyne had lifted from the ancient stone temple. The one that his father had taken on his first visit to Zimbabwe thirty years before had burned in the pyre of Groote Schuur. These six were all that remained.

The soapstone from which each of the birds was carved was of a greenish satiny texture. Each bird crouched on top of a plinth that was ornamented by a pattern of intermeshed triangles like the teeth in a shark's jaw. The statues were not identical: some of the columns supported crocodiles and lizards that crawled up towards the bird image that surmounted it.

Some of the statues had been extensively damaged, chipped and eroded, but the one in the centre of the line was almost perfect. The bird was a stylized raptor, with its long bladelike wings crossed over its back. The head was proud and erect, the cruel beak hooked and the blind eyes haughty and unforgiving. It was a magnificent and evocative work of primitive art, and the crowded auditorium rose as one person in spontaneous applause.

Tungata Zebiwe reached out and touched the head of the central bird. His back was turned to his audience so that they could not see his lips move, and the applause drowned his whisper.

'Welcome home,' he whispered. 'Welcome home to Zimbabwe. Bird of my destiny.'

'Now you do not want to go!' Janine was shaking with fury. 'After all the pains I have gone to, to arrange this meeting. Now you simply do not want to go!'

'Jan, it's a waste of time.'

'Thank you!' She put her face closer to his. 'Thank you for that. Do you realize what it would cost me to face that monster again, but I was prepared to do it for you, and now it's a waste of time.'

'Jan, please—'

'Damn you, Craig Mellow, it's you who are a waste of time, you and your endless cowardice.' He gasped and drew away from her. 'Cowardice,' she repeated deliberately. 'I say that, and I mean it. You were in too much of a blue funk to send that bloody book of yours to a publisher. I had literally to tear it away from you and send it off.' She broke off, panting with anger, searching for words sharp enough to express her fury.

'You are afraid to face life, afraid to leave this cave you have built for yourself, afraid to take the chance of somebody rejecting your book, afraid to make any effort to float this thing you have built.' With a wide, extravagant gesture she indicated the yacht. 'I see it now, you don't really want to get onto the ocean, you prefer to hide here, swilling gin and covering yourself with dreams. You don't want to walk, you prefer to drag yourself around on your backside – it's your excuse, your grand cast-iron excuse to dodge life.'

Again she had to stop for breath, and then she went on. 'That's right, put that little-boy look on your face, make those big sad eyes, it works every time, doesn't it? Well, not this time, buster, not this time. They have offered me the job of curator at the South African Museum. I'm to see the collection safely installed in its new home, and I'm going to take it. Do you hear me, Craig Mellow? I'm going to leave you to crawl around on the floor because you're too damned scared to stand up.' She flung herself out of the saloon and into the forward cabin. She began to snatch her clothes out of the stowage and throw them onto the bunk.

'Jan,' he said behind her.

'What is it now?' She did not look around.

'If we are going to be there by three o'clock, then we'd better leave right away,' Craig said.

'You can drive,' she said and pushed past him and went up in the cockpit, leaving him to follow at his best speed.

They drove in silence until they reached the entrance to the long straight avenue of jacaranda trees. At the far end of it were the white gates of State House, and Janine stared straight ahead at them.

'I'm sorry, Craig. I said things that were hard to say and must have been harder to listen to. The truth is that I am as afraid as you are. I am going to face the man that destroyed me. If I can do it, then perhaps I can retrieve something of myself from the ruins. I lied when I said it was for you. It's for both of us.'

The police guard came to the driver's side of the maroon Land-Rover, and without a word Craig handed him the appointment card. The constable checked it against his visitors' book, and then made Craig fill in his name and address and the reason for his visit.

Craig wrote: 'Visit to Comrade Minister Tungata Zebiwe', and the guard took the book back from him and saluted smartly.

The wrought-iron gates swung open and Craig drove through. They turned left towards the minister's annexe, with just a glimpse of the white gables and blue slate roof of the main residence between the trees.

Craig parked the Land-Rover in the public car park, and slid into the wheelchair. Janine walked beside him to the steps that led up onto the veranda of the annexe, and there was an awkward moment while Craig negotiated them by the sheer strength of his arms. Then they followed the signs down the trestled veranda, beneath the blue wistaria and climbing purple bougainvillaea to the door of the ante-chamber. One of the minister's bodyguards searched Janine's handbag, frisked Craig quickly but expertly, and then stood aside to let them enter the light and airy room.

There were lighter square patches on the walls from where the portraits of previous white administrators and politicians had been removed. The only wall decoration now were two flags draped on either side of the inner double doors, the flags of ZIPRA and of the new Zimbabwe nation.

Craig and Janine waited for almost half an hour, and then the doors opened and another suited bodyguard came through.

'The Comrade Minister will see you now.'

Craig wheeled himself forward and into the inner room. On the facing wall were portraits of the nation's leaders, Robert Mugabe and Josiah Inkunzi. In the centre of the wall-to-wall carpeting stood a huge desk in the style of Louis XIV. Tungata Zebiwe sat behind his desk, and even its size could not belittle him.

Involuntarily Craig stopped halfway to the desk.

'Sam?' he whispered. 'Samson Kumalo? I did not know – I'm sorry—'

The minister stood up abruptly. Craig's shock was reflected in his own face.

'Craig,' he whispered, 'what happened to you?'

'The war,' Craig answered, 'I guess I was on the wrong side, Sam.'

Tungata recovered swiftly, and sat down again. 'That name is best forgotten,' he said quietly. 'Just as what we were once to each other should also be forgotten. You made an appointment through Doctor Carpenter to see me. What was it that you wished to discuss?'

Tungata listened attentively while Craig spoke, and then he leaned back in his chair.

'From what you tell me, you have already made an

application to the exchange control authority for a permit to export this vessel of yours. That permit was refused?'

'That is correct, Comrade Minister,' Craig nodded.

'Then what made you think I would want to or even have the authority to countermand that decision?' Tungata asked.

'I didn't really think you would,' Craig admitted.

'Comrade Minister,' Janine spoke for the first time, 'I asked for this appointment because I believe that there are special circumstances in this case. Mr Mellow has been crippled for life, and his only possession is this vessel.'

'Doctor Carpenter, he is fortunate. The forests and wilderness of this land are thickly sown with the unmarked graves of young men and women who gave more than Mr Mellow for freedom. You should have a better reason than that.'

'I think I have,' Janine said softly. 'Comrade Minister, you and I have met before.'

'Your face is familiar to me,' Tungata agreed. 'But I do not recall—'

'It was at night, in the forest beside the wreckage of an aircraft—' She saw the flare of recognition in those brooding smoky eyes. They seemed to bore into her very soul. Terror came at her again in suffocating overwhelming waves, she felt the earth sway giddily under her feet, and his face filled all her vision. It took all that remained of her strength and courage to speak again.

'You won a land, but in doing so, have you lost for ever your humanity?'

She saw the shift in that dark hypnotic gaze, the almost imperceptible softening of his mouth. Then Tungata Zebiwe looked down at his own powerful hands on the white blotter before him.

'You are a persuasive advocate, Doctor Carpenter,' he said quietly. He picked up the gold pen from the desk set and wrote briefly on the monogrammed pad. He tore off the sheet and stood up. He came around the desk and towards Janine.

'In war there are atrocities committed even by decent men,' he said quietly. 'War makes monsters of us all. I thank you for reminding me of my own humanity.' He handed her the sheet of paper. 'Take that to the exchange control director,' he told her. 'You will have your permit.'

'Thank you, Sam.' Craig looked up at him, and Tungata stooped over him and embraced him briefly but ardently.

'Go in peace, old friend,' he said, in Sindebele, and then straightened up. 'Get him out of here, Doctor Carpenter, before he unmans me completely,' Tungata Zebiwe ordered harshly, and strode to the wide sash-windows.

He stared out across the green lawns until he heard the double doors close behind him, then he sighed softly and went back to his desk.

'It's strange to think that that is the same view of Africa as Robyn and Zouga Ballantyne had in 1860 when they arrived in the slaving clipper *Huron*.' Craig pointed back over the stern at the great massif of Table Mountain standing perpetual guard over the southernmost tip of a continent, wreathed in the silver clouds that spilled over her weathered brow of stark rock. Around the foot of the mountain, like a necklace around the throat, were strung the white buildings with their windows shining in the early sunlight like ten thousand beacon fires.

'This is where it all began, my family's great African adventure, and this is where it all ends.'

'It's an end,' Janine agreed quietly. 'But it's also a new beginning.' She was standing in the stern, with one hand on the back stay for balance.

She wore a thin tee-shirt and blue denim pants with the legs hacked off short, exposing her long brown legs. During the months of final fitting-out of the yacht, in the basin of the Royal Cape Yacht Club, she had put herself on a strict diet: no wine, no gin and no white food. Her waist had fined down, and the buttocks that peeked out from under the ragged bottoms of her pants were round and tight and hard once again.

She had cut her hair as short as a boy's and the salt sea air had made it curl tightly against her scalp. The sun had darkened her face and burned away the blemishes around the corners of her mouth and across her chin. Now she revolved slowly, taking in the wide horizon ahead of them.

'It's so big, Craig,' she said, 'aren't you scared?'

'Scared as hell,' he grinned up at her. 'I am not certain whether out next landfall will be South America or India, but it's exciting also.'

'I'll make us a mug of cocoa,' she said.

'I hate this drying-out period.'

'It's your own rule to have no liquor on board – you'll have to wait until South America or India, or whatever.' She ducked down into the saloon, but before she reached the galley the radio above the chart-table squawked.

'Zulu Romeo Foxtrot. This is Cape Town marine radio. Come in, please.'

'Jan, that's us. Take it,' Craig yelled. 'Someone at the yacht club saying goodbye, probably.'

'Cape Town marine radio, this is Zulu Romeo Foxtrot. Let's go to Channel 10.'

'Is that the yacht *Bawu?*' The operator's voice was clear and undistorted, for they were still on line of sight to the antenna above the harbour.

'Affirmative. This is *Bawu.*'

'We have a radio-gram for you. Are you ready to copy?'

'Go ahead, Cape Town.'

'Message reads: "For Craig Mellow regarding your typescript *A Falcon Flies* STOP we wish to publish and offer advance of $5,000 against 12½ per cent royalties on world rights STOP reply soonest congratulations from Pick chairman William Heinemann Publishers London."'

'Craig,' Janine shrieked from below. 'Did you hear? Did you hear that?'

He could not answer her. His hands were frozen to the wheel and he was staring directly ahead over *Bawu*'s bows as they rose and fell gently across the distant blue horizon of the Atlantic Ocean.

Two days out, the gale came out of the south-east without any warning. It laid *Bawu* over until solid green water came in over the rail and swept Janine out of the cockpit. Only her safety-line saved her, and Craig struggled for ten minutes to get her back on board, while the yacht paid off madly before the wind and the jib sail burst with a crash like cannonshot.

The gale lasted five days and five nights, during which time there seemed to be no clear dividing line between mad wind and wild water. They lived in a deafening cacophony of sound as the gale played on *Bawu*'s hull like a crazed violinist, and the Atlantic grey-beards marched down upon them in majestic succession. They lived with the cold in their bones, soaked to the skin, and with their hands white and wrinkled like those of a drowned man, and the soft skin torn by harsh nylon sheets and stiff unyielding sails. Once in a while they snatched a dry biscuit or a mouthful of cold congealed beans, and washed it down with plain water, then crawled back on deck again. They slept in turns for a few minutes at a time on top of the bundled wet sails that had been stuffed down the companionway into the saloon.

They went into the storm as greenhorns and when the wind dropped as suddenly as it had attacked them, they were sailors – utterly exhausted and gaunt with the terror through which they had lived, but with a new pride in themselves and the vessel that had borne them.

Craig had just sufficient strength to heave the yacht to, and let her ride the smooth but still mountainous swells on her own. Then he dragged himself to his bunk, dropped his stinking wet clothing on the deck and fell back naked on the rough blanket and slept for eighteen hours straight.

He woke to a new tumult of emotions, uncertain of what was fantasy and what was reality. Where before there had been no sensation at all, his lower body was locked in an agonizing spasm. He could feel each separate muscle, and they seemed pitted against each other to the point of tearing or bursting. From the sole of his foot to the pit of his stomach, his nerve-ends felt as though they were scraped raw. He cried out as the pain threatened to swamp him, and then in the pain found suddenly the beginnings of exquisite, almost insupportable, pleasure.

He cried out again, and heard his cry echoed from above him. He opened his eyes and Janine's face was inches above his, her naked body pressed against his from breast to thighs. He tried to speak, but she gagged him with her own lips, and moaned into his mouth. Abruptly he realized that he was buried deeply in her heat and silken elasticity, and they were borne aloft on a wave of triumph higher and fiercer than any that the Atlantic had hurled at them during the gale.

It left them both clinging to each other, speechless and barely able to breathe.

She brought him a mug of coffee once he had *Bawu* sailing again, and she perched on the edge of the cockpit with one hand on his shoulder.

'I want to show you something,' he said.

He pointed at his bare leg that was thrust out in front of him on the deck cushion, and as she watched he wriggled his toes back and forth, then from side to side.

'Oh, darling,' she husked, 'that's the cleverest thing I've ever seen anybody do.'

'What did you call me?' he asked.

'Do you know something?' She did not reply to the question immediately. 'I think that you and I are going to be all right—' Only then, she laid her cheek against his, and whispered in his ear, 'I called you darling, okay?'

'That's okay by me, darling,' he replied, and locked in the yacht's self-steering vane, so that he had both arms free to hold her.

A TIME TO DIE

For my wife
Danielle Antoinette
With all my love
For ever

She had sat for well over two hours without moving, and the need to do so was an almost unbearable affliction. Every muscle in her body seemed to quiver with the craving for movement. Her buttocks were numb and despite being advised to do so, she had not emptied her bladder before they had gone into hiding, for she had been embarrassed by the masculine company and still too nervous in the African bush to go off alone to find a private place. She regretted her modesty and her timidity now.

She was staring out through the eye-slit in the rude grass structure of the hide, down a narrow open tunnel that the gunbearers had meticulously cleared through the thick bush, for even a tiny twig might deflect a bullet flying at 3000 feet a second. The tunnel was sixty yards long, paced out so that the telescopic sight of the rifle could be zeroed on precisely.

Without moving her head, Claudia swivelled her eyes towards where her father waited in the hide beside her. His rifle was propped in the vee of a branch in front of him and his right hand rested lightly on the stock. He needed to lift it mere inches to his cheek to be aiming and ready to fire.

Even in her physical discomfort the thought of her father firing that sinister glistening weapon made her angry. Yet he had always filled her with violent and conflicting emotions, nothing he ever did or said seemed to leave her untouched. He dominated her life and she hated him and loved him for it. Always she was trying to break away, and always he drew her effortlessly back. She knew that the main reason that she was still unmarried at twenty-six years of age, despite the way she looked, despite her own singular achievements, despite having had countless proposals, at least two from men with whom she had believed herself in love at the time, the reason for all this was this man who sat beside her. She had never found another to compare with her papa.

7

Colonel Riccardo Monterro, soldier, engineer, scholar, gourmet, multi-millionaire businessman, athlete, *bon-vivant*, lady-killer, sportsman – how many descriptions fitted him perfectly and yet did not describe him as she knew him. They did not describe the kindness and the strength, that made her love him, nor the cruelty and ruthlessness which made her hate him. They did not describe what he had done to her mother that had turned her into a discarded alcoholic shell. Claudia knew he was as capable of destroying her if she let herself be run down by him. He was the bull and she the matador. He was a dangerous man, and therein lay most of his appeal.

Someone had once told her, 'Some women always fall for real bastards.' She had immediately scoffed at the idea, but then thought about it later and came partially to accept it. The Lord knew, Papa was one. A great rumbustious bastard, with all the charm and flashing golden-brown eyes and shining teeth of his Latin origins. he could sing like Caruso and eat all the pasta she could heap on his plate. But although he had been born in Milano, the greater part of him was American for Claudia's grandparents had emigrated to Seattle from Mussolini's Italy when Riccardo was a child.

She had inherited his physical characteristics, the eyes and teeth and glowing olive skin, but she tried to reject every value of his that offended her and to take the opposite path to his. She had chosen to study law as a direct defiance of the lawless streak in him. and because he was a Republican she had decided long before she could understand what politics meant, that she was a Democrat. Because he set so much store by wealth and possessions, Claudia had deliberately turned down the $200,000 job she was offered after graduating fifth in her law class and had taken instead one at $40,000 in the civil rights agency. Because Papa had commanded a battalion of engineers in Vietnam and still talked of 'gooks'. her work with the indigenous Inuit people of Alaska gave her satisfaction enhanced by his disapproval. He called the Eskimos 'gooks' as well. Yet here she was in Africa at his request, and the true horror of it was that he was here to kill animals and that she was in collusion with him.

At home what spare time she had was devoted to working without remuneration for the Alaskan Nature and Wildlife Conservation Society. The Society devoted most of its resources and efforts to fighting the oil exploration companies and their depredations on the environment. Her father's company, Anchorage Tool and Engineering, was a major supplier of hardware to the drilling rigs and pipeline contractors. The choices she had made had been calculated and deliberate.

Yet here she was in a foreign land waiting submissively for him to assassinate some beautiful wild animal. Her own duplicity sickened her. They called this expedition a safari. She would never have even contemplated becoming an accomplice in such a heinous enterprise, in fact she had indignantly refused the invitations he had made to her in previous years, but for the secret she had learned a scant few days before her father had invited her. This might be the last time, the very last time, she would be alone with him. That thought appalled her more even than the dirty business in which they were engaged.

'Oh God,' she thought, 'what will I do without him? What will my world be without him?'

As the thought struck her she turned her head, her first movement in two hours, and looked over her shoulder. Another man sat close behind her in the small thatch-walled hide. He was the professional hunter. Although her father had hunted with this man on a dozen other safaris, Claudia had met him for the first time only four days previously when they had disembarked from the South African Airways commercial flight at Harare, the capital city of Zimbabwe. The hunter had flown them out from there in his twin-engined Beechcraft Baron to this vast and remote hunting concession near the Mozambique border which he chartered from the Zimbabwe government.

His name was Sean Courtney. She had known him four days but already she loathed him as if she had known him a lifetime. Not strange that thinking of her father had led her instinctively to look back at him. Here was another dangerous man. Hard, ruthless and so devilishly good looking that her every instinct shrieked a warning at her.

He frowned sharply at her with clear bright green eyes in the darkly tanned face, and the crow's-feet at the corners of his eyes puckered with annoyance at her movement. He touched her on the hip with one finger, cautioning her to stillness again. The touch was light, but she felt the disconcerting male strength in his single finger. She had noticed his hands before, trying not to be impressed by their graceful form. 'The hands of an artist or a surgeon or a killer,' she had thought then, but now that peremptory touch offended her. She felt as though she had been sexually violated. She stared fixedly ahead again, through the eye-slit in the grass wall, and she fumed with indignation. How dare he touch her. The spot on her hip burned, as though he had branded her with his finger.

That afternoon before they had left camp, Sean had insisted that each of them shower and bathe with special unscented soap that he provided. He had cautioned Claudia to use no perfume and one of the camp servants had laid out freshly washed and ironed khaki shirt and slacks on her cot in the tent when she returned from the shower.

'Those big cats can smell you from two miles downwind,' Sean had told her. Yet now after two hours in the heat of the Zambezi valley, she could faintly smell him sitting up close behind her, almost but not quite touching her, fresh, male sweat, and she felt an almost irresistible urge to move in the canvas camp chair. He made her feel restless, but she forced herself to sit perfectly still. She found herself breathing deeply, trying to pick up the faint intermittent wafts of his odour, then stopped herself angrily as soon as she realized what she was doing.

Inches in front of her eyes a single green leaf, hanging down into the opening in the grass wall, spiralled slowly on its stalk like a weathercock and almost immediately she felt the shift of the light evening breeze.

Sean had sited the blind below the prevailing wind, and now as the breeze came down to them, it brought a new odour, the stench of the carcass. The bait was an old buffalo cow. Sean had selected her from a herd of two hundred of the huge black animals.

'That old girl is way past breeding,' he had pointed her out. 'Take her low on the shoulder, through the heart,' he had ordered Papa.

It was the first animal Claudia had ever seen killed deliberately. The crash of the heavy rifle had shocked her, but not as deeply as the scarlet gush of blood in the bright African sunlight and the mournful death bellow of the old cow. She had walked back to where they had left the open Toyota hunting car and sat alone in the front seat in a cold sweat of nausea while Sean and his trackers had butchered the carcass.

They had hauled the carcass up into the lower branches of the wild fig tree with the power winch on the front of the Toyota, positioning it with much debate between Sean and his trackers at the exact height which would enable a full grown lion standing on his back legs to reach up and partially satisfy his hunger without enabling a large pride of cats to consume all of it at a sitting and so move on to find other fare.

That had been four days previously, but even then as they worked the metallic-green blow-flies had come swarming to the smell of fresh blood. Now the heat and the flies had done their work, Claudia wrinkled her nose and grimaced at the stench that came down to her on the breeze. The smell seemed to coat her tongue and the back of her throat like slime, and staring at the carcass in the tree, she imagined she could see the black hide undulating softly as the maggots seethed and burrowed into the putrid flesh beneath it.

'Lovely.' Sean had sniffed it before they entered the hide. 'Just like a ripe Camembert. No cat within ten miles will be able to resist it.' While they waited the sun sagged wearily down the sky, and the colours of the bush now glowed with the richer light, in contrast to the washed-out glare of noon.

The faint coolness in the evening breeze seemed to awaken the wild birds from their heat-drugged stupor. In the undergrowth down on the banks of the stream a lourie called 'Kok! Kok! Kok!' as raucously as a parrot, and in the branches directly over their heads a pair of glistening metallic sunbirds flitted busily, with fluttering wings, hanging upside down from the fluffy blooms to suck up the nectar. Claudia lifted her head slowly to watch them with intense pleasure. Though she was so close that she could see their thin tubular tongues thrusting deeply into the yellow flowers, the little creatures ignored her as though she was part of the tree.

She was still watching the birds when she became aware of a sudden tension in the hide. Her father had stiffened, his hand on the buttstock of the rifle clenched slightly. His sense of excitement was almost palpable. He was staring through his peephole, but though she stared as hard she could not see what had excited him. From the corner of her eye, she saw Sean Courtney reach forward between them, his hand moving with infinite stealth, to grasp her father's elbow in a cautionary restraining grip.

Then she heard Sean's whisper, softer than the breeze. 'Wait!' he said.

So they waited, deathly still, as the minutes drew out slowly and became ten and then twenty.

'On the left,' Sean said, and it was so unexpected that she started at the barely audible murmur. Her eyes swivelled left. She saw nothing, just grass and bush and shadows. She stared unblinkingly until her eyes smarted and swam with tears and she had to blink rapidly and then look again, and this time she saw something move like mist or smoke, a drift of brown in the long sun-seared grass.

Then abruptly, dramatically, an animal stepped out into the open killing ground below the reeking carcass in the fig tree.

Despite herself, Claudia gasped, and then her breath choked in her throat. It was the most beautiful beast she had ever seen, a great cat, much larger than she had ever expected, sleek and glossy and golden. It turned its head and looked directly at her. She saw that its throat was a soft cream, and sunlight gleamed on the long white whiskers. Its ears were round and tipped with black and held erect, listening. The eyes were yellow, as implacable and glowing as moonstones, the pupils reduced to black arrowheads as it stared up the long clearing at the wall of the hide.

Still Claudia could not breathe. She was frozen with excitement and dread as the cat stared at her. Only when it turned its head away and looked up at the carcass in the tree, could she let out her breath in a soft ragged sigh.

'Don't kill it. Please, don't kill it,' she almost cried aloud. With relief she saw that her father had not moved a muscle and Sean's hand was still on his elbow restraining him.

Only then did she realize that it was a female, there was no mane, a lioness, and she had listened to the camp-fire conversation enough to know that they were hunting only a full-maned lion and that there were heavy penalties, huge fines and even imprisonment for the killing of a female. She relaxed slightly and gave herself over to the full enjoyment of the moment, to the stunning beauty of this beast. Claudia's pleasure had only just begun, for the lioness looked around her once more and then, satisfied that it was safe, she opened her mouth and gave a low mewling call.

Almost immediately, her cubs came tumbling into the clearing. There were three of them, fluffy as children's toys and dappled with their kitten spots. They tripped over paws that were too large for the tiny bodies, and after a few moments of hesitation

12

during which their mother placed no restraint on them, they launched into boisterous mock combat, wrestling and falling over each other with ferocious baby growls.

The lioness ignored them and rose up on her hind legs to the dangling carcass. She thrust her head into the open belly from which the entrails had been plucked, and she began to feed. The row of black nipples down her belly were sucked out prominently and the fur around them matted with the saliva of her offspring. She had not yet weaned them and the cubs took no notice of her feeding and went on with their play.

Then a second lioness stepped into the clearing, followed by two half-grown cubs. This lioness was much darker in colour, almost blue along the spine and her pelt was criss-crossed with old healed scars, the legacy of a lifetime of hard hunting, the marks of hoof and horn and claw. Half of one ear was torn off and her ribs showed through the scarred hide. She was old. The two half-grown cubs that followed her into the clearing would probably be her last litter. Next year, when the cubs had deserted her and she was too weak to keep up with the pride, the hyena would take her, but now she was still living on her store of cunning and experience.

She had let the young lioness go in first to the bait, for she had seen two mates killed in just such a situation, beneath a succulent carcass dangling from a tree, and she mistrusted it. She did not begin to feed, but prowled restlessly around the clearing, her tail flicking with agitation and every so often she stopped and stared intently down the open lane to the grass wall of the hide at the far end.

Her two older cubs gazed up at the carcass, sitting on their haunches and growling with hunger and frustration for the meat was obviously beyond their reach. At last, the bolder of the two backed off then made a running leap at the bait. Hooking on with its front claws, its back legs swinging free, it tried to grab a hasty mouthful, but the young lioness turned on it viciously, snarling and cuffing it heavily until it fell on its back, scrambled to its feet and slunk away.

The older of the two lionesses made no effort to protect her cub. This was the pride law: the full-grown hunters, the most valuable members of the pride, must feed first. The pride survived on their strength. Only after they had gorged could the young ones feed. In the lean times, when game was scarce or when

13

open terrain made hunting difficult, the young might starve to death, and the adult females would not come into season again until game was once more plentiful. In this way, the survival of the pride was ensured.

The chastened cub crept back to join its sibling beneath the carcass and then to compete eagerly with it for the scraps that the lioness ripped out of the buffalo's belly cavity and unintentionally let fall.

Once the young lioness dropped back on all fours in obvious discomfort, and Claudia was horrified to see that her whole head was swarming with white maggots that had crawled out of the meat as she fed. The lioness shook her head, scattering maggots like rice grains. She pawed frantically at her own head to be rid of the fat worms that were trying to crawl into the furry openings of her ears. Then she extended her neck and sneezed violently, blowing live maggots out of her nostrils.

Her young cubs took this as an invitation to play, or to feed. Two of them launched themselves at her head, trying to hang on to her ears, while the third rushed under her belly and attached himself to a nipple like a tubby brown leech. The lioness ignored them and rose once more on her hind legs to continue eating. The cub at her nipple managed to hang on a few seconds longer and then fell under her back paws, and his dignity was trampled as she tugged and heaved at the bait. He crawled out between her legs crestfallen, dusty and dishevelled.

Claudia giggled, she could not help herself, she tried to muffle it with both hands. Immediately Sean dug her hard in the short ribs.

Only the old lioness reacted to her giggle. The rest of the pride were too preoccupied, but the lioness crouched and flattened her ears against her skull, staring fixedly down the opening at the hide. With these eyes on her, Claudia lost any urge to giggle again and she held her breath.

'She can't see me,' she told herself without conviction. 'Surely she can't see me?' But for long seconds, those eyes bored into hers.

Then abruptly, the old lioness rose and slid away into the thick undergrowth beyond the bait tree. She moved like a serpent, a sinuous flowing and gliding of the brown body. Claudia let out her breath slowly, and gulped with relief.

While the rest of the pride romped and tussled and fed beneath the bait tree, the sun slid below the tree-tops and the short African twilight was on them.

'If there is a tom with them, he will come in now,' Sean breathed softly. The night was the time of the cats, the darkness made them bold and fierce. The light was going even as they watched.

Claudia heard something beyond the grass wall beside her, a furtive brush of some creature in long grass, but the bush was full of such small sounds and she did not even turn her head. Then she heard a distinct and unmistakable sound. The footfall of some heavy creature, soft and stealthy, but very close, and she felt her skin crawl with the insects of fear and the prickle of it up the back of her neck. Quickly she turned her head.

Her left shoulder was pressed up against the thatch wall of the hide, and there was a chink in the thatch an inch wide. Her eyes were at the same level as the hole, and through it, she saw movement. For a moment, she did not recognize what she was seeing, and then she knew that it was a tiny expanse of smooth tawny hide, filling the chink, only inches on the far side. As she stared in horror, the tawny pelt slid past her eyes, and now she heard something else, an animal breathing, snuffling at the far side of the thatch wall.

Instinctively, she reached behind her with her free hand, but never taking her eyes from the chink. Her hand was seized in a hard cool grip. The touch that had offended her only minutes before, now gave her more comfort than she had ever believed possible. She did not even marvel that she had reached for Sean's hand, rather than her own papa's.

She stared into the chink, and suddenly, there was another eye beyond, a huge round eye, glistening like yellow agate, a terrible inhuman eye, unblinking, burning into hers with a dead black pupil in its centre, a hand's span from her face.

She wanted to scream, but her throat was closed. She wanted to leap to her feet, but her legs were dead. Her swollen bladder was like a stone in her lower belly, and before she could control it, she felt a few warm drops escape. That checked her, the humiliation was greater than her terror and she tightened her thighs and buttocks and clung to Sean's hand, still staring into that terrible yellow eye.

The lioness sniffed again loudly, and Claudia started silently but held on. 'I won't scream,' she told herself.

Again the lioness snuffled beyond the grass wall, and her nostrils were filled with the man odour and she let out an explosive grunt that seemed to rock the flimsy grass walls. Claudia caught the scream in her throat before it could escape. Then the yellow eye was gone from the chink, and she heard the pad of great paws circling back round the hide.

Claudia swivelled her head to follow the sound, and she looked straight into Sean's face. He was smiling. That was what shocked her after what she had just lived through, there was that devil-may-care grin on his lips and mockery in those green eyes. He was laughing at her. Her terror subsided, and her anger flared.

'The swine.' she thought. 'The arrogant bloody swine.' And she knew that her face was bloodless and that her eyes were dark and wide with terror. She hated herself for it and she hated him for being witness to it.

She wanted to jerk her hand out of his grip, but she could still hear that great cat out there, still very close, circling them and though she loathed him, she knew that without his grip she would not be able to control herself. So she held on, but she turned her face away, following the furtive sounds of the lioness, so that Sean could not see her face.

The lioness passed in front of the blind. Through the peephole she saw the blur of its golden body, quickly gone, and she saw also that the young lioness and the cubs, alerted by the warning grunt, had disappeared into the undergrowth. The killing ground below the bait tree was deserted.

The light was going swiftly now. Within minutes it would be dark, and the thought of that brute in the darkness was almost too much to bear. Sean reached over her shoulder and pressed something small and hard against her lips. For a moment, she resisted and then she opened and let him slide it into her mouth. It was a cube of chewing-gum.

'The man has gone mad.' She was bewildered. 'Chewing-gum at a time like this?'

Then as she crunched down on to the cube she realized that her saliva had dried out and that the inside of her mouth was seared and puckered as though she had bitten into a green persimmon. At the taste of spearmint, her saliva flowed again, but she was so angry with him that she felt no gratitude. He had known that her mouth was dry with terror and she resented that fiercely.

16

The lioness growled in the semi-darkness behind the hide, and Claudia thought longingly of the Toyota that was parked a mile back up the track. Almost echoing her thought, her father asked softly, 'When did you tell the gunbearers to bring the truck?'

'After the last of the shooting light,' Sean answered him quietly. 'Another fifteen or twenty minutes.'

The lioness heard their voices and growled again threateningly.

'Cheeky bitch,' Sean said cheerfully. 'Snarly Sue in person.'

'Shut up!' Claudia hissed at him. 'She'll find us.'

'Oh, she knows we are here now,' Sean replied, and then raised his voice and called. 'Get away with you, you silly old bitch, go on back to your babies.'

Claudia jerked her hand out of his grip. 'Damn you! You'll get us all killed.'

But the loud human voice had alarmed the cat, and for minutes, there was silence beyond the grass wall. Sean took up the short ugly double-barrelled rifle that was propped against the wall beside him and placed it across his lap. He opened the breech of the .577 Nitro Express, and slid the fat brass cartridges out of the chambers, changing them for two others from the loops on the left breast of his jacket. It was a little superstitious ritual of his, that changing of cartridges, he always performed it at the beginning of a hunt.

'Now, listen to me, Capo,' he addressed Riccardo. 'If we kill that old whore without good reason, the game department is going to pull my licence. "Good reason" is when she has already chewed somebody's arm off, not before. Do you hear me?'

'I hear you,' Riccardo nodded.

'All right, don't shoot until I tell you, or by God, I'll shoot you.'

They grinned at each other in the half light, and Claudia realized with disbelief that the two of them were enjoying themselves. These two crazy oafs were actually having fun.

'By the time Job arrives with the truck, it will be pitch dark, and Job can't get the truck up to the hide. We'll have to go down to it in the riverbed. You go first, Capo, and then Claudia between us. Stay close together, and whatever you do, don't run! For the love of God, don't anybody run!'

Then they heard the lioness again, padding softly around them. She growled once more and almost immediately her growl was

17

answered from the far side of the hide. The young lioness was out there now.

'The gang's all here,' Sean commented. The sound of voices and the old lioness's growls had summoned the rest of the pride, and the hunters had become the hunted. They were trapped in the hide. The darkness was almost complete. The sunset was merely a dull red furnace glow on the western horizon.

'Where is the truck?' Claudia whispered.

Sean said, 'It's coming.' Then his voice changed. 'Down!' he said sharply. 'Get down!' And though she had heard nothing, she dropped out of the canvas chair and crouched on the ground.

The lioness had crept up to the front wall again, almost soundlessly, and now she flung herself at it, roaring furiously as she tore at the flimsy structure with her front claws. With horror, Claudia realized that it was coming in on top of her.

'Keep your heads down,' Sean shouted urgently and lifted the double-barrelled rifle just as the wall burst open.

He fired, a stunning burst of sound as the muzzle blast swept through the hide and lit the interior with flame, brilliant as a flashbulb.

'He's killed the brute.' Despite her hatred of blood sport, Claudia felt a guilty relief, but it was short-lived. The shot had merely startled the cat and driven her off for the moment. Claudia heard the lioness gallop away into the undergrowth snarling viciously.

'You missed,' she accused him breathlessly, with the stink of burnt gunpowder in her nostrils.

'Wasn't trying to hurt her.' Sean opened the rifle and reloaded from the cartridge loops on his breast. 'Just a warning shot over her bows.'

'There's the truck coming.' Riccardo's voice was level and unconcerned. Claudia's ears were still singing from the crash of gunfire, but she could make out the distant beat of the Toyota's diesel engine through it.

'Job heard the shot.' Sean stood up. 'He's coming early. All right, let's get ready to move out.'

Claudia scrambled up eagerly, and then looked over the low grass wall of the roofless hide into the dark forbidding forest around her, and remembered the track that led down to the dry riverbed that served as a road. They would have to travel almost a quarter of a mile in the night to reach the safety of the truck. Her spirit quailed at the prospect.

In the trees not fifty yards away, the lioness roared again.

'Noisy blighter,' Sean chuckled, and took her elbow to guide Claudia to the door. This time she did not try to pull away, but instead found herself clinging to his arm.

'Take hold of Capo's belt.' Gently he disengaged her hand and guided it to her father's belt at the small of his back.

'Hold on,' he told her. 'And remember, whatever happens, don't run. It will pull them onto you instantly. Cat with mouse, they can't resist it.'

Sean switched on the flashlight. It was a big black Maglite, but even that powerful beam seemed puny and yellow in the immensity of the forest as he played it in a circle around them. There were eyes reflected in the beam, they glowed like menacing stars, many eyes out there in the dark bush, impossible to tell cubs from full-grown lionesses.

'Let's go.' Sean said quietly, and Riccardo started down the rough narrow track, dragging Claudia with him.

They went slowly, bunched up tightly. Riccardo covering the van with his lighter rifle and Sean in the rearguard, with the heavy rifle and the flashlight.

Each time the torch beam picked up the flash of cat's eyes in the night, they seemed closer, until Claudia could make out the body of the animal behind the glowing eyes. They were pale as moths in the torchlight, nimble and restless, as they circled, both lionesses closing in now, pacing swiftly through the undergrowth, watching them intently, but turning their heads away whenever the powerful light hit their eyes.

The track was steep and rough, and oh, so long. Each step was an agony of impatience for Claudia as she stumbled along behind her father, not watching her footing, but watching instead those pale feline shapes that paraded around them.

'Here comes Snarly Sue!' Sean warned quietly as the old lioness screwed up her courage and came at them out of the night, grunting like a steam locomotive, deafening gusts of sound surging up her throat and out of her open mouth, her long tail lashing from side to side like a hippo-hide whip. They stopped in a tight group, and Sean swung the torch and the rifle on to the charging animal.

'Get out of it!' he yelled at her. 'Go on, scat!' And the lioness

19

came on, her ears flattened against her skull, long yellow fangs and pink tongue curling between her gaping jaws.

'Yah! Snarly Sue!' Sean howled. 'I'll blow your stupid head off!'

She broke her charge at the last possible moment, skidding to a halt on stiff front legs, ten feet from where they were bunched and the dust swirled around her in the torchlight.

'Piss off!' Sean ordered her sternly, and her ears came erect and she turned and trotted obediently back into the forest.

'That was a game of chicken chicken,' Sean chuckled. 'She was just trying it on.'

'How did you know that?' Claudia's voice was cracked and shrill in her own ears.

'Her tail. As long as she keeps waving it, she's only kidding. When she holds it stiff, then look out!'

'Here's the truck,' Riccardo said, and they could see the Toyota's headlights through the trees as it bumped up the dry riverbed below them.

'Praise the Lord,' Claudia whispered.

'It's not over yet,' Sean warned as they moved off down the track once more. 'There is still Growly Gertie to deal with.'

Claudia had forgotten the younger lioness and now she glanced around fearfully, as she stumbled after her father, hanging onto his belt.

Then at last, they were on the bank of the riverbed, fully lit by the headlights of the parked truck which was standing only thirty yards away with its engine running. She could make out the heads of the trackers in the front seat beyond the blaze of headlights. So close, so very close, and she could not help herself. Claudia let go of her father's belt, and ran for the truck, pelting wildly through the thick loose white sand of the riverbed.

She heard Sean shout behind her, 'You bloody idiot!'

And immediately afterwards the fearsome grunting roar of the lioness as she charged. Claudia glanced sideways as she ran, and the great cat was almost on her, coming in at an angle out of the tall reeds that lined the open riverbed. She was huge and pale in the headlights of the Toyota, snake-swift and her roaring cramped Claudia's belly and her feet dragged in the thick white sand.

Claudia saw that the charging lioness carried her tail high and stiff as a steel ramrod, and even in her terror, she remembered what Sean had said and she thought with icy clarity. 'This time she's not going to stop, she's going to kill me.'

For a vital instant, Sean had not realized that the girl had run. He was backing carefully down the steep path into the riverbed, with the flashlight in his left hand and the double rifle in his right. He held the rifle by the grip with the barrels tilted up over his shoulder and his thumb on the slide of the safety-catch and he was watching the old lioness out there on the edge of the reed bed as she crawled on her belly towards them. But he was sure that she was now merely going through the motions of aggression since he had stared down her mock charge. There were two of the cubs well back behind her, sitting up in the grass and watching the performance with huge eyes and candid fascination, but too timid to take part. He had lost sight of the younger lioness, although he was sure that she was now the main threat, but the river reeds were dense and tall.

He had felt Claudia bump against his hip, but he thought she had stumbled, not realizing that she had bumped him as she turned to run. He was still searching for the younger lioness, probing the reed-beds with the torch beam, when he heard the crunch of Claudia's running feet in the sugary river sand, and he whirled and saw her out there in the dry riverbed alone.

'You bloody idiot!' he yelled in fury. The girl had been a constant source of irritation and dissent since she had arrived four days ago. Now she had flagrantly disobeyed his order, and he knew in an instant, even before the lioness launched her charge, that he was going to lose her. Getting a client killed or mauled was the blackest disgrace that could befall a professional hunter. It meant the end of his career, the end of twenty years of work and striving.

'You bloody idiot!' he vented all his bitterness on the running figure. He barged past Riccardo, who was still standing frozen with shock on the path below him, and at that moment, the lioness burst out of the edge of the reed bed where she had been lying.

The riverbed was brilliantly lit by the lights of the truck, so Sean dropped the torch and swung up the rifle with both hands, but he could not fire. The angle was wrong, the girl was between him and the lioness. Claudia ran awkwardly in the clinging sand, her head twisted away from him to watch the charge, her arms pumping frantically out of time with her legs.

'Down!' Sean shouted. 'Fall flat!' But she kept running, blocking his shot and the lioness swept in on her, sand spurting under her paws from which the curved yellow claws were already fully extended. She was grunting and roaring with each stride and her tail was carried stiff and straight.

In the headlights, the shadows of girl and cat on the stark white sand were grotesque and black, coming together swiftly, and Sean saw the lioness gather herself for the leap and he watched helplessly over the open iron sights of the rifle, impossible to separate them, impossible to fire without hitting the girl.

At the last moment Claudia tripped, her legs weak with fear collapsed under her and with a despairing wail, she sprawled face down in the sand.

Instantly, Sean zeroed his aim on the creamy chest of the lioness. With this rifle, he could hit two penny coins flipped simultaneously into the air at a range of thirty paces, left and right, both coins before they fell to earth. With this rifle, he had killed leopard, lion, rhino, buffalo, elephant by the hundred – and men, many men in the days of the Rhodesian bush war. He never needed a second shot. Now the target was open, he could with supreme confidence send a 750-grain soft-nosed mushrooming bullet through the lioness from her chest to the root of her tail. It would be the end of the cat, and of the safari, and probably his licence. At the least, it would mean months of investigation and trial. A dead lioness would bring all the wrath of the government, and the game department, down upon him.

The lioness was almost on top of the fallen girl, only a scant few feet of white sand between them, and Sean dropped his aim. It was a terrible risk, but he thrived on risk. He was gambling with the girl's life, but she had infuriated him, she deserved to take her chance.

He fired into the sand two feet in front of the lioness' open jaws. The huge heavy bullet ploughed in, sending up an eruption of sand, a solid fountain of flying white grains that for a moment, completely enveloped the animal. Sand filled its mouth and was sucked into its lungs as it roared, sand drove into its nostrils clogging them, and sand lashed into its open yellow eyes, tearing, raking, blinding the lioness, disorientating her, breaking the charge instantly.

Sean raced forward, with the second barrel ready to fire, but it wasn't necessary. The lioness had recoiled, rearing back

22

violently, clawing at her sand-clotted eyes, toppling over and then bounding up again, and careering back into the reed-bed, barging blindly into the sheer bank, rolling and falling, and struggling up again. The sound of her wild run and agonized roars dwindled.

Sean reached Claudia and with an arm around her, jerked her to her feet. Her legs were unable to support her, and he had to half carry, half drag her to the Toyota and bundle her into the front seat.

At the same time, Riccardo scrambled into the back seat of the Toyota, and Sean leapt up onto the running board and with his free hand held the rifle like a pistol, pointed out into the darkness, ready for another charge.

'Go!' he shouted at Job, and the Matabele driver let out the clutch and they flew down the riverbed, lurching and jolting over the heavy going.

Nobody spoke for almost a minute, until they had climbed out of the riverbed onto the smoother track and then Claudia said in a small strangled voice, 'If I can't pee right now, I'm going to burst.'

'We could always point you at Snarly Sue like a fire extinguisher and wash her away,' Sean suggested coldly, and in the back seat, Riccardo let out a delighted guffaw. Even though Claudia recognized the nervous relief and tension in her father's laugh, she resented it bitterly. It aggravated the total humiliation she had suffered.

It was an hour's drive back to camp and when they arrived, Moses, Claudia's camp servant, had the shower filled with piping hot water. The shower was a twenty-gallon oil drum suspended in the branches of a mopane tree, a thatched grass screen, open to the stars, and a cement floor.

She stood under the rush of steaming water and as her body turned bright pink, she felt the humiliation and the nausea of the adrenalin over-dose fade away, to be replaced by that buoyant sense of well-being that comes only from having survived extreme danger.

While she soaped herself, working up a rich lather, she listened to Sean. He was fifty yards away at his makeshift gymnasium at the back of his own tent, but his regular hissing breathing carried clearly as he worked with the iron weights. He had not missed a session in the four days she had been in camp, no matter how long and hard the day's hunting had been.

'Rambo!' She smiled contemptuously at his masculine conceit and yet more than once, during the last few days, she had caught herself surreptitiously contemplating his muscled arms, or his flat greyhound belly or even his buttocks, round and hard as a pair of ostrich eggs in his khaki shorts.

Moses carried the lantern ahead of her, escorting her back from the shower in her silk dressing-gown, with a towel tied like a turban around her hair. He had laid out her mess kit for her, khaki slacks and a Gucci tee-shirt, ostrich-skin mosquito boots, exactly what she would have chosen herself. Moses washed her soiled clothes every day, and his ironing was crisp perfection. Her slacks crackled softly as she pulled them on. They added to her sense of well-being.

She took her time drying her hair and brushing it out. She used an artistic trace of make-up and lipstick, and when she looked in the small mirror, she felt even better.

'Who's the vain one now?' she smiled at herself, and went out to where the men were already at the camp-fire, gratified when they stopped talking, and watched her make her entrance. Sean rose from his camp chair to greet her with those silly limey manners that disconcerted her.

'Sit down!' She tried to sound brusque. 'You don't have to keep jumping up and down.'

Sean smiled easily. 'Don't let her see how she is succeeding in getting up your nose,' he warned himself, and he held the canvas camp chair for her while she sat down with the soles of her mosquito boots to the camp-fire.

'Get the Donna a peg,' Sean ordered the mess waiter. 'You know the way she likes it.'

The waiter brought it to her on a silver tray. It was perfect. A dash of Chivas whisky in a crystal glass, barely enough to colour the Perrier water, and filled right up with ice. The waiter was dressed in a snowy white kanza robe, the hem well below his knee, a scarlet sash over his shoulder to denote that he was the head waiter, and a scarlet pillbox fez on his head. His two assistant waiters stood respectfully in the background, also in scarlet fez and flowing white robes. For Claudia it was mildly embarrassing, there were twenty servants to care for three of them, all so sybaritic and colonial and exploitative. This was 1987, for God's sake, and the empire was long gone – but the whisky was delicious.

24

'I suppose you expect me to thank you for saving my life,' she said, as she sipped it.

'Not at all, ducky.' Sean had learned almost immediately that she hated that form of address. 'I wouldn't even expect you to apologize for your crass stupidity. To be quite frank with you, I was worrying more about having to kill the lioness. Now that would have been tragic.'

They fenced lightly, skilfully, and Claudia found herself enjoying it. Every thrust that went through his guard gave her a satisfied glow, better even than a good day in court. She was disappointed when the head waiter announced in sepulchral tones, 'Chef say dinner she is ready, *Mambo*,' and Sean led them into the dining tent that was lit by candles in a many-branched Meissen porcelain candelabra. The cutlery was solid silver, Claudia had furtively checked the hallmarks, and the Waterford crystal wine-glasses sparkled on the table-cloth of Madeira lacework and a robed waiter stood behind each of their folding canvas safari chairs, ready to serve.

'What do you fancy tonight, Capo?' Sean asked.

'A touch of Wolfgang Amadeus,' Riccardo suggested, and Sean pressed the 'play' button on the tape-deck before going to his seat, and the limpid strains of Mozart's piano concerto number seventeen shimmered in the candlelight.

The soup was made with green peas and pearl barley and buffalo marrow bones, spiced with a fearsome chili sauce that Sean called *Peli Peli Ho Ho*.

Claudia had inherited her father's taste for chili and garlic and red wine, but even she could not face the second course, buffalo tripes in a white sauce. Both men liked their tripes green, which was simply an euphemism for improperly cleaned of the original contents.

'It's only chewed grass,' her father had pointed out, which made her feel squeamish until she turned and caught a whiff of the special dish that chef had prepared for her alone. Beneath a golden pie crust steamed a savoury stew of antelope fillets and kidneys. Chef had shaken his tall white cap when she had suggested the addition of ten cloves of garlic.

'Cook book say no garlic, Donna.'

'My book say plenty garlic, it say very loud ten cloves garlic, okay, chefie?' And the chef had grinned in capitulation. Claudia had almost instantly overwhelmed the entire camp staff with her easy manner and relaxed charm.

25

The wine was a rich and robust South African Cabernet, every bit as good as her favourite Chianti, and she gave both wine and pie her full attention. The day's rigours and the sun and fresh air had honed her appetite. Like her papa, she could eat and drink freely without adding an ounce of flesh or fat to her waistline. Only the conversation was a disappointment. As on every other evening the men were talking about rifles and hunting and the killing of wild animals. The gun talk was mostly unintelligible gibberish to her.

Her father said things like 'The .300 Weatherby can move a 180-grain bullet at 3200 foot per second, that gives you over 4000 foot/lb of muzzle energy and stupendous hydro-static shock.'

And Sean would respond. 'You Yanks are obsessed with velocity. Roy Weatherby has blown up more bullets on African game than you have eaten spaghetti, Capo. Give me high sectional density, Nosler construction and moderate velocity . . .'

No normally intelligent person could keep that up for hour after hour, she told herself, and yet every night of the safari so far she had gone to bed and left the two of them at the camp-fire still at it over their cognac and cigars.

When they spoke of the animals, however, she could take more interest and even participate, usually to vent her disapproval. They talked mostly of particular individual animals, legendary old males for which Sean had pet names, which annoyed Claudia, just the way it irritated her when he called Papa 'Capo', as though he were a mafia don. One such animal he referred to as 'Frederick the Great', or simply 'Fred'. This was the lion they were hunting now, the lion for which they had hung the buffalo carcass.

'I've seen him twice so far this season, one client even had a shot at him. Mind you, he was shaking so much with nerves he missed him by a football field.'

'Tell me about him.' Riccardo leaned forward eagerly.

'Papa, he told you about him last night,' Claudia reminded him sweetly. 'And the night before, and the night before that. . . .'

'Little girls should be seen and not heard,' Riccardo chuckled. 'Didn't I ever teach you anything? Tell me about Fred, again.'

'He's got to be well over eleven foot, and not just length. He's got a head on him like a hippo, and a mane like a black haystack. When he walks, it ripples and tosses like the wind in a msasa tree,' Sean rhapsodized. 'Cunning? Sly? Fred knows it all,

26

he's been shot at at least three times that I know of. Wounded once by a Spanish hunter over in Ian Piercy's concession three seasons ago, but he recovered. He didn't get that big by being stupid.'

'How are we going to get him?' Riccardo demanded.

'I think the two of you are disgusting,' Claudia cut in before Sean could reply. 'After seeing those glorious creatures today, those beautiful little cubs. How can you bring yourself to kill them?'

'I didn't see any cubs shot today,' Riccardo remarked as he nodded to the waiter offering him another helping of tripe. 'In fact, we went to a great deal of trouble and risk to ensure their survival.'

'You are devoting forty-five days of your life to the sole purpose of killing lions and elephants!' Claudia shot back. 'So don't get all righteous with me, Riccardo Monterro.'

'I am always fascinated by the confused thought processes of your average shrieking liberal,' Sean intervened and Claudia turned on him gleefully, lusting for battle.

'There is no confusion in my mind. You are here to kill animals.'

'The same way that a farmer kills animals,' Sean agreed. 'To ensure a healthy flourishing herd, and a place for that herd to survive.'

'You are not a farmer.'

'Oh yes, I am,' Sean contradicted. 'The only difference is that I slaughter them on the range, not in an abattoir, but like any farmer, my chief concern is the survival of my breeding-stock.'

'They are not domestic animals,' Claudia contested. 'Those are beautiful wild animals.'

'Beautiful? Wild? What the hell has that got to do with it? Like anything else in this modern world, the wild game of Africa has to pay its way if it's going to survive. Capo, here, is paying tens of thousands of dollars to hunt a lion and an elephant. He is giving those animals a monetary value far above goats and cattle, so that the newly independent government of Zimbabwe is willing to set aside concessions of millions of acres in which the game can persist. I hire one of those concessions, and I have the strongest incentive in the world for protecting it from the grazers and poachers and making certain I have plenty of game

27

to offer my hunters. No, ducky, legal safari hunting is one of the most effective arms of conservation in Africa today.'

'So you are going to save the animals by shooting them with high-powered rifles?' Claudia demanded scornfully.

'High-powered rifles?' Sean laughed softly. 'Another emotive liberal parrot cry. Would you prefer us to use low-powered rifles? Won't that be rather like demanding that the butcher uses only blunt knives to cut throats? You are an intelligent woman, think with your head, not your heart. The individual animal is unimportant. His life span is limited to a few short years. In the case of this lion we are hunting, probably twelve years at the very most. What is beyond price is the continued existence of the species as a whole. Not the individual, but his entire kind. Our lion is an old male at the very end of his useful life span during which he has protected his females and his young and already added his genes to the pool of his race. He will die naturally within the next year or two. Much better that his death produce ten thousand dollars in cash which will be spent on providing a safe place for his cubs to live, than having this wilderness encroached upon by swarming black humanity and their scrawny herds of goats.'

'My God, listen to you.' Claudia shook her head sadly. '"Swarming black humanity", those are the words of a racist and a bigot. It's their land, why can't they be free to live where they choose?'

'And that is the logic of woolly-headed liberalism,' Sean laughed. 'Make up your mind whose side you are on, the beautiful wild animals or the beautiful wild blacks. You can't have it both ways; when the two come into competition for living space, the wild animals always come off losers, unless we hunters can pay the bill for them.'

He wasn't an easy man to argue with, she conceded, and she was relieved when her father cut in and gave her a moment to gather her wits.

'There can be no doubt on which side my darling daughter stands. After all, Sean, you are talking to a senior member of the commission for the reinstatement of the Inuit people to their traditional lands.'

She smiled at him sweetly. 'Not Inuit, Papa. People will think you are going soft. Not even Eskimos – your usual description is gooks, isn't it?'

Riccardo smoothed back the thick waves of silver at his temples. 'Shall I tell you how my daughter and her commission go about determining how much of Alaska belongs to the Inuits?' he asked.

'He's going to tell you anyway.' Claudia leaned across to stroke her father's hand. 'It's one of his party routines. It's very funny, you'll love it.'

Riccardo went on as though she had not spoken. 'They go down Fourth Street, in Anchorage, that's where all the bars are, and they grab a couple of Eskimos that are still on their feet. They put them in an airplane and fly them down the peninsula, and they say to them: "Now, tell us where your people used to live. Show us your traditional tribal hunting grounds. How about that lake over there, did your people fish there once upon a time?"' Riccardo changed his voice, he was an excellent mimic. '"Sure!!" says the Eskimo in the back seat, squinting out the window, his eyes full of Jack Daniels. "That's where my gran-pappy fished."'

He changed voices, imitating Claudia. '"And what about those mountains over there, the one which we wicked white folk who stole it away from you call Brooks Range, did your gran-pappy ever hunt there?"' He changed to his Eskimo intonation. '"Sure did, man. He shot a whole mess of bears there. I remember my gran-mommy telling me about it."'

'Go on, Papa. You've got a marvellous audience tonight. Mr Courtney is enjoying your wit hugely,' Claudia encouraged him.

'You know something?' Riccardo asked, 'Claudia has never yet had an Eskimo turn down a lake or a mountain she has offered him, isn't that something else? My little girl has got a perfect score, never a single refusal.'

'You are just plain lucky, Capo,' Sean told him. 'At least they might leave you something, here they took the lot.'

* * *

Claudia woke to the clink of crockery outside the flap of her tent and Moses' polite cough. Nobody had ever brought her tea in bed before. It was a luxury that made her feel marvellously decadent. It was still pitch dark and icy cold in the tent. She could hear the crackle of frost on the canvas as Moses opened the flap. She had never expected it to be so cold in Africa.

29

She sat up in the camp-bed with a quilt over her shoulders, cupping her hands around the tea mug and watched Moses fussing about the tent. He poured a bucket of hot water into her wash basin and set a clean white towel beside it. He filled the tooth mug with boiled drinking water and squeezed toothpaste onto her brush for her. Then he brought a brazier of burning charcoal and placed it in the centre of the tent.

'Too cold today, Donna.'

'And too damned early,' Claudia agreed sleepily.

'Did you hear the lions roaring last night, Donna?'

'I didn't hear a thing.' She yawned. They could have had a brass band playing 'America, the Beautiful' beside her bed without waking her.

Moses finished laying out her clothes on the spare bed. He had polished her boots until they shone.

'You want something, Donna, you call me,' he told her as he backed out of the tent flap.

She shot out of the warm bed and stood over the brazier shivering while she held her panties over the coals to warm them before pulling them on.

The stars were still shining when she left the tent. She paused to look up, still amazed by the jewelled treasure chest of the southern sky. She picked out the great cross with a sense of achievement and then went to the camp-fire where the men were, and held her hands out gratefully to the flames.

'You haven't changed since you were little.' Her father smiled at her. 'Do you remember how I used to battle to get you out of bed to go to school every morning?' And a waiter brought her a second cup of tea.

Sean whistled and she heard Job start the Toyota and drive it around to the front gate of the stockade, and they began pulling on their heavy gear. Jerseys and anoraks, caps and woollen scarves.

When they trooped out to the hunting car, they found the rifles in the racks and Job and Shadrach, the two Matabeles, standing in the back with the little Ndorobo tracker between them. The tracker was a childlike figure who came only to Claudia's armpit, but he had an endearing wrinkled grin and bright mischievous eyes. She had been predisposed to like all the black camp staff, but Matatu was already her favourite. He reminded her of one of the dwarfs from *Snow White*. The three blacks were bundled up

30

against the cold in army-surplus greatcoats and knitted Balaclava caps, and they answered Claudia's greeting with white grins in the darkness. All of them had fallen under her spell.

Sean took the wheel and Claudia sat on the front seat between him and her father. She crouched down behind the windscreen and cuddled against Papa for warmth. In the short time she had been on safari, she had come to love this start to the day's adventure.

They drove slowly over the winding bumpy track and as the night retreated before the advance of dawn, Sean switched off the headlights.

Claudia peered into the combretum forest and down the grassy glades that intersected it that Sean called 'vleis', trying to be the first to spot some elusive and lovely creature, but always Sean or her father murmured first, 'Kudu on the left' or 'That's a reed-buck', or Matatu leaned over from the back to tap her shoulder and point out a rarer sight with his tiny pink-palmed hand.

The dusty track was pocked with the spoor of the animals that had crossed in the night. Once they came across the fresh droppings of an elephant, still steaming in the chill of dawn, a knee-high pile which everybody climbed out of the Toyota to examine closely. At first, Claudia had been disconcerted by this avid interest in dung, but now she was accustomed to it.

'Old beggar,' Sean said. 'On his last set of teeth.'

'How do you know that?' she demanded.

'Can't chew his food,' he replied. 'Look at the twigs and leaves in the dung, almost whole.'

Matatu was crouched by the spoor, examining the great round footprints, the size of dustbin-lids.

'See how smooth the pads of his feet are,' Sean told her. 'Worn down like an old set of car tyres. Old and big.'

'Is it him?' Riccardo asked eagerly, and glanced at the .416 Rigby rifle in the gun-rack behind his seat.

'Matatu will tell us,' Sean shrugged, and the little Ndorobo spat in the dust, and shook his head mournfully as he stood up. Then he spoke to Sean in piping falsetto Swahili.

'It's not the one we want. Matatu knows this bull,' Sean translated. 'We saw this one last year down near the river. He has one tusk broken off at the lip, and the other is worn down to a stump. He might once have had a magnificent pair, but he's far over the other side of the hill now.'

'You mean Matatu can recognize a particular elephant by his footprints?' Claudia looked incredulous.

'Matatu can recognize a particular buffalo out of a herd of five hundred, and he'll know that animal again two years later just by a glance at the spoor.' Sean exaggerated a little for her. 'Matatu isn't a tracker, he's a magician.'

They drove on with small wonders occurring all around them: a kudu bull, grey as a ghost, striped with chalky lines, maned and hump-backed, his long corkscrew horns glinting in the gloom, slipped away into the forest; a genet cat caught out from his nocturnal prowling, spotted and golden as a miniature leopard, peering at them with astonishment from the brown grass of the verge. A kangaroo rat hopped ahead of the Toyota. Troops of chittering guinea fowl with waxen yellow helmets on their heads ran through the grass beside the track and Claudia no longer had to ask, 'What is that bird?' or 'What animal is that?' She was beginning to recognize them and this added to her pleasure.

Just before the sunrise, Sean parked the Toyota at the foot of a rocky hill that rose abruptly out of the forest and they climbed out stiffly and took off their heavy outer clothing. They climbed the side of the kopje, three hundred feet of steep uneven pathway, without a pause, and Claudia tried to disguise her ragged breathing as they came out on the summit. Sean had timed the ascent perfectly, and as they reached the top, the sun burst out of the distant forest and lit it all with dramatic colour and brilliance.

They looked out over a panorama of forest and glade that glowed with golden grass to other high sheer kopjes standing like fairy castles, all turreted and towered in the dawn. Other hills were great dumps of black rock, like the rubble left over from the Creation.

They shed their sweaters, for the climb had warmed them and even the first rays of the sun held the promise of the noonday heat and they sat on the front edge of the hill and played their binoculars over the forest below. Behind them, Job laid out the food box that he had carried up and in minutes, he had a fire going. It had been too early to eat breakfast before they left camp, but now at the odour of frying bacon and eggs, Claudia felt her saliva flooding.

While they waited for their breakfast, Sean pointed out the

terrain. 'That is the Mozambique border over there, just beyond the second kopje, only seven or eight miles from here.'

'Mozambique,' Claudia murmured, peering through her binoculars. 'The name has such a romantic ring to it.'

'Not so romantic. It's just another triumph of African socialism and the carefully thought-out economic policy of chaos and ruination,' Sean grunted.

'I can't take racism before breakfast,' Claudia told him icily.

'All right,' Sean grinned. 'Suffice it to say that just across the border there you have twelve years of Marxism, corruption, greed and incompetence, just beginning to bear fruit. You have a civil war raging out of control, famine that will probably starve a million people, and epidemic disease, including Aids, that will kill another million in the next five years.'

'Sounds like a fun place for a vacation,' Riccardo said. 'How about breakfast, Job?'

Job brought them plates of eggs and bacon and fried French bread followed by mugs of strong aromatic coffee. They ate off their laps, glassing the forest through their binoculars between mouthfuls.

'You are a pretty good cook, Job,' Claudia told him.

'Thank you, ma'am,' Job answered quietly. He spoke English with only a slight accent. He was a man in his late thirties, with a tall and powerful physique and wide-spaced intelligent eyes in the handsome moon face typical of the Matabele and their Zulu origins.

'When did you learn?' Claudia asked, and the Matabele hesitated and glanced at Sean before he said in his deep soft voice, 'In the army, ma'am.'

'Job was a captain in the Ballantyne Scouts with me,' Sean explained.

'A captain!' Claudia exclaimed. 'I didn't realize that . . .' she broke off quickly, looking embarrassed.

'You didn't realize there were black officers in the Rhodesian army,' Sean finished for her. 'There is a lot more to know about Africa than what they show you on CBS television.'

Shadrach, the second gunbearer, was sitting fifty yards farther along the crest, where he had a better view towards the north, and now he whistled softly and pointed up that way. Sean wiped the last of the egg yolk off his plate with the toast and stuffed it in his mouth. He passed the plate to Job. 'Thanks, Job, that was great.' And went to join Shadrach. The two of them peered down into the forest.

'What is it?' Riccardo called impatiently.

'Elephant,' Sean replied, and both Riccardo and Claudia sprang up and hurried to join them.

'Where? Where?' she demanded.

'Big one?' Riccardo asked. 'Can you see his tusks? Is it him?'

'Too far to be sure, a couple of miles.' Sean pointed out the indistinct grey blur amongst the trees and Claudia was amazed that such a huge animal was so difficult to see. It took some minutes before it moved slightly and she was able to pick it out.

'What do you think?' Riccardo asked. 'Could it be Tukutela?'

'It could be,' Sean nodded. 'But it's a thousand to one against it.'

Tukutela. Claudia had listened to them discussing this elephant at the camp-fire. Tukutela, the angry one, was one of those legendary animals of which there were only a handful left in the whole length and breadth of Africa. A bull elephant with tusks that weighed over a hundred pounds each. Tukutela was the main reason that her father had come back to Africa for the last time. For he had once seen Tukutela. Three years before, he had been on safari with Sean Courtney, and the two of them had followed the great elephant for five days. Matatu had led them over a hundred miles on the spoor before they had come up with him. They had stalked to within twenty paces of the enormous and ancient beast as he fed on the fruits of a marula tree. They had studied every wrinkle and crease in his riven grey hide. They were so close that they could have counted the remaining few hairs in his tail, the rest worn away over the years, and they had gazed in silent awe upon his ivory.

Riccardo Monterro would have willingly paid any price to possess those tusks as his own trophy. He had asked Sean in a whisper, 'Isn't there any way I can have him?' And he had seen Sean hesitate before he shook his head.

'No, Capo. We can't touch him. More than my licence and my concession are worth.' For around his neck, Tukutela wore a collar, a sturdy thing of nylon, tough as a heavy-duty truck tyre, and suspended from it was a radio transmitter.

Some years previously, the old bull had been darted from a helicopter by members of the government elephant research project, and while he was unconscious, they had riveted the radio collar around his neck. This made Tukutela a 'designated research animal' and placed him beyond the reach of legal safari hunters. Of course, he was still at risk from ivory poachers, but no licensed hunter could legally hunt him.

While the elephant was under the drug, Dr Glynn Jones, the government veterinarian in charge of the project, had measured his tusks. His report was not for general publication, but his secretary was a nubile blonde who thought that Sean Courtney was the most awe-inspiring thing she had ever seen in her young life. She had duplicated a copy of the report for Sean.

'From Jonesy's measurements, one tusk will weigh 130 pounds and the other a few pounds lighter,' Sean had whispered to Riccardo as they studied the old bull, and they had stared at the tusks hungrily.

At the lip, they were as thick as Sean's thigh and there was no taper to them. They were stained almost black with vegetable juice. The tips were rounded off bluntly, according to Doctor Jones, the left tusk was eight foot four and a half inches, the right tusk eight foot six and a quarter, from lip to tip.

In the end, they had walked away and left the old bull to his solitary wandering, and then only six months ago, the blonde secretary had been making breakfast for Sean in her tiny bachelor flat in the Avenues in Harare, when she mentioned quite casually, 'Did you know that Tukutela has thrown his collar?'

Sean was lying naked on her bed, but he sat up quickly. 'What did you say?'

'Jonesy was in an awful pet. They put the radio direction finder on Tukutela and all they got was his collar. He had managed to tear it off at last and had hurled it into the top of a msasa tree.'

'You clever little beauty,' Sean said happily. 'Come here and get your prize.' And the girl had dropped her dressing-gown on the floor and rushed across the room.

So Tukutela had thrown his collar, and was no longer a 'designated research animal'. Once again, he was legal game. That same day, Sean had sent a cable to Riccardo in Alaska, and received the reply the following afternoon.

'I'M COMING STOP BOOK ME FULL SAFARI 1ST JULY TO AUGUST 15TH STOP I WANT THAT JUMBO STOP CAPO'

And now, as Riccardo stood on the crest of the kopje, studying

35

that far-off smudge of elephant grey in the forest below, he was shaking with excitement.

Claudia studied him with open amazement. This was her father, the coolest cat in the business, the master of *savoir faire*. She had seen him negotiating a ten-million-dollar contract and betting a prince's ransom across the tables at Vegas, without any visible emotion, but here he was shivering with excitement like a schoolboy on his first date, and she felt a rush of affection for him.

'I haven't understood just how much this means to him,' she thought. 'Perhaps I am being too hard. This is the last thing in his life that he truly wants.' And she wanted to put her arms around him and hug him and tell him, 'I'm sorry, Papa. I'm sorry that I have been trying to deprive you of this last pleasure.'

Riccardo was not even aware of her existence. 'It could be Tukutela,' he repeated softly, speaking almost to himself, as though he was trying to will it to be so, but Sean shook his head.

'I've got four good trackers watching the river. Tukutela couldn't cross without them knowing, besides it's still too early. I wouldn't expect him to leave the valley until the last waterholes along the escarpment dry up, another week or ten days at the earliest.'

'He could have slipped through.' Riccardo ignored his explanation. 'It's just possible that it is him down there.'

'We'll go down and take a look, of course,' Sean nodded in agreement. Riccardo's passion did not amaze him as it had his daughter. He understood it totally, had seen it in fifty other men like Riccardo, the powerful, aggressive, successful men, who made up his clientele, men who did not try to conceal or check their instincts. The hunting imperative was part of every man's soul; some denied or suppressed it, others diverted it into less blatantly violent avenues of expression, wielding clubs on the golf course or racquets on the court, substituting a little white ball for the prey of flesh and blood, but men like Riccardo Monterro gave their passions full rein and would settle for nothing less than the ultimate thrill of the chase and the kill.

'Shadrach, bring the *Bwana*'s .416 *banduki*,' Sean called. 'Job, don't forget the water-bottles. Matatu, *akwendi*, let's go!'

They went directly down the steep front slope of the kopje, leaping lightly from boulder to boulder, and at the bottom, they dropped naturally into their running formation with Matatu leading to pick up the spoor, followed by Job and Sean with their almost supernatural eyesight to sweep the forest ahead, the clients in the middle, and Shadrach in the drag to hand Riccardo the Rigby when he needed it. They went swiftly, but it was almost an hour through the forest before Matatu picked up the huge dished spoor in the soft earth, and the litter of stripped twigs and branches that the elephant had strewed behind him as he fed. Matatu stopped on it, turning back to roll his eyes, and give shrill piping cries of disgust.

'It's not Tukutela. It's the old one-tusk bull,' Sean told them. 'The same one whose spoor we saw on the road this morning. He has circled back this way.'

Claudia watched her father's face and saw the intensity of his disappointment, and felt her heart squeeze for him.

Nobody spoke on the march back to the Toyota, but when they reached it, Sean said softly, 'You knew it wasn't going to be that easy, didn't you, Capo.' And they grinned at each other.

'You're right, of course. The chase is everything. Once you kill, it's only dead meat.'

'Tukutela will come,' Sean promised him. 'This is his regular beat. He'll be here before the new moon, that's my promise to you, but in the meantime there is the lion. We will go check bait to see if Frederick the Great is going to oblige us.'

It was only another twenty minutes' driving to the dry riverbed below the hide and the buffalo bait. They left the Toyota parked on the white sand, and Claudia felt a tremor of last night's terror as they climbed the path up the far bank and saw the pad marks of the lioness in the earth behind the hide. Then Sean and his gunbearers were talking excitedly and Matatu was chittering like an agitated guinea fowl.

'What is it?' Claudia demanded, but nobody answered her and she had to trot to keep up with them as they hurried down the open tunnel through the bush to where the remains of the carcass hung in the wild fig.

'Somebody tell me what's happening,' Claudia begged them, but she stayed well back from the bait. The stench was just too much for her to bear. The men showed no distaste at all as they prodded and peered at the reeking remains, and even Claudia could see the difference from the previous evening.

Yesterday, the carcass had been virtually untouched, now more than half of it had been devoured. Only the head and forequarters remained, and Sean had to stretch up above his head to reach it. The bones of spine and ribs had been chewed to splinters, and the thick black skin ripped by claw and fang, so that it hung in tatters like a funeral flag.

While Sean and the gunbearers examined the carcass, Matatu searched the earth around the base of the fig tree, giving excited little yaps like a hound questing for the scent. Sean picked something off the jagged white ribs of the carcass and showed it to Riccardo, and both of them laughed excitedly, passing whatever it was from hand to hand.

'Won't somebody talk to me, please?' Claudia insisted, and Sean called to her.

'Come on then, don't stand so far away.'

Reluctantly, holding her nose theatrically, she approached and Sean held out his right hand to her, palm up. On it lay a single hair, almost as long and black as one from her own head.

'What is it?'

Riccardo took the hair from Sean's hand, holding it between thumb and forefinger, and Claudia saw that the back of her father's arms were goose-bumped with excitement, and his dark Italian eyes glowed as he replied.

'Mane hair.'

Then he seized her hand and pulled her across to the base of the fig tree.

'Take a look at that. Look what Matatu has found for us.'

The little tracker was grinning with proprietorial pride as he indicated the churned earth. Five cubs and two lionesses had trampled the soft footing into talcum dust, but one perfect print stood out in the confusion. It was double the size of the other smudged prints, as big as a soup plate, and, looking at it, Claudia felt again the stirring of terror. Whatever animal had left that pad mark must be monstrous.

'Last night, after the lionesses had seen us off, he came. He waited until the moon had set and he came in the darkest hours of the night,' Sean explained. 'And he left again before dawn. He ate damned nigh half a buffalo, and then he took off again before first light. I told you that he is a cunning old devil.'

'A lion?' Claudia asked.

'Not just any old lion.' Riccardo shook his head. 'Frederick the Great has come at last.'

Sean turned away and beckoned his men to come to him. The

three of them, Job and Shadrach and Matatu, squatted around him in a circle and Claudia and Riccardo were forgotten as they planned the hunt, working out their tactics, discussing in detail every aspect, every eventuality. Their concentration was absolute, and it was an hour before Sean stood up and came to where Riccardo and Claudia sat in the shade.

'The trick is going to be getting him to come in before nightfall,' he told them. 'And we all agree that the only way to do that is to set up a fresh bait for him and build a new hide. The lionesses have rumbled this one, and old Fred is going to be as suspicious as all hell. He's going to lurk out there until well after dark or until we can entice him in somehow.'

Sean sat down between them, and was silent for a moment.

'You know, Capo, sometimes for a good friend, someone I can trust, I am prepared to bend the rules a little.' He spoke deliberately, drawing with a twig in the dirt between his feet, and not looking at Riccardo.

'I'm listening,' Riccardo nodded.

'There may be only one way that we will get this lion,' Sean said softly. 'Jack-light him.'

They were silent for a long time, and though Claudia did not know what 'Jack-light' meant, she realized that Sean was suggesting something beyond law or decency, and that her father was tempted. She was angry with Sean for putting temptation in her father's way, but she knew better than to intervene. She kept silent and willed her father to refuse to give in to temptation.

Riccardo shook his head. 'No, let's do it right.'

'We can try,' Sean shrugged. 'But he has been shot at over a bait, and wounded once. It won't be easy.'

They were silent again for almost a full minute, then Sean went on, 'The lion is a nocturnal animal. The night is his time. If you truly want this lion, I think you'll have to take him in darkness.'

Riccardo sighed, and shook his head. 'I want him very badly, but not badly enough to kill him without respect.'

Sean stood up. 'It's your safari, Capo,' he agreed quietly. 'I just want you to know that there are not many men I'd make that offer to. As a matter of fact, offhand I can't think of anyone else I'd do it for.'

'I know,' Capo said. 'Thank you, Sean.' And Sean walked back to the fig tree to help his men to lower the remains of the carcass so the pride could reach it.

As soon as he was out of earshot, Claudia asked her father, 'Jack-light? What is that?'

'Putting a spotlight on an animal after dark, and shooting it in the beam. It's illegal, highly illegal.'

'The bastard,' she said bitterly.

Riccardo did not react to her denunciation, but went on softly, 'He was prepared to put his career on the line for me. That's one of the best things anyone has ever done for me.'

'I'm proud that you refused him, Papa, but he is a bastard.'

'You don't understand,' he said, 'You can't possibly understand.' He stood up and walked away, and immediately she felt a throb of guilt. She did understand. She understood that this was his last lion, and that she was spoiling the pleasure of it for him. She was torn between her love for him, and her protective instinct for that marvellous animal and her sense of right and justice.

'It should be easy to do the right thing,' she thought, 'But it so seldom is.'

So over the days that followed, they hunted the old lion with ethical tactics. They had to provide fresh baits for him and the lionesses, and Riccardo shot the buffalo Sean pointed out to him, another barren cow, and then two days later, a decrepit bull with horns worn down to stumps and his ribs showing through his bald mud-caked hide.

Each day Sean moved the bait or repositioned the thatched hide, trying to find a location which the black-maned male would feel sufficiently confident to approach in broad daylight. Evening after evening, they sat in the hide until an hour after darkness had fallen and then drove back to camp dejected and discouraged. When they visited the bait again the following morning they found that the lion had fed, leaving his mane hairs and his huge pad-marks to tantalize them, and had departed again before dawn.

Cursing the beast bitterly, Sean changed tactics. He lowered the remains of the rotten bait on its chain so that lionesses and cubs could reach it readily. By this stage, it was mostly dried skin and gnawed bone. Five hundred metres up the river, he hung a fresh carcass, at a height that only the big lion could reach in a tree that stood alone in a glade of shoulder-high dry winter grass. He hoped that without the harassment of the females and cubs the lion might come earlier to the bait.

To make him feel even more secure, he placed the hide across the dry riverbed in the fork of a teak tree. It was a machan platform fifteen feet above ground level. From the machan, they had a view across the white sand of the dry riverbed.

Sean did not clear all the grass around the bait tree. He wanted the lion to feel protected by good cover. He merely opened a keyhole in the grass, barely as wide as the body of the lion, through which they could see the carcass.

'If he comes, you'll have to wait until he rears up to feed, Capo,' he explained as they went into the machan an hour after noon, to wait out the long drowsy hot afternoon.

Sean allowed Claudia to bring a paperback copy of Karen Blixen's *Out of Africa* to read.

'Just as long as you don't rustle the pages,' he warned her.

The lionesses and their cubs came early. They were so conditioned to feeding from a bait by now, that they showed not the least trepidation at approaching. First they came to the new bait in the grassy glade, and inspected it wistfully. Both lionesses made attempts to feed from it, but it was just out of their reach.

For the last few days, the eyes of the young lioness, Growly Gertie, had been irritated and infected by the river sand that Sean had fired into them. Tears ran down her cheeks and her eyelids were swollen and inflamed, but now they were healing and clearing, the swelling was abating and there were only smears of yellow mucus in the corners of her eyes.

After a while, they gave up trying to reach the carcass, and led their cubs down the riverbank to the old stinking bait.

From the machan, they could hear the pride growling and ripping at the bait five hundred metres downstream, but as the afternoon passed, so the sounds of feeding dwindled into silence as the lionesses satiated themselves and went to lie up in the shade.

Half an hour before sunset, the small hot breeze that had been blowing all afternoon, dropped abruptly and that peculiar hush of an African evening descended on the veld. The sparse winter growth of leaves on the trees was still, not a blade of yellow grass stirred in the glade across the riverbed, and the fluffy papyrus reeds below the bank ceased their perpetual nodding and bowing and stood as though listening intently. It was so quiet that Claudia looked up from her book, and then closed it softly and sat listening to the absolute silence.

Then suddenly a bush-buck barked on the far bank, an alarm call so clear and loud in the hush that Claudia jumped involuntarily. Immediately, she felt Sean's light firm touch on her hip, a warning, and she heard her father's breathing, quick and deep as though he had just finished a hard rally on the court.

The silence had an ominous weight to it now, as though the world held its breath. Then she heard her father exhale softly, and she glanced sideways at him. His expression was rapt as that of a communicant kneeling for the Sacrament. God, he was a handsome man, she thought. Except for the silver wings at his temples, he looked so much younger than his years, so tanned and lean and fit. As yet, there was no external sign of the treachery of his own body that was destroying itself from within.

His excitement was infectious and she felt her own blood course more swiftly, driven by the quickening of her pulse, and she turned her head slowly to follow the direction of her father's gaze. He was looking off to the right, out across the river, to where the trees of the forest met the tall pale grass at the edge of the glade.

The only living creature out there was a grey parrot-like bird perched on the top branch of a bush willow. Sean had told her it was a grey lourie, the notorious 'go away bird' that plagued the hunter with its raucous warning cry. The bird squawked now, 'G'way! G'way!' But as it fluttered on the high branch, it was twisting its neck, craning to peer down into the long grass below the bush willow.

'Here he comes. The bird can see him.' Sean whispered only inches behind her ear, and Claudia strained her eyes looking for she knew not what.

'Watch the grass.' Sean guided her, and she saw the movement. The tips of the grass trembled and pushed, a stealthy furtive movement that passed slowly down the glade towards the riverbank, and then the grass behind it was still again. It was like the movement of a large trout in a still pool, the creature unseen, just the surface bulging and stirring to mark its passing.

All movement ceased for long minutes at a time.

'He's listening and checking the scent.' Sean explained. She had never expected him to show emotion such as excitement, but his whisper was tight and scratchy.

The movement of the grass tips began again, coming on towards the bait tree, and suddenly her father gave a small breathy gasp, and at the same moment, Sean warned her again. Perhaps he had meant to touch her hip once more, but his fingers closed on her upper thigh instead.

His touch was a shock, made more intense by her first sight of the beast. The lion passed through a gap in the grass, which the lionesses had trampled, and she glimpsed the top of his head, the dense bush of his mane, dark and curling, swaying and rippling to his slow imperial stride, and for an instant she caught the flash of yellow eyes below the mane.

She had never seen any creature so menacing, and yet so majestic. It was the briefest glimpse, before the grass covered him again, but it left her shaken and breathless, and Sean's hand was still on her thigh.

Suddenly, she realized that she was sexually aroused, the tension in her lower belly, the hardening thrust of her nipples against the cotton shirt and the warm flooding of her loins surprised her. She felt an almost irresistible urge to let her thighs relax and fall open under Sean's fingers, even though the folly of it would be monumental. If she had been asked to describe a human being who most offended and angered her, the description would have fitted him perfectly. She knew that if she showed the slightest vulnerability, he would exploit it ruthlessly. 'And I don't even like him,' she told herself desperately. Yet her legs were trembling, he must feel it, and she couldn't move.

Then he took his hand off her leg, but the way he did it was offensive. He did not simply lift it away, he turned it into a caress, drawing his fingers lingeringly over her thigh and hip, a disconcerting sensation for which she was unprepared. She felt her cheeks and her throat turn hot with resentment, but she stared out across the riverbed to that stealthy movement that stopped at last below the bait tree.

The silence drew out while Claudia tried to bring her emotions under control.

'It wasn't him,' she told herself. 'I wasn't reacting to him. He has nothing for me. It was the tension and excitement of the moment, nothing to do with him. He's not the least bit attractive to me. I like sensitivity and subtlety, and he is obvious and overpowering and brutal.'

Across the river, there was an abrupt disturbance in the grass and the sound of a heavy body flopping to earth.

Behind her, she felt Sean shake with soft and silent laughter, and for an incredulous moment, she thought he was laughing at her, then he whispered, 'He's lain down. Can you believe it, he's taking a rest right under the bait. The cocky son-of-a-bitch.'

Sean was thinking about the girl as much as about the lion. The unconcealed antipathy she bore him he returned in full measure, which made it more amusing to tease and plague her. Of course, the lion-hide was always a good place to catch a woman off-balance. He had begun many a memorable affair here. When they were in the hide they were psychologically under his control, like children in a classroom. He was the master and they were conditioned to obey his will, and the tension and nervous excitement made them receptive and compliant, the promise of danger and bloodshed heightened awareness, physical and sexual. It had been fun to find out that this bumptious, spoilt, self-righteous American bitch was no different from any of the others.

She was probably hating herself and him at this moment for that momentary lapse. He smiled thinly as he sat up close behind her. He had judged it with the fine instinct of the gifted philanderer, for it was, of course, a gift. He had read with attention Casanova's memoirs and there the old rogue had described it precisely. When she is receptive, every woman gives out subtle little signs, breathing, flush of skin, change of poise, tiny body movements, even odour, that very few men can even recognize, let alone interpret. It was a gift that only the great lovers possessed. Knowing when to act, and how far to push each stage, that was the trick, he told himself.

From where he sat, he could see her right cheek and the long dark lashes of the eye above, even though she was deliberately keeping her head turned away from him now.

She had bound her jet hair into a thick braid that hung down between her shoulder-blades. So her neck was exposed, an elegant column that supported the small neat head. Her neck and cheek were still flushed with angry arousal beneath skin that was already darkened by the African sun to the tone where she could have modelled for an expensive sun cream in one of the glossy women's magazines.

As he studied her, the flush abated and she regained her composure, but under her thin cotton tee-shirt, the nipple on the one pert, almost girlish, breast that he could see, was in silhouette. It was still standing out, the size and colour of a ripe mulberry, a dark wine colour through the thin material, then it began to shrink and subside; the phenomenon intrigued him and he laughed again soundlessly.

'You've given yourself a blinding hard-on,' he chuckled. 'And you can't even stand the little witch.' He switched his attention from her back to the unseen cat in the grass across the river.

It was almost fully dark before they saw the lion again, there was just a fading memory of the sunset on the western horizon but Sean had positioned the bait and blind so that it back-lit the scene for them. They heard the grass rustle and stir as the lion stood up, and they leaned forward eagerly. Riccardo lifted the buttstock of the rifle to his shoulder and peered into the long tube of the telescopic sight.

Abruptly, the lion reared out of the grass, a great dark, shapeless mass, just visible against the pale sky, and they heard the creak of the chain that held the bait as he swung upon it with all his weight, tearing at the carcass as he began to feed.

'Can you see your sights?' Sean asked Riccardo. The lion was making so much noise that he raised his voice to an almost conversational pitch, but Riccardo did not reply. He was moving the long barrel of the rifle in slow circles, trying desperately to pick up the cross hairs of the sight against the last fading glimmer of the sunset.

'No!' he admitted defeat at last. 'It's too dark.'

Claudia felt a lift of relief that she wouldn't have to witness the slaughter, but Sean said quietly, 'All right, we'll just have to sit it out and try and get a crack at him in the dawn.'

'All night!' Despite his injunctions to silence, Claudia was so startled by the prospect of spending the night in the hide that she protested plaintively.

'You signed on to be tough, didn't you?' Sean smiled at her alarm.

'But, but . . . won't Job bring the truck?' She sounded desperate.

'Not unless he hears a shot.' And she subsided miserably in her chair.

The night was interminable and cold, and the mosquitos came from the stagnant green pool in the riverbed and whined around their heads, ignoring the repellent that Claudia smeared on her exposed skin.

Across the river, the lion fed at intervals, and then rested. A little after midnight, he began to roar, crashing bursts of sound that brought Claudia out of an uncomfortable doze, and made her heart jump against her ribs. The terrible sound ended in a diminishing series of throaty grunts.

'Why does he do that?' Claudia asked breathlessly.

'To let the world know who is boss around here.'

Then the hyena came, shrieking and hooting like a pack of ghouls, gibbering with excitement at the smell of the kill, and the lion drove them off, rushing heavily in the grass, snarling and roaring, but they came edging back as soon as he returned to feed, and they tittered and whooped at him, forming a restless circle around the bait tree.

An hour before dawn, Claudia at last fell into a fitful sleep, hunched down in the chair with her neck twisted at an awkward angle, and she awoke with a start, to find it was light enough to make out the links of the chain that held the buffalo carcass.

In the forest close by, a pair of ground hornbills, grotesque black birds as big as a wild turkey with the same bald red heads, were booming their dawn chorus in a ritual duet. Beside her, Riccardo was stretching and yawning and Sean stood up, rocking the machan.

'What's happened?' Claudia mumbled. 'Where's the lion?'

'He took off an hour ago,' her father told her. 'Long before shooting light.'

'Only one way you are going to get this cat, Capo, and that's with a jack-light, or with a hell of a lot of luck.'

'I'm a lucky guy,' Riccardo grinned and they heard the distant beat of the Toyota's engine growing louder as Job came in to pick them up.

They stayed in camp all that day, catching up on sleep lost the previous night, but when they went into the hide again that evening to wait for the lion, he had disappeared. He did not come to the bait the following night either, and the safari came upon a period of hiatus. Sean and his team worked diligently but fruitlessly to find the lion. There was no report from the scouts whom Sean had placed to watch the elephant crossings on the Chiwewe river which was the northern boundary of Sean's concession. Riccardo Monterro was not interested in hunting lesser plains game, such as sable antelope, or kudu, or eland. These activities would have filled the days of another safari.

Only the two lionesses and their cubs stayed on the banks of the riverbed taking up permanent domicile.

'Courtney's five-star hotel.' Sean complained. 'Gourmet meals delivered daily.'

The pride became so accustomed to their visits, that the lionesses retreated only a hundred yards or so into the forest with a few perfunctory low-key growls and watched with interest as a fresh carcass was hauled into the tree. They barely contained their impatience until the Toyota pulled away, and it was still in full view when they came loping back to inspect the latest offering.

However, Frederick the Great did not return. They saw no sign of his huge distinctive pugmarks around the baits or upon the dirt tracks that Sean patrolled each day, searching the area for forty miles around the camp.

'But why would he just vanish like that?' Riccardo protested.

'Because he is a cat – and who knows how a cat thinks!'

*   *   *

Since that brief but torrid episode in the lion hide, the relationship between Sean and Claudia had altered subtly. Their bickering had become more vindictive and bitter, their overt resentment more intense, and their efforts to discomfort each more spirited.

When she called him a racist, he smiled at her. 'In America that word is dreaded as the ultimate insult that can end a man's political career, or ruin his business or ostracize him from society. You are all so terrified of it, and the blacks know it and exploit it to the full. Even the toughest hard-headed businessman or politician rolls over like a puppy dog and whines if you call him that,' Sean told her gleefully. 'This isn't America, ducky, and here we aren't terrified of that word. Here racism is the same as tribalism, and we are all blatant tribalists, especially the blacks. If you want to experience true dedicated tribalism and racism, then come and live in one of the newly independent African states. If you call your average black politician a racist, he would take it as a compliment, it would be the same as calling him a patriot.'

Her wounded protestations were ample reward for his efforts as he looked for new ways to provoke her.

'Did you know I am a South African?' he asked, and she looked appalled.

'I thought you were a Brit.' He shook his head and smiled in that infuriating way of his.

'I imagine you support your government's sanctions against my country.'

'Of course, every decent person does.'

'Even if it means that a million blacks starve as a direct consequence?' He did not wait for her to reply. 'What about disinvestment of American business from my country, you are all for that too?'

'I campaigned for it on campus,' she told him proudly. 'I never missed a rally or a march.'

'So your plan is to convert a country by withdrawing all your missionaries and burning down the cathedral, that's brilliant!'

'You are twisting it.'

'We should be grateful to you for the success of your efforts, you forced your own citizens to sell our assets back to us at five cents in the dollar. Overnight you created two hundred multi-millionaires in South Africa, and every one of them had a white face. Congratulations and our sincere thanks, ducky.'

But while they argued, they were avidly aware of each other, and that physical contact they had shared lay between them like a poisonous serpent, dangerous, but intriguing.

Claudia had been celibate for almost two years now, ever since she had split from the physician whom she had lived with for a short while until his demands for marriage became intolerable. Celibacy did not suit her affectionate Latin nature, but she was fastidious. She found herself lying awake in her tent at night listening to Sean's voice from the camp-fire as he talked to her father, the soft masculine rumble, just low enough for her to be unable to catch the words. Once she thought she heard her name, and she sat up and strained her hearing, disappointed that she could not hear what he said about her.

Then, when at last he called goodnight to Riccardo and went to his own tent, he had to pass close to hers. She lay rigid in bed, listening to his footsteps and watching the beam of his flashlight through the canvas, preparing an icy dismissal in the most insulting terms, and then experiencing the tiniest prick of disappointment as his footsteps passed on without a check.

On the ninth morning of the safari when they drove out to check the bait on the riverbank, the younger lioness, her eyes now completely healed, ʌas once again violently aggressive, snarling at Sean and mock-charging him from a hundred yards with her tail lashing as soon as he dismounted from the Toyota to inspect the bait. When she backed off and turned to retreat, they saw the pink stain of blood on the soft, pale beige fur beneath her tail.

'Growly Gertie has come into season,' Sean exulted. 'Now we have the one bait that Frederick the Great won't be able to resist. You said you were a lucky guy. Capo, now let's find out just how lucky.'

Sean wanted to get this lion before this extraordinary opportunity passed, there was no time to track down one of the huge buffalo herds along the Chiwewe river for a fresh bait, so Riccardo shot a young kudu bull from a herd of bachelors near the camp. They hung the carcass on the bait tree in the glade where they had last seen the big male lion; this time, low enough for the lionesses to reach it easily; and they climbed into the machan in the early afternoon. Within an hour the lionesses had picked up the scent of fresh blood and came trotting down the dry riverbed, followed by the straggling, squabbling bunch of cubs. While the older lioness fed heartily from the fresh kudu carcass, the younger female ate only lightly and sporadically. In between she prowled restlessly around the area of trampled grass beneath the tree, snarling at her cubs, or rolling on her back, or sitting up to lick at the blood smear beneath her own tail. At intervals, she stood staring into the forest and then held her head low to the ground and let out a long, melancholy moan. It was a sound so full of agonized longing that Claudia felt herself empathizing with the sleek and beautiful creature.

'That's right, Gertie.' Sean whispered behind Claudia's shoulder. 'Call to Big Daddy, tell him what sweets you've got for him here.'

'It's not fair,' Claudia thought fiercely. 'It's not fair to use her like this.'

Suddenly both lionesses leapt up to face into the forest, and the older female snarled softly. Alarmed, the cubs ceased their endless play and huddled behind their dams. Then the young lioness went forward through the grass, slinking and undulating her whole body in a blatantly sexual display, and she emitted a series of low welcoming moans.

'Steady, Capo.' Sean's hand was on Riccardo's arm, preventing him from raising the rifle. 'Take your time.'

Then out of the forest came the lion. At first they saw only the tip of his mane above the grass, as he came forward at an eager trot to meet the lioness. She rushed forward shamelessly, and in a trampled clearing they came together.

'Wait, Capo,' Sean whispered. He wanted the girl to watch it.

The lioness brushed her body against the male, back and forth she stroked him with the full length of her silken flanks, and the lion fluffed out his mane, so that he seemed to double in size, responding to her advances, licking her face as she cuddled into the dense dark bush of his mane.

Then deliberately she turned and presented him with her hind quarters, cocking her tail high, sending a spurt of pink-stained urine out under his nose. The lion groaned and curled his upper lip, exposing his great, yellow fangs in a rictus of passion; his back arched reflexively and Claudia wriggled in her seat as the lion stretched out his neck and licked the female under the tail with a long, curling, pink tongue.

The lioness submitted to his caress for a minute, then whirled flirtatiously and, from across the river, they heard her low purrs of invitation. Sean placed his hand lightly on Claudia's thigh. The gesture was concealed from her father by the side of the chair. She made no attempt to pull away.

The lioness turned from the male, ran a few light mincing paces and then flattened her body against the earth, looking back over her shoulder. The lion came to where she lay, moving with a stiff-legged gait, and he covered her body with his own, standing astride her, and as he lowered his haunches over hers, his penis unsheathed from its pouch, glistening pinkly, and the lioness laid her tail forward along her back.

Sean ran the tips of his fingers up to the juncture of Claudia's thighs, and he could feel the springing mattress of her pubic hair through the cloth of her breeches. Her thighs opened slightly under his hand.

The lion humped his back over the female in a series of convulsive, regular spasms, and then he threw back his huge, maned head and roared and the lioness roared with him and he reached down and bit her lightly in the back of the neck, a fond possessive gesture.

For long moments, they were frozen together like that and then the lion leaped off her, and at the same moment, Claudia reached down and placed her hand over Sean's. She took his little finger and twisted it back against the joint so viciously that she almost dislocated it, and agony shot up his arm to the shoulder.

He almost cried out in protest, but Riccardo was sitting close and though his view of his daughter's lower body was obscured by the canvas side of the chair, he would certainly guess at Sean's advances. With an effort, Sean kept silent, and drew his hand back, surreptitiously massaging the damaged finger, and he could see the corner of Claudia's mouth was curled in a vindictive little smile.

Across the river the lioness stood up and shook herself. Then she walked out with a slow satisfied air on to the open riverbank. There she paused and looked back at the lion where he was sitting on his haunches still half hidden in the long grass.

'Get ready, Capo.' Sean was still massaging his finger.

It was five o'clock in the afternoon, and the sun was at a perfect angle, lighting the far bank as though it were a stage. The range was a measured ninety-six yards from the machan to the bait tree. Riccardo Monterro was the finest rifleman that Sean had ever guided on safari. At that range, he could place three bullets through the same hole.

The lioness mewled seductively and the lion stood up and followed her out onto the open riverbank. He stood behind her, broadside on to the machan across the river, lit by the golden sunlight.

'He's a gift from heaven, Capo,' Sean whispered, and tapped Riccardo's shoulder. 'Take him!'

Slowly Riccardo lifted the buttstock of the rifle to his shoulder. It was a .300 Weatherby Magnum. The massive cartridge under the firing-pin was loaded with eighty grains of powder and a 180-grain Nosler partitioned bullet. It would cross the open riverbed at over three thousand feet per second. When it entered living flesh, it would drive a shock wave ahead of it that would turn the internal organs, lungs and heart, to jelly and suck that jelly out of a massive exit hole, blowing them in a red spray over the grass beyond where the animal stood.

'Take him!' Sean said, and Riccardo Monterro looked through the telescopic sight; the lion's body filled most of the magnified field of the lens.

He could see the individual hairs in the dense curling bush of mane, and the detail of each sculptured muscle beneath the skin. One inch behind the lion's shoulder, on the lateral centre line of its body, was a tiny scar on the sleek hide. It was shaped like a horseshoe, a lucky horseshoe, and it made a perfect aiming point. He aligned the cross-hairs of the sight on the scar, and they bounced slightly to the elevated beat of his own heart. He took up the slack in the trigger, feeling the final resistance under his finger before the sear released and the rifle fired.

Beside her father, Claudia sat rigid with horror. The lion turned his head and looked across the riverbed at her. The mating had touched and moved her deeply.

'He's too glorious to die,' she thought, and almost without conscious effort, she opened her mouth and screamed with all the strength of her lungs.

'Run, damn you! Run!'

The result stunned even her. She had not believed a living creature could react so swiftly. From lazy immobility, all three animals exploded into flight. They dissolved into golden blurs of movement.

The oldest lioness disappeared almost instantaneously into the long grass, with all the cubs rushing after her. The younger lioness raced along the edge of the bank. So swift was her run that she did not seem to touch the earth; like a swallow drinking in flight she skimmed the surface, and the lion followed her. For all his bulk and the dark mass of his mane, he moved as lightly as she did, reaching out those massively muscled legs in full stride.

Riccardo Monterro swivelled in his chair, the rifle to his shoulder, staring into the brilliant glass lens, swinging with the cat's run. The lioness swerved into the grass and was gone. The lion followed her but the instant before he disappeared, the report of the Weatherby rifle drove in on their eardrums, painful and deafening, and even in full sunlight, a long tongue of flame flashed out across the riverbed.

The lion stumbled in his run and with a single, loud cough vanished into the grass. In the silence, their ears sang with the memory of gunfire, and they stared out at the empty clearing, subdued and appalled.

'Nice work, ducky!' Sean said softly.

'I'm not sorry,' she said defiantly, and her father reloaded the rifle with a savage movement that sent the empty brass case

52

spinning and sparkling away in the sunlight. He stood up, rocking the flimsy machan and without a glance at his daughter, climbed down the makeshift ladder.

Sean picked up his .577 double rifle and followed him down. They stood at the bottom of the tree and Riccardo unbuttoned the flap of his breast pocket and offered Sean a Havana from his pigskin cigar-case. Neither of them usually smoked during the day, but now Sean accepted one and bit off the tip.

They lit their cigars and smoked for a while in silence. Then Sean said quietly, 'Call your shot, Capo.'

Riccardo was a marksman of such expertise that he could tell precisely where his bullet had gone the moment after he fired it. Now he hesitated, and then said grudgingly, 'That cat was motoring. I was too quick. I didn't lead him enough.'

'Gutshot?' Sean asked.

'Yeah,' Riccardo nodded. 'Gutshot.'

'Shit,' said Sean. 'Shit, and shit again.'

They both looked across at the dense stand of long grass and tangled thorny patches of undergrowth on the far bank.

It was ten minutes before the Toyota arrived, summoned by that single gunshot. Job and Shadrach and Matatu were grinning with expectation, they had hunted six safaris with Riccardo Monterro and they had never known him to miss. They jumped out of the Toyota, peered across the river, and their grins faded slowly, and were replaced by expressions of deepest gloom as Sean said, 'Intumbu! In the guts!'

The three of them went back to the Toyota and began to prepare for the follow-up in silence.

Sean squinted up at the sun. 'Dark in an hour,' he said. 'We haven't got time to let the wound stiffen.'

'We could leave him until the morning,' Riccardo suggested. 'He'll be sick by then.'

Sean shook his head. 'If he dies in there, the hyena will get him. No trophy. Besides which, we can't leave the poor beggar to suffer all night.'

They fell silent as Claudia climbed down the ladder from the machan. When she reached ground level, she would not look at them, but tossed back the plait of dark hair over her shoulder defiantly and marched across to the Toyota. She climbed into the front seat and folded her arms across her small breasts, staring ahead grimly.

'I'm sorry,' Riccardo said. 'I've known her for twenty-six years. I should have guessed she'd pull one like that.'

'You don't have to come, Capo,' Sean did not answer him directly. 'Stay with Claudia. I'll go across and get the job done. That's what you pay me for.'

It was Riccardo's turn to ignore the remark.

'I'll carry the Rigby,' he said.

'Make sure that you are loaded with soft-nosed bullets,' Sean advised.

'Of course.' They walked side by side to the Toyota, and Riccardo changed the lighter Weatherby for the big Rigby. He opened the breech to check that there were soft-nosed mushrooming bullets in the magazine, then filled the loops on his cartridge belt from a fresh packet.

Sean leaned against the side of the Toyota, and changed the cartridges in his big double rifle for others from the loops on the breast of his bush jacket.

'Poor bloody animal,' he said. Although he was looking at Riccardo, he was speaking to Claudia. 'It would have been a good clean kill, but now he's in the grass there, still alive with half his guts shot away. It's the most painful wound there is.' He saw the girl wince and her cheek pale. She would not look at him.

'We'll be lucky if someone doesn't get killed,' Sean went on with ghoulish relish. 'It will probably be Matatu. He has to go ahead on the spoor, and the little beggar always refuses to run. If it's anybody, it will be Matatu that gets it today.'

Despite herself, Claudia glanced piteously at the little Ndorobo.

'Cut it out, Sean,' Riccardo ordered. 'She knows how stupid she has been.'

'Does she?' Sean asked. 'I wonder.' He snapped the rifle closed. 'Okay, Capo, wear your leather jacket. If the lion gets you down, it may protect you a little, not much, but a little.'

The three blacks were waiting on the edge of the bank. Job carried the eight-bore shotgun loaded with buckshot, but the other two were unarmed. It took a peculiar kind of courage to follow a wounded lion into thick cover without carrying a weapon.

Even in her agitation, Claudia noticed the trust with which they looked at Sean Courtney. She sensed that they had shared mortal danger so many times before that a peculiar bond united their small exclusive group. The four of them were closer than brothers, or lovers, and she felt a sting of envy. She had never been that close to another human being in her life.

In turn Sean touched each of them on the shoulder, a light unsentimental gesture of affirmation, and then he spoke softly to Job. A shadow passed over the Matabele's handsome features, and for a moment it seemed that he might protest, but then he nodded acceptance and crossed to the Toyota, standing guard beside Claudia with the shotgun.

Sean held the double-barrelled rifle across the crook of his arm as he combed his thick glossy hair back from his forehead with his fingers and then bound it up out of his eyes with a strip of plaited leather around his forehead.

Even though she loathed him, she found herself admiring the heroic figure he cut as he made these last preparations to face the terrible danger and gruesome death that she had, in a large measure, prepared for him. The sleeves had been cut out of his bush jacket and he wore short, khaki pants, so that his limbs were bare and tanned. He was even taller than her father, but his waist was slimmer and his shoulders wider, and he carried the squat heavy rifle easily in one hand.

He glanced across at her, and his gaze was level and green and contemptuous. She was possessed suddenly, by a premonition of impending disaster, and she wanted to plead with him not to cross the river, but before she could speak he had turned away.

'Ready, Capo?' he asked, and Riccardo nodded, holding the Rigby at high port across his chest. His expression was solemn. 'All right, let's move out.' Sean nodded at Matatu and the little man led them down the bank.

In the riverbed, they fell into hunting formation with the tracker leading. Sean followed close behind him watching the reed bed ahead. Riccardo came next, leaving a gap of ten paces between them to reduce the confusion in a close-quarter *mêlée*, and Shadrach followed him in the drag position.

As they crossed, they filled their pockets with smooth water-worn pebbles from the riverbed. Below the far bank, they paused to listen, then Sean passed Matatu and went up first. He stood alone in the trampled clearing below the bait tree for almost five minutes, listening and staring intently into the tall grass beyond.

Then he began to lob pebbles into the grass, systematically working the area where the lion had disappeared. The pebbles clattered against other stones or bounced off the stems of shrubs, but there was no challenging growl. Sean whistled softly and the others scrambled up the bank and fell into their positions, and Sean nodded at Matatu.

They went forward slowly. There are many grave-stones in Africa marking the resting places of men who hurried after a wounded lion. Matatu concentrated all his attention on the ground at his feet. He never looked up at the wall of grass ahead. He placed his complete trust in Sean. At the edge of the grass, he hissed softly and with his hand behind his back made a secretive gesture.

'Blood,' Sean told Riccardo softly without looking back at him. 'And belly hair. You were right, Capo. It's a gutshot.'

He could see the wet gleam of blood on the stems of the grass.

'*Akwendi!*' he told Matatu, and drew breath like a diver poised on a cliff above a deep and icy pool. He held that breath as he stepped forward and the tall grass closed around him, limiting his vision like the sinister and murky waters of the pool.

* * *

The impact of the bullet had been a mighty blow in the lion's flank, that slewed him round and numbed his entire body behind his rib-cage.

Then the grass closed about him as he raced forward, and immediately he felt secure and confident. Within twenty strides he stopped and stood looking back over his shoulder, listening and drawing the scent into his flared nostrils, lashing his tail from side to side.

There was no sensation of pain, just a numbness and weight in his entrails as though he had swallowed an ironstone boulder. He smelled his own blood, and turned to sniff at his side. The exit wound the bullet had left was the size of an egg cup and from it oozed blood that was almost tarry black. Mingled with the blood, were the liquid contents of his own bowels. They made a tiny pattering sound as they dribbled onto the dry earth beneath him. He licked at the wound and blood glutted his jaws.

Then he lifted his head and listened again. He heard human voices in the distance, beyond the river and he growled softly, feeling his anger begin to mount, associating the blood and heaviness in his belly with the presence of man.

56

Then the lioness called him, a low gasping moan, and he turned and followed her. He did not run now for the weight in his belly hampered him and his back legs felt numb and heavy. The lioness was waiting for him a little farther on. Eagerly she rubbed herself against him, and then tried to lead him away, trotting off ahead of him. He moved heavily after her, stopping to listen and lick the running wound, and she turned back impatiently and moaned at him and nuzzled his face, sniffing and licking at his wound, puzzled and distressed by his behaviour.

His legs were heavy as tree-trunks now, and ahead of him was a thicket of wild ebony. He turned aside and pushed his way into the dense and tangled undergrowth, and he sighed as he lowered his body, curling the black tuft of his tail under him as he lay down.

The lioness fretted and worried at the edge of the thicket, calling to him with small mewling entreaties. Then when he did not respond, she followed him into the thicket and lay down beside him. She licked at his wound and the lion closed his eyes, and began to pant softly as the pain began.

The pain swelled in his body becoming a vast, suffocating weight that grew and grew within him, seeming to distend his belly until it was on the point of bursting. The lion groaned softly and bit at his own flank, trying to kill this thing within him, this living agony that was feeding on his entrails.

The lioness attempted to distract him. She was confused and worried, and she wriggled around and pressed her hindquarters into his face, offering him her swollen and weeping genitalia, but the lion closed his eyes and turned his head away, and each breath rasped like a wood saw in his throat.

Then he heard voices again, the whispered voices of men, and he raised his head and his eyes burned yellow and fierce as he found a focus for his suffering, and hatred grew out of the agony of his belly, and his rage was dark and all-engulfing.

Something crashed into the branches of the wild ebony thicket above his head and he growled, a rattling exhalation of air through his tortured throat.

* * *

They went forward slowly into the grass, and it reached above their heads, and enclosed them so closely that they could see no more than two or three paces ahead.

The lion's blood was painted on the grass and the stems were pushed over by the passage of his body so the trail was easy to follow. The blood on the grass gave Sean and Matatu the exact height of the wound, and the faeces mixed with the blood told them that the bowels had been penetrated. It was a mortal wound, but death would be slow and agonizing.

Within twenty yards of entering the grass, Matatu paused, and indicated the puddle of dark, tarry blood.

'He stopped here,' he whispered, and Sean nodded.

'He won't have gone far,' Sean guessed. 'He's waiting for us, Matatu, and when he comes, you run back behind me. Do you hear me?'

Matatu grinned at him. They both knew he would not obey. Matatu had never run, he would stand the charge as he always did.

'All right, you stupid little bugger.' Sean was tense. 'Get on with it.'

'Stupid little bugger,' Matatu repeated happily. He knew that Sean only called him that when particularly proud of him, or pleased with him.

They moved along the blood spoor, pausing every three or four paces while Sean lobbed pebbles into the grass ahead of them, and when there was no response, moving forward again cautiously.

Behind him, Sean could hear the click, click of the safety-catch on the Rigby. Riccardo was snapping it on and off as they advanced, a nervous gesture that betrayed his agitation. Although the sound irritated him, Sean felt a stir of admiration for the man. This was probably one of the most dangerous activities in which a man could engage. They don't come much worse than a gut-shot lion in close cover. This was Sean's job, but for Riccardo, it was a once in a lifetime test, and he had not failed it yet.

Sean tossed another pebble into the grass ahead, and listened to it rattle on the branch of a low tree.

As they went on, Sean thought about fear. For some men, fear was a crippling and destroying emotion, but for those like Sean, it was an addiction. He loved the sensation of fear, it was like a drug flowing through his veins, heightening all his senses, so he could feel the chequering on the polished walnut stock of the rifle under his fingers and the brush of each individual blade of grass against his bare legs; his vision was so enhanced that he saw it all through a crystal lens that magnified and dramatized each image, he could taste the very air he breathed and smell the crushed grass under his feet and the blood of the lion they were following. He was vividly, vibrantly alive, and he gave himself up to fear, as an addict would to a syringeful of heroin.

He tossed another pebble into the ebony thicket that stood like an island in the sea of grass just ahead of them, and it fell through the branches, rattling and crackling, and the lion growled from the depths of the thicket.

The fear of death was so pleasurable as to be almost unbearable, an emotional orgasm, stronger than any woman had ever given him, and Sean slid the safety-catch off the rifle and said, 'He's coming, Matatu. Run!' And exultation was in his voice, and time slowed down, another phenomenon produced by fear.

From the corner of his eye, he saw Riccardo Monterro step up beside him, taking his place in the firing line, and he knew what it was costing him.

'Good man!' he said loudly, and at the sound of his voice, the branches of the ebony thicket shook, as a heavy body rushed through them and there was a terrifying, growling, grunting uproar, coming straight at them.

Matatu stood perfectly still, like a guardsman on parade. Matatu had never run. Sean stepped up on one side of him and Riccardo, on the other, and they lifted their rifles and aimed into the wall of grass as that thing rushed in upon them, flattening the tall stems with its charge, roaring now, blasts of sound that were like a physical assault on their senses.

The grass opened in their faces and a huge, tawny body hurled itself upon them.

They fired together and the crash of gunfire drowned the enraged roaring. Sean fired the second barrel, the two shots sounding as one, and the huge 750-grain bullet tore into the charging animal, stopping it as though it had run into a cliff. Riccardo was working the bolt of the Rigby and a rolling echo of gunfire filled all the air about them.

The dead animal fell at their feet, and they stood with rifles raised, staring down at the bleeding carcass, dazed by the swiftness and the savagery and the beat of gunfire in their heads.

In the silence. Shadrach stepped forward. Like Matatu he had stood his ground, and now he stooped to the carcass, and then jerked back and shouted aloud what they had not yet fully realized.

'It's not the lion!'

As he said it, the lion charged. He came straight at them out of the thicket as his mate had done, but even more swiftly, driven by the agony in his belly and the black rage that filled him. He came grunting like a locomotive at full throttle, and they were unprepared, their rifles unloaded, bunched up too closely around the carcass of the lioness, and Shadrach was between them and the lion.

The lion came bursting out of the tall grass in full charge and it seized Shadrach in its jaws, biting into his hip, and the momentum of its charge carried it into the tight knot of men standing close up behind Shadrach.

It knocked them all off their feet, Sean went over backwards, crashing into the earth on his shoulder-blades and the back of his neck with stunning force. He was holding the rifle in front of his chest, instinctively trying to protect it from damage as he went down, and the engraved barrels slammed into his sternum as he hit the earth. Pain shot through his chest but he held on to the weapon and rolled on to his side.

Ten feet away the lion was savaging Shadrach. It had him pinned under its massive paws as it mauled his hip and upper leg.

'Thank God, it's not a leopard,' Sean thought as he broke open the rifle to reload. A leopard will not fix on one man if it attacks a group of hunters. It will bound from one to the other, in rapid succession, maiming and killing all of them with dazzling speed. Furthermore a leopard's main prey is the baboon, so it knows precisely how to despatch a primate. It goes instinctively for the head, taking off the scalp and top of the skull, while its back legs kick down the belly, stripping out the intestines with hooked yellow claws, very quickly, very efficiently.

'Thank God, it's not a leopard.' The great beast was fixed on Shadrach, pinning him with its claws, worrying the leg, and with each growl a scarlet spray of blood puffed out of its jaws. The Matabele gunbearer was screaming and beating ineffectually at the huge maned head with both clenched fists.

Sean saw Riccardo in the grass beyond them scrambling to his knees, crawling towards where the Rigby rifle had been thrown.

60

'Don't shoot. Capo,' Sean yelled at him. In a *mêlée* like this one, an inexperienced man with a loaded rifle was many times more dangerous than the attacking animal. The bullets of the Rigby would crack through the lion's body and smash into anybody beyond.

Sean had two spare cartridges held between the fingers of his left hand. It was the old hunter's trick for the fast reload, and he slid the two cartridges into the empty breeches and snapped the action shut.

The lion was chewing on Shadrach's lower body. Sean could hear the bone crunch and crackle like dry toast under those dreadful fangs. His nostrils were full of the fetid, gamey smell of the lion, of dust and the reek of blood of man and beast.

Beyond them he saw Riccardo had the rifle. He was on his knees, his face ashen with shock, cramming cartridges into the breech of the Rigby.

'Don't shoot!' Sean yelled again. The lion was directly between them. A bullet that hit the animal would come straight on into him.

It takes a special technique to shoot an attacking animal off a prostrate man without killing them both. It was deadly dangerous to run up to them and shoot down into the animal's body with the man lying under it.

Sean made no effort to rise to his feet. He rolled like a log, cushioning the rifle, flipping over three times, the manoeuvre that was second nature from his Scouts' training. Now he was lying alongside the lion, almost touching it, and he thrust the rifle into its lower ribs, aiming upwards, and he fired. It only needed one of those 750-grain bullets.

The shot lifted the lion clear of Shadrach's body, tossing it lightly aside, and the bullet tore out of its back between the shoulders, and went straight on up into the sky.

Sean dropped the rifle and knelt over Shadrach, taking him in his arms, and looked down on the leg. The fangs had inflicted penetrating stiletto wounds. From hip to knee the black flesh was riddled.

'Matatu!' Sean snapped. 'In the Toyota. The medicine box. Get it.' And the tracker vanished into the grass.

Riccardo crawled to Sean's side and looked at the leg.

'Sweet Mother Mary,' he said softly. 'It's the femoral.' Bright arterial blood was pumping up in a regular jet out of the deepest

61

wound, and Sean reached into it, thrusting his fingers into the hot flesh.

He got a grip on the slippery, rubbery, pulsing worm with thumb and forefinger and pinched with all his strength.

'Hurry, Matatu! Run, you little bugger, run!' he bellowed.

It was less than three hundred yards to the Toyota, and Matatu ran like a frightened fawn. He was back within minutes. Job was with him carrying the white chest with the red cross on its lid, and he opened it.

'In the instrument roll,' Sean told Job brusquely. 'Haemostats.'

Job passed him the stainless-steel clamps, and Sean fastened them on the ruptured artery and taped them against the thigh. His hands were wet and bright with blood, but he and Job had done this work fifty times during the bush war, and his movements were swift and confident.

'Rig up a drip set,' he ordered Job. 'We'll give him a bag of Ringers lactate to start with. Rig it.'

As he spoke he was screwing the nozzle on a tube of Betadyne and now he slid the nozzle as deeply as it would go into one of the puncture wounds in Shadrach's thigh and squeezed the thick iodine paste into it until it forced itself out of the mouth of the wound like tobacco-yellow toothpaste. Shadrach lay without protest or any sign of pain, watching them as they worked, replying to Job in monosyllables when he spoke to him in Sinde-bele.

'Drip set is ready,' Job said.

Without a word, Sean took the canula out of his hands. Shadrach was his man, his responsibility. He would allow no one else to do this, not even Job. He twisted Shadrach's arm, exposing the inside of the elbow and worked up a vein with a skilled milking motion, and he hit it with the needle at the first attempt, and nodded to Job to let the plasma flow.

'Hey, Shadrach!' Sean's grin was remarkably convincing as he laid a blood-smeared palm briefly against the Matabele's cheek. 'I think you poisoned that old lion good. He eats your leg and he's dead – poof! Like that!' Shadrach chuckled. It amazed Riccardo to hear it, even though he had fought and worked with tough men before. 'Give Shadrach one of your cigars, Capo,' Sean suggested, and he began to strap the leg with clean white tape from the chest to stop the residual bleeding.

Once he had strapped the leg, he went over the rest of Shadrach's body quickly. He smeared Betadyne into all the rents and tears left by the lion's claws.

'We can't afford to overlook the merest scratch,' he grunted. 'That old lion has been feeding on putrid carcasses. His teeth and mouth are a reeking pit of infection, and there is rotten meat packed in the grooves of his claws. Gangrene kills most of the victims of a mauling.'

Still not satisfied, Sean injected a full ampoule of penicillin into the transfusion bag. That would swamp the body with antibiotic. Sean nodded and stood up. It had taken him less than thirty minutes, and studying the bandages and the drip set that Job was holding over Shadrach's supine form, Riccardo doubted that a trained doctor could have worked more swiftly or efficiently.

'I'm going to fetch the Toyota,' Sean told them. 'But I'll have to bring it around by way of the ford. That will take a little time, it will be dark by the time I get back.' He could have sent Job to fetch the truck, but he wanted to get the girl to himself. 'There are spare blankets in the chest, keep him wrapped and warm.' He looked down at Shadrach. 'Little scratch like that. I want you back at work pretty damn quick, otherwise I'll dock it off your wages.'

He picked up the .577 and he strode back through the grass to the riverbank. As he trudged through the sandy water-course, his anger at last came upon him, more powerful for being so long delayed.

Claudia was sitting alone in the front of the Toyota as he came up the bank. She looked forlorn and abandoned, but he felt no twinge of pity. She stared aghast at his blood-caked hands.

Sean placed the .577 in the gun-rack without looking at her, and then spilled water from the jerry can over his hands and scrubbed them together, washing off most of the blood. He climbed into the driver's seat and started the Toyota, swung it in a tight circle and sent it back along the track that followed the river downstream.

'Aren't you going to tell me what happened?' Claudia asked at last. She had meant to sound unrepentant and full of bravado, but it came out in a small subdued voice.

'All right,' Sean agreed. 'I'll tell you. Instead of a quick merciful kill there was total chaos and confusion. The lioness charged us first. We shot her by mistake in the long grass. Not that we would have had much option anyway. She was coming all the way.' Sean switched on the headlights, for the sun was gone and the forest darkening. 'Okay, so now the lioness is dead. Her cubs are still unweaned, they are goners, all three of them. They'll starve to death inside a week.'

'Oh no!' Claudia whispered.

'Then the lion charged after his mate. He caught us all ends up. We weren't ready for him, and he got Shadrach down. He almost chewed his leg off. The bone is shattered from hip to knee. He may lose the whole leg, I don't know, perhaps he'll get lucky and just end up with a permanent limp. Anyway you look at it, he's not going to be a tracker any more. I'll find him a job as a skinner or camp servant, but he's a Matabele warrior and menial work is going to break his heart.'

'I'm so sorry.'

'You are sorry?' Sean asked. His voice low and furious. 'Shadrach is my friend and my companion. He has saved my life more times than I can count and I've done the same for him. We have fought a war together, we have slept under the same blanket, eaten from the same plate, trekked ten thousand miles together in the heat and the dust and the rain. He is more than a friend. I have two brothers, same mother and father, but Shadrach means more to me than either of them. Now you tell me you're sorry. Well, thanks a lot, ducky. That's a great comfort.'

'You have every right to be angry. I understand!'

'You understand?' he asked. 'You understand nothing. You are an arrogant ignoramus from a different hemisphere. You are a citizen of the land of the quick fix, and you come and try your simplistic naïve solutions here in Africa. You try to save a single animal from his destiny, and you end up by killing a female and sending her three cubs to lingering death and condemning one of the finest men you'll ever meet to the life of a cripple.'

'What more can I say?' she asked. 'I was wrong.'

'At this late hour your new-found humility is most touching.' His low voice lashed her. 'Sure, you were wrong. Just as you and your people are wrong to try and starve an African nation of thirty million souls into acceptance of another one of your naïve solutions. When the damage you have inflicted is beyond repair, will you again say "I'm sorry, I was wrong," and walk away and leave my land and my people to bleed and suffer?'

'What can I do?'

'We have thirty days of safari remaining,' he said bitterly. 'I want you to keep out of my hair for that time. The only reason I don't cancel the show right now, and send you packing back to your Eskimos and your human rights, is that I just happen to think your father is a pretty fine man. From now on, you are under sufferance. Just one more peep out of you and you are on the next plane back to Anchorage. Do I make myself clear?'

'Abundantly.' And there was a trace of spirit in her tone once more. Neither of them spoke again during the rough ride down to the ford and back up the far bank to the glade in which the bait tree stood.

By that time Job and Matatu had a fire going. The glow of the flames guided Sean to where Shadrach lay, and he climbed out of the Toyota and went to him immediately.

'How is the pain?' He squatted beside him.

'It is a little thing,' Shadrach replied, but Sean saw the lie in the grey tone of his skin and the sunken eyeballs, and he filled a disposable syringe from a glass ampoule of morphine. He waited for the drug to take effect before they lifted Shadrach between them and laid him in the back of the truck.

Job and Matatu had skinned out both lions while they waited, and they loaded the bundle of green salted skins onto the bonnet where it would cool in the night wind.

'It's a hell of a lion,' Sean told Riccardo. 'You've got yourself a magnificent trophy!'

Riccardo shook his head and said, 'Let's get Shadrach back to camp.'

Sean drove with care, rolling the truck gently over the rougher spots, trying to protect Shadrach from the worst jolting.

Claudia insisted on sitting in the back with Shadrach, cushioning his head on her lap. Riccardo sat up in front with Sean and he asked quietly, 'What happens now?'

'I'll radio Harare as soon as we get into camp. They will have a private ambulance at the airport to meet him. I'll be gone a couple of days. I'll see Shadrach well taken care of and, of course, I'll have to put in a report to the government game department and try and square it.'

'I hadn't gotten around to thinking about that,' Riccardo said. 'We killed a lioness with cubs and had a man mauled. What will the government do?'

Sean shrugged in the darkness. 'There is a better than even

chance they'll pull my licence and take the concession away from me.'

'Hell, Sean. I didn't realize. Is there anything I can do?'

'Not a thing, Capo, but thanks for the offer. You are out of it. It's between me and the department.'

'I could take full blame for the lioness, say I shot her.'

'No good.' Sean shook his head. 'No blame on the clients. That's departmental doctrine. Whatever you do, I am fully responsible.'

'If they pull your licence . . .' Riccardo hesitated, and Sean shook his head again.

'No, Capo, they won't cancel the safari. That's also departmental doctrine. Finish the safari. Don't offend the paying client. Government needs the hard currency you bring. Only after you have left, they'll bring out the axe for me. You are out of it. I'll be back in two days, and we'll hunt that big elephant together. You don't have to worry.'

'You make me sound like a selfish bastard. I'm worrying about you and your licence, not about enjoying myself.'

'We'll both enjoy ourselves, Capo. After all, if I do lose my licence, it will be the last time that you and I ever hunt together, Capo.'

Claudia could overhear the conversation from where she sat in the back of the truck and she knew why her father did not reply. He knew that it was his last hunt, licence or no licence. Claudia had taken an emotional battering during the last few hours, and thinking about Papa now, she felt the tears well up and scald her eyelids. She fought them back and then it was no longer worth the effort and she wept for all of them, for her father and the lioness and the cubs, for that beautiful male lion, and for Shadrach and his shattered leg.

One of her tears fell on to Shadrach's upturned face, and he stared up at her in perturbation. She wiped the droplet from his cheek with her thumb and her voice was thick and muffled with grief as she whispered to him, 'It's going to be all right, Shadrach.' Even she realized what a crass and fatuous lie that was.

*   *   *

Sean had a scheduled radio contact with his office in Harare at ten o'clock every evening. The journey home was so slow that

66

they reached camp with only minutes to rig the aerial and connect the radio to the Toyota's twelve-volt battery before the schedule.

The contact was good; one of the reasons for the late schedule was the better radio reception in the cool of the evening. Reema's voice with its Gujurati intonation came through clearly. She was a pretty Hindu girl who ran Sean's Harare office with ruthless efficiency.

'We have a casevac.' Sean used the terminology of the bush war for casualty evacuation. 'I want an ambulance standing by to meet me.'

'Okay fine, Sean.'

'Set up a person-to-person telephone call with my brother, Garrick, in Johannesburg for ten a.m. tomorrow.'

'Will do, Sean.'

'Make an appointment for me to see the director of the game department tomorrow afternoon.'

'Director is in New York for the Wildlife Conference, Sean. The deputy director is in charge.'

Sean switched off the hand microphone while he swore bitterly, he had forgotten about the Wildlife Conference. Then he pressed the transmit button again.

'Okay, Reema my love, get me an appointment with Geoffrey Manguza then.'

'Sounds serious, Sean.'

'We just invented the word.'

'What is your ETA? I'll have to file an emergency flight plan for you.'

The security authority was always so jittery about South African hot pursuit of terrorists into Zimbabwe or pre-emptive South African raids on terrorist facilities in Harare itself that they usually required flight plans to be filed forty-eight hours in advance.

'Take off here in fifty minutes. ETA Harare 2300 hours. Pilot and two pax,' Sean told her.

It was half an hour's drive from the camp to the airstrip. Riccardo and Claudia were in the Toyota when they drove out.

Sean took the back seats out of the Beechcraft and placed a mattress on the floor for Shadrach. By this time, Shadrach was feverish and restive. His temperature was 101 and the glands in his groin, hard and lumpy as walnuts. Sean didn't want to look under the dressings on the leg, afraid of what he might find, but one of the minor claw wounds on Shadrach's belly was definitely infected already, weeping watery pus and emitting the first faint odour of putrescence.

Sean administered another dose of penicillin through the canula of the drip set and then he and Job and two of the camp skinners very gently lifted Shadrach into the aircraft and settled him on the mattress.

Shadrach's wife was a sturdy Matabele woman with an infant strapped to her back with a length of trade cloth. They loaded her considerable baggage and then she clambered up and sat beside Shadrach on the mattress, placed the infant on her lap, opened her blouse and gave the child her milk-engorged breast to suckle. The aircraft's empty luggage compartments Job filled with sacks of dried game meat, a valuable commodity in Africa. Then Job drove the Toyota to the far end of the runway to give Sean the headlights for take-off.

'Job will look after you while I am away, Capo. Why don't you take the shotgun and go for dove and sand grouse down at the pools? Best wing shooting you'll ever have, better than white winged dove in Mexico,' Sean suggested.

'Don't worry about us. We'll be just fine.'

'I'll be back as soon as I possibly can. Tukutela won't be crossing before the new moon. I'll be back before then. It's a promise, Capo.'

Sean held out his hand and as Riccardo took it, he said, 'You did good work with the lions, Capo, but then you were never short of bottom.'

'What kind of limey word is that?' Riccardo asked. "Bottom"?'

'How about a good Yankee word then? "Cojones"?'

'That will do,' Riccardo grinned at him.

Claudia was standing beside her father and now she smiled hesitantly, almost shyly, and took a step forward as if to offer her hand.

She had released her hair from its plait and brushed it out into a dense, dark mane around her head. Her expression was soft and her eyes big and dark and lustrous. In the Toyota headlights her classical Latin features went beyond the merely handsome, and Sean realized for the first time that she was truly beautiful. Despite her beauty and her penitent attitude, he kept his own expression cold and forbidding, nodded at her curtly, ignored the tentative offer to shake his hand, climbed up onto the wing of the Beechcraft and ducked into the cockpit.

Sean had cut the airstrip out of the brush himself and levelled it by dragging a bundle of old truck tyres up and down it behind the Toyota. It was narrow, rough and short, with a gradient falling towards the river. He lined up with the Beechcraft's tail-plane backed into the bushes, and stood on the brakes facing down the slope. He aimed at the lights of the Toyota at the far end of the strip while he ran up to full power on both engines and then let the brakes off. Just short of the trees at the end of the strip he pulled on the flaps and bounced the Beechcraft into the air. As always he crossed himself blasphemously with mock relief as he cleared the tree-tops and turned on course for Harare.

During the flight, he tried to plan his strategy. The director of the game department was an old friend, and Sean had successfully dealt with him in equally serious circumstances. However the deputy, Geoffrey Manguza, was a horse of literally another colour. The director was one of the few white civil servants still in charge of a department of government. Manguza would succeed him soon, the first black head of the game department.

He and Sean had fought on opposite sides during the bush war, and Manguza had been an astute guerrilla leader and political commissar. The rumour was that he did not like the safari concession owners, most of whom were white. The concept of private exploitation of State assets offended his Marxist principles, and he had shot too many white men during the war to have any great deal of liking or respect for them.

It was going to be a difficult meeting, Sean sighed.

Reema was waiting for him as he taxied in. As a modern Indian woman, she had abandoned the sari in favour of a neat slacks suit. She was not so modern, however, that she wished to choose her own husband. Her father and her uncles were working on that at the moment, and had already come up with a likely candidate in Canada. A professor of Oriental religions at Toronto University. Sean hated them for it. Reema was an ornament to Courtney Safaris, and he knew that he would never be able to replace her.

She had the ambulance waiting on the tarmac beside the light aircraft hangars. Regularly, Reema bribed the guards on the main gate with dried game meat from the concession. In Africa, meat or the promise of meat opens all gates.

69

They followed the ambulance to the hospital in the Kombi. While Sean sat in the passenger seat glancing through the most urgent mail she had brought for his attention, Reema recited a list of the important developments during his absence.

'Carter, the surgeon from Atlanta, cancelled . . .' That was a twenty-one-day safari, and Sean glanced up sharply, but Reema soothed him. 'I phoned the German soap manufacturer in Munich, Herr Buchner, the one we turned down in December. He jumped at it. So we are full, back to back, for the rest of the season.'

'How about my brother?' Sean interrupted. He didn't tell her that it was touch and go that there was going to be an end to the season.

'Your brother is expecting your call and as at six o'clock this morning the telephone was still working.' In Zimbabwe that was something that couldn't be taken for granted.

At the hospital, there were at least fifty seriously ill patients awaiting admission ahead of them. The long benches were full of huddled, miserable humanity and the stretchers were blocking the aisles and doorways. The admission clerks were in no great hurry and waved Shadrach's stretcher to a far corner.

'Leave it to me,' said Reema, and she took the senior admissions clerk by the elbow and led him aside with an angelic smile, talking to him sweetly.

Five minutes later, Shadrach's admission papers were processed and he was being examined by an East German doctor.

'How much did that cost?' Sean asked.

'Cheap,' Reema answered. 'A bag of dried meat.'

Sean had picked up sufficient of the German language from his safari clients to be able to discuss Shadrach's case with the doctor. The man was reassuring. Sean said goodbye to Shadrach.

'Reema has your money. She will come to see you each day. If you need anything tell her.'

'I will be with you in spirit when you hunt Tukutela,' Shadrach said softly, and Sean had to clear his throat before he could answer.

'We will hunt many more elephant together, old friend.' And he walked away quickly.

The next morning when at last he got through to Johannesburg, the telephone line was crackling with static.

'Mr Garrick Courtney is in a board meeting,' the girl on the switchboard at Centaine House, the Courtney Group head-quarters, told him. 'But he gave orders to put your call through directly.'

In his mind's eye, Sean saw once again the boardroom, panelled in figured walnut, the huge Pierneef canvases framed by the elaborate panels, and his brother, Garry, sitting at the head of the long table, beneath the crystal chandelier that his grand-mother had imported from Murano in Italy, in the chairman's high-backed throne.

'Sean!' Garry's voice cut through the static, bold and assured. How he had changed from the puny little runt who used to pee his bed.

The job could have been Sean's if he had wanted it and had been prepared to work for it. Sean was the eldest son, but he did not want the job. Still he always experienced a twinge of resentment when he thought of Garry's Rolls and Lear jet and holiday home in the south of France.

'Hello Garry. How's it going?'

'All well here,' Garry told him. 'What's the problem?' It was typical of their relationship that any contact meant there was a problem to solve.

'I might need to put a bit of honey with the cheese,' Sean told him diplomatically. It was their private code for money to Switzerland, and Garry would understand that Sean would be bribing somebody for something. It happened often enough.

'Okay, Sean. Just give me the amount and the account num-ber.' Garry was Sean's partner in the safari company, and held forty per cent of the shares.

'Thanks, Garry, I'll call you some time tomorrow. How's the rest of the family?' They chatted for a few minutes longer, and when he hung up Reema came through from the outer office.

'I managed to get through to the game department at last.' Reema had been trying all morning. 'Comrade Manguza will see you at four-thirty this afternoon.'

Geoffrey Manguza was a tall Shona with a very black com-plexion and close-cropped hair. He wore silver-framed eye glasses, and a dark blue suit. However, his neck-tie was Hermès. Sean recognized the horse carriage logo, and his wristwatch was a Patek Philippe with a black crocodile-skin strap. They were not your run-of-the-mill Marxist accessories and Sean found that encouraging. However, the deputy director did not rise from behind his desk to welcome him.

'Colonel Courtney,' he greeted him unsmilingly, using Sean's previous rank to let him know that he knew that Sean had commanded the Ballantyne Scouts, one of the elite Rhodesian groups, after Ballantyne, the founder of the regiment, had been killed in action. It was also a reminder that they had been enemies, and might still be so.

'I prefer plain mister.' Sean smiled engagingly. 'That other business is behind us now, Comrade Manguza.'

The deputy director inclined his head, neither agreeing nor disagreeing. 'What can I do for you?'

'Unfortunately, I have to report an unintentional transgression of the game regulations . . .' And Geoffrey Manguza's expression hardened, and remained like that while Sean described the accidental shooting of the lioness and Shadrach's subsequent mauling. When Sean finished by submitting the written report that Reema had typed for him, Geoffrey Manguza let the document lie untouched on his desk top while he asked a few pertinent and unsympathetic questions.

'You do realize, Colonel Courtney,' he used the rank again deliberately, 'that I am obliged to take a most serious view of this entire business. It seems to me that there has been negligence and serious disregard for the safety of your clients and your own staff. Zimbabwe is no longer a colony, and you cannot treat our people the way you did before.'

'Before you make your recommendation to the director, I would like to clarify a few points for you,' Sean told him.

'You are free to speak, Colonel.'

'It's almost five o'clock now.' Sean checked his watch. 'Won't you allow me to buy you a drink at the golf club, and we can discuss it in more relaxed surroundings?'

Manguza's expression was inscrutable but after a few moments' thought he nodded. 'As you wish. I have a few small matters to attend to before I leave here, but I will meet you at the club in half an hour.'

He kept Sean sitting on the veranda of the golf club for forty minutes before he put in an appearance. It had once been the Royal Salisbury Golf Club. However, the first two words had been dropped from the title lest they perpetuate the colonial past. Nevertheless, the first remark Geoffrey Manguza made after he had taken the chair opposite Sean and ordered a gin and tonic was, 'Strange isn't it, a few years ago, the only way a black man could have got in here was as a waiter, and now I am on the committee and my handicap is five.' Sean let it pass, and changed the subject to that of rhino poaching across the border with Zambia. Manguza made no effort to pursue that topic. He watched Sean through the silver-rimmed spectacles and as soon as he stopped speaking, cut in immediately.

'You wished to clarify a few points for me,' he said. 'We are both busy men, Colonel.'

This directness was disconcerting. Sean was preparing for a typically round-about African approach, but he adapted his pitch.

'First of all, Mr Manguza, I wanted to tell you what a high price I and my associates place on the Chiwewe concession.' Sean used the word 'price' deliberately. 'I telephoned them this morning and explained this unfortunate incident and they are anxious to have it resolved at any price.' Again he used the word, and paused significantly.

There was a certain etiquette to be observed in negotiations such as these. To the western mind it was bribery, but in Africa it was simply the Dash System, a universal and acceptable means of getting things done. Government might put up posters in all public buildings depicting a booted foot crushing a venomous serpent under the slogan 'Stamp out Corruption' but nobody took that very seriously. In fact, in a bizarre fashion, the posters themselves constituted official recognition of the practice.

At this stage, Geoffrey Manguza should have agreed that recompense was due, or given some other indication of his willingness to listen to reason. He said nothing, merely stared at Sean from behind those glinting lens until Sean was forced to speak again.

'If you've finished your drink, why don't we take a stroll down the eighteenth fairway?' The club veranda was crowded and the happy hour in full swing with too many listening ears. Manguza swallowed the last of his gin and tonic, and without a word led the way down the steps to the lawn.

The last four-ball was coming down the eighteenth, but Sean kept to the edge of the rough, and as the players and their caddies straggled past, Sean said softly, 'I told my associates that you are the most powerful man in the department, and that the white director is merely your rubber stamp. I told them that you had it in your power to sidetrack an official enquiry, and dismiss any charges arising from this most unfortunate incident. I was so certain that I laid a bet of ten thousand US dollars with them. If I win my bet, those winnings are yours, Mr Manguza, paid into any account you nominate anywhere in the world.'

Manguza stopped and turned to face him and Sean was taken aback when he saw his expression. Manguza's voice quivered with fury as he said, 'Your assumption that I am open to a bribe is an insult to me personally. That I could tolerate, but it is also an insult to the revolution and the revolutionary heroes who died in the struggle to free this country of the imperial and colonial yoke, it is an insult to the party and our leaders, to the Marxist spirit and ultimately to the African people as a whole.'

'I only suggested a lousy ten grand, not the return of the monarchy, for the love of Allah.'

'You may smile your supercilious white smile, Colonel Courtney, but we know you well. We know about your South African connections, and about the bunch of Matabele hooligans you have gathered about you. We know that all of them fought with you against the forces of revolutionary democracy. They are counter-revolutionaries and capitalist-roaders and you are their leader.'

'I shot a lioness by mistake, and one of my capitalist-roaders got bitten, that's the full extent of my counter-revolutionary activities.'

'We are watching you, Colonel,' Manguza told him ominously. 'You can be certain that I will make the correct recommendation in your case, and that the insult to me and my people will not be forgotten.'

Manguza turned and strode back towards the club-house and Sean shook his head.

'So we say farewell to the beautiful Chiwewe concession,' he murmured. 'I really blew that one!' Despite his levity, he felt a sliding sensation of disaster in the pit of his stomach.

*   *   *

The office of Courtney Safaris was in the Avenues, between Government House and the golf club and Reema was waiting for him in the outer office, its walls decorated with colour posters of

74

wildlife and photographic enlargements of satisfied clients with their trophies.

She jumped up from her desk the moment Sean came in.

'The hospital called an hour ago, Sean. They have amputated Shadrach's leg.'

For long moments, Sean could neither speak nor move, then he crossed slowly to the filing cabinet and took a glass and a half-empty bottle of Chivas from the top drawer. He sagged onto the sofa and poured a three-finger jolt of whisky.

'The ending to a perfect day,' he said, and tossed back the whisky.

Reema left him sitting on the sofa. There were only two more drinks left in the bottle, and when they were gone, Sean went down to the Monomatapa Hotel. The hotel was full of tourists, and amongst them was a blond teutonic Valkyrie in full *Out of Africa* costume. She caught his eye across the lounge the moment that Sean walked in and smiled.

'What the hell!' Sean said to himself. 'It's cheaper than whisky, and no hangover either.'

The German Fräulein laughed delightedly at Sean's rudimentary German, and not long afterwards it transpired that she had the presidential suite on the fourteenth floor all to herself. She ordered a bottle of Mumm from room service and they drank it in bed.

* * *

In the morning, while Reema filed a flight plan for him, taking a bag of dried meat down to air traffic control, Sean returned to the hospital.

They had taken Shadrach's leg off only inches below the hip. The East German doctor showed Sean the X-ray plates. 'Hopeless!' He pointed out the bone fragments. 'Like confetti!'

There was no place to sit in the crowded surgical ward, so Sean stood beside Shadrach's bed for a while and they talked about the battles and the hunts they had shared. They did not mention the leg, and when they had run out of reminiscences, Sean gave the ward sister a hundred dollars to look after him and went out to the airport.

Reema had the flight plan for him and the Beechcraft was

75

refuelled and loaded with everything from fresh fruit and vegetables to toilet paper for the camp.

'You are a heroine, Reema,' he said, and then standing beside the aircraft, he described the meeting with Geoffrey Manguza.

'It doesn't look very cheerful,' he ended. 'You had better begin looking for another job.'

'I'm sorry for you, Sean,' she said. 'But don't worry about me. I was wondering how to break the news to you. I'm leaving for Canada on September 16th. It's all arranged, I'm going to be the wife of a professor.'

'You be happy,' Sean ordered, and for the first time kissed her, and she blushed under her nut-brown skin which made her prettier than ever.

Sean made three low-level passes over the camp and on the third he saw the Toyota pull out towards the airstrip with Job driving and Matatu standing in the back. He landed and taxied the Beechcraft into its cage of galvanized diamond-mesh wire which was designed to discourage the elephant from pulling the wings off and the lions from chewing the tyres.

When Job and Matatu arrived in the Toyota, they transferred the cargo to it, and then Sean told them about Shadrach's leg.

They had fought all through the bush war together and were hardened to casualties, but Sean saw the pain and grief in his eyes as Job murmured, 'We will need a new number two gunbearer. Pumula, the skinner, is a good man.'

'Yes, we will use him,' Sean agreed.

For a while they stood silently, paying tribute to their maimed companion. Then, still without speaking, they climbed into the Toyota and drove back to camp.

*   *   *

Rather than slacks, Claudia Monterro wore a dress for dinner that evening, a floating silk chiffon in pure white with silver and turquoise Seminole jewellery. Against her tanned skin and jet black hair the effect was stunning. However, Sean made certain not to show his admiration and he directed all his conversation at her father.

After he had told Riccardo about Shadrach and his meeting with Manguza, the evening was gloomy and cheerless. Claudia left the men at the camp-fire but they did not sit there long before

Riccardo said goodnight and went off to his tent. Sean took a bottle of whisky from the dining tent and went down towards the servants' village.

Job's tent and those of his two wives were set apart from the others, on the bank of the river overlooking a deep pool where hippo lay like dark rock islands in mid-stream.

When Sean seated himself on the carved native stool across the fire from Job, one of the wives brought two glasses and knelt beside him while he poured a large peg for each of them. The pretty young Matabele girl with Job's infant strapped on her back took the glass to her husband, and Job saluted Sean across the flickering flames.

They drank in silence and Sean watched Job's face in the firelight as he stared out across the river. The silence was companionable and comforting and Sean let his thoughts wander back down the years as he rolled the smoky taste of whisky over his tongue.

He remembered the day he had first met Job Bhekani. It had been on a hill with only a number, Hill 31, a rocky hill, thick with stands of dense wild ebony and Jesse bush where the enemy waited. Job had been on the hill for two days, and his eyes were wild and bloodshot. Sean had parachuted in that morning with five sticks of his own scouts. They fought side by side the rest of that day, and in the dusk when the hill was cleared and those of the enemy still alive had fled down the rocky slopes and disappeared into the forest, Sean and Job had helped each other to where the helicopter waited to take them out. They had gone down the hill slowly, wearily, dragging their weapons, arms around each other's shoulders and their blood mingling when it oozed from under the field dressings.

'Blood brothers whether you like it or not,' Sean had croaked, grinning at Job from under the camouflage cream and soot and dust, and a week later when Job was released from base hospital, Sean had been waiting for him personally with his transfer papers.

'You've been seconded to Ballantyne Scouts, Captain.'

And Job had smiled that rare wide smile and said, 'Let's go, Colonel.'

From his file, Sean knew that Job had been born on the Gwai river and attended the local mission school where he had obtained a bursary to the University College of Rhodesia and Nyasaland from where he had graduated with a first in Politics, History and

77

Social Anthropology. From there he had gone on with another bursary to Brown College in Chicago and got his masters the same year that Ian Smith declared unilateral independence.

Only much later when they had tried and tested their friendship, did Sean learn how Job had herded his father's cattle along the Gwai river and come, even as a child, to know and love the wilds. Job's father was one of the grandsons of King Lobengula, son of great Mzilikazi, so Job was a direct descendant of the royal Zulu line, and this was apparent in his carriage and his features. The powerful jaw and deep forehead, the dark intelligent eyes and domed skull beneath the thick close-cropped curls.

During his studies and his sojourn in America, Job had come to abhor the Communist doctrine and all its works, so it was natural that on his return to Africa, he had enlisted in the Rhodesian African Rifles and within a year had earned his commission.

After the war when the Lancaster House Agreement had given the country over to Robert Mugabe and his people's democracy, Job had sat and passed with honours, the civil service entrance exam, for government and politics was the swift high-road to power and wealth.

However, he was branded a 'sell-out' who had fought the war on the wrong side, the losing side, and he was a Matabele when the power was in the hands of the Shona tribe. Every door to advancement was barred against him. Angry and disillusioned he had come back to Sean.

'Damn it, Job, you are miles too good for any job I could offer you in a safari company.'

'Tracker, skinner, gunbearer, whatever you have, I'll take it,' Job had insisted.

So they had hunted together as they had fought, side by side, and within a year, Sean had made him one of the directors of Courtney Safaris. They always referred to these quiet evenings, drinking whisky around the camp-fire, as directors' meetings.

It amused Job to adopt various roles for different circumstances. In front of safari clients he shifted to what he called, 'Plantation Nigger Mode' when he called Sean *Bwana* and *Nkosi* and acted out the charade of the by-gone colonial era.

'Don't be a prick, Job. You demean yourself,' Sean protested at first.

'It's what the clients expect,' Job had reasoned. 'We are selling

78

them an illusion, man. They are playing eagle scouts and Ernest Hemingway. If they guessed I had a master's in history and politics, it would frighten the hell out of them.' And reluctantly, Sean had gone along with the act.

When they were alone, as they were now, Job changed into what he called his 'Homo Sapiens Mode' and became the thoughtful intelligent educated man he truly was. As they talked, they switched easily from Sindebele to English, each of them as perfectly at ease and comfortable in each other's language as they were in each other's company.

'Look, Sean, don't worry too much about losing this concession. It hasn't happened yet, and even if it does, we'll find a way around it.'

'Give me some comfort. I could do with it.'

'We could apply for another concession, somewhere in Matabeleland where my family still has pull. Down Matetsi way or even on the Gwai river, that's my home turf.'

'No good.' Sean shook his head. 'After this fiasco, I'll have the mark of the beast on me.'

'We'd apply in my name,' Job suggested, and smiled wickedly. 'I'd make you one of my directors and you can call me *Bwana*!'

They laughed together, the mood lightening, and when Sean left Job at his fire and walked back to the main camp in the darkness, he felt cheerful and optimistic for the first time in days. Job had the power to effect that transformation in him.

As he approached his own tent, something pale moved in the moon shadow beneath the trees and he stopped abruptly. Then he heard the tinkle of silver jewellery, and realized that she must have been waiting for him.

'May I speak with you?' Claudia said softly.

'Go ahead,' he invited. Why did that Americanism 'speak with', rather than 'speak to' irritate him so, he wondered.

'I'm not very good at this,' she admitted and he gave her no encouragement. 'I wanted to apologize.'

'You are apologizing to the wrong person, I've still got both my legs.'

She flinched and her voice trembled. 'You are without mercy, aren't you?' Then she lifted her chin. 'All right, I guess I deserved that, I've been an idiot. I thought I knew it all, but it turns out I knew very little, and in my ignorance I've done immense damage. I know it doesn't help much, but I'm desperately sorry.'

79

'You and I are from different worlds, we have not a single thought or feeling in common. We could never hope to understand each other, let alone be friends, but I do know what it took for you to say that.'

'A truce, then?' she asked.

'All right, a truce.' He held out his hand and she took it. Her skin was smooth as the petal of a rose, her hand slim and cool, but her grip was firm as a man's.

'Good-night,' she said, and released his hand and turned away.

He watched her walk back towards her own tent. The moon was two days from full and the white dress was ethereal and misty. Beneath it her body was slim and her limbs long and elegant.

In that moment, he admired her spirit and liked her more than he had ever done in all the time he had known her.

* * *

Sean slept as lightly as a hunter and a soldier. The natural sounds of the bush did not disturb him, not even the shrieks of the hyena pack around the fortified trophy shed, where the lionskins were curing.

However at the light scratch on the canvas of his tent, he was instantly awake and reaching for his flashlight and the .577 propped at the head of his bed.

'Who is it?' he asked quietly.

'It's me, Job.'

Sean glanced at his Rolex wristwatch, the luminous hands pointed to three o'clock.

'Come in, what is it?'

'One of the trackers who we left on the river has come into camp. He has run twenty miles.'

Sean felt the back of his neck prickle and he swung both legs out of bed.

'Yes?' he said eagerly.

'At sunset this evening Tukutela crossed the river out of the National Park.'

'Is it certain?'

'It is certain. They saw him close by. It is Tukutela, the Angry One, and he has no collar around his neck.'

'Where is Matatu?' Sean stood up and reached for his pants,

80

and the little Ndorobo piped at the entrance. 'I am ready, *Bwana*.'

'Good. We leave in twenty minutes. Marching packs and water-bottles. We'll take Pumula in Shadrach's place. I want to be on Tukutela's spoor before it is light enough to see it.'

Bare-chested, Sean strode across to Riccardo's tent, and heard his even snores as he paused at the flap.

'Capo!' The snores cut off abruptly. 'Are you awake? I've got an elephant for you. Get your arse out of the sack. Tukutela has crossed. We leave in twenty minutes.'

'Hot damn!' He could hear Riccardo was still half asleep. He stumbled about in the dark tent. 'Where the hell are my pants? Hey, Sean, wake Claudia, will you?'

There was a lantern burning in Claudia's tent. She must have heard the excitement.

'Are you awake?' Sean asked at the flap, and she opened it and stood with the lantern light behind her. Her nightdress reached almost to her ankles, there was lace at her throat and cuffs, but the cloth was so fine that the light struck through it, and her naked body was in silhouette.

'I heard you telling Papa,' she said. 'I'll be ready. Will we be walking? Should I wear my hiking boots or moccasins?'

He was certain that she was putting on this show deliberately, and he felt a prudish outrage that was totally alien to his nature. 'Today you'll walk further and faster than you ever have in your life before,' he told her harshly. 'She's showing herself off like a tramp,' he thought, ignoring the proven fact that his taste usually ran strongly towards tramps, 'just when I was starting to respect her,' and a reprimand rose to his lips. He bit it off and tried not to look at the flowing shape of her hips, as graceful as the lines of a celadon porcelain vase thrown by a master craftsman of the T'ang dynasty. He wanted to turn away to show his indifference and his contradictory disapproval, but he was still standing there when she let the tent flap drop.

'Truce, be damned,' he muttered furiously as he strode back to his tent. 'She's still in the ring throwing punches.' But his anger puzzled him. With any other woman, even one half as lovely, he would have been delighted by the exhibition.

'She's got more class than that,' he explained to himself, and then remembered how much he despised and disliked her. 'This bimbo is getting you all up a gum-tree,' he warned himself, and then burst out laughing. The dreadful gloom of Shadrach's amputation and the imminent loss of his licence were dispelled.

He was going to hunt one of Africa's legendary beasts, and the presence of this woman, in some unaccountable manner, added spice to his mood of high anticipation.

* * *

There was frost on the grass in the low vleis they crossed. It sparkled in the headlights, and the game they saw was lethargic with the cold, barely moving out of the road to let the Toyota pass in the night. They reached the ford on the Chiwewe river an hour before dawn. The waters were black and shining as anthracite in the last beams of the moon, and the tall trees along either bank were a silvered host, like two opposing armies of mythical giants.

Sean parked the Toyota well off the track, and left one of the skinners to guard it. They fell naturally into established hunting formation, with the clients in the centre. Pumula took up Shadrach's old position in the drag; a muscular taciturn man with a thick woolly bush of a black beard, he carried Riccardo's Rigby on its sling.

All the men, including Riccardo, were under field packs, even Claudia carried her own water-bottles. Job had Riccardo's second rifle, the Weatherby, over his shoulder, and as always Sean lugged the .577 Nitro Express. Once the hunt had begun he never let it out of his hands. They moved out, heading upstream, and within a mile they had warmed up and were pushing harder. Sean noticed that Claudia moved well on those long legs of hers, and was keeping up without difficulty. She gave him a saucy grin as she noticed his appraisal.

The dawn light was hardening when the tracker who had come in with the news of Tukutela's crossing, exclaimed and pointed ahead. It was light enough to make out a fresh blaze on the trunk of a pod mahogany tree which guarded a low place on the riverbank. 'There!' said the tracker. 'I marked the spoor.'

At a glance, Sean saw that this was a natural crossing place for large animals. Troops of hippo had pioneered a pathway through the reed beds, and down the ten-foot riverbank. Herds of buffalo and elephant passing over it had consolidated it and improved the gradient.

The African veld is criss-crossed with a network of game trails, and a dozen or so of these came in through the forest, like the spokes of a wheel, to concentrate on this river crossing. Everyone in the party quickened step at the tracker's exclamation, but Matatu reached the main pathway ahead of them and darted down it, turning his head to use the light of dawn most effectively, dabbing lightly at the earth with the tip of the peeled wild willow wand he carried.

He had not gone five paces before he straightened and looked back at Sean, his features wreathed in wrinkles of happiness and excitement.

'It is him!' he chirped. 'These are the feet of the father of all elephants. It is Tukutela! It is the Angry One!'

Sean looked down at the great dished spoor in the fine dust of the game path and he felt as though a spring tide had begun to flow in his life.

His excitement was replaced by a sense of destiny, an almost religious gravity.

'Matatu,' he said. 'Take the spoor!' Formally, he announced the start of the hunt.

* * *

The spoor was clear as a highway, following the game trail directly into the forest away from the river.

The old bull was striding out briskly as though he knew that the crossing was the danger point. Perhaps that was why he had chosen to cross at sunset, so that darkness would cover him until he was clear.

For five miles he had gone without a check, and then suddenly he had turned aside from the game trail into a thicket of rambling thorn which had come into blossom and new shoot. He had moved back and forth, feeding on the blooms and succulent shoots, and his spoor was confused, the thicket trampled and torn.

Matatu and Job went into the thorn thicket to unravel it, while the rest of the party hung back to let them work unhindered.

'I'm thirsty!' Claudia unhooked one of the water-bottles from her belt.

'No!' Sean stopped her. 'If you drink on your first thirst, you'll want to drink all day, and we have only just begun.'

She hesitated a moment, considering defying him, but then she hooked the bottle back on her belt.

'You are a hard taskmaster,' she said.

Matatu whistled softly on the far side of the thicket.

'He has worked the spoor out,' Sean told them, and let them through the thorn.

'How much have we gained?' he asked Matatu. They had started almost ten hours behind the bull, but every time he had paused to feed, they cut that lead.

'He did not feed long,' Matatu shrugged. 'And now he is going hard again.'

The bull had turned off the game trail and was following a stony ridge, almost as if he was deliberately obscuring his own spoor. He left no indications for the average human eye to follow, but Matatu went after him with complete authority.

'Are you sure he is still on it?' Riccardo asked anxiously.

'Capo, you've hunted with Matatu too often to ask that question,' Sean told him.

'But what can he see?' Claudia wanted to know. 'It's just rocks and gravel.'

'The elephant's pads leave a scuff on the rock, they bruise the lichen, leave smears of dust. There is fine grass growing between the stones, he has disturbed it, bending the stems in the direction of his passing. The disturbed grass catches the light differently.'

'Could you follow it?' Claudia wanted to know, and Sean shook his head.

'No, I'm not a magician.' They had been speaking in barely audible whispers, but Sean said, 'That's enough chatter, let's keep it down to a bellow from now on.'

So they went on in silence; and the forest about them was a perpetually changing show.

There were forty different varieties of the combretum family of trees, and this was not exclusively combretum forest, as many other varieties were mingled with them, each with a distinctive shape of trunk differing in the colour and texture of bark, some with branches denuded by winter, others with dense foliage of a myriad shades of green and gold and orange and cinnabar.

At times, the forest enclosed them like a palisade, then only moments later opened vistas of far hills and weirdly shaped kopjes, of open glades, and vleis from some of which the tall grass had been burned and the tender shoots laid a carpet of green over the black ash.

The new growth of grass had attracted herds of antelope into the vleis. They stood out in the open, sable antelope with long horns curved like scimitars, the proud necks of blood arabs, upper bodies sooty black as the ash of the vlei and their bellies snowy white.

Reed-buck with horns pricked forward inquisitively and tails like white powder puffs, zebra at a distance seeming not striped but a uniform grey colour, and wildebeest with roman noses and scraggly beards chasing each other like clowns in mindless circles, stirring the black ash in a cloud about themselves.

When the lion is not hunting the animals that are his natural prey are amazingly trusting and will stand and stare at him as he slouches past within fifty yards of them. In the same way they seemed to sense that this file of humans was not a threat, and they let them approach closely before moving off at a leisurely trot, and Claudia's delight buoyed her so she felt no fatigue even after four hours of hard walking.

In a gorge between two hills, water had been trapped in a narrow rock-pool. It was stagnant and green and bubbling with the gas of rotting vegetation, but the old bull had drunk from it and left a pile of his spongy yellow dung beside it.

'We'll take ten minutes' rest here,' Sean told them. 'You can have a drink now.' He looked at Claudia. 'But try to limit it to two mouthfuls, unless you'd like to try some of that.' He indicated the foul pool, and she grimaced.

He left her sitting beside her father and went to where Matatu stood alone at the head of the pool.

'What is it?' he asked. After twenty years, he could read the little man's moods. Matatu shook his head and his wrinkles sagged lugubriously.

'Something is not right here,' Matatu told him. 'The bull is unhappy. He goes one way and then the other. He travels swiftly, but without purpose. He does not feed, and he walks as though the ground burns his feet.'

'Why is that, Matatu?'

'I do not know,' he admitted. 'But I do not like it, *Bwana*.'

Sean left him and went back to where Claudia sat. 'Let's take a look at your feet.' He had spotted the slight limp she had developed in the last hour.

'Are you serious?'

She began to smile, but he took one of her feet in his lap, untied the laces, and pulled off her boot and sock. Her feet were long and narrow like her hands, but the skin was delicate and there was a bright pink spot on her heel and another on the ball of her big toe. Sean cleaned the tender spots with cotton wool and surgical spirit. It gave him an intimate and sensuous pleasure to handle those finely formed feet, but he told her severely, 'These must have been hurting you. Don't try and be brave, another few miles and you would have had blisters like a bunch of grapes, and we would have had a cripple on our hands.'

He taped the tender spots. 'Change socks,' he ordered. 'And the next time tell me as soon as it hurts.'

She obeyed him meekly, and they went on.

A little before noon, the spoor changed direction again and ran due east. 'We have gained an hour or two on him,' Sean whispered to Capo. 'But Matatu doesn't like it and neither do I. He's spooky and tense and he's heading straight for the Mozambique border now.'

'Do you think he has sensed us?' Capo was worried, but Sean shook his head.

'Impossible, we are still hours behind him.'

They stopped again briefly at noon to eat and rest, and when they went on again, they had not gone more than a mile before they entered a grove of marula trees. The ripe yellow fruit lay thickly on the ground beneath them and the old bull had not been able to resist that. He had fed heartily, spending at least three hours in the grove, shaking the trees to bring down more fruit, then at last setting off again eastwards as though suddenly remembering a rendezvous.

'At least, we have gained three hours on him,' Sean told them, but he was frowning. 'We are only ten miles from the Mozambique border. If he crosses, we have lost him.'

Sean considered running the spoor. In the old days of the bush war, he and Job and Shadrach never walked in pursuit of the enemy. Running, they had been able to cover sixty or seventy miles in a single day. He glanced back at Claudia; she might surprise him for she moved like an athlete and despite the incipient blisters there was still spring and snap in her step. Then he looked back at Riccardo and abandoned the idea. Capo was wilting in the ninety-five-degree heat of the valley. Sean tended to forget sometimes that Riccardo was only a year or two short of sixty. He had always been so fit, but now he was showing signs of distress, his eyes sunken in plum-coloured hollows and a greyish cast to his skin.

'Old beggar is looking sick,' Sean thought. 'I can't push him harder.'

He had let his attention wander, and now he almost ran into Matatu as the tracker stopped suddenly, still hunched over the spoor.

'What is it?' he demanded. The little man's agitation was obvious. He was shaking his head, and muttering in that obscure Ndorobo dialect that even Sean could not understand.

'What . . . .?' Sean broke off as he saw it. 'Oh shit!' he blurted. Two separate pairs of human tracks had come in from the side and now overlaid the elephant bull's pad marks. Here the earth was sandy and friable, the tracks clear.

Two men, wearing rubber-soled shoes. Sean recognized the distinctive pattern of the soles. Those ubiquitous Bata tennis shoes, locally manufactured, and sold for a few dollars in every street market and general dealer's store.

Even Riccardo picked out the alien human prints. 'Who the hell is that?' he demanded, but Sean ignored him and drew aside with Job to watch Matatu work.

Matatu scurried back and forth picking over the spoor like an old hen, and then came back to them. They squatted down, Job on one side of Sean, Matatu on the other – the council of war, from which only Shadrach was missing.

'Two men. One young and tall and thin, he walks on his toes. The other older, shorter, fatter. Both are carrying packs and *banduki*.' Sean knew he had deduced all this from the length of stride, the different way the two men heeled and toed under packs, and the unbalancing of a heavy weapon carried in one hand. 'They are foreigners. The men of the valley do not wear shoes, and these men came in from the north.'

'Zambian poachers,' Job grunted. 'They are after rhino horn, but they stumbled on the elephant and he is too big to let pass.'

'Bastards!' said Sean bitterly. In 1970 there had been an estimated twelve thousand black rhinoceros left in Zambia across the Zambezi river. Now there were none, not a single animal left. A Yemeni nobleman would pay fifty thousand dollars for a dagger with a rhinoceros-horn handle, and the poachers organized themselves like military expeditions. There were still a few hundred rhinoceros left on the southern side of the Zambezi valley, and from the Zambian side the poachers crossed the river in the night, slipping past the game department patrols. Many of the poachers had been bush fighters in the guerrilla war. They were hard men and killers of men as well as of the great animals on which they preyed.

'They will be carrying AKs.' Job looked at him. 'And there are probably more than two men, they will have out-flankers. We are outnumbered and outgunned, Sean. What do you want to do?'

'This is my concession,' Sean said. 'And Tukutela is my elephant.'

'Then you might have to fight them for both.' Job's noble Matabele features were solemn, but his eyes sparkled; he could not conceal the battle lust in them.

Sean stood up. 'Damned right, Job. If we catch them, we are going to fight them.'

'Then we must hurry.' Matatu stood up beside him. 'They are two hours ahead of us, and Tukutela must stop soon to feed. They will have him before we get there.'

Sean strode across to where Riccardo and Claudia were resting in the shade.

'Poachers!' he told them. 'Probably armed with automatic weapons. Two at least, possibly more, all of them ruthless killers.'

They stared at him wordlessly, and Sean went on. 'We will have to move fast to prevent them getting to Tukutela before we do. I'll leave you and Claudia to follow with Pumula at your own speed. Job and Matatu and I are going to run the spoor, and try to drive them off before they get to the elephant. You keep the Rigby, Capo, and Job will take the Weatherby.'

As he began to turn away, Riccardo caught his arm. 'Sean, I want this elephant. More than anything left in my life, I want this elephant.'

'I will try and save him for you,' Sean nodded. He understood entirely. He felt the same way.

'Thank you.' Riccardo let his hand fall to his side and Sean went to where Job and Matatu were waiting. They had handed over their field packs to Pumula and carried only their water-bottles. Sean glanced at his stainless-steel Rolex. Four minutes since they picked up the poachers' spoor, four minutes wasted.

'Hot pursuit!' Sean ordered. 'And expect ambush!'

Job smiled at him. 'Old times,' he said. 'It makes me feel young again.'

Matatu pulled his loin-cloth up between his legs and tucked the skirt under his belt, then whirled and went away on the spoor at a loping trot. Sean had seen him keep up that pace from sun up to sun down. He went out onto the right flank, and Job who was left-handed took his natural side. Sean changed the cartridges in the .577 and began to run. Within seconds, Riccardo's group was out of sight in the forest behind them, and Sean concentrated all his attention ahead.

It required special skills and vast experience to keep the formation intact in this type of broken country. The flankers had to keep slightly ahead of the tracker, anticipating the line of the spoor, sweeping the terrain for ambush, covering and protecting Matatu, and yet keeping fifty paces out on each side, breaking their own trail, and still maintaining contact with the opposite flanker, all this while on the run and mostly out of sight of each other, with Matatu setting a furious pace in the centre.

When the spoor turned, the man on the outer flank had to wheel on the centre, covering twice the distance of his opposite number, and when the spoor crossed open ground, they had to increase the angle on the flank, forming an inverted spearhead formation, always protecting the centre, keeping contact with subtle bird-calls, the flute of a wood dove, the whistle of a bul-bul, the warble of a shrike, the pipe of a black kite, each had meaning, each a command or a warning.

All this and two other essentials, silence and speed. Job and Sean ran like a pair of kudu bulls, lightly and soundlessly, ducking and weaving under branches through thickets and thorns, quick and vigilant.

After the first hour, Matatu flashed a hand signal down a break in forest, and Sean understood it readily. 'Two more,' the signal said.

Another pair of poachers had joined the first two, and they also were closing swiftly with the elephant.

They ran for another hour, never slackening for a moment, and Matatu signalled again from the centre.

'Very close.' An eloquent flash of his pink palm. 'Beware. Danger.' And Sean whistled like a sand grouse, checking the pace, the signal for imminent contact and they came down to a wary trot.

The trail had led them up the side of a low tableland, along an ancient elephant trail that was well trodden into the iron-hard earth. When they came out on top of the flat plateau they felt the stir of the evening breeze, cool and blessed out of the east, and Sean held his sweaty face up to it.

The plateau was less than a mile wide, and they crossed it quickly and reached the far rim, dropping to their bellies and sliding over the sky line without showing a silhouette against the blue and then crouching below the crest and sweeping the ground below them, a shallow valley with another forested tableland beyond. A riverbed meandered down the centre of the valley, its course marked with a narrow ribbon of dark green riverine bush, and the rest of the valley fairly open: pale, winter grass shining in the sunlight, dotted ant-hills, each the size of a cottage, widely separated umbrella acacia with flat tops, and lemon-yellow trunks. Sean surveyed it all swiftly.

Out on the left, Job gave the penny-whistle snort of a reed-buck, one of the most urgent alarm calls in their repertoire. He was pointing down into the valley, half left from their front. Sean followed the gesture. For a moment he saw nothing, and then suddenly Tukutela, the Angry One, stepped into view.

He had been hidden from Sean by one of the huge ant-hills, but now he strode out into the open meadow, and Sean gasped aloud. Even from almost a mile away, Sean realized that he had only poorly remembered the magnificence of this animal.

Tukutela was the dark grey of volcanic rock, tall and gaunt; even at this distance Sean could make out the folds and tucks of his ancient riven hide, and the knotted outline of his spine beneath it. His ears fanned gently with each stride, and their edges were tattered and eroded, like a pair of battle ensigns torn with shot and blackened with the smoke of cannon.

Tukutela's tusks were black also, stained with age and the sap of the tall trees he had destroyed with them. From his gaping lower lip the tusks flared outwards, and then curved in again towards each other so the tips almost met nine feet from his lip. They were without taper, solid columns of ivory, hanging so low that in the centre they drooped below the level of the winter grass, and they seemed to over-burden even that massive frame.

90

There would probably never be another pair of tusks like that ever again. This elephant was legend and history.

Sean felt a hot flare of guilt. No matter the legality of it, the killing of this beast would be a crime against Africa, an affront to the gods of the wilderness and the very soul of man, yet he knew he would not hesitate to do it, and that knowledge added poignancy to his sense of guilt. As a hunter, the nobler the quarry, the greater the compulsion to take the trophy. Job whistled again, pointing, diverting Sean's attention from the elephant, and only then Sean saw the poachers.

They were already closing in on the bull. He could see all four of them. They had just left the trees at the bottom of the slope, and were moving in single file into the grass meadow. The grass reached to their armpits, and their heads and shoulders bobbed like the cork line of a fishing-net in the pale sea of grass. Each of them carried an AK 47 assault rifle slung over his shoulder.

The light swift bullets those weapons fired were not at all suitable for hunting massive-bodied species, but Sean knew the technique. They would get in close and all four would open fire together, blazing hundreds of rounds into the bull, riddling his lungs with copper-jacketed bullets, bringing him down under the sheer weight of automatic fire power.

The line of poachers was swinging out to flank the elephant, not heading directly towards him, but keeping well below the wind, so that a fluke of the breeze would not carry their scent to him. Despite this detour, they were running hard and gaining on him swiftly. The bull was still totally unaware of their existence, heading with long swaying strides down towards the riverbed, but at this rate, Sean realized that they would intercept him and open fire before he reached it.

The government directive from the game department to the concessionaires was in plain language. Unauthorized armed men in a hunting concession, if apprehended in what was clearly a hunting operation, were presumed to be poachers. Four game department rangers and one concessionaire had been murdered by poachers during the past four years, and the directive was that fire could be opened on poachers without warning. The prime minister, Robert Mugabe, had made it even plainer. 'Shoot to kill,' were his exact words.

The .577 Nitro Express was a devastating weapon at close quarters, but over a hundred yards the heavy bullet dropped away rapidly. The group of poachers was six hundred yards away across the valley floor and Sean jumped up, and crouching low, slipped across the face of the slope to where Job was lying behind a fallen tree-trunk.

He dropped down beside him. 'Give me the Weatherby,' he ordered, and took the lighter weapon from his hands. Job was an excellent shot, but this called for Bisley-standard marksmanship.

Sean jerked the bolt open and checked that there was a cartridge in the chamber. It was a 180-grain Nosler, and Sean tried to estimate how much the bullet would drop over the range of six hundred yards, firing downhill, with a light breeze on his left shoulder. He remembered from the ballistic table that the bullet drop at three hundred and fifty yards would be six inches, at six hundred yards it would probably be four foot or more.

While he worked it out, he stripped off his shirt, rolled it into a bundle and placed it on the fallen tree-trunk behind which he and Job were crouched.

'Back me with the big *banduki*. Shoot very high with it,' he told Job, and settled behind the tree-trunk, resting the fore-end of the Weatherby on the pad of the shirt. He screwed the variable telescopic lens to full power and gazed through it.

He picked up the heads of the file of poachers. With this magnification, he could recognize two of the men as Matatu had described them from their spoor. The tall lean one was leading, and he wore a blue denim jacket, traditional guerrilla uniform from the days of the bush war. Behind him came the shorter heavier man. He had a tiger-striped camouflage cap on his head and wore a plain khaki shirt.

Beyond them Sean could see the elephant. The magnification of the lens foreshortened the range so that the poachers seemed very close to their quarry. Even as he watched them, the leader of the column unslung the automatic rifle from his shoulder and made a gesture with his other hand. Behind him, the other three poachers fanned out into a skirmishing line and slipped their rifles off their shoulders, holding them at high port.

Sean snuggled down behind the Weatherby, digging in his heels, regulating his breathing, his forefinger resting lightly on the trigger. He picked out the tall leader in the denim jacket, and let the cross-hairs of the telescopic sights drift over the man's head.

The image wavered and quivered in the heat, and Sean watched the watery lines of mirage, for they were indicators of the strength and direction of the breeze; when they leaned over, the breeze was gusting, but they rose straight upwards like smoke in the lulls between gusts.

He drew a long breath, let half of it out and held the rest. The mirage steadied in a lull, and he took his aim a full body-length above the poacher's head. The image looked good but he did not pull the trigger. He squeezed the grip of the rifle with his whole hand as though he were modelling clay.

The butt plate slammed back into his shoulder as the barrel jumped high in the typically vicious Weatherby recoil, and he lost sight of the target.

Before he could collect himself, Job exulted, 'Shayile! A hit!' And when Sean brought the lens back there were only three heads showing above the grass.

All three poachers had turned and were firing their weapons back towards the slope where Sean and Job were hidden, blazing wildly on fully automatic, their AKs beating like the rattle of kettledrums.

Beyond them, Sean saw the old bull elephant in full flight. His ears streaming back and his great black tusks lifted high above the grass, he crashed into the narrow ribbon of dark bush and out the other side.

'Run, my beauty,' Sean breathed. 'If I can't have you, nobody else will.' And he turned his full attention back to the band of poachers.

They were a crack unit, that was immediately obvious, two of them were throwing covering fire at the kopje, while the third had run to where the leader had gone down in the grass, and dragged him to his feet. The blue denim-clad leader had lost his rifle, and he was doubled up and clutching his side.

'Nicked him!' Sean muttered, and fired again. He saw dust fly above the grass, as his bullet fell close beside them. The poachers began to pull out, dragging their leader with them, placing an ant-hill between them and the kopje. Both Sean and Job were firing deliberately, but the range was increasing every second, and although Sean saw dust fly very close to the scurrying figures, they could not claim another hit before the band disappeared into the grass and scrub, and the clatter of automatic fire dwindled into silence.

Sean and Job waited fifteen minutes peering down into the

valley, but they did not get another glimpse of them before Sean stood up.

'We'll go and take a look.'

'Careful,' Job warned. 'They could have doubled back to lay an ambush.' That was another old guerrilla trick, and they went down the slope cautiously.

Matatu led them to where the poacher had fallen. It was an area of flattened grass. The man's weapon had disappeared, one of the other poachers must have retrieved it. Matatu picked one of the grass stems and held it out to Sean. The blood on it was almost dry. However, the bleeding had not been profuse and they found less than a dozen droplets on the grass or balled on the dry earth.

'Flesh wound,' Sean grunted. The drift of the breeze must have pushed the bullet off the vital areas of the man's body.

'Who do we follow, Tukutela or the poachers?' Job wanted to know.

'The poachers will be halfway back to Lusaka by now,' Sean grinned. 'Follow the elephant!' he ordered Matatu.

They tracked Tukutela across the riverbed and up the farther side of the valley. After his first panicked rush, the old bull settled down into that swinging stride that ate up the ground at a prodigious rate, and which he could keep up for days. He was boring away towards the east, towards the Mozambique border, only deviating slightly from his course to take a gap in a line of hills, or to climb the easier gradient when there was no pass.

They ran hard on his spoor. Not having to take precaution against ambush, they could push themselves to the limits, but the elephant was pulling away from them, and the day was wasting. The sun was casting their own long shadows ahead of them.

There was no defined border with Mozambique, no fence or cut line through the forest, but a sixth sense warned Sean that they had crossed.

He was about to give orders to halt when Job whistled softly and made a cut-out signal with his left hand. Matatu pulled up and shook his head in agreement, and the three of them bunched up and stood looking along the faint spoor which ran ahead of them into the darkening, eastern forest.

'Mozambique,' Job said. 'He has gone away.' And the others did not deny it.

'He still goes fast.' Matatu spat on the spoor. 'Faster than any man can run. We will not see Tukutela again this year.'

'Yes, but there will be another season,' Sean said. 'Next year, he will range back into the National Park and come again in the new moon across the Chiwewe river. We will be waiting for him.'

'Perhaps.' Matatu took a pinch of snuff from the duiker-horn container that hung around his neck. 'Or perhaps the poachers will find him again, or he will walk onto a land-mine in an old battlefield in Mozambique, or perhaps he will die of his own great age.'

The thought filled Sean with melancholy. Tukutela was a part of the old Africa. Sean had been born too late fully to experience that era. He had only been able to glimpse vestiges of it, yet he had a deep, nostalgic reverence for the history and past of his continent. It was all going so fast, trodden under the greedy rush for power by the thoughtless hordes of the emerging nations, by the unbridled tribal rivalries and the lawlessness of this new age. Once again, Africa was becoming the dark continent, but this time without the glory of its natural treasures, the wild game decimated, the forests hacked down for fuel, the very earth abused by primitive agriculture and animal husbandry, and the Saharan deserts each year marching southwards. Tukutela was one of the very few remaining treasures.

Sean turned back. He had wanted that elephant. He had wanted him with the utmost parts of his being. Now as he turned back into the west, the disappointment weighed down his legs and his heart, and he went heavily.

*   *   *

A little before midnight, they found Riccardo and Claudia sleeping on a mattress of cut grass, under a lean-to shelter beside a fire that had burned down to coals, while Pumula sat guard at the second fire close by.

Riccardo came awake the instant Sean touched his shoulder, and he scrambled up eagerly.

'Did you find him? What happened? What about the poachers?'

'He's gone, Capo. Across the border. We chased off the poachers, but Tukutela got clear away,' Sean told him, and Riccardo sagged back on the grass mattress and listened in silence

95

while Sean described the chase and the contact with the poachers.

Claudia sat close to her father, and when Sean told them how Tukutela had crossed into Mozambique, she slipped her arm around his shoulders in a gesture of comfort.

'All right.' Sean stood up. 'There is one of my hunting tracks that cuts through about five miles south of here. Matatu and I will go back to fetch the truck, and Job will lead you to the track. I'll meet you there. Should take us four or five hours.'

By the light of the stars alone, Matatu led Sean for four hours through forest and dense bush, bringing him at last unerringly to where the truck was parked.

It was another hour's drive to the rendezvous where they found Claudia and Riccardo and the others sitting beside a fire on the verge of the rough track. They climbed wearily into the truck and Sean turned back and headed towards camp. It was four o'clock in the morning, over twenty-four hours since they had set out with such high hopes on the hunt.

They drove in silence for a while with Claudia asleep on her father's shoulder. Then Riccardo asked thoughtfully, 'Do you know where Tukutela has gone?'

'Beyond our reach, Capo,' Sean told him grimly.

'Seriously.' Riccardo was impatient. 'Is there one of his regular haunts where he will be headed?'

'That's rough country in there,' Sean murmured. 'Chaos and confusion. Villages burned and deserted, two armies fighting each other, with Mugabe's lads joining in.'

'Where has that elephant gone?' Riccardo insisted. 'He must have an established range.'

Sean nodded. 'We have worked it out, Job, Matatu and I. We reckon that he holes up from July to September in the swamps below the Cabora Bassa dam. Then in late September or the beginning of October, he crosses the Zambezi and heads north into Malawi, into the dense rain forest around Mlanje. He hides there until after the rains break and then comes south again, crosses the Zambezi near Tete and goes back into the Chiwewe National Park again.'

'So he will be heading for the swamps now?' Riccardo asked.

'More than likely,' Sean nodded. 'We'll get another crack at him next season, Capo.'

They reached camp at dawn, and there were steaming hot showers and freshly ironed clothes ready for them, and a huge breakfast spread in the dining tent. Sean loaded crispy bacon and fried eggs onto their plates.

'When we have finished breakfast, we'll catch up on some of the sleep we missed last night, sack out until lunchtime.'

'Suits me,' Claudia agreed readily.

'Then we'll have a conference. We must work out our plans for the rest of the safari, we still have almost three weeks. We can try for another bull elephant, I can't offer you anything like Tukutela, but we might be able to find a sixty-pounder for you, Capo.'

'I don't want a sixty-pounder,' Riccardo said. 'I want Tukutela.'

'Don't we all, but let's drop it now.' Sean's irritation was undisguised. 'We can't do anything about it, let's just drop the subject.'

'What if we crossed the border and followed him into the swamps?' Riccardo did not look up from his eggs and bacon, and Sean studied his face before he laughed mirthlessly.

'For a moment, you had me worried. I thought you meant it. We'll get Tukutela next season.'

'There isn't going to be another season,' Riccardo told him. 'You know damn well that Geoffrey Manguza is going to pull your licence and take Chiwewe away from you.'

'Thanks, Capo, you certainly know how to make me feel good.'

'No sense fooling ourselves. This is our last chance at that elephant.'

'Correction.' Sean shook his head. 'It's over for this season. We had our chance and we blew it.'

'Not if we follow him into Mozambique,' Riccardo said. 'Follow him into the swamps.'

Sean stared at him. 'My God, you are serious!'

'I told you. There is nothing that I want more in this life than that elephant.'

'So you expect Job and Matatu and me to commit suicide for a whim of yours.'

'No, I don't expect it for a whim – let's say for half a million dollars rather.'

Sean shook his head, but no words came out, and Riccardo went on.

'I feel responsible for you losing your licence. With half a million you could buy a good concession in Zambia or Botswana, or fifty thousand acres of game ranch in South Africa. Half a million. Think about it.'

Sean jumped up from the breakfast table so violently that he knocked his plate to the ground. He strode away without looking back.

He stood alone at the edge of the camp staring down towards the river where a small herd of impala were drinking. and a white-headed fish eagle sat on a dead tree above the green water. He did not see them.

He thought about what it would be like next year without his own concession. He owed his brother. Garry. almost fifty thousand dollars and his overdraft at the bank in Harare was touching ten thousand. Reema had told him that the bank manager was anxious to speak to him, Sean had avoided the appointment on his last visit to Harare.

He was over forty and he had accumulated nothing. His father might be delighted to welcome him back to the family company, but his brother Garry was the chairman now and he would be less enthusiastic.

He thought about air-conditioned offices. neckties and dark business suits. interminable meetings with lawyers and engineers, rush-hour traffic and the smell of the city.

He thought about his father's philosophy. heartily endorsed by his brother. that a man had to start at the bottom of the company and 'work his way up'. Garry had more than twenty years' start on him. Garry loved it and he hated it.

He thought about half a million dollars. With that amount of money in his back pocket. he could thumb his nose at his bank manager. at Geoffrey Manguza. and at Garry Courtney. and at the rest of the world. and tell them all to go and get stuffed.

He turned away from the river. and started down the path to Job's tent. Job was eating alone at his own camp-fire. served by his youngest wife. He gave her a quiet order to leave when he saw Sean coming. then he took the coffee pot off the coals and poured a second mug and dribbled condensed milk from the can into it.

Sean sat on the carved native stool beside him and took the mug from him. He spoke in Sindebele.

'What would you think of a man who followed a great elephant like Tukutela to his secret place in the swamps along the Zambezi?'

'A man of such stupidity does not bear thinking of.' Job blew on his coffee to cool it, and they were silent for a long while.

Matatu, who had been sleeping in his hut nearby, sensed the presence of his master, and came out, blinking and yawning in the early sunlight, to squat at Sean's feet. Sean let his hand rest on the little man's shoulder for a moment. He felt him wriggle with pleasure under the touch. He did not even have to ask Matatu. He would go where Sean went, without question, without a moment's hesitation, so Sean spoke directly to Job.

'Job, old friend of many years, I give you something else to think on. Monterro wants to follow the elephant, he is offering half a million dollars. What do you think of half a million dollars?'

Job sighed. 'I do not have to think too long on that. When do we leave?'

Sean squeezed his arm hard, and stood up.

Riccardo was seated at the breakfast table with a cup of coffee and a cigar. Claudia was beside him, and they had been arguing. The girl's face was still flushed and her eyes asparkle, but she lapsed into silence as Sean entered the tent.

'Capo,' Sean said. 'You have no idea what it will be like across there. It will be Vietnam all over again, but this time without the back-up of the US army. Do you understand that?'

'I want to go,' Capo nodded.

'All right. Here are my terms. You will sign an indemnity, for whatever happens to you. I am not responsible.'

'Agreed.'

'Then I want a written acknowledgement of debt for the full amount, binding on your estate in the event of your death.'

'Give me the paper.'

'You are crazy, Capo, do you know that?'

'Sure,' Riccardo grinned. 'But what about you?'

'Oh, I was born crazy,' Sean laughed with him as they shook hands, and then he sobered. 'I want to fly a reconnaissance along the border to make sure there are no surprises waiting for us. If all is clear, we'll cross tonight. It will mean forced marches and travelling light. I want to be in and out in under ten days.'

Riccardo nodded and Sean told him, 'Get some rest now. You are going to need it.'

He was about to turn away when he caught Claudia's furious gaze. 'I'll radio Reema to send down another charter flight to pick you up tomorrow. She'll wangle you on the first commercial flight back to Anchorage.'

Claudia seemed about to reply when Riccardo laid his hand over hers. 'Okay,' he said. 'She'll go. I'll see to it.'

'Damn right, she'll go,' Sean said. 'She certainly isn't coming into Mozambique with us.'

* * *

Sean taped over the identification markings on the Beechcraft's wings and fuselage, obliterating them from the scrutiny of a ground observer. He made certain that the tape was so firmly adhering to the metalwork that the slipstream could not strip it away. While he worked, Job checked the emergency stores aboard the aircraft, in case they were forced down. Rather than the heavy double-barrelled rifle, he loaded Sean's lightweight 30/06 with the black glass-fibre stock.

They took off and Sean banked onto an easterly heading, keeping barely fifty feet above the treetops. He flew with the map on his lap, checking each landmark as it appeared ahead of them. Job sat beside him in the right-hand seat, while Matatu was in the seat behind Job. Even after all these years, Matatu was terrified of flying, and still occasionally suffered from air-sickness. Sean refused to allow him to sit in the seat behind him.

'Silly little bugger will puke down the back of my neck again.' So Job had to run that risk.

They reached the border and turned northwards along it, searching for troop movements or for any evidence of human presence. They found nothing, until thirty minutes later they saw the sheen of water on the horizon, an inland sea formed by the man-made dam on the Zambezi River. 'Cabora Bassa,' Sean grunted. The hydro-electric scheme, one of the biggest and most expensive in Africa, had been built by the Portuguese before they relinquished the colony to self-government.

Although the South Africans would have taken all the power that the project could supply, transporting it southwards across the grids to their great mines at Palabora in the Transvaal, and the revenue would have gone a long way to alleviating Mozambique's desperate economic plight, Cabora Bassa no longer sold a single kilowatt of electricity. The southbound power lines were continually sabotaged by the rebel forces, and the government troops were so demoralized that they made little attempt to protect the repair crews from attack. Thus it was years since a repair had even been attempted.

'By now the turbines are probably just piles of rust. Score another sweeping triumph for African Marxism,' Sean chuckled, and dropped a wing to turn 180 degrees and head back southwards. On this leg he flew deeper into Mozambique, setting a zigzag course to cover more ground, once again searching for occupied villages or mobile military units.

They found only the patterns of old cultivated lands, now gone back to weed and bush, and burned-out deserted villages, with no sign of human life around the shells of roofless huts.

Sean intersected the road running between Vila de Manica and Cabora Bassa, and flew along it for ten miles. He was so low that he could see the ruts and potholes in the surface and weeds growing in the wheel tracks. No vehicle had used it for months, perhaps years. The culverts and bridges had been destroyed by explosives and the bodies of mined vehicles, burned out and rusted, littered the verges.

He turned back towards the west and the border now, searching for a place that all three of them remembered so well. As they came up ahead, Sean recognized the symmetrical hillocks they called Inhlozane, 'The Maiden's Breasts', and south of them the confluence of two minor rivers, now reduced to strings of green pools in wide sand beds.

Job pointed ahead. 'There it is.' And in the back seat, Matatu forgot his fear and discomfort to cackle with laughter and clutch Sean's shoulder.

'Inhlozane. Do you remember, *Bwana*?'

Sean banked steeply over the junction of the two rivers, circling them, all three of them peering down. They could make out no traces of the old guerrilla camp. The last time they had been here was in the spring of 1976 and they had come as the scouts, Ballantyne's Scouts.

Under interrogation, a prisoner had revealed the existence of a major guerrilla training camp in this area, and the Rhodesian high command had sent one of the Vampire jets over on a high photographic run. The camp had been cunningly concealed, and every artifice of camouflage employed. However, the Rhodesian evaluators were highly skilled, most of them ex-RAF personnel. It is possible to camouflage the dugouts and hutments used by

101

hundreds of men and women, but the pathways between them are the tell-tales. Thousands of feet moving daily between barracks and lecture huts, between mess halls and latrines, going out to forage for firewood or carrying water from the river, beat pathways that from the air look like the veins in a dead leaf.

'Between two and two and a half thousand,' the airforce photographic reconnaissance squadron leader had told the briefing. 'They have been there for approximately six months, so training is almost complete. They are probably just waiting for the rains to break before beginning a major offensive.'

A simultaneous incursion by two thousand trained terrorists would have strained the Rhodesian security forces' capabilities to breaking point.

'Preemptive strike,' General Peter Walls, the Rhodesian Commander-in-Chief, had ordered. 'I want a battle plan prepared within twenty-four hours.' The code name chosen for the attack was 'Popeye'.

Rivalry between the Selous Scouts and the Ballantyne Scouts was fierce, and Sean had been jubilant when he had been given the ground attack role of 'Popeye' in preference to the Selous lads.

They had gone in with the slow and ancient Dakotas, crowded on the benches along the fuselage, fifty men and their equipment to an aircraft, sitting on their parachutes. Almost equal numbers of black and white troopers, but homogeneous in their camouflage paint, they had jumped from three hundred feet, just enough height for the parachutes to flare before they hit the ground. From that height they jokingly referred to themselves as 'meat bombs'.

The jump area was twelve miles from the guerrilla training camp, and ninety-six miles inside the Mozambique border. They were on the ground an hour before sunset. All three hundred Scouts were assembled and ready to move out by nightfall.

They had made the approach march by moonlight, each man carrying a pack that weighed almost a hundred pounds, most of that weight made up of ammunition for the RPD machine-guns. They had reached the fork of the river after midnight and prepared their ambush position along the south bank, overlooking the dry riverbed and its shallow green pools, facing the training camp on the far bank.

Sean, with Job beside him, crept along the bank checking every position personally, speaking to his men in whispers, calling them by name. They had lain for the rest of the night behind their machine-guns, and the small sounds and the smells of the woodsmoke and cooking food had drifted across to them on the night breeze.

At dawn, a bugle had sounded reveille in the dark forest that hid the camps, and they had seen the obscure movement of many persons in the gloom beneath the trees.

Twenty minutes later, precisely at the moment of good shooting light, the Vampires had come whistling in from the west and dropped their napalm canisters. Towering balls of orange flame shot through with evil black smoke had erupted into the sky palling the sunrise; the heat and the chemical stink of the napalm came rolling down to where the Scouts lay in ambush. The Vampires had deliberately dropped their loads of napalm along the northern perimeter of the camp, sealing off that escape route with a wall of fire.

The Canberra bombers came in twenty seconds behind the Vampires, and their bomb loads were fragmentation and high-explosive. They fell into the camp with jarring crumping detonations, sending up fountains of dirt and debris, and the trainee guerrillas who survived came out of the forest, screaming and howling in a panic-stricken mob.

The napalm had cut them off from the north, and they poured into the riverbed, and came running directly at the waiting machine-guns. Sean let them come, studying them with a detached interest. There were almost as many women as men, but it was difficult to differentiate between the sexes. They wore no uniform, some were in khaki shorts and tee-shirts with portraits of guerrilla leaders or political slogans printed on the chests. Others wore blue denim or bush jackets and some were bare-chested and in their underwear. Nearly all of them were young, in their middle or late teens, all of them terrified and running blindly to escape the conflagration of napalm and high-explosive.

They splashed into the pools, and the sand held their feet, slowing them. As they ran, they looked back over their shoulders at the flames and dust of the camp, so none of them saw the gunners that waited for them on the south bank.

The riverbed was filled with struggling humanity, like a pit full of rats, and as the first of them reached the bank on which Sean lay and began to clamber up the steep earthen side, he blew a piercing blast on his whistle. The last note of the whistle was drowned out by gunfire, three hundred automatic weapons opening up together.

Sean had been hardened by years of brutal warfare, but even he found the carnage stunning. At close range, the volleys of machine-gun fire tore a human body to shreds, and went on to destroy the next rank and the next. Shot boiled the white sand of the riverbed, so it rose in a fog waist-high, and turned the running figures to ghostly silhouettes in the dust, and then hid them as they collapsed or were flung carelessly aside by pointblank bursts of fire.

The din lasted for four minutes, and then there were no more targets and the guns fell silent. Between them they had fired fifty thousand bullets into the riverbed and the barrels of the guns were so hot that, like the plate of a stove, they ticked and pinkled as they cooled. Though their ears were dulled and numbed by the roar of gunfire, they could hear the moans and cries of those who still lived in the riverbed.

Sean blew another blast on his whistle and they leaped down the bank, and went forward in a skirmishing line.

Sean's orders were that the only prisoners to be taken were to be officers or political commissars. As they crossed the river, they shot those who showed any signs of life, holding the muzzles against their heads, a single bullet for each, making certain that they would never recover from their wounds to attack another Rhodesian farm house or hack the arms and legs off the black villagers who refused to supply them with food and women. They left nobody alive in the riverbed and then went on to sweep through the camp, tossing grenades into the dugouts, searching the huts for survivors, and more importantly for maps and documents. Like all good Marxists, the guerrillas were obsessed with record-keeping. The capture of the camp archives was one of the major priorities of 'Popeye'.

Racing at the head of his men, Sean was the first to reach the headquarters hut in the centre of the camp. He recognized it by the gaudy flag drooping on its flagpole in front of it.

The doorway was dangerous. He fired a burst through the grass wall and then dived in head first through the window. There was a tall black man in the front office. He was dressed in blue denims, and he was scooping armfuls of documents out of the paraffin boxes that served as filing cabinets and dumping them in the centre of the floor. Clearly he was going to attempt to burn them, but now he dropped his armful of paper and reached for the pistol in the holster on his belt.

Sean kicked his legs out from under him and as he dropped, he slammed the butt of his weapon into the side of his neck just below the ear. As Sean rolled to his feet, Matatu appeared beside him like a grinning gnome and stooped to slit the unconscious guerrilla's throat with his skinning knife.

'No.' Sean stopped him. 'We want that one.' Job was seconds behind him, bursting into the room with the heavy RPD machine-gun held ready across his hip.

'Okay, Captain,' Sean ordered him. 'Get a detail to recover all this bumf.' He glanced at his watch. 'The choppers will be here in twenty minutes.'

The Rhodesian air force was desperately short of helicopters. They were under sanction by every nation in the world except South Africa, and a British warship was blockading the Mozambique channel to deny those ports to them.

They could risk only two helicopters for this operation and one of those was loaded with captured documents, almost five tons of them: lists of the trainees, and their organization, target priorities and supply sheets, equipment dossiers, training manuals, field evaluations of Rhodesian counter measures, communist propaganda, maps of the attack routes and safe corridors, the entire order of battle of the guerrilla army. It was a treasure trove, its acquisition a greater blow to the enemy than the hundreds of bodies lying in the riverbed, but it filled one of the precious helicopters.

The second Alouette helicopter Sean used for 'Casevac' and for ferrying out the prisoners. However, the Scouts had taken more casualties than he had anticipated: three troopers had been injured in the parachute drop, torn cartilages and sprained ligaments, and five others had been wounded by the desultory and quickly suppressed counterfire of the more plucky of the guerrillas. Then one of the guerrillas had feigned dead in the riverbed and thrown a grenade when the Scouts came forward, killing a black trooper and wounding two others. The Scouts always took their dead out for decent burial and the trooper's corpse was already in its green plastic body bag.

In addition to his own casualties, Sean's men had captured eight suspected officers and commissars. The guerrilla leaders wore no insignia of rank but could usually be identified by the superior quality of their clothing, by their sunglasses, wristwatches and by the rows of ballpoint pens in their breast pockets.

They had too many passengers for the helicopters, and Sean was forced to keep five of his prisoners with him for the outward march. He picked those who looked fit enough to survive a forced march with the Scouts, and one of these was the man they had captured in the command hut.

Forty-five minutes after the attack had begun, the last helicopter took off and the Scouts were ready to move out. They could expect the Frelimo counter-attack to be dilatory and unenthusiastic, but Sean was taking no chances. He was on the riverbank surveying the carnage of the killing ground. They couldn't afford the time to make a body count, but the air force would run another reconnaissance later this morning and they would get a fair estimate from the photographs.

'Must be at least fifteen hundred,' Sean decided. They were lying in heaps and windrows like newly cut wheat and already the flies were hanging over them in a grey mist.

Sean turned away from the scene. 'All right,' he called. 'Move them out!'

The first section of fifty men set off at a trot. The troop trucks would race across the border and come in as far as they could to meet them, but the men would still have to run thirty miles or more before they could ride, a full marathon under arms, but most of the ammunition had been shot away and the packs were almost empty.

Job hurried across to where Sean stood on the bank. 'The prisoner you took, Colonel. I have recognized him. It's Comrade China himself.'

'Are you sure?' Sean did not wait for Job to reply. 'Damn, if I had known I would have sent him out on the chopper.'

Comrade China was high on the wanted list of the Rhodesians. He was the area commander of the entire north-eastern sector, the equivalent of a major-general, and one of their most successful commanders, a man with a lot of interesting stories to tell to military intelligence.

'Make sure he gets out safely, Captain,' Sean ordered brusquely. 'Treat him like your new wife.'

'China refuses to march,' Job said. 'We can't shoot him, and we can't carry him. He knows that.'

Sean strode across to where the prisoner was held under guard. He squatted sullenly with his hands behind his head.

'On your feet and march,' Sean ordered, and Comrade China spat on Sean's boots. Sean unbuckled his holster and drew the .357 Magnum revolver. He laid it against the side of the man's head.

'On your feet,' he repeated. 'Your last chance.'

'You won't shoot,' the man sneered. 'You daren't shoot.' And Sean fired. The muzzle was aimed over Comrade China's shoulder, but the barrel was pressed hard against his ear.

Comrade China screamed and clutched at his ear with both hands. A thin trickle of blood from his ruptured eardrum ran out between his fingers. 'On your feet!' Sean said and still holding his damaged ear, Comrade China spat at him again. Sean laid the revolver barrel against his other ear. 'After your ears, we will take out your eyes, with a sharp stick.' Comrade China stood up.

'At the double, move out.' Job took over. He placed his hand between China's shoulder-blades, and sent him tottering down the riverbank.

Sean took one more look around the battlefield. It had been done swiftly and thoroughly, what the Scouts called 'a good kill'.

'All right, Matatu,' Sean said softly. 'Let's go home.' And the little Ndorobo ran ahead of him.

When Comrade China faltered and his knees went rubbery and he collapsed from the agony of his burst eardrum, Sean gave him a subcutaneous shot of morphine from a disposable syringe and a drink from his water-bottle.

'For a soldier of the revolution who shoots babies and chops the feet off old women, this is a stroll in the park,' Sean told him. 'Brace up, China, or I'll blow your other ear out.' And he took one of his elbows and Job the other. Between them, they hoisted him to his feet and half carried him until the morphine had a chance to work, but they kept up the pace of the running column of Scouts through the forest and over the rolling rocky hills.

'You may have killed some of our people today.' After a mile or so the morphine was working and China became loquacious. 'Today you have won a single little battle, Colonel Courtney, but tomorrow we will have won the war.' China's voice was harsh with bitter self-righteousness.

107

'How do you know my name?' Sean asked with amusement.

'You are famous, Colonel, or should I say infamous. Under you, this pack of killer dogs is even more dangerous than when the murderous Ballantyne himself was leading it.'

'Thank you for the pretty compliment, my old China, but aren't you claiming victory a little prematurely?'

'The side which controls the countryside by night wins the war.'

'Mao Tse-tung,' Sean smiled. 'A most appropriate quotation for one of your name.'

'We control the countryside at last, we have you bottled up in your villages and towns. Your white farmers are losing heart, their women are sick of war. The black peasants are openly sympathetic to our cause. Britain and the world are against you. Even South Africa, your only ally, is growing disenchanted with the struggle. Soon, very soon . . .'

They argued as they ran, and despite himself, Sean could not suppress a grudging admiration for his prisoner. He was quick-witted, his command of English impressive and his grasp of politics and military tactics even more so. He was physically strong and fit. Sean could feel the wiry muscle in his arm as he supported him, and few other men with a burst eardrum could have sustained the pace of the march.

'He would make a superb Scout,' Sean thought. 'If we could turn him . . .' Many of his most valuable men were former guerrillas, captured and skilfully turned by Rhodesian intelligence.

So as they ran on he studied Comrade China with renewed interest. He was probably a few years younger than Sean. He had refined Nilotic features, more Ethiopian than Shona, a narrow high-bridged nose and chiselled lips rather than the broadly negroid. Even the morphine could not dim the intelligence of his large dark eyes. He was a handsome man, and of course, he would be tough and utterly ruthless. He would not have reached his rank were he not.

'I want him,' Sean decided. 'My God, he would be worth another full regiment to us.' And he tightened his grip on the man's arm, a proprietorial gesture. 'This little darling is going to get the full treatment.'

The vanguard ran into a Frelimo patrol in the middle of the morning and brushed them aside, hardly slackening their pace to do so. The corpses in their blotched Frelimo camouflage lay beside the track as they trotted past.

They came up with the troop convoy a little after midday. The trucks were guarded by the Eland armoured cars, and they had cans of ice-cold Castle beer in the cool boxes. The Scouts had covered forty-two miles in just over seven hours, and the beer tasted like nectar.

Sean gave a can to Comrade China. 'Sorry about your ear,' he told him, and saluted him with the beer can.

'I would have done the same to you,' China smiled, but his eyes were inscrutable. 'To our next meeting?' he suggested the toast.

'Until we meet again,' Sean agreed, and handed him over to a guard detail under a white sergeant. Then he climbed into the command armoured car to lead the final stage of withdrawal.

Sean extricated his column and had them back across the border ten and a half hours after the attack began. Ian Smith, the prime minister, came on the radio net in person to congratulate him and inform him of his decoration, a bar to his silver cross.

Sean didn't learn about Comrade China's escape until the column went into laager that evening. Apparently, China had slit the canvas hood of the troop truck and slipped through it while his guard was dozing. Undeterred by his manacles, he had dropped off the speeding truck, screened by the dust boiling out from the back wheels, and rolled into the head-high elephant grass along the verge.

Two months later, Sean had seen an intelligence report that placed China in command of the successful attack that had wiped out a supply convoy on the Mount Darwin road.

'Yes, Matatu, I remember it all very well,' Sean answered his question, and made one more steep turn above the site of the old terrorist base before he returned the Beechcraft to straight and level flight on a southerly heading.

He did not, however, fly as far southwards as the railway line that linked the port of Beira to the land-locked Zimbabwe border. This was a focus for all the military and rebel activity in the area, and the countryside would be swarming with Frelimo and Zimbabwean troops, all armed with RPG rockets and eager to get a shot at an unmarked low-flying aircraft with no flight authorization.

'At least,' Sean told Job, 'it looks like a possibility.'

Job agreed. 'The border opposite our camp seems undefended and deserted.'

'Worth a try for half a million?' Sean asked, and Job just grinned at him.

'One more little chore before we go home,' Sean told them.

It required precise navigation and an eye for the terrain, but Sean crossed back into the Zimbabwean side and flying low they were able to pick out the spot where the previous day they had first come across the poachers' tracks; from that point, with Matatu craning his head to see down and calling directions, they found the tableland and valley where they had come up with the band of poachers and taken them under fire. From the air the distances seemed much shorter than they had on foot.

Matatu directed Sean along the trail the old bull had made towards the border. It seemed that his gift for direction and terrain was not impaired by height above the ground, and Sean was following their course on the map he held in his lap.

'We are crossing back into Mozambique now.' Sean was scribbling notes on the map.

'That way.' Matatu leaned over the back of the seat and pointed out a more northerly track. Sean knew better than to argue with him, and turned a few degrees left.

Minutes later Matatu demanded he turn slightly south again.

'Little bugger is actually sensing the old bull's trail, he is thinking like the elephant,' Sean marvelled and at that moment, Matatu gave a squeak of triumph and pointed urgently out of the side window.

As they flashed across another dry riverbed, Sean glimpsed the tracks trodden in the soft sand. They were so deep that they were filled with shadow, a string of dark beads on the white background. Even Sean, who for twenty years had watched Matatu work, was amazed. On instinct alone, Matatu had followed the bull to this river-crossing. It was a supernatural feat.

Sean circled the tracks, his port wing-tip pointing directly at them, so steep was his turn.

'Which way now?' he called to the back seat, and Matatu tapped his shoulder and pointed downstream. Without demur, Sean followed the gnarled black finger.

'There he is!' Job shouted suddenly, and Matatu shrieked with laughter and clapped his hands, bouncing in his seat like a child at the pantomime.

A mile ahead the river ran into a wide vlei that still held water from the last rains. The elephant's humped back showed above the tops of the tall reeds that surrounded the pool, like a grey whale in a sea of green.

As they raced low towards him, the elephant heard the Beechcraft's engine. He lifted his head and spread his ears wide, turning to face them, and they saw his tusks, those legendary shafts of black ivory raised to the sky. The beauty of their curved symmetry struck Sean all over again.

There was just a glimpse of them as they flashed overhead, but the image was printed vividly on his mind's eye. Half a million dollars and those tusks, he had risked his life a hundred times for much lesser prizes.

'Going back for another look?' Job asked, twisting his head to try and see back over the tail-plane.

'No.' Sean shook his head. 'We don't want to disturb him more than necessary. We know where to find him, let's go home.'

* * *

'It's my half-million dollars that you are so gaily throwing around,' Claudia told her father.

'How do you work that out?' Riccardo asked. He was lying on his camp-bed dressed in a pair of silk pyjama bottoms, his chest and his feet bare. Claudia noticed that most of his body hair was still crisp, curly and black, with only a patch of fuzzy grey in the centre of his chest.

'My inheritance,' she explained sweetly. 'You are blowing my inheritance. Papa.'

Riccardo chuckled. She had the sass of a divorce lawyer, coming bursting into his tent to renew the argument which he thought he had finalized in the mess tent over breakfast.

'If I'm not going to get it in your will, the very least you can do is let me enjoy it with you now.'

'According to the last audit, young lady, you will have a little over thirty-six million coming to you after taxes, and after I have allowed myself this small extravagance. I hasten to add that every cent is tied up in a trust fund that not the most crafty lawyers

111

will ever break. I don't want you handing my hard-earned loot out to one of your bleeding-heart charities.'

'Papa, you know the money has never interested me. What interests me is coming with you on this crazy jaunt after the elephant. I came to Africa with you on the understanding that I was to be included in everything. That was our bargain.'

'I'll say it one more time, *tesoro*, my treasure.' He only called her by that baby name when he was feeling very affectionate or very exasperated. 'You are not coming into Mozambique with us.'

'You'd go back on your solemn promise?' she accused.

'Without a qualm,' he assured her. 'If your safety or happiness was involved.'

She jumped up from the canvas camp-chair and began to prowl around the tent. He watched her with secret pleasure. Her arms were folded over those pert little breasts, and she was frowning heavily, but the frown left no lines on her smooth plastic skin. In looks she reminded him of the young Sophia Loren, his favourite actress. Now she stopped beside the camp-bed and glared down at him.

'You know I always get my way,' she said. 'Why don't you make it easier for both of us, and just say I can come.'

'I'm sorry, *tesoro*. You aren't coming.'

'All right.' She drew a deep breath 'I don't want to do this, Papa, but you leave me no choice. I have begun to understand what this means to you, why you are prepared to pay such a vast sum for a chance to do it, but if I can't go with you, as is my right and my duty, then I will prevent you from going.'

He chuckled again, easily and unconcernedly.

'I am serious, deadly serious, Papa. Please don't make me do it.'

'How can you stop me, little girl?' he asked.

'I can tell Sean Courtney what Doctor Andrews told me.'

Riccardo Monterro came to his feet in one lithe swift movement and seized her arms.

'What did Andrews tell you?' he asked in a voice as thin and cutting as a razor blade.

'He told me that last November you had a little black spot on your right arm,' she said. Instinctively, he put his right arm behind his back, but she went on. 'It had a pretty name, melanoma, like a girl's name, but it wasn't pretty at all, and you left it too late.

112

He cut it out, but the pathologist graded it Clarke 5. That's six months to a year, Papa. That's what he told me.'

Riccardo Monterro sat down on the bed and his voice was suddenly very weary.

'When did he tell you?'

'Six weeks ago.' She sat down beside him. 'That is why I agreed to come to Africa with you. I didn't want to be apart from you for one day of the time we have left. That is why I am coming with you into Mozambique.'

'No.' He shook his head. 'I can't let you.'

'Then I will tell Sean that at any moment it may reach your brain.'

She did not have to elaborate. Andrews had been most graphic as he described the many possible directions the disease could take. If it went to the lungs, it would be death by suffocation, but if it affected the brain or nervous system, it would be either general paralysis or total derangement.

'You wouldn't,' he said, shaking his head. 'The last thing in my life that I really want. You wouldn't deny it to me?'

'Without a qualm,' she repeated his own words. 'If you refuse me my right to be with you for every one of these last days, and to be with you at the end as is the duty of a loving daughter.'

'I can't let you.' He let his face sink into the cup of his hands, a gesture of defeat that hurt her, and it required all her resolve to keep her tone firm.

'And I can't let you die alone,' she replied.

'You don't understand how much I want this thing, it's the last thing in my life. The old bull and I will go together. You don't understand, if you did you wouldn't prevent me.'

'I'm not preventing you,' she said gently. 'I want you to have it, if you will let me come with you.' As she said it, they both became aware of a faint vibration in the air, and they looked up together.

'The Beechcraft,' Riccardo murmured. 'Sean is on his way back to the airstrip.' He glanced at his wristwatch. 'He'll be here within the hour.'

'And what will you tell him?' Claudia asked. 'Will you tell him that I am coming with you?'

*   *   *

'No!' Sean let out a bellow. 'No bloody fear! Forget the idea, Capo. She can't come and that's absolutely bloody final!'

'For half a big M, I get to call the shots,' Riccardo told him quietly. 'I say she's coming, so she's coming.'

They were standing beside the Toyota. Riccardo and Claudia had met Sean as he drove into camp. Sean drew a breath and glared at father and daughter as they stood side by side confronting him. He saw that both their expressions were set and determined.

Sean had been on the point of bellowing again, but with an effort he checked himself. 'Be reasonable, Capo.' He moderated his tone. 'You know it's impossible.'

They stared at him grimly, closed against argument or reason.

'It's war out there. I can't take her.'

'Claudia comes with us.'

'The hell she does.'

'What are you making a fuss about, is it because I am a woman?' Claudia spoke for the first time. 'There is nothing a man can do that I can't.'

'Can you pee standing up?' He wanted to disconcert her, make her lose her temper, but she ignored the crude jibe and went on as though he had not spoken.

'You've seen me hike. I can stand the heat and the tsetse fly. I'm as good as my father.'

He turned from her deliberately and spoke to Riccardo.

'As her father you can't allow it. Can you imagine what would happen to her if she were caught by a gang of Renamo cutthroats?'

He saw Riccardo flinch, but Claudia had seen it also and before he could weaken, she took his hand and spoke up firmly.

'Either I go, or nobody goes, and you can kiss your half a million good-bye, Colonel Sean Courtney.'

That was the key, the half-million dollars. She had him, and they both knew it. He couldn't afford to pass it by, but he made one last effort.

'Is she in charge around here, Capo? Do I take my orders from you or from her?'

'That won't work either.' Claudia tried to keep her tone placatory, although she longed to tear into him with tooth and nail. That crude sally of his rankled. 'My father and I are agreed on this. Both of us go, or we call the deal off. Isn't that right, Papa?'

114

'I'm afraid that's it, Sean.' Riccardo looked tired and discouraged. 'It's not negotiable. If you want your money, you take Claudia along with us.'

Sean turned on his heel and strode away towards his own tent, but after a few paces, he stopped and stood with his hands on his hips.

Sean's shouts had attracted the camp servants, and they hovered around the mess tent and peered out of the doorway and windows of the kitchen hutments, apprehension mingled with curiosity.

'What the hell are you all gawking at?' Sean roared. 'Have you got no work to do around here?' And they disappeared with alacrity.

Sean turned and walked slowly back to where the two of them stood beside the Toyota.

'Okay,' he agreed, staring coldly at Claudia. 'Cut your own throat, but don't come to me for a bandage.'

'I won't, that's a promise.' Her voice was honey dripping, more irksome to him than straightforward gloating would have been, and they both knew that their declared truce was at an end.

'We've got some paperwork to do, Capo.' Sean led the way to the mess tent without looking back at them.

With two fingers, Sean typed out the indemnity statements on his old portable Remington, one for Riccardo and one for his daughter. Each began; 'I acknowledge that I am fully aware of the danger and the illegality . . .' Then he typed an acknowledgement of debt for Riccardo to sign and called Job and the chef to witness the signature. He sealed all the copies in an envelope addressed to Reema at the Harare office and locked it in the small steel safe at the back of the mess tent.

'Let's do it, then,' he said.

*   *   *

The poaching expedition would consist of the three whites, Job, Matatu, Pumula and the stocky, bearded tracker who had picked up Tukutela's spoor at the river-crossing. His name was Dedan.

'It's too many, but each of those tusks weighs 130 pounds,' Sean explained. 'Matatu is too small to act as a porter. We need four big men to bring them back.'

Before the equipment was loaded into the Toyota, Sean ordered it laid out, and he opened and checked each pack. Claudia protested when he opened her personal pack. 'That is an invasion of my privacy!'

'So take me to the supreme court, ducky,' he challenged as he went through it remorselessly, throwing out most of the tubes and bottles of cosmetics, allowing her only three tubes of moisturizer and sunscreen.

'One change of underwear,' he ordered, discarding half a dozen pairs of panties. 'But you'll need two more pairs of thick socks. Get them.'

He pulled out her box of Tampax. 'Everything a man can do, and then some,' he remarked coldly. 'You don't need the box, it takes up too much space. Pack them loose.' Her poorly suppressed fury gave him a sour pleasure.

By the time he had finished, they were down to the barest essentials, and the packs were carefully weighed and apportioned depending on the strength and physical condition of each bearer. Sean, Job, Pumula and Dedan carried sixty pounds each, Riccardo and Matatu forty, while Claudia was down to twenty-five pounds.

'I can carry more,' she protested. 'Give me forty, the same as Matatu.' Sean did not bother to answer her.

'And what's more, I eat half as much as any of you!' But he had already turned away to supervise the loading of the Toyota.

* * *

There were still four hours of daylight remaining when they left Chiwewe camp, but Sean drove the first section very fast, jouncing them around in their seats. It was partly an expression of his objection to Claudia's presence but mostly an urgent desire to be at the jump-off point before nightfall.

As he drove, he spoke in a tightly controlled voice. 'Before we commence this guided tour of the Mozambiquan paradise of the proletariat, this shining gem of African socialism, will you bear with me while I give you a few facts and figures.' Nobody protested, so he went on. 'Until 1975 Mozambique was a Portuguese colony. For almost five hundred years it had been under Portuguese control and had been a reasonably happy and prosperous community of some fifteen million souls. The Portuguese, unlike the British or German colonists, had a relaxed attitude towards miscegenation and the result was a large mulatto population, and an official policy of "Assimilado" under which any person of colour, if he attained certain civilized standards, was considered to be white and enjoyed Portuguese nationality. It all worked very well, as indeed did most colonial administrations, especially those of the British.'

'Bullshit,' said Claudia demurely. 'That's limey propaganda.'

'Limey?' Sean smiled thinly. 'Careful, your prejudice is showing, nonetheless your average Indian or African living today in a former British colony is a damned sight worse off now than he was then. Certainly that goes one hundred times more for your average black man living in Mozambique.'

'At least they are free,' Claudia cut in, and Sean laughed.

'This is freedom? An economy managed under the well-known socialist principles of chaos and ruination which has resulted in a negative growth rate of up to ten per cent per annum for every year since the Portuguese withdrawal, a foreign debt amounting to double the gross national product, a total breakdown in the educational system, only five per cent of children regularly attending a recognized school, one doctor per forty-five thousand persons, only one person in ten with access to purified drinking water, infant mortality at 340 per 1000 births. The only worse countries in the world are Afghanistan and Angola, but as you say, at least they are free. In America, where everybody eats three huge meals a day, freedom may be a big deal, but in Africa a full belly counts for a hell of a lot more.'

'It can't be as bad as that,' she protested.

'No,' he agreed. 'It's a lot worse. I haven't mentioned two other factors, the civil war and Aids. When the Portuguese were pushed out, they handed over to a dictator named Samora Machel and his Frelimo party. Machel was an avowed Marxist. He didn't believe in the nonsense of elections, and his rule was directly responsible for the present condition of the country, and for the emergence of the National Mozambiquan Resistance or as it is known to its friends and admirers, Renamo. Nobody knows much about it, what its objectives are, who its leaders are, all we know is that it controls most of the country, especially the north, and that it is made up of a pretty ruthless bunch of characters.'

'Renamo is a South African front organization, directed,

supplied and controlled from Pretoria,' Claudia helped him out. 'Committed to the overthrow of sovereign government and the destabilization of the southern continent.'

'Well done, ducky.' Sean nodded approval. 'You've been studying the wisdom and erudition of the Organization of African Unity and the non-aligned nations. You have even mastered their jargon. If only South Africa had the military and technological capability to commit half the skulduggery it is accused of, it would not be simply the most powerful country in Africa, it would be running the entire world.'

'I keep forgetting you are one of them, which is silly of me. You don't attempt to conceal your bigotry. The simple fact is that your government and apartheid are the scourge and the curse of Africa.'

'Of course, we are responsible for everything, the Aids epidemic, the famines of Ethiopia and Angola and Mozambique, the breakdown of government in Uganda and Zambia, the corruption in Nigeria and Zaire, it's all a dirty South African plot. We even killed Samora Machel, we fed vodka to the Russian crew of his Tupolev jet and with our incredibly sophisticated technology, lured them over the border. Machel hit one of our racist mountains with such force that his brains and major organs were instantly expelled from his body, nevertheless our apartheid doctors kept him alive long enough to torture state secrets out of him. That is the truth as determined by UNO and OAU.'

'Shut up,' said Riccardo Monterro. 'I've had enough. Shut up, both of you.'

'Sorry,' Sean grinned at him. 'I get carried away. I just wanted to let you know what to expect when we cross the border. We can just hope that we aren't going to meet any of the lads from either Frelimo or Renamo, there is not a lot to choose between them. They both shoot the same bullets.'

The thought made the back of his own neck prickle, and he felt his mood lighten. He was going into mortal danger again, and the thrill of it began. Somehow having the girl with him no longer irked but rather heightened that anticipation, and he felt his resentment of her begin to fade. He was glad she was here rather than jetting back to Alaska. Sean drove on in a silence that gripped them all, even the men standing braced against the roll-bar in the back of the Toyota. The closer they came to the border, the deeper the silence became.

At last Sean turned and looked over his shoulder, and Job nodded in agreement.

'This is it, ladies and gentlemen,' Sean said quietly. 'All change!' He let the Toyota trundle to a halt where the track crossed a stony ridge.

'Where are we?' Riccardo asked.

'As close as we can safely get to the border, about three miles. From here, it's shanks' pony.'

Riccardo swung one leg out of the truck, but Sean said sharply, 'Hold it, Capo, step onto that slab of rock, leave no tracks.'

One at a time, each carrying their own pack, they alighted from the truck, at Sean's instruction stepping precisely in the footsteps of the person in front. Matatu was the last off, and he came backwards brushing over the sign with a switch of dried grass, wiping out every trace of their departure from the truck.

The chef had come with them to drive the truck back to the camp.

'Go in peace, *Mambo*!' he called to Sean as he pulled away.

'Fat hope,' Sean laughed, and sent him off with a wave. Then to Job, 'Anti-tracking, let's go!'

Neither Riccardo nor Claudia had ever watched anti-tracking procedure, for while hunting they had always run free in pursuit. The formation for anti-tracking was Indian file, Job leading and everyone else stepping in his footprints. Behind them all, Matatu, the old maestro, was covering the sign, replacing a pebble lichen-side up, stroking a blade of grass into its original position, flicking at the earth with his grass switch, picking up a leaf dislodged from a low-hanging branch or the bruised blade of grass on which a foot had trodden.

Job avoided the game paths and soft ground, choosing always the line of march which was most obscure and yet moving surprisingly fast, so that within half an hour, Claudia felt the chill of fresh sweat between her shoulder-blades and at the cleavage of her shirt-front.

Job led them to the top of a low kopje, and Sean motioned them to conceal themselves below the skyline with the sunset behind them.

Watching them work, Riccardo remarked softly, 'Pumula and Dedan seem to know what they are doing.' The two of them had moved out to guard the flanks without being ordered to do so.

119

'Yes.' Sean settled down between him and Claudia, using the same low bush for cover. 'They were both non-coms in the Scouts, they've done this before.'

'Why are we stopping here?' Claudia asked.

'We are sitting on the border,' Sean explained, 'and we'll spend the last of the daylight studying the ground ahead. As soon as the moon comes up, we'll move in. You can relax until then.'

He lifted his Zeiss binoculars and stared through them; a few yards away Job lay on his belly and focused his own pair of binoculars in the same direction. They lowered the binoculars from time to time to blink their vision clear or polish an imaginary speck from the lens. Claudia had noticed how they protected and looked after these most essential tools of their craft, but apart from that, their concentration on the terrain ahead was absolute, and ended only when the last gleam of the sunset faded. Then Sean buttoned the binoculars into his top pocket and turned to her.

'Time for your make-up,' he said. For a moment she did not understand and then she felt the greasy touch of camouflage cream on her cheek and instinctively pulled away.

'Hold still,' he snapped. 'Your white face shines like a mirror. It's good for insects and sunburn also.'

He daubed her face and the backs of her hands.

'Here comes the moon.' Sean finished working on his own camouflage and screwed the top back on the tube of cream. 'We can go in now.'

Sean changed the formation once again, putting out flankers, Job and Pumula, while he led the centre and, once again, Matatu brought up the rear, diligently sweeping their tracks.

Once Sean stopped and checked Claudia's equipment. A loose buckle on her pack had been tapping regularly in time with her stride, a noise so small that she had not noticed it.

'You sound like the charge of the Light Brigade,' he breathed in her ear, as he adjusted it.

'Arrogant bastard,' she thought, and they went on in silence, an hour and then another hour without pausing. She never knew the exact moment when she crossed the border. The moonlight through the forest was silvery, and the shadows of the trees flickered over Sean's broad shoulders ahead of her.

Gradually the silence and the moonlight gave the march a

120

'dream-like unreality, and she found herself mesmerized by it, her movements were like those of a sleep-walker, so that when Sean stopped abruptly she bumped into him and might have fallen had he not whipped a hard muscular arm around her and held her.

They stood frozen, listening, staring into the dark forest. After almost five minutes Claudia moved slightly to free herself from his arm, but instantly his grip tightened and she submitted to it. Out on the right flank, Job gave a bird call, and noiselessly Sean sank to the ground drawing her down with him, and her nerves strained tighter as she realized that there must be real danger out there. Now his arm no longer annoyed her. Instinctively she relaxed and pressed a little closer to him. It felt good.

Another soft bird call from the darkness, and Sean put his lips to her ear.

'Stay!' he breathed, and she felt lonely and exposed as he released her, and she watched him disappear like a ghost into the forest.

Sean moved in a low crouch, rifle in one hand, reaching forward to touch the earth with the fingers of his left hand, brushing away the dry twigs and leaves that might crackle under his foot before stepping forward. He sank down ten feet from where Job lay and glanced across at his dark shape. The pale palm of Job's hand flashed a signal, and Sean concentrated on the left front that Job had indicated.

For long minutes, he neither saw nor sensed anything untoward, but he trusted Job completely and he waited with the hunter's patience. Suddenly he caught a taint on the night air and he lifted his nose and sniffed at it. Both his confidence and his patience were repaid. It was the acrid stink of burning tobacco, one of those cheap black Portuguese cigarillos. He remembered them so well, they had been issued to the guerrillas in the days of the bush war, and were probably Frelimo issue still.

He signalled Job and they went forward, leopard-crawling, absolutely silently, forty paces, and Sean picked out the glow of the cigarette as a man drew upon it. Then the man coughed, a soft phlegmy sound, and spat. He was at the base of one of the large trees directly ahead; now Sean could make out his shape. He was sitting with his back to the trunk.

'Who is he? Local tribesman? Poacher? Bee hunter? Refugee?' None of those seemed likely. This one was awake and alert, almost certainly a sentry. As Sean reached that conclusion, he sensed other movement farther out, and he flattened against the earth.

Another man emerged from the forest, and came directly to where the sentry was rising to his feet to meet him. As soon as he stood, Sean could make out the AK 47 rifle slung over his shoulder, muzzle down. The two men talked softly together.

'Changing the guard,' Sean thought as the new sentry leaned against the tree and the other man sauntered back into the forest.

'That is where the camp is,' Sean guessed.

Still on his belly, he leopard-crawled forward, passing well wide of the sentry who would be fresh and vigilant. Once he was within the perimeter, Sean rose into a crouch and went forward swiftly.

He found the camp in a fold of ground up against the hills. It was a fly-camp, no huts nor shelters, only two small fires that had burned down to coals. He counted eleven men lying around the fires, all of them with a blanket pulled completely over their heads in typical African fashion. There might be five or six others on guard duty, but it was a small band.

Even lacking automatic weapons Sean and his men could have dealt with them. All of Sean's men still carried their piano-wire nooses and Matatu his skinning knife with the blade so sharp that it was honed down to half its original width. Nobody in the camp would have even woken up.

Sean shook his head with regret, he was certain now that these were either Frelimo regular troops or Renamo guerrillas. He had no quarrel with them, whoever they were. Just as long as they did not interfere with his elephant hunt. Sean backed away and Job was waiting for him at the perimeter.

'Eleven of them at the fires,' Sean breathed.

'I found two more sentries,' Job agreed.

'Frelimo?'

'Who knows?' Job shrugged, and Sean touched his arm and they crept away, farther out of earshot of the camp so they could speak more freely.

'What do you think, Job?'

'A small group, they mean little. We can go around them.'

'They could be the advance guard for a bigger party,' Sean suggested.

'These are not crack troops,' Job muttered contemptuously.

'Smoking on guard duty, sleeping next to a fire, they aren't soldiers, they are tourists.' Sean smiled at the term of derision. He knew that Job's determination was more Anglo-Saxon than African. Once he had decided, it was difficult to dissuade him.

'You want to go on?' he asked.

'For five hundred thousand dollars,' Job whispered, 'you're damned right I want to go on!'

*   *   *

Claudia was afraid. The African night was so charged with mystery, with uncertainty and menace. The wait aggravated her feeling of apprehension. Sean had been gone for almost an hour, and though her father was close beside her, she felt alone and very vulnerable.

Then suddenly, Sean was back, and she experienced a rush of relief. She wanted to reach out for him and cling to him, and was ashamed of herself for the weakness. Sean was whispering to her father, and she drew close to listen. Her arm touched Sean's bare arm, but he did not seem to notice, so she left it there for the feeling of security and comfort it gave her.

'Small party of armed men camped up ahead,' Sean was explaining. 'Not more than twenty of them. We don't know who the hell they are, but we can circle around them and keep going, or we can turn back. It's up to you, Capo.'

'I want that elephant!'

'This is probably your last chance to pull out,' Sean warned him.

'You are wasting time,' Riccardo said. Claudia was torn by her father's decision. It would have been such an anti-climax to turn back now, and yet her first taste of the real flavour of Africa had been disconcerting. She realized as the march resumed and she fell in behind Sean, that this was the first time in her life that she had been beyond the trappings and buttresses of civilization, the first time that there was no police force to protect her, no recourse to law or justice or mercy. Here she was as vulnerable as an antelope to the leopard, in a forest full of predators.

She quickened her step, closing up behind Sean and found to her surprise that in some bizarre fashion she was more alive and aware than she had ever been before. For the first time in her life, she was on the bottom rung of existence, the level of survival. It was a novel and quite overwhelming sensation. She was glad that her father had not decided to turn back.

Claudia had long lost all sense of direction for Sean led unpredictably. They turned and twisted through the forest, sometimes moving swiftly and at others, creeping forward a stealthy pace at a time and then freezing into absolute stillness at a signal from the flank which often she had not even heard. She noticed Sean look up at the night sky every few minutes and guessed that he was navigating by the stars, but to her their whorls and blazes and fields were as confused as the lights of a foreign city.

Then after a while, she realized that they had not turned nor paused for a long while, and were once again heading in a straight line. Obviously, they were clear of danger for the moment. With the excitement over, she soon felt the weight of her legs and the weariness in the small of her back. The pack between her shoulders seemed to have quadrupled in weight, and she glanced at her wristwatch. The luminous dial showed her that they had been going for almost five hours since circling around that hidden camp.

'When will we rest?' she wondered, but made it a point of honour to keep close behind Sean, and not to lag by a single pace. Almost as though a refrigerator door had opened, the temperature plunged and when they crossed another open glade, the dew on the long grass soaked the legs of her trousers, and her boots squelched. She shivered, for the first time in real discomfort.

'When will he rest?' She stared at Sean's back, resenting him, willing him to stop. On he went and still on, and she had the feeling that he was deliberately trying to humiliate her, to break her down, to force her to squeal for mercy.

'I'll show you.' She did not slacken her pace as she reached back and unstrapped her Gortex ski jacket from the top of her pack. It was really cold now, the frost crackled underfoot, and her feet were numb but she kept her station in the line and quite suddenly she realized that she could see clearly each thick glossy tress of hair down the back of Sean's neck.

'Dawn. I thought it would never come.' And as she thought it, Sean stopped at last, and she pulled up beside him with the nerves in her legs jumping and trembling with fatigue.

'Sorry, Capo,' Sean spoke softly past her. 'I had to push a

124

little. We had to get well clear of that bunch before light. How are you making out?'

'No problem,' Riccardo muttered, but in the grey dawn light, his face looked pale and drawn. He was suffering as she was, and she hoped she didn't look as bad. He went to find a place to sit, and lowered himself stiffly.

Sean glanced at Claudia still standing beside him. Neither of them spoke, but he had a faint enigmatic smile on his lips.

'Don't ask me how I feel,' she thought. 'I'd rather drink Drain-o than tell you the truth.'

He inclined his head slightly, condescension or respect, she wasn't sure.

'First day and the third are always the worst,' he said.

'I feel fine,' she said. 'I can go on quite happily.'

'Sure,' he grinned openly. 'But you'd better go and look after Papa rather.'

Sean brought mugs of tea to where she sat beside her father, wrapped in her lightweight down-filled sleeping-bag against the dawn chill. Job had brewed on a tiny smokeless fire which he extinguished immediately the billy boiled. The tea was strong and sweet and scalding, she had never tasted anything more welcome. With it, he handed her a stack of maize cakes and cold cuts of venison. She tried not to wolf them.

'We'll move on in a few minutes,' he warned her, and when he saw the dismay in her eyes, he explained.

'We never sleep next to a cooking-fire, it can attract the uglies.'

They went on five miles and in the middle of the morning, on higher ground in a place secure and easily defended, Sean showed her how to scoop a hollow for her hip and use her pack as a pillow. She fell asleep as though she had been sandbagged.

She could not believe it when he shook her awake only a minute later. 'It's four o'clock.' He handed her a mug and another stack of maize cakes. 'You've slept six hours straight, we are moving out in five minutes.'

Hastily she rolled her sleeping-bag and then peered at herself in the metal hand-mirror which she had surreptitiously retrieved after Sean had thrown it out of her pack.

'Oh God,' she whispered. The camouflage cream had caked and striped with her sweat. 'I look like Al Jolson in drag.' She tidied her hair, dragging her comb through the tangles, and then tied a scarf around it.

125

With short breaks every two hours, they kept going all that night. At first, Claudia's legs felt as though they were in plaster casts, but soon she walked the stiffness out of them and she kept her place in the line without lagging, though the pace Sean set was every bit as hard as the previous night.

In the dawn, they drank tea. Claudia had begun to depend on the brew. She had always been a coffee-drinker, but now on the march, she found herself fantasizing over her next scalding mug of tea.

'It's the only thing keeping me going,' she confided to her father, only half joking.

'They say the limeys conquered their empire on the stuff.' Riccardo nodded agreement, as Sean came across from where he had been in deep discussion with Matatu and Job.

'We are only a few hours' march from the reed-beds where we saw Tukutela from the air.' He looked pointedly at Claudia. 'I'd like to try and get there before we sleep, but, of course, some of us are a little bushed . . .' He let it hang between them, a dare and an accusation.

'I need a little stroll to settle my breakfast,' she said amiably, but she wished her face was not coated with black cream. She hated conceding even the slightest advantage to him.

As Sean walked away, her father swilled the tea leaves in his mug and flicked them out.

'Don't fall for him, *tesoro*. He'd be too big a handful even for you.'

She stared at him, outraged and appalled. 'Fall for him? Are you out of your skull, Papa? I can't stand the sight of him.'

'That's what I mean,' he chuckled.

She jumped up and threw her pack onto her back with unnecessary strength, and then told her father with disdain. 'I could cope with him and five others like him, with my eyes closed and one hand tied behind my back, but I've got better taste than that.'

'Which is fortunate for you,' he murmured just low enough so she was uncertain what he had said.

A little before noon that day, Matatu led them into the papyrus beds which surrounded the green pool which they had seen from the air. He led them directly to the great dished spoor, printed in the mud, and they gathered round to inspect it.

'See!' Matatu told them. 'This is where Tukutela stood when

he heard the *indeki* coming. Here and there he turned to look up in the sky and challenge us.' Matatu imitated the old bull, holding his head at the same angle, humping his back and cupping his hands at each side of his head. It was such a faithful impression, that for a moment, he seemed to become the old bull, and they all laughed. Claudia forgot her fatigue and clapped in applause.

'Then what did the old bull do?' Sean demanded, and Matatu spun and pointed along the run of the spoor.

'He went away with all his speed, he went fast and very far.'

'Well,' Sean said. 'That puts us almost exactly forty-eight hours behind him and we have to sleep now, we'll be fifty-five hours behind him when we march again.'

* * *

Tukutela's dam had been the matriarch of a herd of over one hundred beasts. She had come into her last period of oestrus in her fifty-second year, and over the days that it lasted, she had been mounted and serviced by six of the herd bulls, all young animals, vigorous and at the height of their powers.

It was the ideal formula for the conception of an extraordinary calf, old cow and young bull. Although it was uncertain which seed had taken root in her, the old cow had carried the genes of great elephants, big in body and tusk, in natural intelligence and the urge to dominate. These same genes had made her the leader of her herd, and now she transferred them to the foetus she carried in her womb.

She carried him twenty-two months and then in the year when the German askaris under General von Lettow-Vorbeck were ravaging eastern Africa, the year 1915, she had left the herd and accompanied only by another old female past calf-bearing, her companion of forty years, she had gone deep into the fastnesses of the swamps that lie on the south bank of the Zambezi river and there on an islet fringed with ivory nut palms, surrounded by miles of papyrus beds, and with the white-headed fish eagles chanting overhead, she had cleared an area of sandy earth for her couch. When her time came, she had spread her back legs and squatted over the open area, squealing in the agony of her labour, her trunk rolled up on her chest.

Her eyes had no tear ducts to drain them so the tears poured

127

freely down her withered cheeks as though she wept, and the spasms racked her huge gaunt frame.

The other old cow stood close beside her like a midwife, caressing her with her trunk, stroking her back and rumbling with sympathy. She had forced out the calf's head, and then rested for a minute, before the last violent effort expelled the purple-pink foetal sac and the calf had fallen to the earth, rupturing the umbilical cord. Tukutela had begun to struggle immediately, still trapped in the glistening mucus-coated membrane and the old cow, her companion, had stood over him and, with the prehensile tip of her trunk, delicately stripped it away.

Then with her trunk his dam had gently and lovingly lifted him to his feet, and placed him between her front legs, making the deep purring rumble of elephant contentment. Still wet and smooth and shining pinkly from his birthing, covered in copious gingery hair, almost blind, Tukutela had rolled his little trunk back onto his forehead and reached up instinctively to the twin breasts on his mother's chest.

While he tasted for the very first time the rich creamy milk, his dam picked up the foetal sac and afterbirth and stuffed them into her mouth, chewing and swallowing and, at the same time, using her trunk to cover the damp and blood-stained spot upon the earth with sand.

The three of them, his mother, her companion and Tukutela, had remained on the island for almost two weeks while the calf had mastered the use of his legs and trunk, the pigment of his skin had darkened and his eyes adjusted to the harsh African sunlight. Then, when she considered him strong enough, she had taken him to find the herd, pushing him ahead of her and lifting him over the steep and difficult places.

The din of a hundred elephant feeding had carried to them from afar, the crack and crash of breaking branches and the pig-like squeals of the calves at play. Tukutela's dam trumpeted her return and the herd had come rushing up to greet her. Then, discovering the new calf, they had crowded around to touch him with their trunks, puffing his scent into their mouths, so that they would recognize it always thereafter.

Tukutela cowered between his mother's front legs, overwhelmed by the huge bodies that surrounded him, making little baby noises of terror, but his mother draped her trunk over him and rumbled to reassure him. Within hours rather than days, he ventured out from her protection to join the other calves, and to begin carving for himself a niche in the hierarchy of the breeding herd.

The herd was a close-knit-group, almost all its members blood relatives, mutually reliant upon each other so that the education and discipline of the young was a concern of all.

The calves were always kept in the centre of the herd, and their antics were strictly supervised by the old barren cows who were their self-appointed nursemaids. Their care and protection was intense but any infringement of the herd law was punished instantly: a tree branch wielded with gusto across the recalcitrant's back and hind-quarters would ensure terrified squeals and instant obedience.

Tukutela learned his place in every situation; at the centre when the herd was relaxed and feeding; between his mother's front legs when they were on the march, or in flight from danger. He learned to react instantly to the alarm signal, learned to recognize it even when given by an animal on the further outskirts of the group.

At the signal, the instantaneous silence, in contrast to the preceding happy uproar of the herd, was an eerie phenomenon of elephant behaviour.

Tukutela's development was closely parallel to the ages of a human being: his infancy lasted two years during which time he shed the tiny milk tusks with which he had been born and then entered on his juvenile years when his true tusks emerged beyond his lips. At first, these were covered by a cap of smooth enamel, but as soon as he was weaned and began to use his tusks to feed with and in mock combat with his peers, this was worn away and the true ivory beneath exposed.

His tusks would continue to grow in length and girth throughout his entire life even into his extreme old age, but the genes which dictated their extraordinary development came down from his dam along with all her other gifts of strength and bulk and intelligence.

By the age of three, Tukutela had learned the attitudes of threat and submission towards others, and his play was boisterous with much ear-flapping and threatening and barging which further developed his unusually robust frame.

Once his dam weaned him, her care became less intensive and he was allowed more range and freedom, though he still came under her fierce protection at the first threat, and on the march his place was close beside her in the lead, so very early on he learned the herd's territory.

This was a vast area, from the shores of Lake Nyasa in the north to the rain forests of the Chimanimani mountains in the south, west to the deep gorge where the Zambezi river forces itself between narrow rock cliffs with the roar of perpetual thunder and east five hundred miles to where the same mighty river spread out across wide flood plains and swampy littoral before debouching through multiple mouths into the Indian Ocean.

He learned the mountain passes and the ancient elephant roads, he learned the groves where succulent fruits grew and the seasons when they ripened. She led him to burned-out savannahs just as the first tender green shoots pushed through the ashes and to the salt licks where for thousands of years the elephants had come to prise out lumps of mineral-rich earth with their tusks and eat it with all the relish of small boys with sticks of candy, over the centuries quarrying deep excavations in the red African earth.

The herd was on the Mavuradonha mountains in the south when the msasa forests put out new leaf and their sap began to flow; they were in the dense rain forests on Mount Mlanje when the rest of the range baked in the long African droughts. Always the old cow led them to water, for the herd was totally dependent upon that precious fluid. They must drink each day or experience terrible hardship, they needed copious quantities to nurture their great bodies, to cleanse their hides and, more simply, for the luxurious pleasure of the wallow. The watering hole was an important gathering place for the herd, a place where their bonds were reaffirmed and where many of the rituals of their social behaviour were played out. Even the act of procreation usually took place in the water, and when the cows chose the place for their birthing, it was nearly always near water.

Sometimes there was abundant water, the great green African rivers, the mountains upon which the perpetual drizzling rains fell, and the wide swamplands where they waded belly deep through papyrus beds to reach the islands. At other times, they had to dig for it in the dry riverbeds, or patiently wait their turn at the seeps to thrust their trunks into the deep eye of the secret well and suck up a bitter brackish mouthful at a time.

Their range was wide, and their contact with human beings infrequent. There was a great war raging in a far-off land and it had sucked most of the white men to its centre. The men that the herd encountered were usually half-naked and primitive tribesmen who fled before them. Yet Tukutela learned very early that a special aura of dread surrounded these strange hairless baboon-like beings. At five years of age he could identify their peculiar acrid odour on a light breeze from many miles away, and even the faintest taint of it made him and the entire herd uneasy.

Yet Tukutela was eleven years of age before he had his first memorable encounter with human beings. One night while following their time-honoured route along the south bank of the Zambezi, his dam had stopped abruptly at the front of the herd and lifted her trunk at full stretch above her head to scent the air. Tukutela had imitated her and become aware of a tantalizing odour. He had puffed the taste of it into his mouth and his saliva poured down and dribbled from his lower lip. The rest of the herd bunched up behind them and were almost immediately consumed by the same appetite. None of them had ever smelled sugar cane before.

The old matriarch led them up the wind and within a few miles they came out on an area of the riverbank that had been recently cleared and irrigated and planted with cane. The long sword-shaped leaves glistened in the moonlight, and the aroma was rich and sweet and irresistible. The herd rushed into the new fields, pulling up the plants and stuffing them down their throats in a greedy passion.

The destruction was immense, and in the midst of it suddenly the herd was surrounded by lights and the shouts of men's voices and the beating of drums and metal cans. Panic and pandemonium overtook the herd and as they charged out of the field there was a shocking series of loud reports and the bright flash of gunfire in the night. It was the first time Tukutela had ever smelled burned cordite smoke. He would remember it always and associate it with the squeals of those elephants who had been mortally hit.

The herd ran hard at first and then settled into the long stride that covered the ground at the speed of a cantering horse. By morning, one of the young cows, her first calf under her belly, could no longer keep up with the herd and slumped down on her front knees, bright blood trickling from the bullet wound in her flank.

The matriarch turned back to assist her, calling and encouraging her, but the cow could not rise, and the matriarch moved up beside her. Using tusks and trunk, she lifted the fallen animal to her feet and attempted to lead her away. It was in vain, for the dying animal slumped down and lay with her legs folded up under her, and the smell of her blood upset the herd and they milled about her, swinging their trunks and flapping their ears.

One of the herd bulls, in a desperate effort to revive the fallen cow, mounted her in a stylized attempt at copulation, but a gout of arterial blood spurted from her wound and with a groan she toppled over on her side.

Unlike most animals, the elephant recognizes death, especially in one of its own group, and even the immature Tukutela was affected by the strange melancholy that followed the cow's death. Some members of the herd approached the carcass and touched it with their trunks, almost a gesture of farewell, before they wandered away into the grey thorn scrub.

The matriarch stayed on when the others had left, and Tukutela stayed with her. He watched as his dam began to strip the surrounding trees of their branches and pile them over the carcass of the dead cow. Only when it was completely hidden under a great mound of vegetation, was she satisfied.

The dead cow's unweaned calf had stayed beside its mother's corpse, and now the matriarch shooed it ahead of her as she followed the herd. Twice the calf tried to double back to where its mother lay, but the matriarch blocked it, turning it with her trunk and pushed it along.

A mile away, the rest of the herd was waiting in a grove of yellow-stemmed fever trees. Many of the younger calves were suckling, and the matriarch pushed the orphan calf towards where one of the older calves, one almost due to be weaned, was showing only perfunctory interest in his mother's dugs. She shoved the orphan between the cow's front legs and instinctively the little animal rolled its trunk onto its forehead and reached up for the teat. The cow made no objection, accepting the role of foster mother with equanimity. The matriarch stood beside the pair rumbling to them encouragingly, and when she led the herd on, the orphan calf had displaced the older calf between the cow's front legs.

It seemed that from then on the herd's contact with men bearing firearms became every season more frequent, especially when the bulls were with the breeding herd.

The mature bulls kept a loose liaison with the breeding herd. They found the noisy and boisterous behaviour of the young animals annoying, and the competition for food demanding. No sooner would one of the bulls shake down a rain of ripe pods from the top branches of a tall thorn tree but a dozen youngsters would rush over to gobble them, or he would push over a msasa tree to get at the new leaf, leaning with his forehead against the trunk, and snapping the three-foot diameter of hard wood with a report like a cannon shot. Immediately four or five greedy young cows would push themselves in front of him before he could sample the juicy pink leaves.

So the bulls would wander away from the herd, singly or in bachelor groups of three or four. Perhaps also they realized instinctively that the herd was likely to attract the hunters, and they would be safer away from it. Sometimes they were only a few miles away, sometimes as far as thirty or forty, but they seemed always to be aware of the herd's location and would return when the cows were in season.

When the bulls were with the herd, was the time that there was most likely to be that sudden crash of gunfire, and the squeal of wounded animals and the headlong rush of huge panic-stricken bodies through the brush.

When Tukutela was a juvenile, under ten years of age, there had been six huge bulls associated with the herd, animals carrying thick shafts of ivory, but over the years that he grew towards maturity these were gradually whittled down. Each dry season one or more of them fell to the sound of riflefire, and only the mediocre bulls, or those with worn or damaged ivory, remained.

By this time, Tukutela had grown into an unusually large young bull, and his tusks were beginning to develop, clean and white and sharp-pointed, already showing promise of what they would one day become. As he grew, so the matriarch, his dam, declined. Slowly the outline of her bones appeared through the folds and hangs of her wrinkled grey hide, so she became a gaunt and skeletal figure. Her sixth and last molar was already chipped and half worn away, she ate with difficulty, and the slow starvation of age had begun. She relinquished her place at the head of the herd to a younger more robust cow, and shambled along behind.

On the steep places where the elephant road climbed the mountain passes Tukutela would wait for her at the crest, rumbling to bring her up over the difficult places, and he stood close to her in the night as he had as a calf.

It had been a dry season and the waterholes were less than half full. The approaches to the water had been churned by the elephant herds and rhinoceros and buffalo to glutinous black mud, in some places deep as an elephant's belly, and it was here that the old matriarch stuck.

Lunging in an attempt to free herself, she fell over sideways and the mud sucked her down until only part of her head was clear.

She struggled for two days. Tukutela tried to help her, but even his enormous strength was of no avail. The mud held her fast, and gave him no footing nor purchase. The old cow's struggles became weaker, her wild screams more feeble, until at last she was still and silent except for the hiss of her breathing.

It took two more days, and Tukutela stood beside her all that time. The herd had long ago departed, but he remained. She gave no outward sign of passing from life to death, other than the cessation of her harsh breathing, but Tukutela knew it instantly and he lifted his trunk high and bugled out his grief in a cry that startled the wild fowl from the waterhole in a cloud of noisy wings.

He went to the edge of the forest and plucked the leafy boughs and he brought them to the waterhole and he covered his dam's muddy carcass with them, building for her a high green funeral bier. Then he left her and went into the veld.

He did not rejoin the herd for almost two years. By that time, he was sexually mature and he could no longer resist the scent of oestrus that the breeze brought down to him.

When he found them, the herd was gathered on the bank of the Kafue river, ten miles upstream from where it makes its confluence with the great Zambezi. Some of the herd members came out to meet him as he approached, and they entwined their trunks with his and pushed their foreheads together in greeting, and then allowed him to join the main body.

There were two cows in season and one of them was an animal of similar age to Tukutela. She was prime, fat with good grazing and browsing that the rains had raised. Her ivory was thin and very white, as straight and sharp as knitting needles, and her ears

134

had not yet been torn or tattered by thorn and sharp twigs. She spread them now as she recognized Tukutela as her peer, and came to twine her trunk with his.

They stood with their heads together rumbling gently at each other, and then disentangled their trunks and began to caress each other lightly with the tips, moving down the length of each other's bodies until they stood head to tail.

The tips of the trunk are as sensitive and dextrous as the fingers of the human hand and Tukutela reached down between her back legs and groped for her vaginal opening. She began to sway from side to side, rocking her whole body, an expression of extreme pleasure. As he manipulated her, so her oestrus discharge flowed down freely drenching his trunk and the aroma of it filled his head. His penis emerged from its fleshy sheath, as long as a man is tall and as thick as one of his legs; the tip of it brushed the earth below his belly. Its length was variegated with blotches of pink and black but the skin was smooth and shining and the head flared like the mouth of a trumpet. Elephants belong to the testiconda group, and his testicles were contained deep in the body cavity so there was no external evidence of them.

When both of them were fully aroused Tukutela nudged her gently down the bank and into the river. The green waters closed over them, intensifying their pleasure in each other, supporting their great bodies, buoying them up so they were light and nimble.

They submerged until only their trunks were above the surface, sporting together, breaking out again like blowing whales, and the water poured off them in sheets, cleansing their grey hides of dust and dirt, darkening them to the colour of coal.

Tukutela reared over her, and placed his forelegs on each side of her back. In the water, she supported him easily. Her vagina was placed far forward between her back legs, and he needed all of his length to reach it. His penis took on a life of its own, pulsing and jerking and twisting as it flared upwards to conform to the angle of her opening. Only the first third of its length was able to bury itself in her. His whole body shuddered and convulsed and both creatures trumpeted together and thrashed the waters to white foam.

He stayed with the herd three days, and then the female's oestrus ended and Tukutela became restless. He had inherited

135

his dam's instinct for survival, and he sensed danger with the herd. On the third day, he ghosted away into the grey thorn scrub. He went alone, with no other bull for company.

Each season, when he returned to the herd he was stronger, his tusks longer and thicker, darkening to the colour of alabaster with vegetable juices. On occasion there were other bulls competing to service the females, and he had to fight for his right.

At first, he was driven off by older more experienced males, but each season his tusks and his cunning grew, until none of the other herd bulls stood up against him, and he had his pick of the cows. However, he never stayed more than a few days with the herd, and always he departed alone and sought out fastnesses which his dam had showed to him, the swamps inaccessible to man, the thickest forests, the tallest beds of elephant grass. It was as though he realized the danger that those tusks would bring upon him.

In his thirty-fifth year, he was a huge animal, weighing seven tons and standing over twelve feet at the shoulder. His tusks, though not anywhere as heavy as they would one day be, were perfectly symmetrical and long and pointed.

For days after leaving the herd that season he had been unaccountably nervous. He moved restlessly, testing the air often, raising his trunk high and then puffing it into his mouth. Once or twice he detected it, but the acrid scent was faint, just a tiny shadow on his consciousness.

However, he could not keep moving endlessly. His huge frame each day required over a ton of grass and leaves and fruit and bark to sustain it. He had to stop to feed. In the early morning, he stood in a dense grove of combretum trees, stripping bark. He used the point of a tusk to prise a gash in the bark, then he gripped the tag end in his trunk and with an upward jerk ripped loose a strip of bark fifteen feet up the bole of the tree. He rolled the bark into a ball and stuffed it into his mouth.

Intent on his task, he relaxed his vigilance. An elephant has poor eyesight, he cannot distinguish stationary objects only a few yards distant, although he can instantly detect movement. Furthermore, his eyes are placed well back in the skull, impeding his forward view and the spread of his ears tends to block his peripheral vision to the rear.

Using the small morning wind to negate the bull's marvellous sense of smell, moving with extreme stealth so that his fine hearing was frustrated, the hunters approached him from behind, staying in his blind spot. There were two of them and they had followed him ever since he had left the herd. Now they crept up very close to him.

The bull turned broadside to the hunters, ready to move on to the next tree and he showed them the long curved gleam of his tusks.

'Take him!' said one man to the other, and the Spanish maker of fine sherries lifted his double-barrelled rifle which was engraved and inlaid with gold and he aimed for Tukutela's brain.

Over his sights, he picked out the dark vertical cleft in the front of the ear and followed it down to its lowest point. That was where the actual opening of the eardrum was situated. Having found it he moved his aim forward three inches along an imaginary line from the aperture of the ear towards the elephant's eye.

The Spanish sherry-maker was on his first African safari. He had shot chamois and moufflon and red deer in the Pyrenees, but a wild African elephant is none of these timid creatures, and the Spaniard's heart was thudding into his ribs and his spectacles were fogged with his sweat and his hands shook. The professional hunter with him had patiently instructed him how and where to place his shot, but now he could not hold his aim upon it, and every second his breathing became more laboured, his aim more erratic. In desperation he jerked the trigger.

The bullet hit Tukutela a foot above his left eye and fifteen inches from the frontal lobe of the brain, but the honeycombed bony sponge of his skull cushioned the shock. He reeled back on his haunches and flung his trunk straight up above his head and gave a deep roaring growl in his throat.

The Spanish hunter turned and ran, and Tukutela whirled to face the movement, launching himself off his haunches. The professional hunter was directly under his outstretched trunk, and he flung up his rifle and aimed into Tukutela's head, into the roof of his open mouth between the bases of the long curved tusks.

The firing-pin fell on a dud primer with a click, the rifle misfired and Tukutela swung his trunk down like the executioner's axe, crushing the man to the earth.

The Spaniard was still running and Tukutela went after him, overhauling him effortlessly. He reached out his trunk and curled it around his waist. The man screamed and Tukutela tossed him thirty feet straight up into the air. He screamed all the way down until he hit the earth and the air was driven from his lungs. Tukutela seized him by one ankle and swung his body against the trunk of the nearest tree with a force that burst the man's internal organs, spleen and liver and lungs.

Tukutela raged through the forest with the corpse held in his trunk, beating it against the trees, lifting it high and slamming it down upon the earth, until it disintegrated and he was left with only the stump of the leg in his grip. He flung that aside and went back to where he had left the professional hunter.

The blow from the trunk had shattered his collar-bone, broken both his arms and crushed in his ribs but the hunter was still alive and conscious. He saw Tukutela coming back for him, the long trunk dangling, the huge ears extended and blood from his wound dribbling down to mingle with the blood of the Spaniard that splattered his chest and front legs.

The hunter tried to drag his mangled body away. Tukutela placed one great foot in the centre of his back, pinning him down, then with his trunk, he plucked off his limbs, one at a time, legs and arms, tearing them away from the joints of hip and shoulder, and throwing them aside. Finally he wrapped his trunk around the man's head and pulled it away from the shoulders. It rolled like a ball bouncing across the ground as Tukutela hurled it from him. His rage abated, overtaken by the pain in his head, and Tukutela stood over the bodies that he had destroyed, rocking from one foot to the other, rumbling in his throat as first the pain and then the melancholy of death came over him.

Despite the pain in his head and the slow drip of blood into his eye from the wound above it, he began the ritual of death that he had learned from his dam so many years previously. He gathered the parts of his victims, the squashed trunks and mutilated limbs and piled them in a heap. He picked their accoutrements out of the grass – rifles, hats, water-bottles – and added them to the bloody pile. Then he began to strip the trees of leafy branches and to cover it all with a mound of green.

The bullet wound healed cleanly, but soon there were other scars to add to the little white star that it left above his eye. A weighted spear from a dead-fall trap opened his thick grey hide from shoulder to knee, and he almost died from the infection that followed. The spread of his ears caught on thorn and hooked twigs, the edges became tattered and eroded. He fought for the cows when he joined the breeding herd, and although none of the other bulls could prevail against him, their tusks slashed and cut and marked him. Then there were other encounters with men.

Despite the dire danger associated with it, that first taste of the sweet juice of the sugar cane so long ago had been addictive. Tukutela became a compulsive garden raider. Sometimes he would lurk for days in the vicinity of a patch of cultivation, getting up his courage. Then when there was no moon, in the deepest hours of the night, he would go in stepping soundlessly as a cat on his big padded feet. Millet, maize, papaya, yams, he loved them all, but sugar cane he could never resist.

At first, he allowed himself to be driven off by the flaming torches and the shouting and the drums, but then he learned to answer the shouts with his own wild screams and to charge at the guardians of the forbidden gardens.

On separate occasions over the next ten years, he killed eight human beings in the course of his raids, pulling their bodies to pieces like a glutton dismembering a chicken carcass. He grew reckless in his greed for the sweet cane. Whereas after previous raids, he would travel a hundred miles in a single non-stop march to distance himself from retribution, this season he began to return to the same field on consecutive nights.

The villagers had sent a message to the *Boma* of the colonial district commissioner, begging for assistance. The D.C. had sent one of his askari armed with a .404 rifle and the askari was waiting for Tukutela. The askari was a policeman and neither a great hunter nor marksman. He hid himself in a pit in the middle of the field, quite happy in his own mind that the elephant would not return to the field that night; for Tukutela had already made a reputation for himself across his vast range and his habits were known: he was notorious as the garden raider who had killed so many villagers, and who never returned to the scene of his crime.

The askari awoke from a deep sleep in the bottom of his pit to find Tukutela blotting out the stars over his head, munching on the standing cane. The askari snatched up his .404 and fired a bullet upwards into Tukutela's belly. It was not a mortal wound and Tukutela hunted the askari remorselessly, quartering downwind until he picked up the scent and following it to the pit where the man crouched paralysed with terror. Tukutela put his trunk down into the pit and plucked him out.

The wound took many weeks to heal. The pain gnawed at his guts and Tukutela's hatred of man grew upon it.

Though Tukutela did not understand the reason for it, his contact with man became ever more frequent. His old range was being whittled down; every season there were more tracks and roads cutting through his secret places. Motor vehicles, noisy and stinking, buzzed through the silent places of the veld. The great forests were being hacked down and the earth turned to the plough. Lights burned in the night, and human voices carried to him wherever he wandered. Tukutela's world was shrinking in upon him.

His tusks were growing all this time, longer and thicker, until in his sixtieth year, they were great dark columns.

He killed another man in 1976, a black man who tried to defend his few wretched acres of millet with a throwing spear, but the head of the spear lodged in Tukutela's neck and formed a chronic source of infection, a constantly suppurating abscess.

Tukutela had long ago ceased to seek out the breeding herd. The scent of oestrus on the wind awakened in him only a sweet fleeting nostalgia, but the driving force of the procreative urge had dulled and he pursued his solitary ways through the shrinking forests.

There were some areas of his old range that remained untouched, and from experience Tukutela came to recognize them and to realize that they formed a sanctuary where he was safe from man's harassment. He did not understand that these were the national parks, where he was protected by law, but he spent more and more of his time in these areas, and over the years learned their precise boundaries, and became reluctant to venture across them into the dangerous world beyond.

Even in these sanctuaries he was wary, driven always by his hatred and fear of them to attack men wherever he found them, or to fly from the first acrid taint of them on the breeze. His faith in the safety of the sanctuary was tested when the hunters found him even there. He heard the report of a firearm and felt the sting of the missile, not differentiating between the sound of a rifle and a dart gun, but when he tried to locate and destroy his attackers, a strange lethargy overtook him, a terrible weakness in his thick columnar legs and he slumped unconscious to the earth. He awoke to the terrifying stench of men all around him, thick and repulsive on the air, even on his own skin where they had touched him. When he lumbered unsteadily to his feet, he found a strange serpentine device suspended around his neck and the chronic abscess on his neck caused by the spear wound was burning with the fires of antiseptics. He tried to wrench off the radio collar, but it defied even his might and so, in frustration, he devastated the forest around him, smashing down the tall trees and ripping out the bushes.

The men who watched his rage from afar laughed and one of them said, 'Tukutela, the Angry One.'

It took Tukutela many long seasons before he at last succeeded in ripping that hateful collar from around his neck, and hurling it into the top branches of a tree.

Although he recognized the sanctuary of the parks in which he now spent most of his days, Tukutela could not deny his deepest instincts and at certain seasons of the year, he became restless. The wanderlust came upon him, the urge to follow once again the long migratory road that his dam had first taken him over as an infant. He would be drawn to the boundary of the park by this irresistible longing and he would feed along it for days gathering his courage until he could no longer contain himself and he would set out fearfully and nervously, but with high anticipation for the far-off fastnesses to the east.

Of these, the vast Zambezi swampland was his favourite. He did not recognize it as his birthplace, he only knew that here the waters seemed cooler and sweeter, the grazing more luxuriant and his sense of peace deeper than any other place in his world. This season as he crossed the Chiwewe river and headed east, the urge to return to that place seemed even greater.

He was old now, long past his seventieth year and he was weary. His joints ached so he walked with a stiff exaggerated gait. His old wounds pained him, especially the bullet which had driven through his bony skull and lodged beneath the skin above his right eye. It had formed a hard encysted lump of gristle which he touched occasionally with the tip of his trunk when the pain was bad.

His craggy old head was weighed down by those huge ivory shafts; each day their burden was less supportable. Those tusks alone were a monument to his former glory. For the old bull was going back rapidly now. The sixth set of molars, the last and largest of his teeth, were all but worn away and the starvation of age was upon him. Every day, he was a little weaker, slowly his food was limited more and more to the softer more readily masticated grasses and shoots, but he could not take enough of them.

His huge frame was gaunt and his skin hung in bags at his knees and around his neck. There was a sense of melancholy in him, such as he had experienced only seldom in his life, the same feeling that had encompassed him as he waited for his dam to die beside the waterhole. He did not recognize that feeling as the premonition of his own impending death.

It seemed to Tukutela that as soon as he crossed out of the park, the pursuit began. He sensed that it was more determined, more persistent than ever before. It seemed to him that the forest was full of the human creatures, following him, waiting for him at each turn, and he could not head directly eastwards but must jink and twist to avoid the imaginary and real dangers that beset him.

However, when the sudden cacophony of gunfire roared out close behind him, Tukutela fled directly eastward at last, instead of doubling back towards the sanctuary of the park. It was a hundred miles and more to where the swamps began and the route was perilous; but he could not deny the deep instinct that drove him on.

Ten hours later, he stopped to bathe and drink and feed in an isolated marshy place, still a great distance from the true swamps. This was one of the way-stations on the old migratory road.

He had not been there for more than a few hours before the aircraft had rushed low overhead, filling the air with its buzzing roar, startling and angering Tukutela. In some vague way, he associated this machine with the deadly danger of the hunters. It left the same foul stench upon the air as the hunting vehicles which he had encountered so often before, and he knew he could rest no longer in this place, the hunters were closing in.

The great swamps were his refuge and he fled towards them.

*   *   *

'He won't stop now until he is into the swamps.' Sean Courtney was squatting beside the spoor. 'He's thoroughly alarmed, and we can't hope to catch him before he gets into them.'

'How far?' Riccardo asked, and Sean stood up and studied him as he replied.

'Eighty or ninety miles, Capo. Just a stroll.' Riccardo wasn't looking well. There were dark sweat patches soaking through his shirt and he seemed to have aged ten years in the last four days.

'What will we do if the old bugger keels over on us?' Sean wondered, and then thrust that thought aside. 'Okay, gang, we'll eat and sleep here. Move on again at four.'

He led them to the edge of the marsh, onto firm dry ground. Fatigue and heat had dulled their appetites. They needed sleep more than food and soon they were sprawled out in the shade like dead men.

Sean woke with the feeling that something was amiss; he sat up quickly, his hand already on the rifle, and swept a glance around him.

'Claudia.' He jumped to his feet. She was gone. Her pack lay ten paces away where she had slept. He wanted to shout for her, flouting his own security rules, and that was a measure of his concern.

He strode out of the perimeter, and whistled for the sentry. Pumula came in immediately.

'The donna,' Sean demanded in Sindebele. 'Where is she?'

'That way.' Pumula pointed towards the river.

'You let her go?' Sean demanded.

'I thought she was going to the bush . . .' Pumula excused himself, '. . . to relieve herself. I could not stop her.'

Sean had already started to run down the hippo path into the reeds that surrounded the largest and deepest of the pools, when he heard the splash of water ahead.

'This dilly bitch is going to drive me crazy,' he told himself as he burst out on the edge of the pool.

The pool was a hundred yards across, deep and green and still. For all its comical appearance the hippopotamus is the most dangerous animal in Africa. It has probably killed more human beings than all the other dangerous species put together. The old bulls are cantankerous and aggressive, a cow with a new calf will attack without provocation and a bite from those gaping jaws whose tusks are adapted to shearing coarse river reeds will cut a man in two. The crocodile is a sly and efficient killer. This pool was the ideal haunt of both hippo and crocodile and Claudia Monterro was in it up to her waist.

Her wet clothing, shirt and panties and socks, all freshly washed, were draped over the reeds at the edge, and Claudia was facing away from him leaning forward and with both hands working up a lather of soap in her hair.

The skin of her back was lightly tanned and flawless except for the paler line left by the strap of a bikini top across her shoulder-blades. Her flanks were lean but elegantly shaped into the waist, and the knuckles of her spine just showed between the ridges of fine athletic muscle on each side of it.

'What the hell do you think you're doing?' Sean snarled, and she turned to face him, hands still in her soapy hair, eyes screwed up against the suds.

'Is this how you get your jollies?' she demanded, but making not the slightest effort to cover her bosom. 'You pervert, creeping and peeping?'

'Get your arse out of there, before you get it bitten off by a croc.' Her jibe had stung him, but even in his anger he saw that her breasts were better than he had guessed. The cold water made the points stick out at him.

'Stop gawking,' she yelled back at him. 'And get lost.' She ducked her head under and then stood erect once again with soap lather streaming down her body, her hair shining and slick as a sheet of black silk over her shoulders.

'Get out of there, damn you, I'm not going to stand here arguing,' he ordered.

'I'll get out when I'm good and ready.'

Sean plunged straight into the pool, and reached her before she could avoid him. He seized her arm, and though it was slippery with soap, he dragged her towards the bank; kicking and lashing at him with her free hand, spitting with fury.

'You bastard, I hate you. Leave me alone.'

He controlled her easily with one hand. In the other, he still held his big double-barrelled rifle. His khaki shorts ran water and his velskoen boots squelched as he dragged her out. He snatched up her wet shirt and threw it at her.

'Get dressed!'

'You've got no right, I'm not going to accept this, you brutal ham-handed . . . you've hurt my arm.' She proffered her upper arm, exhibiting his red fingermarks on the skin, holding the wet shirt loosely at her side, shaking and pale with rage.

Strangely it was her navel that drew his eyes. It stared accusingly at him from the flat plain of her midriff, like a cyclopean eye, a perfect dimple at that moment more erotic than even the dense triangular bush of sodden hair beneath it. He dragged his eyes away, and she was so angry that she seemed totally oblivious of her nudity. He thought she might actually attack him, and he stepped back. As he did so he looked beyond her and saw a tiny arrow-head of ripples slipping silently across the still green surface of the pool towards them. At the apex of the vee-shaped ripple were two black lumps: gnarled and no bigger than a pair of large walnuts, they came at surprising speed.

Sean grabbed her arm, the same arm about whose injuries she was complaining, and jerked her back past him, away from the water's edge so viciously that she sprawled on her hands and knees in the mud.

He swung up the .577 Express rifle and aimed between the black eye lumps of the approaching crocodile. The eyes were at least nine inches apart, he calculated as he rode the pip of the foresight between them, a big old mugger.

The thunder of the rifle was stunning in the silence of the reeds and the bullet flicked an ostrich feather of spray from the surface, dead centre between the eye protuberances. The crocodile rolled sluggishly onto its back, its tiny brain mangled by the shot.

Claudia scrambled to her feet and stared over his shoulder as the reptile flashed its butter-yellow saurian belly. Sixteen feet from chin to the tip of its long crested tail, its jaws clicked as its nerves spasmed from the brain shot. The fangs as long and thick as a human forefinger overlapped the grinning scaly lips. It sank slowly back into the pool, the creamy belly fading into the green depths.

Claudia's fury had evaporated. She was staring into the pool, shivering uncontrollably, shaking her wet hair.

'Oh God, I didn't realize . . . how horrible.' She swayed towards him, shattered and vulnerable. 'I didn't know.' Her body was cold from the pool, long and sleek and wet as she pressed against him.

'What is it?' Riccardo Monterro shouted from the edge of the reed-bed. 'Sean, are you all right? What happened? Where's Claudia?'

At the sound of her father's voice, she jumped back from him guiltily and for the first time tried to cover her breasts and crotch.

'It's all right, Capo,' Sean yelled back. 'She's safe.'

Claudia snatched up her panties and pulled them on hastily, hopping on one foot in the mud, turning her back to him as she picked up her shirt and thrust her arms into the sleeves. When she turned back to him she had recovered her anger.

'I got a fright,' she told him. 'I didn't mean to grab you like that. Don't make any big deal out of it, buster.'

She zipped up the fly of her jeans and lifted her chin. 'I would have grabbed the garbageman if he'd been handy.'

'Okay, ducky, next time I'm going to let them bite you, lion or croc, what the hell.'

'You shouldn't have any complaints,' she said over her shoulder as she marched back up the path. 'You got yourself a big eyeful and I noticed you made a meal of it, Colonel.'

'You're right. You gave me a good peep. Not bad, a bit skinny perhaps – but not bad.'

And his grin expanded as he saw the back of her neck turn angry red.

Riccardo ran down the path to meet them, frantic with worry, and he seized Claudia and hugged her with relief.

'What happened, *tesoro*? Are you all right?'

'She tried to feed the crocs,' Sean told him. 'We are moving out in exactly thirty seconds from now, that shot will have alerted every ugly within ten miles.'

*　　*　　*

'At least I got that filthy black muck off my face,' Claudia told herself as they struck out away from the marshes. Her damp clothing felt cool and clean on her skin, and she was invigorated by her perilous bathe.

'No harm done,' she thought. 'Except I got ogled.' Even that no longer troubled her. His eyes on her naked body had not been altogether offensive, and in retrospect there was a satisfaction in having tantalized him.

'Eat your heart out, lover boy.' She watched his back as he strode out ahead of her. 'That was the best you are ever likely to lay eyes on.'

Within a mile her clothes had dried and there was no energy for any extraneous activity. The whole of her existence became the act of picking up one foot and swinging it forward after the other.

The heat was fierce and became fiercer still as they reached

146

the rim of the escarpment of the Zambezi valley and started down. The air changed its character. It lay on the earth in silvery streams like water, it quivered and shimmered like curtains of crystal beads and changed the form and shape of things at a distance so that they squirmed and wriggled, doubled in size, assuming monstrous shapes in the mirage, or disappeared from view, swallowed up by the cascades of heated air.

Farther off the air was blue, so when she looked back, the escarpment down which they were climbing was washed with pale blue, misty and ethereal. The sky was a different blue, deep and vigorous, and the clouds stood upon the firmament in towering ranges the colours of lead and silver, their bottoms cut cleanly horizontal to the earth, their heads shaped like full-rigged ships, mainsail and topsail, royal and skysail piled up into the blue heavens. Under the cloud ranges the air was trapped and lay upon the earth so that it felt as heavy as hot syrup. They trudged along beneath its weight.

From the forest around them the minute black mopane flies came swarming and gathered at the corners of their eyes and mouths, crawled up into their nostrils and into their ears to drink the moisture from their bodies. Their insistence was exquisite torture.

As each long mile fell behind them, so vistas of the valley floor opened ahead and on the horizon they could at last make out the dark belt of riverine vegetation which marked the course of the great Zambezi. Always Matatu danced along ahead of them like a wraith, following a trail that no other eye than his could discern, tireless and unaffected by the heat, so that Sean had to call him back for the regular periods of rest with which he interrupted the march.

'There is no sign of game,' Riccardo remarked, peering ahead through his binoculars. 'We haven't seen so much as a rabbit since we crossed into Mozambique.'

It was the first time he had spoken in hours and Sean was encouraged. He had begun seriously worrying about his client. Now he responded quickly.

'This was once a paradise of big game. I hunted here before the Portuguese pulled out and the buffalo were running in herds ten thousand strong.'

'What happened to them?'

'Frelimo fed the army with them. They even offered me the

147

contract for the slaughter, they couldn't understand why I refused. In the end they did it themselves.'

'How did they do it?'

'From helicopters, they flew low over the herds and machine-gunned them. They killed almost fifty thousand buffalo in three months. For all that time the sky was black with vultures and you could smell the killing fields from twenty miles off. When the buffalo were finished they started on the other game, the wildebeest and the zebra.'

'What a cruel and savage land this is,' Claudia said quietly.

'Surely you don't disapprove?' Sean asked. 'It was done by black men, not whites. It couldn't possibly be wrong.' He glanced at his Rolex wristwatch. 'Time to move on.'

He put out his hand to help Riccardo to his feet, but the older man shrugged the hand away. Nevertheless, Sean fell in beside him as the march resumed and let Claudia move up directly behind Matatu, while he chatted quietly to her father, jollying him along, trying to distract him from his weariness.

He recounted anecdotes from the bush war. He pointed out the site of the guerrilla training camp as they passed a few miles north of it and described the raid by the Ballantyne Scouts. Riccardo was interested enough to ask questions.

'This Comrade China sounds like a good field commander,' he commented. 'Did you ever find out what happened to him, after he escaped?'

'He was active right up to the end of the war. A tough cookie, all right. His men had to back-pack all their munitions into Rhodesia and a Russian T.5 anti-tank landmine weighs almost seventy pounds. The story goes that Comrade China brought in one of them at enormous cost in sweat and blood and laid it on the main Mount Darwin road for one of our regular armoured patrols. However, the local blacks had hired a bus that same weekend to go into town to watch the football match and they touched off the landmine. There were sixty-five of them on the bus and twenty-three of them survived the explosion. Comrade China was so incensed by the waste of his precious T.5 that he sent for all the next-of-kin of the victims, and the survivors who were still able to walk, and fined them each ten dollars to cover the cost of another landmine.'

Riccardo had to stop and double over with laughter and Claudia turned on them furiously.

'How can you laugh? That is the most outrageous story I have ever heard.'

'Oh, I don't know,' Sean replied evenly. 'I don't think ten dollars was so outrageous. I think old China was being fairly lenient.'

She tossed her head and lengthened her stride to catch up with Matatu, and Riccardo asked still chuckling, 'After the war, what happened to this character?'

Sean shrugged. 'He was in the new government in Harare for a while but then he disappeared in one of the political purges. He might have been liquidated, the old revolutionaries are always looked on with distrust when the regime they fought for comes to power. Nobody likes sharing a bed with a trained killer and toppler of other rulers.'

Sean called a halt an hour before dark for a brew of tea and their frugal evening meal. While Job cooked it over his small smokeless fire, Sean took Matatu aside and talked to him quietly. The tracker watched Sean's face as he spoke, nodding eagerly, and as soon as he finished Matatu slipped away, heading back the way they had come.

Riccardo looked a question as Sean came back to join them and he explained.

'I sent Matatu to back-track us. Make sure we aren't being followed. I'm worried about that shot. It could have called up those uglies we found near the border.'

Riccardo nodded and then asked, 'Have you got a couple of aspirin, Sean?'

Sean opened the side flap of his pack and shook three Anadin tablets from their bottle.

'Headache?' he asked as he passed them to Riccardo, and he nodded as he popped them into his mouth and washed them down with a swallow of hot tea.

'The dust and sun glare,' he explained, but both Sean and Claudia were studying him and Riccardo bridled.

'Damn it, don't look at me like that. I'm fine.'

'Sure,' Sean agreed smoothly. 'Let's eat and move on to find a place to sleep.' He went across to the cooking-fire and squatted beside Job. They talked softly.

'Papa,' Claudia moved a little closer to her father and touched his arm, 'how are you feeling, honestly?'

'Don't worry about me, *tesoro*.'

149

'It has started, hasn't it?'

'No,' he replied too swiftly.

'Doc Andrews said there might be headaches.'

'It's the sun.'

'I love you, Papa,' she said.

'I know, baby, and I love you too.'

'An ocean and a mountain?' she asked.

'The stars and the moon,' he confirmed, and put his arm round her shoulders. She leaned against him.

As soon as they had eaten, Job doused the fire and Sean got them up and moving again. Tukutela's spoor was easy to follow in the soft earth and he and Job had no need of Matatu for this stage. However, at dark they were forced to stop for the night.

'We'll reach the swamps tomorrow afternoon,' Sean promised Riccardo as they stretched out on top of their sleeping-bags.

Claudia lay awake worrying about her father long after the others were asleep. Riccardo snored softly, lying on his back with arms extended like a crucifix. When she raised herself on one elbow to look at him in the starlight, she heard Sean's light breathing alter subtly and sensed that he was awakened by her movement. He slept as lightly as a cat, sometimes he frightened her.

Even her concern for her father was at last overcome and she fell into that dark drugged sleep of exhaustion. Waking was like coming back from a faraway place.

'Wake up, come on, wake up.' Sean was slapping her face lightly, and she pushed his hand away and sat up groggily.

'What?' she mumbled. 'God, it's still dark.'

He had left her and gone to her father. 'Come on, Capo, wake up, man, wake up.'

'What the hell, what is it?' Riccardo's voice was slurred and grumpy.

'Matatu has just come into camp,' Sean told them quietly. 'We are being followed.'

Claudia felt the icy wind of dread blow across her skin.

'Followed? By whom?'

'We don't know,' Sean said.

'The same bunch that were camped at the border?' Riccardo asked. His voice was still slurred.

'Possibly,' Sean said.

'What are you going to do?' Claudia asked, and was annoyed that her tone sounded afraid and confused.

'We are going to give them the slip,' Sean said. 'Get up on your hind legs.'

They had slept with their boots on. They had simply to roll their sleeping-bags and they were ready to move out.

'Matatu is going to lead you away and cover your spoor,' Sean explained. 'Job and I are going to lay a false trail for them in the original direction. As soon as it's light we'll break away and circle back to join you.'

'You aren't going to leave us alone?' Claudia blurted fearfully, and then bit it off.

'No, you won't be alone. Matatu and Pumula and Dedan will be with you,' Sean told her disdainfully.

'What about the elephant?' Riccardo demanded. His voice had firmed. 'Are you breaking off the hunt? You going to let my elephant get away?'

'For a few lousy gooks armed with a couple of lousy AK 47s?' Sean chuckled. 'Don't be ridiculous, Capo. We will shake them off and be after Tukutela again before you know it.'

* * *

Sean and Job waited while Matatu assembled his group and then shepherded them away. By now Riccardo and Claudia had learned the basics of anti-tracking and went swiftly under Matatu's direction, while the tracker brushed and covered the sign behind them.

Once they were clear, Sean and Job trampled the area around the camp, back and forth and round in circles until they had confused any remaining spoor and then they fell into single file, Sean leading, and went away at a run. They did not make it too apparent that they were laying a false trail, but adopted all the usual precautions, which would not fool a good tracker.

It was the old Scouts' pursuit pace that Sean set, seven miles an hour, and gradually he began to veer off in a southerly direction. Matatu was heading northwards towards the river and Sean would lead the pursuit directly away from them.

While he ran, Sean puzzled over the identity of his pursuers – government soldiers or rebels, poachers or simply armed bandits looking for plunder – it was impossible to guess. However, Matatu had been worried when he came into camp.

'They are good, *Bwana*,' he had told Sean. 'They have done well to follow the spoor we left, and they were coming on fast. They move in formation like bush fighters, with flankers out.'

'Didn't you get a good look?' Sean had asked, and the little Ndorobo shook his head.

'It was getting dark, and I wanted to get back to warn you. They were closing in swiftly.'

'Even the best tracker won't be able to follow us in darkness, we've got the rest of the night to get clear of them.'

It was a strange reversal of roles, Sean thought grimly, as he and Job trotted through the dark bush. They, the hunters, were now being hunted just as remorselessly.

At first he had considered breaking off the chase after the elephant and doubling back for the border. Riccardo Monterro's condition was causing him real concern, and so was Matatu's warning that their pursuers were skilled and appeared dangerous. However, he had swiftly rejected the idea; they were beyond the point of no return.

'No turning back,' Sean said aloud, and grinned as he admitted to himself the true reasons for his determination, two ivory tusks and half a million dollars in cash. By now he was honestly not certain which of those were the most compelling. Those tusks were beginning to loom large in his imagination. They represented the old Africa, a symbol of a better world that had vanished. He wanted them more than he had ever wanted anything in his life, except perhaps half a million dollars, and he grinned again.

In the first light of dawn, they were running directly southwards and they had covered twenty miles since splitting off from the rest of the party.

'Time to disappear, Job,' he grunted, without breaking stride. There must be no indication to the trackers following them that they were about to split again.

'Good place just ahead,' Job agreed. He was running exactly in Sean's footsteps.

'Do it,' Sean said, and as they ran under the low branches of a grevia tree Job reached up and swung himself off the ground. Sean did not look back, did not alter his stride. Job would work himself through the branches of the closely growing grevia until he found a good place to drop off and anti-track away.

Sean ran on for twenty minutes, once again curving away into the south-west, heading for a low ridge that just showed in the dawn ahead of him. He crossed the ridge and as he had anticipated from the lie of the terrain found a small river in the valley beyond. He drank at the edge of the pool, and milled around, splashing water onto the bank as though he were bathing.

A tracker would expect him to choose this as a breakaway point, wading either upstream or downstream before leaving the river again. They would send scouts along both banks to search for sign. Sean waded downstream supporting himself on over-hanging branches to give them a trail to confirm their suspicions. Then without leaving the water he returned to the exact spot where he had entered the stream, and on the bank he carefully dried his feet and legs, replaced his dry velskoen shoes that he had hung around his neck on their laces, and back-tracked on his incoming spoor.

He retraced his footsteps to the crest of the ridge, walking backwards, stepping precisely on his original footprints and at the top of the ridge he employed the same trick that Job had. He swung himself into the air from a branch and over-handed himself well clear of the spoor before lowering himself to the edge of a rock slab and anti-tracking away.

'Even Matatu wouldn't be able to unravel that,' he thought with satisfaction, as he struck off back towards the north at a run.

Two hours later he joined up with Job at the rendezvous, and in the early afternoon they came up with the other party waiting for them five miles north of the point where they had split up.

'Good to see you, Sean. We were beginning to worry,' Riccardo told him as they shook hands, and even Claudia smiled as he flopped down beside her and said, 'My kingdom for a cup of tea.'

As he sipped at the mug which Matatu brought him, he listened attentively to the little tracker. Matatu squatted beside Sean and chattered in his excited falsetto.

'Matatu went back and kept an eye on the camp we left,' Sean translated for Riccardo and Claudia's benefit. 'He didn't dare approach too closely but he saw the gang that was following us arrive. This time he counted twelve of them. They searched the

153

area of the camp, and then took the bait and followed the false trail that Job and I had laid for them.'

'So we are clear then?' Riccardo asked.

Looks like it,' Sean agreed. 'And if we push along we should be able to reach the beginning of the swamps either this evening or early tomorrow.'

'What about Tukutela?' Riccardo asked.

'Well, we know from his track approximately where he would have reached the swamps. We'll just cast along the edge until we find where he went in, but we've lost a lot of ground on him. We'll have to go hard if we don't want him to get away from us. Do you feel up to it, Capo?'

'Never better,' Riccardo said. 'Lead on, man.'

Before they set off again, Sean went quickly over their packs. They had consumed a great deal of the provisions and he redistributed the remainder. By giving both Job and himself an extra ten pounds or so, he was able to reduce Riccardo's pack to twenty pounds and Claudia's to a mere ten pounds, just her sleeping-bag and personal items.

They both responded well to their reduced burdens but Sean once again marched beside Riccardo to encourage him and watch over him. Claudia was still going surprisingly well, he needn't have worried about her at all. Under her light pack she was stepping out lithely. He took pleasure in watching her long legs driving and her hard little buttocks oscillating in those tight blue jeans. They reminded him of the cheeks of a chipmunk chewing a nut.

They were on the valley floor now, and there were open vleis and baobabs, those trees with bloated trunks, bark like a reptile's skin, and crooked bare branches from which a few late cream of tartar pods still hung. It was easy to see why the Zulus said that the gods had accidentally planted the baobab upside down with its roots in the air.

Far ahead of them a slow standing cloud of evaporation marked the position of the swamps, and the alluvial soil was sandy and yielding under foot.

'Just think of this, Capo.' Sean was trying to divert him. 'You are probably one of the last men who will ever hunt a great elephant in the classical tradition of the long chase. This is the way it should be done, man. Not grinding around in a Land-Rover and then leaning out of the window to kill him. This is how

Selous and "Karamojo" Bell and "Samaki" Salmon hunted their elephant.'

He saw Riccardo's expression light up at the idea of being compared to those grand masters of the chase, men from another age when all elephant had been fair game. 'Samaki' Salmon had hunted and killed four thousand elephant in his lifetime. There had been a different morality in those days. Today a man with a bag of those dimensions would be accounted a villain and a criminal but in his day, 'Samaki' Salmon had been respected and honoured. He had even hunted with Edward, Prince of Wales, as his client.

Sean knew that Riccardo had an avid interest in the old-time elephant hunters, so he enlarged on their careers.

'If you want to do it the way "Karamojo" Bell did it, Capo, you have to walk like this. Bell wore out twenty-four pairs of boots a year and had to replace his porters and gunbearers every few weeks. They just couldn't keep up with him.'

'That was the golden age.' Riccardo extended his stride a little as he thought about it. 'You and I should have lived then, Sean. We were born after our time.'

'A true hunter should kill a great elephant with his legs. He should walk him down. That's the respectful and proper way and that is what you are doing now, Capo. Enjoy every step you take, for you are treading in old Bell's footsteps.'

Unfortunately the effects of Sean's encouragement were not enduring; within an hour Riccardo was flagging again and Sean noticed a new disconcerting unsteadiness in his gait. He stumbled and would have fallen had not Sean caught his arm.

'We all need a five-minute break and a cup of tea.' Sean led him to the shade.

When Job brought the tea mugs, Riccardo mumbled, 'Have you got a couple more aspirins for me?'

'You all right, Capo?' he asked, as he handed him the tablets.

'Damned headache again, that's all.' But he would not meet Sean's eyes.

Sean looked across at Claudia who was sitting close beside her father, but she also avoided his gaze.

'Do you two know something I don't?' Sean demanded. 'You both look guilty as hell.' He didn't wait for an answer but stood up and went to join Job at the small fire where he was baking a fresh batch of maize cakes for their evening meal.

'The aspirin will make you feel better,' Claudia told her father softly.

'Of course, aspirin is a sure-fire cure for cancer once it reaches the brain,' he agreed, and then as he saw her agonized expression be blurted, 'I'm sorry, I don't know why I said that. Self-pity isn't my usual style.'

'Is it bad, Papa?'

'I can tolerate the headache, but I'm getting a little double vision that worries me,' he admitted. 'Damn it, I was feeling so well a few days ago, it's all happened so quickly.'

'The exertion,' she said, pitying him. 'Perhaps that is what has aggravated it. We should turn back.'

'No,' he said with utter finality. 'Don't even talk about that again.' She inclined her head in aquiescence.

'The swamps are not far ahead. Perhaps we'll have a chance to rest,' she said.

'I don't want to rest,' he said. 'I realize just how little time I have left. I don't want to waste a moment of it.'

Sean came back to them. 'Are you ready to go on?'

Claudia glanced at her wristwatch. They had rested for less than half an hour. It was too short and she would have protested but her father pushed himself to his feet.

'All set,' he said, and she could see that even that short break had refreshed him.

They had been going only a few minutes when Riccardo said quite cheerfully, 'Those hamburgers that Job has cooked smell just great. Makes me feel hungry.'

'Those hamburgers are maize cakes,' Sean chuckled. 'Sorry to disappoint you.'

'You can't bullshit me,' Riccardo chuckled with him. 'I can smell the fried onions and beef.'

'Papa.' Claudia looked back over her shoulder and frowned sharply, and Riccardo stopped chuckling and looked distraught.

'There might be hallucinations,' Doc Andrews had warned Claudia. 'He may begin to see things, or imagine various odours. I can't give you an exact progress of the disease, of course, and there may be periods of swift deterioration followed by longer periods of remission. Just remember, Claudia, that his fantasies will be very real to him, and episodes of hallucination can be followed by periods of complete lucidity.'

That evening Sean would not stop to brew tea. 'We have to

156

try and make up the ground we've lost,' he told them, and they ate the cold maize cakes and biltong – slivers of salted, air-dried venison – on the march.

'One large hamburger with fried onions and all the trimmings coming up, Capo,' Sean teased him. Claudia glared at him, but Riccardo laughed uneasily and munched on the unappetizing fare as he walked.

They no longer had a spoor to follow, so Sean kept going long after night had fallen. The long tortuous miles fell slowly behind them and the brilliant southern stars burned over their heads. It was almost midnight before they stopped and unrolled their sleeping-bags.

Sean let them sleep until the dawn light was strong enough to make out the way ahead. The landscape had changed. During the night they had entered the region that was held in thrall by the great Zambezi. These were ancient flood plains that were inundated when the river broke its banks during the torrential rainy season. They were dry now, although almost devoid of trees; a few long-dead mopane and acacia thorn trees drowned by the floods still held up twisted bare branches to the hazy blue sky, standing out on the empty plains like lonely sentinels.

As they moved out into the open, the dried mud had cracked into bricklets beneath their feet, the edges curling up, and the clumps of swamp grass were brown and matted and dead from drought. When the breeze switched fitfully they could smell the swamps still out of view ahead, the odour of mud and rotting vegetation.

The mirage shimmered across the plains, so there was no clear horizon; land and sky merged into each other like water. When they looked back the tree-line crawled like a long black serpent below the milky sky, undulating and vibrating softly in the mirage, and the dust devils spun upon themselves twisting and swaying like belly-dancers.

Out on the plain Sean felt exposed and vulnerable. There was just the scant chance of a Frelimo patrol plane passing this way searching for Renamo bands and they were as obvious as fleas on a white sheet. He wanted to hurry but then glanced back at Riccardo and knew that they would have to rest again soon.

Ahead of Sean, Matatu gave a cry that made his nerves jump. Sean knew what it meant and he ran forward, passing Claudia, and stopped beside Matatu.

'Well, all right!' He clapped Matatu's shoulder and then went down on one knee to examine the earth.

'What is it?' Riccardo sounded alarmed, but Sean lifted his head and grinned at him.

'It's him. Tukutela. We've cut his spoor again just where Matatu predicted that we would.' And he touched the marks of the huge pads whose weight had crushed the bricklets of dried mud to talcum powder. The spoor was so clear that the difference between the bull's rounded front feet and the more oval hind feet was immediately apparent, and the forward edges of each footprint were nicked by his toe-nails.

'Still heading straight for the swamps.' Sean stood and shaded his eyes against the glare as he followed the direction of the spoor. Not far ahead another line of trees was drawn like a pencil along the horizon where a narrow curved finger of higher ground reached out across the plains.

'In a way we are fortunate,' Sean remarked. 'A few years ago there were so many herds of buffalo and game on these flats that Tukutela's spoor would have been wiped out in a few hours by their hooves. Now, since the Frelimo government converted them all to army rations, Tukutela is the only living thing for miles around.'

'How far behind him are we?'

'We've made up a bit of ground.' Sean lowered his hand from his eyes and turned to him. 'But not enough, and if the uglies catch us out here in the open . . . Luckily Tukutela's spoor is headed straight for the line of trees ahead. They will give us some cover.' He gestured to Matatu to take the spoor once again.

Now the expanse of the wide plain was dimpled with old ant-hills, mounds of clay thrown up by colonies of termites, some of them the size of a large cottage. Tukutela's spoor meandered between them. However, the line of growth was by now so close that they could make out the individual trees. The finger of high ground formed a natural causeway from the edge of the forest across the wide plains to the beginning of the true swamps. There were ivory nut palms, bottle-stemmed palms, and the low ilala palms with their fan-shaped leaves, mixed with wild fig and on the highest ridge of the long causeway grew a few massive baobab, with trunks of elephantine grey bark.

With relief Sean followed the spoor of the old bull off the plain and into the trees of the isthmus. Here the elephant had stopped to dig out the juicy roots of an ilala palm, and drop a pile of spongy yellow dung.

'The elephant rested here,' Matatu explained, lowering his voice to a whisper. 'He is an old man now and he tires easily. Here he stood to sleep, see how he shuffled his feet in the dust, and when he awoke he dusted his body. See where he scooped it up with his trunk and threw it over his back.'

'How long did he stay here?' Sean asked, and Matatu put his head on one side as he considered the question.

'He rested here until late yesterday afternoon when the sun was there.' Matatu pointed ten degrees above the western horizon. 'But when he went on he went more slowly. He feels safer now that he is close to the swamps. We have gained on him.'

Sean exaggerated Matatu's estimate as he passed it on to Riccardo and Claudia. He wanted to encourage them. 'We are making really good gains on him now.' He put on a cheerful and confident air. 'We might even catch up with him before he gets into the deep swamps, if we don't waste any time.'

The spoor headed down the isthmus and the old bull had fed quietly as he moved along it, keeping up on top of the low ridge where the bush was thickest. Directly ahead of them stood another gigantic baobab tree. Its bark was grey and folded and riven as the old bull's hide.

For the moment Sean had left Riccardo's side and moved up to his original position behind Matatu. He wanted to caution the tracker not to set too fast a pace, but before he could speak he heard a strange guttural cry behind him and he whirled around.

Riccardo's face was swollen and congested with blood, his eyes blazed and seemed to start from their sockets. Sean thought he was suffering from some kind of seizure, but Riccardo was pointing ahead, his hand shaking with violent emotion.

'There he is,' he croaked, in a thick unnatural voice. 'For God's sake, can't you see him?'

Sean whirled and followed the direction of his outstretched arm.

'What is it, man?'

He was looking ahead, and he did not see Riccardo turn to Pumula and snatch the Rigby rifle off his shoulder, but he heard the metallic clash of the bolt as Riccardo chambered a cartridge.

'Capo, what the hell are you doing?' He reached out to restrain him, but Riccardo shoved him backwards. Sean was unprepared and off balance, and he staggered and almost fell.

Riccardo ran forward to the head of the line and then he stopped and threw up the rifle.

'Capo, don't do it.' Sean was sprinting to catch him, but the Rigby crashed out and the barrel jumped high, driving Capo back a pace with the heavy recoil.

'Have you gone crazy?' Sean could not reach him before he fired again, and the heavy bullet tore a flurry of white wet bark from the trunk of the baobab. The echoes of the shot rolled across the plains.

'Capo.' Sean reached him and seized the rifle, forcing the muzzle up towards the sky just as Capo fired the Rigby for the third time.

Sean wrested the weapon out of his grip.

'In the name of all that's holy, man, what on earth do you think you're doing?'

All their eardrums were numbed by the thunder of gunfire, and Sean's angry outraged voice sounded small and hollow after it.

'Tukutela,' Riccardo mouthed. 'Don't you see? Why did you stop me?' His face was still flushed and he was shaking like a man with malarial fever. He reached once more for the Rigby in Sean's grasp, but Sean jerked it away from him.

'Pull yourself together,' he shouted angrily and tossed the empty rifle to Job. 'Don't let him get it again.' And turned back to Riccardo.

'Are you out of your mind?' He seized him by the shoulders. 'The sound of those shots will carry for miles.'

'Leave me!' Riccardo struggled. 'Don't you see him?' And Sean shook him viciously.

'Snap out of it, you're shooting at a tree. You've blown your lid!'

'Give me the rifle.' Riccardo was pleading, and Sean shook him again and roughly turned him to face the baobab.

'Look at it, you bloody madman! There's your elephant!' He shoved him towards it. 'Take a good look!'

Claudia ran forward and tried to restrain Sean. 'Leave him alone, can't you see he's sick?'

'He's gone crazy!' Sean pushed her aside. 'He's calling up

every Frelimo and Renamo thug within fifty miles, and he's chased any elephant . . .'

'Leave him,' Claudia came back at him, and Sean let go of her father and stepped back.

'All right, ducky, he's all yours.'

Claudia rushed to her father and embraced him. 'It's all right, Papa! It's going to be all right!'

Riccardo was staring uncomprehendingly at the deep raw wounds in the bark of the baobab from which sap was oozing.

'I thought it was . . .' he shook his head weakly. 'Why did I do that? I don't . . . I thought it looked like an elephant.'

'Yes, Papa, yes.' Claudia was hugging him. 'Don't upset yourself.'

Job and the rest of the hunting team were quiet and unhappy, watching this strange episode that none of them could fathom. Sean turned away in disgust. It took him a few seconds to get full control of himself, then he asked Matatu, 'Do you think we are close enough for Tukutela to have heard the shooting?'

'The swamps are close, and the sound carries over this flat earth as it does over water,' Matatu shrugged. 'Perhaps the elephant heard, who knows?'

Sean looked back the way they had come. From the ridge they could see out across the flood plain into the dusty distances.

'Job, what chance that the terrs heard?'

'We'll find out the hard way, Sean. It depends how close behind us they are.'

Sean shook himself, trying to rid himself of his anger the way a spaniel shakes off water.

'We'll have to rest here. The *mambo* is sick. Brew a billy of tea, and we'll decide what to do,' he ordered.

He walked back to where Claudia was still holding her father. She faced Sean defiantly, turning her body to shield Riccardo from him.

'Sorry I pushed you around, Capo,' Sean said mildly. 'You gave me a hell of a fright.'

'I don't understand,' Riccardo mumbled. 'I could have sworn it was him. I saw him so clearly.'

'We will break for a cup of tea,' Sean told him. 'I think you've got a touch of the sun. It can turn a man's brain to jelly.'

'He'll be fine in a few minutes,' Claudia said confidently, and Sean nodded coldly at her.

'Let's get him into the shade.'

Riccardo leaned back against the bole of the baobab and closed his eyes. He looked pale and bewildered, a rash of sweat droplets sparkled on his chin and upper lip. Claudia knelt beside him and dabbed them away with the corner of her scarf, but when she looked up at Sean he jerked his head in a peremptory gesture and she stood up and followed him.

'This doesn't come as any surprise to you, does it?' he accused, as soon as they were beyond earshot. She did not reply and he went on, 'Just what kind of daughter are you anyway? You knew he was sick and you let him come out on this jaunt.'

Her lips were trembling and as he stared into them he saw that her honey-coloured eyes were swimming, he had not expected tears from her. They took him by surprise. He felt his fury slipping away and he had to make an effort to bolster it.

'It's too late to start blubbering now, ducky. We've got to find a way to get him home. He's a sick man.'

'He's not going home,' she murmured, so low that he barely caught the words. Her tears were hanging on thick dark lashes and he stared at her in silence. She swallowed hard and then said, 'He's not a sick man, Sean. He's dying. Cancer. It was diagnosed by a specialist before we left home. He predicted that it could attack the brain like this.'

Sean's fury crumpled.

'No,' he said. 'Not Capo.'

'Why do you think I agreed to let him come and insisted on coming with him? I knew that this was his last hunt – and I wanted to be with him.'

They were silent, staring at each other, then she said, 'You care. I can see that you truly care for him. I didn't expect that.'

'He's my friend,' Sean said, puzzled himself by the depth of his own sadness.

'I didn't think you were capable of gentleness,' she went on softly. 'I may have misjudged you.'

'Perhaps we misjudged each other,' he said, and she nodded.

'Perhaps we did,' she said. 'But thank you anyway. Thank you for caring about my father.'

She began to turn away to go back to Riccardo but Sean stopped her.

'We still haven't settled anything,' he said. 'We haven't decided what we are going to do.'

'We go on, of course,' she answered. 'Right to the bitter end. That's what I promised him.'

'You've got guts,' he told her softly.

'If I have, then I got them from him,' she replied, and went to her father.

The mug of tea and a half dozen Anadin tablets revived Riccardo. He was acting and talking completely rationally again, and none of them made any further reference to his wild behaviour, although quite naturally it had thrown a pall over all of them.

'We must move on, Capo,' Sean told him. 'Tukutela is walking away from us every minute we sit here.'

They followed the ridge of high ground, and now the odour of the swamps was stronger, brought to them by the fitful inconstant wind.

'That's one of the many reasons the elephant like the swamps,' Sean explained to Riccardo. 'There the wind is always shifting, turning and switching. It makes it much more difficult to get close to them.'

There was a gap in the trees ahead, and Sean stopped and they gazed out through it.

'There they are,' he said. 'The Zambezi swamplands.'

The ridge on which they stood was like the back of a sea serpent, swimming across the open flood plains. Now just ahead of them it ducked below the surface and disappeared at the point where the open plains gave way to endless expanses of papyrus and reeds.

Sean raised his binoculars and surveyed the swamps ahead. The reed-beds seemed limitless, but he had flown over them and he knew that they were interspersed with shallow lagoons of open water and narrow winding channels. Farther out, almost on the horizon, he could see the loom of small islets, dark patches of almost impenetrable bush-crowned islands and through the lens of the binoculars he could just make out the curved palm stems with their high fluffy heads.

The past season had been particularly dry and the water level would be low, in most places not more than waist deep, but the mudbanks would be black and glutinous and the channels much deeper. The going would be arduous, and apart from the mud and water, reeds and water plants would impede each step they took, winding themselves around their legs as they tried to move.

For them each mile through the swamps would be the equivalent of five on dry land, while the elephant would be in his element. He loved mud and water. It supported his great bulk and his foot pads were designed by nature to expand as he put his weight upon them, forcing a wide opening, and then they would shrink in diameter as he lifted them, freeing themselves readily from the clinging mud.

Tukutela could gorge on reeds and soft water plants and swamp grass, and the dense bushy islets would afford variety to his diet. The suck of mud and the splash of water would warn him of an approaching enemy and the fitfully turning wind would protect him, bringing the scent of a pursuer down to him from every quarter. In all Tukutela's wide range, this was the most difficult place to hunt him.

'It's going to be a Sunday-school picnic, Capo,' Sean lowered the binoculars. 'Those tusks are as good as hanging over the fireplace in your den already.'

The old bull's spoor went out to the very end of the land bridge, and then down into the papyrus beds, where the undulating sea of green fronds swallowed the trail and left not a sign.

'Nobody can follow a trail in there.' Riccardo stood at the line where dry friable earth ended and damp swamp mud began. 'Nobody can find Tukutela in there,' he repeated, staring at the wall of swamp growth higher than his head. 'Surely they can't?'

'You are right, nobody can find him in there,' Sean agreed. 'That is, nobody except Matatu.'

They were standing in the remains of a village that had been built on the end of the isthmus. Clearly the previous occupants had been fishermen, members of one of the small tribes who live along the banks of the Zambezi and make their livelihood from her abundant green waters. Only the racks on which they had dried their catches of tilapia bream and barbeled catfish still stood, but their huts had been burned to the ground.

Job was searching the outskirts of the village and he whistled for Sean. When Sean went to join him he was standing over an object which lay in the short grass. At first glance Sean thought it was a bundle of rags and then he saw the bones protruding from it. They were still partially covered by shreds of dried skin and flesh.

'When?' Sean asked.

'Six months ago, perhaps.'

'How did he die?'

Job squatted beside the human skeleton and when he turned the skull it snapped off the vertebrae of the neck like a ripe fruit. Job cupped it in his hands, and it grinned at him with empty eye-sockets.

'Bullet through the back of the head,' Job said. 'Exit-hole this side.' It was like a third eye in the bone of the forehead.

Job replaced the skull and walked deeper into the grass. 'Here's another,' he called.

'Renamo has been through here,' Sean gave his opinion. 'Either looking for recruits or dried fish or both.'

'Or else it was Frelimo looking for Renamo rebels, and they decided to question them, with an AK.'

'Poor buggers,' Sean said. 'They get it from both sides. There will be plenty more of them lying around, they are the ones who escaped from the huts before they burned.'

They started back towards the village and Sean said, 'They were fishermen, they would have had their canoes here. They will probably be hidden, but we could certainly use one. Go through the edge of the papyrus beds and then search the bush behind the village.'

Sean crossed to where Riccardo and Claudia were sitting together. As he came up, he looked at her enquiringly and she nodded and smiled optimistically.

'Papa's doing fine, what is this place?'

He explained their reasoning as to the fate of the village.

'Why would they kill these innocent people?' Claudia was appalled.

'In Africa these days you don't have to have a reason for killing somebody, other than a loaded gun in your hands, and a fancy to fire it off.'

'But what harm could they have done?' she insisted.

Sean shrugged. 'Harbouring rebels, withholding information, hiding food, refusing the services of their women, any one of those crimes, or none of them.'

The sun was a red ball through the swamp haze, so low above the tops of the papyrus that Sean could look directly at it without screwing up his eyes.

'It'll be dark before we can leave,' he decided. 'We'll have to sleep here tonight and start again at first light tomorrow. One consolation is that now Tukutela has reached the swamps, he will

165

slow down. He's probably not more than a couple of miles ahead of us right now.' But as he said it he thought about those shots that Riccardo had fired. If the bull had heard them, he would still be running. There was, however, no point in telling that to Riccardo. He looked shaken and despondent, and he had been almost silent since the incident.

'He is just a husk of the Capo I knew, poor old devil. The last thing I can do for him is to get him that elephant.' Sean's sympathy was genuine and unaffected and he sat down beside him, and began to draw him out, describing what lay ahead, and how they would hunt for the old bull in the papyrus beds.

The hunt was all that now seemed to interest Riccardo, and for the first time that day he became animated and once he even laughed.

Claudia flashed a grateful smile at Sean, and then stood up and said, 'I've got a little private business to attend to.'

'Where are you off to?' Sean demanded immediately.

'The little girls' room,' she told him. 'And you are definitely not invited.'

'Don't go wandering off too far, and no swimming this time,' he ordered. 'You'll get enough of that tomorrow.'

'I hear and obey, O great white *Bwana*.' She gave him a sarcastic curtsy and set off out of the perimeter of the burned village. Sean watched her go uneasily and was about to call another warning after her when there was a shout from the papyrus bed and his attention was diverted from Claudia.

He jumped up.

'What is it, Job?' he yelled, and went down to the water's edge.

There were more confused shouts and splashing from the depths of the papyrus, and then Job and Matatu emerged, dragging something long and black and waterlogged between them.

'Our first bit of luck.' Sean grinned at Riccardo and slapped him on the shoulder.

It was a traditional *mokorro* dugout canoe, about seventeen foot long, hewn from a single log of the sausage tree, *Kigelia africana*. The body of the dugout was just wide enough for a person to sit in it, but it was usually propelled by a man standing in the stern and wielding a long punt pole.

Job tipped the water out of the craft and they examined it

carefully. The hull had been repaired and caulked in a few places, but seemed reasonably sound.

'Search the village,' Sean ordered. 'They must have had caulking material here. See if you can find it, and then send Dedan and Pumula to cut a couple of punt poles.'

Claudia screamed, and they all spun to face the sound. She screamed again, the sound was strangely muffled and far off, and Sean began to run, snatching up his rifle from where he had left it beside the nearest burnt-out hut.

'Claudia!' he yelled. 'Where are you?' Only his echo mocked him from the forest. 'Where are you? . . . are you?'

*   *   *

When Claudia stood up and rebuckled her belt, she found that it came in easily a full two notches shorter around her waist. She smiled down at her own belly with approval. Now it was no longer flat but definitely concave. The long march and frugal rations had stripped every last ounce of fat from her frame.

'Strange how in an age of plenty we set out to starve ourselves.' She smiled again. 'I'm going to enjoy putting on those lost pounds, plenty of pasta and red wine when I get home.'

She started back towards the village, and then realized that in her search for privacy she had gone further than she had intended and that a thicket of wiry thorn brush blocked her way back. She turned aside to circumvent it and came upon a broad pathway running directly down through the bush towards the edge of the swamp. She followed it thankfully.

Claudia did not realize that she was following a hippo road, one of the wide thoroughfares that the great amphibians followed on their nightly forays into the forest. However, the road had not been used for many months. The hippopotamus in the area had been decimated along with the other game. She was in a hurry to get back to her father, and she was feeling slightly uneasy at her isolation from the rest of the party. She strode down the pathway, just short of a run.

Ahead of her an old mat of dried papyrus stems was spread across the road from side to side. It had obviously been placed there by the previous occupants of the village, and although it served no purpose that Claudia could imagine, it was no obstacle to her progress and she stepped on to it without slackening her pace.

The pitfall had been dug for the express purpose of trapping a hippopotamus. It was ten feet deep with funnel-shaped sides, that would tumble one of the huge beasts down into its depth and wedge it securely between the earthen walls. The opening was covered by branches strong enough to carry the weight of a man or a lesser animal, but not that of a hippo. Over these branches the builders had spread the papyrus stems.

However, the pitfall had been built a long time previously and both branches and mat had rotted and weakened. They collapsed under Claudia's weight, and she screamed as she dropped through into the pit beneath, and screamed again as she hit the sloping side and bounced off it. The bottom of the pit was covered with a few inches of stagnant water that had seeped into it. Claudia landed awkwardly with one leg twisted up under her and then rolled on to her back in the mud.

The breath had been driven from her lungs and there was a fierce pain in her left knee. For a few minutes she could not respond to the faint shouts she heard from above. She sat up, clutching her injured knee to her chest and gasping wildly to fill her agonized lungs. At last she managed a strangled shout.

'Here! I'm here.'

'Are you all right?' Sean's head appeared above her, peering down anxiously.

'I think so!' she gasped, and tried to stand up, but the pain shot through her knee and she fell back. 'My knee,' she said.

'Hold on. I'm coming down.' Sean's head withdrew. She heard voices. Job and Matatu and her father. Then a coil of nylon rope dropped down towards her, unfurling as it fell. Sean lowered himself swiftly down the rope and dropped the last few feet to land with a splash in the mud beside her.

'I'm sorry,' she said contritely. 'I guess I've done it again.'

'Don't apologize,' he grinned. 'I'm not conditioned to it. For once, it's not your fault. Let's take a look at your leg.'

He squatted beside her. 'Move your foot. Capital! Can you bend your knee? Splendid! At least no bones broken. That's a relief. Let's get you out of this hole.' He tied a loop in the end of the rope and slipped it over her head and shoulders and settled it under her armpits.

168

'Okay, Job,' he called up. 'Take her up. Gently, man, gently.'

As soon as they reached ground level, Sean made a more thorough examination of her knee.

He rolled up the leg of her jeans and said, 'Shit!'

As a Scout commander he had extensive experience of the type of injury that a paratrooper is prone to, broken bones, torn cartilage, sprained ligaments in ankle and knee. Already Claudia's knee was ballooning and the first tinge of bruising coloured the smooth tanned skin.

'This might hurt a little,' he warned, and manipulated her leg gently.

'Ouch!' she said. 'That's damned sore.'

'Okay,' he nodded. 'It's the medial ligament. I don't think you've torn it, it would be more painful if you had. Probably just sprained it.'

'What does that mean?' she asked.

'Three days,' he replied. 'You won't be walking on it for at least three days.'

He put his arm around her shoulders. 'Can you stand up?' he asked, and when she nodded he helped her to her feet. She leaned against him, standing on her good leg.

'Try putting a little weight on it,' he said, and immediately she exclaimed with pain.

'No, I can't use it.'

He stopped and picked her up in his arms as though she were a child and carried her back to the village. She was surprised by his strength and then, although her knee was beginning to throb, she relaxed in his arms. It was a good feeling. Papa had carried her like this when she was a little girl, and she had to resist the urge to lay her head against Sean's shoulder.

When they reached the village he set her down in the clearing, and Matatu ran to fetch his pack. Her injury had diverted Riccardo's attention from his own troubles, and he came to fuss over his little girl in a way which ordinarily would have annoyed her. Now she submitted to it, thankful for his revived animation and attention.

Sean strapped the knee with an elastic bandage from his first-aid kit and then gave her an anti-inflammatory tablet to swallow with hot tea.

'That's about all we can do for it,' he told her, and sat back. 'Only thing that will fix it is time.'

'Why did you say three days?'

'It takes that long. I've seen a hundred knees just like yours, except that they were usually a lot more hairy and not nearly as pretty.'

'That's a compliment.' She raised an eyebrow. 'You are getting soft, Colonel.'

'Part of the treatment, and of course, totally insincere,' he assured with a grin. 'The only question now, ducky, is what on earth are we going to do with you?'

'Leave me here,' she said promptly.

'Are you out of your mind?' he asked, and Riccardo backed him up immediately.

'That's out of the question.'

'Look at it this way,' she reasoned calmly. 'I cannot move for three days, by which time your elephant will be long gone, Papa.' She held up her hand to forestall his argument. 'We cannot go back. You can't carry me. I can't walk. We would have to sit here anyway.'

'We cannot leave you alone, don't be ridiculous.'

'No,' she agreed. 'But you can leave someone to look after me while you go on after Tukutela.'

'No.' Riccardo shook his head.

'Sean,' she appealed to him. 'Make him see that it is the sensible thing to do.'

He stared at her and the admiration she saw in his gaze gave her a full warm feeling in her chest.

'Damn it,' he said softly. 'You're all right.'

'Tell him it will only be for a few days, Sean. We all know how much that elephant means to Papa. I want to give it to him as my . . .' she almost said 'last gift', but then she changed it, 'as my special gift to him.'

'I can't accept it, *tesoro*.' Riccardo's voice was gruff but blurred and he lowered his head to hide his feelings.

'Make him go, Sean,' Claudia insisted, and gripped his forearm firmly. 'Tell him I'll be as safe here with Job to look after me as I would be in the swamp with the two of you.'

'She just may have a point, Capo,' Sean said. 'But, hell, it's not my business. It's between the two of you.'

'Will you leave us alone, Sean?' Claudia asked, and then without waiting for a reply, she turned to her father. 'Come and sit here next to me, Papa.' She patted the ground beside her.

Sean stood up and walked away, leaving them together in the gathering darkness.

He went to sit beside Job. They sat in the companionable silence of old friends, drinking tea and smoking one of Sean's last cheroots, passing it back and forth between them.

An hour passed. It was entirely dark before Riccardo came to where the two of them sat. He stood over them and his voice was rough and drawn with sadness.

'All right, Sean,' he said. 'She has convinced me to do as she wants. Will you make the arrangements to go on with the hunt first thing tomorrow morning? And, Job, will you stay here and look after my little girl for me?'

'I'll look after her for you, sir,' he agreed. 'You just go kill that elephant. We'll be here when you come back.'

*   *   *

Working in the moonlight they moved out of the burned-out village and built a fly camp a few hundred metres back in the forest.

They made a lean-to shelter for Claudia and under it placed a mattress of cut grass. Sean left the medical kit and most of their remaining provisions in the shelter with her. He detailed both Job and Dedan to remain with Claudia. Job would keep the light 30/06 rifle with the fibreglass stock, and Dedan had his axe and skinning knife.

'Send Dedan back to keep an eye on the isthmus. Any Frelimo or Renamo patrols will come that way. At the first sign of trouble, get the girl into the swamp and hide out on one of the islands.' Sean gave Job his final orders, and then sauntered across to where Riccardo was taking leave of his daughter.

'Are you ready, Capo?'

Riccardo stood up quickly and walked away from Claudia without looking back.

'Don't get into any more trouble,' Sean told her.

'You neither.' She looked up at him. 'And Sean, take care of Papa for me.'

He squatted down in front of her and offered her his hand as he would have if she had been a man, and he tried to think of something witty to say, but he could not.

'Okay, then?' he asked instead.

'Okay, then,' she agreed, and he stood up and walked down to the edge of the swamp where Matatu and Pumula and Riccardo were waiting for him beside the dugout canoe.

Matatu took up his position in the bows of the frail craft, Sean and Riccardo were amidships, sitting on their depleted packs and holding their rifles across their laps. Pumula stood in the stern with one of the freshly cut punt poles and propelled the dugout in response to Matatu's hand signals.

Within seconds of pushing off from the bank, they were surrounded by a high palisade of papyrus, and their view was restricted to the wall of reeds and the small patch of lemon-yellow dawn sky overhead. As they passed, the sharp pointed leaves of the reeds were dashed into their faces, threatening their eyes, and the webs that the tiny swamp spiders had spun between the stems of the reeds wrapped over their faces, sticky and irritating. The night's clammy chill hung over the swamp and when they came out suddenly into an open lagoon, there was a heavy mist lying over the surface and a flock of whistling duck alarmed the dawn with the clatter of their wings.

The dugout was heavily overloaded with the four men aboard. There was only an inch or so of freeboard and if any one of them moved suddenly, water slopped on board and they were forced to use the tea billy to bail almost continually, but Matatu signalled them on.

The sun rose above the papyrus and immediately the mist twisted into rising tendrils and then was gone. The water lilies opened their cerulean blossoms and turned them to face the sunrise. Twice they saw large crocodiles lying with just their eye-knuckles exposed. They sank below the surface as the dugout slid towards them.

The swamps were alive with birds. Bitterns and secretive night herons lurked in the reed-beds, little chocolate-brown jacanas danced over the lily pads on their long legs, while goliath herons as tall as a man fished the back waters of the lagoons. Overhead winged formations of pelicans and white egrets, cormorants and darters with serpentine necks, and huge flocks of wild duck of a dozen different species.

The heat built up swiftly and was reflected from the surface of the water into their faces so that the two white men were soon sweating through their shirts. At places the water was only a few inches deep and they were forced to climb out and drag the dugout through to the next channel or lagoon. Under the matted reeds the mud was black and foul-smelling and reached to their knees.

In the shallower places the elephant's pads had left deep circular water-filled craters in the mudbanks. The spoor of the old bull led them deeper and ever deeper into the swamplands, but there was consolation in the swift progress that the dugout made across the lagoons and channels, thrust on by the long punt pole. For a while, Sean spelled Pumula in the stern but soon Pumula could no longer abide his clumsy strokes and took the pole away from him.

There was only room for one man to stretch out in the bottom of the dugout. Riccardo slept in it that night, while the others sat waist-deep in the mud, leaning against the hull of the canoe and took what rest the clouds of mosquitoes allowed them.

Early the following morning, when Sean stood up out of the mud, he found that his bare legs were swarming with black leeches. The repulsive worms were attached to his skin, bloated with the blood they had sucked from him. Sean used a little of their precious supply of salt to rid himself of them. To pull them loose would leave a wound into which the leech had injected anti-coagulants and which would continue to bleed profusely and probably become infected. However, a dab of salt on each leech made them twist and contort with agony and fall off leaving only a sealed wound on the skin.

When he opened his trousers, Sean found that they had crawled up into the cleft between his buttocks and were hanging like black grapes from his genitalia. He shuddered with horror as he worked on them, while safely in the dugout Riccardo watched with interest and made facetious comment:

'Hey, Sean, this must be the first time you've ever objected to a bit of head!'

* * *

Sean set the end of the punt pole in the mud and steadied it while Matatu shinned up it like a monkey and peered ahead. When he came down he told Sean, 'I can see the islands. We are very close. We will be there before noon, and unless Tukutela has heard us, he will be on one of the islands.'

Sean knew from flights over the area and from study of his

large-scale map that the islands formed a chain between the swamplands and the main channel of the Zambezi. They dragged the dugout through the shallows, Sean hauling on the nylon rope tied to the bows, and Pumula and Matatu shoving in the stern. When Riccardo offered to assist, Sean told him, 'Take a free ride, Capo. I want you nicely rested so that you don't have any excuses if you mess up your shot at Tukutela.'

At last Sean saw the fronds of the palm trees rising above the screen of papyrus ahead, and abruptly the water deepened, and he went under to his chin. He dragged himself out and they all clambered back on board. Pumula poled them through to the first island. The vegetation was so dense that it overhung the water, and they had to push their way through to reach the shore.

The earth was grey and sandy, leached by a million floods, but it was good to have dry land under foot. Sean spread out their wet clothing and equipment to dry while Matatu slipped away to make a circuit of the island. The water had just boiled in the billy when Matatu was back.

'Yes,' he nodded at Sean. 'He passed here yesterday early, while we were leaving the village, but he has settled down now. The peace of the river is upon him, and he feeds quietly. He left this island at sunrise this morning.'

'Which way did he go?' Sean asked, and Matatu pointed.

'There is another larger island close by.'

'Let's take a look.'

Sean poured a mug of tea for Riccardo and left him with Pumula, while he and Matatu skirted the northern shore, forcing their way through the dense growth until they reached the base of the tallest tree on the island and climbed into its top branches.

Sean settled into a high crotch of the tree, snapped off the few leafy twigs that obscured his view and gazed out on a scene of magnificent desolation.

He was sixty feet above the island and could see to the misty horizon. The Zambezi flowed past the island. Its waters were an opaque glassy green so wide that distance had reduced the great trees that lined the far bank to a dark band that separated green water from the high alps of cumulus cloud that soared anvil-headed into the blue African sky.

The Zambezi flowed so swiftly that its surface was ruffled by eddies and whirlpools and wayward counter currents. Floating carpets of swamp grass had been torn loose by the current and

174

sailed past, seeming as substantial as the island beneath him. Sean thought about crossing that forbidding river in the frail dugout. It would take more than one trip to get them all across and he abandoned the idea. There was only one way out, and that was back the way they had come.

He transferred all his attention to the chain of islands which stood like sentinels between the mother river and her spreading swamps. The nearest island in the chain was three hundred metres away; the channel between was clogged with reeds and water hyacinth and lily pads. The blooms of the water lilies were spots of electric blue against the green water and even in the tree-top Sean could catch wafts of their perfume.

Sean raised his binoculars and meticulously swept the channel and the nearest shore of the island, for even a great elephant could be swallowed up by the sweep and magnitude of this land- and waterscape.

Suddenly his nerves jumped as he saw movement weighty and ponderous in the reeds and the gleam of wet hide in the sunlight. His excitement was stillborn, followed by the pull of disappoint- ment in his guts, as he recognized the broad misshapen head of a hippopotamus emerging from the swamps.

In the lens of his binoculars he could see the pink-shot piggy eyes and the bristles in the disproportionately tiny ears. The hippo fluttered them like the wings of a bird, shaking off the droplets that sparkled like diamond chips, forming a halo above its huge head. It plodded through the mud, crossing from one lagoon to another, pausing only to loose an explosive jet of liquid dung that it splattered with a violent stirring motion of its stubby tail. The force of this discharge flattened the reeds behind the obese animal.

With relief, Sean watched it move on and submerge itself in the further lagoon. The rotten hull of the dugout would have offered no protection from those heavy curved tusks in the gape of huge jaws.

At last Sean glanced across at Matatu in the fork beside him, and the little Ndorobo shook his head.

'He has moved on, so must we.'

They scrambled down to the ground and went back to where they had left Riccardo. The voyage in the *mokorro* and a good night's sleep had invigorated him. He was on his feet, impatient and eager for the hunt, the way Sean had known him before.

'Anything?' he demanded.

'No.' Sean shook his head. 'But Matatu reckons we are close. Absolute silence from now on.'

While they loaded the dugout, Sean gulped a mug of the scalding tea and kicked sand over the fire.

They punted and pushed the canoe across the channel to the next island, and once again Sean climbed into a tree-top while Matatu scurried into the dense undergrowth to pick up the elephant's spoor again. He was back within fifteen minutes and Sean slid out of the tree to meet him.

'He has moved on,' Matatu whispered. 'But the wind is bad.' He looked grave, and took the ash bag from his loin-cloth and shook out a puff of powdery white ash to demonstrate. 'See how it turns and changes like the fancy of a Shangane whore.'

Sean nodded and before they crossed to the next island he stripped off his sleeveless bush shirt. Naked from the waist up he could feel instantly the slightest vagary of the breeze on the sensitive skin of his upper body.

On the next island they found where Tukutela had left the water to go ashore, and the mud he had smeared on the brush as he passed was still slightly damp. Matatu shivered with excitement like a good dog getting his first whiff of the bird.

They left the canoe and crept forward, feeling their way through the heavy bush, thankful for the breeze that clattered the palm fronds overhead to cover the small sounds of their footfalls in the dead leaves and dry twigs. They found where the old elephant had shaken down the nuts from one of the palms and stuffed them down his throat without chewing them with his last worn set of molars, but he had moved on again.

'Run?' Sean whispered, fearful that the bull might have sensed their presence, but Matatu reassured him with a quick shake of his head and pointed to the green twigs that the elephant had stripped of bark and left scattered along his tracks. The raw twigs had not completely dried out, but the spoor led them on a meandering beat across the island and then once more plunged into the channel on the far side. They sent Pumula back to bring the dugout around to where they waited and when he arrived piled Riccardo into it and pushed him across, wading waist-deep beside him, moving stealthily and silently until they reached the next island.

Here they found a pile of dung, spongy and soft with reeds

and hyacinth that the bull had eaten, and beside it the splash mark of his urine as though a garden hose had been played upon the earth. It was still so wet that Sean scooped a handful of the dirt and moulded it into a ball like a child's mud cake. The pile of dung had a dry crust but when Matatu thrust his foot into it, it was moist as porridge and he exclaimed with delight at the body heat still trapped within.

'Close, very close!' he whispered excitedly.

Instinctively Sean reached for the cartridges looped on his belt and he changed them for those in the double-barrelled rifle, careful to mute the click of the rifle's sidelock as he closed it. Riccardo recognized the gesture, he had seen it so often before and he grinned with excitement and clicked the Rigby's safety-catch on and off, on and off. They crept forward in single file, but disappointment dragged them down again as the spoor led them across the island, and then on the far side once more entered the papyrus beds.

They stood facing the wall of reeds, staring at the point where Tukutela had pushed down the stems as he went through. One of the flattened stems quivered and began slowly to rise into its original position. The elephant must have passed only minutes ahead of them. They stood in a frozen group, straining to listen beyond the susurration of the wind in the papyrus.

Then they heard it, the low rumble like summer thunder heard at a great distance, the sound that an elephant makes in his throat when he is content and at peace. It is a sound that carries much farther than its volume would suggest, but nevertheless Sean knew that the bull was not more than a hundred yards ahead of them and he laid his hand on Riccardo's arm and drew him gently up alongside him.

'We have to be careful of the wind,' he began in a whisper, and then they heard the swish and rush of water sucked up in the bull's trunk and squirted back over his own shoulders to cool himself, and they caught a brief glimpse of the black tip of his trunk as he lifted it high above the tops of the papyrus ahead of them.

Their excitement was so intense that Sean felt his throat closed and dry, and his whisper was rough.

'Back off!'

He made a cut-out hand signal which Matatu obeyed instantly, and they backed away, a stealthy pace at a time, Sean leading

177

Riccardo by the arm. As soon as they were into the undergrowth Riccardo demanded in a furious whisper, 'What the hell, we were so close.'

'Too close,' Sean told him grimly. 'Without any chance of a shot in the papyrus. If the wind had swung just a few degrees it would have been over before it began. We have to let him get across to the next island before we can close in.'

He led Riccardo back faster, and then stopped below the outspread branches of a tall strangler fig.

'Let's take a look,' he ordered. They propped their rifles at the base of the trunk, and Sean helped Riccardo to reach the first branch and then followed him as he climbed upwards from branch to branch.

Near the top of the fig they found a secure stance and Sean steadied Riccardo with a hand on his shoulder, and they stared down into the papyrus beds.

They saw him immediately. Tukutela's back rose above the reeds. It was wet and charcoal-black from the spray of his trunk, the spine was curved and prominent beneath the rough wrinkled hide. He was faced away from them, his huge ears flapping lazily, the edges torn and tattered, the thick veins twisted and knotted like a nest of serpents beneath the smoother skin behind their wide spread.

A row of four egrets rode upon his back, perched along his spine, brilliant white in the sunlight with yellow bills, sitting hunched up but attentive, bright-eyed sentinels who would warn the old bull at the first approach of danger.

While he was in the water, there was no way that they could come at him and he was well over three hundred yards away, far beyond effective rifle shot. So they watched him from the tree-top as he made his slow majestic way across the channel towards the next island.

When Tukutela reached the deepest stretch of open water he submerged completely; only his trunk rose above the surface, waving and coiling in the air like the head of a sea-serpent. He emerged on the far side of the channel with water streaming down his darkly mountainous sides.

Standing together on the branch of the fig, Riccardo and Sean were savouring this high point in both their hunting experience. Never again would there be another elephant like this. No other man would ever gaze upon such a beast. He was theirs. It seemed

178

that they had waited their lifetimes for this moment. The hunter's passion eclipsed all other emotion, at that moment rendering everything else in their lives effete and tasteless. Here was something primeval, sprung from the very wells of the soul and it affected them as great music might affect others.

The old bull lifted his head and turned aside for a moment, affording them just a brief glimpse of his dark-stained ivory, and they stirred unconsciously, affected by the sight of those long perfectly curved shafts as by the creation of a Michelangelo or the body of a beautiful woman. At that moment, there was nothing else in their universe. They were perfectly in tune, a bond of companionship and shared endeavour welded them.

'He's beautiful!' Riccardo whispered.

Sean did not reply, for there was nothing to add.

They watched the old bull reach the far island and heave his body from the water, climb the low bank and stand for a moment, tall and gaunt and shining wet in the sun, before he pushed his way into the undergrowth and it swallowed up even his bulk. The egrets were brushed from his back and rose up like snowy scraps of paper in a whirlwind. Sean tapped Riccardo on the shoulder and he shook himself as though awaking from a dream.

'We'll cross in the canoe,' Sean whispered, and sent Pumula to bring the craft around the islet.

They sat flat in the bottom of the *mokorro* so that their heads would not show above the tops of the reeds and they propelled themselves across the narrow neck of swamp by pulling on the stems of the papyrus. Soundlessly they slid through the reed-beds, and the light breeze held true and steady. Sean felt every light touch of it on his bare shoulders.

They reached the shore and Sean helped Riccardo out of the canoe, and they pulled it up onto the bank, careful not to make the faintest sound.

'Check your load,' Sean whispered, and Riccardo turned the bolt of the Rigby and drew it back just far enough to expose the shining brass cartridge in the chamber. Sean nodded approval and Riccardo closed the bolt silently. They went forward.

They were forced to move in single file, following the path that the bull had opened through the otherwise impenetrable growth. Matatu led them a few paces at a time, and then they all froze to listen.

Suddenly there was a loud crackling uproar in the bushes just ahead of them, and they saw the branches sway and toss and shake. Riccardo swung up the Rigby, but Sean restrained him, grabbing his forearm and pushing the muzzle of the rifle down.

They stood stonily, staring ahead, hearts pounding, and listened to the old bull feeding. Only thirty paces from them he was ripping down branches, swinging his ears back and forth to a leisurely rhythm, rumbling contentedly, and they could not catch even the barest glimpse of grey hide.

Sean still had hold of Riccardo's arm and now he drew him onwards. Step by step they edged through the green press of leaves and vines and drooping branches. Ten paces, and then Sean halted. He eased Riccardo forward, pushing him ahead, and Sean pointed over his shoulder.

For long seconds Riccardo could make out no details in the jumbled growth and confused shadows. Then the bull flapped his ears again, and Riccardo saw his eye through a hole in the vegetation. It was a small rheumy eye, with the slightly opaque blue cast of age, and the tears oozed down the wrinkled cheek below it, giving it a look of great wisdom and infinite sorrow.

That sorrow was contagious, it engulfed Riccardo in a black wave, it weighed down his soul, transforming his ardent predatory passion to a devastating sadness and mourning for this life that was about to end. He did not lift the rifle.

The elephant blinked its eye, the lashes surrounding it were thick and long, and the eye looked deep into Riccardo's own, seemed to pierce his very soul, seemed to mourn for him as he mourned for the old bull. Riccardo did not realize that the evil thing in his brain was once more bending and reshaping reality, he knew only that the sorrow in him was as insupportable as the black oblivion of death.

He felt Sean lightly tap him between the shoulder-blades, screening even that tiny movement from the bull. It was the urgent command to fire, but it was as though Riccardo had left his own body and hovered just above it, looking down upon himself, watching both the man and the beast with death in them and death all about them, and the tragedy engrossed him and robbed him of his will and power of movement.

Once again Sean tapped him. The elephant was fifteen paces away, standing perfectly still, a looming grey shadow in the undergrowth. Sean knew that Tukutela's sudden stillness was the

180

old bull's response to the premonition of danger. He would stand only for a few seconds longer, and then plunge away into the dense undergrowth.

He wanted to seize Riccardo's shoulder and shake him, he wanted to cry out, 'Shoot, man, shoot!' But he was helpless, the slightest movement, the faintest sound would trigger the old bull into flight.

Then it happened as Sean had known and feared it would. It seemed that Tukutela had been snatched away, had disappeared in a puff of grey smoke. It was impossible that such a huge beast could move so quickly and so silently in such dense bush, but he was gone.

Sean seized Riccardo's arm and pulled him along with him, dragging him after the vanished bull. Sean's face was contorted with rage and dark rage filled his chest and made it difficult for him to breathe. He wanted to vent that rage on Riccardo. He had risked his very life to put him in the position to take this animal, and the man had not even raised his rifle.

Sean ran forward, his grip upon Riccardo's arm was savage, and he dragged him through dense scrub and thorn, oblivious to his discomfort. He was certain that Tukutela would try to reach the next island in the chain, and he hoped for another chance at him as he crossed the open channel. He would force Riccardo to take even a long shot, hoping to cripple and slow the bull, so that Sean could follow and finish him off.

Behind him Matatu screamed something that was unintelligible, a warning, a cry for help perhaps, and Sean came up short, and stood listening. Something was happening that was totally unexpected, for which he was unprepared.

He heard the sudden crash and crackle in the undergrowth, and then the wild trumpeting squeal of an enraged elephant, but the sound was from behind him, not the direction in which Tukutela had vanished. For an instant Sean did not understand, and then the reality dawned upon him and he felt the goose bumps rise upon his naked back.

Tukutela had done something that no elephant he knew of had ever done before. The old bull had not fled, but instead had circled downwind of them to get their scent. Even as he stood now, Sean felt the wind touch his naked back, like the caress of a treacherous lover bearing his scent down to where the great bull was rushing through the dense bush, hunting for him.

'Matatu,' Sean yelled. 'Run! Run across the wind!' He shoved Riccardo roughly against the trunk of a towering teak tree.

'Get up there,' he snarled at him. The lower branches were easy to climb, and Sean left him and raced back to protect Matatu.

He charged headlong through the bush, jumping over fallen logs, his rifle held across his chest, and the forest rang to the elephant's wild and angry squeals.

He was closing swiftly, like an avalanche of grey rock. Tukutela rolled through the forest, splitting and dashing the smaller trees that stood in his way, seeking out the evil acrid smell of humanity, following it down so that once again he could wreak upon them the accumulated hatred of his long lifetime.

Suddenly Matatu darted out of the bush just a few paces ahead of Sean. He would stand to meet any odds with Sean beside him, and now instead of running across the wind as Pumula had done, his instinct had led him directly back to his master's side.

As he saw him, Sean changed direction in mid-stride, signalling urgently for Matatu to follow him. He ran a hundred swift paces out to one side, across the wind, trying to deny their scent to Tukutela.

He stopped and crouched with Matatu beside him. His tactic had been successful, Pumula also must have got out of Tukutela's wind. For the moment Tukutela had lost their scent. The forest was absolutely still, the silence so intense that Sean could hear his pulse beating in his own head.

He sensed that the old bull was very close to them, standing as still as they were, listening with ears spread wide, only that long trunk questing for the smell of them. There had never been an elephant like this, he thought, a bull who actively hunted his persecutors. How many times has he been hunted, Sean wondered, how many times has man inflicted hurt upon him that he attacks so fiercely at the first hint of human presence?

'Tukutela, the Angry One, now I know why they named you.'

Then there was a sound in the forest, one that Sean had not expected, a human voice, raised loudly, and it took him a moment to realize that it was Riccardo Monterro.

'Tukutela, we are brothers!' he was calling to the elephant. 'We are all that is left from another age. Our destiny is linked. I cannot kill you!'

The bull heard him and squealed again, a sound so loud and

pitched so high that it was like an auger driven into their eardrums. Tukutela charged the sound of the human voice, like a grey battle-tank. He crashed through the undergrowth, going straight for it, and within fifty yards the scent of man, loathsome and infuriating, filled his head once again and he followed it down to its source.

Riccardo Monterro had made no effort to climb the teak tree where Sean had left him, he simply leaned against the trunk and closed his eyes. The pain in his head came upon him as suddenly as the blow of an axe, and it blinded him, filling his vision with bursting stars of light, but through the pain he heard the old bull elephant squeal and the sound filled him with remorse and bitter despair.

He let the Rigby slip from his hands and fall into the leafy trash at his feet and he reached out his empty hands and staggered blindly to meet the elephant, wanting in some desperate way to placate and make recompense to the great beast, calling to it. 'I mean you no harm, we are brothers.' And ahead of him the bush crackled and burst open and Tukutela bore down on him like a collapsing cliff of granite.

Sean raced back to where he had left Riccardo, ducking under branches and bounding over obstacles in his path, and he heard the terrifying rush of the bull and the voice of the man just ahead of him.

'Here!' he screamed. 'Here, Tukutela! Come! Come this way!' trying to pull the elephant off Riccardo and onto himself, but he knew it was of no avail. Tukutela had fixed on his victim, and nothing would deter him. He would carry his charge through to the death.

The centre of Riccardo's vision cleared, and he looked through an aperture in his head that was surrounded by shooting white lights and catherine wheels of spinning fire. He saw Tukutela's vast grey head burst out of the green forest wall above him, and the long stained tusks came over him like the cross-ties of a roof about to fall.

In that moment, the elephant came to embody all the thousands of animals and birds that Riccardo had slaughtered in his lifetime as a hunter. He had a confused notion that the tusks and long trunk poised above him were the symbols of some semi-religious benediction that would absolve him and redeem the blood that he had spilled and all the life he had destroyed. He reached up both hands to them, joyfully and thankfully, and he remembered a phrase from his early religious instruction.

'Forgive me, Father, for I have sinned,' he cried.

Sean saw the bull's head rear out of the thicket ahead of him. It was facing almost directly away from him with ears cocked and rolled along the top edge. He heard Riccardo's voice though he could not understand the words, and he realized that Riccardo must be almost directly beneath the bull's out-thrust tusks and reaching trunk.

Sean plunged from his headlong run to a dead stop in a single pace and threw up the .577 Express rifle. It was the most difficult angle for the brain shot, with the elephant angled away from him, and the bulk of its shoulder covering the spinal column.

The target was no bigger than a ripe apple and there was no indication of where exactly it lay buried in the huge bony casket of the skull. He had to trust his experience and his instinct. For a moment, it seemed as he looked over the open Express sights of the rifle that he could see into the skull, where the brain seemed to glow in the bony depths like a firefly.

Without conscious effort his trigger finger tightened as the pip of the foresight covered that glowing spot. The bullet bored through the sponge of bone as though it were air, it cleaved the old bull's brain, and he felt nothing. His passage from full enraged life to death was a fleeting instant and his legs collapsed and folded under him. He dropped on his chest with an impact that jarred the earth and shook loose the dead leaves from the branches above him. A cloud of pale dust swirled around his massive carcass and his head dropped forward.

His right tusk drove into Riccardo Monterro's body, entering his belly a hand's-breadth below the sternum of his rib cage, and it passed through him at the level of his kidneys and came out through his spine just at the point where it merged with his pelvis.

The shaft of ivory which Riccardo had coveted and risked both fortune and life to obtain, now pinned him to the earth, skewered him as cleanly as a whaler's harpoon. He looked down at the tusk in surprise. There was no pain, no sensation in his lower body which was twisted up under the bull's coiled trunk, no pain even in his head.

For a moment his vision was clear and bright as though everything he looked at was lit by brilliant floodlights, and then it

184

began to fade and darkness closed in upon him. Just before the darkness engulfed him completely, he saw Sean Courtney's face floating before him, and heard his voice fading as though he were sinking away into an abyss.

'Capo, Capo,' it echoed in his ears, and Riccardo Monterro made a huge effort and said, 'She loves you. Look after my little girl.' And then the darkness swallowed him and he saw and heard nothing more, ever again.

* * *

Sean's first impulse was to free Riccardo Monterro's body. He tugged at the tusk which impaled him, but it was so thick that he could not get a fair grip upon it, and Riccardo's blood was oozing from the terrible wound. It coated Sean's hands so that he left sticky red prints upon the ivory as he strained at it.

Then he realized the futility of his efforts, and stepped back. The full weight of Tukutela's huge head and body was resting on those tusks. After piercing Riccardo's torso the ivory point had gone on to bury itself deep in the soft sandy earth. It would take half a day's work to free the body.

In death, the man and the beast were locked together, and suddenly Sean realized how appropriate that was. He would leave them like that.

First Matatu and then Pumula appeared from out of the forest and stood beside Sean staring in awe at the grim spectacle.

'Go!' Sean ordered. 'Wait for me at the canoe.'

'The ivory?' Pumula asked diffidently.

'Go!' Sean repeated, and at the tone of his voice, they crept quietly away.

Riccardo's eyes were wide open. Sean closed them with a gentle stroke of his thumb and then unknotted the cotton scarf from around Riccardo's neck and bound up his jaw to prevent it sagging into an expression of idiocy. Even in death, Riccardo Monterro was still a handsome man. Sean leaned against the elephant's head and studied Riccardo's face.

'It happened at just the right time, Capo. Before the disease turned you into a vegetable. While you still had most of your zest and vigour, and it was a fitting end for a man like you. I'm glad you didn't die between soiled sheets. I only pray that I will be as fortunate.'

185

Sean laid his hand upon one of the tusks and stroked it. It had the texture of precious jade beneath his fingertips.

'We'll leave them for you, Capo,' he said. 'These tusks will be your headstone. God knows, you paid for them in full.'

Sean straightened up and followed Riccardo's tracks back into the forest until he found the Rigby lying in the dead leaves. He brought it back and placed it in the crook of Riccardo's right arm.

'A warrior should be buried with his weapons,' he murmured, but there was still something missing. He could not go and leave Riccardo like this. He could not leave him lying exposed to an uncaring sky. He must cover him decently.

Then Sean remembered the legend of this elephant and how he disposed of the dead. He drew the heavy knife from the sheath on his belt and turned to the nearest green bush. He slashed off a leafy branch and covered Riccardo's face with it.

'Yes,' he murmured. 'That's right, that's proper.'

Working swiftly, he hacked down the branches and covered Riccardo's corpse and the head of the old bull under a mound of green leaves.

At last he stood back and picked up the .577. He tucked it under his arm and he was ready to leave.

'No regrets, Capo,' he said. 'For you, it was a good life right up to the very end. Go in peace, old friend.'

He turned away and went down to where the canoe was moored.

* * *

The reeds scraped softly along the hull of the canoe as Pumula poled it along. None of them spoke.

Sean sat amidships, hunched forward with his chin in the cup of one hand. He felt numbed, emptied of all emotion except sadness. It was like coming back from a raid in the days of the bush war with every man silent and sad.

He looked at his right hand in his lap and saw the little half moons of dark red under his fingernails. 'Capo's blood,' he thought, and trailed his hand over the side of the canoe, letting the warm swamp waters wash away the stain.

He let the hunt replay itself through his mind, as though it were a silent recording. He saw it all again very vividly from their

186

first sighting of the old bull to the moment that he rushed forward to find Riccardo Monterro impaled beneath the huge grey head.

Then for the first time, he heard sound. Riccardo's voice echoed in his head, faint and breathless, fading swiftly.

'She loves you,' he had said, and the rest trailed away unintelligibly. 'She loves you.' The meaningless words of a dying man, the wanderings of a diseased brain. Riccardo could have been harking back to any one of the hundreds of women who had filled his life.

Sean lifted his hand out of the water. It was clean, the blood washed away.

'She loves you.' He could have been trying to tell Sean of one particular woman.

Sean looked up from his wet hand and stared ahead. Her memory had been with him these last few days, always there in the recesses of his conscience yet coming to the fore at unexpected moments. Often while thinking of the great elephant, he had suddenly smiled at something she had said. This morning during the final stages of the hunt he had reached outboard from the canoe, and picked the bloom of a water lily. He had held it to his face and smelled the perfume, felt the silky touch of the petals on his lip and thought of Claudia Monterro.

Now he stared ahead and for the first time admitted to himself how much he looked forward to seeing her again. It seemed that she was all that could cancel out his grief for her father. He thought about the sound of her voice and the way she held her head when she was about to challenge him. He smiled at the bright specks of anger he could so readily kindle in her eyes, and the way she pursed her lips when she was trying to prevent herself laughing at one of his own digs.

He thought about the way she walked, and the way she felt when he had carried her in his arms, and he remembered the texture of her skin like the petals of the water lily when he touched her under pretext of helping or guiding her.

'We are absolutely and completely wrong for each other,' he smiled, and the melancholy of a few moments previously loosened its grip. 'If Capo was talking about her, then he had definitely gone completely round the bend.' But his anticipation was honed to a sharper edge.

He looked up at the sky. The sun had set. It would be dark in a short while. Even as he watched, Venus as the evening star appeared with a miraculous suddenness and twinkled low down in the west. One after another, the fixed stars followed her entrance, popping through the darkening canopy of night in strict order of their magnitude.

Sean looked up at the stars and he thought of Claudia, and he wondered why she evoked such contrary feelings in him. He compared her to some of the other women he had known, and realized how shallow and fleeting those experiences had been. Even his marriage had been inconsequential, a wild impulse based on simple-minded lust. It had been swiftly consummated, satiated and terminated, a disastrous mistake which he had never repeated. He could only vaguely remember what the woman who had been his wife looked like now.

He thought about Claudia and realized with a small shock that her image was so clear in his mind that he could almost count the individual lashes around those big honey-brown eyes, and the tiny laughter lines at the corners of her mouth. Suddenly he very much wanted to be with her again, and as he acknowledged that fact he began to worry.

'I must have been crazy to leave her alone,' he thought, and as he stared ahead into the dark swamps a multitude of horrid chances that might have befallen her began to plague him.

'Job is with her,' he tried to console himself. 'But I should have stayed to care for her and sent Job with Capo.' Even though he realized that had been impossible, still he fretted.

He felt the canoe check under him as Pumula rested on his pole, hinting at permission to stop for the night.

'I'll take her for a while,' Sean said. 'We'll keep going until we get back to the village.'

While Pumula and Matatu curled up in the bilges, Sean stood in the stern and swayed to the monotonous thrust and reach of the punt pole. He steered by the cross and the pointers, reckoning true south at the intersection of their extended centre lines.

The papyrus stems hissed softly against the hull in strict rhythm to his thrusts, and soon the work became so repetitive and automatic that he could let his mind wander, and all those wanderings seemed to return in the end to Claudia Monterro at the centre.

He thought about her bereavement, how although she had been expecting it, yet it would still devastate her. He composed the words he would use to tell her and then to comfort her. She knew of his own feelings for her father, and the companionship that they had shared in the hunting veld. She knew of their mutual regard for each other.

'I am the right person to help her through the first sorrow. I knew him so well. I will help her to remember all that was good about him.'

He should have dreaded bearing the sad tidings, but instead he found himself looking forward to taking the role of her comforter and protector.

'Perhaps we will be able to drop the postures of antagonism that we have both forced upon ourselves. Instead of accentuating our differences, perhaps we'll be able to explore what we have in common.' He found himself lengthening and quickening his stroke with the punt pole and he had to force himself to slow down.

'You won't last the night at that pace,' he thought, but his eagerness to be with her kept him going long after fatigue demanded a halt.

Hour after hour he kept it up, until Pumula woke of his own accord and came to spell him, but Sean slept fitfully and was back in the stern as the coming of day turned the eastern sky to a murky ruby and then to pale lemon, and the water fowl flighted overhead, their wings whistling softly as they stabbed at the dawn.

Two hours later, Sean sent Matatu up the punt pole and he had not reached the top before he pointed gleefully ahead. However, it was early afternoon before the prow of the canoe knifed through the last dense stand of papyrus and ran ashore on the sand below the burnt village.

Sean leapt onto dry land and strode through the ruins of the village, trying not to break into a run.

'Job should have kept a better watch,' he thought angrily. 'If we can arrive unseen . . .' he did not finish the thought. Just ahead was the thicket in which they had built Claudia's shelter, and Sean stopped abruptly.

It was too quiet. His sixth sense of danger warned him. Something was wrong. He went down fast and hard, falling flat and rolling quickly into cover with the .577 held in front of him.

He lay and listened. The silence was a physical weight. He wet his lips and imitated the clucking sound of a francolin, one of the Scouts' assembly calls that Job would recognize. There was no

189

reply. He went forward at a leopard crawl, and then stopped again. Something sparkled in the short grass just in front of his face. He picked it up and felt his stomach chill.

It was the empty brass case of a 7.62mm cartridge, and it was head-stamped in Cyrillic script, Soviet military issue for firing in the AK assault rifle. Sean held it to his nose, and smelt the burnt powder. It had been fired very recently. He glanced around him quickly and saw other empty shells lying in the grass, evidence of a fierce fire-fight.

He rolled to his feet and was running, jinking and twisting as he sprinted towards the thicket to throw off the aim of a hidden gunman.

As he reached the edge of the thicket, he dropped to earth again, flicking over as he hit the ground. Immediately, he saw the corpse, it lay face down under a low thorn bush only a few yards ahead. It was a black man. The body had been stripped of clothing and boots.

'Job!' The name ripped from his throat. He crawled forward, until he lay side by side with the body. A single bullet had ploughed out of the man's back, and the flies crawled over the wound. The blood had dried to a black crust and he smelt the whiff of corruption.

'Dead twenty-four hours,' he estimated, and rose to his knees. No further need for caution now. Gently he lifted the dead head. The corpse's neck was stiff with *rigor mortis* and he grunted with vast relief and let the head drop with a thud. The man was a stranger.

'Job!' he called. 'Claudia!' It was a despairing cry, and he ran forward to the lean-to in which he had left her. It was deserted.

'Job!' He looked around him wildly. 'Claudia!'

There was another naked black body lying at the edge of the clearing, and he ran to it. It was another stranger, a skinny little runt of a man with the top shot off his skull. He was also starting to stink, his belly blowing up like a shiny black balloon.

'Two of the bastards,' Sean said bitterly. 'Nice shooting, Job.'

Matatu had followed Sean and was checking the lean-to. He left it and began to work out in circles, darting back and forth like a gun dog quartering for a sitting grouse. Sean and Pumula stood and watched him, not joining his search so that they would not trample the sign.

Within minutes Matatu scurried back.

'They are the same *shifta* who followed us before. There are fifteen of them, they surrounded the hut and came in at a rush. Job shot these two with the 30/06 *banduki*.' He offered Sean the empty cartridge cases. 'There was much struggling, but they took them.'

'The memsahib?' Sean dreaded the reply.

'*Ndio*,' Matatu replied in Swahili. 'Yes, they took her also. She is still limping, but they led her away, one on each side. She was fighting them all the way. Job was hurt, and so was Dedan. Perhaps they were beaten, and I think their arms are bound. They walk unsteadily.' Matatu pointed towards the corpses. 'They stripped their dead of uniforms and boots and *banduki* and then went back.' He pointed along the isthmus.

'When?' Sean asked.

'Yesterday, early. Perhaps they rushed the camp at dawn.'

Sean nodded grimly, but inside he cried, 'Claudia, oh God, if they touch you, I'll rip their guts out.'

'Hot pursuit,' he said aloud. 'Let's go!'

Pumula ran back to grab the equipment and water-bottles from the canoe, and Sean was still shrugging into the shoulder-straps of his pack when he started to run. The near exhaustion of the long night of poling the canoe faded away. He felt strong and angry and indefatigable.

Within the first mile, they settled into the pursuit pace of a Scout raiding party. The spoor was still cold and Sean dispensed with any precautions against ambush. He relied entirely on Matatu to pick up any sign of a booby trap or anti-personnel mine that might have been laid on the tracks to hinder pursuit, but apart from that they went in single file at a speed not much below that of an Olympic marathon.

Claudia's image seemed to dance ahead of Sean and winged his feet.

Fifteen of them, Matatu had said, and they would be tempted by Claudia's sweet white body. There were no signs yet that they had stopped to have sport with her. He accepted without reservation Matatu's interpretation that they had crept up on the camp in the dawn, and taken it at a rush, willing to accept casualties without inflicting them. It seemed that they had wanted prisoners rather than kills. Other than a few blows with a rifle butt, it looked as though both Dedan and Job had come through it unscathed, but it was Claudia who had his full concern.

They were forcing her to march on her injured leg. That would only aggravate the knee, and perhaps cause permanent damage. If she slowed them down too much, they would start to become impatient and threatening. It all depended on just how much they needed a white prisoner as a hostage, probably as a bargaining chip with western governments. It depended on who they were, Frelimo or Renamo or free-lance bandits, it depended on how much control there was over them, on who commanded them, and how strong was his authority, but any way he considered it, Sean knew that Claudia was in terrible danger.

Did they realize that there was a pursuit? They must have read the sign going into the village and known that three men – no, four with Capo – were missing from the original party. The answer was, yes. They probably anticipated a pursuit by this group. That would make them nervous and excitable.

Claudia would be no great advocate for her own safety. He could just imagine her arguing with them, demanding her human and legal rights, refusing to follow their orders. Despite his concern, he grinned without humour, as he thought about it. They probably believed they had caught a pussy-cat, but they would soon realize that they had instead a full-grown female tiger on their hands.

His grin faded. He was certain she would deal with them in precisely the fashion best designed to antagonize them and jeopardize her chances of survival. If the leader of the group was a weak man, she would push him to the point where he had to demonstrate his authority to his own men. African society was patriarchal and he would resent a woman who refused to bow to his will. If they were the same group that had wiped out the village they had amply demonstrated their brutality.

'Just for once, ducky, button those lovely lips of yours,' he pleaded with her silently.

Ahead of him, Matatu checked his run and made a sweeping gesture, and Sean pulled up.

'Here they rested.' Matatu pointed to where the group had sat in the shade of a grove of young mopane.

There were the crushed butts of black cigarettes in the dust, and Matatu pointed to the raw white slashes on the mopane from which branches had been chopped. The smaller twigs had been trimmed from them and discarded. The leaves on these were already wilted, confirming Matatu's estimate of time, yesterday morning.

The cutting of branches puzzled Sean for a moment and then Matatu explained, 'They have built a *mushela* for the mem.' And Sean nodded with relief. Claudia on her injured leg had been holding up the march, but rather than ridding themselves of her through the simple expedient of a bullet in the back of the head, they had built a litter of mopane poles on which to carry her. That was a welcome development, and it changed Sean's estimate of Claudia's chance of survival. They had placed a higher value on her than Sean had dreaded they might.

However, the most crucial period would have come yesterday evening when they decided to camp for the night. Her captors would have had a full day to study her, to ogle her body and puff up their imagination and their courage. Sean found he could not bear to face the possibility of what might have happened to her if the leader had lost control of his men.

'Come on, Matatu,' he growled. 'You are wasting time.' If it had happened at all, it would have happened last night. He was already too late but still every second of delay galled him.

The spoor led them back up the isthmus retracing their own route across the dry flood plains heading towards the south. The trail was broad and easy to follow, fifteen men and their captives making no attempt at anti-tracking. Matatu read the spoor and reported that they were forcing Dedan and Job to carry the litter with Claudia on it, and Sean was happy that the two of them were able to do so. Whatever injuries they had sustained in the attack must have been superficial, and he could be certain that Job would employ every ruse to slow down the march, and allow them to catch up.

Even as he thought it, Matatu exclaimed and pointed to the marks in the soft earth where Job had dropped his end of the litter and sprawled theatrically on his hands and knees, only crawling up after he had been surrounded and hectored by his captors.

'Good man,' Sean grunted without checking his stride. 'But don't push them too far.' It was a delicate game Job was playing.

At pursuit speed they were overhauling the clumsy and slow-moving group so rapidly that Sean was beginning to hope they might catch up with them before nightfall.

'That's going to be interesting,' he decided. 'Three of us with only the .577 against fifteen thugs armed with AKs.'

So far they had found no booby traps set for them. It was usually terr tactics to mine their own spoor and Sean pondered their failure to do so. These could be untrained bandits, or they might lack the light plastic anti-personnel mines, or they could be unaware of the pursuit or, worst thought, they could be planning some surprises later.

'We'll deal with that one also when we come to it.'

Matatu pulled up again. 'They cooked here last night.' He pointed to the remains of a camp-fire, and there were the marks where they had sat while they rested and ate. A few black safari ants were scurrying about the site foraging for the scraps of food that they had spilled and there were more cigarette butts.

'Search,' Sean ordered. 'Job will have tried to get a message to us.' While Matatu and Pumula went over the area carefully but quickly, Sean glanced at his watch: 1600 hours, they had been going just over three hours, they still had plenty of daylight and a good chance to catch them before dark.

'Here is where they put the mem's litter.' Matatu pointed out the marks in the earth. 'Here she stood.'

Sean studied her footprints, smaller, neater and narrower than the boot prints of her captors. When she walked she had favoured her leg, dragging the toe.

'Did you find anything?' he demanded roughly. 'Did Job leave a message?'

'Nothing.' Matatu shook his head.

'All right. We'll drink now,' he ordered, and handed out salt tablets from his pack. He didn't have to caution them to self-control. Three swallows each from the bottles, and then they screwed the stoppers tightly closed. They had paused for less than five minutes.

'Let's go,' said Sean.

An hour later, they found where the raiders had slept that night. The fact that they had moved on after eating and not slept beside their cooking-fire told Sean that they were trained troops.

'Search again,' Sean ordered. Any information that Job could have left for them would be valuable.

'Nothing,' Matatu reported back a few minutes later, and Sean felt a prick of disappointment.

'All right. Keep going,' he ordered, and was about to turn

194

away when something made him pause and he glanced around the camp-site.

'Where did the memsahib sleep?' he demanded.

'There.' Matatu pointed. Somebody, probably Job, had cut an armful of leaves and grass for her mattress. Her body had flattened the pile. Sean squatted beside it, and carefully sifted through it, searching for any clues.

There was nothing. He lifted away the last few leaves and was beginning to rise to his feet. He was disappointed, the feeling that she had left something for him had been very powerful.

'So much for ESP,' he grunted, and then noticed the button, half buried in the dust under the mattress of straw.

He picked it out and stood up. It was a brass button from the waistband of her denim jeans, engraved 'Ralph Hutton'.

'Designer jeans, that's my ducky.' He slipped it into his pocket. 'But it doesn't tell me anything,' he broke off, 'unless . . .' He knelt again and gently brushed aside the dust under where the button had lain. He was right, she had used the button as a marker and beneath it had buried a scrap of cardboard, the flap torn from the lid of a packet of cheap Portuguese cigarillos. It was not more than two inches long and half as wide, very little space for the message she had written with a charcoal stick scavenged from the fire.

'Fifteen Renamo.' That was invaluable intelligence, confirming Matatu's estimate of numbers, and now at least he knew who they were dealing with, Renamo.

'Cave.' The next word puzzled him. 'Cave?' Then suddenly he realized it was the old public schoolboy warning from the Latin 'caveat' – beware.

He smiled despite himself. 'Where did she ever learn a limey expression like that?' Then he remembered she was a lawyer and read on.

'Cave. They expect you.' She and Job would have overheard them discussing the pursuit. That information was just as valuable.

'All OK.' And she had signed it, 'C.'

He stared at the scrap of cardboard, holding it in the palm of his hand as though it were a relic of the true cross.

'You little beauty, you,' he whispered. 'You've got to be the brightest, gutsiest . . .' He shook his head in wonder, a choking sensation in his throat. For the very first time, he admitted his longing for her and then suppressed it firmly as he came to his feet. There was no time nor opportunity for such self-indulgence now.

'Renamo,' he told Matatu and Pumula. 'You were right, there are fifteen of them. They know we are following. We can expect an ambush.'

They both looked grave, and Sean glanced at his wristwatch. 'We can catch them before dark.'

Within an hour they came upon the first ambush that the Renamo had set for them. Four men had lain beside the trail at the point where the causeway across the flood plains joined the main forest on the higher ground. The ambush had been cunningly sited on the far edge of a narrow vlei, across open ground with a good field of fire. It had been abandoned only a short time before they came up to it.

'They are putting down a rolling rearguard.' Sean felt queasy at the risk he had taken with such a reckless pursuit.

In the dust were the distinctive double marks left by the bipod of an RPD light machine-gun, one of the simplest and yet the most deadly effective of all guerrilla weapons. If he had led his men into the vlei while that gun was still in position, it would have all been over in a few hellish seconds. He had been pushing too hard, not taking even elementary precautions. His concern for Claudia had unbalanced his judgement.

Renamo had pulled out just before they reached the vlei, they had judged the time of his arrival with disconcerting accuracy, the margin had been far too narrow. The crew of the RPD would have moved back, and resited the ambush farther along the trail in order not to fall too far behind their main party.

'Flankers out,' Sean ordered reluctantly. 'Ambush precautions.' It would slow them to half their previous speed. Now it would be impossible to catch up with Renamo before nightfall.

Three men were too few. It left only Matatu on the spoor, and Sean and Pumula on the flanks. They had a single weapon between them, the big-bore, slow-firing double. They were going in against trained bush fighters armed with automatic weapons, and they were expected.

'Just another name for suicide,' Sean told himself, but despite the odds he had to restrain himself from quickening the pace.

In the centre, Matatu whistled. At that moment, he was out of Sean's line of sight. Even though it was not a warning signal,

Sean fell flat and carefully checked his front and both flanks before he stood up again and went to join him.

Matatu was squatting beside the trail with his loin-cloth drawn up modestly between his legs, but his expression was worried. He stabbed a finger at the spoor without speaking, and Sean saw immediately what was troubling him.

'Where the hell did they come from?' It was a protest more than a question. The odds against them had just been multiplied many times, and for the first time. Sean felt the lead weight of despair on his shoulders.

The original band of Renamo had been reinforced by an even larger group; at a glance it looked like a full company of infantry.

'How many?' he demanded of Matatu, and this time, even he could not give an exact figure. The tracks were overlapped and confused.

Matatu took a little snuff, using the ritual to disguise his uncertainty. He sneezed, and his eyes ran with tears which he wiped away with his thumbs. Then he held up the spread fingers of both hands and shut them four times.

'Forty?'

Matatu grimaced apologetically and showed another set of fingers.

'Between forty and fifty.' Sean unscrewed his water-bottle and took a mouthful. The water was hot as soup, but he gargled with it before he swallowed.

'I will count them later,' Matatu promised, 'when I have learned them all, but now . . .' He spat on the trampled earth, mortified by his failure.

'How far behind are we?' Sean demanded, and Matatu used his forefinger like the hour hand of a clock to indicate a segment of the sky.

'Three hours,' Sean translated. 'We'll never catch them before nightfall.'

When it was dark Sean said, 'We'll eat while we wait for the moon.' But when it rose, it was only a sliver of silver, soon blotted out by cloud, and there was not enough light to follow even that broad clear spoor. Sean thought of keeping going blindly through the night, trying to get ahead of them and then shadowing them hoping for some fortuitous opportunity to reach Claudia and Job and release them.

'That's dreaming in Technicolor,' he told himself.

They had been going hard for days now and were all of them tottering on the edge of exhaustion. Blundering around in the dark, they would either run on top of the Renamo night guards or would miss them completely.

'We'll sleep now.' He was forced to give up at last. As Renamo knew they were being followed they might send a detachment back to try and surprise them.

Sean went into laager for the night well off the trail, in a thicket of thorn that would snag an attacker attempting to sneak up on them. They all desperately needed rest and he would rely on the thorn rather than posting sentries. The night was icy cold and they lay in a huddle sharing each other's body warmth. Sean was already sliding into the black hole of exhaustion when Matatu's whisper called him back.

'There is one of them,' Matatu began, then broke off and Sean opened his eyes with resignation.

'Tell me,' he invited drowsily.

'There is one of these Renamo I have seen before.'

'You know one of them?' Sean came fully awake.

'I think so, but it was long ago, and I cannot remember where.'

Sean was silent as he considered that simple statement, and what it really entailed. Sean would have had difficulty remembering the faces of every person he had met in, say, the last ten years. Here was Matatu bemoaning the fact that he could not instantly recognize a single set of footprints, which he had last seen years previously out of a jumble of other tracks.

Though he had seen Matatu perform similar feats so many times before, yet even he felt a creep of doubt at Matatu's claim.

'Go to sleep, you silly little bugger.' He smiled in the darkness, and took him by the scruff of the neck and shook the little man's woolly head with rough affection. 'Perhaps you'll dream his name in your sleep.'

Sean dreamed of Claudia. She was running naked through a dark forest. The trees were black and leafless with crooked limbs. A pack of wolves pursued her. They also were black as night but with glistening white fangs and red lolling tongues. Claudia called his name as she ran and her skin was pale and luminous as the moon. He tried to go to her but his legs dragged as though he waded through a pool of treacle. He tried to call her name, but his tongue was lead in his mouth and no sound came from his throat.

He awoke with a hand roughly shaking his shoulder, and he tried to shout again but it came out in a garbled slur.

'Wake up!' Matatu shook him. 'You were crying and moaning. Renamo will hear you!'

He sat up quickly. The cold seemed to have frozen the muscles in his legs, and the terror of the dream was still upon him. It took him seconds to focus on reality and remember where he was.

'You're getting past it, boyo.' He was humiliated. A Scout slept soundlessly and awoke to immediate awareness or had his throat cut while he was grunting and snoring.

'It will be light enough soon,' Matatu whispered. Already the dawn chorus of bird calls tinkled and chirruped through the forest and he could make out the lattice-work of thorn branches against the sky.

'Let's go.' Sean stood up.

While the sun was still low and the dew was on the grass, they came up to the dry riverbed in which Renamo had bivouacked for the night. The band had moved on again at first light but could not be far ahead.

Matatu picked Claudia's footprints out of the ruck in the soft sand of the riverbed. 'She moves with less pain,' he told Sean. 'The leg is healing but Job and Dedan are still carrying her. Here she climbed into the litter.'

Matatu left the distinctive feminine prints and hovered over another set of larger male tracks that to Sean were indistinguishable from all the others, except that whoever had made them wore boots with a double herring-bone pattern on the sole.

'I know him,' Matatu whispered. 'I know the way this one walks . . .' He shook his head in frustration and turned away.

They went forward with extreme caution now. The trail led them directly towards the higher ground along the escarpment of the valley, and soon they entered the foothills. Whoever commanded the Renamo column knew exactly where he was headed.

Sean was expecting at any moment to make contact with the rearguard of the column. He dreaded the thought that the first warning they might receive could be the wicked crackle of an RPD light machine-gun, firing at a cyclic rate of six hundred rounds a minute.

Here in the hills every boulder, every fold of ground was a

possible enemy redoubt and had to be minutely inspected before they could move on. Sean fretted with impatience but forced himself to gear his advance to the difficult terrain.

They turned the corner of another low hill and through a frieze of graceful msasa trees an open vista stretched ahead to where the massif of the central escarpment rose above its foothills.

'There it is,' Sean murmured. 'That's where they'll be laying for us.'

The spoor was pointed directly at a pass through the escarpment. The entrance was guarded by cliffs of red stone, and the gut of the pass was almost devoid of trees or cover and yet the sides were heavily bushed. It was a natural trap, a perfect killing ground.

Matatu whistled in the centre, and Sean doubled over, keeping off the crest as he ran down to join him. From the centre, there was an unimpeded view up the gut of the valley and Sean saw movement against the scree and yellow grass. He lifted the binoculars to his eyes and the line of dark moving specks resolved through the lens into a column of men.

They were toiling up the incline in single file. Most of them wore tiger-striped camouflage and jungle hats, although a few were dressed in a motley of denim and khaki. The front of the column was already into the bush at the head of the valley at least three miles distant, but through his binoculars, Sean counted twelve men.

The litter was in the centre, four of them were carrying it. Two men on the front poles and two on the back. Sean tried to pick out Claudia's form but before he could refocus his binoculars, the litter and the bearers had reached the tree line and disappeared.

Sean lowered his binoculars and polished the lens with his handkerchief. Pumula had come in from the other flank, and now he and Matatu crouched in the jumble of rock and coarse bush and studied the lie of the land in gloomy silence. Again Sean raised the glasses and studied the steep bushy sides. It was a perfect site for an ambush, they could catch Sean's party in enfilade and crossfire as they tried to climb the valley.

'How many did you see?' Sean asked without lowering his binoculars. 'Have they all gone into the trees at the head of the valley?'

'I saw only a few,' Pumula murmured.

'*Masesh*,' Matatu spat unhappily. He was referring to the lees of the millet beer that after fermentation the Batonka fishermen use as a ground bait to lure the shoals of bream into Lake Kariba's shallows.

He spat again. 'That valley is the mouth of the crocodile. They want us to put our heads into it.'

Sean studied the sides of the valley, taking his time, every few minutes lowering the binoculars to rest his eyes and then lifting them again. He began at the top of the slope and swept gradually downwards. When he reached the bottom, he began at the top again, going over the same ground time and again. He tried not to think of that sighting of the litter, or the tiny figure he thought he had seen upon it. He concentrated entirely on his search and, ten minutes later, he was rewarded.

It was a single flash of sunlight reflected from the lens of a wristwatch or the lens of a pair of field-glasses.

'There they are.' He lowered his own glasses. 'Yes, Matatu, you are right. They have put out the bait, now they are waiting for us.'

He sat down behind the boulder and tried to think it through logically, but Claudia's memory kept intruding and deflecting his reasoning. There was only one certain conclusion, and that was that it was hopeless to continue the pursuit. He looked up. Matatu and Pumula were watching him with expressions of blind faith. In almost twenty years, they had never seen him at a loss. They waited patiently for him to perform the miracle yet again.

Sean found it infuriating. He jumped up and went back down the hill to think without those trusting eyes upon him. He found a spot that was well concealed and yet had a good all-round view so that nobody could sneak up on him and he settled down with the .577 across his lap to consider his options.

The first one he crossed from his mental list was an attack on the Renamo column. Even leaving aside the puny forces he had available, he had to consider the hostages that Renamo had in their hands. Even with a company of fully armed Scouts, he would still have been unable to attack.

'So what can I hope to achieve by following them?' he asked himself. 'Apart from gratifying this new and mawkish desire to be as close as possible to Claudia Monterro.'

Probably the best chance of release of the captives from Renamo clutches was not his own intervention but diplomatic negotiations through Renamo's reputed allies, the South African government in Pretoria. However, even the South Africans would not be able to achieve anything if they were unaware that an American citizen had been captured by Renamo.

'Okay.' Sean made his first firm decision. 'I have to get a message back to the American embassy in Harare.' Immediately he realized that this took care of his other major worry. Matatu and Pumula were his responsibility. Up to now he had been leading them into a suicidal situation. They had been more and more on his conscience the closer they drew to the Renamo column. This was the excuse he had been looking for.

'I'll send both of them back to Chiwewe with a message for Reema.' He opened the flap of his back-pack and found his small leather-covered notepad. He began to compose the message.

Reema had all Riccardo's and Claudia's personal details on the safari files, everything from their physical descriptions to their passport numbers. Riccardo was an important and influential man. Sean would not tell her that he was dead, but implied in his message that both father and daughter were captives of Renamo. The US embassy could be relied on to react swiftly and he would be in contact with Pretoria within hours of receiving the news.

Of course, since the imposition of US sanctions on that country the relations between Washington and Pretoria were at a historically low ebb, and the influence of the US in southern Africa was no longer the overriding factor that it had once been. Nonetheless, the South Africans could be relied on to intercede with Renamo on the simplest humanitarian grounds.

'Okay, that takes care of Matatu and Pumula.' Sean signed the message, tore the pages out of his notepad and folded them. Then as an afterthought he filled another page of instructions for Reema covering the $500,000 that Riccardo's estate owed them. She was to pass these on to Sean's lawyer.

Then, at last, he had to make his own decision. He could run back across the border, carrying the message himself, and within two or three days he could be drinking Castle lager in the Meikles Hotel and working out how to spend Capo's half-million bucks. That was the sensible and logical thing to do but he had already dismissed the idea before he considered it.

'So I'll follow the column and wait for an opportunity.' He grinned at the absurdity of his decision. 'What opportunity?' he wondered at himself. 'A chance to shoot my way into an encampment of fifty-plus terrs with the old .577, free the three prisoners, and with one mighty bound whip them a hundred miles to the border, carrying Claudia with her injured leg on my back!'

He stood up and resettled his pack between his shoulders, and crept back up to the slope where Matatu and Pumula were lying watching the escarpment. He dropped down beside Matatu.

'Anything?' he asked, and Matatu shook his head. They were silent for many minutes while Sean plucked up his courage to tell the little man he was sending him back.

While he did so, he scowled through the binoculars at the spot up the long valley where he knew Renamo had set their ambush. Matatu seemed to sense that something unpleasant was brewing. He kept glancing at Sean with a troubled expression, but when Sean finally turned to him, he burst into a sunny ingratiating grin and wriggled his entire body in his eagerness to please and to stave off whatever was coming.

'I remember,' he said eagerly. 'I remember who he is.'

Side-tracked for the moment, Sean frowned at him in puzzlement. 'Who? Who are you talking about?'

'The leader of the Renamo,' Matatu told him happily. 'I told you yesterday I knew his footprints. Now I remember who he is.'

'Who is he then?' Sean asked suspiciously, ready to reject the information.

'Do you remember when we jumped from the *indeki* to attack the training camp at the fork of the rivers?' Matatu twinkled at him and Sean nodded guardedly. 'Do you remember how we killed them in the riverbed?' Matatu chuckled with the delightful memory of it. 'Do you remember the one we caught while he was trying to burn the books. The one who refused to march, and you blew his ear in?' Now he giggled at that fine joke. 'The blood came out of his earhole and he squeaked like a virgin.'

'Comrade China?'

'China.' Matatu had a little difficulty with the pronunciation. 'Yes, that is the one.'

'No!' Sean shook his head. 'It isn't China. That's not possible!'

Now, Matatu had to cover his mouth to muffle his delighted squeals of laughter. He loved it when he was able to confound and astound his master. There was no better joke than that.

'China!' He spluttered with mirth and stuck his forefinger in his own ear. 'Pow!' he said, and it was so funny he almost choked. 'Comrade China.'

Sean stared at him unseeingly, while he adjusted his mind to this extraordinary intelligence. All his instincts were to reject it out of hand, but Matatu didn't make mistakes of that nature.

'Comrade China!' Sean breathed softly. 'That changes the odds a little.'

He cast his mind back to that distant day. The man had made such an impression upon him that even from the crowded and confused events of that bloody little war, he retrieved a clear image of Comrade China. He remembered his fine Nilotic head and the dark intelligent eyes, but his physical features were hazy compared to Sean's memory of the sense of confidence and purpose that the man exuded. He had been a dangerous man then, and Sean expected that now he would be even more experienced and formidable.

Sean shook his head. At one time his nickname in the Scouts had been 'Lucky Courtney'; it looked as though he had used up his ration of that commodity. He couldn't have chosen anybody he would have wanted less to command the column of Renamo than Comrade China.

Matatu had almost exhausted his mirth, and was now battling with the hiccoughs that followed, clutching at his naked belly and throat to hold them down, while occasional spasms of laughter interspersed the loud hiccoughs.

'I'm sending you back to Chiwewe.' Sean told him harshly, and the laughter and hiccoughs were instantly extinguished. Matatu stared at him in disbelief and utter despair. Sean could not face those eyes, and their tragic accusation.

He turned to Pumula and brusquely called him across to where he lay. 'This note is for the chef at camp. Tell him to radio the message to Miss Reema in Harare. Matatu will guide you back. Don't stop to pick your nose on the way, do you understand me?'

'*Mambo.*' Pumula was an old Scout. He would obey without argument or question.

'All right, go,' Sean ordered. 'Go now.' And Pumula held out his right hand. They shook hands the African way, gripping palms and then thumbs and then palms again. Pumula crawled down off the ridge, and once he was clear, jumped to his feet and trotted away. He did not look back.

At last Sean forced himself to look at Matatu. He crouched

204

low to the ground, trying to make his small frame smaller still to escape Sean's notice.

'Go!' Sean ordered brusquely. 'Show Pumula the way back to Chiwewe.'

Matatu hung his head and shivered like a whipped puppy.

'Get the hell out of here!' Sean growled at him. 'Before I kick your black butt!'

Matatu lifted his head and his eyes were tragic, his expression abject. Sean wanted to pick him up and hug him.

'Get out of here, you stupid little bugger!' Sean made a face of terrifying ferocity, and Matatu crept away a few paces and then paused and looked back imploringly.

'Go!' Sean lifted his right hand threateningly. At last the little man accepted the inevitable and slunk away down the slope. Just before he disappeared into the coarse scrub at the foot of the slope, he paused and looked back one more time, seeking just the faintest sign of encouragement or weakness. He was the epitome of dejection.

Deliberately, Sean turned his back on him and raised the binoculars to study the terrain ahead, but after a few seconds the image blurred and he blinked his eyes to clear them and despite himself, glanced quickly over his shoulder. Matatu had vanished. It was a strange feeling not to have him there. After a few minutes, Sean lifted the binoculars again and resumed his study of the escarpment line, pushing Matatu out of his mind.

On either side of the mouth of the long valley, the red rock cliffs stretched away unbroken for as far as Sean could see. They were not particularly high; at the lowest points they were only a few hundred feet, but they were vertical and some stretches were even overhanging where softer strata of rock had been eroded from under the harder superimposed upper layers, and formed a shallow horizontal cave.

The entrance of the valley was as inviting as the mouth of a carnivorous plant to an insect, and the cliffs were forbidding and inaccessible, but Sean concentrated upon them. He swept them with the binoculars, in both directions as far as he could see. Of course, it might be necessary to move some miles along the cliff to find a route that was scalable, but that would burn up precious time. He kept swinging the binoculars back to the same point.

A quarter of a mile to the right-hand side of the nearest rock portal of the valley, there was a route that looked as though it might just go, but it wouldn't be easy without a companion and lacking even basic rock-climbing equipment. He would be burdened by the rifle and his pack, and he would have to make the attempt in the dark. To go out on that exposed cliff in daylight would be to invite a little AK target practice.

Through the binocular lens, he picked out a rocky buttress which was faulted like a fire escape. It seemed to offer a way round the overhanging section of cliff, and above that it led to a narrow horizontal ledge running several hundred feet in either direction. From that ledge there appeared to be two possible routes to the top of the cliff, one was a narrow crack or chimney and the other an open face down which grew the exposed serpentine roots of a huge ficus tree that stood tall and massive on the skyline. The roots crawled and twined against the sheer red rock, like a nest of mating pythons, that formed a ladder to the top of the cliff.

Sean glanced at his wristwatch. He had three hours to rest before it was dark enough to make the attempt and suddenly, he felt exhausted. He realized that it was not only the physical exertion of the chase, but also the emotional drain of having glimpsed Claudia and Job in the Renamo column, and the parting with Matatu.

He anti-tracked meticulously back off the ridge and searched for a secure place to hole-up during what was left of daylight. When he found a hidy-hole amongst rock and scrub with a safe line of retreat, he loosened his bootlaces to rest his feet, but kept the rifle in his lap and slumped down over it. He munched a maize cake and protein bar from his emergency pack and drank a few careful mouthfuls from his water-bottle.

He knew he would wake when the sun touched the horizon. He closed his eyes and fell almost instantly asleep.

* * *

On the journey back to Chiwewe camp, Matatu led Pumula at a steady trot. They kept going through the night and the next afternoon stopped to refill their water-bottles in the marsh where they had spotted Tukutela from the air.

Pumula wanted to rest. Matatu did not bother to argue with him. He faced towards the west and went away at that swaying trot on his skinny knob-kneed legs and Pumula was forced to follow. They crossed the border between Mozambique and Zimbabwe during the dark hours c ' the night, and ran into the safari camp in the middle of the following afternoon.

The consternation caused by their arrival was tremendous. In his agitation, the chef even forgot to don his tall cap and snowy apron before rushing out of his hut to greet them and demand the news of the *mambo*.

Matatu left Pumula to hand over Sean's written message and answer the barrage of questions. He went to his own hut and curled up like a puppy on his bed, an ancient iron frame with a lumpy coir mattress, a gift from Sean and his most treasured possession. He slept through all the subsequent excitement, even chef bellowing into the microphone of the VHF radio, attempting by volume alone to reach Reema in Harare almost three hundred miles distant.

When Matatu awoke, he had slept five hours. The camp was dark and silent. He repacked the small leather pouch that was his only luggage, retrieved his remaining store of precious snuff from under his mattress and refilled the horn that hung around his neck.

He crept quietly from the sleeping camp. When he was well clear, he straightened up and faced towards the east.

'Silly little bugger,' he said happily, and began to run, going back to his rightful place beside the man he loved more than a father.

* * *

Sean woke with the first chill of evening in the air. Ahead the cliffs of the escarpment were fading into the smoky purple dusk. Sean stretched and looked around for Matatu. When he remembered he was gone, it gave him a physical jolt in the pit of his stomach. He tied his bootlaces and drank again. When he stoppered the water-bottle, he held it to his ear and shook it. Still half full.

He opened the breech of the .577, slipped the cartridges out of the twin chambers and exchanged them for two others from the loops on his bush-jacket. He squeezed an inch of black camouflage cream from the crumpled tube and rubbed it over his face and the backs of his hands. That completed his preparation and he stood up and moved quietly up the slope.

He spent the last twenty minutes of daylight glassing the entrance to the valley and the top of the cliffs through his binoculars. As far as he could see, nothing had changed. Then he studied and memorized the route up the cliff face.

As the night spread its cloak over the escarpment, he slipped quietly over the ridge and crept up towards the base of the cliff. The bush grew dense and tangled there and it took him much longer than he had anticipated to reach the rocky wall.

It was almost completely dark by then, but he was able to identify the starting point of the climb by a small bush growing in a crack of the cliff which he had marked through the binoculars.

Sean had never used a carrying sling on his rifle. It could be mortally dangerous in thick bush when the sling caught on a branch just as the buffalo or wounded elephant began its charge. He lashed the short-barrelled weapon under the flap of his back-pack with his sleeping-bag. The butt stuck out on one side of his shoulders and the muzzles on the other, making an awkward unbalanced load. He went to the cliff face and laid his hands on it, getting the feel of it. The stone was still hot from the sun and the texture was smooth, almost soapy under his fingers.

Before the war, rock-climbing had been one of his passions. He loved the risk, the terror of the open face and drop sucking at his heels. He had climbed in South America and Europe, as well as on the Drakensberg and Mount Kenya. He had the requisite sense of balance and the strength in his fingers and arms. He could have been one of the top international climbers but for the intervention of the bush war. However, he had never attempted a climb like this before.

His boots were soft velskoen without reinforced toes. He had no ropes, no anchorman, no pitons nor karabiner, and he would be opening this route in darkness, barely able to see the next hold above, following a pitch which he had studied from a mile distant, going blind on red sandstone, the most treacherous of rock.

He stepped up on the face and began to climb. He used his toes, and his fingers, leaning back from the rock, keeping in fine balance, never stopping, never jerking or fighting the holds, smoothly as molten chocolate, flowing upwards.

At first the holds were solid, the kind he called 'jug handles', then the face leaned out slowly and the holds were mere flakes and indentations. He used them lightly and briefly, a touch of his fingers, a nudge of his toes and he was past, putting the minimum of weight on each but even then feeling the frailer flakes of stone grate and creak threateningly under his fingers – but he was gone before the hold could fail.

In places, he could not see above his head and he climbed by instinct, reaching up in the darkness, his fingertips as sensitive as those of a pianist as they brushed the rock and then locked into it. Without check or pause, he covered the first pitch and reached the ledge a hundred feet up from the base.

The ledge was narrower than it had appeared through the binoculars, no more than nine inches wide. With the pack strapped on his back and the rifle protruding on each side of his shoulders, it was impossible for him to turn his back to the rock and use the ledge as a bench to sit upon.

He was forced to stand facing the cliff, with his heels hanging over the edge, and the weight of pack and rifle pulling on his shoulders, trying to drag him backwards. He was less comfortable on the ledge than he had been on the face. He began to shuffle along it, spreading his arms like a crucifix to steady himself, his fingers groping for irregularities in the rock face, the sandstone an inch from the tip of his nose.

He went left along the ledge, seeking the vertical crack that he had spotted through the binoculars. It had been his first choice of the two possible routes. Sean had the rock-climber's instinctive distrust of roots and branches and tufts of grass. They were always unreliable, too treacherous to risk life upon.

He counted his shuffling crablike paces along the ledge, and by the time he reached a hundred the ledge under his toes had narrowed dangerously and the muscles in his thighs were burning and quivering from the unnatural strain of counter-balancing the rifle and pack.

Twenty paces more and the cliff face was beginning to bulge out towards him, forcing him further backwards and he had to thrust his hips forward to keep himself from toppling out over the sheer drop. It was only a hundred feet to the bottom, but it would crush and kill just as surely as a fall from the top of Eiger north face.

The strain on his legs was intolerable now. He thought of going back and trying the roots of the ficus but he doubted that he still had that choice. He wanted to stop, just to rest his legs a moment and gather himself but he knew that would be the end of it. To stop on a pitch like this was defeat and certain death.

He made himself take another pace and then another, now he was forced backwards so his back was arched and his legs were numb to the ankles; he could feel them juddering under him, he knew they were going. Then suddenly the fingers of his left hand touched the crack, and it was as though a syringeful of adrenalin had been squirted into one of his arteries.

His legs steadied under him, and he managed another pace. His fingers danced over the crack, exploring it swiftly. It was not wide enough to get his shoulder into it, and it narrowed quickly.

Sean thrust his hand into it as deep as it would go and then bunched his fist, jamming it securely into the crack. Now he could hang back on his arm and rest his back and his aching legs. His breathing hissed and sawed in his chest and the sweat was streaming down his body, soaking his shirt. Sweat melted the camouflage cream from his face and burned his eyes, blurring his vision.

He blinked rapidly and lifted his head. He was surprised to see that the cliff face above him was visible against the night sky, and that he could make out the crack running vertically up its side.

He turned his head and saw that while he climbed the moon had cleared the horizon in the east and its beams turned the forest below to a frosty silver.

He could not wait any longer. He had to keep moving. He reached up with his free hand and thrust it into the rock crack above the other and made another jam-hold. Then he twisted his foot and pressed the toe into the crack three feet up from the ledge; he straightened his foot and it wedged securely. He put his weight on it and, with the other foot, stepped up and repeated the action. Hand over hand, foot over foot, he walked up the crack, hanging back from the rock face, once more in balance, the strain removed from his legs and back and his weight evenly distributed.

He could see the top of the cliff now, only a hundred feet above his head, and then he felt the crack begin to open wider; his fists and feet were no longer finding secure jams. One of his feet slipped under him, rasping harshly over the rock until it caught again.

He turned his body, trying to wedge his shoulder into the

crack, but the barrel of the rifle clanged against the face, blocking his turn. He hung there for a few seconds before he could force himself back into balance on his legs and then groped above his head searching the depth of the crack for another secure hold. He found only smooth sandstone, and he knew he was stuck.

He had about fifteen seconds before his legs gave in under him. He understood clearly what he had to do, but it went contrary to all his instincts.

'Do it,' his voice grated in his own ears. 'Do it, or die.'

He reached down and opened the quick release buckle on the waistband of his back-pack. Then he straightened one arm and reached backwards and downwards; the carrying strap slid off his shoulder and down his arm, catching in the crook of his elbow. The altered weight of the pack and the rifle slewed his whole body around and he had to fight to stay on the cliff face.

He thrust his head into the crack, trying to hook onto the rock with his chin and the back of his head, the strap of the back-pack locking his arm behind him. He gathered all his strength, braced his neck muscles, his head jammed in the crack and let go. Now he was held only by his head and feet, he straightened both arms behind him. For an aching moment, the strap caught on a fold of his bush jacket, and then it slipped down over his arm.

The pack dropped off his back and fell away into the darkness. Relieved of the weight, Sean tottered and swayed and then with both arms free, he grabbed wildly at the edges of the rock crack and managed to hold himself from plunging after his pack into the abyss.

He clung to the rock and listened to the pack striking the cliff as it fell, the steel of his rifle barrel ringing like a bronze bell off the rock, waking the echoes and sending them bounding from kopje to cliff, a terrifying sound in the night. Long after the pack and rifle had come to rest at the base of the cliff, the echoes still reverberated against the hills.

Sean swung himself sideways and was able at last to wedge his shoulder into the crack. He rested like that, panting wildly, the terror of death for the moment unnerving him. Then slowly his breathing eased and his terror was replaced by the familiar glow of adrenalin in his blood. Suddenly, it felt very good still to be alive.

'Right to the very edge,' he whispered hoarsely. 'You have been there again, boyo.' The greater the terror, the more intense

211

the thrill. He no longer amazed himself, but here he was again gloating at just how close he could get without going over the edge.

The thrill was too fleeting, within seconds it began to fade, to be replaced by realization of his position. His pack was gone. The rifle, his water-bottles, sleeping-bag, food, all gone. All that remained were the contents of his pockets, and the tiny emergency pack and hunting-knife looped to his belt.

He whispered, 'We'll worry about that when we get to the top.' And he began to climb again. With one shoulder wedged into the crack, he was able to push and drag himself upwards an inch at a time, paying for it with skin from his knuckles and bare knees.

Gradually the crack continued to open wider, until it became a full chimney, and he could get his whole body into it and double one leg under him to propel himself upwards more swiftly. At the top the chimney had eroded and crumbled. One side wall of the chimney had broken away, but it had left a narrow buttress with a flat top. Sean was able to transfer his weight across the chimney until he was standing on this precarious pinnacle.

The top of the cliff was still ten feet above his head. When he reached up to the full stretch of his arms standing on the tips of his toes the ledge was still just out of reach. The chimney wall had broken away clearly leaving a smooth almost polished surface, without even the minutest hold or purchase. A good safe climber moved from hold to hold, with never a single moment when he was totally insecure. In a situation such as this that hypothetical climber would have driven an iron piton into the rock to give him the hold he needed.

'Look Mummy, no pitons,' Sean said grimly. 'We'll have to jump for it.' He would only have one chance at it. If he missed his hold on the ledge once he had launched himself, then the next stop would be the base of the cliff.

He set both feet firmly and sank down at the knees, but he was so cramped on the tip of the buttress that he could not get low enough before his face touched the rock and his backside stuck far out over the drop.

He took a breath and used both arms and legs to propel himself straight upwards. It was an awkward hampered jump but he got high enough to hook both his hands over the edge. For a moment, they began to slide back and then his fingers gripped and held.

He kicked both legs and drew himself upwards by the main strength of his arms. His chin came level with the ledge, and in the moonlight he saw in front of him a false crest, simply another ledge below the true top of the cliff.

The ledge was obviously occupied by a colony of rock hyrax. The stink of their droppings, sharp and ammoniacal, filled Sean's lungs as he gasped from the effort of holding himself. The hyrax is a plump fluffy animal. Although it is only the size of a rabbit, it is a remote relative of the elephant, and as endearing in appearance as an infant's soft toy. These hyrax were deep in their rocky burrows now and the ledge seemed deserted. Sean hoisted himself up smoothly and hooked one elbow over the edge; he kicked again, gathering himself for the final effort and then froze.

The silence of the night was cut by a loud high-pitched hiss, like the leaking valve of a truck tyre. In the moonlight what he had taken for a pile of rock lying directly in front of his face, altered shape, seeming to melt and flow.

In an instant, Sean realized that it was a snake. Only one of the adders would hiss as loudly, and only one adder was that large.

It was coiled upon itself, loop after loop of its thick scaly body glistening softly, and as it cocked its neck into the menacing 'S' shape, its eye caught the light of the moon and winked at him sardonically. The huge flat head was the distinctive spade shape of the gaboon adder, the largest of all the adders and one of the deadliest of all Africa's venomous snakes.

Sean could drop back and try to regain his stance on the narrow pinnacle of rock, but that was a slim chance and if he missed it, he would plunge down the cliff face. A much better chance would be to try and brave it out.

He hung with legs free, trying to control his breathing, staring in horror at the loathsome creature. It was cocked to strike, less than two feet from his face, and he knew it could lunge out almost its full body length, seven feet or more. The slightest movement would trigger it.

He hung on his arms, every muscle of his body rigid, staring at the adder, trying to dominate it by the force of his will. The seconds drew out slowly as spilled molasses, and he thought he detected the first relaxation in the taut 'S' of its neck.

At that moment, his left hand slipped, his fingernails rasped

213

on the rock and the adder struck with the force of a blacksmith's hammer.

Sean rolled his head to the side, like a boxer avoiding a punch. The adder's cold scaly nose jarred against his jawbone and there was a fierce tug against his neck and shoulder, so powerful that it jerked one hand loose from its hold on the rock, and spun him half around. He was sideways to the ledge, holding on with only his left arm.

He knew that the adder had hooked its fangs into his shoulder or the side of his throat and he expected the exquisite fire of its venom to kindle in his flesh. The serpent was locked onto him, dangling down the front of his body, thick as a salami sausage; it squirmed and thrashed, hissing explosively in his ear. The cold loathsome touch of its slippery scales brushed against his bare flesh.

Sean almost screamed with the sheer horror of it. The adder's weight threw him about as it lashed from side to side, and its loud hisses deafened him. He felt his single-handed grip on the ledge slipping, but the prospect of the drop below him was suddenly insignificant when compared to this foul creature fastened to his neck.

He felt an icy spray of liquid on the side of his throat and his jaw; it dribbled down the opening of his bush jacket, and with a rush of relief he knew that the adder had missed his throat and had fastened into the collar of his jacket. Its fangs were fully two inches long and viciously recurved, designed to penetrate and hang on to its prey. Hooked into the khaki cotton material of his collar, its violent struggles were forcing the venom out of the hollow bony needles, squirting onto his throat and bare skin.

The realization that the fangs had not penetrated his flesh rallied him, firmed his grip on the ledge and arrested his slow slide into the drop. His right hand was still free. He reached up and seized the adder's neck just at the back of its flat diamond-shaped head. His fingers could barely span the massive body, and he felt the enormous power of its muscles beneath the glassy scales.

He tried to pull it free, but the fangs were like fish hooks in the heavy cloth, and the serpent hissed more viciously and its grotesque body, patterned like a patchwork quilt, coiled around his forearm. He used all his strength, holding onto the ledge with his left arm, heaving at the adder with his right, and he tore the fangs from the roof of its gaping mouth so that its dark blood mingled with the copious flow of its venom, and he flung the twisting coiling body far out over the drop. Then he swung back and grabbed with his right hand at the rock of the ledge.

He was sobbing softly with horror and exertion, and it was fully half a minute before he could gather himself sufficiently to pull himself up and crawl onto the ledge.

He knelt on the rock floor and shrugged out of his bush jacket. The front of it was wet with venom, and one of the adder's fangs was broken off and still buried in the cloth of the collar. He worked it loose and, careful to avoid the needle point, flicked it out over the cliff. Then with his handkerchief he wiped his skin dry.

He considered the danger of wearing the jacket again. The venom might be absorbed through the pores of the sensitive skin under his jaw, it could cause ulcers or worse, but to discard the jacket would expose his body to tomorrow's tropical sun. He hesitated and rolled the jacket and fastened it onto his belt. He would wash it out at the first opportunity.

The thought of water made him aware of his thirst. The climb had dehydrated him, and his water-bottle was with his pack at the bottom of the cliff. He had to find water before tomorrow's noon, but now his first concern must be to get off the exposed face of the cliff and into cover.

He stood up, and felt the night breeze cold on the sweat of his bare upper body. From the ledge on which he stood, it was an easy pitch to the crest, more a scramble than a climb. However, he took it carefully and when he reached the top he lay for a few minutes with just his head peering over the crest.

A haze of light cloud had veiled the moon and Sean could see very little. The bush that grew so densely up the sides of the valley had spread across the tops of the cliff and formed a dark wall just ahead. There were probably forty yards of rocky ground, open except for coarse knee-high grass, and then he would be into the cover of the bush.

He rose to his feet, and ran forward crouching as low as possible as he crossed the skyline, and he was halfway to the edge of the bush when the light hit him.

It stopped him dead as though he had run into the rock cliff, and he flung up his hands instinctively to protect his eyes for his vision had been shattered and starred by the brilliance of the

215

light beamed full into his face. Then he flung himself face forward into the grass and flattened his body against the stony earth.

The beam of light threw long black shadows behind each boulder and cast a bright reflective glow from the pale winter grass. Sean dared not raise his head. He pressed his face to the earth, exposed and vulnerable and helpless in that fierce white beam.

He waited for something to happen but the silence was unbroken. Even the usual night sounds of nocturnal birds and insects were quenched, so that the voice when at last it boomed out of the trees, magnified and distorted by an electronic bullhorn, was as shocking as a blow in the face.

'Good evening, Colonel Courtney.' It was spoken in good English, barely touched by an African accent. 'You made excellent time. Twenty-seven minutes fifteen seconds from the base of the cliff to the top.'

Sean did not move, but he lay and absorbed the bitter humiliation of it. They had been toying with him.

'But I cannot give you high marks for stealth. What was it you threw down the rock? It sounded like a bunch of old tin pots.' The speaker chuckled sardonically and then went on, 'And now, Colonel, if you are sufficiently rested, would you be gracious enough to stand up and raise both hands above your head?'

Sean did not move.

'I beg of you, sir. Don't waste your time and mine.'

Sean lay still, considering wildly the possibility of dashing back over the crest behind him.

'Very well, I see you have to be convinced.' There was a brief pause and Sean heard a soft order given in dialect.

The burst of automatic fire tore into the earth three paces from where he lay. He saw the fiery blur of the muzzle flashes amongst the dark trees and heard the distinctive rush of the RPD light machine-gun, like a strip of heavy-duty canvas being ripped through. The stream of bullets scythed the grass and raised a mist of yellow dust in the bright light.

Sean came slowly to his feet. The beam of light fastened on his face but he refused to turn his head away or shield his eyes.

'Hands at full stretch above the head please, Colonel.'

He obeyed, His naked upper body was very white in the light.

'I am delighted to see you have kept yourself in good shape, Colonel.'

Two dark figures detached themselves from the tree line. Keeping well clear of the light beam, they circled out on either side of him and came up in Sean's rear. From the corner of his eyes, Sean saw they wore tiger-striped battle dress and that their AK rifles were aimed at him. He ignored them until suddenly the steel butt plate of one of the rifles crashed into his spine between the shoulder-blades and he fell to his knees.

The voice on the bull-horn gave a sharp order in dialect to prevent them striking him again and they closed on either side of him and forced him to his feet. One of them searched him swiftly, stripping him of knife, belt and emergency pack and patting his pockets. Then they backed off, leaving him naked except for his khaki shorts and velskoen, but they kept their AKs aimed at his belly.

The light bobbed as the man carrying it advanced out of the wall of bush. Sean saw that it was one of those portable battle lights powered by a heavy rechargeable battery pack that the man carried on his back. Slightly behind him, keeping back in the shadow, came the man with the bull-horn.

Even through the dazzling beam of the battle light Sean saw that he was tall and lean, and that he moved with a cat-like grace.

'It's been a long time, Colonel Courtney.' He was close enough not to have to use the bull-horn and Sean recognized his voice.

'Many years,' Sean agreed.

'You'll have to speak up.' The man stopped a few paces in front of Sean and jokingly cupped one hand to the side of his head. 'I am deaf in one ear, you know,' he said, and Sean grinned sardonically at him through his black camouflage cream.

'I should have done a better job, and blown your other ear out while I was about it, Comrade China.'

'Yes,' China agreed. 'We really must discuss old times together.' He smiled and he was even more handsome than Sean remembered, relaxed and charming and debonair. 'However, I'm afraid you have delayed me a little, Colonel. Pleasant though it is to renew acquaintance, I cannot afford more time away from my headquarters. There will be an opportunity to talk later, but now I must leave you. My men will take good care of you.'

He turned and disappeared into the darkness beyond the beam of light. Sean wanted to call after him, 'My men, the girl, are they safe?' but he restrained himself. With a man like this, it was best to show no weakness, to give him nothing he could use to his advantage later. Sean forced himself to remain silent when the guards urged him forward with practised use of their gun butts.

'We'll join the main column soon,' Sean comforted himself. 'And I'll see for myself how Claudia and Job are doing.'

The thought of Claudia was a refreshing draught that he craved even more than sweet cool water.

*   *   *

There were ten men in his guard detail under the command of a sergeant.

Obviously they were picked troops, powerful and lean as the pack of wolves of his nightmare. Soon they intercepted a well-beaten footpath and they closed up around him and urged him to a jog-trot, heading southwards into the night.

None of his captors spoke. It was an eerie experience, just the sound of their light footfalls and quick shallow breathing, the creak of equipment and the hot feral smell of their bodies close around him in the night.

After an hour, the sergeant signalled a pause, and they stopped beside the track. Sean reached across to the nearest guerrilla and tapped the water-bottle on his belt.

The man spoke to the sergeant. The first words since they had started and Sean understood him. He was speaking Shangane. The Shanganes were the remnants of one of the tiny Zulu tribes that had been defeated by King Chaka's impis at the battle of Mhlatuze River in 1818. Unlike so many of the other lesser chieftains, Soshangane had resisted incorporation into Chaka's empire and fled northwards with his shattered impis to found his own kingdom along the borders of present day Zimbabwe and Mozambique.

So the Shangane language was Zulu-based, and over the years many of Sean's camp staff had been Shangane for, like their Zulu ancestors, they were a fine and noble people. Sean spoke their language fluently for it contained many similarities to Sindebele.

He did not, however, make the mistake of letting his captors know this and gave no indication of having understood as the trooper said, 'The *mabunu* wants to drink.'

'Give it to him,' the sergeant replied. 'You know the *inkosi* wants him alive.'

The man handed Sean the bottle and though the water was brackish and was tainted by swamp mud, to Sean it tasted like chilled Veuve Clicquot served in a crystal glass.

'The *inkosi* wants him alive,' the sergeant had said. Sean pondered that as he handed the bottle back. The *inkosi*, or chief, was obviously Comrade China, and they had orders to care for him. That gave him a little comfort, but he did not have long to savour it. After only a few minutes, the sergeant gave the order and they resumed that mile-eating jog-trot towards the south.

They ran up the dawn and at any moment Sean expected them to overhaul the main column which was holding Claudia and Job captive, but mile succeeded mile without any sign of them. Now that it was light, Sean could look for the tracks of the column on the footpath ahead but there were none. They must have taken a different route.

The sergeant in charge was a veteran. He had flankers out sweeping the verges of the footpath ahead for an ambush by Frelimo, but what seemed to concern him more than attack from the forest was the menace from the sky. At all times they attempted to keep under the canopy of the forest, and whenever they were forced to cross open ground, they stopped and searched the sky, listened for the sound of engines, before venturing out, and then they crossed to the next line of trees at a full run.

Once during the first morning they heard the sound of a turbo-aircraft engine, faint and very far off, but instantly the sergeant gave an order and they all dived into cover. A trooper lay on each side of Sean and forced him to keep his head down and his face to the ground until the last murmur of the aircraft engine faded.

This preoccupation with aerial attack puzzled Sean; all he had heard and read indicated that Frelimo's air force was so weak and scattered as to be almost non-existent. The types of aircraft they possessed were obsolete and unsuited to ground attack, and a shortage of skilled technicians and spares only compounded their ineffectuality. These men, however, were taking the threat very seriously indeed.

At midday the sergeant ordered a halt. One of the troopers prepared food on a small fire, which he doused as soon as it was cooked. They moved on a few miles before stopping once more to eat the meal. Sean was given an equal share. The maize meal was cooked stiff and fluffy and was well salted, but the meat was

219

rancid and on the point of putrefying. In the average white man it would have caused an immediate attack of enteritis, but Sean's stomach was as conditioned as any African's. He ate it without relish, but without trepidation either.

'The food is good,' the sergeant told Sean in Shangane as he sat beside him. 'Do you want more?' Sean made a pantomine of incomprehension and said in English, 'I'm sorry I don't know what you are saying.' The sergeant shrugged and went on eating. A few minutes later he turned back to Sean and said sharply, 'Look behind you, there's a snake!' Sean resisted the natural impulse to jump to his feet and instead grinned ingratiatingly and repeated, 'I'm sorry I don't understand.'

The sergeant relaxed and one of his men remarked, 'He does not understand Shangane. It is all right to speak in front of him.'

They ignored him for the remainder of the meal and chatted amongst themselves, but as soon as they had finished, the sergeant produced a pair of light manacles from his pack and locked one side on to Sean's wrist and the other onto his own. He delegated sentry duty to two of his men and the rest of them settled down to sleep.

Despite Sean's exhaustion, he had been going for days now on only brief snatches of sleep, he lay awake and pondered all he had learned, and the missing pieces of the puzzle. He was still not certain that he was in Renamo hands, he had only Claudia's brief note to suggest that. On the other hand, Comrade China had been a commissar in Robert Mugabe's Marxist ZANLA army, but Renamo was a rabidly anti-communist organization committed to the overthrow of the Marxist Frelimo government. That didn't add up correctly.

Furthermore, China had fought the Rhodesian army of Ian Smith. What was he doing here across the border, involved in another struggle in a foreign country? Was China a soldier of fortune, a turncoat, or an independent warlord taking advantage of the Mozambiquan chaos for his own private ends? It would be interesting to find out.

With all this to think about, still his last thought before sleep finally overcame him, was of Claudia Monterro. If China wanted him alive, then it was highly probable that he wanted the girl alive as well. With that thought, he fell into a deep, dark sleep with a faint smile on his lips.

He woke to the ache of abused muscles and the bruises left by

220

gun butts, but the sergeant had him up and running immediately southwards again into the cool shades of evening. Within a mile, his muscles warmed and the stiffness evaporated. He settled into the run, matching his escorts easily. Always he looked ahead, hoping at any moment to see the tail of the main column emerge from the darkness ahead, and to see Job and Dedan carrying Claudia's litter.

They ran through the night and when they stopped again to eat, his captors began to discuss him through their mouthfuls of maize and high-smelling meat.

'They say that in the other war, he was a lion, an eater of men,' the sergeant told them. 'It was he that led the attack at Inhlozane, the training camp at the Hills of the Maiden's Breasts.'

The troopers looked at him with interest and dawning respect.

'They say that it was veritably he, in person, who destroyed one ear of General China.'

They chuckled and shook their heads, that was a fine joke.

'He has the body of a warrior,' said one of them, and they considered him frankly, discussing his physique as though he were an inanimate object.

'Why has General China ordered this?' another asked, and the sergeant grinned and picked a shred of meat from his back teeth with a fingernail.

'We must run the pride and the anger out of him,' he grinned. 'General China wants us to change him from a lion into a dog who will wag his tail and do his bidding.'

'He has the body of a warrior,' the first man repeated. 'Now we must discover if he has the heart of a warrior.' And they all laughed again.

'So it's a contest, then.' Sean kept his face impassive. 'All right, you bastards, let's see which dog wags its tail first.'

In a perverse fashion, Sean began to enjoy himself. The challenge was much to his taste. There were ten of them, all in their twenties. He was just over forty years of age, but that handicap made it even sweeter and helped him to endure the monotony and hardship of the days that followed.

He was careful not to let them know that he understood that this was a contest. He knew it was dangerous to antagonize or humiliate them. Their goodwill and respect would be more valuable than their hatred and resentment.

Sean had spent his entire adult life in the close company of black men. He knew them as servants and as equals, as hunters and soldiers, as good and loyal friends and as bitter cruel enemies. He knew their strengths and weaknesses and how to exploit them. He understood their tribal customs, their social etiquette, he knew how to flatter and please and impress them, how to gain their respect and make himself agreeable to them.

He showed them just the right degree of respect, but not enough to make them contemptuous. He took especial care not to challenge the sergeant's authority or force him to lose face in front of his men. He made the most of their sense of humour and of fun. With sign language and a little clowning he made them laugh, and once they had laughed with him their whole relationship altered subtly. He became more a companion than a captive and they no longer used the steel-edged gun butts as instruments of casual persuasion. Most importantly, he was every day picking up little snippets of information.

Twice they passed burned-out villages. The cultivated lands around them had gone back to weeds, the black ashes blowing in the wind.

Sean pointed at the ruins. 'Renamo?' he asked, and his captors were outraged.

'No! No!' the sergeant told him. 'Frelimo! Frelimo!' And then he tapped his own chest.

'Me Renamo,' he boasted, and pointed at his men. 'Renamo! Renamo!'

'Renamo!' they agreed proudly.

'Well, that settles that,' Sean laughed.

'Frelimo. Bang! Bang!' He made the gesture of shooting a Frelimo and they were delighted, joining in the pantomime of slaughter enthusiastically. Their attitude towards him improved even further and at their next meal the sergeant handed him an extra-large cut of rotten meat. While he ate it, openly they discussed his performance to date, agreeing that he was acquitting himself admirably.

'But,' the sergeant asked, 'he can run and we know he can kill men, but can he kill a *henshaw*?'

Henshaw was the Shangane word for a falcon, and Sean had heard them use it many times over the last five days of their trek, and each time as they said the word, they looked up at the sky with a troubled expression. Now, once again at the mention of that bird, they looked unhappy and as a reflex glanced upwards.

'General China thinks so,' the sergeant went on. 'But who knows, who knows?'

By now, Sean was confident that his position was fairly secure, his relationship with the band would allow him to take the first liberty, and force a resolution of this trial by attrition.

On the next stage, he began to force the pace. Instead of keeping his station in the file of trotting men two paces behind the Shangane sergeant who led the column, he closed up until he was running on his heels, not quite touching him with each stride, and exaggerating his breathing so that the sergeant could feel it on the back of his thick sweaty back. Instinctively the sergeant lengthened his own stride and Sean matched him, keeping close, too close and pushing him.

The sergeant glanced over his shoulder irritably and Sean grinned at him, breathing into his face. The sergeant's eyes narrowed slightly as he realized what was happening, then he grinned back at Sean and extended his stride into a full run.

'That's it, my friend,' Sean said in English. 'Now let's see whose tail wags.'

The rest of the column had fallen behind. The sergeant called a sharp order to them to close up, and they went away at a killing pace. Within an hour, there were only three of them left, the others were straggled back over a mile of the forest floor and ahead of them the path climbed a steep incline to the crest of another tableland.

Sean moved up slightly until he was running shoulder to shoulder with the tall sergeant, but when he tried to pull ahead the man kept with him. The hillside was so steep that the path went up it in a series of hairpins, and the sergeant forged ahead of Sean at the first bend, but Sean caught him and passed him on the straight.

They ran at the top of their speed now, the lead changing back and forth between them and the third man dropped out before they were halfway up the hillside. They ran grimly, in a wash of sweat, their breathing harsh as the exhaust of a steam engine.

Suddenly Sean darted off the path, scrambling straight upwards, cutting across the bend and coming out fifty feet ahead of the Shangane. The sergeant shouted angrily at this ruse and cut the next bend himself. Now both of them abandoned the pathway and ran straight at the steep slope, jumping over boulders and roots, like a pair of blue kudu bulls in flight.

Sean came out on the crest three feet in front of the sergeant, and threw himself down on the hard earth and rolled onto his back moaning for breath. The sergeant dropped beside him with his breath sobbing in his chest. After a minute, Sean sat up uncertainly and they stared at each other in awe.

Then Sean began to laugh, it was a harsh painful cackle, but after a few seconds the Shangane laughed with him, though clearly each gust of laughter was an agony. Their laughter grew stronger as their lungs regained function, and when the rest of the party struggled to the crest of the hill, they found them still sitting in the grass beside the track, roaring at each other like a pair of lunatics.

When the march resumed an hour later, the sergeant left the endless footpath and struck off across country towards the west and there was at last direction and purpose in the way he led the column.

Sean realized that the trial was over.

* * *

Before dark they ran into a Renamo line of permanent defences.

They were entrenched along the bank of a wide but sluggish river that flowed green between sand bars and round water-polished boulders. The dugouts and trenches were revetted with logs and sandbags and meticulously camouflaged against aerial discovery. There were mortars and heavy machine-guns dug in, with commanding fields of fire across the river and sweeping the northern bank.

Sean had the impression that these fortifications were extensive and he guessed that this was the perimeter of a large military area, certainly battalion and possibly even division strength. Once they had crossed the river and been passed through the defences, Sean's appearance in the ranks of his escort created a stir of interest. Off-duty troopers turned out of their dugouts and crowded around them and his captors were clearly enjoying the elevated status that a white prisoner bestowed upon them.

The crowd of interested and jocular onlookers abruptly thinned and parted as a tubby bespectacled officer strode through them. His escort saluted him with theatrical flourishes which he returned by touching the rim of his maroon beret with the tip of his swaggerstick.

'Colonel Courtney,' he greeted Sean in passable English. 'We have been warned to expect you.'

For Sean, it was refreshing to notice that Renamo wore conventional badges of rank, based on the Portuguese army conventions. This man had red field officer flashes and the single crowns of a major on his epaulettes. During the bush war the terrs had eschewed the capitalist imperialist traditions, and dispensed with the symbols of an elitist officer class.

'You will spend the night with us,' the major told him. 'And I look forward to having you as our guest in mess tonight.'

This was extraordinary treatment, and even Sean's captors were impressed and in a strange way rather proud of him. The sergeant himself escorted Sean down to the river and even produced a fragment of green soap for him to wash out his bush jacket and shorts.

While they dried on a sun-heated rock, Sean wallowed naked in the pool and then used the last of the soap to wash his hair and rid his face of camouflage cream and ingrained dirt. He had not shaved since he had left Chiwewe camp almost two weeks previously and his beard felt thick and substantial.

He worked up a lather of suds in his armpits and crotch and looked down at his own body. There was not a vestige of fat on him, each individual muscle was outlined clearly beneath the sun-darkened skin. He had not been in this extreme condition since the closing days of the war. He was like a thoroughbred racehorse brought up to its peak by a skilful trainer on the eve of a major race. -

The sergeant lent him a steel comb and he brushed his hair out. It fell almost to his shoulders, thick and wavy and sparkling from the wash. He put on his damp clothes and let them dry on his body. He felt good, that charged restless feeling of being at the very pinnacle of physical fitness.

The officers' mess was an underground dugout devoid of ornament or decoration. The furniture was crude and hand-hewn. His hosts were the major, a captain and two young subalterns.

The food made up for its lack of artistic presentation by its abundance. A huge steaming bowl of stew made with sun-dried fish and chillis, the fiery *peri-peri* that was a relic of the Portuguese colonialists, and great mounds of the ubiquitous maize-meal porridge.

It was the best meal Sean had eaten since leaving Chiwewe,

but the highlight of the evening was the drink that the major provided, unlimited quantities of real civilized beer in metal cans. The labels read 'Castle Lager' and in small print at the bottom, 'Verwaardig in Suid Afrika, Made in South Africa'. It was an indication as to which country was Renamo's good friend.

As the guest in mess, Sean proposed the first toast. He stood and raised his beer can.

'Renamo,' he said. 'And the people of Mozambique.'

The major replied, 'President Botha, and the people of South Africa,' which settled it conclusively. They knew Sean was from the south and was, therefore, an honoured guest.

He felt so secure in their company that he could relax and for the first time in months allow himself to get moderately drunk.

The major had fought for the Rhodesians during the bush war. He told Sean that like Job Bhekani he had been a subaltern in the Rhodesian African Rifles, the elite black regiment which had fought so effectively and inflicted such slaughter amongst the ZANLA guerrillas. They soon established the camaraderie of old brothers-in-arms. Without obviously pumping him, Sean was able to nudge the conversation along and pick up the crumbs of information that the major let fall more freely as the cans of beer were consumed.

Sean's estimation had been correct. This was part of the northern perimeter of a Renamo army group. The fortifications were deep and dispersed as a precaution against aerial bombardment. From this base, they marauded southwards, hitting the Frelimo garrisons and strafing and raiding the railway line between Beira on the coast and Harare, the capital of Zimbabwe.

While they were still working on the first case of beer, Sean and the major discussed with seriousness the significance of that rail link. Zimbabwe was a completely land-locked nation. Its only arteries to the outside world were the two railway lines. The major one was southwards, into South Africa, via Johannesburg to the major ports of Durban and Cape Town.

Mugabe's Marxist government bitterly resented being reliant on the nation which, for them, epitomized all that was evil in Africa, the bastion of capitalism and the free-market system, the nation which had for the eleven long years of the bush war propped up the white regime of Ian Smith. Mugabe's hysterical rhetoric against his southern neighbour was incessant and yet the foul hand of apartheid was curled around his jugular vein. His instinct was to look eastward into Mozambique for salvation. During his struggle for independence Mugabe had been nobly assisted by the Frelimo President of Mozambique, Samora Machel, whose own struggle against the Portuguese had only just culminated in freedom from the colonial yoke.

Frelimo, his brother Marxists, had provided Mugabe with recruits and arms and full support for his guerrillas. Without reservation, they had offered him the use of bases within their territory from which to launch his attacks on Rhodesia. It was only natural now that he turned once more to Mozambique to provide an escape from this awful humiliation of being seen by the rest of Africa, by his brothers in the Organization of African Unity, to be dealing with the monster of the south, not only dealing with, but totally dependent upon it for every litre of gasoline, for every ounce of the daily stuff of survival.

The railway line to the port of Beira on the Mozambique channel was the natural solution to his predicament. Of course, the port facilities and the main-line system under the African socialist management had been allowed to fall into almost total disrepair. The solution to that was simple and well-tried: massive aid from the developed nations of the West. As every good African Marxist knew, they were fully entitled to this, and any attempt to withhold it could be countered by the equally simple and well-tried expedient of dubbing it blatant racism. That dread accusation would force immediate compliance. The estimate of the costs of work needed to restore the port and main line to full efficiency was four billion American dollars. However, as actual costs in Africa usually exceeded estimates by a hundred per cent, the sum of eight billion dollars was more realistic. A mere bagatelle, nothing more than their due, a fair price for the West to pay for the pleasure and prestige that Mugabe would derive from being able to thumb his nose at the monster of the south.

There was only one small obstacle in his way, the army of Renamo. It sat astride that vital rail link, attacking it almost daily, blowing up bridges and culverts, ripping out the tracks and shooting up rolling stock.

The actual damage they caused was minor compared to the fact that their depredations gave the Western governments a fine excuse for withholding the funds needed to restore the main line to the condition in which it would be able to carry all of Zimbabwe's imports and exports.

The Frelimo government's efforts to protect the line were so fumbling and inept that the Zimbabweans themselves were forced to assist them. Over ten thousand of Mugabe's own troops were tied up in trying to fend off Renamo attacks on the line. Sean had heard estimates of the cost of these operations to Zimbabwe's economy, already one of the shakiest in sub-Saharan Africa, as high as a million dollars a day.

It was ironic that Mugabe, once the guerrilla, was now forced into the role of passive defender of fixed hardware and permanent positions. He was experiencing the stings of the flea, that he had once so merrily dispensed.

Sean and the Renamo major laughed at the joke, and began on the second case of good apartheid lager. This marked the passing of the time for serious conversation.

Now they reminisced happily about the days of the bush war and they soon discovered that they had both been at the same contact in the Mavuradonhas on the day when they had killed forty-six guerrillas, 'a good kill', as a successful action was always referred to. Sean's Scouts had lain in wait in the gulleys and re-entrances to the hills, acting in the role of stop group, while the RAR had dropped by parachute on the far side and formed the sweep line to drive the terrorists onto the Scouts.

'You drove out as many bush-buck as gooks,' Sean remembered. 'I didn't know which to shoot first.' And they laughed and talked of other dangerous sorties, of crazy ops and of wild chases and 'good kills'.

They drank to Ian Smith, the Ballantyne Scouts and the Rhodesian African Rifles. There was still plenty of beer remaining so they drank to Ronald Reagan and Margaret Thatcher. When they ran out of conservative leaders to toast, Sean suggested, 'Damnation to Gorbachev!'

This was enthusiastically adopted, and the major countered immediately with, 'Damnation to Frelimo and Chissano.' The list of left-wingers was longer than that of conservatives, but they worked their way steadily down it, damning them all from Neil Kinnock to Teddy Kennedy and Jesse Jackson.

When they finally parted, Sean and the major embraced like brothers. Sean had filled all his pockets with cans of beer, so that when he returned to his Shangane guards they too greeted him affectionately as he distributed the cans amongst them.

In the morning, the Shangane sergeant shook him awake while

228

it was still dark. Sean's headache was terrifying and his mouth tasted as though a hyena had slept in it. It was one of the penances of being superbly physically fit. The body's reaction to the abuse of alcohol was proportionately violent, the hangovers more fierce, and he had not a single aspirin for solace.

However, by the middle of the morning Sean had sweated out the last drops of stale beer. Their route was still south and west, and as they ran they saw many more fortifications and strong points. As the major had told him, they were cunningly dispersed and hidden. He saw light field artillery in sandbagged emplacements, together with mortars in their redoubts, and detachments armed with RPG rockets, the mobile hand-held stalwarts of the guerrilla arsenal. All the troops he saw seemed to be cheerful and of high morale, well-fed and equipped. Nearly all of them wore the tiger-striped camouflage and combat boots with rubber soles and canvas uppers.

His escort had replenished their packs from the garrison stores. When they stopped to eat, the maize meal was in two-kilo paper sacks marked 'Premier Mills', and the matches with which they lit the fire were 'Lion Matches' and the new bars of soap 'Sunlight', all with the familiar double legend beneath the name, 'Verwaardig in Suid Afrika, Made in South Africa'.

'It's almost like being home again,' Sean chuckled.

* * *

The Renamo defensive lines were in concentric rings like the ripples on a pond, and soon Sean realized they were approaching the centre. They passed what were obviously training areas, where fresh-faced black recruits, both male and female, some of them in their early teens, sat in rows under thatched sun shelters like schoolchildren in a classroom studying the makeshift blackboard so attentively that they barely glanced up as Sean's detachment trotted by.

From the blackboards, Sean saw that the subjects they were being taught ranged from the infantry field manual to political theory.

Beyond the rear training areas they entered what appeared to be a series of low sparsely-manned kopjes. It was only when they were within a few metres of the side of one of these hills, that Sean spotted the entrances to the dugouts.

They were more elaborately constructed and cunningly concealed than the others that they had been passing all day. These would be invisible from the air and impervious to aerial bombardment, and Sean could tell, by the changed deportment of his guards and their more severe posture towards him, that they had reached the headquarters area of the Renamo army group.

Still, he was taken by surprise when without ceremony they turned aside and drew up at the entrance to one of the underground bunkers. There was a brief exchange while the Shangane sergeant handed Sean over to the guards at the entrance, before Sean was hustled down the steps into the subterranean maze of corridors and caverns hacked out of the earth. The bunker was lit by bare electric bulbs and somewhere far-off, he heard the hum of a generator. The side walls were revetted with sandbags that had been dressed neatly and the roof was reinforced with hewn logs.

They entered a communications room. Sean saw at a glance that the radio equipment was sophisticated and well maintained. A large-scale map of the whole northern and central Mozambique provinces of Zambezia and Manica covered one wall.

Sean studied the map surreptitiously. He saw at once that the broken mountainous ground in which this Renamo army group was ensconced was the Serra da Gorongosa, the mountains of Gorongosa, and that the river they had crossed which formed the Renamo defensive line was the Pungwe river. The main railway line ran only thirty or forty miles further south of this position, but before he could glean more information from the map, he was hurried down another short passageway at the end of which there was a curtained-off doorway.

His escort called a respectful request to enter and the reply was sharp and authoritative. One of them prodded Sean and he pushed the curtain aside and stepped into the room beyond.

'Comrade China,' Sean smiled. 'What a pleasant surprise.'

'That form of address is no longer appropriate, Colonel Courtney. In future, please address me as General China, or simply as "Sir".'

He sat at a desk in the centre of the dugout. He was dressed in the ubiquitous tiger-striped battledress, but it was adorned with silver paratrooper wings and four rows of gaudy ribbons across his left breast. A yellow silk scarf was knotted at his throat and his maroon beret and webbing belt hung on a peg behind him. The butt of the automatic pistol in the webbing holster was ivory-handled. General China was obviously taking his conversion from Marxism to capitalism very seriously.

'I understand that you have acquitted yourself well during the last few days and that you are sympathetic towards Renamo, its allies and its objectives.' His attitude towards Sean was benign, and it made him uneasy.

'How do you know that?' he demanded.

'We do have radio, you know, Colonel. We aren't total barbarians.' China indicated the VHF set on the bench along the side wall of the dugout. 'You passed a pleasant evening with Major Takawira, at my suggestion.'

'Now would you like to tell me what the hell this is all about, General. You have abducted the citizens of two friendly and powerful nations, South Africa and America.'

General China held up his hands to stop him. 'Please spare me your outrage, Colonel. Our people in Lisbon and elsewhere have already received complaints from both the Americans and the South Africans. Of course, we have denied abducting anybody, and adopted an attitude of injured innocence.' He paused and studied Sean for a moment. 'Very enterprising of you to have got a message to the American embassy so soon, but then I wouldn't have expected anything less of you.'

Before Sean could reply, he lifted the hand-set of the field telephone on his desk and spoke quietly in a language that Sean recognized as Portuguese but could not understand. He hung up and glanced expectantly towards the screen doorway, and instinctively Sean did the same.

The canvas curtain was drawn aside and three persons ducked through the dugout. There were two uniformed black women carrying sidearms and AK rifles and between them, escorted closely, dressed in sun-bleached but freshly laundered khaki shirt and loose-fitting shorts, the same clothes she had worn when last he saw her, was Claudia Monterro.

She was thin. That was the first thing that struck Sean. Her hair was drawn back and tied in a plait at the back of her head, and she was tanned to the colour of melba toast.

Her eyes were huge in her thin face and he had never before truly noticed the fine structure of her cheek and jaw bones. At the sight of her his heart seemed to stop and swell against his ribs, and then race away again.

'Claudia!' he said, and her head jerked towards him. The blood drained from her face, leaving a *café-au-lait* colour beneath her tan.

'Oh my God,' she whispered. 'I was so afraid . . .' she broke off, and they stared at each other, neither of them moving for a dozen beats of his heart, then she said his name. 'Sean.' And it sounded like a sob. She swayed towards him and lifted her hands, palms upward in a gesture of supplication, and her eyes were filled with all the suffering and hardship and longing of these last days. With two long strides, he reached her and she threw herself against him and closed her eyes and pressed her face against him. She had both arms locked around his chest, the strength of her grip hampered his breathing.

'Darling,' he whispered, and stroked her hair; it felt thick and springing under his fingers. 'My darling, it's all right now.'

She lifted her face to him and her lips quivered and parted. Blood had flowed back under the smooth brown skin. She seemed to glow and the light in her eyes had changed to the sparkle of dark yellow topaz.

'You called me darling,' she whispered.

He lowered his head over her and kissed her. Her lips opened under his and the inside of her mouth was hot and lubricious. He probed it deeply with his tongue and it tasted like the sap of sweet young grass.

From the desk, General China said quietly in Shangane, 'Very well, now take the woman away.'

Her guards seized Claudia and plucked her out of his embrace. She gave a small despairing wail and tried to resist, but they were powerful heavily built women, and between them they lifted her feet off the ground and hustled her back through the screen doorway.

Sean shouted, 'Leave her,' and started after them, but one of the guards drew the pistol from her webbing holster and pointed it at his belly. The canvas screen dropped between them and Claudia's cries of protest dwindled as she was dragged away. In the silence, Sean turned slowly back to the man at the desk.

'You bastard,' he whispered furiously. 'You set that up.'

'It went better than I could possibly have hoped for,' General China agreed, 'although some previous conversation that I had with Miss Monterro concerning you gave me the idea that she

232

was more interested in you as a man than as a professional hunter.'

'I'd like to twist your head off your shoulders. If you hurt her . . .'

'Come, come, Colonel Courtney. I'm not going to hurt her. She is far too valuable. She is a bargaining chip, surely you realize that.'

Slowly Sean's fury abated and he nodded stiffly.

'Okay, China, what do you want?'

'Good.' General China nodded. 'I was waiting for you to ask that question. Sit down.' He indicated one of the stools facing his desk. 'I'll order a pot of tea and we can talk.'

While they waited for the tea, General China busied himself with the papers on his desk, reading and signing a batch of orders. It gave Sean a chance to recover himself. When an orderly brought the tea, General China gestured for him to clear the papers from the desk.

When they were alone again, China sipped at his mug and regarded Sean over the rim. 'You ask what it is that I want. Well, I must confess that at first, it was nothing more complicated than simple retribution. After all, Colonel, it was you that destroyed my command that day at the camp at Inhlozane. You put the only blemish on my professional career, and you inflicted permanent physical damage on my person.' He touched his ear. 'Reason enough for me to want revenge. I'm sure you will agree.'

Sean remained silent. Although he had not tasted tea in days and craved it, he had not touched the mug which stood on the edge of the desk in front of him.

'Of course, I knew that you were operating the Chiwewe hunting concession. In fact, as a junior minister of Mugabe's government, I was one of those who gave approval to the grant. I thought, even then, that it might be useful to have you so close to the border.'

Sean forced himself to relax. He realized that he might learn more, achieve more by a show of co-operation rather than defiance. It was difficult to do, for he could still taste Claudia's mouth. He picked up the tea mug and took a mouthful.

'You certainly get around,' he smiled. 'Comrade one day, general the next. Marxist government minister one day, Renamo warlord the next.'

China waved a hand deprecatingly. 'The dialectics of Marxism never truly interested me. Looking back now, I realize that I enlisted in the guerrilla army for the very good capitalistic reason. At the time it was the best way to get on in life – does that make any sense to you, Colonel?'

'Perfect sense,' Sean agreed. This time his smile was genuine. 'It's a well-known fact that the only way communism can be made to work is if you have capitalists to pay the bill and manage the show.'

'You phrased that very well.' China nodded his appreciation. 'I only found that out later, once ZANLA had ousted Smith and taken over the government in Harare. I discovered that as a former guerrilla I was feared and mistrusted by the soft fat cats who had avoided the actual fighting but now had taken control of the show. I saw that far from receiving my just rewards, I was more likely to end up in Chikarubi prison so I allowed my capitalistic instinct to guide me. With a few other like-minded citizens, we were arranging another change of government, and we were able to convince some of my old comrades-in-arms, who occupied senior positions in the Zimbabwe army, that I would make a suitable replacement for Robert Mugabe.'

'The good old African game of coup and counter-coup.' Sean suggested.

'It is refreshing to talk to someone who follows the reasoning so readily,' China nodded approval. 'But then you are an African, albeit of the less fashionable hue.'

'I'm flattered to be recognized as one,' Sean told him. 'But to return to your altruistic desire to put the best man in charge . . .'

'Ah, yes . . . well, somebody boasted to a woman, and she told her other lover who just happened to be Mugabe's Chief of Intelligence, and I was forced to cross the border in some haste, and here I fell in with yet others of my former comrades who now had joined Renamo.'

'But why Renamo?' Sean asked.

'It is my natural political home. I am good at what I do and Renamo welcomed me. You see, I am part Shangane. As you know our tribe sprawls over both sides of the artificial line imposed by surveyors of the colonial era, who took no consideration of demographic realities when they agreed on borders.'

'If you are now a capitalist, General China, as you claim to be, then there must be more in it than that. Some future reward in store for you?'

'You do not disappoint me,' China said. 'You are as perceptive and devious as any African. Naturally, there is something in it for me. When I have assisted Renamo to form the new government of Mozambique with South Africa as its ally, between them they will be able to apply irresistible pressure on Zimbabwe. They will be able to force a change of government in Harare . . . a new president to replace Mugabe.'

'From General China to President China in one mighty bound,' Sean cut in. 'I'll give you one thing, General, you don't think small.'

'I'm touched by your appreciation of my aspirations.'

'But where does all this leave me? You talked earlier of revenge for your impaired hearing – what made you so forgiving?'

China frowned and touched his ear. 'To tell the truth I would have enjoyed that. In fact, I had already planned a nocturnal raid on your camp at Chiwewe. I had moved up a unit of my men to the border opposite your concession, and was awaiting only an opportunity to escape from my duties here for a few days personally to pay you a visit, when a change of plan was forced upon me.'

Sean raised an eyebrow to signal his interest and attention.

'Very recently there has been a drastic alteration in the balance of power here in the central province. We of Renamo had fought ourselves into a dominant position. In fact, we control all the country except the major towns, we have reduced food production to the point where Frelimo must rely almost entirely on foreign aid, we have virtually strangled their transport system. We raid the roads and railways at will, and our forces move freely about the countryside recruiting from the villages. We have, in fact, set up our own alternative administration. However, all that changed very recently.'

'What happened?'

China did not answer immediately, but stood up from the desk and went to stand in front of the wall map. 'As a distinguished counter-guerrilla fighter, Colonel Courtney, I do not have to explain our strategy to you nor do I have to lecture you on the weapons that we employ in the "war of the flea". We don't fear nuclear bombs, heavy artillery or modern pursuit planes. We chuckled when Robert Mugabe purchased two squadrons of fighters from his Soviet friends, obsolete MIG 23. Floggers that the Russians were pleased to be rid of and which Mugabe cannot afford to keep in the air. There are few, very few modern weapons that we fear except . . .' China paused and turned to face Sean again, 'but you are the expert, Colonel. You know as much as any man alive about anti-guerrilla operations. What do we fear most?'

Sean did not hesitate. 'Helicopter gunships,' he said.

China sat down heavily in his seat again. 'Three weeks ago the Soviets delivered a full squadron of Hind helicopters to the Frelimo air force.'

Sean whistled softly. 'Hinds!' he said. 'In Afghanistan they call them the Flying Death.'

'Here we call them *henshaw* – the falcons.'

'There is no air force in Africa that could keep a squadron of Hinds in the air for more than a few days, they simply don't have the back-up,' Sean shook his head, but China contradicted him quietly.

'The Russians have supplied technicians and munitions and spares, as well as pilots. They aim to smash Renamo in six months.'

'Will they succeed? Can they succeed?'

'Yes,' China said firmly. 'Already they have severely limited our mobility. Without mobility, a guerrilla army is defeated.' He made a gesture that took in the dugout. 'Here we cower underground like moles, not warriors. Our morale, which was so high just a month ago is crumbling away. Instead of looking proudly ahead, my men cringe and look to the skies.'

'It's not an easy life, General,' Sean commiserated with him. 'I'm sure you'll come up with something.'

'I already have,' China nodded. 'You.'

'Me against a squadron of Hinds?' Sean chuckled. 'I am flattered, but include me out.'

'That is not possible, Colonel. As the Americans say, you owe me one.' He touched his ear. 'And I owe you one, Miss Monterro.'

'All right,' Sean nodded with resignation. 'Spell it out for me.'

'The plan that I have in mind requires a white face and a trained officer who understands black troops and speaks their language.'

'Surely, General China, you don't subscribe to old General von Lettow-Vorbeck's theory that the best bush troops in the

236

world are black soldiers with white officers. Why the hell don't you do whatever this is yourself?'.

'I know my own limitations,' China said. 'I am a better administrator than a soldier. Besides, I have explained, I need a white face.' He held up one hand to prevent Sean interrupting again. 'Initially you'll be working with a small group. Ten men.'

'My Shangane escort,' Sean got ahead of him. 'That's the real reason you sent me off on that little jaunt with them.'

'Perceptive, Colonel. Yes, your reputation seems to be well founded. In just a few days you have gained their respect and, dare I say it, loyalty. I think that they'll follow you on the most hazardous assignment.'

'I'll need more than ten Shanganes, there are two others I want with me.'

'Of course, your Matabeles,' China agreed readily. 'They are definitely part of my calculations.'

This was the opportunity to enquire about Job and Dedan for which Sean had been waiting.

'Are they both safe?' he demanded.

'Quite safe and well, I assure you.'

'I won't even discuss anything further until I have seen them and spoken to them,' he said flatly, and China's eyes narrowed.

'I beg you not to adopt that attitude, Colonel. It will only make our future relationship difficult and unpleasant.'

'I mean it,' Sean repeated stubbornly. 'I want to speak to my men.'

General China glanced at his wristwatch and then sighed theatrically.

'Very well.' He lifted the hand-set of the telephone and spoke into it again, then looked up at Sean. 'The two of them will be required to work with you, you can explain that to them. There is an excellent chance that, with all your co-operation, I will be persuaded to give you your freedom. Of course that offer of freedom includes the nubile Miss Monterro.'

'You are very generous,' Sean was ironic.

'Wait until you hear my full terms. You might think I drive a hard bargain.' General China turned to the lieutenant who came through the doorway in response to his summons and said in Shangane, 'Take this man to visit the two Matabele prisoners,' he ordered. 'You may allow them to talk for –' again he glanced at his wristwatch – 'ten minutes. Then bring him back here.'

There were three men in the escort that marched Sean down the underground passages and out into the dazzling sunshine.

The prison barracks consisted of a single hut of mud daub and thatch surrounded by a stockade of poles and barbed wire, the whole covered by a spread of camouflage net. A warder unlocked the gate to the stockade and Sean went in. He walked to the door of the hut.

Over an open fireplace in the centre of the floor stood a black three-legged pot. Two thin mattresses of split reeds on each side of it were the only other furnishings. Dedan was asleep on the one mattress, while on the other Job sat cross-legged and stared into the smouldering coals.

'I see you, old friend,' Sean said softly in Sindebele, and Job came slowly to his feet, and just as slowly began to smile.

'I see you also,' he said, and then they laughed and embraced, clapping each other on the back. Dedan jumped up from the other mattress, grinning with delight, and seized Sean's hand, pumping it brutally.

'What took you so long, Sean?' Job asked. 'Did you find Tukutela? Where is the American? How did they catch you?'

'I'll tell you all that later,' Sean cut him off, 'there are more important things now. Have you spoken to China, did you recognize him as the one we caught at Inhlozane?'

'Yes, the one with the ear. What are our chances with him, Sean?'

'Too early to be sure,' Sean warned. 'But he is talking about some sort of deal.'

'What?' Job broke off, and they both spun to face the door of the hut.

Outside there was the abrupt shrilling of alarm whistles and wild shouts.

'What's going on?' Sean demanded, and strode to the doorway. The gate to the stockade was still wide open, but the guards were scattering, unslinging their weapons and peering up at the sky. The lieutenant was blowing shrill hysterical blasts on his whistle as he ran.

'Air raid,' said Job at Sean's shoulder. 'Frelimo gunships, there was one two days ago.'

Sean heard the engines now, very faint and distant, and the whistling whine of the rotors, growing swiftly shriller and more penetrating.

'Job!' Sean grabbed his arm. 'Do you know where they are holding Claudia?'

'Over there.' Job pointed through the doorway. 'A stockade like this one.'

'How far?'

'Five hundred metres.'

'The gates are open, and the guards are gone. We are going to make a bolt for it.'

'We are in the middle of an army, and what about the gunships?' Job protested. 'Where can we go?'

'Don't argue, let's go.'

Sean raced through the doorway and out of the stockade gates. Job and Dedan were close behind him.

'Which way?' Sean grunted.

'Over there, beyond that clump of trees.'

The three of them ran in a bunch. The camp was almost deserted as Renamo took to their dugouts and bunkers, but Sean saw that there were crews manning the light anti-aircraft guns in the fixed emplacements, and they passed a small detachment armed with the portable RPG rocket-launchers heading for the nearest kopje. Elevation would give them a good field of fire from which to launch. However, the RPG was not an infra-red seeker and had very limited surface-to-air capability.

The Renamo were so preoccupied that not one of them even glanced at Sean's white face as they scurried to take up their positions. Now the whistle of approaching rotors was punctuated by the crackle and rap of ground fire.

Sean did not even look round. Ahead, he saw the glint of barbed wire. The women's stockade was also well camouflaged under brush and netting, and it too seemed deserted by the female wardens.

'Claudia!' he shouted, as he came up to the fence and gripped the wire. 'Where are you?'

'Here, Sean, here!' she yelled back. There were two huts inside the stockade wire. The doors were locked and there were no windows. Claudia's voice came from the nearest building, and was almost drowned out by the thunder of engines, the shriek of rotors, and the roar of ground fire.

'Give me a boost,' Sean ordered, and backed away from the wire. The fence was seven feet high, he judged. Job and Dedan ran forward and crouched below it. Sean sprinted straight at

239

them and as he leapt up, he drove his feet into the cupped hands they had formed for him with interlocking fingers. In unison, they bobbed up and flung their arms high, flipping Sean forward and over. He cleared the wire easily, somersaulted in the air and landed on his feet. He cushioned the shock, tumbling like a paratrooper, and rolled smoothly back onto his feet, using his momentum to hurl himself forward.

'Clear the door!' he yelled at Claudia, as he built up speed and crashed into the crude hand-hewn panel.

It was too solid and heavy to shatter under the drive of his shoulder, but the hinges ripped clean out of the daubed wall, and crashed inwards in a cloud of dust and flying fragments of dried mud.

Claudia was crouched against the far wall, but as he burst into the hut behind the falling door panel, she rushed forward to meet him. He caught her in his arms, but when she tried to kiss him, he whirled her round by one arm, and ran with her to the door.

'What's happening?' she gasped.

'We are making a break.' As they ran out into the sunlight again he saw that Job and Dedan had a hold on the bottom strand of the fence. With all the strength of their arms and legs, they were dragging it upwards, opening a narrow gap between the wire and the sun-baked earth. Sean stooped to the same strand from the inside, settling his grip between the clusters of spikes and he heaved upwards. Under the combined strength of the three of them the ground at the foot of the nearest fence pole cracked and gave, the pole was lifted a few inches out of the hole in which it was planted, and the strand of wire came up in their hands.

'Down on your belly!' Sean grunted at Claudia. 'Get under it!'

She was lean and nimble as a ferret, and the barbs cleared her back with inches to spare as she wriggled through.

'Hold it!' Sean barked at Job, and they strained up, black muscles knotting, faces contorted with the effort.

Sean dropped flat and pushed himself under the wire. Halfway through he felt one of the steel spikes snag in his flesh and stop him dead.

'Pull me through,' he ordered, and while Dedan continued to hold up the wire, Job stooped and they linked hands in a fireman's grip.

'Pull!' Sean ordered, and Job heaved. Sean felt his flesh tear and the blood spurt down his back, then he was free.

As he rolled to his feet Claudia gasped, 'Your back!' But he seized her arm again and demanded of Job, 'Which way?' He knew that Job would have studied the camp during the days he had been imprisoned here. He could rely on his judgement.

'The river,' Job responded immediately. 'If we can float down, clear of the camp.'

'Lead the way,' Sean ordered, and he had to shout to make himself heard. All around them rose the stutter of automatic small arms fire. The deeper clatter of heavy machine-guns, sounding like a stick drawn sharply across a sheet of corrugated iron, and then even that din was drowned out by a thunder like the Victoria Falls in flood. Sean knew exactly what it was, although he had never heard it before. The sound of the Gatling-type, multi-barrelled cannon mounted in the nose of a Hind helicopter, firing 12.7mm bullets like the jet of a fire hose.

He felt Claudia falter beside him at the gut-melting terror of that sound, and he jerked her arm.

'Come on!' he snarled at her. 'Run!' She was still limping slightly from her injured knee ligament, as they followed Job and Dedan down towards the river. Though they were still under the spread branches of the forest, just ahead of them was open ground.

A small party of Renamo were doubling across this opening, coming up the track towards them, eight or nine men in Indian file and each of them carried an RPG mobile rocket-launcher. As they ran, their faces were turned up towards the sky, seeking a target for their rockets.

The detachment of rocketeers was still two hundred metres from them when suddenly the earth around them erupted. Sean had never in all his war experience seen anything like it. The ground dissolved, seemed to turn to a liquid that boiled into a fog of dust under the jet of 12.7mm cannon shells.

Along a wide swathe of cannon fire all was destroyed, even the trees disappeared in a whirlwind of wood fragments and shredded leaves; only the shattered stumps still stood as the storm of fire passed on. The ground was left like the furrows of a freshly ploughed field and on it was scattered the remains of the party of RPG rocket men. They were hacked and minced as

241

though they had been fed through the cogs of some fearsome machinery.

Sean still had a grip on Claudia's arm and he pulled her down into the grass beside the track just as a shadow swept over them. However, the canopy of branches overhead must have screened them from the eyes of the gunner in the helicopter. Job and Dedan had also dived for cover in the grass verge beside the path and avoided detection.

The Hind cruised overhead, barely fifty feet above the tops of the trees, and abruptly they had a full view of the machine as it crossed over the open ground where the torn corpses of the rocket men lay scattered.

Sean felt a physical shock at the sight of it. He had not expected it to be so large and so grotesquely ugly. It was fifty feet long.

The Russians themselves called it 'Sturmovich', the humpback. It was a deformed monster: aberrant and ungainly, the green and brown splotches of tropical camouflage gave it the appearance of disease and leprous decay. The bulging double canopies of armoured glass looked like malevolent eyes and so fierce was their gaze that Sean instinctively flattened himself in the grass and flung a protective arm over Claudia's back.

Below the gross body of the gunship hung an assembly of rocket pods, and as they stared at it in awe the machine hovered and rotated on its own axis, lowered its blunt unlovely nose and fired a spread of rockets.

They launched with fiery sibilance on plumes of white smoke, streaking across the river and bursting on the ant's nests of sandbagged bunkers in fountains of flame and smoke and dust.

The noise was deafening and the shrill whine of the gunship's rotors was like an awl screwing into their eardrums. Claudia covered both her ears and sobbed.

'Oh God! Oh God!'

The Hind revolved slowly, seeking fresh targets, and again they cowered away from it. It moved away from them, hunting along the bank of the river. The Gatling-cannon in its remotely controlled turret in the nose fired blasts of solid metal into the forest, destroying all in its path.

'Let's go!' Sean shouted above the uproar and dragged Claudia to her feet. Job and Dedan ran ahead of them, and the earth ploughed by the gunship's cannons was soft and spongy under their feet.

As they passed the dead men, Job stooped without breaking his run and snatched up one of the undamaged RPG launchers. At the next stride he stooped again and grabbed a fibreglass back-pack that contained three of the finned projectiles for the RPG, and then went bounding away, on towards the riverbank. With her injured knee, Claudia could not match that pace, and even with Sean pulling her along they fell almost a hundred yards behind.

Job and Dedan reached the riverbank. It was steep and rocky, fractured cliffs of water-polished black stone. A gallery of tall riverine trees spread their branches out over the swiftly flowing apple-green waters.

Job looked back at them anxiously, for they were still out in the open. His face contorted as he screamed a warning and dropped the fibreglass pack at his feet and swung the short squat barrel of the RPG up to his shoulder, pointing it at the sky above Sean's head.

Sean did not look up, he knew there was no time for that. He had not isolated the shrieking rotors of the second incoming Hind from the deafening uproar caused by the first machine, but now the din was escalating to the point of pain.

Running beside them was a narrow donga, eroded by the storm waters of the rainy season, but now dry and sheer-sided. Sean swept Claudia off her feet and jumped with her in his arms. The earthen gulley was six feet deep and they hit the bottom with an impact that clashed Sean's teeth together in his jaws just as the lip of the gulley dissolved under a jet of cannon fire.

The earth on which they lay shuddered like a live thing beneath them, as though they were insects being shaken from the flanks of a gigantic horse. Earth, ripped from the lip of the gulley by the sheets of cannon fire, fell on them in clouds, heavy clods raining on their backs, knocking the breath out of them, dust choking them, burying them alive.

Claudia screamed and tried to fight herself out from under the layer of dust and dry earth, but Sean held her down.

'Lie still,' he hissed at her. 'Don't move, you dilly bird.' The Hind swivelled and cruised back, now directly over the gulley, searching for them, the gunner traversing the thick stack of multi-barrels of the Gatling-cannon in its remote turret.

Sean turned his head slightly, looking up from the corner of one eye. His vision was obscured by dust, but as it cleared, he

243

saw the great splotched nose of the Hind hanging in the air only fifty feet directly overhead. The gunner must have picked out their white skins, which made them targets of preference. Only the thin layer of fresh earth protected them from his scrutiny through the gunsight of his cannon.

'Hit him, Job,' Sean pleaded aloud. 'Hit the bastard.'

On the cliff above the river, Job dropped on one knee. The RPG 7 was one of his favourite weapons. The huge gunship was hovering over the gulley only fifty yards away.

He aimed twelve inches below the edge of the pilot's canopy. The RPG was highly inaccurate, and even at point-blank range he gave himself latitude should the missile fly off track. He held the cross-wire steady for a beat of his pumping heart and then pressed the trigger. The exhaust of white smoke blew back over his shoulder and the rocket streaked away, flying fair and true, to strike only inches higher than he had aimed on the rim where the armoured glass canopy joined the camouflaged metal fuselage.

The rocket burst with the force which would blow the engine block out of a Mac truck, or burst the boiler of a railway locomotive. For an instant, the front of the Hind was obliterated by flame and smoke, and Job whooped triumphantly, jumping to his feet, expecting the hideous monster to crash out of the sky in a sheet of its own smoke and fire.

Instead the huge helicopter jumped higher, as though the pilot had flinched at the rocket-burst close beside him, but when the smoke blew away, Job realized with disbelief that the fuselage was unscathed. There was only a sooty black smear on the painted metal to mark the spot where the rocket had struck.

As he stared the ugly nose of the Hind swivelled towards him, and the many-eyed muzzles of the cannon sought him out. Job hurled the RPG launcher away, and jumped out from the cliff top, dropping twenty feet to hit the water, just as the cannon tore the great branches from the tree under which he had stood. Cannon fire chewed through the trunk as cleanly as a lumberjack's cross-saw and the whole tree leaned outwards and then toppled down the cliff and hit the surface of the river in a cloud of spray.

The Hind pulled away, lifting and banking, cruising on down the riverbank. Unharmed by the rocket hit and as deadly as before, it sought its next target.

Sean crawled to his knees, coughing and gasping.

'Are you all right?' he croaked, but for a moment Claudia could not answer him. Her eyes were blinded with sand, and her tears cut wet runnels through the dust that caked her cheeks.

'We've got to get into the water.' Sean pulled her to her feet, and half-pushed half-pulled her up the side of the gully.

They ran together to the top of the cliff and looked down. The felled tree was floating away on the current, a huge raft of leafy branches.

'Jump!' Sean ordered, and Claudia did not hesitate. She threw herself far out, and dropped away to strike the water feet first. Sean followed while she was still in the air.

He surfaced with Claudia's head bobbing beside him. The dust was washed off her face, and her hair was slicked over her eyes, shiny with streaming water.

Together they struck out for the floating mass of branches and leaves. She was a strong swimmer, and even with boots on her feet and fully dressed, she kicked out powerfully and dragged herself through the water with a full over-arm crawl.

As she reached the floating tree trunk, Job stretched out a long arm and drew her in beneath the branches. Dedan was already there and Sean ducked in a second later. They each clung to a branch and the leaves formed a low green bower over their heads.

'I hit him,' Job complained angrily. 'I hit him right on the nose with a rocket. It was like hitting a bull buffalo with a slingshot. He just turned and came straight at me.'

Sean wiped the water from his eyes and face with the palm of his hand. 'Titanium armour plate,' he explained quietly. 'They are almost invulnerable to conventional fire, both pilot's cockpit and the engine compartment are tight and solid. The only thing you can do when one of those bastards comes at you is run and hide.'

He flicked his sodden hair back out of his eyes. 'Anyway, you pulled him off us. He was just about to blast us with that dirty great cannon.' Sean swam across to Claudia.

'You shouted at me,' she accused. 'You were quite rude. You called me a dilly bird.'

'Better abused than dead,' he grinned at her, and she smiled back.

'Is that an invitation, sir? I wouldn't mind a little abuse – from you.' Under water, he slipped an arm around her waist and hugged her.

'My God, how I have missed your cheek and sauce.'

She pressed herself against him. 'I only realized after you were gone . . .' she whispered.

'Me too,' he confessed. 'Up to then, I thought I couldn't stand you. Then I realized I just couldn't do without you.'

'I feel weak when you say that, tell me you really mean it.'

'Later,' he hugged her. 'First let's just try and get out of here alive.' He left her and paddled across to Job's side of the leafy cavern.

'Can you see the bank?'

Job nodded. 'Looks like the raid is over. They are coming out of the bunkers.'

Sean peered out from under the concealing branches. He saw troops moving cautiously about on the near bank.

'They'll be picking up the pieces for a while before they realize that we've scarpered, but keep an eye on them.'

He paddled across to Dedan who was watching the far bank.

'What do you see?'

'They are busy with themselves.' Dedan pointed. A stretcher party was working along the bank, picking up the dead and the wounded, while work details had already begun repairing the damaged fortifications and replacing destroyed camouflage. Nobody looked out across the river.

There was other debris floating downstream with them, severed branches and damaged equipment, empty oil drums, enough to draw attention away from their flimsy refuge.

'If we can avoid discovery until nightfall, we should have floated down beyond the army. Just keep both eyes wide open, Dedan.'

'*Mambo*,' he acknowledged, and concentrated his attention on the bank.

Sean swam quietly back to Claudia and hung on to the branch beside her. She reached out for him immediately.

'I don't like you to be away for even a moment,' she whispered. 'Did you really mean what you said?'

He kissed her and she kissed him back so fiercely that her teeth bruised his lower lip. He enjoyed the mild pain.

She broke the embrace at last and immediately demanded again, 'Did you mean it?'

'I can't do without you,' he answered.

'You can do better than that.'

'You are the most magnificent woman I've ever known.'

'That's not bad, but it's still not what I want to hear.'

'I love you,' he admitted.

'That's it, oh Sean, that's it. And I love you too.' She kissed him again, and they were oblivious to all else, their mouths blending and their bodies clinging wetly together below the surface.

Sean did not know how long it was until Job disturbed them. 'We are going ashore,' he called.

The push of the current had forced the floating tree to the outside of the next river bend and it was already dragging on the submerged sand bar. When Sean lowered his feet, he touched bottom.

'Walk it into deeper water,' Sean ordered, and still concealed beneath its leafy bulk, they heaved and pushed it out until they felt it come free of the sand bar and the current picked it up again and drifted it into the next stretch of the river.

Sean was panting from the effort as he hung on to a branch above his head, only his head above the surface. Claudia paddled across to him and hung on to the same branch.

'Sean,' she said, and her mood had changed. 'I haven't been able to ask you, mostly because I don't want to hear the answer.' She broke off and drew a deep breath. 'My father?' she asked.

Sean was silent as he sought the words to tell her, but it was Claudia who spoke again.

'He didn't come back with you, did he?'

Sean shook his head and his sodden locks dangled into his face.

'Did he find his elephant?' she asked softly.

'Yes,' Sean answered simply.

'I'm glad,' she said. 'I wanted that to be my last gift to him.'

Now she let go of the branch and slipped both her arms around Sean's neck, laying her cheek against his so she did not have to watch his face as she asked the next question.

'Is my father dead, Sean? I must hear you say it before I will believe it.'

With his free arm he held her tightly and gathered himself to reply.

'Yes, my darling. Capo is dead, but he died a man's death – the kind he would have wanted, and Tukutela, his elephant, went with him. Do you want to hear the details?'

'No!' She shook her head, holding him tightly. 'Not now, perhaps not ever. He is dead, and a part of me and my life dies with him.'

He could find no word of comfort and he held her as she began to weep for her father. She wept silently, clinging to him, the grief shaking her. Her tears mingled with the droplets of river water on her face, but he tasted their diluted salt on his lips as he kissed her again and his heart went out to her.

So they floated down on the wide green river, with the smoke and the smell of battle drifting over them from the bombarded banks and the faint cries and groans of the wounded carrying to them across the water. Sean let her expend her silent grief, and slowly the sobs that rocked her abated and at last she whispered throatily:

'I don't know how I could have borne it without you to help me. You were so much alike, the two of you. I think that's what attracted me to you in the first place.'

'I take that as a compliment.'

'It was meant as one. He gave me a taste for men of power and strength.'

Floating beside them, almost within touching distance, was a corpse. Trapped air ballooned the tiger-striped camouflage battle jacket and the body floated on its back. The face was very young, a boy of fifteen years perhaps. His wounds were washed almost bloodless, just a faint pinky discharge like smoke in the green water drifted from them, but it was enough.

Sean saw the gnarled saurian heads, scaled like the bark of an ancient oak, coming swiftly down the current following the taint of blood. Ripples spreading from the hideous snouts, long tails fanning, two big crocodiles, racing each other for the prize.

One of the reptiles reached the corpse and reared out of the water; its jaws, lined with uneven rows of yellow fangs gaped wide, then closed over the corpse's arm. The fangs met through dead flesh with a grinding sound that carried clearly to them, and Claudia gasped and turned her head away.

Before the crocodile could pull the body below the surface the second reptile, even larger than the first, fastened its jaws into the dead belly, and began a gruesome tug-of-war.

The fangs of the crocodile are not designed to shear cleanly through meat and bone, so they held on with locked jaws and used their great combed tails to spin in the water, twisting viciously in a lather of white foam, rending the corpse between them, dismembering it, so they could hear the sinews tear and the joints of shoulder and groin separate.

In fascinated horror, Claudia looked back and gagged as one of the giant reptiles rose high out of the water with an arm in its jaws, and gulped at it convulsively. The creamy yellow scales of its throat bulged as the limb slid down and then it lunged back to tear another morsel from the body.

Tugging and fighting over the pathetic human fragments, they worked away from the floating tree and Sean, remembering the long tear in his back from the barbed wire, felt a lift of relief, for his own blood must be scenting the green waters.

'Oh God, it's all so horrible,' Claudia whispered. 'It's becoming a terrible nightmare.'

'This is Africa.' Sean held her, trying to give her courage. 'But I'm here with you now, it's going to be all right.'

'Will it, Sean? Do you think we will get out of this alive?'

'There is no money-back guarantee,' he admitted, 'if that's what you are asking for.'

She gave one last sob, and then leant back in his arms and looked steadily into his eyes.

'I'm sorry,' she said. 'I'm acting like a baby. I nearly let go there, but it won't happen again. I promise you that. At least I've found you, before it's too late.' She smiled at him with forced gaiety, bobbing with water up to her chin. 'We'll live for today, or what is left of it.'

'That's my girl.' He grinned back at her. 'Whatever happens, I'll be able to say I loved Claudia Monterro.'

'And was loved by her in turn,' she assured him, and she kissed him again, a long lingering kiss, warm and spiced with her tears, an expression not of lust but of longing, for both of them a pledge and an assurance, something true and certain in a world of dangerous uncertainty.

Sean was not even aware of his own pervading physical arousal, until she broke the kiss and demanded breathlessly, 'I want you now, this minute. I won't . . . I dare not wait. Oh God, Sean, my darling, now we are alive and in love, but by tonight we could both be dead. Take me now.'

He glanced quickly around their leafy arbour. Through the chinks he could see the banks. They seemed to have drifted below the Renamo fortifications. There was no further sign of

249

life below the galleries of tall riverine trees, and the silence of the African noon was heavy and somnolent. Closer to them, just beyond arm's length, floated Job and Dedan, but only the backs of their bare heads were visible as they surveyed the riverbanks.

Sean looked back at Claudia, looked into her honey-gold eyes, and he wanted her. He knew that he had never wanted anything in his life so desperately.

'Just say it one more time,' she breathed huskily.

'I love you,' he said, and they kissed again, but a different type of kiss, hard where the first had been soft, hot where it had been warm, and savagely urgent where it had been gentle and lingering.

'Quickly,' she said into his mouth. 'Every second is precious.' And her hands below the surface of the water were tearing at their clothing. He had to use one hand to keep them from slipping under the green water, but with the other he helped her as best he could.

She opened the front of his bush jacket and then her own shirt to the waist and pressed herself to him. Her breasts were lubricated by the cool water. Her nipples were hard with wanting him, he could feel them distinctly sliding over his chest, they felt as big as ripe grapes.

He tugged the tongue of the leather belt that held her khaki shorts and she lifted herself to make it easier for him to un-zip the fly, and then kicked to free her legs as he worked the clinging wet cloth down over her buttocks. He slipped the garment over his arm to prevent it floating away and she was naked from the waist down. In frantic haste she opened the front of his trousers and thrust in both hands to scoop him out.

'Oh Sean,' she blurted. 'Oh God, my darling. You are so big, so hard. Oh please, quickly, quickly!'

In the water they were both weightless and as lithe as mating otters. Her long legs closed around his body wrapping him, her knees up under his armpits, her ankles locked across the small of her back as she searched for him blindly. He angled his hips to meet her thrusts and they almost succeeded but it slipped away harmlessly between their tense naked bellies.

She groaned softly with frustration and reached down and seized him again. Then with a lewd and beautiful arching of her back she took in just the tip of him. They strained against each other and suddenly her body went rigid and her golden eyes opened so wide they seemed to fill her face, as he went sliding full length into her. After the cold green water she was so hot that it was almost unbearable and he cried out involuntarily.

Both Job and Dedan glanced around in surprise, then looked away in embarrassment but Sean and Claudia were oblivious to all the world.

It was over very swiftly and she hung around his neck exhausted as a marathon runner at the end of a gruelling race.

Sean recovered his voice first. 'I'm sorry,' he said. 'It was so quick. I couldn't wait. Did you . . . ?'

'I was there long before you.' She grinned up at him, a lopsided and uncertain grin. 'It was like being in an auto accident, quick, but devastating!'

They remained locked together by the embrace of her legs and arms, for a long time, quiet and resting, until she felt him shrivel and slip away and only then she released the grip of her legs and reached up with her mouth to kiss him tenderly.

'Now you belong to me, and I to you. Even if I die today, it won't matter so much. I have had you in me.'

'Let's try for a little more than one day.' He smiled gently down at her. 'Get dressed now, my love.' He handed her back her clothing. 'While I check on what's happening in the real world out there.'

He swam away from her and went to Job. 'What do you see?' he asked.

'I think we are clear of the lines,' Job answered, avoiding Sean's eyes tactfully. Strangely, it did not embarrass Sean that Job knew what had happened between Claudia and himself. He still felt elated and triumphant at the consummation of their love, and nothing could degrade it.

'As soon as it's dark enough, we'll swim the tree in towards the bank and get ashore.' Sean glanced at his Rolex. Not more than two hours to sunset. 'Keep your eyes open,' he said, and swam across to Dedan to repeat the warning.

He tried to estimate the rate of the current by watching the bank, and decided it was not more than two miles an hour. They would still be dangerously close to the Renamo lines when the sun set, and the river was flowing eastwards towards the sea, so they would have to work their way round or through General China's forces to reach the Zimbabwe border in the west. It was a formidable task but Sean still felt optimistic and invulnerable. He left Dedan's side and swam back to Claudia.

'You make me feel good,' he said.

'That's going to be my job in future,' she assured him. 'But what do we do now?'

'Nothing until dark, except steer this liner down the river.'

She cuddled against him under the water, and they held each other and watched the riverbanks drift slowly by.

After a while she said, 'I'm getting cold.'

They had been in the water for almost two hours, Sean realized, and though it was only a few degrees below their body temperature it was gradually chilling them through.

She slanted her eyes at him and gave him a naughty grin. 'Can't you think of something to prevent hypothermia?' she asked. 'Or do I have to make a suggestion?'

'Well,' he pretended to reflect, 'we can't light a fire.'

'Can't we?' she asked. 'Do you want a bet?' And she reached down and after a few seconds she whispered, 'See, nothing to it, and I didn't even use matches.'

'It's a miracle!' he agreed, and began to unbuckle her belt again.

'This time let's see if we can make the miracle last longer than ten seconds,' she suggested.

As the sun set, it turned the surface of the river to a luminous serpent with scales of furnace orange and glowing crimson.

'Now we can begin working in towards the bank,' Sean ordered, and they began to swim the floating tree across the current. It was heavy and ungainly, most of its bulk below the surface, and it resisted their efforts to move it closer to the bank. All four of them kept at it, kicking out strongly, and ponderously it began to swing across the wide waters.

The sun slipped below the horizon and the waters turned black as crude oil, the trees along them were dark cut-out silhouettes against the last glow of the sunset, but they were still thirty metres from the southern bank.

'We'll swim from here,' Sean decided. 'Keep close together. Don't get separated in the dark. Is everybody ready?'

They bunched up, clinging to the same branch. Sean reached for Claudia's hand and opened his mouth to give the order, and then closed it again, and cocked his head to listen.

He was surprised that he had not heard it before, perhaps the sound had been muffled by the high banks of the river and the tall trees that lined its winding course. However, it was suddenly loud and unmistakable, the sound of an outboard motor running at high speed.

'Oh shit,' he whispered bitterly, and looked towards the near bank. Only thirty metres away, it could just as well have been thirty miles.

The whine of the motor rose and fell as the acoustics of water and trees played tricks, but it was clearly coming downstream fast, running down from the direction of the Renamo lines. Sean ducked his head to gaze through a chink in the vegetation, and he saw a glow in the darkness, a beam of light that shafted briefly across the night sky and then bounced from the dark trees along the bank, glinted from the water, and swept boldly along the banks.

'Renamo patrol boat,' Sean said. 'And they are looking for us.'

Claudia tightened her grip on his hand, and no one else spoke.

'We'll try to hide in here,' Sean said, 'though I don't see how they can miss us. Get ready to duck under when the light hits us.'

The sound of the motor changed, slowing down, and then the craft swept round the upstream bend of the river a few hundred yards distant but coming down swiftly on the current towards them.

The beam of the spotlight played alternately along each bank, lighting them like day. It was an enormously powerful beam, probably one of the portable battle lights similar to the one which had trapped Sean at the top of the cliffs.

As the beam switched from bank to bank it briefly illuminated the craft and its crew. Sean recognized it as an eighteen-foot inflatable Zodiac driven by a fifty-five-horsepower Yamaha outboard, and though he could not count the occupants, there were at least eight or nine of them and they had a light machine-gun mounted in the bows. The man with the battle light was standing amidships.

The beam of light glanced over their refuge, dazzling them for an instant with its malevolent white eye, passing on and leaving them blinded by its brilliance, then coming back remorselessly and holding them captive. Sean heard someone give an indistinct order in the Shangane language, and the Zodiac altered course towards them, the beam of the battle light still fastened on them.

All four of them sank low in the water, until only their nostrils were exposed and they cowered behind the branch to which they were clinging.

The helmsman of the Zodiac throttled back, and slipped the engine into neutral. The black rubber craft drifted on the current, level with them but twenty feet off; the battle light darted and probed the leafy mass.

'Turn your face away,' Sean told Claudia in a tight whisper, and took her in his arms below the surface. Even their tanned faces would shine in the light and he screened her and turned the back of his head towards the Zodiac.

'There is nobody there,' somebody said in Shangane. Although spoken at conversational level the voice carried clearly across the water to where they were hiding.

'Go around!' another voice ordered in a tone of command, and Sean recognized the Shangane sergeant who had been his escort. A white wake spread out behind the Zodiac as it began to circle the floating tree.

The light beam cast stark black shadows from the tangled branches and struck dazzling reflections when it touched the water. As the Zodiac circled, they paddled quietly to the further side of their leafy refuge, and when the beam fastened on them, they slid softly below the surface, trying not to gasp for breath as they came up again.

The deadly game of hide and seek lasted all of eternity, before the voice in the Zodiac said again, 'There is nobody there. We are wasting time.'

'Keep circling,' the sergeant's voice answered, and then after another minute, 'Gunner, fire a burst into the tree.'

In the bows of the Zodiac, the muzzle flashes of the RPD light machine-gun twinkled like fairy lights, but a storm of shot tore into the floating tree with brutal and stunning savagery. It cracked in their eardrums, and thumped into the branches over their heads cutting loose a shower of leaves and twigs, it ripped away slabs of bark and kicked spray from the surface of the water, odd shots ricocheting into the night, wailing like demented spirits.

Sean pulled Claudia below the surface, but still could hear the bullets plunging into the water above them or striking the trunk of the tree. He kept down until his lungs burned as though they were filled with acid and only then pulled himself to the surface to catch another breath.

The gunner in the Zodiac was firing taps, not a single continu-

254

ous burst. Like a Morse operator on the key, an expert gunner has his own distinctive style that others can recognize. This one fired double taps, five rounds each, it needed a concert pianist's touch on the trigger to achieve such precision.

As Sean and Claudia came back to the surface, straining for the sweet taste of air, Dedan also came up only three feet in front of them. The reflection of the battle light lit his head clearly. His short woolly beard streamed water, his eyes were like balls of ivory in his ebony face and his mouth was open, drinking in air.

A bullet touched his temple, just above the ear. His head flinched to the shot, and it opened his scalp cleanly as a sabre cut. Involuntarily he cried out, a glottal bellow like that of a heart-shot bull buffalo, then his head fell forward and he sank face down into the dark waters.

Sean lunged out and caught his upper arm, pulling him back to the surface before he drifted away, but his head lolled and his eyes had rolled back in their sockets, exposing only the whites.

However, the men in the Zodiac had heard his cry and the Shangane sergeant shouted to one of his men, 'Get ready to throw in a grenade,' then to them, 'Come out of there. I'll give you ten seconds.'

'Job, answer him,' Sean ordered with resignation. 'Tell him we are coming out.'

Matabele and Shangane could understand each other, and Job shouted to them not to fire again.

Claudia helped Sean keep Dedan's head above the surface and between them they pulled him towards the Zodiac. The battle light dazzled them, but hands reached down from out of the glare and one at a time dragged them on board.

Shivering like half-drowned puppies, they huddled in the centre of the boat. They had Dedan's body stretched out between them and Sean lifted his head gently into his lap. He was unconscious, barely breathing, and gently Sean twisted his head to examine the bullet wound across his temple.

For a moment, he did not recognize what he was seeing. From the long shallow wound bulged something white and glistening in the lamp light.

Beside him, Claudia shuddered violently, and whispered, 'Sean, it's his, it's his . . .' She could not bring herself to say it,

255

and only then Sean realized that Dedan's brain, still contained in the tough white membrane of the *dura mater*, was bulging out through the rent in his skull like an inner tube through a hole in an auto tyre.

The Shangane sergeant gave an order and the helmsman gunned the outboard motor and swung the Zodiac upstream. They ran at full throttle back towards the Renamo lines.

Sean sat on the floorboards with Dedan's head in his lap. There was nothing he could do, except clasp his wrist and feel Dedan's pulse grow weaker and more erratic, then finally fade away altogether.

'He's dead,' he said quietly. Job said nothing and Claudia turned her face away.

Sean held the dead head in his lap all the long return. Only when the helmsman cut the engine and coasted in to the bank did he look up. There were lighted lanterns and dark shapes awaiting them at the landing.

The Shangane sergeant gave a brusque order and two of his men lifted Dedan's corpse off Sean's lap and dumped him face down on the muddy bank. Another trooper grabbed Claudia's arm and dragged her to her feet. He shoved her roughly ashore and when she whirled on him furiously to protest, he lifted his AK butt to strike her in the centre of her chest.

Sean was close beside him and he caught the man's arm and stifled the blow.

'Do that again, you son of a syphilitic hyena,' he said softly in Shangane, 'and I'll hack off your *mtondo* with a blunt axe and make you eat it without salt.'

The trooper stared at him, amazed more by his perfect Shangane than the threat itself, and on the bank the Shangane sergeant let out a bellow of delighted laughter.

'Better do what he says,' he warned his trooper, 'unless you are very hungry. This one means what he says.' Then he grinned at Sean. 'So you talk Shangane like one of us, and you understood everything we said!' He shook his head ruefully. 'I won't let you fool me again!'

* * *

Wet, cold and dishevelled they were dragged unceremoniously into General China's bunker and paraded before his desk. One

256

glance at his face and Sean recognized that the man was in a cold fury.

For almost a full minute he stared at Sean without rising from his seat, and then he said, 'The woman is being moved to another camp, well away from here. You will have no further opportunity to see her, until I order it.'

Sean kept his expression neutral but Claudia gave a little cry of protest, and seized Sean's arm as though she could prevent the threatened separation. General China nodded with satisfaction at her distress, and went on quietly, 'She no longer merits the special treatment which she has been given up until now, and I have ordered that she be placed in irons to prevent any further attempts at escape. She will also be kept in solitary confinement.'

The two female gaolers were standing against the wall beside his desk, and he glanced at them and nodded. The taller of the two wore sergeant's stripes on her sleeve. She gave an order to the squat toad-faced trooper beside her, and the woman came forward. The stainless-steel manacles dangled from her hand.

Claudia tightened her grip on Sean's arm and shrank away from her. The woman hesitated, and the tall sergeant gave another sharp command. The gaoler grabbed Claudia's wrist and without apparent effort plucked her away from Sean's side.

With the expertise of long practice, she spun Claudia around and thrust her face hard against the sandbagged wall of the bunker, snapping the manacles on one wrist as she did so, then pulling both Claudia's arms behind her back and locking the second cuff on her other wrist.

She stepped back and the tall female sergeant stepped up and took Claudia's hands and lifted them high between her shoulder-blades. Claudia gasped with pain as she was forced onto her toes. The sergeant inspected the manacles; they were closed snugly around Claudia's wrists, but she was not satisfied. Deliberately the sergeant tightened them two more notches and Claudia gasped again.

'That's too tight, they are cutting into me.'

'Tell that bitch to loosen them,' Sean snapped at General China, and he smiled for the first time that evening and leaned back in his chair.

'Colonel Courtney, I have given orders that the woman is not to be allowed another chance to escape. Sergeant Cara is only doing her duty.'

'She is cutting off the circulation. Miss Monterro could lose her hands to gangrene.'

'That would be unfortunate,' General China agreed. 'However, I will not interfere, unless . . .' he paused.

'Unless?' Sean demanded savagely.

'Unless I am assured of your complete co-operation and unless I have your parole that you will not attempt another escape.'

Sean looked down at Claudia's hands. Already they were beginning to swell and change colour, darkening to a leaden hue, the bright steel bands cutting into her wrists, the veins puffing up into dark blue cords below the manacles.

'Gangrene is a dangerous condition and unfortunately our facilities for amputation of limbs are very primitive,' General China remarked.

'All right,' Sean said heavily. 'I give you my parole.'

'And your co-operation,' he prompted.

'And I promise co-operation,' Sean agreed.

General China gave an order and the sergeant used the key on the manacles, letting them out two notches each and immediately the swelling of Claudia's hands dissipated and her skin colouring began to return to its normal creamy tan as the blood drained away.

'Take her away!' China ordered in English and the sergeant nodded to her assistant gaoler. They each seized one of Claudia's arms and dragged her to the door.

'Wait!' Sean shouted, but they ignored him and when he tried to follow her, the big Shangane sergeant seized his arms from behind in a hammer lock.

'Sean!' Claudia's voice had a note of hysteria. 'Don't let them take me!' But they pushed her out of the bunker and the canvas curtain fell between them.

'Sean!' Her voice came back to him.

'I love you!' he shouted after her, struggling against the sergeant's grip. 'It will be all right, darling. Just remember I love you. I'll do what I have to do to get you out of here.'

The promise rang hollowly in his own ears and her voice was a despairing wail. 'Sean!' And then again very faintly. 'Sean!' Then silence beyond the curtain.

Sean found he was panting with emotion but he forced himself to cease struggling and stand quietly. The sergeant relaxed his

258

grip and Sean shrugged him away and turned to General China.

'You bastard!' he said. 'You rotten bastard!'

'I see that you are in no mood for sensible discussion,' China told him, and glanced at his wristwatch. 'And it's well after midnight. We'll let you cool off.' He looked at the sergeant and changed to Shangane. 'Take them,' he indicated Sean and Job, 'feed them, give them dry clothes and a blanket, let them sleep and bring them to me at dawn tomorrow.' The sergeant saluted and pushed them towards the door.

'I have work for them to do,' China warned him. 'Make sure they are in condition to do it.'

* * *

Sean and Job slept side by side on the floor of a dugout with a guard sitting over them. The floor was of hard-packed damp earth and the blankets were verminous, but neither the discomfort, nor the tickle of insects crawling over his skin, nor even thoughts of Claudia could keep Sean awake.

The sergeant woke him in the dark of pre-dawn from a profound and dreamless sleep by dumping an armful of clothing on his prostrate body.

'Get dressed,' he ordered.

Sean sat up and scratched the bite of a bed bug.

'What's your name?' It was a relief to be able to speak Shangane freely.

'Alphonso Henriques Mabasa,' the Shangane told him proudly, and Sean smiled at the unlikely combination. The name of a Portuguese emperor, and the Shangane name for one who strikes with a club.

'A war club on your enemies and a meat club on their wives?' Sean asked, and Alphonso guffawed.

Job sat up and grimaced at Sean's ribald sally.

'At five in the morning, before breakfast!' he protested, and shook his head sadly, but Sean heard Alphonso delightedly repeating the joke to his men outside the dugout.

'With the Shangane, it doesn't take much to establish the reputation of being a wag,' Job remarked in Sindebele as they sorted through the bundle of clothing Alphonso had brought them. It was all secondhand but reasonably clean. Sean found a military-style cloth cap and a suit of tiger-striped battledress, and discarded his bush jacket and shorts which were by now in rags. He kept on his comfortable old velskoen.

Breakfast was a stew of kapenta, the fingerling dried fish he thought of as African whitebait, and a porridge of maize meal. 'What about tea?' Sean asked, and Alphonso laughed.

'You think this is the Polana Hotel in Maputo?'

Dawn was just breaking when Alfonso escorted them down to the riverbank where they found General China and his staff inspecting the damage done by the Hind gunships.

'We lost twenty-six men killed and wounded yesterday,' China greeted Sean. 'And almost as many deserters during the night. Morale is sinking fast.' He spoke in English and it was clear that none of his staff understood. Despite the circumstances, he looked dapper and competent in his beret and crisply ironed battledress, medal ribbons across his chest and general officer's stars on his epaulettes. The ivory-handled pistol hung on his webbing belt and he wore aviator-style mirrored sunglasses with thin gold frames.

'Unless we can stop those gunships, it will be over in three months, before the rains can save us.'

The rains were the time of the guerrilla when head-high grass, impassable roads and flooded rivers hamstringed the defender and afforded concealment and sanctuary to his tormentor.

'I watched those Hinds in action yesterday,' Sean told him cautiously. 'Captain Job here borrowed one of your RPG 7 rocket-launchers and scored a direct hit with an AP rocket.'

China looked at Job with new interest. 'Good,' he said. 'None of my own men have been able to do that yet. What happened?'

'Nothing,' Job answered simply.

'No damage,' Sean confirmed.

'The entire machine is encased in titanium armour plate,' China nodded, and looked up at the sky, a nervous gesture as though he were expecting one of the humpbacked monsters to appear miraculously. 'Our friends in the south have offered us one of their new Darter missile systems, but there is the difficulty of bringing in the launch vehicles, heavy trucks over these roads and through Frelimo-controlled territory.' He shook his head. 'We need an infantry weapon, one that can be carried and used by foot soldiers.'

'As far as I know there is only one effective weapon of that kind. The Americans developed a technique in Afghanistan.

They adapted the original Stinger missile and worked out a way of getting through the armour. I haven't any idea of the details,' Sean added hastily. He knew it was unwise to set himself up as an expert, but the problem was intriguing and he had allowed himself to be carried away.

'You are quite correct, Colonel. The modified Stinger is the only weapon that has proved effective against the Hind. That's your task, the price of your freedom. I want you to procure a shipment of Stingers for me.'

Sean stopped dead on the riverbank and stared at him, and then he began to smile. 'Certainly,' he said. 'A piece of cake. Do you have a preference for colour and flavour, how about baboon-ball blue and kiwi fruit?'

For the first time that morning China smiled back at him. 'The Stingers are here already, it's simply a matter of picking them up.'

Sean's grin faded. 'I hope, most fervently, that this is a joke. I know that Savimbi has been given Stingers by the Yanks, but Angola is on the other side of the continent.'

'Our Stingers are much closer than that,' China assured him. 'Do you remember the old Rhodesian Fire Force base at Grand Reef?'

'I should,' Sean nodded. 'The Scouts operated out of there for almost a year.'

'Of course, I remember.' China touched the lobe of his ear beneath the gaudy beret. 'It was from there you launched the attack on my camp at Inhlozane.' His expression was suddenly bleak.

'That was in another war,' Sean reminded him.

China's expression relaxed. 'As I was saying, the Stingers we want are at Grand Reef.'

'I don't understand.' Sean shook his head. 'The Yanks would never give Stingers to Mugabe. He is a Marxist and there is no deep love between Zimbabwe and the US. It doesn't make sense.'

'Oh yes, it does,' China assured him. 'In a roundabout African way, it makes good sense.' He glanced at his watch. 'Tea time,' he said. 'I believe you were asking for a brew this morning. No matter what side we were on, the war made us all tea addicts.'

China led them back to his command bunker and an orderly brought in the smoke-blackened kettle immediately.

'The Americans dislike Mugabe, but they dislike the South Africans more,' China explained. 'Mugabe is harbouring and assisting ANC guerrillas operating across his borders into South Africa.'

Sean nodded grimly. He had seen photographs of the carnage created by a limpet mine detonated in a South African supermarket; it had happened on the last Friday of the month, payday for monthly workers, when the store was crowded with housewives and their offspring both black and white.

'The South Africans have vowed to pursue the guerrillas wherever they run. They have already repeatedly made good that threat, hot pursuit across the borders of all their neighbours. The ANC have announced their intention of stepping up their bombing of soft civilian targets. Mugabe knows what the consequences will be, so he wants a weapon to deal with the South African Puma gunships when they cross his border to cull the ANC.'

'I still don't believe the Yanks would supply him with Stingers,' Sean said flatly.

'Not directly,' China agreed. 'But the British are training Mugabe's army for him. They are the middle men. They have got the Stingers from the Americans and they are training Mugabe's crack Third Brigade to use them at Grand Reef.'

'How the hell do you know all this?'

'You must remember that I was once a minister, albeit a junior one, in Mugabe's cabinet. I still have good friends in high places.'

Sean thought about it. 'You are right,' he nodded. 'It is all typically African. So the Stingers are at Grand Reef.'

'They were delivered by a Royal Air Force Hercules fourteen days ago, and are scheduled to be deployed along the South African and Zimbabwe border by the beginning of next month. They will be aimed at your countrymen, Colonel Courtney.'

Sean felt a stirring of patriotic outrage, but he kept his expression neutral.

'The training is being conducted by Royal Artillery personnel, a captain and two NCOs, so you will begin to understand why I require a white face for my plans.'

'It certainly begins to sound ominous,' Sean muttered. 'Tell me what it is exactly that you require.'

'I want you to go back to Zimbabwe and bring me those Stinger missiles.'

262

Sean showed no emotion as he asked, 'In exchange?'.

'Once the missiles are delivered to me, I will remove the manacles from Miss Monterro and transfer her to quarters where you will be able to visit her regularly,' he paused and allowed himself a knowing smile, 'and spend some time with her each day or evening in private.'

'What about our release?'

'Yes,' China agreed. 'All three of you will be released after you have performed one additional service for me – after first obtaining the Stingers.'

'And what is that service?'

China held up both hands. 'One thing at a time, Colonel Courtney. The missiles first. Once you have delivered them, we will discuss the final part of our bargain.'

Sean scowled into his tea mug as he turned it over in his mind, trying to find some vantage point to adopt, but China interrupted him.

'Colonel, every minute you waste merely prolongs Miss Monterro's –' he searched for the correct word – 'her discomfort. Until I have those missiles, she will wear her manacles night and day, waking or sleeping, eating or performing all the other essential functions of life. I suggest you begin immediately laying out your plans to procure them for me.'

Sean stood up and went to the large-scale wall map behind China's desk. He didn't really need to study it. He could have closed his eyes and visualized every valley and peak, every wrinkle of land along the border between Mozambique and Zimbabwe. The railway line crossed the border near the little town of Umtali, and twenty kilometres beyond it on the Zimbabwe side a tiny red aircraft symbol marked the position of the Grand Reef airfield and base.

Sean touched the stylized aircraft symbol with his forefinger, and Job came to stand beside him. They both stared at it thoughtfully. How many times had they sortied from that field, shambling out to the rumbling Dakota transports under the burden of parachute and battle packs and weapons. Each of them could picture clearly the position of every building, the hangars and barracks and perimeter defence.

'Twenty Ks from the border post,' Job said softly, 'fifteen minutes by truck, but we'll never get there on foot.'

'You spoke of a plan, General China. What do you have in

mind? Can you provide us with vehicles?' Sean asked without looking round.

'Some time ago my men captured three Unimog trucks, with authentic Zimbabwe army paintwork and papers. We have them hidden,' China answered, and Sean breathed a sigh of relief.

'My plan is for you to cross the border disguised as Zimbabwean troops.'

'I'll bet there is a huge volume of military traffic through the border post.'

'There is,' China affirmed.

'We'll need Zimbabwe army uniforms for all the black troops and something for me.' Sean tapped his finger on the map. 'We will have to wheedle our way into the base without firing a shot.'

'I have a British field officer's uniform for you,' China said softly. 'It's genuine and I have the papers to go with it.'

'How the hell did you get that?'

'Three months ago we attacked a Zimbabwe column near Vila de Manica. There was a British observer with the column and he got caught in the crossfire. He was a major in one of the guards regiments, seconded to the high commissioner in Harare as a military attaché, according to his papers.

'The uniform has been cleaned of blood and the tears made by fragmentation grenade have been patched most expertly. The tailor who did the work made my own uniform.' China smoothed the fit of his tunic over his lean flanks and looked pleased with it. 'He will alter the captured uniform to fit you, Colonel. The British major was about your height, but a great deal larger around the waist and backside.'

'A guards regiment,' Sean smiled. 'I don't know about my accent, any Englishman would pick me out as a colonial the instant I open my mouth.'

'You will have to deal only with the Third Brigade guards at the base gates. I assure you they will not have such discerning ears.'

'Okay,' Sean said. 'So we may be able to get in, but how the hell do we get out?' He was beginning to enjoy himself, becoming absorbed with the problem.

'Not so fast, Sean.' Job was studying the map. 'We can't just pitch up at the gates without an invitation and demand entry. With the Stingers there the security will be at a maximum.'

'That is correct,' China concurred. 'However, I have more

good news for you. I actually have a man inside the base. He is a nephew of mine, we are a large family.' He looked complacent as he went on. 'He is in signals, a warrant officer, second in command of the Grand Reef communications centre. He will be able to fake a signal from the Zimbabwe high command authorizing an inspection of the Stinger programme by the military attaché. So the guards at the base will be expecting you. They won't scrutinize your pass too closely.'

'If you have a man inside the base, he'll know exactly where the Stingers are stored,' Job suggested eagerly.

'Right,' China nodded. 'They are in number three hangar. That's second from the left.'

'We know exactly where number three hangar is,' Sean assured him, and frowned as he tried to anticipate the other problems they would encounter.

'I will want to know the packaging of the missiles, sizes and weights.' China scribbled a note on his pad. 'And there must be instruction manuals covering their operation. Those will certainly be in the office of the Royal Artillery captain. I must know exactly where that is.' He ticked off each item on his fingers as it occurred to him, and Job added his own ideas.

'We'll need a diversion,' he suggested. 'A second unit to stage an attack on the base perimeter furthest from the hangar and training centre, plenty of tracer and RPG rocks and white phosphorus grenades – we will need another squad for that.'

It was like old times, how often had they worked together like this, each stimulating the other, their excitement kept under tight rein, but sparkling in their eyes.

Once Job remarked, 'I'm glad it's the Third Brigade we'll be going against, that bunch of nun-killers and child-rapers, they led the purge in Matabeleland.' The slaughter and atrocity that had accompanied the brigade's sweep through the tribal areas from which the Matabele political dissidents had been operating was fresh in both their memories.

'Two of my brothers, my grandfather . . .' Job's voice dropped to a deathly whisper. 'The Third Brigade threw their bodies down the old shaft at Antelope Mine.'

'This isn't personal vengeance,' Sean warned him. 'All we want is those Stingers, Job.' The intertribal hatred of Africa was as fierce as any Corsican vendetta, and Job had physically to shake himself to break the spell of it.

265

'You're right, but a few Third Brigade scalps would be a nice little fringe benefit.'

Sean grinned. Despite his admonition, the thought of taking on ZANLA again gave him equal satisfaction. How many good men, and women, how many dear friends had he lost to them over the eleven long years of the bush war, and how complex were the lines of hatred and loyalty that held together the very fabric of Africa. Only an African could ever understand it.

'Okay.' Sean brought them back to hard reality. 'We have got in. We have the Stingers, say two loaded Unimogs. I have found the manuals. We are ready to pull out. The diversion has lured most of the guards to the southern perimeter of the base, on the far side of the airfield. Now we have to get out. They aren't going to be so happy about letting us go.'

'We charge the gates,' Job said. 'Use one truck to break down the barricades.'

'Yes,' Sean nodded. 'And then? We aren't going to be able to get out of the country through the border post at Umtali. By that time the whole Zimbabwe army and Frelimo will all be after us.'

They both turned back to the wall map again. Sean reached up and traced the road that branched northwards, just before it reached the town of Umtali, and then ran parallel with the border as it traversed the rugged eastern highlands towards Inyanga National Park, an area of misty peaks and wet densely forested valleys. He touched one of the valleys, a green wedge driven deeply into the barrier of mountains.

'Honde Valley,' he read the legend. The road crossed the head of it and the valley itself was a funnel that led down to the border and the Mozambique uplands. It formed a natural re-entrance to the highlands, a gateway which had been one of the major infiltration routes of the ZANLA guerrillas from their training bases in Mozambique. The hard way, Sean and Job had learned all its secrets, the hidden trails and strong points, the false ports and the concealed passes.

'The track down to St Mary's mission,' Sean said and they stared at it. 'That's as far as we can take the trucks.'

'From there is only six Ks to the border,' Job murmured.

'Six hard Ks,' Sean qualified. 'And we won't be clear just because we have crossed into Mozambique. We will still have them after us until we get into Renamo-held ground.'

Sean turned back to General China. 'I'll want porters waiting for us at St Mary's mission. How far does your control of territory extend?'

'The porters will present no problem.' China came to stand between them and pointed to a speck on the map marked Mavonela. 'And I can have trucks waiting at this village. Once you reach Mavonela, I will consider that you have made good delivery of the missiles.'

'I suggest we don't try and bring out forty Stingers with one column of porters,' Job cut in. 'It will make a perfect target for Mugabe's MIGs. One load of napalm is all it would take.'

'And of course, Frelimo can call in their Hinds.' Sean added. 'You are right, Job. Once it is light enough for air-attack, we will bombshell.' He was referring to the old guerrilla trick of splintering the column and offering numerous small elusive targets, rather than a single large ungainly one. 'Can you arrange for a series of RZs rather than a single RZ at Mavonela village?' He used the old Scouts' abbreviation for a rendezvous.

'Yes,' China nodded. 'We will disperse the transport along the Mavonela road.' He traced it out. 'One truck every kilometre, hidden under camouflage netting, and we'll move the Stingers out on the last stage under cover of darkness.'

'All right, let's draw up a timetable,' Sean said. 'Let's get it all down on paper. I'll need writing material.'

China opened a drawer of his desk and brought out a cheap notebook and ballpoint pen. While they worked, China sent for his quartermaster, a chubby little man who had run a men's outfitters in Beira before economic necessity rather than ideological commitment had forced him to leave the town and seek employment in the deep bush with China's guerrillas.

He arrived carrying the uniform for a staff officer of the Irish Guards in the field, complete with insignia, headgear, webbing and boots in his arms. Sean donned the uniform for a fitting without interrupting their planning session. The tunic and trousers had to be taken in, and the boots were a size too large.

'Better too big than too small,' Sean decided. 'I'll wear a couple of pairs of socks.'

The tailor tucked and pinned and crawled around Sean's feet as he let the trouser bottoms down an inch.

'Fine.' Sean examined the guards major's papers that China

laid out on the desk top. From the photograph, Sean saw that the major had been a fleshy fair-haired individual in his late forties.

'Gavin Duffy,' Sean read the dead man's name aloud. 'You'll have to alter the ID photograph.'

'My propaganda officer will take care of that,' China told him.

The propaganda officer was a mulatto, half Portuguese, half Shangane, and he was armed with a polaroid camera. He took four mug shots of Sean and then spirited away the deceased guards major's ID card to doctor the photograph.

'All right.' Sean turned back to China. 'Now I want to take command of the men who will make up the raiding party and see them properly kitted out. You'll have to explain to them that they are to take their orders from me in future.'

China smiled and stood up. 'Follow me, Colonel. I'll take you to meet your new command.'

He led the way out of the bunker, but once they were on the path through the forest that led down to the river, Sean fell in beside him and they continued to discuss the raid.

'Obviously I am going to need more than the original ten men in Sergeant Alphonso's squad, at least another detachment to make the diversionary attack on the base,' Sean broke off as the mournful wail of the hand-operated sirens rose from the camp around them, and instantly all around them was turmoil and confusion.

'The Hinds!' shouted China. 'Take cover!' And he sprinted for a sandbagged emplacement amongst the trees nearby. There was a twin-barrelled 12.7mm anti-aircraft weapon mounted in the emplacement. It would be a prime target for the Hind gunners and Sean looked around quickly for alternative cover.

In the long grass on the opposite side of the track, he spotted a less conspicuous shell-scrape and ran for it. As he tumbled into it, he heard the oncoming roar of the Hind gunships and the cacophony of ground fire built up swiftly. Job jumped down into the fox-hole and squatted beside him, and then another smaller figure appeared above them and as nimble as a hare leapt into the hole.

For a moment, Sean did not realize who it was, not until the wrinkled face creased like a used napkin into a wide black smile and the man said happily, 'I see you, *Bwana*.'

'You! You silly little bugger!' Sean stared at him in disbelief. 'I sent you back to Chiwewe. What the hell are you doing back here?'

'I went back to Chiwewe, as you commanded,' Matatu said virtuously. 'Then I came back to look for you.'

Sean still stared at Matatu in awe as he considered what that statement entailed. Then he shook his head and began to smile, immediately the little man's answering grin seemed to split his face in two.

'Nobody saw you?' Sean demanded in Swahili. 'You came through the lines into the headquarters of an army, and nobody saw you?'

'Nobody sees Matatu, when Matatu does not want to be seen.'

The earth trembled under them, and the sound of rockets and gunfire forced them to put their heads close together and shout into each other's faces.

'How long have you been here?'

'Since yesterday.' Matatu looked apologetic. He pointed to the sky where the Hinds were circling. 'Since those machines attacked yesterday. I was watching when you jumped into the river. I followed you along the bank when you used the tree as a boat. I wanted to come to you then, but I saw crocodiles. Then in the night the bad men, the *shifta*, came in the boat and brought you back here. I waited and watched.'

'Did you see where they took the white woman?' Sean demanded.

'I saw them take her away last night.' Matatu showed little interest in Claudia. 'But I waited for you.'

'Can you find out where they took her?' Sean asked.

'Of course.' Matatu's grin faded and he looked indignant. 'I can follow them anywhere they took her.'

Sean unbuttoned his tunic pocket and pulled out his new notebook. Crouched in the bottom of the shell-scrape with an air-raid thundering overhead, he composed the first love letter he had written in years. Filling the single tiny sheet of cheap notepaper with all the assurances and comfort and cheer that he could muster, he ended it, 'Be strong, it won't be for much longer and remember I love you. Whatever happens, I love you.'

He ripped the page out of the notebook and folded it carefully.

'Take this to her.' He handed it to Matatu. 'See that she gets it and then come back to me.'

Matatu tucked the scrap of paper into his loin-cloth and waited expectantly.

'Did you see the hole in which I slept last night?' Sean asked.

'I saw you come from there this morning,' Matatu nodded.

'That will be our meeting-place,' Sean told him. 'Come to me there, when the *shifta* are asleep.' Sean looked up at the sky. The raid had been fierce but short-lived. The sound of engines and gunfire was dwindling, but dust and smoke drifted over their shelter.

'Go now,' Sean ordered, and Matatu jumped to his feet eager to obey, but Sean took his arm. It was thin as a child's and Sean shook it affectionately. 'Don't let them catch you, old friend,' he said in Swahili.

Matatu shook his head and twinkled with amusement at the absurdity of that thought and then like a puff of smoke from the genie's lamp, he was gone.

They waited a few minutes to let Matatu get clear and then climbed out of the shelter. The trees around them were torn and shattered with shell and rocket fire; across the river an ammunition store was burning and RPG rockets and phosphorus grenades were exploding, sending dense white smoke towering into the sky.

General China came striding down the path to meet them. There was a sooty stain on the sleeve of his uniform and dust on his knees and elbows. His expression was furious.

'Our position here is totally compromised,' he fumed. 'They raid us at will and we have no response.'

'You'll have to pull your main force back out of range of the Hinds,' Sean shrugged.

'I can't do that.' China shook his head. 'It will mean that we can no longer maintain our stranglehold on the railway. It will mean conceding control of the main road system to Frelimo, and inviting them to come on the offensive.'

'Well then,' Sean shrugged again, 'you are going to take a hammering if you remain here.'

'Get me those Stingers,' China hissed. 'Get them, and get them quickly!' And he strode away down the path.

Sean and Job followed him to the bunker complex on the

riverbank where a company of guerrillas, forty men, obviously forewarned of the general's approach, were drawn up in a makeshift parade ground of beaten earth the size of a tennis court. They seemed oblivious of the air-raid damage, the smoke and debris, and the scurrying first-aid parties and damage control teams around them.

Sean recognized Sergeant Alphonso and his Shanganes in the first rank. He came forward and saluted General China, then wheeled and gave the order for the detachment to stand easy. General China wasted few words and little time. He raised his voice and addressed them brusquely in Shangane.

'You men are being given a special task. You will, in future, take your orders from this white officer.' He indicated Sean beside him. 'You will follow those orders strictly. You all know the consequences of failing to do so.' He turned to Sean. 'Carry on, Colonel Courtney,' he said, then strode away back up the path towards the command bunker. Instinctively Sean almost saluted him and then checked himself.

'Screw you, China,' he muttered under his breath, and then gave his full attention to his new command.

Of course, he already knew Sergeant Alphonso's squad well, but the additional men that China had found for him were as likely a looking bunch as he had seen in the Renamo ranks. China had given him of his very best. Sean moved slowly down the front rank, inspecting each of them. They were all equipped with AKM assault rifles, the more modern version of the venerable AK 47. In places the blueing was worn from the metal with long usage, however the weapons were meticulously clean and well maintained. Their webbing was in first-class order, and their uniforms, although again well worn, were neatly patched and repaired.

'Always judge a workman by the state of his tools,' Sean thought. These were top soldiers, proud and hard. He stared into each of their eyes as he came level with them and saw it there. Of all the people of Africa, Sean felt the greatest rapport with the Zulu-originated tribes, the Angoni and Matabele and Shangane. If he had been given his choice these were exactly the type of men he would have chosen for this assignment.

Once he had finished the inspection, he went back to the front and addressed them for the first time in Shangane. 'You and I together are going to burst the balls of the dung-eating Frelimo.'

he said quietly, and in the front rank Sergeant Alphonso grinned wolfishly.

*   *   *

With her hands still manacled behind her back, the two female wardresses and an escort of five troopers marched Claudia Monterro through the darkness over a rough track. Often she stumbled and when she fell and sprawled full length, she was unable to use her hands to protect herself from the rocky surface. Soon her knees were raw and bleeding, and the march became a torturous nightmare.

It seemed without end, hour after hour it went on and every time she fell the tall sergeant harangued her in a language she could not understand. Each time it required more of an effort to regain her feet, for she was unable to use her hands and arms to balance herself.

She was so thirsty that her saliva had turned to a sticky paste in her mouth, her legs ached and her hands and arms held so long in such an unnatural position were numb and cold. Sometimes, she heard voices in the darkness around her and once or twice smelled smoke and saw the glow of a camp-fire or a feeble paraffin lantern so she knew that she was still within the Renamo lines.

The march ended abruptly. She guessed that they were still near the river, she could feel the chill of its waters in the air and see the taller riverine trees silhouetted against the stars and she could smell humanity around her: stale ash of the cooking-fires and woodsmoke, human sweat in unwashed clothing, and human body wastes and the sour odours of garbage. At last, they led her through a barbed wire gate into another prison compound, and dragged her towards one of a row of dugouts.

The two wardresses took her arms and hustled her down a set of earthen steps and pushed her into the darkness so she tripped and fell once more on her injured knees. Behind her, she heard a door being closed and barred, and the darkness was absolute.

After a short struggle she regained her feet, but when she tried to stand full height, the top of her head bumped on the low roof. It felt like a roof of undressed wooden poles still in their bark. She shuffled backwards, stretching out her fingers behind her until she touched the door. It was of hand-sawn planks, rough and sharp with splinters. She pressed her weight upon it but it was solid and unmoving.

Bent over to protect her head, she shuffled around her prison. The walls were damp earth. Her cell was tiny, about six feet square, and in the far corner she stumbled over the only furnishing it contained. It was metal and she explored it with her foot and found that it was an iron bucket. The ripe stench from it left no doubt of its purpose. She completed the circuit of her cell and came back to the door.

Her thirst was an agony now, and she called through the door. 'Please I need water.' Her voice was a harsh croak and her lips felt tight and dry, ready to split. 'Water!' she called, and then remembered the Spanish word and hoped it was the same in Portuguese. 'Agua!'

It was futile. The earthen walls seemed to swallow and deaden the sound of her voice. She shuffled to the far corner and sank down to the dark floor. Only then she realized just how physically exhausted she was, yet the manacles on her wrists prevented her lying on her back or side. She tried to find a position in which she could rest comfortably and at last by wedging herself upright in a corner of the cell she succeeded.

The cold and something else woke her, and she was confused and disorientated. For a moment she believed she was back in her father's home in Anchorage and she cried out for him.

'Papa! Are you there?'

Then she smelled the damp and the sewage bucket, and felt the cold in her joints and her pinioned arms, and she remembered. Despair swept over her like a black wave and she felt herself drowning in it. Then she heard again the sound that had awakened her, and she went rigid and felt the cold sweat burst out on her neck and forehead.

She knew what it was instantly. Claudia had none of the more usual feminine phobias, she had no terror of spiders or snakes, there was just one unnatural terror which afflicted her. She sat rigid and listened to the scampering sounds of a creature moving about her cell. That sound was the stuff of her nightmares, and she stared into the darkness trying to will it away from herself.

Then suddenly she felt it on her. The sharp little claws pricking her skin, the cold touch of paws on her flesh. It was a rat and by the weight of it on her, it must have been huge, as big as a rabbit, and she screamed wildly and lunged to her feet and kicked out blindly at it. When she stopped screaming at last, she shrank into the corner and found she was trembling in wild spasms.

'Stop it!' she told herself. 'Pull yourself together!' And by an enormous effort of will, she regained control. There was complete silence in the darkness, her screams had frightened the creature away for the time being but she still could not bring herself to sit on the dirt floor again, for she was terrified that it would return.

Despite her exhaustion she stood propped in the corner and waited out the rest of the night. She dozed, almost fell asleep on her feet, then jerked awake again. That sequence happened many times, and then as she came awake for the last time, she realized that the darkness was no longer total and she could see.

Light was filtering into the cell and she blinked and found the source of it. There were slits and gaps between the poles of the low roof. These had been daubed with clay and grass, but in one or two places the dried clay had fallen out of the cracks allowing chinks of light through. Stems of coarse elephant grass hung down untidily from the cracks.

Fearfully she looked around the cell, but the rat had disappeared, it must have squeezed through one of the gaps between the poles.

Claudia stumbled across to the reeking galvanized sewage bucket, and only as she stood over it she realized her predicament. Her hands were locked behind her back and with that realization her need became irresistible.

Her fingers were almost devoid of feeling, but in desperate haste she was able to grip her leather belt and gradually work it through the loops of her trousers until the buckle was in the small of her back. She was whimpering with the effort of self-control needed to delay her bodily functions while she clumsily unclasped the belt.

She had lost so much weight that as soon as her belt was loosened her trousers fell around her ankles and she was able to hook a thumb under the elastic of her panties and drag them down as far as her knees.

Always fastidious, Claudia experienced the worst hardship of her captivity when her efforts to cleanse herself properly failed. She found herself sobbing with humiliation as she finally managed to dress again. Her wrists were rubbed raw and her arms ached from the strenuous efforts needed to perform this simple task.

She huddled in the corner of her cell and the stench of the bucket seemed to permeate the very depth of her soul.

A single ray of sunlight shot through a chink in the roof poles and pinned a brilliant silver coin on the far wall. She watched it move infinitely slowly down the earthen wall, and somehow it seemed to warm and cheer her enough to dull the cutting edge of her despair.

Before the coin of light reached the floor of the cell, she heard a scraping at the door as the bars were drawn and the door forced open against its primitive hinges. The tall sergeant stooped into the cell and Claudia scrambled to her feet.

'Please,' she whispered. 'You must let me wash,' she said in her schoolgirl Spanish, but the wardress showed no sign of having understood. In one hand she carried a metal billy-can of water and in the other a bowl of stiff maize cake. She placed the billy-can on the floor and then tipped the lump of maize cake into the dirt beside it.

Claudia's thirst, which she had managed temporarily to subdue, returned in even greater agony, and she almost whimpered at the sight of the billy. It contained almost two litres of clear water.

She sank down on her knees before it like a worshipper and looked up at the wardress.

'Please,' she said in Spanish. 'I must use my hands, please.' The wardress chuckled, the first animation she had shown, and she nudged the billy dangerously with the toe of her boot; a little water slopped over the rim.

'No,' Claudia croaked. 'Don't spill it.'

On her knees she bent over and tried to reach the water with her tongue, thrusting it out as far as it would reach, and felt the blessed wetness on the very tip, but the rim of the metal billy was cutting into her face.

She looked up again. 'Please, help me.'

The wardress laughed again and leaned against the wall watching her efforts with amusement.

Claudia stooped again and gripped the rim of the billy between her teeth. Carefully she tilted it and a few drops trickled between her lips. The pleasure was so intense that her vision clouded. She drank a sip at a time until the level in the billy had fallen to where the liquid could no longer flow into her mouth. However, the vessel was still more than half full and her thirst seemed only to have been aggravated by what she had managed to drink.

Still holding the rim between her teeth, she carefully raised her head, and tilted it backwards. It was too quick. She choked as the water flooded into her mouth, and the billy slipped from between her teeth, water splashed down her chest and puddled on the floor to be quickly absorbed into the dirt.

The wardress let out a shrill shriek of laughter, and Claudia felt the tears of despair fill her eyes. She only just managed to smother the sob that came up her throat.

The wardress deliberately stepped onto the white maize cake, smearing it into the dirt, then with another snort of laughter snatched up the empty billy and left the cell. Claudia heard her still giggling as she rebarred the door of the cell.

She could judge the passage of time by the angle of the sunlight through the chinks in the roof. The first day seemed interminable. Despite the discomfort of the manacles, she was able to sleep fitfully but while she was awake she occupied herself by planning to increase her chances of survival.

Water was her most pressing need. The little she had drunk might just see her through this day, but she knew that she was already suffering from dehydration.

'I have to find some method of drinking from that billy,' she told herself, and spent most of that afternoon wrestling with the problem. When the solution came to her, she lurched to her feet so hastily that she bumped the back of her head on the log roof. She ignored the hurt and examined the untidy tufts of elephant grass that hung down from between the chinks of the roof. She selected one of the grass stems and took it carefully between her teeth, worried it loose and let it drop to the floor. She knelt over it and by straining backwards managed to get a hand to it. Fortunately it was dry and brittle and snapped readily between her fingers. She broke it into four equal lengths each about nine inches long and, once again by backward contortions, planted them upright in the loose earth of the floor. She turned round, knelt and picked up the first of them between her lips. She tried to blow through it, but it was blocked with pith and dirt. She discarded it and went on to the next.

When she blew through this one, a tiny cork of dirt flew out of the end like a blow-pipe and then it was hollow and clear. She flopped onto her backside and sat in the middle of the dirt floor with the straw still stuck in her mouth, laughing around it with triumph. Her sense of elation and achievement dispelled the

276

corroding sense of despair which had almost destroyed her will to keep on living.

She crawled to the corner and carefully hid the precious straw, and then for the rest of that day planned how she would use it.

The rays of sun no longer penetrated to her cell, and the heavy gloom of evening was on her before she heard the wardress at the door. She huddled in her corner when the sergeant stooped into the cell and carelessly dumped the stodgy lump of boiled maize meal into the dirt and stood the metal billy beside it.

She leaned back expectantly against the door jamb and waited for Claudia to scramble for the food and drink like an animal on all fours. Claudia crouched motionlessly in the furthest corner of the cell and tried to show no expression, but her throat contracted in an involuntary swallowing reflex and her thirst was a raging beast within her.

After she had not moved for a few minutes, the sergeant said something irritable in Portuguese and gestured to the billy. With an immense effort Claudia prevented herself from looking down at it and the woman shrugged and once again stepped onto the maize cake and ground it into the dirt. She gave a snort of unconvincing laughter and backed out through the door, dragging it shut behind her, but the billy-can was left standing at the threshold.

Claudia forced herself to wait until she was certain that the wardress had truly left and was not watching her through a spy hole. Once she was sure she was not observed, Claudia crawled in frantic haste to the corner where she had hidden the straw and picked it up between her lips. Still on her knees she crossed to the billy-can and stooped over it.

She drew the first mouthful through the straw and let it trickle down her throat, closing her eyes with pleasure. It was as though she were drinking down a magic potion. She felt new strength and resolve flow through her veins.

She drank most of the contents of the billy-can, drawing out the pleasure of it until it was almost totally dark in the cell, but she could not bring herself to eat the sticky mess of maize cake smeared into the dirt.

She hoarded the remains of the water, taking the wire handle of the billy-can between her teeth and carefully moving it to the far corner of the cell where she could ration herself to small sips during the long hours ahead. She settled down for the night feeling almost cheerful and a little light-headed as though she had drunk of champagne rather than plain unboiled river water.

'I can endure anything they do to me,' she whispered to herself. 'They aren't going to break me. I won't let them, I won't.'

Her mood did not last. Almost as soon as it was fully dark in the cell, she realized her terrible mistake in leaving the uneaten maize cake on the floor.

Last night there had been only one rat, and it had fled when she screamed at it. This night the odour of food brought them pouring through the gaps in the roof. To her frenzied imagination, it seemed that the floor of the cell was swarming with furry bodies. The smell of them clogged her nostrils, the nauseating ratty smell like boiling horns and hooves in a glue pot. She cowered in her corner, shivering with cold and horror, and they brushed against her legs and scurried over her feet, squeaking and squealing as they fought for the scraps of spilled porridge.

At last, Claudia succumbed to panic. Screaming, on the edge of hysteria, she kicked out at them wildly; one of them whipped round and bit her naked ankle, the sharp little teeth were like a razor cut She screamed again and kicked, trying to dislodge it, but for a few dreadful seconds its curved teeth were buried in her flesh, and then at last she sent it flying into the darkness.

The rat hit the billy-can containing her treasured water and she heard the metal clank against the wall and the liquid splash onto the earthen floor. She crawled to the overturned container and wept with despair.

After long hours of horror and dark terror, the rats consumed the last of the maize and disappeared back through the roof. Claudia sank to her knees, exhausted both physically and emotionally.

'Please God, let it end. I can't go on.

She toppled over on her side and lay in the dirt, shivering and sobbing softly to herself, and at last dropped into the dark void of oblivion.

She woke with something tugging at her hair, and a strange grinding sound very close to her ear. Still groggy with sleep it took her long seconds to realize what was happening to her. She had slumped over sideways and one cheek was pressed to the dirt floor. She lay for a moment, enduring the sharp pulls on her hair and the grinding crunching in her uppermost ear and then the terror came back to her in full force.

A rat was chewing off her hair, cutting it with those sharp curved incisors, gathering it for nesting material. So great was her horror that it paralysed her. She could not move. Her whole body tingled, her stomach knotted with cramps and her toes and fingers curled with the strength of revulsion.

Suddenly she was no longer terrified. Her fear changed to anger. In one lithe movement she rolled to her feet and began to hunt the loathsome creature.

Relentlessly she pursued it around the cell, following it only by sound, the tiny scratch and patter of its feet. She no longer kicked out wildly, but deliberately aimed each blow at the sound. Twice the creature tried to climb to safety, but each time Claudia heard it and used her whole body to sweep it from the wall and knock it back to the floor.

This killing anger was an emotion she had never experienced before. It heightened all her senses, it rendered her hearing so acute that she could visualize each movement of her prey; it quickened her physical responses so her kicks were fast and powerful and when one of them landed on the warm furry body, the shrill squeal of pain and fear from the rat inflamed her.

She cornered it against the door of the cell and again stamped on it. She felt the small bones break under her heel, and she stamped again and again, sobbing with the effort, keeping it up until the carcass was soft and mushy under her feet.

When, at last, she backed away and sank down in her corner, she was still trembling, but no longer with terror.

'I've never killed anything before,' she thought, amazed at herself and this secret savage side to her nature which she had never suspected existed.

She waited for the familiar feeling of guilt and disgust to overwhelm her. Instead she felt as strong as though she had come through some ordeal which had armed her and equipped her to overcome whatever dangers and hardships lay ahead.

'I'm not going to give in, not ever again,' she whispered. 'I'm going to fight and to kill if I have to. I shall survive.'

*   *   *

In the morning when the wardress came for the billy-can, Claudia confronted her resolutely, thrusting her face only inches from the black woman's, and keeping her voice measured but firm.

'Take this out.' She indicated the rat's carcass with her foot. The woman hesitated and Claudia said, 'Do it, now!' And the wardress picked up the mangled carcass by the tip of the tail, and glanced back at Claudia with a measure of respect in her dark eyes.

Carrying the empty billy and the dead rat she left the cell. When she returned a few minutes later with the billy-can refilled and the bowl of maize meal, Claudia subdued her thirst and maintained her new attitude of calm authority as she indicated the sewage bucket.

'That has to be cleaned,' she said, and the woman snapped a retort in Portuguese.

'I'll do it.' Claudia did not waver, holding the woman's gaze until she broke the eye contact. Only then did she turn her back and offer her manacled hands to the wardress.

'Undo these,' she ordered, and obediently the wardress un- clipped the key from her webbing belt.

Claudia almost cried out as the handcuffs came away. The blood rushed back to her hands and Claudia held them to her chest and massaged them tenderly, biting her lips against the pain, horrified by the condition of her swollen hands and torn bruised wrists.

The wardress prodded her in the small of the back and gave an order in Portuguese. Claudia took up the handle of the sewage bucket and, brushing past the woman, climbed the stairs. The sunlight and warmth and clean dry air were like a benediction.

Claudia looked around the stockade quickly. It was obviously a women's prison, for a few dispirited feminine figures lolled in the dust beneath the single ebony tree in the centre. They were in ragged loin-cloths, their naked upper bodies so painfully thin that the ribs stood out clearly beneath the dusty dark skin and their breasts, even those of the younger women, were empty and dangled loosely as the ears of a spaniel. Claudia wondered what their crimes had been, or if their mere existence had caused their captors offence.

She saw that her own bunker was only one of a row of a dozen or so. It was obvious that these were reserved for the more important or dangerous prisoners.

The gates of the stockade were guarded by a pair of burly black females dressed in the usual tiger stripes and toting AK assault rifles. They peered curiously at Claudia and discussed her

280

with animation. Beyond the gates, Claudia had a glimpse of the broad green flow of the Pungwe river, and for a moment entertained fanciful visions of plunging into it to bathe her battered body and wash her filthy clothes, but the wardress prodded her painfully in the back and urged her towards the screened latrines at the rear of the stockade.

When they reached them the wardress made hand signals for Claudia to empty her bucket into the communal pit, and then turned away to chat with one of the other wardresses who had sauntered across to join them with her AK 47 rifle over her shoulder.

The back wall of the latrine was also the rear wall of the stockade. However, it offered no avenue of escape. The poles were as thick as her leg, lashed securely together with bark rope, and their tops were several feet higher than she could reach.

She abandoned the idea of escape before it was fully formed and tipped the contents of the bucket into the deep pit. Immediately a humming cloud of flies rose from the depths and circled her head.

Wrinkling her nose with disgust, Claudia was backing towards the exit when a soft whistle stopped her dead. It was a low-pitched mournful note, so unobtrusive that she would have ignored it completely if she had not heard it so often before. It was one of the clandestine signals that Sean and his trackers used. Sean had told her once that it was the call of a bird called a bou-bou shrike, and because of its associations rather than its pitch, it electrified her.

She glanced quickly towards the screened entrance to the latrine, but it was safe. She heard the voices of the wardress and her colleague still chatting outside, and she pursed her lips and tried a soft unconvincing imitation of the whistle.

Instantly it was repeated from just beyond the back wall of the latrine and Claudia's hopes soared. She dropped the bucket and ran to the wall of poles, putting her eye to one of the larger chinks. She almost screamed when an eye looked back at her from only the thickness of the poles and then a voice, a well-remembered voice, whispered, '*Jambo*, memsahib.'

'Matatu,' she gasped.

'Silly little bugger.' Matatu gave her the only words of English he knew, and she had to fight to prevent herself bursting out with the laughter of relief and hope and amusement at the incongruity of that greeting.

'Oh Matatu, I love you,' she blurted, and a folded scrap of paper was thrust through the chink into her face. The instant her fingers closed on it, Matatu's eye was snatched away from the peep-hole as though on a fishing line.

'Matatu,' she whispered desperately, but he was gone. She had spoken too loudly and she heard the wardress call out, and her footsteps at the entrance.

Claudia spun round and with the same movement crouched over the reeking pit. The wardress looked round the thatched screen and Claudia snapped at her furiously, 'Get out, can't you see I'm busy.'

And the woman involuntarily jerked her head back. Claudia was trembling with excitement as she unfolded the note and recognized the handwriting, and at the same time she was stricken with terror that it would be taken from her before she could read it. She refolded it quickly and slipped it deeply into the back pocket of her trousers, where she would be able to retrieve it even with her hands cuffed behind her.

Now she was eager to return to the privacy of her cell. The wardress pushed her down the stairs, but without the viciousness of before.

Claudia replaced the sewage bucket in the corner and then when the wardress pointed at her wrists, she held them out obediently. The touch of the metal on her abraded and bruised skin seemed even more galling than it had been before. The muscles and tendons of her upper arms and shoulders knotted in protest.

Once Claudia was manacled the wardress seemed to recapture her harsh mood of authority. She tipped the contents of the maize bowl onto the floor and lifted her boot to grind it into the dirt.

Claudia flew at her. 'Don't you dare!' she hissed, thrusting her face close to the woman's, glaring into her eyes so viciously that she recoiled involuntarily.

'Get out!' Claudia told her. '*Allez*! Vamoose!' And the wardress backed out of the cell with a muttered but unconvincing show of defiance, and dragged the door closed behind her.

Claudia was amazed at her own courage. She leaned against the door trembling with the effort that the contest of wills had cost her, only then realizing the risk that she had taken – she could have been brutally beaten or deprived altogether of her precious supply of water.

It was Sean's letter that had given her the strength and bravado to defy the wardress. Leaning against the door, she reached back into her pocket and touched the scrap of folded notepaper, merely to reassure herself that it was safe. She would not read it yet. She wanted to delay and savour that pleasure. Instead, she retrieved her drinking straw from its hiding-place.

After she had drunk from the billy, she ate the maize cake, delicately picking it out of the dirt with her teeth and trying to shake loose the earth and dirt that clung to the sticky lumps of porridge. She was determined not to leave a scrap of it, not only because she was hungry but because she knew she would have need of all her strength in the days ahead, and because she had learned that food scraps attracted the rats. Only when she had eaten and drunk, did she allow herself the luxurious pleasure of reading Sean's note.

She took it out of her pocket and carefully smoothed it between her swollen fingers. Then she squatted and placed it in the beam of sunlight that fell in a corner of the cell, and at last turned and knelt over it.

She read slowly, moving her lips like a semi-literate, forming every word that he had written as though she could taste it on her tongue.

'Be strong, it won't be for much longer and remember, I love you. Whatever happens, I love you.' Her vision swam with tears as she read his last words, and then she sat back and whispered softly, 'I'll be strong. I promise you that I'll be strong for you, and I love you too, with my very existence, I love you.'

* * *

'They may fight like women,' said Sergeant Alphonso, as he surveyed the piles of captured Zimbabwean army equipment. 'But at least they dress like warriors.'

The uniforms had been supplied by Britain as part of their aid commitment to Mugabe after the capitulation of Ian Smith's white regime. They were the finest quality, and Alphonso and his men stripped off their old faded and patched tiger-striped battledress with alacrity. In particular they were delighted with the gleaming black leather paratrooper boots with which they replaced their eclectic collection of tattered joggers and grubby tennis shoes.

Once they had decked themselves out in this captured finery

and fallen in on the beaten-earth parade ground, Sean and Job went down their ranks checking and instructing them on the correct way to wear each item of uniform. The quartermaster tailor followed behind them, correcting any gross discrepancy in size and fit.

'They don't have to be perfect,' Sean said. 'They won't be on parade, just good enough to pass a casual glance. We haven't got time to waste on the niceties of dress.'

After the men were fully kitted out, Sean and Job worked on their plan of Grand Reef base for the rest of that day and most of the night. First they sat on opposite sides of a desk in the headquarters communications room and brain-stormed for every detail of the base lay-out that they could dredge from their memories. By nightfall, they were satisfied that they had the most accurate picture that they could hope for. However, Sean had learned from experience that it was difficult for an illiterate to visualize physical reality from a two-dimensional drawing, and discreet enquiry had revealed that almost all his new command, although battle-tried warriors, could neither read nor write.

Most of the rest of that night, they worked on building a scale model of the base, setting it out on the beaten surface of the parade ground, working by lantern light. Job had an artistic flair and whittled model buildings from the soft balsa-like wood of the baobab tree, and used water-washed pebbles of various colours from the sandbanks of the river to lay out the airstrip and roads and perimeter fences of the base.

The following morning the raiding party was paraded and inspected by Captain Job and Sergeant Alphonso and then seated around the model in a ring. The model proved to be a major success, provoking lively comment and query.

First Sean described the raid, moving matchboxes down the pebble roadways to represent the column of Unimogs, illustrating the diversionary attack on the perimeter, the withdrawal of the loaded trucks and the rendezvous on the Umtali road. Once he had finished he handed his pointer to Sergeant Alphonso.

'All right, Sergeant, explain it to us again.' The ring of attentive troopers delighted in correcting the occasional mistakes and omissions that Alphonso made. When he was finished he handed the pointer to his senior corporal to repeat the lecture. After five repetitions, they all had it perfectly memorized and even General China was impressed.

'It only remains to see if you can do it as well as you explain it,' he told Sean.

'Just give me the trucks,' Sean promised.

'Sergeant Alphonso was with the unit that originally captured them. He knows where they are hidden. Incidentally the guards major whose uniform you will use was killed in the same action.'

'How long ago was that?' Sean asked.

'About two months ago.'

'Beauty!' said Sean bitterly. 'That means that those trucks have been lying in the bush all that time. What makes you think they are still there, or that they are still in running order?'

'Colonel,' China gave that thin cold smile that Sean was coming to know and loathe so well, 'for Miss Monterro's sake you had better pray they are.' The smile vanished. 'Now, while the men draw their rations and ammunition, you and I will have a final discussion. Come with me, Colonel.'

Once they were in the communications room of the command bunker, China turned to Sean with his expression bleak. 'During the night, I received a radio message from my agent in Grand Reef base. He only transmits in an emergency, otherwise the risk is too high. This is an emergency. Training on the Stinger systems is complete. They have orders to move the missiles out of Grand Reef within the next seventy-two hours, depending on availability of transport aircraft.'

Sean whistled softly. 'Seventy-two hours – in that case we won't make it.'

'Colonel, all I can tell you is that you had better make it. If you don't, you will have no further value to me and I will begin thinking of old times.' He touched his damaged ear significantly. Sean stared him out silently until China went on, 'However, not all the news is bad, Colonel. My agent will meet you in Umtali and give you full intelligence on the buildings where the Stingers are being held, the room used as a lecture theatre, and the training manuals. He will accompany you to the base. He is well-known to the guards at the gates. He will assist your entry and guide you to the training centre.'

'That's something,' Sean growled. 'Where will I meet him?'

'There is a night club in Umtali. The Stardust, a gathering place for pimps and whores. He will be there every evening from eight until midnight. Alphonso knows the Club. He will take you to it.'

'How will I recognize your agent?'

'He will wear a tee-shirt with a large portrait of the comic book hero, Superman, on the chest,' China said, and Sean closed his eyes as though in pain while China went on. 'The man's name is Cuthbert.'

Sean shook his head and whispered, 'I don't believe this is happening to me. Superman and Cuthbert!' He shook his head again as if to clear it. 'What about the RZ with the porters at St Mary's mission?'

'That is arranged,' China assured him. 'The porters will cross the border tomorrow night as soon as it is dark and conceal themselves in the caves in the mountains above the mission station to await your arrival.'

Sean nodded and changed the thread of the discussion.

'If we leave now, how long will it take for us to reach the spot where the Unimogs are hidden?'

'You should be there before noon tomorrow.'

'Is there anything else we should discuss?' Sean asked, and when China shook his head, Sean stood up, slung his AKM assault rifle on one shoulder and with his free hand lifted the small canvas duffel bag that contained the dead guards major's uniform and his personal kit.

'Until we meet again, General China.'

'Until we meet again, I will take good care of Miss Monterro. Never fear, Colonel.'

* * *

The column was heavily laden. Each man carried food and water for two days together with ammunition, the extra belts for the RPD machine-guns, grenades and rockets for the RPG 7 launchers.

Though they could not run under that weight, Sergeant Alphonso in the van set a cracking pace. Before nightfall they passed through the Renamo lines into the 'destruction area', a free-fire zone where there was a possibility of encountering Frelimo patrols, and Sean ordered a change of formation. They opened up to intervals of ten metres between the men in the single file of the main column and he posted flankers at the head and tail to guard against surprise attack.

They kept going hard during the night with ten-minute breaks every two hours, and by dawn they had covered almost forty miles. During the dawn break, Sean moved up to the head of the column and squatted between Alphonso and Job.

'How much further to the trucks?' Sean demanded.

'We have done well,' Alphonso replied, and pointed ahead. 'The trucks are there in that valley.'

They were on the foreslope of another area of hilly forested ground and below them the terrain was broken and bad. Sean appreciated why General China had chosen this area of the Serra da Gorongosa to defend. There were no roads in this wilderness and an attacking army would have to fight its way past an endless series of natural strong points and fortresses.

The valley that Alphonso pointed out was some miles ahead of them and beyond it the country changed from its savage mood and flattened into a broad gentle plain. Down there the dark forest was broken up and blotched with paler grasslands.

Alphonso pointed to the horizon. 'Over there are the railway line and the road to the coast . . .' He was about to speak again when Sean caught his arm to silence him and cocked his head in a listening attitude.

It was some seconds before the sound separated itself from the gentle susurration of the dawn wind in the forest below them and hardened into the whine of turbo engines and spinning rotors.

'There!' Job's eyesight was phenomenal and he picked out the approaching specks even against the dark background of hills and forests.

'Hinds.' Sean spotted them and Alphonso shouted a warning. 'Take cover.' The column scattered into cover and they watched the gunships come on, rising and dropping as they kept low over the hills, sailing northwards towards the Renamo lines in an extended formation.

Sean watched them through the Russian-made binoculars he had acquired from the Renamo stores. It was the first opportunity he had had to study a Hind at leisure. There were four of them and Sean surmised that there would be three flights of four machines to a full squadron of twelve.

'My God, they are grotesque,' he murmured. It seemed impossible that anything so heavy and misshapen could ever break the ties of gravity. The engines were housed in the top of the fuselage below the main rotor and formed the humpback that gave the machine its nickname. The air intakes to the turbos were situated

287

above the cockpit canopy. The belly drooped like that of a pregnant sow. The nose was deformed by the hanging turret which housed the Gatling-cannon and from the stubby wings and bloated belly were suspended an untidy array of rocket systems and ordnance stations and radar aerials.

At the rear of the engine mountings the ungainly lines of the machine were further disturbed by another extraneous structure which seemed to have been tacked onto it as an afterthought.

'Exhaust suppressor boxes.' Sean remembered an article he had read in one of the flying magazines to which he subscribed. These structures masked the exhaust emissions of the twin turbo engines and shielded them from the infra-red sensors of hostile missiles. The author of the article had lauded their efficacy, but although they made the machines almost invulnerable to heat-seekers, the weight of the devices combined with that of the titanium armour to reduce severely the Hind's speed and range. Sean wished he had read the article with more attention, for he could not recall the figures for airspeed and range that the author had quoted.

The flight of gunships passed a mile or so to the east of them boring steadily northwards.

'General China is in for a breakfast show,' Job remarked as he rose from cover to reassemble the column and continue the march.

Although they had been going all night the pace never slackened and even Sean was impressed by the condition and training of Alphonso's company. 'Almost as good as the Scouts,' he decided, and then grinned to himself. 'Nobody could be that good.'

More than once, Sean dropped back to check that the men he had in the drag were anti-tracking and covering spoor. For now there was real danger that a Frelimo patrol might find them. He had fallen only a few hundred metres behind the rear of the column and was down on one knee studying the earth intently, when suddenly he knew that he was not alone, that he was being watched.

Instantly Sean threw himself forward, the rifle coming off his shoulder as he rolled over twice into the cover of a fallen log beside the path and froze, his finger on the trigger, his gaze raking the bush where he thought he had seen the flirt of movement.

It was closer than he had imagined. From the clump of grass

right beside him came a mischievous giggle and Sean raised his head and whispered furiously, 'I've warned you not to sneak up on me like that.'

Matatu's head popped out of the grass and he grinned merrily.

'You are getting old, my *Bwana*. I could have stolen your socks and boots without you knowing.'

'And I could have shot your brown backside full of holes. Did you find the mem?'

Matatu nodded and his smile slipped.

'Where is she?'

'Half a day's march upstream, in a stockade with many other women.'

'Is she well?'

Matatu hesitated, torn between telling the truth and telling Sean what would please him. Then he sighed and shook his head.

'They keep her in a hole in the ground, and there are marks on her arms and legs. They force her to work with the shit-buckets . . .' He broke off as he saw Sean's expression and went on hurriedly, 'but she laughed when she saw me.'

'Did you give her the paper?'

'*Ndio*. She hid it in her clothing.'

'Nobody saw you?'

The reply was beneath Matatu's dignity and Sean smiled. 'I know, nobody sees Matatu unless Matatu wants them to . . .' Sean broke off and both of them looked upwards.

Faintly, from far away, came the now familiar whistle of turbo engines and rotors.

'The Hinds, returning from clobbering the Renamo lines,' Sean murmured. The machines were out of sight beyond the canopy of the forest trees, but the sound passed swiftly southwards.

'With their limited range, their base can't be too far,' Sean thought and looked at Matatu thoughtfully. 'Matatu, those *indeki*, could you find the place where they come from, and where they return to?'

Matatu's gaze flickered with a moment's doubt, and then he grinned, once again brimming with bravado.

'Matatu can follow anything, man or animal or *indeki*, anywhere it goes,' he boasted confidently.

'Go!' Sean ordered. 'Find the place. There will be trucks and many white men. It will be well guarded. Don't let them catch you.'

Matatu looked affronted and Sean clasped his shoulder with affection. 'When you have found the place, come back to General China's camp at the Pungwe river. I will meet you there.'

As unquestioningly as a gun dog sent to retrieve a downed pheasant, Matatu bounded to his feet and tucked up the folds of his loin-cloth.

'Until we meet again, go in peace, my *Bwana*.'

'Go in peace, Matatu,' Sean called softly after him as the little man trotted away into the south. Sean watched him out of sight and then hurried to catch up with Alphonso's column

'They keep her in a hole in the ground, and there are marks on her arms and her legs.' Matatu's words echoed in his head, fuelling his imagination and his anger and his determination.

'Hold on, my love. Stick it out. I'll come to get you . . . soon,' he promised her, and himself.

*   *   *

They crossed the rim of another line of rocky kopjes, using a screen of jesse bush to conceal their movements against the skyline, and from good cover on the foreslope Alphonso pointed down into the valley below.

'That is how we brought the trucks in,' he explained, and Sean saw that the dry river-course would be the only access for a vehicle into this bad country. Even then it must have been a laborious task negotiating the rocky chutes and barriers that broke up the stretches of smooth river sand in the depths of the gorge.

'Where did you hide the trucks?' Sean asked without lowering his binoculars, and Alphonso chuckled.

'Unless Frelimo is cleverer than I think they are, I will show you.'

They left sentries posted along the ridge, to warn of the approach of an enemy patrol, then Alphonso led the rest of the column down into the gorge. The lower they descended, the steeper became the sides, until there were sheer cliffs on each side and they were forced to traverse along a narrow game trail to reach the river bottom. It was suffocatingly hot in the narrow gorge, no breeze reached down here, and the rock absorbed the sun's heat and threw it back at them.

'The trucks?' Sean demanded impatiently, and Alphonso pointed to the cliffs opposite.

'In there,' he said, and Sean was about to snarl irritably at him when he realized that the cliffs had been carved by wind and flood water over the ages.

'Caves?' he asked, and Alphonso led him through the ankle-deep river sand to the cliff face.

Some of the cave entrances were merely scooped shallowly into the red rock, others had collapsed or were clogged with debris brought down by the summer floods. Alphonso indicated one of these and gave an order to his men. They stacked their weapons and began to clear the debris from the mouth of the cavern.

Within an hour they had opened it sufficiently for Alphonso and Sean to scramble through into the cave. Deep in the gloomy gut, Sean made out the shape of the first truck. His eyes accustomed themselves to the poor light as he moved towards it and he saw others parked beyond it.

'How the hell did you get them in here?' he asked incredulously.

'We pushed and carried them,' Alphonso explained.

'I hope to hell we'll be able to get them out again,' Sean muttered, and climbed onto the running board of the nearest vehicle.

It was coated with a thick layer of red dust. He yanked open the door on the driver's side and sneezed in the dust, but saw with relief that the key was still in the ignition.

He reached in and turned it. Nothing happened. The ignition light stayed dark and the needles on the dashboard instruments never flickered.

'I disconnected the batteries,' Alphonso told him, and Sean grunted.

'Bright lad, but how the hell did you know to do that?'

'Before the war, I was a bus-driver in Vila de Manica,' Alphonso explained. It was odd to think that he had ever had such a prosaic occupation.

'All right,' Sean said. 'Then you can help me get this one started. Is there a tool box?'

Each of the trucks was equipped with two spare tyres, hand

pump, tool box, tarpaulin and long-range fuel tank. Once Sean had reconnected the battery of the first truck, there was sufficient charge to produce a dull red glow in the ignition lamp on the dashboard and to raise the needle of the fuel gauge to the 'half' position but insufficient to kick the engine over.

'Find the crank handle,' Sean ordered. It was secured behind the passenger seat in the cab. Two hefty Shanganes swung the engine over with such gusto that it fired and stuttered and then burst into a steady roar. Thick blue exhaust smoke filled the cavern and Sean lifted his foot off the accelerator pedal. Two of the tyres were flat and had to be pumped by hand. While this was being done, the troopers cleared the last of the rocks and tree trunks from the mouth of the cave and with the transmission in four-wheel drive, Sean reversed sharply down the incline and bounced and jolted over the rough ground.

When the truck hung up on the boulders of the river bank and the wheels spun without purchase, twenty men flung their combined weight on it, and by brute force shoved it through. The Unimog crashed over the lip of the bank and into the riverbed. Sean drove it clear and parked under the opposite cliffs. He left the engine running to charge the depleted battery and they climbed back to the cavern and started work on the second truck.

Apart from flat tyres and batteries, they found no serious defects in any of the vehicles. One after the other, they coaxed the engines to life and then manhandled them down into the riverbed. It was the middle of the afternoon by the time all three trucks were lined up on the white river sand.

'Get the men to change uniforms now,' Sean ordered. 'Leave their other gear in the cave.'

Joking and laughing, they stripped off their Renamo tiger stripes and donned the British-pattern battledress of the Zimbabwean army. While they were busy, Sean went over the vehicles again. He found the army registration papers in a plastic wallet in the cubby-holes of each of the Unimogs.

'Hope we never have to show them,' he grumbled to Job. 'They are probably listed as stolen or destroyed.'

He opened the caps on the fuel tanks and physically checked the contents of each.

'Enough to get us to Grand Reef and back to St Mary's,' he estimated. 'With not much to spare.'

292

He ordered the windscreen and side windows of the cabs to be cleaned, but the bodywork to be left as it was, caked with mud and dust. It gave them the appearance of a patrol returning from a sortie into the deep bush and, more importantly, partially obscured the military markings and registration numbers.

Once the men had changed into their disguise and cached their Renamo uniforms, Sean and Job inspected each man and his equipment minutely, before allowing him to board one of the Unimogs.

It was almost five o'clock before they were ready to leave. Both Job and Alphonso had heavy-vehicle driver's licences and one of the Renamo troopers who gloried in the name of Ferdinand da Costa claimed driving experience. Sean took the passenger seat beside him to check his performance.

Job drove the leading truck, Alphonso in the middle and Sean and the learner driver in the rear. Apart from a heavy foot on the accelerator pedal, Ferdinand da Costa proved himself an adequate driver, but Sean took the wheel from him at the difficult places.

In line astern, they churned through the heavy sand, following in the wheel ruts of Job's Unimog, winding up the river-course for half a mile before they reached the first obstacle.

It required the combined efforts of all forty men to heave and shove the trucks up the first rocky chute in the riverbed, and even then they had to cut twenty-foot-long mopane poles and use them as levers to prise the wheels up over the larger boulders.

The powerful truck motors bellowed in high revolutions, blue diesel smoke billowed from the exhausts and Sean remarked to Job, 'An open invitation to every Frelimo within twenty miles to join the party.' Then he checked his wristwatch. 'We are falling behind our schedule.'

They tried to make up time along the easier stretches of the river-course, but the sunset and darkness caught them still almost twenty kilometres from the main east-to-west road between the sea and the border post at Umtali.

Nightfall made the journey more arduous. Sean dared not use the trucks' headlights, and they had to proceed in darkness alleviated only by starlight and a moon in its last quarter.

It was after midnight before they could at last leave the riverbed by negotiating a low spot in the bank. With four men walking ahead of the lead truck to guide it around ant-bear holes and other concealed obstacles, they struck out directly southwards and within two hours had intersected the overgrown disused track that Alphonso had told Sean about.

Sean called a halt and they spread the field map on the bonnet of the lead truck and by flashlight studied it anxiously.

'We are here,' Alphonso told him. 'This track runs up to an old asbestos mine, it was abandoned by the Portuguese in 1963 at the start of the Frelimo war.'

'We'll rest up here,' Sean decided. 'Get the trucks off the road and covered with branches. We must expect the Hinds to over-fly us sometime tomorrow. No cooking-fires, no smoking.'

At four o'clock that afternoon, they woke those still asleep and ate a hasty meal of cold rations. Sean ordered the journey to be resumed and they stripped the camouflage from the trucks. They boarded the entire raiding party except for the four men who walked ahead of the leading truck, examining the ancient overgrown wheel-ruts of the track for Frelimo anti-vehicle land-mines, probing any suspicious lump or hollow with a bayonet before waving the column forward.

The sun was just setting when they at last came in sight of the main road, its macadamized surface snaking through the open forest and winding around the scattered kopjes. Sean halted the column well back out of sight of the road and went forward with Job, leaving Alphonso in command.

From the top of a commanding hillock they kept the road under observation until it was fully dark. During that time two patrols passed, both heading eastwards, each comprised of three or four battered and dusty Unimogs packed with armed men in Zimbabwean combat gear, and with an RPD light machine-gun mounted above the cab.

They rumbled along with strict intervals of a hundred metres between vehicles and watching them through the binoculars Sean remarked, 'Well, at least we look like the real thing.'

'Except for your pale face,' Job pointed out.

'A birth defect,' Sean apologized. 'But I'll keep it out of sight until it's needed.'

They scrambled down from the hilltop and trudged back along the track to the hidden trucks.

'From here you are on your own,' Sean told Ferdinand, the driver. 'Do try to remember to put the clutch in before you change into bottom gear, you'll find it a great help.'

Dressed in the uniform of the deceased guards major, Sean climbed into the back of the cab, behind Job's driving seat. The space was barely sufficient to contain him; he had to twist his shoulders at an angle from his hips and sit flat on the metal floorboards. It was uncomfortable to begin with, but Sean knew that within a few hours it would become agony. However, he was out of sight and yet able to communicate with Job merely by raising his voice.

Without headlights, the column drove the last mile to the juncture with the main road. The scouts they had sent ahead whistled that the road was clear and they raced forward and swung onto the metalled surface, heading westwards towards the border.

As soon as they were safely onto the highway, they switched on the headlights and dropped their speed to fifty kilometres an hour, and adjusted their spacing to the regulation hundred-metre intervals. To an observer they were just another Zimbabwean mechanized patrol.

'So far, so good,' Job called over the back of the seat to where Sean was hiding.

'What's the time?'

'Seven minutes past eight.'

'Perfect, we'll hit the border post just after ten, when the guards are thinking of going off duty.'

The hundred kilometres to the border seemed much further. The metal floorboards of the cab were corrugated and cut into Sean's buttocks, transferring the impact of every pothole in the neglected highway up his spine into his skull.

'Get under the tarp! Border post ahead!' Job called at last.

'Not too bloody soon,' Sean assured him as the truck slowed and the overhead floodlights flooded the cab. Sean pulled the tarpaulin over his head and sank down as low as he could below the seatback.

He felt the truck brake and trundle to a halt. Job switched off the engine and opened the door of the cab.

'Wish me luck,' he muttered, as he stepped down from the cab.

Neither of them knew what to expect. The border formalities must surely be relaxed to accommodate the interchange of troops guarding the railway line. Job was dressed for the part and in possession of a genuine army pay book and ID. The truck's registration papers were likewise genuine and yet they could be compromised by some small unforeseen detail or by an alert border guard.

If anything went wrong, Job would give a single long blast on his whistle and they would shoot their way out. All the rifles and rocket-launchers were loaded, and the RPD machine-guns on the cabs were manned.

As the minutes drew out so Sean's nerves stretched tighter. He expected at any moment the shrilling of Job's whistle and the shouting and the gunfire.

Then at last there was the crunch of footsteps in gravel and the voices of Job and a stranger approaching the truck. Both doors of the cab opened and Sean tried to shrink himself as the truck tipped slightly under the weight of more than one man climbing aboard.

'Where do you want me to drop you off?' Job asked casually in Shona, and a voice Sean had never heard before replied, 'At the edge of town. I'll tell you where.'

Sean turned his head a stealthy inch and through the gap between the seats saw the blue serge cloth of a customs inspector's uniform. With horror, he realized that Job was giving an off-duty inspector a lift into Umtali.

The truck pulled forward and the inspector lowered the side window and shouted to the guards on the barrier.

'It's all right, open!' And as they accelerated ahead, Sean had a glimpse of the raised barrier through the window. He had to cover his mouth to prevent himself laughing aloud with relief and triumph.

On the back of the Unimog, the troopers seemed infected by the same reckless spirit of abandon. They were singing as the column wound down the hill to the town of Umtali. Job was casually discussing with the customs inspector the merits of the Stardust Night Club, and the price of a short time with one of the bar girls.

'Tell Bodo, the barman at the Stardust, that you are a friend of mine,' the inspector advised Job when they dropped him off on the outskirts of.the town. 'He'll get a special price for you, and tell you which of the girls have the clap and which ones are clean.'

As they pulled away, Sean could at last crawl out from behind the seat and slump gratefully into the passenger seat.

'What the hell kind of trick was that?' he complained. 'You damn nearly gave me a hernia.'

'What better way to get VIP treatment,' Job chuckled, 'than to have the head of the customs service as a pal. You should have seen the guards at the border saluting us!'

'Where is this night club?'

'Not far, we'll be there before eleven.'

They drove in silence for a few minutes while Sean rehearsed the next order he had to give. He waited until Job turned the truck into a dimly lit side street and switched off the engine. In the side mirror, Sean watched the other two Unimogs pull in behind them, cut their engines and switch off their headlights.

'Back home again,' Job chuckled. 'Nothing to it.'

'Back home,' Sean agreed. 'And back home is where you are going to stay.'

There was a long silence and then Job turned his head and looked at Sean thoughtfully.

'What do you mean by that?'

'This is the end of the road for us, Job. You aren't coming to Grand Reef, you aren't high-jacking any Stingers, and you sure as hell aren't coming back to Mozambique with me.'

'You're firing me?' Job asked.

'That's it, pal. I've got no more use for you.'

Sean took a small wad of Zimbabwe dollars, part of the expense money General China had provided, and offered it to Job. 'Get rid of that uniform as soon as you can. If they catch you in it, they'll shoot you. Take the next train back to Harare and go see Reema at the office. She's holding about four thousand dollars in back pay and bonus for you. That will be enough to tide you over until Capo Monterro's estate pays out the money it owes us. My lawyers will handle that. You will be entitled to half of that . . .'

Job ignored the proffered money. 'You remember that day on Hill 31?' he asked quietly.

'Shit, Job, don't pull that sob stuff on me.'

'You came back for me,' Job said.

'Because sometimes I'm just a bloody fool.'

'Me too,' Job smiled. 'Sometimes I'm just a bloody fool.'

'Listen, Job, this is not your shauri any more. There is nothing in it for you. Get out. Go back to your village, buy yourself another couple of pretty young wives with Capo's dollars. Sit in the sun and drink a few pots of beer.'

'Nice try, Sean. Pity it didn't work. I'm coming back with you.'

'I'm giving you a direct order.'

'I'm refusing to obey it, so convene a court-martial.'

Sean laughed and shook his head. 'She's my woman, so it's okay for me to risk my life.'

'I've been nursemaiding you for almost twenty years and I'm not giving up now,' Job said, and opened the cab door. 'Let's go and find Cuthbert in his Superman suit.'

Sean left his cap and tunic on the seat, the insignia of a famous regiment would be out of place in a cheap night club. The Stardust was at the end of the lane in a converted furniture factory, a barn-like building with all its windows blacked out. They could hear the music from a hundred paces out, the hypnotic repetitive beat of the new wave African jazz.

Women clustered around the entrance. In the overhead light their dresses were as colourful as butterfly wings. Their hairstyles were flocculent afros, or the intricate beaded dreadlocks of the Rastafarians, their faces painted into death masks of rouge and purple lipsticks with iridescent green eyelids like iguana lizards.

They swarmed around Sean and Job, rubbing themselves against them like cats.

'Hey man, get me in!' they pleaded. 'Give me five dollars to get in, darling, I'll dance with you and jig-jig, man. Everything.'

'Come on, whitey.' A child with a tender immature body in a shiny dress of cheap nylon, the face of a black Madonna and ancient weary eyes, seized Sean's arm. 'Take me with you and I'll give you something you've never had before.' She reached down the front of Sean's body and cupped her hand to fondle him. Sean took her wrist and restrained her.

'What have you got that I've never had before, sweetheart? Aids?'

They pushed their way through the rustling nylon skirts and clouds of cheap perfume and at the door paid their five dollars. The doorman stamped their wrists with an indelible dye in lieu of an entrance ticket and they ducked through the black curtain.

The music was a stunning, painful assault, the lights were revolving strobes and ultra-violet. The dance floor pulsated with humanity transformed into a single primitive organism, like some gigantic amoeba.

'Where is the bar?' Sean bellowed into Job's ear.

'I'm a stranger here myself.' Job seized his arm and they struggled through the engulfing sea of light and sound and gyrating bodies.

The faces around them were transported as in religious fervour, eyeballs rolled glaring white in the rays of the ultra-violet lamps, sweat glistened on upraised arms and streamed in rivulets down jet-black cheeks.

They reached the bar. 'Don't risk the whisky!' Job yelled. 'And make them open the beer in front of you.'

They drank directly from the cans, besieged in a corner of the bar with the ocean of humanity pressing hard against them.

There were a few white faces, all male, tourists and peace corps and military advisors, but most of the clientele were black soldiers still in uniform so that Sean and Job blended into their surroundings.

'Where are you, Cuthbert, in your Superman shirt?' Sean pushed away one of the more persistent bar girls, and peered over the heads of the dancers. 'We'll never find him in here.'

'Ask one of the barmen,' Job suggested.

'Good thinking.' Sean reached across and grabbed the front of the barman's shirt to get his attention, and then stuck a five-dollar bank note into his top pocket and shouted the question in his ear.

The barman grinned and yelled back, 'Wait! I find him.'

Ten minutes later, they saw Cuthbert working his way down the bar towards them, a skinny little man and the Superman tee-shirt was at least two sizes too large for him.

'Hey, Cuthbert, anybody ever tell you that you look like Sammy Davis Junior?' Sean greeted him.

'All the time man, man.' Cuthbert looked pleased, Sean had obviously picked out his pet vanity.

'Your uncle sends his love, can we go somewhere to talk?' Sean suggested as they shook hands.

'Best place to talk is here,' Cuthbert answered. 'Nobody else going to hear a thing you say. Get me a beer, can't talk with a dry throat.'

Cuthbert downed half his beer at a draught and then asked, breathless from the effort, 'You were supposed to be here last night. Where you been, man?'

'We were delayed.'

'You should have been here last night. Would have been easy, man. Tonight, well, tonight is different.'

'What has changed?' Sean asked with a sink of dread in his chest.

'Everything changed.' Cuthbert said. 'The Hercules arrived 1700 hours. Come to pick up the goods.'

'Has it left yet?' Sean demanded anxiously.

'Don't know for sure. She was still there when I left the base at 2000 hours. Sitting out there in front of number three hangar. Perhaps she still there now, perhaps she long gone. Who knows?'

'Thanks a lot,' Sean said. 'That's a great help.'

'That's not all, man.' Cuthbert clearly enjoyed being the bearer of evil tidings.

'Hit us with it, Cuthbert.'

He finished the beer in another long swallow and held up the empty can. Sean ordered another and Cuthbert waited for it, drawing out the suspense masterfully.

'Two full para-commandos of the Fifth Brigade came down from Harare in the Hercules. They real cool, those Fifth Brigade cats,' Cuthbert said with relish. 'They real mean dudes, no shit.'

'Cuthbert, you've been watching too much "Miami Vice" on television,' Sean accused, but he was worried. The Fifth Brigade were the elite of the Zimbabwean army, converted by their North Korean instructors into ruthlessly efficient killing machines. Two full para-commandos of a hundred men each, added to the standing garrison of Third Brigade troops, almost a thousand crack veterans on base.

'Your uncle says you are going to take us in, Cuthbert. Pass us through the gates.'

'No way, man!' Cuthbert was vehement. 'Not with those Fifth Brigade cats in there.'

'Your uncle will be pissed off with you, Cuthbert. He's a pretty cool cat himself, man, Uncle China is.' Sean imitated Cuthbert's hip jargon.

Cuthbert looked worried. 'Man, I've fixed your pass,' he explained hurriedly. 'You'll have no trouble getting in. The guards are expecting you. You don't need me, man. No sense I should compromise myself, no sense at all.'

'You've got the pass here?'

'Right on. The password too. You'll have no trouble.'

'Let's go.' Sean took Job's arm and steered him towards the door. 'That Hercules could take off any time.'

Cuthbert hurried between them down the lane to where the three Unimogs were parked.

'Here's the pass.' He handed the plastic-covered card to Sean, it was slashed with a scarlet 'Top Priority' cross.

'The password is a number, "fifty-seven", and your reply is "Samora Machel". Then you show the pass and sign the book. Simple as a pimple, man. You in like Flynn.'

'I'll tell your uncle that you couldn't bring yourself to come with us.'

'Hey, give me a break, will you? No sense me getting culled, man. I'm more use to my uncle alive and kicking than dead meat.'

'Cuthbert, you are wasted in signals, you definitely should be on television.' Sean shook hands with him and watched him scurry back into the Stardust Club.

There were clusters of women around the back of each of the three trucks, giggling and joking with the troopers who hung out over the tail-gates. One of the girls was climbing aboard, boosted by eager hands, her mini-skirt rucked up high on her long thin black legs.

'Get those whores out of there, Sergeant,' Job snapped at Alphonso, and the women around the tail-gates scattered and three or four others descended hastily from the backs of the Unimogs with their skimpy clothing in varying stages of disarray.

Sean and Job climbed into the cab of the lead truck and as they drove off Sean buttoned on his tunic and tipped his cap at a rakish angle over one eye.

'What are we going to do?' Job asked.

'Number three hangar at Grand Reef is in full view of the main road. We will drive up the highway. If the Hercules is still there, we go in. If not, well, we'll go back the way we came.'

'What about the Fifth Brigade?'

'They're just a bunch of ex-gooks,' said Sean. 'You weren't afraid of them before, so what's changed?'

'Just asking to pass the time,' Job grinned at him sideways. 'You want to tell Alphonso about them?'

'What Alphonso doesn't know, won't hurt him,' Sean said. 'Just keep going.'

The column of three trucks drove sedately through the sleeping town of Umtali. The streets were deserted but Job obeyed the traffic lights punctiliously and then they were out on the open highway.

'Twelve minutes past eleven.' Sean checked his watch, and then read the road sign in the beam of the headlights.

'Grand Reef Military Base, fifteen kilometres.'

He felt the familiar tightness in his stomach muscles, the shortness in his breath and consciously slowed and regulated his breathing. It was always like this before a scene.

'There she is,' Job said softly as they topped a rise in the highway.

The airfield was fully lit, the beacon lights glowing orange and the blue and green dotted lines of the taxi-ways and runway beyond them.

In the stark white light of the floods, even at a distance of almost two miles, the Hercules looked gigantic. Its forty-foot-high tail-fin towered above the roof of number three hangar.

Sean recognized immediately that it was one of the Marshall stretched-out conversions of Lockheed's Hercules original C MK3 transports for the Royal Air Force.

The RAF roundels were painted on the monstrous silver fuselage and on the high tail-fin.

'Pull over,' Sean ordered, and Job flicked his tail-light indicators and pulled into the side of the road. He switched off his headlights and one after the other the following Unimogs did the same.

In the silence Sean said softly, 'So the Hercules is still here. We are going in.'

'Let's do it,' Job agreed.

Sean jumped down from the cab and ran back to the second truck just as Alphonso climbed down to the roadside.

'Sergeant, you know what to do. I'll give you forty-five minutes to get into position. Then I want exactly ten minutes of diversionary fire, everything you've got.'

'The first plan was twenty minutes of diversion.'

'That's changed,' Sean told him. 'We expect a much stronger response than we first thought possible. Ten minutes and then pull out fast. Head straight back for St Mary's mission, we are abandoning the RZ on the Umtali pass. Hit them hard and then get out. Understood?'

'Yehbo.'

'Go!' Sean said, and Alphonso jumped up into the cab. Through the open window he saluted Sean and gave him a cheery grin.

'Break a leg,' Sean said softly, and the Unimog pulled out and headed down the highway towards the brightly lit base.

Sean watched the headlights turn off the main highway onto the secondary road that by-passed the perimeter fence of the airfield, then he lost them amongst the trees. Sean marked the time with the bevel ring on his Rolex and walked back to join Job in the leading truck.

He lay back in the passenger seat, pushed his cap to the back of his head and focused his binoculars through the open window at the huge aircraft that squatted on the tarmac under the floodlights.

The tail ramp at the rear of the fuselage was lowered like a drawbridge. He could see into the cavernous cargo hold.

There were four or five human figures moving about inside the hold and two more at the foot of the ramp. As he watched, a forklift truck trundled out of the open doors of number three hangar. Its fork arms were loaded with a stack of long wooden cases, four of them, one on top of the other. The cases were of raw white wood, and stencilled on them in black paint were letters and numerals which he could not decipher. He did not need to, the shape and size of the crates were unmistakable.

'They are loading the Stingers,' Sean said, and Job sat up straight in the driver's seat.

The forklift truck wheeled around the stern of the Hercules, and then climbed the open ramp and disappeared into the cargo hold. Minutes later it reappeared, drove down the ramp and wheeled into the hangar. Sean glanced at his watch, only five minutes had passed since Alphonso had driven ahead to set up the mock attack.

'Come on,' Sean muttered, and shook the Rolex on his wrist as if to speed up the mechanism.

Twice more, they watched the loaded forklift truck make the journey from out of the hangar, up into the belly of the Hercules and return empty.

Then it turned aside and parked at the far end of the hangar. The driver in blaze orange overalls climbed down from his seat and sauntered back to stand with the two other stevedores at the tail ramp.

'Loading completed,' Sean whispered again, and checked his watch. 'Seven minutes to go.'

Job unbuttoned the flap of his holster and drew the Tokarev 7.62 pistol. He withdrew the magazine and checked the load, then slapped the magazine back into its recess in the pistol grip and returned the pistol to its holster.

Through the binoculars, Sean saw the men who had been working in the cargo hold come down the ramp in a group. Three of them were white men, two of those in flying overalls and the other in British regulation battledress. Two pilots and one of the Royal Artillery instructors, Sean guessed.

'Start up!' he said, and Job kicked the engine to life.

'We should try to knock out those floodlights,' Sean muttered. 'We can't load the truck in the full glare, not with the Fifth Brigade breathing down our necks.'

He was looking at his watch, tilting the dial to catch the glow of the instrument panel.

'Okay, Job. Here we go!' he said, and the Unimog pulled forward. In the rear-view mirror, Sean watched the second truck driven by Ferdinand fall in behind them.

As they drove parallel to the main runway of the airfield Sean was assailed with a thousand memories. It all seemed exactly as it had been ten years before. No hangars nor buildings had been added. He picked out the windows of his old office in the main admin block beyond the control tower, and as Job slowed the truck and turned onto the short driveway that led from the highway to the base gates, Sean almost expected to see the insignia of the Ballantyne Scouts between that of the Rhodesian Light Infantry and the Rhodesian African Rifles on the arch above the gates.

Job halted the truck under the lights facing the wire-mesh gates and two guards came to each of the side windows of the cab. They carried their AK rifles at the trail and peered in at Job and Sean.

Job lowered the side window and exchanged the passwords with the commander of the guard and handed him the plastic-covered pass. The man took it to the guard house and made an entry in the register, then two of his men opened the main gates and he waved the convoy through.

Casually Sean returned the salute that the guards threw him as he passed, and he told Job quietly, 'Just like Cuthbert said, simple as a pimple. Now head straight down towards the admin block, but turn behind the control tower as you reach it.'

Job drove slowly, obeying the on-base fifteen mph speed limit and Sean unbuttoned the flap of his webbing holster and drew his pistol. He withdrew the magazine, pressed two cartridges out into the palm of his hand and then reloaded them in reverse order and slapped the magazine back into its recess in the pistol grip.

'Why do you always do that?' Job asked.

'Just for luck,' he said, as he saw Job watching.

'Does it work?' Job wanted to know.

'Well, I'm still alive, aren't I?' Sean grinned tightly. He pulled back the slide, pumping a round into the chamber of the pistol, engaged the safety and slipped the weapon back into its holster.

'Pull in behind the number three hangar,' he told Job, and he swung the truck across the hard stand in the full glare of the overhead floodlights into the shadowy area at the back of the hangar where they were screened from the control tower and the admin block.

As the truck stopped Sean jumped down and glanced around him quickly. The second Unimog pulled in beside the first, and armed men in battledress swarmed out over the tail-gates of both. With three quick strides Sean reached the back door in the corrugated metal wall of the hangar. It was unlocked and he stepped through. Job followed him immediately.

The hangar was empty except for a single light aircraft parked in the far corner. The bleak concrete floor half the size of a football field was stained with old oil spills, and the steel girders of the roof arched high overhead. It was brightly lit.

The forklift driver and the stevedores in their blaze orange overalls were halfway across the floor, coming directly towards Sean in a group, chatting and smoking cigarettes in direct defiance of the huge prohibition notices in red letters on the hangar walls. They stopped in confusion as they saw Sean come through the door with the armed men behind him.

'Secure them,' Sean ordered. As Job rounded them up swiftly, Sean looked beyond them.

Along the opposite wall of the hangar were a line of office cubicles with side walls of painted chipboard and glass windows. Through a lighted window, Sean saw the head and shoulders of one of the pilots in his blue RAF overalls. He had his back towards Sean, and he was gesticulating as he spoke to somebody out of sight.

By now the stevedores were lying spread-eagled on the concrete floor, each with a man standing over him and the muzzle of an AKM pressed into the back of each of their necks. It had been done swiftly and silently.

With the pistol in his hand, Sean ran to the door of the office cubicle and jerked it open. Two men, one of the pilots and the Royal Artillery captain, were lolling in a pair of dilapidated armchairs under a wall which was covered with a collection of ancient girlie pin-ups which Sean guessed were relics of the bush war. The senior pilot sat on a cluttered desk in front of the lit window. All three of them stared at Sean in amazement.

'This is a commando raid,' Sean told them quietly. 'Stay exactly where you are.'

On the floor between the Royal Artillery captain's feet stood a square black bag with substantial locks and a Royal Artillery decal stuck on the side.

The gunner dropped a hand on it protectively, and Sean knew immediately what the bag contained. The gunner was in his mid-twenties, well built and competent-looking. The name tag on his breast read 'Carlyle'. He had blue eyes and thick sandy-coloured hair.

The senior pilot was a flight lieutenant, but he was middle-aged and over-weight. His flight engineer was balding and nondescript, with real fear in his eyes as he stared at the pistol in Sean's hand. Sean anticipated no trouble from either of them, and transferred his attention back to the gunner. He knew instinctively that this was the main man. He had the shoulders of a boxer, and he hunched them aggressively and scowled at Sean. He was young enough to be foolhardy and Sean held his gaze and warned him.

'Forget it, Carlyle. Heroes are out of fashion.'

'You are a South African,' Carlyle growled as he recognized the accent. 'Whose side are you on?'

'My own,' Sean told him. 'Strictly self-employed.' He glanced down at the black bag and Carlyle pulled it an inch closer to him.

'Captain Carlyle, you are guilty of gross dereliction of duty,' Sean told him coldly, and the gunner reacted to the accusation with the indignation of a professional soldier.

'What do you mean?'

'You should have posted guards while you were loading the

306

missiles. You let us swan in here . . .' It distracted Carlyle as Sean had intended and gave Job the few seconds he needed to get his men into the office.

'Stand up,' he ordered the airmen, and they obeyed quickly, raising their hands and Job hustled them out of the office.

Carlyle remained in the armchair with the bag between his legs.

'Stand up!' Sean repeated the order.

'Screw you, Boer.'

Sean stepped up to him and seized the handle of the bag. Carlyle grabbed at it to prevent him and Sean brought the barrel of the pistol down across his knuckles. The skin split and Sean heard one of his fingers snap. He had misjudged it, he had not intended to inflict that kind of injury, but he kept his expression fierce.

'You have had your warning,' he said. 'My next offer is a bullet in the head.'

Carlyle was holding his injured hand to his chest, but his face was set and dark with fury as he watched Sean place the bag on the desk.

'Keys!' Sean said.

'Get stuffed,' said Carlyle. His voice was tight and hoarse with pain and Sean saw that his broken finger was standing out at an odd angle and swelling like a purple balloon.

Job reappeared in the door of the office cubicle. 'All secure,' he said, and glanced at his wristwatch. 'Four minutes to diversion.'

'Give me your knife,' Sean told him, and Job slid the trench knife from its sheath and passed it to Sean, hilt first.

Sean slashed the leather along the edge of the bag's steel frame and then pulled open the concertina hinge. There were half a dozen large loose-leaf folders filling the interior of the bag and Sean selected one. The file was covered in War Office red plastic and marked 'Top Secret'; he glanced at the title page:

FIELD MANUAL FOR INFANTRY USE OF THE 'STINGER'
MODEL G4X
SURFACE-TO-AIR MISSILE

'Jackpot.' Sean turned the file so that Job could read it. It was a stupid thing to do. They were both distracted, turned towards the desk, studying the file.

Carlyle launched himself out of the chair. He was young and fast. The injury to his hand did not hamper him in the least, and he was across the narrow floor space before either of them could move to stop him and he dived head first into the frosted window in the middle of the far wall. It exploded in a sparkling shower of glass and Carlyle flipped over in mid-air like an acrobat.

Sean leapt to the empty window. Outside on the brightly lit tarmac of the hard stand, Carlyle rolled to his feet and ran. Job pushed Sean aside and stepped up to the window; lifting his AKM and taking deliberate care, he aimed at Carlyle's broad back as he sprinted across open ground towards the base of the control tower.

Sean grabbed the rifle and jerked the barrel down before Job could fire.

'What the hell are you doing?' Job snarled at him.

'You can't shoot him!'

'Why not?'

'He's an Englishman,' Sean explained lamely, and for a moment Job stared at him uncomprehendingly and Carlyle covered the last few yards and dived into the doorway at the base of the control tower.

'Englishman or Eskimo, we are going to have the whole Fifth Brigade down our throats in about ten seconds from now.' Job was obviously trying to control his anger. 'So what do we do now?'

'How long to diversion?' Sean asked to buy time. He had no answer to Job's question.

'Still four minutes,' Job answered. 'And it might as well be four hours.'

As he said it, the sirens began to howl like wolves, bringing the base to full alert. Obviously Carlyle had reached the ops room in the control tower. Sean stuck his head out of the shattered window and saw the guard turning out of the main gate-house on the far side of the runway. They were dragging the spike boards across the approaches to the gates, to cut the tyres of an escaping vehicle to ribbons, and Sean saw the barrels of the 12.7mm heavy machine-guns depressing and traversing to cover the approaches. They were never going to get the trucks out that way.

'You should have let me sort him out,' Job fumed. How could Sean explain it to him? Carlyle had been a brave man doing his duty, and although the lines of loyalty to the old country had become blurred, Sean had the same blood in his veins; it would have been worse than murder to allow Job to shoot him down. It would have been a kind of fratricide.

Outside the hangar, the perimeter lights went on abruptly flooding the high security fence around the runway and taxi-way. The entire base area was lit like daylight.

If the commandos of the Fifth Brigade were in barracks and asleep when the alarm sounded, how long would it take them to come into action? Sean tried to make an estimate and then with self-disgust, realized that he was simply avoiding facing up to his own indecision and lack of any plan. He had lost control, and it was all blowing up in his face.

In a few minutes from now, he and Job and the twenty Shanganes of his commando were going to be overwhelmed. The lucky ones amongst them would be killed outright and so avoid interrogation by the Zimbabwe central intelligence organization.

'Think,' he told himself desperately, and Job was expectantly watching his face, waiting for orders. He had never seen Sean at a loss before. His unquestioning trust irritated Sean and made it even more difficult for him to reach any decision.

'What shall I tell the men?' Job prodded him.

'Get them . . .' Sean broke off as heavy gunfire broke out on the southern perimeter of the base on the opposite side to the hangar and out of their field of vision. Alphonso had been bright enough to realize that the plan had been derailed and he had started his attack a few minutes early.

They heard the whoosh-boom of RPG 7 rockets coming in through the perimeter wire and the duller thud-thud of mortar shells dropping in the base area. The 12.7mm machine-gun at the gates opened up, sluicing green tracer in pretty parabolas high into the darkness.

'How are we going to get out of here?' Job demanded.

Sean stared at him stupidly. He felt confused and uncertain. Panic welled up from deep inside him, he had never suspected such a source existed. He didn't know what order to give next.

'Forget the bloody Stingers, just get us out of here.' Job grabbed his arm and shook it. 'Come on, Sean, snap out of it! Tell me what to do!'

'Forget the Stingers!' The words were like a slap with an open hand across his face. Sean blinked and shook his head. Forget the Stingers and forget Claudia Monterro. Without the missiles, Claudia would stay in the hole in the ground where Matatu had last seen her.

Sean glanced out of the open window again. He could see the gigantic tail-plane of the Hercules and part of the fuselage, the rest of the aircraft was obscured by the angle of the hangar wall. The metallic silver skin of the Hercules glittered in the arc lights.

Sean clamped down hard on the hot effervescence of panic that threatened to swamp him, and felt it subside.

'The lights,' he said, and glanced around him quickly. He spotted the fuse box on the office wall beside the door and he reached it in two strides and jerked open the cover.

The hangar had been built during Hitler's war when the RAF had used Rhodesia as one of its overseas training centres. The electrical wiring dated from that era and utilized the old-fashioned ceramic type fuse-holders.

'Give me an AK round,' Sean snapped at Job. His voice was crisp and decisive and Job obeyed instantly. He flicked one of the brass 7.62mm cartridges from the spare magazine in the pouch on his webbing.

Sean identified the main phase in the fuse box. The in-coming current would be distributed directly from the transformer at the gates, if he could over-load that he would blow the flying fuse on the transformer box.

He pulled out the ceramic fuse-holder and the hangar was plunged into darkness, but the light of the floods through the open window gave him sufficient light to see what he was doing. He jammed the AK cartridge into the lugs of the ceramic fuse-holder and snapped at Job.

'Stand back!'

The last vestiges of his panic were gone. He felt cold and resilient as a knife-blade. His mind was clear and he knew exactly what he was going to do.

He thrust the loaded fuse-holder back into its slot, and a blinding blue explosion of light like a photographer's flash bulb lit the darkened room, and Sean was sent flying backwards. He crashed against the office wall, half stunned, shaking his head, his vision starred with memories of the blue flash.

It took him a few moments to realize that the floodlights

beyond the windows were extinguished and except for fiery bead necklaces of tracer flying across the dark sky and the brief glare of exploding grenades and rockets, the base was in darkness.

'Get the men into the Hercules,' he shouted.

Job was just a dark shadow behind the whirling catherine wheels of fire that still disturbed his vision.

'What? I don't understand?' Job stammered.

'We are getting out in the aircraft.' Sean grabbed his shoulder and thrust him towards the door. 'Get Ferdinand and his boys on board and move your arse.'

Job ran, and Sean blundered blindly after him. His vision was returning swiftly. He turned towards the paler square of light that was the hangar doors.

'What about the prisoners?' Job called from the dark depths of the hangar.

'Turn them loose,' Sean yelled back, and ran for the doors.

Although he did not have the Hercules conversion endorsed on his licence, Sean had flown the type before. In fact, he had accumulated almost 200 hours in the right-hand seat when he had flown with the South African air force in Angola and Namibia on anti-terrorist ops. It all came back to him now. He had enjoyed flying the Hercules and he remembered the remark a Senior pilot had made.

'She's a lamb. I wish my wife was so docile.'

At the hangar door, Sean stopped suddenly.

'Matatu is right, you're getting old, Courtney,' he castigated himself and spun around. He charged back into the dark hangar and almost collided with Job.

'Where you going?'

'I forgot the bag,' Sean yelled. 'Get the men on board.'

He found the gunner's bag on the desk where he had left it and stuffed it under his arm. Job was waiting for him at the foot of the Hercules' loading ramp.

'All the men are on board,' he greeted Sean. 'You should have let me keep the pilot.'

'We didn't have time to convince him to co-operate,' Sean snapped. 'The poor bastard was in a blue funk.'

'Are you going to fly?'

311

'Sure, unless you want a shot at it.'

'Hey, Sean, have you ever flown one of these things?'

'There is a first time for everything.' Sean pointed forward. 'Come on, help me clear the chocks.'

They ran forward and dragged the wheel chocks clear, then Sean led the way up the steep angle of the ramp and stopped at the top.

'Here is the control for the ramp.' He showed Job the rocker switch in the side wall of the fuselage. 'Move it to the "up" position when I have got the first engine started and the red light goes on in that panel. It will switch to green when the ramp is up and locked.'

Sean left him and ran down the length of the Hercules' body. The Shanganes were milling about uncertainly in the darkness.

'Ferdinand!' Sean shouted. 'Get them to sit in the side benches and show them how to strap in.'

Sean groped his way towards the flight deck. He found the wooden missile cases loaded over the Hercules' centre of gravity between the wings. They were piled against the fuselage on wooden pallets and covered with heavy cargo netting. He eased past them and reached the door to the flight deck. It was unlocked and he burst through it and dumped the heavy gunner's bag into the map bin under the flight engineer's steel table. Through the cockpit windows, he saw that the mock attack on the south perimeter was still in full swing, but that the volume of fire from within the base was now much heavier than from the raiders out in the bush beyond the wire.

'The Fifth Brigade has woken up,' Sean muttered, and climbed into the left-hand seat and switched on the lights of the Hercules instrument panel. The vast array of glowing dials and switches was intimidating and confusing, but Sean would not allow himself to be daunted.

It was a lot simpler than starting the old Baron. He merely switched on and ran a finger along the rows of circuit breakers to ensure that they were all in.

'The hell with start-up checks.' He said and hit the start switch for the No. 1 engine. The starter motor whined and he watched the needle creep around the rev counter.

'Come on!' He pleaded. As revolutions touched 10% she automatically primed her combustion chamber with fuel and the

312

engine ignited. He wound her up to 70% of power while he adjusted the earphones of the radio set on his head.

'Job, do you read?'

'Loud and clear, man.'

'Get the ramp up.'

'It's on its way.'

Sean waited impatiently for the ramp warning lamp on the panel to switch from red to green, and the moment it did so, he kicked off the wheel brakes and the Hercules rolled ponderously forward.

He was taxiing on one engine, and had to use gross opposite rudder to meet the asymmetrical thrust. However, as he followed the pale strip of the taxi-way, he worked on the other three engines, and one after the other coaxed them to life, adjusting the controls as the power thrust altered.

'No wind,' he muttered. 'Makes no difference which direction for take-off.'

The main runway had been extended to accommodate the excessive take-off and landing requirements of modern jet fighters. However, the Hercules was STOL – short take-off and landing. It required only a fraction of the available distance and Sean steered her for the main intersection directly in front of the control tower.

So far the Hercules had drawn no fire. The heavy machine-guns at the gates were still firing wildly into the night sky. Poor fire control was always one of the problems with African troops who in all other respects made excellent soldiers.

On the other hand, at the southern perimeter the crack veterans of the Fifth and Third Brigades were showing what well-trained African troops were capable of. Their fire was going in deadly professional sheets, and already they had almost entirely extinguished Alphonso's initial onslaught. Apart from a few desultory mortar shells there was no longer any return fire from the dark sea of bush and forest beyond the base security fence.

It was only a short time before Carlyle managed to alert fully the garrison to the enemy within, and the flight controllers in the blacked-out tower realized that there was an unauthorized take-off in progress.

Sean was taxiing the Hercules at a reckless speed, so fast that she was already developing lift and wanting to fly. He knew that if he came off the concrete taxi-way onto the grass, there was a

313

chance of bellying her or getting her stuck, but not as good a chance as having her shot up by the 12.7mm if he delayed the take-off a moment longer than was necessary.

'Job,' he spoke over the tannoy again, 'I'm going to give you cabin lights so you can make sure the lads are seated and strapped in. Take-off in forty seconds.'

He switched on the cabin lights to prevent chaos in the dark belly of the fuselage and then flicked his headset to the control tower frequency 118.6.

They were calling him stridently. 'Air Force Hercules Victor Sierra Whisky. State your intentions. I say again, Air Force Hercules.'

'This is Air Force Hercules Victor Sierra Whisky,' Sean replied. 'Request taxi clearance to avoid hostile ground fire.'

'Sierra Whisky, say again. What are your intentions?'

'Tower, this is Sierra Whisky. Request . . .' Sean mumbled and slurred his transmission deliberately, forcing the tower to ask for a further repetition. He was watching his engine temperature gauges anxiously as the needles crept up infinitely slowly towards the green.

'Tower, I am having difficulty reading your transmission,' he stalled them. 'Please repeat your clearance.'

Behind him Job barged open the door to the flight deck.

'The men are strapped in ready for take-off,' he called.

'Get into the right-hand seat and strap in,' Sean ordered without looking round. The engine temperature gauge needles were touching the bottom of the green. The main runway was coming up fast. Sean toed the wheel brakes, slowing for the turn and line up.

'Air Force Hercules. You are not cleared to taxi or line up. Repeat you have no clearance from tower. Discontinue immediately and take first left. Return to your holding area. I repeat return to your holding area.'

'Up yours, mate!' Sean muttered, as he pulled on ten degrees of flap and revolved the trim wheel to slightly tail heavy.

'Air Force Hercules. Stop immediately or we will fire upon you.'

Sean switched on the landing lights and swung the monstrous aircraft onto the main runway. She handled as lightly as his little twin Beechcraft.

'You are a pussy cat, darling.' He knew that like a woman an aircraft always responded to loving flattery. He advanced the bank of throttle controls smoothly, and at that moment the heavy machine-gun beyond the tower opened up on them.

However, the Hercules was accelerating strongly and the gunner had not learned the art of forward allowance. He was shooting at the place that the aircraft had been seconds before and perhaps his nerves were still rattling for his fire was high as well as behind. The first long burst of tracer curved away over the high tail-fin.

'That cat needs shooting lessons,' Job remarked calmly. Sean always wondered if Job's cool and phlegmatic behaviour under fire was put on.

The next burst was low and ahead, the tracer splashed across the concrete runway just under the Hercules' nose.

'But he learns fast,' Job grunted a reluctant admission.

Sean was leaning forward slightly in the seat, with his right hand holding the bank of quadruple throttles fully open, with his left feeling the control wheel for signs of life, watching the airspeed needle revolve sedately around the dial.

'Here comes your friend,' Job said, and pointed out of the side panel of the canopy. Sean glanced around swiftly.

An open Land-Rover was tearing wildly across the grass verge alongside the main runway, its headlights cutting crazy patterns in the darkness as it bounced over the uneven ground. It was attempting to cut them off, and Sean could just make out the features of the man who stood in the back of the speeding vehicle.

'He doesn't give up easily, does he?' Sean remarked, and gave his attention back to the Hercules.

Carlyle must have commandeered one of the guard Land-Rovers and its black driver. He was standing in the open back, clinging to the mounting of the RPD machine-gun and his face was pale and contorted in the reflection of the Hercules' landing lights as he egged on the driver to greater speed.

'He's really taking it to heart.' Job leaned forward to watch with interest as Carlyle swung the machine-gun in its mountings, aiming up at the cockpit of the Hercules.

The driver swung the Land-Rover over on two wheels, until it was tearing along beside the huge rolling aircraft, only fifty yards away, almost level with the wing-tip.

'Hey, man,' Job shook his head, 'he's aiming at us personally.'

Carlyle braced himself behind the gun and the muzzle flashes blinked rapidly at them. Bullets raked the perspex canopy starring it with silver dollars, and both of them ducked instinctively as shot flew past their heads.

'He's a better shot than the other cat,' Job murmured and with the tip of his finger touched the drop of blood on his cheek where a splinter had cut him.

Sean felt the controls come to life in his hand as the Hercules approached flying speed and the wings developed lift.

'Come on, pussy cat,' he murmured, and Carlyle fired another burst at the same moment the Land-Rover hit concrete culvert and bounced wildly, throwing his fire high and wild. He steadied himself and lined up to fire again.

'He's fast becoming my least favourite cartoon character.' Without flinching Job watched him take aim. 'Okay, here it comes!'

From the off-side the heavy machine-gun at the gates fired again and a stream of 12.7mm bullets skimmed the belly of the Hercules and flew on to pour into the racing Land-Rover beyond. They tore the front wheels off her and she somersaulted forward rolling end over end in a cloud of dust. From the corner of his eye, Sean saw Carlyle's body thrown high and clear.

'And so we say farewell to óne of the last authentic heroes,' he intoned gravely, and eased back the control column of the Hercules. The great aircraft responded willingly, pointing her nose upwards.

Sean switched off the landing lights and cabin lights, plunging the machine into darkness so she no longer offered a target to the ground gunners. He hit the toggle to raise the landing gear and dumped flap. Immediately the airspeed mounted and he put down one wing and went into a tight climbing turn.

Another burst of tracer followed them, floating up slowly and then accelerating as it approached until it sped past their wing-tip. Sean met the turn and banked the opposite way, weaving out of range.

'You want to make me sea-sick?' Job asked, and Sean ignored him as he checked the engine dials for possible damage.

It seemed impossible that the enormous target offered by the Hercules had received only a single burst of fire out of all the hundreds of rounds fired at it, but the needles on the dials all registered normal and responded instantly as he eased back on the boost and set revolutions for climb at five hundred feet a minute. However, the slipstream was whistling through the bullet

316

holes in the canopy, ruffling Sean's hair and making conversation difficult, so that he had to raise his voice as he told Job, 'Go back and see if anyone was hit, then do a visual check for damage in the hold.'

The lights of Umtali town were off to the south and beyond them Sean could just make out the loom of mountains. He knew that the highest peak in the chain was 8500 feet above sea level so he allowed a wide separation and levelled out at 10,000, then checked his heading.

Up until now, he had not thought about his navigation and was unsure of the bearings for a return to the Sierra da Gorongosa lines.

'Won't find them marked on any map,' he grinned. 'But we'll try 030 magnetic.' And he banked the Hercules onto that heading.

The adrenalin was still thick in his blood, the rapture of fear swirling him aloft on eagles' wings and he laughed again, just a little shakily and savoured the glorious thrill of it while it lasted.

The dark mountain tops slid away beneath him, just visible in the starlight like the shape of whales deep in an Arctic sea. He picked out the occasional pin-prick of light in the valleys, an isolated farm or mission station or peasant hut, and then as he crossed the frontier into Mozambique, there was nothing but darkness ahead.

'Nothing but darkness,' he repeated, and it seemed symbolic and prophetic. They were going back into the wasteland.

Sean eased back on power and began a gradual descent towards the lowland forests. Now that the mountain peaks were behind them, he didn't want to stay up high offering an easy target for the attack radar of a pursuing MIG fighter or an intercepting Hind gunship.

Job came back and locked the door of the flight deck.

'Any damage?' Sean asked, and Job chuckled.

'The floor of the cargo hold is ankle-deep in puke. Those Shanganes don't fancy your flying, man, they are up-chucking in all directions.'

'Charming.' Sean groped in the side pocket of the pilot's seat and came up with a packet of Dutch cigars, property of the RAF pilot.

'Well, look what we have here.' He tossed one to Job and they lit up and smoked contentedly for a few minutes before Job asked, 'How long before the MIGs catch up with us?'

Sean shook his head. 'They are based in Harare, I don't think they can catch us even if they scramble immediately. No. I'm not worried about the MIGs, but the Hinds are another story.'

They were silent again, watching the ripe celestial fruit of the stars that from the dark flightdeck seemed close enough to pluck.

'Are you ready to answer an embarrassing question?' Job broke the silence.

'Fire away.'

'You've got us up here, how the hell are you going to get us down again?'

Sean blew a smoke ring which was instantly obliterated by the slipstream through the bullet holes in the canopy.

'Interesting question,' he conceded. 'I'll let you know when I have an answer myself. In the meantime just worry about finding the Renamo lines in general and China's headquarters in particular.'

Five hundred feet above the tops of the forest trees, Sean levelled the Hercules, and reading the throttle and pitch settings from the instruction engraved on the instrument panel set her up for endurance flying.

'Another two hours before it will be light enough to even start looking for an emergency landing field,' he told Job. 'In the meantime, we can try to find the Pungwe river.'

An hour later, they spotted the gleam of water in the black carpet of forest ahead and seconds later the stars were reflected from a large body of dark water directly below them.

'I'm going back to check it,' Sean warned Job, and put the Hercules into an easy turn, watching the gyro compass on the panel in front of him rotate through 180 degrees before levelling out again.

'Landing lights on,' he murmured and flipped the switch. The tops of the trees below them were lit by the powerful lamps and they saw the river, a dark serpent winding away into the night. Sean threw the Hercules into a hard right-hand turn and then levelled out, flying directly along the course of the river.

'Looks like it,' he grunted, and switched off the landing lights. 'But even if it is the right river, we won't be able to judge whether we are upstream or downstream of the lines until sunrise.'

'So what do we do?'

'We fly a holding pattern,' Sean explained, and banked the Hercules into the first of a monotonous series of figures of eight.

318

Around and around they cruised, five hundred feet above the tree-tops, crossing and recrossing the dark river at the same point, marking time, waiting for the dawn.

'Sitting duck for a Hind,' Job remarked once.

'Don't wish it on us,' Sean frowned at him. 'If you have nothing else useful to do, get the gunner's bag, it's in the map bin.'

Job lugged the bag to the front of the cabin and set it beside his seat, then settled himself comfortably.

'Read to me,' Sean instructed. 'Find something in there to amuse me and pass the time.'

Job brought out the red plastic-covered 'Top Secret' folders one at a time and thumbed through them, reading out the titles and chapter headings from each index page.

The first three files were all field manuals for the Stinger SAM Systems, covering their deployment in every conceivable situation from the decks of ships at sea to their use by infantry in every climatic zone on the globe, setting out in tables and graphs the missile's performance figures in all conditions from tropical jungle to high Arctic.

'All you ever wanted to know, but were afraid to ask,' Job observed, and picked out the fourth manual from the bag.

STINGER GUIDED MISSILE SYSTEM
Target Selection and Rules of Engagement
Operational Reports

Job read aloud, and then turned to the index and chapter headings.

1. Falklands Islands.
2. Arabian Gulf. 'Sea of Hormuz'
3. Grenada Landings.
4. Angola Unita.
5. Afghanistan.

Job read it out, and Sean exclaimed, 'Afghanistan! See if they give us anything about the Hind.'

Job set the bulky file on his lap and adjusted the beam of the reading lamp from its recess in the cabin roof above his head. He paged through the manual.

'Here we go! Afghanistan,' he read. '"HELICOPTER TYPES."'

'Find the Hind!' Sean ordered impatiently.

'SOVIET MIL DESIGN BUREAU TYPES
NATO DESIGNATION "H"'

'That's it,' Sean encouraged him. 'Look for the Hind.'

'Hare,' said Job. 'Hoplite. Hound. Hook. Hip. Haze. Havoc
. . . here it is. Hind.'

'Give me the gen,' Sean ordered, and Job read aloud.

'"This flying piece of artillery ordnance nicknamed by the
Soviets, Sturmovich (or hunchback) known to Nato as Hind
and to the Afghan rebels and many others who have encountered it in the field as 'The Flying Death', has gained a formidable reputation which is perhaps not fully justified."'

Sean interrupted fervently, 'Brother, I hope you know what
you're talking about.'

Job went on,

'"1. Impaired manoeuvrability, hovering and rate of climb
characteristics as a consequence of the mass of its armour
plating.

"2. A limited range of 240 nautical miles fully loaded, again
as a consequence of its armour weight.

"3. A low max. speed of 157 knots and cruise speed of 147
knots.

"4. Very high service and ground maintenance requirements."'

'That's interesting,' Sean cut in. 'Even this big baby,' he patted
the Hercules' control column, 'is faster than a Hind. I'll remember
that if we meet one.'

'Do you want me to read to you?' Job asked. 'If so, then shut
up and listen.'

'My apologies, go ahead.'

'"It is estimated that several hundred machines of this type
have been employed in Afghanistan. Generally they have met
with great success against the rebels although in excess of 150
have been destroyed by rebel troops armed with the Stinger

SAM. These figures alone prove that the Hind can be effectively engaged by the Stinger SAM System employing the tactics set out in the following chapters."'

Job read on, giving the engine type and performance, the weapons and other statistics until, at last, Sean stopped him.

'Hold on, Job!' Sean pointed towards the east. 'It is getting light.'

The sky was pale enough to form a distinct horizon where it met the black land mass.

'Put the book away and go call Ferdinand up here. See if he can recognize where we are, and show us the way home.'

A strong odour of vomit surrounded Ferdinand as he stumbled onto the flight deck and the front of his tunic was stained. He leaned for support on the back of the pilot's seat, and Sean moved to put as much distance between them as possible.

'Look out there, Ferdinand.' Sean gesticulated through the bullet-punctured canopy. 'Do you see anything that you recognize?'

The Shangane peered dubiously around him muttering gloomily and then suddenly his expression cleared and lightened.

'Those hills.' He pointed out the side window. 'Yes, I know them. The river comes out between them at a waterfall.'

'Which way is the camp?'

'That way, far that way.'

'How far?'

'Two full days' march.'

'Seventy nautical miles,' Sean translated time into distance. 'We aren't too far out. Thank you, Ferdinand.' Sean broke out of the monotonous figure-of-eight pattern and levelled the Hercules' gigantic wings.

Still low against the forest, he flew westwards, the direction Ferdinand had pointed, while behind them the dawn came on apace turning the eastern sky a hazy carmine. They chased the shades of night as they fled across the dark hills.

Sean aimed the nose of the Hercules at the gap that Ferdinand had pointed out and checked his wristwatch against the panel clock.

'Time for News Desk on the Africa Service of the BBC,' he said, and fiddled with the radio controls. He picked up the familiar signature tune on 15,400 megahertz.

'This is the BBC. Here again are the news headlines. In the United States, Governor Michael Dukakis has convincingly carried the State of New York against Senator Jesse Jackson in his bid for the democratic party presidential nomination. Israeli troops have shot dead two more protestors in the occupied Gaza Strip. One hundred and twenty passengers have died in an airline crash in the Philippines. Renamo rebels have highjacked an RAF Hercules transport from a Zimbabwe Air Force base near the town of Umtali. They have flown it into Mozambique where it is being pursued by aircraft of the Zimbabwe and Mozambiquan air forces. A spokesman said that both President Mugabe and President Chissano have given orders that the aircraft, which has no hostages on board but which contains sophisticated modern weapons intended for use against the rebels, is to be destroyed at all costs.'

Sean switched off the set and smiled across at Job.

'You never thought you'd make the news headlines, did you?'

'I can do without the fame,' Job admitted. 'Did you get the bit about being pursued and destroyed at all costs?'

The Hercules was fast approaching the gap in the line of hills. The light had strengthened so that Sean could make out the pearly gleam in the throat of the pass where the river tumbled down over wet black rock.

'Incoming!' Job yelled suddenly. 'One o'clock low!'

With his extraordinary eyesight, he had picked it up an instant before Sean did. The Hind had been lying in ambush, squatting like some monstrous insect in a hidden clearing in the forest, guarding the entrance to the river pass.

As Sean saw it, he understood clearly the tactics Frelimo had used to cut him off from the Renamo lines. They would have sent the full squadron of Hinds in during the night, as soon as they guessed where he was headed.

Operating at the limits of their range, the Hinds would have settled in a defensive line, landing to conserve fuel, hiding in the forest and sweeping with their pulse radars, listening in the silence for the sound of the Hercules' engines.

Almost certainly they had guessed that he would use the river as a navigational landmark. There would probably be other gunships waiting further upstream, forming an intercepting ring around the Renamo lines, but erring too far south, Sean had run headlong into this one.

322

It leapt out of the forest, rising vertically on the silver blur of its rotor, the deformed nose drooping, like a minotaur lowering its head to charge, blotched with leprous camouflage, obscenely ugly and deadly.

It was still below them but coming up swiftly, swelling in size as they converged. Within moments its Gatling-cannon would bear, already it was training upwards. Sean reacted without thought.

He rammed all four throttle controls fully open and the great turbos screeched as he thrust the nose down, diving straight at the helicopter.

He saw the rockets leaving the weapon pods under the Hind's wings, each one a black dot in the centre of a white wreath of smoke as it dropped clear. He remembered the statistics Job had read him only minutes before. The Hind carried two AT-2 Swatter missiles and four 57mm rocket pods.

He dived the Hercules through the barrage of rockets, they flashed past his head, a storm of smoke and death, and the Hind was only two hundred metres ahead, still rising to meet him, firing rockets at pointblank range but not allowing for his violent manoeuvre.

'Hold on!' Sean shouted at Job. 'I'm going to ram the bastard.'

The killing rage was on him, sweet and hot in his blood, there was no fear at all, just the marvellous urge to destroy.

At the last moment, the pilot of the Hind guessed his intention. They were so close that through the canopy, Sean could clearly make out his features below the helmet. The Russian's face was doughy white and his mouth a shocking red slash like an open wound.

He flicked the gunship over on its side, almost inverting it completely, closing down his collective so the Hind fell like a lead weight, trying to duck under the Hercules' out-spread pinions.

'Got you, you son of a bitch!' Sean exulted, and the Hercules wing hit the tail of the gunship. The shock of impact threw Sean against his shoulder-straps, and the Hercules shuddered and lurched, the airspeed was knocked off her and she quivered on the edge of the stall only two hundred feet above the forest top.

'Come on, pussy cat,' Sean whispered like a lover.

He was babying the controls, coaxing her with gentle fingers. Her damaged wing was down, tatters of torn metal hanging from it, whipping and banging in the slipstream, and the forest tops reached up like the talons of a predator to claw them out of the sky.

'Fly for me, darling,' Sean whispered, and the four engines, howling with the effort, held her up and then gradually lifted her clear.

The needle of the rate-of-climb indicator rose jerkily, they were climbing at two hundred feet a minute.

'Where's the Hind?' Sean yelled at Job.

'She must be down,' Job called back, both of them screaming at each other with terror and excitement and the triumph of it.

'Nothing could take a hit like that.' Then his voice changed. 'No, there she is, she's still flying. My God, will you look at that mother?'

The Hind was hard hit, skittering out to one side, the tail rotor and the rudder torn, almost completely gone. Obviously her pilot was fighting for her life as she lurched and rolled and wallowed about the sky.

'I don't believe it! She's still shooting at us!' Job cried, and a smoking rocket trail blazed across their nose.

'She's steadying.' Job was watching her through the side window. 'She's coming round, she's after us again.'

Sean met the Hercules' climb, and aimed for the pass through the hills. The rocky cliffs seemed to brush their wing-tips and the foaming white waterfall flashed beneath them.

'He has fired a missile.' As Job called the warning, the pass through the hills opened up ahead of them, and Sean lifted the Hercules' maimed wing high in a maximum-rate turn.

The huge aircraft hugged the cliff face, turning the corner just as the Swatter missile locked onto the infra-red emissions of her exhausts and sped down the gut of the pass. The Hercules cut the turn so finely that Sean had to use full power to hold the nose level, and looking upwards through the skylight of the canopy, he felt as though he could have reached out and touched the rockface as the Hercules stood on one wing-tip. The missile tried to follow her round but at the critical instant the Hercules disappeared from its line of sight, and the rocky corner blocked the infra-red emissions of her exhausts.

The missile crashed into the cliff face, gouging out a great fall of rock and filling the pass behind the Hercules with dust and smoke.

Sean brought the Hercules back on even keel once again, gentling her, favouring her damaged wing.

'Any sign of the Hind?'

'No . . .' Job broke off as he saw the dread shape materialize through the dust and smoke. 'She's there, she's still coming!'

The entire rear section of the Hind's fuselage was twisted askew and half her rudder was missing. She staggered and lurched through the air, only barely under control and falling rapidly behind the fleeing Hercules. The pilot was a brave man, serving her, keeping her in action to the end.

'He's fired again!' Job cried, as he saw the missile drop from under the stubby wing roots and boost towards them on a tail of smoke.

'She's down!' Job watched the tail rotor of the gunship break away and spiral upwards while the body dropped like a spine-shot buffalo bull and hit the trees, breaking up in a tall burst of flame and smoke.

'Break right!' Job called desperately. Although the Hind was dead, her terrible offspring blazed across the sky, bearing down on them mercilessly.

Sean put the Hercules over as hard as she would go. The missile almost missed the turn and went skidding wide in overshoot, but it corrected itself and came around hard, spinning out a long billow of silver smoke behind it, and it fastened on the starboard number two motor.

For a moment, they were blinded as the smoke of the explosion swept over the canopy, and was as suddenly swept away. The Hercules convulsed as though in agony. The missile blast threw her wing up, miraculously knocking her back onto even keel and adroitly Sean held her there.

He looked across in horror at the damage. The number two engine was gone, blown out of its mountings, leaving a terrible gaping wound in the leading edge of the wing. It was a mortal blow. In her death throes, the Hercules careered across the sky, dragged around by the asymmetrical thrust of her live engines, the damaged wing flexing and beginning to fold backwards.

Sean eased back the throttles, trying to relieve the strain and balance the thrust. He looked ahead, and there was the river, wide and shallow and tranquil above the turmoil of the falls. The first rays of the sun were buttering the tops of the trees on either bank and the crocodiles lay black on the white sandbanks.

Sean flipped on the internal tannoy and spoke over the loud-speakers into the cargo hold. 'Hold on! We are going to hit hard!' he said in Shangane, and pulled his own harness adjustment in tighter.

The Hercules lumbered down heavily, both wings so badly damaged that Sean was amazed that she was still airborne.

'Too fast,' Sean muttered. She was dropping like an express elevator. They would hit the trees short of the river. He braced himself to lose a wing with disruption of air flow, and gingerly pulled on full flap to slow her down.

Far from destroying herself, the Hercules responded gratefully to the additional lift, and floated in with a semblance of her old elegance. She skimmed the tree-tops on the riverbank and Sean switched off the fuel pumps, mains and magnetos to prevent fire. He held the nose high, bleeding off speed and the needle on the airspeed indicator wound back sharply. The stall warning buzzer sounded, and then the deafening klaxon of the landing-gear chimed in, trying to warn him that his wheels were still up.

The controls went sloppy as the Hercules approached the stall, but they were out in the centre of the river, twenty feet up, dropping swiftly. The crocodiles slid off the sand-bar directly ahead, churning the green water in panic, and Sean kept feeling the control column back and back, fending her off until the last possible moment.

He felt the tail touch the water and the airspeed indicator was right down to forty knots. The Hercules stalled and belly-flopped into the river. A solid green wave broke over the nose and washed the canopy, spurting in through the bullet-holes.

Both Sean and Job were flung forward violently against their shoulder harnesses, and then the Hercules bobbed up and surfed on her belly, slowing down and turning to stop broadside to the current.

'Are you all right?' Sean barked at Job. For reply, Job un-buckled his harness and leapt out of the co-pilot's seat.

The deck was canted under Sean's feet as he stood up. Through the canopy he saw that the Hercules was floating down aimlessly on the current. Her empty fuel tanks and the air trapped in the fuselage were keeping her afloat.

'Come on!' He led Job back into the main hold and saw at a glance that the cases of missiles were still secured in their heavy cargo nets.

The Shanganes were in a panic, at least two of them injured, writhing and moaning in the puddles of drying vomit on the deck, one with the sharp jagged end of bone protruding through the flesh of his broken arm.

Sean spun the locking wheel on the emergency hatch and kicked it outwards. Immediately the nylon escape chute inflated and popped out like a drunkard's yellow tongue to flop onto the surface of the water below.

Sean leaned out of the open hatch. They were drifting towards another sand-bar and he judged that the water under their keel was only shoulder-deep for he could see bottom clearly.

'Ferdinand.' Sean picked him out of the mob of milling Shanganes. 'This way, get them out!' He saw Ferdinand sober and lash out at the panic-stricken troopers around him, driving them towards the hatch.

'Show them how it's done,' Sean ordered Job. 'And once you are down, get them to haul the hull onto the sand-bar.'

Job folded his arms over his chest and jumped feet first onto the chute. He shot down into the water and then floundered to his feet. The water came up to his armpits and, immediately, he waded to the Hercules' side and threw his whole weight against it.

One at a time, the uninjured Shanganes followed him down the chute, and at the bottom, Job took charge of them. Sean shoved the last trooper through the hatch and then leapt out himself.

The water was just a few degrees below blood warm, and as soon as he surfaced he saw that all the men were straining against the Hercules' floating carcass and slowly moving her across the flow of the river. He added his own weight to theirs, and gradually the bottom shelved beneath their feet, and the water dropped to the level of their waists.

The belly of the Hercules ran aground, and she settled heavily as the fuselage flooded. The men dragged themselves onto the sand-bar and collapsed in sodden heaps, their expressions dull and bovine from the after-effects of terror and exertion.

Sean looked around him, trying to assess their position and plan his priorities. The Hercules was stranded high enough to ensure that only the lower part of the fuselage was flooded and that the missiles would not be submerged and have their delicate electronic circuitry ruined.

The current had swept them in under the sheer riverbank and the summer floods had piled dead trees and driftwood high against it. The sand-bar was merely a narrow strip below the bank.

'We must move fast,' Sean told Job. 'We can expect that the Hind was able to transmit a signal to the rest of the squadron, and they'll come looking for us.'

'What do you want to do first?'

'Unload the Stingers,' Sean answered promptly. 'Get them busy.'

Once Sean climbed aboard again he found that the hydraulic rams on the cargo door were still operating off the batteries and he lowered the ramp.

The weight of each wooden case was stencilled upon it. 152 lb.

'They are light, two men to a case,' Sean ordered, and he and Job lifted them onto the shoulders of each pair as they stepped forward. As soon as they received it, they trotted down the ramp onto the sand-bar, and up the bank into the trees. Ferdinand showed them where to stash them and cover them with driftwood.

It took less than twenty minutes to unload the cargo, and every minute Sean was in a ferment of impatience and anxiety. As the last case was carried ashore, he hurried out onto the ramp and peered up at the sky, expecting to hear the approaching whine of rotors and Isotov turbos.

'Our luck isn't going to last,' he told Job. 'We must get rid of the Hercules.'

'What are you going to do, swallow it or bury it?' Job asked sarcastically.

Against the forward bulkhead of the Hercules' hold was a 120-ton loading winch, used to drag cargo aboard. Under Sean's instruction, four Shanganes ran out the winch cable and used the Hercules' inflatable life raft to take the end of it across the river and shackle it to a tree on the far bank.

While they were doing this, Sean and Job searched the Hercules and stripped it of every item of useful equipment, from the first-aid kit to the stores of coffee and sugar in the tiny forward galley. With satisfaction, Sean saw that the tropical first-aid box was substantial and contained a good supply of malarial prophylactics and antibiotics. He sent it ashore with one of the Shanganes and ran back to the loading ramp.

The dinghy was returning and there was still no sound nor sight of marauding Hind gunships. It was too good to bear thinking about.

'Get everybody ashore,' Sean told Job, and went to the winch controls.

As he engaged the clutch, the steel cable came up taut and the Hercules' hull which was heavily beached on the sand-bar lurched and began to swing. He kept the winch running and the sand gritted and scraped under her belly as she was dragged by her own winch into deeper water.

As soon as she was afloat, Sean half closed the ramp to prevent her flooding too rapidly and winched her into the middle of the river, where the current was swiftest. As soon as she took the current and began to drift downstream, Sean grabbed the bolt cutters from their rack on the bulkhead and sheared the cable. The Hercules floated free.

On an impulse Sean cut a four-foot length from the end of the severed winch cable, and the stainless steel strands immediately began to unravel of their own accord. He rolled three of the separate strands into a tight loop and slipped the roll into his back pocket. Job would fit hardwood buttons to the strands. The garrotting wire was one of the Scouts' favourite clandestine weapons, and Sean had felt half-naked since he had lost his in the pack that he had dropped down the cliff. He transferred his full attention back to the Hercules.

'The fuel tanks are almost empty,' he murmured as he watched her progress downstream. 'She should float until she reaches the falls.' He stayed on board while at least two miles of riverbank went by.

In the meantime, he used the bolt cutters to sever the hydraulic pipes and fuel leads that ran along the roof of the cargo hold. A mixture of hydraulic fluid and Avtur dribbled and spurted and puddled onto the floor of the hold. Satisfied at last that he had done everything possible to throw off the pursuit, he balanced in the open escape hatch and pulled the pin from the phosphorus grenade that he had commandeered from Ferdinand.

'Thanks, old girl,' he spoke aloud to the Hercules. 'You have been a darling. The least I can offer you is a Viking's funeral.' He rolled the grenade down the deck of the hold and then leapt out of the hatch and hit the water. He came up swimming, reaching out in a full over-arm crawl with the image in his mind of those fat black crocodiles he had seen on the sand-bar.

Behind him, he heard the muffled bump of the exploding grenade but he never paused nor looked back until he felt the ground under his feet. By then, the Hercules was a quarter of a mile downstream, burning furiously but still afloat. Black oily smoke boiled up into the clear morning sky.

Sean waded the last few yards to the steep bank and crawled up it on hands and knees. While he sat there panting and gulping for breath, he heard the familiar and by now well-hated sound of rotors and Isotov turbo engines coming in fast. The smoke of the burning Hercules was a beacon that the Hinds would have spotted from fifty miles out.

Sean took a handful of mud from the bank on which he sat and smeared his bare arms and face. He crawled under a dense bush on the bank and watched the Hind come sweeping in over the treetops, banking in a wide circle around the burning hulk of the Hercules and then hovering like an evil vampire two hundred feet above it.

The flames reached one of the fuel tanks and the Hercules exploded in a dragon's breath, scattering pieces of itself across the river, the flames hissing into steam as they hit the water.

The Hind hung over the river for almost five minutes, perhaps searching for survivors, and then abruptly it rose high, turned its nose southwards and dwindled to a speck against the blue.

'Limited range and endurance, like the man said.' Sean stood up from his hiding place. 'Now go home like a good little Ruskie and report the target destroyed. Go tell Bobby Mugabe that he doesn't have to worry about his precious Stingers falling into the wrong hands.'

He reached into his top pocket and brought out the packet of Dutch cigars. The cardboard disintegrated in his hands and the leaf had dissolved into a soggy porridge. He tossed it into the river.

'Time I gave up anyway,' he sighed, and trudged along the bank, heading upstream.

Job was working on the two injured troopers.

'This one has got a nice set of cracked ribs and a broken collarbone.' Job finished the strapping and then indicated the other patient. 'I left this one for you.'

'Appreciate it,' Sean grunted, and examined the broken arm. 'It's a bloody mess.'

'Nice adjective,' Job agreed. Two inches of the shattered humerus protruded from dark bruises and blood clots. A buzzing swarm of metallic-blue flies were circling the clots, and Sean brushed them away.

'What have you done, so far?'

'Given him a handful of painkillers from the med box.'

'That should stun an ox,' Sean nodded. 'Get me a piece of nylon line and two of the strongest Shanganes.'

The arm had shortened dramatically and Sean had to get the ends of the broken bone to meet again. He looped the nylon rope around the trooper's wrist and gave the ends to the Shangane strong men.

'When I say pull, you pull, understand?' he ordered. 'Okay, Job, hold him.'

They had done this before, often. Job took up his position sitting behind the patient and slipped his arms under his armpits and locked them around his chest.

'I'm going to hurt you,' Sean promised the patient, and the man stared back at him impassively.

'Ready?' Job nodded, and Sean glanced up at the rope. 'Pull!' They laid back with a will.

The injured man's eyes snapped wide open, and a rash of sweat droplets like blisters burst out on his skin.

'Pull harder!' Sean snarled at Ferdinand, and the arm began to elongate. The sharp point of protruding bone withdrew slowly into the flesh.

The Shangane ground his teeth together in the effort of re-straining himself from screaming. The sound was like two pieces of glass being rubbed together forcibly, and it grated along Sean's nerve ends.

The point of bone popped back into the swollen purple wound and Sean heard the two ends rasp together deep in the flesh.

'That's it! Hold it!' he told Ferdinand, and deftly placed two splints from the first-aid box along each side of the arm. He strapped them in place with surgical tape, binding it up as firmly as he dared without cutting off the circulation, and then nodded at Ferdinand.

'Slowly. Let it go.' Ferdinand released pressure and the splints held the arm straight.

'Another breakthrough for medical science,' Job murmured. 'An elegant and sophisticated procedure, Doc.'

331

'Can you walk?' Sean asked. 'Or do we have to carry you home?'

'Of course, I can walk.' The trooper was indignant. 'Do you think I am a woman?'

'If you were, we would ask a top bridal price for you,' Sean grinned at him, and stood up.

'Let's inspect the loot,' he suggested to Job. It was their first opportunity to examine the crates from the Hercules.

There were thirty-five of them piled haphazardly under the spreading branches of an African mahogany. With Ferdinand and four of his men assisting, they sorted through them, stacking them neatly after noting the lettering on each.

Thirty-three cases, each weighing 154 pounds were marked:

> STINGER GUIDED MISSILE SYSTEM.
> 1 X GRIP STOCK AND ANTENNA
> 1 X INTERROGATOR.
> 5 X LOADED LAUNCH TUBES.

'That gives China 165 shots, and there are eleven Hinds left in the squadron after the one you knocked out of the sky,' Job calculated. 'Sounds good to me.'

'With the way some of these beauties shoot, they are going to need every one of them,' Sean grunted, and then his expression of deliberate pessimism lightened. 'Well, well! Here is one for the book!'

One of the two remaining odd-sized cases was stencilled:

> STINGER GUIDED MISSILE SYSTEM.
> TRAINING SET M. 134.
> TRACKING HEAD TRAINER.

'That will make somebody's life a lot easier,' Job agreed. The captured manuals had discussed this training system which allowed an instructor to monitor a trainee's tracking technique during a simulated missile launch. It would be invaluable equipment for whoever was given the job of teaching the Renamo troops to use the system.

However, it was not until Sean examined the last and smallest case that the full value of the prize dawned on him.

The small wooden crate was stencilled:

'Sweet Trinity,' he whistled. 'It's a post, not a common or garden system, but a ruddy post that we have got ourselves here!'

'Let's take a look!' Job was as excited as he was.

Sean hesitated, like a child tempted to open his gift before the dawn of his birthday. He glanced up at the sky looking for Hinds, strange how he had picked up that nervous habit from his Shanganes.

'We daren't move until dark. Plenty of time to kill,' he capitulated, and leaned over to draw the bayonet from the sheath of Ferdinand's webbing.

Gently he prised open the lid of the crate and lifted away the slabs of white polyurethane packing. The software was contained in a heavy-duty plastic carry pack. He sprang the catches on the lid and opened the case. The dozens of software cassettes were each colour-coded, sealed in transparent glassine envelopes and fitted into tailored slots in the interior. This was what they had read about in the manuals they had borrowed from Carlyle, the British gunnery officer.

'Get the manuals,' Sean told Job. And when he brought them over they squatted beside the open case and pored through the heavy volume which described the post system.

'Here it is! Hind attack system. Colour code red. Numerical code S.42.A.'

Under the post system the Stinger missiles could be programmed to attack various targets by employing tactics and search frequencies specific to that type of aircraft. Simply by inserting one of the micro-cassettes into the console of the launcher, the missile could be instructed to alter its attack technique.

'"System software cassette. S.42.A.,"' Job followed the text with his forefinger as he read aloud from the manual, '"is targeted on the Hind helicopter gunship. The system employs a 'two-colour' seeker which registers both infra-red and ultra-violet emissions in two stages. The initial stage will lock to infra-red from the engine exhaust system.

'"The Hind's exhaust suppressors divert and emit those infra-red rays through heavily armoured outlets below the main fuselage. Missile-strikes on this section of the Hind have proved ineffective.

'''The S.42.A. modification automatically switches the guidance system of the Stinger into ultra-violet seeker mode when range-to-target is reduced to a hundred metres. Ultra-violet is emitted principally from the air-intake ports of the Isotov TV3-117 turbo shaft engines. This area is the only section of the fuselage not encased in titanium armour plate and missile-strikes through the engine intake ports have resulted in hundred per cent kills.

'''To achieve effective ultra-violet acquisition, the initial launch of the missile must be made from below and dead ahead of the aircraft, at a range not exceeding 1000 metres nor less than 150 metres.'''

Job closed the manual with a snap.

'Big casino!' he said. 'China is getting more than he ever hoped for.'

* * *

There were thirty heavy cases to carry and only twenty uninjured men, including Sean and Job. Sean cached the boxes that they were forced to leave. He would send a detail back to fetch them once they reached the Renamo lines.

Carrying what they could, including the trainer and the post modification equipment, they set out along the bank of the Pungwe river at nightfall, groping for a contact with the Renamo front line. They marched all that night.

The extended column, slowed down by the heavy cases of missiles, covered only twelve miles before sunrise. However, the weather had changed and the wind had backed into the east bringing in low cloud and a cold drizzle of rain that would hide them from the searching Hinds. They kept going all that day.

At dusk Sean let them rest for a few hours, and they huddled miserably in the rain until Sean roused them once again and they stumbled on, slipping and sliding in the mud, and cursing the loads upon their backs. An hour after sunrise the clouds rolled away and their sodden battledress steamed as it dried on their backs.

Two hours later they ran into the ambush.

They were moving through light savannah along the riverbank

The flat-topped acacia thorn trees were interspersed with clumps of coarse elephant grass.

Sean heard the metallic snap of the loading handle being jerked back to cock a machine-gun and before the sound had fully registered in his brain, he was diving forward, shouting a warning to his Shanganes. As he hit the sandy earth with his elbows and belly, he saw the muzzle flashes shimmering and dancing like fairy lights in the grass only thirty paces ahead and a blaze of shot passed over his head, making him blink and flinch.

He rolled left to throw the gunner's aim, holding the AKM with one hand as though it were a pistol, firing blindly to further confuse the attackers and groping for the grenade on his belt.

He was on the point of hurling the grenade when behind him Ferdinand shouted a challenge in Portuguese and the firing from the front shrivelled and died away. From the patch of elephant grass just ahead of Sean, a voice replied to the challenge and then Ferdinand was shouting urgently in Shangane, 'Cease fire! Cease fire! Renamo! Renamo!'

There was a long suspicious silence during which Sean kept his right arm cocked back ready to throw the grenade. He had seen too many good men called out to die in a false truce.

'Renamo!' A voice from the front reiterated. 'Friends!'

'All right!' Sean shouted back in Shangane. 'Stand up, Renamo. Let us see your beautiful friendly faces.'

Somebody laughed, and a grinning black face under a tiger-striped camouflage cap popped up out of the grass and ducked back immediately.

After a few seconds, when there was no more firing, another man stood up cautiously, and then another. Sean's Shanganes came to their feet and moved forward, slowly at first and with weapons cocked, and then they were meeting in the open ground, shaking hands and laughing and slapping each other's backs. They had run into the sector held by the battalion under the command of Major Takawira. He recognized Sean immediately and they shook hands with mutual pleasure.

'Colonel Courtney! What a relief to see you alive! We heard on the news from the BBC and Radio Zimbabwe that your aircraft had been shot down in flames with you and all your men wiped out.'

'I need your help, Major,' Sean told him. 'I've left twenty cases of missiles cached out there in the bush. I want you to send a detachment of a hundred men to fetch them in. One of my men will guide them to the cache.'

'I'll send my best men. I'll pick them out personally,' Takawira assured him.

'How far are we from General China's HQ?' Sean asked.

'The Frelimo helicopters have forced him to pull back. His new HQ is only six miles upstream. I have just spoken to him on the radio and the general is most anxious to see you.'

Their progress was a triumphal march, for news of their success flashed through the Renamo lines ahead of them. Men in tiger stripes turned out to cheer them and shake their hands and thump their backs as they passed. The porters bore the cases of missiles aloft as though they were the ark of Jehovah and they, the priests of an arcane religion. They sang the Renamo battle songs as they trotted along proudly under their burdens.

General China was waiting to greet them at the entrance to his newly constructed command bunker, resplendent in crisply laundered battledress and decorations, with the maroon beret cocked jauntily over one eye.

'I knew you would not fail me, Colonel.' For the first time in their acquaintance, Sean had the feeling that his smile was genuine.

'We lost almost thirty men under Sergeant Alphonso,' Sean told him brusquely. 'We were forced to abandon them.'

'No! No, Colonel!' General China clasped his shoulder in an unparalleled display of goodwill. 'Alphonso got out safely. He lost only three men in reaching the mission at St Mary's. I have just had radio contact with them. They will be in our lines by tomorrow evening at the latest. The entire operation was a brilliant success, Colonel.' He dropped his hand from Sean's shoulder. 'Now let us see what you have brought me.'

The porters laid the wooden cases at his feet. A black Caesar receiving the spoils of war, Sean thought ironically.

'Open them!' China beamed. Sean had never expected such childlike excitement from one usually so cold and contained. China was actually performing an ecstatic little jig, and scrubbing his hands together as he watched the junior officers on his staff wielding jemmies and bayonet blades in an attempt to prise up the lid of the first crate. The steel strapping frustrated their efforts.

In the end China could no longer control himself and pushed

his officers away, snatched a jemmy bar out of the hands of one of them and attacked the case himself. He was sweating profusely with excitement and exertion when at last the lid yielded and there were obsequious cries of congratulation from his staff as the contents were revealed.

The Stinger launcher was fully assembled with a missile tube loaded. The IFF interrogator was packed separately in a transparent glassine envelope ready to be plugged into the console head by its short coil of cable. The additional four disposal tubes, each containing a single missile, nestled in the moulded white polyurethane foam packaging. After firing the missile, the empty tube would be discarded and replaced by a fresh tube containing its own sixteen-pound missile.

The laughter and cheering gradually subsided and the general staff crowded forward to examine the contents of the case, albeit with a marked reserve as though they had discovered a nest of poisonous scorpions under a rock and expected that at any second a fanged tail would whip out at them.

General China slowly went down on one knee and reverently lifted the assembled launcher out of its foam nest.

His staff watched in awe as he settled the clumsy weapon on his shoulder. The missile tube extended behind him and the consol with its antenna, looking as mundane as a plastic milk crate almost totally obscured General China's features. He peered studiously into the aiming screen of the console and gripped the triggered pistol stock.

He aimed the Stinger skyward and his staff uttered small sounds of encouragement and admiration.

'Let the Frelimo *henshaw* come now,' China boasted. 'We will see them burn.' And he began to make helicopter and machine-gun noises like a small boy at play, pointing the missile at flocks of imaginary Hind gunships that circled overhead.

'Pow! Pow!' he cried. 'Vroom! Swish! Boom!'

'Ka pow!' With a straight face, Sean joined in and the general's staff howled with delight and tried to out-do each other with the sounds of exploding and crashing helicopters.

Somebody began to sing and they all picked up the refrain, clapping their hands to the rhythm of the Renamo battle anthem, swaying and stamping their feet.

Now there were two hundred men singing, their voices blending and rising into the beautiful melodious sound of Africa that made

337

the goose-pimples rise on Sean's forearms and the hair on the back of his neck prickle. General China stood in the midst of them with the missile on his shoulders and led the chorus. His voice soared above the rest, amazing Sean with its range and clarity, a magnificent tenor which would not have disgraced any of the world's great opera houses.

The song ended with a great shout of defiance, 'Renamo!' and their dark faces were lit by a fierce patriotic ardour.

'In this mood, they'll be hard men to beat,' Sean thought, and General China handed the launcher to one of his men and came to shake Sean's hand.

'Congratulations, Colonel.' He was earnest and happy at the same time. 'I think you have saved the cause. I am grateful.'

'That's fine, China,' Sean was ironical. 'But don't just tell me how grateful, show me.'

'Of course, forgive me.' China put on a little show of repentance. 'In the excitement I almost forgot, there is somebody very anxious to see you.'

Sean felt his breathing shorten and his chest constrict.

'Where is she?'

'In my bunker, Colonel.' General China indicated the carefully concealed entrance to the dugout amongst the trees.

Sean elbowed his way roughly through the ranks of excited soldiers, and as he reached the entrance to the bunker, he could restrain himself no longer and he went down the rough steps three at a time.

Claudia was in the radio dugout, sitting on a bench along the far wall with her two wardresses flanking her. He spoke her name when he saw her and she came to her feet slowly, staring at him, white-faced with disbelief. The bones of her cheeks threatened to burst through the almost translucent skin and her eyes were huge and dark as midnight.

As he crossed to her, Sean saw the marks on her wrists, livid weals crusted with fresh scab and his anger matched his joy. He swept her into his arms and she was as thin and frail as a child. For a moment she stood quiescent in his embrace, and then fiercely she threw her arms around his neck and hugged him. He was surprised by her strength, and she shivered in convulsive spasms as she pressed her face into the hollow of his neck.

They stood locked together, not moving nor speaking for a

long time until Sean felt the wetness soaking through his shirt front.

'Please don't cry, my darling.'

Gently he lifted her face between his hands, and with his thumbs wiped the tears away.

'It's just that I'm so happy now,' she smiled through the last of her tears. 'Nothing else matters any more, now that you are back.'

He took her hands and lifted them to his lips, kissing the broken scabbed skin on her wrists.

'They can't hurt me any more, not now,' she said, and Sean turned his head and looked at the two uniformed wardresses who still sat on the bench.

'Your mothers rutted with the stinking dung-eating hyena,' he said softly in Shangane, and they flinched at the insult. 'Get out! Go! Before I rip out your ovaries and feed them to the vultures!'

They glowered and hung their heads until Sean dropped his hand onto the butt of his pistol. Then they moved with alacrity, jumping up from the bench and sidling to the dugout steps.

Sean turned back to Claudia, and for the first time kissed her mouth. That kiss lasted a long time and when they drew unwillingy apart Claudia whispered, 'When they took off the handcuffs and let me wash, I knew you were coming back.'

Her words conjured up a picture of the degradation and brutality she had come through and Sean's reply was bitter.

'The bastard. Somehow I'm going to make him suffer for what he has done to you. I swear that to you.'

'No, Sean. It doesn't matter any more. It's over. We are together again. That is all that matters.'

They had only a few more minutes alone before General China came bustling into the radio dugout at the head of his staff, still smiling and elated.

He ushered Sean and Claudia through into his private office and seemed not to notice that they both treated his affable hospitality with icy reserve. They sat close together in front of his desk, quietly holding hands, not responding to his pleasantries.

'I have prepared quarters for you,' General China told them. 'In fact I have evicted one of my senior commanders and given you his dugout. I hope you will find it adequate for your needs.'

'We aren't planning on a long stay, General,' Sean told him.
'I want to be on my way back to the border, with Miss Monterro,
tomorrow morning at the very latest.'

'Ah, Colonel, of course I want to accommodate you. From
now on, you are an honoured and privileged guest. You have
certainly earned your release. However, for operational reasons
that happy moment must be delayed for a few days. Frelimo are
moving in large concentrations of troops.'

Reluctantly Sean conceded. 'Fair enough, but in the meantime,
we expect five-star treatment. Miss Monterro needs new clothes
to replace these rags.'

'I shall have a selection of the best we have sent to your dugout
from our stores. However, I cannot promise either Calvin Klein
or Gucci.'

'While we are at it, we'll need a team of servants to do our
laundry and cleaning and cooking.'

'I haven't forgotten your colonial origins, Colonel,' China
answered slyly. 'One of my men was an under-chef at the President Hotel in Johannesburg. He understands European tastes.'

Sean stood up. 'We'll inspect our quarters now.'

'One of my junior officers will escort you,' General China
suggested. 'If there is anything further you need, please let him
know. He has my personal orders to give you whatever he can to
make you comfortable. As I have said before, you are honoured
guests.'

'He gives me the creeps,' Claudia whispered, as the subaltern
ushered them out of the dugout. 'I don't know when he frightens
me more, when he is being charming or menacing.'

'It won't be for much longer.' Sean put his arm round her
shoulders and led her into the open air, but somehow the sunlight
lacked warmth and despite his assurances to Claudia, the chill of
General China's presence persisted.

*   *   *

The dugout to which the subaltern led them was in the bush
above the riverbank, not more than three hundred yards from
the general's HQ. The entrance was screened with a piece of
tattered camouflage net and the interior was freshly dug out of
the hard red clay of the riverbank.

'It's so new that it probably hasn't yet acquired a permanent

340

population of bed bugs and lice and other wild game,' Sean remarked.

The clay walls were damp and cool and there was ventilation through the spaces between the roof poles.

The only furnishings were a table and two stools of mopane poles against one wall, and opposite that a raised bedstead also of mopane poles and a mattress of combed elephant grass covered with a sheet of faded canvas. There was however, one extraordinary luxury, a mosquito net hung above the bed.

The subaltern who was escorting them summoned the domestic staff and the three of them lined up in front of Sean and Claudia. The two camp boys would take care of their laundry and cleaning under the supervision of the chef.

The chef was an elderly Shangane with a pleasant lined face and silver-frosted hair and beard. He reminded Claudia of a black Santa Claus. They both liked him immediately.

'My name is Joyful, sir.'

'So you speak English, Joyful?'

'And Afrikaans and Portuguese and Shona and . . .'

'Enough already.' Sean held up a hand to stop him. 'Can you cook?

'I'm the best damned cook in Mozambique.'

'Joyful and modest,' Claudia laughed.

'Okay, Joyful, tonight we will have Chateaubriand,' Sean teased him, and Joyful looked doleful.

'Sorry, sir, no fillet steak.'

'All right, Joyful.' Sean relented. 'You just make us the best dinner you can.'

'I'll tell you when it's ready, sir and madam.'

'Don't hurry,' said Claudia, and lowered the netting across the doorway, summarily dismissing all of them.

They stood hand in hand and studied the bed thoughtfully. Claudia broke the silence.

'Are you thinking what I am thinking?'

'Before or after dinner?' Sean asked.

'Both,' she replied, and led him by the hand.

They undressed each other with aching deliberation, drawing out the pleasure of truly discovering each other's bodies.

Though they were already lovers, he had only had one fleeting glimpse of her, and she had never seen him naked. She studied him with big solemn eyes, not smiling, taking her time until he

341

was forced to ask. 'Well, do I get the Monterro seal of approval?'

'Oh, boy!' she breathed, still deadly serious, and he lifted her on to the bed.

It was darkening outside the dugout when Joyful coughed politely beyond the screen doorway.

'Dinner is ready, sir and madam.'

They ate at the table of mopane poles by the light of a paraffin lantern that Joyful had scavenged from somewhere.

'Oh my God!' Claudia cried when she saw what Joyful had provided for them. 'I didn't realize how hungry I was.'

It was a casserole of plump green pigeons and wild mushrooms, with side dishes of steamed yellow yams and cassava cakes and banana fritters.

'General China sent this for you,' Joyful explained, and set cans of South African beer on the crowded table.

'Joyful, you are a paragon.'

They ate in dedicated silence, smiling across the table at each other between mouthfuls. At last Claudia groaned softly.

'I think I can just waddle as far as the bed, but definitely no further.'

'Suits me fine,' he said, and reached across to take her hand.

The mosquito net was a tent over them, creating an intimate and secret temple for their loving. The light from the lantern was soft and golden. It washed subtle tones and shadings across the planes of her face and the rounds and hollows of her body.

The texture of her skin fascinated him. It was so fine-pored as to seem glossed like warm wax. He stroked her shoulders and arms and belly, marvelling at the feel of her.

She rasped her fingernails through his short crisp beard, and pressed her face into the springing curls that covered his chest.

'You are as hairy and hard as a wild animal,' she whispered. 'And as dangerous. I should be terrified of you.'

'Aren't you?'

'A little, yes. That's what makes it such fun.'

She was starved to the point where her ribs showed clearly through her pale skin. Her limbs were slender and childlike, and the marks of her suffering upon them threatened to break his heart. Even her breasts seemed smaller, but it was as though their diminution had merely emphasized the sweet and tender shape. She watched him take the nipple of one between his lips and she stroked the thick curls at the back of his neck.

342

'That feels so good,' she whispered. 'But there are two.' And she took a handful of his hair to direct his mouth across to the other side.

Once while she sat astride him, he looked up at her and reached high to stroke the soft skin of her throat and shoulders and said, 'In this light, you look like a little girl.'

'And me trying so hard to prove to you what a big girl I am,' she pouted down at him, then leaned forward to kiss his mouth.

They slept so intricately entwined that their hearts beat against each other and their breath mingled and they woke to find that they had begun again while they still slept.

'He's so clever,' she murmured drowsily. 'Already he can find his way all on his own.'

'Do you want to go back to sleep?'

'Do I, hell!'

Much later she asked him, 'Do you think we could make this last for ever?'

'We can try.'

But at last through the slats above them, the dawn sent orange-gold fingers of light, and Claudia cried softly, 'No. I don't want it to end. I want to keep you inside me for ever and ever.'

When Joyful brought the tea to the bedside, on the tray with the mugs was an invitation from General China to dine in the mess that evening.

*　*　*

General China's mess night was for Claudia and Sean less than an unqualified success, despite the general's continued efforts to charm them.

The buffalo meat he served was tough and rank and the beer made the officers of the general's staff loud and argumentative. The weather had changed and was close and sweltering even after dark and the bunker that served as a mess was thick with the smoke of cheap native tobacco and the odour of masculine sweat.

General China drank none of the beer, but sat at the head of the table ignoring the shouted conversation and hearty eating habits of his staff. Instead, he played the gallant to Claudia, engaging her in a discussion which she at first attempted to evade.

Claudia was unaccustomed to the table manners of Africa. She watched with an awful fascination as the stiff maize porridge was scooped from the communal pot in the centre of the table by many hands, moulded into balls between the fingers and then dipped into buffalo-meat gravy. Greasy gravy ran down their chins, and no attempt was made to moderate the conversation during mastication, so that small particles of food were sprayed across the table when one of them laughed or exclaimed loudly.

Despite the fact that she was still half starved Claudia had no appetite for the meal and it took an effort to concentrate on General China's dissertation.

'We have divided the entire country into three war zones,' he explained. 'General Takawira Dos Alves is the commander of the north. He commands the provinces of Niassa and Cabo Delgado. In the south, the commander is General Tippoo Tip, and of course, I command the army of the central provinces of Manica and Sofala. Between us we control almost fifty per cent of the total ground area of Mozambique, and another forty per cent of the country is a destruction zone over which we are forced to maintain a scorched earth policy to prevent Frelimo growing either food for their troops or cash crops to finance their war effort against us.'

'So the reports of atrocities that we have received in the United States are true then.' He had engaged Claudia's interest at last. Her tone was sharp as she accused, 'Your troops are attacking and wiping out the civilian population in those destruction zones.'

'No, Miss Monterro.' China's smile was icy. 'The fact that we have moved the civilian population out of many of those destruction areas, is unavoidably true, but all the atrocities, all the massacres and tortures, have been committed by Frelimo themselves.'

'They are the government of Mozambique, why would they massacre their own people?' Claudia protested.

'I agree with you, Miss Monterro, sometimes it is difficult to follow the devious working of the Marxist mind. The reality is that Frelimo is unable to govern. They are unable to provide even basic protection to the civilian population outside the cities, let alone give them services of health and education and transport and communications. To draw world attention away from the total failure of their economic policies and their lack of popular support, they have provided the international media with a Roman holiday of slaughter and torture which they blame upon

Renamo and South Africa. It is easier to kill people than to feed and educate them, and the anti-Renamo propaganda is worth a million lives, to a Marxist that is.'

'You are suggesting that a Khmer Rouge style massacre is being conducted here in Mozambique by the government forces?' Claudia was aghast, pale and perspiring with the noise and fug of the subterranean mess, and with the horror of General China's explanations.

'I am not suggesting, Miss Monterro. I am simply stating the literal truth.'

'But, but, surely the world must do something?'

'The world is uncaring, Miss Monterro. It has been left for us, Renamo, to try to bring down the heinous Marxist regime.'

'Frelimo is the elected government,' Claudia pointed out, but General China shook his head.

'No, Miss Monterro, very few governments in Africa are elected. There has never been an election in Mozambique or Angola or Tanzania or any of the other gems of African Socialism. In Africa the trick is to seize power and hang onto to it at all costs. The typical African government plunges into the void left by the exodus of the colonial power and entrenches itself behind a barricade of AK 47 assault rifles. It then declares a one-party system of government which further precludes any form of opposition and it nominates a presidential dictator for life.'

'Tell me, General China,' Claudia raised her voice above the roar of conversation further down the mess table, 'if one day, your military efforts succeed and you and the other generals of Renamo vanquish Frelimo and become the new government of this country, will you then allow free elections and a truly democratic system to evolve?'

For a moment General China stared at her in astonishment and then he laughed delightedly.

'My very dear Miss Monterro, your childlike belief in the myth of the essential goodness of mankind is really rather touching. I certainly have not fought so hard and so long to gain power, simply to hand it over to a bunch of illiterate peasants. No, Miss Monterro, once we have the power it will remain safely in the right hands.' He extended his own elegantly shaped hands, pink palms uppermost, towards her. 'These,' he said.

'So you are every bit as bad as you say the others are.' There were hot red spots of anger on Claudia's cheeks. This was the man who had put chains on her wrists and incarcerated her in that vile pit. She hated him with all her strength.

'I think you are actually beginning to understand at last, even through the haze of your liberal emotions. In Africa there are no good guys and no bad guys, there are simply winners and losers.' He smiled again. 'And I assure you, Miss Monterro, that I intend to be one of the winners.'

General China turned away from her as one of his signals officers ducked through the low entrance to the bunker and hurried down to the head of the table. With an apologetic salute, he handed the general a yellow message flimsy. China read it without change of expression and then looked up at his guests.

'Please excuse me for a few minutes.' China placed his beret at the correct angle over one eye, then stood and followed the signaller out of the bunker.

The moment he was gone, Claudia leaned across the table to Sean. 'Can't we get out of here now? I don't think I can bear another moment of it. God, how I hate that man.'

'Mess tradition doesn't seem very strict,' Sean murmured. 'If we leave, I don't think anyone is going to take offence.'

As they crossed to the doorway, there was a drunken chorus of suggestive catcalls and whistles, and they went up the steps with relief.

The night air had cooled and Claudia breathed it in deeply and gratefully. 'I don't know which was more suffocating, the fug or the dialectic.' She breathed again. 'I never expected Africa to be like this. It's so confused, so illogical, it turns everything I know to be true upside down.'

'But it's interesting, isn't it?' Sean asked.

'Like a nightmare is interesting. Let's go to bed. At least that's something I can believe in completely.'

They turned towards their dugout shelter, but General China's voice halted them.

'You aren't leaving us so soon?' And his tall lithe form came striding towards them out of the darkness. 'I'm afraid I have disappointing news for both of you.'

'You aren't letting us go. You are reneging on our deal,' Sean said flatly. 'I knew this was coming.'

'Circumstances beyond my control,' China assured him smoothly. 'I have just had a radio report from Sergeant Alphonso. As you know I was expecting his return this evening and he and his men would have escorted you and Miss Monterro safely back to the border, however . . .'

'All right, let's hear it from you, China,' Sean snarled angrily. 'What new scheme have you cooked up?'

General China ignored the accusation and the tone in which it was delivered. 'Sergeant Alphonso reports that there is a massive build-up of enemy to the west of our lines. It seems that, emboldened by their gunships, Frelimo, backed by Zimbabwean contingents, are about to launch a full-scale offensive. We are probably already cut off from the Zimbabwe border. The territory that we once controlled seems certain to have been overrun by the enemy advance. Within hours it will become a battlefield, even now Sergeant Alphonso is fighting his way through and has taken some casualties. I am afraid you would not last long out there, Colonel. It would be suicide for you to try to reach the border now. You must remain under my personal protection.'

'What the hell do you want from us?' Sean demanded. 'You are up to something, I can smell the stink of it from here. What is it?'

'Your lack of confidence in my motives is very distressing,' China smiled coldly. 'However, the sooner the Hind gunships are destroyed, the sooner the Frelimo offensive will collapse and you and Miss Monterro will be returned to the civilized world.'

'I'm listening,' Sean told him.

'You are the only one, you and Captain Job, who understand the Stinger. In this our interests coincide. I want you to train a select contingent of my men to handle the Stingers.'

'That's all you want?' Sean stared into his face. 'We train your men to use the Stinger, then you let us go?'

'Exactly.'

'How do I know you won't move the goal posts again?'

'You pain me, Colonel.'

'Not nearly as much as I'd like to.'

'It's agreed then. You will train my men and in exchange I will have you escorted across the border at the very first opportunity.'

'What option do we have?'

:I'm so pleased that you are being reasonable, Colonel. It makes life much easier for all of us.' His voice became crisp and businesslike. 'We must begin immediately.'

'You'll have to let your staff sober up a little,' Sean told him. 'I'll begin first thing tomorrow, and I'll train the Shanganes under

Alphonso and Ferdinand, if Alphonso makes it through the Frelimo offensive intact.'

'How long will it take you?' China wanted to know. 'From now on every hour will be vital to our survival.'

'They are bright lads and willing, I should be able to do something with them in a week.'

'You will not have that long.'

'I'll have the Stingers in action just as soon as I possibly can,' Sean retorted irritably. 'Please believe me, General, I don't want to hang around here a minute longer than I have to. Now we'll bid you good-night.' He took Claudia's arm as he turned away.

'Oh Sean,' she whispered. 'I have the terrible premonition that we are caught up in something from which we are never going to escape.' And Sean squeezed her upper arm to make her stop.

'Look up there,' he ordered softly, and she raised her face.

'The stars?' she asked. 'Is that what you want me to look at?'

'Yes, the stars.' They daubed the night as though a gigantic firefly had been crushed to death and its luminous essence smeared across the vault of heaven.

'They calm the soul,' Sean explained gently.

She breathed softly and deeply. 'Yes, you are right, my darling. Tonight we have our love, let's exploit it to the full and let tomorrow take care of itself.'

She felt safe and invulnerable under the tented mosquito netting. The lumpy grass-filled mattress had taken on the shape of their bodies and she did not notice the harsh touch of the canvas covering against her skin.

'If we made love ten thousand times, it would still not have taken the edge off my need for you,' she whispered, as she slipped over the edge of sleep.

She woke suddenly feeling the tension in his body against hers, and instantly he touched her lips to caution her to silence. She lay frozen in the darkness, not daring to move or breathe, and then she heard it. A soft scraping at the entrance of the dugout as the netting curtain was pushed aside and an animal passed through.

Her heart raced away and she bit her lip to stop herself gasping aloud as she heard the thing crossing the earth floor towards the bed. Its paws were almost soundless, just the faintest tick of grit compressed by the stealthy weight. Then she smelled it, the wild gamey smell of a meat-eating animal and she wanted to cry out.

Beside her, Sean moved suddenly, fast as a striking adder; he lunged through the mosquito net and there was a quick scuffle and squeal and she tried to crawl over Sean's back to escape whatever it was.

'Got you, you little bugger,' Sean said grimly. 'You don't sneak up on me twice and get away with it. Now tell me I'm getting old and I'll wring your neck!'

'You'll be young and beautiful for ever, my *Bwana*,' Matatu giggled, and wriggled like a puppy caught by the scruff of the neck.

'Where have you been, Matatu?' Sean demanded sternly. 'What took you so long, did you meet a pretty girl along the way?'

Matatu giggled again, he loved to be accused by Sean of dalliance and amatory exploits.

'I found the roosting place of the *henshaws*,' he boasted. 'The same way I find where the bees have their hive, I watched their flight against the sun and followed them to their secret place.'

Sean drew him closer to the bed and shook his arm gently. 'Tell me,' he ordered, and in the darkness Matatu squatted down and tucked his loin-cloth between his legs and made little self-important throat-clearing and humming sounds.

'There is a round hill, shaped like the head of a bald man,' Matatu began. 'On one side of the hill passes the *insimbi*, the railway, and on the other side the road.'

Sean propped himself on one elbow to listen and with his other arm, he encircled Claudia's naked waist and held her close. She snuggled against him, listening to Matatu's piping pixie voice in the darkness.

'There are many askari around the hill with big *banduki* hidden in holes in the ground.' Sean formed a vivid mental picture of the heavily garrisoned hilltop as Matatu described it to him. Beyond the outer defensive lines the gunships were laagered in separate sandbagged emplacements. Like battle tanks in hull-down fortifications, they would be impregnable, and yet they had only to rise and hover a few feet above ground level to bring into action their devasting Gatling-cannons and rocket pods.

'Inside the circle of roosting *henshaw*, there are many gharries parked and white men in green clothes who climb on the *henshaw* and look inside them all the time.' Matatu described the mobile workshops and fuel tankers and the squads of Russian mechanics and technicians needed to keep the helicopters flying. The training manuals had pointed up the Hind's excessive requirements of service and maintenance, while those big Isotov turbo engines would guzzle Avgas.

'Matatu, did you see railway gharries on the line near the hill?' Sean asked.

'I saw them,' Matatu confirmed. 'Those big round gharries full of beer – the men who ride in the *henshaw* must be very thirsty.' Once many years ago, on one of his infrequent visits to the city with Sean, Matatu had seen a beer tanker disgorging its load at the main Harare beerhall. He had been so impressed that since that day he was utterly convinced that all tankers of whatever size or type contained only beer. Sean could not change his mind on this, Matatu would never accept that some of them actually carried less noble fluids such as gasoline and he always stared wistfully after any tanker they passed on the road.

Sean smiled now in the darkness at the little man's fixation. Fuel for the gunships was obviously being railed from Harare in bulk tankers, and transshipped into smaller road tankers. It was ironic that the fuel was almost certainly being originally supplied by the South Africans. However, if the helicopter squadron was storing its fuel within the laager itself they were taking a grave risk. It was something to bear in mind.

Matatu remained at the bedside for almost an hour while Sean patiently drew from him every possible detail he could of the gunship laager.

Matatu was certain that there were eleven helicopters in the emplacements, which tallied with his own estimate. Of the original twelve, one had been destroyed in the collision with the Hercules.

Matatu was equally certain that only nine of the gunships were actually flying. Hidden on a nearby kopje, he had watched the helicopters sortie from their laager at dawn, return for refuelling during the day and at nightfall come in to roost. Sean knew that Matatu could count accurately to twenty, but after that, he became vague and any greater number was described progressively as 'many' or 'a great deal' and finally as 'like grass on the Serengeti plains'.

So Sean was now fairly certain that two of the gunships had broken down and were probably awaiting spares, and he accepted Matatu's figure of nine operational gunships, still a formidable force, quite sufficient to turn the tide of the looming battle against Renamo unless they could swiftly be put out of the action.

When at last Matatu had finished his recitation he asked simply, 'Now, my *Bwana*, what do you want me to do?'

Sean considered in silence. There was really no reason why he should not bring Matatu in from wherever he was hiding up in the bush, allowing him openly to join the force of Shangane under his command as a tracker. However, he sensed that there might be some future advantage in keeping Matatu hidden from China's cold reptilian gaze.

'You are my wild card, Matatu,' he said in English and then in Swahili, 'I want you to keep out of sight. Do not let any of the men here see you, except Job and me.'

'I heard you, my *Bwana*.'

'Come to me each night as you have tonight. I will have food for you and I will tell you what to do. In the meantime, watch and tell me all you see.'

Matatu went so silently that they heard only the faint rustle of the netting at the entrance as he passed through.

'Will he be all right?' Claudia asked softly. 'I worry about him. He's so cute.'

'Of all of us, he is probably the most likely to survive.' In the dark, Sean smiled fondly after the little man.

'I'm not sleepy any more.' Claudia snuggled against him like a cat, and then much later she whispered, 'I'm so glad Matatu woke us up . . .'

* * *

It was still dark when Sean turned Job out of his blanket the next morning. 'We've got work to do,' he told him, and while Job laced on his boots, he described his meeting with General China.

'You mean we are now instructors,' Job laughed softly. 'All we know about those Stingers is what we have read in the manuals.'

'That will have to change,' Sean told him. 'The sooner we get the Shanganes into action, the sooner we are going to get the hell out of here.'

'Is that what China told you?' Job raised an eyebrow at Sean.

'Let's get Ferdinand and his boys cracking,' Sean said brusquely to cover his own misgivings. 'We'll sort them into teams of two men, one to serve the launcher and the other to carry the extra missiles. Of course, the number two must be able to take over if the leader is put down.'

Sean pulled out his notebook and drew the candle stump closer, writing in its guttering yellow light.

'When do you expect Alphonso to get here?' Job stuffed his shirt into the top of his tiger-striped pants.

'Sometime today, if at all,' Sean replied.

'He's the best of the bunch,' Job grunted.

'Ferdinand is not bad,' Sean pointed out, and placed their names at the head of the page as his section leaders. 'Okay, we need thirty names for our number ones, give me some.'

It was like the old days, working together this way and Sean found he was beginning to enjoy himself.

As soon as it was light enough, they paraded the men who had returned in the Hercules from the Grand Reef raid. With the two casualties missing there remained eighteen men under Ferdinand. Sean immediately gave Ferdinand a field promotion to full sergeant, and was rewarded with a huge grin and a flourishing salute that almost swept Ferdinand off his feet with his own vigour.

Sean had to find something to occupy them and keep them out of the way while he and Job gave themselves a crash course on the Stinger missile system.

'Sergeant.' Sean addressed Ferdinand by his rank for the first time. 'Do you see that hill over there?' It was just visible through the trees, shaded blue with distance. 'Take your men for a run around it and get them back here in two hours. Weapons and full field-packs.'

As they watched the column of men doubling away, Sean said, 'If Alphonso and his lads don't arrive by this evening, we'll have to recruit replacements. That's no problem; however, China will be keen to let us have his very best men. At the moment, we are right at the top of his list of favourite flavours.'

'In the meantime, let's hit those manuals,' Job suggested. 'I haven't swotted since varsity days. I'm not looking forward to it.'

Claudia joined them in the dugout, helping them sort through the thick loose-leaf red plastic-covered manuals, picking out the information relevant to their situation and discarding the vast body of technical data that they had no need of, and the operational reports and instructions that did not apply to deployment in this altitude and terrain. After two hours' work they had reduced the mass of information to one manageable slim volume.

'All right.' Sean stood up. 'Let's go find a training ground.'

They picked out a spot a few hundred metres downriver from the dugout where the side of a low kopje formed a natural lecture theatre. The tall riverine mahogany trees spread their branches overhead to provide cover from a surprise raid by the Hind gunships. When Ferdinand and his men returned bathed in sweat from their little outing Sean put them to work clearing the amphitheatre of thorn and scrub and digging shell scrapes conveniently close at hand for use when air raids interrupted classes.

'Right,' Sean told Job and Claudia. 'Now we can uncrate the trainer set and one of the launchers. From now on it's "look and learn", "show and tell" time.'

When they opened the first crate, Sean discovered that the battery power pack was discharged. However, each crate contained a small charger set with appropriate connections and transformers.

Ferdinand and his men under Job's supervision carried the power packs up to the headquarters communications centre and at General China's order, they were given priority use of the portable 220 volt 15 kilowatt generator. Sean connected up the power packs in batches of five, but it would take twenty-four hours before they had power available for all the missile launchers.

With the batteries on charge they laid out the trainer set and one of the launchers on the makeshift table that Ferdinand had built on the floor of the open-air theatre under the trees. While Claudia read aloud from the instruction manual, Sean and Job stripped and reassembled the equipment until they were thoroughly familiar with all of it.

Sean was relieved and pleased to discover that with the exception of the IFF, the operation of the equipment was not a great deal more complicated than the conventional RPG 7 rocket-launchers. The RPG 7 was so much a part of the guerrilla arsenal that, as Job remarked, every single man in China's division could load and lock on a pitch-dark night in a thunderstorm.

'Anyway, we don't need the IFF,' Sean pointed out. 'Everything that flies in these skies, apart from the dicky birds, is a foe.' The IFF, 'Identification Friend or Foe', was a system that interrogated the target, determining from the aircraft's on-board transponder whether it was hostile or friendly, and preventing launch of missile against friendly aircraft.

Claudia found the section on the manual dealing with the IFF and under her tutelage, they disarmed the system, converting the Stinger into a free-fire weapon which would attack any aircraft at which it was aimed.

Without IFF fit, the attack sequence for the missile is straight-forward. The target is picked up in the small screen of the aiming sight, and the safety device above the pistol grip is disengaged with the right thumb. The actuator is engaged by depressing the button built into the reverse of the pistol grip. This starts the run up of the navigational gyro and releases a flow of freon gas to cool the infra-red seekers as they become active. With the sights held on the target, all incoming infra-red radiation is magnified and focused on the detector cell of the missile head. As soon as this radiation is of sufficient concentration to allow the missile to track to its source, the gyro stabilizer uncages, and the missile emits a high-pitched tone.

To fire the missile the operator depresses the trigger in the pistol grip with his forefinger which starts the electric ejector motor. The missile discharges from the launch tube through the frangible front seal and ejects to a safe distance, approximately eight metres from the operator. to protect him from rocket back-blast. At this point the solid fuel rocket motor fires and the blast of exhaust gas flares out the retractable tail-fins and the missile accelerates to four times the speed of sound. When an inertial force of twenty-eight times gravity is attained, the fuse shut-out is thrown open and the missile is armed. It tracks towards the target on a fire-and-forget trajectory, guided not by the operator but by its own proportional navigational system.

With the specialized 'Hind' attack cassette inserted in the launcher's RMP – reprogrammable micro processor – the system switches automatically into 'two colour' mode when it is a hundred metres from the infra-red source. At this point it abandons the infra-red radiations emitted by the engine exhaust suppressors and instead focuses on the much weaker ultra-violet emanations from the engine intakes. On this target the high-explosive warhead hits to kill.

'Even a Shangane could learn how to fire one of these.' Job said, and Sean grinned.

'Tut tut, your Matabele tribal racism is showing again.'

'It's like this, when you are genetically superior, there is simply no point in trying to conceal the fact.'

They both glanced expectantly at Claudia, but she did not even look up from the manual as she drawled, 'You are wasting your time, you two bigots. You aren't going to get a rise out of me this time.'

'Bigot,' Job savoured the word. 'It's the first time anybody has ever called me that. I love it.'

'That's enough fooling around.' Sean broke it up. 'Let's take a look at the trainer.'

After they had connected one of the freshly charged battery packs and assembled the trainer equipment, Sean gave his opinion.

'With this stuff, we can have the lads ready to go into action within days, not weeks.'

Once a micro cassette was inserted in the training monitor, the launcher screen simulated the image of a 'Hind' which the instructor was able to manipulate in various flight patterns, climbing, descending, side-slipping or hovering. While he did so he was able to watch the trainee's reactions as he attempted to acquire the ghost ship on his own screen and attack it with a phantom missile.

Sean and Job played with the trainer like a pair of teenagers, flying the image in complicated manoeuvres. 'It's just like a Pac-man game,' Job enthused. 'But what we need is a dum-dum, a pseudo-Shangane to act as a trainee for us.'

Once more both the men looked at Claudia who was still sitting cross-legged on the table studying the manual.

She looked up as she felt their eyes on her. 'A dum-dum?' she demanded. 'I'll show you dum-dum. Give me the launcher.'

She stood in the centre of the floor of the amphitheatre with the launcher balanced on her shoulder, and stared into the sighting screen. The bulky equipment seemed to dwarf her. She had reversed her camouflage cap so the peak stuck out behind her head, and it gave her the gamine air of a little league baseballer.

'Ready?' Sean asked.

'Pull!' she said, concentrating ferociously on the screen, and Sean and Job exchanged smug supercilious grins.

'Incoming!' Sean called sharply. 'Twelve o'clock high. Lock and load.'

He brought the ghost Hind in on a head-on attack at 150 knots.

'Locked and loaded,' Claudia affirmed, and in their screen, they watched the duplicate sight ring of her missile launcher swing up smoothly and centre on the approaching Hind.

'Actuator on,' she said calmly, and a second later, they heard the launcher sob and growl in her grip, and then settle into a steady insect whine, like an infuriated mosquito.

'Target acquired,' Claudia murmured. The Hind was six hundred metres out but coming in fast, swelling dramatically in the sights.

'Fire!' she said, and they saw the red light blink, and then change to green signalling that the rocket motor of the fictitious missile was running, and almost instantaneously the image of the Hind disappeared from the screen to be replaced by the flashing legend.

'Target destroyed! Target destroyed!'

There followed a profound silence. Job cleared his throat nervously.

'Flukes happen,' said Sean. 'Shall we try it again?'

'Pull!' said Claudia, and concentrated on her aiming screen.

'Incoming,' Sean called. 'Six o'clock high. Lock and load.'

He brought the next Hind in from behind her at tree-top level, attack speed. She had three seconds to react.

'Locked and loaded.' Claudia pirouetted like a ballerina and picked the Hind up in the sight ring. 'Actuator on.' As she said it, Sean flung the Hind into a climbing side-slip, giving her deflection in three planes. It would be like trying to hit a high bird in a gale of crosswind.

In their screen, they watched with disbelief as Claudia swung smoothly, keeping the image in the exact centre of her aiming ring and the missile sobbed and then settled into its high-pitched tone.

'Target acquired. Fire!'

'Target destroyed! Target destroyed!' The screen blinked at them, and they fidgeted uncomfortably.

Job murmured, 'Twice on the trot. That ain't no fluke, man.'

Claudia laid the launcher on the table, readjusted the peak of her cap over her eyes, and then placed her fists on her hips and smiled at them sweetly.

'I thought you said you didn't know how to shoot,' Sean accused her with righteous indignation.

'Would a daughter of Riccardo Enrico Monterro not know how to shoot?'

'But you are stridently opposed to blood sports.'

'Sure,' she agreed. 'I've never shot at a living creature. But I'm death to clay pigeons. Papa taught me.'

'I should have guessed when you said "Pull",' Sean groaned softly.

'As a matter of interest,' Claudia examined the fingernails of her right hand modestly. 'I was Alaska State women's skeet champion three years running, and runner-up at the national championships in '86.'

The two men exchanged embarrassed glances. 'She got you with a sucker punch.' Job shook his head. 'And you walked straight into it with both eyes closed.'

'All right, Miss Alaska,' Sean told her sternly. 'You are so damned clever, you've just landed yourself the job of instructor. From here on you are in charge of this equipment Job and I will split the Shanganes into two classes and give them the basics. Then we'll pass them on to you for simulation. It'll speed up the whole works.'

General China interrupted them as he strode into the amphitheatre, beret cocked jauntily, slapping his swagger-stick against his thigh and taking in their preparations with quick inquisitive eyes.

'How soon can you begin training? I expected to be further along than this.'

Sean recognized the futility of trying to explain to him. 'We'll get along better without interference.'

'I came to warn you that Frelimo have launched their offensive. They are coming at us in force from the south and the west, a two-pronged drive, obviously trying to push us out of these hills, away from the river into more open terrain where they can deploy their armour and their helicopters to better advantage.'

'So they are whipping the hell out of you,' Sean needled him with a thinly concealed sneer.

'We are falling back,' China acknowledged the jibe with just a glitter in his eyes. 'As soon as my men attempt to hold up their advance at a natural strong point, Frelimo simply calls in the

Hinds. The Russian pilots are showing us the close-support skills they learned in the mountains of Afghanistan. They simply obliterate our defences. It is not a pleasant experience to listen helplessly on the radio while my field commanders plead for help. How soon can I send them the Stingers?'

'Two days,' Sean said.

'So long? Is there no way you can hurry it up?' Impatiently, China slapped the swagger-stick into the palm of his hand. 'I want you to let me have at least one trained team immediately. Anything to be able to hit back at them.'

'That, General China, would be crass stupidity,' Sean told him. 'With all due respect,' Sean showed none in the tone of his voice, 'if you deploy the Stingers piecemeal, you'll be tipping your hand to the Hind crews.'

'What do you mean?' China's voice cracked like breaking floe-ice.

'Those Ruskie pilots have met the Stingers before, in Afghanistan, you can be pretty damn sure of that. They'll know every counter-measure in the book and then a few more. Right now they are blissfully convinced that they are the only things in the sky. Their guard is wide open, but you let one Stinger fly and all that will change. Okay, you might put one down, but the rest of the squadron will be ready for you.' China's frozen expression thawed and he looked thoughtful.

'So what do you suggest, Colonel?'

'Hit them all at once with everything you've got.'

'When? Where?'

'When they are least expecting it, a full-scale surprise attack on their laager – at dawn.'

'On their laager?' China shook his head irritably. 'We don't know where they laager at night.'

'Yes, we do,' Sean contradicted. 'I have already pinpointed the laager. I'll train Alphonso and Ferdinand and set up the raid for them. Give me two days, and they'll be ready to go.'

China thought for a moment, hands clasped behind his back, staring up at the blue African sky as though he expected at any moment to see those dread humpbacked shapes appear.

'Two days,' he agreed at last.

'Two days, and when I have your missile crews trained and ready to leave on the raid, you let me and my party go. That is my condition.'

'There is a Frelimo column between here and the Zimbabwe border,' China reminded him.

'We'll take our chances,' Sean snapped. 'That is the bargain, do I have your word on it?'

'Very well, Colonel. I agree.'

'That's fine. Now when do you expect Alphonso and his detachment to arrive?'

'They have already reached our lines. I expect Alphonso and his men will be here in another hour or so, but they will be exhausted, they have been in action almost continuously for twenty-four hours.'

'They aren't on a Sunday school picnic.' Sean was callous. 'Send them to me as soon as they arrive.'

They came in at last, moving with the slack stumbling gait of a heavyweight boxer at the end of ten hard rounds. Their tiger-striped camouflage was encrusted with the filth of the battle-field, and their faces were grey with exhaustion.

While his men collapsed on the floor of the amphitheatre and slept where they fell, Alphonso described to Sean in flat prosaic terms the retreat from Grand Reef base and the flight to the mission station in the gut of the Honde Valley where they had abandoned the Unimog truck and crossed into Mozambique on foot.

'The bush is full of Frelimo, and the air is full of *henshaw*.' He paused and wiped his face wearily on a grubby tattered bandanna. 'It is witchcraft, but the *henshaw* can speak from the sky. They taunt us in the Shangane language. They tell us that they have magic that turns our bullets and rockets to water.'

Sean nodded grimly. The Russians must be using sky-shout amplifiers to demoralize the Renamo defenders. That was another trick they had learned in Afghanistan.

'All along the line our men are being shot to pieces, or are running away. We cannot fight against the *henshaw*,'

'Yes, you bloody well can.' Sean seized the front of his tunic. 'I'll show you how. Get your men up. There'll be plenty of time to sleep later, when we have burned those Russian bastards out of the sky.'

* * *

Sean and Job had worked and fought with all these men and had come to know them by name and deed so they had formed a fairly accurate picture of their individual worth and capabilities.

They knew that there were no cowards nor shirkers amongst them. Alphonso had long ago sifted those out. However, there were those whom Job classified as 'oxen', the strong and stupid, the muscle and cannon fodder. The others were of varying degrees of intelligence and adaptability. At the top of the heap were Alphonso and Ferdinand.

Sean and Job sorted them into two groups and concentrated their efforts on the most promising in each group, quickly picking out those who had the image recognition to translate what they saw on the aiming screen of the launchers into finite terms in shape and space.

At the end of almost three hours, they had picked out twenty men who had the potential to assimilate swiftly the necessary training and to act as number ones in the missile teams, and as many again who might be able to fulfil the number two back-up role.

The others who showed no aptitude were allotted to the assault team which would be using conventional weapons in the attack Sean was planning. Of the missile trainees, Sean took one group and Job the other, and they began the monotonous task of familiarizing them with the actual weapons. Once again, they relied on the technique of repetition and reinforcement. Each trainee had his turn at stripping and reassembling, locking and loading, and aiming the launcher. While he did so, he explained to the class exactly what he was doing and Sean and Job corrected their mistakes while the rest of the class taunted them.

It was late afternoon before Sean sent the first group of five men, which included both Alphonso and Ferdinand, to Claudia for simulated attacks with the training equipment.

Alphonso scored three consecutive hits, and was immediately detailed to act as Claudia's assistant and translator. By nightfall, all five members of the first group had scored three consecutive hits which Claudia had arbitrarily decided was her passing standard, and Sean and Job had another ten men ready to begin simulator training as soon as it was sufficiently light the following morning. When it was too dark to continue, Sean dismissed them and Alphonso and his group staggered off wearily into the night, punch-drunk with fatigue and the effort of learning.

Joyful, the chef, had stolen the tripes from the buffalo carcass that had fed the officers' mess the previous evening. After the day's heat, they were a little ripe, but he had disguised that fact with a liberal addition of chopped wild onion tubers and peri-peri sauce. Claudia paled when Joyful proudly placed a steaming bowl of the tripes in front of her. In the end, hunger overcame her fastidiousness.

'Put hair on your chest,' Sean comforted her.

'That, my darling man, isn't high on my list of beauty aids.'

'Okay then,' he smiled at her. 'Put some weight on those skinny little buns of yours.'

'You don't like my buns?'

'I love your buns, that's why I want more of them, as much as I can get.'

When Matatu came creeping in out of the darkness, Sean fed him and he gorged on tripes until his naked belly bulged like a shiny black beach ball.

'All right, you greedy little bugger,' Sean told him. 'Now it's time for you to earn your keep.'

They led him up to the dark amphitheatre where they found that Job was waiting for them. He had already assembled the raw materials for building the scale model of the gunship laager. By the light of two paraffin lanterns, they started to lay it out. Matatu had been a party to these model constructions so many times during the bush war that he understood exactly what was required of him. Like so many who have never acquired the skills of reading and writing, Matatu had a photographic memory.

He strutted about importantly, giving Sean and Job instructions, showing them the topography of the countryside in and surrounding the laager, the shape of the hill on which it had been built, the relationship of it to the main road and the railway line.

Claudia showed a new talent which Sean had not suspected. Using the soft white wood of the baobab tree, she whittled eleven tiny scale models of the Hind gunships. They were fully recognizable as what they represented and when she sat them in their emplacements within the perimeter of the model laager, they added an authentic touch.

It was well after midnight before Claudia and Sean crept naked under the mosquito net in their dugout. They were both weary to their bones but even after they made slow languorous love neither of them could sleep, and they lay close in the darkness and talked. Mention of her father earlier in the day caused

Claudia to hark back to her childhood. Listening to her, Sean was relieved that she was able to speak naturally and easily about her father. She had conquered the initial shock and sorrow and she remembered him now with only a nostalgic melancholy which was almost pleasure in comparison to the pain which had preceded it.

She described to Sean how at the age of fourteen, the very year that her womanhood had first flowered, the wonderfully secure cocoon of her life had burst asunder in the traumatic divorce of her parents. She painted a picture for him of the years that followed. The droughts of loneliness when she was separated from her father followed by the roaring floods of love and conflict when they came together again.

'You can see why I'm such a crazy mixed-up kid,' she told him. 'Why I have to strive to be the best at whatever I do, and why I'm always drawn to try and protect the underdog. Half the time, I'm still trying to win Papa's approval, while the other half of the time, I'm trying to flout and reject his elitist materialistic view of life.' She snuggled against Sean. 'I truly don't know how you are going to handle me.'

'Handling you will always be a pleasure,' he assured her. 'But keeping you in your place looks like a full-time job.'

'That's just the sort of thing that Papa would have said. You and I are in for some rip-roaring fights, mister.'

'Ah, but just think of the reconciliations, what fun they will be.'

In the end, they managed a few hours of sleep, and awoke surprisingly refreshed and clear-headed to take up the training where they had left off at nightfall the previous day.

While Claudia ran the last of the trainees through the attack sequences on the simulator, Sean and Job squatted beside the model of the gunship laager and Sean explained his plans for the attack. Job listened attentively and made the occasional suggestion, until at last they had it all clear in their own minds, the approach march, the attack and the withdrawl with the alternative actions to be taken if there were a hitch anywhere along the line.

'Okay.' Sean stood up. 'Let's give it to the lads.'

The Shangane troopers watched totally absorbed from their perches on the rock slopes of the amphitheatre while Sean and Job described the plans for the raid. They used river pebbles to denote the various units of the raiding party, moving them into place around the laager. When the attack began, Claudia manipulated her model Hinds and there were enthusiastic cheers from the watching Shanganes as one by one they were brought crashing to earth by volleys of Stinger missiles.

'Right, Sergeant Alphonso.' Sean replaced the counters in their original positions. 'Show us the attack again.'

Five times, they went over it. In turn, each of the section leaders described it to them, and the final cheers as the Hinds were destroyed lost none of their gusto for being so often repeated. At the end of the fifth show, Sergeant Alphonso stood up and addressed Sean on behalf of the entire unit.

'*Nkosi Kakulu*,' he began. He had never before used this form of address to Sean. Usually this was reserved for very high-ranking tribal chieftains. Sean was aware of the honour, and this proof that he had at last won the full respect and loyalty of these fiercely proud and hard-bitten warriors.

'Great Chief,' Alphonso said, 'your children are troubled.' There was a murmur of agreement and nodding of heads. 'In all that you have told us of the battle, you have not assured us that you will be there to lead us and to put fire in our bellies as you did at Grand Reef. Tell your children, *Nkosi Kakulu*, that you will be with us in the midst of the fighting and that we will hear you roaring like a lion as the *henshaw* fall burning from the sky, and Frelimo baboons run from us screaming like virgins feeling the prong for the very first time.'

Sean spread his hands. 'You are not my children,' he said. 'You are men of men, just as your fathers were men before you.' There was no higher compliment he could pay them. 'You do not need me to help you to do this thing. I have taught you all I know. The flames in your bellies burn with the same fury as the fire in the tall dry grass of winter. The time has come for me to leave you. This battle is yours alone. I must go, but I will always be proud that we were friends and that we fought side by side as brothers do.'

There was a low chorus of dissent, and they shook their heads and spoke together in low rumbling tones.

Sean turned away, and saw that while he had been speaking General China had come up and now stood quietly amongst the trees at the riverside, watching him. There were a dozen officers and men of his personal bodyguard behind him, all wearing the same maroon berets, but somehow, they seemed insignificant as China stepped forward and instantly commanded the attention of every person in the amphitheatre.

'I see your preparations are complete, Colonel Courtney,' he greeted Sean.

'Yes, they are ready, General.'

'Will you please go over the plans again, for my benefit.'

Sean singled out Sergeant Alphonso. 'Describe the raid for us again,' he ordered, and General China stood in front of the mock-up laager with the swagger-stick clasped behind his back and watched with quick bright eyes, interrupting sharply to ask his questions.

'Why are you using only half the available missiles?'

'The raiding column has to get through the Frelimo lines undetected. The missiles are bulky and heavy, a larger number would be superfluous and make discovery by Frelimo much more likely.'

China nodded, and Sean went on, 'You also have to take into account the possible failure of the raid. If that happens and you have bet all your Stingers on one throw of the dice . . .' Sean shrugged.

'Yes, of course, it's wise to keep half of the missiles in reserve. Even if the raid fails we will not be left entirely helpless. Carry on.'

Alphonso went through the plan step by step, illustrating with the coloured pebbles how the missile teams would move into position and lie in readiness five hundred metres from the perimeter of the gunship laager, two teams confronting each sand-bagged emplacement.

At the signal of a red flare, the assault team would attack in full force from the south, hitting any fuel tankers that might be on the rail spur with RPG 7 rocket fire, sweeping the interior of the laager with mortar fire and then launching a frontal assault on the southern perimeter.

'The *henshaw* will take fright as soon as the shooting begins.' Alphonso explained. 'They will try to escape by flying away, but there will be a moment when they rise from the earth that they will still be low down, standing still in the air, the way a falcon hovers before it stoops. That is the moment we will kill them.'

Sean and China discussed every aspect of the plan until at last, China was satisfied.

'So when will you move out?'

'You keep saying "you".' Sean pulled him up. 'I'm not having anything more to do with it. Sergeant Alphonso will lead the attack. They'll move out this evening two hours before dark to penetrate the Frelimo lines during the night, lay up in cover tomorrow and launch the attack tomorrow night.'

'Very well,' China agreed. 'I'll address the men now.'

He was a compelling orator, Sean admitted, as he listened to China reminding them of the consequences of a Frelimo victory and exhorting them to deeds of valour and self-sacrifice. By the time he ceased speaking their faces were shining and their eyes sparkled with patriotic fervour. General China raised his voice. 'You are warriors so let me hear you sing the Renamo battle anthem.'

The forest echoed and rang to the haunting beauty of their massed voices, and Sean found his vision dissolving into a blur as his eyes filled with emotion. He had not realized how much these men had come to mean to him, until now that he was about to leave them.

'Colonel, I would like to speak to you in private,' General China broke into his sentimental reverie. 'Please come with me.'

With a word to Claudia and Job, Sean excused himself, 'Give them each one more run with the simulator.'

He fell in beside General China and as they set out for the headquarters bunker, Sean took no notice of the fact that China's bodyguard did not accompany them, but remained at the entrance of the amphitheatre in an arrogant manner.

When they reached the command bunker, General China led them through to his underground office. There was tea ready for them and Sean piled brown sugar into his mug and savoured the first steaming mouthful.

'So what did you want to tell me?' he asked.

China was standing with his back to him, studying the wall map of which he had marked the developing Frelimo offensive with coloured pins. He did not answer Sean's question and Sean would not pander to him by asking again. He sipped at the tea and waited.

A signaller came through from the radio room and handed China a message flimsy. As he read it, the General exclaimed with disgust tinged with anxiety and reached up to move a group of coloured pins on the map. Frelimo had broken through in the west and were closing in remorselessly.

'We are not containing them,' China told Sean, without looking around. Another messenger ducked into the bunker. He was one of China's personal bodyguards, wearing the distinctive maroon beret. He whispered something to China and Sean thought he heard the word 'American'. It quickened his interest.

China smiled briefly and dismissed the man with a nod before he turned to Sean.

'It won't work,' he said.

'What won't work?'

'The attack as you have planned it.'

'Nothing is certain in war, as you should know, General. But I disagree. The plan has about a sixty per cent chance of total success. That's pretty good odds.'

'The odds would be considerably higher, perhaps eighty per cent, if you led the attack, Colonel Courtney.'

'I'm flattered by your estimate. However, it's hypothetical. I'm not leading it. I'm going home.'

'No, Colonel. You are leading the attack.'

'We had a bargain.'

'Bargain?' China smiled. 'Don't be naïve. I make bargains and break them as the need arises. The need has arisen I'm afraid.'

Sean sprang to his feet, his face pale as candle wax beneath the deep tan. 'I'm going,' he said. Despite his fury, he managed to keep his voice thin and tight. 'I'm taking my people and I'm leaving now. Right away. You'll have to kill me to stop me.'

China touched his deaf ear, and smiled again. 'That notion is not without its attractions, I assure you, Colonel. However, I don't think it will come to that.'

'We'll see.' Sean kicked back the stool on which he had been sitting and it hit the wall and crashed over on its side. He turned and ducked out of the low doorway.

'You'll be back,' China assured him softly, but Sean gave no sign of having heard him. He came out in the sunlight and strode down towards the river.

He had reached the amphitheatre before he realized that something was desperately amiss.

The Shanganes sat rigid at their places upon the slope, they seemed not to have moved since he had last seen them. Alphonso's features were graven in black ironstone, expressionless and dull, the shield of deliberate stupidity behind which the African distances himself from powers and forces against which he has no other defence.

Job was sprawled across the table in the centre of the amphitheatre. His tunic was floury with dust and his cap still lay in the dirt at his feet. He shook his head in a dazed uncertain fashion and droplets of blood dripped from his nose.

'What happened?' Sean ran to him, and Job stared at him, trying to focus his eyes. He had been brutally beaten. His lips were swollen into purple bruises, his mouth full of blood that stained his teeth like red wine. One eyebrow was cut through, a deep jagged split from which blood trickled down the side of his nose. Blood welled out of both nostrils, swelling into bright pink bubbles as he breathed through it. There were lumps on his forehead like overripe grapes, and the lobe of one ear was torn. Blood dripped onto the front of his dusty tunic.

'Job, what the hell. . .?' Sean caught him by the shoulder. 'Who?'

'I tried to stop them!' Job blurted, his eyes fixed on Sean's face. 'I tried!'

'Take it easy.'

Sean tried to lead him to a seat, but he shook Sean's hands away and said, 'Claudia.'

A flash frost of dread chilled Sean's belly. 'Claudia!' he repeated, and looked around him wildly. 'Where is she, Job? What happened?'

'They took her,' Job repeated. 'China's goons. I tried to stop them.'

Sean reached for the pistol on his webbing belt. 'Where is she, Job?' The pistol grip filled his hand.

'I don't know.' Job wiped the palm of his hand down his face and looked at the blood. 'I was out cold, I don't know for how long.'

'China, you turd-munching bastard, you are going to die.' Sean whirled, ready to go charging back to the headquarters bunker.

'Sean, think first!' Job called urgently, and Sean checked. So often Job had saved him with those two words. 'Think first!'

It required an enormous effort of will, but for seconds, Sean managed to keep his head above the wave of his killing rage.

'The manuals, Job!' he gritted out. 'Burn them!'

Job blinked at him through the blood that spilled from the split eyebrow. 'Burn the manuals!' Sean repeated. 'Insurance, man. We are the only ones who know.'

Job's expression cleared. 'And the cassettes,' he exclaimed.

'Right!' Sean said. 'The cassettes. Give them to me.'

While Job hastily repacked the attack cassettes into their carrying case, Sean walked across to where Alphonso sat at the front of the amphitheatre and unhooked a phosphorus grenade from his belt.

Working swiftly, he used his pistol lanyard and the phosphorus grenade to rig a makeshift self-destruction device in the interior of the case of attack cassettes. He hooked the clip of his pistol lanyard through the pin of the grenade, and laid the grenade itself in the middle of the case. Using the point of a bayonet, he drilled a hole through the lid of the carrying case and threaded the end of the lanyard through it. When he locked the case, he looped the free end of the lanyard securely around his own wrist.

'Let China try and get them away from me now,' he said grimly. If the case were jerked out of his grip, or if he let it fall the lanyard would pull the pin of the grenade, destroying not only the contents but anybody standing nearby. He waited just long enough to watch Job set a match to the pile of instruction manuals.

Once they were fully ablaze he ordered Job, 'Stay here, make certain they are burned to ashes.'

Then lugging the case of cassettes, he started back to the headquarters bunker.

'I said that you would be back,' China greeted him, with that icy sardonic smile which faded swiftly as he saw the case that Sean carried and the lanyard looped around his wrist.

Sean lifted the case in front of him and flaunted it in China's face.

'There is the Hind Squadron, China,' he said, with an effort keeping his voice level. 'Without this your Stingers are useless to you.'

China's eyes flicked towards the entrance of the dugout.

'Don't even think about it,' Sean warned him. 'There is a grenade inside the case, a phosporus grenade. This lanyard is attached to the firing-pin. If I drop it, like if I was to die suddenly or someone were to pull it out of my hand, the whole lot goes up in a nice little bonfire, happy fifth of November.'

They stared at each other across the desk.

'So this is a pretty little stalemate, Colonel,' China's smile was reborn, even colder and more deadly than Sean had seen it before.

'Where is Claudia Monterro?' Sean asked, and China raised his voice, summoning an orderly from the radio room.

'Bring the woman!' he ordered, and they waited, both of them poised and alert, watching each other's eyes.

'I should have thought of the cassettes,' China said in conversational tones. 'That was good, Colonel. Very good. You can see why I want you to lead the attack.'

'While we are on the subject,' Sean replied, 'I have also burned the instruction manuals. There are only the three of us – Job, Claudia and me – who understand the Stingers.'

'What about the Shanganes, Alphonso, Ferdinand?' China challenged, and Sean grinned at him like a death's head.

'Not on, China. They know how to shoot it, but they don't have any idea how to program the micro processors. You need us, China. Without us the Hinds are coming after you, and there's not a damned thing you can do about it. So don't fool with me. I have your survival in my hands.'

There was a scuffle in the outer room, and both of them looked to the entrance as Claudia was pushed through from the radio room.

Her hands were once more manacled behind her back, she had lost her cap and her hair tumbled into her face and down her neck.

'Sean!' she blurted when she saw him, and she pulled against the hands of the two bodyguards who held her, trying to reach him. They jerked her back and threw her against the side wall of the dugout.

'Tell your baboons to knock that off,' Sean snarled, and when they glowered at him, China restrained them with a sharp order.

'Put that woman in the chair!'

They forced her into the solid mahogany seat and at another order from China used the manacles to chain her wrists securely to the heavy arms of the chair.

'I have something of yours, Colonel, and you have something of mine. Shall we work out a deal?' General China suggested.

'Let us go,' Sean said promptly. 'At the border, I'll hand over the cassettes.' And China shook his head regretfully.

'Not acceptable. Here is my counter offer. You lead the attack on the Hind laager. When it is completed successfully, Alphonso will escort you to the border.'

Sean raised the booby-trapped case head high, and China smiled. In retaliation he drew the trench knife from its sheath on his belt. It was ivory-handled with a five-inch blade.

Still smiling he lifted a single hair from Claudia's scalp, and with a sharp jerk pulled it out. He held it up between thumb and forefinger and touched the hair with the blade. Half of the dark strand fell away and floated down to the earthen floor of the dugout.

'That is how sharp it is,' China said softly.

'If you kill her you haven't got anything to bargain with.' Sean's voice was harsh with strain and he was sweating.

'I have this to bargain with,' China replied, and he nodded to his guards at the doorway.

They led in someone whom Sean had never seen before. An apparition with an ancient skull-like head. The hair had fallen out in tufts, leaving shiny black patches on the scalp. The lips had shrunk and peeled back to expose teeth that were too large and white for that ruined head.

At a word from China the guards stripped away the single filthy ragged shift that covered the body, leaving it entirely naked, and for the first time, Sean realized that it was a woman.

Her body reminded him of the horror pictures he had seen of the survivors of Dachau and Belsen. She was a skeleton covered with baggy skin, her empty dugs dangled over the rack of her ribs, her stomach was drawn in so that her pelvic girdle was an empty bony basin. Her arms and legs were fleshless, the bony elbows and knees grotesquely enlarged.

Sean and Claudia stared at her with horror, unable to speak with the shock of it.

'Look at the lesions on her abdomen,' China invited in a pleasant voice, and numbly they obeyed.

They were blind boils, hard and shiny as ripe black grapes beneath the skin, covering her lower belly and disappearing into the wiry mop of her pubic hair.

While all their attention was on this pathetic figure, China reached down quickly with the knife and touched the back of Claudia's hand with the point of the blade. Claudia gasped and tried to jerk her hand away, but it came up short against the manacle chain and she stared down as a thin snake of bright blood trickled down her forefinger and dripped onto the floor.

'What did you do that for, you snot-gobbling bastard?' Sean demanded.

China smiled. 'It's only a scratch.'

Slowly he reached out towards the naked skeletal figure of the black woman, pointing with the knife at her shrunken belly.

'The extreme emaciation, and those characteristic lesions are diagnostic,' he explained. 'The woman is suffering from what we, in Africa, call the "Slim Sickness".'

'Aids,' Claudia whispered, and her voice was filled with the dread that single word conjured up.

Despite himself Sean took a step back from the dreadful figure before him.

'Yes, Miss Monterro,' China agreed. 'Aids in its terminal stage.'

He touched one of the marble-hard chancres on the woman's belly with the point of the blade, and she gave no reaction as it split open and a mixture of pus and dark tarry blood oozed from the wound and trickled down into the matted bush of her pubic hair.

'Blood,' whispered China, and gently scooped it up onto the bright silver blade. 'Warm living blood, swarming with the virus.'

He proffered the blade for Sean's inspection and involuntarily Sean pulled back further as blood dripped from the point.

'Yes,' China nodded. 'Something that even the bravest have reason to fear, the most certain, the most lingering, the most loathsome death of all the ages.'

With his free hand he took hold of Claudia's wrist.

'Consider this other blood. The sweet bright blood of a vibrant, beautiful, young woman.'

The scratch on the back of Claudia's hand was vivid, but the tiny flow of blood from it almost quenched it.

'Blood to blood,' China whispered. 'Sick blood to healthy blood.'

He brought the filthy blade closer to Claudia's hand and she stiffened in the chair, straining silently against the manacle, her face white with horror as she stared at the knife.

'Blood to blood,' China repeated. 'Shall we let them mingle?'

Sean found he could not speak, he shook his head dumbly, staring at the knife.

'Shall we do it, Colonel?' China asked. 'It's all up to you now.' He brought the blade closer to the open wound in Claudia's smooth creamily tanned skin.

'Just another inch, Colonel,' China whispered, and suddenly Claudia screamed; it was a wild ringing release of horror and terror, but China did not flinch. He did not look at her face and his knife hand was steady and tremorless.

'What shall we do, Colonel Courtney?' he asked.

He lowered the knife and touched her wrist with the flat of the blade, leaving a smear of diseased blood on the unblemished skin, only inches from the scratch on Claudia's hand, then slowly he moved the knife downwards.

'Speak quickly, Colonel. In seconds it will be too late.' The knife left a shiny track of blood like the slime trail of some disgusting snail across her skin. Inexorably it moved down towards the open wound.

'Stop it!' Sean screamed. 'Stop it!'

China lifted the blade away, and looked at him enquiringly. 'Does that mean we have reached an agreement?'

'Yes, damn you to hell! I'll do it!'

China tossed the contaminated knife into a corner of the dugout, and then opened one of the drawers in his desk and brought out a bottle of Dettol antiseptic. He soaked his handkerchief in the undiluted fluid, and then carefully wiped the smear of diseased blood from Claudia's skin.

The tension went out of her rigid body and she slumped in the chair. She was panting softly and trembling like a kitten left out in the rain.

'Turn her loose,' Sean croaked, but China shook his head.

'Not until we have made our terms of agreement clear.'

'All right,' Sean snarled. 'And the first of those terms is that my woman comes with me on the mission. No more dugouts filled with rats.'

China pretended to ponder that and then nodded. 'Very well, but the second term is that if you fail me in any way, then Alphonso will kill her immediately.'

'Get Alphonso in here,' Sean demanded. The sweat had not yet dried on his forehead and his voice was still rough and unsteady. 'I want to hear you give him his orders.'

Alphonso stood to attention and listened expressionlessly as China told him, 'However, if the attack fails, if you are intercepted by Frelimo before you reach the laager, or if any of the *henshaw* are allowed to escape . . .'

Sean interrupted. 'No, General, a hundred per cent success is too high to hope for. Let us be reasonable and realistic. If I can destroy all but six of the Hinds, then it must be counted that I have fulfilled my part of the bargain.'

China frowned and shook his head. 'Even six Hinds will be sufficient to ensure our defeat. I'll allow you two. If more than two Hinds escape from the laager your mission will be a failure, and you must pay the price.' He turned back to Alphonso and went on with his instructions. 'And so, Sergeant, you will obey all orders from the Colonel, carrying out the attack exactly the way he has planned it, but if the raid fails, if more than two *henshaw* escape, then you are to take full command, and your very first duty will be to shoot the two whites, and their black servant – you will shoot them immediately.'

Alphonso blinked almost sleepily at the order. He did not turn his head to look at Sean, and Sean found himself wondering if, despite their relationship, the friendship that had grown up between them, despite the fact that Alphonso had called him *Nkosi Kakulu* and *Baba*, and had exhorted him to lead the mission, despite all of this, he would carry out the execution order.

Alphonso was an African Shangane and a warrior with a deep sense of tribal loyalty and a tradition of absolute obedience to his chief and tribal elders.

'Yes,' Sean thought. 'He'd probably have a few regrets, but without question or hesitation, he would do it.'

He raised his voice. 'All right, China, we all know exactly where we stand. Let Miss Monterro come to me now.'

The bodyguard removed her handcuffs and politely General China helped her out of the chair. 'I apologize for the unpleasantness, Miss Monterro, but I'm sure you will understand the necessity for it.'

Claudia was unsteady on her feet, and staggered before she reached Sean and clung to him.

'And so I'll wish you farewell and good hunting.' China gave them a small mocking salute. 'One way or the other, we will not meet again, I'm afraid.'

Sean did not deign to reply. With the case of cassettes in one hand and his other arm around Claudia's shoulders, Sean led her to the doorway.

* * *

They moved out two hours before darkness. It was an unwieldy column and the missile-launchers and the back-up missiles made awkward burdens; apart from their weight, the length of the packs made them cumbersome. They hooked up in thick bush when the path narrowed and slowed down the column's ability to react to threat and danger.

At first, Sean kept the column bunched up in a close cohesive whole. They were still some miles from the tenuous front line of the Renamo army, and would not be seriously menaced until much later in the march.

However, taking no chances, Sean kept the assault troops of the vanguard and rear vigilant and at the utmost degree of readiness to repel any attacks and to give the missile-bearers a chance to escape. To ensure this, Sean sent Job to the head of the column while he stayed in the centre where he could reach any trouble spot quickly and where he could be near to Claudia.

'Where is Matatu?' she asked Sean. 'We've just gone off and left him. I'm so worried about him.'

'Don't worry about leaving him behind. He's like one of those puppies which you can't send home. He'll follow me anywhere, in fact the little bugger is probably watching us out of the bush at this very moment.'

And so it proved, for as darkness descended on the column, a small shadow appeared miraculously at Sean's side.

'I see you, my *Bwana*,' Matatu twinkled.

'I see you also, little friend.' Sean touched his woolly head as he would his favourite gun dog. 'I've been waiting for you to find a way for us through the Frelimo lines, and so lead us to the roosting place of the ugly falcons.' And Matatu swelled with self-importance.

'Follow me, my *Bwana*,' he said.

Now with Matatu to guide them, Sean could rearrange the column into a more streamlined formation for passing through the Frelimo advance and getting into their rear.

To his advantage was the size of the battle being fought ahead

374

of him. There were six thousand Frelimo and Zimbabwean troops advancing against less than half that number of Renamo defenders, and the area of the battlefield was tens of thousands of square miles in extent. The fighting ahead of them was taking place in small isolated pockets, while most of the ground was wild and rugged and deserted.

Sean sent Job and Matatu ahead with a small party of assault troops to find the wide gaps in the line and steer them through. The rest of the column followed at a discreet interval, protected by the conventionally armed assault division of Shanganes.

They kept going steadily through the night, runners coming back from Job and Matatu in the vanguard to guide them whenever it was necessary to make a detour or to change direction.

At intervals during the long cold march, they heard distant gunfire and the sound of mortars and heavy machine-guns as elements of the Frelimo advance ran into the Renamo defence. Occasionally they saw the twinkle of signal flares soar above the dark forest, but there was no sound of Isotov turbos and helicopter rotors in the night. It was clear that the Hinds were limiting their depredations to the daylight hours when they could distinguish friend from foe and make their close-support operations more effective.

An hour before dawn Job came back down the column to find Sean.

'We aren't going to reach our first objective until an hour or so after first light,' he reported. 'The pace has been slower than we expected, what do you want us to do? Shall we take a chance on the Hinds finding us?'

Sean looked up at the sky before he replied. The first lemon-coloured flush of dawn was paling out the stars.

'The forest roof isn't dense enough to hide so many men and so much equipment,' he decided. 'We have to keep going and get them into hiding. Tell Matatu to quicken the pace.'

'What about the Hinds?'

'The main fighting is well behind us now, that is where they will be headed, we have to take the chance, but move fast.'

As the light strengthened so the faces of the men in the long column turned more frequently and fretfully to the sky. The pace was fast, almost a run. Although they had been going all night, still the Shanganes bore their heavy burdens with all the hardiness and fortitude of the African, burdens that would have broken the heart and the back of even a strong white man.

It was light enough to define the tree-tops against the orange blossom of dawn when Sean heard the dread whistle of turbos, faint and distant, passing to the east. The Hinds were flying their first sortie of the day, and the alarm was shouted down the length of the column. The porters dived off the path, seeking the nearest cover, and the section leaders crouched ready to wave the captured Frelimo colours that Sean had provided for each of them should the Hinds spot them and come in to strafe them.

The deception was not necessary for the pair of Hinds passed two miles east of their position. Sean saw their silhouettes, like deformed gnats, black against the oncoming dawn, and minutes later heard the thunder of their Gatling-cannons and the boom of their assault rockets as they pounded another Renamo stronghold amongst the ironstone hills far behind them.

Sean got the column moving again and the glimpse that they had been given of 'the flying death' sped their feet. An hour later, the tail end of the column clambered swiftly down the almost sheer side of the gorge at the bottom of which lay the dry riverbed and the caves where the captured Unimogs had been hidden.

It was almost a home-coming and the men crept thankfully into the gloom of the caverns and laid down the heavy packs.

'No fires,' Sean ordered. 'No smoking.'

They ate their rations of cold stodgy maize cakes and dried fish and then curled on the cavern floor and slept like a pack of hounds exhausted at the end of a day's hunting.

Sean found a private place for Claudia at the back of the cavern, behind a natural screen of tumbled sandstone blocks. He spread a blanket on the rocky floor and she sat cross-legged upon it and munched the unappetizing rations; but before she had half finished, she slumped sideways, asleep before her head touched the floor. Sean spread the other blanket over her for it was chilly in the depths of the cavern, and then he went back to the entrance.

Alphonso had rigged the antenna of the small portable two-way VHF radio. He was crouched beside the set with the volume turned low, listening to the situation reports of the Renamo field commanders as they reported in to General China's headquarters.

'It goes very badly,' he told Sean glumly. 'Frelimo will be on the riverbank by noon tomorrow, and unless the general pulls back, he will be overrun.' Alphonso broke off as he recognized their call sign in the jumbled static of the wave band.

'Banana Bush, this is Warthog,' he replied into the hand mike and then gave the 'primary objective established' code. 'Coca-Cola!' Sean smiled at this subtle commentary on modern Africa, and Banana Bush acknowledged and signed off. Their next report was scheduled for dawn tomorrow by which time the fate of the mission would be decided one way or the other.

Sean left Alphonso rolling up the antenna and packing the radio into its carrying case and from the entrance of the cavern watched the party of five men who under Job's supervision were sweeping the sandy riverbed with thorn branches to obliterate the last traces of their passing.

Job climbed back to the mouth of the cave and Sean asked, 'Sentries?'

'On each of the peaks.' Job pointed to the heights above them. 'I have covered every approach.'

'All right.' Sean led him back into the cavern. 'It's time to arm and program the Stingers.'

It took almost a full hour to assemble the launchers, connect the battery-packs and feed the cassettes into the micro computers in the consoles. Finally each of the launchers was fully armed and programmed for 'Two Colour' attack sequence on the Hind gunships, and they handed them back to the Shangane section leaders.

Sean glanced at his wristwatch, mildly surprised that it was still keeping time after all the abuse he had given it recently.

'We can grab a few hours' shut-eye,' he told Job, but neither of them made a move to do so.

Instead, as if by consent, they moved back to the entrance of the cavern, away from the others, and leaned against the rock wall with their shoulders almost touching, staring thoughtfully out into the riverbed where the early sunlight was sparkling the crystalline sand like powder snow.

'If you had taken my advice, you could be living high in the flesh pots of Harare now,' Sean murmured.

'And never have the chance to bag a Hind?' Job smiled carefully, his damaged lip was crusted with a fragile scab and a drop of blood like a tiny ruby appeared as it split open again. He dabbed at it with the corner of his bandanna, as he went on, 'We have hunted all the dangerous game together, Sean, in all the worst places. Buffalo in the jesse bush, elephant in the Kasaga-saga. This will be another trophy, the best and biggest.'

Sean turned to study his face. It was typical of their friendship that their feelings should be so perfectly in tune. During the long night march, Sean's fury and hatred of General China had abated and given way to this emotion which Job had just articulated, the excitement of the hunter. They were both hunters, the chase was a fire and a passion in their blood which they had never attempted to suppress. They understood each other, recognized and accepted this bond between them which had grown stronger over the twenty years of their friendship. Yet they had seldom spoken of their feelings for each other, Sean realized.

'Perhaps now is the time to do so,' he thought, and said aloud, 'We are more than brothers, you and me.'

'Yes,' Job replied simply. 'We are beyond the love of brothers.'

They were silent then, not embarrassed by what had passed between them, but rather fulfilled and fortified by it.

'As a brother,' Sean broke the silence, 'may I ask a favour of you?'

Job nodded, and Sean went on softly, 'There will be hard fighting at the laager. I would not want Claudia to fall into the hands of Frelimo if I were not there to prevent it. That is the favour I ask.'

A shadow passed behind Job's eyes. 'I do not like to think about that possibility.'

'If I am not there, will you do it for me?'

Job nodded. 'I give you my word.'

'If you have to do it, do not warn her, do not speak, do it unexpectedly.'

'She will not know it is coming,' Job promised. 'It will be quick.'

'Thank you,' Sean said, and clasped his shoulder. 'Now we must rest.'

Claudia was still asleep, her breathing was so gentle and silent that, for a moment, Sean was alarmed. He put his face close to hers and felt the warmth of her breath on his cheek. He kissed her and she murmured in her sleep and reached out, fumbling for him and sighing contentedly as he crept into the circle of her arms.

He seemed only to have closed his eyes for a moment, before

378

a light touch on his cheek woke him again, and he looked up to see Job squatting over him.

'It's time,' Job's lips formed the words, and Sean gently disentangled Claudia's arms.

'Sleep sweetly, my love,' he murmured, and left her lying on the blanket.

The others were already waiting for him at the entrance of the cave, Matatu and Alphonso and the section leaders, only lightly armed so that they could move swiftly and steathily.

'Four o'clock,' Job told Sean, and he saw that the light in the riverbed had mellowed, the shadows were lengthening.

There was nothing more to say. They had both done this half a hundred times before.

'See you around,' Job said, and Sean nodded, as he strapped on his pack.

With Matatu dancing ahead of them like a forest sprite, they slipped out of the cavern and into the trees, turning immediately south and settling into their running formation.

Twice they heard the Hind gunships passing at a distance and once they were forced into cover as one of the helicopters came directly overhead.

However, it was high, over four thousand feet Sean estimated, flying at the top of its speed. Studying the aircraft through his binoculars, Sean guessed it had completed a mission and was racing back to the laager to refuel and rearm. To confirm this, he saw that the racks for the Swatter assault missiles below the fuselage were empty, and the nozzles of the rocket pods were scorched with the back blast of discharged rockets.

The Hind was heading on exactly the same bearing as Matatu was leading them, and even as Sean held it in the field of his binoculars, the Hind reduced power on its turbos and commenced its descent, homing in on its laager.

'Not more than five miles ahead,' Sean guessed, and glanced across at Matatu, who was waiting expectantly for Sean's approbation.

'Like a bee to its hive,' Matatu grinned.

'Your eyes are like those of the vulture,' Sean agreed. 'They see all.' And Matatu hugged himself with pleasure and rocked on his haunches. Sean's praise was all the reward he ever asked for.

Half an hour later they leopard-crawled up onto the crest of a low rocky kopje and slid over the skyline into the dead ground below before Sean raised his binoculars. He used his cap to shade the lens; a reflected ray of sunlight would telegraph their position like a heliograph.

He picked up the railway line immediately, less then two miles distant; the ballast was of blue granite and the single set of tracks gleamed dully in the late sunshine, polished by the steel wheels of rolling stock.

He followed the tracks for a mile and found the spur onto which two railway tankers had been shunted. They were partially hidden by scraggly trees and rank bush, but minutes later a feather of dust rose out of the forest and a fuel bowser came down a dirt track and pulled in beside the leading tanker. Sean watched through the binoculars as overall-clad workers connected up the delivery hose and began pumping fuel between the two vehicles.

While this was happening, a Hind gunship rose with dramatic suddenness from the foreslope of the hill just beyond the railway spur, and at last, Sean had a positive fix on the laager.

The Hind rose to three hundred feet above the hill and then turned and bore away, humpbacked and nose-heavy, for one more mission over the battlefield in the north before the light failed, and the fighting was suspended for the night.

Now that he knew exactly where to look, Sean was able to make out other heavily camouflaged emplacements on the slopes of the hill. He counted six of them and said so to Matatu.

'There are two more,' Matatu grinned patronizingly as he pointed out the hidden emplacements that Sean had overlooked. 'And there are three more on the far side of the hill, you cannot see them from here.'

The wisdom of making this reconnaissance in daylight became clearer, as Sean was able to pick out the discrepancies between the model with which they had planned the raid and the actual topography of the laager and its surroundings.

Sean jotted the amendments in his notebook, making new estimates of the ranges and the fields of fire that his missiles could command. One by one, he called over each of the section leaders and pointed out exactly what positions he wanted them to occupy as soon as their teams arrived and darkness had fallen to cover them.

Satisfied that Matatu could supply no further information, Sean despatched him. 'Go back to Job. As soon as it is dark, guide him and all the other soldiers up here.'

When Matatu was gone, Sean devoted the last hour of daylight to watching the gunships return out of the north. There were eleven of them, ample proof of the efficiency of the Russian maintenance crews who must have repaired the two Hinds that Matatu had reported were not flying. The entire squadron, less the single gunship that Sean had knocked out of the sky, was once again operational and doing dreadful execution amongst the Renamo guerrillas.

As each gunship hovered above the hillock and then settled into its emplacement, Sean pointed out the flying characteristics to his section leaders and urged them to mark well the exact position of each emplacement.

'That one is yours, Tendela.' He reinforced the target allocations. 'See how he stands in the sky. You will shoot from that clump of dark trees at the edge of the vlei. Have you marked it well?'

'I have marked it, *Nkosi Kakulu*,' they affirmed. The sky was washed by the blood of the dying day, and as he watched the red orb sink away beneath the trees, Sean wondered how much more blood the dawn would bring.

There was that short period of African twilight during which it was not yet dark enough to move off the ridge. There was nothing further to discuss and Sean and Alphonso sat close together. The feeling was so familiar. No matter how many times Sean waited like this, he would never be able to control or ignore the tension that pulled like rubber bands across his guts. It was the heady anticipation of the draught of terror which soon he would drink to its dregs. He longed for it as the addict does for the needle, and dreaded it to the limits of his soul.

'We will make a good kill,' Alphonso said quietly. 'It will be a fight for men who are truly men.'

Sean nodded. 'Yes, my friend, it will be a good fight, and if we fail, then you must try to kill me. That also will be a good fight.'

'We will see,' Alphonso growled, his eyes reflecting the smoky red glare of the sunset. 'Yes, we will see.'

The crisp silhouette of the hill on which the Hinds were laagered dissolved with the onset of night. Then Venus appeared as the evening star and its cold unwavering light burned directly above the hilltop, seeming to single it out for them.

Within the first hour of darkness, the leading troopers of the raiding column emerged from the trees behind them. Job was at the head of the column with Matatu guiding him and Claudia beside him. Sean met them with a quiet word and immediately began to marshal the troopers into their various units. The section leaders took charge of their missile teams, and the Stinger launchers were unpacked and assembled; the spare missiles in their sealed frangible tubes were checked and readied.

Sean and Job and Claudia went from team to team, running the final checks on the missile launchers, making certain that the battery packs were fully charged and correctly connected, that the cylinders of freon gas were open-valved and that the sighting screens illuminated when the actuator was engaged.

At last, Sean was ready to deploy the missile teams, but before he did so, he called the section leaders together and, for the last time, made each repeat his orders. Satisfied at last, he began to despatch them to their attack positions. He allowed five-minute intervals between each team leaving the ridge.

Alphonso was in charge of the missile teams attacking the eastern perimeter of the laager and because he had farther to go to get into position, he left first.

When it was time for Job, who would lead the missile attack on the western perimeter, to go, he and Sean shook hands briefly. There was no exchange of good wishes, they were both superstitious about that. Instead Job asked facetiously, 'Listen, Sean, about that four thousand dollars in bonus and back-pay, don't you want to pay me out now?'

'Will you take a cheque?' Sean grinned at him through the dark mask of his camouflage cream. Job answered his grin, punched his shoulder and moved away out of earshot so that Sean could speak to Claudia in private.

'I don't want to leave you,' she whispered, and Sean hugged her fiercely.

'Stay close to Job,' he ordered.

'Come back to me safely.'

'Yes.'

'Promise me.'

'I promise,' he said, and she pulled out of his embrace and turned away, disappearing into the darkness after Job.

382

Sean stared after her, he found that his hands were trembling. He thrust them into his pockets and clenched his fists.

'Love doesn't do much for one's fighting instincts,' he thought, and tried to dismiss her from his mind. 'She'll be all right with Job.'

The assault party was waiting for him patiently, squatting at the edge of the tree-line. Twenty-four men, the cannon fodder, the meat bombs, he thought ruefully, those who had failed the aptitude tests for operating the Stingers. While the missile crews would fire from stand-off positions five hundred metres outside the perimeter of the laager, the assault party would attack it head on and frontal, deliberately drawing fire while trying to flush the Hinds up into the air for the missile gunners to get a fair shot at them. It was this unit who would meet the 12.7mm cannons in their fortified positions, and all the other dangers and obstacles which certainly guarded the laager.

Theirs was the most dangerous task, and for that reason alone, Sean could not delegate the command of them to another. He would lead them in.

'Come on, Matatu,' he said quietly. When there was real danger at hand, wounded game in thick cover or an enemy position to attack, Matatu's self-chosen place was always at Sean's side. Nothing could dislodge him from it.

As a mark of his esteem Alphonso had presented Sean with an AKM assault rifle, the improved and up-dated version of the ubiquitous AK 47 which was much prized and sought after by the Renamo guerrillas. Sean carried this weapon now as he led the assault team down off the ridge, and, with Matatu guiding them through the night, circled out to get in between the main railway line and the laager, as close as was prudent to the spur of line on which the railway fuel tankers stood.

There was no urgency, they had all night in which to get into position, so they went with a stealth which increased the closer they came to the enemy positions.

It was after two o'clock in the morning and the small slice of the moon had set before Sean had them in their jump-off positions, spread out at precise intervals so that at his command, they could sweep forward in skirmishing formation.

He made one final inspection of their dispositions, crawling silently from man to man, personally sighting in the 60mm M4 commando mortars for them, by sense of touch alone checking

383

their equipment, making absolutely certain that each of them clearly understood his objective and then leaving them with a whisper of encouragement and a brief but firm clasp of the shoulder. At last, with everything done that could be done, he settled down to wait.

This was always the worst and the best part of the hunt. As he lay in the silence, he wondered how much of his life he had spent like this, waiting for it to begin, waiting for shooting light, waiting in the blind for that breath-stopping moment when the leopard appeared with magical suddenness in the bait tree, an elegant silhouette against the pale backdrop of the dawn.

His mind went back over the years to those other adventures and wild endeavours, to the terrible risks and almost unbearable thrills, and suddenly it dawned upon him that this was probably the last time it would happen. He was over forty years of age and Claudia Monterro had entered his life, it was time for it to change. There was a sadness and, at the same time, a satisfaction in that thought.

'Let the last be the best of all the game,' he thought, and in the utter darkness of pre-dawn, he heard a sound at once both thrilling and terrifying, the shrill high whine of a mighty turbo engine, howling like a man-eating wolf in the night. It was joined almost at once by another and then another. The Hind squadron was starting engines, warming up for their first sortie in the dawn.

Sean checked his watch and the luminous dial showed eleven minutes before five. It was almost time. Without thinking, he unclipped the curved banana magazine from under the AKM rifle and replaced it with another from the pouch of spare magazines on his webbing. That habitual gesture gave him the comfort of long familiarity, and beside him, Matatu seeing him do it stirred expectantly. The dawn wind came softly as a lover and stroked Sean's cheek.

He turned his head towards the east and held up his hand with fingers spread. He could just make out the silhouette of his fingers against the coming dawn. It was what the Matabele called 'the time of the horns', when a herdsman could first see the horns of his cattle against the sky.

'Shooting light in ten minutes,' Sean reminded himself, and knew how long it would take those minutes to pass.

One after the other, the Hinds shut down their engines to an idle. The ground crews would be completing the refuelling and rearming, the flying crews would be going aboard.

Sean had to judge it exactly, the light must be just right. The Hinds would probably not use landing lights, and missile gunners must be able to see them clearly against the dawn.

The light bloomed swiftly. Sean closed his eyes and counted slowly to ten before he opened them again. Now he could make out the stark outline of the crest of the hill, like a cut-out in black cardboard, the lace-work of the msasa trees stood out against the purple sky, swaying gracefully to the dawn breeze.

'Shoot!' he said, and tapped the shoulder of the mortar man beside him. The trooper leaned forward holding the mortar bomb in both hands and dropped it into the mouth of the mortar tube. The charge in the tail ignited and with a polite pop hurled the signal bomb five hundred feet into the sky above the hilltop. It exploded in a twinkling red flare of lights.

* * *

Claudia Monterro followed Job down off the ridge, keeping so close behind him that she need only reach out her hand to touch him. Job carried one of the missile launchers across his shoulders, and behind Claudia the number two of their team was bowed beneath the weight of the spare rocket tubes.

The footing was loose and dangerous, while quartz pebbles as treacherous as ball-bearings rolled under foot. It pleased her that she was as steady and sure-footed as any of t' m over this difficult ground.

Nevertheless, she was sweating in the night chill as they reached the bottom of the slope and crept forward towards the perimeter of the laager. There was a time, only a few short weeks ago, when she would have felt inept and awkward in these circumstances, but now she orientated herself by the beacon of the evening star above the hilltop and responded instantly to Job's signals, picking her footfalls and anti-tracking almost instinctively.

They reached the dense copse of trees which was their attack position, and crept in amongst them. Claudia helped Job set up the Stinger ready for firing and then found herself a comfortable perch at the base of one of the trees to wait out the night.

Job left her there with just the Shangane number two loader

for company, and he disappeared into the darkness like a hunting leopard. She was unhappy to see him go, but not long ago she would have been panic-stricken. She realized what a measure of self-reliance and fortitude she had been forced to learn in these last few weeks.

'Papa will be proud of me,' she smiled to herself, using the future tense as though her father still existed. 'Of course he does,' she assured herself. 'He's still out there somewhere looking out for me. How else would I have made it this far?' His memory was a comfort, and as she thought about him, he became confused in her mind with Sean, so that they seemed to merge into a single entity as though her father had somehow achieved a new existence in her lover. It was a good feeling that alleviated her loneliness, until suddenly Job returned as silently and abruptly as he had left.

'All the other sections are in position,' he whispered, as he settled down beside her. 'But it's going to be a long night. Try and get some sleep.'

'I'll never be able to sleep,' she answered, keeping her voice so low that he had to lean close to her to catch the words. 'Tell me about Sean Courtney, I want to know everything you know about him.'

'Sometimes he's a hero, and sometimes he's a complete bastard.' Job thought about it. 'But most of the time, he's something in between.'

'Then why have you stayed with him so long?'

'He's my friend,' Job answered simply, and then slowly, haltingly, he began to tell her about Sean, and they talked the night away.

Claudia listened avidly, encouraging him with quiet questions. 'He was married, wasn't he, Job?' Or, 'Why did he leave his home? I have heard that his family is enormously wealthy. Why did he choose this life?'

So the night passed, and in those hours they became friends, the first true friend she had found in Africa, and in the end he said to her in that beautiful deep African voice, 'I shall miss him, more than I can tell.'

'You speak as though the two of you are parting, and that isn't so. It will be the same.'

'No,' Job denied. 'It will never be the same. He will go with you now. Our time together has ended, yours is beginning.'

'Don't hate me for it, Job.' She reached out to touch his arm in appeal.

'You two will be good together,' he said. 'I think your journey with him will be as good as mine has been. My thoughts will go with you, and I wish you both great joy in each other.'

'Thank you, Job,' she whispered. 'You will always be our friend.'

Job lifted his arm and with fingers spread held his open hand against the dawn.

'The time of the horns,' he murmured softly. 'Soon now.' And as he said it, a flower of bright crimson fire burst open in the sky above the hill.

*   *   *

As the signal flare burst in the dawn sky, the battle was born. Sean always thought of it as the birth of a living thing, a monster which he could only try to direct but which had a life and a will of its own, a terrible thing which swept them all up and carried them along willy nilly.

He had placed the RPG 7 rocket-launchers in the hands of his two best remaining gunners, but the expert marksmen had all gone to man the Stingers. The first rocket flew low, striking the earth twenty feet in front of the nearest fuel tanker; it burst in a vivid yellow flash and Sean saw one of the Frelimo sentries cartwheel bodily into the air. The second rocket was high, missing the tanker by six feet, reaching the top of its trajectory five hundred yards out and then dropping into the forest beyond, its detonation screened by trees and scrub.

'Aim, you Shangane oxen!' Sean bellowed at them, and he was up and running as he realized his mistake in not taking the first crucial shot himself.

The Frelimo sentries were screaming and scattering around the fuel tankers and from the perimeter of the laager a 12.7mm cannon opened up, sluicing gaudy strings of fiery tracer across the sky.

The rocketeer was fumbling to reload the RPG 7, but he was panicky and unsure in the dark. Sean snatched the launcher off his shoulder and with two deft movements had removed the protecting nose cap of the missile and cleared the safety-pin. He

387

swung the launcher over his shoulder and dropped on one knee, aiming at the nearest tanker.

'All the time in the world,' he reminded himself, and waited for the puff of the morning breeze on his cheek to abate. The RPG 7 was wildly inaccurate in a crosswind for the push of the wind on its tail-fins would turn its nose into wind.

The breeze dropped and Sean centred the sights on the fuel tanker. The range was just on three hundred metres, the limit of the rocket's accuracy, and he fired. The missile sped true, and the side of the tanker erupted in a tall sheet of volatile Avgas. The sky filled with flames.

Sean snarled at the rocketeer beside him and the man fumbled another missile out of his pack, the cardboard propellant tube already attached to it.

Burning Avgas illuminated the southern slope of the hill like noonday. Sean was kneeling in the open and the gunner on the 12.7mm swung his aim onto him.

The earth around Sean dissolved into billowing clouds of dust and flying clods, and the rocketeer ducked.

'Come on, you yellow bastard!' Sean completed the loading sequence unaided, making no effort to avoid the aim of the 12.7mm gunner.

He lifted the launcher on to his shoulder, and aimed at the second fuel tanker. It was lit up by the flames as though it were a stage effect, but as he was on the point of firing, the tanker was obscured by a dancing curtain of yellow dust and the volley of cannon fire passed so close to Sean's head that his eardrums creaked and popped as though he were in a decompression chamber.

He held his fire for three seconds and then as the curtains of dust blew open he fired through them, and the second tanker burst, blown clear of the railway lines by the explosion of its lethal cargo.

Burning Avgas flowed down the slope like the lava of a miniature Vesuvius, and Sean threw the launcher at the rocketeer's chest. 'Hit them on the head with the bloody thing!' he yelled at him. 'That's the only damage you are going to do with it!'

The mortar men were making better practice. Sean had sighted their weapons for them and they bobbed and weaved over the short mortar tubes as they dropped the finned projectiles into the open mouths. A steady stream of bombs lobbed high into the dawn sky and then rained down into the hilltop laager.

Sean watched the effect of the bursts with a dispassionate, professional eye.

'Good,' he murmured. 'Good.' But they had only been capable of carrying thirty bombs for each of the mortars; they weighed almost two kilos each and they would be expended in a few short minutes. They must rush the perimeter while the exploding bombs distracted the Frelimo gunners. He hefted the AKM rifle and slipped the safety-catch.

'Go!' Sean yelled, and blew a short series of blasts on his whistle. 'Go!'

The Shanganes came to their feet in a single cohesive movement, and swept down the hill, but there were only twenty of them, a puny line of running men, brightly lit by the flames. The 12.7mm gunners on the hill fastened on them, and the tracer flew in clouds about them, thick as a locust plague.

'Shit!' Sean laughed aloud in terror. 'What a way to go!'

One of the Frelimo guns had picked Sean out of the sweep line and was concentrating his fire on him, but Sean was plunging down hill with long flying strides and the gunner was shooting high and a little behind. Shot flashed past Sean so close he could feel the wind of it tugging at his tunic. Impossibly, he lengthened his stride, and beside him Matatu giggled shrilly, keeping pace with him down the hill.

'What's so goddamned funny, you silly little bugger!' Sean yelled at him furiously, and they hit the level ground beside the burning fuel tankers. The Frelimo gunner's field of fire was blanketed by the rolling screen of black smoke, and in the respite Sean marshalled his sweep line of racing Shanganes, pivoting them on the centre and directing them at the perimeter of the laager, pumping his right fist overhead to urge them on.

They used the smoke to cover themselves for the next two hundred metres of their charge. The dawn breeze was spreading it, sooty black and dense and low along the ground.

A Frelimo sentry staggered out of the smoke ahead of Sean. He wore faded and tattered denim jeans and grubby tennis shoes, he had lost his weapon and a rocket splinter must have hit him in the eye. The eye was dislodged from its socket and hung out on his cheek like a huge wet grape, dangling and bouncing on the thick cord of the optic nerve as the man jerked his head.

Without breaking his stride. Sean hit him in the belly with a tap of three from the AKM, firing from the hip. He jumped over the body as it hit the ground.

They came out of the smoke, still in sweep line. Sean glanced along the line and realized incredulously that they had not yet taken a single casualty, the twenty Shanganes were spread out and going hard, offering only fleeting targets through the smoke and flame to the disorientated Frelimo machine-guns.

At that moment, he saw the single strand of wire and the line of round metal discs on short steel droppers only a dozen paces ahead of him. The discs were each emblazoned with a stylized skull and crossbones in scarlet that caught the ruddy glow of the flames, and almost before he realized it, they were into the minefield that guarded the perimeter of the laager.

Two seconds later, the Shangane running on Sean's right-hand side triggered an anti-personnel mine. From the waist down his body was obscured by the dust and flash of the explosion and he dropped to the earth with both of his legs blown to bloody stumps below the knees.

'Keep going!' Sean screamed. 'We are nearly through!' And now his fear was a grotesque black beast upon his back that weighed him down and choked his breathing. To be maimed was a terror far beyond that of death, and the ground beneath his feet was sown with the steel capsules of terrible mutilation.

Matatu ducked in front of Sean, forcing him to check his stride. 'Follow me, my *Bwana*!' he piped in Swahili. 'Tread where I have trodden.' And Sean obeyed, shortening his stride to that of the little mannikin.

So Matatu ran him through the last fifty paces of the minefield, and Sean knew that he had never witnessed such a display of raw courage and devotion of one human being to another. Two more Shangane went down before they were through, their legs blown away beneath them. They left them lying in puddles of their own blood and minced flesh and jumped over the single strand of wire that marked the far side of the minefield.

Even in the terror and exhilaration of the moment. Sean felt his eyelids scalding with the strength of his gratitude and love for the little Ndorobo. He wanted to pick him up like a child's toy and hug him. Instead he gasped at him, 'You're so damned skinny it wouldn't have gone off even if you had stepped on one.' And Matatu twinkled with delight and ran at Sean's side as he charged the 12.7mm machine-gun in its sandbagged emplacement that lay dead ahead of them.

Sean was firing the AKM from the hip, short raking bursts, and he could see the head of the Frelimo gunner in the embrasure of the parapet of sandbags.

The gunner swivelled the barrel of the heavy machine-gun onto him, aiming for his belly and he was so close that Sean could see his eyes reflecting the red light of the fires as he sighted over it. The instant before he fired, Sean hurled himself forward, dropping under the shot like a runner sliding for the base plate; bullets whipped over his head and the muzzle blast beat in his eardrum, but he rolled forward and came up hard against the parapet, flattening himself against it, so close that he could have reached out and touched the muzzle of the machine-gun.

Sean unhooked the fragmentation grenade from his belt, drew the pin, and popped it into the embrasure beside him as though he were posting a letter.

He smiled as he heard the Frelimo gunner scream something unintelligible in Portuguese.

'Happy birthday!' he said, and the grenade exploded, blowing out through the opening in an exhalation of flame and fumes.

Sean jumped up and rolled over the top of the parapet. There were two men in the emplacement, writhing and wriggling on the floor, and half a dozen others had abandoned the position and were sprinting away up the hill, unarmed and screaming with panic.

Sean left Matatu to finish the two wounded men on the floor with his skinning knife, while he seized the abandoned 12.7mm machine-gun and manhandled it to the rear wall of the emplacement. He aimed it up the hill at the fleeing Frelimo and fired a long traversing burst. Two of the runners dropped in their tracks and grinning happily, crooning to himself with the fun of it, Matatu dragged a steel box of spare ammunition belts across the bloody floor, and helped Sean reload.

With a fresh belt of 250 rounds loaded, Sean traversed the heavy machine-gun and his fire lashed the hillside above him, tracer swirling through the groups of running Frelimo and scattering them.

It seemed to Sean as though more than half the Shangane had survived the minefield and the bloody charge and assault. Roaring wildly with triumph, they were pursuing and harrying the routed defenders.

The barrel of the heavy machine-gun was so hot that it crackled like a horseshoe fresh from the blacksmith's forge.

'Come on!' Sean abandoned it and jumped onto the rear parapet, ready to follow his Shanganes deeper into the laager and to begin wrecking the Russian service installations.

As he stood poised on the parapet, backlit by the burning fuel tankers, a monstrous apparition appeared in the dawn sky ahead of him. Rising on its glittering rotor, turbos shrieking, a Hind gunship lifted out of its sandbagged emplacement not two hundred metres from where Sean stood. It looked like some prehistoric behemoth. Supernatural and other-worldly, it rotated ponderously until the mirrored eyes of the canopy stared at Sean and the multiple cannon barrel in the turret below its nose pointed at him like an accuser's finger.

Sean reached down and seized Matatu by the scruff of his neck and hurled him to the floor of the emplacement, and then threw himself full length on top of him, knocking the breath out of the little man just as a gale of cannon fire dissolved the parapet wall and turned it to clouds of driving dust and gravel.

* * *

The suddenness of it all was what shocked Claudia most. One moment the stillness and tranquil darkness of dawn and the next the glare and cacophony of battle, the sky lit by the brilliance of leaping flame and glittering floods of tracers, her ears pounded by bursting mortars, shells and grenades and the blasts of machine-gun fire.

It took long moments for her eyes to adjust to the intensity of light, and to orientate herself to the swift kaleidoscope of the battle. Job had pointed out to her the point on the perimeter of the laager through which Sean would lead the assault and she searched it anxiously. The tiny figures of running men on the exposed slope of the hill were lit by the flames of burning Avgas which cast dark spiderlike shadows that scampered ahead of each man. There were so many of them, little black ants scurrying about, and with a jolt of horror she watched some of them fall and lie very still in the confusion of movement and light and sound.

'Where is Sean?' she whispered anxiously. 'Can you see him?'

'On the left, at the edge of the smoke.' Job told her, and she picked him out by the tiny figure that ran ahead of him like a hunting dog.

'I see him, and Matatu.'

Just in front of the pair the earth seemed suddenly to bloom with dust and flame, and they were gone.

'Oh God. No!' she cried aloud, but as the dust blew aside on the morning breeze, she saw the two of them running on, tracer bullets flickering about them like hellish fireflies.

'Please, please protect him.' she breathed, and lost sight of him as he reached the first emplacement.

'Where is he?' She found that she had seized Job's arm and was shaking it wildly. 'Where is he, can you see him?'

Then suddenly Sean was there again, even at that distance he appeared an heroic figure balancing easily on the sandbagged parapet in the ruddy glow of the flames, and she cried aloud with relief.

Then she saw him cower and from out of the very earth, only a short distance ahead of him, the monstrous shape of a Hind gunship reared into the air and swung its monstrous head towards him, lowering it like a charging bull. She heard the roar of its cannon, and leaping fountains of dust and flying earth obscured Sean's distant figure as cannon shell raked across the hillside.

'Job!' she screamed. 'They have killed him!' She reached out for him again, but Job shook off her hand.

He was down on one knee, the launch tube of the Stinger across his right shoulder, his face in the reflected firelight fixed in a mask of concentration as he stared into the sight screen.

'Quickly!' Claudia whispered. 'Shoot quickly!'

The missile leapt from its long tube, and hot air and stinging particles of dust and dead grass were blown back into Claudia's face as the rocket motor ignited. She slitted her eyes and held her breath as she watched it dart away on its tail of smoke and flame leaving a trail of dazzling smoke behind it as it flew towards the crest of the hill where the Hind hovered against the dark sky.

She saw the slight kick in its trajectory, as the missile changed to the ultra-violet seeker, and lifted its nose fractionally, no longer aiming at the armoured exhaust ports but at the open mouth of the turbo intakes just below the humped gearbox of the rotor.

She thought she saw the missile actually fly squarely into the intake, but the resulting explosion was deceptively mild, contained within the shell of titanium armour plate, so that none of its fury was dissipated. The Hind reeled wildly to the shot, throwing its nose high, falling backwards so that its tail rotor caught the rocky hillside and flipped it over sideways. It tumbled and bounced down the slope, rolling end over end, flames billowing from the throat of the air intake, its huge main rotor thrashing the earth and tearing itself to pieces, fragments hurtling into the night sky.

Claudia sought desperately for Sean, and gasped as she recognized him through the dust and the smoke, leaping back on to the parapet and then plunging on up the hillside with Matatu close behind him.

'Reload!' Job snapped at her, and with a guilty start she reached for the spare missile tube beside her and helped him clip it into the launcher.

The moment the Stinger was reloaded she glanced back at the laager. Sean was gone, but three more of the Hind gunships were airborne, soaring across the dawn, backlit by the flames. They were firing their cannon, some of them seeking targets within the laager where the attackers were in desperate hand-to-hand combat with the Frelimo garrison, others flailing the dark forest beyond the perimeter with their gales of tracer, trying to extinguish the hail of missiles that flew at them from out of the darkness.

Another Hind was hit and fell on its back, bursting into violent flame as it crashed into the rocky crest of the hill, and then another staggered in flight and curved down, mortally wounded, to hit the tree-tops and cartwheel through them to the earth.

As fast as they fell, others rose from their hidden emplacements with cannons blazing, sweeping down upon the attackers. Job leapt to his feet as a gunship tried to break away, climbing steeply up over their heads. He arched his back, pointing the missile almost vertically upwards, like a gun taking on a high-driven pheasant.

The Hind was a thousand feet up, climbing away, seeming to be safely beyond the Stinger's effective range, presenting a difficult angle and impossible trajectory, but the missile darted up, overhauling it effortlessly, and the great machine seemed to wince and tremble to the shot, standing for a moment stationary in the air, before it fell back with its damaged turbos screaming in mortal agony and dived into the valley, striking in a storm of breaking branches and torn tree-trunks.

'Reload.' Job did not even watch the Hind's death agony, and Claudia leaped to help him fit another missile tube to the launcher. She tapped his shoulder as she finished.

'Go!' she said.

Another Hind came out of the forest directly in front of them. The Russian pilot was flying so low that he seemed to be earthbound. He was dodging and ducking the huge machine behind the scattered trees, weaving like a boxer, the down-draught of the rotor flattening the tall elephant grass only a few feet below the Hind's belly.

Job turned to face the oncoming machine, standing out in the open, lit by the flames, and he braced himself, picking up the image of the Hind in the sight screen.

The Hind seemed to steady itself for an instant, and the blast of its Gatling-cannon swept around them like a hurricane wind. Standing beside Job, Claudia was blown off her feet by the force of it, and her ears buzzed with the supersonic shock of passing cannon shells.

Job was thrown on top of her, his weight driving the wind from her lungs, but they had fallen between two round boulders which deflected the rest of the volley of cannon fire, and the Hind passed over them, only feet above where they lay. The blast of its rotors slashed at them, whipping Claudia's hair into her face so that it stung her eyes like a scourge.

Then the Hind slid away like a cruising tiger shark, and Claudia was suffocating by Job's weight on top of her and half-blinded with dust and her own hair. She struggled to free herself and was suddenly aware that her hands were wet, and that hot liquid was spilling over her and soaking her shirt.

'Job!' she blurted. 'Get up! Get off me!' Only when he neither replied nor moved, but lay on her with a heavy loose weight, did she realize that the wetness that was dousing her was Job's blood. That knowledge gave her wild strength and she rolled his body aside, and dragged herself out from under him.

She crawled to her knees and looked down at him. A cannon shell had hit him high in the upper body, and the damage was horrific. It looked as though he had been savaged and mauled by some ferocious beast; his right arm was almost torn from the shoulder and was thrown above his head in a ghastly parody of surrender.

She stared at him numbly and tried to say his name. No sound came from her throat. She reached out and caressed his face, not daring to touch that terribly mutilated body. She felt a terrible sense of loss and opened her mouth again to give vent to her grief with a wail of despair. It came out in a wild shriek of rage. The force of her rage stunned her, and seemed to impel her out of her own body so that she watched herself from afar, amazed by the actions of this savage stranger who had usurped her body and who now lunged for the missile-launcher where it lay beside Job's body.

Then she found herself on her feet with the missile-launcher on her right shoulder, searching the sky for the Hind gunship. It was four hundred metres away, cruising the foot of the hill, sweeping over the forest, picking out its targets from amongst the trees and destroying them with short but terrible blasts of its forward cannon.

As she turned to face it, standing fully upright in the daylight glare of the fires, the pilot must have spotted her, for he swivelled the gunship on its own axis, bringing the cannon in the pod below his cockpit to bear upon her.

'Locked and loaded.' she said, and the voice was strange in her ears as she repeated the litany of death.

'Actuator on.' She saw the image of the Hind appear in the tiny screen before her eyes, and she centred it in the cross hair on the aiming ring and the missile sobbed and then steadied into its high-pitched electronic tone.

'Target acquired.' she whispered, and felt no fear as the silhouette of the Hind altered in her sight screen. Now it was facing her head-on, its cannon almost bearing, the gunner traversing fractionally to pick up her tiny figure in his own sights.

'Fire!' she said quietly, and squeezed the pistol grip. The shoulder pad jolted her as the Stinger launched, and she slitted her eyes against the back blast of the missile as it sped away at four times the speed of sound, running straight and true at the hovering machine.

The cannon in the Hind's nose blazed, but Claudia felt only the disrupted air of shot passing close over her head before the missile jerked almost imperceptibly and arrowed unerringly into the open throat of the machine's turbo intakes. The Hind had only a few feet to drop before it hit the earth and rolled over on to its side. In the moments before it was totally engulfed by burning fuel from the punctured belly tank, Claudia saw the panicky contortions of the pilot trapped under the armoured canopy and then even that was obliterated in a wall of flame.

'That was a human being,' she thought. 'A living and breathing person, and I destroyed him.' She expected a rush of guilt and remorse. How much a part of her was the belief that all life, especially human life, was sacred. The guilt did not come, instead she was borne aloft on a wave of savage triumph, the same berserk fury that had overtaken her so unexpectedly.

She looked around her swiftly, searching the sky for another target, something else to destroy, anything on which to wreak her vengeance. The dawn sky was empty. The burning carcasses of the Hind gunships lay strewn upon the slopes of the hill and amongst the trees of the valley forest.

'They are all down,' she thought. 'We got them all.'

From the forest, the Shanganes of the Stinger sections were swarming up the hill, breaking into the laager to support Sean's assault. She saw the Frelimo defenders throwing down their weapons, and cowering in their dugouts with hands raised pathetically, attempting to surrender, and watched dispassionately as the yelling Shanganes bayoneted and clubbed them like slaughtered chickens.

At her feet Job groaned, and instantly her rage was gone. She flung the empty missile-launcher aside and dropped down on her knees beside him.

'I thought you were dead!' she whispered, as she unwound the scarf from around her own neck with fingers which only now began to tremble. 'Don't die, Job. Please don't die.' The scarf was stained with sweat and dust, and its seams were unravelled and torn but she balled it up and stuffed it into the terrible wound, pressing down on it with her full weight to try and staunch the flood of his life's blood.

'Sean will be here soon,' she told him. 'Don't die, Job. Fight, please fight. I'll help you.'

* * *

Sean and Matatu crouched below the parapet, ducking lower as the storm of cannon fire flew only inches over their heads and filled their eyes and nostrils with dust from the ripped sandbags.

The instant the firing ceased, Sean bobbed up, just in time to see the stricken Hind fall tail-first against the rocky hillside and tear itself to pieces as it rolled down the slope.

'Well, blow me down, those damned Stingers actually work!' he laughed, still flying high on his own fear, and beside him Matatu giggled and clapped his hands.

'Like shooting sand grouse with the .577 *banduki*!' he cried in Swahili, and then leapt to his feet to follow Sean over the parapet.

Three Frelimo troopers bolted out of their dugout as they saw them coming and Sean fired the AKM from the hip, a short tap that caught one of them low in the back and flung him face down. The other two threw down their rifles and fell to their knees, gibbering with terror, hands held high over their heads. Sean ran on past them and they collapsed with relief as he ignored them.

Sean was through the outer defences and into the laager proper with its service areas and hardened helicopter emplacements. The workshops and fuel dumps were heavily sandbagged and covered with camouflage netting. Stray mortar shells were still falling amongst them, kicking up geysers of dust and gusts of whistling shrapnel. One of the Hinds had fallen near the far perimeter of the laager and was burning fiercely, oily black smoke billowing back over the workshops.

In the confusion, human figures scurried about without apparent purpose, unarmed technicians in baggy grey overalls who flung up their arms when they saw Sean, most of them dropping onto their knees to emphasize their surrender. In full camouflage paint and with the blood lust and elation of battle contorting his features, Sean cut a ferocious and terrifying figure.

'Down!' Sean gestured at them with the barrel of the AKM and with transparent relief they fell face down in the dust and clasped their hands behind their heads.

Just ahead he made out the long drooping rotors of a Hind protruding above the sandbagged wall of its emplacement.

'One didn't even get up,' he thought as he raced towards it, and at that moment the rotors began to revolve slowly, building up speed swiftly. Somebody was attempting to start the machine.

Sean darted through the narrow entrance, and into the deep circular emplacement. He checked his charge for a moment to survey the interior.

The Hind in its blotched camouflage towered over him, its

rotors whirling over his head as they built up to start speed on the Isotov turbo engine. Three Russian ground crew were crowded around the front of the machine, and incongruously Sean noticed the crimson arrow emblem painted on the Hind's nose which designated them an 'Excellent Crew'. One of the cherished performance awards of the Soviet air force.

The ground crew turned their white faces towards Sean and gaped at him. He jerked the muzzle of the AKM at them and they fell back.

The canopy of the weapons cockpit of the helicopter was still open, and one of the flight crew was clambering up into it. Only his plump backside in grey flying overalls protruded. Sean reached up between his legs and seized a handful of the man's genitals. The Russian squealed shrilly as Sean used them as a handle to drag him backwards and threw him against the sand-bagged side wall of the emplacement.

The spinning rotors whistled shrilly as the turbo engine caught, and Sean jumped up onto the boarding step of the helicopter. The pilot's canopy was also open, and Sean thrust his AKM forward.

The pilot at the controls was young and thin with pale blond hair cut very short. In his haste to get the Hind away he had not even donned his flying helmet. He turned his head to look at Sean. His complexion was marred by angry purple and red acne and his eyes were very pale blue. They widened dramatically as Sean touched the tip of his acne-scarred nose with the muzzle of the AKM and said, 'Party is over, Ivan. Let's go home.'

It was apparent that this helicopter had not been scheduled for the dawn sortie that morning and the pilot and his crew had only begun their attempt to get the machine airborne once the attack had begun. It was less than ten minutes since the first mortar shells had fallen into the laager, not sufficient time, although they had almost made it.

'Kill the engine,' Sean told the pilot, and enforced the order by jamming the muzzle of the AKM into his nose with sufficient force to bring a smear of blood from one nostril and tears from both his pale eyes.

Reluctantly the pilot pushed the fuel mixture control to fully lean and cut both master switches. The whistle of the turbo died away.

'Out!' said Sean, and the pilot understood the gesture and

tone, if not the word. He unclasped his safety-belt and climbed down into the laager.

Sean lined up the pilot, the flight engineer and the three members of the ground crew against the sandbagged wall.

'Welcome to the capitalist world, comrades,' he greeted them, and then looked back at the helicopter.

'Jackpot!' he grinned, still euphoric with the adrenalin in his blood. 'We've got ourselves a real live, working Hind, Matatu!'

Matatu was having a grand time. 'Let's kill them now,' he suggested merrily. 'Give me the *banduki*. Let me shoot them for you.'

Sean had only seen Matatu fire one shot in his entire life, when as a joke Sean had let him fire the double .577. It had lifted Matatu clear off his feet and deposited him ten feet away.

'You couldn't hit one of them, even at this range, you blood-thirsty little bugger.' Sean grinned down at him, and then once more concentrated all his attention on the Hind. The magnitude of the prize he had taken began to dawn upon him.

The Hind would be a magnificent escape vehicle. He and Claudia, Job and Matatu could get out of here with first-class tickets, and then with a drop of spirits, reality overtook him.

Sean had never flown a helicopter, did not even have the vaguest notion of how to do so. All he knew was that it required a delicate and expert touch on the controls and was entirely different from piloting a fixed-wing aircraft.

He looked back at the Russian pilot calculatingly. Despite the acne and his unprepossessing appearance, he thought he detected a stubborn and proud streak in the man's pale eyes and he knew that the air-force officers were amongst the elite of the Soviet armed forces. The Russian was almost certainly a fanatical patriot.

'Not much chance of getting you to act as ferry pilot,' he guessed, and then spoke aloud. 'All right, gentlemen, let's get out of here.' He indicated the exit from the emplacement, and under the barrel of the AKM, they trooped towards it obediently. As the Russian pilot passed, Sean stopped him and lifted the Tokarev pistol from the holster at his hip.

'You won't need that, Ivan,' he said, and tucked the pistol into his own belt.

There was a fortified workshop almost abutting the Hind's emplacement. It had been excavated into the hillside and roofed

400

with poles and sandbags. Sean herded the Russians down into it and then looked around him.

The battle had fizzled out, although there were still a few desultory shots and the pop and bang of burning ammunition. Through the drifts of smoke and dust, he saw the Shanganes of the Renamo force rounding up the prisoners and searching for loot and booty. He recognized some of the missile crews. Once the Hinds had been destroyed, they must have abandoned their Stingers and rushed up the hill to join the sack of the laager.

He saw one of them bayoneting a Frelimo prisoner in the buttocks and legs and roaring with laughter as the man squirmed in the dirt, kicking and contorting his body in an attempt to avoid the point of the blade. Other Renamo were emerging from the dugouts, rifles slung over their shoulders and arms full of booty.

Sean was accustomed to the ethics of irregular troops in Africa, but still this blatant indiscipline annoyed him. He snarled at them, and it was a measure of the force of his personality and the authority that he wielded over them that even in the heady moments of victory, they obeyed him with alacrity. The Renamo who had been torturing his prisoner paused only to dispatch the maimed victim with a bullet in the back of the neck before hurrying to Sean's bidding.

'Guard these white prisoners,' Sean ordered them. 'If harm comes to them, General China will roast your testicles on a slow fire and make you eat them,' he warned.

Without looking back, he strode through the laager, reasserting his command, getting his triumphant howling shrieking Shanganes back to sanity. He saw Sergeant Alphonso ahead of him.

'We can't carry much loot away, let the men take their pick and then I want limpet mines in the store rooms after everything has been drenched with Avgas from the drums,' he ordered Sergeant Alphonso. Sean glanced at his wristwatch. 'We can expect Frelimo to counter-attack the laager within the hour. I want to be gone by then.'

'No!' Alphonso shook his head. 'General China has moved three companies in between us to hold the Frelimo counter-attack. He has ordered you to hold this position until he arrives.'

Sean pulled up short and stared at Alphonso. 'What the hell are you talking about? China is two days' march away on the river!'

Alphonso grinned and shook his head. 'General China will be here in an hour. He followed us with five companies of his best troops. He has never been more than an hour behind us, not since we left the river.'

'How do you know this?' Sean demanded, and Alphonso grinned again and patted the radio on the back of the trooper who stood beside him.

'I spoke to the general ten minutes ago, as soon as we killed the last of the Russian *henshaw*.'

'Why didn't you tell me before this, you bastard?' Sean growled.

'The general ordered me not to. But now he has ordered me to tell you that he is very pleased with the killing of the *henshaw*, and he says that you are like a son to him. When he arrives he will reward you.'

'All right.' Sean changed his orders. 'If we have to hold the laager, get your men into the perimeter defences, we will use the 12.7mm heavy machine-guns.'

Sean broke off as a Shangane trooper came running up the hill towards him.

'*Nkosi!*' The man panted, and as soon as he saw his face, Sean knew it was bad news.

'The woman?' he demanded, seizing the messenger's arm. 'Is the white woman hurt?'

The Shangane shook his head. 'She is safe. She sent me to you. It's the Matabele. Captain Job. He is hit.'

'How bad?' Sean was already starting to run and he shouted the question over his shoulder.

'He's dying,' the Shangane called after him. 'The Matabele is dying.'

Sean knew where to look, he had himself selected the copse of knob-thorn acacia as Job's attack position. The first rays of the morning sun were turning the tops of the knob-thorns to gold as Sean ran down the hill. With the help of two Shanganes, Claudia had moved Job onto level soft ground beneath one of the trees. She had propped his head on one of the back-packs and had a field dressing over the wound.

She looked up and cried, 'Oh, Sean, thank God!' Her shirt was drenched with drying blood and she saw Sean's expression. 'Not my blood,' she assured him. 'I'm all right.'

Sean transferred all his attention to Job. His face was a sickly blue-grey colour and the flesh seemed to have melted like hot tar from his skull.

Sean touched his cheek and his skin was cold as death. Frantically he searched for a pulse in the wrist of Job's good arm and although it was faint and rapid, Sean's relief was intense.

'He's lost huge quantities of blood,' Claudia whispered. 'But, I have contained the bleeding now.'

'He's in shock,' Sean muttered. 'Let me have a look.'

'Don't lift that dressing,' Claudia warned him quickly. 'It's ghastly. He was hit on the point of the shoulder by a cannon shell. It's just mangled flesh and bone chips. His arm is hanging by a shred of muscle and sinew.'

'Take Matatu with you,' Sean cut in brusquely. 'Go up to the laager. Find where they had their first-aid post. The Russians will have a decent stock. Find it. I want plasma and a drip set. Dressings and bandages, those are the most urgent. But if you can find antiseptic and pain-killers . . .'

Claudia scrambled to her feet. 'Sean, I was so worried about you! I saw . . .'

'You don't get rid of me that easy.' He did not look up from Job's face. 'Now, off you go, and get back here as quick as you can. Matatu, go with Donna, look after her.'

The two of them went at a run. Until they returned with medical supplies, Sean was helpless. But for something to keep himself occupied he wet his bandanna from the water-bottle and began to sponge the blood and dirt from Job's face. Job's eyelids fluttered open and Sean saw that he was conscious.

'Okay, Job. I'm here. Don't try and talk.'

Job closed his eyes for a moment and when he opened them again, he swivelled them downwards, too weak to move his head, yet he was trying to look down at his body, trying to check the extent of his injuries. It was always the first reaction.

'Is it lung blood I'm losing? Are both my feet still here, both my hands. . . ?'

'Right arm and shoulder,' Sean told him. '12.7mm cannon nicked you. Just a little bitty scratch. You are going to make it, lad, written guarantee. Would I lie to you?'

A faint smile tugged up the corners of Job's mouth and he lowered one eyelid in a conspiratorial wink. Sean felt his heart begin to break. He knew he had lied. Job wasn't going to make it.

'Relax,' he ordered cheerfully. 'Lie back and enjoy it, as the bishop said to the actress. I'm in charge here now.'

And Job closed his eyes.

* * *

Claudia picked out the medical dugout by the red cross insignia at the entrance. There were two Shangane Renamo looting the interior, ransacking it for booty, but Claudia shrieked at them so violently that they slunk away guiltily.

The labels on the cartons of medical supplies were all in Russian Cyrillic script. Claudia had to rip the lids open and check the contents of each. She found boxes which contained a dozen plastic bags of clear plasma each, and gave two of them to Matatu. The drip sets were on the shelf below. Field dressings and bandages were easy, but she was flummoxed by the tubes of ointments and pill bottles. However, the contents of one tube were yellow brown and had the characteristic iodine aroma; she selected those and then she found that some of the labels had alternative notations in French and Arabic. She had a smattering of both languages, enough to identify which were antibiotics and pain-killers.

She found two field packs, obviously prepared for use by the Russian first-aid teams and included these in her selection; then she and Matatu, heavily laden, hurried out of the first-aid post.

Before she reached the perimeter of the laager again, a dreadfully familiar figure loomed out of the banks of drifting smoke ahead of her. This was the very last person she had expected to see here.

'Miss Monterro,' General China called. 'What a fortunate encounter. I need your assistance.' China was accompanied by half a dozen officers of his staff.

Claudia recovered swiftly from the shock of the unexpected meeting. 'I'm busy,' she snapped, trying to step around him. 'Job is badly wounded. I have to get back to him.'

'My need is greater than anybody else's, I'm afraid.' China put out an arm.

'Forget it,' Claudia flared at him. 'Job needs this stuff, or he'll die.'

'One of my men will take it to him,' China replied. 'You are coming with me, please. Or I'll have you carried. Not very dignified, Miss Monterro.'

Claudia was still protesting as one of the Renamo officers relieved her of her load of medical supplies, but at last she shrugged with resignation.

'Go with him, Matatu.' She pointed down the hill. The little man nodded brightly and Claudia allowed China to escort her back into the laager.

They picked their way through the shambles of the battle, and Claudia shuddered as she stepped over the charred corpse of one of the Frelimo garrison.

'Colonel Courtney's attack has succeeded beyond even my wildest expectations.' General China was affable and clearly delighted with what he saw around him. 'He even managed to capture a Hind gunship completely intact, together with the Russian air crew and ground crew.'

'I hope you won't keep me long. I have to get back.'

'Captain Job will live or die without you, Miss Monterro. I need your services as a translator in talking to the pilot. '

'I don't speak Russian,' Claudia told him flatly.

'Fortunately the pilot seems to speak Italian, how he learned the language I cannot guess, but he keeps repeating, "*Italiano, Italiano*".' China took her arm and led her down the steps of the sandbagged and camouflaged dugout.

Claudia glanced round the dugout and saw instantly that it was an engineering workshop. A long work-bench ran down each wall. Set up on one of these were a metal lathe and drill press. A wide selection of hand tools was racked in cupboards above the benches and she recognized the electric and gas welding sets at the far end of the workshop. Her father had had his own workshop in the cellar of their home in Anchorage and she had spent so many evenings watching him pottering around down there.

The Russian prisoners, five of them, were at the far end of the underground room.

'Which one of you speaks Italian?' she asked.

A tall thin man stepped forward. He wore grey flying overalls and his face was scarred with acne. His pale blue eyes were shifty and nervous.

'I do, *Signora*.'

'Where did you learn?' Claudia asked.

405

'My wife is a graduate student from Milano. I met her while she was doing her doctorate at Patrice Lumumba University in Moscow.' His Italian was heavily accented and his grammar uncertain, but she understood him without difficulty.

'I am translating for General China,' she told him, 'but I must warn you that he is a savage and cruel man. I am neither his ally nor his friend. I cannot protect you.'

'Thank you, *Signora*. I understand, but I do not need protection. I am a prisoner-of-war under the Convention of Geneva. I have certain rights. So do my men.'

'What does he say?' China demanded.

'He says he is a prisoner-of-war, and he and his men are protected by the Geneva Convention.'

'Tell him that Geneva is far away. This is Africa and I was no signatory to any agreement in Switzerland. Here he has only such rights as I decide he should have. Tell him he will fly the helicopter under my command and that his ground crew will service and maintain the machine in flying condition.'

As Claudia translated, she watched the pilot's jaw set and his pale blue eyes harden. He turned his head slightly and spoke to his men in Russian. Immediately they began to mutter and shake their heads.

'Tell this black monkey that we insist on our rights,' the pilot spoke scornfully. Claudia had heard that many Russians were racists, and the derogatory term the pilot used suggested that for him at least this was true. 'We refuse to fly or fight for him. That would be a traitorous act.'

His refusal was so obvious, that China did not wait for Claudia's translation.

'Tell him,' he cut in brusquely, 'that I have no time for argument, or for subtle persuasion. I ask once more for his co-operation and if he refuses, I will be forced to demonstrate my serious intentions.'

'*Signore*, this man is very dangerous,' Claudia told the Russian officer. 'I have seen him commit the most unspeakable atrocities. I have suffered torture by him, myself.'

'I am a Russian officer and a prisoner-of-war.' The pilot drew himself to attention, his tone stern. 'I know my duty.'

China was watching his face as the pilot replied. He smiled coldly as Claudia translated. 'Another brave man,' he murmured. 'We must now determine just how brave he is.'

Without looking at his staff officers, he gave them a quiet order in Shangane and while they trundled forward the chariot that held the oxyacetylene gas cylinders. China smiled steadily at the Russian officer. The man returned his regard with a cold pale stare as they matched wills.

China was the one who turned away. He went to the workbench and swiftly examined the tools and objects scattered upon it. He gave a grunt of approval as he selected a thin steel rod and weighed it in his hand. It was the length and thickness of a rifle ramrod pierced at each end for a connecting screw, probably a control link from the Hind helicopter.

'This will do very nicely,' he spoke aloud, and then picked up a discarded woven asbestos welding glove. He pulled it onto his right hand, and then turned his attention to the gas welding set. Claudia, who had watched her father work, realized that China was well versed in the use of the apparatus. He lit the welding flame on the torch and swiftly adjusted the flow of oxygen and acetylene from their separate cylinders until the flame was a brilliant blue feather, hot and unwavering. Then he took up the metal rod in his gloved hand and began to heat the tip of it in the blue flame.

All the Russians watched him uneasily. Claudia saw the pilot's hard stare flicker uncertainly, as the shine of nervous sweat dewed on his upper lip.

'This man is an animal,' Claudia said softly in Italian. 'You must believe me when I tell you he is capable of the vilest acts. Please, *Signore*, I do not want to watch this.'

The pilot shook his head, dismissing her appeal, but he was staring at the tip of the metal rod as it began to glow cherry red.

'I will not be intimidated by brutish threats,' he said, but she detected the slightest catch and crack in his voice.

In China's gloved hand, the tip of the rod turned slowly to incandescent crimson and then to translucent white heat. China smiled and turned off the flame of the welding torch. He weaved the glowing tip of the rod in a gentle flourish, like a conductor's baton, and smiled at the pilot. It was the humourless reptilian smile of a cobra.

'I repeat my request. Ask him if he will fly for me.'

'*Nyet*.' Even though his voice cracked, the pilot's reply was decisive, and then he added in Russian, '*Obezyana*, black monkey!'

China stood in front of him and made a slow pass with the tip of the rod a few inches in front of the Russian's eyes.

'Tell him, *Signora*,' the pilot whispered, 'that without my eyes, I cannot fly.'

'Very true,' China nodded as Claudia translated, and he left the pilot and walked on down the line of white prisoners, waving the glowing tip of the rod in a slow mesmeric gesture in each of their faces, studying their reactions carefully. The plump mechanic in oil-stained overalls at the end of the line gave China his most satisfying response. He shrank away from the rod until the wall of the dugout stopped him, and sweat ran down his fat rosy cheeks and dripped from the end of his chin. In a squeaky voice, he said something in Russian, and the pilot answered him with a sharp monosyllabic order.

'You don't like it, do you? My fat little white slug.' China smiled thinly at him and let him feel the radiated heat on his cheek. The back of the flight engineer's head was pressed against the wall, and he swivelled his eyes in their sockets to watch the rod.

The metal was cooling and with a small frown of annoyance, China left him and turned back to the work-bench and relit the welding torch. While he carefully reheated the tip of the rod, the mechanic sagged against the sandbags. He was sweating in dark patches through the cotton of his greasy overalls.

The pilot spoke softly to him in an encouraging tone, and the engineer nodded and straightened up. He glanced at his superior with an expression of patent gratitude and watching this brief exchange between the two men, China smiled again, this time with satisfaction.

When Claudia saw that smile, she realized suddenly that China had just run a selection test. He had chosen his victim. The mechanic was the least courageous of the five Russians, and the pilot had inadvertently disclosed his concern and friendship for the man.

'Please,' she whispered in Italian. 'Your friend is in terrible danger. You must do what this man asks if you wish to save him.'

The pilot looked at her, and from his expression Claudia saw he was beginning to waver.

'Please, for my sake. I cannot bear to watch.' But with despair, she saw the Russian's expression change as his resolve firmed once again. He shook his head and China saw that gesture.

He switched off the welding torch and blew softly on the white tip of the metal rod. He let the moment draw out agonizingly; every eye in the bunker was fixed on the point of glowing steel.

Then abruptly he gave an order in Portuguese and two of his men sprang forward and seized the mechanic by his arms. He gave a little squeal of protest, but they hustled him to the work-bench and threw him face down across its top. One of them jumped up and sat between his shoulder-blades pinning him down. He struggled ineffectually, kicking his legs. Swiftly and expertly, they strapped his ankles to the legs of the work-bench, and he lay helplessly sprawled face downwards with his backside sticking up in the air, stretching the cotton seat of his overalls.

The Russian pilot shouted a protest and stepped forward but one of the Renamo officers thrust a pistol into his belly and forced him back against the wall.

'I ask you again,' China told him. 'Will you fly for me?'

The pilot shouted at him in Russian. It was clearly an insult. His face was flushed now, the acne purple and shiny as buttons on his chin and cheeks.

China nodded at his men. One of them drew the trench knife from its sheath on his webbing belt and slit the waistband of the mechanic's overalls. Then he seized the severed edges of cotton and ripped them downwards, tearing the cloth loose so it hung in tatters around the pinioned man's knees. Under the overalls, the engineer wore a pair of elasticized blue underpants. The Renamo pulled these down as far as they would go.

Claudia stared in fascinated horror at the mechanic's exposed buttocks. They were very white and fat and round, covered with a scraggle of dark curly ginger hair. From between his thighs, his wrinkled hairy scrotum protruded backwards like that of a dog.

The pilot was shouting in Russian and Claudia found herself pleading weakly.

'Please, General China, please let me leave, I cannot bear this.' She tried to turn her head away and cover her eyes, but the dreadful fascination of it compelled her to watch through her fingers despite herself.

China ignored both the pilot's and Claudia's pleas, and spoke crisply to the officer who sat between the Russian's shoulder-blades. Still pinning him to the bench, the Renamo reached over and seized one of his buttocks in each of his hands and drew them sharply apart. Claudia's protests dried in her throat and she found herself staring dry-mouthed at the Russian's puckered rosey-brown anus as it nestled like a blind man's eye between his hairy cheeks.

China reached out towards it with the tip of the rod, then stopped three inches short of it. The mechanic felt the heat of it on his most intimate flesh, and began to struggle so violently that two more of the Renamo officers had to throw their combined weight on to his back to keep him pinned down.

'Yes?' China looked across at the Russian pilot. He was raving like a madman, his face contorted with outrage, shouting threats and accusations.

'I regret the necessity,' China said, and thrust the metal rod forward, his wrist cocked like that of a fencing master going on attack, a *flèche*.

As the glowing metal touched the sensitive skin the Russian screamed, a shattering high-pitched shriek that made Claudia cry out pitifully in sympathy.

The metal smoked and sizzled and spluttered, as China rotated his wrist, twisting the rod deeper and deeper into the Russian's body. Now his screams were great explosive gusts of sound, and Claudia clapped her hands over her ears to shut them out and turned away, running into the corner of the dugout and pressing her face against the rough sandbags.

The smoke filled her nostrils, her throat and her lungs, the obscene odour of burning flesh, of charring fat, coated her tongue and her gorge rose. She tried to contain it, but her vomit shot up her throat and in a projectile stream splashed onto the earthen floor between her feet.

Behind her the screams dropped gradually in volume, and became ghastly rattling groans. However, all the Russians were yelling their protest and fury, and the din was confusing.

Another whiff of burned flesh and spilled faeces made her retch again and then she wiped her mouth with the back of her hand and leaned her forehead against the sandbagged wall. She was trembling wildly, and tears and sweat streamed down her cheeks.

Slowly the uproar behind her subsided, and the only sounds in the bunker were the mechanic's groans and gurgles. They were weaker now but nonetheless harrowing. Claudia could tell without looking at him that the Russian was dying.

410

'Miss Monterro.' China's voice was level and calm. 'Please get a grip on yourself, we still have work to do.'

'You are an animal!' she blurted. 'I hate you! Oh God, how I hate you!'

'Your feelings are not of the slightest interest to me,' China said. 'Now you will tell the pilot that I await his full co-operation.'

The flight engineer's groans distracted her. As she turned to face China, she saw that they had released the stricken man and allowed him to slump to the floor. China had made no effort to withdraw the metal rod from his body, and he was still transfixed. As he rolled weakly about on the earthen floor, he was plucking ineffectually at the protruding end of the rod. The heated metal had adhered to his bowels as it cooled, and was firmly rooted in his flesh. Every time he tugged at it a trickle of liquid faeces bubbled from the terrible wound.

'Speak to the pilot,' China commanded.

Claudia dragged her eyes from the dying man and addressed the pilot. 'Please do what he wants.'

'I cannot, my duty!' the pilot cried.

'The devil with your duty!' Claudia shouted back furiously. 'You and all your men will end up like this!' She gestured to the floor without looking down again. 'That's what will happen to you!' She turned to the other Russians who were shaken and appalled, pale with horror and terror.

'Look at him!' she screamed in English. 'Is that what you want?'

They did not understand the words but her meaning was clear to all of them. They turned their faces towards the pilot.

The pilot resisted their entreaties for a minute, and then at a word from China the Renamo officers seized another one of the ground crew and threw him screaming and kicking face down, across the bench and the Russian pilot threw up both hands in a gesture of resignation.

'Tell him to stop,' he said wearily to Claudia. 'We will do as he orders.'

'Thank you, Miss Monterro.' China smiled at her charmingly. 'You are now free to rejoin Colonel Courtney.'

'How will you communicate with the pilot?' she asked uncertainly.

'Already he understands me.' China transferred the benevolence of his smile to the Russian. 'I assure you that he will learn

411

to speak my language with the utmost fluency in a very short time indeed.' He turned back to Claudia. 'Please convey my respects to Colonel Courtney and ask him to join me at his earliest convenience. I would like to take my leave of him, to thank him and wish him *bon voyage*.' He gave her a mocking bow. 'So God speed, Miss Monterro. I hope that you will remember all of us, your friends in Africa, with affection.'

Claudia could find no words to reply, she turned to the door of the bunker and her legs were shaky and rubbery beneath her.

In a daze of horror, she stumbled down the hill. The sights around her which at another time might have sickened and appalled her, she hardly noticed.

At the foot of the hill, she paused and tried to get a grip on herself. She breathed deeply, trying to quell the intermittent sobs that still caught her unawares and she combed her hair back from her face with her fingers and retied the strip of cloth she was using as a headband. With the tail of her shirt, she wiped the tears and sweat from her face, and was shocked at the grimy smear they left on the cloth.

'I must look like hell,' she whispered, and clenched her hands to hide her broken fingernails, but she braced her shoulders and lifted her chin. 'Sean mustn't see me like this,' she told herself fiercely. 'Pull yourself together, woman.'

Sean looked up as she hurried to where he was still working over Job's blanket-wrapped body.

'What happened?' he demanded. 'What kept you?'

'General China is here. He made me go with him.'

'What did he want? What happened?'

'Nothing, not important. I'll tell you about it later. How is Job?'

'I've got a full litre of plasma into him,' Sean replied. He had suspended the drip set from a branch above them. 'His pulse is better. Job is as tough as an old buffalo bull. Help me dress the wound.'

'Is he conscious?'

'He comes and goes,' Sean warned her.

Beneath the field dressing was such a terrible injury that neither of them could bring themselves to discuss it, especially as Job might be able to hear and understand them.

Sean smothered the entire area with iodine paste, and then bound it up again with pressure pads and clean white bandages from the medical pack. The blood and iodine soaked through the white even as he worked.

Between them they had to roll Job on to his side to pass the bandages over his back. Claudia held the half-severed arm in place, bending the elbow across his chest, and Sean strapped it securely. By the time they finished, Job's entire upper body was swathed in a cocoon of expertly applied bandage from which only his left arm protruded.

'His pulse is going again.' Sean looked up from his wrist. 'I'm going to give him another litre of plasma.'

There was a scattered outbreak of machine-gun and mortar fire from the forest beyond the hill laager, and Claudia looked up apprehensively. 'What's that?'

'Frelimo counter-attack.' Sean was still busy with the drip set. 'But China has three companies in there, and Frelimo are going to be less than enthusiastic now that they have lost their air support. China's lads should be able to hold them off with no trouble. '

'Sean, where did China come from? I thought . . .'

'Yes,' Sean cut in. 'I also thought he was back on the river. The crafty bastard was right on our heels, ready to rush in and grab the spoils.' He finished adjusting the plasma flow in the drip set, and squatted down beside Claudia, studying her face.

'All right,' he said. 'Tell me what happened.'

'Nothing.' She smiled brightly.

'Don't bullshit me, beautiful,' Sean said gently, and put an arm around her. Despite herself she choked on a sob.

'China,' she whispered. 'Right on top of what happened to Job. He made me translate for the Russian pilot. Oh God, I hate him. He's an animal. He made me watch . . .' she broke off.

'Rough stuff?' Sean asked, and she nodded.

'He killed one of the Russians, in the foulest possible way.'

'He's a lovely lad, our China, but try and put it out of your mind, we've got enough troubles of our own. Let the Ruskies worry about theirs.'

'He forced the Russian pilot to agree to fly the helicopter.'

Sean stood up, lifting her to her feet beside him. 'Don't think of China and the Russian any more. All we have to worry about is getting out of here.' He broke off as he saw Sergeant Alphonso and a half dozen of his Shanganes trotting down the hill towards them. All of them were laden with loot.

'*Nkosi!*' Alphonso's broad handsome face was wreathed in a beatific grin. 'What a fight, what a victory!'

'You fought like an impi of lions,' Sean agreed. 'The battle is won but now you must help us to get away to the border. Captain Job is badly hurt.'

Alphonso's smile faded: despite their natural tribal enmity, both men had developed a grudging respect for each other.

'How bad?' Alphonso came to stand beside Sean and looked down at Job.

'There was a fibreglass stretcher in the first-aid post,' Claudia said. 'We can carry Job on that.'

'It is two days' march to the border,' Alphonso murmured dubiously. 'Through Frelimo territory.'

'Frelimo are running like dogs with a hot coal under their tails.' Sean's tone was hard. 'Send two of your men to fetch the stretcher.'

'General China calls for you. He is leaving in the Russian *henshaw*. He wants to speak to you before he goes,' Alphonso said.

'All right, but I want that stretcher here when I get back,' Sean warned him, and glanced at his wristwatch. 'We will march for the border in one hour from now.'

'*Nkosi!*' Alphonso agreed cheerfully. 'We will be ready.' Sean turned back to Claudia.

'I'm going to see China. I'm going to try to talk him into flying Job out in the helicopter, but I don't think my chances are particularly rosy. Please stay with Job and keep an eye on his pulse rate. I've found a disposable syringe of adrenalin in the medic pack, use it only as a last resort.'

'Please don't be long,' she whispered. 'I'm only brave when you're here.'

'Matatu will stay with you.'

Sean climbed the hill swiftly, passing the first string of Renamo porters. Obviously China was taking everything he could carry away, including boxes of helicopter spares and hundreds of jerry cans of Avgas. The lines of porters were heading back into the wilderness towards the river, and Sean paid them scant attention. His role was played. He was eager to get out, reach the border, get Job to where he could receive professional medical attention and get Claudia to safety. However, over all his urgency lay the nagging uncertainty, was China really going to stand by his word,

414

and let them go? Was he not being just a trifle optimistic?

'We'll see,' he told himself grimly, and shouted at one of the Renamo officers who was supervising the loading of the porters. 'Where is General China?'

He found him with his staff and the captured Russians in the laager's command bunker, and China looked up from the map he was consulting and smiled affably as Sean entered.

'Colonel Courtney, my felicitations. You were magnificent. A famous victory.'

'And now you owe me a favour.'

'You and your party wish to leave,' China agreed. 'All debts between us have been paid in full. You are free to go.'

'No,' Sean shook his head. 'By my calculation, you still owe me one. Captain Job has been badly wounded. His condition is critical. I want him flown out to Zimbabwe in the captured Hind.'

'You jest, of course,' China laughed lightly. 'I cannot risk sending such a valuable asset on a non-productive mission. No, Colonel, all debts are paid, please don't persist in extravagant demands. With my defective hearing, it only annoys me and I may be tempted to review my generous offer to allow you and, yours to depart unhindered.' He smiled and held out his hand. 'Come now, Colonel. Let us part as friends. You have the services of Sergeant Alphonso and his men. You are a man of infinite resourcefulness. I am sure that you will contrive to get yourself and all your party to safety without any further assistance from me.'

Sean ignored the outstretched hand and China glanced at it and then lowered it to his side. 'So we part, Colonel. Me to my little war and, who knows, perhaps one day, a country of my very own. You to the tender embraces of your very rich, very beautiful young American.' His smile had a sly and foxy slant to it. 'I wish you joy and I am sure you do the same for me.' He turned back to his map, leaving Sean for an instant nonplussed and taken off balance. It was incomplete, it couldn't end like this. Sean knew there was more to come, but General China began dictating orders to one of his officers in Portuguese, leaving Sean standing uncertainly at the door of the bunker.

Sean waited a few moments longer, and then turned abruptly and ducked out through the entrance. Only after he was gone, China lifted his head and smiled after him, a gloating little smile which if Sean had seen it, would have answered his question.

* * *

Alphonso's men had worked quickly. The litter was a fibreglass stretcher, one of those lightweight body-moulded types used by mountain rescue teams. Nonetheless it would still require four men to carry it over rough ground, and they had a long hard path to the border.

'Less than a hundred kilometres and not that hard,' Sean reassured himself. 'Two days, if we push it.'

Claudia greeted him with relief. 'Job seems stronger. He was conscious, asking for you, he said something about a hill, Hill 31?'

Sean flickered a smile. 'That's where we met. He's wandering a little, help me to get him onto the stretcher.'

Between them they lifted Job gently and settled him onto the fibreglass stretcher. Sean rigged the drip set on a wire frame above his head, and tucked looted grey woollen blankets around him.

'Matatu,' he said as he stood up. 'Take us home.' And he gestured to the first team of stretcher-bearers to take their positions.

It was less than two hours since sunrise, but they seemed to have lived an entire lifetime in that short period, Sean thought as he glanced back at the hilltop laager. Streamers of smoke drifted from its crest and the last column of General China's porters was disappearing into the forest below it, all heavily laden with booty.

The distant sounds of battle had finally dwindled into silence. The half-hearted Frelimo counter-attack had long ago fizzled out, and China was withdrawing his forces into the bad ground below the Pungwe river.

As Sean watched, the captured Hind helicopter rose slowly out of its emplacement and hung above the hill on its glistening rotor; then abruptly it dipped towards them, the sound of its engine crescendoed and suddenly Sean was staring into the multiple mouths of the Gatling-cannon in its nose.

As it raced towards him, he recognized China's face behind the armoured glass canopy. He was perched in the flight engineer's seat, at the controls of the 12.7mm cannon. Sean saw the barrels of the cannon traverse slightly, coming on to aim. The Hind was only fifty feet above them, so close he could see China's teeth flash in his dark face as he smiled.

Their little column had not reached the edge of the forest. There was no cover, no protection from the blast of that terrible weapon, and instinctively Sean reached out and drew Claudia to him, trying to shield her with his own body.

Above them General China lifted his right hand in an ironic salute, and the Hind banked steeply away into the north-west, dwindled swiftly to a speck and was gone. They all stared after it silently, seized by a sense of anti-climax, until Sean broke the spell.

'Let's go, brethren!' And once again the stretcher-bearers started forward at an easy jog-trot, singing very softly one of the ancient marching songs.

Scouting ahead of them, Matatu came across a few scattered parties of Frelimo assault troops, but they were all in headlong retreat from the river wilderness. After the loss of their air support the Frelimo offensive seemed to have collapsed completely and the situation was fluid and confused. Although they were forced to detour further northwards than Sean had planned, Matatu steered them out of contact with any Frelimo and the stretcher-bearers were rotated regularly so they made swift progress.

At nightfall, they stopped to eat and rest. Alphonso made the scheduled radio contact with Renamo headquarters and gave them a position report. He received only a laconic acknowledgement without change of orders.

They feasted on tinned goods looted from the Russian stores, and smoked the perfumed Balkan tobacco in yellow cigarette paper with hollow cardboard filters.

Job was conscious again and complained in a husky whisper, 'There is a lion gnawing on my shoulder.'

Sean injected an ampoule of morphia into his drip set and it eased him, so that he was even able to eat a few mouthfuls of the bland-tasting tinned meat. However, his thirst was far greater than his hunger, and Sean held his head and helped him get down two full mugs of the surprisingly good Russian coffee.

Sean and Claudia sat beside the litter and waited for the moon to rise.

'We are going in through the Honde Valley again.' Sean told

Job. 'Once we get you to St Mary's Mission you'll be fine. One of the Catholic fathers is a doctor, and I'll be able to send a message to my brother, Garry, in Johannesburg. I'll ask him to send the company jet to Umtali. We'll fly you into Johannesburg General Hospital before you know what's hit you, mate. There you'll get the best medical attention in the world.'

When the moon rose they went on, and it was almost midnight before Sean called a halt for the night.

He made a mattress of cut grass beside Job's litter, and as Claudia drifted off to sleep in his arms, he whispered to her, 'Tomorrow night, I'll give you a hot bath and put you between clean sheets.'

'Promise?' she sighed.

'Cross my heart.'

From deeply ingrained habit, he woke an hour before first light and went to rouse the sentries for dawn stand-by.

Alphonso threw aside his blanket, stood up and fell in beside him. When they had made the sentry round, they paused on the edge of the camp and Alphonso offered him one of the Russian cigarettes. They smoked from cupped hands, shielding the glow of burning tobacco.

'What you told me about South Africa, is it true?' Alphonso asked unexpectedly.

'What did I tell you?'

'That men, even black men, eat meat every day?'

Sean smiled in the darkness, amused by Alphonso's concept of paradise, a place where a man could eat meat every day.

'Sometimes they get so sick of eating beef,' he teased, 'that they try chicken and lamb just for a change.'

Alphonso shook his head. That was beyond belief, no African could ever tire of beef.

'How much does a black man earn in South Africa?' he demanded.

'About five hundred rand a month if he is an ordinary unskilled labourer, but there are many black millionaires.' Five hundred rand was more than a man earned in Mozambique in a year, even if he were lucky enough to find employment. A million was a figure beyond Alphonso's powers of imagination.

'Five hundred?' He shook his head in wonder. 'And paid in rands, not paper escudos or Zimbabwe dollars?' he demanded earnestly.

'Rands,' Sean confirmed. Compared to other currencies in Africa the rand was as good as a gold sovereign.

'And there are things in the stores, things for a man to buy with his rands?' Alphonso demanded suspiciously. It was difficult for him to visualize shelves laden with goods for sale, other than a few pathetic bottles of locally produced carbonated soft drinks and packets of cheap cigarettes.

'Whatever you want,' Sean assured him. 'Soap and sugar, cooking oil and maize meal.' Half-forgotten luxuries in Alphonso's mind.

'As much as I want?' he asked. 'No rationing?'

'As much as you can pay for,' Sean assured him. 'And when your belly is full, you can buy shoes and suits and ties, transistor radios and dark glasses . . .'

'A bicycle?' Alphonso demanded eagerly.

'Only the very lowest men ride bicycles,' Sean grinned, enjoying himself. 'The others have their own motor cars.'

'Black men own their own motor cars?'

Alphonso thought about that for a long time.

'Would there be work for a man like me?' he asked with a diffidence that was completely out of character.

'You?' Sean pretended to consider it, and Alphonso waited apprehensively for his judgement. 'You?' Sean repeated. 'My brother owns a gold mine. You could be a supervisor on his mine within a year, a shift boss in two years. I could get you a job the same day you arrived at the mine.'

'How much does a supervisor earn?'

'A thousand, two thousand,' Sean assured him, and Alphonso was stunned. His Renamo pay was the equivalent of a rand a day, paid in Mozambique escudos.

'I would like to be a boss supervisor,' he murmured thoughtfully.

'Better than a Renamo sergeant?' Sean teased, and Alphonso chortled derisively.

'Of course, in South Africa you would not have the vote,' Sean ribbed him. 'Only pale faces get to vote.'

'Vote, what is a vote?' Alphonso demanded, and then answered himself. 'I don't have a vote in Mozambique. They don't have the vote in Zambia or Zimbabwe or Angola or Tanzania. Nobody has the vote in Africa, except perhaps once in a man's life to elect a president for life and a one-party government.' He shook his head and snorted. 'Vote? You can't eat a vote. You can't dress in a vote, or ride to work on it. For two thousand rand a month and a full belly you can have my vote.'

'Any time you come to South Africa, you come and see me.' Sean stretched and looked at the sky. He could see the trees against it. Dawn was only a short time away. He crushed out the butt of the cigarette and began to get to his feet.

'There is something I must tell you,' Alphonso whispered, and his altered tone caught Sean's full attention.

'Yes?' He squatted down again and leaned closer to the Shangane. Alphonso cleared his throat in embarrassment.

'We have travelled a long road together,' he murmured.

'A long hard road,' Sean agreed. 'But the end is in sight. This time tomorrow . . .' He did not have to go on and Alphonso did not reply immediately.

'We have fought side by side,' Alphonso said at last.

'Like lions,' Sean confirmed.

'I have called you *Baba* and *Nkosi Kakulu*.'

'You have honoured me thus,' Sean said formally. 'And I have called you friend.'

Alphonso nodded in the darkness. 'I cannot let you cross the Zimbabwe border,' he said with sudden decisiveness and Sean rocked back on his heels.

'Tell me why not.'

'You remember Cuthbert?' Alphonso asked, and it took Sean a moment to place the name.

'Cuthbert, you mean the one from Grand Reef air base. The one who helped us on the raid?' It all seemed so long ago.

'General China's nephew,' Alphonso nodded. 'That is the one I speak of.'

'Sammy Davis Junior.' Sean smiled. 'The cool laid-back cat. I remember him well.'

'General China spoke to him on the radio. This very morning from the laager of the *henshaw*, after our victory. I was in the outer room of the bunker. I heard everything he said.'

Sean felt a cold wind blow down his spine and the hair at the base of his skull prickled.

'What did China tell him?' he asked, dreading the reply.

'He ordered Cuthbert to let the Zimbabwean army know that it was you who led the raid on Grand Reef and stole the *indeki*

420

full of missiles. He told Cuthbert to tell them that you would be crossing back into Zimbabwe through the Honde Valley at St Mary's Mission, and they must wait for you there.'

Sean's gut knotted with shock and for long moments he was stunned by the enormity and cunning of the trap that China had prepared for him. The cruelty of it was diabolical. To allow them to believe that they were being set free, letting them taste the relief of crossing out of harm, when in fact, they were going to a fate even worse than China himself could have meted out to them.

The fury of the Zimbabwe high command would know no bounds. Sean was the holder of a Zimbabwe passport, a document of convenience but one which would make him a traitor and a murderer beyond any help from outside. He would be handed over to the notorious Zimbabwe Central Intelligence Organization and taken to the interrogation cells at Chikarubi prison, and he would never re-emerge from there alive. Job, despite his wounds, would share the same fate.

Even though Claudia was an American citizen, officially she no longer existed. It was weeks since she had been reported missing. By this time, interest in her case even at the United States embassies in Harare and Pretoria would have cooled. Along with her father, she was presumed dead and so she could expect no protection. She was as vulnerable as they were.

The trap was completely closed, there was no way out. The Renamo army behind them, Frelimo on either hand and the Zimbabwean CIO ahead of them. They were marooned in a devastated wasteland, doomed to be hunted down like wild animals or to slow starvation in the wilderness.

'Think!' Sean told himself. 'Find the way out.'

They could attempt to cross the Zimbabwe border at some other point than the Honde Valley, but the CIO would have the entire country alerted for them. There were permanent army blocks on every road. Without papers, they wouldn't get more than a few miles, and then there was Job, what would he do with Job? How could they transport a wounded man when every police and military post would be looking for somebody in a stretcher.

'We must go southwards,' Alphonso said. 'We must go to South Africa.'

'We?' Sean stared at him. 'You want to come with us?'

421

'I can't go back to General China,' he pointed out philosophically. 'Not after I have betrayed him. I will come with you to South Africa.'

'That's a trek of three hundred miles, through two opposed armies, Frelimo and the southern division of Renamo. And what about Job?'

'We will carry him,' Alphonso replied.

'Three hundred miles?'

'Then we will leave him behind.' Alphonso shrugged. 'He is only a Matabele and he is dying anyway, it will be no great loss.'

Sean caught the angry words that rose to his tongue and remained silent while he thought it out. Every way he twisted it and examined it he saw that Alphonso was right. To the north the dubious haven of Malawi was blocked by the waters of Cabora Bassa and by General China's division. To the east lay the Indian Ocean, and to the west the Zimbabwean CIO.

'All right,' Sean admitted reluctantly. 'South is the only way. Perhaps we can squeeze through between Frelimo and the southern division of Renamo. All we have to do is get across a heavily guarded railway line and the Limpopo river, and find enough to eat while we are doing it in a land that has been burned and devastated by ten years of civil war.'

'In South Africa, we will eat meat every day,' Alphonso pointed out cheerfully.

Sean stood up. 'Will your men follow you?'

'I will kill those that don't.' Alphonso was matter-of-fact. 'We can't let them go back to General China.'

'Right,' Sean agreed. 'And you will report on the radio schedule that I have crossed into Zimbabwe. We'll be able to string China along on the radio for four or five days. He won't realize that we have broken away southwards until we are well on our way and beyond his range. You had better talk to your men now. We'll have to turn south right away. Talk to them before they realize for themselves that we are up to something.'

Alphonso called in the sentries, and in the grey light of dawn the faces of the Shanganes were sober and intent as they squatted in a circle around him and listened to Alphonso describe to them the southern paradise to which he would lead them.

'We are all weary of fighting, of living like animals in the bush. It is time we learned to live like men, to find good wives to bear our sons.' He was filled with the fiery eloquence of the recent convert and before he had finished Sean saw the sparkle of anticipation in most of their eyes and he felt a lift of relief. For the first time, he began to believe that the journey ahead might just be possible, with a great deal of endeavour and an even greater deal of luck.

He went to tell Claudia and Job what lay ahead. Claudia was bathing Job's face with a damp rag. 'He's much better, a good night's rest.' Then she broke off as she saw his face. Claudia's spirits visibly plummeted as he explained to them what they had to do.

'It was too good to be true.' she whispered. 'I knew deep down that it wouldn't be that easy. that General China wasn't Santa Claus in disguise.'

Job lay so still on his stretcher that Sean thought he had once again slipped over the edge of consciousness and he reached out to check his pulse. At his touch. Job opened his eyes.

'Can you trust those Shanganes?' he whispered.

'We don't have much choice.' Sean pointed out, and then went on briskly. 'We . . .'

'Leave me here.' Job's whisper was barely audible, but Sean's expression hardened and his voice was brittle with anger.

'Cut out that sort of bullshit.' he warned Job.

'Without me you might have a chance,' Job insisted. 'If you have to drag this stretcher . . .'

'We've got twelve hefty Shanganes,' Sean pointed out.

'Better some of you get through than all of us die. Leave me, Sean. Save Claudia and yourself.'

'I'm getting angry.' Sean stood up and said to Claudia, 'We leave in ten minutes.'

They travelled cautiously southwards all that day. It was an intense relief not to have to watch the sky for the Hind gunships, although out of habit the Shanganes occasionally turned their faces upward. The closer they drew to the railway line, the slower their progress became and they spent much of their time hiding in the dense wild ebony thickets and clumps of jesse until Matatu came ghosting back to assure them that the coast was clear and to lead them onwards.

In the late afternoon, Sean left the main party hiding in a bushy ravine and went forward with Matatu. He was gone for almost two hours and the sun was setting when he reappeared silently and suddenly at Claudia's side.

'You startled me!' she gasped. 'You're like a cat.'

'The railway line is only a mile ahead. The Frelimo guards seem to be in a state of confusion still. There is a lot of military traffic on the line, and a great deal of panicky activity all around. The crossing is going to be a trifle tricky. As soon as the moon comes up, I'll go up and take another look.'

While they waited for the moon, Alphonso rigged the radio aerial and made his scheduled contact with General China's headquarters.

'The dove is in flight.' He gave the prearranged code so that China would believe that Sean and his party had crossed the border. After a brief pause, presumably while he relayed the message, the radio operator came back to Alphonso with the order to return to the main base on the river. Alphonso acknowledged and signed off.

'They won't expect me to arrive back for another two days.' Alphonso grinned as he packed up the radio. 'It will be that long before they start getting suspicious.'

As the moon pushed its bald silver pate above the trees, Sean and Matatu slipped away into the forest to make a final reconnaissance of the railway line.

A mile south of their position they found the place where the line crossed a narrow stream. Although the stream contained only a few shallow puddles, the banks were thick with riverine bush which would afford them good cover. Originally the bush must have been cleared for a hundred yards on each side of the line, but secondary growth had been allowed to spring up to waist height.

'Sloppy Frelimo bastards,' Sean muttered. 'That will give us some cover, and we'll stay in the riverbed.'

The main line crossed the stream over an embankment and culvert. There was a guard post on the approaches, fifty yards uptrack from the culvert. While Sean watched through his binoculars, a Frelimo sentry with his AK rifle slung on his back sauntered down to the bridge over the culvert. He leaned on the guard rail and lit a cigarette. The glow of the cigarette marked his progress as he ambled back to the guard post. He seemed to Sean to be a little unsteady on his feet, and when he reached the guard post, a faint ripple of feminine giggles carried to where Sean and Matatu lay.

'They are having a party.' Sean chuckled.

'Palm wine and jig-jig,' Matatu agreed enviously, and in the moonlight held up his right hand with his thumb trapped between his first two fingers. 'I would like some of that myself.'

'You randy little bugger.' Sean tweaked his ear. 'When we get to Johannesburg, I'll stand you to the biggest, fattest lady we can flush out.' Matatu's taste in amour ran to the mountainous. 'Like Sherpa Tensing on Everest,' Sean often remarked.

The distractions with which the railway guards had provided themselves promised to make their crossing easier. Sean and Matatu withdrew quietly and started back to where they had left the rest of the party.

They had been gone for three hours and it was a few minutes before midnight, as they approached the camp. At the head of the ravine, Sean paused to give the recognition signal, the liquid warble of a fiery-necked nightjar. He didn't want to be shot by one of Alphonso's Shanganes. He waited a full minute for the reply, and when it did not come, he repeated the signal. Still there was silence and he felt the first tickle of alarm.

Instead of going straight in, they circled the ravine cautiously, and in the moonlight Matatu picked up unexpected spoor and squatted over it, frowning with alarm.

Sean whispered. 'Who? Which way?'

'Many men, our own Shanganes!' Matatu lifted his head and pointed to the north. 'They are going out, leaving camp.'

'Outgoing?' Sean was puzzled. 'Doesn't make sense, unless . . . ! Oh God! No!'

Swiftly, quietly, he closed in on the camp. The sentries he had set before he left were gone, their posts deserted. Sean felt panic rise in a wave that threatened to suffocate him.

'Claudia!' he whispered, suppressing the urge to shout her name aloud. He wanted to rush into the camp and find her, but he drew a series of deep breaths and fought back the panic.

He slipped the AKM on to fully automatic and went down on his belly, creeping in. The five Shanganes he had left asleep in the gut of the ravine were gone, all their equipment and their weapons had disappeared. He went on and made out the shape of Job's stretcher in the dappled moonlight; beside it, exactly as he had left her, Claudia's body wrapped in a blanket, but just beyond her another body lay sprawled. In the moonlight, he saw the sheen of wetness on the back of the man's head.

'Blood!'

Sean threw all caution aside and rushed to Claudia's body, dropping to his knees beside her and sweeping her into his arms.

She gasped and cried out, coming out of deep sleep, beginning to struggle in his arms, and then quieting as she realized who he was.

'Sean!' she blurted, still groggy with sleep. 'What is it? What happened?'

'Thank God,' he murmured fervently. 'I thought. . . !' He set her down gently, and reached across to where Job lay in the litter.

'Job, are you all right?' He shook him carefully, and Job stirred and murmured.

Sean jumped to his feet and went to where Alphonso lay. He touched his neck. The skin was warm, his pulse strong and even.

'Claudia!' he called. 'Bring the flashlight.'

In the beam of the flashlight, he examined the laceration in Alphonso's scalp.

'A nice little ding,' he grunted; although the bleeding had staunched spontaneously, he pressed a field dressing over it and bound it in place. 'Good thing they hit him on the head, or they might have done some serious damage.' He grinned wryly at his own joke.

'What happened, Sean?' Claudia demanded anxiously. 'I was fast asleep, I didn't hear a thing.'

'Lucky for you,' Sean tied the tag ends of the bandage, 'or you might have got the same treatment.'

'What happened, where are the others?'

'Gone,' he told her. 'Flown, deserted. They obviously didn't fancy the walk or the destination. They bashed Alphonso on the noggin and took off back to General China.'

She stared at him. 'You mean there are only the four of us now? All the Shanganes except Alphonso have gone?'

'That's right,' Sean agreed and Alphonso groaned and reached up to touch his bandaged head. Sean helped him sit up.

'Sean!' Claudia tugged at his arm and he turned back to her. 'What are we going to do?' Sean glanced across at Job's stretcher. 'What are we going to do with Job? How are we going to carry him? How are we going to get out of here now?'

'That, my love, is an extremely interesting question,' Sean agreed grimly. 'All I can tell you is that by this time tomorrow, our old pal General China is going to know that we are on the run, and he's going to know exactly where we are headed.'

She stared at him aghast. 'What are we going to do?'

'We don't seem to have much choice,' he said. 'There is only one road still open to us – we keep on the way we are going.'

He hauled Alphonso to his feet.

'That's impossible,' Claudia whispered anxiously. 'Two of you cannot carry the stretcher.'

'You're right, of course. We'll have to make some other arrangement.'

Between them, they lifted Job out of the stretcher and laid him on Claudia's blanket, then, while the others watched, Sean began to dismantle the fibreglass stretcher. Before he had finished, Matatu appeared silently out of the darkness and whispered a brief report to Sean.

Sean barely looked up as he told Alphonso, 'You taught them well. Your Shanganes have bomb-shelled, taken off in eleven different directions. If we followed we might catch one or two of them, but some of them are going to get back to China with the good news.'

Alphonso cursed the deserters bitterly, while Sean explained to Claudia and Job.

'I'm going to use the nylon webbing from the stretcher to improvise a sling seat.'

Claudia looked dubious. 'Job isn't strong enough to sit upright. The movement will reopen his wound, the bleeding . . .' She broke off as Sean glared at her.

'Can you think of a better way?' he snarled, and she shook her head.

Sean doubled the length of heavy green canvas and took the rifle slings from his AKM and Alphonso's AK to make carrying loops.

'We'll have to make adjustments as we go along,' he grunted, and then looked at Claudia. 'Instead of finding difficulties, make yourself useful by gathering all the equipment the Shanganes left. We'll have to make a selection.'

He picked out the equipment swiftly, discarding all but the most vital pieces. 'Alphonso and I will be carrying Job between us. On top of that we'll only be able to manage our basic weapons and a blanket each. Claudia and Matatu must lug the medical pack, the water bottles and a blanket each. Everything else will be left behind.'

'The canned food?' Claudia asked.

'Forget it,' Sean told her brusquely, and set about apportioning their loads. He cut everything down to the barest minimum, knowing that every pound of weight now would seem like ten after the first few miles. He even made Alphonso abandon his AK rifle and gave him the pistol that he had taken from the Russian pilot to replace it. He restricted himself to two spare clips of ammunition for his own AKM and he and Alphonso retained only a pair of grenades each, one fragmentation and the other phosphorus.

The abandoned equipment they piled in the bottom of the ravine and covered with loose earth and branches to conceal it from casual discovery by a Frelimo patrol.

'Okay, lad,' Sean told Job. 'Time to go.' He glanced at his wristwatch and found it was a little before three o'clock. They were well behind schedule and they only had a few hours of darkness left in which to make the crossing.

He knelt beside Job and eased him up into a sitting position, then restrapped his injured arm firmly against his chest.

'This is the bad part,' he warned him, and between them he and Alphonso lifted Job to his feet. Job endured the movement in stoic silence, and stood supported between them.

Sean and Alphonso adjusted the nylon sling seat over their outer shoulders. They lifted Job into it, and he sat with his feet dangling, his good arm draped around Sean's shoulder while Sean and Alphonso linked their arms behind his back to support him.

'Ready?' Sean asked, and Job grunted softly, trying to conceal the pain that every movement caused him.

'If you think it's bad now . . .' Sean warned him cheerfully, 'just give it a couple of hours!'

They started down the ravine towards the railway line. They moved slowly, accustoming themselves to this awkward form of travel, trying to cushion Job between them, but they stumbled over the broken ground and Job swung on his seat and bumped against them. He made no sound, but Sean heard his ragged breathing close to his ear and when the pain stabbed him especially cruelly, he unconsciously dug his fingers into Sean's shoulder.

Slowly they moved down the shallow stream bed towards the culvert beneath the railway line. Matatu was a hundred yards

428

ahead of them, just visible in the moonlight. Once he signalled them to halt and then after a few minutes beckoned them to come on. Claudia trailed fifty paces behind them so that she would have a start if they were discovered and forced to run back.

Carrying Job between them, it was not possible for Sean and Alphonso to move silently. Once they splashed into one of the muddy pools of the stream and they sounded like a herd of cavorting hippos in the silence.

Matatu had reached the culvert ahead of them and he signalled them frantically to hurry. They staggered forward under Job's weight and were in the open, when on the embankment above them, there was the sudden crunch of footsteps in the gravel ballast and the sound of voices.

Trying to keep low, they kept going at a clumsy run. They reached the culvert and carried Job into the dark concrete tunnel. Claudia was running doubled over only a few yards behind them and Sean reached back with his free hand and dragged her in out of the pale moonlight into the blessed darkness of the culvert.

They leaned against the concrete wall, stooped below the curved roof, trying to quiet their breathing, all of them panting wildly from that charge through the mud and sand of the stream bottom.

The footsteps and the voices above them grew louder and finally stopped almost directly overhead. It sounded like a man and a woman. The Frelimo garrison had either brought their own camp-followers with them, or had found lady friends in the refugee camps that had sprung up along the guarded railway line.

There was a spirited argument going on out there, the man's voice slurred with drink and the woman's shrill and shrewish as she protested and haggled. At last, they heard the man's voice raised in exasperation.

'Dollar *shumi*, ten dollars,' he said, and immediately the woman's voice softened and cooed agreement.

Then there was the sound of feet sliding in gravel and a few pebbles rattled down the embankment in the stream bed.

'They are coming down here!' Claudia breathed in horror, and they instinctively drew back deeper into the dark culvert.

'Quiet!' Sean whispered, and stooped to ease Job out of the canvas sling and prop him against the wall of the culvert.

As he drew the trench knife from the sheath on his webbing two figures appeared in the mouth of the culvert, silhouetted by the moonlight.

They were clinging together and laughing softly, the woman half supporting the man as they staggered forward. Sean gripped the knife underhand, the point of the blade belly high, ready to receive them, but they advanced only a few paces into the intimate darkness of the tunnel and then turned to face each other still giggling and whispering, both of them outlined against the moonlit exterior.

The Frelimo sentry pushed the woman against the wall and propped his rifle beside her while he fumbled to open his own clothing. The woman leaned back against the wall and with a practised gesture lifted the front of her skirt above her waist. Laughing and muttering drunkenly the sentry reeled against her and she used one hand to steady and guide him, the other still holding up her skirt.

If Claudia had reached out a hand she could have touched the couple, but they were locked together oblivious of all around them. The man began to push against her, his voice rising as he exhorted himself to greater effort, his movements becoming more frenzied. The woman clucked like a rider urging a mount forward and the Frelimo went from a canter to full gallop, pounding away with abandon.

Suddenly the man threw his head back, stiffening into rigidity, and crowed like an asthmatic rooster. Slowly he drooped and the woman laughed and pushed him away briskly. Still laughing, she smoothed down her skirt and seized the man's arm. The two of them staggered out into the sandy riverbed and disappeared round the corner of the culvert. The sounds of their scrambled ascent of the embankment dwindled and Sean slid the knife back into its sheath on his belt and said softly, 'That's what we call a tumble in the jungle!'

Claudia giggled with nervous relief. 'Two seconds flat, that just has to be a new world record,' she whispered, and Sean hugged her briefly.

'Shall we also be friends?' he whispered. 'Sorry I snarled at you.'

'I was being a dismal Jane, I deserved it. You won't have any more moaning and whining from me.'

'Stay close.' He turned back to grope for Job and found that he had slid weakly down the wall and was sitting on the sandy floor of the culvert.

As he stooped to help him to his feet, Sean's fingers touched his shoulder. The bandage was damp and his smile faded. The bleeding had started again.

'Nothing we can do about it now,' he thought, and gently eased Job to his feet.

'How are you doing, old son?'

'No worries.' Job's whisper was scratchy and faint.

Sean touched Matatu's shoulder and he obeyed the unspoken command, instantly creeping out the far side of the culvert and disappearing into the scrub on the stream bank.

A few minutes later the soft whistle of a night bird carried to them as Matatu gave the all clear. Sean sent Claudia ahead and gave her a full five minutes to get across the open ground of the cut line.

'Let's go.' Sean looked up from the luminous dial of his Rolex and they lifted Job into the sling seat and started forward into the moonlight.

The next hundred paces seemed like the slowest and longest Sean had ever covered, but at last they were into the forest beyond the cut line, and Claudia was waiting for them there.

'We've made it!' she whispered joyfully.

'We sure have, the first mile was a romp, only three hundred more to go,' he answered grimly, and they kept going.

Counting their paces against the second hand of his wristwatch, Sean estimated that they were averaging two miles an hour. Ahead of them, Matatu selected the easiest going. He was always out of sight in the forest ahead, only his soft bird calls guided them. At intervals Sean checked their heading against the stars, catching glimpses of the Southern Cross and its brilliant pair of pointers through the forest canopy ahead of them.

When the dawn paled out the stars, they stopped once again and Sean allowed them to drink for the first time, two swallows each from one of the water-bottles that Claudia carried. Then he turned his attention to Job's shoulder. The dressing was soaked with fresh blood and Job's face was grey as the ashes of a cold camp-fire. His eyes had sunk into dark sockets and his lips were dry and cracked, his breath whistling softly through them. The pain and loss of blood was taking a dreadful toll.

Gently Sean unwound the bandage and then he and Claudia

exchanged a quick glance. The destruction of tissue was horrifying and the field dressing was caked into the wound cavity. Sean realized that if he tried to remove it, he would tear the flesh to which it had adhered and probably restart the bleeding. He leaned forward and sniffed the wound, while Job grinned at him, a skull-like twitching back of the lips.

'Steak tartare?' he asked weakly.

'All it needs is a little garlic,' Sean grinned back at him, but he had caught the first sickly whiff of corruption. He squeezed another half tube of iodine paste over the original field dressing and then stripped the plastic packaging from a fresh dressing and placed it over the wound.

Claudia held it in place as he rewrapped it with a new bandage from the medical pack. He rolled the blood-soaked bandage and stuffed it into a side pocket. He would wash it out at the first water that they came to.

'We must keep going,' he told Job. 'We've got to get well clear of the railway line. Are you up to it?'

Job nodded, but Sean could see the dread in his eyes. Every step they moved him was an agony.

'I'm going to give you another shot of antibiotic —I can give you a jolt of morphine at the same time?'

Job shook his head. 'Keep it for when it gets really bad.' He grinned again, a grimace that tugged at Sean's heart. He could not meet Job's eyes. 'Show us your best side,' he said, and made a performance of pulling down the trousers of Job's battledress and darting the hypodermic needle into one of his glossy black buttocks. Claudia averted her gaze modestly and Job whispered, 'It's okay, Claudia, you are allowed to look. Just don't touch, that's all.'

'You're as bad as Sean,' she said primly. 'Downright vulgar, both of you.'

They lifted Job back into the nylon sling seat and went on. By mid-morning the mirage shimmered and rose in glassy whirlpools from the rocky kopjes over which they were trekking, and the tiny mopane flies hovered in a fine mist around their heads, crawling into their nostrils and ears and eyes with infuriating persistence. With the heat came the thirst, and their sweat dried on their shirts and left irregular outlines in white salt on the cloth.

When they stopped at noon in the sparse dappled shade of an African teak, Sean knew they had all had enough and the worst heat of the day was still to come. They laid Job on a hastily cut mattress of dried grass and he lapsed almost immediately into a state that was more coma than sleep, and snored softly through his dry swollen lips.

The carrying sling had rubbed the skin from both Sean's shoulders, for he and Alphonso had changed sides at each of the hourly stops. The harsh nylon straps had galled Alphonso as badly and he muttered sullenly as he examined his injuries.

'Before this, I hated the Matabele simply because they are a flea-infested, thieving bunch of venereal apes. Now I have another reason to hate them.'

Sean tossed him the tube of iodine paste. 'Smear the *muti* on your grievous injuries, then stuff the empty tube in your garrulous mouth,' he advised, and Alphonso went off still muttering to find a place to lie down.

Sean and Claudia found a hollow screened by a low hook-thorn bush a short distance from where Job lay and Sean spread their blankets to make a nest for them.

He settled into it thankfully. 'I'm bushed.'

'How bushed?' Claudia asked, and knelt over him to nibble his ear.

'Not that bushed,' he qualified, and pulled her down beside him.

At sunset, Sean cooked a pot of maize-meal porridge on a tiny smokeless fire while Alphonso rigged the aerial and tuned the radio to the Renamo command frequency. There was a clutter of garbled broken-up traffic on their wavelength, probably Frelimo transmissions, but at last they heard their call sign through the jumble.

'*N'gulube*! Warthog! Come in, *N'gulube*! This is Banana Tree.'

Alphonso acknowledged and then made a fictitious position report that placed them still far north of the railway line, on a march back to the river area. Banana Tree acknowledged and signed off.

'They fell for it,' Sean gave his opinion. 'Looks like the Shangane deserters haven't reached base and blown the whistle on us, not yet anyway.'

In the last of the daylight, they ate the meal of maize porridge and Sean studied his field map and marked in his dead reckoning position. According to the map, the hilly ground seemed to extend for another thirty miles or so, and then descended gently

433

to a more level plain on which a number of small villages and cultivated lands were marked; beyond that was the first natural barrier, another wide river that ran west to east directly across their route.

He called Alphonso across and asked him, 'The southern division of Renamo under General Tippoo Tip, do you know where his area begins, where his main forces are deployed?'

'Like us, they move all the time to confuse Frelimo. Sometimes they are here, other times down here near the Rio Save.' He shrugged. 'Renamo is wherever the fighting is.'

'And Frelimo? Where are they?'

'They chase after Renamo, and then run like frightened rabbits when they catch them,' he guffawed. 'To us now, it doesn't matter who is who and where they are. Everybody we meet down here is going to try and kill us.'

'Great intelligence report,' Sean thanked him, and folded the map into its plastic wallet.

Quickly they finished the frugal meal and Sean stood up.

'All right, Alphonso. Let's get Job up and moving.'

Alphonso belched softly then grinned wickedly. 'He's your Matabele dog. If you want him, you carry him, I've had enough.'

Sean hid his dismay behind a neutral expression.

'You are wasting time,' he said softly. 'Get on your feet!' And Alphonso belched again and held his eyes, still grinning.

Slowly Sean reached down to the trench knife in its sheath and just as deliberately Alphonso reached and touched the Tokarev pistol tucked into his belt. They stared at each other.

'Sean, what is it?' Claudia asked anxiously. 'What is going on?' She had not understood the exchange in Shangane, but the tension was palpable.

'He's refusing to help me carry Job,' he replied.

'You can't carry him alone, can you?' Claudia said anxiously. 'Alphonso *will* help –'

'– or I'll kill him!' Sean replied in Shangane and Alphonso laughed out loud. He stood up and shook himself like a dog, turned his back on Sean, picked up his radio pack, Sean's AKM rifle and most of the water-bottles.

'I'll carry these,' he chuckled, shaking his head at the joke. 'You can carry your Matabele.' He ambled away southwards along the line of march.

Sean dropped his hand from the hilt of the knife and looked

across at Job. He was watching quietly from his mattress of grass and Sean snarled at him, 'If you say it, I'll kick your black arse for you.'

'I didn't say nothing.' Job tried to smile, but it was a weak and transient grimace.

'Good,' said Sean grimly, and picked up the nylon sling seat and straps.

'Claudia, give us a hand here.'

Between them, they got Job on his feet and Sean rigged the nylon slings around his waist and under his crotch like a parachute harness, and looped them over his own shoulders. Then he supported Job with an arm around the waist.

'One more river, there's one more river to cross,' he sang hoarsely and untunefully, and grinned at Job. They moved forward. Although Job's feet touched the ground and he tried to take as much of his own weight as possible, he was mainly supported by the straps that crossed over Sean's shoulders and they were locked together like a pair in a harness.

Within the first hundred paces they had established some sort of rhythm, but still their progress was unsteady and painfully slow, set by Job's uncertain footsteps. There could be no attempt at stealth or anti-tracking for Sean had to pick the easiest and most obvious route. They stuck to the open game trails, that complex network that like the veins in a dried leaf meshes the African veld.

Behind them Claudia followed laden with the medical pack and the rest of the water-bottles, but still she carried a leafy branch with which she tried to sweep their tracks. Her efforts might conceal their passing from a casual observer, but a Frelimo tracker would follow them as though he were on the M1 motorway. It was hardly worth the effort, but Sean did not discourage her, he knew how important it was to her to feel that she was pulling her weight and making a useful contribution to their escape.

Sean counted their paces against the second hand of his wristwatch and estimated that they were down to less than a mile an hour, eight miles a day was all the progress they could hope for, and he started to divide that into three hundred but gave up before he reached the depressing answer.

Both Matatu and Alphonso had disappeared into the combretum forest ahead of them and Sean glanced at his watch again.

They had only been going a little over thirty minutes, but already their momentum was winding down. Job's weight was heavier, the straps cutting painfully into the flesh of Sean's shoulders, and Job's footsteps were dragging and catching on every irregularity of the game path.

'I'm cutting down to thirty-minute stages,' he told Job. 'We'll take five minutes now.'

When Sean lowered him to a sitting position against the bole of a tree, Job leant his head back against the rough bark and closed his eyes. His breathing sobbed in his chest, and droplets of sweat made slow runnels down his cheeks. Like tiny black pearls, the drops reflected the colour of his skin.

Sean let the five minutes run over to ten and then told Job cheerfully, 'On your feet, soldier, let's eat some ground.'

Getting Job up on his feet again was torture for both of them and Sean realized that trying to be gentle on him, he had allowed Job to rest too long. The wound had begun to stiffen.

The next thirty-minute stage endured so long that Sean was convinced that his watch had stopped. He had to check the sweep of the second hand to reassure himself.

When at last, he lowered him to a sitting position, Job grimaced. 'Sorry, Sean, cramps. Left calf.'

Sean squatted in front of him and felt the knots of tortured muscle in Job's leg. While he massaged it, he spoke quietly to Claudia. 'There are salt tablets in the medic pack, front pocket.'

Job swallowed them and Claudia held the water-bottle to his lips. After two swallows, he pushed it away.

'More,' Claudia urged him, but he shook his head.

'Don't waste it,' he murmured.

'How's that feel?' Sean gave his calf a couple of hard slaps.

'Good for another few miles.'

'Let's go,' Sean said. 'Before it seizes up again.'

It amazed Claudia how the two of them kept going through the night with only those five-minute breaks and the frugal draughts from the water-bottles.

'Three hundred miles of this,' she thought. 'It simply is not possible. Flesh and blood can't take it. It will kill both of them.'

A little before dawn, Matatu popped up like a small black shadow out of the forest and whispered to Sean.

'He has found a waterhole about two or three miles ahead,' Sean told them. 'Can you make it, Job?'

The sun had risen and cleared the tops of the trees and the day's heat was building up like a stoked furnace. When Job collapsed and hung suspended at Sean's side, dangling with his full weight on the cross straps, they were still half a mile from the waterhole.

Sean lowered him to the ground and sat beside him. He was so exhausted himself that, for a few minutes, he could not find the energy to talk or move.

'Well, at least you picked a good place to pass out,' he congratulated Job in a hoarse whisper. They were in a patch of thick thorn bush that would give them shade and cover for the rest of the day.

They made a bed of cut grass for Job in the shade and settled him on it. He was only half conscious, his speech slurred and wandering, and his eyes continually slipping out of focus. Claudia tried to feed him, but he turned his face away. However, he drank thirstily when at last Matatu and Alphonso returned from the waterhole with all the water-bottles refilled. After he had drunk, Job lapsed back into coma and they waited out the heat of the day in the thorn patch.

Sean and Claudia lay in each other's arms, she had become so accustomed to falling asleep in his embrace. She realized that Sean was near the end of his tether. She had never imagined that he could be so finely stretched, that even his strength which she had come to believe was inexhaustible had a limit upon it.

When she woke a little after noon, he lay like a dead man beside her and she studied his face lovingly, almost greedily. His beard was full and beginning to curl and she picked out two curly silver hairs in the dense bush. His features were gaunt, all trace of fat and superfluous flesh burned away and there were lines and weathered creases in his skin that she had never noticed before. She studied them as though his life history were chiselled into them like cuneiform writing on a tablet that she could read. 'God, but I love him,' she thought, amazed at the depth of her own feelings. His skin was burned to the colour of dark mahogany by the sun, and yet it retained a lustre like that of fine leather, well used but polished with care over the years, 'like Papa's polo boots'. She smiled at the simile, but it was somehow apt. She had watched her father in his dressing-room lovingly applying dubbin to the leather with his fingers and polishing it to a dull glow with his own bare palm.

'Boots!' she whispered. 'That's a good name for you,' she told Sean as he slept, and she remembered how her father's boots had flexed and wrinkled at the ankle, almost as supple as silk as he stepped up into the stirrup. 'Wrinkled just like you, my old boot.' She smiled and kissed the lines in his forehead so softly as not to wake him.

She realized then to just what extent the memory of her father had been absorbed in this man who lay for once like a child in her arms. The two men seemed to have merged in one body, and she could concentrate all her love in a single place. Gently she moved Sean's sleeping head until it nestled against her shoulder, and she burrowed her fingers into the dense springing curls at the back of his head and rocked him gently.

Up until this moment, he had succeeded in evoking the full spectrum of her emotions, from anger to sensual passion, everything except tenderness. Now, however, it was complete. 'My baby,' she whispered, as tenderly as a mother. For once she truly felt that he belonged to her completely.

A soft groan shattered her fragile mood, and she raised her head and glanced across at where Job lay beneath the thorn bush nearby, but he relapsed into silence once again.

She thought about the two of them, Job and Sean and their special masculine relationship in which she knew she could never share. She should have been jealous, but instead in some strange way, it made her feel more secure. If Sean could be so constant and self-sacrificing in his love for another man, then she hoped that she could expect the same constancy from him in their own different but even more intense relationship.

Job groaned again and began to thrash about restlessly. She sighed and then gently disentangled herself from Sean's sleeping form, stood up and crossed to where Job lay.

A cloud of metallic-green flies buzzed around the blood-soaked bandage that covered his shoulder. They settled on the soiled dressing and tasted it with their long proboscises, then rubbed their front legs together with delight. Claudia saw that they had laid their rice-grain eggs in thick rafts on the bloody cloth, and with an exclamation of disgust, she fanned them away, and then scraped the loathsome white eggs from the folds of the bandage.

Job opened his eyes and looked up at her. She realized that he was fully conscious once again and she smiled encouragingly at him. 'Would you like another drink?'

'No.' His voice was so low that she had to lean closer to him. 'You have to make him do it,' he said.

'Who? Sean?' she asked, and Job nodded.

'He can't go on like this. He's killing himself. Without him, none of you will survive. You must make him leave me here.' She had begun to shake her head before he stopped speaking.

'No,' she said firmly. 'He would never do it, and I wouldn't let him, even if he wanted to. We are in this together, pardner.' She touched his arm. 'Now, how about that drink?' He subsided, too weak to argue further. Like Sean, Job also seemed to have deteriorated alarmingly in the last few hours. She sat beside him fanning the flies away with an ilala palm frond while the sun slid slowly down the western sky.

In the cool of the afternoon Sean stirred and sat up, instantly wide awake, taking in his surroundings with a quick glance. Sleep revived and fortified him.

'How is he?' he asked, and when she shook her head, he came to squat beside her.

'We'll have to get him up again pretty soon.'

'Give him a few more minutes,' she pleaded, and then went on. 'Do you know what I've been thinking about while I've been sitting here?'

'Tell me,' he invited, and put his arm around her shoulders.

'I've been thinking about that waterhole out there. I've been fantasizing about pouring water over myself, washing my clothes, getting rid of this stink.'

'Have you heard about Napoleon?' he asked.

'Napoleon?' She looked puzzled. 'What does he have to do with bathing?'

'Whenever he returned from a campaign, he would send a galloper ahead of him to Josephine with the message, "*Je rentre, ne te lave pas.*" "I'm coming home, don't bathe." You see he liked his ladies the way he liked his cheese, full bodied. He would have loved you the way you are now!'

'You're disgusting.' She punched his shoulder, and Job groaned.

'Hey, there.' Sean turned his attention to him. 'What's going down, man?'

'I'll take you up on your offer now,' Job whispered.

'Morphine?' Sean asked, and Job nodded.

'Just a little shot, okay?'

'You've got it,' Sean agreed, and reached for the medical pack.

After the injection, Job lay with his eyes closed and they watched the taut lines of pain around his mouth slowly relax.

'Better?' Sean asked, and Job smiled softly without opening his eyes. 'We'll give you a few minutes more,' Sean told him. 'While we make the radio sched. with Banana Tree.'

Sean stood up and went across to where Alphonso was already rigging the radio aerial.

'*N'gulube*, this is Banana Tree.' The response to Alphonso's first call was so strong and clear that Sean started.

Alphonso adjusted the gain and then thumbed the microphone and gave another fictitious position report, as though he were still on the return march to the river area.

There was a pause, filled only by the drone and crackle of static, and then another voice equally clear and loud. 'Let me speak to Colonel Courtney!' The intonation was unmistakable and Alphonso looked up at Sean.

'General China,' he whispered, and he offered Sean the microphone but Sean pushed it aside and frowned with concentration as he waited for the next transmission.

In the silence that followed, Claudia left Job's side and crossed quickly to Sean. She squatted beside him and he placed his arm around her protectively; they both stared at the radio.

'The deserters,' she said softly. 'China knows.'

'Listen!' Sean cautioned. They waited.

'Very well.' China's voice again. 'I can understand that you do not wish to reply. However, I will presume that you are listening, Colonel.'

All their attention was on the radio, and Job opened his eyes. He had heard every word that China spoke quite clearly and rolled his head. Alphonso had left his pack and webbing piled on his blanket not ten paces from where Job lay. The butt of the Tokarev pistol protruded from the side pocket of the pack.

'You have yet to disappoint me, Colonel.' China's voice was mellow and affable. 'It would have been too simple and totally unsatisfying if you had merely blundered into the arms of the reception committee I had arranged for you at the Zimbabwean border.'

Job eased himself up on his good elbow. There was no pain, merely a sensation of weakness and drowsiness. The morphine was working. It was difficult to think clearly. He focused all his attention on the pistol, and he wondered if Alphonso had chambered a round. He began to move towards it extending his legs, digging in his heels, then lifting his buttocks clear and jack-knifing his legs. He made no sound and the others were all concentrating on the voice from the radio.

'So the game is still on, Colonel, or should we rather call it the hunt? You are a great hunter, a great white hunter. You glory in the pursuit of wild animals. You call it sport, and you pride yourself on what you term "fair chase".'

Job was halfway across the clearing. There was still no pain, and he moved a little quicker. At any moment, one of them might turn their head and see him.

'I have never understood your white man's passion for this pursuit. To me it always seemed so pointless. My people have always believed that if you want meat, you should kill it as efficiently and with as little effort as possible.'

Job reached the pile of equipment on Alphonso's blanket and stretched out to touch the hilt of the pistol. However, when he tried to withdraw it from the pocket, his fingertips were numb and it slipped from his hand; but instead of clattering on the hard earth, the pistol dropped soundlessly onto a fold of the blanket and he saw with a rush of relief that the action was cocked and the safety-catch engaged. Alphonso had loaded it, ready for instant use.

Behind him, China's voice still echoed from the radio set, 'Perhaps you have corrupted me, Colonel. Perhaps I am acquiring your decadent European ways, but for the first time, I understand your passion. Perhaps it is simply that at last the game is big enough to excite me. I wonder how you must feel at this change of role, Colonel. You are the game and I am the hunter. I know where you are, but you don't know where I am. Perhaps, I am closer than you believe possible. Where am I, Colonel? You must guess. You must run and hide. When will we meet, and how?'

Job settled his fingers carefully around the butt of the Tokarev. He lifted it and was surprised by the effort it required. He placed his thumb upon the slide of the safety-catch, and it would not budge. He felt panic rising in him. His hand was too weak and numb to move the slide forward into the firing position.

'I do not promise you "fair chase", Colonel. I will hunt you in my own African way, but it will be good sport. I promise you that at least.'

Job exerted all his strength and felt the slide of the safety-catch begin to move under his thumb.

'The time is now 1800 hours Zulu. I will call you on this frequency at the same time tomorrow, Colonel. That is if we have not already met. Until then watch the sky, Colonel Courtney, look behind you. You do not know from which direction I will come. But be sure, I will come!'

There was a faint click as China unkeyed his microphone and Sean reached over and switched off the radio set to conserve the battery. None of them spoke or moved, until another sharper metallic click broke the silence. To Sean the sound was unmistakable, the sound of a safety-catch being disengaged and he reacted instinctively, pushing Claudia flat and whirling round to face it.

For a moment, he was paralysed and then he screamed, 'No! Job, for Christ's sake! No!!' and hurled himself forward, like a sprinter from the blocks.

Job was lying on his side facing Sean, but well beyond his reach. Sean drove himself across the space that separated them, but he seemed to be wading through honey, sticky and slow, it impeded his movements. He watched Job raise the pistol, and he tried to prevent him by the force of his gaze. They were looking into each other's eyes, Sean trying to dominate and command him, but Job's eyes were sad, filled with a deep regret and yet unwavering.

Sean saw him open his lips and heard the muzzle of the pistol click against his teeth as Job thrust it deeply into his own mouth and closed his lips around the muzzle, like a child sucking a frozen lollipop. Sean reached out desperately, straining with all his strength to reach Job's pistol hand and rip the stubby black barrel out of his mouth. His fingertips had only touched Job's wrist when the pistol fired.

The sound was muffled, damped down by the flesh and bone of Job's skull.

In his extremity of effort, Sean's vision was enhanced to unnatural clarity and it seemed that time had been suspended so that everything happened very slowly, like a movie reel run at half speed.

Job's head altered shape, it swelled before Sean's eyes, like a rubber hallowe'en mask filled with high-pressure gas. His eyelids flew wide open and for an instant his eyeballs bulged from their sockets exposing a wide rim of white around their dark iris and then rolling upwards into his skull.

His shattered head changed shape again, elongating backwards, stretching his skin tightly over his cheekbones, and flattening his nostrils as the bullet drew the contents of his skull out through the back of his head, whiplashing his neck to its full stretch so that even in the aftermath of the shot, Sean heard the vertebrae creak and click.

Job was jerked backwards, his arm flung away from his head in a debonair salute with the Tokarev pistol still gripped in his clenched fist, but Sean was quick enough to catch him before his mutilated head hit the hard earth.

He caught Job in his arms and held him to his chest with all his strength. His body was heavy and hot with fever, but slack and plastic as though it contained no bone. It seemed to overflow Sean's enfolding arms, and he held him hard. He felt Job's muscles shiver and shudder, and his legs kicked in a macabre little jigging movement and he tried to hold him still.

'Job,' he whispered, and reached up behind him and cupped his hand over the back of his head, covering the terrible exit wound, as though he were trying to hold it together, to press the spilled contents back into the ruptured skull.

'You fool,' he whispered. 'You shouldn't have done it.' He laid his own cheek against Job's, and held him like a lover.

'We would have made it. I would have got you out.' Still hugging Job's quiescent body, he began to rock him gently, murmuring to him softly, pressing his cheek to Job's, his eyes closed tightly.

'We have come so far together, it wasn't fair to end it here.'

Claudia came to them and went down on one knee beside Sean. She reached out to touch his shoulder and searched desperately for something to say, but there were no words, and she stopped her hand before she touched him. Sean was oblivious of her and everything else around him.

His grief was so terrible to see that she felt she should not watch it. It was too private, too vulnerable, and yet she could not tear her eyes from his face. Her own feelings were overshadowed entirely by the magnitude of Sean's sorrow. She had developed a deep affection for Job, but it was as nothing compared to the love that she now saw laid naked before her.

It was as though that pistol shot had destroyed a part of Sean himself, and she experienced no sense of shock or surprise when he began to weep. Still holding Job in his arms, Sean felt the last involuntary tremors of dying nerves and muscle grow still and the first chill of death sap the heat from this body he hugged so tightly to his chest.

The tears seemed to well up from very deep inside of Sean and they came up painfully, burning all the way, scalding his eyelids when at last they forced their way between them and rolled slowly down his darkly weathered cheeks into his beard.

Even Alphonso could not watch it. He stood up and walked away into the thorn scrub, but Claudia could not move. She went on kneeling beside Sean, and her own tears rose in sympathy with his. Together they wept for Job.

Matatu had heard the shot from a mile out where he was guarding their rear, lying up on their back-spoor to watch for a following patrol.

He came in quickly and from the bush at the perimeter of the camp watched for only a few seconds before he deduced exactly what had happened. Then he crept in quietly and crouched behind Sean. Like Claudia, he respected Sean's mourning, waiting for him to master its first unbearably bitter pangs.

Sean spoke at last, without looking round, without opening his eyes.

'Matatu,' he said.

'Ndio, Bwana.'

'Go and find the burial place. We have neither tools nor time to dig a grave, yet he is a Matabele and he must be buried sitting up facing the direction of the rising sun.'

'Ndio, Bwana.' Matatu slipped away into the darkling forest and at last Sean opened his eyes and laid Job gently back upon the grey wool blanket. His voice was steady, almost conversational.

'Traditionally we should bury him in the centre of his own cattle kraal.' He wiped the tears from his cheeks with the back of his hand, and went on quietly, 'But we are wanderers, Job and I, he had no kraal nor cattle to call his own.'

She was not certain that Sean was speaking to her, but she replied, 'The wild game were his cattle, and the wilderness his kraal. He will be content here.'

Sean nodded, still without looking at her. 'I am grateful that you understand.'

He reached down and closed Job's eyelids. His face was undamaged except for the chips from his front teeth, and with a fold of the blanket, Sean wiped the blood from the corner of his mouth. Now he looked peaceful and at rest. Sean rolled him on his side and began to wrap him in the blanket, using the nylon webbing and the rifle slings to bind his body tightly into a sitting position, with his knees up under his chin.

Matatu returned before he had finished. 'I have found a good place,' he said, and Sean nodded without looking up from his task.

Claudia broke the silence. 'He gave his life for us,' she said quietly. 'Greater love hath no man.' It sounded so trite and unworthy of the moment, that she wished she had not said it, but Sean nodded again.

'I was never able to square the account with him,' he said. 'And now I never will.'

He was finished. Job was trussed securely into the grey blanket, only his head was exposed.

Sean stood up and went to his own small personal pack. He took out the only spare shirt it contained and came back to where Job lay. He knelt beside him again.

'Goodbye, my brother. It was a good road we travelled. I only wish we could have reached the end of it together,' he said softly, and leaned forward and kissed Job's forehead. He did it so unaffectedly that it seemed completely natural and right.

Then with the clean shirt, he wrapped Job's head, hiding the ghastly wound, and he picked him up in his arms and walked with him into the forest, cradling Job's head against his shoulder.

Matatu led him to an abandoned ant-bear hole in the thorn forest nearby. It was the work of a few minutes to enlarge the entrance just enough to slide Job's body down into it. With Matatu assisting him, Sean turned him until he was facing east, with his back to the evening star.

Before they covered the grave, Sean knelt beside it and took the fragmentation grenade from the pocket on his webbing. Matatu and Claudia watched as he cautiously rigged a booby trap with the grenade and a short length of bark twine. As he stood up, Claudia looked at him enquiringly, and he answered her shortly, 'Grave robbers.'

Matatu helped him pack stones around Job's shoulders to hold him in a sitting position. Then with larger boulders, they covered him completely, building a cairn over his grave that would keep the hyena out. When it was done, Sean did not linger. He had said his farewell. He walked away without looking back, and after a few moments Claudia followed him.

Despite her sorrow, in some strange way she felt privileged and sanctified by what she had witnessed. Her respect and love for Sean had been reinforced a hundredfold by the emotions he had displayed at the loss of his friend. She felt that his tears had proved his strength rather than betrayed his weakness, and that rare demonstration of love had only pointed up his manhood. From this terrible tragedy, she had learned more about Sean than she might otherwise have done in a lifetime.

They marched hard that night. Sean forged on as though he were trying to outrun his grief. Claudia did not try to slow him. Although she was now lean and fit as a coursing greyhound, she had to put out all her strength to stay with him, but she did not complain. By sunrise, they had covered almost forty miles from where they had buried Job and ahead of them, lay a wide alluvial plain.

Sean found a grove of tall trees to give them a little shade and while Claudia and Matatu prepared their meal, Sean slung his binoculars across his back and stuffed the field map into his back pocket and went to the base of the tallest tree.

Claudia watched him anxiously as he began to climb, but he was as nimble as a squirrel and as powerful as a bull baboon, using the brute strength of his arms to haul himself up the smooth stretches of the bole where there were no footholds.

When he neared the top of the tree, a white-backed vulture launched herself from her shaggy nest of dried branches and circled anxiously overhead while Sean settled into the fork of a branch only a few feet from the nest.

The vulture's nest contained two large chalky-white eggs and Sean murmured soothingly to the bird still cruising high above. 'Don't worry, old girl. I'm not going to steal them.' Sean did not share the popular distaste for these birds. They performed a vital function in cleansing the veld of carrion and disease, and while grotesque in repose, they were models of elegance and beauty in the air, masters of the sky and of natural flight, revered as gods by the ancient Egyptians and other peoples with a close affinity to nature.

Sean smiled up at the bird. The first smile that had bent his lips since Job had gone, and then he gave his full attention to the terrain spread out below him. The alluvial plain ahead had been intensively cultivated, only scattered groves of trees still stood between the open fields. Sean knew that these would mark the sites of the small family villages shown on his map. He turned his binoculars upon them.

He saw at once that the fields had not been tilled nor planted for many seasons. They were thick with the rank secondary growth that invades abandoned cultivation in Africa. He recognized the tall harsh stems of *Hibiscus irritans* named for the sharp fine hairs that cover the leaves and which brush off on anyone that touches them. He saw castor-oil bush and cotton gone wild, and the orange-coloured blossoms of wild cannabis, whose narcotic properties had first so delighted Jack Kennedy's peace corps boys and girls and which over the years since then, had given solace to the hordes of other European and American youngsters who had followed them out to Africa equipped only with back-packs, dirty blue jeans, good intentions and a hazy belief in beauty, peace and the brotherhood of man. Recently fear of Aids had slowed their arrival to a trickle and Sean was grateful for that. He realized his thoughts were wandering and he pulled himself up and panned his binoculars slowly across the scene of desolation ahead.

He could just make out the roofless ruins of the villages. On some of the huts, the roof timbers were still intact but skeletal and blackened by flames; the thatch burned away. Though he scrutinized the area meticulously, he could make out no sign of recent human presence. The paths between the fields were all overgrown, there was no sign of domestic stock, no chicken nor goat and no tell-tale tendrils of smoke rising from a cooking-fire.

'Somebody, Frelimo or Renamo, has worked this area over pretty thoroughly,' he thought, and then looked away to the east to the distant blue hills of the interior. This early in the morning, the air was still clear and bright and he was able to recognize some of the features and cross-reference them to the topography of his field map. Within fifteen minutes he was able to mark in their position with reasonable accuracy and confidence.

They had made a little better progress than he had estimated. Those mountains out on the right-hand side were the Chimanimani; they formed the border between Mozambique and Zimbabwe but their nearest peaks were almost forty kilometres distant. His map was marked in kilometres, and Sean still liked to work in miles rather than the metric scale.

The larger village of Dombe should be a few kilometres out on his left flank, but he could pick out no indication of its exact whereabouts. He guessed that like the other family villages ahead, it had long ago been abandoned and allowed to return to bush and forest, in which case there would be little prospect of finding food there. With so many feeding from it, the small quantity of maize-meal they had been able to bring with them was almost expended. By tomorrow they would need to begin foraging and that would slow them up. On the other hand, if Dombe was still inhabited, it would certainly be either a Frelimo or a Renamo stronghold. Prudently he resolved to avoid any contact with all other humans. Nobody, not even Alphonso, could say which territory was held by the opposing forces and which was a destruction area devastated equally by both sides. Even those boundaries would be fluid and would alter on a daily, if not an hourly basis, like the amorphous body of an amoeba.

He looked directly southward along their intended route. In that direction, there were no features rising above the plain. This was a part of the littoral that stretched down to the shores of the Indian Ocean, and no mountain nor deep valley ruffled it. The only natural obstacles ahead were the dense hardwood forests, the rivers and the swamps that guarded the approaches to them.

The largest river was the Sabi, or the Rio Save as the Portuguese named it as it flowed in across their border with the land that was to become Zimbabwe and down towards the ocean. It was broad and deep and they would probably need some sort of craft to make the crossing.

The last river, Rudyard Kipling's great grey-green, greasy Limpopo river, all set about with fever-trees, was the final obstacle they would face. It was still three hundred kilometres further south. Three national borders converged and met upon its banks, Zimbabwe, Mozambique, and the Republic of South Africa. If they were able to reach that point then they had reached the northern boundary of the celebrated Kruger National Park, heavily guarded and patrolled by the South African military. Sean studied the map longingly – South Africa and safety, South Africa and home, where the rule of law still held sway and men did not walk each moment in the shadow of death.

A soft whistle brought him out of his reverie, and he looked down. Matatu was at the base of the tree, sixty feet below where he sat. He gesticulated up at Sean.

'Listen!' he signalled. 'Danger!' And Sean felt his pulse trip and accelerate. Matatu did not use the danger signal lightly. He cocked his head and listened, but still it was almost a full minute before he heard it. As a bushman Sean's senses, especially eyesight and hearing, were honed and acute, but compared to Matatu, he was a blind mute.

As he heard and recognized the sound at last, even though it was faint and faraway, Sean's pulse jumped again and he swivelled round in the fork of the branch and looked back northwards, in the direction from which they had come.

Apart from a few high streaks of cirro-stratus cloud, the morning sky was empty blue. Sean put up his binoculars and searched it, looking low along the horizon, close to the tops of the tall hard-wood trees. The distant sound, increasing in volume, gave him a direction in which to search, until suddenly the shape appeared in the field of his binoculars and he felt the slide of dread in his guts.

Like some gigantic and noxious insect, the Hind cruised humpbacked and nose low above the forest tops. It was still some miles distant, but coming on directly towards Sean's tree-top perch.

* * *

General China sat in the flight engineer's seat under the forward canopy of the Hind and looked ahead through the armoured windscreen. This early in the morning the air had a crystalline lucidity through which the rays of the low sun lit every detail of the landscape below him with a radiant golden light.

Although he had already flown many hours in the captured machine, he had not yet grown accustomed to the extraordinary sense of power that his seat under the forward canopy aroused in him. The earth and everything in it lay below him, he could look down on mankind and know that he held the power of life and death over them.

He reached out now and gripped the control lever of the Gatling-cannon. The pistol grip fitted neatly into his right hand, and as the heel of his hand depressed the cocking plunger, the remote aiming screen lit on the control panel directly in front of him. As he moved the control lever, traversing, depressing or elevating, so the multiple barrels of the cannon faithfully duplicated each movement and the image of the target was reflected on the screen.

With the slightest pressure of his forefinger, he could send a dense stream of cannon shell hosing down to obliterate any target he chose. Then by simply throwing a switch on the weapons console, he could select any of the Hind's alternative armaments, the rockets in their pods or the banks of missiles.

It had not taken China long to master the complex weapons control system, for the basic training he had received in the Siberian guerrilla training camp so long ago, at the beginning of the Rhodesian war of liberation, had stood him in good stead down the years. However, this was the most awe-inspiring fire power he had ever had at his fingertips and the most exhilarating vantage point from which to deploy it.

At a single word of command, he could soar aloft like an eagle in a thermal, or plunge like a stooping peregrine, he could hover on high or dance lightly on the leafy tops of the forest. The power that this machine had bestowed upon him was truly godlike.

At first there had been serious problems to surmount. He could not work with the captured Russian pilot and crew. They were sullen and unreliable. Despite the threat of horrible death that hung over them he realized that they would seize the first opportunity to escape, or to sabotage his precious new Hind. One of the Russian ground crew need only drain the lubricant from a vital part of the machine, or loosen a bolt, or burn out a section of wiring, and neither China nor any of his Renamo had the technical expertise to recognize the sabotage attempt until it was too late. In addition, the Russian pilot had from the very beginning made communication between them difficult. He had played dumb and deliberately misunderstood China's commands. Trading on the knowledge that China could not do without him, he had become progressively more defiant and recalcitrant.

China had solved that problem swiftly. Within hours of the destruction of the Russian squadron and the capture of the Hind, he had radioed a long coded message to a station two hundred miles further north across the national boundary between Mozambique and Malawi. The message had been received and decoded at the headquarters of a large tea plantation on the slopes of Mlanje mountain, the proprietor of which was a member of the central committee of the Mozambique National Resistance and the deputy director of Renamo intelligence. He had telexed China's report and requests directly to the director general of the central committee at his headquarters in Lisbon, and within six hours a crack Portuguese military helicopter pilot with many thousands of hours flying experience and two skilled aeronautical engineers were aboard a TAP airliner southward bound for Africa. From Nairobi they changed to an Air Malawi commercial flight scheduled directly for Blantyre, the capital of Malawi. There a driver and Land-Rover from the tea plantation were waiting to whisk them out to the private airstrip on the tea estate.

That night the tea company's twin-engined Beechcraft, made a midnight crossing of Lake Cabora Bassa, a perilous journey that the pilot had undertaken many times before, and a single red flare guided him to the secret bush strip that General China's men had hacked out of the wilderness just west of the mountains of Gorongosa.

A double line of Renamo guerrillas, each holding aloft a burning torch of paraffin-soaked rags, provided a flare path and the Beechcraft pilot landed smoothly and without shutting down his engines deposited his passengers, turned and taxied back to the end of the rough airstrip and then roared away, climbed clear and turned northwards again into the night.

There had been a time not long ago when such a complicated route for bringing in men and material would not have been necessary. Only a year previously China's request would have been radioed southwards, rather than north, and the delivery vehicle, instead of a small private aircraft, would have been a Puma helicopter with the South African air-force markings.

In those days when the Marxist President of Frelimo, Samora Machel, had hosted the guerrillas of the African National Congress, and allowed them to use Mozambique as a staging post for their terror attacks with limpet mines and car bombs on the civilian population of South Africa, the South Africans had retaliated by giving their full support to the Renamo forces that were attempting to topple Machel's Frelimo government.

Then to the dismay of the Renamo command, Samora Machel and P. W. Botha, the South African president, had signed an accord at the little town of Nkomati on the border between their two countries, the direct result of which had been a drastic reduction of South African aid to Renamo in exchange for the expulsion of the ANC terror squads from Mozambique.

Both sides had cheated on the agreement, with a wink and a nudge. Machel had closed the ANC offices in Maputo but allowed them to continue their terror campaign without official Frelimo support or approval, and the South Africans had cut back on their support of Renamo, but still the Pumas made their clandestine cross-border flights.

Then the deck had been reshuffled when Samora Machel died in the wreck of his personal aircraft, an antiquated Tupolev which had been retired from airline service in the USSR and magnanimously given to Machel by his Russian allies. The Tupolev's instrumentation was decrepit, and on the night of the crash both the Russian pilots had been so full of vodka that they had neglected to file a flight plan. They were almost two hundred kilometres off-course when they crashed on the South African border, actually striking on the Mozambique side and then by some improbable chance bouncing and sliding across into South Africa.

Despite the evidence of the flight recorder, the Tupolev's black box, which contained a recording of the two Russian pilots' repeated requests for more vodka from the air hostess and an animated and anatomically precise discussion of exactly what they were going to do to her after they had landed, the Russians and the Frelimo government insisted that the South Africans had lured Machel to his death. The Nkomati accord died with Machel on that remote African hillside, and the Pumas resumed their cross-border flights, ferrying supplies to the Renamo guerrillas.

Then gradually news began to filter out of the Mozambiquan wilderness. At first a few dedicated missionaries emerged from the bush to describe the appalling destruction, the misery and the starvation, and the atrocities that were being perpetrated by the ravaging Renamo guerrilla armies over an area the size of France.

A few intrepid journalists managed to get into the battle zone, and one or two of them survived and emerged to relate their accounts of the holocaust that was raging. Some of their reports put the estimate of civilian casualties as high as half a million dead of starvation, disease and genocide.

Refugees, tens of thousands of them, began to stream across the border into South Africa. Terrified, starving, riddled with disease, they told their harrowing stories. The South Africans realized to their horror that they had been nourishing a monster in Renamo.

At the same time, the more moderate Chissano who had replaced Samora Machel as president of the government of Mozambique and Frelimo began making placatory overtures. The two presidents met and the Nkomati accord was hurriedly revived, this time with honest intent. Overnight, the flow of South African aid to Renamo was cut off.

This had all taken place only months before, and General China and his fellow Renamo commanders were angry and desperate men, their stores of food and weapons dwindling rapidly without prospect of resupply. Soon they would be reduced to surviving on plunder and loot, foraging and scavenging from a countryside already ravaged by twelve years of guerrilla warfare. It was inevitable that they would turn their fury on what remained of the civilian population and on any foreigner that they could capture. The world was against them, and they were against the world.

Sitting up in the high seat of the Hind, General China let all this run through his mind. From here he seemed to have an over-view of the chaos and confusion. The entire country was in a state of flux, and always in a situation such as this, there was opportunity for the cunning and the ruthless to seize upon.

Of the Renamo field commanders, General China had proved himself over the years to be the most resourceful. With each victory and success he had established his power more firmly. His army was the most powerful of the three Renamo divisions. The external central committee was nominally the high command of the resistance movement, but paradoxically General China's prestige and influence was becoming progressively greater with each setback that the movement received. More and more the central committee acceded to his wishes. The alacrity with which they had reacted to his request for a Portuguese pilot and engineers demonstrated this most aptly. Of course, the destruction of the Russian squadron and the capture of the Hind had enormously inflated his prestige and importance, while possession of the extraordinary vehicle in which he now soared over the wilderness placed him in a unique position of power.

General China smiled contentedly and spoke into the microphone of his hard helmet. 'Pilot, can you see the village yet?'

'Not yet, General. I estimate four minutes' more flying time.'

The Portuguese pilot was in his early thirties. Young enough still to have dash and fire, but old enough to have accumulated experience and discretion. He was handsome in a swarthy olive-skinned fashion, with a drooping gun-slinger moustache and the dark bright eyes of a predatory bird. From the first he handled the controls of the Hind with precision and confidence, and his skill had increased with each hour flown as he came to terms with every nuance of the Hind's flying characteristics.

The two Portuguese engineers had taken command of the Russian ground crew and supervised every move they made. One of the Hind's principal advantages was that it could be serviced and maintained in all conditions without the need for sophisticated equipment, and the chief engineer assured General China that the spares and tools he had captured at the laager were sufficient to keep the Hind airborne indefinitely. The only shortages were of missiles for the Swatter system and assault rockets, but this was amply compensated for by almost a million rounds of 12.7mm cannon shells they had captured in the laager.

It had taken a hundred and fifty porters to carry the munitions away, while another five hundred porters had each carried a twenty-five-litre drum of Avgas. Renamo used mainly women porters, trained since girlhood to carry weights on their heads. That quantity of Avgas was sufficient to keep the Hind flying for almost two hundred hours, and by then there would be a good chance of capturing a Frelimo fuel tanker, either on the railway line or on one of the roads nearer the coast that were still open to traffic.

However, General China's main concern at that moment was to keep the rendezvous which he had arranged by radio with General Tippoo Tip, the commander of Renamo's southern division.

'General, I have spotted the village,' the pilot spoke in China's headphones.

'Ah, yes, I see it,' China answered. 'Turn towards it, please.'

As the Hind approached Sean shifted his perch, creeping behind a densely leafed bough and flattening himself against the branch. Although he knew it was dangerous to turn his face towards the sky, he relied on the bush of his beard and his deep tan to prevent the sun reflecting off his face and he watched the helicopter avidly.

He realized that their ultimate survival depended on being able to elude this monster, and he studied its shape to estimate the view that the pilot and his gunner commanded from behind their canopies. It might be vital for Sean to know the blind spots of the flight engineer and the field of fire of his weapons.

He saw the cannon in the remote turret below the nose abruptly traverse left and right, almost as though the gunner was demonstrating them for him. Sean could not know that General China was merely gloating on his own power and playing with the weapon controls, but the movement illustrated the Gatling-cannon's restricted field of fire. The barrel could only swing through an arc of thirty degrees from lock to lock, beyond that the pilot was obliged to swivel the entire aircraft on its own axis in order to bring the cannon to bear.

The Hind was very close now. Sean could make out every minute detail of the hull, from the crimson 'Excellent' logo on the nose to the rows of rivet heads that stitched the titanium armour sheets. He looked for some weakness, some flaw in the massive armour, but in the few seconds, before she was overhead, he saw that she was impregnable, except for the air intakes to the turbo engines, like a pair of hooded eyes above the upper pilot's canopy. The intakes were screened by debris suppressors, bossed light metal discs that inhibited the dust and debris thrown up by the down-draught of the rotors when the helicopter hovered close to the ground from being sucked into the turbines. However, the debris suppressors were not so substantial as to prevent the Stinger missiles flying clearly into the intakes, and Sean saw that there was a necessary gap around the edge of the metal boss wide enough for a man to stick his head through. At the correct angle and from very close range an expert marksman might just be able to aim a burst of machine-gun fire through that gap so as to damage the turbine vanes. Sean knew that even a chip from one of those vanes would unbalance the turbine and set up such vibrations in the engine that it would fly to pieces within seconds.

'A hell of a shot, and a hell of a lot of luck,' Sean muttered, staring upwards through slitted eyes. Suddenly the light reflected from the armoured glass canopy altered so that he could see into the interior of the cockpit.

As he recognized General China, despite the hard plastic flying-helmet and the mirrored aviator glasses shielding his eyes, hatred flushed fiercely through Sean's guts. Here was the man on whom he could firmly set the blame for Job's death and all their other woes and hardships.

'I want you,' Sean muttered. 'God, how badly I want you.'

China seemed to sense the force of his hatred for he turned his head slightly and looked down directly at Sean's perch, staring at him evenly through the mirrored lens of his sunglasses, and Sean shrank down upon the branch.

Then abruptly the Hind banked away, exposing its blotched grey belly. The down-draught lashed the tree-top, shaking the branches, and throwing Sean about in the hurricane of disrupted air, and Sean realized that it had been an illusion and that China had not spotted him in his tree-top bower.

He watched the huge machine skitter away on its new heading and then a few miles distant the engine beat changed, the sound of the rotors whined in finer pitch and the Hind hovered briefly above the forest and then sank from view.

Sean clambered down the tree. Matatu had doused the small cooking-fire at the first sound of the Hind's approach, but the canteen of maize porridge had already cooked through.

'We'll eat on the march,' Sean ordered.

Claudia groaned softly, but pulled herself to her feet. Every muscle in her legs and back ached with fatigue.

'Sorry, beautiful.' Sean put an arm around her shoulders and squeezed her. 'China landed only a mile or two east of here. Probably at the village of Dombe, we can be pretty sure he has troops there. We've got to move on.'

They ate the last handfuls of hot sticky salted maize porridge on the march and washed it down with water from the bottles that tasted of mud and algae. 'From now on, we are living off the land,' Sean told her. 'And China is breathing down our necks.'

*　　*　　*

The Hind hovered a hundred feet above the road that ran through the village of Dombe.

It was the only road, and the village was merely a collection of twenty or so small buildings that had been long abandoned. The glass was broken from the window frames and the white-washed plaster had fallen from the adobe walls in leprous patches. Termites had devoured the roof timbers so that the corroded corrugated sheeting sagged from the roof. Those buildings fronting onto the road had all once been small general dealers' stores, the ubiquitous *dukas* of Africa, owned by Hindu traders. One faded sign hung at a drunken angle. 'Patel & Patel', it proclaimed between the crimson trademarks of the Coca-Cola company.

The road itself was dirt-surfaced and littered with rubbish and debris, weeds growing rankly in the unused ruts.

'Take us down,' China ordered, and the helicopter sank towards the roadway, lifting a whirlwind thick with dead leaves, scraps of paper, discarded plastic bags and other rubbish.

There were men on the verandah of 'Patel & Patel' and armed men amongst the derelict buildings, fifty or more, all heavily armed and dressed in an assortment of camouflage, military and civilian clothing, the eclectic uniform of the African guerrilla.

The Hind settled to the rutted road and the pilot throttled back the turbos; the rotors slowed and the engine noise sank to a low whistle. General China opened the armoured canopy, jumped down lightly to earth and turned to face the group of men on the stoep of the general dealer's store.

'Tippoo Tip,' he said, and opened his arms wide in fraternal greeting. 'How good to see you again.' He raised his voice above the engine whistle.

General Tippoo Tip came down the steps to meet him, his own thick arms held wide as a crucifix. They embraced with the utmost insincerity of two fierce rivals who knew that they might one day have to kill each other.

'My old friend,' said China, and held him at arm's length, smiling warmly and lovingly upon him.

Tippoo Tip was not his real name, he had taken that as his *nom de guerre* from one of the most notorious of the old Arab slave-traders and ivory-runners of the previous century. However, the name and its associations suited him to perfection, China thought as he looked down upon him. Here stood a rogue and brigand cast in the classic mould, a man to admire and to treat with great caution.

He was short, the top of his head on a level with China's chin, but everything else about him was massive. His chest was like that of a bull gorilla, and his thick arms hung in similar fashion, so his knuckles were at the level of his knees. His head was like one of those gigantic Rhodesian granite boulders balanced on the pinnacle of a rocky kopje. He had shaved his pate, but his beard was a thick mattress of woolly black curls, that hung onto his chest. The forehead and nose above it were broad and his lips full and fleshy.

He wore a gaily coloured strip of cotton cloth bound around his forehead, while a gilet of tanned kuku-hide over his naked torso was open down the front to expose his chest. His chest was covered with black peppercorns of wool, and his naked arms protruding from the short sleeves were thick and roped with muscle.

He smiled back at China and his teeth were brilliant as mother-of-pearl, in contrast to the smoky yellow whites of his eyes, laced with a network of veins.

'Your presence has perfumed my day with the scent of mimosa blossom,' he said in Shangane, but his eyes slid past China's face and returned to the huge helicopter from which he had disembarked. Tippoo Tip's envy was so unconcealed that China felt he could smell it and taste it like burning sulphur in the air.

That machine had altered the fine trim and balance of the relationship between these two most powerful of all the Renamo warlords. Tippoo Tip could not keep his eyes off it. It was obvious that he wanted to examine it more closely but China took his arm and led him back towards the shade of the verandah. The pilot had not killed the engines and as China and his host stepped out of the circle of the rotors he gunned the Hind and pulled on his collective. The great machine rose, and turned away.

Tippoo Tip twisted out of China's grip and shaded his eyes to watch it. His smoked yellow eyes were as hungry as though he were watching a beautiful naked woman performing an obscene act. China let him yearn after it until it passed out of sight. He had sent the Hind away purposely because he knew and understood Tippoo Tip. He knew that if the machine had remained, the temptation might have become too strong for him to resist, and treachery was as natural to both of them as breathing was to other men. The Hind was China's joker, his wild card.

Tippoo Tip shook himself and laughed for no apparent reason. 'They told me that you had destroyed the squadron and captured one of those, and I said, "China is a lion among men and he is my brother."'

'Come, my brother,' China agreed. 'It is hot in the sun.'

There were stools ready for them on the verandah in the shade and two of Tippoo Tip's young women brought them clay pots of beer, thick as gruel and refreshingly tart. The girls were both in their teens, pretty little things with eyes like fawns. Tippoo Tip liked women and always surrounded himself with them. It was one of his weaknesses, China thought, and smiled a cold superior smile. He himself could take a boy or a girl with equal enjoyment, but only as a brief diversion and not as a necessity of life, and the women engaged his attention for only a fleeting moment before he turned back to his host.

The bodyguards had retired out of earshot, and Tippoo Tip waved the girls away.

'And you, my brother?' China asked. 'How goes the battle? I hear that you have taken the head of Frelimo and pushed it down between their knees to give them a close-up view of their own fundament. Is that true?'

It was not true, of course. As commander of the southern division of Renamo, Tippoo Tip was closer to the capital and port of Maputo which was the centre of government power. He was, therefore, more prejudiced by the withdrawal of South African military assistance and he stood in the front line of Frelimo counter-attacks and reprisals. China knew that in the last few months Tippoo Tip had experienced heavy reversals and lost many men and much territory in the south, but now Tippoo Tip chuckled and nodded.

'We have eaten everything that Frelimo has sent against us. Swallowed them without a belch or a fart.'

They sparred lightly over the beer pots, smiling and laughing, but watching each other like lions over a kill, on guard and ready at any instant to pounce or defend themselves until, at last, China murmured, 'I am pleased to hear that all goes so well with you. I had come to see if my Hind gunship could assist you against Frelimo.' He spread his hands in a deprecating gesture. 'But I see you have no need of help from me.'

It was a machiavellian ploy, and China watched as the point slid through Tippoo Tip's guard and his expression changed. China knew that it would have been a serious tactical error to ask a man like this for assistance. Tippoo Tip had the nose of a hyena to smell out weakness. Instead China had offered the bait of the Hind, dangled it for an instant before his eyes, and then with a crafty sleight of hand made it disappear again.

Tippoo blinked and behind his grin he searched for a response. He also hated to admit failure or weakness to one who he knew would exploit it ruthlessly, but still he craved and lusted after that fabulous machine.

'The help of a brother is always welcome,' he contradicted pleasantly, 'especially a brother who rides the skies in his own *henshaw*.' And then he went on swiftly, 'And perhaps there is some small service that I can offer in return for your help?'

'Crafty rogue,' China thought, admiring his style. 'He knows I haven't come here out of compassion. He knows I want something.' And both of them retreated, in the African manner, behind another screen of pleasantries and trivialities, coming back only circuitously and almost flirtatiously to the main subject.

'I laid a trap for Frelimo,' Tippoo Tip boasted. 'I pulled back from the Save forests.' In truth he had been driven out of those infinitely valuable indigenous forests only after hard fighting, in the face of the most determined Frelimo attacks since the beginning of the long campaign.

'That was cunning of you,' China agreed, letting the razor edge of sarcasm flash in his tone. 'What a trap to leave the forests to Frelimo and how stupid of them to fall for it.'

The Save forests were a treasure house – seventy-foot-tall leadwoods, which were also called ivory tusk trees for their dense finely grained timber; magnificent Rhodesian mahogany which yielded logs five feet in diameter; and the most rare and valuable of all African trees, the tamboti or African sandalwood with its richly figured and scented timber.

Probably nowhere on the continent was there such a concentration of these precious hardwoods. They constituted the last natural resource of this ravaged land. First the great elephant herds had been wiped out, then the rhinoceros and the buffalo had been machine-gunned from the air. The Soviets and the North Koreans had plundered the vast natural prawn-beds and fisheries of the rich warm Mozambique current along the eastern coast, while foreign adventurers with Frelimo licences and approval had decimated the crocodile population of Lake Cabora Bassa. Only the forests still remained intact.

Even more so than the other newly independent African states, the government of Mozambique was desperately short of foreign exchange. For over a decade they had been fighting a drawn-out guerrilla war that had bled their economy white. Those forests were the last assets they had to sell for hard cash.

'They have moved in with labour battalions, twenty, perhaps thirty thousand slaves,' Tippoo Tip told China.

'So many?' China asked with interest. 'Where did they find them?'

'They have swept the last peasants off the land, they have raided the refugee camps, gathered the vagrants and the unemployed from the slums and streets of Maputo. They call it the "Democratic People's Full Employment Programme", and the men and women work from dawn to sundown for ten Frelimo escudos a day, and the single meal they are fed costs them fifteen Frelimo escudos.' Tippoo Tip threw back his head and laughed, more in admiration than amusement. 'Sometimes Frelimo is not so stupid,' he admitted. 'The labour battalions pay five escudos a day for the privilege of cutting the government timber, a most admirable arrangement.'

'And you have allowed Frelimo to do this?' China asked. It was not the plight of the labour battalions that concerned him. A single sixty-foot log of tamboti was valued at approximately fifty thousand US dollars, and the forests extended for hundreds of thousands of acres.

'Of course I allow them to do this,' Tippoo Tip agreed. 'They cannot move the timber out until the roads and the railway are reconstructed, and until then they are piling the logs in dumps along the old line of rail. My scouts count each log that is added to the stock pile.' Tippoo Tip took a grubby plastic-covered notebook from the pocket of his kudu-skin gilet and showed China the figures that he had neatly noted down in blue ballpoint pen on the back page.

China kept his face impassive as he read the total, but his eyes glittered behind the gold-rimmed sunglasses. That sum of dollars was sufficient to finance the war chest of both armies for a further five years, enough to buy the alliance of nations or to elevate a small warlord to the estate of president over the entire nation for life.

'The time is almost ready for me to return to the forests of Save and collect the harvest that Frelimo has gathered in ready for me.'

'How would you export this harvest? A log of tamboti weighs a hundred tons, who would buy it from you?'

Tippoo Tip clapped his hands and shouted to one of his aides who was squatting in the shade of the building across the street.

The guerrilla jumped up and hurried to where the two generals sat. He knelt to unroll a field map on the cracked concrete floor of the verandah between their stools and placed lumps of broken concrete on the corners of the map to hold it flat. Tippoo Tip and China leaned forward to study it.

'Here are the forests.' Tippoo Tip traced out the boundaries of that vast area between the Rio Save and Limpopo rivers, directly south of their own position. 'Frelimo have set up their timberyards, here and here and here.'

'Go on,' China encouraged him.

'The most southerly dump is only thirty miles from the north bank of the Limpopo, thirty miles from the South African border.'

'The South Africans have disavowed us, they have signed an accord with Chissano and Frelimo,' China pointed out.

'Treaty and accords are merely pieces of paper.' Tippoo Tip waved them aside. 'Here, we are discussing half a billion US dollars' worth of timber. I have already received assurances from our erstwhile allies in the south that if I can make good delivery, they will arrange transport to their border and payment in Lisbon or Zurich.' He paused. 'Frelimo has cut and stacked the goods for me, it remains only for me to collect and deliver.'

'And my new helicopter gunship will assist your collection?' China suggested.

'Assist, yes, although I could achieve the same result with my own forces.'

'Perhaps, but a joint operation would be quicker and more certain,' China told him. 'We share the fighting and the spoils. With my *henshaw* and reinforcements from the north it would take a week or less to drive the Frelimo forces out of the forests.'

Tippoo Tip pretended to consider the proposition, and then nodded and asked delicately, 'Of course, I could reward you for your help, with a modest percentage of the value of the timber we capture.'

'Modest is not a word I greatly favour,' China sighed. 'I prefer the good socialist word equal, let us say an equal share?' And Tippoo Tip looked pained and threw up his hands in protest.

'Be reasonable, my brother.' For an hour longer they haggled and argued, slowly drawing closer to striking a bargain over the private distribution of a nation's wealth and the fate of tens of thousands of wretched individuals in the labour battalions.

'My scouts tell me that the people in the logging camps are near the end of their usefulness,' Tippoo Tip remarked at one point. 'Frelimo have fed them on such rations that nearly all of them are sick and starving. They are dying by hundreds each day and they are cutting half the timber that they were two months ago. Frelimo have run out of replacements for the logging gangs and the whole business is running down. There is not much to be gained by waiting any longer, we should attack immediately, before the beginning of the rains.'

China looked at his digital wristwatch, a badge of rank as significant as the star upon his epaulettes. The Hind would be returning to pick him up within half an hour, he must conclude the negotiations and strike the bargain. Within minutes, they had agreed on the last details of the combined operation and then China mentioned casually, 'There is one other matter.' And his tone alerted Tippoo Tip to the importance of the next request. He leaned forward on the stool and placed his hands, as broad and powerful as the paws of a grizzly bear, on his knees. 'I am chasing a small party of white fugitives. It seems that they are attempting to reach the South African border.' Briefly China sketched out a description of Sean's party and ended, 'I want you to alert all your forces between here and the Limpopo to be on the look-out for them.'

'A white man and a white woman, a young white woman. It sounds interesting, my brother.' Tippoo Tip said thoughtfully.

'The man is the most important. The woman is an American and may have some value as a hostage, but otherwise she means little.'

'To me a woman always has value,' Tippoo Tip contradicted him. 'Especially if she is white and young. I like a change of flesh occasionally. Let us make another bargain, my brother, once again equal shares. If I help you to capture these runaway whites, you may have the man, but I will keep the woman. Is it agreed?'

China thought for a moment and then nodded. 'Very well, you may have her, but I want the man alive and uninjured.'

'That is exactly how I want the woman,' Tippoo Tip chuckled. 'So again, we are in accord.' He stretched out his right hand, and China took it. Both of them knew as they stared into each other's eyes that the gesture was meaningless, that their agreement would be honoured only as long as it favoured both of them, and it could be broken without warning by either of them as circumstances altered.

'Now tell me about this young white woman,' Tippoo Tip invited. 'Where was she last seen, and what are you doing to catch her?'

China returned immediately to the map spread between them and Tippoo Tip took note of the new animation in his expression and the eagerness in his voice as he explained how Sean and his party had avoided the trap he had set on the border and how the Shangane deserters had reported their position and their intention of heading southwards.

'We know their last definite position was here.' China touched a spot just north of the railway line. 'But that was three days ago. They could be anywhere along here.' He spread his hand and drew it down across the map. 'One of the party is badly wounded so they have probably not reached this far south. I have patrols, almost three hundred men quartering the ground south of the railway looking for their spoor, but I want you to lay a net, like this, in front of them. How many men can you spare?'

Tippoo Tip shrugged. 'I have already placed three companies here along the Rio Save keeping watch on the logging in the forests. There are five more companies spread across in here, further north. If these whites are trying to reach the Limpopo border, they will have to pass right through my lines and the Frelimo guards in the forest. I will radio my company commanders to be fully alert for them.'

General China's tone was sharp and authoritative. 'They must cover every trail, every river crossing. They must stake out a stop line with no gaps in it, and my sweep line coming down from the north will drive them onto it. But warn your section commanders that the white man is a soldier and a good one. He commanded the Ballantyne Scouts at the end of the war.'

'Courtney,' Tippoo Tip broke in. 'I remember him well.' And then he chuckled. 'Of course, it was Courtney who led the raid on your base. No small wonder that you want him so badly. You and Colonel Courtney go back many years. You have a long memory, my brother.'

'Yes,' China nodded, and touched the lobe of his deaf ear. 'Many years and a long memory, but then revenge is a dish that tastes best if it is eaten cold.'

They both looked up as the sound of the Hind's turbos whistled in from the north of the village and China checked his wristwatch. The pilot was precisely on time for the pickup and China felt his confidence in the young Portuguese reinforced. He stood up from the stool.

'We will maintain radio contact on 118.4 MHZ,' he told Tippoo Tip. 'Three schedules daily, six a.m., noon and six in the evening.' But Tippoo Tip was not looking at him, he was looking up longingly at the shape of the Hind as it hovered above the village like some mutated monster from a horror movie.

General China settled himself into the flight engineer's seat and closed the armoured-glass canopy. He raised his right thumb towards where Tippoo Tip stood on the verandah of the derelict *duka* and as he returned the salute, the Hind rose vertically above the village and swung its nose towards the north.

'General, one of the patrols has been calling you urgently on the radio.' The pilot spoke in China's earphones. 'They are using the call sign "Twelve Red".'

'Very well, please switch to the patrol frequency,' China ordered, and watched the digital display on the panel of his radio transmitter.

'"Twelve Red" this is "Banana Tree". Do you read?' he spoke into his helmet microphone. 'Twelve Red' was one of his crack scouting groups sweeping for spoor south of the railway line. Glancing at the map on his knee China tried to guess the scouts' exact position. The section leader answered his call almost immediately.

'"Banana Tree", this is "Twelve Red". We have a confirmed contact.'

China felt the excitement and triumph rise in his chest, but he kept his voice level.

'Report your position,' he ordered; and as the section leader read out the co-ordinates China checked them on his field map, and saw that the patrol was about thirty-five miles due north of the village.

'Have you got that, pilot?' he asked. 'Get there as fast as you can.' And as the engine tone of the Hind rose sharply he called ahead, '"Twelve Red", give us a red flare when you have us in sight.'

Seven minutes later the flare arced up out of the forest almost directly under the Hind's nose, and the pilot slowed the machine and let it drift down towards the tree-tops.

The Renamo patrol had cleared a landing zone with their machetes and the pilot manoeuvred the Hind into it and let her settle in a cloud of dust and debris. He saw with satisfaction that the scouts had thrown out a protective screen around the landing zone. They were crack bush fighters. China leapt eagerly out of the cockpit and the section leader came forward to salute him. He was a lean veteran, festooned with weapons and water-bottles and bandoliers of ammunition.

'They passed this way sometime yesterday,' he reported.

'Are you sure it's them?' China demanded.

'The white man and woman,' the section leader nodded. 'But they buried something over there.' He pointed with his chin. 'We have not touched it, but I think it is a grave.'

'Show me.' China ordered, and followed him into the thorn thicket. The section leader stopped beside a cairn of boulders.

'Yes, a grave.' China said with finality. 'Open it up.'

The section leader snapped an order at two of his men and they laid aside their weapons and went forward. They kicked away the top stones and rolled them down the slope.

'Hurry!' China called. 'Work faster!' And the ironstone boulders rang against each other and struck sparks as they were hurled aside.

'There is the corpse,' the section leader called, as Job's bundled head was exposed. He stepped forward and jerked aside the stained shirt that covered it.

'It's the Matabele.' China recognized Job's features immediately. 'I didn't think he'd get this far. Dig him out and feed him to the hyena,' he ordered.

Two of the scouts reached down and seized Job's blanket-wrapped shoulders and China watched with ghoulish interest. Mutilation of the enemy dead was an ancient Nguni custom, the ritual disembowelment allowed the spirit of the vanquished to escape so that it would not plague the victor. There was, however, a vindictive satisfaction in watching his men exhume the Matabele. He understood what grief this act would cause Sean Courtney, and he relished how he would describe it to him on his next radio transmission.

At that moment, he spotted the short length of bark twine. It was twisted lightly around the blanket-wrapped shoulders of the corpse. For a moment he stared at it with puzzlement and then as he saw it tighten and heard the click of the grenade primer, he realized what it was and he screamed a warning and hurled himself face forward to the earth.

The explosion crushed his eardrums and filled his head with pain. He felt the blast wave hit him and something struck him in the cheek with numbing force. He rolled into a sitting position, and for a moment thought that he had lost his eyesight; then the stars and catherine wheels of light that filled his head dissipated, and with a rush of relief he realized that he could see again.

Blood was streaming down the side of his face, and dribbling from his chin onto the front of his battledress blouse. He whipped the kerchief from around his neck and wadded it into the deep gash that a fragment from the grenade had opened across his cheekbone.

Unsteadily he came to his feet and stared down into the grave. The grenade had gutted one of his men like a fish. He was kneeling and trying to push his own bowels back into the hole, but the wet lining was sticking to his bare hands. The second guerrilla had been killed cleanly. The section leader sprang to China's side and tried to examine the gash in his cheek, but China struck his hands away.

'You white bastard,' his voice was shrill. 'You will pay dearly for that, Colonel Courtney. I swear it to you.'

The wounded guerrilla was still fumbling with his own entrails, but they bulged out between his fingers. He was making a dreadful cawing bubbling sound that only increased General China's fury.

'Get that man out of here!' he screamed. 'Take him away and shut him up!'

They dragged the wounded man away and still China was not satisfied. He was shaking wildly with shock and fury, looking around for something on which to vent his rage.

'You men!' He pointed with a trembling finger. 'Bring your pangas.' Two guerrillas ran forward to obey. 'Pull that Matabele dog out of his hole! That's right. Now use the pangas. Chop him into hyena food. That's it. Small pieces, don't stop! Mincemeat! I want him turned into mincemeat!'

* * *

All that morning Matatu led them southwards through the abandoned fields and past the deserted villages. The weeds and rank secondary growth gave them good cover and they avoided the footpaths and skirted the burnt-out huts.

Claudia was having difficulty keeping up. They had been going with only brief rests since the previous evening and she was reaching the limits of her endurance. There was no sensation of pain. Even the devilish little red-tipped thorns that left red weeping lines across the exposed skin of her arms merely tugged painlessly at her as she passed. Her steps were leaden and mechanical, and though she tried to keep the rhythm of the march, she felt herself running down like a clockwork toy. Slowly Sean drew ahead of her and she could not lengthen her stride to hold him. He glanced over his shoulder and saw how she was lagging and slowed for her to catch up.

'I'm sorry,' she blurted, and he glanced at the sky.

'We have to keep going,' he answered, and she toiled on behind him.

A little after midday they heard the Hind again. The sound of its engines were very faint and grew fainter still, dwindling away into the north.

Sean put out an arm to steady Claudia as she swayed on her feet.

'Well done,' he told her gently. 'I'm sorry I had to do that to you, but we've made good ground. China will never expect us to have got so far south. He has headed back northwards, and we can rest now.'

He led her to a cluster of low thorn acacia which formed a natural shelter. She sobbed with exhaustion as she sank to the hard ground and lay quietly as Sean squatted in front of her to remove her shoes and socks.

'Your feet have hardened up beautifully,' he told her as he massaged them gently. 'Not a sign of a blister. You're as tough as a Scout and twice as gutsy.' She couldn't even raise a smile at the compliment. Sean pulled her sock over his hand, stuck one finger through the hole in the toe and wiggled it like a ventriloquist's dummy.

'Okay. She walks good,' he made the sock speak like Miss Piggie, 'but, buster, you should see her in the sack.'

Claudia giggled weakly and he smiled down at her gently. 'That's better,' he said. 'Now go to sleep.'

For a few minutes longer she watched him working on her sock.

'Which of your trollops taught you to darn?' she murmured drowsily.

'I was a virgin until I met you. Go to sleep.'

'I hate her whoever she was,' Claudia said, and closed her eyes. It seemed to her that she opened them again immediately but the light had changed to soft shades of evening and the midday heat had cooled. She sat up.

Sean was cooking over a small fire of dry sticks, and he looked across at her.

'Hungry?' he asked.

'Starving.'

'Dinner.' He brought the metal billy to her.

'What is it?' she asked suspiciously, and peered down at the heap of scorched black sausages, each the size of her little finger.

'Don't ask,' he said. 'Eat.'

Gingerly she picked one out and sniffed at it. It was still hot from the cooking-fire.

'Eat!' he repeated, and to set an example popped one into his own mouth, chewed and swallowed.

'Damned good,' he gave his opinion. 'Go ahead.'

Carefully she bit into it and it squelched between her teeth and burst, filling her mouth with the consistency of warm custard that tasted like creamed spinach. She forced it down.

'Have another.'

'No thanks.'

'They're full of protein. Eat.'

'I couldn't.'

'You won't last out the next march on an empty stomach. Open your mouth.' He fed her and then himself alternately.

When the billy was empty, she asked again, 'Now tell me, what have I been eating?' But he grinned and shook his head and turned to Alphonso who was squatting across the fire devouring his share of the meal.

'Rig the radio,' Sean ordered. 'Let's hear if China has anything to say.'

While Alphonso was busy stringing the radio aerial, Matatu slipped quietly into camp. He was carrying a cylinder of freshly peeled bark whose ends were stoppered with plugs of dried grass. He and Sean exchanged a few words, and Sean looked serious.

'What is it?' Claudia asked with concern.

'Matatu has seen a lot of sign up ahead. It looks like there is a great deal of patrol activity. Frelimo or Renamo, he can't tell which.'

That made her uneasy and Claudia moved a little closer to where Sean sat and leaned against his shoulder. Together they listened to the radio, and here again there seemed to be a much higher level of traffic, most of it in Shangane or African-accented Portuguese.

'There is something brewing,' Alphonso grunted, as he concentrated on the set. 'They are moving patrols into a stop line.'

'Renamo?' Sean asked, and Alphonso nodded.

'Sounds like General Tippoo Tip's men.'

'What does he say?' Claudia asked, but Sean didn't want to alarm her further.

'Routine traffic,' he lied, and Claudia relaxed and watched Matatu at the cooking-fire as he carefully unstoppered the bark cylinder and shook out its contents onto the coals. As she realized what he was cooking, she stiffened with horror.

'Those are the most disgusting. . . !' She couldn't finish and she stared in awful fascination at the huge hairy caterpillars writhing and wriggling on the coals. Their long ginger hair frizzled off in little puffs of smoke and gradually the worms stopped moving and curled into little crisp black sausages.

Claudia let out a tiny strangled cry and clutched at Sean's arm as she recognized them. 'They aren't. . . !' she gasped. 'I didn't! You didn't make me! Oh! No! I can't believe. . . !'

'Highly nutritious,' Sean assured her, and Matatu seeing the direction of her gaze picked one of the caterpillars out of the coals and passing it quickly from hand to hand to cool it, offered it to her with a magnanimous flourish.

'I think I'm going to throw up,' Claudia said faintly, and turned her face away. 'I can't believe I actually ate one of those.'

At that moment the radio crackled sharply and a voice spoke very faintly in a guttural language that Claudia could not understand. However, Sean's sudden interest in the transmission distracted her from her feelings of nauseous disgust and she asked, 'What language is that?'

'Afrikaans,' he replied shortly. 'Quiet! Listen!' But the transmission faded out abruptly.

'Afrikaans?' she asked. 'South African Dutch?'

'That's right,' Sean nodded. 'We must be getting within extreme range. That was almost certainly a South African military transmission. probably a border patrol on the Limpopo.' Sean spoke briefly to Alphonso and then told Claudia. 'He agrees. South African border patrol. Alphonso says they sometimes pick up skip transmissions like that even further north.' Sean checked his wristwatch. 'Well. it doesn't look as though General China is going to entertain us this evening. We had better pack up and get ready to march.' Sean had half risen when suddenly the radio burst into life again. This time the voice was so clear that they could hear every intake of General China's breath.

'Good evening. Colonel Courtney. Please forgive me for the late schedule. but I have had urgent business to attend to. Come in please. Colonel Courtney.'

In the silence that followed Sean made no move towards the microphone. and General China chuckled softly across the ether.

'Still at a loss for words. Colonel. Never mind. I'm sure you are listening. so I will congratulate you on the ground you have covered to date. Quite remarkable. especially in view of Miss Monterro's brake upon your progress.'

'Arrogant bastard.' Claudia whispered bitterly. 'He is everything and a male chauvinist pig to boot.'

'Quite frankly. Colonel Courtney. you took me by surprise. We have been forced to redeploy our stop lines further south to welcome you.'

Again there was a short silence and then suddenly General China's voice was full of malice.

'You see. Colonel. we have found where you buried your Matabele.' Claudia felt Sean stiffen beside her and the silence drew out until China spoke again. 'We dug up the body and we were able to judge how long it had been in the earth by the extent of putrefaction.' Sean began to tremble and China went on affably. 'A Matabele can stink like a dead hyena and your friend was no exception. Tell me. Colonel. did you put that bullet in his head? Very sensible thing to do. He wasn't going to make it anyway.'

'The swine! The bloody swine!' It was wrung out of Sean.

'Oh and by the way. the booby trap didn't work. Very amateurish effort. I'm afraid.' China laughed easily. 'And don't worry about the Matabele. I made it easier for the hyena. I put two of my men to work on him with pangas. Bite-size chunks. Colonel. Matabele goulash!'

Sean lunged for the microphone and snatched it to his mouth.

471

'You depraved bloody animal!' he yelled into it. 'You filthy ghoul! By Christ, you'd better pray I never get my hands on you!'

Sean broke off, panting with the strength of his outrage.

'Thank you, Colonel.' There was a smile in General China's voice. 'I was getting bored with talking to myself. It's good to be in contact again. I've missed you.'

With a huge effort Sean resisted the temptation to reply and instead switched off the set.

'Pack up.' His voice was still trembling with fury. 'China will have us pretty well pinpointed after that little outburst. We've got to move fast now.'

'Like we were dragging our heels before?' Claudia asked with resignation, but stood up obediently.

Yet their progress was slower this night. Twice before midnight Matatu cautioned them to wait, warned by his animal sixth sense of danger ahead. He went forward to scout the track and found the ambush that had been set for them, and each time they were forced to make a slow and stealthy detour to avoid the trap.

'General Tippoo Tip's men,' Alphonso muttered. 'He must be helping General China. There are men waiting for us on every path.'

However, after midnight their luck changed for the better. Matatu came across a well-used path running almost directly southwards, and discovered that only a short time before a large detachment of men had passed along it in the same direction as they were headed.

'We'll use their spoor to cover our own.' Sean seized the opportunity and put Matatu in the lead, with Claudia following him, while he and Alphonso took the drag, deliberately treading over the small distinctive footmarks of the leading pair, obliterating them and losing them in the heavy sign which the party of Tippoo Tip's men had left behind them.

They hurried along the path until Matatu's sharp ears picked out the tiny sounds that the Renamo patrol was making as it moved forward in the silence of the night. Then they moderated their pace and trailed them at a discreet distance, letting the patrol run interference for them.

Keeping in contact with the enemy, maintaining the strict interval that was the line between discovery and concealment was a delicate and eerie business for which they had to rely completely on Matatu's hearing and night sight, but they were moving at almost double the pace they could have hoped for without this assistance.

A little before dawn the Renamo patrol stopped just ahead of them and they crouched in the darkness and listened to them setting up an ambush on both sides of the pathway. Once the ambush party was settled in, Matatu led them on another detour to meet the path again further on and they struck out southwards once again.

'We have covered twenty-five miles by my reckoning,' Sean murmured with grim satisfaction, as the first delicate light of dawn paled the eastern stars. 'But we cannot risk moving further in daylight, the country is crawling with Renamo. Matatu, find us a place to lie up for the day.'

During that night march, they had moved into an area of wet vlei ground on the approaches to the Save river and now Matatu led them deliberately into the tall swamp grass. They waded knee-deep across the flood plains that guarded the river, picking their way between shallow open lagoons from which the mosquitos rose in grey clouds. The water covered their tracks and Sean brought up the rear of the file, meticulously closing the swamp grass and brushing it upright behind him to disguise their passing.

A few hundred yards off the path Matatu discovered a small dry island only inches above the level of the flood waters and as he stepped onto it there was a violent upheaval in the reeds as a heavy body rushed through it.

Claudia screamed with shock, certain they had blundered into another murderous Renamo ambush. However, Matatu whipped out his skinning knife and with a shrill war-cry dived into the grass; there was a wild commotion as he wrestled with a writhing scaly body twice his own size.

Sean rushed forward to help him and between them they clubbed and stabbed the creature and dragged it out of the grass on to the island. Claudia shuddered with horror as she realized that it was a huge grey lizard, almost seven feet long, with a speckled yellow belly and a long whip of a tail that still twitched and lashed from side to side.

With squeaks of glee, Matatu began immediately to peel off the scaly skin.

'What is it?'

'Matatu's favourite delicacy, leguan.' Sean whetted the blade

473

of his trench knife on the palm of his hand and then helped Matatu butcher the monitor lizard.

The flesh from the tail was white as the fillets of Dover sole, but Claudia grimaced when Sean offered her a strip.

'You and Matatu would eat your own offspring,' she accused.

'That from the girl who dines regularly on mopane caterpillars!'

'Sean, I couldn't. I really couldn't force myself. Not raw.'

'We haven't any dry wood for a fire and you have eaten Japanese sashimi, haven't you? You told me you loved it.'

'That's raw fish, not raw lizard!'

'Same difference, think of it as a kind of African sashimi,' he coaxed her gently. When at last she gave in and tasted it, she found it surprisingly palatable, and her hunger overcame her squeamishness.

For once there was no shortage of water and they filled their bellies with sweet white meat and flood water and then curled up on their blankets. With the tall swamp grass swaying over their heads to protect them from the burning sunlight and the eyes in the sky, Claudia felt secure and gave in to her fatigue.

Once in the middle of the day, she woke and lay in Sean's arms to listen to the sound of the searching Hind.

'China is working the riverbanks ahead of us,' Sean whispered. The sound of the Hind's turbos rose and fell as it turned on each leg of the search pattern, and Claudia felt her stomach muscles knotting and contracting as it grew louder, passing only a short distance south of where they lay, and then finally faded into silence.

'He's gone.' Sean hugged her. 'Get some sleep.'

She woke again with a sense of panic upon her, but when she tried to move she found herself held down firmly and the palm of someone's hand clamped painfully across her mouth. She turned her eyes sideways and Sean's face was close to hers.

'Quiet!' he breathed in her ear. 'Not a peep out of you.'

When she nodded he released her and rolled over to look out through the screen of swamp grass. She did the same and peered out across the shallow waters of the lagoon.

At first she saw nothing and then she heard someone singing. It was a sweet girlish treble softly piping a Shangane love song, and with it came the sound of light footfalls in the shallow lagoon water. The singing came very close, so close that Claudia instinctively shrank nearer to Sean and held her breath.

Then suddenly the singing girl stepped into the line of her vision through the aperture in the grass before Claudia's eyes. She was a slim and graceful lass, just past puberty for though her features were sweet and childlike, her breasts were big and round as tsama melons. She wore only a ragged loin-cloth pulled up between her long coltish legs and her skin glowed in the late afternoon sunlight like burnt molasses. She seemed as wild and fey as a spirit of the forest and Claudia was instantly enchanted by her.

In her right hand the girl carried a light reed fishing spear with multiple barbed grains, and as she waded softly through the lucid warm waters she held the spear poised to strike.

Abruptly the song died on her lips and she froze for an instant and then lunged with the grace of a dancer. The shaft of the spear twitched in her hands and with a happy little cry she lifted a long slimy catfish clear of the water. It wriggled on the end of the spear, its wide whiskered mouth gulping and grunting and the girl clubbed its flattened skull and dropped it into the plaited-reed bag at her waist.

She washed the fish slime from her small pink-palmed hands, picked up the spear and resumed her fishing, coming on directly towards where they lay in the patch of swamp grass. Sean reached out and squeezed Claudia's arm, cautioning her not to move, but the black girl was already so close that with a few more paces, she would stumble over them.

Suddenly she looked up, directly into Claudia's eyes. The two of them stared at each other for only a moment, and then the girl whirled and darted away. In an instant, Sean was up and racing after her, and from the grass on either side both Alphonso and Matatu rushed out to join the chase.

The girl was halfway across the lagoon before they caught up with her; she tried to dodge and double back, but each way she turned there was one of them ready to cut her off and, at last, she stood at bay. Wild-eyed and panting with terror, but holding the fishing spear determinedly in front of her. Her courage and spirit were wasted against the three men facing her; like a cat surrounded by alsatians she had no chance of escape.

Matatu feinted at her flank and the instant she turned the point of the spear towards him, Sean knocked it out of her hands and swept her up under his arm. Kicking and clawing, he carried her back to the island and dumped her on the dry land. She had lost both her straw bag and loin-cloth in the struggle, and she crouched naked and trembling, staring up at the men who surrounded her.

Sean spoke to her in soft soothing tones, but at first she would not reply. Then Alphonso questioned her, and as soon as the girl realized that he was of her own tribe, she seemed to relax slightly, and after another few gentle questions, made a hesitant breathless response.

'What does she say?' Claudia could not restrain her concern for the child.

'She is living here in the swamps to hide from the soldiers,' Sean answered. 'Renamo killed her mother and Frelimo took her father and the rest of her family away to cut trees in the forest. She escaped.'

They questioned the girl for almost an hour. How far ahead was the river? Was there a crossing? How many soldiers were there at the river? Where were the Frelimo cutting trees? And as she replied to each question, the girl's terror abated and she seemed to sense Claudia's sympathy and looked towards her with a pathetic childlike trust.

'I speak English a little, miss,' she whispered at last, and Claudia was startled.

'How did you learn?'

'At the mission, before the soldiers came and burned it and killed the nuns.'

'Your English is good.' Claudia smiled at her. 'What is your name, child?'

'Miriam, miss.'

'Don't get too chummy,' Sean warned Claudia grimly.

'She's a darling little thing.'

Sean seemed about to reply but then thought better of it and looked up at the sunset instead. 'Damn it, we have missed China's radio schedule. Let's get ready to move out. Time to get cracking.'

It took only minutes for them to gird up for the march, and with her pack on her back, Claudia asked, 'What about the girl?'

'We'll leave her here,' Sean said, but something in his voice and the way he looked away worried Claudia. She started to follow Sean as he stepped off the island into the water, and then she stopped and looked back. The black girl still squatted naked, staring after Claudia unhappily, but behind her stood Matatu, and he had the skinning knife in his right hand.

Realization dashed over Claudia like a huge wave of icy anger.

476

'Sean!' Her voice shook as she called him back. 'What are you going to do to this child?'

'Don't worry about it,' he told her brusquely.

'Matatu!' She began to tremble. 'What are you going to do?' And he grinned at her. 'Are you going to. . . ?' She drew her finger across her own throat, and Matatu nodded merrily and showed her the knife.

'*Ndio*,' he agreed. '*Kufa*.' She knew that Swahili word. Matatu had used it whenever her father had shot down an animal and Matatu had slit its throat. Suddenly she was shaking with anger. She rounded on Sean.

'You're going to murder her!' Her voice was shrill with outrage and horror.

'Wait, Claudia, listen. We can't leave her here. If they catch her . . . It would be suicide.'

'You bastard!' she screamed at him. 'You're as bad as any Renamo thug, as bad as China himself!'

'It's our lives, don't you understand? It's survival.'

'I can't believe what I'm hearing!'

'This is a hard, cruel land. If we are to survive, we have to live by those standards. We can't afford the folly of compassion.'

She wanted to attack him physically, she balled her fists in the effort of self-control, but her voice was still shrill.

'Compassion and conscience are all that separate us from the animals.' She drew a deep breath. 'If you value what there is between us, you won't say anything more, you won't try to rationalize what you almost did to this child.'

'You prefer to be captured by General China?' he demanded. 'This child, as you call her, won't hesitate to give them our exact whereabouts.'

'Don't, Sean! I'm warning you, everything you say is causing damage to our relationship that can never be repaired.'

'All right then.' Sean reached out to take her hands and draw her to him. 'What do you want us to do with her? I'll do whatever you say. You want us to turn her loose to report to the first Renamo patrol that comes along, I'll do it.'

Claudia was standing rigid in the circle of his arms and though the strident edge was gone from her voice, it was cold and determined.

'We'll take her with us.'

Sean dropped his arms. 'With us?'

'That's what I said. If we can't leave her, then that is the only solution.'

Sean stared at her and she went on firmly, 'You said you'd do whatever I say. You gave me a promise.'

He opened his mouth and then closed it and looked at the black girl. She had understood some of the argument, enough to know that her life was at stake and that Claudia was her champion, her saviour. When Sean saw the expression on the child's face, suddenly he was filled with shame and self-disgust. It was an alien sensation. During the bush war the Scouts had left no witnesses. This woman of his was turning him soft, he thought, and then smiled and shook his head – or perhaps she was simply humanizing him.

'All right.' He was still smiling. 'The girl comes with us, on condition that you forgive me.'

The kiss was brief, cool. Claudia's lips were tightly closed. Sean understood it would take time for her to recover from her outrage. She turned from Sean and lifted the black girl to her feet. Miriam clung to her thankfully.

'Fetch her loin-cloth,' Sean ordered Matatu. 'And put your knife away. The girl is coming with us.' Matatu rolled his eyes in disapproval. But he went to find the girl's single item of clothing.

While Miriam rewound the scrap of rag around her waist, Sergeant Alphonso leaned on his rifle and watched her with interest. It was obvious that he was not unhappy with the decision to spare the girl. Claudia did not approve of his appraisal of her protégée and she opened her small personal pack and dug out her one spare shirt, a camouflage Renamo sweat-shirt from General China's stores.

The shirt hung half down Miriam's thighs and satisfied Claudia's sense of decorum. The black girl was delighted, her terror of a few minutes before forgotten as she preened in her new finery.

'Thank you, Donna, thank you very much. You good lady.'

'All right.' Sean intervened. 'The fashion show is over, let's move out.' And Alphonso took Miriam's arm.

Only then the girl realized that she was being abducted, and she pulled away and broke into a passionate protest.

'Damn it!' Sean exploded. 'Now we are really in trouble!'

'What is it?' Claudia demanded.

'She isn't alone. She's got others with her.'

478

'I thought she had lost her parents!'

'That's right, but she's got a brother and sister hidden in the swamps. Two kids so young that they can't fend for themselves. Damn it! Damn it!' Sean repeated bitterly. 'Now what the hell do we do?'

'We fetch the children and take them with us also,' Claudia stated simply.

'Two brats! Are you crazy? We aren't running an orphanage.'

'Do we have to go over this one more time?' Claudia turned her back on him in exasperation and took Miriam's hand. 'It's all right. You can trust me. We'll look after all of you.'

The black girl quietened and stared at Claudia with a puppy's trust and adoration.

'Where are the children? We'll fetch them.'

'Come, Donna. I show you,' Miriam led her by the hand into the swamp.

It was almost dark when they reached the tiny island where Miriam had hidden the children in a clump of papyrus. When she parted the thick green stems, two pairs of huge dark eyes stared out at them like owlets from the nest.

'A boy.' Claudia lifted him out. He was five or six years of age, skinny and shivering with fright. 'And a girl.' She was younger, not more than four years old and Claudia exclaimed as she touched her.

'She's burning up, this child is very sick!' She was too weak to stand and she lay curled like a dying kitten, trembling and mewling softly.

'Malaria,' said Sean, and squatted beside the child. 'She's riddled with it.'

'We've got chloroquine in the medical pack.' Claudia reached for it briskly.

'This is madness!' Sean growled. 'We can't lumber ourselves with this bunch. It's a nightmare!'

'Do shut up!' Claudia snapped. 'How many chloroquine do I give her? The instructions say, "For children under six years, consult a physician." Thanks a lot, we'll try two tablets.'

As they worked over the child, Claudia asked Miriam, 'What are their names? What do you call the children?'

The answer was so long and complicated that even Claudia looked daunted, but she recovered quickly.

'I'll never pronounce that,' she said finally. 'We'll call them Mickey and Minnie.'

'Walt Disney will sue,' Sean warned, but she ignored him and wrapped Minnie in her own blanket.

'You'll have to carry her,' she told Sean matter-of-factly.

'If the little bugger pees on me, I'll wring her neck,' he protested.

'And Alphonso can carry Mickey.'

Sean could see that Claudia's maternal instincts were thoroughly aroused, and his resentment of this additional burden that had been thrust upon them was tempered by the tonic the new responsibilities had been to her. Claudia had sloughed off her exhaustion and lethargy and was more vigorous and incisive than she had been since Job's death.

Sean lifted the child's almost weightless little body on to his back and strapped it there with a strip of the blanket. The heat of the fever soaked through the blanket as though she were a hot-water bottle. However, it was a familiar experience to the child who had been carried since infancy in this fashion, and she was immediately quiet and somnolent. 'I still can't believe what's happening to me,' Sean muttered. 'A goddamned unpaid nursemaid at my age.' But he plunged once more into the swamp.

Before the night had half run, Miriam had proved an asset that far outweighed the additional burden that the two children had placed upon them. She knew the river area with the intimacy of a swamp creature. She went ahead with Matatu and guided him through the labyrinth of islands and lagoons, picking out the secret pathways that saved them hours of wearisome exploration.

A little after midnight, when Orion the great hunter stood directly overhead with his bow at full draw, Miriam led them out onto the bank of the Rio Save and pointed out the ford through which a man could wade to the far bank.

They rested and the women tended the children and fed them morsels of the leguan meat. The chloroquine had taken effect and the little girl was cooler and less fretful. After a hurried meal, the men concealed themselves in the reed-beds and stared out across the black waters in which the stars were reflected like drowning fireflies.

'This is the most dangerous point,' Sean whispered. 'China was patrolling the river all day yesterday in the Hind and he'll

480

be back at first light. We don't dare waste time here. We have to get across and get clear before sunrise.'

'They'll be waiting on the far side,' Alphonso demurred. 'They'll be expecting us.'

'That's right,' Sean agreed. 'They are here, but we know they are here. We'll leave the women on this side and go across to clear the far bank. We can't use firearms, it will have to be knives and wire. It's wet work tonight.' He used the old Scouts' term for it. 'Sebenza enamanzi. In more ways than one, it will be wet work tonight.'

Sean's wire was a four-foot length of stainless steel, the single strand that he had cut from the winch cable of the Hercules aircraft before abandoning it. Job had carved two hardwood buttons and fixed them to either end of the wire to form grips. It rolled into a coil the size of a silver dollar and slipped easily into the grenade pocket of his webbing. Now Sean fished it out and unrolled it. He tested it, settling the wooden buttons between his fingers and jerking it tight, grunting with satisfaction at the familiar tension in the single resilient strand. Then he recoiled the wire and slipped it over his left wrist like a bangle.

The three of them stripped completely naked, wet clothing dripped water to alert an enemy or give him a hold in a hand-to-hand struggle. Each of them wore his knife on a short cord around his bare neck.

Sean went to where Claudia waited with the children in the reeds. When he kissed her, her lips were soft and warm and she clung to him briefly.

'Have you forgiven me?' he asked. For an answer she kissed him again.

'Come back soon,' she whispered.

The three men slid into the water soundlessly, keeping close contact, and dog-paddled quietly out from the bank letting the current carry them well down below the ford.

They landed in a bed of papyrus on the south bank and slid ashore on their bellies. Sean's naked white body gleamed in the starlight. He rolled in the sticky black swamp mud until it coated every inch of his skin, and then he scooped a double handful and rubbed it over his face.

'Ready?' he asked quietly, and freed the trench knife in its sheath at his throat.

'Let's go!'

They moved out away from the river and circled back upstream towards the ford. The swamps were confined to the north bank, while this side of the river was drier, and the forests grew almost to the river's edge. They stayed in the shadows beneath the trees for concealment. As they drew closer to the ford they moved more cautiously, spreading out, Sean in the middle and Alphonso and Matatu on the flanks.

Sean smelt Renamo before he saw them. It was the odour of stale native tobacco smoke and dried sweat in unwashed clothing and he froze, listening and staring ahead with all his soul concentrated on it.

A little ahead of him in the darkness, a man coughed softly and cleared his throat, and Sean placed him accurately. He sank down and touched the earth, sweeping a clear spot with his fingertips for his next footstep, so that no twig or dry leaf would betray him. One step at a time, he moved forward until he had the Renamo's head silhouetted against the starry sky. He was sitting behind an RPD machine-gun on its bipod, staring out across the river.

Sean waited and the minutes drew out, five then ten, each one a separate age. Then someone else yawned and stretched out on the left flank and immediately a third voice cautioned him to silence in an angry whisper.

'Three of them.' Sean memorized each position, and then withdrew as quietly and cautiously as he had come in.

On the edge of the forest Alphonso was waiting for him, and minutes later Matatu crept back to join them.

'Three,' Alphonso whispered.

'Yes, three,' Sean agreed.

'Four,' Matatu contradicted them both. 'There is another one just below the bank.' Matatu missed nothing and Sean accepted his estimate without reservation.

Only four Renamo in the ambush, Sean was relieved. He had expected more, but China must be spreading his men thinly to cover every path and every ford of the river.

'No noise,' Sean warned them. 'One shot and we'll have the entire army doing a war dance on our backs. Matatu, you take the one you found below the bank. Alphonso, the one in the reeds who spoke. I'll take the two in the centre.' He slipped the wire bangle off his left wrist and unrolled it, once more stretching and testing it between his hands to get the feel of it.

'Wait until you hear my man blow before you strike yours.' He reached out and lightly touched their shoulders, the ritual benediction, and then they separated and drifted away into the night, back towards the river.

The machine-gunner was exactly where Sean had left him, but as Sean moved in behind him a few scattered clouds obscured the stars, and Sean had to wait for them to clear. Every second's delay increased the chance of discovery and he was tempted to work only by sense of touch, but he restrained himself. As the sky cleared, he was glad he had done so. The sentry had removed his cap and was scratching the back of his head; that raised hand would have blocked the wire and prevented a clean kill. There would have been a scream, gunshots, and every Renamo within miles would have come down upon him.

He waited while the sentry relieved his itch, and readjusted his cap, then as he dropped his hands, Sean reached forward and looped the wire noose around his throat in one swift wrap. In the same movement he hauled back with the full strength of both his arms and shot his right knee between the man's shoulder-blades. The wire sliced through flesh and windpipe as though they were cheddar cheese. Sean felt the momentary check as the wire came up hard against the vertebrae of the neck, but he sawed with both hands, keeping all his weight on the wire, pushing with his knee.

The wire found the gap between the vertebrae and snicked clearly through it. The man's head fell forward, and tumbled into his own lap and the man blew. The air from his lungs rushed out through the open windpipe, in a soft sigh. It was the sound he had told Matatu and Alphonso to wait for. He knew they would be taking their victims at this moment, but there was no sound until the man Sean had killed flopped forward and his carotid artery discharged onto the earth with a regular hiss like milk from the teat jetting into the bucket under the milkmaid's practised fingers.

The sound alerted the fourth Renamo, the only one still alive, and he called out in a puzzled tone.

'What is it, Alves? What are you doing?'

The question guided Sean to him, and he had the knife out of its sheath, holding it under-hand so the point went up at an acute angle under the man's ribs. Sean pinned him down with his left hand, holding his throat closed to prevent him screaming, working the knife with his other hand, opening the wound, twisting and turning the blade with all the strength of his right wrist.

In thirty seconds, it was over. The last tremors shook the body beneath him and Sean released him and stood up. Matatu was already beside him, with his skinning knife ready. The knife and his hands were wet. His own work was done and he had come to help Sean, but it was not necessary.

They waited for a full minute, listening for any alarm, perhaps there was another sentry that even Matatu might have overlooked, but apart from the croaking of the frogs in the reed-beds and the whine of mosquitos there was no sound.

'Search them,' Sean ordered. 'Take whatever we can use.'

One of the rifles, all of the ammunition, half a dozen grenades, spare clothing, all the food. They gathered it up swiftly.

'That's it,' Sean said. 'Dump the rest of it.' They dragged the bodies down the bank and pushed them out into the current, then dropped the heavy machine-gun and the rest of the discarded equipment into the deep water beyond the reeds.

Sean glanced at his watch. 'We are running out of time, we must bring the others across.'

Claudia and Miriam and the children were still in the reed-beds on the south bank where they had left them.

'What happened? We didn't hear anything.' Claudia hugged Sean's naked wet chest with relief.

'Nothing to hear,' Sean told her, and picked up the sleeping children, one on each arm.

Across the current, they formed a human stanchion, locking arms together, bracing each other against the heavy pull of the water that was as deep as Claudia's chin. Without this support the women would have been swept away. Even with it the crossing was arduous and they dragged themselves onto the south bank near exhaustion.

Sean would not let them rest longer than the few minutes it took to dry Minnie and wrap her in a jacket they had looted from one of the dead Renamo; then he had them up again and chivvied them onwards into the forest.

'We have to get clear of the river before sunrise. China will be back as soon as it is light.'

*   *   *

General China picked out the group of men on the riverbank at two hundred feet. As the helicopter slanted in towards them, the down-draught of its rotors furred the surface of the Save river with a dark ruffle.

The Portuguese pilot set the machine down at the edge of the forest on the south bank and China clambered out of the weapons cockpit and went striding down towards the river. Although his face was an expressionless mask, his anger boiled behind it and glinted in his eyes. He took the dark glasses from his breast pocket and concealed his eyes behind the lens.

The circle of men opened respectfully and China stepped through and looked down at the disembodied human head that lay on the muddy bank. It had been washed up amongst the reeds, the fresh-water crabs had nibbled it, and the water had leached the exposed flesh white and clouded the open eyes to opaque marbles, but the clean cut that had severed the neck was still as unmistakable as a hand-written signature.

'That's the white man's work,' China said softly. 'His Scouts called it "wet work", the wire was their trade-mark. When did it happen?'

'Last night.' Tippoo Tip tugged at his own beard with agitation. There had been no survivors of the ambush party, no one of which to make an example.

'You let them get through,' China accused coldly. 'You promised me they would never cross the river.'

'These dogs,' Tippoo Tip snarled. 'Those useless pigs.'

'They are your men,' China pointed out. 'And men take after those who command them. Their failure is your failure, General.'

It was said in front of his own staff, and Tippoo Tip growled with humiliation. He had made the promise and failed, and he shook with anger. He glared round at his men, looking for a victim, but they dropped their eyes and their faces were abject and obsequious. There was no relief there.

Suddenly he drew back his foot and swung a vicious kick at the severed head. The steel toe-cap of his boot crushed in the pulpy waterlogged nose.

'Dog!' he shouted, and booted the head again, sending it rolling down the bank. He followed it shouting with anger, aiming wild kicks at it, until it bounced like a football and plopped over the bank into the river.

He came back to General China, panting with rage.

'Very good, General,' China applauded him ironically. 'Very brave, what a pity you could not do the same to the white man.'

'I had every crossing of the river guarded,' Tippoo Tip started, and then broke off as he noticed the crudely stitched gash on China's cheek for the first time and he grinned viciously. 'You have been wounded. What misfortune. It wasn't the fault of the white man, was it? Surely not. You are too cunning to let him injure you, General China, apart from your ear, of course.'

It was China's turn to bridle with fury. 'If only I had my own men here. These stupid dogs of yours couldn't wipe their own backsides.'

'One of your men is a stooge,' Tippoo Tip roared back at him. 'He's running with the white man, my men are not traitors. I have them in my hands.' He showed those great paws, shaking them in China's face, and General China closed his eyes for a moment and drew a deep breath. He realized that they were on the brink of an irretrievable breach, a few more words like those exchanged and he would have no further co-operation from this great bearded ape. One day he would kill him, but he needed him today.

Today the most important thing in General China's world was getting his hands on the white man, alive if possible, but dead if it had to be. Without Tippoo Tip's help, there was no chance of that. His anger and retribution must wait for another time and opportunity.

'General Tippoo Tip,' his tone was conciliatory, almost humble, 'please forgive me. I let my disappointment run over my good sense. I know you did your best for me. We are, both of us, victims of our own people's incompetence. I ask you to ignore my bad manners.'

Tippoo Tip was taken off-balance as China had intended and the angry words died in his open mouth.

'Even though these fools were unable to stop them, now at last we know exactly where they are. We have their fresh spoor, and a full day in which to follow it. Let us make the most of this opportunity. Let's get this tiresome business over with. Then I, and my helicopter, will be entirely at your disposal for the more important task ahead of us.'

He saw that he had picked the right words. Tippoo Tip's rage gradually gave way to that sly and avaricious expression that China knew so well.

'I have already called up my best trackers,' he agreed. 'I'll have fifty of my men on their spoor within the hour, men who can run an eland off its feet. The white man will be in your hands before the sun sets this evening. This time there will be no mistake.'

'Where are these trackers?' China demanded.

'I have radioed.'

'I will send the helicopter to fetch them.'

'That will save valuable time.'

They watched the Hind rise and bore away northwards, low across the darkly flowing waters of the Save river. As it disappeared they both turned to stare towards the south.

'You no longer control the territory south of the river,' China pointed out. 'These are the forests that you so cunningly relinquished to the Frelimo.' He pointed at the dense stands of hardwoods that stood tall against the southern sky.

'The river is my front line,' Tippoo Tip conceded reluctantly. 'But the nearest Frelimo forces are still many miles further south. My patrols cover this ground without interference from them. The men I am sending after the white man will catch him long before he gets into Frelimo-held territory.' Tippoo Tip broke off and then pointed along the riverbank. 'Ah, here they come.' A long double file of heavily armed guerrillas came trotting down the footpath towards them. 'Fifty of my best men. You will eat white chickens for dinner tonight. Don't worry, my friend. They are as good as on your plate already.'

The two platoons of Renamo halted and fell out on the bank, waiting for their trackers. China was a good judge of troops. He walked amongst them, and he recognized in them that eagerness and enthusiasm tempered by discipline and professionalism that is the peculiar mark of first-class bush fighters. For once he agreed with Tippoo Tip. These were hard men who could be relied upon to get the job done. China beckoned the section leaders across to him.

'You know who you are chasing?' he asked, and they nodded. 'The white man is as dangerous as a wounded leopard, but I want him alive. Do you understand?'

'We understand, General.'

'You have a radio. I want a report of your progress every hour on the command frequency.'

'Yes, General.'

'And when you have the quarry in sight, call me. I will come in the *henshaw*. I want to be there at the death.'

The section leaders looked across the river, their expressions alert, and moments later even with his impaired hearing, China picked up the whistle of the Hind's turbos returning from the north.

'If you do your job, you will be rewarded. But if you fail me, you will regret it. You will regret it deeply,' General China promised them.

As soon as the helicopter landed the two trackers clambered down with alacrity from the small rear cabin and Tippoo Tip shouted at them and pointed to the outgoing spoor that Sean and his party had left.

Watching the trackers begin their task. China was even more confident of the outcome. These two were good. They made a quick cast ahead and then came back to the centre and squatted over the spoor, whispering together softly, touching the faint tracks with the supple wands of wild willow they each carried, intent as a pair of bloodhounds taking the scent of the chase. When they stood up again a change had come over them. They were determined and businesslike. They turned to face the southern forests and went away at a run.

Behind them, the two full platoons of camouflaged Renamo assault troopers fanned out into their running formation and set their pace to match the trackers.

'The white woman can never keep up that speed,' Tippoo Tip exulted. 'We will overtake them before they reach the Frelimo lines, we will have them before the end of this day. This time they'll not escape.' He turned back to China. 'Why don't we follow them in the helicopter?'

China hesitated. He did not want to explain the Hind's short-comings. It was better to let Tippoo Tip go on believing in its infallibility. He would not discuss with him the difficulty of bringing up sufficient fuel, nor the Hind's limited range even with full tanks, nor the fact that his Portuguese engineer had warned him that the turbos were long overdue for service, that the pilot had already reported a malfunction and loss of power in the starboard engine.

'I will wait here,' he said. 'When your men catch up with the white man, they will call on the radio. That is when I will follow them.'

China adjusted his dark glasses and sauntered across to the Hind. The pilot was waiting for him, leaning with assumed nonchalance against the camouflaged fuselage below the main cockpit.

'How is the engine behaving?' China asked in Portuguese.

'It is beginning to surge and miss. It needs to be worked on.'

'Fuel?'

'Main tanks are down to quarter. However, I still have the auxiliary.'

'The convoy of porters with the fuel will be at our forward base by tomorrow morning. The engineer can work on her tonight, but I have to have her on standby until dark. I'll need her when they catch up with the runaways.'

The pilot shrugged. 'I'll fly her, if you are willing to take the chance on that engine,' he agreed.

'Keep a listening watch on the radio,' China ordered. 'With luck it will all be over in a few hours.'

* * *

Sean realized that Claudia could not maintain this pace much further. She was running just ahead of him so he could study the changes in her that privation and hard living had brought about. She was so lean and wispy that her scanty threadbare shirt flapped around her flanks, and the legs of her trousers had been reduced by thorns and razor-edged grass to a fringe of tatters that hung halfway down her thighs; below that, the length of her legs was exaggerated by their extreme thinness, yet somehow they had retained their elegant high-bred lines. However, the thorns and sharp grass had wrought havoc on the exposed skin of her arms and legs. It looked as though she had been scourged by a cat-o'-nine-tails, some of the scratches were healed, others scabbed over, but a few still bled.

Her hair had grown into a lank sweat-tangled mop that thumped between her prominent bony shoulder-blades with each pace, and her back was so thin that he could have counted the knobs of her vertebrae beneath her shirt. The perspiration had soaked through in a dark line down her spine, and hard exercise had firmed her buttocks into a pair of Indiarubber balls in the sun-bleached cotton pants; through a tiny three-cornered tear a tender flash of her white bottom winked at him with each pace.

Her legs were floppy with exhaustion, throwing out sideways and her ankles were loose and wobbled under her.

He would have to let her rest very soon and yet she had not complained, not once in all the long tortured hours since they had left the river, and he grinned fondly as he remembered the spoilt arrogant bitch that had stepped off the Boeing at Harare airport so many aeons ago. This was a different woman, tough, determined and with a spirit as resilient as a Damascus steel blade. He knew that she would never give up, she would keep going until she killed herself. He reached forward and tapped her shoulder.

'Ease up, wench. We'll take ten.'

When she pulled up she was unsteady on those long legs and he put an arm around her shoulders to steady her. 'You're a ruddy marvel do you know that?' He eased her down to sit with her back against one of the le 'wood trees and unscrewed the stopper on his water-bottle and passed it to her.

'Give Minnie to me. It's time for her chloroquine.' Claudia's voice was husky with tiredness. Sean swung the little girl off his back and placed her in Claudia's lap.

'Remember, ten minutes, that's all.'

Alphonso had taken the break to rig the radio, Mickey was squatting on one side of him, Miriam on the other. They watched with fascination as he tuned the set and began searching the bands. There was the crackle and buzz of static followed by some faint extraneous snatches of Afrikaans, and then an excited voice speaking in Shangane, very close and loud.

'Very close now,' it said, and the reply came immediately.

'Keep going hard. Push them. Don't let them escape. Call me as soon as you catch them.' That voice was unmistakable and they did not need the acknowledgement to confirm it.

'Very well, General China.'

The transmission ended and Sean and Alphonso exchanged a quick hard frown.

'Very close,' said the Shangane. 'We can't outrun them.'

'You might be able to get away,' Sean said, 'on your own.'

Alphonso hesitated and looked sideways at Miriam. The Shangane maid returned his glance with open trusting eyes and Alphonso coughed and scratched himself with embarrassment.

'I'll stay,' he muttered, and Sean laughed bitterly and said in English, 'Join the club, mate. That little witch didn't take long to hook you. These ruddy sheilas will be the death of all of us yet, you mark my words.'

Alphonso frowned, he did not understand and Sean switched back into Shangane. 'Pack up the radio. If you are going to stand with us, we'd best find a good place to do it. Your dung-eating Renamo brothers are going to be with us very soon.'

Sean turned and looked across at Matatu, and instantly he was on his feet.

'That was China on the radio,' he told him in Swahili.

'He hisses like a cobra,' Matatu nodded.

'His men are on our spoor, they boast to him that they are very close. Are there any more tricks we can use now, old friend?'

'Fire?' Matatu suggested, but without conviction, and Sean shook his head.

'The wind is against us, we'd cook ourselves if we torched the forest.'

Matatu hung his head. 'If we keep the women and children with us, there are no more tricks,' he admitted. 'We are slow, and we leave a spoor that a blind man can follow in a moonless night.' He shook his small grizzled head miserably. 'The only trick we have left is to fight them, and after that we are dead, my *Bwana*.'

'Go back, Matatu. Find how close behind us they really are. We will go ahead and find a good place to fight them.' He touched the little man's shoulder, and then let him go. Sean watched him disappear amongst the tree-trunks and then deliberately altered his expression before he turned to Claudia, striking a lighter more carefree pose and putting a lift in his tone.

'How's our patient?' he asked. 'She looks pretty chirpy to me.'

'The chloroquine has done wonders.' Claudia bounced the child on her lap and as if to confirm her improvement, Minnie stuck her thumb in her mouth and smiled shyly around it at Sean. He felt that smile tug at him with wholly unexpected poignancy.

Claudia laughed. 'No female is immune to your fatal charms. You have collected yourself another fan.'

'Typical woman, all she really wants is a free ride.' But he stroked the child's soft woolly little head. 'All right, sweetness, your horsey is ready to go.'

Trustingly Minnie held out both arms and he swung her up on to his back and strapped her there.

Claudia pulled herself stiffly to her feet and for a moment

leaned against him. 'Do you know something? You are a much nicer person than you pretend to be.'

'Fooled you, didn't I?'

'I'd like to see you with a baby of your own,' she whispered.

'Now you really terrify me. Let's go before you come up with any more crazy ideas like that one.'

But the idea lingered with him as they ran on through the forest, a son of his own from this woman.

He had never even thought about that before, and then, as though to complement the idea, he felt a tiny hand reach across his shoulder from behind and touch his beard, stroking it as lightly as an alighting butterfly. Minnie was reciprocating that caress he had bestowed on her a few minutes earlier and for a moment his throat closed up and made it difficult for him to breathe. He took her tiny hand in his, and it was silken and fragile as the wing of a humming-bird and he was overcome with a feeling of terrible regret. Regret that there would never be a son, he accepted that at last, nor a daughter. It was almost over. The hunting pack was very close behind. They could never outrun them. There was no escape, all they could hope for was a good place in which to make the final stand. After that there was nothing, no escape, no future.

He was so wrapped up in his melancholy that he had run out into the open before he realized it. Claudia pulled up so sharply in front of him that he almost ran into her. He stopped at her side and they looked about them with puzzled uncertainty.

The forest had been laid waste. For as far ahead as they could see the great hardwoods had been swept away as though by a hurricane. Only the stumps remained, raw and bleeding gum as red as heart's blood. The earth was torn and scarred, where the huge trunks had come crashing down. Bright piles of sawdust remained where their branches had been stripped and the logs cut into lengths, and then between the windrows of discarded branches and wilting boughs were the drag roads along which the precious timber had been hauled away.

Miriam stopped beside Sean. 'This is where my people were forced to work,' she said softly. 'Frelimo came and took them to cut the trees. They chained them together and made them work until the meat was torn from the bones of their hands. They beat them like oxen and worked them until they fell and could not rise.'

'How many people?' Sean asked. 'So many trees have been destroyed.'

'Perhaps a man or woman died for every tree,' Miriam whispered. 'They took everybody, thousands upon tens of thousands.' She pointed to the horizon. 'They work far south now and they leave no tree standing.'

Sean felt the anger beginning to rise through his amazement. This was destruction on a scale that affronted the law of nature and the sanctity of life itself. It was not just that those trees had taken three hundred years to reach their full majesty, and had been destroyed with a few hours' callous work with the axe blades. It was more, much more. This forest was the source and fountain of myriad forms of life, insect and bird and mammal and reptile, of man himself. In this vast devastation, all would perish.

It did not end there. With his own fate determined, with a term and a number of the hours that remained of his own life, Sean was overtaken by a prophetic melancholia. He realized that the destruction of this forest was symbolic of the predicament of the entire continent. In a few fleeting decades, Africa had been overtaken by its own inherent savagery. The checks that had been placed upon it by a century of colonialism had been struck off. Chains perhaps those checks had been, but once freed of them, the peoples of Africa were rushing headlong, with almost suicidal abandon, towards their own destruction.

Sean felt himself shaking with impotent rage at the folly of it and at the same time saddened, sickened almost unto death, by the terrible tragedy of it all.

'If I have to die,' he thought, 'then it's best to do so before I see everything I love, the land, the animals, the people, all of it destroyed.'

With his arm round Claudia's thin shoulders and the little black girl strapped on his back, he turned and looked back the way they had come and, at that moment, Matatu came scampering out of the forest behind them.

There was desperate urgency in his gait and the fear of death in his small wizened features.

'They are very close, my *Bwana*. They have two trackers leading them. I watched them work, we will not throw them off. They are good.'

'How many troopers with them?' With an effort Sean cast off the oppressive mantle of dejection.

493

'As many as the grass on the plains of Serengeti,' Matatu replied. 'They run like a pack of wild dogs on the hunt and they are hard men and fierce. Even the three of us will not stand too long against them.'

Sean roused himself and looked around him. The cut line in which they stood was a natural killing ground, devoid of cover except for the knee-high stumps of hardwood. The open ground stretched two hundred metres wide to where the dead wood was piled in untidy windrows, the leaves long withered and browned, the branches forming a natural barricade.

'We'll make our stand there,' Sean decided swiftly and signalled Alphonso forward. They crossed the open ground at a run, bunched up with the two women in the middle. Miriam was dragging her little brother along by one arm. Alphonso ran protectively beside them. The big Shangane was heavily burdened with the radio and the packs of ammunition and stores they had picked up from the ambush at the Save river, nevertheless he had also carried Mickey whenever the boy tired, only setting him down on his own feet for short intervals. The three Shanganes, man, woman and boy child, had very swiftly formed their own distinct core within the band, drawn together by tribal loyalties and natural physical attraction. Sean knew he could rely on Alphonso to take care of his own, and that allowed him to concentrate on his own particular charges, Claudia and Matatu and now the little girl.

Alphonso needed no orders. Like Sean he had a soldier's eye for terrain and he ran unerringly towards a section of the tumble of discarded branches that formed a natural redoubt, and which commanded the best field of fire across the cut line.

Swiftly they settled in, dragging some of the heavier branches into place to strengthen the position, laying out their weapons and spare ammunition, making their very limited preparations to stand off the first rush of the attackers.

Claudia and Miriam had taken the children a little further back to where a hollow in the earth and two especially large tree-stumps formed some sort of shelter. His own preparations complete, Sean crossed to them quickly, and squatted beside Claudia.

'As soon as the shooting starts, I want you to take Miriam and the children and run for it,' he told her. 'Keep heading south.' He broke off as he realized that she was shaking her head, and her jaw was clenched obstinately.

'I've run far enough,' she told him. 'I'm staying with you.' She laid her hand on his arm. 'No, don't argue. It would be a waste of time.'

'Claudia!'

'Please don't,' she forestalled him. 'There isn't much time left, don't spend it arguing.'

She was right, of course. To try and run further on her own was pointless, not with two children to care for and a team of fifty Renamo on her spoor. He nodded.

'All right,' he agreed, and took the Tokarev pistol from his belt, cocked it and carefully engaged the safety-catch. 'Take this.'

'What's that for?' She stared at the weapon with distaste.

'I think you know what it's for.'

'The same way as Job?'

He nodded. 'It would be easier than going China's way.'   •

She shook her head. 'I couldn't,' she whispered. 'If there is no other way, at the end, won't you do it for me?'

'I'll try,' he said. 'But I don't think I'll have the guts. Here, take it, just in case.' Reluctantly she accepted the pistol and tucked it into her belt.

'Now kiss me,' she said.

Matatu's whistle interrupted their embrace. 'I love you,' Sean murmured in her ear.

'I'll love you . . .' she replied, 'through all eternity.'

He left her and crawled back into the piles of dead wood. At Matatu's side he sank down and peered out through the chink between two branches towards the edge of the forest.

For many minutes he saw nothing, and then there was a shadowy flit of movement amongst the boles of the standing hardwood, and Sean laid his right hand on the pistol grip of the AKM rifle and raised it until the buttstock touched his cheek.

The silence drew out in the languorous sunlit afternoon while they waited. No bird sang, no creature moved, until at last there was a muted bird whistle from the edge of the forest and a man shape detached itself and flitted into the opening, showing for just a small part of a second and then disappearing behind one of the thick tree-stumps. As soon as it was gone another broke from the tree-line a hundred metres further to the left and darted forward. This one also disappeared and almost immediately, out on the right, a third Renamo guerrilla emerged.

'Three only,' Sean murmured, they were not going to expose

more men than that and these were good. They advanced in fleeting rushes. never two together. widely spread out and wary as old tom-leopards coming in to the bait.

'What a pity.' Sean thought. 'We are only going to get one out of this lot. I had hoped for a better killing to get us off the mark.' He concentrated on the advancing scouts. trying to pick the most dangerous of their enemies.

'Probably the one in the centre.' he decided. and almost immediately had his choice confirmed as he saw the flick of the man's hand from behind the stump that hid him. He was signalling one of the others forward. co-ordinating the advance and that marked him as the main man. the one to take out first.

. 'Let him come in close.' Sean told himself. The AKM was no sniping rifle and he didn't trust its accuracy over a hundred metres. He waited. willing the man in. watching for him over the sights of the rifle.

The Renamo jumped up and kept coming. Sean saw that he was young. mid-twenties. with bandoliers of ammunition over both shoulders. and a Rastafarian hair-style. ribbons of camouflage rag braided into his hair. There was an Arabian cast to his features. and an amber patina to his skin. a good-looking lad except that his left eye was a little askew and it gave his face a sly knowing expression.

Close enough to see the cast in his eye was close enough. Sean lined up carefully on the tree-stump behind which the Renamo had disappeared and drew a breath. exhaled half of it and let the first joint of his right forefinger rest lightly on the trigger.

The Renamo popped up into his sights. Sean took him low. deliberately declining a clean kill. He knew what damage the 7.62 bullet would do as it plunged through his belly at over three thousand feet a second. and he knew from bitter experience just how unnerving it was to have one of your comrades lying in no-man's land with his guts shot out screaming for water and mercy. In the Scouts they called them 'warblers'. and a warbler in good voice could inhibit an attack almost as effectively as a well-placed RPD machine-gun.

Sean heard the bullet hit the Renamo in the stomach. that meaty thump like a water melon dropped on a stone floor. and he went down out of sight in the trash and debris.

Instantly there was a heavy volley of rifle fire from the edge of the forest. but it was obvious from the wild aim that they had not spotted Sean and the firing stuttered swiftly into silence. Renamo was conserving ammunition, a sure sign of their discipline and training. Second-rate African troops started firing at the beginning of a contact and kept shooting until their last round was expended.

'These lads know their business,' Sean confirmed Matatu's estimate. 'We aren't going to hold them long.' The two guerrillas were still pinned down in the middle of the cut line, and there was a low hollow groan from out there as the first pangs of the belly wound hit the downed man.

'Sing to us, Daddy-oh!' Sean encouraged him. 'Let your pals know how it hurts.' But he was studying the forest edge, trying to get some hint of the next play before it developed.

'Now, they'll make a pincer move to try to out-flank us,' he guessed. 'But which flank, left or right?' And as if in answer he saw a tiny blur of movement in the forest. One of them was moving right.

'Alphonso,' Sean called softly. 'They are going to try the right. Stay here. Hold the centre.'

Sean crawled back, until he was hidden by the high windrow of brush. Then he rose to his feet, and ran doubled over, out to the right flank.

Four hundred metres out he dropped to his knees and crawled forward, finding another position facing the forest wall. He wriggled in behind a protective stump and marshalled his breathing, watching the tree-line, the AKM set on automatic fire, and his thumb on the safety-catch.

He had anticipated the next move almost perfectly, the flanking movement came out of the forest only a hundred metres further to his right. A detachment of eight troopers, they came all together, trying to reach the cover of the windrow in a single concerted rush, and Sean let them get half way across the cut line.

'This is better. I should be able to get a brace out of this covey,' he told himself. He had them in enfilade, his fire would be coming in from their flank and sweeping the line. He picked out the section leader who was running slightly ahead of the line. Sean led him by a man's length so that he would run into the stream of fire, taking him at knee height because the AKM rode up brutally in automatic and he held the trigger down.

The section leader dropped as though he had fallen over a trip

497

wire, and the two men following him ran into the same burst. Sean saw the bullets hit them. One of them took it in the shoulder, and a puff of dust flew from his camouflage tunic to mark the strike. The other was a head shot, a clean hit in the temple and as he went down his base-ball cap fluttered from his head like a maimed dove.

'Three.' Sean changed magazines, pleased with the result. He had expected one and hoped for two.

The rest of them had turned and were racing back for the forest, the attack broken completely. Sean got off another quick burst before they reached the trees, and thought he saw one of them hunch his shoulders and lurch to the shot, but he kept going and disappeared.

Almost immediately there was another burst of firing back in the centre, and Sean jumped up from behind his stump and ran back to help Alphonso.

As he ran somebody opened up on him from the forest. Shot passed close to his head with that vicious whiplashing sound that made his adrenalin spurt hotly into his bloodstream. He ducked his head and ran on. He was enjoying himself, riding the curling wave of his terror.

In the centre there was a sharp fire-fight raging. Renamo was trying to rush the open ground, and they were almost across when Sean fell flat in the brush near Alphonso and added the weight of his fire to the defence. The attack wavered and broke, just short of the row of deadwood behind which they lay. The Renamo went ducking and dodging back between the tree-stumps with AK fire kicking up dust around them.

'Two!' Alphonso shouted across at Sean. 'I put two of them down.' But Matatu was tugging at Sean's arm and pointing out to the left flank. Sean was just able to get a glimpse of another group of Renamo cutting across the cut line and reaching cover on this side. The attacks on the right and centre had been diversions. Now there were a dozen or so Renamo coming in behind them, within minutes they would be surrounded, pinned down helplessly.

'Alphonso, they have got in our rear,' Sean called across.

'There was nothing we could do to stop them,' Alphonso answered. 'There are too many, we are too few.'

'I am going back to hold the rear, I'll be with the women.'

'They won't attack again,' Alphonso told him flatly. 'Now that they have us surrounded they will wait for the *henshaw* to come.'

A burst of automatic fire raked the pile of deadwood, and they ducked instinctively.

'They are only shooting to hold us,' Alphonso called. 'They don't have to risk losing more men.'

'How long until the helicopter arrives?' Sean wanted his own estimate confirmed.

'Not more than an hour.' Alphonso told him with finality. 'Then it will all be over very quickly.'

Alphonso was right. Against the Hind, there was no defence, no more tricks to play.

'I'm leaving you here,' Sean repeated, and crawled back to the hollow in which the women were concealed.

Claudia had Minnie on her lap, but she looked up expectantly as Sean slid down the shallow side of the hollow.

'They've got in behind us,' Sean told her shortly. 'We are surrounded.' He dumped the empty AK magazines in front of her. 'There are boxes of spare ammo in Alphonso's pack. You know how to fill these.'

It would keep her busy. The next hour was going to be difficult to live through. Sean crawled to the back lip of the hollow and peered over the edge.

He saw something move in the dried brown leaves fifty paces ahead of him and he fired a quick burst into the brush. His fire was returned from three or four positions in their rear. AK bullets cracked overhead and behind him Minnie wailed with fright. The minutes dragged past slowly, the silence broken every few seconds by sporadic bursts of holding fire from the Renamo positions.

Claudia crawled up beside Sean and stacked the replenished magazines at his right elbow.

'How many boxes left?' he asked.

'Ten,' she told him, and pressed a little closer to him.

It didn't really matter that there were only two hundred rounds remaining in Alphonso's pack. Sean looked up at the sky, any moment now they would hear the whistle of the Hind's turbos.

Claudia read his thoughts, and she groped for his hand. Lying in the hot African sun, they held hands and waited. There was nothing left to say, nothing more that they could do. No defence, however feeble. All that remained was to wait for the inevitable.

Matatu touched Sean's leg. It wasn't necessary to say anything.

Sean cocked his head and picked up the sound. It was higher and steadier than the soughing of the afternoon breeze in the forest-tops.

Claudia squeezed his hand very hard, digging her fingernails into his palm. She had heard it also.

'Kiss me,' she whispered. 'One last time.' And he laid the rifle down and rolled onto his side to take her in his arms. They strained together, holding with all their strength.

'If I have to die,' Claudia whispered, 'I'm glad it will be like this.' And Sean felt her press the loaded Tokarev into his hand.

'Goodbye, my darling,' she said.

He knew that he had to do it, but he did not know where he would find the courage.

The sound of the Hind's engines was rising into a high penetrating shriek.

He slid the safety-catch to the 'off' position and lifted the Tokarev gently. Claudia's eyes were tightly closed and she had turned her head half away. A little sweat-damp tendril of dark hair hung down in front of her ear, and he could see the artery beating under the creamy skin of her temple that the curl had protected from the sun. It was the most difficult task he had ever set himself, but he raised the muzzle of the Tokarev towards her temple.

There was a shattering explosion of a shell-burst on the lip of their shelter. Instinctively Sean pulled Claudia down to protect her. He thought for a moment that the Hind had opened fire, but that was impossible, it was still out of sight and range.

A further series of explosions crashed out in rapid succession, and Sean lowered the pistol and released Claudia. He rolled to the lip of the hollow, and saw that a heavy barrage of fire was sweeping the Renamo positions. Mortar fire, Sean recognized the characteristic bursts of three-inch mortar shells and then the rushing smoke trails of RPG rockets amongst the trees of the forest. The rattling din of small arms drowned out even the sound of the approaching Hind. The entire situation had changed.

Suddenly they were in the midst of a battle, and Sean saw figures running wildly amongst the windrows and stumps, firing as they ran.

'Frelimo!' Matatu was tugging at Sean's arm and screeching with excitement. 'Frelimo!'

Only then Sean understood. Their desultory exchange of fire

with the Renamo pursuers must have called up a large force of Frelimo troops who had been massed in the immediate vicinity, probably preparing to attack the Save river line.

Now the fifty Renamo guerrillas suddenly found themselves attacked by a vastly superior Frelimo force. Judging by the intensity of fire, Sean estimated that there were several hundred Frelimo out there in the forest, front-line regular troops in battalion strength.

He saw the small party of Renamo who had cut them off abandon their positions amongst the dead wood of the cut line, and scuttle away in wild disorder with mortar shells bursting amongst them. Sean snatched up the AKM and helped them on their way with a long burst. One of the running men fell and flopped around into the brush like a beached catfish.

Then he spotted a sweep line of Frelimo infantry coming in from the left at a run. Their camouflage field dress was East German issue, the blotches of green and brown distinctly different from the Renamo tiger-stripes.

Renamo or Frelimo were equally dangerous for them. Sean pulled Claudia down beside him.

'Don't move. The Frelimo probably don't know we are here. They might just chase off the Renamo and overlook us. We've still got a chance.'

Minnie was wailing loudly, terrified by the uproar. Sean called urgently to Miriam, 'Keep her quiet. Stop her screaming.'

The Shangane girl pulled the child down beside her and covered her mouth and nose with her hand, cutting off her wails abruptly.

Sean raised one eye above the lip of the hollow and saw the Frelimo sweep line still bearing down on them, tough-looking troopers, firing from the hip as they came. They would overrun the hollow within seconds. He raised the AKM. Their salvation had been fleeting, the only real change was that now they would be killed by Frelimo rather than by Renamo.

As he raised the AKM and aimed at the belly of the nearest of the oncoming Frelimo troopers, the target was blotted out by a tall curtain of flying dust and from the sky above came the thunderous roll of the heavy 12.7mm cannon. The Frelimo sweep line dissolved before Sean's eyes, blown away by the Hind's concentrated fire, and the dust rolled over the hollow in which they lay, concealing them from the air in those crucial seconds that the Hind hovered above them.

Now all was chaos, two forces inextricably mixed up in the deep forest, mortar and rocket fire crashing through the trees, while over the battlefield the Hind hovered, sending in rockets and bursts of cannonfire to make the confusion complete.

Sean slapped Matatu on the shoulder. 'Fetch Alphonso,' he ordered, and the little Ndorobo disappeared into the dust and gunfire, to emerge only a minute later with the huge Shangane close behind him.

'Alphonso, get ready to make another run for it,' Sean told him tersely. 'Frelimo and Renamo are giving each other a full go out there. We'll try to sneak away before the Hind spots us.' Sean broke off and sniffed the air, and then raised himself quickly on his knees to look back.

Already the air around them was turning a dirty grey, and above the din of battle and the whine of turbos, Sean heard the first faint crackle of burning brush.

'Fire!' he snapped. 'And it's upwind of us!'

One of the exploding rockets had ignited the rows of piled deadwood, and now a dense cloud of smoke rolled down over the hollow where they lay, stinging their eyes and making them cough and choke.

'Now, we have no choice, it's run or cook.' The crackle and roar of the flames was already drowning out the din of battle. Dimly they heard the shrieks of wounded men caught up in the path of the surging fire.

'Let's go!' Sean swept Minnie onto his back and the child locked both arms around his neck and clung to him like a little black flea. Sean pulled Claudia to her feet. Alphonso had Mickey sitting perched on his shoulders, his legs dangling over the bulky radio pack. Miriam was at his side clinging to the arm which held his rifle.

The smoke rolled over them, thick as oil, and they ran with the wind, bunched up to keep contact with each other. The smoke filled their lungs and blotted out the sky, screening them from the fighting men in the forest around them and from the helicopter gunship that hovered above them, and the fire raged close behind them driving them on wildly, but gaining on them with every second.

Sean felt the heat fan the back of his neck, and Minnie

502

squeaked as a flying spark touched her cheek. Gasping for breath, Claudia stumbled and sank to her knees, but Sean hauled her to her feet and dragged her onwards.

Sean was suffocating, each breath burned all the way down into his lungs. They couldn't go much farther. The heat licked their skin and flying sparks dashed against them and the child on Sean's back screamed in agony and pawed ineffectually at her tortured body as though assailed by a swarm of wasps. She lost her grip and would have fallen, but Sean snatched her off his back and carried her under one arm.

Suddenly, they were into another open cut line. Only dead stumps surrounded them, standing like tombstones in the dense banks of rolling smoke, and the sandy earth beneath their feet had been ploughed up by the teams of loggers.

'Down!' Sean pushed Claudia flat on the ground and placed Minnie in her arms.

The child was struggling wildly. 'Hold her still!' Sean shouted and stripped off his shirt.

'Lie flat, face down!' he ordered and obediently Claudia rolled on her stomach, holding Minnie under her. Sean wrapped the shirt around both their heads to filter out the smoke and sparks and soot. He tore the stopper out of his water-bottle and soaked the shirt, splashing their hair and soaking their clothing.

Minnie was still shrieking and struggling, but Claudia held her down firmly. Sean knelt beside them and scooped loose sand over them, burying them under a mound of earth, like one of those beach games that children play. The smoke was thinner closer to the earth, they could still breathe. Alphonso had seen what he was doing and followed his example, burying Miriam and her little brother in the sand nearby.

Live sparks swirled through the blinding clouds of smoke and settled on Sean's bare skin. They stung like the poisonous bites of safari ants. Sean felt his beard begin to frizzle and his eyeballs drying out in the heat. He emptied his pack on to the ground and pulled the empty canvas bag over his head, poured the contents of the second water-bottle over his torso, and then fell on his back and scooped the loose sand over himself and lay still.

With his head low to the ground the air was breathable, just sufficient oxygen in it to keep him conscious, but his head buzzed and swirled dizzily and the heat came at him in crushing blasts.

He smelled the canvas bag over his head begin to smoulder and the thin layer of sand that covered his body scalded him like a pot fresh from the furnace. He heard the roar of the flames rise to a crescendo, the dry branches crackled like rifle fire in the inferno. The fire was in the windrows all around them, but the wind, generated by its own heat, drove it swiftly onwards.

It swept past them, the roaring subsided, and for an instant the smoke clouds opened allowing them a fleeting gasp of sweet air, but the heat around them was still so fierce that Sean dared not shake off the protective layer of sand that covered his body.

Gradually the heat dissipated, and the gusts of cooler sweeter air became more frequent. Sean sat up and lifted the canvas pack from his head. His skin burned as though acid had been splattered upon it, and the bright red spots where sparks had touched him would soon be blisters.

He crawled to the mound of earth that covered Claudia and the child and scraped it away from their heads. The shirt had kept their mouths and noses clear, and when they sat up and shook off the sand, he saw that they had come off much better than either he or Alphonso had. The fire had run past them, but the air around them was still so thick with smoke that the sky was blotted out.

Sean hauled them to their feet. 'We have to get well away before the smoke clears,' he croaked hoarsely. His throat felt as though he had swallowed a handful of crushed glass, and tears spilled down his sooty scorched cheeks.

Clinging together, picking their way through the blackened, smouldering landscape, like a party of bedraggled soot-covered phantoms, they limped through the swirling fog of smoke. The earth was hot as a flow of volcanic lava, scorching the soles of their boots, but they carried the children, and avoided the piles of glowing ash.

Twice they heard the Hind above them, but although they peered up with red and weeping eyes, they caught not a glimpse of it through the drifting blue clouds and there was no sign of pursuit by either Renamo or Frelimo. The opposing forces had been scattered and swept away by the flames.

'The little bugger has asbestos-lined feet,' Sean muttered, as he watched Matatu dance ahead of them through the thinning smoke. On Sean's back, Minnie whimpered fretfully with the pain of her blisters and at their first rest stop Sean gave her half an aspirin and a swallow from their one remaining bottle of water.

The sunset that evening filled the heavens with flaming crimsons and sombre purples. In the darkness, they lay huddled together, too exhausted and weakened by the smoke to post sentries, and their sleep was interrupted by bouts of painful lung-tearing coughing.

In the dawn, the wind veered into the south but the smoke still hung over the land like a heavy river-mist, reducing visibility to a few hundred feet.

Sean and Claudia treated the children first, smearing their blisters and burns with yellow iodine paste, and though Mickey bore it with the stoicism of a Shangane warrior, the little girl whined with the sting of the iodine and Sean had to take her on his lap and blow on her injuries to cool them.

Once the children were taken care of, the women tended their men. The burns on Sean's chest and back were all superficial, but Claudia treated them with a gentleness that reflected her gratitude and her complete love.

Neither of them spoke of that moment when he had lifted the Tokarev pistol to her temple. They probably never would, but both of them would be conscious of it for ever more. It would always be there between them: for Sean the most horrific moment of his life, worse even than that of Job's death; for Claudia, an affirmation of his devotion to her. She knew that he would have found the strength to do it, but she knew also that it would have cost him dearer than the sacrifice of his own life. She needed no more proof of his love.

The children needed water desperately, they were desiccated by the heat of the flames and the smoke. Sean gave half the remaining water to them, and shared the remainder disproportionately amongst the adults, most of it to the two women and a bare taste to the men.

'Matatu,' he said in a harsh gravelly whisper, 'if you don't find us water before nightfall, then we are as dead as if the *henshaw* had blown us into dust with its cannons.'

They limped on through the blackened and smouldering forest, and in the late afternoon Matatu led them to a shallow clay pan, surrounded by the smoking stumps of burned-out trees. In the centre of the pan, thick with black ash and the charred bodies of small creatures, of snakes and rats and civet cats that had fled there for protection from the flames, was a puddle of filthy water.

Sean strained it through his shirt and they drank it as though it were nectar, groaning with the pleasure through their scorched and smoke-abraded throats. When they had drunk until their bellies ached, they scooped the water over their heads and let it soak their clothing, and they laughed weakly with the joy of it.

A mile beyond the waterhole, they reached the line at which the wind had changed and held the fire, driving it back upon itself. They left behind them the devastation of black ash and smouldering stumps and camped that night amongst the confusion of withered dead branches where the logging gangs had wrought almost as much destruction as the flames had done.

For the first time since the fire, Alphonso rigged the radio aerial, and they gathered round the set and listened for General China's taunts and threats. They all stiffened instinctively as they recognized his voice, but he was talking in Shangane and they could hear the sound of the helicopter's engines in the background. His transmissions were terse and enigmatic, and the replies from his subordinates were equally abrupt and business-like.

'What do you think he is up to?' Sean asked Alphonso, and the Shangane shook his head.

'It sounds like he is moving troops into fresh positions.' But there was no conviction in his tone.

'He hasn't given up?' Sean said. 'He may have lost our spoor in the burn, but I don't think he has given up.'

'No,' Alphonso agreed. 'I know him well. He has not given up. He will follow us all the way. General China is a man who hates very well. He will not let us go.'

'We are in Frelimo-held territory now. Do you think he will follow us in here?'

Alphonso shrugged. 'He has the *henshaw*, he does not have to worry too much about Frelimo. I think he will follow us wherever we go.'

General China made his last transmission and it was obvious he was arranging for refuelling. He had changed to Portuguese and the reply seemed to be from a ground engineer in the same language. Alphonso translated.

'The porters have arrived. We now have reserves of two thousand litres.'

China's voice, 'What about the spare booster pump?'

'It's here, my General,' the engineer again. 'I can change it tonight.'

'We must be airworthy again by first light tomorrow.'

'I will have it ready by then. I guarantee it, General.'

'Very well, I'll be landing in a few minutes. Be ready to begin work immediately,' China ordered and then signed off.

They listened for another ten minutes, until it was fully dark, but there were no further transmissions and Alphonso reached across to turn off the radio. On an impulse Sean prevented him doing so and instead switched frequencies. Almost at once, he picked up the South African military traffic. It was much stronger now, they were that much closer to the border on the Limpopo river, and to Sean the sound of Afrikaans was a comfort and a promise.

After a few minutes, Sean sighed and switched off the set. 'Alphonso, you take the first sentry. Go!' he ordered.

* * *

With the threat of aerial surveillance reduced, Sean decided to resume daylight travel, and every mile they covered towards the south the signs left by the logging gangs were fresher and more numerous.

On the third day after the fire, Matatu led them on a wide detour. The hardwood stumps had been cut very recently and they were still weeping sap. The leaves on the discarded branches piled in tall windrows had not dried out and were still green and pliant. Matatu cautioned them to silence and as they trudged on between the piled rows of trash, they heard not far off, the whine of chain saws, and the doleful work chant of the labour gangs.

The forest around them was full of human activity, and the soft soil carried the prints of thousands of bare feet and the skid marks of heavy logs being dragged and manhandled towards the rough logging roads. However, so skilfully did Matatu shepherd them through the torn and despoiled forests that it wasn't until the fourth day of travel that they actually caught sight of any other human beings.

Leaving the others to eat and rest well concealed under a shaggy pile of newly cut branches, Sean and Matatu sneaked forward to the edge of a natural open glade in the forest and through the binoculars Sean lay and watched the Frelimo logging gangs at work on the far side of the opening. Hundreds of black men and women, some of them no more than children, were toiling in teams, supervised by guards in Frelimo camouflage battledress.

The guards all carried AK rifles slung on their shoulders, but they wielded the long hippo-hide whips, the savage African sjambok, which they plied to the naked backs and legs of their charges. The snap of the lash on bare flesh and the agonized yelps carried across five hundred yards of open ground to where Sean and Matatu lay.

The labour gangs were piling the roughly trimmed logs into tall pyramid-shaped stacks, half of them straining and heaving on the heavy ropes while the others pushed against the huge timber baulks from the lower side. The guards urged them to greater effort, calling out the verses of the work-chant to which the gangs responded with a deep melancholy chorus and a concerted heave on the heavy manila ropes.

While Sean watched through his binoculars, one of the huge logs was laboriously hoisted towards the pinnacle of the stack, but before it could be rolled securely into place, one of the ropes parted and the log slewed sideways and went bouncing and rumbling down the side of the pyramid. Wailing with terror the labour gang broke and fled before it, but some of the weaker ones were not fast enough and the log steamrolled over them. Sean heard their shrill shrieks snuffed out and the crackle of their bones like dried twigs being fed through a clothes mangle.

It was too much even for a soldier's hardened stomach, and he touched Matatu's shoulder and they crept away, back to where they had left the others.

That afternoon they passed close to the labour camps, a vast collection of primitive lean-to huts that stank of wood-smoke, open latrines and human misery.

'The cheapest African commodity these days is black flesh,' Sean told Claudia grimly.

'If you told people back home about this, they just simply wouldn't understand what you were talking about. It's just so contrary to our own experience,' said Claudia.

At this time of day, the camps were almost deserted. All the able-bodied were at work in the forest and only the sick and the dying lay under the crude open shelters. Sean sent Matatu into the camp to scavenge, and he must have found one of the field kitchens and eluded the cooks. He returned with a half sack of uncooked maize-meal slung over his shoulder.

They ate handfuls of maize porridge that evening, huddled round the radio, listening to General China's voice on the Renamo command frequency.

Once again after General China had made his last transmission at nightfall, Sean switched to the South African military frequency and listened for almost half an hour, learning the voices and call signs of the various units within range. At last, he felt he had identified the South African border headquarters. It was using the call-sign 'Kudu', that beautiful spiral-horned antelope of the bushveld.

Sean waited patiently for a lull in the military traffic and then he keyed the microphone and spoke in Afrikaans.

'"Kudu", this is "Mossie". This is a storm sending. Do you read me, "Kudu"? This is "Mossie"!'

A storm sending was the call for a top priority message. It was the radio procedure that they had used back in the days of the Rhodesian bush war. He hoped that the South African commander's military experience went back that far. 'Mossie' in Afrikaans was a sparrow and had been Sean's call-sign in those far-off days.

A long silence followed Sean's transmission, in which the static echoed in the void of the stratosphere, and Sean thought that his call had been lost. He lifted the microphone to call again just as the radio came to life.

'Station calling "Kudu",' said a voice, heavy with suspicion. 'Say again your call-sign.'

'"Kudu", this is "Mossie". I repeat "Mossie". Mike Oscar Sierra Sierra India Echo. I request a relay to General De La Rey, the deputy minister of law and order.'

Lothar De La Rey had been Sean's control back in the seventies. Since then he had risen to high political office. 'Kudu' would surely know who he was, and hesitate to refuse a request for relay to such a source.

It was clear that 'Kudu' must be thinking the same thoughts, but taking longer to reach a decision. At last he called again, '"Mossie", standby. We are relaying you to De La Rey. '

Almost an hour later, long after dark, 'Kudu' called again.

'Mossie, this is "Kudu." De La Rey is unobtainable.'

'"Kudu", this is life and death. I will call you on this frequency every six hours until you reach De La Rey. '

'*Dood reg*, "Mossie". We'll keep a six-hour listening watch for you. *Totsiens*.'

* * *

They had abandoned their blankets when they fled before the fire, and tonight it was frosty. Sean and Claudia lay in each other's arms and whispered together softly.

'I didn't understand what you were saying on the radio. Who were you speaking with?' Claudia used the Americanism 'with', and Sean corrected it as he replied.

'I was speaking to a South African military base, probably on the border where we are headed.'

'Will they give us assistance?' she asked hopefully.

'I don't know. They might, if I can contact someone I know. I have asked them to try, but they can't get hold of him.'

'Who?'

'During the bush war, although I was in command of the Rhodesian Scouts, I was also reporting to the South African military intelligence,' he explained.

'A spy?' she asked.

'No,' he answered too quickly. 'The South Africans and the Rhodesians were allies, both on the same side. I am a South African, so I was neither a spy nor a traitor.'

'A double agent, then?' she teased him.

'Call it whatever you like, but De La Rey was my South African control. Since the war, I have continued sending him reports from time to time; whenever I have been able to pick up pieces of information about ANC terrorist activity or sanctioneering moves by hostile governments, I pass it on to him.'

'He owes you, does he?' she asked.

'He owes me plenty, besides which we are related. He's a cousin, a first cousin on my grandmother's side.' Sean broke off as a small body insinuated itself between them. 'Well, look who's here! If it isn't Minnie Mouse herself!'

Claudia wriggled around to make room for the child and Minnie settled down happily in the warm cradle formed by their bodies and pillowed her head on Sean's arm. He drew the child's body a little closer.

'She's so cute.' Claudia stroked the child's head. 'I could just eat her up.'

They were silent for so long that Sean thought she had fallen asleep, but Claudia spoke again, softly and thoughtfully.

'If we get out of here, do you think we could adopt Minnie?'

The simple question was fraught with snares and pitfalls. It presupposed a life together thereafter, a settled existence with home and children and responsibilities, all the things that Sean had avoided over a lifetime. It should have startled him, but instead it made him feel warm and comfortable.

*   *   *

The portable Honda generator clattered noisily and its light bulbs were strung on poles around the grounded helicopter.

The engine hatches were open and the debris suppressors had been removed from over the turbo intakes. The Portuguese engineer in blue overalls supervised and checked every task performed by his Russian prisoners. The Portuguese had very soon come to know and understand General China, and to appreciate just how vulnerable was his own position. During the short time he had been with the Renamo force he had on more than one occasion been a witness to the punishment that General China dealt out to anyone who failed or offended him, and he was conscious now of those dark fanatical eyes upon him as he worked.

It was after midnight, but General China had not yet retired to rest. He had been flying all the previous day, from first light to dusk, only landing to refuel the helicopter. A normal man would have been exhausted by now, certainly the Portuguese pilot had slouched off to his tent many hours before, but General China was indefatigable. He prowled around the helicopter, watching every move, every action, asking questions, demanding haste, as restless as though he were possessed by some dark passion.

'You must have her ready to fly at dawn,' he repeated, it seemed for the hundredth time that night, and then he went striding back to the open canvas-roofed shelter that he was using as his forward headquarters and pored over the large-scale map, studying once more his troop dispositions, brooding over them and muttering to himself.

On the map he had noted the features he had observed from the air, the location of the Frelimo logging camps and the rough roads they had hacked out of the forest. He had very soon realized the scope of the deforestation, and the numbers employed in the forced labour battalions. He had swiftly realized the futility of trying to find such a small party amongst such multitudes. He knew any sign of Sean's progress would have been obliterated by the intense activity in the area. He dared not send trackers or a pursuit into the logging area. He had already lost almost forty men in the Frelimo attack and the subsequent fire.

'No, I must be patient,' he told himself.

He moved his hand down across the map.

The Frelimo logging operation had not yet reached as far south as the hills that guarded the approaches to the Limpopo river-basin; between the hills and the river the forest thinned out and gave way to open mopane veld. It was a strip fifty kilometres wide, good ground for tracking the fugitives, ground that they would be forced to traverse in order to reach the Limpopo and the border.

General China had decided to set his final stop line there. All that day he had ferried in the fresh troops that Tippoo Tip had placed at his disposal. In its rear cabin the Hind was able to carry fourteen men in full field kit, and they had made eleven sorties. They had hopped over the forest, fully laden with assault troops, and landed them along the line of hills with orders to set up observation posts on each hill crest and to patrol the gaps between them. He now had almost a hundred and fifty men in place to cut Sean Courtney off from the Limpopo.

General China stared at the map as though it were a portrait of the white man's face. Once again he experienced the bitter disappointment and frustration. He had almost had the white man in his grasp, pinned down by his pursuit troops, with no possible avenue of escape, and then had come the Frelimo intervention; the forest below him had been obliterated by the roiling clouds of smoke and the screaming of his men on the radio, crying for help as the flames engulfed them.

Tippoo Tip had tried in vain to convince him that Sean Courtney had perished with them in the forest fire, but General China knew better than that. He had dropped his own trackers from

the Hind into the blackened ashes as soon as they had cooled
sufficiently for men to walk upon them. They had found the spot
where the white man had buried his people to evade the heat,
the marks of their bodies were still imprinted in the soft earth,
and they had found the tracks leading away southwards, ever
southwards.

For the rest of that day, China had searched from the low-flying
Hind, but the smoke had hampered him, limiting his vision to
the small circle directly beneath the Hind's belly.

If anything, this additional failure had intensified his determination. The white man's cunning and his outrageous good fortune
in evading all China's best efforts only aggravated his hatred and
inflamed his longing for revenge. During those long hours when
they had ferried his last line of assault troops into position, China
had sustained himself with fantasies of vengeance, dreaming up
the most bizarre ordeals for Sean Courtney and his woman once
he had them in his power.

There would be no haste then. He would draw out the pleasure,
eking out their suffering and pain as jealously as a miser his
shekels. He would begin with the woman, of course, and the
white man would watch it all. After Tippoo Tip had enjoyed her
to the full, they would hand her over to the men. China would
personally select the most repulsive, those with hideous features,
deformed bodies and elephantine members. Some of his men
were truly remarkable in their physical development. He would
let them have the woman after Tippoo Tip, and when they were
done, he would bring on the sick and diseased, the men with
open venereal ulcers and virulent skin disorders, covered with
scabs and tropical sores. Then at last he would give her to the
men with the slim sickness, the most dreaded of all. Yes, it would
be marvellous sport. He wondered how strong the American
woman was, how many she could take. Would her mind go
before her body? It would be fascinating to find out, and of
course, the white man would be forced to watch every second
of it.

Only when the woman was finished, would he begin on Colonel
Sean Courtney. He had not yet decided what it would be, there
were so many possibilities. However, the man was tough, he
could be expected to last for days, perhaps even weeks. Planning
it, gloating on it, brought a smile to General China's lips and
calmed his frustration enough to allow him to drop into his canvas

chair, draw the lapels of his greatcoat around him and sink at last into sleep.

He awoke in confusion, unable to orientate himself. Somebody was shaking him urgently, and he threw off the hands and struggled out of his chair, glaring around him wildly. It was morning, the trees around his temporary base were grey skeletons against the paler grey of the dawn sky. The light bulbs still glowed on their poles above the squatting helicopter and the radio on the rough table of hand-planed logs in front of him was squawking urgently.

'Contact! General China, we have a live contact!' It was the commander of the line of men that he had placed upon the hills at the approaches to the Limpopo. He was calling in clear language, proof of his agitation.

Still half asleep, China stumbled to the radio set and seized the microphone. 'This is "Banana Tree", report your position and status correctly,' he snapped, and at the sound of his voice the distant patrol leader steadied himself and corrected his radio procedure.

The fugitives had run into his stop line, at almost precisely the point which China had predicted. There had been a brief fire-fight and then the fugitive band had taken refuge on the crest of a small kopje, almost within sight of the Limpopo river.

'I have called for the mortars to come up,' the patrol leader exulted. 'We'll blow them off the top of that hill.'

'Negative.' China spoke very clearly. 'I say again, negative. Do not open fire on the position with mortars. Do not attack. I want them taken alive. Surround the hill and wait for my arrival.' He glanced across at the helicopter. The titanium engine hatches were back in place, and the Portuguese engineer was overseeing the last of the refuelling. A line of porters, each of them with a twenty-five-litre drum balanced on his head, were queued up, waiting their turns to empty the drums into the helicopter's main tanks.

China shouted to the engineer in Portuguese and he came striding across to the tent.

'We must take off immediately,' he ordered.

'I will complete the refuelling in half an hour.'

'That's too long. How much fuel have you got on board right now?'

'Auxiliary tanks are full, main tank is three quarters.'

'That will do. call the pilot. Tell him we must take off right away.'

'I must replace the debris suppressors over the turbo intakes,' the engineer protested.

'How long will that take?'

'Not more than half an hour.'

'Too long!' China shouted with agitation. The pilot was stumbling along the pathway from his tent. Not yet fully awake, he was pulling on his leather flying jacket and the flaps of his helmet dangled loosely around his ears.

'Hurry!' China yelled at him. 'Get her started!'

'What about the suppressors?' the engineer insisted.

'We can fly without them, they are only precautionary.'

'Yes, but. . . !'

'No!' China pushed him away. 'I can't wait! Forget about the suppressors! We fly at once! Get the engines started!'

With the tails of his greatcoat flapping around his legs, General China ran to the helicopter and scrambled up into his seat in the weapons cockpit.

* * *

Sean Courtney lay on his belly between two rocks just below the crest of the kopje and looked out over the tops of the mopane forest. Away towards the south, the dark green belt of trees was just visible in the uncertain light. It marked the position of the Limpopo river.

'So close,' he lamented. 'We so very nearly made it.'

It was against all the odds that they had survived this far, almost three hundred kilometres through a devastated war-torn land and two murderous opposing armies, only to be stopped here in sight of their goal. There was a burst of AK fire from down the slope of the hill, and a ricochet sang away into the dawn sky.

Matatu lay amongst the rocks nearby, and he was still berating himself. 'I am a stupid old man, my *Bwana*. You must send me away and get yourself a clever young one who is not blind and decrepit with age.'

Sean guessed that a Renamo observation post must have spotted them as they crossed one of the open glades between the hills. There had been no warning, no obvious pursuit, no set

515

ambush. Without warning a sweep line of tiger-striped figures had rushed at them from out of the mopane.

They had all been weary after travelling hard all night, perhaps their concentration had been eroded, perhaps they should have stayed in the trees instead of cutting across the open vlei, but it was vain to think about what they might have done.

There had only been sufficient time to snatch up the children and drag the women up the side of the kopje with poorly aimed Renamo fire whining off the rocks around them. Perhaps the Renamo aim had been deliberately wild, Sean pondered. He could guess what General China's orders to his men had been. 'Take them alive!'

'Where is China now?' he wondered. One thing was certain, he was not far away and coming as fast as the Hind would fly. He looked out at the Limpopo river again and there was the foul taste of failure and disappointment on the back of his tongue.

'Alphonso,' he called out. 'Have you got the radio rigged?' It was more for something to occupy his mind than with any real hope of making contact.

Twice during the night he had attempted to make the pre-arranged radio schedule with the South African army. Once he had even heard 'Kudu' calling him very faintly; however, the batteries of their radio had finally begun to fail. The battery test needle had dropped back deeply into the red quadrant of the dial.

'If I try to raise the aerial those baboons down there will shoot my testicles off,' Alphonso growled from amongst the rocks.

'It's almost line of sight to the river,' Sean told him brusquely. 'Give me the aerial.' He raised himself on one elbow and threw the bundle of insulated wire as far out down the slope as he could reach and then stooped to the radio set. When he turned on the power, the control panel glowed feebly.

'"Kudu", this is "Mossie",' he sent out his despairing call, ' "Kudu", do you read me? "Kudu", this is "Mossie"!'

A stray bullet hit the rock above his head, but Sean ignored it.

'"Kudu", this is "Mossie"!'

The two women, white and black, were holding the children and watching him wordlessly.

'"Kudu", this is "Mossie".' He adjusted the gain knob, and

516

then unbelievably, so faintly that he could barely catch the words, a voice answered him.

'"Mossie", this is "Oubaas". I read you strength three.'

'"Oubaas". Oh God,' he breathed. '"Oubaas"!'

Oubaas, the grandfather, was General Lothar De La Rey's code name.

'"Oubaas". We are in deep shit here. Request an immediate hot extraction.' He was asking for a removal while under enemy fire. 'We are seven pax, five adults and two children. Our position is . . .' He read out the map co-ordinates of his dead-reckoning position. 'We are holding a small kopje approximately twenty kilometres north of the Limpopo.' He raised his head and glanced around quickly. 'There are two large kopjes approximately two miles due east of our position. Do you read me, "Oubaas"?'

'I read you "Mossie".' The voice faded and then came back. 'What was your grandmother's maiden name?'

'Oh, sod you!' Sean snarled frustration. Lothar was double-checking his identity at a time like this. 'My grandmother's maiden name was Centaine De Thiry and she is your grandmother also, Lothar, you rotten bastard!'

'Okay, "Mossie". I'm sending a Puma in for a hot extraction. Can you hold out for one hour longer?'

'Pull finger, "Oubaas". We've got gooks all over us.'

'Wilco, "Mossie".' Sean had to put his ear close to the set to catch the last words. 'Give them hell, Sean . . .' And then the signal faded and the last flicker of the battery died.

'They are coming!' Sean looked up from the radio and grinned across at Claudia. 'They are sending a Puma helicopter in to take us out.' Then his grin faded and all their faces turned slowly towards the north. There was a new sound in the dawn, still faint and far off, but they all recognized it. It was the sound of death.

* * * *

They watched the Hind come down from the north, sweeping in low over the forest, a great hunchbacked monster, blotched with camouflage paint, the first rays of the rising sun reflecting off the cockpit canopy like huge glowing red eyes.

Out of the mopane forest at the foot of the kopje a signal rocket sailed up in a lazy red parabola, calling the Hind in, and it altered course slightly and headed directly towards the crest of the hill on which they lay.

Claudia was at Sean's side and he placed his arm over her shoulders.

'It's so cruel,' she whispered. 'It's like dying twice over.' She pulled the Tokarev pistol from her belt and tried to place it in his hand.

'No!' he rejected. 'I can't do it! I can't screw myself up to that again!' He pushed the pistol away.

'What then?' she asked, and he showed her the fragmentation grenade he held in his right hand.

She glanced at the deeply chequered black metal orb. It looked like some evil poisonous fruit, and she shuddered and averted her eyes.

'It will be as quick and more certain,' he whispered reassuringly. 'And we'll go together, at the very same moment.'

He knew what he had to do. He would hold the grenade between them as they lay chest to chest.

He looked up again at the approaching Hind. It was very close. It was almost time. He would not warn her. He would simply kiss her one last time and then . . .

Suddenly Sean's eyes narrowed. Something about the Hind's silhouette was different. It was coming in swiftly, swelling in size before his eyes and he felt the first stirring of a new excitement as he realized what had been changed on the helicopter.

'There is still a chance,' he whispered to her. 'A small chance, but we are going to take it. Come here, Minnie. Come quickly!' he called in Shangane, and the tiny black girl tottered across to where they lay.

'Hold her,' Sean whispered, and lifted the back of the child's short ragged skirt. Under the skirt, she wore a pair of blue knickers.

Sean pulled open the elastic top of the knickers and pushed something down into them, something as round and black as one of her little buttocks between which it nestled.

'Keep that for me, little one,' he whispered to the child in Shangane as he adjusted the waistband. 'It's a secret. Don't take it out. Just keep it there. Will you do that for me, my little flower?'

Minnie stared at him with dark adoring eyes and nodded solemnly and Sean gave her a hug.

The sound of the Hind's turbos was almost unbearably shrill as it came in towards them at the level of the hilltop. When it was two hundred metres out, Alphonso opened fire with his AK rifle, pouring a full magazine into the front canopy. The light bullets left no mark on the armoured glass, and the helicopter slowed and hung motionless on its shining rotor. General China was sitting up in the high-backed seat of the weapons cockpit, so close that they could clearly see the triumphant smirk on his face as he lifted the microphone to his mouth.

His grossly magnified voice boomed out of the speakers of the 'sky shout' system that were slung below the helicopter's stubby wings.

'Good morning, Colonel Courtney. You have led me a merry dance, but the chase is over. Tell your men to lay down their weapons, please.'

'Do it!' Sean shouted at Alphonso, but he snarled a protest and clipped a fresh magazine onto his rifle. 'Do as I tell you!' Sean's voice hardened. 'I have a plan. Trust me.'

Still Alphonso hesitated, and suddenly the Hind's Gatling-cannon thundered, deafening them and kicking a storm of rock chips and dust from the side of the kopje just below where they lay.

'Don't try my patience, Colonel. Tell your men to stand up, with their hands high above their heads.'

'Do it!' Sean repeated, and first Matatu and then Alphonso rose slowly to their feet with arms held high.

'Tell them to turn around. I want to make sure they have no surprises for me.'

They shuffled in a circle and China's voice boomed out again.

'Take your clothes off, all of them.'

Slowly they stripped themselves and stood naked before him.

'All right, now move down the hill into the open.'

Still with their hands held high they walked down into the open ground below the crown of rocks.

'Now the two women.'

'Be brave,' Sean whispered to Claudia. 'We've still got a chance, a good chance.'

Claudia stood up slowly.

'Miss Monterro.' China's voice echoed across the forest tops, 'will you be good enough to remove your clothing?'

Briskly, defiantly Claudia unbuttoned her ragged shirt and

pulled it over her tousled head. Her breasts were white in the early sunlight.

. 'Now your trousers,' China encouraged her. She let them drop around her ankles and kicked them off.

'Very good, and now the rest of it.'

Claudia's lace panties had been washed and worn until they were wispy as spider web, her pubic triangle was a dark shadow under the filmy cloth.

'No.' She shook her head. 'I won't do it.' She crossed her hands in front of her. Her refusal was unmistakable.

'Very well. We'll allow you your modesty for the time being. My men will enjoy it all the more later.' China chuckled. 'Move down into the open, please.'

Claudia walked down the hill, her chin and her small pert breasts held high, and stood between Alphonso and Matatu.

'Now you, woman.' China spoke in Shangane, and Miriam stood up. She did not have a European's shame of nudity and quickly stripped herself naked. Holding her little brother's hand, she went down to join the others.

'And now, Colonel Courtney. The last is the best of all the game.'

Sean rose to his feet and carelessly threw aside his tattered clothing.

'Very impressive, Colonel.' China taunted him. 'For a white man, that is.'

Sean stood and stared up at him impassively, but he was trying to judge the distance to the helicopter. Sixty yards, he estimated, much too far.

'Please come down into the open where I can keep an eye on you, Colonel. We don't want any misunderstanding now, do we?'

Sean took Minnie's hand and led her down the hill. The lump under the little girl's skirt wobbled from side to side like a Victorian bustle, and with her free hand she tugged at the waistband of her knickers to prevent them being pulled down around her knees by the weight.

Ten, fifteen, twenty paces, Sean counted as he moved towards the hovering Hind. He could clearly see the pupils of General China's eyes, forty yards, still too far. He stopped beside Claudia and they stood in a row, naked and vulnerable.

China gave an order in Shangane, and at the foot of the hill his men burst out of the forest and came swarming up the slope.

whooping with triumph. The Portuguese pilot edged the huge machine in closer. and then closer still. showing off his prowess at the controls.

Thirty yards. twenty-five yards. Sean was concentrating on the opening of the air-intakes to the turbo engines. They were the size of garbage bins with the covers missing: he could just make out deep in the circular openings the velvety blur of the rotor blades spinning at incredible speed.

The Hind steadied in the air and hung in front of them. In the cockpit General China twisted his head to peer down the hill at the line of advancing Renamo guerrillas. He was distracted and Sean seized the moment.

He stooped slightly and jerked up the back of Minnie's skirt. In the same movement. he thrust his hand under the waistband of her knickers and closed his hand over the grenade. As it came out. he pulled the pin and let the firing handle fly free. He heard the pin fall on the primer. There was a delay of five seconds. He counted off three under his breath and then reared back like a baseball pitcher just as China looked back at him.

He concentrated on the starboard engine intake. and hurled the grenade. It went up in a flat arc and he willed its flight. trying by sheer force of his mind to steer it into the small circle of the intake.

The grenade struck the bottom of the intake rim. and bounced on the edge. like a million-dollar putt quivering on the lip. Then the tremendous draught of air created by the rotor blades sucked it in. and it popped into the throat of the open duct.

The grenade exploded as it hit the spinning blades. and the great turbo's energy was thrown out of balance. all its mighty power directed upon itself. in an orgy of self-destruction.

As Sean seized Claudia and Minnie under each arm and hurled them face down. the Hind's engine tore itself to pieces in one fatal instant.

The Hind lurched heavily. throwing General China's aim so that the burst he fired from the Gatling-cannon flew almost straight into the sky. and the helicopter rolled on to its back. Smoke and fragments of metal blew in a screaming cloud from its maimed engines.

It struck the side of the hill. and bounced high. fell again. and cart-wheeled down the slope. directly on top of the climbing line of Renamo. They broke and scattered. but most of them could not escape, and the shattered fuselage of the Hind rolled over them and swept them away down the slope.

At last the Hind slithered on its belly like a gigantic toboggan to the bottom of the kopje and came up hard against the tree-line. Avgas, as clear as water, fountained from its ruptured main tanks and sprayed over the hull, sparkling in the sunlight.

Sean and Claudia rose shakily to their knees and watched in awe the magnificent destruction.

Then, incredibly, the canopy of the weapons cockpit opened like the half shell of an enormous oyster and General China crawled out from under it. The Hind's fuel sprayed high in the morning sunlight as innocuous-seeming as a garden sprinkler, and fell upon him in a gentle rain. It soaked his uniform and ran in thin rivulets down his face, but China pushed himself away from the shattered fuselage and set off down the hill at a shambling run.

He had not gone ten shaky paces when the Hind went up in a sheet of flame, and the flames jumped the gap and ignited China's sodden uniform. It turned him into a human torch and he ran on down the slope with the yellow flames streaking out behind him. They could hear his screams even from the top of the hill, it was a high inhuman sound.

China did not reach the trees. He fell at the edge of the forest and his burning flesh touched off the thick brown grass in which he lay. The hillside became his pyre, but still they could hear him screaming in the heart of the flames.

'Back!' Sean shouted, and his voice aroused them from their mesmerized horror. He hauled Claudia to her feet and picked Minnie up in his arms.

In a bunch they fled back into the circle of rocks that crowned the kopje just as a renewed Renamo fusillade whined about them. They lay behind the rocks, not yet bothering to cover their naked bodies and watched the Hind burn, and the flames sweep through the grass at the edge of the forest.

When the flames had passed, a dark charred mound lay on the blackened slope. It might have been merely a pile of discarded sacking, except that when the wind shifted, the odour of burned flesh carried up to them on the crest of the hill.

The shift in the wind carried a new sound to them, and Sean roused himself and looked towards the green Limpopo river on the horizon.

The Puma helicopter was still a dark speck out there, but it was coming on swiftly, the sound of its engines rising on the wind.

'Put your pants on, darling,' Sean hugged Claudia a little closer. 'It looks as though we've got company dropping in on us!'